Ulysses
Annotated

NOTES FOR
JAMES JOYCE'S *Ulysses*

From David A. Chart, *The Story of Dublin* (London, 1907)

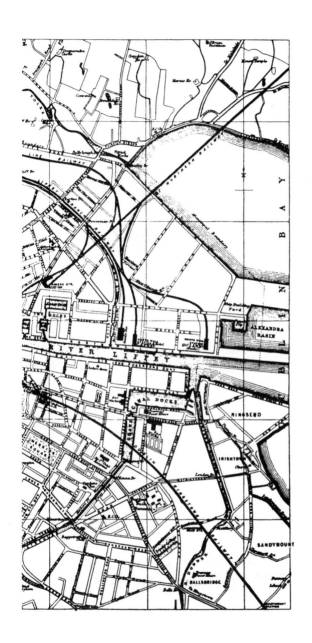

Ulysses Annotated

NOTES FOR
JAMES JOYCE'S *Ulysses*

Don Gifford WITH
ROBERT J. SEIDMAN

SECOND EDITION,
REVISED AND ENLARGED
BY DON GIFFORD

University of California Press
Berkeley   Los Angeles   London

This volume is a revised and expanded edition
of *Notes for Joyce: An Annotation of James Joyce's
"Ulysses,"* by Don Gifford with Robert J. Seidman
(New York: E. P. Dutton, 1974).

The maps were drawn by Beth Gavrilles.

University of California Press
Berkeley and Los Angeles, California
University of California Press, Ltd.
London, England
© 1988 by
The Regents of the University of California
First paperback printing 1989
Second paperback printing 2008

Library of Congress Cataloging-in-Publication Data

Gifford, Don.
  "Ulysses" Annotated.

  Rev. ed. of: Notes for Joyce. 1974.
  Includes index.
  1. Joyce, James, 1882–1941. Ulysses. I. Seidman,
Robert J. II. Gifford, Don. Notes for Joyce.
III. Title.
PR6019.09U647 1988   823'.912   85-22262
ISBN 978-0-520-25397-1

Printed in the United States of America

14   13   12   11   10   09   08
7   6   5   4   3   2   1

I've put in so many enigmas and puzzles that it will keep the professors busy for centuries arguing over what I meant, and that's the only way of insuring one's immortality.

JAMES JOYCE

NOTES FOR JOYCE'S *Ulysses*

CONTENTS

PREFACE TO THE SECOND EDITION

Since publication of the first edition of these annotations in 1974, responses from colleagues, students, correspondents, and innumerable critics have made it clear that, even with the able collaboration of R. J. Seidman and the assistance of many others, I had assembled something less than a definitive working annotation of *Ulysses*. Hugh Kenner sums up the first edition succinctly: "By no means impeccable, but a good place to look first."[1] This revised and enlarged second edition is still, of course, by no means impeccable, but I hope it is a better place to look first.

Some of the revisions report new discoveries that add to the excitement of Joyce's text. Others expand information in the previous edition—providing, for example, plot summaries of operas, plays, and novels frequently alluded to in *Ulysses*. And there remains the indigestible mass of notes identifying inert things, "street furnishings" that require annotation to ensure that they remain inert, that they are overlooked instead of over-exploited. Vico Road, for instance, is in Dalkey, where Stephen teaches in the morning; a single mention of Vico Road as the place where one of Stephen's students resides does not necessarily introduce Giambattista Vico and the "rosary of history" to preside over the whole of *Ulysses*.

Twenty years ago I began this work of annotating Joyce spurred by the pedagogical frustration described in the Preface to the first edition, reprinted below. Now, as I am about not to finish, but to "abandon" (as Paul Valéry would say) these revised notes for publication, there is another sort of frustration: over one thousand additions and corrections since 1974, and still they come—as if from the fabled pot of lentils or, more appropriately, from that inexhaustibly hospitable ancient Irish soup pot, the caulderon of Manannan Mac Lir, the god of the sea.

Richard M. Kain, in his review of the first edition of these notes, quite appropriately quotes Dr. Johnson's sage words: "Notes are often necessary, but they are necessary evils."[2] The annotator's role in accumulating those evils reminds me of Swift's Gulliver in Glubbdubdrib. Offered the opportunity to speak with the

---

1 Hugh Kenner, *Ulysses* (London: George Allen and Unwin, 1980) p. 176.

2 *James Joyce Quarterly* 11, no. 4 [1974]: 423.

ghosts of antiquity, Gulliver is so crippled in imagination that he can think only to ask for mob scenes: Alexander the Great at the head of his army, "Hannibal passing the Alps," and, as a sort of afterthought, Homer and Aristotle— not to speak to them (heaven forbid), but to see them with their commentators; a mob scene that produces not enlightenment, but a crowd the palace of Glubbdubdrib cannot contain.

Robert J. Seidman, who assisted me to the point of co-authorship in the 1974 edition, had to step toward the wings during preparation of this revised and enlarged edition. The demands on his time would simply have been too great; even so, he turned up additional notes, reviewed the accumulation of new and revised notes several times, and was prompt with support throughout.

This new edition obviously had to be keyed to the text of the Critical and Synoptic Edition of *Ulysses* (New York, Garland, 1984). The general editor of the Critical Edition, Professor Hans Walter Gabler of the Institute for English Philology at the University of Munich, has been a model of generosity and cooperation during the past four years. He supplied me with the new reading text as it became available, including a collation with the 1961 Random House text to help me spot changes. With admirable patience and skill, his editorial associate, Claus Melchior, renumbered my lemmata and cross references in accordance with the new edition of *Ulysses*.

Since publication of the first edition of these notes, I have received invaluable corrections and suggestions from colleagues, friends, and correspondents. The desire to list them fills me with trepidation that I might fail to thank all who have offered help or to give to each credit due. Particularly gratifying was help I received from correspondents who volunteered information out of the blue: Edward Stewart of Auckland, New Zealand, who helped considerably with the matter of Dublin from a Dubliner's perspective; and Joan Glasser Keenan of Wellesley, Massachusetts, whose meticulous and voluminous correspondence was an enormous help, as acknowledgments in the notes will attest.

Roland McHugh interrupted the project of revising his monumental *Annotations to Finnegans Wake* (London, 1980) to forward over one hundred suggested emendations to this volume. I can only hope that my far less searching commentary on his project has been some compen-

sation. Correspondence with Vincent Deane, editor-compiler of *A Finnegans Wake Circular,* resulted in eighty-plus emendations and additions.

Other correspondents and commentators deserve my thanks: Professor Bernard Benstock, University of Miami; Professor Richard Ellmann, Emory University; Professor Hugh Kenner, The Johns Hopkins University; Tom Mac Intyre, Irish writer and playwright; Mary T. Reynolds, Yale University; and Professor Nathan Suskind. R. J. Seidman adds to this list: Professor Dorothy Bilik, University of Maryland; Dr. Vivian B. Mann, The Jewish Museum, New York; and Syrl Silberman, Media Producer/Consultant.

Williams College is a "small college," and my colleagues there coped admirably with my preoccupations, nagging questions, and progress reports. Many of them I thanked in the Preface to the first edition; many I must add, and many I must thank again. The first edition was only a few weeks old when Clara and David Park (Department of English and Physics Department, respectively) presented me with a pack of fifty-odd 3 × 5 cards (pink slips, they were) to launch me toward this second installment. And so many others in the interim: from Classics, Professors Maureen Meaney Dietze, Charles Fuqua, and Meredith Hoppin; from German, Professor Edson Chick; from Russian (with asides in Italian), Professor Nicholas Fersen; from Philosophy, Professors Nathaniel Lawrence and Laszlo Versenyi (who helped with the Hungarian as well as with Plato); from English, Professors Robert Bell, Peter Berek, Arthur Carr, Stephen Fix, Lawrence Graver, Sherron Knopp, and John Reichert; from the Sawyer Library, the former librarian Lawrence Wikander and the present librarian Phyllis Cutler as well as that splendidly cooperative research staff, Lee Dalzell, Faith Fleming, Nancy Hanssen, Sarah McFarland, Barbara Prentice, and the assistant librarian Elizabeth Scherr. I must also include Robert Volz, custodian of the Chapin (rare book) Library; Carl Johnson, Associate Curator of the Paul Whiteman Collection; and Paula McCarthy Panczenko, who made field trips to Dublin.

I wish to thank my Joyce classes—all those generations of Williams College students who have used the notes and helped me to develop them. Particular thanks go to Theoharis C. Theoharis, Williams College 1977, who, in the years since his experience of that course, has come to function as a regular contributor to this revision. During the final months of preparation, Susan Reifer (1985) and William Galloway (1984) helped by reviewing the manuscript; Robin Lorsch (1986) and Thomas Lydon (1986) checked the references to *The Odyssey*. I am also grateful to Anne Geissman Canright for her skillful editing.

Throughout the project Williams College has been most generous with research funding assistance.

PREFACE AND ACKNOWLEDGMENTS (1974)

Work on the present volume began in 1962–63 as a continuation of the projects that resulted in the annotations of *Dubliners* and *A Portrait of the Artist as a Young Man*, published as *Notes for Joyce* (New York: E. P. Dutton, 1967).[1] As with those earlier projects, the decision to annotate *Ulysses* was a function of the somewhat frustrating and unrewarding experience of trying to teach the book. I felt that far too much classroom time was given to a parade of erudition, far too little to the actual process of teaching—the discussion that comes to grips with the forms and textures of the book itself. I was in effect encouraging my students to be overdependent on my information and therefore on my readings. As I launched the annotations with a mimeographed and fragmentary set of notes for the first three episodes of *Ulysses* in 1962–63, two things became clear: my students were able to undertake independent readings of those episodes; and my own grasp of the book was spotty—very spotty indeed—because I had relied on a fairly thorough reading of isolated passages to suggest what might be (but clearly was not) a thorough reading of the book as a whole.

In 1966 Robert J. Seidman, a former student, joined me in the enterprise. We declared a moratorium on writing and undertook to complete the factual research. This approach enabled us to develop the basis for the annotations and to identify that wide variety of things we knew we did not know. The actual writing began early in 1967, and in the academic year 1967–68 we photocopied a draft of the notes to the first eight episodes for use with classes at Williams College. That exposure of the notes gave us valuable information; students made helpful contributions to the notes themselves and also helped us clarify what a thorough and essentially pedagogical annotation might ultimately be. The students made it quite clear, for example, that the context from which a literary allusion or a historical moment is taken should not just be cited, but should be briefly described

---

1 A second edition, revised and enlarged, was published as *Joyce Annotated: Notes for "Dubliners" and "A Portrait of the Artist as a Young Man"* (Berkeley and Los Angeles: University of California Press, 1982).

and summarized so the reader could be oriented without consulting the original sources.

The preparation of this volume has naturally involved considerable reliance on the body of Joyce scholarship. Where the annotations are matters of fact from reasonably public realms, we have not tried to identify the original discoverer—in part because there have been innumerable simultaneous and overlapping discoveries, and in part because such identification and the comment it entails would imply a scholarly compilation (an annotation of critical commentaries on *Ulysses*), which has not been the point of this work (an annotation of the text itself). When Weldon Thornton's *Allusions in "Ulysses"* (Chapel Hill, N.C., 1968) was published, it seemed at first that what we had undertaken had already been accomplished. Indeed, Thornton's work and ours do overlap to a considerable extent, but the differences implied by the terms "allusion" and "annotation" do suggest two different approaches and two different end products. Thornton's book has informed us on many points and has helped us immeasurably. At the same time our own questions and investigations have carried us into fields other than those Thornton has defined as "allusions," and the hope is that the two books can be regarded as complementary attempts at different approaches to *Ulysses* rather than as mutually exclusive attempts at the same approach.

It is a challenge to try to acknowledge here our wide-ranging indebtedness to friends and associates and correspondents for their assistance. We would like to thank the following for their varied contributions to this compendium: Theodore Albert, Williams College, 1963; Stephen Arons, Harvard Law School, 1969; M. Amr Barrada, Professor of English, Williams College; Murray Baumgarten, Professor of English, University of California at Santa Cruz; Arthur Carr, Professor of English, Williams College; Loring Coes III, Williams College, 1971; James M. Cole, Williams College, 1968; Padraic Colum, Irish poet and critic; Thomas Foster, Williams College, 1969; John Garvin, Dublin City Commissioner; Marin Haythe; Mathew J. C. Hodgart, University of Sussex, co-author of *Song in the Works of James Joyce;* Sarah Hudson; J. Clay Hunt, Professor of English, Williams College; Nathaniel Lawrence, Professor of Philosophy, Williams College; Nancy MacFayden, Library Assistant, Williams College; Roger McHugh, Professor of Anglo-Irish Literature, University College, Dublin; Holly McLennan; Benedict R. Miles (*d.* 1970), editor and proprietor of the *Gibraltar Directory and Guide Book;* Kathleen A. O'Connell, Secretary to the President, Williams College; Daniel O'Connor, Professor of Philosophy, Williams College; Ulick O'Connor, Dublin Man of Letters; Robert O'Donnell, Professor of English, Hofstra University; Iona Opie, co-author of *The Oxford Dictionary of Nursery Rhymes* and *The Language and Lore of Childhood;* Clara Park, Berkshire Community College, Pittsfield, Massachusetts; Eric Partridge, English authority on slang and unconventional language; Anson Piper, Professor of Romance Languages, Williams College; Christopher Ricks, Professor of English, University of Bristol; Kenneth Roberts, Professor of Music, Williams College; Robert M. Ross, Professor of English, University of Pennsylvania; Charles Schweighauser, Williams College Center for Environmental Studies; Patti Seidman; Juanita Terry, Research Librarian, Williams College; Mabel P. Worthington, co-author of *Song in the Works of James Joyce.*

I would also like to thank the Williams College 1900 Fund for grants in aid of this project.

D. G.

The primary intention of these annotations is pedagogical—to provide a specialized encyclopedia that will inform a reading of *Ulysses*. The rule of thumb I have followed is to annotate all items not available in standard desk dictionaries. As they now stand, the notes, even with the revisions, are not complete. Many of the incompletions I know I do not know; there are undoubtedly other incompletions of which I am unaware; and some of the complete notes are bound to prove inaccurate or inadequate. To the extent that these flaws are part of the formal traditions of history, theology, philosophy, science, literature, and the arts, they should prove correctable. But other limitations derive from a central problem in annotating *Ulysses:* Joyce depended heavily for his vocabularies on the vernacular and oral worlds of 1904 Dublin. Those worlds of slang and gossip, anecdotal (as against formal) history, and popular literature and culture are rapidly passing out of living memory. The effort to catch the nuances of those informal vocabularies before they are lost is consequently of critical importance.

I have tried to balance on the knife-edge of factual annotation and to avoid interpretive remarks. This distinction is something of a legal fiction, since it can hardly be said that the notes do not imply interpretations or that they do not derive from interpretations; but the intention has been to keep the notes "neutral" so that they will inform rather than direct a reading of the novel. The ideal of neutrality, however, has its drawbacks and has tended to overweight the annotations. Joyce was fascinated by what he called "Dublin street furniture," and he included vast amounts of it in *Ulysses*. For the most part that furniture is detail with no suggestive dimension beyond the factual—streets, bridges, buildings, pubs, and shops are there: period. But occasionally something transfactual occurs: when Bloom twice places Wisdom Hely's, where he once worked, at nonexistent addresses (literally wishing Hely's out of existence); or when Stephen passes Henry and James Clothiers and thinks of Henry James; or when Stephen places the physics theater of Jesuit University College in the palace of the archbishop of the Church of Ireland. These occasions and many less obvious ones seemed to me to require that all the "street furniture" be annotated, if only to demonstrate, rather than to assert, that in most cases it is factual and in-

THE NOTES AND THEIR USE

ert, as in life most such furniture inevitably is. On another level, the catalogues, such as those of Irish heroes and saints in Cyclops, present a similar problem. Most of the heroes at the beginning of the list are just that, Irish heroes who make one appearance in the novel; but at least two of them are what Stephen would call the "indispensable informer," so the whole list seemed to require annotation. Similarly, the saints are saints, but the list also includes ringers, such as Molly Bloom and the dog Garryowen; so all were to be included. Because even the well-informed reader needs to know only that the street furniture is *there* and *in place*, that the heroes are heroes, the saints, saints, the notes may appear to labor an abundance of the obvious in order to render a few grains of the subtle and suggestive. Yet I could see no way around simply accepting the overweighting as a problem inherent from the outset in "neutral" annotations.

The annotated passages are presented in order of occurrence—not unlike the notes at the foot of the pages of an edition of Shakespeare or Milton. The numerals before each annotated word or phrase indicate the episode and line number established by the new Critical and Synoptic Edition of *Ulysses*, edited by Hans Walter Gabler et al. (New York: Garland, 1984). The numbers in parenthesis refer by page and line to the 1961 Random House edition, which is virtually identical with the current Modern Library and Vintage texts. Cross references among the notes in this revised edition are indicated by the episode and line numbers of the Critical Edition—for example, 3.259n. References to passages elsewhere in *Ulysses* include the episode and line numbers of the Critical Edition and, in parenthesis, the page and line numbers of the 1961 Random House edition—for example, 3.259 (44:4). Further, the Critical Edition has altered many passages and included several that were omitted in the 1961 and previous editions; the slightly changed passages in the notes are marked with an asterisk and lacunae are additionally marked with a double slash in the Random House page-line reference—for example, **3.79 (39.5//). *Sit down and take a walk.**

This book is thus designed to be laid open beside the novel and to be read in tandem with it. Tandem reading has, however, its disadvantages. It threatens a reader not only with interruption but also with distortion, because details that are mere grace notes in the novel may be overemphasized by the annotations. Several compromises suggest themselves here: one is to accept an interrupted reading and to follow it with an uninterrupted reading; another is to read through a sequence of the notes before reading the annotated sequence in the novel. Perhaps the best compromise would be to skim a sequence of notes, then to read the annotated sequence in the novel with interruptions for consideration of those notes that seem crucial, and then to follow with an uninterrupted reading of the sequence in the novel.

The annotations are designed to be useful on several different levels. The suggestive potential of minor details was, of course, enormously fascinating to Joyce, and the precision of his use of detail is a most important aspect of his literary method. When he was working on the stories that were to form *Dubliners*, Joyce said to his brother Stanislaus:

> Do you see that man who has just skipped out of the way of the tram? Consider, if he had been run over, how significant every act of his would at once become. I don't mean for the police inspector. I mean for anybody who knew him. And his thoughts, for anybody that could know them. It is my idea of the significance of trivial things that I want to give the two or three unfortunate wretches who may eventually read me.[1]

The technical difficulty was how to let the man in fiction skip "out of the way of the tram" and yet give the reader the sense of the "significance of trivial things" consequent on the man's having been "run over." If we are to count ourselves among the "unfortunate wretches," we have to strike a balance between the sense that trivial details are (and should remain) trivial and the sense that they are capable of revelatory metaphoric significance. This balance is difficult to achieve because the excitement of recognizing a significance can so easily make us forget that the man has only figuratively, not literally, been run over by the tram.

Joyce's ideal of artistic detachment makes this striking of a balance even more difficult. Joyce does not point to the significant detail. As readers our attention must be independently informed and focused so that we can catch unstated or understated nuances. The annotations in this volume are thus intended to illuminate and to alert the reader to details that are not necessarily common knowledge. Again, the intention is not to interpret the details or to develop their suggestiveness, but to provide a fac-

1 Quoted from Stanislaus Joyce's *Diary* in Richard Ellmann, *James Joyce*, rev. ed. (New York, 1982), p. 163.

tual point of departure for that interpretation and development.

In a related way the notes should help the reader to understand the perspectives from which the novel's characters and its worlds are to be viewed. On the one hand, for example, Mr. Deasy is dramatized as plausible, if stuffy and square, but he is woefully inaccurate about many details of Irish history, as the notes reveal. And yet these historical lapses should not discredit his relatively sensible approach to the problem of foot-and-mouth disease. The Citizen, on the other hand, is dramatized as an intolerant windbag, and yet, as the notes suggest, much of what he has to say is relevant to Ireland's problems, if in an overstated, violent, and wrongheaded way.

In a more comprehensive sense the notes should help to flesh out Stephen and Bloom and the contexts in which they are trying to find themselves. Stephen's literary ambitions have projected him into an unstable and competitive world, crosshatched with the claims of national self-consciousness and Gaelic revival, with political, moral, and religious prejudice, and with Theosophical mysticism and the apparently contrary impulses of French symbolism, elaborate critical theory, and Ibsenesque naturalism. Ideally, the notes should help to define these conflicting claims and the confusing immediacy they have for Stephen. However, many of the notes bear on Bloom's presence as "distinguished phenomenologist" (12.1822 [343:4]), at the center of the Dublin about which Stephen has "much, much to learn" (7.915 [144:31]). Several commentators have argued that Bloom is badly misinformed, if not ignorant, but the effort to examine his knowledge in detail reveals not an impressive knowledge (or lack thereof) but an impressive curiosity, an appetite for information that has been imperfectly nurtured in the realms of public knowledge (1890–1905) and by the middle-class culture in which he moves.

On another level the notes should help us to perceive more fully the significance of the novel's day (16 June 1904) in the lives of its central characters. Joyce's literary method precluded any overt evaluation of that significance, and it would have been *irrealism* from his point of view to attribute to Stephen or Bloom or Molly a direct access to that significance, quite simply because no individual can see his life in perspective when he is immersed in a day in that life. The analogues to *The Odyssey* provide some clues to significant possibilities of change in the characters' lives, fragments of dream and astrology provide other clues, analogues to Jewish and Christian religious ceremonies and practices still others, and so on. The notes seek to develop these clues, or indicators, as points of departure for a fuller reading of the novel.

In the final analysis the notes will probably suggest minor and local rather than major and comprehensive revisions in established ways of reading and interpreting the novel. But one area of distortion should be guarded against: the notes put considerable emphasis on "street furniture," on the phenomenological presences of Dublin, its real inhabitants and real events; nonetheless, Dublin is a mythical city—a vast concentration of "real" detail adds up to a city that has the presence of a character in a novel, not a city in real life. And as character, Dublin is in its way subject to, but not inevitably destined for, significant and positive change.

Short Titles

A myriad of novels, plays, and poems, and a variety of other books, publications, and reference works are cited in this volume. Many are mentioned only once or a few times, and in these cases a full citation at the appropriate juncture is clear enough. But Joyce is notorious for the range and frequency of the allusions he employs (to Homer, Dante, Shakespeare, Milton, Blake, for example); those I have listed simply by author and title in the text, with appropriate bibliographical information included in the following list. Several works also proved such invaluable resources to me that I refer to them again and again as aids in explaining, filling out, clarifying; others are cited often for purposes of comparison or cross reference. In order to minimize clutter on the page, I have resorted to short-title citations for these works. The following list provides, in the left-hand column, the short title I use in this volume, and in the right-hand column, the corresponding publication information in full:

Adams	Adams, Robert M. *Surface and Symbol* (New York, 1962).
A Portrait	Joyce, James. *A Portrait of the Artist as a Young Man* (New York, 1964).
[Bible]	Authorized King James Version (Oxford, n.d.), unless otherwise specified.
[Blake]	*The Poetry and Prose of William Blake*, ed. David V. Erdman (New York, 1970).

Brandes — Brandes, George. *William Shakespeare* (London, 1898).

CW — Joyce, James. *Critical Writings*, ed. Ellsworth Mason and Richard Ellmann (New York, 1959).

[Dante] — *The Inferno*, ed. and rev. H. Oelsner, trans. John Aitken Carlyle (London, 1937). *The Purgatorio*, ed. H. Oelsner, trans. Thomas Okey (London, 1937). *The Paradiso*, ed. H. Oelsner, trans. Philip H. Wicksteed (London, 1936).

Dubliners — Joyce, James. *Dubliners* (New York, 1969).

Ellmann — Ellmann, Richard. *James Joyce*, rev. ed. (New York, 1982).

Fitzgerald — trans. Fitzgerald, Robert, *The Odyssey* (New York, 1961).

Harris — Harris, Frank. *The Man Shakespeare and His Tragic Life-Story* (New York, 1909).

Hoult — Hoult, Powis. *A Dictionary of Some Theosophical Terms* (London, 1910).

Hyman — Hyman, Louis. *The Jews of Ireland* (Shannon, Ireland, 1972).

JJQ — *James Joyce Quarterly*

Lee — Lee, Sidney. *A Life of William Shakespeare* (London, 1908).

Letters — *Letters of James Joyce*, vol. I, ed. Stuart Gilbert, rev. ed. (New York, 1966); vols. II and III, ed. Richard Ellmann (New York, 1966).

[Milton] — Milton, John. *Complete Poems and Major Prose*, ed. Merritt Y. Hughes (New York, 1957).

Partridge — Partridge, Eric. *A Dictionary of Slang and Unconventional English* (London, 1937).

P. W. Joyce, *English* — Joyce, P. W. *English as We Speak It in Ireland* (London, 1910).

[Shakespeare] — (1) *The Riverside Shakespeare*, ed. G. Blakemore Evans et al. (Boston, 1974). (2) *The Complete Works*, ed. G. B. Harrison (New York, 1952).

Stephen Hero — Joyce, James. *Stephen Hero* (New York, 1963).

Thom's 1904 — *Thom's Official Directory of the United Kingdom of Great Britain and Ireland for the Year 1904* (Dublin, 1904).

Thornton — Thornton, Weldon. *Allusions in "Ulysses"* (Chapel Hill, N.C., 1968).

Ulysses advertises itself as a novel that includes and says it all, yet the experience of annotating the novel and teaching it with the aid of the annotations suggests that often what is not said is central to our experience of the novel. For example, *Ulysses* seems to time itself meticulously by the clock, when in fact it stretches the clock in many ways to place its characters' actions at the intersection of two contrasting orders of literary time.

Likewise, the novel is suffused with Irish political, religious, and social preoccupations and prejudices, but these are nowhere fully stated or deployed. Leopold Bloom, the novel's central character, is Jewish by heritage though not by practice, and he is the outsider, the obvious focus of a constant, for the most part muted, drumfire of anti-Semitism in the course of the day. Not so obvious is that Dublin's anti-Semitism is played against the larger backdrop of the anti-Semitism that was sweeping Europe in the opening decades of this century. A similar observation can be made about the role of women in the novel. Individual women as characters are set against and confined by the position of women in Dublin, that city, as Joyce was fond of saying, on the benighted fringe of Europe. The terms of that confinement are everywhere in the novel by implication but are nowhere explicit.

Money and monetary values are also central to the middle-class world on which Joyce focuses, but the novel's method precludes any direct consideration of the values of money or of the relation of money to individual middle-class lives in that city and at that time.

The intention of the following brief discussions of these matters is therefore pedagogical, as is the intention of the annotations themselves—to help the reader grasp some general issues understated in the novel and therefore treated in a fragmentary way in the specific annotations.

INTRODUCTION

Time in *Ulysses*

The action of Ulysses takes place at the confluence of two orders of literary time: dramatic time and epic time as Aristotle defines them in the *Poetics:* "Tragedy [drama] endeavors, as far as possible, to confine itself to a single revolution of the sun; . . . whereas the Epic action has no limits of time."[1] A modern translator might be inclined to render this passage as applying not to the action imitated but to the time of performance: a drama to be performed in a single day, an epic to be performed over a period of several days.[2] But earlier translators, such as Butcher (a copy of whose translation was in Joyce's Trieste library),[3] assumed Aristotle to mean that drama was to *imitate* the events of a single day, as *Ulysses* does: from 8:00 A.M., 16 June 1904, until sometime during the long summer dawn of 17 June 1904 (sunrise was at 3:33 A.M.). And *Ulysses* enjoys the other unities Aristotle recommended for drama: it has unity of place (Dublin and environs); unity of action (all the action takes place in a single day); and, as good Sophoclean drama, Ulysses has three central characters (Stephen Dedalus, Molly Bloom, and Leopold Bloom) as well as a chorus (of Dubliners) that, as Aristotle said it should, functions collectively as a fourth character.

But the novel's title announces an epic, and Aristotle defines an epic action not as the whole course of a hero's life, because that would lack unity of action, but as the whole course of a major phase in the life. Thus *The Odyssey* traces Odysseus's homecoming from Troy, together with Penelope's faithful waiting and Telemachus's coming of age; in *Ulysses* it is Stephen's coming of age, Bloom's homecoming, Molly's affirmation of her husband, and Dublin (as Ithaca) once more (or for once) properly governed. There is no assurance in *Ulysses* that any of these epic actions are being or will be lived through to completion, but by novel's end we as readers should know what conditions the central characters and the chorus will have to meet if the epic destiny that is "possible" on 16–17 June 1904 is to become "actuality" (*Ulysses* 2.67 [25:35–36]).

In dramatic time, in contrast to the epic's slow development of a phase-in-the-life, the action we anticipate is *peripeteia*, an abrupt or unexpected change that is both revelatory and conclusive. Thus, the action in Sophocles' *Oedipus Rex* is the discovery in the course of one day that Oedipus is the contaminator of Thebes, the

man destined by the gods to kill his own father and to marry and have children by his mother. In the *peripeteia* of drama the entire course of Oedipus's life is abruptly reviewed and changed in a single day, in contrast to the gradual narrative process of *The Odyssey*.

As in a good epic, *Ulysses* begins *in medias res* and fills us in on Stephen's life since the end of *A Portrait of the Artist as a Young Man* by flashback; and by the flashback of memory we are given the story of Molly's and Bloom's lives.[4] *The Odyssey* similarly begins less than three weeks before Odysseus lands on Ithaca, and coils back to tell the story of the years since the departure from Troy before moving forward into the events that take place after Odysseus's arrival on Ithaca. But, as in drama, the action of *Ulysses* stays *in medias res*, in the present tense of one day rather than in a succession of days: to the characters, this is only a day-in-the-life, exceptional in more or less trivial ways as all days are, but not all that different from yesterday and tomorrow. Only we as readers know that the characters are both acting in the dramatic time of a play, complete with *peripeteia*, and, by implication rather than by action, completing a major phase of their lives in the narrative medium of epic time. So while we judge significance in relation to our expectations of dramatic and epic time, the characters move in what might be called mimetic time: various imitations of time, a rich mix of clock time, psychological time, and mnemonic time.

As for clock time, *Ulysses* implies throughout that we ought to be able to clock this day with some precision; but that turns out not to be consistently the case. Nor did Joyce help matters when he suggested differing timetables in the two extant schemas, the one he sent to Carlo Linati in 1920[5] and the one he provided Jacques Benoîst-Méchin in 1921 (published by Stuart Gilbert in 1931).[6] For example, Joyce told Linati that the Lotus-Eaters episode begins at 9:00 A.M.; the other schema gives the time as 10:00 A.M. In either case all of Bloom's activities from the beginning of the hour on Sir John Rogerson's Quay until he exits from the church (5.1–461 [pp. 71–84]) take place in fifteen minutes; Bloom reflects that it's "Quarter past" (5.462 [84:2]) and that he still has time for a

1 S. H. Butcher, *Aristotle's Theory of Poetry and Fine Art with a Critical Text and Translation of the Poetics* (London, 1907), p. 23.

2 Gerald F. Else, *Aristotle, "Poetics"* (Ann Arbor, Mich., 1967), pp. 24–25.

3 Richard Ellmann, *The Consciousness of Joyce* (New York, 1977), p. 99; Joyce used the edition cited in n. 2 above.

4 John Henry Raleigh, *The Chronicle of Leopold and Molly Bloom: "Ulysses" as Narrative* (Berkeley, Calif., 1977).

5 Richard Ellmann, *Ulysses on the Liffey* (New York, 1972), Appendix pp. 186ff.

6 Stuart Gilbert, *James Joyce's "Ulysses,"* rev. ed. (New York, 1952).

bath before the funeral at 11:00 A.M. Bloom's circuitous route from the quayside to the chemist's shop would have taken at least fifteen minutes and would have left no time at all for his pause in church. And after midnight 16–17 June 1904, clock time becomes less and less certain. Midnight strikes just after Bloom arrives at Bella Cohen's brothel (15.1362 [478:16]), and by 16.1603–4 (657:20–21) it's "getting on for one," after an extraordinarily active two hundred pages, or 5,208 lines of text in the Critical Edition.

If the Ithaca episode begins at 2:00 A.M., as the Gilbert schema says, then Stephen and Bloom must part at 2:30-plus. Bloom, left alone, is aware of "the incipient intimations of proximate dawn" (17.1247–48 [704:30]). Sunrise in Dublin on 17 June 1904 was at 3:33 A.M., so, depending on the cloud cover, daylight would have begun to gray things as early as 2:00 A.M. Would it help to move Circe, Eumaeus, and Ithaca back an hour, as the Linati schema does, relocating Ithaca at 1:00 A.M.? That would ease the timetable from the beginning of Ithaca to firstlight to sunrise and almost make it believable that Molly hears the chimes of "George's church" ring "2 oclock" (18.1231–32 [772:27–28]), but it would incredibly clog the hours from 11:00 P.M. to 1:00 A.M.

If elaborate efforts to establish accurate timetables tend to falter, they also tend to mislead our attention as readers and distract us from the variety of ways Joyce imitates time. We are all aware, for example, that we can think and perceive far more in the course of a few minutes of multi-leveled consciousness than we could spell out in words in as many hours. Joyce variously explores that disparity. At 8.481 (164:23) Bloom reflects that it is "five minutes" since he fed the birds from O'Connell Bridge, and it *is* a five-minute stroll from the bridge to the front of Trinity College where Bloom is, but he feeds the birds at 8.75–76 (153:7–8), a good twenty-minute read away. Twenty minutes of prose time is being manipulated to imitate five minutes of half-formed thought-perception time, thought-perception that could be verbalized but usually is not.

There are even more radical experiments with the disparities between clock time, psychological time, and the imitation of time in the Circe and Penelope episodes. Because the Circe episode is cast in the form of a play with speeches and stage directions, we assume that reading time is approximately equal to playing time. But the reverse is the case: there is a radical disparity between reading time and playing time. For example, the hallucination at 15.1354–1956 (pp. 478–99), which we associate with Bloom, actually takes place between the two halves of Zoe's speech: "Go on. Make a stump speech out of it. . . . Talk away till you're black in the face." And again at 15.2750 (527:10), Bella Cohen, the whoremistress, enters with the line, "My word! I'm all of a mucksweat," and continues at 15.3500 (555:2–3), "Which of you was playing the dead march from *Saul*?" The implication is that the hallucinations we associate with Bloom are acted out not for his witness but for ours; what are mere blips on the screen of his consciousness are dramatized and spelled out for us. Psychoanalysts I have consulted about Bloom's hallucinations say that the ones we associate with him would unfold not in the course of one night's dreams, but over a period of about two years for the average patient undergoing analysis. In other words, the hallucinations last only a moment in dramatic time but are spelled out in a dramatic imitation of epic time, the two years or so of this phase-in-the-life.

In the Penelope episode the prose seems to imitate the way Molly might mutter to herself. Read aloud, the duration of the episode is three hours. Is that the order of time Joyce is imitating? Or is the muttering voice of the prose in turn imitating the foreshortened time and kaleidoscopic scatter of image we experience in brief spells of insomnia, an hour or less by the clock? I suspect that the Penelope episode's time is more like the time of hallucination and drama in Circe than it is like the time of a voice overheard and, therefore, that Molly's soliloquy belongs at once in the dramatic and the epic dimensions of time.

Ulysses and Its Times

The outstanding political issues of the time for Dublin and Ireland were land reform and Home Rule. In 1904 land reform was still being resisted by landlords with big holdings, and the peasant-tenants on many estates were still living and laboring in grinding poverty; but in terms of legislation and practice, land reform was at least getting under way. From Joyce's urban point of view the real issue was Home Rule. In 1800 a quasi-independent Irish Parliament had been pressured and bribed by the English into passing the Act of Union and in so doing had dissolved itself and been absorbed into the English Parliament at Westminster. The results were an Ireland ruled politically all-but-directly from London; an Irish economy dominated by absentee landlords who had followed the center of power from Dublin to London; and a century of constitutional agitation and sporadic violence in Ireland for repeal of the Act of Union and for the establishment of an independent Irish parliamentary government.

In the 1880s, under the forceful leadership of Charles Stewart Parnell (1846–91), a nationalist majority of the Irish members of Parliament achieved a well-coordinated coalition that held the balance of power between the Liberal and Conservative (Tory) parties at Westminster. In 1886 Parnell exploited this position to the verge of passage of a Home Rule Bill, a near-miss that, for most Irish, seemed to promise eventual success for constitutional achievement of Home Rule. But Parnell's extraordinary power to unify dissolved in controversy in December 1890, when his ten-year liaison with Katherine O'Shea was revealed in the divorce action brought by her husband, Capt. William Henry O'Shea. Parnell's career was abruptly ruined, and his increasingly strident efforts to recoup ruined his already precarious health. With Parnell's collapse came the Great Split among Irish nationalists and the end of anything resembling unity and accord in Irish politics. John Redmond (1856–1918) emerged from the wreckage as titular leader of the nationalists, but by 1904 he had achieved little more than a semblance of unity in his party, and what many, including Joyce, called the "betrayal" of Parnell continued to haunt that age of splinter-group politics in Ireland.

One of the most important factors in the collapse of Parnell's career (and in the social and political scene of all Ireland) was the Irish Roman Catholic church. Church leaders remained quiet during the divorce trial so as not to appear to be interfering in politics, but once the trial was over and the Great Split had taken place, they were unrelenting in their denunciation of Parnell. The result was a bitter divisiveness in the Catholic community (90 percent of the Irish) that compounded the political dissension. (See *A Portrait of the Artist as a Young Man*, chapter 1:C [the Christmas dinner], for a capsule dramatization of that bitterness and its potential for violence.)

In 1904 the Protestant Anglo-Irish minority (10 percent) was economically and politically dominant and profoundly conservative and defensive. The Catholic majority was in its contrasting way equally conservative—puritanical and censorious—and defensive in ways one does not expect of a 90 percent majority. The result was a bewildering maze of prejudice and intolerance, which was intensified by the infiltration into Dublin of growing continental prejudice against the Jews. That prejudice, although far less virulent in 1904 Ireland than in Germany, France, and Russia, emerges as a major theme in *Ulysses*.

According to the *Oxford English Dictionary*, the terms *anti-Semitic* and *anti-Semite* first appeared in English in a note entitled "Our Library Table" in *The Athenaeum* (London, 3 September 1881):

> Anti-Semitic literature is very prosperous in Germany; there scarcely passes a week without another production on the matter, *pro* or *contra*, without, however, new results for history. But we are glad to mention that at last a serious book has appeared on the present condition of the Jews and their statistics by Herr Richard Andree. . . . The author, apparently an anti-Semite, has honestly collected second-hand information concerning Jews in all countries, which may be usefully consulted since the sources are indicated in the footnotes.

The terms were first coined in German in 1879–80 by the pamphleteer Wilhelm Marr, whose pamphlet *Der Sieg des Judenthums über das Germanenthum* (The Victory of Judaism over Germanism) (Bern, February 1879) was the "first anti-Semitic best-seller."[7] Marr argued that Jews in Germany had already taken over the press, they had become "dictators of the financial system," and they were on the verge of taking over the legislature and the judiciary. These accusations were not original with Marr, nor was his pamphlet a cause so much as a symptom of the stridency and cruelty of anti-Jewish hysteria in late-nineteenth-century Germany and Europe.

In Russia, in the aftermath of the Russo-Turkish War (1877–79), several reactionary newspapers waged a virulent anti-Jewish campaign, and anti-Jewish rioting broke out in the south in 1879–80. The Procurator of the Holy Synod joined the campaign in 1880, and the blood libel (that Jews used the sacrificial blood of a Christian—preferably a child—in the celebration of Passover) was revived (see 6.771–72n). When the relatively liberal Czar Alexander II (1818–81; czar 1855–81) was assassinated in 1881, cruel oppression of the Jews and widespread pogroms became government policy. What Harold Frederic (1856–98) called the

---

7 Jacob Katz, *From Prejudice to Destruction: Anti-Semitism, 1700–1933* (Cambridge, Mass., 1980), p. 260.

"New Exodus" began:[8] within a single generation some 2.5 million eastern European Jews were forced to seek new homes overseas.

German propaganda and Russian cruelty soon infected the Austro-Hungarian Empire and, with the violent public controversy over the Dreyfus case (1894–1906),[9] France. Even England, although it carried on its tradition of tolerance and offered sanctuary to many of those displaced in the New Exodus, was infected— witness Haines's remark in the first episode of *Ulysses:* "I don't want to see my country fall into the hands of German jews either" (1.666–67 [21:20–21]).

In the irony of retrospect, this new wave of persecution began only a few decades after the Jews had achieved considerable legal, political, and economic emancipation in western Europe and, to a surprising extent, even in Russia. And it differed from past waves in that it involved not only a reinvigoration of the old Christian prejudice against the Jews[10] but also the new "patriotic" prejudice of the modern nation- state; the Jews now represented the threat of international conspiracy within the "Christian" nation-state's borders. That prejudice was to go supranational in the "Protocols of the Elders of Zion," supposedly the protocols of a Jewish conspiracy aimed at an international power- grab but in fact a 1905 forgery by Russian secret police in Paris for home consumption at the court of a czar who was perceived as "soft on Jews." The protocols did not turn up in western Europe until 1918–19 (see 15.249n).

The shift in the 1880s from the term *anti- Jewish* to the term *anti-Semitic* was a foretaste of just how sinister this new wave of persecution was to become. The term *Jewish* means a people with a specifically religious identity, if dispersed among many nations. The idea of religious com- mitment and belief thus implies the possibility of change and reform, including renewal of faith and new idealism. *Semitic* (which refers to the ancient Babylonians, Assyrians, and Phoeni- cians as well as Arabs and Jews) suggests instead a racial identity—complete with the nine- teenth-century assumption that each race had biologically innate characteristics that dictated a predetermined racial superiority, mediocrity, or inferiority. The biology of race held that in- dividuals could behave variously, but only in very limited ways because racial characteristics (what we would call stereotypes), while they could be controlled or held in check, could never be eradicated.

Anti-Jewish prejudice in Great Britain and Ireland was not nearly as virulent as on the Con- tinent, but it was certainly alive and well at the beginning of this century, in the stereotypes of the Jew as anti-Christian and as cupidity per- sonified and in vituperative language and derog- atory epithets, such as sheeny and Jewboy in England and Jewman in Ireland. And there was an abundance of caricature imagery, from Dick- ens's Fagan in *Oliver Twist* to Ikey Moses in *Ally Sloper's Half-Holiday*, a London illustrated weekly (see 9:607n).

As a result of the New Exodus from eastern Europe, "the number of Jews in England, esti- mated in 1880 at 65,000, more than trebled by 1905,"[11] amounting to approximately 0.6 per- cent of the population of England. In Ireland the Jewish population increased about eight- fold, from 472 in 1881 to 3,769 in 1901,[12] but the 3,769 amounted to only 0.08 percent of the population of Ireland.

In 1906 Edward Raphael Lipsett, a Jew re- siding in Dublin, published his impressions of what it was to be Jewish in Ireland at the begin- ning of this century:

> You cannot get one native to remember that a Jew may be an Irishman. The term "Irish Jew" seems to have a contradic- tory ring upon the native ear; the idea is wholly inconceivable to the native mind. . . . Irish Jews feel that if they spoke of each other as Jewish Irishmen,

---

8 Harold Frederic, *The New Exodus: A Study of Israel in Russia* (New York, 1892). The book was forceful enough that Frederic was banned as *persona non grata* in Russia, and since Frederic was the Lon- don correspondent for the *New York Times*, the ban was extended to all of that newspaper's reporters.

9 Alfred Dreyfus (1859–1935), a Jewish officer in the French army, was arrested in October 1894 on charges of conveying military secrets to a foreign power. He was tried in secret and convicted on the basis of evidence that proved ultimately to have been forged. Retried in 1899 by court-martial, he was again (and somewhat evasively) found guilty. Dreyfus was finally declared innocent and vindicated in 1906, but an abiding, and well-founded, suspicion of anti- Semitism in the military and in the government was not that readily allayed.

10 Martin Luther's accusations, although wild, were more or less typical of his time and were shared alike by western Catholicism and Russian orthodoxy: that Jews were guilty of the "blood libel," of desecrat- ing the host, and of sucking the teats of sows. Mr. Deasy's summary dismissal of the Jews in *Ulysses* is that accusation drawn mild: "They sinned against the light" (2.361 [34:3]).

---

11 Cecil Roth, *A History of the Jews in England* (Oxford, 1964), p. 270.

12 Louis Hyman, *The Jews of Ireland: From the Earliest Times to the Year 1910* (Shannon, Republic of Ireland, 1972), p. 160.

it would meet with a cutting cynicism from the natives that the two elements can never merge into one for any single purpose. . . . The Jews understand the Irish little; the Irish understand the Jews less. Each seems a peculiar race in the eyes of the other; and, in a word, the position of Jews in Ireland is peculiarly peculiar.[13]

Louis Hyman prefaces this quotation from Lipsett with the remark: "The mere concept of the Irish Jew raised a laugh in the Ireland of Joyce's day"; and he sums up: "Lipsett's impressions may have truly represented the situation of Jews in the unsympathetic social climate of Ireland at the turn of the century, at best grudgingly neutral to them and at worst openly hostile."[14]

The want of sympathy in that social climate extended in less overt but no less demeaning ways to women. Dublin and Ireland were dominated by the cult of the aggressive and competitive male—a dominion both sustained and dramatized by a pub culture that was essentially *for men only*.[15] Women had little place in the public and political life of the city, and the exceptions, such as Lady Augusta Gregory and Maud Gonne, were upper-class exceptions who proved the rule. If Dublin women did take to the streets in political protest, it was not to fight for votes for women and women's rights as their London sisters were doing, but for Home Rule for Ireland.

A middle-class woman's horizons in Dublin at the beginning of this century were severely limited. Apart from marriage or a convent there were precious few careers open to her, and some of those, such as clerking in a shop or going into domestic service, implied a loss of social status. If she were skilled, dressmaking and millinery were open to her. With some vocational schooling (a relatively new idea), she might become a typist, a stenographer, or even (though rarely) a secretary. If educated, she could seek employment as a governess, companion, or teacher, but one statistic reveals how very limited that alternative apparently was: of the 3,409 students enrolled in colleges and universities in Ireland in 1901, only 91 (2.66 percent) were women. Molly thought that it would be a good idea for Milly to attend Skerry's "shorthand, typewriting, and commercial college" (see 18.1006n) instead of being apprenticed to a photographer as Bloom insisted. And yet Milly's career as photographer, following in the footsteps of her grandfather's cousin, would have made her unique among young women in Ireland.

Marriage itself was by no means something that could be expected in due course. After the Great Famine of the 1840s the population of Ireland declined, and it continued to decline well into the twentieth century. The birth and marriage rates declined, and the average age at which people married rose into the mid-thirties. In 1901 more than 80 percent of men between twenty-five and thirty years of age and more than 60 percent between thirty and thirty-five were unmarried; of the women of marriageable age in the population (fifteen years of age and older), 52.7 percent were unmarried, 37.7 percent were married, and 9.6 percent were widowed. The percentage of unmarried increased from 47.7 percent in 1881 to 50.8 percent in 1891, and to 52.7 percent in 1901.[16] These are very high rates, and they mean that young women like Gerty MacDowell could have little hope—or even consolation, unless one regards a twenty-two-year-old woman's daydreams of romance with a sixteen-year-old boy (she a Catholic and he a Protestant in *that* Ireland) as some consolation.

For most women the only alternative was some form of dependency: in a convent, in the homes of parents or near relatives. Even if employed, women were generally regarded as "temporary employees" and were not paid wages that would enable them to be self-supporting, on the assumption that they would live at home and contribute to the family purse.

A Note on Monetary Values[17]

Joyce uses monetary values (among other incidental "hard facts") as indicators of and clues to

---

13 Quoted in ibid., p. 176.

14 Ibid, p. 176.

15 The pub as *mise-en-scène* is everywhere in *Ulysses:* Davy Byrne's in Lestrygonians, the bar of the Ormond Hotel in Sirens, Barney Kiernan's in Cyclops, and Burke's at the end of Oxen of the Sun. These are all but matched as pub environments by the carriage in Dignam's funeral procession (no women at the funeral?), by the newspaper office in Aeolus, by the librarian's office in Scylla and Charybdis, by the residents' and interns' commons room in the National Maternity Hospital in Oxen of the Sun, and by the cabman's shelter in Eumaeus. Even the brothel in Circe seems to enjoy its version of pub atmosphere.

16 "Statistics of Ireland," in *Thom's Official Directory of the United Kingdom of Great Britain and Ireland for the Year 1904* (Dublin, 1904), p. 688.

17 The pound (£) is still the basic monetary unit of the United Kingdom and the Republic of Ireland,

his characters' attitudes and status. Since Joyce's technique dictates that he withhold evaluatory comment, these clues can easily be overlooked or misinterpreted. The value of money in 1904 Ireland (or in any country foreign in space and time) presents difficult problems for the reader. Stephen, for example, receives a monthly salary of three pounds, twelve shillings (£3 12s.; 2.221 [30:6]). A direct and rough approach to translation would suggest that in 1904 the dollar was worth at least five times what it is worth in 1985; thus, the pound, worth $5 in 1904, would be worth $25 in 1985, and so Stephen's monthly wage would amount to $90. The school does not provide Stephen with bed and board, so in those terms $90 implies a grinding poverty. However, a somewhat different line of calculating exchange rates leads to quite different answers. *Thom's Official Directory of the United Kingdom of Great Britain and Ireland* (Dublin, 1904), p. 1345, lists the Dublin market prices of four Irish staples: bacon, bread, potatoes, and oatmeal.[18] A comparison of those 1904 prices with today's prices gives the British penny (1904) the buying power of about 45¢ (U.S., 1985). In these terms Stephen's salary translates into a respectable, if modest, $388.80.

But the relation of money to everyday life was quite different in 1904 Dublin from what it is in the United States in 1985. Dubliners then did not face the range and variety of consumer goods or the pressures to spend that so influence the meaning of money in 1985. In effect, staples were much closer to the backbone of a family budget in 1904 than that vague yardstick, "standard of living" (with its central heating and air-conditioning, automobiles, household appliances, leisure expenses, vacations, and so on), implies in 1985.

This suggests that Stephen could live quite comfortably within his income. It also suggests that his behavior with money is not mildly but wildly prodigal on 16–17 June 1904. He sets out with £3 12s., and at the end of his day of pub crawling Bloom returns £1 7s. to him from safekeeping (17.1475 [711:33]). This does not count the half-crowns (2s. 6d.) Stephen discovers in his pocket (16.191–94 [618:11–14]), one of which he lends to Corley. Assuming he had two half-crowns left (5s.), he ends the day having spent roughly £2, or, using the price of staples as a measure of exchange, over $200 (1985). Considered in this way, the evidence relates strikingly to Stephen's larger financial dilemma: his total indebtedness, not including "five weeks' board" (2.255–59 [31:1–5]), amounts to £25 17s. 6d.—in other words, he owes a bit more than he could earn in seven months.

Bloom's financial situation also undergoes a significant change if we view it in a similar manner. Bloom's Dublin contemporaries are dubious about his financial state, and as readers we might accept their doubts if we neglected the evidence given in the novel and if we undervalue the currency. In the financial terms of his time, Bloom enjoys a relatively secure, though of course not affluent, position in the middle class. He has savings of £18 14s. 6d. (17.1863 [723:10]), more than five times Stephen's monthly wage and, since Bloom's house is valued at an annual rent of £28, sufficient to pay his monthly rent for at least eight months. In terms of the relative value of staples, Bloom's 1904 savings would be worth about $2,000 in 1985; his rent, about $250 per month. Bloom receives a commission from the *Freeman's Journal* for £1 7s. 6d.—more than half a month's rent and roughly equivalent to $150. His endowment insurance policy will be worth £500 ($53,000 in staples?) when it matures. His stock holdings have a face value of £900 ($95,580?) and would give him an annual income of £36 ($3,825). Inevitably distorted as they are, these figures do not suggest that Bloom is financially insecure, but that he is at least holding his own.

To hold one's own was no mean feat in the Dublin middle-class world of 1904. One serious side effect of British economic (in effect, anti-industrial) policy for Ireland was the economic disenfranchisement of the Irish middle class.

---

but the units that make up the pound have been changed in both countries. In 1904 twelve pence (12d.) made a shilling (1s.); twenty shillings, a pound. In 1904 fashionable shops and services quoted their prices in guineas (now discontinued): a guinea was £1 1s. or 21s.

18 Bacon was 7d. (sevenpence) a pound in Dublin, 1904; a comparable lean or Canadian bacon in the United States (1985) would be at least $3.00 a pound, making the British penny (d.) worth 43¢. Bread, 5½d. for a four-pound loaf in 1904; U.S. 1985, $2.36: d. = 43¢. Potatoes, .36d. per pound in 1904; U.S. 1985, 25¢: d. = 69¢. Oatmeal, 1.8d. per pound in 1904; U.S. 1985, 39¢: d = 22¢. Average: one penny (1904) = 44.25¢ (1985); or one shilling (1904) = $5.31 (1985); or one pound sterling (1904) = $106.20 (1985). These figures may seem way out of line; yet even when we adjust them by recognizing that food was heavily subsidized in the United Kingdom of Great Britain and Ireland in 1904, we still have to take into account a profound change in monetary values (as well as in the meaning of money) in the last eighty years.

Outside of the church, law, medicine, civil service, and merchandising, there was precious little employment for members of the middle class, and the number of Bloom's contemporaries who are on their way down (and out) in the novel is not only testimony to Joyce's disaffection with middle-class Dublin, it is also a function of the hard realities that were the conditions of that Dublin world.

Don Gifford

WILLIAMSTOWN, MASSACHUSETTS
1 JUNE 1985

PART I

The Telemachiad

(1.1–3.505, PP. 2–51)

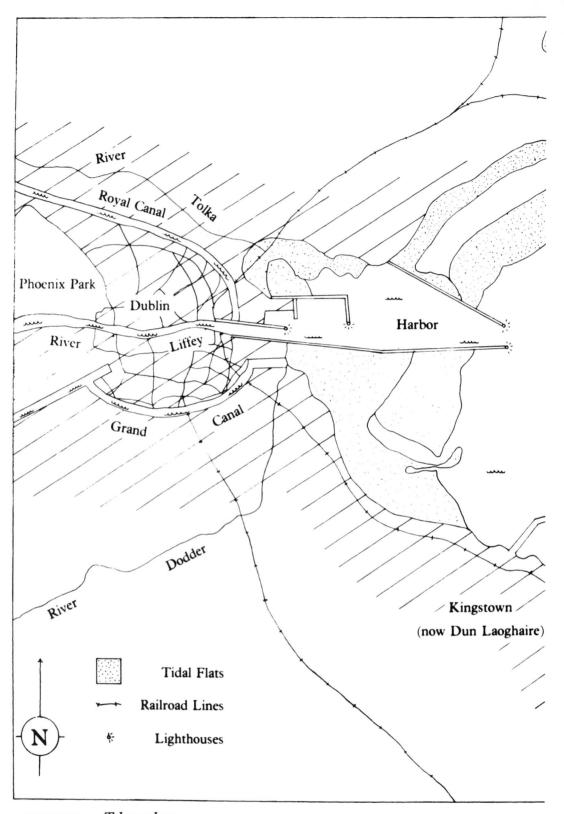

River

Royal Canal

Tolka

Phoenix Park

Dublin

River

Liffey

Harbor

Grand

Canal

Dodder

River

Kingstown
(now Dun Laoghaire)

Tidal Flats

Railroad Lines

Lighthouses

N

EPISODE I. *Telemachus*

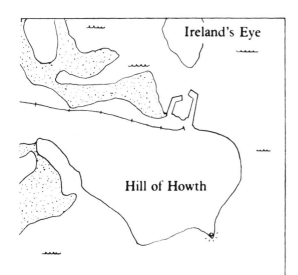

Ireland's Eye

Hill of Howth

Dublin Bay

Kingstown Harbor

East Pier

Martello Tower
The Forty Foot

Bullock Harbor

Maiden's Rock
Sandycove   The Muglins

Dalkey   Dalkey Island

EPISODE I

Telemachus

(1.1–1.744, PP. 2–23)

Episode 1: *Telemachus,* 1.1–1.744 (2–23). Book 1 of *The Odyssey* opens with an invocation of the muse, followed by an account of a council of the gods on Olympus at which Zeus decides that it is time for Odysseus to return home. The scene then shifts to Ithaca, where we find Telemachus, Odysseus's son, "a boy, daydreaming" of his father's return (1:115; Fitzgerald, p. 17).[1] He is unhappy, threatened with betrayal and displacement by the suitors who have collected around his mother, Penelope, during his father's absence. These arrogant men, led by Antinous (whose name means "antimind") and Eurymachos ("wide fighter"), mock the omens sent by Zeus, going so far as to plot Telemachus's death and to boast that they will kill Odysseus should he return alone. (See headnote to Ithaca, p. 566.)

In the council on Olympus, Pallas Athena (the goddess of the arts of war and peace, of domestic economy, and of human wit and intuition) is revealed as Odysseus's patron. In Book 1 she appears to Telemachus disguised as Mentes, king of Taphos and an old friend of the family, and advises him to assert his independence of his mother and journey to the mainland in search of news of his father. In Book 2, now disguised as Mentor, the guardian of Odysseus's house and slaves during his absence, Athena encourages Telemachus and helps him find ship and crew for the voyage to the mainland.

According to the schema that Joyce gave to Stuart Gilbert,[2] the Time is 8:00 A.M., Thursday, 16 June 1904. Scene: a Martello tower at Sandycove, on the shore of Dublin Bay seven miles southeast of the center of Dublin. Organ:

none; Art: theology; Colors: white, gold; Symbol: heir; Technique: narrative (young). Correspondences: *Telemachus, Hamlet*–Stephen; *Antinous* [and, by implication, Hamlet's uncle, *Claudius*]–Mulligan; *Mentor*–the milkwoman.

Another, and somewhat different, schema, which Joyce gave to Carlo Linati, lists as Symbols: Hamlet, Ireland, and Stephen; and under Persons (without identifying Correspondences) adds: Mentor, bracketed with Pallas [Athena], the Suitors, and Penelope [Muse].

S, the initial letter of Part I, is Stephen Dedalus's initial; as the initial letter of Part II, *M* (4.1[p. 54]) is Molly Bloom's; and *P,* the initial letter of Part III (16.1[p. 612]), is Poldy's (Leopold Bloom's). The initial letters thus suggest the central character in each of the three parts—Stephen self-preoccupied in Part I; Bloom preoccupied with Molly in Part II; and both Molly and Stephen preoccupied with Bloom in Part III.

S, M, and *P* are also conventional signs for the three terms of a syllogism: *S,* subject; *M,* middle; *P,* predicate. While the three terms do not necessarily appear in the same sequence in all syllogisms, medieval pedagogy regarded the sequence *S-M-P* as the cognitive order of thought and therefore as the order in which the terms should initially be taught. Medieval pedagogy also established an initial order for the syllogism's three propositions: Proposition 1 would combine terms *M* and *P;* Proposition 2 would combine terms *S* and *M;* Proposition 3 (the conclusion) would combine terms *S* and *P.* *S* and *P* are subject and predicate of the conclusion-to-be but not necessarily the subject and predicate of the propositions themselves. *M,* the middle term, drops out when the conclusion is formed. In the original edition of *Ulysses* (restored in the Critical Edition) there was a large black dot or period at the end of Episode 17 (17.2331[p. 737]). A dot or period is a conventional sign for Q.E.D. (*quod erat demonstrandum,* Latin: "which was to be proved"). The analogue of the syllogism (as the overall analogue to *The Odyssey*) suggests a logical and narrative structure, which the reader can grasp but of which the characters in the fiction are essentially unaware.

1.2 (3:1). bowl – The bowl will become the chalice in the mockery of the Mass[3] in the scene

---

1 The numbers 1:115 refer to book and line numbers in the Greek text of *The Odyssey;* English translations (unless otherwise noted) are from *The Odyssey,* trans. Robert Fitzgerald (New York, 1961).

2 Joyce produced two schemas for his novel and in effect had them published through the good offices of friends who were also commentators and critics. The first schema was sent to Carlo Linati in September 1920; the second was loaned to Valery Larbaud late in 1921 and circulated (somewhat secretly) by Sylvia Beach during the 1920s. The second schema was first published in part in Stuart Gilbert's *James Joyce's "Ulysses"* (New York, 1930; revised, 1952) and finally published in full, edited by H. K. Croessmann, in *James Joyce Miscellany,* 2d ser., ed. Marvin Magalaner (Carbondale, Ill., 1959). The headnotes to the episodes in this volume summarize this second schema and introduce variants from the Linati schema where appropriate. For a complete outline of the Linati schema, see the appendix to Richard Ellmann, *Ulysses on the Liffey* (New York, 1972), pp. 186ff.

3 On the meaning of the ceremonies of the Mass, the *Layman's Missal* (Baltimore, Md., 1962) remarks: "At the heart of every Mass there occurs the account

that follows (as the "stairhead" becomes the altar steps). The chalice contains wine, which in the ceremony of the Mass becomes the blood of Christ.

1.2 (3:2). razor – The sign of the slaughterer, the priest as butcher. See 9.1048–50n.

1.2 (3:2). yellow – 16 June is the feast day of St. John Francis Regis (1597–1640), a little-known French saint much venerated in the south of France. Since it is the feast day of a confessor, the appropriate vestments for the Mass are white with gold optional.[4] But the gold of liturgical vestments is not a yellow fabric but cloth of gold, a fabric woven wholly or in part with threads of gold. Liturgically, the color yellow has many negative connotations: "Yellow is sometimes used to suggest infernal light, degradation, jealousy, treason, and deceit. Thus, the traitor Judas is frequently painted in a garment of dingy yellow. In the Middle Ages heretics were obliged to wear yellow" (George Ferguson, *Signs and Symbols in Christian Art* [New

___

of the Last Supper, because every Mass renews the sacramental mystery then given to the human race as a legacy until the end of time: 'Do this in memory of me.' The liturgical rites which constitute the celebration of Mass—taking bread (offertory), giving thanks (preface and canon), breaking the bread and distributing it in communion—reproduce the very actions of Jesus. The Mass is an act in which the mystery of Christ is not just commemorated, but made present, living over again. God makes use of it afresh to give Himself to man; and man can use it to give glory to God through the one single sacrifice of Christ. In the missal there are certain central pages used over and over again in practically the same way at every Mass, and therefore they are called the 'ordinary' of the Mass."

Around the core of the ordinary the ceremonies of the Mass vary in accordance with the different phases of the liturgical year; thus, there are sequences of masses for the yearly anniversaries of "Christ in His Mysteries" and "Christ in His Saints," as well as votive masses, masses for the sick and for the dead, and various local masses for special feast days.

4 The outer vestments of the priest have distinctive colors symbolically related to the feast being celebrated: *white*, for Easter and Christmas seasons and for feasts of the Trinity, Christ, the Virgin Mary, and angels and saints who are not martyrs; *red*, for Pentecost and for feasts of the cross and of martyrs; *violet*, for Advent, Lent, and other penitential occasions (*rose* is occasionally substituted for violet); *green* is used at times when there is no particular season of feasts; *gold* can substitute for white, red, or green; and *black* is the color for Good Friday and for the liturgy of the dead.

York, 1954], p. 153; cited by Joan Glasser Keenan).[5]

1.3 (3:3). ungirdled – When a priest celebrates Mass, the alb, the long white linen robe with tapered sleeves that he wears, is secured by a girdle, a narrow band ending in tassels. "Ungirdled" suggests violation of the priestly vow of chastity; see 15.4689–90n and 15.4691–93n.

1.5 (3:5). *Introibo ad altare Dei* – Latin, from Psalms 43:4 (Vulgate 42:4): "I will go up to God's altar." The Latin is what the celebrant used to say in the opening phase (the entrance and preparatory prayers, "Prayers at the Foot of the Altar") of the Mass. The minister or server responds, "Ad Deum qui laetificat juventutem meam" (To God who giveth joy to my youth); cf. 15.122–23n. In the biblical context of the Introit, the psalmist prays to be delivered from the oppression and affliction of his enemies and to be restored to the temple and altar of God. Stephen reluctantly plays the part of server to Mulligan as celebrant in the mockery of the Mass that follows. Also, the invocation of God is a mocking reminder that epics conventionally begin (as *The Odyssey* does) with an invocation of the Muse, "daughter of Zeus" at 1:10 (Fitzgerald, p. 13).

1.8 (3:8). Kinch – After *kinchin*, or child (William York Tyndall, *A Reader's Guide to James Joyce* [New York, 1959], p. 139); or "in imitation of the cutting sound of a knife" (Ellmann, p. 131). In an essay, "James Joyce: A Portrait of the Artist," Oliver St. John Gogarty remarks, "Kinch calls me 'Malachi Mulligan.' . . . 'Mulligan' is stage Irish for me and the rest of us. It is meant to make me absurd. I don't resent it, for he takes 'Kinch'—'Lynch' with the Joyces of Galway, which is far worse" (In *Mourning Became Mrs. Spendlove* [New York, 1948], p. 52).

1.8 (3:8). jesuit – The Jesuits, members of the Society of Jesus, a religious order of the Roman Catholic church, were noted for their uncompromising intellectual rigor (and hence were popularly regarded as "fearful" in their seriousness).

1.9 (3:9). gunrest – A raised circular platform in the center of the tower's flat roof, once used as a swivel-gun mount.

___

5 This and subsequent suggestions from Joan Keenan derive from an extensive correspondence during Fall and Winter 1983–84.

1.19 (3:20). Back to barracks – The military command sometimes used to dismiss troops after a parade, in this case morning parade, when troops are assembled and accounted for at the beginning of the day.

1.21 (3:22). *for this . . . genuine christine – A parody of Jesus' words to his disciples at the Last Supper (Matthew 26:26–28): "And as they were eating, Jesus took bread, and blessed it, and brake it, and gave it to the disciples, and said, Take, eat; this is my body. And he took the cup, and gave thanks, and gave it to them, saying, Drink ye all of it; for this is my blood of the new testament, which is shed for many for the remission of sins." Jesus' words are recited in the canon of the Mass as the host is consecrated. "Christine," the Eucharist, feminine here, is Mulligan's joking allusion to the Black Mass, which is irreverently celebrated with a woman's body as altar. See 15.4688–4781 (pp. 599–600).

1.22 (3:23). blood and ouns – An abbreviation of "God's blood and wounds," a blasphemous oath from the late Middle Ages.

1.23 (3:24–25). trouble . . . white corpuscles – Mulligan, in mocking scientism, alludes to the process of transubstantiation when the wine is transformed into the blood of Christ in the mystery of the Mass.

1.26 (3:28). Chrysostomos – Mulligan's gold-capped teeth suggest the Greek epithet "golden-mouthed," after the Greek rhetorician Dion Chrysostomos (c. 50–c. 117) and St. John Chrysostomos (c. 345–407), patriarch of Constantinople and one of the Fathers of the early Church. Joan Keenan points out that a passage from the sermons of St. John Chrysostomos would have been included in the Mass for this feast day (*The Roman Breviary*, trans. John, marquess of Bute [Edinburgh, 1908], vol. 3, p. 457). Hugh Kenner (*Ulysses* [London, 1980], p. 35) says that the pope who sent the "English mission" was called in Ireland Gregory Golden-mouth," that is, Pope Gregory I, Gregory the Great (c. 540–604); pope 590–604). The story is that, struck by the beauty of some English youths he saw in the slave market in Rome (c. 575), Gregory resolved to convert their land to Christianity. He eventually entrusted that mission to St. Augustine of Canterbury (d. 604).

1.26 (3:28–29). Two strong shrill whistles – At the consecration of the host during Mass, the server rings a handbell to announce that the

bread and wine have been transubstantiated into the body and blood of Christ.

1.32–33 (3:34–35). a prelate, patron of the arts in the middle ages – The face described suggests that of the Spanish-Italian pope, Alexander VI (c. 1431–1503; pope 1492–1503). He was born Roderigo Borgia, and his career, together with that of his children, Lucrezia and Cesare Borgia, has long been cited as a model of Renaissance high corruption. He was also a dedicated patron of the arts, attempting to outshine his predecessors and to leave a monument to himself and his family for posterity. See Thornton, p. 12.

1.34 (3:37). Your absurd name – *Stephen:* after the first Christian martyr, St. Stephen Protomartyr (first century), a Jew educated in Greek (see Acts 6–7). He was the dominant figure in Christianity before Paul's conversion. *Dedalus:* Daedalus in Greek means "cunning artificer," and in Greek mythology Daedalus was the archetypical personification of the inventor-sculptor-architect. Exiled from Athens after murdering his nephew Talus out of jealousy for Talus's promising inventiveness, Daedalus went to bull-worshiping Crete, where he was attached to the court of King Minos. There he constructed an artificial cow for Queen Pasiphaë to satisfy her lust for a semidivine bull, and a labyrinth to house her half-bull–half-man offspring, the Minotaur. When Minos, angered by the discovery of Daedalus's role as pander to the queen, confined him and his son, Icarus, in the labyrinth, Daedalus contrived their escape by fashioning wings of wax and feathers. Icarus, in the excitement of being able to fly, flew too near the sun; his wings melted, and he fell into the sea. Daedalus escaped to Sicily, where he found security and was able to live out his life creatively. As son, Stephen is Icarus (Telemachus) to Daedalus (Odysseus), the father—just as Stephen plays Hamlet, the son, through this day.

1.41 (4:4). Malachi – Hebrew: "my messenger." Malachi is the prophet (c. 460 B.C.) of the last book of the Old Testament who foretells the second coming of "Elijah the prophet before the coming of the great and dreadful day of the Lord" (Malachi 4:5). The name also recalls Malachy the Great, high king of Ireland in the late tenth century, and St. Malachy (c. 1094–c. 1148), an Irish prelate and reformer who according to tradition had the gift of prophecy.

1.49 (4:13). Haines – Possibly a pun on the

French *la haine*, "hate" (since he is anti-Semitic, etc.).

1.59 (4:25). funk – Fear, excessive nervousness, depression.

1.66 (4:34). scutter – A scurrying or bustling about.

1.77–78 (5:5–6). *Algy . . . great sweet mother – Algernon Charles Swinburne (1837–1909), in "The Triumph of Time" (1866), lines 257–58: "I will go back to the great sweet mother, / Mother and lover of men, the sea." In 1904 Swinburne was, in Yeats's phrase, the "King of the Cats," the grand old man of the preceding century's *avant-garde*.

1.78 (5:7). Epi oinopa ponton – Homeric Greek: "upon the wine-dark sea." An epithet that first occurs at 1:183 (Fitzgerald, p. 15) in *The Odyssey* and recurs throughout.

1.80 (5:8). Thalatta! Thalatta! – Attic Greek: "The sea! The sea!" From Xenophon's (c. 434–c. 355 B.C.) *Anabasis* (IV.vii.24), which records the exploits of the ten thousand Greek mercenaries in the employ of Cyrus the Younger against his brother Ataxerxes, king of Persia. Betrayed and stripped of their chief officers by Persian treachery, the ten thousand cut their way out of a hostile Persia back to the Black Sea, the Bosporus, and safety. "Thalatta! Thalatta!" was thus their shout of victory.

1.83–84 (5:11–12). *the mailboat clearing the harbourmouth of Kingstown – Kingstown (now Dun Laoghaire) Harbor, an artificial harbor on the southern shore of Dublin Bay, is approximately one mile northwest of the tower at Sandycove. Daily at 8:15 A.M. and P.M., express mailboats linked England and Ireland through this port, which is fifteen minutes by rail from Dublin and two and a half hours by boat from the railroad terminal at Holyhead in northwest Wales.

1.85 (5:13). Our mighty mother – A favorite phrase of the Irish poet-Theosophist-economist George William Russell (pseudonym AE; 1867–1935). In an essay, "Religion and Love" (1904), he effectively defines the Mighty Mother as "nature in its spiritual aspect."

1.86 (5:14). his grey searching eyes – "Grey-eyed goddess" is a Homeric epithet for Athena that first occurs at 1:178 (Fitzgerald, p. 19) in *The Odyssey* and recurs throughout.

1.92 (5:20). hyperborean – In Greek legend, a mythical people who dwelt beyond the north wind in a perpetual spring without sorrow or old age. More specifically, the reference is to the German philosopher Friedrich Nietzsche (1844–1900) in *Der Wille zur Macht* (The Will to Dominate) (1896). In Part I, "The Antichrist," section 1, Nietzsche uses the term *hyperborean* to describe the *Übermensch* (superman), "above the crowd" and not enslaved by conformity to the dictates of traditional Christian morality, whereas the moral man who lives for others is a weakling, a degenerate.

1.112 (6:2). dogsbody – Colloquial for a person who does odd jobs, usually in an institution; cf. 15.4711n. Since the dog's epithet in Celtic mythology is "Guard the Secret" (see 9.953n), the term here also identifies Stephen as secretive.

1.113 (6:3). breeks – Slang for trousers.

1.117 (6:7). bowsy – Or bowsey, Dublin slang: "an unemployed layabout who loves nothing better than to shout abusive remarks, usually of a sexual nature, after passing girls" (Gerry O'Flaherty, quoted in *Dublin*, ed. Benedict Kiely [New York, 1983], p. 3).

1.120 (6:11). I can't wear them if they are grey – Stephen's behavior recalls Hamlet's insistence on dressing in black and continuing to mourn his father's death after the rest of the court has ceased to do so (I.ii). In the mid-Victorian world, the period of a son's deep mourning for his mother (black suit, shoes, socks, and tie and a sharply limited social life) would have been a year and a day. By 1904 the rules had been considerably relaxed, but Stephen is adhering to the letter of the old law. His mother was buried on 26 June 1903 (17.952 [695:25–26]); if the period between her death and burial was the traditional three days, she must have died on 23 June 1903, and Stephen would be free to go into "second mourning" (gray would be acceptable) on 24 June 1904, or in eight days.

1.127 (6:19). the Ship – A hotel and tavern at 5 Abbey Street Lower, in the northeast quadrant of Dublin not far from the Liffey.

1.128 (6:20). g.p.i. – Abbreviation for *general paresis of the insane*, the genteel medical term for syphilis of the central nervous system. Among medical students in the British Isles, "g.p.i." was slang for eccentric.

1.128 (6:20). Dottyville – A mocking name for the Richmond Lunatic Asylum, which with its attached farm was located in the northwest quadrant of Dublin. It was erected in 1815 during the lord lieutenancy of the duke of Richmond and was originally for the benefit of paupers. The facilities have been expanded, and it is now known as the Grangegorman Mental Hospital.

1.128 (6:21). *Connolly Norman – (1853–1908), a famous Irish alienist who made a special study of insanity and instituted improved methods for treatment of the insane while he was superintendent of Richmond Asylum from 1886 to 1908.

1.136 (6:28–29). As he and others see me – After Robert Burns's (1759–96) much-quoted lines in "To a Louse; on seeing one on a Lady's bonnet at Church" (1786): "O wad some Power the giftie gie us / To see oursels as ithers see us! / It wad frae monie a blunder free us, / An' foolish notion" (lines 43–46).

1.138 (6:31). skivvy's – As slavey, a maid of all work; see 6.319n.

1.139–40 (6:33). *Lead him not into temptation – After the Lord's Prayer: "And lead us not into temptation, but deliver us from evil" (Matthew 6:13).

1.140 (6:34). Ursula – An early Christian saint whose legendary career involved the abhorrence of marriage. She led a pilgrimage of eleven thousand virgins around Europe in honor of virginity. She was, along with her cohorts, martyred at Cologne. The official year of her martyrdom is A.D. 237; other sources give it as 283 or 451.

1.143 (6:37). the rage of Caliban . . . mirror – Paraphrased from the preface (a prose poem) to Oscar Wilde's (1854–1900) novel *The Picture of Dorian Gray* (1891): "The nineteenth century dislike of Realism is the rage of Caliban seeing his own face in a glass. / The nineteenth century dislike of Romanticism is the rage of Caliban not seeing his own face in a glass" (lines 8–9). Wilde used Caliban, the evil-natured brute of Shakespeare's *The Tempest*, as a symbol for the nineteenth-century Philistine mentality.

1.146 (6:40–41). a symbol . . . of a servant – Paraphrased from Oscar Wilde's dialogue (essay) *The Decay of Lying* (1889): "CYRIL: I can quite understand your objection to art being treated as a mirror. You think it would reduce genius to the position of a cracked looking glass. But you don't mean to say that you seriously believe Life imitates Art, that Life in fact is the mirror, and Art the reality? VIVIAN: Certainly I do."

1.154 (7:8). oxy – Not only an ox but also an Oxonian and a Saxon.

1.155 (7:9). a guinea – See 1.291n.

1.158 (7:13). Hellenise it – The verb to *Hellenise* was coined by Matthew Arnold (1822–88) in his attempt to distinguish what he regarded as the two dominant impulses of Western culture. To *Hebraise* (by which he meant to *do* in the light of "the habits and discipline" of a revealed dogmatic truth) and to *Hellenise* (to *know* in the light of a "disinterested" and "flexible" humanism) are concepts central to Arnold's *Culture and Anarchy* (1869), particularly chapter 4, "Hebraism and Hellenism." Arnold argued that the English had Hebraized to excess and should Hellenize in pursuit of "our total perfection." Arnold's essentially intellectual distinction underwent a series of modulations as it was popularized in the closing decades of the nineteenth century, modulations informed in part by Swinburne's poetic development of the opposition between the sensual-aesthetic freedom of the pagan Greek world and the repressiveness of late-Victorian "Hebraism." By 1900 *Greek* had become Bohemian slang for those who preached sensual-aesthetic liberation, and *Jew* had become slang for those who were antagonistic to aesthetic values, those who preached the practical values of straightlaced Victorian morality.

1.159 (7:14). Cranly's arm – Cranly is presented as a friend of Stephen's in *A Portrait*, chapter 5. Cranly and Stephen are estranged; so Stephen is linking arms with Mulligan in the present as he has with Cranly in the past. Cranly's name derives from Thomas Cranly (1337–1417), a monk of the Carmelite order who succeeded to the archbishopric of Dublin in 1397 but did not arrive in Dublin until October 1398. He was also lord chancellor of Ireland. The combination in one man of Church and State authority implies yet another Anglo-Irish betrayal.

1.163 (7:18). Seymour – Apart from the context, identity and significance unknown.

1.163–64 (7:19–20). Clive Kempthorpe – Apart from the context, identity and significance unknown.

1.166 (7:22). **Palefaces** – Irish slang for the English, from "paleface," what North American Indians were supposed to have called their white English conquerors, at least according to the novels of James Fenimore Cooper (1789–1851). Also, as "Palemen," the English were kept outside Irish society, just as their ancestors had been confined to the pale, the relatively small coastal area around Dublin to which English rule was limited, off and on, before Cromwell's reconquest of the island in the mid–seventeenth century.

The episode Mulligan and Stephen recall took place in England, not Ireland. The scene was Oxford, where Mulligan's real-life counterpart, Oliver St. John Gogarty, spent a term at Worcester College in early 1904 (interrupting his career at Trinity College, Dublin, where he took his degree).

1.167 (7:23). **Break the news to her gently** – After an American popular song, "Break the News to Mother" (1897), by Charles K. Harris. The song records the battlefield death of a son who "gave his young life, / All for his country's sake." Chorus: "Just break the news to Mother; / She knows how dear I love her / And tell her not to wait for me, / For I'm not coming home; / Just say there is no other / Can take the place of Mother / Then kiss her dear sweet lips for me, / And break the news to her."

1.167 (7:24). **Aubrey** – A name regarded as effeminate and frequently used to express the sort of scorn the context implies.

1.169 (7:26). **Ades of Magdalen** – Apart from the context, the significance of "Ades" is unknown. Magdalen is one of the Oxford colleges.

1.170–71 (7:28). **to be debagged** – To have one's trousers taken off.

1.173 (7:30–31). **Matthew Arnold's** – Arnold's emphasis on restraint, poise, and taste, and on what his contemporaries called the "ethical element" in literature, was regarded as Philistinism incarnate by turn-of-the-century aesthetes, even though many of their terms were derived from Arnold and Arnold's influence was (from an academic point of view) still paramount in English criticism. See. 1.158n.

1.175 (7:32). **grasshalms** – Stems of grass.

1.176 (7:33). **To ourselves** – Irish: *Sinn Fein* ("We ourselves"). First the motto of Irish patriotic groups formed in the 1890s for the revival of Irish language and culture, the phrase was subsequently adopted by Arthur Griffith (1872–1922) c. 1905–06 as the name of a political movement for national independence; see 3.227n. Stephen is thinking of efforts to produce an Irish literary revival.

1.176 (7:33). **new paganism** – A slogan associated with the avant-garde "younger generation" of the 1890s, defined and also questioned as somewhat "misleading" in the foreword to William Sharp's (1855–1905) *Pagan Review*, no. 1 (Rudgwick, England, August 1892), the only issue of the magazine, written entirely by Sharp under various pseudonyms. Sharp's foreword proclaims that "the religion of our forefathers" has ceased to be a vital force and that "a new epoch is about to be inaugurated," an epoch that will be characterized (figuratively, at least) by cessation of the "duel between Man and Woman" and a final realization of the ideal of "copartnery" (p. 2). Given this point of departure, "it is natural that literature dominated by the various forces of sexual emotion should prevail" (p. 3). The foreword ends by qualifying "sexual emotion" as only "one among the many motive forces of life," all of which, "the general life and interest of the commonwealth of soul and body," are the province of the "new paganism" (p. 4).

1.176 (7:33). ***omphalos** – Greek: "navel." In *The Odyssey*, one of Homer's epithets for Ogygia, Calypso's island where Odysseus is stalled at the beginning of the epic, is "navel of the sea" (1:50; S. H. Butcher and Andrew Lang, trans. [London, 1879]). The oracle at Delphi was also an omphalos (the navel of the earth) and center of prophecy in ancient Greece. Some late-nineteenth-century Theosophists contemplated the omphalos variously as the place of the "astral soul of man," the center of self-consciousness and the source of poetic and prophetic inspiration.

1.181 (7:39). **Bray Head** – The headland that rises abruptly 791 feet above the shoreline approximately seven miles south of, but not visible from, the tower at Sandycove.

1.192–93 (8:11–12). **I remember only ideas and sensations** – This proposition echoes the essentially mechanistic concept of the human psyche developed by the English philosopher David Hartley (1705–57) and derived from the work of John Locke (1632–1704) and Sir Isaac Newton (1642–1727). Hartley, in his major work, *Observations of Man, His Frame, His*

Duty, and His Expectations (London, 1749), defines memory as "that faculty by which traces of sensations and ideas recur, or are recalled, in the same order and proportion, accurately or nearly, as they were once present." In effect Hartley argues that literal recall is (as Mulligan implies) an illusion; the only real presences in the memory are sensations and ideas.

1.205–6 (8:27). the Mater and Richmond – The Mater Misericordiae Hospital in Eccles Street, the largest hospital in Dublin. It was under the care of the Sisters of Mercy (Roman Catholic) and provided "for the relief of the sick and dying poor." The Richmond Lunatic Asylum (see 1.128n) was associated with the Mater Misericordiae in the treatment of poverty cases.

1.211 (8:34). *sir Peter Teazle – Elderly and exacting but kindhearted old gentleman, a character in *The School for Scandal* (1777) by Richard Brinsley Sheridan (1751–1816).

1.213–14 (8:36–37). hired mute from Lalouette's – Lalouette's, a "funeral and carriage establishment" in Dublin, advertised itself as supplying "funeral requisites of every description," including professional mourners called mutes.

1.231 (9:14). Loyola – St. Ignatius of Loyola (1491–1556), founder of the Society of Jesus and noted for the militancy of his dedication to religious obedience, not only in outward behavior but also obedience of the will.

1.232 (9:14). Sassenach – Irish for the Saxon (or English) conqueror.

1.235–36 (9:19). Give up the moody brooding – Recalls Antinous's blustering speech to Telemachus after the suitors refuse Telemachus's appeal in the Ithacan assembly that they end the state of siege in Odysseus's house: "High-handed Telemachus, control your temper! / Come on, get over it, no more grim thoughts, / but feast and drink with me, the way you used to" (2:303–5; Fitzgerald, p. 40). This is in effect what Gertrude says to Hamlet on her and Claudius's behalf (I.ii. 68–73).

1.239–41 (9:22–24). *And no more . . . the brazen cars* – Lines 7–9 of W. B. Yeats's "Who Goes with Fergus?" (*Collected Poems* [New York, 1956], p. 43). The poem was included as a song in the first version of Yeats's play *The Countess Cathleen* (1892). The song, accompanied by harp, is sung to comfort the countess, who has sold her soul to the powers of darkness

that her people might have food: "Who will go drive with Fergus now, / And pierce the deep wood's woven shade, / And dance upon the level shore? / Young man, lift up your russet brow, / And lift your tender eyelids, maid, / And brood on hopes and fears no more. // And no more turn aside and brood / Upon love's bitter mystery; / For Fergus rules the brazen cars, / And rules the shadow of the wood, / And the white breast of the dim sea / And all dishevelled wandering stars." At 1.242 (9:25) and 1.244–45 (9:28) Stephen echoes lines 10 and 11 of the poem.

1.249 (9:33). a bowl of bitter waters – Numbers 5:11–31 outlines the "trial of jealousy," the trial of a woman suspected of an unproven adultery. The priest presents the woman with the "bitter water," cursing her so that if she is guilty "this water that causeth the curse shall go into thy bowels, to make thy belly to swell, and thy thigh to rot." If she is not guilty, the curse will have no effect.

1.256 (9:41). a gaud of amber beads – In modern English, "gaud" suggests something showy, a trinket; but it is also Middle English for "bead," specifically one of the large ornamented beads used to punctuate the decades of the rosary (see 5.270n). (Suggested by Joan Keenan.)

1.257 (10:2). Royce – Edward William Royce (1841–?), an English comic actor famous for his roles in pantomimes. The pantomime was a popular form of theatrical entertainment consisting of a loose story frame that allowed considerable latitude for improvisation, topical jokes, specialty acts, and vaudeville turns.

1.258 (10:3). *Turko the Terrible – (1873) A pantomime by the Irish author-editor Edwin Hamilton (1849–1919), adapted from William Brough's (1826–70) London pantomime *Turko the Terrible; or, The Fairy Roses* (1868). Hamilton's version was an instant success at the Gaiety Theatre in Dublin during Christmas week 1873. It was repeatedly updated and revived in the closing decades of the century. Its frame was essentially a world of fairy-tale metamorphoses and transformations—as King Turko (Royce) and his court enjoyed the magic potential of the Fairy Rose.

1.260–62 (10:4–6). *I am the boy / That can enjoy / Invisibility* – A song from *Turko the Terrible*, "Invisibility is just the thing for me," which King Turko sings when he discovers that the Fairy Rose can give him that gift.

1.265 (10:9). the memory of nature – What the English Theosophist Alfred Percy Sinnett (1840–1921), in *The Growth of the Soul* (London, 1896), called the Theosophical concept of a universal memory in which all moments and thoughts are stored. See Akasic records, 7.882n; and cf. 1.192–93n.

1.266–67 (10:10–11). Her glass of water . . . the sacrament – That is, on mornings when she went to mass she had scrupulously observed the injunction to fast until after the ceremony.

1.269 (10:14). lice – Infestation with lice was chronic among Dublin's poor, thanks to the appalling lack of sanitation and a general want of cleanliness of body and clothes.

1.273–74 (10:20). On me alone – When the ghost of Hamlet's father appears and beckons to Hamlet, Horatio says: "It beckons you to go away with it, / As if it some impartment [communication] did desire / To you alone" (I.iv.58–60).

1.276–77 (10:23–24). *Liliata rutilantium . . . chorus excipiat* – Latin: "May the glittering throng of confessors, bright as lilies, gather about you. May the glorious choir of virgins receive you." The *Layman's Missal* (Baltimore, Md., 1962) quotes this as one part of Prayers for the Dying and remarks, "In the absence of a priest, these prayers for commending a dying person to God, may be read by any responsible person, man or woman" (p. 1141).

1.279 (10:26). No, mother. Let me be and let me live – In Book 1 of *The Odyssey*, after Athena has urged Telemachus to become more manly Penelope intervenes in the hall to suggest that the bard sing something less distressing than the sad songs about the return of the heroes from Troy. Telemachus surprises her with a mild rebuke, asserting himself as master of the house and suggesting that she retire to her chamber. In *Hamlet*, Hamlet's mother urges him to give up mourning the death of his father: "And let thine eye look like a friend on Denmark [i.e., on his uncle-stepfather, Claudius]" (I.ii.69). Hamlet resents and resists his mother's requests. In Act I, scene v, the Ghost appears and urges on the prince a radically different course of action.

1.284 (10:32). mosey – Someone who strolls slowly or shuffles.

1.291 (10:40). quid . . . guinea – The guinea (21s.) is not only more money than the twenty-shilling quid (pound), it is also more fashionable, a *gentlemanly* sum of money.

1.293 (11:2). kip – Has various slang meanings, which Mulligan exploits in his repeated use of the word: "that which is seized or caught; the catch," and "a brothel, lodging house, lodging, or bed."

1.293 (11:2–3). four quid – Stephen's monthly wage as paid (2.222 [30:6]) is £3 12s., not £4, and while not sizable in modern terms, would still compare favorably with the salaries of instructors in all but the wealthiest of modern preparatory schools.

1.300–305 (11:10–15). *O, won't we have a merry . . . On Coronation day! – One of several variants of an English street song popular in 1902 during the months of waiting before the coronation of Edward VII. J. B. Priestly[6] recalls one version: "We'll be merry / Drinking whiskey, wine, and sherry. / Let's all be merry / On Co-ronation Day." "Coronation Day" was also slang for payday because the pay could be reckoned in crowns (five-shilling pieces).

1.311 (11:21). the boat of incense – In the ceremony of the Mass. Stephen has performed as a server, a boy who assists at the altar and holds the container of incense for the priest (as here he performs a similar role for Mulligan, who is acting the part of priest in this parody of the Mass).

1.311 (11:22). Clongowes – Clongowes Wood College, a Jesuit school for boys, regarded as the most fashionable Catholic school in Ireland. Stephen is a student at Clongowes in chapter 1 of *A Portrait*.

1.312 (11:23). A server of a servant – Stephen was a server in the Mass at Clongowes to the priest, who was a servant of God and the Church. The phrase also recalls the curse Noah

---

6 "Good Old Teddie," *Observer* (London, 1 November 1970), p. 25. Matthew J. C. Hodgart and Mabel P. Worthington (*Song in the Works of James Joyce* [New York, 1959], p. 62), list this as a combination of "On Coronation Day" and "De Golden Wedding" (1880), a song by the American black, James A. Bland (1854–1911). The chorus of Bland's song does contain the lines "Won't we have a jolly time / Eating cake and drinking wine," but there are several other songs with "Won't we have a jolly time" in their choruses, and this direct attribution seems doubtful.

imposed on his son Ham, "the father of Canaan," because Ham had seen Noah naked and drunk, "Cursed be Canaan; a servant of servants shall he be unto his brethren" (Genesis 9:25). The Latin phrase *Servus Servorum Dei* (A Server of the Servants of God) is a title once used by bishops and rulers, but since the twelfth century it has been used exclusively by the popes and is now part of the superscription of papal bulls.

1.323 (11:36). Janey Mack – A common imprecation, as in the nursery rhyme: "Janey Mac, me shirt is black, / What'll I do for Sunday? / Go to bed and cover me head / And not get up till Monday." "Janey Mack" is also what the Irish call "dodging the curse," a euphemistic form of *Jesus Jack*.

1.333 (12:6). I'm melting . . . candle remarked when – Obviously, as it was being consumed by the flame; almost as obviously, the prelude to a dirty joke about female masturbation.

1.335 (12:8–9). Bless us . . . thy gifts – A conventional blessing before meals.

1.336 (12:9). O Jay – Dodging the curse *O Jesus*.

1.351 (12:27). *In nomine . . . Spiritus Sancti* – Latin: "In the name of the Father and of the Son and of the Holy Spirit"; a formula of blessing and consecration.

1.357 (12:33). mother Grogan – Appears as a character in an anonymous Irish song, "Ned Grogan." First verse: "Ned Grogan, dear joy, was the son of his mother, / And as like her, it seems, as one pea to another; / But to find out his dad, he was put to the rout, / As many folks wiser have been, joy, no doubt. / To this broth of a boy oft his mother would say, / 'When the *moon* shines, my jewel, be making your hay; / Always ask my advice, when the business is done; / For two heads, sure, you'll own, are much better than one.'"

1.361 (12:37). *Mrs Cahill* – Her (comic?) origin and identity are unknown.

1.365 (12:41). folk – One aspect of the somewhat self-conscious Irish attempt to achieve a national cultural identity in the late nineteenth and early twentieth centuries was a revival of interest in Irish folklore and folk customs. At times this interest ran to hairsplitting scholarship and at times to gross sentimentality. The revival of Irish as "the language" was another aspect of this national-identity crusade. See 1.424–35 (14:26–40).

1.366–67 (13:1–2). the fishgods of Dundrum . . . weird sisters . . . big wind – Nonsense folklore. The fishgods are associated with the Formorians, gloomy giants of the sea, one of the legendary peoples of prehistoric Ireland. One Dundrum, on the east coast of Ireland sixty-five miles north of Dublin, was famous as the "strand of champions" where ancient Irish tribes held a folk version of Olympic games. But another Dundrum, a village four miles south of the center of Dublin, was the site of a lunatic asylum, and it was at this Dundrum that Yeats's sister Elizabeth established the Dun Emer Press (1903, name changed to Cuala Press in 1908). The press was to publish Yeats's new works and works by other living Irish authors in limited editions on handmade paper. Lily Yeats, Yeats's other sister, became active in the Dun Emer Guild, which produced handwoven embroideries and tapestries. *Weird sisters:* what the witches in Shakespeare's *Macbeth* call themselves as they wind up their "charm" at Macbeth's approach (I.iii.32). *The year of the big wind:* there is a big wind in *Macbeth* (II.iv), but this allusion is to the Irish habit of dating events as before and after 1839, when an incredible January storm blew down hundreds of houses across Ireland. In the Dun Emer Press's edition of W. B. Yeats's *In the Seven Woods* (1903), the colophon announces that the book was finished "the sixteenth day of July in the year of the big wind, 1903."

1.371 (13:6). Mabinogion – Welsh: "instructions to young bards." The title of a mixed bag of Welsh prose tales, some from early Celtic tradition, others from late medieval French Arthurian romance, published by Lady Charlotte Guest in 1838.

1.371 (13:6). Upanishads – Hindu: the name of a class of Vedic works devoted to theological and philosophical speculations on the nature of the world and man—associated here with the Theosophical interests of Yeats, AE (George William Russell; see 2.257n), and other Irish intellectuals.

1.382–84 (13:20–22). *For old Mary . . . her petticoats* – An anonymous bawdy Irish song; only a clean, relatively recent version, "Mick McGilligan's Daughter, Mary Anne" by Louis A. Tierney, is available in print. First verse: "I'm a gallant Irishman, I've a daughter Mary

Anne, / She's the sweetest, neatest, colleen in this Isle, / Though she can't now purchase satin, she's a wonder at bog Latin, / In a fluent, fascinatin' sort of style. / When she's selling fruit or fish, sure, it is her fondest wish / For to capture with her charm some handsome man; / Ah no matter where she goes, sure, and everybody knows / That she's Mick McGilligan's daughter, Mary Anne. [Chorus:] She's a darling, she's a daisy and she's set the city crazy, / Though in build, and talk, and manner, like a man; / When me precious love draws near, you can hear the people cheer / For Mick McGilligan's daughter, Mary Anne." The remaining eight verses of Tierney's version are devoted to comic elaboration of Mary Anne's boisterous "masculine" charms. Mabel Worthington has found one bawdy version that ends with the line, "She pisses like a man," an appropriate fourth line to cap the three Mulligan quotes.

1.394 (13:33). collector of prepuces – God, in the light of the commandment that all male children were to be circumcised (Genesis 17:10–14).

1.399 (13:38). tilly – A small quantity over and above the amount purchased.

1.400 (13:39). messenger – The milkwoman appears in the role of Mentes-Mentor (Pallas Athena's disguises) in Books 1 and 2 of *The Odyssey;* see 1.406–7n.

1.403 (14:2–3). Silk of the kine . . . poor old woman – Two traditional epithets for Ireland. "Silk of the kine" (the most beautiful of cattle; allegorically, Ireland) is a translation of the Irish phrase *a shíoda na mbó,* from an old Irish song, "Druimin Donn Dílis" (suggested by Vincent Deane). "The poor old woman," from the Irish ballad "The Shan Van Vocht" (see 1.543–44n), in legend looks like an old woman to all but the true patriots; to them she looks like a "young girl" with the "walk of a queen," as in the closing lines of Yeats's play *Cathleen Ni Houlihan* (Poor Old Woman) (1902). Legend also has it that during the Penal Days in the eighteenth century, the Irish were forbidden to mention their nationality or to display the national color (green) or wear the national emblem (the shamrock), so they used allegorical circumlocutions instead.

1.405 (14:5). cuckquean – A female cuckold; a woman betrayed by those who should be faithful to her.

1.406–7 (14:6–7). To serve or to upbraid . . . to beg her favour – In Books 1 and 2 of *The Odyssey,* Pallas Athena appears disguised as Mentes and Mentor to encourage Telemachus to assert himself if not actually to upbraid him for his boyish lassitude. She also organizes the ship and crew for his voyage to the mainland. Since Telemachus realizes that he is in the presence of one of the gods, he can hardly be said to "scorn to beg her favour."

1.421–22 (14:22–23). woman's unclean loins . . . serpent's prey – Woman was regarded as "unclean" after childbirth (Leviticus 12:2, 5) and during menstruation (15:19–28). Woman was made of man's flesh ("And the rib, which the Lord God had taken from man, made he a woman" [Genesis 2:22]), and she was "the serpent's prey," deceived into sin by Satan disguised as a serpent in Genesis 3. A woman's "loins" are not anointed in the Roman Catholic sacrament of extreme unction.

1.427 (14:30). Is there Gaelic on you? – A west-of-Ireland, peasant colloquialism for "Can you speak Irish?"

1.428 (14:32). from the west – From the Gaeltacht, those remote areas in the west of Ireland where Irish was still in everyday use among the peasants (some of them still monoglot in 1900). Education and commerce in nineteenth-century Ireland had been so dominated by the English language that Irish had all but disappeared from most accessible parts of the country by 1900.

1.455–56 (15:20). *Ask nothing . . . I give* – Lines 1 and 2 from Swinburne's "The Oblation" (*Songs Before Sunrise* [1871]). The poem continues: "Heart of my heart, were it more, / More would be laid at your feet: / Love that should help you to live, / Song that should spur you to soar. // . . . // I that have love and no more / Give you but love of you sweet: / He that hath more, let him give; / He that hath wings, let him soar; / Mine is the heart at your feet / Here, that must love you to live."

1.463–64 (15:27–28). *Heart of my . . . at your feet.* – See preceding note.

1.466 (15:30). stony – Slang: short for stony broke.

1.467–68 (15:32–33). Ireland expects . . . do his duty – After words attributed to Lord Nelson ("England expects . . .") at the battle of Trafalgar (1805) and part of the refrain from

"The Death of Nelson," words by S. J. Arnold, music by J. Braham. See 10.232n.

1.469–70 (15:35). your national library – The National Library of Ireland, founded in 1877. The nucleus of its books was donated by the Royal Dublin Society. In the nineteenth century, when the Irish language and culture were in eclipse, the society and later the library were identified with efforts to preserve records and keep the Irish language and culture alive. Ironically, in 1904 the more distinguished collection of ancient Irish MSS, etc., was housed in Trinity College library. See 7.800–801n.

1.476 (16:1). All Ireland is washed by the gulfstream – Technically, Ireland is "washed" not by the Gulf Stream but by the North Atlantic Drift, into which the Gulf Stream disperses off Newfoundland.

1.481 (16:7–8). Agenbite of inwit – Middle English: "remorse of conscience." *Ayenbite of Inwyt* (1340) is a medieval manual of virtues and vices, intended to remind the layman of the hierarchy of sins and the distinctions among them. The manual was translated into Middle English (Kentish dialect) by Dan Michel of Northgate from the French of Friar Lorens's *Somme des Vices et Vertus* (1279).

1.482 (16:8). Yet here's a spot – From *Macbeth* (V.i.35), as Lady Macbeth walks in her sleep and, hallucinating, struggles to cleanse her hands of the blood of Duncan, the murdered king.

1.491 (16:18). holdfast – In context, one of the hooks or rings from which the hammock is suspended.

1.499 (16:26). I blow him out about you – Obsolete or colloquial for "I make him feel proud (or vain) of your acquaintance."

1.510 (16:39). Mulligan . . . garments – A reference to the Way of the Cross, the fourteen stations representing Christ's Passion on the Via Dolorosa (Street of Sorrows) in Jerusalem, along which Jesus passed on his way to Golgotha and the Crucifixion. The motto of the tenth station is, "And Jesus was stripped of his garments" (based on Matthew 27:28 and John 19:23–24).

1.516 (17:4–5). puce gloves and green boots – This sort of idiosyncratic costume was associated with late-nineteenth-century decadence and aestheticism.

1.517 (17:5–6). Do I contradict . . . contradict myself – From Walt Whitman's (1819–92) "Song of Myself" (1855, 1891–92), section 51, lines 6–7. Whitman's reputation in England at the end of the nineteenth century is reflected in Swinburne's praise of him as the poet of the "earth-god freedom" in "To Walt Whitman in America" (1871).

1.518 (17:6). Mercurial Malachi – As Malachi is Hebrew for "my messenger" (see 1.41n), so Mercury was the messenger of the gods in Roman mythology. His Greek counterpart, Hermes, plays a key role in *The Odyssey*, intervening at Zeus's behest to rescue Odysseus from bondage on Calypso's isle in Book 5 and to make Odysseus immune to Circe's magic in Book 10; see the headnotes to those episodes, pp. 70 and 452, respectively.

1.519 (17:8). Latin quarter hat – A soft or slouch hat associated with the art and student worlds of the Latin Quarter in Paris, as against the "hard" hats (bowlers or derbies) then fashionable in Dublin.

1.527 (17:16). And going forth he met Butterly – After Jesus had been arrested and Peter for the third time had denied any association with him, "Peter remembered the word of Jesus which he had said: Before the cock crow, thou wilt deny me thrice. And going forth, he wept bitterly" (Matthew 26:75 [Douay]). A "Maurice Butterly, farmer," is mentioned at 15.1611 (486:31); *Thom's* 1904 lists a Maurice Butterly, Court Duff House, Blanchardstown (a village four and a half miles west of Dublin). Another Maurice Butterly was proprietor of the City and Suburban Race and Amusement Grounds on Jones Road, in the northern outskirts of Dublin.

1.528 (17:17). ashplant – An inexpensive walking stick made out of the unbarked sapling of an ash tree. In Celtic tradition the ash was associated with kingmaking and " 'half the furniture of arms'; that is, the handles of spears were made of it" (P. W. Joyce, *A Social History of Ancient Ireland* [London, 1913], vol. 2, p. 247).

1.535 (17:25). leader shoots – The shoot that

grows at the apex of the stem or of a principal branch of a plant.

1.539 (17:29). Twelve quid – The actual rent was £8, paid by Oliver St. John Gogarty, who sat for his partial portrait as Mulligan.

1.540 (17:30). To the secretary of state for war – The rent was paid in quarterly installments to His Majesty's Secretary of State for the War Department at the War Office in London. The secretary was a cabinet official in charge of what would now be called the Defense Department.

1.542 (17:34). Martello – After Cape Martello in Corsica, where in 1794 the British had great trouble taking a similar tower. The towers were constructed at key points on the Irish coast (1803–6) as defense against the possibility of a French invasion during the Napoleonic Wars.

1.543 (17:36). Billy Pitt – William Pitt the Younger (1759–1806), prime minister of England when the Martello towers were built.

1.543–44 (17:36–37). when the French were on the sea – From a late-eighteenth-century Irish ballad, "The Shan Van Vocht" (The Poor Old Woman; i.e., Ireland herself). Between 1796 and 1798 the French made four ill-starred attempts to lend naval and military support to the Irish revolution: "Oh! the French are on the sea, / Says the Shan Van Vocht, / The French are on the sea, / Says the Shan Van Vocht; / Oh, the French are in the Bay, / They'll be here without delay, / And the Orange will decay, / Says the Shan Van Vocht. [Fifth and final stanza:] And will Ireland then be free? / Says the Shan Van Vocht; / Will Ireland then be free? / Says the Shan Van Vocht; / Yes! Ireland shall be free / From the centre to the sea; / Then hurrah for Liberty! / Says the Shan Van Vocht." A later version substitutes the line "Oh Boney's [Napoleon's] on the sea."

1.544 (17:37). *omphalos* – See 1.176n.

1.546–47 (17:40). Thomas Aquinas – St. Thomas Aquinas (1225–74), called the Angelic Doctor, the Common Doctor, and (by his schoolmates) the "dumb ox"; a Dominican, a theologian, and a leading Scholastic philosopher, he is famous for synthesizing the philosophy that in 1879 was made the required text for Roman Catholic seminaries. The goal of his work was to summarize all learning and to dem-

onstrate the compatibility of faith and intellect. In *A Portrait* 5:A, Stephen expounds a theory of aesthetics that he asserts is "applied Aquinas."

1.547 (17:40). fifty-five reasons – Mulligan's phrase recalls Aristotle's cosmological assertion in the *Metaphysics* that the universe consisted of fifty-nine concentric spheres: the four mutable spheres of the earth and fifty-five immutable celestial spheres, each with its prime mover (or reason). The natural movement of the fifty-five was circular and changeless.

1.554 (18:9–10). Wilde and paradoxes – Paradox was a staple of Oscar Wilde's wit; see 1.143n for an example.

1.561 (18:17). Japhet in search of a father – Refers to an 1836 novel by Capt. Frederick Marryat (1792–1848), an English naval officer and novelist. The novel deals with the adventures of a foundling who is trying to find his father; the father, when finally found, turns out to be a testy old East India officer. Japhet was also the youngest of Noah's three sons and the legendary ancestor of a varied group of nations including the Greeks.

1.567–68 (18:25). Elsinore. *That beetles o'er his base into the sea* – Elsinore is the seat of the Danish court in *Hamlet*. In Act I, Horatio warns Hamlet of the dangers involved in following the Ghost: "What if it tempt you toward the flood, my lord, / Or to the dreadful summit of the cliff / That beetles o'er [juts out over] his base into the sea, / And there assume some other horrible form / Which might deprive your sovereignty of reason / And draw you into madness? Think of it. / The very place puts toys of desperation, / Without more motive, into every brain / That looks so many fathoms to the sea / And hears it roar beneath" (I.iv.69–78).

1.574 (18:33). The sea's ruler – As in song, "Britannia rules the waves" (see 12.1347n), but also an allusion to the international predominance of Britain's navy and merchant marine in the decades before 1914. And it is Poseidon, the god of the sea, who harasses Odysseus and attempts to prevent him from reaching Ithaca and home.

1.575 (18:34). the mailboat – See 1.83–84n.

1.576 (18:35). the Muglins – A shoal off Dalkey, the southeastern headland of Dublin

Bay; the light on the Muglins thus marks the southeastern limit of the bay.

1.577–78 (18:36–38). a theological interpretation . . . atoned with the father – Source unknown. But it is notable that Haines's description could be fitted to Stephen's interpretation of Hamlet. See Scylla and Charybdis (9.1–1225 [pp. 184–218]).

1.584–87, 589–92, 596–99 (19:3–6, 8–11, 16–19). *I'm the queerest . . . Goodbye, now, goodbye* – These stanzas, which Stephen calls "The Ballad of Joking Jesus" (1.608 [19:30]), are quoted with some adaptations from a longer poem by Oliver St. John Gogarty, "The Song of the Cheerful (but Slightly Sarcastic) Jesus." The poem was apparently circulated in manuscript and by word of mouth in Dublin 1904–5. See Ellmann, pp. 205–6.

1.585 (19:4). *My mother's a jew* – Catholic tradition has consistently avoided allusion to the Virgin Mary's Jewishness in order to emphasize her role as Queen of Heaven and as intercessor with her son for the "peace and salvation" of the devout who pray for her redeeming influence. This emphasis approached a climax in 1854, when Pope Pius IX proclaimed as dogma and an article of faith that Mary had been immaculately conceived, born free of any taint of original sin.

1.585 (19:4). *my father's a bird* – The dove is a traditional symbol of the Holy Ghost. When the Virgin Mary asks the Archangel Gabriel how she shall conceive "seeing I know not a man," the archangel replies: "The Holy Ghost shall come upon thee, and the power of the Highest shall overshadow thee: therefore also that holy thing which shall be born of thee shall be called the Son of God" (Luke 1:34–35).

1.586 (19:5). *Joseph the joiner* – The husband of the Virgin Mary was a carpenter in Nazareth in Galilee (Matthew 13:55).

1.590 (19:9). *when I'm making the wine* – In John 2:1–11 Jesus achieves his first miracle when at his mother's request he turns water into wine for a wedding feast in Cana of Galilee.

1.599 (19:19). *Olivet's breezy* – Olivet, or the Mount of Olives, is just east of Jerusalem. The Garden of Gethsemane, where Jesus prayed and was arrested on the eve of the Crucifixion, was located on its western slope; but "breezy" suggests an allusion to the site of the Ascension,

which Christian tradition has located on the summit of the mount.

1.600 (19:20). the forty-foot hole – A bathing place at Sandycove; according to the *Official Guide to Dublin* (1958), "a popular resort of swimmers (men only)."

1.601 (19:21). Mercury's hat – A broad-brimmed hat was one of Mercury's attributes; see 1.518n.

1.610 (19:32). Three times a day, after meals – Like a prescribed medicine.

1.612 (19:33–34). Creation from nothing – The Nicene Creed (the uniform creed, or Profession of Faith, evolved at the first Council of Nicaea in 325) is repeated as part of the ordinary of the Mass every Sunday and at more important feasts of the Catholic church. It begins: "I believe in one God, the Almighty Father, maker of heaven and earth, and of all things, visible and invisible."

1.612–13 (19:35). miracles – Not only the miracles of healing the sick, casting out devils, and raising the dead that Jesus performed, but also the miracles of the Immaculate Conception and the Resurrection and Ascension.

1.612 (19:35). a personal God – In theological terms, the Trinity is three *persons:* the Father, the Son, and the Holy Ghost; but in Haines's mouth the phrase may have a peculiarly Protestant emphasis: that each Christian must realize a direct personal relationship to God (without a mediating presence), since God has a personal interest in each individual soul.

1.626 (20:14). free thought – Thought free from the dictates of "Christian revelation," a position eloquently stated by the English theologian and philosopher Anthony Collins (1676–1729) in his *Discourse of Freethinking* (London, 1713).

1.628–29 (20:17). My familiar – "A spirit who accompanies, and often helps, a magician, sorcerer or witch" (*Dictionary of Mysticism*, ed. Frank Gaynor [New York, 1953], p. 62).

1.631 (20:20). Now I eat his salt bread – From Dante's *Paradiso*. Dante's great-great-grandfather, Cacciaguida, predicts the future course of Dante's life and the bitterness of his exile: "Thou shalt abandon every thing beloved most dearly; this is the arrow which the bow of exile shall first shoot. Thou shalt make trial of how salt doth taste another's bread, and how hard the path to descend and mount upon another's stair. And that which most shall weigh thy shoulders down, shall be the vicious and ill company with which thou shalt fall down into this vale, for all ungrateful, all mad and impious shall they become against thee; but, soon after, their cheeks, and not thine, shall redden for it" (17:55–65).

1.636–37 (20:25–26). I should think you able to free yourself. You are your own master – Compare the closing lines of Virgil's valediction to the now spiritually cleansed Dante in the *Purgatorio*, 27:140–142: "Free, upright, and whole, is thy will, and 'twere a fault not to act according to its prompting; wherefore I do crown and mitre thee over thyself."

1.638 (20:27). servant of two masters – From the Italian, *Il servitore di due padroni*, a play by Carlo Goldoni (1707–93). The play is a conventional Roman comedy with a girl disguised as a boy, a pair of lovers separated by an unfortunate marriage pledge, and a servant, Truffaldino ("trickster"), who plies his trade for two masters. Cf. the Sermon on the Mount, when Jesus says: "No man can serve two masters: for either he will hate the one, and love the other; or else he will hold to the one and despise the other. Ye cannot serve God and mammon" (Matthew 6:24).

1.651 (20:42–21:1). et in unam . . . ecclesiam – Latin: "and in one holy catholic and apostolic church." This phrase is from the last portion of the Nicene Creed, which was an attempt to resolve the theological speculation and controversy over Arianism; see 1.657n. Some of these early Christian speculations (particularly those concerning the nature of the Trinity and of the Son's consubstantiality with the Father) Stephen contemplates in the lines that follow.

1.652–53 (21:2). a chemistry of stars – Alchemy, the study and poetry of which fascinated late-nineteenth- and early-twentieth-century Theosophists, including W. B. Yeats. In *The Key to Theosophy* (London, 1893), Helena Petrovna Blavatsky (see 7.784n) dismisses the "Kabalist-Alchemist" (as preoccupied with the "purely material" effort to transmute base metals into gold) in favor of the "Occultist-Alchemist [who], spurning the gold of the earth, gives all his attention to, and directs his efforts only towards, the transmutation of the baser *quaternary* [which includes the physical plane of hu-

man existence] into the divine upper *trinity* [the spiritual, mental, and psychic planes] of man, which, when finally blended, is one" (p. 201).

1.653 (21:3). Symbol of the apostles – The Apostles' Creed in the Mass (so called because each of the twelve clauses is traditionally attributed to one of the apostles): (1) Peter—I believe in God the Father Almighty, Maker of heaven and earth; (2) John—And in Jesus Christ, His only Son, our Lord; (3) James (the Elder)—Who was conceived of the Holy Ghost, born of the Virgin Mary; (4) Andrew—Suffered under Pontius Pilate; was crucified, dead, and buried; (5) Philip—He descended into hell; (6) Thomas—The third day He rose again from the dead; (7) James (the Younger)—He ascended into Heaven, and sitteth on the right hand of God the Father Almighty; (8) Matthew—From thence He shall come to judge the quick and the dead; (9) Nathaniel—I believe in the Holy Ghost; (10) Simon—the Holy Catholic Church, the Communion of Saints; (11) Matthias—the forgiveness of sins; (12) Jude—the resurrection of the body, and the life everlasting.

1.653 (21:3). the mass for pope Marcellus – Pope Marcellus II (1501–55) lived only twenty-two days after his coronation in 1555. The Italian composer Giovanni Pierluigi da Palestrina (1525–94) wrote the *Missa Papae Marcelli*, first performed 27 April 1565. The Credo of the Missa parallels in places the Apostle's Creed (see preceding note). Thanks largely to the encouragement and generosity of Edward Martyn (see 9.306–7n), there was a considerable revival of interest in Palestrina and his contemporaries during the 1890s in Dublin. The first Dublin performance of the *Missa Papae Marcelli* was at St. Teresa's Church in 1898.

1.654–56 (21:4–6). behind their chant the vigilant . . . menaced her heresiarchs – The "angel of the Church Militant" is the Archangel Michael, a presence the Church invoked in its struggle against the spread of the Protestant heresy in the sixteenth century. The struggle culminated in the Council of Trent (1545–63) and included even strictures against "all music in which anything lascivious or impure was mixed" (1551). Purists in the council argued that this dictate excluded all music except plainsong and Gregorian chant. When Pope Julius III (pope 1551–55) appointed Palestrina master of the Cappella Giulia in 1552, he was expressly repudiating the purists in favor of the "new" polyphonic music. After Julius's death, Pope Marcellus II continued to support Palestrina, but the purist Pope Paul IV upon his accession in 1555 promptly dismissed Palestrina. In 1564 another musically liberal pope, Pius IV, asked Palestrina to compose a polyphonic mass that would be free of all "impurities" and would thus silence the purists. The *Missa Papae Marcelli* was that mass, and its performance succeeded in establishing polyphonic music (and Palestrina) as the voice of the Church.

1.656 (21:7). Photius – (c. 820–c. 891), appointed patriarch of Constantinople (857) against the pope's wishes and in the midst of political and religious controversy. Photius was excommunicated (863) and in turn convened a church council at Constantinople and excommunicated the pope and his partisans (867). Photius was subsequently restored to the Church, only to be excommunicated once again. Photius is regarded by the Roman church as "one of its worst enemies" because the eastern schism, which he initiated, climaxed in 1054 in the separation of the Eastern Orthodox and Roman Catholic churches.

1.656–57 (21:7). the brood of mockers – Those who dissent from orthodox concepts of the nature of the Trinity. Photius's dissent was his assertion that the Holy Ghost proceeded not "from the Father and from the Son" (Roman Catholic orthodoxy) but "from the Father."

1.657 (21:8). Arius – (c. 256–336); his heresy: he taught that the Word, or Logos (Christ), was God's first creation, that God created him out of nothing; and then Christ created the Holy Spirit; and then the Holy Spirit created our world. Thus Christ is God's first creation and inferior to God; and the Holy Spirit, as Christ's creation, is inferior to Christ. The first Council of Nicaea (325) condemned Arius as a heretic and used the term *consubstantial* to underscore the equality of the three persons of the Trinity in refutation of Arius's speculations.

1.658 (21:9–10). Valentine – (d. c. 166), an Egyptian Gnostic who preached in Rome 135–60. His heresy: he taught that the Demiurge, creator of the material world, was not a member of the Trinity but a "demon," remote from the unfathomable God. Hence the material world and its creator were regarded as antispirit and all men as diverse compounds of spirit and matter. Christ was sent by God to lead men to gnosis, or pure knowledge, which is spiritual and which transports man to the kingdom of light and enables him to escape the material

world, a kingdom of darkness destined to remain "forever darkness." Valentine argued that Christ had no "terrene body" but was pure spirit.

1.659 (21:11). Sabellius – (Third century); his heresy: he maintained that the names "Father," "Son," and "Holy Spirit" were merely three names for the same thing (or three different aspects or modes of one Being).

1.661 (21:13). the stranger – An Irish expression for the English (the invaders and overlords).

1.662 (21:14). weave the wind – After Isaiah 19:9, "and they that weave networks shall be confounded," and John Webster (c. 1580–c. 1625), song from *The Devil's Law Case* (1623): "Vain the ambition of kings / Who seek by trophies and dead things / To leave a living name behind, / And weave but nets to catch the wind."

1.663 (21:15). Michael's – The archangel symbolic of the Church Militant.

1.665 (21:18). *Zut! Nom de Dieu!* – French: "Damn it! In the name of God!"

1.667 (21:20–21). into the hands of German jews – See the brief account of Wilhelm Marr's pamphlet, *The Victory of Judaism over Germanism*, in the Introduction, p. 4.

1.671 (21:25). Bullock harbour – Near Dalkey on the southeast headland of Dublin Bay. The castle of Bullock overhung a creek that had been converted into an artificial harbor.

1.673 (21:28). five fathoms out there – To the north in the offshore area of Dublin Bay, an area two miles wide that extends five and a half miles from the south shore of the bay across the seawalled mouth of the Liffey to the north shore. See 3.470n.

1.673–74 (21:29). when the tide comes in about one – High tides in Dublin, 16 June 1904, were at 12:18 A.M. and 12:42 P.M.

1.674 (21:29–30). It's nine days today – In superstition, a drowned body that sinks and is not recovered will surface after nine days.

1.683 (21:40). Westmeath – A county forty miles west and west-northwest of Dublin.

1.684 (21:41). Bannon – Alec Bannon, a minor character in the novel, is an associate of Mulligan's. He has met Milly Bloom in Westmeath.

1.689 (22:5). garland of grey hair – The swimmer is tonsured, as a Catholic priest or member of a monastic order would have been. The tonsure was abolished by Pope Paul VI in 1972. (Suggested by Joan Keenan.)

1.693–94 (22:8–9). crossed himself piously . . . and breastbone – The gesture in honor of the Father (forehead), Son (lips), and Holy Spirit (breast) that prefaces the reading of the Gospel in the ceremony of the Mass and with which the celebrant concludes his participation in the Mass after he has dismissed the congregation.

1.698 (22:14). to stew – To sweat, to work doggedly and unimaginatively.

1.698 (22:14–15). that red Carlisle girl, Lily – Apart from the context, identity and significance unknown.

1.700 (22:18). rotto – Slang for rotten.

1.701 (22:19). up the pole – Slang for crazy or in difficulties (and in some cases, as here, pregnant).

1.706 (22:24). Redheaded women buck like goats – Red hair has been superstitiously associated with treachery and deceit since ancient Egypt. The icon of the traitor (Judas, for example) is traditionally represented as redheaded. Thus redheaded women are assumed to be untrustworthy and, it follows, oversexed.

1.708 (22:27). My twelfth rib . . . Uebermensch – *Übermensch*, German: "superman"; after Nietzsche's *Thus Spake Zarathustra* (1883). Zarathustra (Zoroaster), a Persian religious leader who flourished in the sixth century B.C., was expropriated by Nietzsche and converted into the prophet of the superman. In "Zarathustra's Prologue": "*I teach you the superman.* Man is something that is to be surpassed"; and in section 5 Zarathustra asserts: "The most contemptible thing . . . is *the last man.*" Thus, since Mulligan's "twelfth rib is gone," he is Adam, first man, least contemptible man—in other words, superman. See 1.92n.

1.727 (23:7). He who stealeth . . . to the Lord – After Proverbs 19:17, "He that hath pity upon the poor lendeth unto the Lord."

Mulligan's view of Nietzsche as advocate of the radical egoist who exploits others and uses them as stepping stones to his own higher goals was a view fashionable at the turn of the century, one now regarded by students of Nietzsche as pseudo-Nietzsche.

1.732 (23:12). Horn of a bull, hoof of a horse, smile of a Saxon – A version is listed as Proverb 186 under "British Isles: Irish," in Selwyn Gurney Champion, *Racial Proverbs* (New York, 1963): "Beware of the horns of a bull, of the heels of a horse, of the smile of an Englishman."

1.733 (23:13). The Ship – At the end of Book 2 of *The Odyssey*, Telemachus eludes the suitors, whom Athena has put to sleep, and sails for the mainland to seek news of his father. There he visits Nestor and Menelaus and Helen. When he is about to return to Ithaca (at the end of Book 4), twenty of the suitors, led by Antinous, sail to a strategically located islet to lie in ambush, but Telemachus, guided by Athena, eludes their deadly grasp. See 1.127n.

1.736–38 (23:16–18). *Liliata rutilantium . . . te virginum* – See 1.276–77n.

1.739 (23:19–20). the priest's grey nimbus . . . dressed discreetly – The priest, who has been swimming, dresses as the celebrant of the just concluded mock mass would divest himself.

1.741–43 (23:21–23). A voice, sweettoned and sustained . . . a seal's – Traditionally, seals are symbolic of wide-ranging curiosity, and in *The Odyssey* they constitute the "flock" of which Proteus is "shepherd" and from which he gets some of his all-seeing knowledge; see headnote to Proteus, p. 44 below. In *The Odyssey*, when Proteus's daughter, a sea-goddess, tells Menelaus how to trap her father and gain a prophecy from him, "her voice sang . . . 'How can you linger in this island, aimless / and shiftless, while your people waste away?'" (4:369–73; Fitzgerald, p. 76).

1.744 (23:24). Usurper – In effect, what Telemachus calls Antinous, Eurymachos, and the other suitors in the hall of Odysseus's house at the end of Book 1 and in the assembly at the beginning of Book 2 of *The Odyssey*. Hamlet has similar feelings about his uncle Claudius, who, Hamlet says, "killed my King and whored my mother, / Popped in between the election and my hopes" (V.ii.64–65).

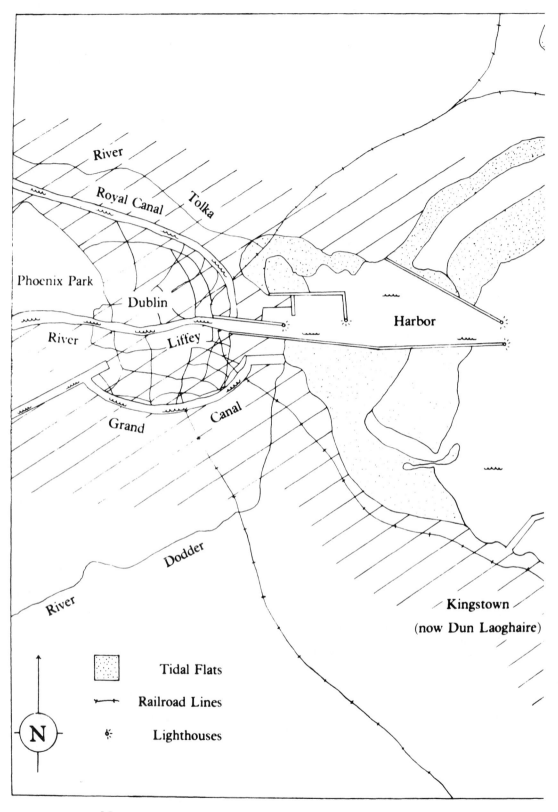

River

Royal Canal

Tolka

Phoenix Park

Dublin

River

Liffey

Grand

Canal

Harbor

Dodder

River

Kingstown
(now Dun Laoghaire)

Tidal Flats

Railroad Lines

Lighthouses

N

EPISODE 2. *Nestor*

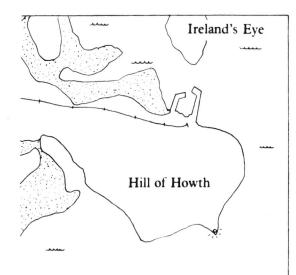

Ireland's Eye

Hill of Howth

Dublin Bay

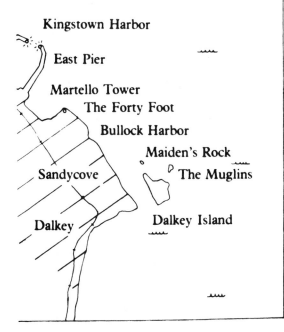

Kingstown Harbor

East Pier

Martello Tower
The Forty Foot

Bullock Harbor

Maiden's Rock

Sandycove   The Muglins

Dalkey   Dalkey Island

EPISODE 2

Nestor

(2.1–449, PP. 24–36)

Episode 2. *Nestor*, 2.1–449 (24–36). In Book 2 of *The Odyssey*, Telemachus faces the suitors in council, is repudiated by them, and sails for the mainland to seek news of his father, as Athena in the guise of Mentor had counseled him. In Book 3 Telemachus arrives on the mainland and approaches Nestor, the "master charioteer" (3:17; Fitzgerald, p. 48), for advice. Pisistratus, the youngest of Nestor's sons, greets Telemachus; Nestor, though he knows only that Odysseus's homecoming is fated to be hard, affirms Telemachus's emergent manhood and recites part of the history of the homecoming of the Greek heroes, including the story of Agamemnon's homecoming and death and his son's punishment of the murderers, a story suggestive of what might be in store for Odysseus and Telemachus. In Book 4 Pisistratus guides Telemachus to the court of Menelaus, where Telemachus meets Helen and hears the story of Menelaus's homecoming.

Time: 10:00 A.M. Scene: a private school for boys in Dalkey, a village on the southeast headland of Dublin Bay, approximately one mile southeast of the Martello tower at Sandycove. Organ: none; Art: history [in Book 3 of *The Odyssey* Athena urges Telemachus: "Go to old Nestor, master charioteer, / so we may broach the storehouse of his mind. / Ask him with courtesy, and in his wisdom / he will tell you history and no lies" (3:17–20; Fitzgerald, p. 48)]; Color: brown; Symbol: horse; Technique: catechism (personal). Correspondences: *Nestor*—Deasy; *Pisistratus*, Nestor's youngest son—Sargent; *Helen*—Mrs. O'Shea [Parnell's mistress and, later, wife; see 2.394n].

The Linati schema, without specifying correspondences, adds Telemachus to the list of Persons.

2.1 (24:1). Cochrane – A Charles H. Cochrane, solicitor and commissioner for oaths, had offices at 29 Frederick Street in Dublin; residence, Cambridge House, 38 Ulverton Road, Dalkey (*Thom's* 1904, p. 1834).

2.2 (24:2)/2.12 (24:13)/2.18 (24:22). Tarentum/ Asculum/Pyrrhus – Stephen is questioning his class about Pyrrhus (318–272 B.C.) and his campaigns against the Romans on behalf of the Tarentines (a Greek colony in lower Italy). Pyrrhus had had a checkered career as a minor king and successful general before he took up the Tarentine cause in 280 B.C. He was reasonably successful against the Romans, winning battles at Siris in 280 B.C. and at Asculum in 279 B.C., but he won in such a costly way that the collapse of the Tarentines became inevitable.

2.7 (24:7). Fabled by the daughters of memory – William Blake (1757–1827), from *A Vision of the Last Judgment* (1810): "Fable or Allegory is Form'd by the daughters of Memory. Imagination is surrounded by the daughters of Inspiration, who in the aggregate are call'd Jerusalem." In a wider context, the daughters of Zeus and Mnemosyne (memory) are the nine muses of Greek mythology; see 15.1707n.

2.8–9 (24:9). Blake's wings of excess – A compound of two of the Proverbs of Hell from Blake's *The Marriage of Heaven and Hell* (c. 1790): "The road of excess leads to the palace of wisdom" and "No bird soars too high, if he soars with his own wings."

2.9–10 (24:9–11). the ruin of all space . . . time one livid final flame – Blake repeatedly predicts "the world . . . consumed in Fire" (as in *The Marriage of Heaven and Hell*), and he asserts in a letter to William Hayley, 6 May 1800, that "every Mortal loss is an immortal gain. The ruins of Time build mansions in Eternity." Stephen fuses fragments from Blake with a vision of the fall of Troy, a lost cause not unlike the efforts of the Tarentines under Pyrrhus to resist the dominion of Rome. From this apocalyptic vision arises a question about the nature of history: if, as Blake predicts in *The Marriage of Heaven and Hell*, the moment of transformation is "the livid final flame," then will "the whole creation . . . be consumed and appear infinite and holy, whereas it now appears finite & corrupt"?

2.12 (24:14). gorescarred – Not gore in the sense of thickened blood or to pierce by spear or horn, but in the obsolete sense of dirt, filth, stain.

2.14 (24:15–16). *Another victory like that and we are done for* – After the battle of Asculum "it is said, Pyrrhus replied to one that gave him joy of his victory, that one other such would utterly undo him" (Plutarch's *Lives*, "Pyrrhus," trans. Arthur Hugh Clough [Boston, 1863], vol. 3, p. 29.

2.18 (24:21). Armstrong – Apart from the context, the significance of this name is not known. (There was no Armstrong family resident in Vico Road, Dalkey, in 1904.) See Ellmann, p. 153.

2.18 (24:21–22). the end of Pyrrhus . . . ? – After Asculum, Pyrrhus continued to barnstorm around the Mediterranean world. That world was in a limbo of small-state anarchy with rivalries and lost causes enough for all the ambitious. His "end" came in 272 B.C.: Pyrrhus had undertaken to assist one of the leading citizens of Argos in a town feud. His opponent was Antigonus II of Macedon. Pyrrhus was trapped inside the town; when he attempted to slip out, he was caught up in a street fight and was about to kill one of his assailants when the assailant's mother threw a tile from a housetop. Pyrrhus was stunned, thrown from his horse, and killed by one of Antigonus's henchmen. See 2.48 (25:14).

2.20 (24:24). Comyn – There was no family of this name resident in Dalkey in 1904, but Comyn was the name of a powerful and prominent family in Scotland after the Norman Conquest. It spent itself in a futile (Pyrrhus-like) struggle to preserve the Scots' independence in the course of the thirteenth century.

2.25 (24:31). *Vico road, Dalkey – This has been repeatedly cited as an allusion to the Italian philosopher Giambattista Vico (1668–1744), whose concept of history as an endless *ricorso*, or "rosary," Joyce found fascinating. But there is room for doubt about this allusion because there is a Vico Road in Dalkey; because one of the models for Armstrong (Clifford Ferguson; see Ellmann, p. 153) lived in Vico Terrace; and because Stephen's free associations on Blakean and Aristotelian concepts of the nature of history put him in an essentially pre-Viconian position.

2.33 (24:40). Kingstown pier – For the pier as a metaphoric bridge, see 1.83–84n. The two L-shaped seawalls that form the artificial harbor at Kingstown (now Dun Laoghaire) are called East Pier and West Pier. East Pier, almost a mile long, was a fashionable promenade, complete with band concerts on summer evenings and opportunities for flirtation among groups of unattached young men and women.

2.48–49 (25:15). Julius Caesar not been knifed to death – Caesar (100–44 B.C.), Roman general, statesman, and dictator, was the victim of a conspiracy of sixty aristocrats who resented and feared his personal concentration of political power. Nineteenth-century historians insisted that his murder by stabbing was disastrous for the Roman Empire, since, in retrospect, it seems to have been prelude to a particularly unstable period in Roman history.

2.50–51 (25:17–18). the infinite possibilities they have ousted – A distinction based on Aristotle's discussion (in the *Metaphysics*) of the antithesis between "potential" (that which can move or be moved) and "actuality" ("the existence of the thing" which cannot move or be "dislodged"). In effect Aristotle argues that at any given moment in history there are a number of "possibilities" for the next moment, but only one of the possibilities can become "actual," and once it becomes actual, all other possibilities for that given moment are "ousted."

2.52 (25:19). Or was that only possible which came to pass? – This echoes another of Aristotle's distinctions, that between poetry and history in the *Poetics* (8:4–9:2): "From what we have said it will be seen that the poet's function is to describe, not the thing that has happened, but a kind of thing that might happen, i.e., what is possible as being probable or necessary. The distinction between historian and poet . . . consists really in this, that the one describes the thing that has been, and the other a kind of thing that might be."

2.52–53 (25:20). weave, weaver of the wind – In ancient Irish tradition weaving is connected with the art of prophecy; cf. 1.662n.

2.57 (25:25); 2.64–66 (25:32–34); 2.78 (26:7). *Weep no more . . . watery floor / Through the dear . . . walked the waves – From John Milton's (1608–74) "Lycidas" (1638), lines 165–93. The following is the whole passage from Milton's pastoral elegy on the death by drowning of his friend Edward King:

> Weep no more, woeful Shepherds weep
>   no more,   165
> For *Lycidas* your sorrow is not dead,
> Sunk though he be beneath the wat'ry
>   floor,
> So sinks the day-star in the Ocean bed,
> And yet anon repairs his drooping head,
> And tricks his beams, and with new-
>   spangled Ore,   170
> Flames in the forehead of the morning
>   sky:
> So *Lycidas*, sunk low, but mounted
>   high,
> Through the dear might of him that
>   walk'd the waves,
> Where other groves, and other streams
>   along,
> With *Nectar* pure his oozy Locks he
>   laves,   175

And hears the unexpressive nuptial
  Song,
In the blest Kingdoms meek of joy and
  love.
There entertain him all the Saints above,
In solemn troops, and sweet Societies
That sing, and singing in their glory
  move,   180
And wipe the tears for ever from his
  eyes.
Now *Lycidas*, the Shepherds weep no
  more;
Henceforth thou art the Genius of the
  shore,
In thy large recompense, and shalt be
  good
To all that wander in that perilous flood. 185

  Thus sang the uncouth Swain to
    th'Oaks and rills,
While the still morn went out with
  Sandals gray;
He touch't the tender stops of various
  Quills,
With eager thought warbling his *Doric*
  lay:
And now the Sun had stretch't out all
  the hills,   190
And now was dropt into the Western
  bay;
At last he rose, and twitch't his Mantle
  blue:
Tomorrow to fresh Woods, and Pastures
  new.

2.58 (25:26). Talbot – For one association with
this name, see 10.156–58n. There was no Talbot family resident in Dalkey in 1904, according to *Thom's* 1904.

**2.67 (25:35–36). a movement . . . an actuality
of the possible as possible** – From Aristotle's
definition of motion in the *Physics* 3:1: "The
fulfillment of what exists potentially, in so far as
it exists potentially, is motion—namely, of what
is alterable *qua* alterable, alteration."

**2.69–74 (25:37–26:2). *the library of Saint Ge-
nevieve . . . dragonscaly folds** – The library,
in Paris on the Place du Panthéon, was, according to Baedeker (*Paris and Its Environs* [Lon-
don, 1907], p. 285), "frequented almost exclusively by students" in the evening hours. The
iron girders that support the vaulting of the
large reading room do give the effect of a cave.
The passage also alludes to Blake, *The Marriage
of Heaven and Hell:* "I was in a Printing house
in Hell, & saw the method in which knowledge
is transmitted from generation to generation.

"In the first chamber was a Dragon-Man,
clearing away the rubbish from a cave's mouth;
within, a number of Dragons were hollowing
the cave."

**2.70–71 (25:39–40). a delicate Siamese
conned a handbook of strategy** – Siam corresponded roughly to modern Thailand. France,
through its presence in French Indochina
(roughly modern Vietnam, Laos, and Cam-
bodia), put increasing pressure on Siam for
territorial and other concessions in the closing
decades of the nineteenth century. The Franco-
Siamese convention of 1904 exacted further
concessions west of the Mekong River (once the
eastern boundary of Siam), and the Anglo-
French convention of the same year resolved
spheres of influence (British to the west of Siam
in Burma and Malaysia, French to the east). In
short, Siam was an embattled, quasi-colonial
state, its territorial integrity diminished but
"guaranteed" by the Anglo-French convention.

**2.74–75 (26:3–4). Thought is the . . . form of
forms** – From Aristotle's *On the Soul* 3:432a:
"As the hand is the instrument of instruments,
so the mind [*nous*, soul] is the form of forms and
sensation the form of sensibles." In *Metaphysics*
Aristotle argues that the prime mover is thought
thinking on itself.

2.72 (25:41). glowlamps – Incandescent light
bulbs, in this case made of clear glass, their fil-
aments visible.

**2.78 (26:7). *of Him that walked the waves* ** –
In Matthew 14:22–33, Jesus walks on the sea to
join and comfort his disciples whose ship is
"tossed with the waves: for the wind was contrary."

**2.86 (26:15–16). To Caesar . . . what is
God's** – Jesus has argued that man should pay
tribute only to God. The Pharisees attempt to
"entangle Jesus in his talk" by showing him a
Roman penny marked with Caesar's "image and
superscription" and asking, "Is it lawful to give
tribute to Caesar, or not?" Jesus' answer is a
riddle; he argues that the image on the "coin of
tribute" is Caesar's: "Render therefore to Caesar the things that are Caesar's; and to God,
the things that are God's" (Matthew 22:15–22
[Douay]; Mark 12:17; Luke 20:25).

**2.88–89 (26:19–20). *Riddle me . . . seeds to
sow* ** – The opening lines of a riddle that continues: "The seed was black and the ground was
white. / Riddle me that and I'll give you a pipe

(or pint)." Answer: writing a letter. Compare with the actual opening lines of the riddle Stephen propounds in 2.102–7 (26:33–38) (see note below).

2.92 (26:23). Hockey – The boys play the English game of field hockey instead of the recently revived Irish sport of hurling; see 12.58n and 12.645n.

2.102–7 (26:33–38); 2.115 (27:8). *The cock crew . . . to go to heaven . . .* The fox burying . . . *hollybush* – Stephen's riddle is a joke at the expense of riddles, since it is unanswerable unless the answer is already known. See P. W. Joyce, *English*, p. 187: "Riddle me, riddle me right: / What did I see last night? / The wind blew, / The cock crew, / The bells of heaven / Struck eleven. / 'Tis time for my poor soul to go to heaven." Answer: "The fox burying his *mother* under a holly tree."

2.123 (27:16). Sargent – Apart from the context, identity and significance are unknown. (There was no Sargent family resident in Dalkey, according to *Thom's* 1904.)

2.131 (27:25). Mr Deasy – The headmaster of the school (see Ellmann, pp. 152–53). His name may owe something to the Deasy Act (1860), an act ostensibly intended for land reform in Ireland but in practice a ruthless regulation of land tenancy in favor of landlords (i.e., in favor of the pro-English, anti-Catholic Establishment). In keeping with his name, Mr. Deasy is a "west Briton," one who regards Ireland as the westernmost province of England and who mimics English manners and morals. Ironically, there was a Rev. Daniel Deasy, resident as curate-in-charge of the Roman Catholic church in Castle Street, Dalkey, in 1904, and chaplain of the Loretto Abbey Female Boarding and Day School.

2.143 (27:38). The only true thing in life? – Stephen's friend Cranly has remarked in *A Portrait* 5:C: "Whatever else is unsure in this stinking dunghill of a world a mother's love is not."

2.144 (27:39). the fiery Columbanus – (543–615), Irish saint, one of the most learned and passionately eloquent of the Irish missionaries to the Continent. Columbanus is reputed to have left his mother "grievously against her will" (*Butler's "Lives of the Saints*," ed. Herbert Thurston, S.J., and Donald Attwater [London, 1956]).

2.155 (28:11). morrice – A Moorish dance. The Moors (2.157 [28:14]) were reputed to have introduced algebra into Europe during the Renaissance.

2.158 (28:14–15). Averroes and Moses Maimonides – Averroës (1126–98), a Spanish-Arabian philosopher and physician noted for his commentaries on Aristotle, which provided much of the background of medieval Christian Scholasticism. While he strove to reconcile Aristotle with Moslem orthodoxy (with heavy emphasis on God the Creator), he was suspected by the Moslem world of heterodoxy, and his reputation implied that both his Christian and Jewish adherents were likewise somehow heterodox.

Moses Maimonides (1135–1204), a Jewish rabbi, Talmudic scholar, and philosopher. Like Averroës, he had considerable influence on medieval Christian thought, notably on Aquinas; he was called the Light of the West. Maimonides' primary effort was at a reconciliation of Aristotelian rational thought with the revealed truth of orthodox Judaism.

Aquinas (1225–74) completes the triad because he sought much the same goal, a reconciliation of Aristotelian thought with the revealed truth of Christianity.

2.159 (28:15–16). flashing in their mocking mirrors – That is, Averroës and Maimonides (non-Christians) were "guilty" of scrying, divination by the "mirror of the sorcerers" (a crystal ball or other shining surface, such as a vessel filled with water).

2.159 (28:16). soul of the world – The Italian philosopher-mystic Giordano Bruno (1548–1600), whom the young Joyce regarded as the "father of what is called modern philosophy" (*CW*, p. 133), was indebted to, among others, Averroës. Bruno postulated an *anima del mondo* (Italian: "soul of the world") as both principle and cause of nature, the indwelling presence in the light of which form and matter, being and the capacity to be, are not separable as Aristotle thought them, but one, a unity.[1] Bruno began life as a Dominican monk and became, as Joyce described him, "a gipsy professor, a commentator of old philosophies and a deviser of new ones, a playwright, a polemist, a counsel for his

---

1 For this and other allusions to the presence of Giordano Bruno behind the scenes throughout *Ulysses*, I am indebted to a doctoral dissertation by Theoharis Constantine Theoharis, "The Unity of *Ulysses*," University of California, Berkeley, 1983.

own defence, and finally, a martyr burned at the stake in the Campo dei Fiori" (*CW*, p. 133). In late-nineteenth-century Theosophy (very much in vogue in avant-garde literary circles in Dublin and London; see 7.784n and 7.786–87n, and Scylla and Charybdis, passim) the *anima mundi* (Latin: "soul of the world") was the "divine essence which pervades, permeates, animates and informs all things from the smallest atom of matter to man and god" (H. P. Blavatsky, *The Key to Theosophy* [London, 1893], p. 203).

2.160 (28:16–18). a darkness shining . . . not comprehend – "In [God] was life; and the life was the light of men. And the light shineth in darkness; and the darkness comprehended it not" (John 1:4–5).

2.165 (28:25). *Amor matris:* **subjective and objective genitive** – Latin: "mother love." Ambiguous to Stephen because the phrase could mean the mother's love for her child (subjective) or the child's love for its mother (objective).

2.190 (29:12). Halliday – Apart from the context, identity and significance unknown. (*Thom's* 1904 does not list a Halliday family in residence in Dalkey.)

2.200–204 (29:24–28). As it was in the beginning, is now . . . and ever shall be . . . world without end – From the Gloria Patri, "Glory be to the Father, and to the Son, and to the Holy Ghost; as it was in the beginning, is now and ever shall be, world without end."

2.201 (29:25). Stuart coins – James II of England (1633–1701; king 1685–88), a Catholic, invaded Ireland and accepted Irish allegiance after being deposed from the English throne in 1688. In 1689 he debased the Irish currency by coining money out of inferior metals. The coins, though initially as worthless as the Stuart attempt to use Ireland (a bog) as a base from which to retake England, are, of course, rare. The coins bore the motto CHRISTO—VICTORE—TRIUMPHO (Christ in Victory and in Triumph).

2.202–3 (29:26–27). snug in their spooncase . . . all the gentiles – Mr. Deasy has a spooncase containing twelve spoons whose handles represent the figures of the twelve apostles. The spoons were the traditional present of sponsors at christenings. In Matthew 10, Jesus gives the twelve apostles "power to work miracles" and sends them out into the world with the admonition: "Go not into the way of the Gentiles, and

into any city of the Samaritans enter ye not: But go rather to the lost sheep of the house of Israel" (Matthew 10:5–6). In Acts 10–11 the apostles determine to preach to the Gentiles.

2.215 (29:39–40). *the scallop of saint James – The scallop is the attribute of St. James the Greater, whose shrine at Compostella, Spain, was one of the major goals of medieval pilgrimages. Pilgrims who had been to the shrine wore a scallop as a sign of their achievement.

2.226–27 (30:12). Symbols too of beauty and of power – In heraldry, shells are symbolic of the beauty, goodness, and wisdom of God; and the murex shell, which provided the Greeks with royal purple dye, is symbolic of sovereignty and the power of the gods.

2.238 (30:24–25). *If youth but knew* – Proverb: "If youth but knew what age would crave, it would at once both get and save."

2.239 (30:25–26). *Put but money in thy purse* – At the end of Act I, scene iii of *Othello*, Iago says to his dupe Roderigo, "put money in thy purse," repeatedly and with considerable cynicism, because Iago intends to use both Roderigo *and* his money.

2.242 (30:29–30). He knew what money was . . . He made money – Most of the sources on which Stephen (and Joyce) rely for biographical information about Shakespeare in Scylla and Charybdis assert that Shakespeare had a large professional income from shares in the Globe Theatre and its company and from the sale of his plays. The sources also cite in proof the considerable real estate holdings that Shakespeare acquired in and around Stratford after 1599. See 9.741–42nff.

2.249 (30:36). French Celt – The germ of the sun-never-sets image is in Herodotus (Xerxes brags about the glory of the Persian Empire). Subsequent reworkings of the phrase can be found in Capt. John Smith, Sir Walter Scott, Friedrich von Schiller, and Daniel Webster, none of them "French Celts."

2.256 (31:2). Curran – Constantine P. Curran, a Dublin friend of Joyce's. See Ellmann.

2.256 (31:2). *McCann – MacCann appears as a character in *A Portrait* 5:A.

2.256 (31:2–3). Fred Ryan – (1876–1913), an

Irish economist, journalist, and editor who wrote for and edited the magazine *Dana*, which began publication in 1904. W. K. Magee (under the pseudonym of John Eglinton; see Scylla and Charybdis) was coeditor of the magazine. Ryan also had aspirations as a playwright and was secretary of the Irish National Theatre Society, which eventually established the Abbey Theatre.

2.257 (31:3). Temple – Appears as a character in *A Portrait* 5:A and 5:C.

2.257 (31:3). Russell – George William Russell (AE; 1867–1935), a dominant figure in the Irish literary renaissance of the late nineteenth and early twentieth century. He was profoundly committed to the truths of mystical (Theosophical) experience, and he combined in one career the activities of prophet, poet, philosopher, artist, journalist, economic theorist, and practical worker for agrarian reform. See Scylla and Charybdis.

2.257 (31:4). Cousins – James H. Cousins, a Dubliner. Ellmann records his relation to Joyce and remarks that he was a "Theosophical poetaster" (Ellmann, p. 151 and passim).

2.257–58 (31:4). Bob Reynolds – Identity and significance unknown, unless this is W. B. Reynolds, "the music critic of the *Belfast Telegraph*, who had set some of his [Joyce's] poems to music" (Ellmann, p. 302).

2.258 (31:4). *Koehler – Identified as T. G. Keller, a Dublin literary friend of Joyce's (Ellmann, pp. 164, 200).

2.258 (31:5). *Mrs MacKernan – A Dubliner from whom Joyce rented a room in 1904 (Ellmann, p. 151 and passim).

2.266–67 (31:15–16). *Albert Edward, prince of Wales – (1841–1910), Queen Victoria's son and successor as Edward VII (king of England 1901–10).

2.269 (31:18). O'Connell's time – Daniel O'Connell (1775–1847), an Irish political leader known as "the Liberator" because he successfully agitated for the 1829 repeal of the laws that limited the civil and political rights of Catholics. His chief political weapon was "moral force" within the limits of constitutional procedures, though his followers pressed him to use illegal and violent means. He agitated for the repeal of the Act of Union, which united the parliaments

of England and Ireland in 1800, in a series of "monster meetings" (1841–43), but his efforts were interrupted when he was tried and sentenced to one year in prison for "seditious conspiracy." The end of his career was marred not only by his failing health but also by dissensions and oppositions between the partisans of "old" and "new" Ireland within his own party.

2.269 (31:19). *the famine in 46 – The disintegration of the Irish economy in the nineteenth century had condemned at least half of Ireland's population of eight million to abysmal poverty and to dependence on the potato as staple food. (At least three-quarters of the land under cultivation in Ireland was devoted to cattle and to crops, primarily wheat for export, which the poor simply could not afford.) The potato blight appeared in 1845, destroying the potato crop and reducing the poor to famine. The ruin of the tottering Irish economy was now complete. Since English policy had suppressed industry in Ireland, the agrarian collapse was a deathblow, not only to the peasantry but also to the many landlords who tried to tide their peasants over the famine and were ruined in the process. The population of Ireland declined from 8,295,061 in 1841 to 6,574,278 in 1851 through death by starvation and epidemic as well as immigration to America, and it continued to fall through the rest of the nineteenth century, until by 1903 it was 4,413,655 (*Thom's* 1904, p. 686). The famine has been repeatedly described as the worst event of its kind recorded in European history at a time of peace.

2.270 (31:19). the orange lodges – Emerged as Protestant nuclei of anti-Catholic violence in the 1790s and united to form the Orange Society after 1795. The society was anti-Union at its inception, but it became pro-Union shortly after 1800. The Orangemen were concentrated in Ulster, the northernmost counties of Ireland, and regarded themselves as "an organization for the maintenance of British authority in Ireland." When the English Parliament came close to granting Home Rule for Ireland in 1886, it was to the tune of anti–Home Rule riots in the Orangemen's stronghold of Belfast.

2.270 (31:20). repeal of the union – The Act of Union of 1800 dissolved the Irish Parliament and merged it with the English Parliament. It required that the Irish Parliament, which had attained a measure of legislative independence in the so-called Grattan Constitution of 1782, vote itself out of existence; this it did, encouraged by considerable bribery and skulduggery.

Union resulted in the displacement of political power from Dublin to London and a radical increase in absentee landlordism (and agrarian misrule) because the landlords moved to England to secure an influence in politics. Repeal of the Act of Union by the English Parliament thus became one of the central political issues in nineteenth- and early-twentieth-century Ireland.

2.271–72 (31:21–22). the prelates of your communion . . . as a demagogue – The Irish Roman Catholic bishops were far more energetic in their support of O'Connell's successful campaign for Catholic emancipation than they were of his subsequent campaign for repeal of the Act of Union. While some bishops were suspicious of O'Connell and his methods, it is hardly accurate to say that they "denounced" him.

2.272 (31:22). fenians – The Fenians (nicknamed the "hillside men") took their name from the Fianna of Irish legend, a standing force of warriors under Finn MacCool in the third century. The Fenian Society (Irish Republican Brotherhood), organized in 1858 by James Stephens, was committed to the achievement of Irish independence through terrorist tactics and violent revolution (rather than through parliamentary or constitutional reform). As Mr. Deasy uses the term, it is slang for radical republicans, those who favored an immediate end to English rule and the establishment of an independent Irish state with civil and religious liberties for all.

2.273 (31:23). Glorious, pious and immortal memory – The Orangeman's toast to the memory of William of Orange, William III (1650–1702); king of England (1689–1702), the patron "saint" of the radically Protestant Irish because he saved Ireland from James II and completed the English conquest of Ireland (effectively reducing it to the penal colony it was in the eighteenth century). "To the glorious, pious and immortal memory of the Great and Good King William III, who saved us from popery, slavery, arbitrary power, brass money and wooden shoes."

2.273–75 (31:23–26). The lodge of Diamond . . . true blue bible – Stephen contemplates a capsule version of an incident in Irish history. In the 1790s the northern Irish (from the "black north," after black or reactionary Protestants) organized a series of persecutions that were intended to drive all the Catholics out of Armagh, one of the northern counties. The Catholic ten-

ants organized a resistance, the Defenders. When a group of Defenders gathered at the lodge of Diamond, 21 September 1795, they were massacred for having "experimented with resistance" after the notice "To Hell or Connaught" had been nailed to the lodge door.

Planter's Covenant: the plantation system was developed in Queen Elizabeth's reign as a method of organizing land management in Ireland and as a way of pacifying the rebellious population. Roman Catholic Irish were declared in forfeit of their lands, and large, quasi-feudal plantations were granted to English and to loyal Anglo-Irish planters. A planter who received a grant of forfeited lands was required to "covenant" his loyalty to the English Crown by acknowledging the English sovereign as head not only of the State but also of the Church. The punitive potential of the plantation system was effectively exploited during the reign of James I of England (1566–1625; king 1603–25) and during the Protectorate under Cromwell, so effectively that the Roman Catholic population of Ireland was virtually reduced to feudal peasantry.

A *true blue* was originally a seventeenth-century Scottish Presbyterian or Covenanter (from the color blue they adopted in opposition to the Royalists' red during the English Civil War). Many of the colonists whom the English transported into northeastern Ireland (Ulster) in order to subdue or displace the Irish Catholic population and stabilize that province in the seventeenth century were fundamentalists of the "true blue" sort. For "Armagh the splendid," see 12.85n.

2.276 (31:26). Croppies lie down – "Croppy" after the close-cropped heads of the Wexford rebels in 1798; subsequently a term for any Irish rebel. The phrase itself is the refrain of several "loyal" (i.e., Orangeman's) ballads, among them "When the Paddies of Erin". First verse and chorus: "When the paddies of Erin took a pike in each hand, / And wisely concerted reform in the land; / Ough, and all that's before them they'd drive, to be sure, / And for conjured up grievances each had a cure. / But down, down, Croppies, lie down." The refrain is also quoted in the chorus of "The Old Orange Flute," a ballad about an Orangeman who is converted to Roman Catholicism but whose flute insisted on playing "Croppies Lie Down."

2.279 (31:29). sir John Blackwood – (1722–99), was offered a peerage to bribe him to vote for Union; he refused and, to quote a letter from Henry N. Blackwood Price to Joyce (1912), "died in the act of putting on his top boots in order to go to Dublin to vote against the Union" (quoted in Ellmann, pp. 326–27). Blackwood's son, Sir J. G. Blackwood, is however included by Josiah Barrington (1760–1834), in *The Rise and Fall of the Irish Nation* (1833), on the "black list" as having voted for Union and having been made Lord Dufferin in the transaction.

2.279–80 (31:30). all Irish, all kings' sons – Proverb: "All Irishmen are kings' sons" (after the ancient kings of Ireland). There is a similar Jewish proverb.

2.282 (31:32). *Per vias rectas* -- Latin: "by straight roads"; Sir John Blackwood's motto.

2.283 (31:33–34). the Ards of Down -- An arm-like peninsula on the Irish Sea in County Down, eighty miles north-northeast of Dublin. The district is just west of the Orangeman's stronghold of Belfast.

2.284–85 (31:35–36). *Lal the ral . . . road to Dublin* – From "The Rocky Road to Dublin," an anonymous Irish ballad that describes the adventures of a poor Catholic peasant boy from Connacht as he travels through Dublin to Liverpool. He is mocked, robbed, and housed with pigs during the crossing. In Liverpool, when his country is insulted he answers with his shillelagh and is joined by Galway boys (thus he finally wins respect in the rough world). Chorus: "For it is the rocky road, here's the road to Dublin; / Here's the rocky road, now fire away to Dublin."

2.286 (31:37). *Soft day – A usual Irish greeting, meaning a misty or drizzly day.

2.299 (32:13–14). the princely presence – That is, beneath the portrait of Edward VII, who was an ardent horse fancier; see 2.266–67n. Also, Stephen as Telemachus is in the presence of Nestor, master charioteer and king of Pylos.

2.301–3 (32:15–17). *lord Hastings' *Repulse . . . prix de Paris*, 1866 – Henry Weysford Rawdon-Hastings, marquess of Hastings (1842–68); his horse Repulse won the One Thousand Guineas (1866), an annual race at Newmarket in England. Hugh Lupus Grosvenor, first duke of Westminster (1825–99); his filly Shotover won the Two Thousand Guineas (1882), another of the annual races at Newmarket, and the Derby at Epsom Downs (1882). Henry Charles Fitzroy Somerset, eighth duke

of Beaufort (1824–99); his horse Ceylon did win the Grand Prix de Paris (1866), the most famous of French horse races, run annually at Longchamps outside of Paris.

2.309–10 (32:25). *Fair Rebel! . . . **Even money the favorite: ten to one the field** – The bookie offers ten to one odds that no other horse in the field can defeat the favorite. Fair Rebel ran at the odds Stephen recalls and won the Curragh Plate (4 June 1902), an annual race at Leopardstown, a racecourse six miles southeast of Dublin.

2.310 (32:25–26). thimbleriggers – Professional gamblers who run a variant of the shell game.

2.312 (32:28). clove of orange – A section of an orange, as in "a clove of garlic."

2.316 (32:33). crawsick – Ill in the morning after a drunken bout the night before.

2.321–22 (32:41). the foot and mouth disease – Aphthous fever, a virus disease that affects cattle, pigs, sheep, goats, and frequently man. In the early twentieth century there was no dependable cure for animals afflicted with the disease, and attempts to develop methods of immunizing cattle had had inconstant results. The occasion of Mr. Deasy's letter is somewhat anachronistic, since there was no outbreak of foot-and-mouth disease in Ireland in 1904, indeed not until 1912. The *Irish Daily Independent* for 16 June 1904 reported on the "Diseases of Animals Acts for 1903" (just issued by the Department of Agriculture) and remarked, "The Irish cattle, however, continued practically immune from the more serious contagious diseases. There was no cattle plague, foot and mouth disease, pleuro pneumonia, or sheep louse in 1903" (p. 4, col. 7).

2.325–26 (33:3). The way of all our old industries - See below, 12.1242–47nn inclusive.

2.326 (33:3–4). Liverpool ring . . . Galway harbour scheme – In the 1850s a group of English and Irish promoters proposed to transform Galway Harbor on the west coast of Ireland into a transatlantic port. Their first step was to establish a Galway–Halifax steamship line, but the enterprise was plagued by accidents that, as they mounted in number, were widely rumored to be the result of sabotage. The hard-luck story began in 1858, when one of the company's ships, the *Indian Empire*, struck Marguerite Rock in Galway Harbor, the only obstacle in a channel nine miles wide. The ship was not seriously damaged, but the episode prefigured six years of accidents and mismanagement. The company closed shop in 1864. There is no evidence that a "Liverpool ring" (Liverpool shipping interests fearing the competition of Galway) plotted to frustrate the plan; the evidence, on the contrary, points to the maritime incompetence of the promoters.

2.327–28 (33:4–5). European conflagration . . . of the channel – In the event of a European war, transatlantic shipping would not have to run the gamut of St. George's Channel between Ireland and Wales or the North Channel between Ireland and Scotland, but could enter Galway directly from the Atlantic.

2.329 (33:7). Cassandra – Someone who prophesies doom and is not heard. After Cassandra, daughter of Priam of Troy, who refused Apollo's love and was condemned by him to speak true prophecies that would not be believed. Her predictions of the destruction of Troy thus went unheeded.

2.329–30 (33:7–8). woman who . . . should be – Helen of Troy, whom Telemachus is to meet at Menelaus's palace when he leaves Nestor. See 2.391–92n.

2.332 (33:11). Koch's preparation – For the prevention of anthrax (not foot-and-mouth disease). The German physician and bacteriologist Robert Koch (1843–1910) developed a method of preventing anthrax by inoculation in 1882. In the early twentieth century two of his assistants attempted to apply Koch's methods to immunize cattle against foot-and-mouth disease, but their success was minimal.

2.332–33 (33:12). Serum and virus – A reference to what were in the early twentieth century new methods of developing antitoxins for treatment of various diseases.

2.333 (33:12). Percentage of salted horses – Horses that had been treated with T.C., a substance derived from the "virus of tuberculosis" in 1905 by the German physician Emil Adolph von Behring (1854–1917). T.C. was supposed to render animals immune to tuberculosis, but initial claims proved somewhat overoptimistic. The production of T.C. involved the use of saline solutions, hence "salted."

2.333 (33:12). Rinderpest – Another cattle disease for which there was no known cure.

2.333–34 (33:12–13). Emperor's horses at Murzsteg, lower Austria – The Austrian emperor did maintain a hunting lodge and stable at Mürzsteg, but Dr. Richard Blaas, director of the House, Court, and State Archives in Vienna, can find no evidence of veterinary experiments at Mürzsteg between the years 1895 and 1914. Cf. Henry N. Blackwood Price's letter, quoted in Ellmann, pp. 326–27n.

2.334 (33:13). Veterinary surgeons – A relatively new branch of medical science at the turn of the century. Mr. Deasy's letter apparently claims that cures for foot-and-mouth and other diseases were being developed; that claim is premature. But the central argument of his letter is sound: that epidemic diseases among animals should be investigated and treated in the light of the latest scientific methods.

2.334 (33:14). Mr Henry Blackwood Price – Corresponded with Joyce in 1912 about an outbreak of foot-and-mouth disease in Ireland. See Ellmann, pp. 325ff.

2.346–47 (33:28–29). England is in the hands of the jews – See 1.667n.

2.355–56 (33:38–39). *The harlot's cry . . . winding sheet* – Lines 115–16 from William Blake's "Auguries of Innocence" (c. 1803). In context: "The Whore and Gambler, by the State / Licenc'd, build that Nation's fate. / The Harlot's cry from street to street / Shall weave Old England's winding sheet. / The Winner's Shout, the Loser's Curse, / Dance before dead England's Hearse."

2.357–58 (33:40–41). the sunbeam in which he halted – Cf. *The Odyssey*: "While Nestor talked, the sun went down the sky / and gloom came on the land" (3:329; Fitzgerald, p. 57).

2.361 (34:3). They sinned against the light – In the first chapter of the Gospel of John, John the Baptist is "sent to bear witness of that Light [Jesus]. That was the true Light which lighteth every man that cometh into the world" (1:8–9). Mr. Deasy's phrase rests on the assumption that the Jews not only refused that Light (Jesus' presence and message) but also demanded that it be extinguished by crucifixion.

2.362 (34:5). wanderers on the earth – The Jews were driven out of their homeland and dispersed by the Romans under the emperor Vespasian (A.D. 9–79; emperor 69–79) after the capture and destruction of Jerusalem in 70. Subsequently they suffered a series of dispersions at the hands of the Christian European nations. Figuratively, the allusion is to the legend of the Wandering Jew. Christian versions of the legend revolve around a Jew who rejects or reviles Jesus at the time of the Crucifixion and who is condemned to wander the earth until the Last Judgment or until the last of his race is dead (or, in some versions, until he repents).

2.364 (34:6). the Paris stock exchange – The bourse (stock exchange) in Paris was an early-nineteenth-century copy of the temple of Vespasian in Rome (see preceding note). The scene Stephen recalls is not outside but inside the hall; the "steps" are "the *parquet*, at the end, a railed-off space which the sworn brokers . . . are alone privileged to enter" (Karl Baedeker, *Paris and Its Environs* [London, 1907], p. 208). Baedeker warns visitors that, while admission is free, "the crush is anything but pleasant."

2.365–66 (34:8). They swarmed . . . the temple – An allusion to the Gospel accounts of the money changers in the temple at Jerusalem. Each of the four Gospels records Jesus' expulsion of the moneychangers (Matthew 21:12–13; Mark 11:15–17; Luke 19:45–46; John 2:13–16).

2.377 (34:22–23). History . . . trying to awake – After Jules Laforgue (1860–87), *Mélanges posthumes* (Paris, 1903), "Lettres à Mme.?," p. 279: "La vie est trop triste, trop sale. L'histoire est un vieux cauchemar bariolé qui ne se doute pas que les meilleures plaisanteries sont les plus courtes" (Life is very dreary, very sordid. History is an old and variegated nightmare that does not suspect that the best jokes are also the most brief).

2.380–81 (34:27–28). *All human history moves toward one great goal, the manifestation of God – In Mr. Deasy's mouth this expresses the Victorian faith in the inevitability of man's moral and spiritual progress. By the end of the century this faith, summed up by Alfred, Lord Tennyson (1809–92), at the end of *In Memoriam* (1850) as "one far-off divine event, / To which the whole creation moves," was widely regarded as a feeble substitute for vital spiritual commitment. As a philosophy of history, however, it has enjoyed a rigorous heritage, from St. Augustine of Hippo (354–430) through Giordano Bruno (see 2.159n) to the German philosopher Georg Wilhelm Friedrich Hegel (1770–1831) and his attempt to render scientific the revealed truths of religion.

2.386 (34:33). A shout in the street – "Wisdom crieth without; she uttereth her voice in the streets . . . saying, How long, ye simple ones will ye love simplicity? and the scorners delight in their scorning, and fools hate knowledge?" (Proverbs 1:20–22).

2.390 (34:39–40). A woman brought sin into the world – The biblical account of the Fall in the Garden of Eden is not as antifeminine as Mr. Deasy's remark implies: "And when the woman saw that the tree was good for food, and that it was pleasant to the eyes, and a tree to be desired to make one wise, she took of the fruit thereof, and did eat, and gave also unto her husband with her; and he did eat" (Genesis 3:6). However, the antifeminine version of the Fall has been a strong component of Christian tradition.

2.391–92 (34:41–42). Helen, the runaway . . . war on Troy – In Greek mythology, Aphrodite awarded Helen, the wife of Menelaus, king of Sparta, to Paris, the son of King Priam of Troy, when Paris adjudged Aphrodite more beautiful than Hera and Athena. Then Menelaus, with the help of his brother Agamemnon, the king of Mycenae, organized a Greek invasion of Troy, which fell to the Greeks after ten years of war.

2.393–94 (35:1–2). MacMurrough's . . . Breffni – Dermod MacMurrough, the king of Leinster (1135–71). Deposed in 1167, he fled to England, where he solicited the aid of Henry II and was joined by several of Henry's lords for the first Anglo-Norman invasion of Ireland, in 1169. A quaint nineteenth-century history describes him as follows: "Owing to his youth and inexperience . . . he became an oppressor of the nobility. . . . This of itself brought him trouble, which another circumstance contributed to increase for he eloped [in 1152] with Devorgilla, the wife of O'Ruarc [O'Rourke] Prince of Briefny [Breffni] and East Meath." "Leman" archaically meant husband, but Mr. Deasy is using the word in the modern sense and thus has the relationship muddled.

2.394 (35:2–3). A woman . . . Parnell low – Parnell was named as correspondent in a divorce case as a result of his liaison with Mrs. Katherine O'Shea, and this resulted in the collapse both of Parnell's career and of Irish hopes for the achievement of Home Rule under his leadership.

2.394–95 (35:3). but not the one sin – That is, the Irish have not been guilty of the sin against the Light. See 2.361n.

2.397–98 (35:6–7). *For Ulster will . . . will be right* – Ulster was the northern of the four provinces of early Ireland, together with Leinster (east), Connacht (west), and Munster (south). Today (1985) the political entity of Northern Ireland is frequently called Ulster, but the predominantly Protestant and Unionist six counties of Northern Ireland are really a gerrymandered reduction of the old province of Ulster's nine counties. During the late nineteenth century the majority of people in Ulster were violently opposed to Home Rule for Ireland. Lord Randolph Spencer Churchill (1849–95) capitalized on the sentiments of Ulster in his campaigns against Gladstone and the Home Rule Bill. Lord Churchill first used what Winston Churchill called "the jingling phrase" in a letter of 7 May 1886. The phrase became a battle cry for anti-Catholic, anti-Home Rule forces.

2.412 (35:22). *Telegraph. Irish Homestead* – The *Evening Telegraph* was a four-page, nine-column daily newspaper in Dublin. The *Irish Homestead* was a weekly Dublin newspaper with which AE (George William Russell) was associated. In 1904 the paper was edited by H. F. Norman; Russell was editor from 1905 to 1923. The paper emphasized agrarian reform and was self-consciously addressed to rural Ireland. "The pig's paper" is Stephen's epithet for the *Irish Homestead* (9.321 [193:2]).

2.415 (35:26). Mr Field, M.P. – William Field, member of Parliament and president of the Irish Cattle Traders and Stock Owners Association in 1904.

2.416–17 (35:26–27). a meeting of the cattle-traders' . . . **City Arms Hotel** – The Irish Cattle Traders and Stock Owners Association

held meetings every Thursday at its offices in the City Arms Hotel, owned by Elizabeth O'Dowd, at 54 Prussia Street (near the cattle market in northwestern Dublin).

2.431 (36:2–3). bullockbefriending bard – An allusion to Homer, because Homer "befriended" the cattle of the sun-god by condemning the members of Odysseus's crew who violated the god's prohibition and slaughtered some of the cattle (Book 12 of *The Odyssey*). The phrase also alludes to Stephen's preoccupation with Thomas Aquinas, who was called the "dumb ox" by his fellow students at Cologne. Albertus Magnus (1193–1280), Aquinas's teacher, is supposed to have said, "We call him the dumb ox, but he will one day give such a bellow as shall be heard from one end of the world to the other."

2.442 (36:14). Because she never let them in – Jews are first mentioned as resident in Ireland in eleventh-century documents; Henry II acknowledged their presence (and legitimated it) by assigning custody of the King's Judaism in Ireland to one of his lords in 1174. From the time of the Norman Conquest the King's Judaism meant that the Jews were literally the king's chattel, but in practice they were protected, their rights to free exercise of their religion guaranteed and their businesses as merchants and moneylenders relatively secure. Jews were expelled from Ireland, as from England, in 1290 and were resettled in both countries under Cromwell in the mid–seventeenth century. There is no evidence that Ireland "never let them in" and considerable evidence to the contrary, including various legislative attempts to provide civil rights for Jews, which were finally successful in the course of the nineteenth century (see 14.906–7n). *Thom's* 1904 reports in "Statistics of Ireland" (p. 693) that there were 3,898 Jews resident in Ireland in 1901, an increase of 2,119 since 1891.

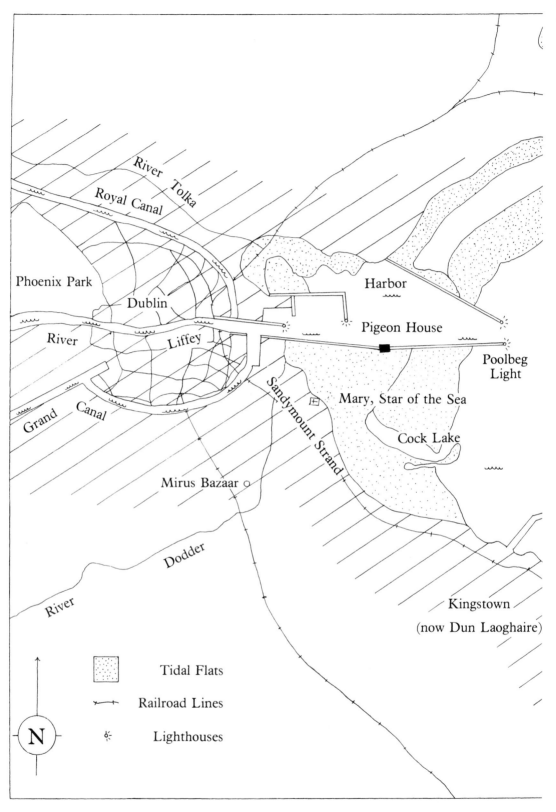

River Tolka

Royal Canal

Phoenix Park

Dublin

River

Liffey

Grand Canal

Sandymount Strand

Harbor

Pigeon House

Poolbeg Light

Mary, Star of the Sea

Cock Lake

Mirus Bazaar

Dodder

River

Kingstown
(now Dun Laoghaire)

Tidal Flats

Railroad Lines

Lighthouses

N

EPISODE 3. *Proteus*

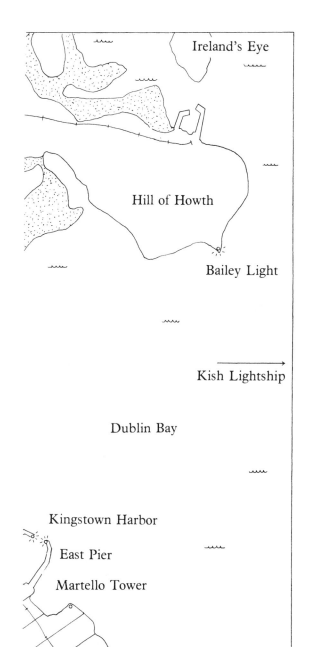

Ireland's Eye

Hill of Howth

Bailey Light

Kish Lightship

Dublin Bay

Kingstown Harbor

East Pier

Martello Tower

Sandycove

Dalkey

Dalkey Island

Dalkey
Hill

EPISODE 3

Proteus

(3.1–505, PP. 37–51)

Episode 3: *Proteus,* **3.1–505 (37–51).** In Book 4 of *The Odyssey,* Telemachus is at the court of Menelaus, and Menelaus recounts the story of his journey home from Troy. Forced by adverse weather to detour by way of Egypt, when he set sail again he was becalmed on Pharos, a rocky island just west of the Nile delta. Menelaus did not know which of the gods had him "pinned down" (4:380; Fitzgerald, p. 76) for, it turned out, neglect of the rules of sacrifice; nor did he know how to continue his voyage home. The daughter of the "Ancient of the Sea," Proteus, second in command to Poseidon, took pity on Menelaus and intervened to tell him that her father had the power of prophecy. To get Proteus to speak, Menelaus would have to grasp and hold him even though he would "take the forms / of all beasts, and water, and blinding fire" in the attempt to escape (4:417–18; Fitzgerald, p. 77 [cf. 3.477–79n]). Menelaus did succeed, and Proteus answered his questions, telling him how to break the spell that bound him to Egypt and telling him also of the deaths of Ajax and Agamemnon and of the whereabouts of Odysseus, marooned and in bondage on Calypso's island.

Time: 11:00 A.M. Scene: Sandymount Strand, the beach just south of the mouth of the Liffey and the Pigeon House breakwater, which extends the south bank of the Liffey out into Dublin Bay. Stephen has come from Dalkey to Dublin by public transportation, and he now idles away the hour and a half before his scheduled meeting with Mulligan at 12:30 (which he ends up skipping). Organ: none; Art: philology; Color: green; Symbol: tide; Technique: monologue (male). Correspondences: *Proteus*— primal matter [impenetrability in space and inevitable or uninterrupted extension in time];[1] *Menelaus*—Kevin Egan [Telemachus's visit to the palace of Menelaus is reflected in Stephen's recall of his mission to Paris and of Kevin Egan's "palace"]; *Megapenthus*—Cocklepicker [Megapenthus was born before the walls of Troy, the son of Menelaus by a slave girl. Megapenthus's wedding feast is being celebrated when Telemachus arrives at Menelaus's mansion].

The Linati schema in addition lists under

---

[1] Compare Walter Pater's vision of the "whirlpool," the "eager and devouring flame" of "our physical life" that is "a perpetual motion" of combining and recombining "natural elements." "Or if we begin with the inward world of thought and feeling, the whirlpool is still more rapid, the flame more eager and devouring" (in conclusion to *The Renaissance* [London, 1873]).

Persons (without specifying correspondences) Helen and Telemachus.

3.1 (37:1). Ineluctable modality of the visible – Exact source unknown, but Aristotle does argue in *De Sensu et Sensibili* (Of Sense and the Sensible) (see 3.4n) that the substance of a thing perceived by the eye is not present in the form or color of the perceptual image (in contradistinction to sound and taste, which involve a "becoming," or an intermixture of substance and form, in the perceptual image). In effect, Aristotle says that the ear participates in (and thus can modify) the substance of what it hears, but the eye does not.

3.2 (37:2–3). Signatures of all . . . to read – Jakob Boehme (1575–1624), a German mystic, maintained that everything exists and is intelligible only through its opposite. Thus, the "modality" of visual experience stands (as signatures to be read) in necessary opposition to the true substances, spiritual identities. As John Sparrow put it in his prefatory notes to translations of Boehme's *The Forty Questions of the Soul* and *The Clavis* (1647; reprinted London, 1911), p. xi: "Boehme, not being yet sufficiently satisfied with two visions of 'the divine light,' went forth into the open fields, and there perceived the wonderful or wonderworks of the Creator in the *signatures,* shapes, figures and qualities or properties of all created things, very clearly and plainly laid open; whereupon, being filled with exceeding joy, kept silence, praising God." In *The Clavis* (p. 19) Boehme remarks that Mercury, "the word or speaking," means "the motion and separation of nature, by which everything is figured with its own signature." Boehme begins chapter 1 of his *Signatura Rerum* (The Signature of All Things) with proposition 1: "All whatever is spoken, written or taught of God, without the knowledge of the signature is dumb and void of understanding; for it proceeds only from an historical conjecture, from the mouth of another, wherein the spirit without knowledge is dumb; but if the spirit opens to him the *signature,* then he understands the speech of another; and further, he understands how the spirit has manifested and revealed itself (out of the essence through the principle) in the sound of the voice."

3.4 (37:4). coloured signs – The Irish educator, philosopher, and Church of Ireland bishop of Cloyne George Berkeley (1685–1753) argued in *An Essay Towards a New Theory of Vision* (Dublin, 1709) that we do not "see" objects as such; rather, we see only colored signs and then take these to be objects: "Sitting in my study I hear a coach drive along the street; I look through the casement and see it; I walk out and enter into it. Thus, common speech would incline one to think I heard, saw, and touched the same thing, to wit, the coach. It is nevertheless certain the ideas intromitted by each sense are widely different, and distinct from each other; but, having been observed constantly to go together, they are spoken of as one and the same thing" (section 46).

3.4 (37:4–5). Limits of the diaphane. But he adds: in bodies – Aristotle's theory of vision, as developed in *De Sensu et Sensibili* (Of Sense and the Sensible) and *De Anima* (On the Soul). In *De Anima* Aristotle argues that color is the "peculiar object" of sight, as sound is that of hearing. In *De Sensu* he postulates that the "Translucent" (diaphane) is "not something peculiar to air or water, or any of the other bodies usually called translucent, but is a common 'nature' and power, capable of no separate existence of its own, but residing in them, and subsisting likewise in all other bodies in a greater or less degree. . . . But it is manifest that, when the Translucent is in determinate bodies, its bounding extreme [limit] must be something real; and that colour is just this 'something' we are plainly taught by facts—colour being actually either *at* the external limit, or being itself that limit, in bodies. . . . It is therefore the Translucent, according to the degree in which it subsists in bodies (and it does so in all more or less), that causes them to partake of colour. But since the colour is at the extremity of the body it must be at the extremity of the Translucent in the body" (from 439a, b, *The Works of Aristotle*, trans. J. A. Smith, ed. W. D. Ross [Chicago, 1952], vol. 1, p. 676).

3.5–6 (37:6–7). By knocking his sconce against them – Aristotle has proven the existence of "bodies" in a manner similar to Dr. Samuel Johnson's (1709–84) refutation of "Bishop Berkeley's [see 3.4n] ingenious sophistry to prove the non-existence of matter, and that everything in the universe is merely ideal" (James Boswell, *Life of Johnson*, 6 August 1763). Boswell reports, "I shall never forget the alacrity with which Johnson answered, striking his foot with mighty force against a large stone, till he rebounded from it, 'I refute it thus.'"

3.6 (37:7–8). Bald he was and a millionaire –

Medieval embellishments of the rather sparse biographical information about Aristotle.

3.6–7 (37:8). *maestro di color che sanno* – Italian: "master of those that know." From Dante's description of Aristotle in the *Inferno* (4:131).

3.8 (37:9). adiaphane – The opaque.

3.8–9 (37:9–10). If you can put your five fingers through it, it is a gate, if not, a door – A parody of Dr. Johnson's manner of definition in his *Dictionary of the English Language* (1755). Johnson's entry on "Door": "*Door* is used of house, and *gates* of cities and public buildings except in the license of poetry."

3.13, 15 (37:14, 17). *Nacheinander . . . Nebeneinander – German: "One after another . . . Side by side." In his book *Laocoön* (1766), the German dramatist and critic Gotthold Ephraim Lessing (1729–81) set out to distinguish between subjects appropriate to the visual arts and those appropriate to poetry: "In the one case the action is visible and progressive, its different parts occurring one after the other (*nacheinander*) in a sequence of time, and in the other the action is visible and stationary, its different parts developing in co-existence (*nebeneinander*) in space." Lessing implies that the first is the subject of poetry and asserts that the second is the subject of painting (*Laocoön*, trans. Edward Allen McCormick [Indianapolis, Ind., 1962], p. 77).

3.14 (37:16). a cliff that beetles o'er his base – *Hamlet* I.iv.70–71. See 1.567–68 (18:25).

3.16 (37:18). My ash sword – See 1.528n.

3.16–17 (37:19). My two feet . . . his legs – Stephen has on shoes and trousers that Mulligan has thrown away.

3.18 (37:20–21). *Los demiurgos. Am I walking into eternity – "Los, the creator," one of William Blake's symbolic figures, is central to "The Book of Los" (1795): "all was / Darkness round Los" (1:9–10), and "Incessant the falling Mind labor'd / Organising itself" (2:9–10). Los, for Blake, is related to the Four Zoas, the primal faculties, and is the embodiment of the creative imagination. The "Demiurge" was both Plato's name for the creator of the material world and, in Gnostic theory and Theosophy, the "architect of the world" (see 1.658n). Compare also the moment in Blake's *Milton* when

Milton enters Blake through the left foot: "And all this Vegetable World appear'd in my left foot / As a bright sandal form'd immortal of precious stones and gold. / I stoop'd down and bound it on to walk forward thro' Eternity" (Book the First. Plate 21).

3.19 (37:22). Wild sea money – "Shells" is slang for money.

3.19–20 (37:22–23). Dominie Deasy kens them a' – Scots dialect: *dominie*, "teacher, schoolmaster, pedagogue"; *kens*, "knows." Source unknown.

3.21–22 (37:24–25). *Won't you come to Sandymount / Madeline the mare?* – A play on one of two names: Madeleine Lemaire (1845–1928), a French watercolorist whose portraits, floral themes, and illustrations (particularly those for Ludovic Halévy's *L'Abbé Constantin*, 1882) were much in fashion between 1880 and 1910. Or Philippe-Joseph Henri Lemaire (1798–1880), a French sculptor who created a well-known relief of the Last Judgment in the tympanum of Paris's Madeleine (the church of St. Mary Magdalene). If the pun holds, he could have come to Sandymount and similarly improved the Church of Mary, Star of the Sea, in Leahy's Terrace, which Stephen has just passed on his way to Sandymount strand.

3.26 (37:29). *Basta!* – Italian: "Enough!"

3.27–28 (37:31–32). and ever shall be, world without end – See 2.200–204n.

3.29 (37:33). Leahy's terrace – Runs from Sandymount Road to Beach Road (and the shore of Dublin Bay) between Sandymount and Irishtown, one-half mile south of the mouth of the Liffey.

3.30 (37:34). *Frauenzimmer* – German: originally, "a lady of fashion," subsequently, and in contempt, "a nitwit, drab, sloven, wench."

3.31–32 (37:35–36). like Algy . . . our mighty mother – That is, like Swinburne; see 1.77–78n and 1.85n.

3.32 (37:36–37). lourdily – Heavily, after the French *lourd*, "heavy."

3.32 (37:37). gamp – A large, bulky umbrella, after Mrs. Sairey Gamp in Dickens's *Martin Chuzzlewit* (1843–44). Mrs. Gamp not only carries a large, badly wrapped umbrella, she is also nurse and midwife in the novel.

3.33 (37:38). the liberties – In 1904, a run-down section, largely slum, in central Dublin south of the Liffey. The area was originally called "the Liberties" because it was formed by the estate of the earl of Meath and the landholdings of the two medieval cathedrals, Christ Church and Saint Patrick's, properties exempt from city jurisdiction and taxation. In the eighteenth century the area's privileges made it a textile and manufacturing center, but it also became a breeding ground for civic disorder thanks to the Liberty Boys (gangs of immigrant Protestant workers).

3.33–34 (37:38–39). Mrs Florence MacCabe, relict of the late Patk MacCabe – A Patrick J. MacCabe, a "meat purveyor" at 8 Talbot Street, was high sheriff of Dublin in 1902 (*Thom's* 1904, pp. 1604, 1798).

3.34 (37:39–40). Bride Street – A street of tenements in the Liberties in south-central Dublin.

3.35 (37:41). Creation from nothing – As in the Judeo-Christian concept of the Creation: "In the beginning God created the heaven and the earth" (Genesis 1:1).

3.38 (38:2–3). why mystic monks – That is, are fascinated by the navel and gaze at it in the discipline of contemplation.

3.38 (38:3). Will you be as gods? – A version of Satan's approach to Eve: "For God doth know that in the day ye eat thereof, then your eyes shall be opened, and ye shall be as gods, knowing good and evil" (Genesis 3:5).

3.38 (38:3). omphalos – See 1.176n.

3.39 (38:4). Aleph, alpha – Initial letters of the Hebrew and Greek alphabets, respectively.

3.39–40 (38:5). nought, nought, one – Creation (as only God can create) from nothing.

3.41 (38:6). Adam Kadmon – In Theosophical lore, man complete (androgynous) and unfallen. "Starting as a pure and perfect spiritual being, the Adam of the second chapter of Genesis, not satisfied with the position allotted to him by the Demiurgos (who is the eldest first-begotten, the Adam-Kadmon), Adam the second, the man of dust, strives in his pride to become Creator in his turn" (H. P. Blavatsky, *Isis Unveiled* [New York, 1886], vol. 1, p. 297).

3.41–42 (38:6–7). Heva, naked . . . no navel – *Cheva*, Hebrew: "Life"; an early version of Eve's name. Cabalistic tradition held that Eve had no navel because she was not born of woman (see H. P. Blavatsky, *Isis Unveiled* [New York, 1886]).

3.42 (38:7). Belly without blemish – Cf. Song of Solomon 4:7: "Thou art all fair, my love; there is no spot in thee" (Christ in praise of his spouse, the Church).

3.43 (38:8). whiteheaped corn – "Thy navel is like a round goblet, which wanteth not liquor: thy belly is like an heap of wheat set about with lilies" (Song of Solomon 7:2).

3.43–44 (38:8–9). corn, orient . . . everlasting to everlasting – The opening phrase of a childhood vision of Eden from Thomas Traherne's (1637–74) *Centuries of Meditations* (first published, London, 1908), Century III, section 3: "The Corn was Orient and Immortal Wheat, which never should be reaped, nor was ever sown. I thought it had stood from everlasting to everlasting."

3.44 (38:9). Womb of sin – Eve's belly, because through her (and through Adam) sin came into the world.

3.45 (38:10). made not begotten – The Nicene Creed (325) maintains that Jesus, unlike all other men, was "begotten, but not made, of one essence consubstantial with the Father." The creed forms part of the ordinary of the Mass on all Sundays and on more important feast days.

3.47 (38:12–13). the coupler's will – God is the "coupler" who joins man and woman together in the sacrament of marriage. His "will," according to Catholic doctrine, is that humankind should "increase and multiply" (Genesis 1:28) by having as many children as possible.

3.47–49 (38:13–14). *From before the ages He . . . A *lex eterna* stays about Him – *Lex eterna*, Latin: "eternal law." In the *Summa Theologica*, Prima Secundae, Query 91, article 1, "Varieties of Law," St. Thomas Aquinas says: "The ruling idea of things which exists in God as the effective sovereign of them all has the nature of law.

Then since God's mind does not conceive in time, but has an eternal concept . . . it follows that this law should be called eternal. Hence: 1. While not as yet existing in themselves things nevertheless exist in God in so far as they are foreseen and preordained by Him; so St. Paul speaks of God summoning *things that are not yet in existence as if they already were*. Thus the eternal concept of divine law bears the character of a law that is eternal as being God's ordination for the governance of things he foreknows" (trans. Thomas Gilby, O.P., for Blackfriars, Cambridge, England, *Law and Political Theory* [New York, 1963], vol. 28, pp. 19, 21).

3.50–52 (38:16–19). Arius to try . . . breathed his last – See 1.657n. Arius died of "hemorrhage of the bowels" (intestinal cancer?) on the eve of what would have been a great triumph for him and his followers. He had journeyed to Constantinople in 336 to make an apparently orthodox confession of faith to the emperor. The emperor then ordered Alexander, bishop of Constantinople, to administer Holy Communion to Arius on the following Sunday. That ministration would have been public evidence that Arius was no longer excommunicant, but Arius died before it took place. The manner, timing, and place (in a public toilet) of his death were exploited by the defenders of the faith as a way of further refuting his heresies by *argumentum ad hominum* and as evidence of God's displeasure with the heretic. Epiphanius (c. 315–403), in *Adversus Haereses*, gives a splendidly one-sided account.

To try conclusions: Hamlet, in the bedroom scene, mocks his mother and suggests that she will, against all better judgment, betray him to his uncle Claudius, "and like the famous ape, / To try conclusions, in the basket creep / And break your own neck down [by leaping out of the basket in imitation of the birds that have escaped]" (III.iv.194–96).

The compound "contransmagnificandjewbangtantiality" includes *consubstantiality* (of the Father and the Son and the Holy Spirit), which Arius denied, and *transubstantiality* (of the Son over the Holy Spirit and of the Father over the Son), which Arius affirmed. "Magnific" suggests *Magnificat* (the Blessed Virgin Mary's song of thanksgiving for her role in the Word-made-flesh, Luke 1:46–55) plus *magnificent* and *magnify*. "Jew" is a reminder that the Son was born of a Jew and rejected by the Jews. "Bang" suggests both the controversial origin of Christianity and the sustained controversy over Arianism. See 14.307–8n.

3.53–54 (38:20). widower of a widowed see – Arius, presbyter and pastor of a church in Alexandria when the controversy over his beliefs began, was deposed in 321 by a council of Egyptian and Libyan bishops. From that time until his death in 336, Arius, banished by the Church hierarchy, had a considerable following, but he never achieved the bishopric his importance suggests he deserved.

3.54 (38:21). *omophorion* – The distinctive vestment of bishops, an embroidered strip of white silk worn around the neck so that the ends cross on the left shoulder and fall to the knee.

3.55 (38:22). nipping and eager airs – Horatio to Hamlet as they watch on the battlements for the appearance of the Ghost (I.iv.2).

3.56–57 (38:24). the steeds of Mananaan – The waves are the white manes of the horses of Mananaan MacLir, the Irish god of the sea, who had Proteus's ability for self-transformation.

3.58 (38:25). The Ship – See 1.127n. In *The Odyssey*, when Menelaus finishes the account of his wrestling match with Proteus he invites Telemachus to stay longer. Telemachus thanks him and refuses: "But time hangs heavy on my shipmates' hands / at holy Pylos if you make me stay" (4:598–99; Fitzgerald, p. 82).

3.61 (38:28). *aunt Sara's – Sara Goulding, the wife of Richie Goulding, Stephen's mother's brother. They are modeled on Joyce's aunt and uncle, Mr. and Mrs. William Murray. See Ellmann.

3.63 (38:30–31). Strasbourg terrace – Or Irishtown strand, in Irishtown, then a "maritime and suburban village" just southeast of Ringsend and the mouth of the Liffey (*Thom's* 1904, pp. 1710, 1712). Reclamation projects to the north and east have since moved the terrace inland.

3.64 (38:31–32). Couldn't he fly a bit higher than that? – That is, without the risk of becoming an Icarus; see 1.34n.

3.66 (38:34). costdrawer – A cost accountant, similar to a certified public accountant.

3.67 (38:35). Highly respectable gondoliers – Like characters in the comic opera by Gilbert and Sullivan, *The Gondoliers* (1889), in which the phrase occurs several times in a song sung by Don Alhambra in Act I: "I stole the Prince,

and brought him here, / And left him gaily prattling / With a highly respectable gondolier, / Who promised the Royal babe to rear / And teach him the trade of timoneer / With his own beloved bratling." The bratling and the prince look so much alike that not even the highly respectable gondolier could tell them apart when he was alive; and he has died of gout and drink. Who is to distinguish between the prince and the pauper?

3.68 (38:36–37). Jesus wept – The shortest verse in the Bible (John 11:35), as Jesus approaches the tomb of Lazarus.

3.71 (38:39). coign of vantage – As Duncan and his courtiers approach Macbeth's castle, they compliment its beauties, and Banquo remarks of the martelet (a kind of swallow): "No jutty, frieze, / Buttress, nor coign of vantage but this bird / Hath made his pendant bed and procreant cradle. / Where they most breed and haunt, I have observed / The air is delicate" (I.vi.6–10).

3.76 (39:2). nuncle – Archaic: "uncle."

3.79 (39:5//). *Sit down and take a walk – A cliché bit of Irish comedy and a much-quoted example of an "Irish bull," a verbal blunder in which apparent congruity masks obvious incongruity; see 14.579n.

3.81 (39:7). Goff – One who is awkward, stupid, a clown, an oaf.

3.81 (39:7). *master Shapland Tandy – Combines the Irish revolutionary Napper Tandy (1740–1803) (see 3.259–60n) and Laurence Sterne's eccentric hero from *Tristram Shandy* (1760–67).

3.82 (39:8–9). *Duces Tecum* – Latin: "Bring with you"; the name of certain writs requiring a summoned party to appear in court with some document, piece of evidence, etc., to be used or inspected by the court.

3.83 (39:9–10). Wilde's *Requiescat* – Latin: "let her rest"; Oscar Wilde's poem (1881) on the death of his sister.

3.90 (39:16). lithia – Bottled spring water.

3.92 (39:19). by the law Harry – "Law" dodges the curse *by the Lord;* "Old Harry" is the Devil.

3.99–100 (39:27–28). *All'erta! . . . aria di sortita* – *All'erta*, Italian: "beware, look out, take care"; an aria from Act I, scene i of Giuseppe Verdi's (1813–1901) opera *Il trovatore* (1852). It is Ferrando's *aria di sortita* (the song on which he enters), explaining the family history of witchcraft and vengeance that sets the stage for the opera's action. Ferrando is the faithful retainer (a sort of active Horatio) in a "house of decay" torn by the feuding of Cain-and-Abel brothers who do not know they are brothers until it is too late.

3.107–8 (39:36). **in the stagnant bay of Marsh's library** – St. Sepulchre Library in the close of St. Patrick's Cathedral in south-central Dublin. Founded in 1707 by Narcissus Marsh, Church of Ireland archbishop of Dublin, it is the oldest public library in Ireland. Its collection consists chiefly of theology, medicine, ancient history, and Hebrew, Syriac, Greek, Latin, and French literature. *Stagnant bay:* in 1907 the interior was still as it had been when the library was first constructed, with wire-cage alcoves where readers could be locked while they read particularly valuable books, and some books and manuscripts still secured by chains to rods. Most guidebooks regard it as "charming" and "quaintly picturesque" (D. A. Chart, *The Story of Dublin* [London, 1907], p. 192).

3.108 (39:37). **Joachim Abbas** – Father Joachim of Floris (c. 1145–c.1202) was an Italian mystic whose visions were essentially apocalyptic. He prophesied that the history of man would be covered by three reigns: that of the Father, from the creation to the birth of Christ; that of the Son, from the birth of Christ to 1260; and that of the Holy Spirit, from 1260 onward. This prophecy developed into the belief that a new gospel would supersede the Old and New Testaments (as the Old Testament was of the Father, the New of the Son, the New New would be of the Holy Spirit). Apparently spurred by W. B. Yeats's short story "The Tables of the Law" (1897; see 3.113n), Joyce visited Marsh's Library on 22 and 23 October 1902 to consult a volume in Italian and Latin that includes a text purportedly by Joachim as well as biographical notes of uncertain reliability.[2]

_____

2 *Vaticinia, siue Prophetiae Abbatis Joachimi & Anselmi Episcopi Marsicani, cum adnotationibus Paschalini Regiselmi, Latine et Italice* (Predictions or Prophecies of the Abbot Joachim & Anselm, Bishop of Potenza, with annotations by Paschalini Regiselmi, Latin and Italian) (Venice, 1589).

3.109 (39:37–38). **The hundredheaded rabble of the cathedral close** – In the opening sentence of "The Day of the Rabblement" (1901) Joyce quotes what he calls a "radical principle of artistic economy" from Giordano Bruno of Nola (see 2.159n): "No man, said the Nolan, can be a lover of the true or the good unless he abhors the multitude; and the artist, though he may employ the crowd, is very careful to isolate himself" (*CW*, p. 69). At the beginning of this century St. Patrick's close was at the heart of a teeming slum.

3.109–10 (39:38–39). **A hater of his kind ran from them to the wood of madness** – Jonathan Swift (1667–1745), dean of St. Patrick's Cathedral from 1713, was widely regarded in the late nineteenth and early twentieth centuries as a misanthrope, his hatred of mankind the product of a diseased mind that gradually disintegrated into madness. However, this misrepresents Swift, who remarked in a letter to Pope that he loved individuals but hated mankind in general because man was only an "animal capable of reason," and not a truly "rational animal." Nor did Swift go "mad." He suffered from a disturbance of the inner ear that caused dizziness, nausea, and bouts of deafness, and by the time he was seventy-two years old, all but completely cut off from the world by deafness, he suffered the final indignity of a rapidly advancing senility.

3.111 (39:40). **Houyhnhnm, horsenostrilled** – The Houyhnhnms are the rational horses in Part IV of Swift's *Gulliver's Travels* (1726). Brutish in form but entirely reasonable in behavior, they are contrasted with the Yahoos, their utter opposites. Throughout the nineteenth century and until fairly recently, most readers of Swift assumed that the Houyhnhnms represented the rationality and culture of Swift's idea of a utopia, and the Yahoos were frequently cited as evidence of Swift's devastating misanthropy. Modern readers tend to regard the Houyhnhnms as satiric speculation on just how sterile and reductively simpleminded utterly rational behavior would be.

3.112 (39:41–42). **Foxy Campbell, Lanternjaws** – Nicknames for Father Richard Campbell, S.J., one of the teachers at Belvedere College when Joyce (and Stephen) were students there; see *A Portrait* 4:B.

3.113 (39:42). **furious dean** – That is, Jonathan Swift. The connection between Swift and Joachim derives from W. B. Yeats's story "The

Tables of the Law" (1897). In the story, Owen Aherne, a believer in Joachim's prophecies, searches for the "secret law" (of the Holy Spirit), which is to displace Christ's "law" (to love God, and love thy neighbor as thyself), which in turn has displaced the Ten Commandments. Aherne links Swift's fervor with Joachim's: "Jonathan Swift made a soul for the gentlemen of this city by hating his neighbor as himself" (Yeats, *Early Poems and Stories* [New York, 1925], p. 509).

3.113–14 (40:1–2). *Descende, calve . . . decalveris* – Latin: "Descend, bald one, lest you be made excessively bald." Transposed from *Vaticinia Pontificum*, attributed (but spuriously) to Joachim Abbas (Venice, 1589): "Ascende, calve ut ne amplius decalveris, qui non vereris decalvere sponsam, ut conam ursae nutrias (Ascend, bald man, so that you do not become more bald than you are, you who are not afraid to sacrifice your wife's hair [but, by implication, are so self-conscious about your own baldness] so that you nourish the female bears' hair)." The allusion is to II Kings 2:23–24: "And [Elisha] went up from thence unto Beth-el: and as he was going up by the way, there came forth little children out of the city, and mocked him, and said unto him, Go up, thou bald head; go up, thou bald head. And he turned back, and looked on them, and cursed them in the name of the Lord. And there came forth two she bears out of the wood, and tare forty and two children of them."

3.114 (40:2). his comminated head – To comminate is to threaten, as with anathema. Although Joachim of Floris's opinions were not censured during his lifetime, some were condemned by the Lateran Council of 1215, and in 1254 Gherardino of Borgo's enthusiastic advocacy of Joachim's "Everlasting Gospel" led to thirty-one condemnatory propositions by the University of Paris. In 1255 a papal commission examined the alleged heresies and censured Gherardino and the Joachimites, but not Joachim. The *Catholic Encyclopedia* says of Joachim: "The holiness of his life is unquestionable; . . . and, though never officially beatified, he is still venerated as a *beatus* [among the blessed] on 29 May" ([New York, 1910], vol. 8, p. 407a).

3.117 (40:5). the altar's horns – Associated with sacrifice. "And thou shalt take of the blood of the bullock, and put it upon the horns of the altar with thy finger, and pour all the blood beside the bottom of the altar" (Exodus 29:12). "God is the Lord, which hath shewed us light: bind the sacrifice with cords, even unto the horns of the altar" (Psalms 118:27). "The Lord is God, and he hath shone upon us. Appoint a solemn day with shady boughs, even to the horn of the altar" (Psalms 117:27 [Vulgate]).

3.117 (40:6). jackpriests – *Jack Catholic* is slang for Catholic in name only; thus, "jackpriests" are priests in name only.

3.118–19 (40:7–8). fat of kidneys of wheat – God's generosity to Jacob is celebrated in the Song of Moses: "And he made him to suck honey out of the rock, and oil out of the flinty rock; Butter of kine, and milk of sheep, with fat of lambs, and rams of the breed of Bashan, and goats, with the fat of kidneys of wheat; and thou didst drink the pure blood of the grape" (Deuteronomy 32:13–14).

3.121 (40:10). Dringdring – During the celebration of the Mass a bell (the sacring bell) is rung several times, at the Sanctus, at the elevation of the host (as here), and at the Communion (when the celebrant used also to genuflect). (Suggested by Joan Keenan and Thomas Arsenault.)

3.123 (40:13). Dan Occam – The English Scholastic, philosopher, and theologian William of Occam (c. 1285–1349), noted for the remorseless logic with which he dissected every question. Occam had, in *Tractatus de Sacramento Altaris*, argued that after the host is consecrated, its quantity and quality are unchanged; therefore, the body of Christ is not in the host in quantity or quality (i.e., the host is not the body of Christ by "reason," but by "faith"), so there is only *one* body of Christ and not several—as Stephen speculates, no matter how many elevations of the host are celebrated simultaneously, there is still only one body of Christ.

3.124 (40:13). invincible doctor – Occam was given the epithet *doctor singularis et invincibilis*.

3.124 (40:13–14). A misty . . . morning – From the nursery rhyme: "One misty moisty morning, / When cloudy was the weather, / I chanced to meet an old man, / Clothed all in leather. / He began to compliment, / And I began to grin: / How do you do, and how do you do, / And how do you do again."

3.124 (40:14). hypostasis – The whole personality of Christ as against his two natures: human and divine. As a matter of faith, the whole person of Christ is indivisibly present in the consecrated host.

3.128 (40:19). Cousin Stephen . . . be a saint – After a remark of John Dryden (1631–1700) to Swift: "Cousin Swift, you will never be a poet."

3.128 (40:19). Isle of saints – A medieval epithet for Ireland that recalls the key role played by Irish churchmen and missionaries in western European Christianity after the fall of Rome.

3.130 (40:22). Serpentine avenue – In Sandymount on the southeastern outskirts of Dublin.

3.131–32 (40:23). O si, certo! – Italian: "Oh yes, certainly."

3.133 (40:25). the Howth tram – The village of Howth is on the north side of the Hill of Howth, the northeast headland of Dublin Bay, nine miles from Dublin center. Stephen probably means one of the electric trams that plied between Dublin and Howth, making numerous stops en route. There was also an electric tramline to convey sightseers around the Hill of Howth (*Thom's* 1904, pp. 1706–7).

3.141 (40:34). epiphanies – In *Stephen Hero*, Stephen defines an epiphany as "a sudden spiritual manifestation" when the "soul" or "whatness" of an object "leaps to us from the vestment of its appearance," that is, when the metaphoric potential of an object (or a moment, gesture, phrase, etc.) is realized (p. 211).

3.143 (40:36). Alexandria – The greatest and most famous library of the ancient world. Severely damaged by fire when Julius Caesar was besieged in Alexandria in 47 B.C., it was finally destroyed by another fire during the Arab conquest of Egypt in A.D. 641.

3.144 (40:37). mahamanvantara – Hindu: "great year"—a "Day of Brahma," or a thousand *maha-yuga*s. Each maha-yuga is 4,320,000 years, so a Day of Brahma is 4,320 million years (Hoult, pp. 77, 78).

3.144 (40:37–38). Pico della Mirandola – (1463–94), an Italian humanist, philosopher, and scholar with a Renaissance mastery of Greek, Latin, Hebrew, and Arabic, plus an interest in alchemy and the cabala. His flair is shown in the title he gave his theses: *De Omni Re Scibili* (On Everything That Can Be Known). Stephen's pretension is like Pico's in that Pico at twenty-three is described (Giovanni

Francesco Pico, *Giovanni Pico della Mirandola: His Life by His Nephew*, trans. Sir Thomas More, ed. J. M. Regg [London, 1890], pp. 9–10) as "full of pryde and desyrous of glory and mannes prayse. . . . He went to Rome and there covetynge to make a shew of his connynge: (& lytel consideringe how grete envye he sholde reyse agaynst hymselfe)" set out to publicize the scope and breadth of his obscure and esoteric learning. He was subjected to humiliation and partial defeat.

3.144 (40:38). Ay, very like a whale – Polonius's ready agreement to Hamlet's "mad" demonstration ("camel . . . weasel . . . whale") of the Protean form of a cloud (III.ii.399).

3.144–46 (40:38–40). When one reads . . . one who once – Echoes the style of an essay by Walter Pater (1839–94), "Pico della Mirandola," in *The Renaissance* (1873): "And yet to read a page of one of Pico's forgotten books is like a glance into one of those ancient sepulchres, upon which the wanderer in classical lands has sometimes stumbled, with the old disused ornaments and furniture of a world wholly unlike ours still fresh in them." And: "Above all, we have a constant sense in reading him . . . a glow and vehemence in his words which remind one of the manner in which his own brief existence flamed itself away."

3.148–49 (41:1). that on the unnumbered pebbles beats – In *King Lear*, Gloucester, blind and broken in spirit, wants to commit suicide by throwing himself from Dover Cliff. Edgar, his son but in disguise, tricks his father into believing that the level beach is indeed the top of the cliff: "The murmuring surge / That on the unnumbered idle pebbles chafes / Cannot be heard so high" (IV.vi.20–22).

3.149 (41:2). lost Armada – The Spanish Armada, after its defeat in 1588 in the English Channel, sailed north in an attempt to circle the British Isles and escape back to Spain. The fleet was scattered by storms, and many of the ships were wrecked on the coasts of Ireland and Scotland.

3.150–51 (41:2–3). Unwholesome sandflats . . . sewage breath – Much of Dublin's sewage was emptied untreated into the Liffey and its tributaries, so the streams in the metropolis were little better than open sewers, and the inshore waters of Dublin Bay, particularly just south of the mouth of the Liffey, where Stephen is walking, were notoriously polluted; see 8.1000n.

3.151 (41:3//). *seafire – Phosphorescence at sea.

3.153 (41:4). stogged – Stalled in mire or mud.

3.153–54 (41:5–6). isle of dreadful thirst – Ireland; also, in Book 4 of *The Odyssey*, Menelaus remarks that he and his men, becalmed on Pharos, were about to run out of provisions when Proteus's daughter intervened with advice about her father's powers of divination.

3.156–57 (41:9). Ringsend: wigwams of brown steersmen and master mariners – Stephen associates the present scene with an imaginary scene out of the historic past. *Wigwams:* temporary dwellings.

3.160 (41:13). Pigeonhouse – Formerly a hexagonal fort ("an apology for a battery"), now the Dublin electricity and power station, located on a breakwater that projects out into Dublin Bay as a continuation of the south bank of the Liffey. The dove, related to the pigeon, is also a traditional symbol of the Holy Ghost.

3.161–62 (41:14–15). *Qui vous a mis . . . le pigeon, Joseph* – French: "Who has put you in this wretched condition? / It's the pigeon, Joseph." From *La vie de Jésus* by Léo Taxil (Paris, 1884), p. 15; see 3.167n below. In chapter 5, "Où Joseph, après l'avoir trouvé mauvaise, en prend son parti" (In which Joseph, having discovered evil, takes a stand), Taxil facetiously describes Joseph with his suspicions aroused: "Could he imagine, this good man of naive soul, that a pigeon had been his only rival?" Joseph then confronts Mary in response to her assertion that no man has been allowed to touch as much as her fingertips: "Ta, ta, ta, je ne prends pas des vessies pour les lanternes . . . Qui donc, si ce n'est un homme, vous a mis dans cette position?" (Tsk, tsk, tsk, I don't mistake bladders for lanterns. . . . Who in the world, if it wasn't a man, has put you in this wretched condition?); and Mary replies, "C'est le pigeon, Joseph!" Taxil cites Matthew 1 for evidence of this "incident," and suggests that it is unfortunate that the Gospel has omitted the text of these "recriminations."

3.163–64 (41:16–17). Patrice . . . Son of the wild goose, Kevin Egan – "Wild geese" are Irish who have purposefully become expatriated rather than live in an Ireland ruled by England.

The name was first applied to the Irish insurgents who supported the Stuart cause (James II of England) and who accepted exile after William III of England defeated James II at the Battle of the Boyne (1690) and the Treaty of Limerick was signed in 1691. Kevin Egan is a portrait of Joseph Casey, an active Fenian who was imprisoned for his alleged involvement in the so-called Manchester rescue of September 1867, when two Fenian leaders were rescued from a police van in Manchester, England, leaving a police sergeant dead. Thus Casey was in London's Clerkenwell (a maximum-security prison) in December 1867 when the Fenians made another ill-fated attempt at rescue by exploding a keg of gunpowder at the base of the prison wall. Twelve Londoners were killed and thirty others badly wounded by the explosion, sparking widespread public outrage. See 3.247–48n.

3.164 (41:17). the bar MacMahon – Named for one of the outstanding descendants of the Wild Geese, Marie Edmé Patrice Maurice de MacMahon, duke of Magenta (1808–93), marshal of France, and second president of the Third Republic (1873–79). MacMahon enjoyed a distinguished military career until the Franco-Prussian War (1870–71), when he was responsible for a series of costly defeats that led to the French army's collapse. After the war he was chosen as president because he seemed aloof from politics, but his tenure was marred by bitter conflict between the imperialists (or monarchists) on the one hand, who tried to use MacMahon as a stalking-horse, and their republican opponents on the other, who did see MacMahon as having imperialist leanings.

3.165 (41:18). *lait chaud* – French: "warm milk."

3.166 (41:19). *lapin* – French: "rabbit."

3.166 (41:20). *gros lots* – French: "le gros lot"—first prize in a lottery.

3.167 (41:21). Michelet – Jules Michelet (1798–1874), a French historian "of the romantic school." Michelet is noted not for his objectivity but for picturesque, impressionistic, and emotional history. In *La Femme* (Woman) (Paris, 1860; trans. J. M. Palmer [New York, 1890])—presumably the book Patrice has been reading—Michelet traces woman's growth and "education" toward her ideal and eventual role: "Woman is a religion" and her function is "to *harmonize* religion" (p. 78), just as "her evident vocation is love" (p. 81) and her indispensable gracefulness is "a reflection of love on a ground-work of purity" (p. 83). Properly "cultivated by man" in the light of this ideal, woman will become "superior to him" to the point where he is "strong; [but] she is divine . . . practical and . . . spiritual . . . a lyre of ampler range" than man—and yet not "strong" (pp. 200–201).

3.167 (41:21–22). *La Vie de Jésus* **by M. Léo Taxil** – French: "The Life of Jesus" (Paris, 1884) by Léo Taxil (pseudonym of Gabriel Jogand-Pages, 1854–1907), *dessins comiques* (cartoons) by Pépin. The tone of Jogand-Pages's book is not angry denunciation but chaffing humor in an attempt to develop the absurdities in traditional Christian versions of the life of Jesus. The book plays with three propositions: (1) that Jesus was a god who spent some time on earth in the form of a man; (2) that he was deified by those who embraced his ideas of social emancipation; (3) that he never existed and that the legends were fabricated by exploiters. Jogand-Pages's approach to religion is implicit in some of his other titles: *The Amusing Bible* (1882); *Pius IX, His Politics and Pontificate, His Debaucheries, His Follies, and His Crimes* (1883); *The Secret Loves of Pius IX* (1884). His books were regarded as so scandalously anticlerical that he was pressured into recanting to the papal nuncio in 1885 and into journeying to Rome for a well-publicized papal absolution. But there remained considerable doubt about how firmly Jogand-Pages's tongue had been in his cheek— whether he had meant his recantation or his books or neither or both.

3.169–72 (41:23–26). *C'est . . . oui* – French, Patrice speaking: "It's side-splitting, you know. Myself I am a socialist. I do not believe in the existence of God. Don't tell my father.
—He is a believer?
—My father, yes."

3.173 (41:27). *Schluss* – German: "end, conclusion," or, as here, the mild exclamation "enough!"

3.175 (41:29). puce gloves – See 1.516n.

3.176 (41:30). Paysayenn – As the letters *P.C.N.* would be pronounced in French; see following note.

3.176–77 (41:31). *physiques . . . naturelles* – French: "physics, chemistry, and biology" (premedical studies).

3.177 (41:32). *mou en civet* – French: a stew made of lungs, the cheapest of restaurant dishes.

3.177–78 (41:32). fleshpots of Egypt – The children of Israel "murmured against Moses and Aaron in the wilderness: And the children of Israel said unto them, Would to God we had died by the hand of the Lord in the land of Egypt, when we sat by the flesh pots, and when we did eat bread to the full" (Exodus 16:2–3).

3.179 (41:34). *boul' Mich'* – Slangy Paris contraction of *Boulevard Saint-Michel*, a street on the left bank of the Seine in Paris and the café center of student and bohemian life at the turn of the century. Arthur Symons (1865–1945), in "The Decadent Movement in Literature" (1893), speaks of the "noisy, brainsick young people who haunt the brasseries [beer shops] of the Boulevard Saint-Michel and exhaust their ingenuities in theorizing over the works they cannot write."

3.181–82 (41:36–37). On the night of the seventeenth . . . seen by two witnesses – On Friday, 19 February 1904, the *Irish Times* reported: "CHARGE OF MURDER. Yesterday in Southern Police Court before Mr. Swift, Patrick McCarthy, who was on remand, was charged with the wilful murder of his wife Teresa, by having violently assaulted her at their residence in Dawson's Court, off Stephen Street." Two witnesses did appear for the prosecution, but not to identify the prisoner or to place him at the scene of the crime on 17 February; they detailed instead a long history of marital violence, which presumably culminated in the death of the victim on 10 February. The *Irish Times* continues: "Dr. O'Hare, of the Holles Street [Maternity] Hospital, stated that deceased had been brought there in an unconscious condition. On the ninth instant she gave birth there to a child still-born, and died the following day. A post mortem examination showed that there was an abcess on the membranes of the brain. The assaults described might have set up the abcess.
"The prisoner was committed for trial at the next commission."

3.182–83 (41:38). *Lui, c'est moi* – French: "I am he." A parody of Louis XIV's "L'état, c'est moi" (I am the state).

3.187 (42:1). *Encore deux minutes* – French: "still two minutes left."

3.187 (42:2). *Fermé* – French: "closed."

3.193 (42:8). Columbanus. Fiacre and Scotus – Three of the most famous Irish missionaries to the Continent. For Columbanus, see 2.144n. St. Fiacre, born in Ireland in the latter part of the sixth century, journeyed to France, where his hermit cell expanded into a sanctuary (a sort of informal monastery) and his shrine after his death (c. 670) had the reputation of working miracles. John Duns Scotus (c. 1266–1308), an important Scholastic, was known as the Subtle Doctor. Joyce regarded him as the "notorious opponent" of St. Thomas Aquinas. (There is some dispute about his Irish origin, since both England and Scotland also claim him.)

3.193 (42:8–9). creepystools – Scots and English dialect for a three-legged stool (the sort used as the chair of repentance in the Scottish Kirk).

3.194 (42:10). *Euge! Euge!* – Latin: "Well done! Well done!" But in several biblical contexts the words are spoken ironically by mockers, as they are here.

3.196 (42:12). Newhaven – Channel port on the south coast of England, a rail terminus with channel steamers twice daily to Dieppe, its French counterpart.

3.196 (42:12). *Comment?* – French: "What?"

3.196–97 (42:12–13). *Le tutu* – A short ballet skirt; also, a light weekly Parisian magazine.

3.197 (42:13–14). Pantalon Blanc et Culotte Rouge – French: "White Underclothes and Red Breeches" (though *culotte rouge* is also slang for a camp follower). As Thornton (p. 53) points out, this title seems to be Joyce's variant of a light Parisian magazine, *La vie en coulette rouge* (Life in Red Breeches, or Among the Camp Followers).

3.201–4 (42:18–21). *Then here's a health . . . The Hannigan famileye* – After a song by Percy French (1854–1920), Irish songwriter and parodist, "Matthew Hanigan's Aunt." First verse: "Oh, Mat Hanigan had an aunt, / An uncle too, likewise; / But in this chant, 'tis Hanigan's aunt / I mean to eulogize. / For when young lovers came / And axed her to be theirs, / Mat Hanigan's aunt took each gallant, / And fired him down the stairs. [Chorus:] So here's a health to Hanigan's aunt! / I'll tell you the reason why, / She always had things dacent / In the Hanigan family. / A platther and can for every man, / 'What more do the quality want? / 'You've yer bit and yer sup, / 'What's cockin' yees up!' / Sez Matthew Hanigan's aunt."

3.206 (42:23). the south wall – The seawall that extends the south bank of the Liffey out into Dublin Bay.

3.210 (42:28). farls – In Ireland and Scotland, scones or small cakes.

3.210 (42:28). froggreen wormwood – Absinthe; see 3.217–18n.

3.211 (42:29). Belluomo – Italian: "handsome man"; also slang for a prankster.

3.212 (42:30–31). saucer of acetic acid – For cleansing stone or marble surfaces?

3.212 (42:31). Rodot's – A patisserie at 9 Boulevard Saint-Michel in Paris (c. 1902).

3.214 (42:33). *chaussons* – French: "puff pastry."

3.214 (42:33). *pus* – French: "pus"; that is, yellow liquid.

3.214 (42:33–34). *flan breton* – A custard tart (Breton style).

3.215 (42:34). pleasers – A literal translation of the French word *favoris*: "sideburns."

3.215 (42:35). conquistadores – French slang: "lady-killers."

3.216 (42:36). Noon slumbers – In *The Odyssey*, Proteus's daughter tells Menelaus that each day, "When the sun hangs at high noon in heaven," Proteus comes ashore to rest among crowds of seals "in caverns hollowed by the sea" (4:400–403; Fitzgerald, pp. 76–77).

3.216 (42:36). gunpowder – The cigarettes Kevin Egan rolls remind Stephen of the fuses Egan once made and employed (or that were employed on his behalf); see 3.163–64n.

3.217 (42:37). fingers smeared with printer's ink – Joseph Casey, the real Fenian after whom Kevin Egan is drawn, was a typesetter on the *New York Herald* of Paris.

3.217–18 (42:37–38). sipping his green fairy as Patrice his white – "Green fairy's fang" is slang for absinthe, considerably more intoxicating than ordinary liquors and containing wormwood, a substance that causes deterioration of the nervous system. Absinthe has been banned in France since 1915. *White:* unlike his father, Patrice drinks milk.

3.218–19 (42:39). *Un demi setier!* – A Parisian colloquialism for a demitasse; a *setier* is an obsolete measure for liquids, about two gallons.

3.220–21 (42:40–43:1). *Il est irlandais . . . savez? A oui!* – French: "He is Irish. Dutch? Not cheese. Two Irishmen, we, Ireland, do you understand? Oh yes!"

3.224 (43:4). *slainte!* – Irish toast: "good health!"

3.226 (43:7). green fairy's fang – See 3.217–18n.

3.227 (43:8). Dalcassians – A tribe that made up the household troops for the medieval Irish kings of Munster. It is also a tribal name of the O'Briens, whose patrimony was County Clare on the west coast of Ireland.

3.227 (43:8). Arthur Griffith – (1872–1922), an Irish patriot instrumental in the final achievement of Ireland's independence in 1921–22 and, briefly, first president of the newly formed Irish Free State (1922). In 1899 he founded the Celtic Literary Society with William Rooney and the *United Irishman*, a newspaper that crusaded for Irish independence. In the early twentieth century he organized Sinn Fein ("We Ourselves"), a movement that agitated for independence by disrupting the British government of Ireland (largely by civil disobedience). In 1906 he founded a newspaper named *Sinn Fein*.

3.227–28 (43:8). *AE, pimander, good shepherd of men – For AE (George William Russell), see 2.257n. For "pimander," see 15.2269n. In John 10, Jesus in parable speaks of himself as the "door" of the sheepfold: "I am the good shepherd, and know my sheep and am known of mine" (10:14); the shepherd image also alludes to AE's role as agrarian reformer.

3.228–29 (43:9). his yokefellow, our crimes our common cause – In Shakespeare's *Henry V*, Pistol proposes to join Henry's expedition to France: "Yokefellows in arms, / Let us to France, like horseleeches, my boys, / To suck, to suck, the very blood to suck!" (II.iii.56–58).

3.229 (43:10). You're your father's son. I know the voice – In *The Odyssey*, Nestor comments on how surprisingly similar Telemachus's and Odysseus's voices are (3:123–24), and Helen and Menelaus comment on how much father and son look alike (4:141–50).

3.230 (43:11). Spanish tassels – The pompoms that decorate a matador's suit of lights.

3.230–31 (43:12). M. Drumont – Edouard Adolphe Drumont (1844–1917), a French editor and journalist whose newspaper, *La Libre Parole* (Free Speech), was distinguished chiefly for the bitterness of its anti-Semitism.

3.232–33 (43:13–14). *Vieille ogresse . . . dents jaunes* – French: "Old ogress . . . yellow teeth." In folklore, cannibalism turns people's teeth yellow.

3.233 (43:14). Maud Gonne – (1866–1953), a famous Irish beauty who became a minor Irish revolutionary leader before seeking refuge in Paris. She is a dominant presence in the poetry of Yeats, who lamented the waste of her classic "Ledaean" beauty in revolutionary pursuits. The juxtaposition of her name and Millevoye's may allude to the fact that she was his mistress for several years. She had two children by Millevoye, a boy who died in childhood and a girl, Iseult Gonne (1895–1954), after whose birth she and Millevoye apparently lived apart (see W. B. Yeats, *Memoirs*, ed. Denis Donoghue [London, 1972], pp. 132–33).

3.233 (43:15). *La Patrie, M. Millevoye* – *La Patrie* (French; "the fatherland") was a political periodical founded in 1841. Lucien Millevoye (1850–1918) became editor of the periodical in 1894.

3.233–34 (43:15). Felix Faure, know how he died? – Faure (1841–99), president of the French Republic (1895–99), died suddenly of a cerebral hemorrhage at the Elysée, the presidential residence. The obvious innuendo is that his death was the result of sexual excess, a rumor then current in Paris.

3.234 (43:16). *froeken* – *fröken*, Swedish: "an unmarried woman."

3.234 (43:16). *bonne à tout faire* – French: "maid of all work."

3.235–36 (43:17–18). *Moi faire . . . tous les messieurs* – French: "I do . . . all the gentlemen."

3.238 (43:20–21). Green eyes, I see you. Fang, I feel – Iago to Othello: "Oh, beware, my lord, of jealousy. / It is the green-eyed monster which doth mock / The meat [victim] it feeds on" (III.iii.165–67). For "fang," see 3.217–18n.

3.241 (43:24). peep of day boy's – Precursors of the Orangemen (see 2.270n). They were late-eighteenth-century Ulster Protestants named for their early-morning raids on the cottages of Catholic peasants, whom they sought to displace from Ulster.

3.241 (43:25). How the head centre got away – James Stephens (1824–1901), an Irish agitator, was Chief Organizer and subsequently Head Centre of the Fenian Society (Irish Republican Brotherhood; see 2.272n). In November 1866 Stephens was betrayed by a spy planted in his organization's Dublin offices; he was arrested, tried, and sentenced, but a few days later he was "rescued" from Dublin's Richmond Gaol by a group of Fenians, with the help of sympathetic guards on the inside. Stephens went into hiding in Dublin (just across the street from the Kildare Street Club). In February 1867 he was smuggled out of the country, and he made his way to America, where he was elected Head Centre of the American branch of the Fenians.

In 1866 many in the society had split off, urging an immediate insurrection. Stephens's resistance to their pressures earned him the reputation of being a good organizer but not a man of action. The split in the society was apparently responsible for the apocryphal (and denigrating) story that Stephens assumed the disguise of a woman to effect his escape, "betraying and abandoning" his lieutenants in Ireland in the process. See 8.459–61n.

3.243 (43:27). Malahide – A village and seaside resort nine miles north of Dublin on the coast of the Irish Sea. Stephens made his escape to sea by this route.

3.243 (43:27). Of lost leaders – Reference is to Robert Browning's (1812–89) "The Lost Leader" (1845). The poem expresses regret (and some irritation) at the defection of Wordsworth (1770–1850) from the ranks of the revolutionaries to those of the Establishment. Though Wordsworth is not named in the poem, the suggestion is clearly that his receipt of a government pension in 1842 and of the position of Poet Laureate in 1843 influenced the reversal of his political opinions. "Just for a handful of silver he left us, / Just for a riband to stick in his coat" (lines 1–2).

3.245 (43:29). gossoon – A boy, a servant boy, a lackey; rustic, inexperienced.

3.247 (43:31). colonel Richard Burke – Richard O'Sullivan Burke, a colonel in the United States Army during the Civil War and an Irish-American member of the Fenian Society. Burke led a Fenian group in the successful rescue of two Fenian leaders in Manchester, England, in September 1867. He was arrested soon thereafter for other Fenian activities, and he was among the Fenian leaders who were supposed to have been freed by the abortive gunpowder plot against Clerkenwell Prison. See 3.163–64n.

3.247 (43:32). tanist of his sept – A sept was an ancient and medieval Irish tribal division. Among the ancient Irish, a tanist was the heir apparent to the tribal chief, elected during the chief's lifetime. The implication here is that Burke was to be James Stephens's successor as Head Centre.

3.247–48 (43:32–33). under the walls of Clerkenwell and crouching – The plot to blast the wall of the prison yard and rescue Burke and Casey hinged on their scheduled exercise time. (They were supposed to crouch down against the yard's outer wall to avoid injury.) But the prison authorities, warned by informers that a rescue was to be attempted, changed Burke and Casey's exercise time and thus foiled the plot. See 3.163–64n.

3.249 (43:34). Shattered glass and toppling masonry – See 2.9–10n.

3.250 (43:35–36). Making his day's stations – See 1.510n.

3.251 (43:36–37). Montmartre – A poor, run-down section in north-central Paris, at the turn of the century a favorite haunt of avant-garde artists, bohemians, and students.

3.252 (43:37–38). *rue de la Goutte-d'Or,* **dam-ascened with flyblown faces of the gone** – Rue de la Goutte d'Or (Street of the Golden Drop or Golden Liquor) in Montmartre was named for the golden wine from long-since displaced vineyards. The "gone" whose faces "damascene" the street are several of Emile Zola's (1840–1902) characters: Gervaise Macquart, the protagonist of *L'assommoir* (The Grog Shop or Gin Mill) (1877), lives in what Zola calls the *quartier de la Goutte d'Or* and, with her husband, declines into dereliction, filth, inanition, and finally death as a result of alcoholism. Gervaise's daughter Nana (*Nana*, 1880) is born and comes of age in the *quartier;* she is en route to supreme success as a grand *cocotte* (prostitute) when she meets a premature, and symbolic, death from smallpox. The second to the last paragraph of *Nana* is a particularly vigorous description of the face of Nana's corpse, devastated by smallpox as though the "virus" with which she had "poisoned a people had mounted into her face and rotted it" (my translation). Stephen's adjective "flyblown" is mild in comparison with Zola's prose.

3.254 (43:40). *rue Gît-le-Coeur* – (Street Sacred to the Memory of the Heart, or Here Lies the Heart), roughly parallel to the Boulevard Saint-Michel, near the Seine on the Left Bank.

3.257 (44:1). *Mon fils* – French: "my son."

3.257–58 (44:2–3). *The boys of Kilkenny are stout roaring blades* – Anonymous Irish song that praises the town of Kilkenny for its scenery, its young men, and particularly its young women: "Oh! the boys of Kilkenny are nate [neat] roving blades, / And when ever they meet with dear little maids, / They kiss them, and coax them, and spend their money free. / Oh! of all towns in Ireland, Kilkenny for me. / Oh! of all towns in Ireland, Kilkenny for me."

3.258–59 (44:3). Old Kilkenny – A county and a town on the River Nore in southeastern Ireland, named after St. Canice (St. Kenny); *kil:* "church or cell."

3.259 (44:4). saint Canice – (d. c. 599), Irish, he preached in Ireland and Scotland and accompanied St. Columba (or St. Columcille; see 12.1699n) on a mission to convert Brude, king of the Picts. St. Canice's Cathedral (now Protestant) from the thirteenth century and a round tower mark the site of the sixth-century monastery that gave Kilkenny its name.

3.259 (44:4). Strongbow's castle on the Nore – Richard de Clare or Richard FitzGilbert, earl of Pembroke, called "Strongbow" (d. 1176). He was a Norman adventurer and one of the key leaders of the Anglo-Norman invasion of Ireland in 1169. As a son-in-law of MacMurrough, he claimed succession as king of Leinster—comprising the central counties of eastern Ire-

land, including Dublin—after MacMurrough's death in 1171. See 2.393–94n. His castle on the Nore was built in 1172 near the site of St. Canice's monastery to command the strategic river crossing.

3.259–60 (44:5). O, O. He takes me, Napper Tandy, by the hand – From "The Wearing of the Green," an anonymous Irish ballad from the 1790s, as "formalized" by Dion Boucicault (1822–90), an Irish-American songsmith, playwright, and actor: "Oh, Paddy dear, and did you hear the news that's going round? / The shamrock is forbid by law to grow on Irish ground; / Saint Patrick's day no more we'll keep, / His colour can't be seen, / For there's a cruel law agin the wearin' of the green. / I met with Napper Tandy, and he tuk me by the hand, / And said he, 'How's poor ould Ireland, and how does she stand? / She's the most distressful country that ever yet was seen; / They're hanging men and women there for wearin' of the green.'" James Napper Tandy (1740–1803) was an Irish revolutionary and reformer. He supported Grattan (see 7.731n) and was a co-founder and secretary of the United Irishmen in the 1790s. A sympathizer with the French Revolution, he was a key figure in the attempt to secure French aid and support in the Irish struggle for independence.

3.261–62 (44:6–7). O, O the boys of Kilkenny – See 3.257–58n.

3.264 (44:9). Remembering thee, O Sion – A phrase of mourning associated with the Jews in captivity (and hence with all exiles), as in Psalms 137:1–2: "By the rivers of Babylon, there we sat down, yea, we wept, when we remembered Zion. We hanged our harps upon the willows in the midst thereof."

3.266–67 (44:12). wind of wild air of seeds of brightness – See 14.242–43n and 14.244n.

3.267 (44:13). the Kish lightship – A lightship moored at the northern end of Kish Bank, two miles east of Kingstown (now Dun Laoghaire). The bank forms a dangerous obstacle at the southern entrance to Dublin Bay.

3.279 (44:25–26). the mole of boulders – The seawall, topped by Poolbeg Road, that extends the south bank of the Liffey east into Dublin Bay for more than two miles. The Pigeon House sits astride the wall a mile and a half in from Poolbeg Light at the wall's end.

3.280 (44:26–27). form of forms – See 2.74–75n.

3.281 (44:28). in sable silvered . . . tempting flood – Horatio reports to Hamlet about his midnight encounter with the Ghost (I.ii), and in response to one of Hamlet's questions he describes the Ghost's beard as "A sable silvered" (line 242). Later when the Ghost appears to Hamlet, Horatio attempts to keep Hamlet from following the Ghost, lest it be an evil spirit and tempt or deceive Hamlet into throwing himself into the sea. "What if it tempt you toward the flood, my lord, / Or to the dreadful summit of the cliff" (I.iv.69–70).

3.283 (44:30). Poolbeg road – See 3.279n.

3.285 (44:32). grike – A crevice, chink, crack.

3.286 (44:33). bladderwrack – A species of seaweed (*Fucus vesiculosus*) with air bladders in its fronds.

3.287 (44:34–35). *Un coche ensablé* – French: "A coach mired in sand." From an essay by Louis Veuillot, "Le vrai poète Parisien" (The True Parisian Poet), included in his *Les odeurs de Paris* (The Paris Flavor) (Paris, 1867), pp. 230–46. The essay rejects the French romantics on the grounds that they are hardly French, let alone Parisian. Veuillot is particularly hard on Gautier, who he says "provides us with a perfect example of bad writing . . . such incongruities! Young men, avoid . . . all those superlatives which give to a sentence the look of a coach mired in sand" (pp. 234–35).

3.287 (44:35). Louis Veuillot – (1813–83), a French journalist and leader of the Ultramontane party, which opposed nineteenth-century political efforts to curtail the secular powers of the Church of Rome in France. Veuillot was a notoriously uncompromising anti-romantic (because the French romantics were traditionally anti-Church).

3.288 (44:35). Gautier's – Théophile Gautier (1811–72), a French poet, critic, and novelist famous for a "flamboyant" romanticism with overtones of frank hedonism and a "pagan" contempt for traditional morality.

3.291–93 (44:39–45:2). Sir Lout's toys . . . oldz an Iridzman – A scrambled free association that includes the nursery rhyme: "Fee, fi, fo, fum, / I smell the blood of an Englishman, / Be he alive, or be he dead, / I'll grind his bones

to make my bread." *Stepping stones:* the jumble of boulders on the beach recalls the Giant's Causeway, a great pile of basaltic pillars on the northeastern coast of Ireland. One legend accounts for the causeway by crediting it to the giant Finn MacCool, who, irritated by a braggart Scottish giant, pitched the rocks into the sea so that he could cross and humiliate the Scot. Frank Budgen (*James Joyce and the Making of "Ulysses"* [Bloomington, Ind., 1960], p. 52) implies that Sir Lout is Joyce's contribution to legend, but in Irish myth, "Lug of the long arm—the *Ildana* or 'master of many arts'" (P. W. Joyce, *A Social History of Ancient Ireland* [London, 1913], vol. 1, p. 241) was also a rock thrower, one of whose exploits was the rock death of Balor of the Evil Eye (the giant chief of the Formorians). See 12.197–98n.

3.297 (45:7). The two maries – "Mary Magdalene, and Mary the mother of James and Joses," followers of Jesus who in Matthew and in Mark watch at the Crucifixion, "ministering unto him [Jesus]," and who also watch at the sepulcher after the entombment and are thus the first to receive the news: "He is not here: for he is risen" (Matthew 27–28; Mark 15–16).

3.298 (45:8). tucked it safe among the bulrushes – In Exodus, the infant Moses is hidden by his mother to avoid the Pharaoh's command, "Every son that is born ye shall cast into the river" (1:22). "And when she could not longer hide him, she took for him an ark of bulrushes, and daubed it with slime and with pitch, and put the child therein; and she laid it in the flags by the river's brink" (2:3).

3.298 (45:8). Peekaboo. I see you – From a nursery rhyme or children's song that accompanies a game of hide-and-seek.

3.300 (45:10). Lochlanns – Literally, "lake dwellers," the Irish name for the Norwegians, who constituted the first waves of the Scandinavian invasions of Ireland c. 787. "Dane vikings" (3.301 [45:12]) were involved in subsequent invasions. Scandinavian power was not broken until the early eleventh century.

3.301–2 (45:12). torcs of tomahawks aglitter on their breasts – A "torc" (torque) is a collar of twisted metal worn by ancient Gauls, Britons, and Irish. The Danish invaders of Ireland wore metal bodyarmor (coats of mail and helmets with visors), thereby outmatching the Irish, and what the Irish called the "dark blue" or "blue-green coats" of mail frequently had reversed battle-axes emblazoned on the chest (like a collar of tomahawks?).

3.302–3 (45:12–13). when Malachi wore the collar of gold – From Thomas Moore's (1779–1852) "Let Erin Remember the Days of Old": "Let Erin remember the days of old / Ere her faithless sons betrayed her; / When Malachi wore the collar of gold / Which he won from the proud invader; / When her kings, with standard of green unfurled, / Led the Red Branch Knights to danger / Ere the emerald gem of the western world / Was set in the crown of a stranger." Malachi (948–1022), high king of Ireland, was instrumental in the tenth- and eleventh-century struggle to dislodge the Scandinavian invaders. Malachi took the "collar of Tomar" from the neck of a Danish chieftain whom he had defeated.

3.303–6 (45:13–17). A school of turlehide whales . . . green blubbery whalemeat – In 1331 Dublin was suffering from a great famine, when "a prodigious shoal of fish called Turle-hydes was cast on shore at the mouth of the Dodder near the mouth of the Liffey. They were from 30 to 40 feet long, and so thick that men standing on each side of one of them could not see those on the other. Upwards of 200 of them were killed by the people" (*Thom's* 1904; p. 2092).

3.306 (45:17). Famine, plague and slaughters – For famine, see the preceding note and 2.269n. *Plague:* the major European epidemic of the Black Plague occurred between 1334 and 1351. In the "Dublin Annals" section of *Thom's* 1904, the entry for 1348 cites "a great pestilence [that] raged through many parts of the world, and carried off vast numbers in Dublin" (p. 2092). Some authorities estimate that the population of Ireland, already ravaged by indiscriminate slaughter during the Bruce invasion (1314–18) and in the prolonged anarchy of its aftermath (see 3.313–14n), was reduced by one-half in the second half of the fourteenth century.

3.307–8 (45:18–20). on the frozen Liffey . . . among the spluttering resin fires – In 1338 there was "a severe frost from the beginning of December to the beginning of February, in which the Liffey was frozen so hard that the citizens played at foot-ball, and lit fires on the ice" (*Thom's* 1904, p. 2092). Though this seems to be the date Stephen has in mind, the Liffey was again frozen over in 1739 "so that the people amused themselves on the ice" (p. 2096).

3.308–9 (45:20). I spoke to no-one: none to me – After the English folk song: "There was a Jolly Miller / Once lived on the River Dee . . . I care for nobody, no not I / And nobody cares for me."

3.311 (45:22). stood pale, silent, bayed about – Stephen envisions himself as Acteon, who, because he interrupted Diana while she was bathing, was transformed into a deer and hunted down by his own dogs. The deer or roebuck is also a traditional symbol of the hidden secret of the self. In Celtic mythology its epithet is "Hide the Secret." See 3.336–37n and 9.953n. Compare lines 83–88 of Joyce's "The Holy Office" (1904): "Where they have crouched and crawled and prayed / I stand, the self-doomed, unafraid, / Unfellowed, friendless and alone, / Indifferent as the herring-bone, / Firm as the mountain-ridges where / I flash my antlers on the air."

3.311 (45:22–23). Terribilia meditans – Latin: meditating on terrible things.

3.312 (45:23). fortune's knave – Rosencrantz and Guildenstern describe themselves to Hamlet as fortune's "privates" (II.ii.238), and they are, of course, at least dupes if not knaves. In *Antony and Cleopatra*, after Antony's death (and Octavius Caesar's victory), Cleopatra contemplates the meaninglessness of high rank: " 'Tis paltry to be Caesar. / Not being Fortune, he's but Fortune's knave, / A minister of her will" (V.ii.2–4).

3.313–14 (45:25). The Bruce's brother – Edward Bruce (d. 1318), younger brother of Robert the Bruce (1274–1329). Robert was king of Scotland (1306–29), and as king he won Scotland's independence from England. Edward, after the battle of Bannockburn (1314), invaded Ireland in an ultimately unsuccessful attempt to likewise free Ireland from the English. He was "elected" king of Northern Ireland and subsequently murdered by the Irish as a "pretender."

3.314 (45:26). Thomas Fitzgerald, silken knight – (1513–37), Lord Offaly, tenth earl of Kildare, called "Silken Thomas" because his retainers wore tokens of silk. He was left in charge as vice-deputy of Ireland when his father, who was lord deputy, went to England. Falsely informed that his father had been slain, Thomas renounced his allegiance to Henry VIII and declared war on England—a quixotic revolt, because his power was limited and he had no powder and shot, at that time modern and necessary military supplies. The English caught up with him, and with five of his uncles he was hanged, drawn, and quartered at Tyburn.

3.314 (45:26). Perkin Warbeck – (c. 1474–99), a Yorkist pretender to the throne of Henry VII of England (by fraudulently claiming that he was Richard, duke of York, second son of Edward IV). He was supported by the Anglo-Irish lords of Ireland (particularly the Kildares). Captured by the English, he confessed his imposture and was semipardoned; but he couldn't leave well enough alone and got involved in another conspiracy, thereby earning his ticket to Tyburn.

3.315–16 (45:28). Lambert Simnel – The Simnel conspiracy (1486), also Yorkist. Richard Simons, a priest of Oxford, palmed off his ward, Lambert Simnel, aged eleven and the son of an Oxford joiner, as Edward, earl of Warwick, son of George, duke of Clarence, and thus heir to the throne of England. Simnel was crowned king as Edward VI in 1487 at the instigation of the Anglo-Irish lords (with a diadem borrowed for the occasion from a statue of the Virgin Mary in Christ Church Cathedral, Dublin). He invaded England and was captured by Henry VII on 16 June 1487 at the battle of Stoke; instead of being put to death he was made turnspit boy in the royal kitchen and later became royal falconer.

3.316 (45:28). nans – English dialect: "serving maids."

3.316 (45:29). All king's sons – See 2.279–80n.

3.317 (45:29). Paradise of pretenders – That is, Ireland, which supported the Yorkist pretenders to the throne of England in the fifteenth century and the Stuart pretenders from 1688 to 1745.

3.317 (45:30). He – Mulligan.

3.318–19 (45:31–32). But the courtiers . . . House of . . . – After Boccaccio's (1313–75) *Decameron*, Day 6, story 9. Guido Cavalcanti (c. 1250–1300), an Italian poet and a friend of Dante's, walks from the Church of San Michele in Florence to the Church of San Giovanni, where some acquaintances find him brooding among the tombs. They say: "Let us go and plague him" (to ally himself with them). "Guido you refuse to be of our society; but, when you have found out that there is no god, what good will it have done you?" Guido answers: "Gentle-

men, you may use me as you please in your own house." After Guido leaves, his mockers finally understand the nature of Guido's witty rebuke: "Consider, then, these arches are the abode of the dead, and he calls them our house to show us that we . . . are, in comparison with him and other men of letters, worse than dead men." Thus, the word Stephen omits, "House of . . . ," is *decay* or *death*.

3.321 (45:34). *Natürlich* – German: "Naturally."

3.322 (45:36). Maiden's rock – One of a small group of rocks near the north shore of Dalkey Island in Dublin Bay. The island is just off the southeast headland of the bay.

3.336–37 (46:12–13). On a field tenney a buck, trippant, proper, unattired – Stephen translates the dog on the beach into the language of heraldry: *tenney:* tenne, orange, or tawny; *trippant:* applied to a buck or stag when *passant*, or walking; *proper:* in natural colors; *unattired:* without antlers (unusual in heraldry because it would imply impotence). By contrast, the crest of Ireland: on a wreath *or* (gold) and *azure* (blue) a tower triple towered of the first; from the portal a *hart* (stag, buck) springing (hindlegs on ground, forelegs extended), *argent* (silver), *attired* (with antlers), and hoofed gold.

3.339 (46:15). seamorse – Obsolete for walrus.

3.340 (46:17). every ninth – In Irish mythology the ninth wave out from land was considered to be a magical boundary.

3.351 (46:30). moves to one great goal – See 2.380–81n.

3.360–61 (46:40–41). Something he buried there, his grandmother – See 2.102–7n.

3.363 (47:2–3). *a pard, a panther got in spousebreach – *Spousebreach:* adultery. John de Trevisa, *Bartholomeus (de Glanvilla) De Proprietatibus Rerum* 18:66 (trans. 1398): "Leopardus is a cruel beast and is gendered in spousebreche of a parde and of a lionas" (quoted in the *Oxford English Dictionary*).

3.366 (47:5–6). Haroun al Raschid – (763–809), caliph of Baghdad, enlightened monarch and Oriental despot whose reign was for the most part successful, his empire prosperous. He was a lover of luxury and pleasure and a patron of learning and the arts. He is reputed to have disguised himself and wandered among his people to keep himself aware of their moods and concerns. Many of the tales of the *Arabian Nights* are set during his caliphate.

3.367–69 (47:6–9). That man led me . . . rule, said. In. Come. Red carpet spread – Stephen's dream involves the Hebraic "rule" that the firstfruits of the land were to be brought to the holy place of God's choice and there presented to the priest, whose perquisite the firstfruits were (Deuteronomy 26:2–11). During their wanderings in the wilderness, the children of Israel complain, "our soul is dried away"; the standard gloss suggests that "the people lust for flesh," and among other fruits, they long for melons (Numbers 11:4–6). See 4.210–11n.

3.370 (47:10). the red Egyptians – Gypsies, once thought to have been Egyptian in origin. In the passage that follows Stephen associates gypsy language with seventeenth-century cant; see 3.381–84n.

3.373 (47:13). mort – A "free woman" held in common by a tribe of gypsies.

3.375 (47:16). bing . . . Romeville – "Go away to London"; *Rome* (or *rum*) means "first-rate."

3.377 (47:18). fancyman – A man who is fancied as a sweetheart; or a man who lives on the income of a prostitute.

3.377 (47:18–19). two Royal Dublins – Two soldiers from the Royal Dublin Fusiliers.

3.377 (47:19). O'Loughlin's of Blackpitts – Apparently a "shebeen," an unlicensed bar or public house, in Black Pitts, a street in south-central Dublin (in the run-down area called the Liberties).

3.378 (47:19–20). wap in . . . dell – "Wap" means to make love; "rum lingo" is noted talk; "dimber, wapping dell" is a pretty, loving wench.

3.379 (47:21). Fumbally's lane – Also in the Liberties in south-central Dublin.

3.379–80 (47:22). the tanyard – Kelly, Dunne & Co., tanners, fellmongers, and woolmerchants, 26–27 New Row South, just around the corner from Fumbally's Lane.

3.381–84 (47:23–26). *White thy . . . kiss* – The second stanza of "The Rogue's Delight in

Praise of His Strolling Mort," in Richard Head's *The Canting Academy* (London, 1673). In seventeenth century underworld cant "fambles" means hands; "gan" is mouth; "quarrons," body; "Couch a hogshead" is to lie down and sleep; "darkmans" is night. First stanza: "Doxy oh! Thy Glaziers shine / As Glymmar by the Salomon, / No Gentry Mort hat prats like thine / No Cove ere wapp'd with such a one." Seventh stanza: "Bing awast to Romeville then / O my dimber wapping Dell, / We'el heave a booth and dock agen / Then trining scape and all is well."

3.385 (47:27). Morose delectation – The sin of letting the mind dwell on evil thoughts. See St. Thomas Aquinas, *Summa Theologica*, Prima Secundae, Query 31, article 2, and Query 74, article 6.

3.385 (47:27). tunbelly – Because the St. Thomas of medieval legend was so big-bellied that tables had to be cut out to fit around his stomach.

3.385 (47:27–28). *frate porcospino* – Italian: "the porcupine monk" or "Brother Porcupine"; that is, Aquinas's argument is prickly and difficult to attack.

3.386 (47:28). Unfallen Adam . . . not rutted – According to tradition, before the Fall sexual intercourse was without lust.

3.387 (47:30). marybeads – The beads of their rosaries, since the rosary includes a cycle of fifteen Hail Marys among its prayers.

3.390 (47:33). my Hamlet hat – See 3.487–88n.

3.391–92 (47:34–36). Across the sands of all the world . . . trekking to evening lands – This passage begins a poetic improvisation on the closing phase of the lyric drama *Hellas* (1821) by Percy Bysshe Shelley (1792–1822), and on Adam and Eve's departure westward from Eden after the Fall in Genesis 3. In his drama, Shelley celebrates the "intense sympathy" he feels for the cause of Greek liberty and the promise of the Greek war of independence, which began in March of 1821 and in which Shelley saw the dawn of a new Golden Age (though the war was to conclude with only ambiguous liberty for the Greeks ten years after Shelley's death). Lines 1023–49 (of the 1101-line drama): "SEMICHORUS I: Darkness has dawn'd in the East / On the noon of time: / The death-birds descend to the feast, / From the hungry clime. / Let Freedom and Peace flee far / To a sunnier strand, / And follow Love's folding star / To the Evening land! // SEMICHORUS II: The young moon has fed / Her exhausted horn, / With the sunset's fire: / The weak day is dead, / But the night is not born; / And, like loveliness panting with wild desire / While it trembles with fear and delight, / Hesperus flies from awakening night, / And pants in its beauty and speed with light / Fast flashing, soft and bright. / Thou beacon of love! thou lamp of the free! / Guide us far, far away, / To climes where now, veil'd by the ardour of day / Thou art hidden / From waves on which weary noon, / Faints in her summer swoon, / Between Kingless continents sinless as Eden, / Around mountains and islands inviolably / Prankt on the sapphire sea." The final chorus of Shelley's lyric drama celebrates the "golden years" that are to "return" with the liberation of Greece: "A new Ulysses leaves once more / Calypso for his native shore" (1075–76). The "sun's flaming sword" suggests the aftermath of the Fall in Genesis 3:24: "So he [God] drove out the man; and he placed at the east of the garden of Eden Cherubims, and a flaming sword which turned every way, to keep the way of the tree of life."

3.392–93 (47:36). She trudges, schlepps, trains, drags, trascines her load – The verbs are all synonyms; in sequence: English (Anglo-Saxon root), Yiddish, from Shlepn, French, English (Anglo-Saxon root), and Italian. The reference is to Eve, whose load of "sorrow" was "greatly multiplied" by the Fall (Genesis 3:16).

3.394   (47:38). *oinopa   ponton* – Homeric Greek: "wine-dark sea"; see 1.78n.

3.395 (47:39). Behold . . . moon – Transposed from the Angelus (a prayer offered by peasants at 6:00 A.M., noon, and 6:00 P.M.): "Behold, the handmaid of the Lord. Be it done to me according to Thy will," after Luke 1:38. The sea (the "mighty mother") is, of course, the "handmaid of the moon" as Mary (*Stella Maris*) is the Star of the Sea.

3.396–97 (48:1). *Omnis caro ad te veniet* – Latin: "All flesh will come to thee"; after Psalms 65:1–2 (Vulgate 64:1–2): "Praise waiteth for thee, O God, in Sion: and unto thee shall the vow be performed. O thou that hearest prayer, unto Thee all flesh shall come." This passage is part of the Introit (the entrance chant) of the requiem, or funeral, mass.

3.397–98 (48:1–3). He comes . . . mouth's kiss – Stephen's poem (see 7.522–25 [132:12–15]) is a souped-up (Canting Academy) version of the last stanza of "My Grief on the Sea," a poem translated from the Irish by Douglas Hyde (1860–1949) in his *Love Songs of Connacht* (Dublin, 1895), p. 31. Hyde's stanza reads: "And my love came behind me— / He came from the South; / His breast to my bosom, / His mouth to my mouth." *Bat:* in the Middle Ages the bat was symbolic of black magic, darkness, and rapacity and was a portent of peril or torment. In Finno-Ugric tradition, the bat is one of the forms the soul takes when it leaves the body during sleep, and in alchemy the bat is the dragon, the primordial enemy.

3.399 (48:4). My tablets – Hamlet, momentarily deranged by the psychological impact of the Ghost and its message, writes an aphorism about villainy and his uncle in his notebook: "My tables—meet it is I set it down" (I.v. 107).

3.409–10 (48:18). darkness shining in the brightness – After John 1:5; see 2.160n.

3.410 (48:18). delta of Cassiopeia – Delta is a relatively inconspicuous star (of the third magnitude) in the constellation Cassiopeia, a W in the northern skies. See 9.928–32n. Delta is at the bottom of the left-hand loop of the W.

3.410–11 (48:19). augur's rod of ash – The Roman augur's rod, the *lituus*, was a staff without knots, curved at the top. It was one of the principal insignia of the augur's office and was used to define the *templum*, the consecrated sectors of the sky within which his auguries (observations of the omens given by birds) were to be made. For "ash," see 1.528n. Stephen has, as he recalls (9.1206 [217:31]), "watched the birds for augury" in *A Portrait* 5:C.

3.414 (48:23). form of my form – See 2.74–75n.

3.414–15 (48:24). Who ever anywhere . . . these written words? – Answer: 13.1246–47 (381:18–19).

3.415 (48:24–25). Signs on a white field – Not only writing on paper but also birds (as the augur sees them) against the sky.

3.416 (48:26). bishop of Cloyne – George Berkeley; see 3.4n. In his *Essay Towards a New Theory of Vision* (Dublin, 1709), Berkeley argued that "the proper objects of sight are not without the mind; nor the images of anything without the mind," and that since what we actually see we see as "flat," distance is not something that is *seen* but something that is *thought*.

3.416–17 (48:26–27). the veil of the temple . . . shovel hat – As described in Exodus 26:31–35, the veil acts as a multicolored screen between the outer "holy place" and "the most holy" (behind the veil). And the veil is rent at the moment of Jesus' death (Matthew 27:51). Berkeley argued that "Vision is the Language of the Author of Nature" (*The Theory of Vision* [London, 1733], section 38); in other words, the visible world is like a screen with signs on it, a screen that God presents to be *read* and *thought* rather than *seen*. Thus, the signs on the screen could be regarded as something taken out of one's head (or hat). A "shovel hat" was worn by some Church of Ireland and Church of England clergy in the eighteenth century.

3.425–26 (48:37). the ineluctable modality of the ineluctable visuality – See 3.1n.

3.426–27 (48:38). Hodges Figgis' window – Hodges, Figgis & Co., Ltd., booksellers and publishers, 104 Grafton Street (in the southeast quadrant of Dublin between Trinity College and St. Stephen's Green).

3.429 (48:41). Leeson park – A street (and the local name of an area) south of the Grand Canal on the then-suburban outskirts of metropolitan Dublin.

3.430 (48:42–49:1). Talk that to . . . a pickmeup – Echoes Stephen's friend Davin, whose notable experience with a pick up is recalled by Stephen in *A Portrait* 5:A. Davin addresses Stephen as Stevie, "the homely version of his christian name."

3.431 (49:1). those curse of God stays suspenders – A corset with garters; "curse of God" because it functioned as a chastity belt (?).

3.432 (49:3). *piuttosto* – Italian: "rather."

3.435 (49:5). What is that word known to all men? – See 9.429–30n and 9.430–31n.

3.439–40 (49:10). sabbath sleep, *Et vidit . . . bona* – The Latin (from Genesis 1:31) reads, "And God saw [the works he had made] and they were exceedingly good": God's words at the end of the six days of creation, before the "first sabbath." "And on the seventh day God

ended his work which he had made; and he rested on the seventh day from all his work which he had made" (Genesis 2:2).

3.440–41 (49:11). *Welcome as the flowers in May – From the song "You're as Welcome as the Flowers in May," words and music by Dan J. Sullivan: "Last night I dreamed a sweet, sweet dream; / I thought I saw my home, sweet home, / And oh! how grand it all did seem, / I made a vow no more to roam. / By the dear old village church I strolled, / While the bell in the steeple sadly tolled, / I saw my daddy old and gray, / I heard my dear old mother say: [Chorus:] You're as welcome as the flowers in May, / And we love you in the same old way; / We've been waiting for you day by day / You're as welcome as the flowers in May."

3.441–44 (49:11–15). Under its leaf he watched . . . Pain is far – This passage improvises on Stéphane Mallarmé's (1842–98) eclogue "L'après-midi d'un faune" (1876–77). Mallarmé's poem evokes an atmosphere thick with the heat of "l'heure fauve" (the tawny hour) and "heavy with foliage." The faun dreams of nymphs "traced by / my shuttered glances." At the poem's end: "Oh certain punishment . . . // But no, / the spirit empty of words, and this weighed-down body late succumb / to the proud silence of midday; / no more—lying on the parched sand, / forgetful of the blasphemy, / I must sleep, in my chosen way, / wide-mouthed to the wine-fostering sun!" (trans. Frederick Morgan, in *An Anthology of French Poetry from Nerval to Valéry in English Translation*, ed. Angel Flores [New York, 1958], p. 156). Stephen's "pain is far" counters the ambiguous presence of pain-in-pleasure in Mallarmé's poem. Noon is "Pan's hour" because that is when the Greek nature-god reached the peak of his daily activity. Noon is also Proteus's hour because it is then, as he composes himself for sleep, that Menelaus seizes him (*The Odyssey*, Book 4).

3.445 (49:16). *And no more turn aside and brood* – From W. B. Yeats; see 1.239–41n.

3.447 (49:18). *nebeneinander* – See 3.13, 15n.

3.448 (49:20). tripudium – Latin: literally, "a triple beat or stroke"; figuratively, "a measured stamping, leaping, jumping, dancing"; in ritual, "a solemn religious dance."

3.449 (49:21). Esther Osvalt's – Apart from the context, identity and significance unknown.

3.450 (49:22). *Tiens, quel petit pied!* – French: "My, what a small foot!"

3.451 (49:23). Wilde's love that dare not speak its name – After a poem by Oscar Wilde's friend Lord Alfred Douglas, "Two Loves," published in *The Chameleon*, a little magazine at Oxford: " 'I am true Love, I fill / The hearts of boy and girl with mutual flame.' / Then sighing said the other, 'Have thy will, / I am the Love that dare not speak its name.' " In 1895 Wilde brought a libel action against the eighth marquess of Queensberry, Lord Alfred Douglas's father, claiming that the marquess had accused him of homosexual practices—at that time a serious criminal offense. The marquess's lawyer exploited the poem in a successful defense against the libel suit. In the course of the trial Wilde said: "The 'Love that dare not speak its name' in this century is such a great affection of an elder for a younger man as there was between David and Jonathan. . . . It is that deep, spiritual affection that is pure as it is perfect." After he lost the libel suit, Wilde was arrested, tried, convicted, and sentenced to two years in prison.

3.452 (49:24). All or not at all – In Henrik Ibsen's *Brand* (1866; trans. G. M. Gathorne Hardy [Seattle, 1966]), Brand announces at the end of Act II, scene ii, "My claim is 'nought or all,' " a claim Joyce labeled "will-glorification" (*CW*, p. 54). In Act III, scene i, armed with his "awful slogan," Brand refuses to visit and absolve his dying mother, just as Stephen has refused to pray at his mother's deathbed in the interim between *A Portrait of the Artist as a Young Man* and *Ulysses*. In Act IV, Brand's refusal to compromise causes first his son's death, and then his wife's while he is en route to his final estrangement from his congregation in Act V. At the end of the play, as the avalanche wipes Brand out, a voice-over proclaims: "GOD IS LOVE!"

3.453 (49:25). Cock Lake – A tidal pool off Sandymount.

3.462 (49:36). *hising up their petticoats – See 1.382–84n.

3.465 (49:39). Saint Ambrose – (c. 340–97), bishop of Milan and one of the most famous of the church fathers, particularly noted as a hymnologist and composer of church music.

3.466 (49:41–42). *diebus ac noctibus . . . ingemiscit* – Latin: "day and night it [the Creation] groans over wrongs"; from St. Ambrose's *Commentary on Romans*, specifically on Romans 8:22, "For we know that the whole creation groaneth and travaileth in pain together until now."

3.468–69 (50:2). a naked woman shining in her courts – John Dryden (1631–1700) in *Mac Flecknoe* (1682) describes the "brothel houses" of the Barbican in London: "Scenes of lewd loves, and of polluted joys / Where their vast courts the mother-strumpets keep, / And, undisturbed by watch, in silence sleep" (lines 71–73). The mock-heroic of Dryden's lines is sustained by a parody of two lines from Abraham Cowley's (1618–67) unfinished biblical epic *Davideis* (1656): "Where their vast Courts the Mother-Waters keep, / And undisturb'd by Moon in Silence sleep."

3.470 (50:4). full fathom five thy father lies – From Ariel's song about drowned Alonso (who has actually been rescued) in *The Tempest* (I.ii.397–403): "Full fathom five thy father lies, / Of his bones are coral made, / Those are pearls that were his eyes. / Nothing of him that doth fade / But doth suffer a sea change / Into something rich and strange. / Sea nymphs hourly ring his knell."

3.470–71 (50:4–5). At one, he said . . . High water at Dublin bar – See 1.673–74n. "High Water at Dublin Bar" is the phrase *Thom's* 1904 uses in its tidetables (pp. 5ff.).

3.471 (50:5). Found drowned – The coroner's official verdict for an accidental drowning, and hence the newspaper headline.

3.473 (50:8). a pace a pace a porpoise – This sounds suspiciously like an allusion or part of a nursery rhyme, but I've been unable to locate a satisfactory source. Two possibilities: in Milton's *Paradise Lost*, as Sin and her son Death approach earth after the Fall: "behind her [Sin] Death / Close following pace for pace, not mounted yet / On his pale horse" (10:588–90). In Shakespeare's *Pericles*, when Pericles enters "wet" from shipwreck, three fishermen speak briefly of the "poor souls" they could not save from the wreck, and one of them says he knew the storm was coming "when I saw the porpas how he bounc'd and tumbled" (II.i.23–24).

3.474 (50:9). Sunk though he be beneath the watery floor – Line 167 of Milton's "Lycidas"; see 2.57n.

3.477–79 (50:13–14). God becomes man . . . goose becomes featherbed mountain – Stuart Gilbert (*James Joyce's "Ulysses"* [New York, 1952], p. 128) cites this as "a variant of the kabalistic axiom of metempsychosis" (as well as an allusion to the protean ebb and flow of living matter): "a stone becomes a plant, a plant an animal, an animal a man, a man a spirit, and a spirit a god." But Stephen's sequence also has an internal logic of its own: "God becomes man" (as God in one of the three persons of the Trinity became man as Jesus Christ); "man becomes fish" (as the fish is an iconographic symbol for Christ in the early Christian church); "fish becomes barnacle goose" (after the medieval belief that barnacle geese were not born from eggs but from barnacles, "at first gummy excrescences from pine beams floating in the waters, and then enclosed in shells to secure a free growth. . . . Being in process of time well covered with feathers, . . . they take their flight in the free air") (Giraldus Cambrensis, *Topography of Ireland*, quoted in T. H. White, *The Bestiary: A Book of Beasts* [New York, 1960], pp. 267–68); "barnacle goose becomes featherbed mountain" (as goose feathers are used to make featherbeds, and Featherbed Mountain is in the Dublin Mountains south of Dublin).

3.482 (50:19). a seachange – See 3.470n.

3.482 (50:19). Seadeath – The death Tiresias prophesies for Odysseus, "a seaborne death, soft as this hand of mist" (*The Odyssey*, 11:134–35; Fitzgerald, p. 201).

3.483 (50:20). Old Father Ocean – Homeric epithet for Proteus.

3.483 (50:20). *Prix de Paris* – *Grand Prix de Paris*, French: "Great Prize of Paris"—the most important event in the French horseracing calendar. The prize itself in 1904 amounted to 250,000 francs; see 2.301–3n. Stephen is, of course, punning on "the prize of Paris," because Paris, by giving the golden apple to Aphrodite, started the Trojan War and ultimately faced Odysseus with the possibility of "sea death." However, another version of the Helen of Troy story, derived from the Greek poet Stesichorus (c. 632–c. 552 B.C.), may be relevant in view of 3.483–84n. In that version only a ghost, or "imitation," of Helen went to Troy with Paris, while

the real Helen remained faithful to Menelaus and sat out the Trojan War under the protection of King Proteus of Egypt.

3.483–84 (50:21). beware of imitations. Just you give it a fair trial – These advertising slogans suggest that the phrase *Prix de Paris* is also a trade-fair award, which a manufacturer will then use in promotion of his product.

3.485 (50:23). I thirst – Jesus says this on the cross "that the scripture might be fulfilled" (John 19:28). Thus, "thunderstorm" (3.486 [50:24]) is suggested by the cataclysm after the Crucifixion; and the thunderstorm in turn suggests the fall of Satan.

3.486 (50:24–25). Allbright he falls . . . of the intellect – *Lucifer* means the bearer of light, thus "allbright." "I beheld Satan as lightning fall from heaven" (Luke 10:18).

3.486–87 (50:25). *Lucifer, dico, qui nescit occasum* – Latin: "The morning star, I say, who knows no setting." Stephen borrows the phrase from the Catholic service for Holy Saturday, the Easter vigil, "a festival of light, and a festival of baptismal water and of baptism itself." The phrase occurs near the end of the Exultet, a chant in praise of the paschal candle, "acclaiming the light of the risen Christ" (*Layman's Missal* [Baltimore, Md., 1962], pp. 492, 495). But there is some ambiguity here, as Joan Keenan points out, because the morning star sometimes refers to Christ—"I [Jesus] am . . . the bright and morning star" (Revelation 22:16)—and sometimes to Satan—"How art thou fallen from heaven, O Lucifer, son of the morning" (Isaiah 14:12).

3.487–88 (50:25–26). My cockle hat . . . my sandal shoon – Cf. the ballad Ophelia sings when she runs mad: "How should I your true love know / From another one? / By his cockle hat and staff / And his sandal shoon" (*Hamlet* IV.v. 23–26). The cockle hat (with a scallop shell as a sign of pilgrimage) and the staff suggest the conventional metaphor of the lover as pilgrim. Another allusion to Ophelia's ballad may be relevant here, namely the last stanza, in effect the *envoi*, of George Gordon, Lord Byron's (1788–1824) *Childe Harold's Pilgrimage* (1818): "Farewell! a word that must be, and hath been / A sound which makes us linger;—yet—farewell! / Ye! who have traced the Pilgrim to the scene / Which is his last, if in your memories dwell / A thought which once was his, if on ye swell / A single recollection, not in vain / He wore his sandal-shoon and scallop-shell; / Farewell! with *him* alone may rest the pain, / If such there were—with *you*, the moral of his strain!" (canto 4, stanza 186).

3.488 (50:26–27). To evening lands – See 3.391–92n.

3.491 (50:30–31). Tuesday will be the longest day – Summer began in Dublin on Tuesday, 21 June 1904, at 9:00 P.M.

3.491–92 (50:31). Of all the glad new year, mother – From Alfred, Lord Tennyson's "The May Queen" (1833). First verse: "You must wake and call me early, call me early mother dear; / Tomorrow'll be the happiest time of all the glad New-year; / Of all the glad New-year, mother, the maddest merriest day; / For I'm to be Queen o' the May, mother, I'm to be Queen o' the May." The poem, retitled "Call Me Early, Mother Dear (For I'm to Be Queen of the May)," was set to music by Dempster.

3.492 (50:32). Lawn Tennyson – Lawn tennis was a genteel version of the modern game—in contrast to court tennis, which was then regarded as a rigorous, demanding, and masculine game. Alfred, Lord Tennyson (1809–92), the official "great poet" of the Victorian age, succeeded Wordsworth as Poet Laureate. Critical reaction to the disproportion of elaborate prosody to often rather flimsy subject matter caused his reputation to rapidly decline in his last years, and his stature as an important poet has only been reestablished in recent times.

3.493 (50:32). *Già* – Italian: "Already." As Stephen uses the word here, "Già . . . Già," it is an expression of impatience: "Let's go . . . Let's go."

3.493 (50:32–33). For the old hag with the yellow teeth – See 3.232–33n.

3.493 (50:33). Monsieur Drumont – See 3.230–31n.

3.494–97 (50:34–38). My teeth are very bad . . . does it mean something perhaps? – Teeth are the "primigenial weapons of attack"; thus their loss or decay is symbolic of "fear of castration or of complete failure in life, or inhibition" (J. E. Cirlot, *A Dictionary of Symbols*, trans. Jack Sage [New York, 1972], p. 332).

3.496 (50:37). the superman – See 1.708n.

3.503 (51:4). rere regardant – In the language of heraldry: "with head turned, looking back over the shoulder." See 3.336–37n.

3.504–5 (51:5–7). high spars . . . ship – The schooner *Rosevean*, announced in "Shipping News," *Freeman's Journal*, 16 June 1904, as "from Bridgewater with bricks"; see 10.1098–99 (249:35–36) and 16.450–51 (625:13–14). Bridgewater is just west of Bristol in southwestern England; it was well known for its manufacture of Bath bricks (scouring bricks used to clean knives and polish metal). The three "crosstrees" recall Calvary Hill, where Jesus was crucified: "Then were two thieves crucified with him, one on the right hand, and another on the left" (Matthew 27:38).

PART II

The Wanderings of Ulysses

(4.1–15.4967, PP. 54–609)

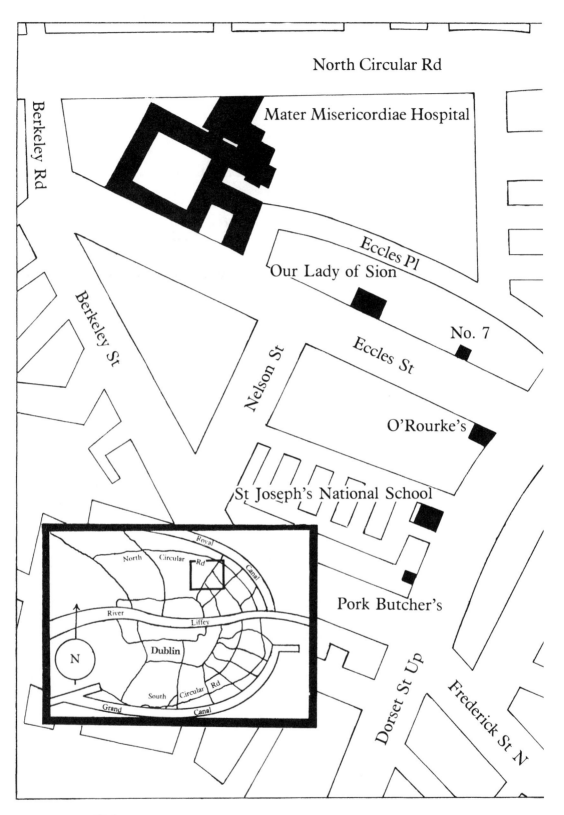

North Circular Rd

Berkeley Rd

Mater Misericordiae Hospital

Eccles Pl

Our Lady of Sion

No. 7

Berkeley St

Nelson St

Eccles St

O'Rourke's

St Joseph's National School

Pork Butcher's

Royal

North Circular Rd

Canal

River

Liffey

N

Dublin

South Circular Rd

Grand

Canal

Dorset St Up

Frederick St N

EPISODE 4. *Calypso*

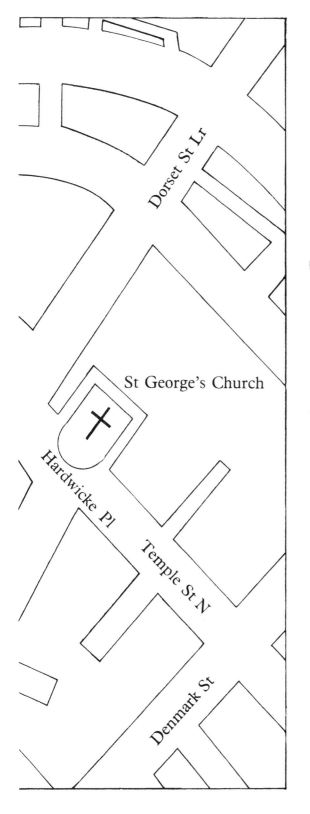

EPISODE 4

Calypso

(4.1–551, PP. 54–70)

Episode 4: Calypso, (4.1–551, pp. 54–70). In book 5 of *The Odyssey*, Odysseus is discovered in bondage to the goddess Calypso (whose name means "the Concealer") on the island of Ogygia in "the sea's middle" (1:50; Fitzgerald, p. 15; S. H. Butcher and Andrew Lang [1879] render the phrase "the navel of the sea"—see *omphalos*, 1.176n). Athena intercedes with Zeus on behalf of Odysseus, and Zeus sends Hermes to instruct Calypso to free Odysseus for his voyage home (i.e., to recall Odysseus to Ithaca and his own people). Odysseus has meanwhile been on the island for seven years, mourning his thralldom and longing for home. "Though he fought shy of her, and her desire, / he lay with her each night, for she compelled him" (5:154–55; Fitzgerald, p. 97). Calypso promises Hermes: "My counsel he shall have, and nothing hidden, / to help him homeward without harm" (5:143–44; ibid.). Odysseus is prepared for his voyage and sets out, only to be intercepted once again by Poseidon's antipathy in the form of "high thunderheads" (5:291; Fitzgerald, p. 101). Athena intercedes, calming the storms and sustaining Odysseus with the "gift of self-possession" (5:437; Fitzgerald, p. 105).

Time: 8:00 A.M., Thursday, 16 June 1904. Scene: Leopold Bloom's house at 7 Eccles Street in the northwest quadrant of Dublin. The house was one of a row of three-story over-basement houses on the north side of the street. Eccles Street in 1904 was regarded as a sedate and respectable neighborhood, solidly middle class and not at all as shabby as what is left of it today is (see Austin Clarke, *Twice Around the Black Church* [London, 1962], p. 38). The street was named after the family that included Ambrose Eccles (d. 1809), a distinguished Irish editor of and commentator on Shakespeare's plays. The *Annual Register* for 1810 memorialized him as "a profound scholar, a perfect gentleman, an ornament to society." Organ: kidney;[1] Art: economics [the useful art of household management]; Color: orange; Symbol: nymph; Technique: narrative (mature). Correspondences: *Calypso*—the Nymph [the print of the Bath of the Nymph over the Blooms' bed]; *The Recall* [as Hermes is sent to recall Odysseus]—Dlugacz; *Ithaca*—Zion.

The Linati schema also lists as Persons "(Penelope 'wife'), Ulysses, Callidike" but does not specify correspondences. Callidike in story is the queen of Thesprotia, whom Odysseus marries in the course of his further voyagings after the end of *The Odyssey* (in a lost continuation, *The Telegonia*, by the Cyclic poet Eugammon of Cyrene who flourished c. 568 B.C.). Symbols listed in addition to Nymph are "Vagina, Exile, Family, Israel in bondage."

4.1 (55:1). Leopold – Means "the people's prince" and implies birth under the "constellation of the Northern Crown" (17.2018–19 [728:4–5]): the sign of ambition, beauty, dignity, empire, eternal life, glory, good fortune, history, honor, judgment, and the female principle.

4.9 (55:9). peckish – Inclined to eat.

4.26–27 (55:28–29). They understand what we say better than we understand them – Compare Michel de Montaigne (1533–92) in the "Apology for Raimond Sebond" (1568): "When I play with my cat, who knows but that she regards me more as a plaything than I do her?" (*The Essays of Montaigne*, trans. E. J. Trechmann [Oxford, 1935] vol. I, p. 444).

4.36 (56:1). Hanlon's milkman – *Thom's* 1904 lists three Hanlons under "Registered Dairies" in Dublin, 1904. The one nearest Bloom's house was S. Hanlon, dairyman, 26 Lower Dorset Street.

4.40–41 (56:5–6). Wonder is it true . . . can't mouse after – No, it is not true; it is only an old wives' tale. Nor do the whiskers shine in the dark, though they do act as "feelers" (4.42 [56:7]), helping the cat to perceive spatial relationships.

4.45 (56:10). Buckley's – John Buckley, victualler, 48 Dorset Street Upper, a short walk east and south from 7 Eccles Street.

4.46 (56:11). pork kidney – See n. 1 below, except, of course, that pork is tref (not kosher).

4.46 (56:11). Dlugacz's – The only pork butcher in Dorset Street Upper, where Bloom goes to buy his kidney, was Michael Brunton at 55A (*Thom's* 1904, p. 1479). The Polish-Jewish name Dlugacz is an irony, since Jewish dietary laws forbid the eating of pork. The butcher took his name, and his "enthusiasm," from Moses Dlugacz (1884–1943), a Jewish intellectual and ardent Zionist whom Joyce knew in Trieste (see Hyman, pp. 184–85).

---

1 In ancient Jewish rites (as in "the sacrifice and ceremonies of consecrating the priests," Exodus 29:1–28), kidneys were regarded as "the special parts to be burned upon the altar as a gift to Yahweh" (*The Interpreter's Dictionary of the Bible* [New York, 1962]; suggested by Joan Keenan).

4.47 (56:12–13). Then licking the saucer clean – After the seventeenth-century nursery rhyme: "Jack Sprat could eat no fat, / His wife could eat no lean, / And so between them both, you see, / They licked the platter clean." In the sixteenth and seventeenth centuries "Jack Sprat" was an epithet for "dwarf."

4.50–51 (56:18). Thin bread and butter – Nursery rhyme: "Little Tommy Tucker / Sings for his supper: / What shall we give him? / White (or, in a variation, thin) bread and butter. / How shall he cut it / Without any knife? / How will he be married / Without any wife?"

4.59 (56:27–28). brass quoits of the bedstead – The quoits are the brass discs that decorate the metal rods supporting the bedstead.

4.60 (56:29). Gibraltar – Molly (Marion) Bloom, née Tweedy, was born (8 September 1870) and brought up in Gibraltar, the daughter of (Sgt.-?) Maj. Brian Cooper Tweedy (Irish, Royal Dublin Fusiliers) and Lunita Laredo (Spanish Jew). Technically, the fusiliers were stationed on the Rock from January 1884 to February 1885. Presumably Molly and her father moved to Dublin in May or June of 1886. Re Tweedy's rank, see 11.508n and 18.766–67n.

4.62 (56:31). a short knock – That is, the auctioneer cut the bidding short in favor of Tweedy.

4.63 (56:32). Plevna – During the Russo-Turkish War (1877–78), a Turkish army under Osman Pasha defended Plevna, a city in northern Bulgaria, for 143 days (20 July–10 December 1877), first against a series of Russian assaults and then against siege. The Turks came within an ace of success at Plevna in a war that was for them a losing cause. The English maintained an attitude of strict neutrality, though they did rattle the naval saber and approach intervention in 1878 when the Russian military victory was capped with a diplomatic victory that gave Russia more territorial aggrandizement in the Balkans than the English favored. Tweedy would not have been "at Plevna" in fact, though he was apparently fascinated with the action and might have been placed there by the omnipotent hand of fiction. One of Bloom's books (17.1385–87 [709:5–7]), Sir Henry Montague Hozier's *History of the Russo-Turkish War* (London, 1877–79), which contains an extended account of Plevna, by implication belonged to Tweedy because it came from the Garrison Library at Gibraltar.

4.63–64 (56:33). rose from the ranks – Far more unusual in the British army in the late nineteenth century than it would be today.

4.65 (56:34). corner in stamps – Tweedy, a stamp collector, had apparently bought up all available copies of an unusual stamp before the stamp was recognized as valuable.

4.67 (56:37). lost property office – Railroad stations had periodic sales to dispose of unclaimed lost articles.

4.68 (56:38–39). in the swim – In league with each other in schemes to make money.

4.69 (56:40). Plasto's – John Plasto, hatter, 1 Great Brunswick (now Pearse) Street in the southeast quadrant of Dublin.

4.70 (56:41). White slip of paper – The card with Bloom's pseudonym, Henry Flower.

4.73 (57:2). Potato – A talisman, symbolic of the continuity of life and, in Jewish tradition, a central dish in the ritual meal after a funeral. The potato is also a reminder of the staple food of the Irish peasant and of the potato blight that triggered the famine; see 2.269n. It was given to Bloom by his mother.

4.77–78 (57:7–8). He crossed to the bright . . . of number seventyfive – Eccles Street angles from southeast to northwest, and Bloom's house is on the northeast side, which would be in shadow in the early morning. Joyce assumed (apparently from *Thom's* 1904) that "seventyfive" was opposite number seven, but it was actually slightly to the right, and Bloom turns left (see Clive Hart and Leo Knuth, *A Topographical Guide to James Joyce's "Ulysses"* [Colchester, England, 1975], pp. 24–25).

4.78 (57:9). George's church – St. George's (Church of Ireland, Protestant), in Hardwicke Place, near Hardwicke Street and just east of the southeastern end of Eccles Street, in the northeast quadrant of Dublin.

4.79–80 (57:10–11). Black conducts . . . the heat – Answer: absorbs.

4.80 (57:11). But I couldn't go in that light suit – See 1.120n.

4.82 (57:13). Boland's – Bolands, Ltd., a bakery at 134–136 Capel Street and on Grand Canal Quay in Dublin.

4.82 (57:13). our daily – After the Lord's Prayer (Matthew 6:11; Luke 11:3): "Give us this day our daily bread."

4.87 (57:19). ranker – A soldier who has risen from the ranks to become an officer; see 4.63–64n.

4.89 (57:22). Turko the terrible – A pantomime popular in Dublin and a character in that pantomime; see 1.258n.

4.99–100 (57:33–34). in the track of the sun – Frederick Diodati Thompson, *In the Track of the Sun: Diary of a Globe Trotter* (London, 1893), in Bloom's library (17.1395–96 [709:16–17]). Thompson traveled west from New York (October 1891) and returned via England (May 1892). Thompson concentrates on his travels in the Orient and the Near East, as Bloom's reverie suggests.

4.100 (57:34). Sunburst on the titlepage – The title page of the book (missing from Bloom's copy) depicts an Oriental girl playing a stringed instrument—"dulcimers" (4.98 [57:32]).

4.101 (57:35). Arthur Griffith – See 3.227n.

4.101–3 (57:35–37). the headpiece over . . . bank of Ireland – For Home Rule, see p. 3. The *Freeman's Journal and National Press*, a daily morning newspaper in Dublin, was editorially pro–Home Rule but essentially moderate-conservative in its point of view. The headpiece does depict a sunburst over the Bank of Ireland (and given the position of the bank, sunrise would be in the northwest). Under the headpiece is the motto Ireland a Nation. The symbolism of the headpiece involves the fact that the conservative Bank of Ireland occupied the building that, before passage of the Act of Union in 1800, had housed the Irish Parliament.

4.103 (57:38). Ikey – Jew or Jewish; smart, alert, artful, clever.

4.105 (57:40). Larry O'Rourke's – Laurence O'Rourke, grocer and tea, wine, and spirit merchant, 74 Dorset Street Upper, on the corner of Eccles Street.

4.108 (58:2). M'Auley's – Thomas M'Auley, grocer and wine merchant, 39 Dorset Street Lower, north of Eccles Street.

4.108 (58:2). n.g. – Slang: "no good."

4.109–10 (58:3–4). North Circular . . . to the quays – North Circular Road starts at the western side of Dublin near the Liffey; it describes a semicircle around the northern outskirts of metropolitan Dublin and links with streets that complete the semicircle back to the mouth of the Liffey at the quays. The cattle market was off North Circular Road on the western side of the city.

4.112–13 (58:7). my bold Larry – Larry is a faintly comic name to the Dublin ear; see "The Night Before Larry Was Stretched," 12.542–43n.

4.114 (58:8). curate – Literally, a clergyman who assists a vicar or a rector in the celebration of the Mass; thus, slang for bartender.

4.116–17 (58:11–12). the Russians, they'd . . . for the Japanese – The aggressive and expansionist policies of both Russia and Japan in Manchuria and Korea (beginning in 1895) climaxed in the Russo-Japanese War (February 1904–September 1905). O'Rourke's prediction of the outcome, while a little too pro-Japanese (as the English tended to be), was not entirely inaccurate. The Japanese had the advantage of much shorter supply lines than the Russians; they also enjoyed naval and military superiority. Japanese successes in the opening months of the war would have made O'Rourke's prediction look sound on 16 June 1904.

4.119 (58:14). Dignam – The fictional Patrick Dignam and his family "lived" at 9 Newbridge Avenue in Sandymount, a maritime village three miles east-southeast of the center of Dublin.

4.127 (58:22). the county Leitrim – The county, in north-central Ireland, seemed remote and agrarian to Dublin, and its inhabitants were regarded as country bumpkins.

4.127 (58:22–23). old man in the cellar – Saving the drink ("old man") that the customer leaves in his glass instead of throwing it out.

4.128 (58:23–24). Adam Findlaters – Adam S. Findlater, M.A., J.P., with offices in Alexander Findlater & Co., Ltd., tea, wine, and spirit and provision merchants, 29–32 Sackville Street Upper (now O'Connell Street). The company had five other branches in Dublin and six in County Dublin. Findlater was a successful businessman with political aspirations. Arthur Griffith's newspaper, the *United Irishman*, criticized him for encouraging foreign manufacture in Ireland, for being a "west Briton," and for angling for a knighthood.

4.128 (58:24). Dan Tallons – Daniel Tallon, grocer and wine merchant, 46 George's Street South and 57 Stephen Street. A successful publican, he was lord mayor of Dublin in 1899 and 1900.

4.132–33 (58:28–29). double shuffle . . . town travellers – A trick, a piece of fakery (after a hornpipe step that involves shuffling both feet twice). "Town travellers" are traveling salesmen. The "double shuffle" would thus amount to some manipulation of wholesale prices by getting the salesman to overcharge and then split the proceeds.

4.136 (58:33). Saint Joseph's, National School – At 81–84 Dorset Street Upper. The National Schools were the Irish counterpart of the American public schools, although they bore more resemblance to trade or vocational schools because their emphasis was on practical education for the working and lower middle classes. The National Schools were dominated by an English Protestant point of view and were regarded by the Irish as part of an English plot to control Ireland religiously and socially as well as politically.

4.138 (58:36). Inishturk, Inishark, Inishboffin – Three small islands in the Atlantic off the west coast of central Ireland (actually off a small area of Galway called "Joyce's Country"). *Inishboffin:* "the island of the white cow"; *Inishturk:* "the boar's island"; *Inishark:* "the ox's island." The islands are not named in geographical sequence but in a lilting, mnemonic sequence.

4.139 (58:37). Slieve Bloom – A range of mountains in central Ireland, fifty-five miles west-southwest of Dublin. *Slieve:* after the Irish *sliabh,* "mountain."

4.140 (58:38). Dlugacz's – See 4.46n.

4.141 (58:39). polonies, black and white – A polony sausage is made of partially cooked pork and thus looks mottled, black and white.

4.148 (59:6). Denny's sausages – Henry Denny & Son, meat-product manufacturers, had their factory in Limerick from the early nineteenth century.

4.148 (59:7). Woods – *Thom's* 1904 (p. 1482) lists a Mr. R. Woods at 8 Eccles Street, next door to Bloom's house. He is listed again under "Nobility, Gentry, Merchants, and Traders" (p. 2043), but his vocation is not identified.

4.155 (59:16). the model farm at Kinnereth . . . Tiberias – The Sea of Galilee is variously known as the Sea of Tiberias and the Sea of Kinneret. Kinneret, apparently on the southwest shore of the sea, is mentioned once in the Bible (Joshua 19:35) as a fortified city of the tribe of Naphtali. Smith's *Dictionary of the Bible* (Philadelphia, 1884) remarks: "No trace is found in later writers and no remains by travellers." The farm was founded and advertised by "the Palestine Land Development Company on 8 June 1908, to train Jewish workers and to prove that a farm employing Jewish workers could be profitable" (Hyman, p. 338).

4.156 (59:17). Moses Montefiore – Sir Moses Haim Montefiore (1784–1885), born Anglo-Italian, became a wealthy English philanthropist who used his influence and wealth to secure political emancipation of Jews in England, to alleviate Jewish suffering elsewhere in Europe, and to encourage the colonization of Palestine (at the beginnings of the Zionist movement in the latter half of the nineteenth century). Among the Jews of Europe his name became a synonym for orthodox sanctity.

4.159 (59:21). mornings in the cattlemarket – In 1893–94 Bloom worked for Joseph Cuffe as a clerk superintending cattle sales in the cattle market; see 17.483–86 (680:25–29). The cattle market is located off North Circular Road in northwestern Dublin.

4.176 (59:41). Brown scapulars – See 15.2227–28n.

4.178 (60:2). Eccles lane – Gives into the Mater Misericordiae Hospital complex on the north side of Eccles Street toward its western end.

4.178 (60:2–3). They like them sizeable – The minimum height requirement for the Dublin Metropolitan Police in 1904 was five feet nine inches, well above the stature of the ordinary Dubliner.

4.179 (60:3–4). O please Mr. Policeman . . . in the woods – This apparently combines a music-hall song with the catch phrase "lost in the wood" (from the story "The Babes in the Wood"). The song "Oh Please, Mr. P'liceman,

Oh! Oh! Oh!" was written by E. Andrews and popularized in the 1890s by the Tillie Sisters: "To London Town we came, you know, a week ago today, / And 'tis the first time we've been out, and quickly lost our way; / We got somewhere near Leicester Square, when a p'liceman bold / Cried out, 'Move on!' and how he laughed as we our story told. [Chorus:] Oh, please, Mr. P'liceman, do be good to us; / We've not been long in London, and we want to take a 'bus. / They told us we could go by 'bus to Pimlico, / Oh, what a wicked Place is London—Oh! Oh! Oh!"

4.191–92 (60:16–17). Agendath Netaim – Hebrew: "a company of planters" (though the more proper spelling would be *Agudath*), an advertisement for a Zionist colony. "It was established in Palestine only in the summer of 1905 . . . its aim was to save the prospective settler the initial hardships involved in setting up a farm by itself buying land, developing it, and planting trees for him" (Hyman, p. 339). See 17.759n; and cf. 4.155n.

4.192–93 (60:18). Turkish government – Palestine was part of the Turkish empire from 1516 until the end of World War I. During the closing decades of the nineteenth century the Zionist movement, headed by Theodore Herzl (1860–1904), undertook to purchase lands and establish Jewish colonies in Palestine, to which the Turkish government was largely amenable. However, at the time of Herzl's death (3 July 1904), the attempt to establish "for the Jewish people a *politically* and *legally* assured home in Palestine" by creating an autonomous Jewish state under Turkish suzerainty and guaranteed by the "great powers" of Europe was inconclusively stalled in negotiation.

4.194 (60:20). Jaffa – A seaport in Palestine (incorporated into Tel Aviv in 1949).

4.195 (60:20). *eighty marks – The German mark in 1904 was roughly equivalent to the English shilling (eighty 1904 marks in modern currency: $400?). The offer is that the company of planters will buy the land for an investor or prospective settler, plant, and harvest for him, and ship him a portion of the crop as a return on his investment; see 4.191–92n.

4.195 (60:21). dunam – A unit of land area (one thousand square meters, or approximately one-quarter of an acre) used especially in the modern state of Israel.

4.199 (60:25–26). Bleibtreustrasse 34, Berlin, W. 15 – The Palestine Land Development Company's Berlin address was Bleibtreustrasse 34–35 (Hyman, p. 338). *Bleibtreu*, German: "remain true."

4.203 (60:30). Andrews – Andrews & Co., tea and coffee dealers, wine and spirit merchants, and Italian warehousers, 19–22 Dame Street, in central Dublin south of the Liffey.

4.205 (60:33). Citron . . . Saint Kevin's parade – J. Citron, of 17 St. Kevin's Parade, a "neighbor" of Bloom when Bloom lived in Lombard Street West in south-central Dublin. St. Kevin's Parade was just around the corner. Hyman (p. 329) says that the J. in *Thom's* 1904 is a misprint for "I(srael) Citron (1876–1951)."

4.205 (60:33). Mastiansky – Julius Mastiansky, a grocer at 16 St. Kevin's Parade and a "neighbor" of Bloom's. Hyman (p. 189) identifies him as P. Masliansky.

4.209–10 (60:38–39). Moisel . . . Arbutus place: Pleasants street – The two streets are also near Lombard Street West. An M. Moisel lived at 20 Arbutus Place in 1904 and thus had been a "neighbor" of Bloom's. Citron, Mastiansky, and Moisel are Jews in the novel and are therefore "spiritual" as well as physical neighbors. Hyman (p. 190) identifies Moisel as Nisan Moisel (1814–1909), "with whose two sons and their families Bloom was acquainted": Elyah Wolf Moisel (see 8.391–92n) and Philip Moisel (see 17.1254n).

4.210–11 (60:39). Must be without a flaw – Refers to the Feast of Tabernacles (Sukkoth) in the seventh month of the Hebrew calendar, a festival that was both a thanksgiving for the completed harvest and a commemoration of the time when the Israelites lived in tents during their passage through the wilderness. One phase of the observance involves the carrying of palm branches entwined with myrtle and willow, together with a specimen of citron, into the synagogue. The citron to be used for this purpose, according to the elaborate instructions of the *Babylonian Talmud*, was to be not only without physical flaw but perfect in every way, including the legal, moral, and religious conditions under which it was grown. Together the citron (*ethrog*) and the twined branches (*lulav*) represent all the scattered tribes of Israel and are symbolic of the coming redemption that will reunite all the tribes.

4.215 (61:3–4). His back is . . . Norwegian captain's – Ellmann (p. 23) reports the story "of a hunchbacked Norwegian captain who ordered a suit from a Dublin tailor, J. H. Kerse of 34 Upper Sackville Street. The finished suit did not fit him and the captain berated the tailor for being unable to sew, whereupon the irate tailor denounced him for being impossible to fit."

4.216–17 (61:5–6). On earth as it is in heaven – From the Lord's Prayer (Matthew 6:10; Luke 11:2): "Thy kingdom come. Thy will be done in earth, as it is in heaven."

4.219–20 (61:9–10). Vulcanic lake, the dead sea – In the mid–nineteenth century, the Dead Sea was assumed to occupy the giant crater of a dead or inactive volcano, but by 1903 the *New International Encyclopedia* could announce: "The region is not, as has been supposed, volcanic." ([New York, 1903], vol. 6, p. 16a).

4.221–22 (61:12–13). Brimstone they called . . . Sodom, Gomorrah, Edom – The five "cities of the plain" ("in the vale of Siddim which is the salt [Dead] sea") were Sodom, Gomorrah, Admah, Zeboiim, and Bela (subsequently Zoar) (Genesis 14:2–3). In Genesis 18:20, the Lord determines to destroy the cities, "Because the cry of Sodom and Gomorrah is great, and because their sin is very grievous." In Genesis 19, Lot and his family, faithful to the Lord, are warned and escape; "Then the Lord rained upon Sodom and upon Gomorrah brimstone and fire . . . And he overthrew those cities, and all the plain, and all the inhabitants of the cities, and that which grew upon the ground." Bloom mistakenly includes "Edom" as one of the cities. In Genesis 25:30 Esau, Jacob's brother, has his name changed to Edom, and in Genesis 36:9 Esau ("who is Edom") becomes the father of the Edomites.

4.223–24 (61:14–15). the first race – Genesis 5 traces "the genealogy of the patriarchs" from Adam to Noah. The traditional Judeo-Christian view is that after the Flood and, literally or figuratively, the destruction of the race except for Noah and his family, "Noah is clearly the head of a new human family, the representative of the whole race" (William Smith, *A Dictionary of the Bible* [Philadelphia, 1884], p. 454b).

4.224 (61:15). Cassidy's – James Cassidy, wine and spirit merchant, 71 Dorset Street Upper.

4.224 (61:15). naggin – A small quantity of liquor, usually a quarter of a pint.

4.225–26 (61:17). captivity to captivity – A reference to the history of the Jews, in captivity in Egypt in the second millennium B.C., in various captivities in Assyria and Babylon in the eighth through the sixth centuries B.C., dispersed by the Romans in the first century A.D. (thus in "captivity," prevented from returning to their native land), and most recently, from Bloom's point of view, subjected to the "captivity" of waves of anti-Semitism in the late nineteenth century.

4.232 (61:23–24). age crusting him with a salt cloak – When Lot and his family escaped from Sodom, they were instructed not to look back (Genesis 19:17). "But [Lot's] wife looked back from behind him, and she became a pillar of salt" (Genesis 19:26); here, then, Bloom has looked back on the destruction of Sodom and Gomorrah.

4.234 (61:25–26). Sandow's exercises – Eugene or Eugen Sandow (Frederick Muller, 1867–1925), a strong man who advertised himself as capable of transforming the puny into the mighty. Bloom's bookshelf contains a copy of his book *Physical Strength and How to Obtain It* (London, 1897) (17.1397 [709:18–19]). It includes a program of exercises and a chart for recording measurements, as Bloom apparently did (17.1815–19 [721:33–38]). Sandow also did a self-advertising turn in vaudeville at the Empire Theatre of Varieties in Dublin, 2–14 May 1898. His pursuit of publicity eventually destroyed his health when he lifted a motorcar out of a ditch single-handedly.

4.235–36 (61:27–28). Number eighty . . . only twenty-eight – In point of fact, no. 80 was valued at £17 and was occupied in 1904; Bloom's house was valued at £28 and was vacant in 1904. The assessed value of real estate in 1904 Dublin was based on net rent or net annual value.

4.236 (61:28). Towers, Battersby, North, MacArthur – Four Dublin house (real-estate) agents who have signs on the vacant house, advertising it as among their offerings.

4.237–38 (61:29–30). To smell the gentle smoke of tea – Early in Book 1 of *The Odyssey*, Athena describes Odysseus's state on Calypso's isle to Zeus: "But such desire is in him / merely to see the hearthsmoke leaping upward / from his own island, that he longs to die" (1:52–59; Fitzgerald, p. 15).

4.240–42 (61:32–34). Quick warm sunlight ... slim sandals ... a girl with gold hair on the wind – Bloom is walking west along Eccles Street (from Dorset Street, which crosses the east end of Eccles Street) toward Berkeley Road. As the cloud moves eastward on the prevailing westerly wind, sunlight moves along Eccles Street toward Bloom, and he has a momentary vision of his blond daughter, Milly, running to greet him. Cf. *The Odyssey*, Book 5, when Zeus orders Hermes to Calypso's isle to tell her to release Odysseus for his voyage home. Hermes, "the Wayfinder," prepares to comply: he "bent to tie his beautiful sandals on, / ambrosial, golden, that carry him over water / or over endless land in a swish of the wind" (5:43–46; Fitzgerald, p. 94).

4.244 (61:36). Mrs Marion Bloom – In 1904 an ill-mannered mode of address to a married woman who is living with her husband. She should be addressed as "Mrs. Leopold Bloom."

4.250 (62:1). Mullingar – The county town of County Westmeath, Ireland, forty-six miles west-northwest of Dublin.

4.256 (62:7–8). his backward eye – An allusion to the one-eyed Malbecco, the cuckold husband of Hellenore in Edmund Spenser's (c. 1552–99) *The Faerie Queene*. While Hellenore lies with a group of satyrs, Malbecco is eternally unable to escape the presence of the past, "Still fled he forward, looking backward still" (Book 3, canto 10, stanza 56).

4.276–77 (62:29–30). Give her too much ... won't eat pork – The bit about meat is folk-wisdom about cats; the "won't eat pork" is folk-nonsense.

4.281 (62:35). Mr Coghlan – The photographer in Mullingar for whom Milly works.

4.281 (62:35). lough Owel – A lake in Westmeath near Mullingar. Black's rather outspoken *Tourist Guide to Ireland* (Edinburgh, 1888) remarks that it is "attractive but not overwhelming."

4.281 (62:36). young student – Alec Bannon; see 1.684n.

4.282 (62:36). seaside girls – A song written and composed by Harry B. Norris (1899; quoted in Zack Bowen, *Musical Allusions in the*

Works of James Joyce [Albany, N.Y., 1974], pp. 89–90).

> Down at Margate looking very charming
>   you are sure to meet
> Those girls, dear girls, those lovely
>   seaside girls,
> With sticks they steer and promenade
>   the pier to give the boys a treat,
> In pique silks and lace, they tip you
>   quite a playful wink.
> It always is the case you seldom stop to
>   think,   5
> You fall in love of course upon the spot,
> But not with one girl, always with the
>   lot.
>
> *Chorus:*
> Those girls, those girls, those lovely
>   seaside girls,
> All dimples smiles and curls, your head
>   it simply whirls,
> They look all right, complexions pink
>   and white,   10
> They've diamond rings and dainty feet,
> Golden hair from Regent Street,
> Lace and grace and lots of face, those
>   pretty little seaside girls.
>
> There's Maud and Clara, Gwendolen
>   and Sarah where do they come
>   from?
> Those girls, dear girls, those lovely
>   seaside girls.   15
> In bloomers smart, they captivate the
>   heart, when cycling down the
>   prom.
> At wheels and heels and hose, you must
>   not look 'tis understood,
> But ev'ry Johnnie knows, it does your
>   eyesight good,
> The boys observe the latest thing in
>   socks,
> They learn the time by looking at the
>   clocks.   20
>
> When you go to do a little boating just
>   for fun you take,
> Those girls, dear girls, those lovely
>   seaside girls,
> They all say 'we so dearly love the sea.'
>   Their way on board they make.
> The wind begins to blow. Each girl
>   remarks 'how rough today,
> It's lovely don't you know,' and then
>   they sneak away.   25
> And as the yacht keeps rolling with the
>   tide,
> You'll notice hanging o'er the vessel's
>   side

Second Chorus:
Those girls, those girls, those lovely
    seaside girls,
All dimples smiles and curls, each head
    it simply whirls,
They look a sight, complexions green
    and white,   30
Their hats fly off, and at your feet
Falls golden hair from Regent Street,
Rouge and puffs slip down the cuffs of
    pretty little seaside girls.

4.283–84 (62:37–38). moustache cup . . . Milly's birthday gift – "Sham crown Derby" is a cheap imitation of an expensive English china made since 1773 in Derby under royal patent and thus marked with a crown. Victoria changed the name from Crown Derby to Royal Crown Derby in 1890. In the Homeric parallel, Alcinous, Nausicaa's father, gives Odysseus a present: "My own wine-cup of gold intaglio / I'll give him, too; through all the days to come, / tipping his wine to Zeus or other gods / in his great hall, he shall remember me" (8:430–32; Fitzgerald, pp. 149–50).

4.287–90 (63:1–4). *O Milly Bloom . . . ass and garden* – After Samuel Lover (1787–1868), an Irish poet, novelist, playwright, painter, etcher, and composer: "O Thady Brady you are my darlin', / You are my looking glass from night till mornin' / I love you better without one fardin / Than Brian Gallagher wid house and garden" (*Legends and Stories of Ireland* [Philadelphia, 1835], vol. 2, p. 206). See Ellmann, p. 31.

4.291 (63:5). professor Goodwin – A pianist who was Molly's accompanist from 1888 or 1889 to 1895. The concert Bloom recalls took place in 1893.

4.305–6 (63:22–23). The warmth of her . . . fragrance of the tea – In *The Odyssey*, as Hermes approaches Calypso's cave: "Upon her hearthstone a great fire blazing / scented the farthest shores with cedar smoke / and smoke of thyme, and singing high and low / in her sweet voice, before her loom a-weaving" (5:59–62; Fitzgerald, p. 95).

4.308 (63:24–25). A strip of torn envelope . . . dimpled pillow – Molly, in her *Odyssey*-role as Calypso, the Concealer.

4.314 (63:31). *Là ci darem* – *Là ci darem la mano*, Italian: "Then we'll go hand in hand"; a duet in Act I, scene iii, of Mozart's opera *Don Giovanni* (1787–88). Don Giovanni comes upon some villagers "merrymaking," is "smitten" by the "innocent" Zerlina, and attempts to seduce her away from her peasant fiancé, Massetto: "This summer house is mine; we shall be alone, / and then, my jewel, we'll be married. / Then we'll go hand in hand, / Then you'll say yes. / Look, it isn't far; / Let's be off from here, my darling." Zerlina answers, "Vorrei e non vorrei": "I would like to and I wouldn't like to; / My heart beats a little faster. / It's true I would be happy, / But he can still make a fool of me."

4.314 (63:31). J. C. Doyle – See 6.222n.

4.314 (63:31–32). *Love's Old Sweet Song* – (1884), words by G. Clifton Bingham (1859–1913), set to music by the Irish composer James Lyman Molloy (1837–1909): "Once in the dear, dead days beyond recall, / When on the world the mists began to fall, / Out of the dreams that rose in happy throng, / Low to our hearts, Love sang an old sweet song; / And in the dusk where fell the firelight gleam, / Softly it wove itself into our dream. [Chorus:] Just a song at twilight, / When the lights are low / And the flick'ring shadows / Softly come and go; / Though the heart be weary, / Sad the day and long, / Still to us at twilight, / Comes love's sweet song, / Comes love's old sweet song. [Second stanza:] Even today we hear Love's song of yore, / Deep in our hearts it dwells forevermore; / Footsteps may falter, weary grow the way, / Still we can hear it, at the close of day; / So till the end, when life's dim shadows fall, / Love will be found the sweetest song of all."

4.316 (63:34). flowerwater – Distilled water scented with the essential oil of one or more flowers.

4.327 (64:4). *Voglio e non vorrei* – Italian: "I want to and I wouldn't like to." Bloom misquotes Zerlina's line from the duet in Act I, scene iii, of *Don Giovanni;* see 4.314n. Zerlina sings the more delicately ambiguous line "Vorrei e non vorrei" (I would like to and I wouldn't like to). Bloom changes the conditional *would* to the unconditional *want.*

4.330 (64:7). orangekeyed – Decorated with a geometrical pattern of interlocking lines or bands called Greek fret, "which characterized much Greek pottery of the Geometric Period, the ninth to seventh centuries B.C.: pottery of the lifetime (if he lived) of Homer" (Hugh Kenner, *Ulysses* [London, 1980], p. 144).

4.339 (64:18). metempsychosis – The mystical doctrine that the soul after death is reborn in another body. In ancient India (and in the Orphic cult in ancient Greece) rebirth could take place not only in another human body but also in any other animate (animal or vegetable) body. Late-nineteenth-century theosophists modified metempsychosis with the concept of progressive evolution. They held that the human soul could only be reincarnated in another human body and denied the possibility of the soul's migrating down the scale of evolution. They also held that the purpose of reincarnation was evolutionary, to test and refine the soul through a sequence of human embodiments until it emerged as "pure spirit." See 3.477–79n. According to Mary Power, who has discovered the novel Joyce had in hand (see 4.346n), the word *metempsychosis* does not appear in the text.

4.345 (64:24). Dolphin's Barn – An area on the southwestern outskirts of Dublin, where Molly was living with her father when she first met Bloom.

4.346 (64:25–26). *Ruby: the Pride of the Ring* – After *Ruby. A Novel. Founded on the Life of a Circus Girl* by Amye Reade (London, 1889). The novel, an exposé of the cruelties of circus life, has overt reform intentions. The story: after a checkered childhood, the heroine, Ruby, her family finally broken, is indentured (sold into slavery) at age thirteen to Signor Enrico, a circus master whom Joyce improves from Mr. Henry to Signor Maffei (echoing *maffioso*). Ruby is worked to exhaustion, beaten when she falters, and hounded to her death before the eyes of her father, who has been returned from Australia (by sentimental convention) just in time. See Mary Power, "The Discovery of Ruby," *JJQ* 18, no. 2 (1981): 115–21.

4.346–49 (64:26–29). Illustration. Fierce Italian . . . *from him with an oath* – The illustration (as reproduced in *JJQ* 18, no. 2 [1981]: 119) is much as Bloom sees it, though the "carriagewhip" may be a cane and the fallen figure of the woman is discreetly draped. The text, which Bloom has apparently not read, reveals that the victim is Ruby's heroine-friend, not Ruby. The caption of the illustration reads, " 'The monster desisted and threw his victim from him with an oath.' Chap. xxxi."

4.347 (64:27–28). Sheet kindly lent – Zack

Bowen (*Musical Allusions in the Works of James Joyce* [Albany, N.Y., 1974], p. 88) suggests a punning allusion to John Henry Cardinal Newman's (1801–80) "The Pillar of Cloud" (1833). First of three verses: "Lead, Kindly Light, amid the encircling gloom, / Lead Thou me on! / The night is dark, and I am far from home— / Lead Thou me on! / Keep Thou my feet; I do not ask to see / The distant scene,— one step enough for me."

4.349 (64:30). Hengler's – The brothers Charles (1820–87) and Albert Hengler ran "permanent circuses" (i.e., not traveling or tent shows) in Edinburgh, Glasgow, Liverpool, Hull, Dublin, and London. Bloom has apparently witnessed a trapeze accident at the circus.

4.351 (64:32). Bone them young – In circus tradition, children of trapeze acrobats are intensively trained from a very early age.

4.358 (64:39). Paul de Kock's – Charles Paul de Kock (1794–1871), a popular French novelist whose books dealt with shopgirls, clerks, etc.—that is, with the democratic bourgeoisie. An Edwardian evaluation: "His novels are vulgar but not unmoral."

4.360 (64:42). Capel street library – At 166 Capel Street in central Dublin north of the Liffey. The Dublin public libraries were established in 1884 under the Public Libraries Act of 1855. The Capel Street branch has a lending department, a reference library, and a news room.

4.361 (65:1). Kearney – Joseph Kearney, book and music seller, 14 Capel Street across from the Library.

4.369 (65:11). *The Bath of the Nymph* – Source unknown; probably fictional.

4.370 (66:12). *Photo Bits* – A London penny-weekly magazine (est. 1898) published on Tuesdays. It presented itself as a photography magazine but was closer to soft pornography in effect. Its advertisers set the tone by offering everything from "Aristotle's Works" to "Flagellations and Flagellants," "Rare Books and Curious Photographs," "Rose's Famous Female Mixture . . . will Positively Remove the most Obstinate Obstructions," "Bile Beans For Biliousness," and innumerable books and pills that promised "Manhood Restored."

4.371 (65:13–14). Not unlike her with her hair down: slimmer – In Book 5 of *The Odyssey*, "the beautiful nymph Calypso" offers Odysseus immortality if he will remain with her, and then she asks about Penelope: " 'Can I be less desirable than she is? / Less interesting? Less beautiful? Can mortals / compare with goddesses in grace and form?' // To this the strategist Odysseus answered: / 'My lady goddess, here is no cause for anger. / My quiet Penelope—how well I know— / would seem a shade before your majesty, / death and old age being unknown to you, / while she must die' " (5:205–18; Fitzgerald, p. 99).

4.391 (65:37). the toothsome pliant meat – Just before the discussion quoted in the preceding note, Calypso gives Odysseus "victuals and drink of men" and dines herself on "nectar and ambrosia" (5:199; Fitzgerald, p. 99).

4.402–3 (66:7–8). all the beef to the heels – "When a woman has very thick legs, thick almost down to the feet, she is 'like a Mullingar heifer, beef to the heels.' The plains of Westmeath round Mullingar are noted for fattening cattle" (P. W. Joyce, *English*, p. 136).

4.403 (66:8). lough Owel – See 4.281n.

4.404 (66:9). a scrap picnic – Picnics in the late nineteenth century were more formal and elaborate than they tend to be today; so a "scrap picnic" is an exception, an informal, last-minute outing.

4.406 (66:12). Greville Arms – A hotel in Mullingar.

4.409 (66:15). those seaside girls – See 4.282n.

4.417 (66:22–23). Mrs Thornton in Denzille Street – A Dublin midwife, 19A Denzille Street, near the lying-in hospital on Holles Street—see Oxen of the Sun (14.1–1591 [pp. 383–428])—and that would locate her approximately one and a half miles northeast of Bloom's residence in Lombard Street West *if* the Blooms were living there in 1889.

4.419 (66:25). little Rudy – Son of Molly and Leopold Bloom, born 29 December 1893, died 9 January 1894 (aged eleven days). The name Rudolph derives from two Old German words, *hrothi* (fame) and *vulf* (wolf) (*Oxford Dictionary of Christian Names;* suggested by Joan Keenan).

4.419 (66:25). Well, God is good, sir – A staple cliché of Irish fatalism. It masks the inscrutability of God's omniscience and omnipotence: even what seems disastrous to human beings can be "good" in the divine order of things.

4.422–23 (66:29). XL Café – Refreshment rooms, 86 Grafton Street, in the southeast quadrant of Dublin.

4.425 (66:32). Twelve and six a week – Milly's salary, 12s. 6d., while far from lavish, was not bad—Dublin shopgirls who lived at home were apparently paid as little as 7s. a week (see "Eveline," *Dubliners*). Stephen's salary at Mr. Deasy's school (£3 12s. a month) is only approximately 16s. a week.

4.426 (66:33). Musichall stage – Not very well paid and possibly morally compromising, since music-hall *artistes* were regarded as living on the permissive fringes of middle-class society.

4.433–34 (67:2). Anaemic . . . given milk too long – It was an old wives' tale that anemia could result if the milk in a baby's diet were not supplemented early enough with solid foods, particularly meat.

4.434 (67:3). *Erin's King* . . . the Kish – The *Erin's King* was an excursion steamer that took sightseers on two-hour trips around Dublin Bay, circling the Kish lightship to the south (see 3.267n) or Ireland's Eye, an island just north of the Howth peninsula, to the north. During the summer it sailed several times a day from Custom House Quay in central Dublin; fare, one shilling.

4.435 (67:4). Not a bit funky – "Funky" is slang for afraid, timid, or excessively nervous; *Cf.* "Seaside Girls" (4.282n) lines 24–33.

4.437–38, 442–43 (67:6–7, 11–12). *All dimpled cheeks . . . seaside girls* – See 4.282n.

4.439 (67:9). jarvey – Slang for the driver of a hackney coach or an Irish outside car; see 5.98n.

4.440–41 (67:10). Pier with lamps, summer evening, band – See 2.33n.

4.445–46 (67:14–15). her hair . . . braiding – One Homeric epithet for Calypso in *The Odyssey* is "the softly-braided nymph" (5:28; Fitzgerald, p. 94).

4.447 (67:16). A soft qualm, regret – *Cf.* Odysseus, marooned on Calypso's isle: "But when day came he sat on the rocky shore / and broke his own heart groaning, with eyes wet / scanning the bare horizon of the sea" (5:156–58; Fitzgerald, p. 97).

4.452 (67:22–23). August bank holiday – A long holiday weekend not unlike Labor Day weekend in the United States.

4.454 (67:24). M'Coy – Appears as a character in "Grace," *Dubliners*, where he is described as having been, among other things, a clerk in the Midland Railway. See Ellmann, p. 375.

4.463 (67:35). to fag – To drudge, to work hard at an unrewarding task.

4.467 (67:39). Titbits – *Titbits from All the Most Interesting Books, Periodicals and Newspapers in the World*, a sixteen-page penny-weekly (published on Thursdays, dated Saturday). Some historians of journalism suggest that modern popular journalism ("oddments and persiflage") was born with the first issue of *Titbits* in 1881.

4.474 (68:7). The maid was in the garden – After the nursery rhyme: "Sing a song of sixpence, / A pocket full of rye; / Four-and-twenty blackbirds, / Baked in a pie. / When the pie was opened, / The birds began to sing; / Was not that a dainty dish, / To set before the king? // The king was in his counting-house / Counting out his money; / The queen was in the parlor, / Eating bread and honey. / The maid was in the garden, / Hanging out the clothes. / There came a little blackbird, / And snapped off her nose."

4.480 (68:15). oilcakes – The mass of compressed seeds (rapeseed, linseed, cottonseed, or other kinds) left after pressing out as much of the oil as possible; the cakes are used as a fattening food for cattle or sheep or as manure.

4.484 (68:19). Whitmonday – The day after Whitsunday (the seventh Sunday after Easter). Whitmonday is a bank holiday, providing a long weekend. In 1904 Whitmonday fell on 23 May, when Bloom was stung by a bee.

4.488 (68:23). Drago's – A hairdresser at 17 Dawson Street in the southeast quadrant of Dublin, approximately a mile and a half south of Bloom's home.

4.490 (68:26). Tara Street – Dublin Corporation Public Baths, Wash Houses, and Public Swimming Baths, J. P. O'Brien, superintendent, in Tara Street, just south of the Liffey in east-central Dublin.

4.491 (68:27). James Stephens . . . O'Brien – James Stephens, Chief Organizer and first Head Centre of the Fenian Society (see 3.241n). The O'Brien Bloom mentions could be one of two O'Briens associated with Stephens, but neither was directly involved in Stephens's escape from Richmond Gaol in 1865: William Smith O'Brien (1803–64)—see 6.226 (93:11)—or James Francis Xavier O'Brien (1828–1905)—see 17.1648 (716:15–16); and neither of them was the J. P. O'Brien of the Tara Street baths. W. S. O'Brien joined with Daniel O'Connell's Repeal Association in 1843, but then withdrew and formed the more activist Irish Confederation in 1847. During the famine of 1848 he attempted to "raise the country," and he, with Stephens and others, attacked a police garrison in County Tipperary. The attack was unsuccessful; Stephens, slightly wounded, escaped by feigning death. O'Brien was apprehended and found guilty of high treason. His death sentence was commuted to penal servitude, and he was released in 1854 and fully pardoned in 1856, but he took no further part in politics. J. F. X. O'Brien studied medicine in Paris, participated in Walker's filibuster in Nicaragua in 1856, met Stephens in New Orleans in 1858, and joined the American branch of the Fenian Society. He was an assistant surgeon in the Union army during the Civil War. After the war he went to Ireland, where he was arrested for his involvement in the abortive Fenian uprising in Cork in 1867. His death sentence was commuted, and he was released in 1869. He became a member of Parliament (1885–1905) and supported Parnell until the Great Split in 1891. As general secretary of the United Irish League he advocated an independent economic (as well as political) policy for Ireland.

4.493 (68:29). Enthusiast – The name was applied to a fourth-century Christian sect in the Near East and to a splinter group of seventeenth-century Puritans who preached an anarchistic agrarian utopia. Here Bloom uses the word to describe the religiously committed Zionist Dlugacz, who wanted to establish "for the Jewish people a *politically* and *legally* assured home in Palestine."

4.494 (68:30). crazy – Archaic: "cracked, flawed, liable to disintegrate."

4.498–99 (68:35–36). The king was in his counting house – Nursery rhyme; see 4.474n.

4.500 (68:37). cuckstool – Obsolete: a chair used to punish dishonest tradesmen and other offenders. The victim was fastened in the chair in front of his own door to be hooted at and pelted by the community.

4.502 (68:39–40). *Matcham's Masterstroke* – The magazine *Titbits* did print a "Prize Titbit" in each issue with the payment quoted, as here. This particular story appears to have been Joyce's private joke at the expense of his own adolescence. Apparently Joyce wrote a story, intended for *Titbits* and money, that included the sentence Bloom reads: *"Matcham often thinks . . . who now. . . . Hand in hand"* (4.513–15 [69:12–14]).

4.502–3 (68:40–41). Mr Philip Beaufoy, Play-goers' club, London – A real person who contributed (terrible?) stories to *Titbits* in the 1890s. The joke resides in the contrast between Beaufoy's literary stature on the one hand and his name, which means "good faith," and his fashionable London address on the other. The story attributed to him here is fictional.

4.510 (69:9). cascara sagrada – Spanish: literally, "sacred bark"; as advertised, a mild laxative made from the bark of the buckthorn tree.

4.522 (69:22). Roberts – Unknown.

4.522 (69:23). Gretta Conroy – A central character in "The Dead," *Dubliners*.

4.526 (69:27). May's band – Maintained and supplied by May & Co., music sellers and professors of music and piano, 130 St. Stephen's Green West in the southeast quadrant of Dublin.

4.526 (69:28). Ponchielli's dance of the hours – Amilcare Ponchielli (1834–86), *La gioconda*. The opera's plot is complicated by two villains and by two heroines who are in love with one hero. In Act III, "The House of Gold," one of the villains determines to avenge his honor by poisoning his heroine-wife, who has had a rendezvous with the hero. The other heroine substitutes a narcotic. Meanwhile, there is a festival with an elaborate ballet, "The Dance of the Hours," which represents the passing of the hours from dawn till dark. A sequence of costumes marks the progression, as Bloom recalls at 4.534–35 (69:38–39). In the dark climax of the ballet the villain reveals the "corpse" of his drugged wife, and confusion is reestablished before the paired happy and pathetic endings of Act IV.

4.542 (70:6–7). The houghs of the knees – Or hock; here, the back of the knee (as for the knee of a bird's leg).

4.544 (70:10). George's church – See 4.78n.

4.546–48 (70:11–13). *Heigho! . . . Heigho!* – The bells sound the time in the Westminster pattern: each phrase of four notes indicates a quarter hour, and at the end of the hour, after four phrases, a low bell tells the number of hours.

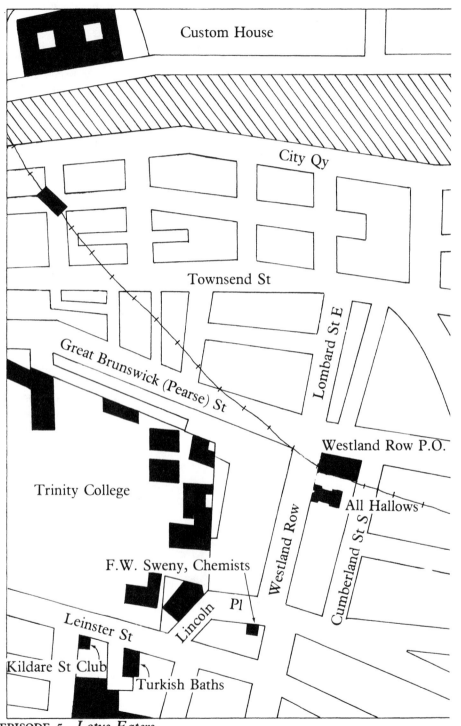

Custom House

City Qy

Townsend St

Lombard St E

Great Brunswick (Pearse) St

Westland Row P.O.

Trinity College

Westland Row

All Hallows

Cumberland St S

F.W. Sweny, Chemists

Lincoln Pl

Leinster St

Kildare St Club

Turkish Baths

EPISODE 5. *Lotus-Eaters*

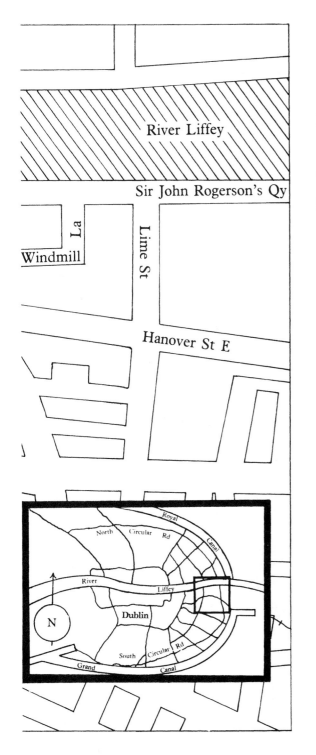

EPISODE 5

Lotus-Eaters

(5.1–572, PP. 71–86)

Episode 5: *The Lotus-Eaters*, 5.1–572 (71–86). After Odysseus escapes from Calypso's island and from the sea, he lands on Scheria (Book 6) and is entertained at King Alcinous's court (Books 7 and 8); in Book 9 he reveals himself to Alcinous and begins to recount the adventures of his voyage from Troy, "years of rough adventure, weathered under Zeus" (9:37–38; Fitzgerald, p. 158). Early in his voyage he and his men were driven by a storm to the land of the Lotus-Eaters, "who live upon that flower" (9:84; Fitzgerald, p. 159), and Odysseus disembarked to take on water. Some of Odysseus's men met the friendly Lotus-Eaters, ate the Lotus, and longed "to stay forever, browsing on that native bloom, forgetful of their homeland" (9:96–97; Fitzgerald, p. 160). Odysseus drove the infected men back to the ships and set sail.

Time: 10:00 A.M. Scene: Bloom has traveled approximately one and a quarter miles southeast from his home in Eccles Street to Sir John Rogerson's Quay on the south bank of the Liffey near its mouth. He circles south toward the Westland Row post office (as though he were approaching it surreptitiously rather than directly) and then turns sharply southwest toward the Leinster Street baths (see 5.549n). His wanderings take place within a triangle about a third of a mile on a side. Organ: genitals; Art: botany-chemistry; Color: none; Symbol: the Eucharist; Technique: narcissism. Correspondences: *Lotus-Eaters*—the cabhorses, communicants, soldiers, eunuchs, bather, watchers of cricket.

The Linati schema lists as Persons (without specifying correspondences): "Eurylochus [one of Odysseus's companions, the only one of the advance-patrol on Circe's island who escapes being turned into a swine]; Polites [one of Priam's sons, killed by Achilles' son Pyrrhus (or Neoptolemus) in a "murderous rage" during the fall of Troy (Virgil, *Aeneid*, 2:526)]; Ulysses; Nausicaa (2) [Martha Clifford?]." It also lists as Symbols: "Host, Penis in Bath, Foam Flower, Drugs, Castration, Oats."

5.1 (71:1). lorries – Waterside cranes.

5.1 (71:1). sir John Rogerson's quay – On the south bank of the Liffey at its mouth. The quayside was reclaimed by Sir John Rogerson, an early-eighteenth-century barrister and alderman who eventually became chief justice of the King's Bench.

5.2 (71:2). past Windmill lane – On Bloom's right, as he walks east along Sir John Rogerson's Quay.

5.2 (71:2–3). Leask's the linseed crusher – H. M. Leask & Co., linseed crushers, oil and linseed cake manufacturers, 14–15 Rogerson's Quay.

5.2 (71:3). the postal telegraph office – 18 Rogerson's Quay.

5.3 (71:3–4). Could have given that address too – Town Sub–Post Office, Savings Bank, and Money Order Office at 18 Rogerson's Quay. Bloom reflects that he could have used this post office as a blind in addition to the one in Westland Row toward which he is circling.

5.3 (71:4). the sailor's home – And Shipwrecked Mariner's Society, 19 Rogerson's Quay.

5.4 (71:5). Lime street – Bloom has turned right and is walking south.

5.5 (71:6). Brady's cottages – An alley of tenements that intersects Lime Street.

5.5 (71:6). a boy for the skins – A boy who has been making the rounds of trash heaps and garbage cans.

5.5 (71:7). linked – Held by a chain or cord rather than a handle.

5.7 (71:9). caskhoop – Her toy is a piece of trash, the discarded hoop from a barrel.

5.10 (71:12). Townsend street – Bloom has turned to his right at the foot of Lime Street and has walked west along Hanover Street East, which gives into Townsend Street. Bloom turns left (south), crosses Townsend Street, and walks south through Lombard Street East.

5.1 (71:13). Bethel. El – Hebrew: *Beth*, "House of"; *El*, "God." After the city and holy place twelve miles north of Jerusalem, where the ark of the covenant was kept (Judges 20:26–28; 21:4). This is the name of a Salvation Army hall that Bloom passes in Lombard Street East.

5.11 (71:14). Nichols' the undertaker's – J. and C. Nichols, funeral and job carriage proprietors and undertakers, 26–31 Lombard Street East.

5.12–13 (71:15). Corny Kelleher ... O'Neill's – Kelleher, a fictional character, works for Henry J. O'Neill, carriage maker and undertaker, 164 North Strand Road (in the northeast quadrant of Dublin near Newcomen

Bridge over the Royal Canal). See 10.207–26 (224:33–225:14).

5.13–16 (71:16–20). Met her once . . . tooraloom, tooraloom – Song associated with Kelleher, source unknown. A "tout" is a spy or informer.

5.17 (71:21). Westland row – Extends south from Lombard Street East.

5.17–18 (71:21–22). Belfast and Oriental Tea Company – 6 Westland Row.

5.20 (71:24). Tom Kernan – Tea merchant; an Ulsterman who accepted conversion to Catholicism when he married, he appears as a character in "Grace," *Dubliners*, and frequently in *Ulysses*. He is a fictional agent for Pulbrook Robertson & Co., 5 Dame Street, Dublin, and 2 Mincing Lane, London, E.C.

5.32 (71:37). Cinghalese – Singhalese, one of the ethnic groups of Sri Lanka (formerly Ceylon).

5.32 (71:37–38). lobbing – Lounging.

5.32 (71:38). *dolce far niente* – Italian: literally, "sweet doing nothing"; thus, pleasant idleness or inactivity.

5.33 (71:39). Sleep six months out of twelve – According to post-Homeric Greek mythology, the Lotus-Eaters slept half the year.

5.34 (71:41). Azotes – French: "nitrogen." The French chemist Antoine Laurent Lavoisier (1743–94) called nitrogen "azote" and noted that, though it was present in air, it was unable to support life.

5.35 (71:41). Hothouse in Botanic gardens – In Glasnevin, a little less than two miles north of Dublin center.

5.35 (71:42). Sensitive plants – Suggests Shelley's "The Sensitive Plant" (1820), which contrasts the immanence of the plant's decay against "love, and beauty and delight," for which "there is no death or change." If this is indeed an allusion to Shelley, then "Botanic gardens" (5.35 [71:41]) would recall Erasmus Darwin's (1731–1802) poem *Botanic Garden* (1791), with its two parts, "The Economy of Vegetation" and "The Loves of the Plants." And "Flowers of Idleness" might echo Byron's first series of poems, *Hours of Idleness* (1807).

5.38 (72:3). dead sea – Because the waters of the Dead Sea contain approximately twenty-five percent salt in solution, their specific gravity is approximately 1.16; thus, a human body floats easily on the surface.

5.41 (72:7). a law – Bloom is trying to recall Archimedes' (c. 287–212 B.C.) principle: a solid body immersed in a liquid undergoes an apparent loss of weight equal to the weight of the liquid displaced.

5.42–43 (72:8–9). Vance in high school . . . The college curriculum – Vance, a (fictional?) teacher at Erasmus Smith High School. "Roygbiv," his nickname (13.1075 [376:23]), derives from the initial letters of the spectrum: *r*ed, *o*range, *y*ellow, *g*reen, *b*lue, *i*ndigo, *v*iolet. High schools in the national school system were primarily vocational in their emphasis, but the possibility of a "college curriculum" (i.e., college preparatory course) was enhanced in 1878 (when Bloom was twelve) by the establishment of a Board of Intermediate Education, which held annual examinations and distributed subsidies to secondary schools according to the results.

5.44 (72:10–11). *Thirty two feet per second per second – The approximate rate of acceleration of falling bodies, represented as g in the full statement of the law: $v = gt$, where v is velocity and t is time (in seconds).

5.45–46 (72:12–13). It's the force . . . is the weight – An oversimplification of Newton's law, which holds, instead, that weight is a function of the relation between the mass of the earth and the mass of the body in question.

5.49 (72:16). Freeman – The *Freeman's Journal;* see 4.101–3n.

5.53 (72:21). postoffice – Substation, 49–50 Westland Row.

5.62 (72:31). Henry Flower, Esq – An assumed name of Bloom's. He has struck up this correspondence with Martha Clifford by inserting an advertisement in the *Irish Times:* "Wanted smart lady typist to aid gentleman in literary work." Martha was one of forty-four respondents. See 8.326–27 (160:11–12). The name Henry entered English from the Old High German *Heimrich* (ruler of the house).

5.66–68 (72:36–37). Tweedy's regiment? . . . No, he's a grenadier – Bloom is looking at recruiting posters. Tweedy's regiment was the Royal Dublin Fusiliers, founded in 1881, disbanded in 1922. Uniform: a raccoon hat, six inches high, smaller and flatter on top than that of the Grenadier Guards (nine inches high, bear or raccoon, decorated in front with a flaming grenade in metal). The fusiliers wore the hackle on the left side, green over blue; the collar, shoulder strap, and "pointed cuffs" (5.68 [72:37]) were blue; the trousers were blue with red piping. The grenadiers wore slashed rather than pointed cuffs. Bloom's confusion of the two uniforms was a common mistake.

5.68 (72:38). Redcoats – By the end of the nineteenth century, battle dress for the British army was khaki, but redcoats remained the off-duty and dress uniform of many infantry regiments until World War I.

5.70 (72:40–41). Maud Gonne's letter . . . off O'Connell street – Early in the Boer War (1899–1902), in an effort to encourage enlistments, the British army suspended the rule that troops in Dublin spend the nights in barracks. The result was a considerable number of troops prowling O'Connell Street and vicinity in search of "companionship." Maud Gonne (see 3.233n) rallied her Daughters of Ireland to campaign against enlistment in the British army; as part of their campaign the women distributed a leaflet (attributed to Maud Gonne) "on the shame of Irish girls consorting with the soldiers of the enemy of their country" (Maud Gonne MacBride, *A Servant of the Queen* [London, 1938], p. 292). The issue was sporadically revived in the Dublin press, particularly in May and early June of 1904 after army authorities refused to take action on a Dublin Corporation resolution against the army's allowing troops the freedom of the city.

5.71 (72:41). Griffith's paper – Arthur Griffith (see 3.227n), founder and editor of the *United Irishman* (1899–1906).

5.72 (73:1). an army rotten with venereal disease – A frequently quoted (and largely unfounded) bit of demagoguery at the British army's expense.

5.72 (73:2). overseas or halfseasover empire – Britain's overseas empire. *Halfseasover:* intoxicated.

5.73–74 (73:3). Table:able. Bed:ed. – Like

"left, right; left, right": a cadenced chant that troops or their drill sergeants use to establish the rhythm of their drill or march.

5.74 (73:3–4). The King's own – A phrase that could be applied to a regiment if the king, Edward VII, had presented it with its colors or if the regiment had inducted him into honorary membership. The phrase could also be applied to the Grenadier Guards because, as the first of the "household regiments," they would be attached to the person of the king.

5.74–75 (73:4–5). Never see him . . . A mason. Yes – One would see Edward VII (1841–1910; king 1901–10) dressed in various military (regimental) uniforms but never in uniform as an honorary fireman or policeman. Edward VII was a bencher and officer of the Middle Temple and served as the grand master of English Freemasons from 1874 until he became king in 1901.

5.93 (73:26). badge – A token of membership in a Catholic church organization, regarded as a charm by the superstitious; see 13.639n.

5.96 (73:29). Holohan – Appears as a character in "A Mother," *Dubliners:* "He had a game leg and for that his friends called him Hoppy Holohan."

5.98 (73:32). outsider – Also called a "jaunting car"; a two-wheeled horse-drawn vehicle on which the driver faces ahead, but the passengers, their seats at right angles to the axle with a well for luggage in between, sit with their backs to each other and thus face "outside."

5.99 (73:33). the Grosvenor – A then-fashionable hotel at 5 Westland Row.

5.104–5 (73:39–40). Handsome is and handsome does – Bloom's version of the proverb "Handsome is as handsome does."

5.105–6 (73:41). Brutus is an honourable man – Marc Antony, in his oration over Caesar's body, speaks this phrase in scorn of Brutus's "honourable" motives for killing Caesar (*Julius Caesar* III.ii.87).

5.107 (74:1). Bob Doran – Appears as a character in "The Boarding House," *Dubliners.* His "bender" in *Ulysses* provides one of the minor odysseys of the novel's day.

5.108 (74:2). Bantam Lyons – Appears as a

character in "Ivy Day in the Committee Room," *Dubliners*.

5.108 (74:3). Conway's – A public house, James Conway & Co., grocers and wine merchants, 31–32 Westland Row.

5.112 (74:7). braided drums – The ridges of cord on the back of the woman's glove.

5.117 (74:13). Broadstone – That is, off to the country by way of the Broadstone terminus of the Galway or Midland Great Western Railway. The terminus was in the northwest quadrant of Dublin.

5.118 (74:14). *foostering – Anglicized Irish for to bustle about.

5.119–20 (74:16). Two strings to her bow – A popular proverb dating at least from the Elizabethan age, it applauds the thoughtfulness of providing a reserve that can be drawn on in an emergency.

5.128 (74:25). the Arch – A public house, 32 Henry Street, just north of the Liffey in central Dublin (Molloy and O'Reilly, grocers and spirit merchants).

5.132–33 (74:30). Paradise and the peri – A catch phrase for "so near to paradise and yet prevented." The phrase is the title of an interpolated poem in Thomas Moore's *Lalla Rookh, an Oriental Romance* (1817). In Persian mythology the peri were originally malevolent superhuman beings, but they later became good genies, endowed with beauty and grace; hence, "fair ones," deserving of and hidden in paradise. Moore's poem recounts the struggles of a peri ("Nymph of a fair but erring line!") and her efforts to gain access to paradise: "One morn a Peri at the gate / Of Eden stood, disconsolate; / And as she listen'd to the Springs / Of Life within, like music flowing, / And caught the light upon her wings / Through the half-open portal glowing, / She wept to think her recreant race / Should e'er have lost that glorious place." A "glorious Angel" informs her: "'One hope is thine. / 'Tis written in the Book of Fate, / *The Peri yet may be forgiv'n / Who brings to this Eternal gate / The Gift that is most dear to Heav'n!*'" The peri has a good deal of trouble discovering what that gift is, but it turns out to be "Blest tears of soul-felt penitence!" And with one tear "The Gates are pass'd and Heav'n is won!"

5.133–34 (74:31). Eustace street – In central Dublin south of the Liffey, approximately one-half mile west of Bloom's present position in Westland Row.

5.135 (74:32). *Esprit de corps* – French: "spirit of association; fellow feeling." Also a pun on *corps*, "body": "spirit of the body."

5.138 (74:36–37). the Loop Line bridge – The City of Dublin Junction Railway (the Loop Line) linked the Dublin and Southeastern Railway terminus in Westland Row with the Amiens Street station, the terminus of the Great Western Railway north of the Liffey. The Loop Line is bridged over Westland Row; thus, "they" drive north up Westland Row.

5.144–47 (75:1–4). *What is home . . . abode of bliss* – This advertisement and its position under the obituaries, front page, left column of the *Freeman's Journal*, is a fiction, but a George W. Plumtree was listed as a potted-meat manufacturer at 23 Merchant's Quay in Dublin. "To pot one's meat" is crude slang for to copulate.

5.148 (75:5). My missus – Mrs. M'Coy, "who had been a soprano, still taught young children to play the piano at low terms" in "Grace," *Dubliners*.

5.149 (75:7). Valise tack – Bloom regards M'Coy as a sponger who has borrowed (and not returned) suitcases "to enable Mrs. M'Coy to fulfill imaginary engagements in the country" ("Grace," *Dubliners*).

5.151 (75:10). swagger – Like "swank," for very stylish and important.

5.151–52 (75:11). Ulster hall, Belfast – A concert room and hall for public meetings built in 1862, seating 2,500 people "with all the modern improvements"; in south-central Belfast, eighty-five miles north and slightly east of Dublin.

5.154–55 (75:14–15). Queen was in . . . bread and – After a nursery rhyme; see 4.474n.

5.155–56 (75:15–16). Blackened court cards . . . and fair man – "Court cards," a corrupted form of *coat cards*, the cards bearing the coated figures of king, queen, and knave. In fortune telling, the coat cards indicate people, the numbered cards, events. "Dark lady and fair man" combines one of two queens and one of two kings. The queen of spades: a very dark woman, a false and intriguing woman; a widow. The queen of clubs: a brunette, agreeable and intelligent; marriage; a woman in middle life. The king of hearts: a fair or brown-haired man, good-natured but hasty. The king of diamonds: a very fair-complexioned or gray-haired man, a protector but quickly angered.

5.157–61 (75:18–22). *Love's. / Old. / Sweet. / Song. / Comes loo-ve's old . . . – See 4.314n.

5.171 (75:35). the coroner and myself – M'Coy is "secretary to the City Coroner" in "Grace," *Dubliners*.

5.178 (76:4). wheeze – A theatrical "gag," especially if repeated; an antiquated fabrication— hence, a frequently employed trick or dodge.

5.180 (76:7). Bob Cowley – A "spoiled priest," that is, a priest who has drifted out of his calling but not flamboyantly enough to be unfrocked by the Church and not courageously enough to request that he be released from his vows. Cowley appears later in the novel.

5.181 (76:7). Wicklow regatta – Held each year at Wicklow (a coastal town twenty-six miles south of Dublin) during the August bank holidays, which start on the first Monday in August. There were various races for different classes of ships and boats.

5.183 (76:10). towards Brunswick street – Great Brunswick Street, now called Pearse Street. Bloom walks north along Westland Row and then turns right (east) along Great Brunswick Street.

5.188 (76:16–17). that smallpox up there – There was an outbreak of smallpox in Belfast in May–June 1904, but it subsided without reaching epidemic proportions.

5.190 (76:18). Your wife and my wife – See 11.972n.

5.193 (76:21). Cantrell and Cochrane's – Advertising themselves as "mineral and table water manufacturers, by special appointment to His Royal Highness, Edward VII," the firm was based in London with "works" in Dublin and Belfast.

5.194 (76:22). Clery's – A major department store, 21–27 Sackville Street Lower (now O'Connell Street), a shopping district in the center of Dublin, north of the Liffey.

5.194–95 (76:23). *Leah tonight: Mrs Bandmann Palmer – Millicent Palmer (1865–1905), an American actress who made her first tour of the British Isles in 1883. Her performance in *Leah* at the Gaiety Theatre in Dublin was advertised in the *Freeman's Journal*, 16 June 1904.

Leah the Forsaken (1862) was a translation and adaptation by the American playwright John Augustin Daly (1838–99) of the German *Deborah* (1850) by Salomon Hermann Mosenthal (1821–77), a German-Austrian playwright and archivist. The play is set in an Austrian village in the early eighteenth century; its central theme involves an attack on anti-Semitism. The villain, Nathan (5.203 [76:33]), is an apostate Jew who masquerades as a pharisaical and anti-Semitic Christian to protect his place in the village. Leah, the Jew, is hounded by Nathan and "forsaken" by her Christian lover, achieving peace only by self-immolation at the play's end. The part of Leah lent itself to flamboyant performance; hence the list of important actresses in this paragraph.

5.195–96 (76:24). *Hamlet* she played last night – It was not unusual for "heavy" nineteenth-century actresses to assume male roles in Shakespeare's plays (because the female roles are comparatively thin and because sustained, flamboyant, operatic performance was the actor's ideal). Mrs. Palmer did play Hamlet at the Gaiety Theatre on 15 June 1904, and the *Freeman's Journal* of 16 June notes that she played the part of the prince and "to say the least sustained it creditably."

5.196–97 (76:25–26). Perhaps he was a woman. Why Ophelia committed suicide? – Bloom (unconsciously?) echoes Edward P. Vining's speculation about Hamlet (see 9.518–19n) and adds a further twist: that Ophelia's (offstage) discovery that Hamlet was a woman drove her to madness and suicide (IV.vii).

5.197 (76:26). Poor papa – Bloom's father, Rudolph Virag (Bloom), committed suicide 27 June 1886; see 17.622–32 (684:33–685:8).

5.197–99 (76:26–28). Kate Bateman in that! . . . was: sixty-five – Kate Bateman (1843–1917), a member of a famous English stage family, had a great success in *Leah* in 1863 (not 1865) at the Adelphi Theatre, 411 Strand, North Side, London, a theater that specialized in melodramas and farces.

5.198–99 (76:28). year before I was born – Bloom was born in 1866, ambiguously either an

Aquarius (20 January–19 February, as Joyce on 2 February 1882) or a Taurus (19 April–20 May), because he had "just turned fifteen" (wrong by a year) in May 1882 at the time of the Phoenix Park murders (see 5.378n). See 16.608n.

5.199 (76:29). Ristori in Vienna – Adelaide Ristori (1822–1906), the Marquesa Capranica del Grillo (after 1847), was an Italian actress celebrated for her tragic roles. A version of *Leah* was "adapted expressly for Mme Ristori," and though there is no available record, she undoubtedly did perform it in Vienna.

5.200 (76:29–30). *Mosenthal . . . Rachel – "*Rachel*" is Bloom's mistake for "*Deborah*"; see 5.194–95n. The mistake may be a function of Bloom's (or his father's) association of the role of Deborah with the Alsatian-Jewish actress Elisa Rachel (1821–58).

5.200–205 (76:30–35). The scene he was . . . God of his father – From *Leah the Forsaken* (III.ii):

ABRAHAM: I hear a strange voice, and yet not a strange voice.
NATHAN [*to Sarah*]: Who is this old man?
SARAH: Abraham, sir—a poor old blind man. . . . This is our benefactor, Abraham! Go kiss his hand—
NATHAN: This is no time for idle acts! Come, away, away!
ABRAHAM: That voice! I know that voice! There was at Presburg, a man whose name was Nathan. He was a singer in the synagogue. It is his voice I hear.
NATHAN: . . . The man is mad.
ABRAHAM: It was said he became a Christian and went out into the world.
NATHAN [*angrily*]: Silence!
ABRAHAM: He left his father to die in poverty and misery since he had forsworn his faith, and the house of his kindred.
NATHAN: Silence! silence, I say.
ABRAHAM: I will not be silent. I hear the voice of Nathan. [*Passing his hand over Nathan's face.*] And I recognize the features of Nathan.
NATHAN [*terrified*]: The Jew is mad! Silence, or I'll do you injury!
ABRAHAM: With my fingers I read thy dead father's face, for with my fingers I closed his eyes, and nailed down his coffin! Thou art a Jew!
NATHAN [*flying at him*]: Another word! [*Seizes him by the throat.*] . . .

SARAH: Oh, spare the old man. He's mad, sir, I know.
NATHAN [*bewildered, knocking on door*]: Coming? Ha! What's this? [*Loosens his grasp from which Abraham sinks supinely; at the same moment a thunder-bolt strikes the cabin, and the storm increases.*]
SARAH [*screams*]: He is dead!
NATHAN [*at first confused, but recovering, as the Peasants all run in affright from the storm, and stand gazing around the dead body of Abraham*]: Aye—dead! by the hand of heaven!—[*Tableau.*]

5.210–11 (76:41). the hazard – A cabstand on Great Brunswick Street near Westland Row.

5.215 (77:4). jugginses – A "juggins" is a simpleton or a fool, someone easily imposed upon.

5.222 (77:11). The lane – That part of Cumberland Street South that passes beneath Westland Row (now Pearse) station.

5.223 (77:13). the cabman's shelter – Cabman's Shelter and Coffee Stand on Great Brunswick Street between Cumberland Street South and Westland Row.

5.224 (77:15). *Voglio e non* – See 4.327n.

5.227 (77:17). *Là ci darem la mano* – See 4.314n.

5.229 (77:19). Cumberland street – Bloom turns right and walks south. Cumberland Street is parallel to Westland Row.

5.230 (77:20–21). Meade's timberyard – Michael Meade & Son, builders; steam-sawing, planing, and moulding mills; and merchants, 153–159 Great Brunswick Street (on the corner of Cumberland Street).

5.232 (77:23). pickeystone – Pickey is hopscotch, played with a flat stone on a diagram on pavement.

5.232 (77:23). Not a sinner – That is, Bloom did not step on a line as he crossed the hopscotch court; if he had, he would have been disqualified to the tune of the child's chant: "You're a sinner; you're a sinner."

5.233 (77:24). shooting the taw with a cunny thumb – *The taw:* the marble that the player shoots, a large choice marble, usually streaked or variegated. *Cunny thumb:* the marble is held in the bent forefinger and shot by flicking it with the thumb.

5.235 (77:26–27). Mohammed cut a piece out of his mantle not to wake her – One of the *hadith,* or traditions about Mohammed, is this story about his extraordinary kindness to animals. It was not included in the great anthology of *hadith, Al-Jami al-Sahih*—after the Koran the most sacred book of Islam—compiled by Abu Muhammad ibn-Ismail al-Bukhārī (810–70) after he had examined some six hundred thousand *hadith* and selected as valid more than seven thousand; but it survived in other anthologies compiled in the ninth and tenth centuries.

5.237 (77:28–29). Mrs Ellis's. and Mr? – Mrs. Ellis ran a "dame's school" or "juvenile school" (a sort of nursery school–kindergarten or pre–grammar school), which Bloom attended when he was a child (17.1494 [712:13]); see 17.570n. *And Mr?:* the child's question about the woman titled Mrs. (widow?) when the husband is not in evidence.

5.258 (78:12). what kind of perfume does your wife use – Answer: opoponax. See 13.1010 (374:29).

5.261 (78:15–16). Language of flowers – Florigraphy: various traditional symbolic meanings were attached to flowers. The western Greco-Roman traditions were revived and expanded in the iconography of the medieval Church and further developed in chivalric and heraldic conventions. The Victorians elaborated and codified the traditions with sentimental thoroughness. An anonymous dictionary, *The Language of Flowers* (London, n.d.; dedication dated 1913) lists meanings for over seven hundred flowers.

5.264–66 (78:19–21). Angry tulips with you . . . all naughty nightstalk – *Tulips:* dangerous pleasures; *manflower:* an obvious pun; *cactus:* not only the phallus but also touch-me-not; *forget-me-not:* as the name suggests and also true love; *violets:* modesty; *roses:* love and beauty; *anemone:* frailty, anticipation; *nightstalk:* in addition to the phallic pun, nightshade; falsehood.

5.270 (78:27). Sunday after the rosary – The rosary is a form of prayer usually comprising fifteen decades of Ave Marias (a prayer to the Virgin Mary: "Hail Mary, full of Grace . . . "). Each decade is preceded by a Paternoster (the Lord's Prayer) and followed by a Gloria Patris ("Glory be to the Father . . ."). The prayers are counted on beads as they are being said, and a mystery is contemplated during the recital of each decade. The rosary is divided into three parts, each consisting of five decades and known as a corona or chaplet. What Bloom apparently means is "after mass," since the rosary was not a conventional part of Sunday mass or Sunday vespers. At the beginning of this century it was conventional for the celebrant and the people to say the Hail Mary three times together with a longer prayer to the Virgin Mary after low mass but not necessarily on Sundays, great feast days, etc.

5.279 (78:36). Flat Dublin voices – A lower-class Dublin accent is frequently described as "flat," such as "cometty" for *committee.*

5.280 (78:37). the Coombe – A street in south-central Dublin, and also the rather dilapidated area around St. Patrick's Cathedral (Protestant). It was once a fashionable and thriving quarter in the city.

5.281–84 (78:38–41). *o Mairy lost . . . To keep it up* – The source of this street rhyme is unknown.

5.285 (79:1). her roses – A euphemism for the menstrual period.

5.289–91 (79:6–9). Martha, Mary . . . that picture . . . He is sitting . . . would listen – Martha and Mary, sisters of Lazarus and friends of Jesus (the "he" who is "sitting in their house, talking"), in the painting Bloom recalls having seen. (*Christ at the House of Martha and Mary* by Peter Paul Rubens [1577–1640] was hanging in Dublin's National Gallery, but it is not the picture Bloom has in mind.) "The other one" (5.295 [79:13]) is Martha, whose spirit was "cumbered about with much serving . . . careful and troubled about many things." Martha complained about the indolence of her sister Mary—"She" (5.298 [79:17]). "Mary sat at Jesus' feet and heard his word." Jesus reproves Martha: "Mary hath chosen that good part, which shall not be taken away from her" (Luke 10:38–42). Medieval and Renaissance tradition confused Mary, Lazarus's sister, with Mary Magdalene, the prostitute whom Jesus cures of evil spirits; hence Bloom's thought, "the two sluts in the Coombe would listen," is appropriate.

5.296–97 (79:15–16). *a well, stone cold like the hole in the wall at Ashtown – Ashtown is on the north side of Phoenix Park, adjacent to the gate that led to the Viceregal Lodge; hence the district's association with bribery at election time. The "hole in the wall" was a place where the virtuous voter could pass his empty hand through an aperture and withdraw it filled with guineas—thus he could conscientiously swear ignorance of the identity of the person who bribed him (and therefore of the fact that bribery was even involved). Apparently Bloom (or Joyce?) recalls that a well with a reputation for extremely cold water is near the Ashtown gate of Phoenix Park, but according to Dr. Wright of the Geological Survey in Dublin (1984), maps dating back as far as the 1890s show no evidence of a well near the Ashtown gate. The two wells in the vicinity of the park are the Poor Man's Well, near the Cabra gate almost a mile east of the Ashtown gate, and the Baker's Well, near the Knockmaroon gate at the southwest corner of the park. There was also a pub, the Blackhorse Tavern, known popularly as the Hole in the Wall, in Blackhorse Lane (now Avenue) on the northern boundary of the park east of the Ashtown gate.

5.297–98 (79:16–17). the trottingmatches – At the end of the nineteenth century trotting-pony matches were held at the Phoenix Park Race Course (just outside the Ashtown gate) in conjunction with the annual Dublin Horse Show, one of the more important events in the Dublin social calendar. The trotting races have since disappeared from the show. See 7.193n.

5.300 (79:19). the railway arch – Beneath Westland Row station; the arch supports the elevated tracks of the Dublin and Southeastern Railway.

5.304 (79:24). Lord Iveagh – Edward Cecil Guinness, earl of Iveagh (1847–1927), a philanthropist and one of the family partners in the Guinness Brewery in Dublin.

5.305 (79:25–26). the bank of Ireland – See 4.101–3n.

5.306 (79:27). Lord Ardilaun – Sir Arthur Guinness (1840–1915), a politician, president of the Royal Dublin Society, and another of the family partners in the brewery. Joyce speaks of him as "morose and charitable" (*Letters* 1:225). Apparently his morose demeanor, plus his

wealth and conservative politics, gave rise to rumors of the sort Bloom recalls.

5.318 (79:41). All Hallows – Or St. Andrew's, a Roman Catholic church at 46 Westland Row. Bloom enters the church from its rear porch in Cumberland Street.

5.322–23 (80:3–4). the very reverend John Conmee S.J. – (1847–1910), rector of Clongowes Wood College (1885–91) during Stephen's days as a student, then prefect of studies at Belvedere College in the early 1890s, when Stephen was there. He was the superior of the residence of St. Francis Xavier's Church, Gardiner Street Upper, Dublin, from 1898 until 16 June 1904. In August 1905 he was named Rome provincial of the Irish Jesuits.

5.323 (80:4). *saint Peter Claver S.J. – (1581–1654), a Spanish Jesuit missionary who worked for forty-four years in Cartagena, Colombia, as chaplain to the slaves arriving from Africa. He is patron saint of missionary work among black peoples.

5.323 (80:4). the African mission – The *Catholic Encyclopedia* (New York, 1907–14) lists extensive Jesuit missionary activity in Africa during the latter half of the nineteenth century.

5.323–24 (80:7). Prayers for the conversion of Gladstone – William Ewart Gladstone (1809–98), four times prime minister of England and popular with the Irish because of his qualified support for Irish Home Rule. Gladstone was regarded as a liberal in his attitude toward Catholics, and the fact that his sister Helen had been converted also seemed to imply his sympathies. This was something of a misapprehension, however, for Gladstone was by conviction anti-Catholic, though his tract "Vaticanism" (criticizing the doctrine of papal infallibility) was characteristically moderate and far from rabid in tone. Archbishop Walsh of Dublin (see following note) did address a letter to the "faithful of the diocese" suggesting prayers for Gladstone on the eve of his death, 19 May 1898. The letter did not overtly ask for prayers for Gladstone's conversion, but it might easily have been so taken since it concluded by suggesting "a prayer that God, in whom he always trusted, may now in his hour of suffering be pleased to send him comfort and relief to lighten his heavy burden, and to give him strength and patience to bear it, in so far as in the designs of Providence it may have to be borne *for his greater good*" (italics added).

5.325 (80:9). Dr William J. Walsh D.D. – The Reverend William J. Walsh (1841–1921), Catholic archbishop of Dublin (1885–1921).

5.326 (80:5). Save China's millions – In the nineteenth century the Jesuits maintained missions in several cities in China in spite of rather intense Chinese xenophobia. One crisis in the resistance to the missionaries and their efforts was the death of five Jesuit priests at Nanking during the Boxer Rebellion in 1900.

5.326–27 (80:6). the heathen Chinee – The title of two song versions of a ballad, "Plain Language from Truthful James: (Table Mountain, 1870)" by Bret Harte (1836–1902). The ballad observes, "For ways that are dark, / And for tricks that are vain, / The heathen Chinee is peculiar" (lines 3–5), and goes on to "explain" this observation by citing the card-sharping career of one "Ah Sin."

5.327 (80:6). Celestials – The Chinese.

5.328 (80:10). Buddha their god . . . in the museum – The Buddha (meaning the wise or enlightened one) is the title of Siddhartha Gautama (c. 563–c. 483 B.C.); he is not "their god," but the Indian philosopher who founded Buddhism. At the beginning of this century Buddhism with its many sects was the dominant religion of eastern and central Asia. Among the statues in the main entrance hall of the National Museum (off Kildare Street, not far south of where Bloom now is) was a reclining Buddha, acquired in 1891.

5.329 (80:11). josssticks – Thin cylinders of fragrant tinder mixed with clay, used by the Chinese as incense.

5.329–30 (80:12). Ecce Homo. Crown of thorns and cross – The cross wreathed with a crown of thorns is a traditional Christian symbol. Three of the Gospels describe a crown of thorns as one phase of the torture Jesus underwent at the hands of the Roman soldiers who mocked him as "king of the Jews" (Matthew 27:29ff.; Mark 15:16ff.; John 19:2ff.). *Ecce Homo*, Latin: "Behold the man," Pontius Pilate's words in John 19:5 when he presents Jesus to the people: "Behold, I bring him forth to you, that ye may know that I find no fault in him. . . . Behold the man!" A painting of Jesus crowned with thorns, entitled *Ecce Homo*, by

the Hungarian Michael Munkácsy (1844–1900), was exhibited at the Royal Hibernian Academy in Abbey Street Lower in 1899. The young Joyce wrote a brief essay about the painting in September of that year (*CW*, pp. 31–37).

5.330 (80:12–13). Saint Patrick the shamrock – St. Patrick (c. 385–c. 461), one of three patron saints of Ireland. He was carried into slavery in Ireland but escaped to Gaul, where he studied at Tours before he returned to Ireland as a missionary. His mission settlement at Armagh is still the primatial city of Ireland. The trifoliate shamrock was (according to an apocryphal legend) used by St. Patrick to illustrate the doctrine of the Trinity; it was subsequently adopted as the national emblem of Ireland. See 12.573–74n.

5.331 (80:13–14). Martin Cunningham – Appears as a character in "Grace," *Dubliners*. Cunningham's character was modeled on that of Matthew F. Kane (d. 1904), chief clerk of the Crown Solicitors' Office (like a district attorney's office) in Dublin Castle. See Adams, p. 62.

5.332 (80:15). about getting Molly into the choir – Bloom is apparently unaware that women's participation in church choirs had been called into question by Pope Pius X's (1835–1914; pope 1903–14) papal rescript *motu proprio* ("of his own accord"; i.e., not on the advice of cardinals or others) *Inter Sollicitudines* (With Solicitude), 22 November 1903: "Singers in churches have a real liturgical office, and . . . therefore women, as being incapable of exercising such office, cannot be admitted to form part of the choir or of the musical chapel. Whenever, then, it is desired to employ the acute voices of sopranos and contraltos, these parts must be taken by boys, according to the most ancient usage of the church."

5.332–33 (80:15–16). Father Farley – *Thom's* 1904 lists the Reverend Charles Farley, S.J., as in residence at the Presbytery, Gardiner Street Upper (i.e., associated with St. Francis Xavier's Church and therefore with Father Conmee). Obviously Bloom has tried to get Molly into the choir in that church, which was not far from the house in Eccles Street. Molly thinks (18.381–82 [748:34–35]) the trouble was that the Jesuits had found out Bloom was a Freemason.

5.333 (80:16). They're taught that – The lay suspicion that Jesuits are taught to be devious and deceptive.

5.334 (80:17). bluey specs – Sunglasses.

5.339 (80:22). rere – For *rear*, usually appearing in combined forms, as in *reredos*, the screen or wall behind the altar in a church.

5.340 (80:23). sodality – In the Roman Catholic church, a religious guild or brotherhood (sisterhood) established for purposes of devotion and mutual help or action.

5.341 (80:24). Who is my neighbour? – In Luke, "a certain lawyer stood up and tempted [Jesus], saying, Master, what shall I do to inherit eternal life?" The answer: to love God "and thy neighbor as thyself." The lawyer then asks, "Who is my neighbor?" Jesus responds with the parable of the good Samaritan (Luke 10:25–37).

5.342 (80:26). Seventh heaven – This stock phrase for "perfect heaven" derives from the belief in seven as a perfect number, signifying the complete whole; in both Jewish and Moslem traditions there are seven heavens, the highest of which is the abode of God.

5.343 (80:26–27). crimson halters – Scapulars, insignia or badges of membership in a religious society or sodality. The communicants are probably celebrating a monthly meeting of their society.

5.344–45 (80:29). the thing – The ciborium, the vessel in which the priest carries the consecrated "bread" during Communion.

5.346 (80:30). (are they in water?) – Answer: no.

5.349 (80:33). murmuring all the time. Latin – The priest repeats the formula of administration as each participant in the communion receives "the Lord's body." The formula begins: "Corpus Domini nostri"—"May the body of our Lord Jesus Christ keep your soul and bring it to everlasting life. Amen."

5.349–50 (80:34). Shut your eyes and open your mouth – After the jingle "Open your mouth and shut your eyes, And I'll give you something to make you wise."

5.351 (80:36). Hospice for the dying – Our Lady's Hospice for the Dying at Harold's Cross, south of Dublin, maintained by the Roman Catholic Sisters of Charity "for those whose illness is likely to terminate fatally, within a limited period."

5.351 (80:36). don't seem to chew it – Tradition dictates that the "sacred species" should not be touched with the teeth but that it should be broken against the roof of the mouth.

5.358–59 (81:3–4). mazzoth . . . unleavened shewbread – *Matzo:* the unleavened bread used in the Jewish Feast of Passover. "This is the poor bread which our fathers ate in the land of Egypt." "And they shall eat flesh in that night, roast with fire, and unleavened bread; and with bitter herbs they shall eat it" (Exodus 12:8). At the Last Supper Jesus was celebrating Passover with his disciples. Bloom confuses the Passover matzoth with shewbread, the unleavened twelve cakes of "fine flour" (Leviticus 24:5–9; Exodus 25:30) that ancient Jewish priests placed on the altar each Sabbath (to be eaten by them alone at the end of the week).

5.360 (81:5–6). bread of angels – A literal translation of the Latin *panis angelorum*, a reverential name for the Eucharist.

5.362 (81:7–8). Hokypoky – Charlatanism. A traditional (and anti–Roman Catholic) derivation of this slang term occurs in John Tillotson's (1630–94) *Works*, volume 1, sermon 26: "a corruption of *hoc est corpus* (this is [my] body) by way of ridiculous imitation of the priests of the Church of Rome in their trick of transubstantiation." "Hokeypokey" also occurs in nursery rhymes with many variants: "Hokeypokey five a plate" or "Hokeypokey / Penny a lump. / That's the stuff / To make you jump" or "Hokeypokey, whiskey, thum."

5.364 (81:10–11). Then come out a bit spreeish – Common Protestant prejudice about the behavior of Catholics right after mass.

5.365 (81:12). Lourdes cure, waters of oblivion – Lourdes in southern France, one of the chief Catholic pilgrim shrines in Europe. The fame of Lourdes dates from the reputed appearance of the Virgin Mary to fourteen-year-old Bernadette Soubirous (St. Bernadette) in 1858. Near the grotto where the miracle occurred is a spring whose waters are diverted into several basins in which the ailing pilgrims bathe. The waters are "waters of oblivion" in the sense that they are believed to have the power of effecting miraculous cures.

5.365–66 (81:12). the Knock apparition –

Knock is a village six miles from Claremorris, County Mayo (in the west of Ireland). The apparitions are detailed in *The Apparition at Knock, with the Depositions of the Witnesses and the Conversion of a Young Protestant Lady by a Vision of the Blessed Virgin*, by Sister Mary Frances Clare (London, 1880). The first apparition, on 21 August 1879, the eve of the octave of the Assumption, was experienced by Mary McLoughlin and Mary Byrne. They saw some "figures," which at first they took to be statues, surrounded "by a light brighter than that of any earthly sun" (p. 42). Mary had her hands raised, and St. Joseph inclined toward her. St. John also appeared carrying a small mitre and a small altar, above which a lamb was haloed "with gold-like stars" (p. 43). Subsequent apparitions, early in 1880, witnessed by others, were associated with a series of miraculous cures.

5.366 (81:13). statues bleeding – A miracle called "*The Blood of Christ*. Alban Butler says that this relic 'which is kept in some places, of which the most famous is that of Mantua, seems to be what has sometimes issued from the miraculous bleeding of some crucifix, when pierced in derision by Jews or Pagans, instances of which are recorded in authentic histories'" (Clara Erskine Clement, *A Handbook of Legendary and Mythological Art* [Boston, 1891], p. 302).

5.367 (81:14–15). Safe in the arms of kingdom come – After the revival hymn "Safe in the Arms of Jesus," words by Fanny Crosby, music by W. H. Doane, *Songs of Devotion* (1869): "Safe in the arms of Jesus, / Safe from corroding care; / Safe from the world's temptations, / Sin cannot harm me there." *Kingdom come:* from the Lord's Prayer, Matthew 6:9–13, "Thy kingdom come. Thy will be done in earth as it is in heaven" (6:10).

5.372 (81:20). I.N.R.I. – Latin initials for Jesus of Nazareth, King of the Jews (*Iesus Nazarenus Rex Iudaeorum*), the inscription on the cross.

5.372 (81:20). I.H.S. – These Latin initials derive from a Greek abbreviation of the name Jesus and are variously interpreted as standing for *Jesus Hominum Salvator* (Jesus the Savior of Man) and *In Hoc Signo—Vinces* (In This Sign—Thou Shalt Conquer). The latter is what the angel said to the Roman emperor Constantine as he went into battle with the cross as his standard for the first time (when the Roman Empire was being converted to Christianity).

5.375 (81:23). Sunday after the rosary – See 5.270n.

5.376 (81:24–25). Dusk and the light behind her – In Gilbert and Sullivan's *Trial by Jury* (1876), the judge describes his problem and its cynical solution: how he was once "as many young barristers are, / An impecunious party / . . . , / So I fell in love with a rich attorney's / Elderly, ugly daughter." The judge then quotes the rich attorney's recommendation: "'You'll soon get used to her looks,' said he, / 'And a very nice girl you'll find her! / She may very well pass for forty-three / In the dusk, with a light behind her!'" (W. S. Gilbert, *Original Plays* [London, 1876], pp. 333–34).

5.378 (81:27). the invincibles – Sometimes called the Invincible Society or Irish National Invincibles, a small splinter group of Fenians organized late in 1881 with the object of assassinating key members of the then militantly repressive British government in Ireland. On 6 May 1882 the Invincibles assassinated Lord Frederick Cavendish (1836–82), the new chief secretary of Ireland, and Mr. Thomas Henry Burke, an undersecretary in Dublin Castle whom the Irish regarded as the principal architect of the so-called coercion policy, the policy of assuring Irish compliance with English rule by punitive restriction of Irish civil liberties. Burke was apparently the assassins' primary target, not only on account of his policies but also because he was an Irish Catholic from the west of Ireland (and thus a traitor to the Irish cause). The assassinations (by stabbing) took place in Phoenix Park not far from the Viceregal Lodge; hence, "the Phoenix Park murders."

5.379 (81:28). Carey – James Carey (1845–83), a builder and Dublin town councillor, apparently pious and public-spirited, became in 1881 one of the leaders of the Dublin branch of the Invincibles. Arrested after the Phoenix Park murders, he turned queen's evidence during the trial in February 1883, and his comrades were hanged. In July he attempted (with English help) to escape to South Africa, but he was recognized and shot on shipboard by Patrick O'Donnell, who was, of course, hanged for his pains. James Carey did have a brother named Peter, also associated with the Invincibles.

5.380 (81:29). Peter Claver – See 5.323n.

5.381 (81:30). Denis Carey – Unknown.

5.381 (81:30–31). Wife and six children at home – At the time of the Phoenix Park murders in May 1882, James Carey and his wife had six children; a seventh was born late in the year.

5.382 (81:32). crawthumpers – Ostentatiously devout people. The Irish *crawtha* means "mortified, pained" (P. W. Joyce, *English*, p. 241).

5.386 (81:37). rinsing out the chalice – In the ceremony of the Mass the chalice has contained wine that has become "the blood of Christ." The priest receives this in Holy Communion, and in one of the closing phases of the ceremony (the ablution) cleanses the chalice of any remaining drops of the "blood" by rinsing it with wine, which he then drinks.

5.388 (81:39). Guinness's – Dublin's (and Ireland's and Europe's) largest brewery (stout and Dublin porter), and one of the most famous. In 1904 it occupied about forty acres in the southwest quadrant of Dublin and was the city's largest industry.

5.389 (81:40). Wheatley's Dublin hop bitters – A "temperance beverage" because it was a non-alcoholic imitation of an alcoholic beverage; advertised in the day's *Freeman's Journal*: "When Ordering / Hop Bitters / Ask for Wheatley's / *Caution* / Please note label, as Sometimes / A low-priced and Inferior / Article is Substituted for the / Genuine Wheatley's Hop Bitters."

5.389 (81:41). Cantrell and Cochrane's – See 5.193n.

5.390 (81:41–42). Doesn't give them . . . shew wine – The communicants receive only the consecrated wafer (the consecrated wine is reserved for the priest's communion). *Shew wine:* after the ancient Jewish ceremony of shewbread, which was also consumed only by the priests; see 5.358–59n.

5.392 (82:2). cadging – Begging.

5.395 (82:6). old Glynn – Joseph Glynn; apart from the context, identity and significance unknown.

5.396 (82:7–8). fifty pounds a year – A handsome fee for the organist's part-time job.

5.396–97 (82:8). in Gardiner street – That is, in the Church of St. Francis Xavier, just east and slightly north from Bloom's house in Eccles Street.

5.397–98 (82:9). *Stabat Mater* of Rossini – *Stabat Mater:* "the Mother Was Standing" (as the Virgin Mary stood at the foot of the cross). The hymn commemorates Mary's "compassion" and "her suffering with" her son at that moment. The melody of the *Stabat Mater* is intact in its ancient form, and the text is probably by the Italian Jacopone da Todi (d. 1306). There are several famous Renaissance settings of the hymn by Josquin, Palestrina, and Pergolesi. The "romantic" one Bloom recalls is by the Italian composer Gioacchino Rossini (1792–1868); it was first performed in 1842.

5.398 (82:9–10). Father Bernard Vaughan's . . . or Pilate? – Father Conmee recalls a moment from this sermon at 10.33–38 (219:39–220:3). The sermon apparently contrasted Jesus' insistence on principle with the worldly compliance of Pilate, who objected that he found "no fault" in Jesus and yet allowed himself to be swayed by the mob into decreeing the Crucifixion.

5.399 (82:11–12). Footdrill stopped – "Footdrill" (or Kentish fire) is the prolonged rhythmic stamping of the feet in protest, but for the context Bloom recalls the term is used only figuratively to suggest an audience's impatient rustling.

5.402 (82:15). *Quis est homo. – Latin: "Who is the man?" or "Who is there?"; the opening line of the third stanza of the *Stabat Mater:* "Who is there who would not weep were he to see Christ's mother in such great suffering?" In Rossini's *Stabat Mater*, the "Quis est homo" is a duet for two sopranos.

5.403–4 (82:16–17). Mercadante: seven last words – Giuseppe Saverio Raffaelo Mercadante (1795–1870), Italian composer. *Le sette ultime parole* ("The Seven Last Words of Our Savior on the Cross"), an oratorio. First word: "Father, forgive them" (Luke 23:34); second: "Verily I say unto thee, To day shalt thou be with me in paradise" (Luke 23:43); third: "Woman, behold thy son" (John 19:26); fourth: "My God, my God, Why hast thou forsaken me?" (Matthew 27:46); fifth: "I thirst" (John 19:28); sixth: "It is finished" (John 19:30); seventh: "Father, into thy hands I commend my spirit" (Luke 23:46).

5.404 (82:17). Mozart's twelfth mass: the *Gloria* – Wolfgang Amadeus Mozart (1756–91). The true Twelfth Mass is Köchel listing 262; a spurious work, popularized as the *Gloria* by the Novello Publishing Company, was discredited by Köchel and included in an appendix as K. *Anhang* 232. However, his listings, which appeared in 1862 with a supplement in 1889, did not immediately reduce the popularity of the spurious work. It is not clear which of the two masses Bloom has in mind. The *Gloria*, the Greater Doxology or Angelic Hymn, is apparently a third-century expansion of the song of the angels in Luke 2:14, and it is an integral part of the music of the Mass, its position in the Mass varying in accordance with the liturgical calendar. It begins, "Gloria in excelsis Deo" (Glory to God in the highest).

5.405 (82:19). Palestrina – Giovanni Pierluigi da Palestrina (1525–94), a celebrated and prolific Italian musician; see 1.653n and 1.654–56n.

5.406–7 (82:20–21). chanting, regular hours – Bloom generalizes away from the Mass and church music to the round of the Monastic Day and the chanted celebration of the Divine Office (prayer for various hours of the day; see 10.184n) in choir.

5.407 (82:21). Benedictine. Green Chartreuse – *Benedictine:* a liqueur similar to chartreuse, first brewed by the monks of a Benedictine monastery in southern France. *Green Chartreuse:* one of three (with yellow and white) liqueurs made from a complex formula at the Carthusian monastery La Grande Chartreuse, near Grenoble, France.

5.407–8 (82:22). having eunuchs in their choir – The practice of castrating boy sopranos so that their voices would not change was prohibited by law in the early eighteenth century but was still relatively common in the Papal Choir until the accession of Pope Leo XIII in 1878. One of Leo's first acts was to dismiss the castrati from the choir and forbid the practice.

5.410–11 (82:25). fall into flesh – One common aftereffect of prepubertal castration is the accumulation of fatty tissue.

5.413–14 (82:28–29). the priest bend down . . . all the people – After the ablution the priest reads the *Communio* antiphon, then kisses the altar and blesses the people.

5.416 (82:31). gospel – If there were a proper last Gospel, the people would stand at the end of the post-Communion and then kneel again during the last Gospel.

5.417–18 (82:34). holding the thing out from him – That is, holding the missal from which he repeats the last Gospel.

5.420 (82:37). O God, our refuge and our strength – After low mass, the celebrant was required to recite or read from a card two prayers in the vernacular prescribed by Leo XIII in 1884 and 1886 and renewed by Pius X in 1903. The first of the prayers was "O God, our refuge and our strength, look down in mercy on Thy people who cry to Thee; and by the intercession of the glorious and immaculate Virgin Mary, Mother of God, of Saint Joseph her spouse, of Thy blessed apostles Peter and Paul, and of all the saints, in mercy and goodness hear our prayers, and for the liberty and exaltation of our holy mother the Church: through the same Christ our Lord. Amen." For the second prayer, see 5.443–47 (83:22–27).

5.422 (82:39–40). How long since your last mass? – Bloom's version of a standard opening question in the confessional: "How long since your last confession?"

5.423 (82:40–41). *Glorious and immaculate virgin. Joseph her spouse. Peter and Paul – Bloom is catching phrases from the first of the closing prayers; see 5.420n. "Glorious and immaculate virgin" is a reference to an article of faith proclaimed in 1854: "that Mary, in the first instant of her conception in her mother's womb, was kept free from all stain of original sin" (*Layman's Missal* [Baltimore, Md., 1962], p. 870).

5.425 (83:1). Confession – The Catholic church regards penance as a sacrament instituted by Christ, in which forgiveness of sins is granted through the priest's absolution of those who, with true sorrow, confess their sins. In the process of confession, the penitent is at once the accuser, the accused, and the witness, while the priest pronounces judgment and sentence. The grace conferred is deliverance from guilt of sin. Confession is made to an ordained priest with requisite jurisdiction and with power to forgive sins, this power being granted by Christ to his Church. The priest is bound to secrecy and cannot be excused either to save his own life or that of another, or to avert any public calamity. No law can compel him to divulge the sins confessed to him. The violation of the seal of confession would be a sacrilege, and the priest would be subject to excommunication.

5.429–30 (83:5–7). Whispering gallery walls . . . God's little joke – Bloom imagines that the confessional could be like a whispering gallery, that the whispered confession might (by "God's little joke") be overheard at some distance. In the most famous whispering gallery, the cupola of St. Paul's Cathedral in London, a low whisper near one wall can be distinctly heard at the opposite wall 108 feet away.

5.431 (83:8). Hail Mary and Holy Mary – That is, her penance might involve a number of repetitions of the Angelic Salutation: "Hail Mary, full of grace, the Lord is with thee. Blessed art thou among women, and blessed is the fruit of thy womb, Jesus. Holy Mary, Mother of God, pray for us sinners, now, and at the hour of our death. Amen."

5.432–33 (83:9–10). Salvation army blatant imitation – One phase of the militant evangelicalism of the Salvation Army (established 1865) was the exploitation of public confession.

5.434 (83:11). Squareheaded – Not readily moved or shaken in purpose.

5.435 (83:13). P.P. – Parish priest.

5.437–38 (83:16). *The priest in that Fermanagh will case – Unknown.

5.440 (83:18–19). The doctors of the church – A rare title formally conferred by the pope on saints whose theological learning has been outstanding. In the early Middle Ages many saints and scholars were informally so called; the formal tradition was established by Pope Boniface VIII in 1295 when he named SS. Gregory the Great, Ambrose, Augustine, and Jerome as *the* four "doctors" of the early Christian church.

5.443–47 (83:22–27). Blessed Michael . . . ruin of souls – The second of the prescribed vernacular prayers at the close of the Mass (see 5.420n).

5.450 (83:30). Brother Buzz – "Buzz" is variously slang for gossiping, telling stale news, and picking pockets.

5.451 (83:31). Easter duty – Involves not money but the obligation to receive Holy Communion during the Easter season (between the first day of Lent—forty days and six Sundays before Easter—and Trinity Sunday, eight weeks after Easter). Since it is considered a mortal sin to receive communion when not in a state of grace, an obligation to confess is implied as well.

5.455 (83:36). Glimpses of the moon – Hamlet speaks to the ghost of his father: "What may this mean, / That thou, dead corse, again, in complete steel, / Revisit'st thus the glimpses of the moon, / Making night hideous, and we fools of nature / So horridly to shake our disposition / With thoughts beyond the reaches of our souls" (I.iv.51–56).

5.458–60 (83:40–41). cold black marble bowl . . . holy water – The font in the porch of the church. Traditionally, worshipers dip the first and second fingers of the right hand in the water and touch their foreheads or cross themselves on entering and leaving the church.

5.460 (83:42). a car of Prescott's dyeworks – William T. C. Prescott, dyeing, cleaning, and carpet-shaking establishment at 8 Abbey Street Lower, had several branches in Dublin and environs. Molly recalls (18.1342 [775:33]) that Bloom has sold Prescott's an advertisement, and it duly appears in the *Freeman's Journal*, 16 June 1904, p. 1, col. 2: "*IMPORTANT. LACE CURTAINS* are now very carefully cleaned and finished with our New Dust Resisting process. By this System they keep clean longer than if done in the old way. In Three Days 1 / –Per Pair PRESCOTT'S DYE WORKS Carriage Paid One Way."

5.463 (84:4). Sweny's in Lincoln place – F. W. Sweny, dispensing chemists (pharmacy), 1 Lincoln Place, a street that enters the southern end of Westland Row (where Bloom is) from the west.

5.464 (84:5). beaconjars – Large hanging jars of colored liquid used to decorate (and advertise) chemists' shops.

5.464–65 (84:5). Hamilton Long's – Hamilton, Long & Co., Ltd., state apothecaries, perfumers, and manufacturers of mineral waters, had several shops in and around Dublin. The one Bloom has in mind is at 107 Grafton Street, just north of St. Stephen's Green.

5.465 (84:6). Huguenot churchyard – At 10 Merrion Row, east of St. Stephen's Green about one-third mile south of Bloom's present position. Three congregations of French Protestant refugees flourished in Dublin in the seventeenth century. They were assigned special burying places, the principal one being the one Bloom intends to visit "some day."

5.473–74 (84:15–16). Quest for . . . The alchemists – In medieval alchemy, the "philosopher's stone" was the mysterious object of unrewarded search, believed to transmute base metals into gold and silver and to be a universal panacea.

5.476–77 (84:19–20). alabaster lilypots . . . Laur. Te Virid – Bloom looks at the apothecary's jars of ingredients ("lilypots," or ornamental jars) and reads some of the abbreviations that served as labels: *Aq. Dist.:* distilled water; *Fol. Laur.:* Laurel leaves; *Te [The] Virid:* green tea.

5.478 (84:21). *Doctor Whack – In other words, the curative power of a heavy, smart, resounding blow.

5.479 (84:22). Electuary – A medicine consisting of a powder or other ingredient mixed with honey, jam, or syrup.

5.481 (84:25). turns blue litmus paper red – An acid; alkalines turn red litmus blue, and chloroform would produce neither reaction, since undiluted it is relatively inert.

5.482 (84:26). Laudanum – In early use, any of various preparations in which opium was the main ingredient; now, the simple alcoholic tincture of opium.

5.482–83 (84:26–27). Paragoric poppysyrup . . . or the phlegm – Paregoric did contain a bit of opium, thus it could be called poppy syrup. Although opiates were then commonly used in cough syrups, paregoric was most widely used as a specific against diarrhea because it constipates. Bloom assumes, vaguely but correctly, that paregoric would constipate the mucous membranes rather than anesthetizing them as an opiate would.

5.488 (84:33). loofahs – The fibrous substance of the pod of the plant *Luffa aegyptiaca*, used as a sponge or flesh brush.

5.496–97 (84:42–85:1). strawberries for the . . . steeped in buttermilk – Variations of these "recipes" occur in the "Medical Department" of *Dr. Chase's Recipes; or, Information for Everybody* (20th ed., Ann Arbor, Mich., 1864).

5.497–99 (85:1–2). One of the old . . . Leopold, yes – Queen Victoria's youngest son, Prince Leopold, duke of Albany (1853–84). Regarded by his contemporaries as "very delicate," the prince was in fact suffering from hemophilia; the disease was mysterious enough to warrant the old wives' diagnosis: "He only has one skin."

5.500 (85:4–5). *Peau d'Espagne* – French: "Spanish skin."

5.502 (85:7). Hammam. Turkish – The Hammam Family Hotel and Turkish Baths, 11–12 Sackville (now O'Connell) Street Upper.

5.512 (85:17). Lemony – "The lemon is a symbol of fidelity in love" (George Ferguson, *Signs and Symbols in Christian Art* [New York, 1954], p. 33; cited by Joan Keenan). The odor of the ceremonial citron is also "lemony"; see 4.210–22n.

5.524–25 (85:31–32). Good morning . . . Pear's soap? – An advertising slogan for a famous English soap.

5.529 (85:37). Tight collar he'll lose his hair – Another popular medical superstition.

5.532 (85:40). Ascot. Gold cup – The Gold Cup, one of the two main annual events of the British racing calendar, was to be run that day at Ascot Heath, twenty-six miles from London, at 3:00 P.M. "*The Gold Cup*, value 1,000 sovereigns with 3,000 sovereigns in specie in addition, out of which the second shall receive 700 sovereigns and the third 300 sovereigns added to a sweepstakes of 20 sovereigns each . . . for entire colts and fillies. Two miles and a half. The field: M. J. de Bremond's Maximum II; age 5. Mr. W. Bass's Sceptre; age 5; A. Taylor. Lord Ellesmere's Kronstad; age 4; J. Dawson. Lord Howard de Walden's Zinfandel; age 4; Beatty. Sir J. Miller's Rock Sand; age 4; Blackwell. Mr. W. Hall Walker's Jean's Folly; age 3; Robinson. *Mr. F. Alexander's Throwaway*; age 5; Braime. M. E. de Blashovits's Beregvolgy; age 4. Count H. de Pourtale's Ex Voto; age 4. Count H. de Pourtale's Hebron II; age 4. M. J. de Soukozanotte's Torquato Tasso; age 4. Mr. Richard Croker's Clonmell; age 3." "*Selections for Ascot Meeting.* Gold Cup—Zinfandel." "*Tips from 'Celt':* Gold Cup—Sceptre" (as reported in the *Freeman's Journal*, 16 June 1904, p. 7.) The race was won by the dark horse Throwaway, a twenty-to-one shot; see 14.1128–33n.

5.534 (85:42). throw it away – See preceding note. The point is that Bloom has just unwittingly given a tip on the Gold Cup race.

5.542 (86:8). Conway's corner – A public house; see 5.108n.

5.542 (86:8). scut – The tail of a rabbit, a term often applied in scorn to a contemptible fellow (P. W. Joyce, *English*, p. 318).

5.545 (86:11). to put on – To bet on.

5.546–47 (86:13–14). Jack Fleming . . . to America – A circumstantial story that Bloom recalls in relation to Bantam Lyons's gambling fever. The story is a fragment not developed in the novel.

5.548 (86:15). Fleshpots of Egypt – See 3.177–78n.

5.549 (86:16). mosque of the baths – Bloom walks around the corner from Lincoln Place into Leinster Street, where he proceeds to the Leinster Street Turkish and Warm Baths at no. 11.

5.550 (86:17–18). College sports – The poster advertises a "combination meeting of Dublin University Bicycle and Harrier Club" to be held that afternoon in College Park.

5.551–52 (86:19). cyclist doubled up like a cod in a pot – After the song "Johnny, I Hardly Knew Ye." Johnny's Peggy sings the song as Johnny returns crippled from the wars. Chorus: "Wild drums and guns, and guns and drums, / The enemy fairly slew ye; / My darling dear, you look so queer; / Och! Johnny, I hardly knew ye." Endless repetitive verses review the nature of that "look so queer," including "you're an eyeless, noseless, chickenless egg" and "like a cod you're doubled up head and tail."

5.555 (86:23). Hornblower – The porter at the south (Lincoln Place) gate of Trinity College.

5.555–56 (86:24). on hands – That is, keep renewing the speaking (or nodding) acquaintance.

5.556 (86:24). take a turn in there on the nod – That is, Hornblower might nod Bloom through the college gates and give him the privileges of the grounds, as he has done before; see 18.1257–58 (773:17–19).

5.558 (86:26–27). Cricket weather – Frank Budgen (*James Joyce and the Making of "Ulysses"* [Bloomington, Ind., 1960], p. 84) remarks that "cricket still had its agreeable lotus flavour in 1904."

5.559 (86:27). Over after over. Out – When the starting bowler (pitcher) has delivered six "fair balls" from his end, the umpire calls, "Over." A man at the other wicket then becomes the bowler, bowling to the batter at the opposite wicket. Similarly, when an "out" is made the bowling changes hands.

5.559 (86:28). They can't play it here – A commonplace about the Irish, that they have no taste for or skill at cricket.

5.560 (86:28). Duck for six wickets – If a batsman fails to score a single run before he is retired, he has been "bowled for a duck." It would be an extraordinary feat for a bowler to accomplish "six wickets," six outs in sequence, in that fashion.

5.560 (86:28–29). *Captain Culler – Apart from the context, identity and significance unknown.

5.560–61 (86:29). the Kildare Street club – At the entrance of Kildare Street across from Trinity College Park. The club was fashionable and expensive, and its membership was dominated by wealthy Irish landlords well known for their pro-English sentiments. It was reputedly the only place in Dublin where one could get decent caviar.

5.561 (86:29–30). a slog to square leg – "Square leg" is one of the defensive positions in cricket, to the left of the batsman and nearly in a line with the wicket; a "slog" is a hit that is both hard and not particularly well aimed.

5.561 (86:30). Donnybrook fair – Donnybrook, formerly a village, now a southeastern suburb of Dublin. The Donnybrook Fair, established in the reign of King John (1167–1216), abolished in 1855, was so distinguished for its debaucheries and brawls that its name became synonymous with any scene of uproar.

5.562 (86:30–31). And the skulls we were acracking when M'Carthy took the floor – From the song "Enniscorthy" by Robert Martin, celebrating the prowess of "Demetrius O'Flannigan McCarthy, . . . the pride of balls and parties and the glory of a wake." The third of the song's four stanzas begins: "When they gurgled all the whiskey, faith, a desperate row arose. / McCarthy sure he levelled them, he fought them to a close." But McCarthy's luck doesn't hold, and by the song's end he is "the fragments of the man they call McCarthy. [Chorus:] Miss Dunne said they did crowd her then, / Miss Murphy took to powther then / For fear the boys might say that she was swarthy: / And the sticks they all went whacking / And the skulls, faith, they were cracking / When McCarthy took the flure in Enniscorthy." Enniscorthy is a market town in County Wexford, southeastern Ireland.

5.563–64 (86:32–33). *Always passing, the stream . . . dearer thaaan them all – From *Maritana* (1845), an opera, libretto by Edward Fitzball (1792–1873), music by the Irish composer William Vincent Wallace (1813–65). "Rousing" and "sentimental," it has all the stock theatrical bravado of the mid-nineteenth-century light-opera tradition.

Plot outline: in Act I, the nobleman-hero Don Caesar, irrepressibly cheerful though down on his luck and hounded by creditors, rescues Lazarillo, a persecuted apprentice, from the guard, and offends the captain of the guard into a duel. The captain is killed, and Don Caesar is condemned to death by hanging. Another plot takes over in the second act, urged by the villain Don Jose's elaborate schemes to divert the king (who is smitten by the gypsy charmer, Maritana) and ensnare the queen. Don Jose offers Don Caesar an "honorable" death by firing squad if Don Caesar will marry a secret candidate (Maritana veiled) and thus ennoble her. Don Caesar accepts: "Yes, let me like a soldier fall." Lazarillo saves Don Caesar's life by removing the bullets from the firing squad's muskets, and Don Caesar, honor-bound, goes in search of his wife—not knowing that she is Maritana, whom he too adores. In Act III Don Jose maneuvers Maritana into a rendezvous with the king, but Maritana manages to resist the king's advances. Don Caesar survives further murderous plots until, in the end, Don Jose is dead, the king's shame is averted, and Maritana and her hero are united, all in time for the finale, "With Rapture Glowing."

In the middle of Act II, scene i, as Don Jose's schemes seem about to succeed, he sings of his first love-vision of the queen, "In Happy Moments Day by Day": "[Second stanza:] Though anxious eyes upon us gaze, / And hearts with fondness beat, / Whose smile upon each feature plays, / With truthfulness replete. / Some tho'ts none other can replace, / Remembrance will recall; / Which in the flight of years we trace, / Is dearer than them all."

5.566 (86:35). This is my body – Jesus at the Last Supper: "And he took bread, and gave thanks, and brake it, and gave it unto them, saying, This is my body which is given for you: this do in remembrance of me" (Luke 22:19). This passage is regarded as scriptural authority for the Communion ceremony. It is repeated at the Consecration in the Mass when "the celebrant does what Christ did and says what Christ said at the Last Supper" (*Layman's Missal* [Baltimore, Md., 1962], p. 811).

5.571–72 (86:41–42). the limp father of thousands, a languid floating flower – After the plant *Saxifraga stolonifera,* called "mother of thousands" because it spreads by runners that seem to float its flowers. It is used as a ground cover in moist, shady places in the south of England and Ireland.

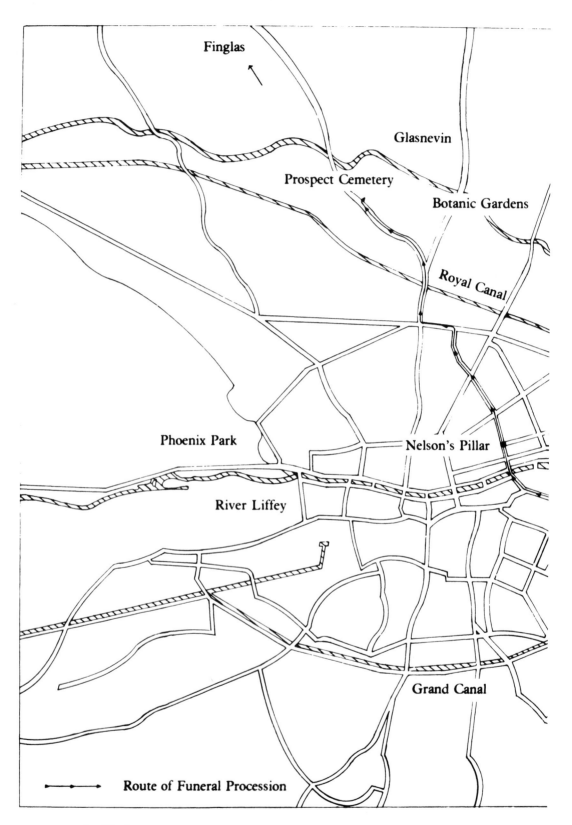

Finglas

Glasnevin

Prospect Cemetery

Botanic Gardens

Royal Canal

Phoenix Park

Nelson's Pillar

River Liffey

Grand Canal

→ Route of Funeral Procession

EPISODE 6. *Hades*

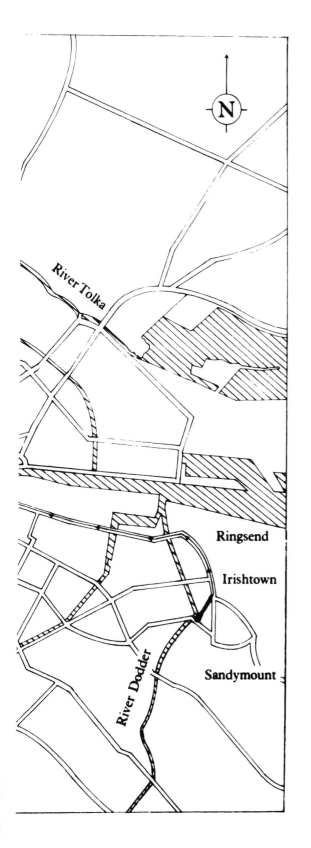

EPISODE 6

Hades

(6.1–1033, PP. 87–115)

Episode 6: *Hades,* **6.1–1033 (87–115).** In Book 9 of *The Odyssey,* Odysseus recounts his adventures in the lands of the Cicones, the Lotus-Eaters, and the Cyclopes. In Book 10 Odysseus and his men reach the isle of Aeolus, the "wind king"; then they meet disaster in the land of the Lestrygonians and finally arrive at Circe's island. Circe advises Odysseus to go down to Hades, the world of the dead, to consult the shade, or spirit, of the blind prophet Tiresias before continuing the voyage. In Book 11 Odysseus descends into Hades; the first shade he meets is that of Elpenor, one of his men who, drunk and asleep, had fallen to his death in Circe's hall. Elpenor requests that Odysseus return to Circe's island and give his corpse a proper burial; Odysseus so promises. Odysseus then speaks with Tiresias, who tells him that it is Poseidon, god of the sea and the earthquake, who is preventing Odysseus from reaching his home. Tiresias warns Odysseus: if his men violate the cattle of the sun god, Helios, the men will all be lost, the difficulties of Odysseus's voyage will be radically increased, and upon his arrival home he will find his house beset with suitors, "insolent men" whom he will have to make "atone in blood" (11:116, 118; Fitzgerald, p. 200). Tiresias closes his prophecy by promising Odysseus a "rich old age" and "a seaborne death soft as this hand of mist" (11:134, 137; Fitzgerald, p. 201). Odysseus then speaks with the shade of his mother and sees the shades of many famous women. He speaks with Agamemnon and learns of Agamemnon's homecoming and of his death at the hands of his wife, Clytemnestra, and her lover. Odysseus speaks with Achilles and approaches Ajax, who, driven mad by the gods, had died by his own hand after Odysseus was awarded the dead Achilles' armor as the new champion of the Greeks. Ajax refuses to speak. Odysseus glimpses other shades, including that of Sisyphus, condemned to push a boulder up a hill eternally. He then speaks to Hercules, who is not a shade but a "phantom," because Hercules himself rests among the immortal gods. Hercules, reminded by Odysseus's presence in the flesh, tells the story of his twelfth labor, his own descent into Hades while he was still alive, when he had to capture the "watchdog of the dead," Cerberus (11:623; Fitzgerald, p. 217). Odysseus then returns to his ship and to Circe's island.

Time: 11:00 A.M. Scene: Prospect Cemetery in Glasnevin, north of Dublin. The cemetery is notable as the "open air Pantheon or Westminster Abbey of Catholic and Nationalist Ireland" (D. A. Chart, *The Story of Dublin* [London, 1907], p. 321). In the course of the episode

Bloom travels with the funeral procession from Dignam's house in Sandymount, a suburb of Dublin on the coast southeast of the city, across Dublin to Glasnevin. Organ: heart; Art: religion; Colors: white, black; Symbol: caretaker; Technique: incubism [after *incubus,* an evil male spirit said to produce nightmares]. Correspondences: *the four rivers of Hades* [*Styx, Acheron, Cocytus, Pyriphlegethon*]—the Dodder, the Grand and Royal Canals, and the Liffey; *Sisyphus*—Martin Cunningham; *Cerberus* [the two- or three-headed dog that fawns on new arrivals in Hades but that also prevents their escape]— Father Coffey; *Hades,* the god who rules the underworld—Caretaker [John O'Connell]; *Hercules*—Daniel O'Connell; *Elpenor*—Dignam; *Agamemnon*—Parnell; *Ajax*—Menton.

The Linati schema lists several additional Persons without identifying correspondences: *Ulysses. Eriphyle:* the wife "who betrayed her lord for gold" (11:326; Fitzgerald, p. 207); Aeneas also sees her when he descends into the underworld—she is among "those whom cruel love has wasted," displaying the wounds her son inflicted when he avenged his father's death (*Aeneid* 6). *Orion:* the great hunter whom Odysseus sees herding the ghosts of all the animals he has killed (11:572ff.). *Laertes, etc.:* Odysseus's father who, in *The Odyssey,* is still alive but in retirement on Ithaca; the shade of Odysseus's mother describes the "sackcloth and ashes" of Laertes' mourning for his absent son. *Prometheus:* both Odysseus (11:576ff.) and Aeneas (*Aeneid* 6) see Tityos, a traitor to the gods, whose liver is being perpetually consumed by two vultures, as Prometheus's was. *Tiresias. Proserpina:* Roman counterpart of the Greek Persephone, the "iron queen" of Hades (11:212; Fitzgerald, p. 203). *Telemachus:* during their interview, Odysseus asks his mother for news of his wife and son on Ithaca and is partially reassured about his wife's faithfulness and his son's manly behavior. *Antinoos:* Odysseus's mother does not mention the suitors in her account of how things were on Ithaca when she died (though Tiresias foretells their presence), and Simon Dedalus will mention Mulligan who is playing the part of Antinoos [Antinous].

6.2 (87:2–3). Mr. Power – Jack Power, fictional, is attached to the offices of the Royal Irish Constabulary in Dublin Castle; he appears as a character in "Grace," *Dubliners.* Gladstone called the R.I.C. a "semi-military police"; it modeled itself after Scotland Yard, but its members were armed and, charged with the control and suppression of Irish political dissidents and thus with the maintainence of British overlordship in Ireland, its functions were much more political than the Yard's.

6.11–12 (87:13–14). the lowered blinds of the avenue – In Irish tradition, blinds were lowered and shops closed during a funeral in a village or, as here, on a street or in a neighborhood. The "avenue" is Newbridge Avenue in Sandymount; see 4.119n.

6.15 (87:17–18). Job seems to suit them – The job of laying out the corpse is traditionally the woman's job.

6.15 (87:18). Huggermugger – Secretly. Claudius uses this expression in *Hamlet* in speaking of the burial of Polonius: "And we have done but greenly / In huggermugger to inter him" (IV.v.83–84).

6.16 (87:18–19). slipperslappers – Old Mother Slipperslapper is a type of the "poor old woman" who personifies Ireland; see 1.403n. She appears in the folk song "The Fox" to announce: "John, John, the grey goose is gone / And the fox is on the town, O." First verse: "Old Mother Slipper Slapper jumpt out of bed, / And out at the casement she popt her head, / Crying the house is on fire, the grey goose is dead, / And the fox is come to the town, O!"

6.16–17 (87:19). Then getting it ready – Namely, the corpse of the Blooms' eleven-day-old son, Rudy.

6.17 (87:20). Mrs Fleming – A part-time domestic in the Blooms' employ.

6.27 (87:32). number nine – Dignam's house at 9 Newbridge Avenue, Sandymount.

6.30 (87:35). Tritonville road – Runs north from Sandymount into Irishtown.

6.34 (87:40–41). Irishtown . . . Ringsend. Brunswick street – The funeral takes a route parallel to the shore of Dublin Bay; it continues north from Tritonville Road into Irishtown Road and then into Thomas Street in Irishtown. There it turns west into Bridge Street, just south of the mouth of the Liffey, and continues west over the River Dodder, along Ringsend Road over the Grand Canal, and into Great Brunswick (now Pearse) Street toward the center of Dublin, where it will again turn north and cross the city to Glasnevin.

6.36 (88:1). a fine old custom – Namely, the custom of the funeral procession taking a route through the center of the city that all might see and by implication "pay their last respects."

6.39 (88:5). Watery Lane – Now Dermot O'Hurley Avenue off Irishtown Road in Ringsend.

6.39–40 (88:6). a lithe young man, clad in mourning, a wide hat – Stephen has come north on the Dalkey tram as far as Haddington Road where, instead of going on into Dublin, he apparently changes to the Sandymount tram and travels east toward Irishtown, where the Gouldings live; but instead of calling on them he walks south and east toward Leahy's Terrace and Sandymount Strand, where he spends the Proteus episode.

6.49 (88:15). *fidus Achates* – Latin: "the faithful Achates" (*Aeneid* 1:188); Aeneas's friend and companion. As Mr. Dedalus uses it, the phrase is a cliché, but in the context of Hades it alludes to Achates' role in support of Aeneas as Aeneas gets ready for the fearful voyage to the underworld (*Aeneid* 6).

6.52 (88:18). costdrawer – See 3.66n.

6.53 (88:19–20). the wise child that knows her own father – Proverbial. One version occurs in *The Odyssey* when Telemachus says: "My mother says I am his son; I know not / surely. Who has known his own engendering?" (1:215–16; Fitzgerald, p. 20).

6.54 (88:21). Ringsend road – West from Ringsend toward central Dublin.

6.54–55 (88:21–22). *Wallace Bros: the bottleworks – At 34 Ringsend Road.

6.55 (88:22). Dodder bridge – The River Dodder flows north and enters the Liffey just west of Ringsend and Irishtown.

6.56 (88:23–24). Goulding, Collis and Ward – The fictional Goulding (see 3.61n) has been added to the real firm of Collis and Ward, solicitors, 31 Dame Street, in the southeast quadrant of Dublin.

6.58 (88:25). Stamer street – In south-central Dublin near the Grand Canal.

6.58 (88:25). Ignatius Gallaher – Appears as a character in "A Little Cloud," *Dubliners*. In

Aeolus (7.732–33 [139:4–5]) he is identified as an employee of the Irish-born English publisher Alfred C. Harmsworth on either the *London Daily Mail* or the *London Evening News*. A notable story is told about Gallaher at 7.629–81 (135:33–137:16).

6.60 (88:28). ironing – Massaging.

6.67–68 (88:36–37). I'll tickle his catastrophe – In *II Henry IV*, the hostess, Fang (the sheriff's sergeant), and his boy attempt to arrest Falstaff, who is accompanied by Page and Bardolph. Page threatens the hostess with his drawn sword: "Away, you scullion! You rampallian! You fustilarian! I'll tickle your catastrophe [buttocks]!" (II.i.65–66).

6.70–71 (88:40). counterjumper's son – The son of a shop clerk.

6.71 (88:40–41). selling tapes in my cousin, Peter Paul M'Swiney's – For a time Oliver St. John Gogarty's father worked in Clery & Co. (formerly M'Swiney & Co.), drapers, silk mercers, hosiers, glovers, haberdashers, jewelers, boot and shoe makers, tailors, woolen drapers, and general warehousers, 21–27 Sackville (now O'Connell) Street. Peter Paul M'Swiney, a cousin of Joyce's grandmother's, was a successful merchant-politician and lord mayor of Dublin in 1864 and 1875.

6.76 (89:5). Eton suit – A fashionable costume for young boys (in imitation of the "uniform" worn by the students at Eton, one of the most exclusive and establishmentarian of the English public schools): a short, waist-length jacket with broad lapels and a shirt with a broad white linen collar.

6.78 (89:7). Raymond terrace – That section of South Circular Road (nos. 22 to 34, including St. Kevin's Church) opposite the Wellington (now Griffith) Barracks in south-central Dublin, not far north of the Grand Canal and not far west of Lombard Street West. Apparently Rudy was conceived there early in 1893, shortly before the Blooms moved to Lombard Street West.

6.79 (89:8). The cease to do evil – "Cease to do evil—learn to do well" was the motto over the door of the Richmond bridewell (jail) in South Circular Road, where Daniel O'Connell was briefly imprisoned in 1844. By the late nineteenth century the jail had been absorbed into

the Wellington (now Griffith) Barracks complex.

6.80 (89:10). a touch – Slang for sexual intercourse.

6.82 (89:12). the Greystones concert – Greystones, a small fishing village on the coast eighteen miles south-southeast of Dublin, was also a fashionable summer resort.

6.92 (89:24). yoke – "Any article, contrivance, or apparatus for use in some work" (P. W. Joyce, *English*, p. 352).

6.93 (89:26). that squint – After the tailor who lacks material and therefore "squints," or skimps.

6.111 (90:3). Ned Lambert – A fictional character who works in a seed and grain store in Mary's Abbey in central Dublin.

6.111 (90:4). Hynes – The fictional Joe Hynes appears as the loyal Parnellite in "Ivy Day in the Committee Room," *Dubliners*. In *Ulysses* he seems still relatively unemployed and down on his luck, though he does do a paragraph on Dignam's funeral for the *Freeman's Journal*.

6.120 (90:14). The grand canal – The most important canal in Ireland; it skirts the southern perimeter of central Dublin and links Dublin with the west coast of Ireland. The carriage stops at Victoria Bridge over the canal.

6.121 (90:15). Gas works – The Alliance and Consumer Gas Company at 110 Great Brunswick (now Pearse) Street, just southwest of the bridge over the Grand Canal. The works, notoriously odoriferous, transformed coal into gas for lighting and heating.

6.124 (90:18). Flaxseed tea – A tea made of flaxseed (from which linseed oil is also derived). Linseed oil was a popular "natural remedy," and flaxseed tea shared this popularity.

6.125 (90:19–20). Dog's home – On Grand Canal Quay, the Dog's and Cat's Home, established and maintained by the Dublin Society for the Prevention of Cruelty to Animals. The home advertised its interest in strays and proclaimed: "The diseased painlessly destroyed."

6.125–27 (90:20–22). Poor old Athos! . . . took it to heart, pined away – Athos, Bloom's father's dog, was apparently named after one of the three musketeers (Aramis, Athos, and Porthos) from Alexandre Dumas *père*'s (1802–70) popular novel *Les trois musquetaires* (Paris, 1844). In *The Odyssey*, when Odysseus first approaches his manor house he weeps at the sight of his old dog Argos, "abandoned" on a dung heap outside the gates. The dog struggles to greet his master, "but death and darkness in that instant closed / the eyes of Argos, who had seen his master / Odysseus, after twenty years" (17:326–27; Fitzgerald, pp. 331–32).

6.126 (90:21). Thy will be done – After the Lord's Prayer (Matthew 6:10; Luke 11:2): "Thy kingdom come. Thy will be done in earth, as it is in heaven."

6.142 (90:39–40). Paddy Leonard – Appears as a character in "Counterparts," *Dubliners*, in Lestrygonians, and elsewhere in *Ulysses*.

6.145 (91:1–2). Ben Dollard's singing of *The Croppy Boy* – Ben Dollard appears as a character in the Wandering Rocks and sings the song in Sirens (11.991ff. [pp. 282ff.]); see 11.29n for the song's text.

6.151 (91:8). Dan Dawson's speech – Reviewed at length in Aeolus (7.243 ff. [pp. 123ff.]). It does not appear in the *Freeman's Journal* for 16 June 1904. Charles (Dan) Dawson was a successful baker who owned the Dublin Bread Company in Stephen's Street. He became one of Dublin's merchant-politicians: member of Parliament for County Carlow, lord mayor of Dublin (1882, 1883), and, in 1904, collector of rates (taxes) for the Dublin Corporation.

6.157 (91:15). down the edge of the paper – The *Freeman's Journal* carried obituaries at the top of the left-hand column on page one. The names Bloom reads do not appear in the 16 June 1904 edition, and none seems to have any significance except momentarily Peake, who is mentioned as "hounded . . . out of the office" in "Counterparts," *Dubliners*.

6.159 (91:18). Crosbie and Alleyne's – C. W. Alleyne, a solicitor, had offices at 24 Dame Street (on the corner of Eustace Street) in central Dublin just south of the Liffey (*Thom's* 1904, p. 1468). No Crosbie is mentioned in *Thom's*. However, the same Mr. Alleyne appears in "Counterparts," *Dubliners*, and repeatedly mentions his absent partner Mr. Crosbie. See Ellmann, pp. 16, 39.

6.161–63 (91:19–22). Thanks to the little . . . Jesus have mercy – Typical snippets of obituary-column prose. "The Little Flower" is a popular name for St. Teresa of Lisieux (St. Teresa-of-the-Child-Jesus, 1873–97), whose cultus grew with such rapidity and intensity after her death that *Butler's "Lives of the Saints"* (ed. Herbert Thurston, S.J., and Donald Attwater [London, 1956]) calls it "the most impressive and significant religious phenomenon of contemporary times" (4:12). St. Teresa (beatified in 1923, canonized in 1925) promised: "After my death I will let fall a shower of roses" (4:15); hence her nickname, "the Little Flower."

Another "little flower," a poem by Tennyson titled "Flower in the Crannied Wall" (1869), appears at the top of the right-hand column of the *Evening Telegraph* of 16 June 1904 under the heading "Gleaned from All Sources": "Flower in the crannied wall, / I pluck you out of the crannies, / I hold you here, root and all, in my hand, / Little flower—but *if* I could understand / What you are, root and all, and all in all, / I should know what God and man is." *Month's mind:* a commemorative requiem mass said on the thirtieth day after death.

6.164–67 (91:23–26). It is now a month . . . meet him on high – Typical of the sort of verse that appeared under "In Memoriam" in the obituary columns of daily newspapers (inserted in this case as an advertisement of the month's mind). The linkage of Henry with "Little Flower" above recalls Bloom's assumed name.

6.171 (91:30). National School. Meade's yard. The hazard – In sequence along Great Brunswick (now Pearse) Street: 114–121, St. Andrews Boys' and Girls' National School; 153–159, Michael Meade & Son, builders and contractors, sawing, planing, and moulding mills, and joinery works; the hazard, Cabman's Shelter and Coffee Stand outside Westland Row station.

6.175 (91:34). pointsman's – A man who has charge of the "points" on a railway, the tapering, movable rails that direct vehicles from one line of rails to another.

6.180 (91:40). Antient concert rooms – A hall where privately sponsored concerts were given, 42 Great Brunswick Street.

6.180–81 (92:1). with a crape armlet – A small band of black cloth worn on the arm in token of mourning, usually for a person who was not a close relation.

6.183 (92:3). the bleak pulpit of St. Mark's – The church (c. 1737) is on Mark Street, just off Great Brunswick (now Pearse) Street. Built in a neoclassical style so severe as to be bleak, the west front is typical: rugged and black, the sweeping curve of the walls unrelieved by the slit windows that are intended to light the staircases within.

6.183–84 (92:3–4). the railway bridge – Carries the City of Dublin Junction Railway (the Loop Line) over Great Brunswick Street; see 5.138n.

6.184 (92:4). the Queen's Theatre – At 209 Great Brunswick (now Pearse) Street, one of the three major theaters in Dublin at the turn of the century. The Theatre Royal was primarily used for dramatic presentations, the Gaiety for the more socially prominent musical events, and the Queen's for productions that fit neither category.

6.184 (92:5). Eugene Stratton – Billed by the Theatre Royal as "The World Renowned Comedian in a series of Recitals from his Celebrated Repertoire," Eugene Stratton was the stage name of Eugene Augustus Ruhlmann (1861–1918), an American who became a music-hall star as a Negro impersonator. He toured primarily in the British Isles, first with a minstrel group and then as a solo performer. His routine involved "coon songs" with whistled refrains and soft-shoe dancing "on a darkened, spotlighted stage, a noiseless, moving shadow."

6.185 (92:5–6). *Mrs. Bandmann Palmer . . . Leah – At the Gaiety Theatre; see 5.194–95n.

6.186 (92:6–7). the *Lily of Killarney?* Elster Grimes Opera company – The Queen's Royal Theatre advertised the Elster-Grimes Grand Opera Company in that "Irish" opera (1862)— a melodramatic, musical version of *The Colleen Bawn* (see 12.194n), libretto by Dion Boucicault (1822–90) and John Oxenford (1812–77), music by the German-English composer Sir Julius Benedict (1804–85).
    Plot summary: Eily, the Colleen Bawn (Irish: "the blond"), is a peasant girl secretly married to a gentleman, Hardress Creegan. Creegan and his mother are in financial straits, but these are apparently to be resolved because Creegan is apparently betrothed to a rich gentlewoman, Anne, the Colleen Ruaidh ("the red-

head"). Then Creegan's best friend, Kyrle, falls in love with Anne and she with him, but she mistakenly thinks that he, not Creegan, is Eily's husband. The melodramatic tangle is compounded by Creegan's pride; by a pettifogging lawyer with a mortgage to foreclose unless Mrs. Creegan marries him; by Creegan's faithful servant, whose mistaken zeal leads him to attempt to murder Eily; by the lawyer, who has Creegan arrested for the murder that has not been committed; etc. All is resolved by revelation and confession: Creegan is reunited with Eily, Anne marries Kyrle, the mortgage blows away, and the lawyer is ducked in the horsepond.

6.187 (92:8). *Fun on the Bristol – The New York musical-comedy version of Henry C. Jarret's "American Eccentric Comedy-Oddity," *Fun on the Bristol; or, A Night on the Sound*, was advertised as "funnier than a pantomime" and was enormously popular in the provinces in the late nineteenth century; together with Eugene Stratton's recital, it constituted the Theatre Royal's "double feature" for 16 June 1904.

6.188 (92:9). the Gaiety – See 6.184n.

6.189 (92:10). As broad as it's long – Proverb; in this context: it would cost Bloom as much to stand the drinks as it would to buy the tickets.

6.191 (92:12). Plasto's – Hatter at 1 Great Brunswick (now Pearse) Street, where Bloom purchased his hat.

6.191 (92:12). Sir Philip Crampton's . . . bust – The Crampton Memorial, a bust above a fountain and surmounted by a cascade of metal foliage, stood in College Street at the west end of Great Brunswick (now Pearse) Street. The procession angles north at this point, toward O'Connell Bridge over the Liffey. Crampton (1777–1858) was a Dublin surgeon whose "fame was almost European" and who served for several years as surgeon general of Her Majesty's Forces. The memorial has been removed.

6.196 (92:19). airing his quiff – That is, with his hat off. "Quiff" can mean an oiled lock of hair plastered on the forehead; but it can also mean smartly dressed, in which case Boylan is showing off.

6.198 (92:21–22). the Red Bank – Burton Bindon's Red Bank Restaurant, 19–20 D'Olier Street.

6.216–17 (92:42). the county Clare – On the

west coast of Ireland. Bloom's goal is the town of Ennis, where his father committed suicide 27 June 1886.

6.219 (93:3). Mary Anderson – Ulster Hall, Belfast, 16 June 1904, advertised a visit of "the World-Renowned Actress, Miss Mary Anderson (Madame de Marano) in the Balcony Scene from 'Romeo and Juliet,' etc. etc." Other "eminent and celebrated artists" (vocal and instrumental, including Clyde Twelvetrees, cellist) were also to appear.

6.221 (93:6). Louis Werner – Billed as "Conductor and Accompanist" with Miss Anderson and company in Belfast.

6.222 (93:7). topnobbers – After *nob*, notable person.

6.222 (93:7). J. C. Doyle and John Mac-Cormack – Doyle, a baritone, won the award at the 1899 Feis Ceoil (annual Dublin music festival and competition). MacCormack (1884–1945), a tenor, also won a gold medal at the Feis Ceoil. He was a member of the Palestrina Choir of the Metropolitan Procathedral (temporary Roman Catholic cathedral in Dublin) and in 1904 sang with that choir at the St. Louis Exposition, St. Louis, Missouri. The two were regarded as among the cream of contemporary Irish musicians in the early twentieth century.

6.226 (93:11). Smith O'Brien – A statue of William Smith O'Brien (hero of 1848; see 4.491n) stood at the intersection of Westmoreland and D'Olier streets where they converge at O'Connell Bridge. The statue (1869) was the work of Sir Thomas Farrell (1827–1900), Irish sculptor. See 6.228 (93:13).

6.227 (93:12). his deathday – It was; O'Brien died on 16 June 1864.

6.227 (93:12–13). For many happy returns – A salutation appropriate to birthdays and anniversaries but hardly to deathdays.

6.232 (93:18). struck off the rolls – Disbarred from the practice of law.

6.232–34 (93:19–20). Hume street . . . solicitor for Waterford – Henry R. Tweedy, Crown solicitor for County Waterford (in southern Ireland), 13 Hume Street, in the southeast quadrant of Dublin.

6.234 (93:20–21). Relics of old decency –

From the chorus of an Irish song, "The Hat My Father Wore," by Johnny Patterson: "It's old, but it's beautiful, / The best was ever seen, / 'Twas worn for more than ninety years / In that little isle of green. / From my father's great ancestors / It's descended with galore, / 'Tis the relic of old decency, / The hat my father wore."

6.235 (93:22). Kicked about like snuff at a wake – Popular expression for indiscriminate use, after the assumption that snuff would be in demand at a wake to mask the odor of death.

6.236 (93:22–23). O'Callaghan on his last legs – I do not know whether the disbarred attorney now selling bootlaces was named O'Callaghan, but *His Last Legs* (London, 1839) is the title of a brief and once-popular two-act farce by the American William Bayle Bernard (1807–75). The charlatan-hero of the farce is a stage-Irishman (see 15.1729n), Felix O'Callaghan, who, as the play opens, is "shabby genteel" and down on his luck. Once a landed gentleman and "the reigning star of Cheltenham [a fashionable resort town in England]," he has for ten years been the "football of Fortune," a failure at everything he has touched. The farce repairs all that through an elaborate pattern of coincidence aided by what playwright and audience apparently assumed was O'Callaghan's all-too-Irish skill as an impostor and manipulator of others. He winds up about to marry the wealthy widow whom he had courted and lost before his fall from fortune. (Quotations from New York, 1847, edition.)

6.238 (93:25–26). *voglio e non vorrei*. No: *vorrei e non* – Bloom corrects his previous mistake; see 4.327n.

6.239 (93:27). *Mi trema un poco il—cor!* – Italian: "My heart beats a little faster!" Zerlina to Don Giovanni in the "Là ci darem" duet; see 4.314n.

6.247 (93:36). Crofton – The "decent Orangeman," appears as a character in "Ivy Day in the Committee Room," *Dubliners*. In real life he was J. T. A. Crofton (1838–1907), an associate of John J. Joyce's (Simon Dedalus's) in the Dublin Rates Office (the Collector General's Office) in 1888 (see Adams, p. 6).

6.248 (93:38). Jury's – Jury's Commercial and Family Hotel, 7–8 College Green, in the southeast quadrant of Dublin.

6.248 (93:38). the Moira – Moira Hotel, 15

Trinity Street, in the southeast quadrant of Dublin.

6.249 (93:39). Liberator's form – A twelve-foot statue of Daniel O'Connell on a twenty-eight-foot pedestal (see 2.269n) by the Irish sculptor John Henry Foley (1818–74) stands in the northern approach to O'Connell Bridge. The procession moves north along Sackville (now O'Connell) Street.

6.251 (93:41). the tribe of Reuben – That is, Jewish, after Reuben, the eldest son of Jacob and Leah (Genesis 29:32) and the patriarch of one of the twelve tribes of Israel (Numbers 1:5 and 21). He distinguished himself by saving and protecting his younger half-brother, Joseph, and (known for his impetuosity) disgraced himself by his adulterous relationship with his father's concubine, Bilhah. The tribe of Reuben, composed of herdsmen and warriors, occupied a remote part of the Promised Land and eventually renounced its Judaism. In Christian tradition Judas, the betrayer of Jesus, is frequently identified as "of the tribe of Reuben."

6.253 (94:1). *Elvery's Elephant house – 46–47 Sackville Street Lower, advertised themselves as "Waterproofers," selling "Waterproofs for Fishing, Shooting, Riding, Walking."

6.258 (94:8). Gray's statue – On a pedestal in the middle of Sackville Street, also by Sir Thomas Farrell (see 6.226n). Sir John Gray (1816–75) was a Protestant Irish patriot, owner and editor of the *Freeman's Journal*. He advocated disestablishment of the Church of Ireland (accomplished in 1869), land reform, and free denominational education.

6.259 (94:9). We have all been there – That is, we have all felt the animosity of "Jewish" moneylenders. See Ellmann, pp. 37–39, 366.

6.264–65 (94:16). *Reuben J and the son – Reuben J. Dodd, solicitor, 34 Ormond Quay Upper, agent for the Patriotic Assurance Company and Mutual Assurance Company of New York. The *Irish Worker* of 2 December 1911 carried an article headlined, "Half-a-Crown for Saving a Life." The story describes the son's jump into the Liffey: "Whatever his motive, suicide or otherwise—we care not." A "common docker" named Moses Goldin saved his life. Goldin fell ill, losing work and wages, but when Mrs. Goldin went to Dodd Senior she was told curtly "that her husband should have minded his own business." She received 2s. 6d.

from Dodd. In real life Dodd was not Jewish, though he is so portrayed in the novel. See Ellmann, p. 38n.

6.270 (94:21). *the Isle of Man – In the Irish Sea, a port of call on Dublin–Liverpool steamship routes; an out-of-the-way but not expensive place of exile.

6.271 (94:23–24). hobbledehoy – A boy not yet a man.

6.274 (94:27). Drown Barabbas – Pilate, sitting in judgment of Jesus, offers the Jews a choice between the release of Barabbas (a thief and rebel leader) and the release of Jesus. "But the chief priests and elders persuaded the multitude that they should ask Barabbas and destroy Jesus" (Matthew 27:20). In Christopher Marlowe's *The Jew of Malta* (1589), the treacherous central character, Barabas, dies at the end of Act V in a caldron of scalding water, which he has prepared as a trap for his enemies.

6.278 (94:32). piking it – Slang for to leave or depart (also, to die).

6.293 (95:9). Nelson's pillar – In the middle of Sackville (now O'Connell) Street, a column 121 feet tall, surmounted by a thirteen-foot statue of Admiral Lord Nelson (1758–1805). In the early twentieth century most of the electric trams that served Dublin and its suburbs started from Nelson's Pillar. The monument was rather ineptly destroyed by Irish patriots in 1966 on the fiftieth anniversary of the Easter 1916 Uprising.

6.303 (95:20). As decent a little man as ever wore a hat – See 6.234n.

6.307 (95:24). John Barleycorn – Slang for whiskey.

6.308 (95:25). adelite – A gray or grayish-yellow mineral.

6.316 (95:35–36). land agents – In the nineteenth century land agents were important in the management of Irish landlords' (many of them absentee) large land holdings. A succession of land reforms in the late nineteenth century, climaxing in 1903, dismantled these estates and displaced the land agents as a class.

6.317 (95:36). temperance hotel – The Edinburgh Temperance Hotel, 56 Sackville Street Upper.

6.317 (95:36). Falconer's railway guide – At 53 Sackville (now O'Connell) Street Upper: John Falconer, printer, publisher, wholesale stationer, depot for the sale of Irish national school books; office of the *Irish Law Times*, the *Solicitor's Journal*, and the *ABC Railway Guide*.

6.317 (95:36–37). civil service college – Maguire's Civil Service College (a tutoring school for the British civil-service examinations), 51 Sackville (now O'Connell) Street Upper.

6.317 (95:37). Gill's – M. H. Gill & Son, Ltd., wholesale and retail booksellers, publishers, printers, and bookbinders, depot for religious goods, 50 Sackville (now O'Connell) Street Upper.

6.318 (95:37). catholic club – Catholic Commercial Club, 42 Sackville (now O'Connell) Street Upper.

6.318 (95:37). the industrious blind – Richmond National Institution for the Instruction of the Industrious Blind, 41 Sackville (now O'Connell) Street Upper.

6.319 (95:38). Chummies and slaveys – That is, young boys with poor employment (after *chum*, a chimney sweep's boy), and girls employed as maids of all work (i.e., with no defined job status, in contrast to upstairs and downstairs maids, etc.).

6.319–20 (95:39). the late father Mathew – The procession passes a statue of the Reverend Theobald Mathew (1790–1861), the "Apostle of Temperance," famous for his work in the cholera epidemic of 1832 and the Great Famine (1846–49).

6.320 (95:39–40). Foundation stone for Parnell. Breakdown. Heart – The procession passes the base (erected 8 October 1899) on which the Parnell monument by the American sculptor Augustus Saint-Gaudens would eventually be placed (in 1911). "Breakdown. Heart" refers to Parnell's death. As his leadership of the Irish Nationalists disintegrated following the divorce scandal (1889–90), Parnell intensified his efforts to regain control, and in so doing he seriously undermined his already precarious health. He finally broke down after being soaked in the rain during a speaking engagement and died of a complex of causes (rheumatism, pneumonia, etc.) simplistically diagnosed as "heart attack."

6.321–22 (95:41–42). White horses with white . . . A tiny coffin – Burial customs dictated that "white and not black should be used in token of mourning" for a child (*Catholic Encyclopedia* [New York, 1908], vol. 3, p. 76a).

6.321–22 (95:42). Rotunda corner – Where Sackville (now O'Connell) Street Upper gave into Cavendish Row, a group of houses on Rutland (now Parnell) Square East. "The Rotunda" was a series of buildings that housed, variously, a maternity hospital, a theater, a concert hall, and "assembly rooms."

6.323–24 (96:1–2). Black for the married. Piebald for bachelors. Dun for a nun – I have not found a source for these funeral traditions.

6.327 (96:5–6). Burial friendly society pays – The Friendly Societies were mutual insurance societies that paid sick benefits and funeral expenses to their members. Apparently Rudy's funeral expenses were paid by this kind of insurance.

6.329 (96:7–8). If it's healthy . . . not the man – After the ancient Jewish belief that the health of a child is a reflection on the virility of the male. Jewish law asserts that a man should "fulfill the precept of propagation," that is, he should beget a son and a daughter, each in turn capable of having children.

6.332 (96:11–12). Rutland square – Now Parnell Square. The procession continues northwest along the east side of the square and into Frederick Street.

6.332–33 (96:12–13). Rattle his bones . . . Nobody owns – From "The Pauper's Drive," a song by Thomas Noel. "[First verse and chorus:] There's a grim one-horse hearse in a jolly round trot— / To the churchyard a pauper is going I wot; / The road it is rough, and the hearse has no springs; / And hark to the dirge which the sad driver sings: // Rattle his bones over the stones! / He's only a pauper, whom nobody owns! [Fifth and last verse with final chorus:] But a truce to this strain; for my soul it is sad, / To think that a heart in humanity clad / Should make, like the brutes, such a desolate end, / And depart from the light without leaving a friend! // Bear soft his bones over the stones! / Though a pauper, he's one whom his Maker yet owns!"

6.334 (96:14). In the midst of life – We are in death. This aphorism is included in "The Burial

Service" in the Book of Common Prayer (Church of England). It is derived from a tenth-century Latin aphorism and from Martin Luther's antiphon "De Morte."

6.335 (96:15–16). But the worst . . . his own life – St. Augustine defined suicide as a sin, and Church councils from the fifth century onward decreed that a suicide could not be buried with Church rites. Medieval law throughout Europe decreed confiscation of the suicide's property, and burial customs traditionally involved indignities to the corpse.

6.346 (96:29). Refuse christian burial – Bloom is both right and wrong. The Catholic church did continue to refuse religious services and burial in consecrated ground, but English law (which technically included Ireland) provided for burial in consecrated ground in 1823 and permitted religious services in 1882.

6.347 (96:29–30). to drive a stake of wood through his heart in the grave – The superstition was that suicides (like witches) would return to haunt the living; a stake through the heart and burial at a crossroads were supposed to prevent that. The custom persisted in Ireland until the early nineteenth century.

6.348–49 (96:31–32). Found in the riverbed clutching rushes – Recalls Ophelia drowned, as described by Gertrude (*Hamlet* IV.vii.167ff.); cf. the infant Moses, 3.298n.

6.352–53 (96:36–37). *Monday morning. Start afresh. Shoulder to the wheel – Martin Cunningham in the role of Sisyphus, whom Odysseus sees in Hades (11:593–600; Fitzgerald, p. 216).

6.355–57 (96:40–42). *And they call . . . the geisha – A song, "The Jewel of Asia," from the light opera *The Geisha*, music by James Philip and libretto by Harry Greenbank: "A small Japanese once sat at her ease / In a garden cool and shady / When a foreigner gay who was passing that way / Said 'May I come in, young lady?' / So she opened her gate, and I blush to relate / That he taught Japan's fair daughter / To flirt and to kiss like the little white miss / Who lives o'er the western water. // He called her the Jewel of Asia, of Asia, of Asia / But she was the Queen of the Geisha, the Geisha, the Geisha; / So she laughed, 'Tho' you're ready today, Sir / To flirt when I flutter my fan, / Tomorrow you'll go on your way, Sir, / Forgetting the girl of Japan. [Second verse:] But when he came back

(Alas! and Alack!) / To the garden cool and shady, / The foreigner bold was decidedly cold, / And talked of an English lady. / With his heart in a whirl for the little white girl / He declared how much he missed her, / And forgot if you please, his poor Japanese, / For he never even kissed her. // But she was the Jewel of Asia, of Asia, of Asia, / The beautiful Queen of the Geisha, the Geisha, the Geisha, / And she laughed, 'It is just as they say, Sir, / You love for as long as you can! / A month, or a week, or a day, Sir, / Will do for a girl of Japan.'"

6.358 (97:1). Rattle his bones – See 6.332–33n.

6.361 (97:5). Boots – In a hotel, one who cleans the shoes guests leave outside the doors of their rooms at night; hence, a general term for a hotel's odd-job boy.

6.365 (97:9). Nobody owns – See 6.332–33n.

6.366 (97:10). Blessington street – The procession has moved northwest up Frederick Street from Rutland (Parnell) Square and then angled west-northwest along Blessington Street.

6.366 (97:10–11). Over the stones – See 6.332–33n.

6.370 (97:15). in Germany. The Gordon Bennett – An annual international road race instituted by the American sportsman and journalist, James Gordon Bennett (1841–1918), and first run in 1900. In 1904 it was scheduled to be held outside of Homberg, a village near Frankfurt, Germany, on 17 June. The race was to be run against time over a 275- to 300-mile course. The *Evening Telegraph* for 16 June 1904 billed the race a test of the drivers' skill and endurance and, mechanically, a test of brakes. Top automobile speeds for a "flying kilometer" in 1904 were 85 to 90 m.p.h., but such speeds could not even be approached in a road race.

6.372 (97:18). Berkeley street – The procession turns north-northwest out of Blessington Street into Berkeley Street and thence north into Berkeley Road (which crosses the west end of Eccles Street).

6.372 (97:18–19). the Basin – The City Basin, a rectangular reservoir just west of Berkeley Street.

6.373–74 (97:20). Has anybody here . . . double ell wy – An American adaptation (1909), by William J. McKenna ("Has Anybody Here Seen Kelly?"), from the English song "Kelly from the Isle of Man" (1908) by C. W. Murphy and Will Letters. The English song tells the story of an Irishman from the Isle of Man who is taken in hand by a lady of leisure only to abandon her for a rival. The American version: "Michael Kelly with his sweetheart came from County Cork / And bent upon a holiday, they landed in New York. / They strolled around to see the sights, alas, it's sad to say, / Poor Kelly lost his little girl upon the Great White Way. / She walked uptown from Herald Square to Forty-second Street, / The traffic stopped as she cried to the copper on the beat: [Chorus:] Has anybody here seen Kelly? / K-E-double-L-Y? / Has anybody here seen Kelly? / Have you seen him smile? / Sure his hair is red, his eyes are blue, / And he's Irish through and through. / Has anybody here seen Kelly? / Kelly from the Emerald Isle. [Second verse:] Over on Fifth Avenue, a band began to play, / Ten thousand men were marching for it was St. Patrick's Day, / The 'Wearing of the Green' rang out upon the morning air. / 'Twas Kelly's favorite song, so Mary said, 'I'll find him there.' / She climbed upon the grandstand in hopes her Mike she'd see, / Five hundred Kellys left the ranks in answer to her plea."

6.374 (97:21). *Dead March from *Saul* – George Frederick Handel (1685–1759)'s *Saul*, an oratorio (1739). In Act III Saul's implacable jealousy of David drives David away and divides the Israelites, who are then defeated by the Philistines at the battle of Gilboa. Saul's son Jonathan is killed, and Saul is wounded and commits suicide. The Dead March occurs when the Israelites recover the bodies and carry them in just before the climactic Elegy. Handel's Dead March is traditionally played in British military funerals (pointed out by Joan Keenan).

6.374–75 (97:21–22). He's as bad . . . on my ownio – A song about an Italian ice-cream merchant who treats his benefactors much as Kelly from the Isle of Man treated his. The song was a forerunner of all the Kelly songs. See 6.373–74n.

6.375–76 (97:22). The *Mater Misericordiae* – In 1904, the largest hospital in Dublin (at the intersection of Berkeley Road and Eccles Street). The hospital did have a ward for incurables.

6.377 (97:24). Our Lady's Hospice for the dying – See 5.351n.

6.378 (97:25). Mrs Riordan – Appears as a character (called "Dante") in chapter 1:A and C of *A Portrait*. See Ellmann, pp. 24–26, 33–44, and Stanislaus Joyce, *My Brother's Keeper* (New York, 1958), pp. 8–9.

6.381–82 (97:29). the lying-in hospital – The National Maternity Hospital, 29–31 Holles Street, the scene of [Oxen of the Sun] (14.1–1591 [pp. 383–428]). The student involved is Dixon.

6.385–91 (97:33–39). drove of branded cattle . . . raddled sheep . . . drover's voice . . . Out of that! – In the realm of the dead, Odysseus sees Orion, the fabulous hunter, driving the "wild beasts he had overpowered in life" with an "unbreakable" club (11:572–75; Fitzgerald, p. 215).

6.392 (97:40). Springers – A cow in calf (Irish).

6.392 (97:41). Cuffe – Joseph Cuffe, associated with Laurence Cuffe & Sons, cattle, corn, and wool salesmen, at 5 Smithfield (in the northwest quadrant of central Dublin), near the cattle market.

6.393–94 (97:42). *Roastbeef for old England – Suggests the song "The Roast Beef of Old England": "When mighty roast beef was the Englishman's food / It ennobled our hearts and enriched our blood. / Our soldiers were brave, and our courtiers were good. [Chorus:] Oh, the Roast Beef of old England, / And oh for Old England's Roast Beef!"

6.397 (98:4–5). dicky meat – In bad condition, of inferior quality.

6.398 (98:5). Clonsilla – A junction in the Midland Great Western Railway, seven miles west of Dublin.

6.400 (98:7). the corporation – The Dublin Corporation is the ruling body of the city, including the lord mayor, sheriffs, aldermen, councilmen, and their various committees and the bureaucracies that answer to those committees.

6.400–401 (98:8). from the parkgate to the quays – Along the north bank of the Liffey, from the western side of Dublin at the Parkgate, southeast entrance of Phoenix Park, to the eastern side of the city and the quays at the mouth of the Liffey. See 4.109–10n.

6.406 (98:13). municipal funeral trams like they have in Milan – A belt electric railway seven miles long passed from the center of Milan to a point near the graveyards outside the sixteenth-century walls. Special funeral cars were provided to alleviate traffic congestion in the old city.

6.416 (98:23). Dunphy's – Dunphy's Corner, the intersection of North Circular and Phibsborough roads. From Berkeley Road the procession turns left (west) into North Circular Road and then right (north) into Phibsborough Road. The corner was named after a pub once owned by Thomas Dunphy. In 1904 the owner was John Doyle (*Thom's* 1904, p. 1569).

6.430–31 (98:42). Elixir of life – A translation of the Irish *usquebaugh:* "whiskey."

6.436 (99:6). Phibsborough road – Part of a main north–south thoroughfare that gives into Prospect Road beyond the Royal Canal.

6.438 (99:8). Crossguns bridge: the royal canal – Phibsborough Road leads into Crossguns Bridge over the Royal Canal, which traces the northern perimeter of metropolitan Dublin and circles south toward the mouth of the Liffey. The canal was once a major link between Dublin and central Ireland.

6.439–40 (99:9–10). A man stood on his dropping barge – The barge is being lowered in the lock just above (west of) Crossguns Bridge. The Correspondences (headnote, p. 104) imply that the bargeman is cast in the role of Charon, who ferries Aeneas across the Styx for his visit to the underworld (*Aeneid* 6:299ff.).

6.441 (99:11). Aboard of the *Bugabu* – A satirical ballad by J. P. Rooney about the difficulty of navigating a turf barge. The barge is threatened by seas that "ran mountains high," and it is steered by a helmsman who is asleep and commanded by a captain who sets fire to the cargo. The voyage reaches a climax when the crew discovers that the barge is not on the high seas at all but in a canal.

6.444–45 (99:15). Athlone, Mullingar, Moyvalley – On the Royal Canal system: Athlone is 78 miles from Dublin and 48½ miles from Galway on the west coast; Mullingar, 50 miles from

Dublin, 76½ from Galway; Moyvalley, 30½ miles from Dublin, 96 from Galway.

6.446 (99:17). crock – A worthless animal.

6.446 (99:17). Wren – P. A. Wren of Wren's Auction Rooms, 9 Bachelor's Walk, in central Dublin, northwest quadrant.

6.447–48 (99:18–19). James M'Cann's hobby to row me o'er the ferry – James M'Cann (d. 12 February 1904) was chairman of the court of directors of the Grand Canal Company, which maintained a regular fleet of trade boats on the Grand Canal (to central and southern Ireland). Thus M'Cann, who has already arrived in Hades, is another candidate for the role of Charon; cf. 6.439–40n.

6.450 (99:22). Leixlip, Clonsilla – Leixlip, eleven miles west of Dublin, is on the Liffey (not on the Royal Canal); Clonsilla, seven miles west, is on the Royal Canal.

6.453 (99:25). Brian Boroimhe house – A pub at 1 Prospect Terrace, on the corner of Prospect Road north of the Crossguns Bridge; J. M. Ryan, proprietor and family grocer, tea, wine, and spirit merchant. The pub is named after Brian Boru (Boroimhe) (926–1014), king of Munster from c. 978, principal king of Ireland from c. 1002. He achieved a major victory over the Danes at Clontarf (on the northeastern outskirts of Dublin) on Good Friday 1014. Although Brian was too old to participate in the battle, tradition holds that he remained in his tent at prayer and that he was killed at the end of the day by Danes fleeing the battle they had lost.

6.454 (99:26). Fogarty – "A modest grocer" and a friend of Kernan's with "a small shop on Glasnevin Road" in "Grace," *Dubliners*.

6.456 (99:29–30). Left him weeping – In "Grace," *Dubliners*, "There was a small account for groceries unsettled" between Kernan and Fogarty. The implication is that what was once "small" has grown and that Kernan has left Fogarty "weeping at the church door," that is, has not paid him and avoids him.

6.457 (99:31). Though lost to sight . . . to memory dear – "To Memory You Are Dear," song (1840) with words by George Linley (1798–1865): "Though lost to sight, to memory dear, / You ever will remain; / One only hope my heart can cheer, / The hope to meet again. /

Oft in the tranquil hour of night, / When stars illumine the sky, / I gaze upon each orb of light / And wish that you were by. / Yes, life then seemed one pure delight, / Though now each spot looks drear / Yet though your smile be lost to sight, / To memory you are dear."

6.458 (99:32). Finglas road – The southern boundary of the cemetery, angling northwest from Prospect Road.

6.460 (99:34–35). silent shapes . . . holding out calm hands – At the beginning of Book 11 of *The Odyssey*, when Odysseus arrives in Hades and fills a sacrificial pit with blood, crowds of the shades of the dead gather around the pit in supplication. Odysseus fends them off with his sword until he has had a chance to consult Tiresias.

6.462 (99:37). Thos. H. Dennany – His "stonecutter's yard" and display of cemetery sculpture was just off Finglas Road on Prospect Avenue in Glasnevin.

6.464 (99:39). *Jimmy Geary, the sexton's – J. W. Geary's address: Prospect Cemetery, Glasnevin.

6.467 (99:42). Gloomy gardens – Recall the *Lugentes Campi* (Latin: "Fields of Mourning") where Aeneas sees the souls of those whom love has cruelly wasted (*Aeneid* 6:440ff.).

6.469 (100:2). where Childs was murdered – Samuel Childs was tried for and acquitted of the murder of his seventy-six-year-old brother, Thomas, in October 1899. The murder took place on 2 September 1898 at 5 Bengal Terrace in Glasnevin.

6.470 (100:4–5). Seymour Bushe – Ellmann (pp. 91–92) characterizes him as "one of the most eloquent Irish barristers" of his time. See 7.741n.

6.473 (100:7). Only circumstantial – In the course of the trial Bushe had spoken on the law of evidence, arguing that "the evidence that Samuel Childs had murdered his brother Thomas rested chiefly on the fact that only Samuel had a key to the house, and that there was no evidence for the murderer's having entered by force" (*Evening Telegraph*, 21 October 1899, quoted in Ellmann, p. 756, n. 49).

6.474–75 (100:8–9). Better for ninety-nine . . . to be wrongfully condemned – This combines mild misquotations of Jesus—"Joy shall be in heaven over one sinner that repenteth, more than over ninety and nine just persons, which need no repentance" (Luke 15:7)—and Sir William Blackstone (1723–80), commentator on English law—"It is better that ten guilty persons escape than that one innocent suffer" (*Commentaries on the Laws of England* [1765–69], volume 4, chapter 27).

6.477 (100:11). unweeded garden – Hamlet, in his first soliloquy, contemplates his mother's marriage to Claudius (who only later is revealed as a murderer) and complains of the world: "'Tis an unweeded garden, / That grows to seed, things rank and gross in nature / Possess it merely" (I.ii.135–37).

6.478 (100:12–13). The murderer's image . . . the murdered – Refers to the superstition that the image of the murderer would be fixed on the retina of his victim and therefore could be "seen."

6.482 (100:16–17). Murder will out – Proverbial wisdom, as in Chaucer's "The Nun's Priest's Tale." The prideful cock, Chantecleer, arguing the prophetic validity of dreams, concludes an elaborate example with the tag: "Mordre wol out, that se we day by day" (l. 3052). The idea is echoed in Hamlet's soliloquy on the possible effectiveness of the play *The Mouse-trap* (III.ii.247) as a way of catching "the conscience of the King." "For murder, though it have no tongue, will speak / With most miraculous organ" (II.ii.622–23).

6.486 (100:22). Prospect – The cemetery in Glasnevin is called Prospect Cemetery.

6.486–89 (100:22–25). Dark poplars, rare . . . gestures on the air – The description of the cemetery recalls Aeneas's initial vision of the underworld (*Aeneid*, 6:282ff.) when Aeneas sees "throngs" of "faint bodiless lives, flitting under a hollow semblance of form . . . in the midst an elm, shadowy and vast." In fear, Aeneas threatens "vainly" to draw his sword.

6.501 (100:37). Simnel cakes – A kind of rich plumcake, enclosed in a very hard dough crust (especially for Mothering Sunday in mid-Lent, when parents were visited and presented with a gift); see 3.315–16n.

6.501 (100:38). Dogbiscuits – Not only because simnel cakes are hard but also after the *Aeneid* (6:417ff.) when the sibyl, guiding Aeneas into the underworld, throws "a morsel drowsy with honey and drugged meal" to the three-headed dog Cerberus.

6.507 (101:4). Finglas – A village northwest of the cemetery. There are quarries in the area.

6.510 (101:8). Got here before us, dead as he is – Namely, Dignam in his role as Elpenor (whose name can be rendered "the fiery faced"). Odysseus, on seeing Elpenor in Hades, asks "how could you journey to the western gloom / swifter afoot than I in the black lugger?" (11:57–58; Fitzgerald, p. 199).

6.511 (101:9). skeowways – Askew.

6.513 (101:12). Mount Jerome – The Protestant cemetery at Harold's Cross, south-southwest of central Dublin.

6.521 (101:21). The mutes – See 1.213–14n.

6.529–30 (101:32–33). the Queen's hotel in Ennis . . . Clare – Ennis is an inland town in County Clare in western Ireland, 140 miles west-southwest of Dublin. The hotel that Bloom's father "owned" was and is located in Church (now Abbey) Street, where "it still enjoys a thriving business," according to Mr. Vincent McHugh, chairman of the Ennis Urban District Council (1970).

6.534 (101:37). the cardinal's mausoleum – Edward Cardinal MacCabe (1816–85), the archbishop of Dublin (1879–85), created cardinal in 1882. From an Irish point of view he was a "townsman," with little interest in land reform or Home Rule, the two central political issues of his time.

6.537 (101:41). Artane – The village of Artane, in the parish of Donnycarney, is three miles north of the center of Dublin. The institution Martin Cunningham has in mind (see 10.3–5 [219:3–6]) is the O'Brien Institute for Destitute Children in Donnycarney, the Reverend Brother William A. Swan, director.

6.539 (102:2). Todd's – That is, get her employment in Todd, Burns & Co., Ltd., silk mercers, linen and woolen drapers, tailors, and boot and shoe and furnishing merchandisers in Dublin. (May Joyce, one of Joyce's sisters, was at one point employed in Todd's.)

6.546–47 (102:9–10). Wise men say . . . in the world – After a song by Murray and Leigh, "Three Women to Every Man": "Women are angels without any wings, / Still they are very peculiar things; / Men who have studied the ladies a lot, / Know what peculiar notions they've got. / Soon as a maiden gets married, you know, / She wants at once to be 'boss' of the show; / I think, though perhaps my opinion is small, / She ought to feel lucky she's married at all. [Chorus:] Wise men say there are more women than men in the world, / That's how some girls are single all their lives, / Three women to every man / Oh, girls, say if you can, / Why can't every man have three wives?"

In Book 11 of *The Odyssey*, Persephone (11:225ff.) sends the shades of "great women" to talk to Odysseus and then (11:385ff.) those of great men. All told, including his mother, who has died in his absence, and Tiresias, Odysseus talks to sixteen women (plus Persephone) and sees or talks to twelve men.

6.548 (102:11–12). For hindu widows only – That is, suttee, the Hindu practice of the wife immolating herself on her husband's funeral pyre, abolished by the British rulers of India in 1829.

6.549 (102:13–14). Widowhood not . . . old queen died – Queen Victoria (1819–1901; queen 1837–1901) had made the perpetual mourning of a dedicated widowhood fashionable after the death of Albert, duke of Saxe-Coburg-Gotha, her husband and prince consort, on 14 December 1861. But Victoria's protracted mourning led gradually to a widespread feeling that she was overdoing it; and by 1904 the rigid rules of mid-Victorian mourning had been considerably relaxed. See 1.120n.

6.550 (102:14–15). Frogmore memorial – At the Frogmore Lodge at Windsor Castle, where Victoria had a special mausoleum constructed for herself, her husband, Prince Albert, and her mother, the duchess of Windsor. For her own funeral Victoria had commanded full military observance: her body was "drawn in a gun carriage" in a remarkable funeral procession on 2 February 1901 and lay in state in St. George's Chapel in Windsor. On 4 February the coffin was privately removed to the Frogmore mausoleum and there placed in the sarcophagus that already held the remains of Prince Albert.

6.550–51 (102:15–16). But in the end . . . in her bonnet – Queen Victoria's self-imposed seclusion after her husband's death, together with her insistence on a protracted mourning, caused much controversy. Late in her life she did relax the strictures of her mourning somewhat.

6.551–52 (102:16–17). All for a shadow . . . was the substance – Bloom echoes a common criticism of Queen Victoria's excessive mourning for the "shadow" of her dead husband, who was, as prince consort, only the shadow of a king in real life. Bloom also echoes a related criticism of Queen Victoria's refusal to share the responsibilities of the Crown with her mature son, who was allowed to cool his heels until her death, when, at the age of sixty, he finally became a king in substance as Edward VII.

6.558 (102:23). Cork's own town – The title of a song (1825) by Thomas Crofton Croker (1798–1854): "They may rail at the city where first I was born, / But it's there they've the whisky, and butter, and pork, / And a little neat spot for to walk in each morn— / They call it Daunt's Square, and the city is Cork. / The square has two sides—why one east and one west, / And convenient's the region of frolic and spree, / Where salmon, drisheens, and beefsteaks are cooked best: / Och! Fishamble's the Eden for you, love, and me!"

6.559 (102:24). Cork park races – An annual race meet held on a track in the city of Cork's public park. The most fashionable day of the meet (and the day of the principal purses) was Easter Monday (4 April in 1904).

6.560 (102:25). Same old six and eightpence – A usual and unchanging thing, after the usual fee for carrying back the body of an executed malefactor and giving it Christian burial.

6.560 (102:26). Dick Tivy – Identity and significance unknown.

6.561 (102:27). solid – Sedate, steady, trustworthy.

6.564 (102:32). get up a whip – A "whip" was slang for money subscribed by a military mess for additional wine; therefore, to take a collection.

6.568 (102:37–38). John Henry Menton – A solicitor and commissioner of affidavits. In fiction, a former employer of Dignam, but he was also "real," with offices at 27 Bachelor's Walk, in central Dublin just north of the Liffey.

6.578–79 (103:7–8). I owe three shillings to O'Grady – A parody of Socrates' last words, "I owe a cock to Asclepios; see that the debt is paid," as recorded in Plato's *Phaedo*. Jane S. Meehan (*JJQ* 16, no. 4 [1979]: 512–13) suggests an allusion to the Irish comic song "I Owe $10 to O'Grady," written by Harry Kennedy (1887). The singer is down on his luck, out of work, and in debt to "the little tailor-man," Pat O'Grady. Chorus: "I owe ten dollars to O'Grady, / You'd think he had a mortgage on my life; / He calls to see me early every morning, / At night he sends his wife. / He tried to have me pawn my girl's piano. / I think O'Grady has a dreadful gall; / Unless he wants to wait, / I'll rub it off the slate, / And the devil a cent he'll ever get at all."

6.580 (103:9). Which end is the head? – Traditionally, the corpse is borne head-first, and oriented with the head toward the altar in the church and toward the headstone in the grave.

6.585 (103:15). *prayingdesks – With a lectern for a prayer book and a step on which to kneel.

6.585 (103:15). The font – At the chapel entrance, contains holy water with which worshipers moisten their fingers and touch their brow or cross themselves in blessing.

6.589 (103:20). a brass bucket with something in it – The vessel contains holy water and a rod (sprinkler) for shaking it over the coffin.

6.591–92 (103:23–24). Who'll read the book? I, said the rook – After the nursery rhyme: "Who killed Cock Robin? / I, said the sparrow, / With my bow and arrow, / I killed Cock Robin. // Who'll be the parson? / I, said the rook, / With my little book, / I'll be the parson."

6.595 (103:27). Father Coffey – The Reverend Francis Coffey, curate-in-charge and chaplain, 65 Dalymount. Father Coffey is to perform the absolution, the final phase of the funeral before the burial.

6.595 (103:27–28). *Dominenamine – Apparently the priest has said, *"In nomine Domini"* (Latin: "In the name of the Lord"), and Bloom has not heard it clearly.

6.596 (103:28). Bully about the muzzle – Too large and thick in the mouth. The dog imagery identifies Father Coffey as Cerberus; see 6.501n.

6.596 (103:29). Muscular christian – A term applied since about 1857 to a brand of Christian opinion and practice that had its origins in the Church of England and put particular stress on the importance of a healthy body as conducive to morality and true religion. One of the principal advocates of muscular Christianity was the English clergyman, novelist, and poet Charles Kingsley (1819–75).

6.597 (103:30). Thou art Peter – Jesus changes Peter's name from Simon ("hearer") to Peter ("rock") and says, "And I say also unto thee, that thou art Peter, and upon this rock I will build my church; and the gates of hell shall not prevail against it" (Matthew 16:18).

6.601 (103:34). *Non intres . . . tuo, Domine* – Latin: "Do not weigh the deeds of your servant, Lord"; the opening phrase of the prayer that begins the absolution. The sentence continues: "for no one is guiltless in your sight unless you forgive him all his sins." The absolution is usually pronounced after the funeral mass and just before the coffin is carried to the grave.

6.602–3 (103:36). Requiem mass – Or funeral mass, customarily precedes the absolution in the funeral rites. In Dignam's case the funeral mass seems to have been omitted, his body brought directly from the house in Sandymount to the mortuary chapel at Glasnevin.

6.603 (103:36). Crape weepers – Professional mourners, who dressed in crape because the material was cheap.

6.603 (103:37). altarlist – The list or book signed by those who attend a funeral.

6.609 (104:1). *Mervyn Browne – A Mervyn A. Browne is listed in *Thom's* 1904 as "professor of music and organist." A Mr. Browne appears as a character in "The Dead," *Dubliners*.

6.609 (104:2). vaults of saint Werburgh's – The church on Werburgh Street in south-central Dublin is one of the oldest in Dublin, built during the reign of Henry II (1133–89; king 1154–89) by the "men of Bristol" who colonized the city. It was dedicated to St. Werburgh, daughter of Wulfhere, king of Mercia. The original building was destroyed in 1301, then repaired and enlarged in 1662. The twenty-seven vaults beneath the church are part of the original building. One of the vaults houses Lord Edward Fitzgerald's coffin. See 10.785–86n.

6.610 (104:2). lovely old organ – St. Werburgh's was rebuilt in 1712, destroyed by fire in 1754, and restored in 1759 (when the organ Bloom has in mind was installed). Before the fire and after its restoration the church was the scene of regular concerts of Handel's music, organized after Handel's triumphant visit to Dublin in 1742. (Handel's visit came to a climax when he conducted the first performance of his *Messiah* as a reward for Dublin's appreciative, as against London's cold, reception.) The church's organ was regarded as one of the finest eighteenth-century organs in the British Isles.

6.614–15 (104:7–8). a stick with a knob . . . over the coffin – That is, the aspergill with which the celebrant sprinkles holy water on the bier to recall "the water that flowed over the deceased person's head at baptism" (*Layman's Missal* [Baltimore, Md., 1962], p. 1044).

6.618 (104:12). *Et ne nos . . . tentationem* – Latin: "And lead us not into temptation," from the Lord's Prayer (Matthew 6:13). As the celebrant sprinkles the bier with holy water he intones the Paternoster (the Lord's Prayer) in a low voice. When he has finished sprinkling the bier, he takes up the prayer at the quoted line and is answered by the server: "But deliver us from evil. [CELEBRANT:] From the mouth of Hell. [SERVER:] Rescue his soul, Lord. [CELEBRANT:] May he rest in peace. [SERVER:] Amen."

6.628 (104:25). *In paradisum* – Latin: "Into paradise"; the opening words of the anthem that is said or sung as the coffin is being carried to the grave, "May the angels lead you into Paradise."

6.641 (104:41). The O'Connell circle – Near the center of the cemetery, a round platform of earth surrounded by a deep ditch. O'Connell was originally buried in the circle, but in 1869 his remains were removed to a crypt in the O'Connell monument, a 160-foot-tall replica of an Irish round tower near the mortuary chapel. Mr. Dedalus is apparently referring to this monument, because "the lofty cone" (6.642 [104:42]) is the round tower.

6.643–44 (105:2). his heart is buried in Rome – O'Connell died in Genoa in 1847 when he was returning from a pilgrimage to Rome. His heart was taken to Rome and placed in the church of St. Agatha (the Irish College). His body was brought back to Ireland for burial in the O'Connell circle.

6.645 (105:4). Her grave – Simon Dedalus's wife, Stephen's mother, Mary Goulding Dedalus. Buried 26 June 1903.

6.657 (105:16–17). a treacherous place – Odysseus and his men approach Hades with "a bitter and sore dread upon" them (11:5; Fitzgerald, p. 197).

6.663 (105:23). In the same boat – That is, Bloom and Kernan are the only mourners present who are not practicing Catholics.

6.665 (105:26). The service of the Irish church – The Church of Ireland (disestablished in 1869) was the Irish counterpart of the Church of England. The service was, of course, in English, not Latin.

6.670 (105:31). *I am the resurrection and the life* – Jesus in mild reproof to Martha, the sister of Lazarus, when she doubts that her brother will "rise again" before "the resurrection at the last day." Jesus continues, "He that believeth in me, though he were dead, yet shall he live: And whosoever liveth and believeth in me shall never die" (John 11:24–26). The irony, at Kernan's expense, is that these words, which play a prominent part in the English funeral service of the Church of Ireland, play an equally important part (in Latin) in the Roman Catholic burial service that he is witnessing.

6.677–78 (105:41). last day idea – That is, at the Resurrection and Last Judgment (the "last day") the dead will be raised in the flesh. One key biblical passage on this "idea" is John 6:40. Jesus says: "And this is the will of him that sent me, that everyone which seeth the Son, and believeth on him, may have everlasting life: and I will raise him up at the last day."

6.678 (105:42). Come forth, Lazarus! – Jesus, at the tomb of Lazarus, prays, giving thanks to God, "And when he thus had spoken, he cried with a loud voice, Lazarus come forth" (John 11:43).

6.679 (105:42). And he came fifth and lost the job – A commonplace pun on the biblical "Come forth"; in its more usual form: And the Lord commanded Moses to come forth but Moses slipped on a banana peel and came in fifth.

6.679–80 (106:1). fellow mousing around for his liver – See Tityos under notes on the Linati schema, p. 104. The humor is also at the ex-

pense of those who believe that when the dead rise at the Last Judgment they will be physically reconstituted just as they originally were.

6.681–82 (106:3–4). Pennyweight . . . Twelve grammes one pennyweight. Troy measure – The English system of weight measure, named after Troyes in France. The original measure was based on the weight of a grain of wheat; hence the smallest unit is a "gramme," meaning grain. Troy weight is currently used for precious metals and jewels. Twenty-four (not twelve) grammes (grains) make a pennyweight; twenty pennyweights, one ounce (oz.t.); twelve ounces, one pound (lb.t.).

6.684 (106:6). A 1 – First class, after its use in *Lloyd's Register*, where the letter *A* denotes a new or renovated ship and the vessel's stores are graded *1* or *2* to denote that they are in good condition.

6.686 (106:8). tooraloom tooraloom – See 5.13–16n.

6.696–97 (106:19). fifteen seventeen golden years ago – May 1887, seventeen years ago.

6.697 (106:19–20). at Mat Dillon's in Roundtown – Roundtown is an area named after a circle of houses in Terenure, a village in the parish of Rathfarnham on the southern outskirts of Dublin.

6.701 (106:23). fell foul – Got into a dispute.

6.703 (106:26). Wisdom Hely's – A stationer and printer at 27–30 Dame Street, Dublin. The sequence of Bloom's employments is hardly clear, but at 8.158 (155:20–21) Bloom remarks that he got the job in Hely's the year he and Molly were married (1888) and had it for (roughly) "six years."

6.704 (106:29). coon – In English idiom, a sly, knowing fellow; in American slang, derogatory and offensive for a black.

6.710 (106:37). John O'Connell – Superintendent of Prospect Cemetery, Glasnevin.

6.714 (107:2). custom – That is, business, after the customary patronage of a particular shop or tradesman.

6.717 (107:6–7). Mulcahy from the Coombe – Apart from the context, Terence Mulcahy's identity and significance are unknown. For the Coombe, see 5.280n.

6.741 (107:35). Keyes's ad – Alexander Keyes, a client of Bloom's; see 7.25n.

6.742 (107:37). Ballsbridge – An area on the southeastern outskirts of Dublin (to disguise Martha Clifford's address in the southwest quadrant of the city).

6.746 (107:42). Silver threads among the grey – After the song "Silver Threads Among the Gold" (1874), words by Eben E. Rexford, music by Hart Pease Danks (1834–1903): "Darling, I am growing old / Silver threads among the gold / Shine upon my brow today, / Life is fading fast away. / But, my darling, you will be / Always young and fair to me. / Yes, my darling, you will be / Always young and fair to me."

6.750 (108:5). when churchyards yawn – Hamlet soliloquizes after *The Mouse-trap* and before he goes to visit his mother: "'Tis now the very witching time of night, / When churchyards yawn and hell itself breathes out / Contagion to this world" (III.ii.406–8).

6.750 (108:5). Daniel O'Connell – See 2.269n.

6.751–52 (108:6–7). a queer breedy man – Alludes to the rumors still persistent in Dublin that Daniel O'Connell had a number of illegitimate children and was thus literally as well as figuratively the "father of his country."

6.752 (108:7–8). like a big giant in the dark – Daniel O'Connell in his role as the "phantom" of the giant Hercules; see headnote to this episode, p. 104.

6.757 (108:13). Whores in Turkish graveyards – Nineteenth-century travelers reported the extensiveness of Turkish graveyards and their cypress groves and noted with surprise that some areas of the graveyards were treated as "fashionable lounges," other areas as "a common resort for *idlers* of both sexes among the Franks, Greeks, and Armenians"—not to mention "the convenience of comfortable seats, afforded by the flat tombstones" (James Ellsworth DeKay, *Sketches of Turkey by an American* [New York, 1833], p. 160).

6.758–59 (108:15). Love among the tombstones. Romeo – Combines allusions to the title of Browning's poem "Love Among the Ruins" (1855) and to the final scene of *Romeo and Juliet*, with the star-crossed love-deaths of Romeo and Juliet in the Capulet mausoleum (V.iii).

6.759 (108:16). In the midst . . . are in life – A reversal of the common line; see 6.334n.

6.760 (108:16–17). Tantalizing for the poor dead – See 6.460n.

6.761 (108:18). to grig – Anglicized Irish: "to excite desire or envy, to tantalize."

6.765 (108:22). Standing? – Ancient Irish kings and chieftains were occasionally buried in a standing posture in full armor, facing toward the lands of their enemies.

6.768 (108:26). Major Gamble – Maj. George Francis Gamble, registrar and secretary, Mount Jerome Cemetery, Dublin.

6.770 (108:29). The Botanic Gardens – See 5.35n.

6.771–72 (108:30–31). those jews they said killed the christian boy – Anachronism? In 1913 the Western world was outraged by a particularly rabid instance of Russian anti-Semitism, the trial in Kiev of a Jew named Mendel Beilis accused of killing a Christian child so that the child's blood could be used in a Passover ceremony. The jury acquitted Beilis, thanks in large part to the international uproar occasioned by the trial. The legend Bloom recalls, however, has a fertility twist to it and has been current since early Christian times: the child is "sacrificed" that his blood may reinvigorate a garden. See the song Stephen sings at 17.802–28 (690:16–691:24).

6.774 (108:33–34). William Wilkinson, auditor and accountant – The Prospect Cemetery records reveal only two *W. W.*'s—one died in 1865 at age sixteen, the other in 1899 at age six months. *Thom's* 1904 lists no such "auditor and accountant." A Mr. Wilkinson appears as a friend of the Daedalus (*sic*) family in *Stephen Hero* (pp. 159–60) and is present at Stephen's sister's funeral (p. 168).

6.780 (108:41). Deathmoths – The death's-head moth has a skull-like marking on the upper part of its thorax and is superstitiously regarded as a harbinger of death.

6.784–85 (109:4–5). swurls . . . gurls – Boylan's pronunciation; see 4.282n.

6.788 (109:10). (closing time) – The time when bars and public houses were required by law to close their doors.

6.792 (109:14). Gravediggers in *Hamlet* – In Act V, scene i, two "clowns" digging Ophelia's grave are involved in an elaborate low-comic scene.

6.792–93 (109:15). the profound knowledge of the human heart – Shakespeare's strength as seen through the eyes of sentimental nineteenth-century academicism.

6.794 (109:16). *De mortuis nil nisi prius* – Latin: Bloom misquotes *De mortuis nil nisi bonum*—"Of the dead speak nothing but good." Bloom's substitution, *nisi prius*, is a legal term for a civil action tried in a court of record before a judge and jury.

6.803 (109:27). We come to bury Caesar – The second (and ironic) line of Marc Antony's (Marcus Antonius's) funeral oration: "I come to bury Caesar, not to praise him" (*Julius Caesar* III.ii.79).

6.803 (109:27–28). His ides of March or June – In *Julius Caesar* (I.ii.18) a soothsayer warns Caesar: "Beware the ides of March" (15 March). Dignam died on the ides of June, 13 June 1904.

6.805 (109:29). galoot – An awkward, ungainly person.

6.809–10 (109:34–35). Only man buries. No, ants too – Popular natural history, in part because many ants hollow out underground nests, in part because many, but not all, species of ants do remove debris, including dead bodies, from their nests.

6.811 (109:36). Robinson Crusoe . . . Friday – Refers to Daniel Defoe's (1660–1731) *Strange Surprising Adventures of Robinson Crusoe* (1719). Crusoe, marooned on an island, acquires the faithful services of a native whom he calls Friday.

6.813–14 (109:38–39). *O, poor Robinson . . . possibly do so* – From a song, "Poor Old Robinson Crusoe," by Hatton (?). An American version: "Poor old Robinson Crusoe was lost / On an island they say, O / He stole him a coat from an old billy-goat / I don't see how he could do so."

6.819 (110:4). Bit of clay from the holy land – An allusion to a Jewish burial custom. The soil of Palestine was popularly believed to have a special holiness; thus Jews longed to be buried in Palestine or, if that were impossible, to have a handful of soil from Palestine put in the coffin under their head.

6.819–20 (110:4–5). Only a mother . . . in the one coffin – Bloom is right that Jewish burial customs allow a mother who dies in childbirth to be buried in the same coffin with her child if it is stillborn. But Jewish burial customs are far more elaborate and not quite so strict as Bloom recalls. Thus, a young child can be buried *in the same grave* with its parents, provided that the child has slept in the same bed with the parents and that they all die in time to be interred in one burial.

6.821–22 (110:7). The Irishman's house is his coffin – After the proverb: "An Englishman's (Irishman's) house is his castle."

6.825–26 (110:10–11). I'm thirteen . . . Death's number – Thirteen, an unlucky number in both pre-Christian and Christian worlds, though one Christian tradition holds that the ill luck of the number stems from the thirteen who sat at the Last Supper (Judas, the betrayer, being the thirteenth guest).

6.831 (110:17). Mesias – In fiction, Bloom's tailor; in life, George R. Mesias, tailor, 5 Eden Quay (on the north bank of the Liffey, just short of its mouth).

6.831–32 (110:17–19). Hello. It's dyed . . . those threads – That is, the "tinge of purple" was not in the wool from which the cloth was woven but had been dyed in after the suit was made. The telltale "threads" would be bright with the dye, which the wool would absorb and diffuse.

6.837 (110:25). a donkey brayed. Rain – The ancient Romans regarded the donkey as a beast of ill omen. Bloom associates that belief with the Irish superstition that a donkey braying at midday forecasts rain.

6.837–38 (110:25–26). No such ass. Never see a dead one, they say – After an Irish saying, "Three things no person ever saw: a highlander's kneebuckle, a dead ass, a tinker's funeral" (P. W. Joyce, *English*, p. 111).

6.846 (110:36). Light they want – Recalls "Light! More light!" the last words of the German poet, playwright, and philosopher Johann Wolfgang von Goethe (1749–1832). It also recalls Anticlea's closing remarks to her son, Odysseus, in Hades: "You must crave sunlight soon" (11:223; Fitzgerald, p. 204).

6.849–50 (110:40–41). Watching is his . . . his feet yellow – Three indications of imminent death (popular superstition).

6.850–51 (110:41–42). Pull the pillow . . . since he's doomed – In Emile Zola's (1840–1902) *La Terre* (The Earth) (1887), this is how the old peasant father dies at the hands of his son and daughter-in-law, who covet his property.

6.851–52 (110:42–111:2). Devil in that . . . in his shirt – Source unknown.

6.852–53 (111:2). *Lucia. Shall I nevermore behold thee?* – *Lucia di Lammermoor* (1835), an opera by Gaetano Donizetti (1797–1848) after Sir Walter Scott's novel *The Bride of Lammermoor* (1819). The opera deals with the "tragic fate" of two lovers separated by family strife. In Act III, scene i, the heroine, Lucia, married against her will, goes mad; then Edgar, the hero, learns that Lucia is dead as he waits in a graveyard to duel with Lucia's villainous brother. He declares, "Yet once more shall I behold thee," and, on the wings of an appropriate aria, commits suicide while the chorus in the background prays heaven to be merciful and forgiving.

6.855 (111:5). Even Parnell. Ivy day dying out – Parnell died 6 October 1891; on the anniversary of his death his partisans wore a leaf of ivy (evergreen, symbolic of fidelity) in his memory. See "Ivy Day in the Committee Room," *Dubliners*.

6.857 (111:70). for the repose of his soul – The dead who are doing penance in purgatory before entrance into heaven are, according to Catholic doctrine, aided by the prayers of the living.

6.861 (111:11). Someone walking over it – The superstition is that when you shiver in the sun someone has walked over your grave, that is, has reminded you that you will die.

6.862 (111:12) towards Finglas – The village of Finglas is northwest of Prospect Cemetery.

6.862–63 (111:13). Mamma, poor mamma, and little Rudy – After Odysseus has consulted with Tiresias, his mother, who unbeknownst to Odysseus has died during his absence from Ithaca, drinks of the sacrificial blood, recognizes her son, and talks to him (11:155–224). She tells him that his wife and son are alive and well but that she died of "loneliness" for him (11:202–3). Odysseus longs to embrace her, "but she went sifting through my hands, impalpable / as shadows are," and this, Odysseus says, "embittered all the pain I bore" (11:207–8; Fitzgerald pp. 202–3).

6.874 (111:26). grace – Grace is that love of God for man that makes repentance and redemption possible. It is also the time allowed a debtor for the payment of his debts.

6.877 (111:29–30). the dismal fields – See 6.467n.

6.885 (111:39–40). Louis Byrne – Louis A. Byrne, M.D., coroner of the City of Dublin.

6.887 (111:42). Levanted – To "levant" is to run away from debts or to make a wager without intending to pay.

6.888 (111:42–112:1). Charley, you're my darling – After the Scottish folk song "Charlie Is My Darlin'," words by Lady Nairne (in honor of Charles Stuart, Bonnie Prince Charlie [1720–88], pretender to the throne of England): "Twas on a Monday morn, / Right early in the year, / When Charlie came to our town, / The young chevalier. [Chorus:] Oh Charlie is my darlin', my darlin', my darlin', / The young chevalier. / Oh Charlie is my darlin', my darlin', my darlin', / The young chevalier. [Second verse:] As he came marchin' up the street, / The pipes played loud and clear, / And all the folk came runnin' out / To meet the chevalier. [Third verse:] With Highland bonnets on their heads, / And claymores bright and clear, / They came to fight for Scotland's right, / And the young chevalier."

6.900 (112:14–15). Has anybody . . . double ell – See 6.373–74n.

6.919 (112:35). the chief's grave – That is, Parnell's grave, opposite the door of the mortuary chapel. In 1904 no tombstone had been erected, but the grave was "surrounded by iron railings, and almost covered by artificial wreaths and crosses" (*Dublin and Its Environs* [London, n.d.; after 1910], p. 84). Parnell is cast in the role of Agamemnon, the chief of the Greeks, to whose shade Odysseus talks at length (*The Odyssey* 11:385ff.).

6.923–24 (112:40–41). Some say . . . That one day he will come again – Rumor that Parnell was alive persisted, in part because he died relatively young (at 45) and in part because his body was not put on view but was almost immediately sealed in its coffin. One of the more popular rumors was that he was hiding out in South Africa (a rumor apparently excited by Irish sympathy for that territory's reluctance to accept Britain's imperial ambitions).

6.930 (113:5). old Ireland's hearts and hands – A song by Richard F. Harvey from W. W. Delaney, *Delaney's Irish Song Book* (New York, n.d.): "Oh Erin, home of lovely scenes, / Oh land of love and song, / In joy once more my fond heart leans / On thee so true and strong: / For like a restless bird I've strayed, / And oft on far-off strands / I dreamed of love knots years have made / With Ireland's hearts and hands. [Chorus:] O sweetheart Erin, good old land, / Though near or far I stray, / I love them all, thy heart and hand, / I love thy shamrock spray: / Old Ireland's hearts and hands, / Old Ireland's hearts and hands, / Oh sweetheart Eire, good old land, / I love thy hearts and hands."

6.931 (113:7). Pray for the repose of the soul – See 6.857n.

6.933 (113:9). All souls' day – In the Roman Catholic church, 2 November, a holy day for the liturgical commemoration of the souls of the faithful dead still in purgatory.

6.933–34 (113:9–10). Twenty-seventh . . . at his grave – Each year on 27 June Bloom visits his father's grave in Ennis.

6.939 (113:16). cork lino – A floor covering made by laying hardened linseed oil mixed with ground cork on a canvas backing. Gerty McDowell's father "travels for" (sells) cork lino (10.1206–7 [253:1–2], 13.321–24 [355:6–9]).

6.939 (113:16–17). paid five shillings in the pound – Went bankrupt and could only pay each creditor one-quarter of what was owed.

6.940–41 (113:18–19). Eulogy in a country . . . Thomas Campbell – The English poet Thomas Gray's (1716–71) "Elegy Written in a Country Churchyard" (1751). Not William Wordsworth (1770–1850) or Thomas Campbell (1777–1844), poet and critic.

6.942–43 (113:20–21). Old Dr. Murren's . . . called him home – Apparently that saying was Dr. Murren's cliché for death. Apart from the context here and at 8.397 (162:8–9), the doctor's identity and significance are unknown.

6.943 (113:21). it's God's acre for them – That is, for Protestants, since "God's acre" is a standard Englishman's phrase for a cemetery.

6.945 (113:23). the *Church Times* – A weekly Church of England newspaper, quite conservative and High Church in its views, but it did contain an impressive number of genteel personal want ads (as Bloom recalls).

6.948 (113:27). Immortelles – French: literally, "the immortals"; the meaning here is of a plant whose flowers may be dried without losing their form or color.

6.950 (113:29). alderman Hooper – Alderman John Hooper (from Cork) gave the Blooms a stuffed owl as a wedding present (17.1338–39 [707:26]). He was a real person and the father of Paddy Hooper, a reporter on the *Freeman's Journal* who is mentioned at 7.456 (130:7).

6.951 (113:30). catapults – Slingshots.

6.953 (113:33). chainies – Damaged chinaware.

6.954 (113:34). the Sacred Heart that is: showing it – The Blessed (in 1904; since 1920, St.) Margaret Mary Alacoque (1647–90) experienced repeated visions in which Jesus took his heart, showed it to her, and placed it in hers. Eventually she consented to establish the festival of the Sacred Heart (since 1882, the second Sunday in July) and the Litany of the Sacred Heart, a method for practicing Christian devotion.

6.954 (113:34). Heart on his sleeve – Proverbial phrase applied to a person so candid that he cannot conceal his thoughts and motives. In

Othello, Iago cynically declares, "I am not what I am," and implies that when he *seems* outwardly what he *is* inwardly "I will wear my heart upon my sleeve / For daws to peck at" (I.i.64–65).

6.957–59 (113:37–40). Would birds then come . . . Apollo that was – Bloom confuses the name Apollo with that of the Greek painter Apelles, a contemporary of Alexander the Great (356–323 B.C.). Similar stories are associated with Apelles, but the story Bloom recalls is of another Greek painter, Zeuxis (d. c. 400 B.C.), who painted grapes so realistically that birds tried to eat them. Pliny the Elder (A.D. 23–79) remarks in his *Natural History* (c. 77): "It is said that Zeuxis subsequently painted a child carrying grapes and when birds flew to the fruit with the same frankness as before, he strode up to the picture in anger with it and said, 'I have painted the grapes better than the child, as if I had made a success of that as well, the birds would inevitably have been afraid of it'" (Book 35, section 36).

6.960 (113:41). How many! – After Dante: "So long a train of people, I never should have believed death had undone so many" (*Inferno* 3:55–57).

6.961 (113:42). As you are now so once were we – A common line in epitaphs. One example: Edward, the Black Prince of England (1330–76), "Who passeth here with closed lips, near to where this body reposeth, let him hear what I shall say, saying only what I know. Even as thou art so once was I: and as I am so thou shalt be."

6.974 (114:14). an old stager – That is, a veteran, a person of experience.

6.977–78 (114:17–18). Robert Emery. Robert . . . wasn't he? – Robert Emery's name reminds Bloom of Robert Emmet (1778–1803), an Irish patriot who attempted to get Napoleon's assistance for an Irish uprising. He led an attempt to seize Dublin Castle in 1803, but the help Napoleon (and Emmet's Irish allies) had promised did not materialize. Robert Kee remarks (*The Green Flag* [New York, 1972], p. 164) that "the plan itself was reasonable and practical, its execution lamentable to the point of farce." The revolt disintegrated into a riot in the course of which "Lord Kilwarden, the Lord Chief Justice . . . was savagely piked to death" (p. 167). After a month underground Emmet was captured (because, legend has it, he returned to bid his fiancée, Sara Curran, farewell). He was hanged and beheaded in a bru-

tally botched public execution. His fame was enhanced by his "last words" (see 11.1275n). But the mystery remains: how and why did this disastrous farce get transformed into one of the most potent Irish-hero myths? As Kee puts it: "Why was it Robert Emmet's portrait above all others that was to go up along with the crucifix in countless small homes in Ireland for over a century and may even be seen there still? . . . The proximity of the crucifix may provide a clue. The success of the Emmet myth lay in the very need to ennoble failure. For tragic failure was to become part of Ireland's identity, something almost indistinguishable from 'the cause' itself" (p. 169).

The whereabouts of Emmet's remains are unknown. After execution he was buried in Bully's Acre near Kilmainham Hospital in Dublin. Rumors abound that his remains were secretly removed to either St. Michan's Church in Dublin or Prospect Cemetery, Glasnevin. Both places have uninscribed tombstones that are said to mark his grave. In 1903, at the centennial of Emmet's death, the *United Irishman* carried a number of stories about renewed attempts to locate his grave; but its whereabouts are still a matter of conjecture.

6.983 (114:24). *Voyages in China* – By "Viator," in Bloom's bookshelf (17.1379 [708:35–36]). The pseudonym Viator was used by several travel writers at the turn of the century, but none of the standard-book catalogues lists this title by a Viator. One of the more prominent Viators was the Presbyterian missionary E. F. Chidell, and the missing *Voyages in China* might have been his, along with *The Way-Farer; Africa and National Regeneration* (London, 1903) and *Overland to Persia* (London, 1906).

6.984 (114:25–26). Priests dead against it – That is, against cremation because it implies a challenge to the doctrine that the flesh is to be resurrected on "the last day."

5.984 (114:26). Devilling – A "devil" is a junior legal counselor who works for a barrister in the preparation of law cases; also the pun.

6.985 (114:27). Time of the plague – Bodies were burned or buried in pits with quicklime in an effort to forestall the contagion.

6.985–86 (114:27). Quicklime fever pits – Not only for plague victims but also for the bodies of executed murderers.

6.986 (114:28). Ashes to ashes – In the *Book*

of *Common Prayer*, "Burial of the Dead. At the Grave": "Earth to earth, ashes to ashes, dust to dust; in sure and certain hope of the Resurrection unto eternal life."

6.987 (114:29). Where is that . . . Eaten by birds – After the Parsi custom of exposing the dead in towers. One of the books in Bloom's library contains an illustration of a Parsi tower: Frederick Deodati Thompson, *In the Track of the Sun: Diary of a Globe Trotter* (London, 1893), p. 156.

6.988 (114:30). Drowning they say is the pleasantest – See 3.482n.

6.995 (114:39). The gates glimmered in front – At the end of Book 6 of the *Aeneid*, Aeneas approaches the exit from the underworld accompanied by his sibyl guide and the shade of his father, who has prophesied his future: "Two gates of Sleep there are, whereof the one is said to be of horn, and thereby an easy outlet is given to true shades; the other gleaming with the sheen of polished ivory, but false are the dreams sent by spirits to the world above. There then . . . Anchises attends both his son and the sibyl, and dismisses them by the ivory gate" (lines 893–98); trans. H. Rushton Fairclough, *Virgil* [London, 1930], vol. 1, p. 571).

6.997 (114:41). Mrs Sinico's funeral – Mrs. Sinico's death by accident in "A Painful Case," *Dubliners,* is a near-suicide occasioned by her alcoholism, which was occasioned in turn by disappointment in love. See Adams, pp. 52–53.

6.1002 (115:6). she wrote – That is, Martha Clifford wrote; see 5.241–59 (77:32–78:12).

6.1004 (115:9). this innings – A cricket inning, much more extended than one in baseball.

6.1010 (115:15). Tantalus glasses – A stand containing three cut-glass decanters that, though apparently free, cannot be withdrawn until the grooved bar engaging the stoppers is raised; after Tantalus, whose torment (*The Odyssey* 11:582ff.) is to suffer hunger and thirst, with water up to his chin and boughs of fruit suspended over him.

6.1010 (115:16). Got his rag out – Slang for blustered, grew angry.

6.1011–12 (115:17–18). Sailed inside him . . . the bias – A player scores in bowls by placing a ball closer to the target-ball, or "jack," than his opponent does. Apparently Bloom put an accidental twist on the ball that made it curve ("the bias") inside Menton's, though Menton's ball blocked straight balls from the jack.

6.1015 (115:21). dinge – A dent or depression.

6.1025 (115:32–33). John Henry Menton jerked his head down in acknowledgment – Toward the end of Book 11 of *The Odyssey* (11:541ff.), Odysseus encounters the shades of several of his former comrades in arms, including Ajax, who refuses to speak to Odysseus because he is still "burning" (angry) over the fact that in the contest over who was to bear Achilles' arms after his death (i.e., who was to be the leading hero of the Greeks), the Lady Thetis (Achilles' mother) and Athena awarded the honor to Odysseus. Ajax then, according to "The Little Iliad," "becomes mad and destroys the herd of the Achaeans and kills himself" (trans. Hugh G. Evelyn-White, *Hesiod: The Homeric Hymns and Homerica* [London, 1914], p. 509).

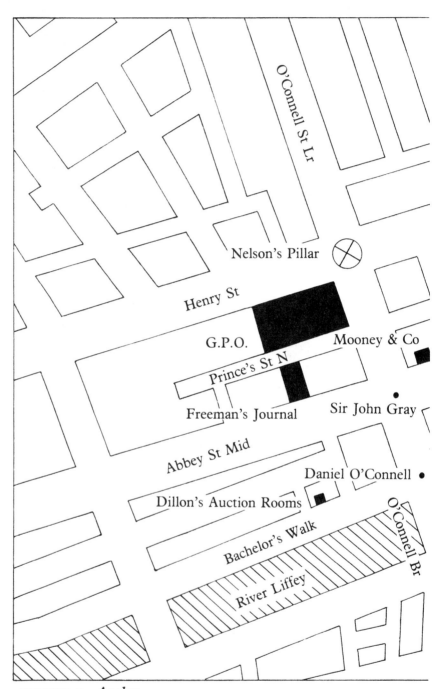

EPISODE 7. *Aeolus*

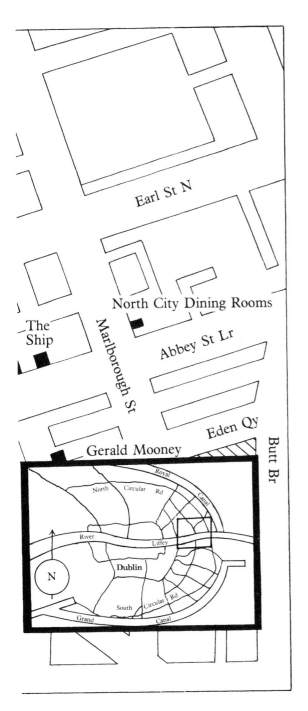

Episode 7: *Aeolus* 7.1–1075 (116–150). In Book 10 of *The Odyssey,* after the unfortunate encounter with the Cyclops (see headnote to Cyclops, p. 314), Odysseus reaches Aeolia, ruled by Aeolus, whom Zeus had made "warden of the winds" (10:21; Fitzgerald, p. 178). Aeolus entertains Odysseus and tries to help him by confining all the unfavorable winds in a bag, which Odysseus stows in his ship. Within sight of Ithaca, Odysseus "nods" at the tiller. His men suspect him of having hidden some extraordinary treasure in the bag; they open it, release the winds, and the ships are driven back to Aeolia, where Aeolus refuses any further help to Odysseus and drives him away as "a man the blessed gods detest" (10:74; Fitzgerald, p. 179).

Time: 12:00 noon. Scene: the newspaper offices of the *Freeman's Journal* (and the *Evening Telegraph*), 4–8 Prince's Street North in the northeast quadrant of Dublin near the General Post Office and Nelson's Pillar. Organ: lungs; Art: rhetoric;[1] Color: red; Symbol: editor; Technique: enthymemic [in logic an *enthymeme* is a syllogism in which one of the premises is only implicit or is based on probability instead of true for all cases; an enthymeme thus resembles a syllogism but is more rhetorical than it is logical]. Correspondences: *Aeolus*—Crawford; *Incest* [since Aeolus gave his six daughters to his six sons in marriage]—Journalism; *Floating Island* [Homer describes Aeolus's island as "adrift upon the sea, ringed round with brazen ramparts on a sheer cliffside" (10:3–4; Fitzgerald, p. 177)]—the Press.

The Linati schema lists as Persons: "Aeolus, Sons, Telemachus, Mentor, Ulysses (2)," and remarks that the Sense (Meaning) of the episode is "The Mockery of Victory."

7.3 (116:3). Nelson's pillar – See 6.293n. The area around the pillar in Sackville (now O'Connell) Street functioned as the central terminal and departure point for most of Dublin's trams (all electric by 1904; the last line stopped service in July 1949).

7.4–13 (116:4–14). Blackrock, Kingston and Dalkey . . . Harold's Cross . . . Rathgar and Terenure . . . Palmerston Park – These are the names of some of the tramlines that started from Nelson's Pillar. Many of the final destinations were near one another (as Sandymount Green and tower), but the trams followed different routes in a system that in 1904 was re-garded as the most efficient and "modern" in Europe.

7.4 (116:4). Blackrock, Kingstown and Dalkey – Suburban communities on Dublin Bay southeast of Dublin five, six, and eight miles, respectively.

7.4–5 (116:4–6). Clonskea, Rathgar . . . Upper Rathmines – All in the inland area south of central Dublin (two to two and a half miles from Nelson's Pillar).

7.5–6 (116:6–7). Sandymount Green . . . Ringsend and Sandymount Tower – Ringsend is on the south bank of the Liffey at its mouth, Sandymount Green is in Sandymount less than a mile to the south, and the tower is one-half mile south-southeast of the green.

7.6 (116:7). Harold's Cross – On the southern outskirts of metropolitan Dublin.

7.6–7 (116:7–8). Dublin United Tramway Company's – The usual term for three companies that shared the same offices and were united under a common board of directors and a common manager: Dublin United Tramways Co., Ltd.; The Dublin United Tramways Co.; and Dublin Southern District Tramways Co.

7.15 (116:16). general post office – Fronts on Sackville (now O'Connell) Street between Henry Street and Prince's Street North, just southwest of Nelson's Pillar, which stood in the middle of the street.

7.17 (116:19). E.R. – Initials for *Edward Rex* (Edward VII of England).

7.21–22 (116:24). Prince's stores – A warehouse at 13 Prince's Street North, halfway between the General Post Office and the newspaper offices of the *Freeman's Journal* and the *Evening Telegraph.*

7.22 (116:24). float – A flat-topped wagon with a low body for carrying heavy objects.

7.25 (116:27). Red Murray – Joyce's uncle John Murray's nickname; see Ellmann, p. 19.

7.25 (116:27). Alexander Keyes – An Alexander Keyes is listed at 5–6 Ballsbridge under "Grocers &c.," "Trades Directory, Dublin & Suburbs," in *Thom's* 1904 (p. 2066). Keyes is not listed in "List of the Nobility, Gentry, Merchants, and Traders, Public Offices &c &c."

---

1 See Appendix, pp. 635–43, for an annotation of the "Art" of this episode.

(pp. 1795ff.); and the "County Dublin Directory" (p. 1635) lists not Keyes but "Fagan Bros. Grocers, wine and spirit merchants" at 5–6 Ballsbridge. Under "List of the Nobility" (p. 1866), Fagan Brothers appear as grocers at 103–104 and 212 Great Britain Street; under "Dublin Street Directory" (p. 1433), 103–104 Great Britain Street, "Fagan Brothers, family grocers and wine merchants, 'The Blue Lion' . . . Bernard P. Fagan," and (p. 1434) 202 Great Britain Street, "Fagan Brothers, grocers, tea, wine and spirit merchants; James J. Fagan." This suggests that the real Keyes was manager of Fagan Brothers' branch in Ballsbridge; and that fiction has elevated Keyes to ownership of the company, including the company's "house in Kilkenny" (which Bloom mentions 7.155–56 [120:38–39]). Adams (p. 174) notes that "Keyes was a member of the jury that tried the Childs murder case," though Joyce does not use this circumstance in the novel.

7.26–27 (116:29). the *Telegraph* office – The offices of the *Evening Telegraph* (evening daily) were in the same large rambling building as the offices of the *Freeman's Journal and National Press* (morning daily). The two newspapers were closely associated, both owned by the same company, Freeman's Journal, Ltd., which also published the *Weekly Freeman and National Press, Sporting News,* and *Sport.*

7.28 (116:30). Ruttledge's office – Ellmann (p. 289) describes him as the "cashier of the newspaper"; Adams (p. 216) describes him as the "advertising manager." The combination of the two would make him business manager of Freeman's Journal, Ltd.

7.28 (116:30). Davy Stephens – A conspicuous Dublin character who styled himself the "prince of the news vendors" and was called "Sir" Davy Stephens. He kept a newsstand at Kingstown (now Dun Laoghaire) and had a de facto monopoly on newspaper sales to mailboat passengers. He was witty and uninhibited, and anecdotes about an amusing confrontation between Stephens and King Edward VII when the latter visited Ireland in 1903 provide for the epithet "a king's courier."

7.34 (117:5). a par – A paragraph; that is, a short feature story as a sort of free advertisement.

7.38–39 (117:9–10). WILLIAM BRAYDEN . . . SANDYMOUNT – William Henry Brayden (1865–1933), an Irish barrister and editor of the *Freeman's Journal* (1892–1916). Address: Oaklands, Serpentine Avenue, Sandymount.

7.52–53 (117:28–29). Our Saviour . . . Mary, Martha – See 5.289–91n.

7.53 (117:30). Mario the tenor – Giovanni Matteo Mario, cavaliere de Candia (1810–83), an Italian tenor, made his last stage appearance in 1871 (when Bloom was five years old).

7.58 (117:35). *Martha* – A light opera (1847) in five acts by the German composer Friedrich von Flotow (1812–83). Plot: In Act I, Lady Harriet Durham, maid of honor to Queen Anne of England, disguises herself as "Martha," a servant girl, and with her maid Nancy, also disguised, goes to Richmond Country Fair to escape for a moment the stultifying life of the court. Act II: At the fair "Martha" and Nancy meet Lionel and Plunkett, two well-to-do farmers who have come to the fair to hire servant girls. "Martha" and Nancy unwittingly enter a binding contract as their servants. Act III: At the farmhouse, confusions of work and love: boisterously Plunkett-Nancy; touchingly, Lionel-"Martha," whose relationship is characterized by Martha's song "'Tis the Last Rose of Summer." Then the girls escape back to court. Act IV: Lionel mourns appropriately ("M'appari"; see Simon Dedalus's song (11.587–751 [271:25–276:6]), and Plunkett and Lionel accidentally meet Lady Harriet and the fashionable Nancy. The girls again escape. Act V: Lionel loses his reason as the result of his grief and does not even respond when he becomes (!) earl of Derby or when Lady Harriet visits him. Nancy and Plunkett stage a repeat performance of Richmond Fair; Lionel meets his "Martha"; his reason is restored; marriage; happy ending.

7.59–60 (117:36–37). *Co-ome thou lost . . . dear one* – From Lionel's Lament (Act IV), as freely translated into a popular nineteenth-century song: "Forever lost, I love you! / Sweet as a dream, / Quickly come, as quickly gone. / You are all I'm longing for! / Come thou lost one, / Come thou dear one, / Bring the joys I knew before; / Come thou lost one, / Come thou dear one, / You must be mine evermore."

7.62 (118:2). His grace phoned down twice this morning – The Most Reverend William J. Walsh (1841–1921), the archbishop of Dublin (unless "his grace" is slang for the editor, or for the publisher, Thomas Sexton). Ellmann (p. 288) notes that Sexton, a dedicated Parnellite, carried on a prolonged feud with Archbishop Walsh after the archbishop had roundly condemned Parnell at the time of the divorce scandal. Sexton's newspapers, the *Freeman's Journal* and the *Evening Telegraph,* played down Archbishop Walsh's activities and played up the activities of Michael Cardinal Logue (1840–1924), the archbishop of Armagh.

7.74 (118:15). clanking drums – The sound effects are reminiscent of the daily "royal feast / . . . and winds that pipe / 'round hollow courts" in Aeolus's palace in *The Odyssey* (10:10–11; Fitzgerald, p. 177).

7.75 (118:16). Nannetti's – Joseph Patrick Nannetti (1851–1915), the Irish-Italian master printer and politician. He was member of Parliament from the College Division of Dublin (1900–1906)—thus, "Member for College green" (7.87–88 [118:31])—as well as a member of the Dublin Corporation. He was lord mayor of Dublin in 1906–7. According to the *Evening Telegraph,* at 2:00 P.M., 16 June 1904, Nannetti was asking questions in Parliament about the prohibition of Irish games in Phoenix Park. Joyce moves this occurrence to the following day.

7.87 (118:30). Ireland my country – Who qualified as Irish was a question much discussed in the columns of Arthur Griffith's *United Irishman* (founded in 1901). The purists argued that "only Gaels" were truly Irish; the more liberal view was that any "Irish-born man," in Thomas Osborne Davis's (1814–45) phrase, should be affirmed as Irish. It is interesting that the purist position would deny the distinction "Irish" to many outstanding Irish-born people, including Swift, Sheridan, and Burke, Grattan and the members of his Parliament, Wolfe Tone and most of the United Irishmen, Parnell, Yeats and Synge, the Irish-born Italian Nannetti, and of course, the Irish-born Bloom. A landmark purist document in this controversy is Daniel Corkery's *Synge and Anglo-Irish Literature* (Dublin, 1931), and the controversy has continued to this day. Many Irish still ask: "Why do you Americans have such a high regard for Yeats when he's not one of us?"

7.88 (118:31–32). workaday worker tack – Nannetti argued that he was not a professional politician but a workingman who pursued a political career on the side.

7.89–90 (118:33). the official gazette – The *Dublin Gazette,* printed and published under the authority of His Majesty's Stationery Office on Tuesday and Friday each week. It printed legal notices, etc., in addition to what Bloom regards as "stale news."

7.90 (118:33–34). Queen Anne is dead – Queen Anne (1665–1714; queen of Great Britain and Ireland 1702–14). Addison announced this news in the *Spectator* long after it had become publicly known. The sentence thus became a famous example of and proverbial expression for stale news.

7.91–92 (119:1–2). Demesne situate . . . barony of Tinnahinch – Tinnehinch House on the Dargle in the parish of Rosenallis in County Laois (formerly Queens County) twelve miles south-southeast of Dublin, was presented to Henry Grattan (1746–1820), Irish statesman and orator, by the Irish Parliament in 1797 "in appreciation of his noble exertions on behalf of Irish Independence and in order that he might end in peace a life that had been so laborious." Grattan had been a leader in the successful Irish campaign for increased legislative independence in 1782. He retired in 1797 but came out of retirement to oppose the Act of Union (1799–1800) and to serve as a member of Parliament when the passage of the act had displaced Irish political power to London. In Ireland "townlands" are subdivisions of parishes varying considerably in area. They are regarded as delineations of ancient land-holdings. The phrases Bloom recalls have the official ("stale news") flavor of the public announcements the *Dublin Gazette* published.

7.92–93 (119:2–4). To all whom . . . exported from Ballina – The *Weekly Freeman* carried a column entitled "Market News" that listed, in prose of the sort Bloom recalls, sales of livestock in Dublin and environs. Ballina is a market town and seaport of relatively little importance on the west coast of Ireland in County Mayo.

7.94 (119:4). Nature notes – The *Weekly Freeman* carried a page devoted to "nature notes" and to advice on agriculture and animal husbandry.

7.94 (119:4). Cartoons – The *Weekly Freeman* carried a feature entitled "Our Cartoon." It was not a caricature but a verse or jingle, usually political and satiric.

7.94 (119:4–5). Phil Blake's weekly Pat and Bull story – After Pat and Mike, traditional Irish-American comic figures, and cock and bull, or an Irish bull—a mental juxtaposition of incongruous ideas that provides the sensation but not the sense of a connection; see 3.79n.

7.94–95 (119:5). Uncle Toby's page for tiny tots – In 1904 the *Weekly Freeman* carried a feature entitled "Uncle Remus' Address to his Nieces and Nephews," which included puzzles, games, and essay competitions for children.

7.95–96 (119:6–7). Country bumpkin's queries . . . cure for flatulence – One of the features in the *Weekly Freeman* was entitled "Our Letterbox." It carried replies to questions of the sort Bloom contemplates.

7.97 (119:8). M.A.P. – M(*ainly*) A(*bout*) P(*eople*), a penny weekly published every Wednesday, edited by T. P. O'Connor; see 7.687m. The weekly advertised itself as "Best, Brightest, Most Brilliant of all the Society Weeklies . . . Without M.A.P. your Daily Paper is—WHAT? Well, just a string of names. With M.A.P. it becomes a fascinating panorama of the personalities of notable people with whom M.A.P. has put you on as intimate and friendly a footing as you are with your next-door neighbor—possibly a little more so." Bloom's "mainly all pictures" refers not to O'Connor's weekly but to the photo-engraved supplements that were a popular feature of Sunday newspapers like the *Weekly Freeman and National Press* in the opening decades of this century.

7.99 (119:11). Double marriage of sisters . . . Cuprani too, printer – A second-generation Dubliner of Italian extraction, Menotti Vincent (Tony) Caprani (not Cuprani) (c. 1869–1932) was a member of the chapel (the printer's union) of the *Freeman's Journal* in the early 1900s. According to an article by his grandson Vincent Caprani ("James Joyce and the Grandfather," *Ireland of the Welcomes* [Dublin, Jan.–Feb. 1982]), he and a brother married two O'Connor sisters in the double wedding Bloom recalls (suggested by Vincent Deane).

7.100 (119:11–12). More Irish than the Irish – Dog Latin: *Hibernicis ipsis Hibernior*, a phrase traditionally quoted against those guilty of Irish bulls; see 7.94n.

7.106 (119:20). Soon be calling him my lord mayor – Nannetti became lord mayor of Dublin in 1906.

7.106 (119:20). Long John – Fanning (fictional), subsheriff of Dublin, described in

"Grace," *Dubliners*, as "the registration agent and mayor maker of the city."

7.119 (119:33). Meagher's – A public house at 4 Earl Street North, in the center of Dublin just north of the Liffey.

7.141 (120:20). HOUSE OF KEY(E)S – The lower house of the Parliament of the Isle of Man. The island was governed by the king or queen in council, the governor in council, and the House of Keys; in other words, the island enjoyed (as Ireland did not) a qualified home rule. The House was originally an oligarchy, but after 1866 its members were chosen by popular election. "Keys" also suggests the "Power of the Keys," the supreme power of Church government vested in the pope as the successor of St. Peter (see Matthew 16:19).

7.142 (120:21). Two crossed keys – The emblem of the House of Keys.

7.152 (120:34–35). that *voglio* – See 4.327n.

7.155 (120:38). Kilkenny – A county and a cathedral town seventy-four miles south-southwest of Dublin.

7.173 (121:21). phiz – Physiognomy.

7.175 (121:23). flyboard – The board on which the printing press deposits the printed sheets.

7.175 (121:23). quirefolded – Four sheets folded into eight pages.

7.181 (121:30). the archbishop's letter – Appears in fiction but does not appear in the day's *Freeman* or *Evening Telegraph*; see 7.62n.

7.184 (121:33). Monks – Apart from the context, identity and significance unknown.

7.184 (121:33). castingbox – A box used for taking casts for stereotyping.

7.193 (122:4–5). August . . . horseshow month. Ballsbridge – Ballsbridge is on the southeastern outskirts of Dublin. The *Official Guide to Dublin* (1958) describes the "great Horse Show" in August as the "most celebrated event in Dublin's social and sporting calendar." The show is held at the Royal Dublin Society's Agricultural Premises in Ballsbridge and "attracts sportsmen and lovers of horseflesh from every corner of the earth." The society was founded in 1731 for "the advancement of agriculture and other branches of industry and for the advancement of science and art." The Horse Show was held 23–26 August in 1904.

7.195 (122:6). DAYFATHER – Father of the chapel for the day staff—in effect, a shop steward; the chapel was an association of the workers in a printing office for dealing with questions that affected their interests.

7.199 (122:10–11). found drowned – See 3.471n.

7.201 (122:13). working the machine in the parlour – Working at a sewing machine. The implication is that she did piecework or was self-employed as a seamstress.

7.201 (122:14). Plain Jane – Proverbial for a woman whose manners and dress are simple to the point of severity; after jane or jean, the twilled cotton cloth used in the manufacture of overalls, etc.

7.203 (122:15–16). AND IT WAS THE FEAST OF THE PASSOVER – Biblical, after John 2:13, "And the Jews' passover was at hand"; see also John 6:4 and 11:55 and elsewhere in the Gospels.

7.206 (122:20). his hagadah book – The Hebrew word *haggadah* means "a telling," after the injunction "and thou shalt tell thy son on that day"; that is, at the first seder, on the first day of the Feast of Passover when the story of the exodus of the children of Israel from Egypt is brought "into present immediacy" by being retold and acted out with ritual gestures in a religious ceremony in the home.

7.207 (122:21). Pessach – Passover.

7.207 (122:21). Next year in Jerusalem – The final phrase of the home ceremony on the first night of Passover. It climaxes a prayer to God to "rebuild . . . Jerusalem, the city of holiness, speedily in our days and bring us up into its midst."

7.208–9 (122:22–23). that brought us . . . house of bondage – In the *Haggadah* this central theme of the feast recurs three times, at the beginning, toward the middle, and toward the end: "by strength of hand the Lord, our God, brought us out of Egypt, from the house of bondage . . . and because Thou, the Lord, our God, didst bring us forth from the land of Egypt, and didst redeem us from the house of

bondage. . . . Thou, O Lord, our God, didst redeem us from Egypt and deliver us from the house of bondage." Cf. Exodus 13:3, 13–14.

7.209 (122:23). alleluia – The Latin and Greek form of the Hebrew *Hallelujah,* "Praise ye the Lord."

7.209 (122:23–24). *Shema Israel Adonai Elohenu* – Hebrew: "Hear, oh Israel, the Lord our God." The words *Adonai Echad* ("the Lord is One") complete the chant, which is known as the Shema (Deuteronomy 6:4).

7.210 (122:24). the other – That is, the Shema, which Bloom associates with the ceremonies of the second seder, although it is not actually included in either seder. It is mentioned by name in both, in a little story about several rabbis who got so engrossed in telling about the exodus from Egypt that their pupils had to remind them: "Our teachers, the time has arrived for the recitation of the morning Shema!" The Shema is part of the daily morning and evening worship services in the synagogue.

7.210 (122:24–25). Then the twelve brothers, Jacob's sons – Bloom associates Jacob's twelve sons (Genesis 35:22–27) with the twelve tribes of Israel. The second seder includes a cumulative chant: "Who Knows One?" which ends with the question, "Who knows thirteen?" and the answer: "I know thirteen. Thirteen are the attributes of Divinity; twelve are the tribes of Israel; eleven are the stars of Joseph's dream; ten are the commandments; nine are the months of pregnancy; eight are the days of circumcision; seven are the days of the Sabbath-count; six are the orders of the Mishnah; five are the books of the Torah; four are the mothers; three are the fathers; two are the tables of the covenant; one is our God in the heavens and in the earth."

7.210–13 (122:25–28). And then the lamb . . . kills the cat – After the chant *Chad Gadya* ("One Kid"), which closes the second seder. Another cumulative chant, this one ends with the verse: "And the Holy One, blessed is He, came and killed the Angel of Death that slew the slaughterer that slaughtered the ox that drank the water that quenched the fire that burned the stick that beat the dog that bit the cat that ate the kid that father bought for two zuzim. One kid, one kid."

7.213 (122:28). Sounds a bit . . . into it well – "*Chad Gadya* (One Kid), in outward seeming a childish lilt, has been interpreted as the history of successive empires that devastate and swallow one another (Egypt, Assyria, Babylon, Persia, etc.). The kid, bottommost and most injured of all, is, of course, the people of Israel. The killing of the Angel of Death marks the day when the kingdom of the Almighty will be established on earth; then, too, Israel will live in perfect redemption in the promised Land" (Abraham Regelson, *The Haggadah of Passover, A Faithful English Rendering* [New York, 1944], p. 63).

7.219–20 (122:35). Citron's house – Cf. 4.205n. *Thom's* 1904 lists only twenty-five house numbers in St. Kevin's Parade and lists Citron at no. 17.

7.224 (123:5). Thom's – Alexander Thom & Co., Ltd., printers and publishers; the *Dublin Gazette*, published by the king's authority every Tuesday and Friday; office for the sale of parliamentary papers and acts of Parliament; office of *Thom's Official Directory;* government printing and book-binding establishment; 87–89 Abbey Street Middle, next door but one to the offices of the *Freeman's Journal* (*Thom's* 1904, p. 1409).

7.226–27 (123:6–7). Citronlemon? Ah, the soap – The odor associates the soap with the citron (*Ethrog*) central in the ritual of the Jewish Feast of Tabernacles (Sukkoth); see 4.210–11n.

7.236 (123:17). ERIN, GREEN GEM OF THE SILVER SEA – See "Let Erin Remember the Days of Old" (3.302–3n), and compare John Philpot Curran's (1750–1817) "Cuisle Mo Chroidhe" (*Cushla Ma Chree;* "pulse of my heart"), first stanza: "Dear Erin, how sweetly thy green bosom rises! / An emerald set in the ring of the sea! / Each blade of thy meadows my faithful heart prizes, / Thou queen of the west! the world's *Cuisle mo chroidhe.*" This headline may also involve an allusion to John of Gaunt's praise of England in Shakespeare's *Richard II:* "This precious stone set in the silver sea" (II.i.46).

7.237 (123:18). the ghost walks – Theatrical and journalistic slang for "salaries are being paid." "On payday Ruttledge [7.28n] carried a money box around with him, paying out from office to office of the old building; and his coming was announced by the phrase, 'the ghost walks'" (Ellmann, p. 289). Also (and unbeknownst to him) Bloom is playing the part of the Ghost in *Hamlet;* see 8.67–68 (152:39–40).

7.237 (123:18). professor MacHugh – A par-

tial portrait of Hugh MacNeill, whom Ellmann characterizes as "a scholar of the classical modern languages, clever and lazy" (p. 289); in other words, not quite a "professor."

7.243–47 (123:25–30). *Or again, note . . . giants of the forest* – Source, if any outside the language of fiction, unknown.

7.250 (123:33). Changing his drink – Popularly regarded as a sure and speedy way to get intoxicated.

7.254–55 (124:1–3). And Xenophon looked . . . on the sea – After Byron's lines, "The mountains look on Marathon— / And Marathon looks on the sea," from a lyric interpolated in *Don Juan*, "Canto the Third" (1821), between stanzas 86 and 87. The Greek historian Xenophon (c. 434–c. 354 B.C.) was one of the leaders of the Ten Thousand (see 1.80n) as well as the chief historian of the expedition; thus he did look on the sea and join in the victory cry, "Thalatta! Thalatta!" Marathon, on the east coast of Attica twenty-two miles from Athens, was the scene of a decisive battle in 490 B.C. in which the Athenians defeated the Persians. Marathon does physically "look on" the sea. If Xenophon "looked upon Marathon," he did so in retrospect, as historian and as yet another Greek involved in a military struggle against the Persians.

7.260 (124:9). Bladderbags – Nonsense; a silly, foolish person; a babbler.

7.262 (124:11). Old Chatterton, the vice chancellor – Hedges Eyre Chatterton (1820–1910), queen's counsel (1858), solicitor general (1866), attorney general (1867), also member of Parliament for Dublin University and vice-chancellor of Ireland, a judge appointed to act for, or as the assistant to, the chancellor.

7.263 (124:13). Subleader – In newspaper practice the account of a well-known person's life and accomplishments is kept on file. For the obituary it would be updated and added to the "leader," the paragraph announcing the death, its time, place, and, if relevant, cause.

7.264–65 (124:14–15). Johnny, make room for your uncle – In the late nineteenth century, a common saying addressed to the younger man or men in a group. The saying derived from a popular song and patter routine in which one "Fred Jones, Hatter, of Leicester Square" complains of the difficulties caused by a "spoiled boy" whose widowed mother is the object of Jones's attentions. The mother introduces Jones to the boy as "your uncle." Chorus: "Tommy, make room for your uncle, / There's a little dear, / Tommy, make room for your uncle, / I want him to sit here."

7.266 (124:17). gale days – Days when periodical or installment payments are due.

7.270 (124:20). *fragment of Cicero – (106–43 B.C.), Roman orator and statesman. The irony turns on Cicero's reputation as an extraordinary rhetorician who tried to hold a middle ground between the studied simplicity of diction associated with the Greek orator Demosthenes (384?–322 B.C.) and an "Asiatic" floridity then popular in Rome.

7.276 (124:26). Dan Dawson's – See 6.151n.

7.282 (124:32). J. J. O'Molloy – A solicitor down on his luck, apparently fictional, though Stanislaus Joyce (*My Brother's Keeper* [New York, 1958], p. 188), tells the story of a conversation Joyce had with the dean of studies at Belvedere, a conversation that provided some of the material for *A Portrait* 5:A. Stanislaus says that the "successful" Mr. Moonan, whom the dean cites as an example to Stephen in *A Portrait*, is "named in the Aeolus episode in *Ulysses*"; if so, Mr. Moonan and J. J. O'Molloy may both be partial portraits of the same unknown person.

7.300 (125:10). Lenehan – Appears as a character in "Two Gallants," *Dubliners*.

7.301–2 (125:12). the pink pages – The *Evening Telegraph*, Last Pink Edition, printed, as the name suggests, on light pink paper.

7.303–4 (125:14). Debts of honour – Debts not recoverable by law, such as gambling debts, personal obligations to relatives and friends, etc.

7.304 (125:14). Reaping the whirlwind – The prophet Hosea threatens Israel with destruction for its idolatry and impiety: "For they have sown the wind, and they shall reap the whirlwind" (Hosea 8:7); see 7.995n.

7.304–5 (125:15). D. and T. Fitzgerald – Solicitors, 20 St. Andrews Street, in north central Dublin. Senior partner: Thomas Fitzgerald, J.P. County Limerick, crown solicitor for County Donegal and the County and City of Londonderry, commissioner of affidavits, and law agent for the commissioner of Irish Lights.

7.305–6 (125:15–17). Their wigs to . . . statue in Glasnevin – Barristers wear wigs as emblems of their intelligence the way the statue Bloom noticed in the cemetery wore a heart as a symbol of devotion.

7.306–7 (125:17). the *Express* – The *Daily Express*, an Irish newspaper (1851–1921), essentially conservative and opposed to Irish aspirations; its announced policy involved "the development of industrial resources" and a reconciliation of "the rights and impulses of Irish nationality with the demands and obligations of imperial dominions."

7.307 (125:18). Gabriel Conroy – The central character in "The Dead," *Dubliners*, who writes occasional book reviews for the *Daily Express* in fiction, as Joyce did in real life.

7.308 (125:19). the *Independent* – The *Irish Daily Independent*, a Dublin newspaper founded by Parnell after his fall, though it did not begin to be published (18 December 1891) until over two months after Parnell's death. It quickly passed into the hands of anti-Parnellites and was acquired in 1900 by William Martin Murphy (see 12.237n). In effect, the *Independent* veered from a radical, pro-Parnell policy to a conservative, even reactionary, anti-Parnellite stance.

7.309–10 (125:21). Hot and cold in the same breath – In Aesop's fable "The Man and the Satyr" (late sixth century B.C.), a man, lost on a cold winter night, is rescued by a satyr. The man blows on his hands, to warm them he says when the satyr inquires. When they reach the satyr's home the satyr gives the man a dish of hot porridge, which he blows on to cool it. The satyr throws the man out, saying he will have nothing to do with someone who can blow hot and cold with the same breath.

7.311 (125:22–23). Go for one another bald-headed – Impetuously, wholeheartedly; when men wore wigs, they frequently discarded them when the going got rough. See 13.247n.

7.326 (126:1). HIS NATIVE DORIC – A dialect, especially Scots dialect as opposed to English.

7.325 (126:2). The moon . . . He forgot Hamlet – That is, the "logic" of the speech will inevitably carry Dawson to a rhetorical flourish about Ireland by moonlight (as it does), but Dawson "forgot" to continue the progression to Ireland at dawn, as Horatio does in *Hamlet*, "But, look, the morn, in russet mantle clad, / Walks o'er the dew of yon high eastward hill" (I.i. 166–67).

7.332 (126:9). welshcombed – A "Welsh comb" is the thumb and four fingers (because the Welsh were popularly regarded as a wild and unkempt people).

7.336 (126:13). Doughy Daw – See 6.151n.

7.337 (126:14). WETHERUP – "Evidently he was W. Wetherup of 37 Gloucester Street Upper, who served for a while in the office of the Collector-General of Rates with John S. Joyce" (Adams, p. 217).

7.338–39 (126:16). like hot cake – To "sell like hot cakes" is to sell extraordinarily well.

7.341 (126:18–19). inland revenue office – In the Custom House, Dublin. The office was responsible for the collection of "duties" (excise, income, and stamp taxes and death duty) in Ireland.

7.341 (126:19). the motor – Automobiles were not numerous enough to require registration and license numbers in Ireland before 1903, and in 1904 automobiles were still something of an event in Dublin's streets.

7.348 (126:26). the sham squire – Francis Higgins (1746–1802), so called because, though he was an attorney's clerk in Dublin, he married a respectable young woman by palming himself off as a country gentleman. He went from that to the ownership of gambling houses and eventually to the ownership of the *Freeman's Journal*, which he used to libel Henry Grattan and other Irish patriots. He was also an informer and accepted a bribe of £1,000 for revealing Lord Edward Fitzgerald's hiding place to Major Sirr in 1798; see 10.785–86n.

7.359–63 (127:2–6). North Cork militia! . . . In Ohio! – It is doubtful whether this bit of scrambled history can ever be unscrambled. The North Cork Militia (loyal to the Crown in the Rebellion of 1798) enjoyed the dubious distinction of having disgraced itself and suffered humiliating defeats in every action it was involved in during the rebellion. Apparently the editor's recall of this "famous" militia is triggered by the professor's mention of the Sham Squire, another anti-Irish Irishman whose behavior during the rebellion was less than glorious. The link between that militia and Ohio can only be called dubious. Territorial militias were not subject to service outside their home countries until 1827, and then only in the British Isles. But when the Anglo-Irishman Gen. Edward Braddock (1695–1755) attempted the ill-fated invasion of the Ohio Valley in June 1755, he had as the backbone of his expeditionary force two British regiments, the 44th and the 48th, which had been stationed in Cork and had been allowed to recruit themselves up to strength from the Cork and North Cork militias before they embarked for America in January 1755. To say the least, those regiments did not win "every time." "Spanish officers" is even more troublesome: the 44th and the 48th were commanded by men named Halkett and Dunbar, and the North Cork Militia in 1798 was commanded by men named Foote, Jacob, Boyd, and Le Hunt. It is just possible that the editor's excursion into mid-eighteenth-century wars involves a fantastic association of the North Cork Militia with the Irish Brigade (expatriate Irish who served with the French in the eighteenth century). The Irish Brigade did distinguish itself in action and did have a rather tenuous tradition of being commanded by officers of Spanish-Irish descent.

7.366 (127:9). jigs – After *jig*, to hop or skip around, referring to the inconsistent mental processes of advanced alcoholism.

7.367–68 (127:10–11). Ohio! . . . My Ohio! – Source in song or rhyme unknown.

7.369 (127:12). cretic – A foot composed of one short syllable between two long syllables: /˘/.

7.370 (127:13). HARP EOLIAN – An aeolian harp is a stringed instrument designed to be played by the winds (of Aeolus) rather than by human fingers. The harp was the instrument of the Celtic bards and is a national symbol for Ireland. "Harp" is also slang for an Irish Catholic.

7.383 (127:28). Canada swindle case – A man known as (i.e., alias) Saphiro, Sparks, or James Wought was accused, tried, and convicted of swindling, among others, one Zaretsky by promising to secure passage to Canada for 20s.

(The lowest advertised fare for steerage passage in 1904 was £2.) The case was remanded 17 June 1904, and Saphiro was convicted and sentenced 11 July.

7.387 (128:2). *Sport's tissues – Racing forms prepared by *Sport*, a weekly penny paper, published on Saturday by the Freeman's Journal, Ltd., advertised as containing "all the sporting news of the week."

7.388–89 (128:4). O. Madden – Sceptre's jockey that day, contrary to the *Freeman's Journal*'s morning announcement of A. Taylor. Cf. 5.532n.

7.399–400 (128:16). a hurricane blowing – When Odysseus's men open the bag in which Aeolus has confined the winds (10:46–49), the ensuing storm frustrates their homecoming and drives them back to Aeolus's island. "Then every wind / roared into hurricane" (Fitzgerald, p. 178).

7.403 (128:20). Pat Farrell – Apart from the context, identity and significance unknown.

7.412 (128:30). auction rooms – Joe Dillon, auctioneer, 25 Bachelor's Walk, a section of the north quay of the Liffey, just east of the center of Dublin.

7.422 (129:7). *anno Domini* – Latin: "in the year of our Lord"; hence, "years."

7.427–28 (129:13–14). *We are the boys . . . heart and hand* – From an Irish ballad of 1798, "The Boys of Wexford." The Boys of Wexford earned part of their reputation at the expense of the North Cork Militia: "In comes the captain's daughter, / The captain of the yeos [militia], / Saying, 'Brave United Irishmen, / We'll ne'er again be foes, / A thousand pounds I'll give you / And fly from home with thee. / I'll dress myself in man's attire / And fight for liberty.' [Chorus:] We are the Boys of Wexford / Who fought with heart and hand, / To burst in twain the galling chain / And free our native land." The ballad goes on to cite the total defeat of the North Cork Militia by the Boys of Wexford at Oulart, and then ascribes the subsequent collapse of the boys to alcoholic excesses.

7.435 (129:22). Begone! . . . The world is before you – In *Paradise Lost*, when Adam and Eve are expelled from paradise, their state is described: "The World was all before them, where to choose / Thir place of rest, and Provi-

dence thir guide" (12:646–47). Miles Crawford is also playing the part of Aeolus, who at the beginning of Book 10 of *The Odyssey* sends Odysseus on his way home with kind words.

7.440 (129:27). crossblind – A window shade that pulls up from a roller at the bottom of a window.

7.448 (129:36). spaugs – Big, clumsy feet.

7.448–49 (129:36). Small nines – Up to all the dodges, all the little tricks (i.e., the newsboys).

7.449 (129:36). Steal upon larks – That is, they are clever enough to creep up on something as difficult to surprise or catch as a lark.

7.455 (130:7). the Oval – A public house at 78 Abbey Street Middle, just south of the *Freeman* offices; John J. Egan, wine and spirit merchant.

7.456 (130:7). Paddy Hooper – Patrick Hooper, a Dublin journalist who worked as a reporter for the *Freeman's Journal* and who was to be its last editor. He was the son of Alderman John Hooper of Cork; see 6.950n.

7.456 (130:7). Jack Hall – J. B. Hall, a Dublin journalist with a considerable local reputation as a raconteur.

7.461 (130:14). pretty well on – Half drunk.

7.464 (130:19). CALUMET – The American Indian peace pipe.

7.471–72 (130:28–29). *'Twas rank and . . . charmed thy heart* – From an aria in Act III of *The Rose of Castile* (1857) (see 7.591n), an opera by the Anglo-Irish composer Michael William Balfe (1808–70). The aria is sung by Manuel, the king of Castile in disguise as a muleteer, to Elvira, the Rose of Castile: "'Twas rank and fame that tempted thee, / 'Twas empire charmed thy heart; / But love was wealth, the world to me, / Then false one, let us part. / The prize I fondly deemed my own, / Another's you may be; / For ah! with love, life's gladness flown, / Leaves grief to wed, to wed with me, / Leaves grief alone to me, / With love, life's gladness flown, / Leaves grief alone to me. // Tho' lowly bred and humbly born, / No loftier heart than mine, / Unlov'd by thee, my pride would scorn / To share the crown that's thine. / I sought no empire save the heart, / Which mine can never be; / Yes, false one, we had better part, / Since love lives not in thee."

7.478 (130:35). *Imperium romanum* – Latin: "the Roman Empire."

7.479 (130:36). Brixton – A London suburb regarded at the turn of the century as the prototype of the drab machine-made life of the urban-industrial world. George Moore (see 9.274n) remarked, on England and her language: "To begirdle the world with Brixton seems to be her ultimate destiny. And we, sitting on the last verge, see into the universal suburb, in which a lean man with glasses on his nose and a black bag in his hand is always running after his bus" (quoted in Edward Gwynn, *Edward Martyn and the Irish Revival* [London, 1930], pp. 242–43).

7.483 (131:5). THE GRANDEUR THAT WAS ROME – From Edgar Allan Poe's (1809–49) "To Helen" (1831, 1845), stanza 2: "On desperate seas long wont to roam, / Thy hyacinth hair, thy classic face, / Thy Naiad airs have brought me home / To the glory that was Greece, / And the grandeur that was Rome."

7.489 (131:12). *Cloacae* – Sewers or toilet bowls.

7.490–91 (131:13–14). *It is meet . . . altar to Jehovah* – This seems less a direct quotation than a generalization of the ancient Jewish belief that an altar must be constructed as witness or testimony to the taking of new lands or to release from captivity. In Matthew 17:4, after Peter and two of the other disciples have seen Jesus "transfigured," Peter says, "Lord, it is good for us to be here: if thou wilt, let us make here three tabernacles; one for thee, and one for Moses, and one for Elias."

7.493 (131:16). (on our shore he never set it) – There is considerable evidence that the Mediterranean world knew of Ireland and carried on some commerce with the island (see 12.1248–50n and 12.1251n). But the Romans were apparently content with commercial relations and did not attempt to establish a foothold for conquest. Irish historians have debated this point, some arguing that it was not Roman policy but Irish valor that kept the Romans away. But Roman forbearance was consistent with Roman imperial policy, which preferred direct overland communication with conquered territories. Furthermore, from a Roman point of view the conquest of Ireland would have meant diverting troops much needed in Britain and elsewhere in the empire, a cost not balanced by the potential returns.

7.493 (131:16). cloacal obsession – As Thornton (p. 114) points out, this phrase has been borrowed from the English novelist-critic H. G. Wells (1866–1946), whose review of *A Portrait of the Artist as a Young Man* was rather severe ("James Joyce," *New Republic* 10 [10 March 1917], p. 159). "Like Swift and another living Irish writer, Mr. Joyce has a cloacal obsession. He would bring back into the general picture of life aspects which modern drainage and modern decorum have taken out of ordinary intercourse and conversation."

7.497 (131:20). Guinness's – Lenehan's pun (a common pun in Dublin) conjoins Genesis with Guinness's, the famous Dublin brewery. Since Genesis 1 is the story of the Creation, the pun involves the triad: as the Jews were to their altars, and the Romans to their waterclosets, so the Irish are to their drink.

7.500 (131:23). Roman law – The blend of common law and legislation that governed the citizens of Rome. In modern English usage, the term "civil law" designates all the existing systems of private law that are in the main based on Roman law.

7.501 (131:24). Pontius Pilate is its prophet – As Jesus was the prophet whose "kingdom is not of this world" (John 18:36), so Pilate is the prophet whose kingdom is of this world. When asked to condemn Jesus, Pilate asserts: "I find in him no fault at all" (John 18:38). In spite of this legal finding, Pilate condemned Jesus in order to forestall what Pilate regarded as the threat of insurrection in Jerusalem. MacHugh's remark echoes the Moslem profession of faith: "There is no god but God [Allah]; and Mohammed is his Prophet."

7.502 (131:26). *chief baron Palles – Christopher Palles (1831–1920), Irish barrister and lord chief baron of the Exchequer, that is, the chief judge in the court of Exchequer, a division of the High Court of Justice in Ireland.

7.503 (131:27). the royal university – Not an institution of higher learning, but an examining and degree-granting institution in Dublin. It was established by the University Education Act of 1879 and organized in 1880 to align higher education in Ireland with English academic standards.

7.505 (131:30). Mr. O'Madden Burke – Appears as a character in "A Mother," *Dubliners.*

7.505 (131:30). Donegal tweed – Donegal, the northwesternmost county in Ireland was (and still is) the principal producer of hand-woven tweeds. The richly colored tweeds of 1904 were considerably rougher in texture and heavier than modern tweeds because they were woven with hand-spun yarn, not with machine-spun yarn as today.

7.507 (131:33). *Entrez, mes enfants!* – French: "Enter, my children!"

7.511 (131:37). governor – Slang: "father."

7.521 (132:10). pelters – Archaic: "whoremonger, tramp, paltry person."

7.522–25 (132:12–15). On swift sail . . . to my mouth – Stephen's version of the last stanza of Douglas Hyde's "My Grief on the Sea"; see 3.397–98n.

7.535 (132:25). the Star and Garter – A hotel at 16 D'Olier Street in the southeast quadrant of Dublin near the Liffey.

7.536–37 (132:26–28). A woman brought . . . prince of Breffni – See 2.390–94 (34:39–35:2) and accompanying notes.

7.539 (132:30). a grass one – A grass widower: in 1904, a man separated from his wife. This portrait of Mr. Deasy's estranged wife suggests an ironic contrast to his role as Nestor who, Menelaus says, "had true felicity, marrying and begetting!" (*The Odyssey* 4:208; Fitzgerald, p. 71).

7.540 (132:31). Emperor's horses – See 2.333–34n.

7.540 (132:31). Habsburg – The imperial royal house of Austria-Hungary, at that time headed by Francis Joseph (1830–1916; emperor 1848–1916).

7.540–42 (132:31–33). *An Irishman saved . . . Tirconnell in Ireland – Maximilian Karl Lamoral Graf [Earl or Count] O'Donnell von [of] Tirconnell (b. 1812), the Austrian-born son of an Irish expatriate, was aide-de-camp to Emperor Francis Joseph. On 18 February 1853 he attended the emperor on his daily walk around the bastions that encircled old Vienna. When the emperor was attacked and wounded by a knife-wielding Hungarian tailor, O'Donnell knocked the would-be assassin down and prevented further attack. The emperor subse-

quently asserted that he owed his life to O'Donnell.

7.542–43 (132:34–35). Sent his heir . . . Austrian fieldmarshal now – Edward VII made several attempts to exploit his friendly relations with Emperor Francis Joseph in the hope of loosening the Austrian alliance with Germany. On a state visit to Vienna in 1903, Edward VII announced his appointment of the emperor as a field marshal of the British army. On 9 June 1904, Francis Joseph's heir, Archduke Francis Ferdinand, in the course of a state visit to England, handed Edward VII the baton of an Austrian field marshal "without any kind of ceremony."

7.543 (132:35). Wild geese – The O'Donnells in Spain and Austria were one of the most famous of the wild-goose families; see 3.163–64n.

7.546 (133:2–3). *a thankyou job – A job that is sure to merit a substantial reward.

7.549 (133:6–7). A Hungarian it was – See 7.540–42n.

7.553 (133:10). We were always loyal to lost causes – See 6.977–78n.

7.556 (133:14). time is money – The maxim, apparently coined by the Greek philosopher Theophrastus (c. 372–287 B.C.), Aristotle's favorite pupil, was popularized by Benjamin Franklin in "Advice to a Young Tradesman" (1748). Victor Hugo, in *Les Misérables* (1862), Book 4, chapter 4, wrote: "Take away *time is money* and what is left of England?"

7.557 (133:15). *Domine! – Latin: "master, possessor, ruler, lord, proprietor, owner."

7.557–58 (133:16). *Lord Jesus? Lord Salisbury? – Reference is to the fact that the spiritual and the temporal "masters" both have the same title. Robert Arthur Talbot Gascoyne Cecil, third marquess of Salisbury (1830–1903), was leader of the Conservative party in England and hence anti-Gladstone and against any concession to the Irish. He was prime minister of England 1885–86, 1886–92, and 1895–1902.

7.558 (133:16). A sofa in a westend club – Lord Salisbury asserted his "dominion" from the comfortable seclusion of an aristocratic and fashionable club in London.

7.559 (133:18). KYRIE ELEISON – Greek: "Lord have mercy [upon us]." The Kyrie forms a regular part of the Mass.

7.562 (133:21). *Kyrios!* – Greek: "a lord or a guardian."

7.562–63 (133:22). vowels the Semite and the Saxon know not – Namely, the twentieth letter of the Greek alphabet, the vowel *upsilon*, for which there is no equivalent in Hebrew or English. It is rendered in English by the inexact equivalents *u* and *y* (as in *Kyrie*). MacHugh is alluding indirectly to the controversy about the traditions of Greek pronunciation, which were under attack in Germany around 1880 and were to be defended in an extraordinary outbreak at Oxford (1905–6).

7.566 (133:26). the catholic chivalry of Europe that foundered at Trafalgar – Napoleon's bid for mastery of the sea (and with it a firmer hold on his imperial mastery of Europe) foundered when the British fleet under Admiral Lord Nelson defeated the combined French and Spanish fleets, 21 October 1805, off the Cape of Trafalgar, twenty-nine miles northwest of the western entrance to the Strait of Gibraltar; the British thus effectively deprived Napoleon's continental empire of overseas trade and hastened its collapse. The phrase "catholic chivalry" is something of an irony when applied to the secular and leveling energies of the French Revolution and the "new aristocracy" of its Napoleonic aftermath; and, if the phrase is misread as "Catholic chivalry" (reflecting the persistent Irish misapprehension that beneath his apparent atheism Napoleon was still a Catholic at heart), the irony is even more pointed.

7.567 (133:27). *imperium* – Latin: "dominion, realm, empire."

7.567–68 (133:27–28). that went under . . . fleets at Aegospotami – The Spartans under Lysander (d. 395 B.C.) surprised the unguarded Athenian fleet and destroyed its ships and three thousand of its men at Aegospotami in Thrace in 405 B.C. This disaster virtually brought the Peloponnesian War to an end and ensured the fall of Athens.

7.568–69 (133:29–30). Pyrrhus, misled by . . . fortunes of Greece – Late in his career and after failures in Italy and Sicily, Pyrrhus launched a campaign against Sparta that appeared to have as its goal the capture of all of the Peloponnesus. The "oracle" that misled

Pyrrhus was a dream that he read as promising him success in his attempt to reduce Lacedaemon (Sparta), the capital of Laconia. He could have bypassed the town with considerable profit, but the continued effort to reduce the city depleted his forces, gave the Spartans time to bring up reinforcements, and resulted in his defeat.

7.572–73 (133:32–33). They went forth . . . they always fell – The title of a poem by William Butler Yeats in *The Rose* (1893). The poem, rewritten and retitled "The Rose of Battle," appears in the *Collected Poems* (New York, 1956), p. 37. Yeats took the initial title from Matthew Arnold's epigraph to the *Study of Celtic Literature* (London, 1867): "They came forth to battle, but they always fell."

7.574–75 (133:34–134:2). Owing to a brick . . . poor Pyrrhus! – See 2.18n.

7.582 (134:9). the *Joe Miller* – Slang: "the joke." Joe Miller was a comedian who flourished during the reign of George I of England; his jokes, published in a book that was repeatedly revised and reissued in the nineteenth century, came to be regarded as old chestnuts, corny stories.

7.583 (134:10). In mourning for Sallust – Mulligan's quip at the expense of MacHugh. Sallust, Gaius Sallustius Crispus (86–34 B.C.), was a Roman historian and active partisan of Caesar. The point of Mulligan's quip is that, while Sallust became a distinguished, though not especially accurate, historian after his retirement from public life, his public career, in the course of which he acquired a large fortune, was apparently marked by corruption and a willingness to oppress those under his command and governance.

7.591 (134:19). *The Rose of Castile – A light opera (1857) by Michael William Balfe. Plot: The queen of Leon, Elvira, is betrothed to Don Sebastian, the brother of the king of Castile. Elvira is under the impression (mistaken) that Don Sebastian has disguised himself as Manuel, a muleteer, so she disguises herself as a peasant girl in order to meet him as one belonging to his class. A group of inept conspirators, led by one Don Florio, plot to seize the throne of Castile, and to further their plot they disguise Elvira, the queen-turned-peasant-girl, as queen. (Faced with this transformation, Manuel sings "'Twas rank and fame that tempted thee"; see 7.471–72n.) The conspiratorial farce collapses, and Elvira and Manuel are reunited as peasant girl and muleteer—except that he turns out to be the king of Castile in disguise.

7.591 (134:19). wheeze – A gag or joke.

7.599 (134:29–30). communards – Members of the Commune of Paris, the left-wing insurrectionary force that held Paris from March 1871, when the German occupation troops departed, to May 1871, when the insurrection was put down by the republican government of France.

7.600 (134:31). *blown up the Bastile – The Bastille St.-Antoine, a fortress-prison in Paris, was stormed and destroyed by a revolutionary mob 14 July 1789. The date is usually regarded as marking the beginning of the French Revolution.

7.601–2 (134:32–34). Or was it you . . . General Bobrikoff – Nikolai Ivanovitch Bobrikoff (1857–1904), a Russian general, governor-general, and commander in chief of the military district of Finland (1898–1904). He was given dictatorial powers, and he used them ruthlessly to suppress Finland's constitutional liberties and to carry out the policy of Russianizing Finland. The *New York Times*, 17 June 1904, characterized him as "a typical Russian tyrant." He was assassinated by Eugene Schaumann, the son of a former Finnish senator, on 16 June 1904 at 11:00 A.M. Helsinki time; since it would have been 8:35 A.M. Dublin time, the news would have reached Dublin in the course of the morning. See 8.109n.

7.604 (135:1). OMNIUM GATHERUM – A mock-Latin cliché for a gathering of all sorts of persons or things, a confused medley.

7.617 (135:16–17). *In the lexicon of youth* – From *Richelieu* (1838), a play by the English novelist-playwright-politician Edward Bulwer-Lytton. In Act III, scene i, Richelieu sends his page, Francois, on a dangerous mission; Francois asks, "If I fail—" and Richelieu responds, "Fail—Fail? In the lexicon of youth, which fate reserves / For a bright manhood, there is no such word / As 'fail.'"

7.618 (135:18–19). See it in your face . . . idle little schemer – In *A Portrait* 1:D, Stephen, at Clongowes, has broken his glasses and cannot work. He is unjustly punished by Father Dolan, the prefect of studies, who says: "Out here, Dedalus. Lazy little schemer. I see schemer in

your face. . . . Lazy idle little loafer! . . . Broke my glasses! An old schoolboy trick! Out with your hand this moment."

7.619–20 (135:21). Great nationalist meeting in Borris-in-Ossory – Borris-in-Ossory is a fair town sixty-six miles south-southwest of Dublin. Its name is associated with pre-English Catholic Ireland and with the riches of that cultural past. In 1843 Daniel O'Connell held one of his "monster meetings" for repeal of the Act of Union there, because the town was associated with an ancient and *free* Ireland. In 1904 the Nationalists toyed with the idea of imitating O'Connell's campaign. After the deposition of Parnell in 1890, the Nationalist (Parliamentary or Home Rule) party was divided against itself under the titular leadership of John Redmond (1856–1918). Redmond's aides, Timothy Healy, William O'Brien, and John Dillon, were rivals as much as they were aides. It was not until 1900 that Redmond was able to restore a semblance of unity to the party, and even then he was not able to restore its vitality and effectiveness.

7.620 (135:22). Bulldosing – Or bulldozing, slang for a severe flogging, and, from the 1870s, for bullying or coercing by intimidation.

7.622 (135:24). Jakes McCarthy – A "jakes" is an outdoor toilet or privy; Jakes McCarthy was a pressman on the *Freeman's Journal*.

7.626 (135:29). GALLAHER – See 6.58n.

7.629 (135:32). on the shaughraun – Wandering about, unemployed.

7.629 (135:33). billiardmarking – Taking charge of a billiard room as a combination clerk and janitor.

7.629 (135:33). the Clarence – Clarence Commercial Hotel at 6–7 Wellington Quay, on the south bank of the Liffey just east of the center of Dublin.

7.631 (136:2). the smartest piece of journalism – The story Crawford tells raises questions about the legality of Gallaher's behavior. English law severely limits what can be published about a crime after individuals have been charged and before they come to trial; thus, Gallaher's device of transforming a newspaper page into a map of the decoy and escape routes may border on violation of the law. But whether Crawford's story is about the time of the crime or of the trial is far from clear. See 7.652n.

7.632–33 (136:3–4). That was in eighty-one . . . the Phoenix park – See 5.378n and 5.379n. Crawford is mistaken about the year; it was not 1881, but 1882. Also, the identities of the Invincibles involved were not revealed until Peter Carey, a member of the group, turned queen's evidence on Saturday, 10 February 1883.

7.633 (136:4). before you were born – Stephen was presumably born in 1882, as was Joyce (on 2 February); see 17.447–48 (679:22–23).

7.635 (136:7). The *New York World* – A daily New York newspaper owned by the financier Jay Gould from 1876–83. Gould used the paper to manipulate stock prices, paying little attention to its handling of the news, which was dull enough to earn the comment: "Page one was about as exciting as Gray's 'Elegy in a Country Churchyard.'" The *World* did, however, devote considerable space on 7 and 8 May 1882 to the Phoenix Park murders. When it was acquired by Joseph Pulitzer in May 1883, the *World* rapidly achieved an international reputation for hard-hitting and sensational, though accurate, reporting and for aggressive, muckraking journalism. This latter reputation seems to be the one associated with the *World* in this passage.

7.639 (136:11–12). Tim Kelly, or Kavanagh . . . Joe Brady – All three were members of the Invincibles. Joe Brady earned, whether rightly or wrongly, the reputation of having been the chief assassin. According to the evidence given at the trial, he stabbed the victims to the ground, and "Young Tim" Kelly then cut their throats. It was Brady who revealed that the primary target of the plot had been Burke (on account of his key role in the English policy of coercion). Michael Kavanagh drove the getaway cab, and it was he who was on the stand and whose testimony was broken when Carey turned queen's evidence.

7.640 (136:12–13). Where Skin-the-Goat drove the car – "Skin-the-Goat" James Fitzharris did not drive the getaway cab (Kavanagh did, taking the circuitous route Crawford describes); Fitzharris drove a decoy cab over a direct route from Phoenix Park to the center of Dublin. He was sentenced to life imprisonment but was paroled in 1902. He was nicknamed "Skin-the-Goat" because he was said to have skinned his pet goat and sold its hide to pay his drinking debts. Skin-the-Goat was not the proprietor of the cabman's shelter that Bloom and Stephen visit in the Eumaeus episode; he had

Gumley's job, minding a pile of paving stones for the Dublin Corporation (7.645–46 [136:18–19]).

7.641–42 (136:15). that cabman's shelter – See headnote to Eumaeus, p. 534.

7.642 (136:15). Butt bridge – In 1904, the easternmost of Dublin's bridges over the Liffey.

7.645 (136:18). Gumley – Whether fictional or real, another declining member of the Irish middle class.

7.652 (136:27). 17 March – St. Patrick's Day and so significantly Irish, but the date is a misleading flourish. The *Weekly Freeman* was published on Sundays, but St. Patrick's Day fell on Friday in 1882, and it is not clear whether the story Crawford tells took place at the time of the murders in May 1882 or in February 1883 during the trial, when the full story of the two cab routes became known.

7.654 (136:30). Bransome's coffee – A widely advertised coffee distributed by Bransome & Co., Ltd., of London.

7.659 (136:35). parkgate – At the southeastern entrance to Phoenix Park; the gate nearest the center of Dublin.

7.661 (136:37). viceregal lodge – The residence of the lord lieutenant of Ireland, in the northwest quadrant of the park.

7.661–62 (136:38). Knockmaroon gate – At the western extremity of Phoenix Park.

7.667–68 (137:6–7). Inchicore, Roundtown, Windy Arbour, Palmerston Park, Ranelagh – This sequence of placenames describes not the direct decoy route that Skin-the-Goat drove but the roundabout route the murderers took, looping south from Phoenix Park, then east and north to the center of Dublin. Inchicore is south of the Liffey on the western outskirts of Dublin; thus it is south of Phoenix Park. Roundtown is in Terenure, a village south of Dublin and west of the city's center, and Windy Arbour is east and slightly south of Terenure. In Windy Arbour the fugitives turned north toward Palmerston Park and Ranelagh, on the southeastern outskirts of metropolitan Dublin.

7.669 (137:7). Davy's publichouse – The Invincibles did stop for a drink at the public house of J. and T. Davy, 110A–111 Leeson Street Upper, on the outskirts of Dublin just northeast of Ranelagh.

7.678 (137:17). Nightmare from which you will never awake – See 2.377n.

7.679 (137:18–19). Dick Adams – Richard Adams (b. 1846) was a journalist on the *Cork Examiner* and later on the *Freeman's Journal*. He became a member of the Irish Bar in 1873 and gained fame for his defense of some of those, including James Fitzharris, charged with complicity in the Phoenix Park murders. In 1894 he became a judge of the county courts of Limerick and Down. He was a noted wit and humorist.

7.680 (137:19–20). the Lord ever put the breath of life in – "And the Lord God formed man of the dust of the ground, and breathed into his nostrils the breath of life; and man became a living soul" (Genesis 2:7).

7.683 (137:22). Madam, I'm . . . I saw Elba – Two well-known palindromes. Elba is, of course, the Mediterranean island on which Napoleon was confined (May 1814–February 1815) after his first fall from power.

7.684 (137:23–24). the Old Woman of Prince's street – A nickname for the *Freeman's Journal*. It combines "old woman" (an epithet for Ireland) with a suggestion of the *Journal's* rather fussy and cautious editorial support of Home Rule.

7.685 (137:24–25). weeping and gnashing of teeth – What Jesus prophesies for those barred from "the kingdom of heaven. But the children of the kingdom [of Israel] shall be cast out into outer darkness: there shall be weeping and gnashing of teeth" (Matthew 8:12).

7.686 (137:25). Gregor Grey – *Thom's* 1904 (p. 1886) lists Gregor Grey, artist (and George Grey, engraver) at 1 Sherrard Street Lower in Dublin.

7.687 (137:27). Tay Pay – From the Irish pronunciation of *T.P.*, for Thomas Power O'Connor (b. 1848), the Irish journalist and politician who founded and edited several newspapers and weeklies in London, including the *Star* and the *Sun* and the *Weekly Sun*, *M.A.P.*, and *T.P.'s Weekly*.

7.687 (137:27). the *Star* – Founded in 1888 by T. P. O'Connor and edited by him for two years.

7.688 (137:28). Blumenfeld – Ralph D. Blum-

enfeld (1864–1948), an American-born newspaperman and editor who in 1904 became the expatriate editor of the *Daily Express* in London.

7.688 (137:28). Pyatt – Félix Pyat (1810–89), a French social revolutionary and journalist, had a checkered career on the European Revolutionary Committee in Belgium and England; he was involved in the Paris Commune in 1871 (see 7.559n) before escaping to London. He contributed to several newspapers and edited several revolutionary journals.

7.690 (137:30). the father of scare journalism – That is, Pyat. An overstatement and an oversimplification.

7.690–91 (137:31). the brother-in-law of Chris Callinan – That is, Gallaher. Callinan was "a Dublin journalist famous for his gaffes, bloopers and Irish bulls" (Adams, p. 216).

7.698–99 (138:2). some hawkers were up before the recorder – The recorder was the chief judicial officer of Dublin; in 1904 the Honourable Sir Frederick Richard Falkiner (1831–1908) was recorder of Dublin (1876–1905). The hawkers involved did not appear in so august a presence as the recorder's but rather in police court, 8 June 1904. They had been arrested for selling postcards and mementoes of the Phoenix Park murders. The *Freeman's Journal*, 9 June 1904, p. 2, col. j, reports that in spite of repeated police warnings beginning in November 1903, the hawkers had not desisted. Lady Dudley and the recorder are flourishes of fiction, not fact. See Adams, p. 230.

7.700 (138:3). Lady Dudley – Née Rachel Gurney, the wife of William Humble Ward, earl of Dudley (1866–1932), lord lieutenant of Ireland (1902–6).

7.701–2 (138:5). that cyclone last year – 26–27 February 1903, one of the most severe gales in Dublin's history (compared at the time to that of 1839; see 1.366–67n). The gale caused great damage to property and particularly to trees in Phoenix Park.

7.703 (138:7). Number One – The leader of the Invincibles, identity uncertain.

7.705 (138:9). in the hook and eye department – That is, involved in inconsequential dealings.

7.707 (138:11). Whiteside – James Whiteside (1804–76), an Irish barrister famous for his forensic eloquence and for his defenses of Daniel O'Connell in 1844 and of Smith O'Brien in 1848. He became lord chief justice of Ireland in 1866.

7.707 (138:11–12). Isaac Butt – (1813–79), an Irish barrister and politician. He is reputed to have been a great orator and a kindly man; known as the "father of Home Rule," he was also famous for his participation in the defenses of Smith O'Brien in 1848 and of the Fenian Conspirators (1865–68). His leadership of the Home Rule movement was balanced and moderate, though not so "conservative" as it seemed in retrospect after he was displaced by Parnell.

7.707 (138:12). silvertongued O'Hagan – Thomas O'Hagan (1812–85), a barrister and a jurist. In the 1840s he was associated with O'Connell in lawsuits bearing on Irish national rights, but his reputation in Ireland was mixed because he defended the union of the Irish and English parliaments and because he seemed to benefit from what was regarded as a pro-English stance. He was the first Catholic to be appointed lord chancellor of Ireland (1868–74; 1880–81). Raised to the House of Lords in 1870, he was famous for his eloquent, pro-Irish appeal for the Irish Land Bill in 1881.

7.708 (138:13). Only in the halfpenny place! – Only second rate.

7.715–16 (138:21). two men dressed the same, looking the same – In view of the freewheeling associations from Dante that follow, these phrases suggest the closing phrases of Dante's vision of the Divine Pageant (*Purgatorio* 29:134–35): "I saw two aged men, unlike in raiment, but like in bearing, and venerable and grave." Cf. 7.720–21n and 7.722–23n.

7.717–19 (138:23–25). *la tua pace . . . che parlar ti piace . . . mentrechè . . . si tace* – The closing words of lines 92 and 94 and all of line 96 in canto 5 of Dante's *Inferno*. Francesca da Rimini, one of the carnal sinners, is speaking to Dante (the phrases Stephen recalls are italicized): "If the King of the Universe were our friend, we would pray him for *thy peace:* seeing that thou hast pity of our perverse misfortune. Of that which *it pleases thee to speak* and to hear, we will speak and hear with you, *while the wind, as now, is silent for us.*"

7.720–21 (138:26–27). He saw them three . . . in russet, entwining . . . in mauve, in purple – This transition from the idealized image of the sinner Francesca da Rimini (*Inferno*) to the idealized image of the Virgin Mary (*Paradiso*) is made by way of fragments from Dante's vision of the Divine Pageant in *Purgatorio* 29. The girls approach in bands, "Three by three" (110), "one so red that hardly would she be noted in the fire" (122–23), "the next . . . as if her flesh and bone had been made of emerald" (124–25); "four clad in purple, made festival" (130–31).

But the "approaching girls" in the threes of *terza rima* involve another allusion. Benvenuto, one of the earliest commentators on Dante, reports the "quaint conceit" of another admirer of Dante: "When Dante first set about the composition of his poem, all the rhymes in the language presented themselves in the guise of lovely maidens, each petitioning 'to be granted admission' into *The Divine Comedy*. In answer to their prayers, Dante called first one and then another, and assigned to each its appropriate place in the poem, so that, when at last the work was complete, it was found that not a single one had been left out" (Paget Toynbee, *Dante Studies and Researches* [London, 1902], p. 233; suggested by Clara Claiborne Park).

7.721 (138:27). *per l'aer perso* – Italian: "through the black (ruined) air" (*Inferno* 5:89). Francesca da Rimini addresses Dante when she first recognizes that he is a living creature.

7.721–22 (138:28). *quella pacifica oriafiamma* – Italian: "that peaceful oriflamme [gold flame]" (*Paradiso* 31:127). In Dante's vision the oriflamme is intensified in its center, and he sees first a concentration of "more than a thousand angels making festival"; then in their midst he sees the Virgin Mary, "smiling on their sports."

7.722 (138:28–29). *di rimirar fè più ardenti* – Italian: "more ardent to regaze" (*Paradiso* 31:142). St. Bernard, Dante's guide in the final stage of his journey, watches Dante's inarticulate wonder at this vision of the Virgin Mary; and then Bernard "turned his eyes to her, with so much love that he made mine more ardent to regaze."

7.722–23 (138:29–30). But I old men . . . underdarkneath the night – At the close of the Divine Pageant Dante reemphasizes the penitence that is the inescapable precondition of Christian festivity: "Then saw I four of lowly semblance; and behind all, an old man solitary, coming in a trance, with visage keen" (*Purgatorio* 29:142–44).

7.726 (138:32). SUFFICIENT FOR THE DAY – Jesus, in the Sermon on the Mount: "Take therefore no thought for the morrow: for the morrow shall take thought for the things of itself. Sufficient unto the day is the evil thereof" (Matthew 6:34).

7.729–30 (139:1). the third profession – Law; the other two: divinity and medicine.

7.730 (139:2). your Cork legs – The pun combines the fact that Crawford is from Cork with an Ulster ballad, "The Runaway Cork Leg." The ballad tells the story of a Dutch merchant, "full as an egg," who tries to kick a poor relation who has come to beg. The merchant kicks a keg instead of the relative; he loses his leg and substitutes a cork one that won't stop running: "So often you'll see in the dim half light / A merchant man and cork leg tight, / And from these you may learn that it's wrong to slight, / A poor relation with a keg in sight!"

7.731 (139:3). Henry Grattan – (1746–1820), Irish statesman and orator, a leader in Ireland's struggle for increased legislative independence (1782) and a leader of opposition to the Act of Union. He also helped organize the political movement for Catholic emancipation, which was not accomplished until nine years after his death. See 7.739n.

7.731 (139:3). Flood – Henry Flood (1732–91), Irish statesman and orator, played a prominent part in Irish political opposition to English dominion. Flood was, for a time, a supporter of Grattan but eventually quarreled with him.

7.731 (139:3). Demosthenes – (c. 384–322 B.C.), reputed to have been the greatest of the Greek orators. He was also a patriot and a leader of the opposition to the opportunistic and expansionist policies of Philip II of Macedon.

7.732 (139:3–4). Edmund Burke – (1729–97), an Irish-born English parliamentarian, orator, and essayist. He advocated policies of conciliation toward both Ireland and prerevolutionary America. He was noted not only for his eloquence but also for the thoroughness of his research and the precision of his logic. A moderate and a purist in politics, he earned a reputation as a conservative late in his career, when his opposition to the French Revolution

appeared to contradict his emphasis on conciliation.

7.732–33 (139:4–5). His Chapelizod boss, Harmsworth – Alfred C. Harmsworth, Baron Northcliffe (1865–1922), an English editor and publisher, was born at Chapelizod, just west of Dublin. In 1888 he started a weekly journal, *Answers;* in 1894 he gained control of the *London Evening News,* and in 1896 he founded the *London Daily Mail.* He also published *Harmsworth's Magazine* (from 1898) and several popular magazines for children. He regarded himself as a champion of the "newspaper of the future."

7.733 (139:5). the farthing press – Cheap and sensational journalism.

7.733–34 (139:5–6). *his American cousin of the Bowery guttersheet – That is, Harmsworth's personal friend, the American publisher Joseph Pulitzer (1847–1911). Pulitzer's *New York World* (see 7.635n) had its offices in Park Row, not in the Bowery; but when Pulitzer took over the *World* in 1883, he told its genteel staff, "A change has taken place in the *World.* Heretofore you have all been living in the parlour and taking baths every day. Now I wish you to understand that, in future, you are all walking down the Bowery." Pulitzer and Harmsworth were close enough for Pulitzer to have Harmsworth edit a special edition of the *World* for 1 January 1900; but they were estranged in 1907 when Harmsworth, despite a no-raid agreement, hired away one of Pulitzer's protégés. *Our American Cousin* (1858), a comedy by Tom Taylor (1817–80), is a play with one distinction: Lincoln was watching it when he was assassinated.

7.734 (139:6). *Paddy Kelly's Budget* – (November 1832–January 1834), a humorous weekly newspaper published in Dublin. Its humor was essentially topical and was regarded as vulgar by its Dublin audience.

7.734 (139:7). *Pue's Occurrences* – The first daily newspaper in Dublin, founded in 1700 and published for half a century.

7.735 (139:7–8). *The Skibbereen Eagle – A general weekly newspaper, published in Skibbereen, County Cork (c. 1840–1930); originally the *Skibbereen Eagle,* it became the *Munster Eagle* after the 1860s, and by 1904 it was being published as the *Cork County Eagle.* The newspaper that replaced the *Eagle* after the 1930s is called the *Southern Star.* The original change of name was occasioned by the fact that "Skibbereen Eagle" became a laughing-stock phrase for the obscure provincial newspaper that overreached itself in political bluster, as the *Eagle* once portentiously informed the prime minister of England and the emperor of Russia that it "had got its eyes" on them.

7.736 (139:8–9). Whiteside – See 7.707n.

7.736 (139:9). Sufficient for the day is the newspaper thereof – See 7.726n.

7.738 (139:11). Grattan and Flood – Did contribute articles to the *Freeman's Journal* (founded in 1763). See 7.731n.

7.739 (139:12). Irish volunteers – First formed locally by private subscription in 1778 to guard against the possibility of a French invasion of Ireland after regular army troops had been withdrawn for service in America. Within a year the Volunteers had become a national force, Protestant (though Catholics were eventually admitted) and loyal to the English Crown, though committed to the proposition that the Irish Parliament should have full legislative authority under the Crown. The articulate and wellarmed Volunteers helped bring about English acceptance of that legislative independence in 1782 in a political victory known as Grattan's Parliament. However, that victory has been frequently overstated: the unreformed nature of both the English and the Irish parliaments at the time, the narrowness of the franchise in both countries, and the fact that administrative officers at all levels in Ireland answered not to the Irish Parliament but to the Crown rendered Irish legislative independence an independence in name only.

7.739 (139:13). Dr. Lucas – Charles Lucas (1713–71), an Irish physician and a patriot, of whom Grattan said: "He laid the groundwork of Irish liberty." He was a frequent contributor to the *Freeman's Journal,* over the bylines "Civis" or "A Citizen."

7.740 (139:13–14). John Philpot Curran – (1750–1817), an Irish barrister, patriot and orator who had a reputation for animating every debate he was involved in. His theme was universal emancipation, and he was famous for his defenses of the prisoners of 1798 and of other "traitors."

7.741 (139:15). Bushe K. C. – Seymour Bushe (1853–1922), King's Counsel. Bushe was an Irish barrister who was senior Crown Counsel for the County and City of Dublin (1901) before he moved to England and became King's Counsel in 1904.

7.743 (139:17). Kendal Bushe – Charles Kendal Bushe (1767–1843), an Irish jurist and orator, was an ally of Grattan in opposing the Act of Union. He was reputed to have been the most eloquent orator of his day.

7.744–45 (139:19–20). He would have been on the bench . . . only for – Seymour Bushe's career was clouded by a "Matrimonial tangle" that finally prompted his departure from Ireland. Mr. Colum Gavan Duffy, librarian of the Incorporated Law Society of Ireland, reports in a letter dated 23 October 1970: "It seems that a certain Sir ——— Brook and his wife were rather estranged, and that on a certain occasion the husband followed his wife to Dublin. He eventually found his wife in the room of Mr. Bushe and threatened to take proceedings against him. As there was no divorce in Ireland, these proceedings would consist in the tort of 'Criminal Conversation,' whereby the husband would sue the alleged co-respondent for damages for adultery. It is for this reason that I understand Mr. Bushe left. . . . He also drank heavily."

7.748–49 (139:25). the Childs murder case – See 6.469n.

7.750 (139:26). *And in the porches of mine ear did pour* – The Ghost, as he tells Hamlet the manner of his death at the hands of his brother Claudius. Claudius "stole" upon King Hamlet when the king was "Sleeping within my orchard, / My custom always of the afternoon . . . / And in the porches of my ears did pour / The leperous distilment" (I.v.59–63).

7.751–52 (139:27–28). By the way . . . with two backs? – The question involves the assumption that the Ghost could not have known the manner of his death unless it had been revealed to him after his death. *The other story:* the Ghost tells Hamlet that Claudius is an "adulterate beast" and that the queen has been only "seeming virtuous" (I.v.42–46). This Stephen interprets to mean that before King Hamlet's death Claudius and the queen had committed adultery—had made, in Iago's words, "the beast with two backs" (*Othello* I.i.117–18). But the question remains: how did King Hamlet find these two things out?

7.754 (139:30). ITALIA, MAGISTRA AR-TIUM – Latin: "Italy, Mistress of the Arts."

7.755–56 (139:31–33). He spoke on the law of evidence . . . Roman justice . . . *lex talionis* – Seymour Bushe did speak on the laws of evidence during the trial, but to contrast Irish laws of evidence, which precluded Mrs. Childs from testifying in defense of her husband, with English laws, which would have allowed her testimony. The Mosaic code as propounded in the Old Testament (Exodus 21:23–25) is the law of retaliation: an eye for an eye, a tooth for a tooth, etc. *Lex talionis* is the Latin phrase for that law, "the law of punishment similar and equal to the injury sustained." Roman justice gradually rejected *lex talionis* in favor of uniform rather than retaliatory punishment for crimes. Bushe did not mention that contrast; see 7.500n.

7.756–57 (139:33–34). *the Moses of Michelangelo in the vatican – Michelangelo (1475–1564) carved the *Moses* (1513–16) as part of a mausoleum for Pope Julius II. The mausoleum stood (and still stands) not in the Vatican but in San Pietro in Vincoli (St. Peter in Chains) in Rome. A statue of Moses, flanked by figures of Justice and Mercy, also dominated the central portico of the Four Courts, the building that housed the higher courts of Ireland (in the center of Dublin on the north bank of the Liffey).

7.762 (140:4). Messenger – J. J. O'Molloy is about to deliver a message; and in a much higher sense, Moses was "God's messenger," receiving the tables of the Law on Mount Sinai and being charged with transmitting them to the children of Israel.

7.763–65 (140:6–9). I have often thought . . . of both our lives – This stylistic intrusion echoes the Dickens of *David Copperfield* (1849–50) and *Great Expectations* (1861); as, for example, David on the wedding of Peggoty and Barkis: "I have often thought, since, what an odd, innocent, out-of-the-way kind of wedding it must have been! We got into the chaise again soon after dark, and drove cosily back, looking up at the stars and talking about them" (chap. 10).

7.768 (140:12). *frozen music* – The German philosopher Frederick von Schelling (1775–1854), in *Philosophy of Art* (trans. London, 1845), said of architecture that it was "music in space, as it were a frozen music."

7.768–69 (140:13). *the human form divine* –

The phrase occurs twice in Blake's "The Divine Image," *Songs of Innocence;* the third and fourth stanzas of the poem: "For Mercy has a human heart / Pity, a human face; / And Love, the human form divine, / And Peace, the human dress. // Then every man of every clime, / That prays in his distress, / Prays to the human form divine / Love Mercy Pity Peace."

7.782 (140:27). Professor Magennis – William Magennis, a professor at University College, Dublin. He was something of an arbitrator on the Irish literary scene at the turn of the century and apparently recognized Joyce's distinctiveness and treated him in a friendly fashion when Joyce was a student at the college. Richard M. Kain thinks that Magennis "knew his man well enough to wonder whether" Joyce's approach to Russell "might have been a leg-pull" (*A James Joyce Miscellany*, 3d ser., ed. Marvin Magalaner [Carbondale, Ill., 1962], p. 156).

7.783 (140:28–29). that hermetic crowd – The literary avant-garde of the late nineteenth and early twentieth centuries was fascinated by hermetic and Theosophical lore. AE (George William Russell) was a member of the Second Dublin Lodge, chartered in 1904 by Madame Blavatsky's Theosophical Society. In 1909 the lodge reestablished itself as the independent Hermetic Society.

7.783–84 (140:29). the opal hush poets – "Opal" and "hush" were two of AE's favorite poetic words, and some of the young poets whom Russell encouraged in *New Songs: A Lyric Selection Made by A.E.* (Dublin, 1904) apparently caught the infection; for example, Ella Young in "The House of Love" (p. 12): "house of dream . . . pearly light . . . opal gleam." See 9.290–91n.

7.784 (140:30). That Blavatsky woman – Helena Petrovna Blavatsky (1831–91) was a Russian traveler and Theosophist who expanded her interest in spiritualism and the occult with rather impressionistic studies of the esoteric doctrines of India, the Middle East, and the medieval cabalas, both Christian and Jewish. She founded the Theosophical Society in 1875 and in 1876 published a "textbook" for her followers, *Isis Unveiled, A Master Key to the Mysteries of Ancient and Modern Science and Philosophy.* She was a controversial figure, frequently investigated and discredited because she made fanciful claims about her Indic scholarship (she knew practically no Sanskrit) and about her capacity to perform miracles (including the miracle of reappearing in the flesh after her death).

7.785 (140:31). A. E. has been telling some yankee interviewer – As Richard M. Kain has pointed out, the interviewer was Professor Cornelius Weygandt of the University of Pennsylvania, who visited Russell in the summer of 1902 and reported the substance of their conversation in *Irish Plays and Playwrights* (Boston, 1913), pp. 121–22. Joyce is not named but is identifiable as "a boy . . . not yet twenty-one" who waits in the street and accosts Russell at night, not to ask him about "mysticism" (or "economics") but about "literary art." Russell discovers that the "boy [is] an exquisite who thought the literary movement was becoming vulgarized"; he also discovers that the boy was "infected with Pater's relative. . . . Finally the boy turned questioner and found that 'A. E.' was seeking the Absolute. Having found this out, he again sighed, this time regretfully, and said decidedly that 'A. E.' could not be his Messiah." For Pater's subjective relativism, see 9.376–78n.

7.786–87 (140:33). planes of consciousness – Theosophical doctrine conceived the phenomenon of life as a function of seven planes of consciousness: (1) elemental or atomic, a simple consciousness of the elements of matter; (2) mineral or molecular consciousness, the consolidating of the elements into form according to a definite principle of design; (3) vegetable or cellular consciousness, a recombining of matter through growth and expansion by the principle of life; (4) animal or organic consciousness, the direction of life and matter by the principle of desire; (5) human, "I-am-I," the self-identifying consciousness; (6) universal consciousness, "I-am-thee-and-thou-art-I," the relating of all elements and souls together, thus overcoming the sense of separateness; (7) divine consciousness, that which sees no separateness but unites all as one.

7.793 (141:3–4). *John F Taylor – (c. 1850–1902), an Irish barrister, orator, and journalist. He was Dublin correspondent for the *Manchester Guardian* and "in the opinion of good judges, the finest Irish orator of his time." On 24 October 1901 Taylor did make the speech that MacHugh attempts to recall; see 7.823–24n.

7.793 (141:4). college historical society – The Trinity College Historical Society, founded in 1770, describes itself as "the oldest University Debating Society in Ireland or Great Britain."

Its membership has included most of the famous orators and patriots Miles Crawford has cited above. The meeting in question was held Thursday evening, 24 October 1901.

7.794 (141:4). Mr Justice Fitzgibbon – Gerald Fitzgibbon (1837–1909), Irish, but a devoted Freemason and a staunch Conservative (hence anti-Home Rule). He was made lord justice of appeal in 1878; and as commissioner of national education, he was regarded as one of those who were attempting to Anglicize Ireland.

7.796 (141:7). revival of the Irish tongue – Part of a movement that had gained considerable momentum by the early twentieth century. The aim was, in Douglas Hyde's phrase, to "de-Anglicise Ireland" and to re-create an *Irish* Ireland. Ostensibly cultural, the movement was political and revolutionary in its overtones. See 9.323n.

7.800 (141:11). Tim Healy – Timothy Michael Healy (1855–1931) was an Irish politician and patriot who first distinguished himself as Parnell's "lieutenant" and later, when he became one of the leaders of the move to oust Parnell from leadership of the Irish Nationalist party, as Parnell's "betrayer." He did work consistently, however, for the achievement of Irish independence.

7.800–801 (141:12). the Trinity College estates commission – The commission was appointed on 9 June 1904 by the lord lieutenant of Ireland. Its purposes, according to its report (Dublin, 1905), were: "(1) To inquire into and report upon the relations subsisting between the Grantees and Lessees and the Occupying Tenants, since the date of the passing of the Trinity College, Dublin, Leasing and Perpetuity Act, 1851; and (2) To inquire into and report upon the means by which the Purchase by the Occupying Tenants of the Holdings pursuant to the provisions of The Land Purchase Acts may be facilitated without diminishing the Average New Rental derived by Trinity College as Head Landlord." In other words, the operating funds of Trinity College were derived from its landholdings, and the commission was charged with determining how the university might comply with Irish land reform legislation and yet retain its income.

7.802 (141:13). a sweet thing in a child's frock – The innuendo is at the expense of Healy, whose opposition to Parnell involved ringing denunciations of Parnell's "immorality" after the divorce scandal became public. Crawford implies that the denunciations were all too innocent (and vicious) to be perfectly credible as outraged morality. In the nineteenth century, small boys wore frocks or pinafores until the age of three or four.

7.805–6 (141:17). the vials of his wrath – "And I heard a great voice out of the temple saying to the seven angels, Go your ways, and pour out the vials of the wrath of God upon the earth" (Revelation 16:1).

7.806 (141:18). the proud man's contumely – Hamlet, in the "To be or not to be" soliloquy, asks "who would bear . . . the proud man's contumely . . . /When he himself might his quietus make / With a bare bodkin?" (III.i.70–76).

7.807 (141:19). It was then a new movement. We were weak – Something of a misstatement. By 1901 the Gaelic League (formed in 1893) and its campaign for revival of the Irish language had made considerable headway, though obviously not among Anglo-Irish Conservatives of Fitzgibbon's stripe.

7.823–24 (141:38–39). Briefly, as well . . . words were these – Taylor's speech was never written out or taken down. MacHugh's version of the speech is just that, a version, as is Yeats's quotation from the speech in *The Autobiography of William Butler Yeats* (New York, 1958), pp. 64–65, and as was the "pallid" account published by the *Freeman's Journal* on 25 October 1901 (quoted in Ellmann, p. 91n).

7.833 (142:11). the youthful Moses – Moses, born when the Israelites were in captivity in Egypt, was automatically condemned to die: "And the Pharaoh charged all his people, saying, Every son that is born ye shall cast into the river" (Exodus 1:22). To evade this dictum Moses' mother hid him in an "ark of bulrushes . . . by the river's brink" (Exodus 2:3), where he was found by the daughter of the pharaoh, and "he became her son" (2:10). Thus, Moses, though an Israelite, was brought up as an Egyptian; he was to become the leader of the Israelites in their struggle to achieve release from captivity in Egypt.

7.835–36 (142:13–14). *And let our crooked smokes* – At the end of Shakespeare's *Cymbeline*, when peace and tranquillity have been restored, Cymbeline determines: "Laud we the gods, / And let our crooked smokes climb to

their nostrils / From our blest altars. Publish we this peace / To all our subjects" (V.v.476–79).

7.841 (142:20). FROM THE FATHERS – That is, from the Fathers of the Church, a title of honor applied to the early leaders and writers of the Christian church, in this case St. Augustine.

7.842–44 (142:21–23). It was revealed . . . could be corrupted – From St. Augustine's (354–430) *Confessions* (397), 7:12. The passage continues: "Therefore, if things shall be deprived of all good, they shall no longer be. So long therefore as they are, they are good: therefore whatever is, is good."

7.847–48 (142:28). *galleys, trireme and quadrireme* – Galleys with three and four banks of oars. The allusion to the world-dominating presence of the British navy and merchant marine is obvious.

7.852 (142:34). Child, man, effigy – Moses' progress from the ark of bulrushes to Michelangelo's statue.

7.853 (142:35). babemaries – Moses was hidden by two women (his mother and her sister), as the "two Maries" watched at Jesus' sepulcher; see 3.297n and 3.398n.

7.853–54 (142:36). a man supple in combat – "And it came to pass in those days, when Moses was grown, that he went out unto his brethren, and looked upon their burdens: and he spied an Egyptian smiting an Hebrew, one of his brethren. And he looked this way and that way, and when he saw that there was no man, he slew the Egyptian, and hid him in the sand" (Exodus 2:11–12).

7.854 (142:36). stonehorned – Michelangelo's statue represents Moses as having horns, as do most medieval depictions of Moses. The tradition of this distinctive mark derives from a mistranslation of the Hebrew verb *qāran*, which originally meant "to put forth horns [*qeren*]" but metaphorically came to mean "to emit rays." The mistake is preserved in the King James Bible's "he had horns coming out of his hand" (Habakkuk 3:4), which should read, "he had bright beams coming out of his hand." St. Jerome (c. 340–420) made a similar mistake in translating Exodus 34:29: "when Moses came down from mount Sinai with the two tables of testimony . . . the skin of his face shone." St.

Jerome rendered it "his face was horned" and established the iconographic tradition.

7.855 (142:38). *a local and obscure idol* – Late-nineteenth-century biblical scholars generally believed that Jewish monotheism had its origins among clans living near Mount Sinai who shared a cult that regarded the mountain as the sacred dwelling place of the deity Yahweh. The scholars also thought that Moses was not so much an individual as a symbolic representative of these clans.

7.856 (142:39). *Isis and Osiris* – The central deities of the Egyptian pantheon in the centuries just before the beginning of the Christian era. Isis represented the feminine, receptive, productive principles of nature. Osiris, her brother and husband, was the male god of the fructification of the land; he represented the death and resurrection cycle of the natural world and was lord of the underworld.

7.856 (142:39). *Horus* – The son of Isis and Osiris. He avenged his father's death and was regarded as the victorious god of light who overcame darkness, winter, and drought.

7.856 (143:1). *Ammon Ra* – In Egyptian mythology, the sun-god and supreme deity, protector of humans and conqueror of evil.

7.864–65 (143:10–11). *he would never . . . house of bondage* – The familiar phrase about Moses' leadership of the children of Israel (Exodus 13:17–20, 20:2); see 7.208–9n.

7.865–66 (143:11–12). *nor followed the pillar of cloud by day* – After the passage of the Israelites through the Red Sea: "And the Lord went before them by day in a pillar of cloud, to lead them the way" (Exodus 13:21).

7.866–67 (143:12–13). *He would never have spoken . . . on Sinai's mountaintop* – In Exodus 19 the children of Israel come to Mount Sinai, and Moses experiences a three-day communion with God that climaxes in the appearance of "the fearful presence of God upon the mount."

7.867–69 (143:13–15). *nor ever have . . . tables of the law* – In the course of his experience on Mount Sinai Moses received and recorded the Ten Commandments and other laws (Exodus 20–31). "And Moses turned, and went down from the Mount and the two tables of the testimony were in his hand. . . . And the tables

were the work of God, and the writing was the writing of God, graven upon the tables" (Exodus 32:15–16). And "when Moses came down from mount Sinai . . . the skin of his face shone" (Exodus 34:29).

7.873 (143:20–21). And yet he died . . . land of promise – "And Moses went up from the plains of Moab unto the mountain of Nebo, to the top of Pisgah, that is over against Jericho. And the Lord shewed him all the land. . . . And the Lord said unto him, This is the land which I sware unto Abraham, unto Isaac, and unto Jacob, saying, I will give it unto thy seed: I have caused thee to see it with thine eyes, but thou shalt not go over thither. So Moses the servant of the Lord died there in the land of Moab, according to the word of the Lord" (Deuteronomy 34:1–5).

What Moses' transgression was and why God denied him entry into the Promised Land has been the subject of considerable speculation. Some commentators suggest that Moses suffered with and for the people as a consequence of their faithlessness (when they erected and worshiped a golden calf during Moses' absence on Mount Sinai [Exodus 32–33]) and their rebelliousness (during the wandering in the wilderness [Numbers 13–14]). Others suggest that Moses himself broke faith when he and Aaron brought forth water out of the rock, but not as God had directed: "And the Lord spake unto Moses and Aaron, Because ye believed me not, to sanctify me in the eyes of the children of Israel, therefore ye shall not bring this congregation into the land which I have given them" (Numbers 20:12). Still others cite Moses' surreptitious murder of the Egyptian who was beating a Jewish slave; see 7.853–54n. And some commentators suggest that the reasons Moses was denied entry into the Promised Land remain obscure because later editors of the Pentateuch wanted to tone down criticism of men as holy as Moses.

7.880 (143:28). Gone with the wind – From Ernest Dowson's (1867–1900) "Non Sum Qualis Eram Bonae Sub Regno Cynarae" (1896). (Latin, from Horace, *Odes* IV.i.3: "I am not what I once was under the rule [or spell] of kind Cynara.") The phrase occurs in the third stanza of Dowson's poem: "I have forgot much, Cynara! gone with the wind, / Flung roses, roses riotously with the throng, / Dancing, to put thy pale, lost lilies out of mind; / But I was desolate and sick of an old passion, / Yea, all the time, because the dance was long: / I have been faithful to thee, Cynara! in my fashion."

7.880–82 (143:28–31). Hosts at Mullaghmast . . . within his voice – The "tribune" in this passage is Daniel O'Connell, who so styled himself, identifying with "the People of Ireland . . . in their wishes and wants, speaking their sentiments and [seeking] to procure them relief" (*Nation*, 19 August 1843). The association of O'Connell with Moses is obvious. "A people Sheltered within his voice" because as "a constitutional lawyer" his insistence was on legal and nonviolent achievement of repeal of the Act of Union. His theme was "No man shall find himself imprisoned or persecuted who follows my advice. . . . Ireland is a country worth fighting for, it is a country worth dying for, but above all it is a country worth being tranquil, determined, submissive, and docile for" (*Nation*, 7 October 1843). The "hosts" whom Stephen recalls were present at the two most famous of O'Connell's "monster meetings." The occasion for these Sunday-morning meetings was provided in the spring of 1843 by a plain-talk English rejection of O'Connell's constitutional arguments for repeal. O'Connell intended to demonstrate in a series of meetings throughout Ireland that the people were united in civil-disobedient support of repeal. The meeting at the Hill of Tara (twenty-one miles northwest of Dublin, associated with the ancient high kings of a united, golden-age Ireland) was held Sunday, 13 August 1843; patriotic Irish estimates put the crowd at seven hundred fifty thousand to one million people! Conservative (English) estimates put it at two hundred fifty thousand. Next to the Tara meeting, the most impressive was held at the Rath of Mullaghmast, thirty-five miles southwest of Dublin, 1 October 1843. The rath was famous as the site in 1577 of a particularly perfidious massacre, executed by the English at the expense of a then-pacified and loyal section of the O'More clan. O'Connell's words have been "scattered" in the sense that his reliance on and hope for an orderly constitutional achievement of repeal (and a measure of independence for Ireland) were, to say the least, blasted, and his words, for all their oratorical success, wasted. O'Connell himself was one of the first to fall victim to his own advice: he was imprisoned 14 October 1843 for the "seditious conspiracy" of the monster meetings. For "miles of ears of porches," see 7.750n.

7.882 (143:31). Akasic records – In Theosophical lore, the Akasa is an all-embracing medium, the infinite memory of eternal nature in which every thought, silent or expressed, is immortalized.

7.883 (143:32). Love and laud him – See 7.835–36n.

7.887 (143:36–37). a French compliment – A compliment that is essentially objectionable; an empty gesture or promise.

7.892 (144:4). *Mooney's* – Mooney & Co., wine and spirit merchants, a pub at 1 Abbey Street Lower, near the corner of Sackville (now O'Connell) Street. Mooney's was not far east of the *Freeman's Journal* offices and was only four doors from the Ship at 5 Abbey Street Lower, where Stephen was to have met Mulligan and Haines at 12:30 P.M.

7.898 (144:10). Lay on, Macduff – After Macbeth has learned that Macduff is, according to the witches' prophecies, to be his executioner, he says: "Lay on, Macduff / And damn'd be him that first cries 'Hold, enough!' " (V.viii. 33–34); in this context it is a cliché.

7.910 (144:25). *Fuit Ilium!* – Latin: "Troy has been"; that is, "Troy is no more" (Virgil, *Aeneid* 2:325, when Aeneas, at Dido's request, recounts the fall of Troy).

7.910 (144:25–26). windy Troy – A Homeric epithet as rendered by Tennyson in his poem "Ulysses" (1842). Ulysses speaks of himself as having "drunk delight with my peers, / Far on the ringing plains of windy Troy" (lines 16–17). It is notable that Tennyson's Ulysses yearns "To follow knowledge like a sinking star, / Beyond the utmost bound of human thought" (lines 31–32), and that Telemachus is presented as the reverse of his father, as he who "by slow prudence" (line 36) will master and reform Ithaca, a kingdom of this world.

7.910–11 (144:26). Kingdoms of this world – Jesus remarks in answer to Pilate's questions about his being "king of the Jews," "My kingdom is not of this world" (John 18:36).

7.911 (144:26–27). The masters . . . are fellaheen today – The Greeks, who became "masters of the Mediterranean" after the fall of Troy, were, in 1904 as seen from western Europe, more like their enemies the Turks (and the Arabs) than they were like western Europeans. Bulgaria, Rumania, Albania, and half of modern Yugoslavia were still part of the Turkish Empire, and Greece was decidedly weaker than its Turkish adversary, as a brief war in April–

May 1897 proved with disastrous conclusiveness.

7.916 (144:32). left along Abbey street – Abbey Street was on the southern side of the *Freeman's Journal* building. They turn east toward Sackville (now O'Connell) Street and Mooney's.

7.921 (145:1). DEAR DIRTY DUBLIN – A phrase coined by the Irish woman of letters Lady Sydney Morgan (1780–1859).

7.923 (145:3). Two Dublin vestals – The vestal virgins were priestesses of Vesta, the Roman goddess of hearth and home whose temple was the hearth of Rome, the oldest temple in the city. The six priestesses of the temple dedicated themselves to lives of chastity and were charged with maintaining the eternal flame of Vesta's sacred fire.

7.924–26 (145:4–6). Fumbally's lane . . . Off Blackpitts – Both streets are in the Liberties, in the southwest quadrant of central Dublin.

7.927–29 (145:7–9). Damp night reeking . . . Quicker, darlint! – Stephen's recall of a street encounter with a prostitute. For "Akasic records," see 7.882n.

7.930 (145:10). Let there be life – Enforcing the analogy between artistic creation and divine creation, after Genesis 1:3: "And God said, Let there be light: and there was light."

7.931:18 (145:12). Nelson's pillar – See 6.293n. Spiral stairs led to a platform 120 feet in the air, at the base of the statue of Nelson; admission was threepence.

7.937 (145:18). Wise virgins – After Jesus' parable of the ten virgins (Matthew 25:1–13). The ten virgins "went forth to meet the bridegroom." The five foolish virgins took their lamps but no oil; the wise virgins took both lamps and oil. Thus, when the bridegroom came at midnight, the wise virgins "were ready [and] went in with him to the marriage: and the door was shut." The foolish virgins were left out. "Watch therefore, for ye know neither the day nor the hour wherein the Son of man cometh."

7.939 (145:20). brawn – Similar to headcheese.

7.939 (145:21). panloaf – A small loaf of bread.

7.939–41 (145:21–22). at the north city . . . Collins, proprietress – *Thom's* 1904 lists Kate Collins as the proprietor of the North City Dining Rooms at 11 Marborough Street. The street runs parallel to Sackville (now O'Connell) Street, one block east; the two "vestals" have not taken a direct route to Nelson's Pillar but have circled from the southwest around to a point east of the pillar.

7.948 (145:31). Anne Kearns and Florence MacCabe – A Mrs. Kearns was a pawnbroker at 7 Great George's Street North (*Thom's* 1904, p. 1916). For Florence MacCabe, see 3.33–34n.

7.949 (145:32). Lourdes water – See 5.365n.

7.950 (145:33–34). a passionist father – A member of the Roman Catholic order "Barefooted Clerks of the Holy Cross and Passion of Our Lord," founded in 1737 by St. Paul of the Cross (the Italian Paolo Francisco Danei, 1697–1775). The Passionists vowed not only to live in poverty, chastity, and obedience but also to meditate continually on the sufferings of Christ. Their interest was primarily in the conversion of sinners through preaching missions.

7.951 (145:34). crubeen – A pig's foot.

7.951 (145:35). double x – The standard Dublin pub beer manufactured by Guinness, as distinct from "triple x," which Guinness manufactures for export.

7.962 (146:10). RETURN OF BLOOM – As Odysseus is driven back to the island of Aeolus; see headnote to this episode, p. 128.

7.964 (146:13–14). the *Irish Catholic* and *Dublin Penny Journal* – Two weekly newspapers, both published on Thursdays. Their offices were at 90 Abbey Street Middle.

7.975–76 (146:26–27). the *Kilkenny People* – A weekly newspaper published on Saturdays in Kilkenny.

7.976 (146:27–28). House of keys – See 7.141n.

7.981 (146:32). kiss my arse – The way the Devil's disciples demonstrate their obeisance.

7.983 (147:1). squalls – Reminiscent of the hurricane of contrary winds that escapes from the sack just as Odysseus reaches home, and of

Aeolus's peremptory dismissal of Odysseus when the winds blow his ship back to Aeolia. See headnote to this episode, p. 128.

7.987 (147:6). Irishtown – See 6.34n.

7.990 (147:10). K.M.R.I.A. – Obviously the initial letters of Crawford's abusive outburst, but the initials *M.R.I.A.* also stand for Member of the Royal Irish Academy.

7.995 (147:15). RAISING THE WIND – Raising money by pawning, borrowing, etc.

7.996 (147:16). *Nulla bona* – Latin: "No goods or possessions." The expression is used in law to assert that an individual has no possessions that could be mortgaged or sold to pay his debts.

7.997 (147:17). through the hoop – In financial difficulties.

7.997 (147:18). back a bill – Countersign a note.

7.1008–9 (147:30–31). Out for the waxies' Dargle – "Waxies" are cobblers (after their use of wax for the preparation of thread). The Dargle is a picturesque glen near Bray, twelve miles south of Dublin, where Powerscourt, one of the most fashionable of Irish great houses, was situated. The "waxies' Dargle" may thus have been an annual (?) cobblers' picnic that was either held at the Dargle or staged in a manner that aspired to the fashionableness associated with Powerscourt. In the latter case the picnic may have been held at Ringsend on the south bank of the mouth of the Liffey, and not exactly a fashionable "park".

7.1011 (148:1). Rathmines Blue Dome – Our Lady of Refuge, Rathmines (1850), two miles south of Nelson's Pillar. Designed by Patrick Byrne, it is a cruciform church, "conspicuous by its large copper dome." It was destroyed by fire in 1921, but the original dome was restored.

7.1012 (148:1). Adam and Eve's – A Franciscan church five-eighths of a mile west-southwest of the pillar, off Merchant's Quay on the south bank of the Liffey, west of the center of Dublin. See 17.757–58n.

7.1012 (148:1–2). saint Laurence O'Toole's – A Roman Catholic church (1863) in Seville Place, just north of the Liffey near its mouth and three-quarters of a mile east and slightly north of the pillar. The church is named after an Irish saint (1132–80), archbishop of Dublin (1162–80) and eventually Dublin's patron. He was a popular saint because he had resisted the Anglo-Norman invasion of Ireland.

7.1015–16 (148:7). the archdiocese – The diocese of an archbishop, in this case the archbishop of Dublin.

7.1018 (148:9). onehandled adulterer – Lord Nelson lost an arm in an unsuccessful assault on Santa Cruz de Tenerife in the Canary Islands (1797). In 1798 Nelson formed a liaison with Emma Hamilton (c. 1765–1815), the wife of Sir William Hamilton (1730–1803), the British minister at Naples. The liaison was widely publicized and became one of the "great scandals" of the period.

7.1021–22 (148:12–14). DAMES DONATE DUBLIN'S CITS / SPEEDPILLS VELOCITOUS / AEROLITHS, BELIEF – In Matthew 13:3–9, Jesus tells the parable of the sower and the seed: many seeds are unproductive because they "fell by the wayside" or "upon stony places" or "among thorns." "But other fell into good ground and brought forth fruit, some an hundredfold, some sixtyfold, some thirtyfold. Who hath ears to hear, let him hear."

7.1035 (148:30). Antisthenes – (c. 444–370 B.C.), a Greek philosopher and a pupil of Gorgias (see following note), he attached himself to Socrates; Plato disliked him. Antisthenes asserted that without virtue there could be no happiness and that virtue alone was sufficient to happiness. He was committed to ascetic self-denial and was scornful of power, honor, and fame. His philosophical and rhetorical works are lost, except for two small and disputed declamations. The *Of Helen and Penelope* to which MacHugh alludes has been lost for over a thousand years. In it Antisthenes apparently argued that Penelope's virtue made her more beautiful than Helen, whose virtue was somewhat less solidly demonstrated. Antisthenes was only a half-citizen of Athens because his mother was Thracian, "a bondwoman."

7.1035 (148:31). Gorgias – (fl. c. 427–c. 399 B.C.), a Greek Sophist and rhetorician known as "the Nihilist" for his three propositions: (1) nothing exists; (2) if anything existed, it could not be known; (3) if anything did exist, and could be known, it could not be communicated. Thus philosophy (and life) were matters of persuasion, not of communication.

7.1040 (149:5). Penelope Rich – Née Devereux (c. 1562–1607), Sir Philip Sidney's (1548–86) love; the object of his devoted attentions, literary and otherwise. She is the Stella of Sidney's sonnet sequence *Astrophel and Stella* (1591). Her life contrasts sharply with that of *The Odyssey*'s Penelope. Married to Robert, Lord Rich (c. 1581), apparently unhappily and against her will, she eventually revolted into an open liaison with Lord Mountjoy (c. 1594) by whom she bore several children. When Lord Rich abandoned her after the execution of her brother Robert Devereux, the second earl of Essex (1566–1601), she lived openly with Lord Mountjoy, and they married after her divorce in 1605.

7.1042 (149:7). CENTRAL – A telephone operator.

7.1044–46 (149:9–12). Rathmines . . . Upper Rathmines – These trams serviced areas of Dublin and environs south of the Liffey; see 7.4–13nn. Rathfarnum is a suburban village area three miles south of Dublin center; Donnybrook was a village two miles southeast of the pillar.

7.1047 (149:13). becalmed in short circuit – Power failures in the tram system were not unusual before a central generating plant was built in Ringsend in 1906. In 1904 the Dublin United Tramways Co. had two power plants, one in Shelbourne Road on the southeastern outskirts of the city and one in Clontarf to the northeast. Apparently the Shelbourne Road plant is out.

7.1054 (149:21–22). OLD MAN MOSES – Zack Bowen (*Musical Allusions in the Works of James Joyce* [Albany, N.Y., 1974], p. 126) remarks that this is the title of a song "about a degraded flower salesman with a red nose who spends his time smelling flowers while he is alive, and when he dies spends eternity smelling the roots." In the Bible, Acts 6 and 7, the charges and disputations that lead to St. Stephen Protomartyr's death by stoning (see 1.34n) include the testimony of "suborned men which said, We have heard him speak blasphemous words against Moses" (6:11).

7.1056 (149:24). *Deus nobis haec otia fecit – Latin: "god has made this peace [leisure, comfort] for us" (Virgil, *Eclogues* 1:6). Virgil's pastoral poem contrasts in dialogue the peace within the "spreading beech's covert" with the "unrest on all sides in the land."

7.1057 (149:25). A Pisgah Sight of Palestine – That is, the vision that was granted Moses; see 7.873n. Also: Thomas Fuller (1608–61), *A Pisgah-Sight of Palestine and the Confines Thereof with the History of the Old and New Testament Acted Thereon* (London, 1650).[2]

7.1057–58 (149:26). *The Parable of the Plums – Jesus relies heavily on parables to teach his followers. See, for example, 7.1021–22n. In Christian art "the plum is symbolic of fidelity and independence" (George Ferguson, *Signs and Symbols in Christian Art* [New York, 1954], p. 37; cited by Joan Keenan).

7.1061 (149:29–30). Moses and the promised land – Canaan, a rich and fertile land, was promised to Abraham and his seed (the children of Israel) in Genesis 12:7; the promise is renewed to Moses in Exodus 12:25.

7.1067 (150:6). sir John Gray's pavement island – See 6.258n.

7.1070–71 (150:10). WIMBLES . . . WANGLES – Joyce told Stuart Gilbert that "wimbles" was an example of *Hapax legomenon*, a term used in Greek lexicons to denote words found only once in extant literature (there are several such words in Homer). The *Oxford English Dictionary* lists a Yorkshire-Lancashire usage of *wimble* as "active, nimble," and remarks: "The immediate source is unknown. (Scand. words of appropriate form, e.g., Norw. *vimmel* giddy, confused, have not the required sense.)" And yet the sense Joyce apparently intended is giddy, confused. To "wangle" is dialect for to move or go unsteadily.

---

2 There is a copy of Fuller's book in Marsh's Library in Dublin (see 3.107–8n), but there is no evidence that Joyce consulted the book when he visited the library, 22 and 23 October 1904.

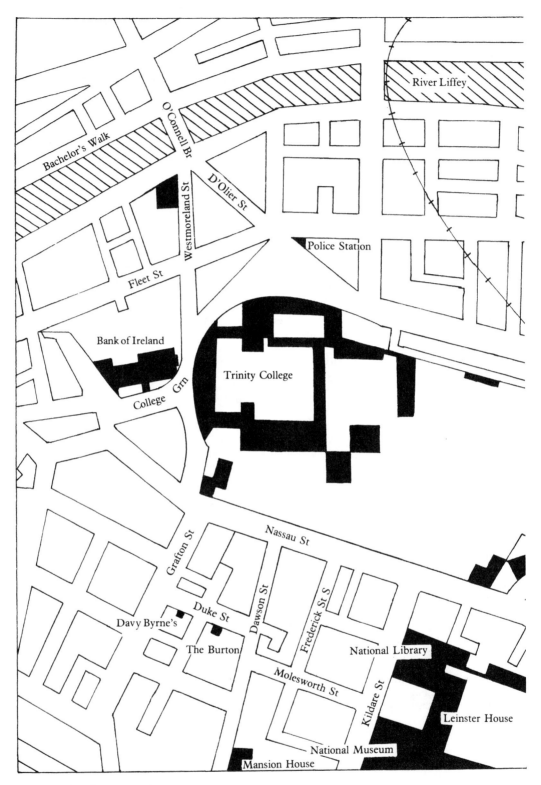

EPISODE 8. *Lestrygonians*

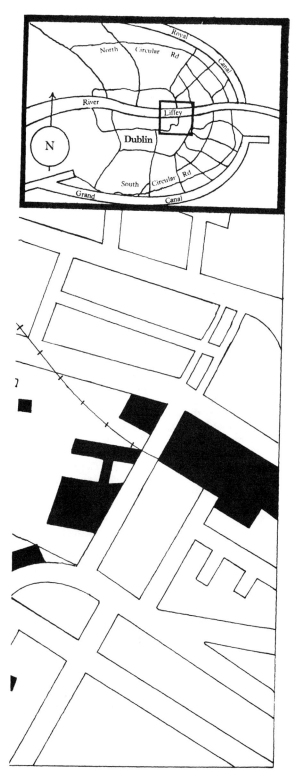

EPISODE 8

Lestrygonians

(8.1–1193, PP. 151–83)

Episode 8: *Lestrygonians*, 8.1–1193 (151–183).   In Book 10 of *The Odyssey*, Odysseus recounts his disappointing adventures with Aeolus, the wind king (see headnote to Aeolus, p. 128); rebuffed by Aeolus, Odysseus and his men take to the sea once more. They reach the island of the Lestrygonians, where all the ships except Odysseus's anchor in a "curious bay" (10:87; Fitzgerald, p. 180) circled "with mountain walls of stone" (10:88; ibid.). Odysseus cannily anchors "on the sea side" (10:95–96; ibid.). A shore party from the ships anchored in the bay is lured by a "stalwart / young girl" (10:105–6; ibid.) to the lodge of her father, Antiphates, king of the Lestrygonians. The king turns out to be a giant and a cannibal, who promptly eats one of the shore party and then leads his tribe in the destruction of all the landlocked ships and the slaughter of their crews. Only Odysseus and his crew escape—to Circe's island.

Time: 1:00 P.M. Scene: the Lunch; Bloom moves south and across the Liffey to Davy Byrne's pub at 21 Duke Street and thence to the National Library, not far to the east. Organ: esophagus; Art: architecture; Color: none; Symbol: constables; Technique: peristaltic. Correspondences: *Antiphates*—hunger; *The Decoy* [Antiphates' daughter]—food; *Lestrygonians*—teeth.

The Linati schema lists as Persons: "Antiphates, The seductive daughter, Ulysses," and remarks that the Sense (Meaning) of the episode is "Dejection."

8.1 (151:1). lemon platt – Candy made of plaited sticks of lemon-flavored barley sugar.

8.2 (151:2). a christian brother – A member of a teaching brotherhood of Roman Catholic laymen, bound under temporary vows. The Christian Brothers ran schools and were supported by public contributions; they charged very low fees for their services and were more interested in practical than in academic education, in contrast to the Jesuits whose educational emphasis was academic and whom Dubliners regarded as of a better, less common, and more worldly class.

8.3–4 (151:3–4). Lozenge and comfit manufacturer to His Majesty the King – The familiar and somewhat exclusive English licensing (and advertising) formula displayed outside the confectionery store of Lemon & Co., Ltd. (called "Graham Lemon's" in *Ulysses*) at 49 Sackville (now O'Connell) Street Lower.

8.4 (151:4). God. Save. Our – From the unofficial "national anthem" of Great Britain, "God Save the King [or Queen]." The song, with its recast folk- and plainsong elements, appeared as early as the sixteenth century: "God save our gracious King, / Long live our noble King, / God save the King! / Send him victorious, / Happy and glorious, / Long to reign over us, / God save the King."

8.5 (151:6). Y.M.C.A. – Young Men's Christian Association. In 1904 individual societies of the association were composed of an active controlling membership, identified with evangelical churches, and of a more numerous associate membership not connected with the churches. The societies sought to promote "the physical, social, mental and spiritual wellbeing of their members and of all other young men"; and the active members were regarded as energetic, if not always tactful, proselytes.

8.9 (151:11). Blood of the Lamb – The throwaway's question, "Have you been washed in the Blood of the Lamb" (i.e., in the blood of Christ), echoes Revelation 7:14–15: "These are they which came out of great tribulation, and have washed their robes, and made them white in the blood of the Lamb. Therefore are they before the throne of God." This passage was the scriptural basis for the well-known nineteenth-century revival hymn "Holiness Desired," or, popularly, "Washed in the Blood of the Lamb," by Elisha Hoffman.

8.11–12 (151:13–15). God wants blood victim . . . sacrifice – The throwaway Bloom is scanning sounds much more like Y.M.C.A. "hell fire and damnation" evangelism than it does like Dowie, whose rhetorical emphasis was on the "restoration" of primitive Christianity, on "Divine Healing," and on "the kind words given by Christ, 'Peace be to this house'" (Rolix Harlan, *John Alexander Dowie and the Christian Catholic Apostolic Church in Zion* [Evansville, Wisc., 1906], pp. 97, 99, 104). As Dominic Manganiello (*Joyce's Politics* [London, 1980], pp. 102–3) has pointed out, Bloom's scansion of the throwaway not only echoes Y.M.C.A. rhetoric but also owes a (perhaps unconscious) debt to the anarchist Mikhail Bakunin (1814–76): "Then, remembering that he was not only a God of vengeance and wrath, but also a God of love, after having tormented the existence of a few milliards of poor human beings and condemned them to an eternal hell, he took pity on the rest, and, to save them and reconcile his eternal and divine love with his eternal and divine anger, always greedy for victims and blood, he sent into the world, as an expiatory victim, his only son, that he might be killed by men" (*God and the State* [1882; New York, 1970], p. 11). "All religions are cruel, all founded on blood; for all rest principally on the idea of sacrifice—that is, on the perpetual immolation of humanity to the insatiable vengeance of divinity" (ibid., pp. 25–26).

8.11 (151:14). hymen – The god of marriage or (rare) marriage itself.

8.12 (151:14). foundation of a building – "One of Mr. Dowie's promoting schemes" (1903–5) was to raise money for a new "Shiloh Tabernacle" in Zion City, "a concrete and steel temple to seat 16,000." He claimed that the "foundation" of the building had been laid, though in actuality "the only thing that had been done was to plow a line around the temple site, and with a great demonstration to remove a few shovels of earth with a steam shovel" (Harlan [see 8.11–12n], p. 13).

8.12 (151:15). kidney burntoffering – See p. 70, n. 1.

8.13 (151:15). *druids' altars – Bloom associates ancient Jewish sacrificial customs with druidic ceremonies; see 7.835–36n and 9.1224–25 (218:8–12). At the end of the nineteenth century the revival of interest in Irish antiquities led to a reexamination of the druids and their lore. Early Christian polemicists had accused the druids of human sacrifice in order to discredit them, but Irish historians of the early twentieth century argued that such sacrifices, if they had ever been the practice among Irish druids, had been sublimated to animal sacrifice well before the beginning of the Christian era in Ireland.

8.13 (151:15). Elijah is coming – Recalls the closing words of the Old Testament (Malachi 4:5–6): "Behold, I will send you Elijah the prophet before the coming of the great and dreadful day of the Lord: And he shall turn the heart of the fathers to the children, and the heart of the children to their fathers, lest I come and smite the earth with a curse." This passage has become the scriptural basis for the Jewish tradition that the second coming of Elijah will signal the coming of the Messiah (in Christian tradition, the second coming of Christ). When Passover is celebrated in Jewish households, it is traditional to set an extra place for Elijah in case this year's feast were to be the occasion for Elijah's return.

8.13 (151:16). John Alexander Dowie – (1847–1907), a Scottish-Australian-American evangelist who began life in sober piety but found such success as a revivalist that he proclaimed himself "Elijah the Restorer" (Harlan [see 8.11–12n], p. 4) and finally "First Apostle of the Christian Catholic and Apostolic Church in Zion" (i.e., the modern reincarnation of the apostle Paul). He said that he was "the third manifestation of Elijah" after Elijah and John the Baptist (p. 57), and he undertook to "restore" the church in Zion by founding Zion City, near Chicago, in 1901. In October–November 1903 he made news by leading his "hosts" (three thousand of them) to New York City to "regenerate" that metropolis. He was not in Dublin on Bloomsday, nor was he scheduled to appear there in 1904, though he was in Europe 11–18 June. In 1906 Zion City revolted against him, accusing him of misuse of funds, of "tyranny and injustice . . . polygamous teaching, and other grave offenses" (p. 24).

8.17 (151:20). Torry and Alexander – A team of American revivalists who carried out an extensive "Mission to Great Britain" in 1903–5, including a mission to Dublin in March–April 1904. Reuben Archer Torrey's (1856–1928) publications speak for him: *How to Promote and Conduct a Successful Revival; Revival Addresses; How to Study the Bible for the Greatest Profit*. Charles McCallom Alexander (1867–1928) was a minister who handled the musical side of the revival mission.

8.17 (151:20). Polygamy – What Dowie's followers accused him of "teaching"; see 8.13n. Bloom apparently associates Dowie's teaching with that of Joseph Smith (1805–44), the founder of the Mormon church. Smith founded several "new Zions" and did preach and practice polygamy, as did his followers.

8.18–19 (151:22). Birmingham firm the luminous crucifix – Meaning unknown.

8.20 (151:24). Pepper's ghost idea – Padraic Colum, in an interview in 1968, recalled this as a circus or stage trick developed by an Englishman named John Pepper in the 1870s. It involved the manipulation of phosphorescent costumes, lighting, and dark curtains to produce the dramatic illusion of ghostly presences on stage.

8.20 (151:24). *Iron Nails Ran In – Bloom's version of I.N.R.I.; see 5.372n.

8.27 (151:32). Butler's monument house corner – George Butler, manufacturer of musical instruments, 34 Bachelor's Walk, the quay side, north bank of the Liffey just west of Sackville [now O'Connell] Street, where it enters O'Connell Bridge; thus "monument house corner" because it was adjacent to the monument to O'Connell that stands at the entrance to the bridge.

8.28 (151:33–34). Dillon's auctionrooms – Joseph Dillon, auctioneer and valuer, 25 Bachelor's Walk, eleven doors in from the corner where Bloom pauses.

8.30 (151:35). Lobbing – To slip, give way; therefore, to lounge.

8.32–33 (151:38–39). the confession, the absolution – The priest would not refuse to hear the unfruitful woman's confession, but might very well withhold absolution (formal remission of sin) until the woman had done penance to demonstrate her contrition and her renewed willingness to dedicate herself to a life of fruition.

8.33 (151:39). Increase and multiply – "And God blessed them, saying: Increase and multiply, and fill the earth, and subdue it, and rule over the fishes of the sea, and the fowls of the air and all living creatures that move upon the earth" (Genesis 1:28 [Douay]). This passage has been repeatedly cited as one of the key scriptural bases for Roman Catholic condemnation of birth control.

8.34–35 (151:41). Living on the fat of the land – The pharoah tells Joseph to urge his brothers and his father and all of Israel to come and settle in Egypt: "I will give you the good of the land of Egypt, and ye shall eat of the fat of the land" (Genesis 45:18). The biblical account implies that the pharaoh's action was truly generous and benign and that Egypt only became a "house of bondage" for the Israelites under "a new king over Egypt, which knew not Joseph" (Exodus 1:8).

8.35–36 (152:1). black fast Yom Kippur – Yom Kippur, the Jewish Day of Atonement, is the only fast commanded in Mosaic law. It occurs five days before the Feast of Tabernacles (see 4.210–11n). The method of its observance, including the sacrifice of the scapegoat, is de-

scribed in Leviticus 16, and the conduct of the people is enjoined in Leviticus 23:26–32 with the command, "and ye shall afflict your souls"; thus the fast is "black." The twenty-four-hour fast, from sundown to sundown, originally climaxed in celebration and feasting, but ever since the destruction of the temple and the dispersion of the Jews in A.D. 70 the day has been strictly one of solemn penitence.

8.36 (152:2). Crossbuns – Small cakes prepared especially for Good Friday and appropriately marked with a cross. Bloom associates the fast of Good Friday (with Jesus as scapegoat) with the fast of Yom Kippur and regards the crossbuns as a violation of strict fast.

8.36 (152:2). collation – A light meal permitted for fast days.

8.37–38 (152:3–4). A housekeeper of one . . . out of her – A commonplace expression of Protestant suspicion of the chastity and poverty of the Roman Catholic clergy.

8.38 (152:4). £. s. d. – That is, pounds, shillings, and pence; short for money.

8.39–40 (152:6). Bring your own bread and butter – The first line of a street rhyme that continues: "Bring your own tea and sugar, / But you'll come to the wedding, / Won't you come?"

8.41 (152:8). flitters – Tatters, rags, fragments.

8.42 (152:9). Potatoes and marge, marge and potatoes – Margarine and potatoes, the staple diet of the poverty-stricken city dweller in the British Isles and the chant protesting that diet.

8.42–43 (152:10). Proof of the pudding – "The proof of the pudding is in the eating" (*Don Quixote*, Part I, Book 4, chapter 7).

8.45 (152:13–14). Brewery barge with export stout – From Guinness's Brewery, which is just south of the Liffey on the western side of Dublin. The stout would be moved by barge from the brewery to the mouth of the river for shipping.

8.46 (152:15). Hancock – Identity and significance unknown.

8.46–47 (152:15). the brewery – In 1904, Guinness's Brewery occupied approximately forty acres in southwestern Dublin. It employed three thousand people, and its numerous buildings were connected by a miniature narrow-gauge railway system. It is curious that Bloom should need a pass—in 1904 a limited number of visitors (twenty) were conducted through the brewery every hour from 11:00 A.M. to 3:00 P.M. on weekdays, and on Saturdays at 11:00 and 12:00.

8.49 (152:18). puke again like Christians – To "puke like a Christian" is low slang for to "take one's drink like a man," to stand up without flinching in competition with other heavy drinkers.

8.53 (152:24). that sewage – The estuarine Liffey, which bisects Dublin, was little better than an open sewer in 1904. See 3.150–51n and 8.100n.

8.57–58 (152:28–29). Elijah thirtytwo feet per sec – The attraction the earth exerts on bodies on its surface and the acceleration thus produced is a uniform quantity at any one point, an average value of approximately 32.2 feet per second squared. See 8.13n.

8.60 (152:32). Erin's King – See 4.434n.

8.62–63 (152:34–35). *The hungry famished . . . waters dull* – Apparently Bloom's own composition.

8.64–65 (152:37). Shakespeare has no rhymes – This generalization is, of course, woefully inaccurate.

8.67–68 (152:39–40). *Hamlet, I am . . . walk the earth* – The Ghost speaks to Hamlet: "I am thy father's spirit, / Doomed for a certain term to walk the night" (I.v.9–10).

8.71 (153:3). Australians they must be this time of year – In 1904 most fresh fruits and vegetables were only seasonally available in markets. Apples in June would therefore be imports from the southern hemisphere; the Australian harvest peaked in April.

8.74–76 (153:7–8). Banbury cakes . . . down into the Liffey – Banbury is a town in Oxfordshire, England, once noted for the excessive zeal of its Puritan inhabitants, and still noted for its cakes, pastry with mince filling. Bloom's gesture invites comparison with Elijah, who retired into the wilderness "and dwelt by the brook Cherith" after he had prophesied against King Ahab. "And the ravens brought him bread and

flesh in the morning and bread and flesh in the evening; and he drank of the brook" (I Kings 17:5–6). Ravens, gulls, and swans are classified as unclean fowl in Leviticus 11:13ff. (Douay).

8.76–77 (153:9–10). from their heights pouncing on prey – When the Lestrygonians attack the landlocked ships of Odysseus's squadron, they destroy the ships, throwing rocks from the heights surrounding the "curious bay," and they spear the men like fish (*The Odyssey* 10:121–24).

8.79 (153:12). Manna – In Exodus 16, when the children of Israel are wandering hungry in the wilderness and murmuring "against Moses," God sends manna, a miraculous "bread," to feed them.

8.80 (153:14). Anna Liffey – The River Liffey, since "Anna" is close to the Irish for river; "Anna Liffey" suggests "river of (the district called) Life." The term is usually applied not to the estuarine Liffey but to the attractive upper reaches of the river west and south of Dublin.

8.81–82 (153:15–16). Wonder what kind . . . live on them – Swan meat, classified as unclean in the Bible, was regarded as such a delicacy in medieval and Renaissance England that all swans were "birds royal," reserved exclusively to the king's use. In Daniel Defoe's (1660–1731) *Robinson Crusoe* (1719), Crusoe eats goat meat, fowl, and turtles; he remarks on fowl that are "like ducks" and "like geese," as well as on "a large bird that was good to eat, but I know not what to call it." He never explicitly mentions swan meat, though he does at one point call the shot that he uses to hunt birds "swan shot."

8.84–85 (153:19). They spread foot and mouth disease – Foot-and-mouth disease is spread largely by contact and by infected water. There is no evidence that gulls are involved.

8.90–92 (153:25–27). *Kino's / 11/– / Trousers* – J. C. Kino, a London clothier, had an outlet in Dublin, the West End Clothiers Co., 12 College Green, where Kino's ready-made trousers were sold, 11s. a pair.

8.94–95 (153:29–30). It's always flowing . . . stream of life we trace – See 5.563–64n.

8.97 (153:32). greenhouses – Public urinals.

8.97–98 (153:33). Dr Hy Franks – Franks is not listed under "Registered Medical Practioners in Ireland" in *Thom's* 1904. Hyman (p. 168) identifies him as an "English Jew . . . Henry Jacob Franks, born in Manchester in 1852, arrived in Dublin in 1903 after deserting his Turkish-born wife Miriam (née Mandil) and their four children," and confirms, or at least accepts, Bloom's (Joyce's) assertion that Franks was a quack who advertised "treatment for venereal diseases," as described in *Ulysses*.

8.98 (153:34). cost him a red – That is, a red cent.

8.98 (153:34). Maginni the dancing master – Denis J. Maginni (born Maginnis), professor of dancing, 32 Great George's Street North, a well-known character around Dublin. "Everyone knew his costume of tailcoat and dark grey trousers, silk hat, immaculate high collar with wings, gardenia in buttonhole, spats on mincing feet, and a silver-mounted silk umbrella in hand" (Ellmann, p. 365).

8.109 (154:4–5). Timeball on the ballast office . . . Dunsink Time – The Ballast Office, at the southern end of O'Connell Bridge on the corner of Westmoreland Street and Aston's Quay, was headquarters for the supervision of Dublin Harbor and its works; Dubliners regarded its clock, controlled by a direct wire from Dunsink Observatory (see 12.1858–59n), as the most reliable public timepiece in the city. A "time ball" is a ball on a pole rigged to drop at a specific mean time, in this case 1:00 P.M. Greenwich time, so that ships' chronometers could be checked. Since Dunsink time, twenty-five minutes behind Greenwich time, was standard time for Ireland, Bloom's "after one" is inaccurate because the dropped time ball would mean only that it is after 12:35 P.M. in Dublin, and from where he is in the street Bloom could not have seen the clock face that would tell him Dublin time.

8.110 (154:5–6). sir Robert Ball's – (1840–1913), astronomer royal and director of the observatory at Cambridge, England. Ball was born and educated in Dublin; he was a popular lecturer and the author of many books on astronomy. The book that Bloom recalls is *The Story of the Heavens* (1885); it is among the books in his library (17.1373 [708:27]).

8.110 (154:6). Parallax – The apparent displacement or the difference in apparent direction of an object as seen from two different points of view; in astronomy, the difference in direction of a celestial body as seen from some point on the earth's surface and from some other

conventional point, such as the center of the earth or the sun.

8.111 (154:7). Par it's Greek – Bloom is right. *Parallax* does derive from the Greek root *par(a)*, meaning "beside, close to," as in parallel, parable, parabola, etc.

8.112 (154:7–8). *Met him pike hoses – See 4.339n.

8.119 (154:16). big Ben – After the extraordinarily large bell in the clocktower of the Houses of Parliament in London.

8.121 (154:18). baron of beef – A double sirloin of beef.

8.121 (154:19). number one Bass – A strong ale brewed by Bass, Ratcliff, and Gretton, Ltd., Burton-on-Trent, England. The import of Bass into Ireland was to become, by the 1920s, controversial to the point of riot.

8.125 (154:23–24). we have sinned: we have suffered – See 5.372–73 (81:20–21).

8.126 (154:25). Wisdom Hely's – Hely, Ltd., manufacturing stationers, letterpress and lithographic printers, and bookbinders, 27–30 Dame Street, where Bloom was once employed. Charles Wisdom Hely was the managing director of the firm in 1904.

8.130 (154:29). skilly – Gruel, a soup-like concoction of oatmeal and water.

8.130 (154:30). Boyl: no: M'Glade's – The fictional Boylan ran an advertising firm, as did the real M'Glade (at 43 Abbey Street).

8.136 (154:37). Pillar of salt – See 4.232n.

8.142 (155:2). 85 Dame Street – A nonexistent address; in 1904 the numbers on Dame Street stopped at 82.

8.142 (155:2). ruck – Mess, jumble, tangle.

8.143–44 (155:3). Tranquilla convent – Carmel of the Nativity, Tranquilla, in Rathmines, a suburb south of the center of Dublin. The convent was founded in 1833 by the Order of Our Lady of Mount Carmel (the Carmelites).

8.148 (155:9). Feast of Our Lady of Mount Carmel – The feast occurs on 16 July or the Sunday following, celebrating the founding of the Carmelite order (on Mount Carmel in Syria, c. 1156).

8.152 (155:13). My heart's broke eating dripping – "Dripping" is fat left over from cooking meat, particularly bacon. The saying seems a stock expression of poverty, because dripping was even less expensive than margarine (let alone butter); see 8.42n.

8.153–54 (155:15). Pat Claffey, the pawnbroker's daughter – Patricia (?), the daughter of Mrs. M. Claffey, pawnbroker, 65–66 Amiens Street, became a nun (at least so Bloom thinks).

8.154 (155:15–16). a nun . . . invented barbed wire – Imaginative but unsound history of technology. Barbed wire itself was invented and patented by three Americans (Smith, Hunt, and Kelly) simultaneously in 1867–68, and it became practicable when the American inventors Glidden and Vaughan obtained a patent on a machine for its manufacture in 1874.

8.155 (155:17). Westmoreland street – O'Connell Bridge, over which Bloom crosses the Liffey, gives south into Westmoreland Street, which continues south to the west front of Trinity College and College Green.

8.156 (155:18). Rover cycleshop – 23 Westmoreland Street.

8.156 (155:18). Those races are on today – See 5.550n.

8.156–57 (155:19). Year Phil Gilligan died – The causes of the fictional Mr. Gilligan's death are given at 17.1252–53 (704:35).

8.157 (155:20). Thom's – See 7.224n.

8.159 (155:22). the big fire at Arnott's – On 4 May 1894 "the block of buildings owned by the firm of Arnott & Co. (Ltd.) which extends from Henry st. to Prince's st., totally destroyed by fire" (*Thom's* 1904, p. 2105).

8.159 (155:22). Val Dillon – Valentine Dillon, lord mayor of Dublin in 1894–95, died early in 1904.

8.160 (155:23). The Glencree dinner – An annual fund-raising dinner at St. Kevin's Reformatory (now the Glencree Reconciliation Center), Glencree, County Wicklow, an institution for Roman Catholic males located at the headwaters of the Glencree River in the hilly country

ten miles south of the center of Dublin; see 10.536ff. (234:3ff.).

8.160 (155:23–24). Alderman Robert O'Reilly – A merchant tailor by trade (8 Parliament Street) and a small-time Dublin politician, listed as an alderman on the markets committee in the 1890s.

8.161 (155:24). before the flag fell – Before the race began.

8.161–62 (155:25). for the inner alderman – To "feed the inner man" is to take spiritual sustenance.

8.162 (155:25–26). Couldn't hear what the band played – A stock joke at the expense of a noisy eater.

8.162–63 (155:26–27) For what we . . . Lord make us – An inversion of the standard blessing: "For what we are about to receive may the Lord make us thankful."

8.163 (155:27). Milly – Born 15 June 1889.

8.166 (155:30). Sugarloaf – A mountain fourteen miles south-southeast of Dublin.

8.171 (155:36). Dockrell's – Thomas Dockrell & Sons, Ltd., contractors, window glass, oil color, cement, and wallpaper dealers, and decorators, 47–49 Stephen Street, south of the Liffey in central Dublin.

8.171 (155:36). one and ninepence a dozen – One shilling, ninepence, an inexpensive but by no means low-grade wallpaper.

8.174 (155:39–40). daguerreotype atelier – Belonged not to Bloom's father but to Bloom's father's cousin, Stefan Virag, in Szésfehérvár, Hungary; see 17.1876–77 (723:26–28).

8.176 (155:42). Stream of life – See 5.563–64n.

8.178 (156:2). Citron's saint Kevin's parade – See 4.205n.

8.178–79 (156:3). Pendennis? . . . Pen . . . ? – Answer: Penrose, identity and significance unknown (8.1114 [181:32]). *The History of Pendennis* (1850) is a novel by William Makepeace Thackeray (1811–63). The hero, Arthur Pendennis, begins life as a weakling spoiled by an indulgent mother; he nearly ruins himself in imprudent love affairs before he gets straightened out.

8.180 (156:4–5). if he couldn't . . . sees every day – In other words, if Nannetti couldn't remember Monks's name; see 7.182–85 (121:31–34).

8.181 (156:6). Bartell d'Arcy – Fictional; appears as a character in "The Dead," *Dubliners*.

8.183 (156:8–9). *Winds that blow from the south* – Song, source unknown. The song continues: "Shall carry my heart to thee / . . . / And the breath of the balmy night / Shall carry my heart to thee." Parnell and Mrs. O'Shea were supposed to have used this song as a code during the early years of their liaison.

8.184–85 (156:10–11). that lodge meeting on about those lottery tickets – Fictional; Bloom was almost arrested in 1893 or 1894 for attempting to sell tickets for "The Royal and Privileged Hungarian Lottery" and was apparently rescued by members of his Masonic Lodge (see 12.772–79 [313:23–26] and 18.1224–25 [772:20–21]). The factual source for this detail appears in the *Illustrated Irish Weekly Independent and Nation*, 16 June 1904, p. 4, col. 7: "From a prosecution which took place at the Clerkenwell Police Court [in London] the other day it would appear that the authorities have decided on the adoption of strong measures for the purpose of putting a stop to the circulation of announcements relating to foreign lotteries. A printer was summoned by the Treasury for publishing a certain proposal and scheme for the sale of tickets and chances, and shares in certain tickets, in a lottery called 'The Privileged Royal Hungarian Lottery' authorized by the Government of the State of Hungary."

8.185–86 (156:12). *the supper room or oak room of the Mansion house – The Mansion House, the official residence of the lord mayor of Dublin, is in Dawson Street, between Trinity College and St. Stephen's Green in the southeast quadrant of Dublin. The Oak Room, paneled in oak from floor to ceiling and with an intricately carved oak cornice, was the smaller and more intimate of the two spaces for public entertainment in the Mansion House in 1904. The larger was the Round Room.

8.187 (156:14). High school – The Erasmus Smith High School (founded in 1870) was at 40 Harcourt Street, south of St. Stephen's Green and on the route the Blooms take from the Man-

sion House to their home in Lombard Street West. Bloom was a student at the school until 1880 (when he started is not known). Perhaps the school's most distinguished alumnus (1880–83) was William Butler Yeats, who in "Reveries over Childhood and Youth" (1914) describes the school as much more rigorous and demanding than his school in London, though his description suggests considerable emphasis on sheer quantity of work, on memorization, and on the mechanics of grammar (*The Autobiography* [New York, 1958], pp. 36–38).

8.190 (156:17–18). May be for months and may be for never – A paraphrase of the chorus of the song "Kathleen Mavourneen," words by Annie Barry Crawford, music by Frederick N. Crouch. First verse: "Kathleen Mavourneen, the grey dawn is breaking, / The horn of the hunter is heard on the hill. / The lark from her light wing the bright dew is shaking / Kathleen Mavourneen—what, slumb'ring still? [Chorus:] Oh, hast thou forgotten how soon we must sever? / Oh, hast thou forgotten, this day we must part? / It may be for years, and it may be forever. / Oh, why art thou silent, thou voice of my heart? / It may be for years, and it may be forever / Then why art thou silent, Kathleen Mavourneen?"

8.191–92 (156:19). Corner of Harcourt road – South of the high school, at the junction of Harcourt Street and Harcourt Road, where the Blooms would have turned west toward their home.

8.203 (156:32). Mrs Breen – As the former Josie Powell, Mrs. Breen was a friend (and potential rival) of Molly when Bloom and Molly were courting. She subsequently married the eccentric Denis Breen.

8.211 (156:40). on the baker's list – Able to eat bread or solid food; therefore, well.

8.216 (157:3). Turn up like a bad penny – Proverbial expression of the superstitious belief that it is almost impossible to rid oneself of a small, meaningless, and annoying detail.

8.221–24 (157:10–13). *Your funeral's tomorrow . . . Diddlediddle . . .* – Bloom juxtaposes lines from two songs, "His Funeral's Tomorrow," by Felix McGlennon, and "Comin' through the Rye," by Robert Burns. "His Funeral's Tomorrow," first verse: "I will sing of Mick McTurk. / Mick one day got tight / And he roamed about the street / Dying for a fight; /

Mickey said to me, / He would put me on the fire / And because I said he'd not, / He called me a liar. [Chorus:] And his funeral's tomorrow / My poor heart aches with sorrow / I hit him once that's all / Then he heard the angels call / And we're going to plant him tomorrow." "Comin' through the Rye," chorus: "O, Jenny's a'weet, poor body, / Jenny's seldom dry; / She draigl't a' her petticoatie, / Comin thro' the rye! [First verse:] Comin' thro' the rye, poor body / Comin' thro' the rye, / She draigl't a' her petticoatie, / Comin' thro' the rye. [Second verse:] Gin a body meet a body / Comin' thro' the rye / Gin a body kiss a body / Need a body cry?"

8.229 (157:20–21). a caution to rattlesnakes – So remarkable or extreme as to astonish a rattlesnake.

8.230 (157:22). He has me heartscalded – A still-current Dublinism: "He'll be the death of me."

8.232 (157:23). jampuffs – A puff pastry filled with jam.

8.232 (157:24). rolypoly – A kind of pudding consisting of a sheet of paste covered with jam or preserves, formed into a roll and boiled or steamed.

8.233 (157:24). Harrison's – Harrison Co., confectioners, 29 Westmoreland Street.

8.234–35 (157:26). Demerara sugar – A raw cane sugar in the form of yellowish-brown crystals, named after a region of Guyana.

8.237–38 (157:29–30). Penny dinner . . . to the table – Dublin Free Breakfasts for the Poor in the Christian Union Buildings, Lower Abbey Street: "free breakfasts on Sunday mornings, penny and halfpenny dinners during the winter months." Charity customers ate standing up at counters to which the flatware was literally chained.

8.242 (157:34). barging – To "barge" is to speak roughly or abusively.

8.245 (157:38). new moon – Mrs. Breen is right; on Monday, 13 June 1904, at 8:45 a new moon rose over Dublin. Popular superstition regarded the new moon as a positive time, associating derangement with the waning moon. One notable exception: werewolves were assumed to be excited into activity by the new

moon (and to wane back into their human alter egos as the moon developed through its phases).

8.252 (158:6). Indiges. – Bloom attributes Breen's nightmare to indigestion.

8.253 (158:7). the ace of spades – In fortunetelling, a card of ill omen: malice, misfortune, perhaps death.

8.258 (158:12). U. p: up – In Charles Dickens's *Oliver Twist*, chapter 24, the expression *U.P.* is used by an apothecary's apprentice to announce the imminent death of an old woman. In the French edition of *Ulysses* the postcard is translated *fou tu*, "you're nuts, you've been screwed, you're all washed up." Richard Ellmann suggests: "When erect you urinate rather than ejaculate" (letter, 3 October 1983; see also Ellmann, p. 455n). Another possibility is the designation *u. p.* for whiskey, meaning underproof, below the legal standard (suggested by Robert T. Byrnes, in 1983 a graduate student in the English Department at UCLA). Still another speculation has to do with the initials that precede the docket numbers in Irish cemeteries; see Adams, pp. 192–93.

8.273 (158:31). Josie Powell – Mrs. Breen's maiden name.

8.274 (158:31–32). In Luke Doyle's . . . Dolphin's Barn – Luke and Caroline Doyle, friends of the Blooms, lived in Dolphin's Barn on the southwest outskirts of metropolitan Dublin. Their wedding present to the Blooms is mentioned at 17.1337–38 (707:24–26).

8.277 (158:36). Mina Purefoy – Takes her name, appropriately, from Richard Dancer Purefoy, M.D., a Dublin obstetrician who in 1904 was former master of the Rotunda Lying-in Hospital on Rutland (now Parnell) Square. Her husband in fiction, the Methodist Theodore Purefoy, was "conscientious second accountant, Ulster Bank. College Green Branch," in Dublin (14.1324–25 [421:5–6]).

8.278–79 (158:37–38). Philip Beaufoy . . . the masterstroke – See 4.502n and 4.502–3n.

8.281–82 (159:1). lying-in hospital – See 6.381–82n.

8.282 (159:1). Dr Horne – Andrew J. Horne, former vice-president of the Royal College of Physicians in Ireland and one of the two "masters" of the National Maternity Hospital in Holles Street.

8.282 (159:2). three days bad – She has been in labor for three days.

8.296 (159:17). glass – Monocle.

8.302 (159:24–25). Cashel Boyle O'Connor Fitzmaurice Tisdall Farrell – A Dublin eccentric nicknamed "Endymion" ("whom the moon loved") Farrell. Oliver St. John Gogarty (*As I Was Going Down Sackville Street* [New York, 1937] pp. 1–10) describes him as an appropriate opening image of topsy-turvy Dublin-Ireland and renders his name "James Boyle Tisdell Burke Stewart Fitzsimmons Farrell." See also Ellmann, p. 365.

8.304 (159:26). Denis – That is, her husband, Denis Breen. *Thom's* 1904 lists a Denis Breen as proprietor of the Leinster Billiard Rooms in Rathmines Road.

8.310 (159:34). Harrison's – See 8.233n.

8.311 (159:35). Blown in from the bay – Breen is so skinny that he looks as though he could be blown away by a gust of wind.

8.314 (159:38). Meshuggah – Yiddish: "eccentric, crazy."

8.314 (159:38). Off his chump – Very eccentric, utterly mad.

8.315–16 (159:40–41). the tight skullpiece . . . umbrella, dustcoat – Farrell's costume, which Ellmann describes (p. 365) as including two swords, a fishing rod, an umbrella, and a "small bowler hat with large holes for ventilation."

8.316 (159:41). Going the two days – Dublin slang for behaving with extraordinary flair or flourish.

8.318 (160:1). mosey – Hairy, especially having soft h⸴ like down.

8.320 (160:3). Alf Bergan – (d. 1951 or 1952), another Dublin character and practical joker, a solicitor's clerk in the offices of David Charles, solicitor, Clare Street, Dublin. *Thom's* 1904 does not list a David Charles, but it does list an Alfred Bergan, Esq., as resident in Clonliffe Road, and it is this Bergan whom Joyce mentions in a letter, 14 October 1921 (*Letters* 1:174).

In 1904 Bergan was assistant to the subsheriff of Dublin.

8.321 (160:4). the Scotch house – A pub, 6–7 Burgh Quay, on the corner of Hawkins Street, south bank of the Liffey; James Weir & Co., Ltd., tea dealers, wine and spirit merchants.

8.323 (160:7). the *Irish Times* – At 31 Westmoreland Street (Bloom is walking south). The *Times* was and is a daily morning newspaper. In 1904 its handling of the news was sober and reliable; its editorial policy was consistently, but not stridently, Protestant Anglo-Irish conservative, in favor of the status quo and dubious about the campaign for Irish nationhood. The ad that Bloom placed in the *Times* put him in touch with Martha Clifford.

8.330–31 (160:16). Lizzie Twigg – Adams (p. 55) notes that she was a real person, "a protégé of A.E.'s . . . an ardent Irish Nationalist." She had published poetry under her own name in the *Irish Rosary* and the *United Irishman* and was in 1904 to publish a volume, *Songs and Poems*, under her Gaelic name, Elis ni Chraoibhin.

8.334 (160:20). by long chalks – "Chalks" are scores or tabulations; therefore, by a considerable degree or distance.

8.334 (160:20–21). Got the provinces now – That is, since the paper enjoyed a wide circulation outside Dublin, it was used for the publication of legal notices in the provinces.

8.335 (160:21). Cook and general, exc. cuisine, housemaid kept – Wanted: a cook and general housekeeper, with the assurance that the kitchen over which she will preside is excellent and that she will have the assistance of a housemaid.

8.336 (160:22). Resp. – Respectable.

8.337 (160:23). James Carlisle – In *Thom's* 1904 spelled as both "Carlisle" and "Carlyle"; the manager and a director of the *Irish Times*.

8.337 (160:23–24). Six and a half per cent dividend – The Irish Times, Ltd., was a "public corporation"; its annual dividend in 1903 was six and a half percent.

8.338 (160:24–25). Coates's shares . . . old Scotch hunks – James and Peter Coats, a thread-manufacturing firm based in Paisley,

Scotland, merged in 1896 with its foremost rival, Clark & Co. The monopoly thus created resulted in spectacular economic growth for the company and a corresponding rise in the value of its stocks.

8.338 (160:25). Ca'canny – Scots: literally, "drive gently"; figuratively, "move slowly and cautiously."

8.338 (160:25). hunks – Miser.

8.339 (160:26). the *Irish Field* – A weekly newspaper "devoted to the interests of country gentlemen," published in Dublin on Saturdays.

8.340 (160:27). Lady Mountcashel – Bloom's version of the kind of news the *Irish Field* indulged in. There was, however, no Lady Mountcashel. Edward George Augustes Harcourt (1829–1915), Earl Mountcashell and Baron Kelsworth (1898–1915), did not marry and died without an heir.

8.341 (160:28). Ward Union staghounds – The staghound or buckhound, the first variety of dogs now classed under the general term *foxhound*. The Ward Union Staghounds, one of the more famous of the Irish fox hunts, met two and occasionally three times weekly during the season (November to mid-April).

8.341 (160:28–29). enlargement – When the fox to be pursued is released from a cage at the beginning of the hunt.

8.341 (160:29). Rathoath – A village twenty-five miles northwest of Dublin. Fairyhouse, the "home" of the Ward Union Staghounds hunt, is near Rathoath.

8.342 (160:29). uneatable fox – In Act I of Oscar Wilde's play *A Woman of No Importance* (1893; 1894), Lord Illingworth describes fox hunting as "the unspeakable in full pursuit of the uneatable" (Patrick A. McCarthy, *JJQ* 13, no. 1 [1975]: 54).

8.342 (160:29). Pothunters – A "pothunter" is one who hunts game only for the food it represents; hence, a poor person who steals food to prevent himself from starving.

8.342–43 (160:30). Fear injects juices make it tender enough for them – Even though fox is inedible, its flesh might be transformed by fear so that at least a starving man could eat it?

8.343 (160:31). Weightcarrying – A "weight-carrier" is a horse that can run well under a heavy weight.

8.344 (160:32). not for Joe – After an anonymous popular song of the 1860s: "Not for Joseph, / If he knows it; / Oh, no, no, / Not for Joe!"

8.344–45 (160:33). in at the death – Or in at the kill: present when the hounds overtake and kill the fox. It usually means that one has ridden extraordinarily well, courageously, if not recklessly.

8.346 (160:35). while you'd say knife – Proverbial expression for very quickly or suddenly.

8.347 (160:35). the Grosvenor – See 5.99n.

8.348 (160:37). five-barred gate – Between five and six feet high; a formidable obstacle.

8.349–50 (160:38–39). Mrs Miriam Dandrade – Apart from the context, identity and significance unknown. She is to appear in one of the hallucinations in Circe.

8.351 (160:40). Shelbourne Hotel – A posh tourist hotel at the junction of Kildare Street and the northern mall of St. Stephen's Green.

8.351–52 (160:41). Didn't take a feather out of her – Obviously, didn't disturb her in the least, but Partridge also cites "feather" as slang for female pubic hair.

8.353 (160:42–161:1). Stubbs the park ranger – Until 1901, Henry G. Stubbs was overseer, Board of Public Works, the Cottage, Phoenix Park, Dublin.

8.353 (161:1). Whelan – Identity and significance unknown.

8.353 (161:1). the *Express* – The *Daily Express;* see 7.306n.

8.356–57 (161:5). No nursery work for her – In other words, she would avoid conceiving a child.

8.358 (161:6–7). Method in his madness – When Hamlet pretends to be mad but is actually mocking Polonius, Polonius responds in an aside: "Though this be madness, yet there is method [order, sense] in it" (II.ii.207–8).

8.359 (161:7–8). the educational dairy – The Educational Dairy Produce Stores, Ltd., purveyors of "health foods" and "temperance beverages," had several shops with lunch counters in Dublin.

8.361–62 (161:10). Theodore's cousin – In fiction, if not in fact, Mortimer Edward Purefoy, a third cousin, is in the Treasury Remembrancer's Office in Dublin Castle; see 14.1335–36 (421:18–19). The Remembrancer's Office was the government paymaster for Ireland, but *Thom's* 1904 (p. 834) does not cite the third cousin's presence in that office.

8.362 (161:10). Dublin Castle – The lord lieutenant of Ireland, appointed by England, used the castle as his town residence, and it also housed the offices of the chief secretary, the law offices of the Crown, the Royal Irish Constabulary, and other administrative offices.

8.362 (161:10). tony – Stylish, high-toned.

8.363 (161:12). the Three Jolly Topers – A public house north of Dublin on the River Tolka.

8.364 (161:13). squallers – Babies, young children; also, tramps.

8.366 (161:15). t.t.'s – Teetotalers.

8.366 (161:15). Dog in the manger – A churlishly selfish person, after Aesop's fable about the dog that took over the manger and kept the cattle from eating the hay in spite of the fact that he obviously had no use for it himself.

8.368 (161:17). Fleet street crossing – Fleet Street intersects Westmoreland Street halfway between O'Connell Bridge and the west front of Trinity College in College Green.

8.369 (161:18). Rowe's – Andrew Rowe, vintner and publican, 2 Great George's Street South, not far west of where Bloom is walking (the National Library is, however, south and east of Bloom's position).

8.369–70 (161:19). the Burton – The Burton Hotel and Billiard Rooms advertised "Refreshment Rooms" at 18 Duke Street (on Bloom's route to the library).

8.371 (161:20). Bolton's Westmoreland house – William Bolton & Co., grocers and tea, wine, and spirit merchants; 35–36 Westmoreland Street.

8.374 (161:23). vinegared handkerchief – For reducing fever and alleviating headache.

8.378 (161:28). Twilight sleep – A partial anesthetic prescribed for women in childbirth. In April 1853, when she was giving birth to Prince Leopold, Queen Victoria did allow her doctors to experiment with "twilight sleep" in the form of a light dose of chloroform. Anesthesiology was then in its pioneering stages, and the queen's willingness to experiment was widely publicized.

8.379 (161:29). Nine she had – Queen Victoria had four sons and five daughters.

8.379 (161:29). A good layer – A phrase used to describe a productive hen.

8.379–80 (161:29–30). Old woman that . . . so many children – After the nursery rhyme: "There was an old woman who lived in a shoe. / She had so many children she didn't know what to do; / She gave them some broth without any bread; / She whipped them all soundly and put them to bed."

8.380 (161:30–31). Suppose he was consumptive – Bloom speculates (incorrectly) that Prince Albert had tuberculosis (after the popular assumption that tubercular individuals were sexually hyperactive). In reality Prince Albert died of typhoid fever.

8.381–82 (161:32–33). the pensive bosom of the silver effulgence – Bloom combines two phrases from Dan Dawson's speech (7.246–47, 253 [123:29, 36] and 7.328 [126:4–5]).

8.382 (161:33). Flapdoodle – Empty talk, transparent nonsense.

8.383–88 (161:35–40). give every child . . . more than you think – £5 at five percent interest, compounded annually, would almost treble to £13 18s. in twenty-one years.

8.391–92 (162:2). Mrs Moisel – According to Hyman (p. 190), Nisan Moisel (1814–1909) was among Bloom's neighbors in or near Lombard Street West. "He was the father of Elyah Wolf Moisel (1856–1904), whose wife Basseh (née Hodess), gave birth to a daughter, Rebecca Ita, on 28 June 1889, thirteen days after Molly Bloom's daughter, Milly, was born."

8.392 (162:2–3). Phthisis retires . . . then returns – Phthisis, medically, means a wasting or consumption of tissue; it was formerly applied to many wasting diseases, but by the early twentieth century it was usually applied to pulmonary consumption and tuberculosis. As Bloom observes, tuberculosis may be quiescent for several months or even for more than a year.

8.394 (162:5). a jolly old soul – After the nursery rhyme: "Old King Cole was a merry old soul, / And a merry old soul was he. / He called for his pipe and he called for his bowl, / And he called for his fiddlers three."

8.396 (162:7). old Tom Wall's – Adams (p. 235) regards this as "a reference, no doubt, to Thomas J. Wall, K.C. [King's Counsel], chief divisional magistrate of the City of Dublin Police District."

8.397 (162:8). snuffy – Obsolete for sulky, angry, vexed.

8.397 (162:8–9). Dr Murren – See 6.942–43n.

8.401 (162:13). the Irish house of parliament – That is, the Bank of Ireland. The building had housed the Irish Parliament until its dissolution by the Act of Union in 1800.

8.404 (162:16). Apjohn – Percy Apjohn, fictional, a childhood friend of Bloom's; Apjohn was killed in the Boer War (17.1251–52 [704:34]).

8.404 (162:17). Owen Goldberg – Another of Bloom's childhood friends; *Thom's* 1904 lists him at 31 Harcourt Street, not far from the Erasmus Smith High School, which both he and Bloom attended.

8.404 (162:17). Goose green – Goosegreen Avenue is in Drumcondra on the northern outskirts of Dublin.

8.405 (162:18). Mackerel – The fish, of course; but also a mediator or agent, and slang for a pimp or bawd.

8.406 (162:19). A squad of constables debouched from College street – College Street intersects the southern end of Westmoreland Street from the east. There was a police station and barracks across from the east end of College Street, a short block from where Bloom is walking.

8.409 (162:22–23). Policeman's lot is oft a happy one – After a song from Gilbert and Sullivan's *The Pirates of Penzance* (1880); the Sergeant and Chorus sing antiphonally. Sergeant: "When a felon's not engaged in his employment / Or maturing his felonious little plans / His capacity for innocent enjoyment / Is just as great as any honest man's. / Our feelings we with difficulty smother / When constabulary duty's to be done. / Ah, take one consideration with another— / A policeman's lot is not a happy one."

8.413 (162:27–28). Prepare to receive cavalry – A command to infantry threatened by a cavalry charge. In response to the command, troops in the front rank go down on one knee, the rifle with fixed bayonet angled forward, its butt braced against the ground.

8.414 (162:29). Tommy Moore's roguish finger – A statue of the Irish poet Thomas Moore (1779–1852) stands over a public urinal near Trinity College, opposite the east front of the Bank of Ireland. A fragile eroticism is characteristic of Moore's early verse. His most famous series, *Irish Melodies* (intermittently, 1807–1834), was to be found on the bookshelf of every properly sentimental Irish household. Moore left Ireland in 1798 and advanced himself in the drawing rooms of the influential in London. His laments for "poor old Ireland" were, therefore, not vital Irish rebellion but sentimental complaints acceptable to English ears. Moore's reputation was tarnished by his apparent willingness to compromise his artistic integrity and by the scandal that ensued when he abandoned his admiralty post in Bermuda and left an embarrassingly dishonest deputy in charge. His "roguish finger" is, however, an allusion to a famous literary hoax perpetrated by "Father Prout," pen name of the witty Irish priest Father Francis Mahony (1804–66), in an article, "Rogueries of Tom Moore," in *Frazier's Magazine*. Father Prout's hoax involved the charge that several of Moore's most popular songs were "literal and servile translations" of French and Latin "originals"; Father Prout duly "quoted" in evidence the "originals," complete with circumstantial historical background.

8.415–17 (162:30–32). meeting of the waters . . . There is not in this wide world a vallee – Thomas Moore's "The Meeting of the Waters," in *Irish Melodies;* the poem celebrates the beauty of the vale of Avoca, the confluence of the Avonmore and Avonbeg, near Rathdrum in County Wicklow thirty-five miles south of Dublin. First verse: "There is not in the wide world a valley so sweet / As that vale in whose bosom the bright waters meet; / Oh! the last rays of feeling and life must depart, / Ere the bloom of that valley shall fade from my heart."

8.417 (162:33). Julia Morkan's – Julia Morkan appears as a character in "The Dead," *Dubliners*.

8.418 (162:34). Michael Balfe's – Michael William Balfe (1808–70), a Dublin musician who sang, played virtuoso violin, conducted, and composed operas, including *The Rose of Castile* (1857), *The Bohemian Girl* (1843), and *Il talismano* (1874).

8.420 (162:36). could a tale unfold – The Ghost speaks to Hamlet: "But that I am forbid / To tell the secrets of my prison-house, / I could a tale unfold whose lightest word / Would harrow up thy soul" (I.v.13–16).

8.420 (162:36). a G man – A member of the "G," or plainclothes intelligence division of the Dublin Metropolitan Police.

8.421 (162:37). lagged – Arrested.

8.421 (162:38). bridewell – House of correction; loosely, jail or prison. After the Bridewell, a house of correction in London (until 1864). The Dublin bridewell was located in Chancery Street behind the Four Courts on the north bank of the Liffey.

8.422 (162:39). hornies – Constables (policemen).

8.423–24 (162:40–41). the day Joe Chamberlain was given his degree in Trinity – Joseph Chamberlain (1836–1914), an English politician and statesman. Originally a member of Gladstone's government, Chamberlain was antagonistic to Gladstone's policy of Home Rule for Ireland; in 1886 Chamberlain resigned and formed the Liberal Unionist party (splitting Gladstone's Liberal party and ensuring both its defeat and the defeat of Home Rule). In 1895 the Liberal Unionists and Conservatives joined forces under Lord Salisbury, and Chamberlain became secretary for the colonies (1895–1903). Once regarded as a "radical republican," Chamberlain emerged as an aggressive imperialist; his name was particularly associated with the En-

glish policy that resulted in the Boer War (1899–1902) and the extinction of the South African republics. Thus, Chamberlain was doubly unpopular in Ireland when he came to Dublin on 18 December 1899 to receive an honorary degree at Trinity College. On the same day John O'Leary, Maud Gonne, and other radical leaders had organized a pro-Boer meeting in Beresford Place, just across the Liffey from Trinity College. The protest meeting was interrupted by the police, but the protesters followed their leaders across the Liffey to College Green, where the demonstration continued with appropriate police harassment.

8.425 (162:42). Abbey street – 150 yards north of and parallel to the Liffey in central Dublin.

8.426 (163:1). Manning's – A pub, 41 Abbey Street Upper, on the corner of Liffey Street, one block east of Sackville (now O'Connell) Street; T. J. Manning, grocer and wine merchant.

8.426 (163:1). souped – In the soup: in difficulty, in trouble.

8.428 (163:4). the Trinity jibs – First-year undergraduates.

8.429 (163:6). Dixon – *Thom's* 1904 (p. 872) lists under "Registered Medical Practitioners in Ireland" a Joseph F. Dixon, M.D. from Dublin University (Trinity College), residing at 12 Conyngham Road, on the southern border of Phoenix Park.

8.430 (163:6). the Mater – The Mater Misericordiae Hospital; see 1.205–6n.

8.430 (163:7). in Holles street – At the National Maternity Hospital.

8.431 (163:7). Wheels within wheels – A cliché for complex interrelationships, after Ezekiel's vision of God's creation as four great wheels, "and their appearance and their work was as it were a wheel in the middle of a wheel" (Ezekiel 1:16).

8.432 (163:9). Give me in charge – That is, the policeman had formally told Bloom that he was under arrest.

8.434 (163:10). Up the Boers! – Committed Irish nationalists were pro-Boer because the South African Boer War seemed so clearly another and all-too-familiar instance of English suppression of the legitimate national aspirations of a people who stood in the way of the "course of Empire." Irish radicals even raised volunteer brigades to fight for the Boers against the English.

8.435 (163:11). De Wet – Christian R. De Wet (1854–1922), a distinguished Boer commander noted for his gallantry, for his extraordinarily clever field tactics in the Boer War, and finally, for his dignity in defeat.

8.436 (163:12). We'll hang Joe . . . sourapple tree – After one of the many improvised verses of "John Brown's Body," a Civil War Union army song: "We'll hang Jeff Davis to a sourapple tree! / As we go marching on!"

8.437 (163:13–14). Vinegar hill – At Enniscorthy in County Wexford, the headquarters of the Wexford rebels in the Rebellion of 1798 and the site of their defeat at the hands of the English on 21 June 1798. The final stanza of the ballad "The Boys of Wexford" recalls the battle: "And if for want of leaders, / We lost at Vinegar Hill, / We're ready for another fight, / And love our country still." See 7.427–28n.

8.438 (163:14). The Butter exchange band – The Butter Exchange was a dairyman's guild with branches in several Irish cities and towns. The Dublin branch maintained a band for the recreation of its members. The band sometimes played at political rallies; it was present at the demonstration Bloom recalls.

8.438–39 (163:14–15). few years time . . . and civil servants – Bloom reflects that half of the young students demonstrating against England will ultimately go straight and accept positions in the British civil service, which included not only the Home Service but also the administrative bureaucracy of the British Empire. *Magistrates:* in the late nineteenth century there were sixty-four "resident magistrates" functioning as resident judges in every part of Ireland except Dublin. The well-paid magistrates were traditionally portrayed as living the ideal life of the hunting-shooting-fishing country gentleman.

8.440 (163:16–17). *Whether on the scaffold high – After the chorus of the song "God Save Ireland," by T. D. Sullivan (1827–1914). Chorus: " 'God Save Ireland!' said the heroes; / 'God save Ireland!' said they all. / 'Whether on the scaffold high / Or on the battlefield we die, / O, what matter when for Ireland dear we fall!' "

8.441–42 (163:19). Harvey Duff – An informer

(a police sergeant disguised as a peasant) in *The Shaughraun* (1874), a play by the Irish-American playwright Dion Boucicault (1822–90).

8.442–43 (163:19–20). Peter or Denis . . . on the invincibles – See 5.378n and 5.379n.

8.443 (163:20–21). Member of the corporation too – Peter Carey was a councillor and therefore a member of the Dublin Corporation.

8.444 (163:22). secret service pay from the castle – Dublin Castle housed the offices of the British government in Ireland and, in this case, the offices of the Royal Irish Constabulary. Peter Carey was not in the "employ" of the Castle, though after he turned queen's evidence the Castle did make an ineffectual effort to aid his escape from Ireland and from retribution at the hands of Irish nationalists.

8.446 (163:24). slaveys – A slavey was a maid of all work with no defined job status on a household staff.

8.446 (163:24). twig – Notice, detect, discern, understand.

8.446 (163:24–25). Squarepushing – A squarepusher is a masher, usually with the implication that he is all dressed up or sporting a uniform.

8.449 (163:27). Peeping Tom – He figures in the eleventh-century legend about Lady Godiva, the wife of Leofric, earl of Mercia. Lady Godiva begged her husband to relieve the people of Coventry of an onerous tax that he had imposed. He agreed, on the condition that she ride naked through the town's marketplace, which she did. In gratitude and out of respect for her courage and modesty, the townspeople stayed indoors and did not look; they were rewarded by being relieved of the tax. But Tom the Tailor did peep, and he was miraculously struck blind.

8.449 (163:28). Decoy duck – Slang for a person employed to decoy others into some form of entrapment. In John Gay's (1685–1732) *The Beggar's Opera* (1728), Act II, scene iv, the highwayman-hero Macheath is deprived of his pistols and embraced (in effect, held) by several women so that Peachum and the constables can take him. In scene v Macheath responds: "Women are decoy ducks; who can trust them!"

8.454 (163:33). There are great . . . till you see – A variant of the opening line of the song "There's a Good Time Coming" by the English songwriter Henry Russell (1813–1900). First verse: "There's a good time coming, boys, / A good time coming, / We may not live to see the day. / But Earth shall glisten in the ray / Of the good time coming. / Cannon balls may aid the Truth, / But thought's a weapon stronger, / We'll win our battle of its aid, / Wait a little longer. [Chorus:] There's a good time coming, boys, / A good time coming, / Wait a little longer."

8.457–58 (163:36–38). James Stephens' idea . . . his own ring – For Stephens, see 3.241n. Stephens organized the Irish Republican Brotherhood (Fenian Society) in circles of ten, which divided when more than ten members had been initiated. Each circle of ten had a circle master, or "center," who was the only leader the ordinary member came in contact with unless the circle was mobilized for political action. The centers were responsible to a District Center; the District Center to a Divisional Center; the Divisional Centers to an eleven-member Supreme Council. Only the top members of the organization knew anything substantial about the organization and its personnel. As Stephens conceived it, the organization was proof against the plague of ordinary informers, but in practice it proved amazingly vulnerable, particularly in the abortive Fenian uprising of 1867.

8.458 (163:38). Sinn Fein – Irish: "We ourselves," with the added implication, "Stand Together." Bloom uses the term (as it was so often used) to mean the underground organization of the Irish Republican Brotherhood (see 2.272n) in the early twentieth century. More accurately, the term applies to the separatist policies articulated by Arthur Griffith late in 1905 and early in 1906. The Sinn Fein policy advocated that the Irish should refuse to support English economic and political institutions and should create their own, whether or not the English were willing to recognize them as constitutional. As originally conceived, Griffith's Sinn Fein did not have a secret or underground military arm, but many Irish republicans with outspoken paramilitary attitudes rallied to Sinn Fein's cause. See 1.176n.

8.458–59 (163:38–39). Back out you . . . The firing squad – James Stephens's original organization was designed primarily to frustrate informers. By the early twentieth century the discipline of the Irish Republican Brotherhood was so tight that summary execution by the "Hidden Hand" was threatened if any attempt was made to withdraw from membership. The "firing squad" was, of course, the British answer to the organization's activities. *The Hidden Hand* (1864) was the title of a popular melodrama by the English playwright Tom Taylor (1817–80). The play is an elaborate tangle of intrigues in the course of which the "hidden hand" poisons its victims with arsenic.

8.459–61 (163:39–41). Turnkey's daughter got . . . their very noses – For the story of Stephens's escape from Richmond Jail, see 3.241n. Lusk is a small village on the Irish Sea eleven miles north of Dublin. The collier on which Stephens and his associates were smuggled out of Lusk in 1867 was blown off course to Scotland. They landed there and took a train to London, where they put up for a night at the Palace Hotel near Victoria Station before traveling on to France and then America. The addition of "Buckingham" to the hotel's name is Bloom's flourish; Buckingham Palace was Queen Victoria's London residence.

8.461 (163:41). Garibaldi – Giuseppe Garibaldi (1807–1882), a revolutionary leader (notably in Uruguay and Italy) famous for his quasi-successful efforts to establish a unified, independent Italy. Like Stephens, he endured several periods of political exile from Italy (even after heroic contributions toward a measure of unity for Italy) and relied heavily, and daringly, on popular sympathies. In 1860, accompanied not by his army but by two companions, he openly entered a Naples that was in hostile hands. Unlike Stephens, who was regarded as a good organizer but not a man of action, Garibaldi was an excellent and courageous military leader.

8.463 (164:1). squareheaded – Honest and forthright.

8.463 (164:1–2). no go in him for the mob – Griffith quite frankly admitted that his separatist policies could not hope for anything like unanimous popular support in Ireland. Consequently, he couched his appeal in rational argument to the "one quarter" who could be expected to understand and support his policies and consciously rejected a rabble-rousing approach. Bloom contrasts Griffith with the more charismatic figure of Parnell.

8.464 (164:2–3). Gammon and spinach – Slang for the everyday round of things, after the folk song. First verse: "A frog he would a-wooing go, / Heigh ho! say Rowley, / A frog he would a-wooing go, / Whether his mother would let him or no. / With a rowley powley, gammon and spinach / Heigh ho! says Anthony Rowley." (A "rowley powley" is a plump fowl.)

8.464 (164:3). Dublin Bakery Company's tea-room – *Thom's* 1904 lists this as the Dublin Bread Co., Ltd., with restaurants at 3–4 St. Stephen's Green North; 6–7 Sackville Street Lower; 33 Dame Street; and the National Library, Kildare Street. It is not clear which of these Bloom associates with "gas about our lovely land," though it is at the one in Dame Street that Mulligan and Haines see Parnell's brother, John Howard Parnell (10.1045–53 [248:15–26]), and thus the tearoom near Dublin Castle may be the one Bloom has in mind; or perhaps it is the one near the National Library because it was frequented by students.

8.465 (164:3–4). Debating societies – See 7.793n.

8.466–67 (164:5–6). That the language . . . the economic question – That is, that the cause of Irish independence could best be served by the revival of the Irish tongue (see 10.1006–12 [247:16–23]) rather than by efforts to establish an independent Irish economy.

8.468 (164:7–8). Michaelmas goose – It is customary in Ireland (and England) to eat goose on Michaelmas (29 September).

8.469 (164:8). apron – The fat skin covering the belly of a goose or duck.

8.470–71 (164:10). Penny roll and walk with the band – The Salvation Army (formed in 1865) offered a penny's worth of bread to anyone who would march through the streets in witness to his "conversion."

8.471 (164:11). No grace for the carver – A pun on "grace," the blessing that precedes a meal and the time allowed a debtor to pay his debts. In effect, the person who carves will have little or no time to eat before he has to carve again for those who want second helpings.

8.473–74 (164:14). *Homerule sun rising up in the northwest – See 4.101–3n.

8.476 (164:16). Trinity's surly front – The great facade of the college was erected in 1759. "Surly" in this context has its original meaning of "proud" or "haughty" from the relatively unrelieved 300-foot neoclassical front of the college, which is severe, dark, and heavy-stoned; Bloom and his contemporaries would have called it "Corinthian" (as twentieth-century architectural historians would label it "Georgian").

8.483 (164:24–25). washed in the blood of the lamb – See 8.9n and 8.11–12n.

8.487 (164:30). notice to quit – A landlord's eviction notice.

8.490 (164:33). bread and onions – The classical diet of slaves.

8.490 (164:33–34). Chinese wall. Babylon – Together with the pyramids, these are examples of massive public monuments built at immense cost of labor and now fallen into a decay that reveals their essential pointlessness. The Great Wall of China, the present form dating substantially from the Ming dynasty (1368–1644), averages 25 feet high and 21 feet thick and extends some 1,500 miles along the Chinese-Mongolian border. The walls and hanging gardens of ancient Babylon (reduced to a series of mounds by the early twentieth century) were one of the Seven Wonders of the classical world.

8.490–91 (164:34). Big stones left. Round towers – That which remains of the architecture of ancient Ireland. "Big stones" are the "standing stones" and "stone circles" of prehistoric Ireland. Their functions remain a mystery, though some standing stones are apparently associated with Bronze Age burial sites, and many archaeologists speculate that the stone circles were laid out according to astronomical relationships and used to establish a calendar. "Round towers," many of which are still standing, were the most striking features of the pre-Norman Irish monasteries. The towers were constructed from the ninth through the twelfth centuries and were used as watchtowers and as places of refuge when the monasteries were being harassed by Scandinavian invaders.

8.491–92 (164:35). Kerwan's mushroom houses – Michael Kirwan (not Kerwan) was a Dublin building contractor who built low-cost housing for the Dublin Artisans' Dwellings

Co., Ltd., in the area just east of Phoenix Park in western Dublin.

8.496 (164:40). *Provost's house. The reverend tinned Salmon – The Reverend George Salmon (1819–1904), D.D., D.C.L., F.R.S. (Doctor of Divinity, Doctor of Civil Law, and Fellow of the Royal Society), a distinguished mathematician, was provost of Trinity College from 1888 to 1902. *Thom's* 1904 (apparently mistakenly) lists him as in residence in the provost's house (corner of Grafton and Nassau streets); the provost in residence (appointed in 1904) was Anthony Traill, M.D. (1838–1914). "Tinned" is also Dublin slang for having money or being wealthy.

8.497 (164:41//). *Like a mortuary chapel – That is, the provost's house reminds Bloom of the mortuary chapel in Prospect Cemetery, Glasnevin. The two-story sandstone facade of the provost's house (built in 1769) is heavy-handed in its eighteenth-century symmetry and weighed down by overstated arches above the windows and the entry door. The interior, by contrast, is rich and elegant, with "the finest private reception room in Dublin" (Maurice Craig, *Dublin 1660–1860* [Dublin, 1969], p. 182).

8.500 (165:2). Walter Sexton's window – Across the street from the provost's house. Walter Sexton, goldsmith, jeweler, silversmith, and watchmaker, 118 Grafton Street.

8.500 (165:2–3). John Howard Parnell – (1843–1923), brother of Charles Stewart Parnell. J. H. Parnell was member of Parliament for South Meath (1895–1900) and in 1904 was city marshal of Dublin and registrar of pawnbrokers.

8.504–5 (165:7). Must be a corporation meeting today – Bloom is right; see 10.1004–12 (247:13–23). One of the city marshal's duties was to establish and keep order at meetings of the Dublin Corporation (though J. H. Parnell skips the meeting in favor of his chess game).

8.506 (165:9). *Charley Kavanagh – Former city marshal of Dublin.

8.509 (165:12–13). his brother's brother – Bloom plays with the superstition that the brilliance of one of two brothers will be compensated by the dullness of the other.

8.510 (165:14). D.B.C. – Dublin Bread (or Bakery) Co. The smoking room of the company's restaurant at 33 Dame Street was a meeting place for chess players.

8.513 (165:17). Mad Fanny – C. S. Parnell's sister, Frances Isabel Parnell (1849–82), was active in the Irish nationalist movement. She worked closely with her brother and is reputed to have been an effective public speaker and a good organizer. Toward the end of her life she went into self-imposed exile in the United States and poured out a flood of patriotic verse, which she called "Land League Songs."

8.513 (165:18). Mrs Dickinson – Née Emily Parnell (1841–1918), another of Parnell's eight siblings, was married to a Capt. Arthur Dickinson. After C. S. Parnell's death she wrote an ambiguously sympathetic biography entitled *A Patriot's Mistake;* the *Irish Times* remarked that it should have been called *A Patriot's Sister's Mistake.*

8.514 (165:19). surgeon M'Ardle – John S. M'Ardle, Fellow of the Royal College of Surgeons in Ireland, was a surgeon at St. Vincent's Hospital in Dublin.

8.515 (165:19–20). David Sheehy beat him for South Meath – David Sheehy (1844–1932), Nationalist member of Parliament from South Galway (1885–1900), stood against and defeated John Howard Parnell for the seat of South Meath in 1903, a seat that Sheehy held until 1918.

8.515 (165:20). Apply for the Chiltern Hundreds – The Chiltern Hills, between Bedford and Hertford in England, were once notorious as a highwaymen's refuge, until Crown Stewards were appointed to patrol the area. Although the necessity for the patrol disappeared, the offices of the stewards remained; thus when a member of Parliament wished to vacate his seat, he could accept the office of Steward of the Chiltern Hundreds. Because this advanced him to a government office, his seat in Parliament was ex officio vacated. This device was occasionally used to cover what might otherwise have been an ignominious retreat (see Dickens, *Our Mutual Friend,* "Chapter the Last"). Bloom regards the office of city marshal of Dublin as a similar sinecure.

8.516–17 (165:21–22). The patriot's banquet. Eating orangepeels in the park – At patriotic assemblies and celebrations in Phoenix Park, Irish nationalists ate oranges as a symbolic gesture calculated to annoy Orangemen (who were Protestant, pro-Union, and antipatriot) with the suggestion that they were about to be swallowed in a united and independent Ireland.

8.520–22 (165:25–27). Of the two headed . . . with a Scotch accent – This may refer to George William Russell's uneasy relation with his friend and colleague in Theosophy S. Liddell MacGregor Mathers (1854–1918). Mathers was a wild professional Scot, resident in Dublin; his "two heads" were a fanatic interest in the occult and an equally fanatic interest in what Yeats (*The Autobiography* [New York, 1958], p. 225) called "the imminence of immense wars" (i.e., Armageddon, "the end of the world"). This warlike phase of Mathers's fanaticism upset Russell, a dedicated pacifist. Russell's remark about the two heads could also allude to Walter Pater's description of the Mona Lisa in *The Renaissance* (1873), "The presence that rose thus so strangely beside the waters, is expressive of what in the ways of a thousand years men had come to desire. Hers is the head upon which all 'the ends of the world are come' [I Corinthians 10:11], and the eyelids are a little weary." Hugh Kenner argues (*JJQ* 18, no. 2 [1981]: 205) that what Bloom overhears is not a fragment of the occult but a fragment of economics—to the effect that "British economic power, its tentacles stretched toward Ireland, its two heads, London and Edinburgh," are strangling the Irish economy. As Kenner notes, Russell's metaphors for "fiscal invective" include "elephant, tiger, plesiosaurus," and why not octopus? Another candidate for the "Scotch accent" might be Arthur James Balfour, Conservative prime minister of England in 1904; see 12.865n.

8.526 (165:31). Coming events cast their shadows before – From "Lochiel's Warning" (1802), a ballad by Thomas Campbell (1777–1844). In the poem the wizard predicts the defeat of Bonnie Prince Charlie, the Young Pretender (1720–88), at the battle of Culloden (1745) and further predicts Lochiel's death. In spite of the warning, Lochiel chooses honor over expediency, supports the foredoomed campaign of his prince, and goes to his death. The wizard's last warning begins: "Lochiel, Lochiel, beware of day! / For, dark and despairing my sight I may seal, / But man cannot cover what God would reveal: / 'Tis the sunset of life gives me mystical lore, / And coming events cast their shadows before" (lines 52–56).

8.527–28 (165:33). A.E.: What does that mean? – George William Russell's pen name,

which, according to one witty Dublin version, meant "Agricultural Economist." But Russell himself tells the story of its choice and meaning: he had attempted a picture of "the apparition in the Divine Mind of the Heavenly Man," and the title for it was mysteriously supplied by a disembodied whisper—"Call it the birth of Aeon." Some time later, in the National Library, his eye caught the word *aeon* in a book left open on a counter. He took this as a sign that his pen name had been chosen for him; but when he used it for the first time, the compositor misread it as *AE*, and with this final sign from the Divine Mind the revelation of the pen name was complete. For "Heavenly Man," see 9.61–62n; for "aeon," see 9.85n.

8.528 (165:34). Albert Edward – Edward VII of England was christened Albert Edward (an ironically unlikely pen name for an Irish patriot).

8.528 (165:34). Arthur Edmund – For Arthur Edmund Guinness, Lord Ardilaun, see 5.306n.

8.533 (165:39). homespun – Russell wore homespun as a sign of his belief in peasant Ireland and the potential of its cottage industries.

8.533 (165:40). bicycle – One of Russell's trademarks because he traveled all over Ireland on a bicycle while organizing farmers' cooperative societies. Dublin wit at his expense: "he rode that bicycle right into the editorship of the *Irish Homestead*."

8.534 (165:40–41). the vegetarian – Bloom assumes (correctly) that Russell is a vegetarian and that he has lunched at a nearby vegetarian restaurant (unidentified).

8.535–36 (165:42–166:1). the eyes of that cow . . . through all eternity – Bloom's version of the rationale behind Theosophical vegetarianism. The actual Theosophic argument was that animals had "desire-bodies," which were "astral," capable of "a fleeting existence after death." "In 'civilized' countries then animal astral bodies add much to the general feeling of hostility . . . , for the organized butchery of animals in slaughter houses and by sport sends millions upon millions of these annually into the astral world, full of horror, terror, and shrinking from men . . . and from the currents set up by these there rain down influences" that are extraordinarily destructive (Annie Besant, *The Ancient Wisdom* [London, 1897], p. 84).

8.537–38 (166:2). a bloater – "Bloat" is a condition in cattle or sheep in which the first stomach becomes painfully distended as a result of gas. Bloat is most frequent among animals unaccustomed to grazing on green legumes.

8.539 (166:4). nutsteak – A vegetarian meat substitute made of ground nuts.

8.539 (166:4). Nutarians. Fruitarians – Two subspecies of vegetarians. Nutarians believed in subsisting on a diet primarily of nuts; fruitarians, primarily of fruit.

8.540 (166:5). They cook in soda – Vegetarian manuals at the end of the nineteenth century did advise cooking in soda because it was believed the vegetable would then retain its original color (and presumably all its original virtue). The fact that cooking with soda depletes the vegetables of their vitamins was not known in 1904 because vitamins were not discovered until 1912.

8.546 (166:12). Irish stew – Basic ingredients: mutton, potatoes, onions, water, salt, and pepper.

8.551 (166:17). Nassau street – Along the south side of Trinity College, intersects Grafton Street (which Bloom now enters) from the east.

8.552 (166:18). Yeates and Son – On the west side of Grafton Street, opposite the intersection of Nassau and Grafton streets. Yeates & Son, opticians and mathematical instrument makers to the university and to the Dublin Port and Docks Board, were at 2 Grafton Street.

8.552 (166:19). old Harris's – Morris Harris (c. 1823–1909), dealer in works of art, plate, and jewelry, 30 Nassau Street. See Ellmann, p. 230n; *Letters* 1:242 and 2:194n; and Hyman, p. 148.

8.553 (166:19). young Sinclair – William Sinclair (1882–1938), Morris Harris's grandson, was, at his grandfather's insistence, raised as a Jew; see Hyman, pp. 148–49.

8.554 (166:21). Goerz lenses – Technically not lenses but prisms; Goerz, a German optical firm, enjoyed considerable success in developing and marketing prism binoculars.

8.555–56 (166:21–23). Germans making their way . . . Undercutting – Germany's expansionist policies in the years before World War I

included not only an all-out effort to enlarge its navy and its colonial empire but also to capture international markets. The German government granted impressive subsidies to key industries (such as the optical industry) to ensure a favorable competitive position in world markets. See 15.4455n.

8.556 (166:23–24). the railway lost property office – The office held personal belongings that had been left in trains for a limited period of time during which they could be reclaimed by their owners. After that period, the items were placed on sale to the general public.

8.560 (166:28). Limerick junction – In County Tipperary, a major railroad junction 123 miles southwest of Dublin and 48 miles southeast of Ennis (where Bloom's father died and was buried in 1886).

8.560–61 (166:28–30). little watch up there . . . test those glasses by – On the roof of the Bank of Ireland, 150 yards to the north across College Green. Many doubt that the watch ever existed, but it still constitutes a Dublin myth.

8.566 (166:36–37). the tip of his little finger blotted out the sun's disc – The druids regarded this gesture and its effect as symbolic of man's capacity for divination; see 8.526n.

8.568–69 (166:39–40). sunspots when we were in Lombard street west. Terrific explosions they are – Sunspots reach a maximum frequency in an eleven-year cycle; the maximum Bloom has in mind occurred in August 1893. In 1904 sunspots were generally regarded as fairly large and deep depressions in the sun's surface. Bloom here confuses sunspots with what were called "prominences," eruptive jets of red hydrogen flame that burst outward from the solar surface. But Bloom's "mistake" is not a serious confusion, because the two phenomena, while not explicable in 1904, were recognized as interrelated.

8.570 (166:40–41). total eclipse this year: autumn some time – 9 September 1904, visible in the United States but not in Dublin.

8.571 (167:1–2). that ball falls at Greenwich time – The time ball on the Ballast Office; see 8.109n. Bloom has corrected his initial mistake: the ball did fall at Greenwich rather than Dunsink time.

8.572 (167:2–3). Dunsink – The observatory,

northwest of Phoenix Park, was owned and operated by Trinity College from 1783 to 1946. It was "open to the general public on the first Saturday of each month from October to March inclusive from 7 to 9 P.M. and from 8 to 11 P.M. other months." The clocks in the Ballast Office were controlled by an electric current transmitted each second from the mean-time clock at the Dunsink Observatory.

8.573–74 (167:4). professor Joly – Charles Jasper Joly (1864–1906), astronomer royal of Ireland, Andrews Professor of Astronomy at Trinity College, and director of the observatory at Dunsink.

8.576 (167:7). foremother – A bastard is technically fatherless.

8.577 (167:8). Cap in hand goes through the land – An Irish proverb that suggests that humility will get one much further than arrogance or self-assertion.

8.582–83 (167:15–16). *Gas: then solid . . . frozen rock – A version of Laplace's nebular hypothesis about the origins of the earth and the universe: that the original gaseous materials concentrated into a hot solid that cooled, allowing the process of evolution ("world"), and will continue to cool to the point where temperatures approach absolute zero, eliminating the possibility of life. The moon (this theory held) is already such a body, and the earth will follow its example. Pierre Simon, marquis de Laplace (1749–1827), was a French astronomer.

8.584 (167:17). new moon – See 8.245n.

8.586 (167:18). *la maison Claire – "Court dressmaker," 4 Grafton Street.

8.587 (168:19). The full moon – Sunday, 29 May 1904.

8.588 (167:20–21). the Tolka . . . Fairview – The Tolka is a small river that meanders along the northern outskirts of metropolitan Dublin and empties into Dublin Bay at Fairview, which in 1904 was a tidal mudflat north of the reclaimed area at the mouth of the Liffey and has since been reclaimed as Fairview Park.

8.589–90 (167:21–23). The young May moon she's beaming, love. / Glowworm's la-amp is gleaming, love – A song entitled "The Young May Moon" by Thomas Moore, from *The Dandy, O!* Verse: "The young May moon is beaming, love, / The glow-worm's lamp is gleaming, love, / How sweet to rove, / Through Morna's grove, / When the drowsy world is dreaming, love."

8.591 (167:23–24). Touch. Fingers – Not just literally, since "touch" is slang for sexual intercourse. In the finger code Bloom suspects Molly and Boylan of having used, the questioner touches the palm of the person being questioned with the third finger; an answer of *yes* is conveyed by the same gesture in response.

8.593 (167:26–27). Adam court – A small street off Grafton Street.

8.596–97 (167:31). *cherchez la femme* – French: literally, "look for the woman"; figuratively: "expect a woman to be the hidden cause."

8.597 (167:31). the Coombe – See 5.280n.

8.597 (167:32). chummies – In context, slang for pimps; cf. 6.319n.

8.599 (167:34). Sloping – To "slope" is to saunter or loiter.

8.599 (167:34). the Empire – The Empire Buffet, a public house and restaurant at 1–3 Adam Court.

8.600 (167:35). Pat Kinsella – In the 1890s, the proprietor of the Harp Musical Hall, a cabaret, formerly at 1–3 Adam Court.

8.600 (167:36). Whitbred – *Thom's* 1904 lists James W. Whitbread (not Whitbred) as manager of the Queen's Royal Theatre, Great Brunswick (now Pearse) Street. Whitbread became manager after the demise of the Harp Musical Hall, with which he had been associated.

8.601 (167:36). Broth of a boy – The essence of boyishness, as broth is the essence of meat (P. W. Joyce, *English*, p. 137).

8.601–2 (167:36–37). Dion Boucicault business with his harvestmoon face – Dion Boucicault (1822–90), the "moonfaced" Irish-American playwright and actor, was regarded by contemporary critics as lacking "marked histrionic talent" but as making up for it "by his keen sense of humor"; so when Pat Kinsella did the "Dion Boucicault business," he was imitating Boucicault's manner of hamming it up in the entr'actes in female costume, with falsetto songs, etc.

8.602 (167:38). Three Purty Maids from School – After Gilbert and Sullivan's "Three Little Maids from School," *The Mikado* (1885), Act I. Sung by Yum-Yum, Peep-Bo, and Pitti-Sing, with Chorus. "THE GIRLS: Three little maids from school are we, / Pert as a school-girl well can be, / Filled to the brim with girlish glee, / Three little maids from school! YUM-YUM: Everything is a source of fun. [*Chuckle.*] PEEP-BO: Nobody's safe, for we care for none. [*Chuckle.*] PITTI-SING: Life is a joke that's just begun. [*Chuckle.*] THE GIRLS: Three little maids from school. CHORUS AND GIRLS: Three little maids who, all unwary, / Come from a ladies' seminary, / Freed from its genius tutelary. THE GIRLS [*demurely*]: Three little maids from school."

8.604 (167:40–41). More power – In other words, more whiskey, in reference to John Power & Son, Dublin distillers.

8.605–6 (167:42). Take off that white hat – A catch line developed by Moore and Burgess, minstrel show comics; see 15.410n.

8.606 (167:42). parboiled eyes – Overheated eyes, that is, eyes reddened by drinking.

8.606–7 (168:1). The harp that once did starve us all – After Thomas Moore's song "The Harp that Once Through Tara's Halls": "The harp that once through Tara's halls / The soul of music shed / Now hangs as mute on Tara's walls / As if that soul were fled. // So sleeps the pride of former days, / So glory's thrill is o'er, / And hearts, that once beat high for praise, / Now feel that pulse no more." The harp was the instrument of the Celtic bards and is a traditional symbol for Ireland; "harp" is also low slang for an Irish Catholic.

8.608–9 (168:2–3). Twentyeight . . . She twentythree – Bloom was born sometime between early February and early May in 1866 (see 16.608n); Molly on 8 September 1870. If Bloom's recall is accurate, the move would have taken place in mid-1894, after February–May and before September.[1]

---

[1] Timetables of Bloom's jobs, Molly's concerts, and the Blooms' residences are at best somewhat uncertain; see John Henry Raleigh, *The Chronicle of Leopold and Molly Bloom: "Ulysses" as Narrative* (Berkeley, Calif., 1977), pp. 273–74; and cf. 8.608–9n.

8.614 (168:10). Grafton street – "At that time the 'smartest' of the shopping thoroughfares of Dublin" (Frank Budgen, *James Joyce and the Making of "Ulysses"* [Bloomington, Ind., 1960], p. 102).

8.616 (168:12). causeway – The street was paved with granite blocks.

8.617 (168:14). chawbacon – A yokel.

8.617–18 (168:14). All the beef to the heels – See 4.402–3n.

8.620 (168:17). Brown Thomas – Brown, Thomas & Co., silk mercers, milliners, costumers, mantle makers, and general drapers, 15–17 Grafton Street, advertised itself in 1904 as having been famous for "the best quality" of Irish laces and linens for one hundred years.

8.622–23 (168:20). The huguenots brought that here – That is, the silk- and poplin-weaving industries. The Huguenots, who sought shelter in Ireland in the late seventeenth century and established colonies in Dublin and in the Protestant north, brought with them improved textile machinery and dyes, notably the red dyes, as Bloom remarks.

8.623–24 (168:20–22). *Lacaus esant . . . bom bom bom – Bloom recalls a passage from an opera by the German composer Giacomo Meyerbeer (1791–1864), *Les Huguenots* (1836). The original opera was written in French, but performances in Italian were common in the late nineteenth century. The opera deals in a rather ahistorical way with the massacre of the Huguenots in Paris on St. Bartholomew's Day, 24 August 1572. In Act IV, St. Bris, one of the leaders of the Catholic faction, pledges to do his part in the massacre in an impressive solo, "Pour cette cause sainte" (For this sacred cause [the massacre]), which Bloom recalls from the Italian, "La cause è santa" (The cause is sacred). Strictly speaking, it is not a "chorus," as Bloom thinks, though St. Bris's solo is later taken up by the full chorus.

8.623–24 (168:21–22). Must be washed in rainwater – Bloom sees in the window part of a sign with instructions for the care of the cloth. Rainwater was widely used with delicate materials and unstable dyes because it was ideally soft (i.e., contained no minerals). Cf. 8.9n.

8.629 (168:27). september eighth – Molly's

birthday (by coincidence) is also celebrated as the birthday of the Blessed Virgin Mary.

8.630 (168:28–29). Women won't pick . . . cuts lo – Refers to the superstition that if a girl picks up a pin, she will make a staunch new boyfriend; therefore, a woman avoids picking up pins because it would divide her affections— it would "cut love."

8.635 (168:35). Jaffa – See 4.194n.

8.635–36 (168:35). Agendath Netaim – See 4.191–92n.

8.640 (168:39). Duke street . . . The Burton – Bloom turns east from Grafton Street into Duke Street and walks past Davy Byrne's pub (at 21) to the Burton Hotel and Billiard Rooms at 18; the Burton advertised its "Refreshment Rooms" in *Thom's* 1904.

8.641 (168:41). Combridge's corner – Combridge & Co., picture depot, print sellers, and picture-frame makers, artists and color men, at 20 Grafton Street, on the corner of Duke Street.

8.662 (169:22). See ourselves as others see us – After Robert Burns's (1759–96) "To a Louse; on Seeing One on a Lady's Bonnet at Church" (1786): "O wad some Power the giftie gie us / To see oursels as ithers see us! / It wad frae monie a blunder free us, / An' foolish notion: / What airs in dress an' gait wad lea'e us, / An' ev'n devotion" (lines 43–48).

8.663–66 (169:23–27). That last pagan king . . . him to Christianity – Garbled history and legend. The poem Bloom recalls is "The Burial of King Cormac" by Sir Samuel Ferguson (1810–86), Irish poet and antiquary. The lines Bloom vaguely remembers: "He choked upon the food he ate / At Sletty, southward of the Boyne." King Cormac was not, however, "that last pagan king." Cormac, who reigned c. 254-c. 277, was the son of Art, whose father was Conn of the Hundred Battles. Irish tradition holds that Cormac was the first founder and legislator of Ireland, the shaper of the nation; it was he who made the hill of Tara the capital of the country and shaped Ireland's Golden Age. Legends of his reign picture him as having been the first person in Ireland to accept the Christian faith (139 years before the arrival of St. Patrick). His conversion caused the druids to become irritated and let loose a group of demons who arranged for Cormac to choke on a salmon bone while he was eating his dinner. St. Patrick

(c. 385–c. 461) did not begin his mission to Ireland until 432 or 433. There is a famous legend of a meeting at Tara between St. Patrick and (then) high king Laeghaire; the legend holds that, though Laeghaire himself did not accept conversion, he did agree not to interfere with St. Patrick's mission—as Bloom puts it, he "couldn't swallow it all" (8.666–67 [169:27]).

8.666 (169:26). galoptious – For *goluptious*, slang: "very enjoyable, delicious."

8.674 (169:34). tootles – A nursery word for a child's teeth.

8.675 (169:36). Look on this picture then on that – In Act III, Hamlet berates his mother and urges her to compare the image of his father with that of Claudius, his uncle and his mother's present husband: "Look here upon this picture, and on this, / The counterfeit presentment of two brothers" (III.iv.53–54).

8.676 (169:36). Scoffing – To "scoff" is to devour.

8.683 (170:2). Good stroke – Cricket slang for a well-hit ball.

8.683–84 (170:3). Safer to eat from his three hands – After the conventional saying used to reprove a child for eating with his fingers: "You could eat faster if you had three hands."

8.684–85 (170:4). Born with a silver knife in his mouth – After the proverbial expression for born to inherit wealth: "Born with a silver spoon in his mouth."

8.687–88 (170:7–8). *Rock, the head bailiff – I have been unable to determine whether anyone named Rock was in the bailiff's office in early-twentieth-century Dublin, but if he had been, his name would have appealed as something of a joke: underground land-reform organizations in the nineteenth century traditionally identified their leaders pseudonymously as "Captain Rock," and one of Captain Rock's key duties was to take the lead in terrorizing or assassinating the bailiffs who, as collectors and evictors for the landlords, were the omnipresent instruments of oppression for the Irish peasantry.

8.692 (170:13). Table talk – In context obviously a cliché, but also (for possible comparison) the title of several notable volumes of essays and conversation: William Cowper's (1731–

1800) comments, written in heroic couplets, on the poetry of his century (1782); a collection of essays (1821–22) by William Hazlitt (1778–1830); and conversations of Samuel Rogers (1763–1855), recalled and edited by others in 1856, and of the scholar-jurist John Selden (1584–1654), compiled and edited by his secretary in 1689.

8.693 (170:14). Unchester Bunk – Garbled version of Munster (and Leinster) Bank in Dublin.

8.696 (170:18). Out. I hate dirty eaters – Bloom shuns the Burton, as in *The Odyssey* Odysseus avoids the entrapment of the "curious bay" in the land of the Lestrygonians; see p. 156.

8.697 (170:19–20). Davy Byrne's – David Byrne, wine and spirit merchant, 21 Duke Street.

8.701 (170:24). gobstuff – "Gob" is close to the Irish word for mouth.

8.705 (170:28). tommycans – A "tommy" is something (usually food) supplied to a worker in lieu of wages.

8.706–7 (170:30). every mother's son – In *A Midsummer Night's Dream*, Peter Quince warns his fellow players that the lion must not be so impressively real as to frighten the ladies in the audience. If he were, the players would all be hanged. The "rude mechanicals" reply: "That would hang us, every mother's son" (I.ii.80).

8.707, 713 (170:30–31, 38–39). Don't talk of . . . provost of Trinity / Father O'Flynn would make hares of them all – After the ballad "Father O'Flynn" by Alfred Percival Graves (1846–1931), in *Father O'Flynn and Other Lyrics* (1879). (To "make a hare" of someone is to render him ridiculous, to expose his ignorance.) Second verse: "Don't talk of your Provost and Fellows of Trinity / Famous for ever at Greek and Latinity, / Faix! and the divils and all at Divinity— / Father O'Flynn'd make hares of them all! / Come, I vinture to give you my word, / Niver the likes of his logic was heard, / Down from mythology Into thayology, / Troth and conchology if he'd the call."

8.708–9 (170:32–33). Ailesbury road, Clyde road – Fashionable suburban streets, respectively two and a half and one and a half miles southeast of Dublin center.

8.709 (170:33). artisans' dwellings, north Dublin union – Residences of the poor. The artisans' dwellings were in the area just east of Phoenix Park in western Dublin. The North Dublin Union Workhouse was a poorhouse in Brunswick Street North in northwest-central Dublin.

8.710 (170:34). gingerbread coach – The highly decorated, antique coach that the lord mayor of Dublin used on ceremonial occasions.

8.710 (170:34–35). old queen in a bathchair – In her declining years, Queen Victoria "took the air" in a so-called bathchair (after the basket-weave chairs on wheels used for invalids at the health resorts in Bath, England).

8.711 (170:35–36). incorporated drinking-cup – A cup that belonged to or was issued by the Dublin Corporation.

8.711 (170:36). like sir Philip Crampton's fountain – See 6.191n. The fountain beneath the statue was equipped with community drinking cups. (The fountain is no longer in existence, and the statue has been removed.)

8.713 (170:38–39). Father O'Flynn would make hares of them all – See 8.707n.

8.715–16 (170:40–42). a soup pot as big . . . hindquarters out of it – In 1904, Phoenix Park was advertised as the biggest urban park in the world: 1,760 acres, seven miles in circumference. For the allusion to *The Odyssey*, see 8.76–77n.

8.716 (170:42). City Arms hotel – A residence hotel owned by Elizabeth O'Dowd at 54 Prussia Street, near the cattle market in western Dublin. The Blooms lived there in 1893–94 or 1894–95 (see p. 176, n. 1) while Bloom was working for the cattle dealer Joseph Cuffe. Boarding at the City Arms or living nearby would have been a near-necessity, since the cattle market opened at 2:00 A.M.

8.717 (171:1). Soup, joint and sweet – A crude and less fashionable way than *table d'hôte* of describing a three-course meal. *Joint:* the main or meat course; *sweet:* dessert.

8.719 (171:3). feeding on tabloids – That is, on pills, after the commonplace science-fiction vision of the synthetic diet of the future.

8.723 (171:8). cattlemarket – See 4.159n.

8.724 (171:10). bob – A calf less than one month old. "Bob veal" is veal too immature to be suitable for food; its sale is usually prohibited by statute, though the implication of "staggering bob" in context is illicit slaughterhouse procedure.

8.724–25 (171:10). Bubble and squeak – Beef and cabbage fried together.

8.725 (171:11). Butcher's buckets wobble lights – That is, the "lights" (lungs) of slaughtered animals wobble in the buckets into which they are dropped.

8.726 (171:12). Rawhead and bloody bones – A nightmare figure out of Irish folklore invoked to frighten children into obedience.

8.728 (171:14). Top and lashers – The tops children once kept spinning by whipping them with leather thongs, or "lashers."

8.729 (171:16). decline – A wasting disease, such as tuberculosis.

8.730 (171:17–18). Famished ghosts – The ghosts Odysseus meets in Book 11 of *The Odyssey* must drink from the blood-filled trench before they can achieve the power of speech.

8.736 (171:24). Shandygaff? – A drink made by mixing beer with ginger beer or ginger ale (sometimes, when it is called "shandy," with lemon bitters).

8.737 (171:25). Nosey Flynn – Appears as a character in "Counterparts," *Dubliners*, where he is discovered "sitting up in his usual corner of Davy Byrne's."

8.741–42 (171:29–30). *Sandwich? Ham and his descendants musterred and bred there – A comic rhyme from C. C. Bombaugh, *Gleanings for the Curious from the Harvest Fields of Literature* (Philadelphia, 1890), p. 158: "Why should no man starve on the deserts of Arabia? / Because of the sand which is there. / How came the sandwiches there? / The tribe of Ham was bred there and mustered" (quoted by Fritz Senn, *JJQ* 12, no. 4 [1975]: 447). The joke involves Ham, one of Noah's three sons and traditionally regarded as the tribal father of the Negroid races. Ham, on seeing his father drunken and naked, was cursed by Noah and condemned to be "a servant of servants . . . unto his brethren" (Genesis 9:22–27).

8.744 (171:34). up a plumtree – Slang for cornered, done for; or, trapped in an unwanted pregnancy.

8.745–46 (171:35–36). White missionary too salty – Legendary (and quasi-cynical) explanation for the survival of missionaries.

8.751 (171:42). Kosher – Food regarded as ceremonially clean under Jewish law. Bloom uses the term (as it is so often used) to include Jewish dietary laws generally.

8.751 (171:42). No meat and milk together – One of the Jewish dietary laws.

8.751 (172:1). Hygiene that was – Bloom quite rightly observes that many of the dietary laws were originally for reasons of hygiene: for example, the law against pork reflects the fact that hogs were scavengers (in graveyards); the laws against shellfish suggest the pollution of inshore waters, etc.

8.752 (172:1–2). Yom kippur fast spring cleaning – See 8.35–36n. Yom Kippur now occurs in early autumn; thus "spring" is hardly appropriate except that in Jewish tradition the year is renewed four times in agricultural feasts: at the Feast of Tabernacles (Sukkoth), five days after Yom Kippur; at Passover in the early spring; at the midwinter Feast of the Trees; and at Shavuot, the Feast of Weeks, in early summer. See 3.367–69n.

8.754 (172:3–4). Slaughter of innocents – When Herod heard the prophecies accompanying the birth of Jesus, he determined to eliminate this new rival by a stratagem that failed: "Then Herod . . . was exceeding wroth, and sent forth, and slew all the children that were in Bethlehem, and in all the coasts thereof" (Matthew 2:16). Joseph, meanwhile, had been warned by a vision and had escaped with Mary and her child to safety in Egypt. In the Catholic liturgical calendar, Holy Innocents' Day, or Childermas, is celebrated just after Christmas, on 28 December.

8.754 (172:4). *Eat drink and be merry – The writer of Ecclesiastes contemplates the "vanity which is done upon the earth" and continues, "Then I commended mirth, because a man hath no better thing under the sun, than to eat, and to drink, and to be merry; for that shall abide with him of his labour the days of his life, which God giveth him under the sun" (Ecclesiastes 8:15).

8.754 (172:4). casual wards – Outpatient clinics.

8.755 (172:5). Cheese digests all but itself – A saying that originated in the sixteenth century. The process of making cheese was popularly regarded as a process of digestion because it involved the use of rennet, a substance derived from animal stomachs and used to curdle milk.

8.755 (172:5–6). *Mity cheese – The minute cheese mite infests and "digests" cheese, leaving a brown, powdery mass of shed skins where it has traveled.

8.761–62 (172:13–14). God made food, the devil the cooks – After John Taylor (1580–1653), an English writer who styled himself "the king's water poet": "God sends meat, and the Devil sends the cooks" (*All the Works of John Taylor, The Water Poet, being 63 in Number* [1630], vol. 2, p. 85).

8.771 (172:24). a big tour – Only one concert is scheduled for Belfast (on 25 June).

8.774 (172:27). curate – See 4.114n.

8.789 (172:42). *hanched – To "hanch" is Scots dialect for to snap or bite greedily or noisily.

8.790–91 (173:2). Pub clock five minutes fast – The closing time of public houses was strictly enforced. The clocks in pubs were traditionally set a few minutes fast to avoid inadvertent error.

8.800 (173:13). Jack Mooney – Bob Doran's brother-in-law appears as a character in "The Boarding House," *Dubliners*.

8.800–801 (173:14). *that boxingmatch Myler Keogh won against that soldier – An advertisement in the *Freeman's Journal* (28–29 April 1904) announced a civil and military boxing tournament to be held at the Earlsfort Terrace Rink on Friday and Saturday, 29–30 April. In the second event on Friday night's card (M. L. Keogh of Dublin *vs.* Garry of the 6th Dragoons), Keogh knocked out Garry in the third round with a right hand to the pit of the stomach. Joyce changed the date to Sunday, 22 May, made this preliminary event the main event, and substituted the thoroughly English "sergeant-major Percy Bennett," an artilleryman. See 12.939–87 (318:6–319:19).

8.801–2 (173:15). Portobello barracks – (Now Cathal Brugha Barracks), a British army barracks due south of the center of Dublin on the outskirts of the city. It was the headquarters of the South Dublin Division of the Dublin Military District.

8.802 (173:15). kipper – A young Australian aborigine male who has passed through the puberty rites; hence, any young or small person.

8.802 (173:16). county Carlow – About fifty miles south-southwest of Dublin.

8.807 (173:21). hairy – Shrewd, cautious, clever.

8.810 (173:24). Herring's blush – Connotations unknown.

8.811 (173:24–25). Whose smile upon each feature plays with such and such replete – After a passage in Don Jose's song in the opera *Maritana;* see 5.563–64n.

8.811–12 (173:25). Too much fat on the parsnips – After the proverb "Soft or fair words butter no parsnips" (i.e., saying "Be thou fed" does not feed a hungry man); butter on parsnips was considered a delicacy. "Too much fat" suggests an excess that is inferior in quality (to butter); hence, a person who is excessively unctuous.

8.813 (173:26). here's himself and pepper on him – In other words, he's in good form.

8.814 (173:27). the Gold Cup – See 5.532n.

8.820 (173:33). logwood – An astringent used in medicines.

8.826 (173:39). Vintners' sweepstake – Literally, the owners of licensed pubs own the race to be run; figuratively, they have a surer bet than anyone playing the horses.

8.826–27 (173:39–40). Licensed for the sale . . . on the premises – Official language of a public-house license.

8.827 (173:40–41). Heads I win tails you lose – A cliché meaning "I win either way the coin turns."

8.829–31 (174:2–3). He's giving Sceptre . . . Morny Cannon – See 5.532n. The *Freeman's Journal*, 16 June 1904, was not entirely accurate in its report of the field in the Gold Cup. Flynn is right: the odds on Sceptre (ridden by O. Madden) were seven to four against; odds on Zinfandel (ridden by Mornington Cannon), five to four. Zinfandel did win the Coronation Cup at Epsom Downs on 3 June 1904 (the day after the Derby); Sceptre finished second in that race.

8.831–32 (174:4–5). seven to one against Saint Amant a fortnight before – The Derby was run on 2 June 1904. St. Amant, a colt (not a filly, as Flynn thinks) by St. Frusquin out of Lady Loverule, owned by M. Leopold de Rothschild (whose racing colors were blue and gold), did win the Derby under the conditions Flynn describes below. On 20 May 1904, the odds against St. Amant were six to one; they shortened to approximately four to one in late May but lengthened again just before the race.

8.839 (174:13). John O'Gaunt – Another of the entries in the 1904 Derby, owned by Sir John Thursby and named after King Edward III's son John of Gaunt (1340–99), duke of Lancaster and earl of Derby. The odds against the horse were quoted at four to one on 1 June 1904, the day before the race. The favorite before the start of the Derby was Gouvernant, a horse Flynn does not mention.

8.845 (174:19–20). Fool and his money – Are soon parted; a saying current since the sixteenth century.

8.860 (174:37). Johnny Magories – Johnny MacGorey or Magory, the fruit of *Crataegus oxyacantha*, the dog rose or hawthorn.

8.865–66 (175:2–3). Fizz and Red bank oysters . . . He was in the Red Bank – The combination of champagne and oysters was supposed to be an aphrodisiac. Oysters from the red-bank beds in County Clare on the west coast of Ireland were advertised in Dublin as the best of Irish oysters by Burton Bindon's Redbank Restaurant at 19–20 D'Olier Street, outside of which Bloom saw Boylan earlier in the day (6.196–99 [92:19–22]).

8.867 (175:3–4). Was he oysters old fish at table perhaps he young flesh in bed – Source unknown.

8.868 (175:5). June has no ar no oysters – Traditional and proverbial since at least 1599, when Butler wrote in *Dyet's Dry Dinner:* "It is unseasonable and unwholesome in all months that have not an R in them to eat an oyster." Oysters

are in fact edible year round, but they do not taste as good in spawning season, which almost corresponds to the months of the no-*R* rule.

8.869 (175:6). Jugged hare – Seethed or stewed in an earthenware pot or casserole.

8.869 (175:6). First catch your hare – A stock joke, popularly (and mistakenly) supposed to have been a blooper, from a recipe for hare soup in Mrs. Hannah Glasse's *The Art of Cookery Made Plain and Easy* (1747) (William D. Jenkins, *JJQ* 15, no. 1 [1977]: 91).

8.869–70 (175:6–7). Chinese eating eggs . . . and green again – The Chinese preserve duck eggs by burying them in the ground for ten to twelve months; the eggs undergo a peculiar fermentation in which the hydrogen sulfide formed by the rotting egg breaks the shell and escapes; the egg itself becomes hard in texture, and the white changes color to blue, the yolk to green. The final product is not disagreeable in odor or taste. Its worth seems to have been measured by its rarity, or, more accurately, its age, since the eggs are "ripe" and edible after a year. The few saved for up to fifty years were highly prized as being "exceptional."

8.871 (175:9). That archduke Leopold – Bloom understandably confuses Leopold von Bayern (1821–1912), prince regent of Bavaria from 1886 to 1912, with King Otto of Bavaria (see following note). Leopold's career was intimately related to King Otto's; Leopold became prince regent in the same year that Otto, who was adjudged insane as early as 1872, became king.

8.872 (175:9–10). Otto one of those Habsburgs – Otto I (1848–1916; king of Bavaria, 1886; deposed 1912). He went insane in 1872 and lived the remainder of his life under a strict surveillance that gave rise to a number of lurid stories of the sort Bloom recalls. Otto I was not a Habsburg, though the Habsburg emperor of Austria, Francis Joseph I (1830–1916), did have a nephew named Otto.

8.875–76 (175:13–14). Half the catch . . . keep up the price – An unfounded but widespread suspicion of economic malpractice.

8.876–77 (175:15–16). Hock in green glasses – Hock, after Hochheimer, a delicate white Rhine wine, was traditionally bottled and served in colored glasses to prevent its being affected by light.

8.880 (175:19). Royal sturgeon – All sturgeon in English territorial waters was declared the legal property of the Crown by Edward II, king of England from 1307 to 1327.

8.882 (175:19–21). *high sheriff, Coffey . . . from his ex. – His excellency, the lord lieutenant of Ireland, has instructed the high sheriff (of County Dublin? or of all counties?) that William Coffey, butcher and victualler, 10 Arran Quay and 35 Cuffe Street in Dublin, has permission to sell venison in his markets. The high sheriff of each county had responsibility for the enforcement of game laws.

8.882 (175:22). Master of the Rolls – The Right Honorable Sir Andrew Marshall Porter, Bart. (1837–1919), master of the rolls for Ireland (1883–1907), had a residence in Dublin at 42 Merrion Square East. Bloom has apparently looked through the kitchen windows, which gave onto an open area below street level between the house and the sidewalk. The master of the rolls was president of the chancery division of the High Court of Justice in Ireland, in rank next to the lord chief justice and the lord chancellor.

8.882–83 (175:22–23). whitehatted chef like a rabbi – The cylindrical white hat that rabbis wear on certain ceremonial occasions resembles a chef's cap.

8.883 (175:23). Combustible duck – Duck prepared in a sauce and flamed with brandy just before it is served. Several distinguished French recipes for duck (e.g., duck with black cherries) call for this treatment.

8.883 (175:23–24). Curly cabbage *à la duchesse de Parme* – Baked savoy cabbage with a stuffing of ground veal, herbs, bread crumbs, etc.

8.884–85 (175:25). *Too many drugs spoil the broth – After the saying "Too many cooks spoil the broth" (the converse of "Many hands make light work").

8.885–86 (175:26). Edward's dessicated soup – Widely advertised as a substitute for freshly prepared broth.

8.886 (175:27). Geese stuffed silly for them – Geese were confined in cages and force-fed to produce the highly enriched and outsized livers used in making *pâté de foie gras*.

8.889 (175:30). miss Dubedat – *Thom's* 1904 lists the Misses Du Bedat, Wilmount House, Killiney. Adams (p. 74) notes that at a benefit held at the Queen's Royal Theatre for J. W. Whitbread (see 8.600n) a Miss Du Bedat sang "Going to Kildare" (*Freeman's Journal*, 3 February 1894).

8.889–90 (175:31). Huguenot name – Origin of the name Dubedat or Du Bedat is unknown, but its French form makes Bloom's assumption logical.

8.890 (175:32). Killiney – An attractive village on the coast nine miles southeast of Dublin.

8.890 (175:32). *Du de la – French: "of the"; *du* is a contraction of *de* ("of") and the masculine definite article *le; de la* includes the feminine definite article.

8.891 (175:33). Micky Hanlon – M. and P. Hanlon, fishmongers and ice merchants, 20 Moore Street, Dublin. It was from his fish store that the last holdouts of the Easter 1916 Uprising surrendered; see 15.4661n.

8.894 (175:36–37). Moooikill A Aitcha Ha – That is, Michael . . . A . . . H . . . A . . . (toward Hanlon).

8.894 (175:37). *ignorant as a kish of brogues – A "kish" is a large square basket used for measuring turf. The expression suggests that if having one's brains in one's feet means stupidity, how much more stupid a basket full of empty, rough shoes.

8.900–902 (176:1–3). Howth . . . the Lion's head . . . Drumleck . . . Sutton – Howth Head projects out into the Irish Sea to form the northeastern arm of Dublin Bay. The peninsula is dominated by 583-foot Ben (mountain peak) Howth. Lion's Head is a promontory on the southeastern side of Howth. Drumleck Point is on the southern shore of Howth; Sutton is on the spit of land between Howth and the mainland. The progression of colors marks the progression from the deeper waters off Lion's Head through the shallower waters (five fathoms) off Drumleck to the shallow waters over the tidal flats of Sutton strand.

8.902–3 (176:4). buried cities – The configuration of algae and deeper channels in the bay as seen from above suggests cities buried in the sea, such as Atlantis, a large island that, according to classical tradition (as articulated by

Plato), existed in the Atlantic off Gibraltar. Plato, in the *Critias*, credits the island with a fabulous history of cultural achievement before its inundation. Ireland's legendary Atlantis is buried beneath the waters of Lough Neagh; see 12.1454n.

8.920 (176:26). Venus, Juno – Bloom is almost cast in the role of Paris, judge of the beauty contest among Venus (Aphrodite), Juno (Hera), and Minerva (Athena)—the latter unmentioned because she was Ulysses' (Odysseus's) patron? See 2.391–92n.

8.921–22 (176:26–27). library museum . . . naked goddesses – The National Library and National Museum are matching buildings that face each other across a quadrangle on the east side of Kildare Street. Plaster casts of various famous classical statues, including the Venus of Praxiteles, stood in the entrance rotunda of the National Museum. They have since been retired in favor of Celtic crosses, etc.

8.922 (176:27–28). Aids to digestion – Significance unknown.

8.924 (176:30). Pygmalion and Galatea – In Greek mythology, Pygmalion, a sculptor and the king of Cyprus, fell in love with his own handwork, the ivory statue of a maiden. He prayed to Aphrodite, who breathed life into the statue (Galatea). The transformation was climaxed by the marriage of Pygmalion and Galatea. *Pygmalion and Galatea* is also the title of a popular play (1871) by Sir William S. Gilbert, a satire of sentimental-romantic attitudes toward myth. Gilbert's Galatea is born so innocent that she appears wayward and disrupts the lives she touches (including those of Mr. and Mrs. Pygmalion) during her less-than-twenty-four hours in the flesh.

8.926 (176:32). a tanner lunch – That is, a sixpenny lunch, inexpensive but hot and filling.

8.927 (176:33). Allsop – A popular and inexpensive bottled beer made by Allsopp & Son, Ltd., brewers, 35 Bachelor's Walk.

8.927–29 (176:33–36). Nectar . . . gods' food . . . and we stuffing food in one hole – In *The Odyssey*, "the divine Kalypso placed before him [Odysseus] / victuals and drink of men; then she sat down / facing Odysseus, while her serving maids / brought nectar and ambrosia to her side. / Then each one's hands went out to each one's feast" (5:196–200; Fitzgerald, p. 99).

8.929–30 (176:36–37). food, chyle, blood, dung, earth, food – In *Cause, Principle, and Unity* (1584), Giordano Bruno discusses the dynamics of the "soul of the world" (see 2.159n) and its endless proliferation of material forms: "Don't you see that what was seed becomes stalk, and what was stalk becomes corn, and what was corn becomes bread—that out of bread comes chyle, out of chyle blood, out of blood the seed, out of the seed the embryo, and then man, corpse, earth, stone, or something else in succession–on and on, involving all natural forms?" (trans. Jack Lindsay [New York, 1962], p. 102).

8.934 (176:41–42). A man and ready . . . to the lees – Echoes lines 6–7 of Tennyson's "Ulysses" (1842): "I cannot rest from travel; I will drink / Life to the lees." Compare with the opening lines of *The Odyssey* as translated by S. H. Butcher and A. Lang (London, 1879): "Tell me, Muse, of that man, so ready at need, who wandered far and wide."

8.935 (176:42–177:1). manly conscious – Shakespeare, in *Venus and Adonis* (1593), describes Venus as essentially masculine in her approach to the youthful Adonis: as she "like a bold-faced suitor 'gins to woo him" (line 6), and "Backward she push'd him, as she would be thrust" (line 41).

8.935–36 (177:1). a youth enjoyed her – If Bloom is thinking about Venus and Adonis, then he is mistaken. Adonis does not "enjoy" Venus; the pivot of Shakespeare's poem is that Venus is unable to overcome the resistance of Adonis's "unripe years" (line 524).

8.950–51 (177:17–18). that Irish farm . . . in Henry street – Fiction has substituted Mrs. Nolan for Mrs. J. W. Power, manager, Irish Farm Produce Company, 21 Henry Street. Adams (p. 68) identifies Nolan (who appears later in *Ulysses*) as a journalist named "Power in real life."

8.952 (177:20). Plovers on toast – Some of the large plovers are prized as game birds in Europe. The expression turns on the plover as "rare good eating," but as slang it means full-breasted in an attractive way.

8.955–56 (177:23–24). You can make bacon of that – "Bacon" is slang for money, so the phrase means "You can bet on that."

8.960 (177:28). in the craft – The "craft" is

Freemasonry, so called in allusion to the heritage of the ancient guild of craftsmen; the express object of the Freemasons was the creation of an undefiled spiritual temple in the individual heart and public striving for the brotherhood of humanity in a brighter and more beautiful world. Bloom has in fact been a Mason. See 8.184–86 (156:10–12).

8.962–63 (177:30–31). Ancient free and . . . love, by God – Flynn is echoing phrases from the Masonic ritual; the order regarded itself as practicing "Ancient and Accepted Rites," to which all "free men could be admitted." Three symbols of light dominate the Masonic temple: the Volume of the Sacred Law (the Bible), symbolic of the light from above; the square, symbolic of the light within man; and the compass, symbolic of fraternity, the light around man. The Masonic ritual, as articulated in the *Antient Charges* (1723), expresses a commitment to the creation of "the Temple of Human Love, the foundations of which are Wisdom, Strength and Beauty." Flynn's "by God" is his own Irish interpolation: the Masonic formula dictated tolerance under "the Great Architect of the Universe."

8.963 (177:31–32). They give him a leg up – The popular suspicion was that Masons gave excessive preference to members of their order, even to the point of handing out money. The order is committed to help and support its members and families in time of disease and personal crisis, but the *Antient Charges* is quite specific on preference: "All preferment among Masons is grounded upon real worth and personal merit only."

8.967–68 (177:36). They're as close as damn it – Another expression of popular suspicion of Freemasonry, reflecting not only the exclusive nature of the order but also the assumption that the order involved a profound and conspiratorial "secret." According to its own principles, the order was open to any man at least twenty-one years of age and in body "a perfect youth"; no man could be admitted to membership if he was "a stupid atheist or an irreligious libertine."

8.971–74 (177:40–178:1). There was one woman . . . Legers of Doneraile – There are several (exceptional) histories of women who were initiated into Masonic lodges. The one Flynn cites is traditionally regarded not as the only but as the first. She was Elizabeth Aldworth (d. 1773), the only daughter of Arthur St. Leger, first Viscount Doneraile. She is sup-

posed (at age seventeen) to have been a witness to a Masonic meeting in her father's house and to have been initiated to ensure secrecy. A portrait of her in Masonic apron with her finger on a passage in the Volume of the Sacred Law (the Bible) is reproduced in Eugen Lennhoff, *The Free-Masons* (New York, 1934), opp. p. 336. There are three symbolic degrees in Freemasonry: Entered Apprentice, Fellowcraft, and Master Mason; the last is the highest degree, and it is obviously Flynn's flourish of exaggeration in the story he tells.

8.982 (178:11). safe – In the obsolete sense of sane and dependable, mentally and morally sound.

8.988 (178:19). Nothing in black and white – Combining the suspicion of Bloom's secretiveness as a Mason with a suspicion of Bloom as a Jew (on the assumption that all Jews were averse to swearing an oath on signing a contract).

8.989 (178:20). Tom Rochford – Appears as a character elsewhere in *Ulysses*. In real life he lived at 2 Howth View, Sandymount, and was, on 6 May 1905, involved in the attempt to rescue a sanitation worker overcome by sewer gas (in a sewer at the corner of Hawkins Street and Burgh Quay, near the Scotch House). In the newspaper accounts of the incident, Rochford is described variously as "clerk of the works" and an "engineer" formerly in the employ of the Dublin Corporation. In the real-life rescue Rochford was the third of twelve men down the sewer; all twelve were overcome by gas and dragged out unconscious—two died. Rochford lived, but his eyes were at least temporarily injured by the gas. Joyce radically transformed the story for inclusion in *Ulysses*. See Adams, pp. 92–94.

8.997 (178:28). a stone ginger – A nonalcoholic Irish drink regarded as a temperance beverage.

8.1000 (178:31). How is the main drainage? – Combines references to Rochford's dyspepsia and his adventure in the sewer with an allusion to Dublin's long-delayed and controversial project for an adequate sewage system. The Main Drainage Committee's duties had been absorbed by the Improvements Committee late in 1903 (apparently because the special committee's handling of the project was not above suspicion). The Dublin Main Drainage Works was finally inaugurated 24 September 1906. See 8.53n.

8.1007 (178:40). suck whiskey off a sore leg – Whiskey was applied as an antiseptic for wounds and sores.

8.1008 (178:41). snip – Racing slang for a good tip.

8.1025 (179:17). Jamesons – A well-known Irish whiskey distilled by John Jameson & Sons in Dublin.

8.1028 (179:20). Dawson street – Runs north and south across the east end of Duke Street; Bloom will turn south and then east into Molesworth Street.

8.1029–30 (179:21–23). Something green it . . . searchlight you could – A troublesome fragment because we reenter Bloom's thoughts when they are in full flow. Röntgen rays, or X rays, were discovered in 1895 by the German physicist Wilhelm Konrad von Röntgen (1845–1923). The discovery was greeted with widespread, if speculative, enthusiasm. X rays were initially produced by relatively low-powered equipment, so neither the immediate danger of burns nor the long-range danger of radioactivity was recognized. The practical applications of X rays in medicine and dentistry were recognized from the outset, but popular journalistic accounts went well beyond modest applications (such as the location of dental caries) to speculate on phototherapeutic uses of X rays, as Bloom here speculates that X rays could be used to trace the progress of "something green" through the digestive tract.

8.1031 (179:24). Duke lane – Intersects Duke Street between Davy Byrne's and Dawson Street.

8.1034 (179:28). Their upper jaw they move – Recalls Oliver Goldsmith's (1728–74) quip at the expense of "Society": that everyone else chewed with the lower jaw (as ruminants do), but he alone chewed with the upper.

8.1035 (179:29). that invention of his – See 10.465–83 (232:4–22).

8.1040–41 (179:35–36). *Don Giovanni, a cenar teco / M'invitasti* – The line continues "e son venuto!" Italian: "Don Giovanni, you invited me to sup with you and I have come." Act II, scene iii of Mozart's *Don Giovanni* takes place in a moonlit graveyard, where Don Giovanni mocks the statue of his dead enemy, Il Commendatore, by inviting it to supper. In scene v (the final scene of the opera) the statue enters, singing the quoted lines, to keep the engagement and to inform Don Giovanni that he must repent because the last moment of his life is at hand. Don Giovanni refuses and is engulfed in the flames of hell.

8.1042 (179:37). Who distilled first? – The process was apparently known to Aristotle and his contemporaries and has from the first century A.D. been employed in much the same way as it is at present.

8.1043 (179:38). in the blues – In a state of depression; also, gone astray.

8.1043 (179:38). Dutch courage – Courage produced with the help of an alcoholic beverage.

8.1043 (179:38). *Kilkenny People* – A weekly Kilkenny newspaper published on Saturdays.

8.1045–46 (179:40–41). William Miller, plumber – And sanitary contractor, 17 Duke Street.

8.1052 (180:7). What does that *teco* mean? – Italian: "with you."

8.1059 (180:14//). *If I get Billy Prescott's ad – That is, if Bloom convinces Prescott to renew the ad that has already appeared; see 5.460n.

8.1060 (180:15). On the pig's back – In luck, in luck's way.

8.1064–65 (180:20). Brighton, Margate – Brighton, in Sussex, England, on the English Channel, was advertised as the "Queen of Watering Places." Margate, on the Isle of Thanet, in Kent, England, was Brighton's principal competition at the turn of the century.

8.1065–66 (180:21). Those lovely seaside girls – See 4.282n.

8.1066 (180:21). John Long's – A pub, 52 Dawson Street (on the corner of Duke Street); P. J. Long, grocer and wine merchant.

8.1069 (180:24). Gray's – Katherine Gray, confectioner, 13 Duke Street, at the intersection of Dawson Street; Bloom turns south to Molesworth Street, where he will turn east toward the National Library.

8.1070 (180:25–26). the reverend Thomas Connellan's bookstore – 51B Dawson Street; the shop specialized in Protestant propaganda.

8.1070–71 (180:26). *Why I left the church of Rome* – A thirty-page pamphlet (London, 1883) by the Canadian Presbyterian minister Charles Pascal Telesphore Chiniquy (1809–99). Chiniquy was ordained a Roman Catholic priest in 1833 and switched allegiance to the Presbyterian church in 1858. He was styled the "veteran Champion of Pure Religion and Temperance" and was reputed to have converted twenty-five to thirty thousand of his countrymen. Chiniquy's specific objection was to the Roman Catholic concept of the Virgin Mary as intercessor; as he put it, "Mary cannot have the power to receive from Jesus the favors she asks." On a more general level Chiniquy argued that laymen should have their own Bibles and should read and think out their faith for themselves.

8.1071 (180:26–27). Birds' nest women – *Thom's* 1904 lists the Birds' Nest institution at 19–20 York Street in Kingstown (now Dun Laoghaire). It was a Protestant Missionary Society with accomodation for 170 "ragged children"; Miss Cushen, secretary. "Birds' nest" was also a generic term for institutions of that sort.

8.1071–73 (180:27–28). They say they . . . the potato blight – The practice of bribing potential converts with food was, as Bloom suggests, all too common, not only during the Great Famine (see 2.269n) but throughout the nineteenth century.

8.1073 (180:29–30). Society over the way . . . of poor jews – Church of Ireland Auxiliary to the London Society for Promoting Christianity Among the Jews, 45 Molesworth Street (which enters Dawson Street where Bloom is walking).

8.1080 (180:36–37). Molesworth street – Half a block south of Duke Street, runs east from Dawson Street into Kildare Street.

8.1083 (180:41). Drago's – Adolphe Drago, Parisian perfumer and hairdresser, 17 Dawson Street.

8.1088 (181:5). South Frederick street – Runs north and south across Molesworth Street, a short distance east of Dawson Street.

8.1100 (181:18). Behind a bull: in front of a horse – Safety maxim, since a bull cannot kick backwards and a horse can.

8.1114 (181:32). Penrose – See 8.178–79 (156:3).

8.1120 (181:39). Dark men – Irish dialect: "blind men."

8.1126 (182:4). the Stewart institution – For Imbecile Children and Hospital for Mental Diseases, 40 Molesworth Street.

8.1132 (182:11). Postoffice – Town Sub–Post Office, Money Order and Savings Bank Office, 4 Molesworth Street.

8.1133 (182:12–13). Stationer's – E. F. Grant & Co., scriveners, typewriters, law and general stationers, 1–2 Molesworth Street.

8.1139 (182:19). Levenston's dancing academy – Mrs. Philip M. Levenston, dancing academy; Mr. P. M. Levenston, professor of music, 35 Frederick Street South, just off Molesworth Street.

8.1140 (182:21). *Doran's publichouse – Michael Doran, grocer, wine and spirit merchant, 10 Molesworth Street, on the corner of Frederick Street South.

8.1146–47 (182:28–30). All those women . . . in New York. Holocaust – The *Freeman's Journal*, 16 June 1904, carried the story on page 5: "Appalling American Disaster . . . Five hundred persons, mostly children, perished today by the burning of the steamer *General Slocum*, near Hell Gate, on the East River. The disaster is the most appalling that has ever occurred in New York Harbour, and the fact that the victims were almost entirely of tender age, or women, renders it absolutely distressing. The annual Sunday School excursion of the St. Mark's German Lutheran Church was proceeding to Locust Grove, a pleasure resort on Long Island Sound. As the steamer made its way up the East River, with bands playing and flags flying, every deck was crowded with merrymakers.

"When she was off Sunken Meadows a fire broke out in the lunch room. The crew endeavoured to extinguish the flames, but they quickly became uncontrollable and made rapid headway. A panic ensued. The Hell Gate rocks hemmed the steamer in, and she was unable to turn. The vessel, consequently, went on at full speed, and was finally beached on North Brothers Island, where the Municipal Charity Hospital's physicians and nurses were immediately available for the injured. No attempt was made to lower the lifeboats." Estimates of the death toll varied between 500 and 1,000 in the course of the day, 16 June, and the final toll was 1,030, mainly women and children—in effect, almost all of the women and children of the German Lutheran community on New York's Lower East Side.

8.1147 (182:30). Karma – See 9.70n.

8.1148 (182:31–32). Met him pike hoses – See 4.339n.

8.1151 (182:34). Sir Frederick Falkiner – See 7.698–99n.

8.1151 (182:34). the freemason's hall – 17–18 Molesworth Street.

8.1151–52 (182:35). Solemn as Troy – After the pro-British Roman Catholic archbishop of Dublin, the most Reverend John Thomas Troy (1739–1823), who issued a "solemn condemnation" of the Rebellion of 1798. His subsequent support of the Act of Union (indirectly, support of the political repression of Catholic Ireland) made his solemnity something of a local legend.

8.1152 (182:35). in Earlsfort terrace – Falkiner lived at 4 Earlsfort Terrace, just south of the southeastern corner of St. Stephen's Green.

8.1153 (182:36–37). Tales of the bench . . . bluecoat school – Falkiner was on the board of governors of the Bluecoat School and wrote a *History of the Blue Coat School, Literary Miscellanies: Tales of the Bench and Assizes*, published posthumously in 1909. The Bluecoat School (the Hospital and Free School of King Charles II, Oxmantown, Blackhall Place, Dublin) was a fashionable school modeled after the famous English public school Christ's Hospital, which was also called the Bluecoat School. In context, "bluecoat school" implies an education befitting a member of the Protestant Anglo-Irish Establishment.

8.1156 (182:40). the recorder's court – The highest of the Dublin city courts; see 7.698–99n.

8.1156–58 (182:41–183:1). Police chargesheets . . . to the rightabout – To "send someone to the rightabout" is to effect a radical

change in his behavior. Bloom recalls Falkiner's reputation as a judge who was severe with police whom he suspected of making arrests for petty crimes (cramming the chargesheets) in order to secure advancement (get their percentage).

8.1158–59 (183:1–2). Gave Reuben J a great strawcalling – That is, Reuben J. Dodd (see 6.264–65n). A "strawcalling" is a tongue-lashing, with the added implication that the lashing is in excess of what is merited. There is no factual record of Falkiner so treating Dodd, but Falkiner did create a furor in Dublin in January 1902 when he launched an anti-Semitic tirade from the bench. Public indignation was so sharp that it reached the floor of the House of Commons, and Falkiner is said to have retracted. See Adams, p. 105.

8.1160 (183:3–4). Bear with a sore paw – Proverbial for a brooding and irritable person.

8.1160–61 (183:4). And may the Lord have mercy on your soul – The formula a judge used when imposing the death penalty.

8.1162 (183:5). Mirus bazaar – In fiction the bazaar opens on 16 June 1904; in fact it opened on Tuesday, 31 May 1904, and the lord lieutenant did not parade through Dublin as described in Wandering Rocks but arrived in haste from the south of Ireland. The site of the bazaar was Ballsbridge, on the southeastern outskirts of Dublin. The bazaar was given to raise funds for Mercer's Hospital.

8.1163 (183:6–7). Mercer's hospital – Located where Mercer Street Lower gives into William Street, in central Dublin south of the Liffey. The hospital was incorporated by act of Parliament in 1734.

8.1163.64 (183:7). *The *Messiah* was first given for that – Handel's oratorio was given its first performance on 13 April 1742 at Dublin's Musick Hall, Fishamble Street, with Handel conducting. Handel presented the *Messiah* "to offer this generous and polished nation something new" (because he regarded Dublin as more friendly and receptive than London). The performance was a charity benefit for the then newly organized Mercer's Hospital.

8.1165 (183:8). Ballsbridge . . . Keyes – See 7.25n.

8.1167 (183:11). Kildare street . . . Library – Molesworth Street, through which Bloom has been walking, enters Kildare Street across from the quadrangle (now a parking lot), flanked by the facades of the National Museum to the south (on Bloom's right) and the National Library to the north.

8.1168 (183:12). Turnedup trousers – Boylan wears the very latest in flashy clothes: trousers with cuffs.

8.1174 (183:19–20). Sir Thomas Deane designed – Sir Thomas Deane (1792–1871), an Irish architect, designed the Trinity College Museum building (1857) and the Ruskin Museum at Oxford with Benjamin Woodward (1815–61). The National Library (1883) and the National Museum (1884) are replicas of one another and were not designed by Sir Thomas Deane but by his son, Sir Thomas Newenham Deane (1830–99), and grandson, Sir Thomas Manly Deane (1851–1933); the latter is reputed to have dominated the father-son partnership. The buildings are variously regarded as "impressive" and "pedestrian" in design.

8.1176–77 (183:22–23). Quick . . . Safe in a minute – The manner of Bloom's escape recalls Odysseus's precipitate departure from the land of the Lestrygonians; see p. 156. Odysseus's ship goes unnoticed because it is not anchored with the other ships of his squadron. Odysseus cuts his ship's cable: " 'Men,' I shouted, / 'man the oars and pull till your hearts break / if you would put this butchery behind!' " (10:128–29; Fitzgerald, p. 181).

8.1180–81 (183:27). Sir Thomas Deane was the Greek architecture – Sir Thomas Deane the elder practiced solidly in the traditions of nineteenth-century eclecticism and was praised by Ruskin for the "Lombardo-Venetian style" of his buildings. Ruskin was in effect praising Deane for his reaction against the cold simplicities of early-nineteenth-century Greek-revival architecture. Sir Thomas Newenham Deane and Sir Thomas Manly Deane practiced in a rather restrained and heavy way the "Renaissance style" taught and advocated by the Ecole des Beaux Arts in Paris; while it is technically incorrect to call this style "Greek," the handling of columns and pediments is somewhat reminiscent of Greek architecture.

8.1184 (183:30). Agendath Netaim – See 4.191–92n.

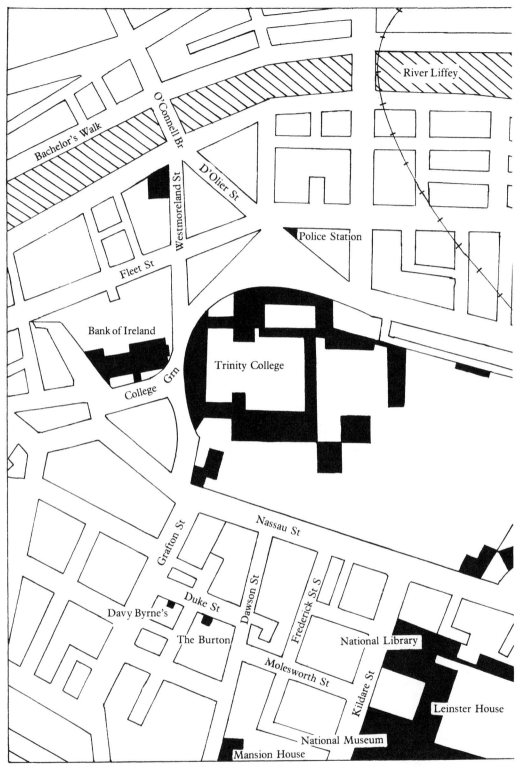

EPISODE 9. *Scylla and Charybdis*

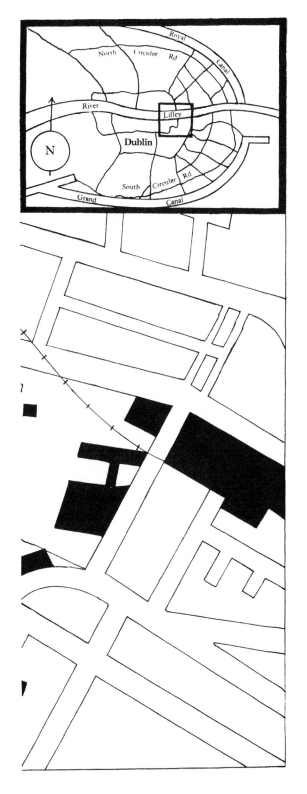

EPISODE 9

Scylla and Charybdis

(9.1–1225, PP. 184–218)

Episode 9: *Scylla and Charybdis*, 9.1–1225 (184–218). In Book 12 of *The Odyssey*, Odysseus and his men return from the Land of the Dead (see headnote to Hades, p. 104) to Circe's isle, where they fulfill Odysseus's promise to bury Elpenor's body. Circe gives Odysseus "sailing directions" (12:24; Fitzgerald, p. 222). She tells him about the Sirens (*Ulysses*, Episode 11) and offers him a choice of routes: one by way of the Wandering Rocks (*Ulysses*, Episode 10)—"not even birds can pass them by" (12:62; Fitzgerald, p. 223); and the other by way of the passage between Scylla and Charybdis. The latter route, which Odysseus chooses, offers a second choice: the ship that sails the side of the channel overlooked by the six-headed monster Scylla, that lives on "a sharp mountain peak" (12:74; ibid.), does so at the sacrifice of "one man for every gullet" (12:99; Fitzgerald, p. 224). But the ship that chooses the other side of the channel risks being totally engulfed by the "whirling / maelstrom" (12:104; ibid.) of Charybdis. Circe advises Odysseus to "hug the cliff of Scylla" (12:108; ibid.), which he does. But she also urges him not to try to combat Scylla, a "nightmare [that] cannot die" (12:118; Fitzgerald, p. 225). When the time comes to face Scylla, Circe's bidding slips his mind, and try to combat Scylla he does—but in vain, because at the moment of her strike Odysseus and his men are distracted by the terrifying vision of the "yawning mouth" of Charybdis (12:243; Fitzgerald, p. 230).

Time: 2:00 P.M. Scene: the National Library. Organ: the brain; Art: literature; Color: none; Symbol: Stratford, London; Technique: dialectic. Correspondences: *The Rock* [on which Scylla dwells]—Aristotle, dogma, Stratford; *The Whirlpool* [Charybdis]—Plato, mysticism, London. *Ulysses*—Socrates, Jesus, Shakespeare.

The Linati schema lists as Persons: "Scylla and Charybdis, Ulysses, Telemachus, Antinoos," and as Symbols: "Hamlet, Shakespeare, Christ, Socrates, London and Stratford, Scholasticism and Mysticism, Plato and Aristotle, Youth and Maturity."

The principal sources for the free-wheeling and largely fictional biography that Stephen performs in this episode are George Brandes, *William Shakespeare* (London, 1898), cited as Brandes in the notes to this episode; Frank Harris, *The Man Shakespeare and His Tragic Life-Story* (New York, 1909), cited as Harris; and Sidney Lee, *A Life of William Shakespeare* (London, 1898), cited as Lee.

George Morris Cohen Brandes (1842–1927) was a Danish literary critic and one of the lead-

ers of the "new breaking through" in Scandinavian and European thought in the nineteenth century. In 1871 he began to formulate the principles of a new realism and of naturalism, condemning abstract idealism and fantasy in literature and championing the works of Ibsen and Zola, among others. His scholarship ranged through the literatures of Germany, France, and England as well as Scandinavia. He was praised in his own time as "a scientific critic to whom literature is in itself 'a criticism of life.'"

Frank Harris (1856–1931) was an English editor and man of letters. Most of the materials for his biography of Shakespeare had appeared in the *Saturday Review,* under his editorship, in the 1890s. He is better known in our time as the author of *My Life and Loves* (New York, 1963), an autobiographical account, spiced apparently with some wishful thinking, of his experiments with Don Juanism.

Sidney Lee (1859–1926), the elder son of Lazarus Lee, was originally named Solomon Lazarus Lee. He changed his name to Sidney L(ancelot) Lee in 1880 and subsequently dropped the middle initial. His career as man of letters included the editorship of the prestigious *Dictionary of National Biography,* biographies of Shakespeare and Queen Victoria, and his work *Great Englishmen of the Sixteenth Century.* He was, as he aspired to be, a pillar of the English political as well as literary establishment—and he devoted himself to seeing Shakespeare's inclusion in that exalted circle.

These three biographies (and other of Stephen's sources, notably Oscar Wilde) remind me of Samuel Schoenbaum's observation that "biography tends toward oblique self portraiture" (*Shakespeare's Lives* [New York, 1970], pp. viii–ix) and tempt me to add that the less solid the data about the biographee, the greater the latitude for obliquity.

9.1 (184:1). the quaker librarian – Thomas William Lyster (1855–1922), librarian of the National Library of Ireland (1895–1920). Among his writings was a translation of Dunster's *Life of Goethe* (1883), which he revised, enlarged, and annotated. He was also editor of a series of volumes, *English Poems for Young Students* (1893ff.). During his tenure as librarian the oddity of his religious faith made him the object of suspicion and considerable mockery.

9.2 (184:2–3). *Wilhelm Meister* – *Wilhelm Meister's Apprenticeship and Travels* (1796) by Johann Wolfgang von Goethe (1749–1832), the giant of German letters both in his own time and in retrospect. The "priceless pages" Lyster mentions comprise Book 4, chapter 13, through Book 5, chapter 12, of Goethe's novel, in the course of which Wilhelm translates and revises (remolds) *Hamlet* and participates in a production of his version of the play. Lyster and his contemporaries assumed that Goethe's "pages" are not so much fiction as they are Goethe's thinly disguised personal commentary on and response to Shakespeare's *Hamlet*.

9.3–4 (184:3–5). A hesitating soul . . . conflicting doubts – The passage to which Lyster alludes occurs at the end of Book 4, chapter 13 of *Wilhelm Meister;* Meister is speaking: "To me it is clear that Shakespeare meant in *Hamlet* to represent the effects of a great action laid upon a soul unfit for the performance of it. In this view the whole piece seems to me to be composed. There is an oak-tree planted in a costly jar, which should have borne only pleasant flowers in its bosom; the roots expand, the jar is shivered.

"A lovely, pure, noble, and most moral nature, without the strength of nerve which forms a hero, sinks beneath a burden which it cannot bear and must not cast away. All duties are holy for him; the present is too hard. Impossibilities have been required of him; not in themselves impossibilities, but such for him. He winds and turns, and torments himself; he advances and recoils; is ever put in mind, ever puts himself in mind; at last does all but lose his purpose from his thoughts; yet still without recovering his peace of mind" (trans. Thomas Carlyle [Boston, 1876], vol. 1, p. 232). Lyster continues this allusion to *Wilhelm Meister* with a quotation from Hamlet's "To be or not to be" soliloquy: "Whether 'tis nobler in the mind to suffer / The slings and arrows of outrageous fortune, / Or to take arms against a sea of troubles, / And by opposing end them" (III.i.57–60).

9.5 (184:6). a sinkapace forward on neatsleather – Combines allusions to lines in two Shakespeare plays. In *Twelfth Night* Sir Toby Belch advises Sir Andrew Aguecheek on the manners of a fop: "Why dost thou not go to church in a galliard and come home in a coranto? My very walk should be a jig; I would not so much as make water in a sink-a-pace" (I.iii.136–39). A "coranto" is a running dance; a "sink-a-pace" (after the French *cinque pace*) is a dance of five steps; and a "galliard" is a lively dance in triple time. In *Julius Caesar*, a cobbler who came to see Caesar enter Rome in triumph brags about his trade: "I am indeed, sir, a surgeon to old shoes; when they are in great danger, I recover them. As proper men as ever trod

upon neat's leather have gone upon my handiwork" (I.i.26–29). "Neat's leather" is oxhide. George Fox (1624–91), the founder of the Society of Friends, was apprenticed to a shoemaker in his youth and frequently spoke of sinful behavior as "disorderly walking."

9.9–10 (184:10–12). The beautiful ineffectual . . . against hard facts – This paraphrases Wilhelm Meister's remarks about Hamlet (see 9.3–4n). But it is also a remark about Wilhelm Meister himself, since Goethe regards Meister's flirtation with the theater as placing him in danger of becoming "a beautiful ineffectual dreamer" instead of the active moralist he is destined to become. Goethe enforces the temporary analogues between Hamlet's and Meister's characters: when Meister is acting the part of Hamlet, the ghost that appears on stage is impressively acted by the ghost of Meister's father, who warns Meister to escape from the lure of the theater. The phrase "beautiful and ineffectual" is borrowed from Matthew Arnold's final dictum in his essay "Shelley," in *Essays in Criticism: Second Series* (1888). "And in poetry, no less than in life, he is a beautiful 'and ineffectual' angel, beating in the void his luminous wings in vain." The implication of Lyster's remark is that Shelley was another Hamlet.

9.12 (184:14). he corantoed off – From *Twelfth Night;* see 9.5n.

9.16–17 (184:18–19). Monsieur de la Palisse . . . before his death – A famous example of ridiculous statement of obvious truth, attributed to the soldiers of the French Maréchal de la Palisse, who died after a heroic effort in a losing cause at the battle of Pavia in 1525. The Maréchal's soldiers, protesting that their leader had done nothing to contribute to the debacle, were supposed to have said: "Un quart d'heure avant sa mort il est en vie" (A quarter of an hour before his death he was alive).

9.18 (184:20). six brave medicals – Recalls a line from Blake's *Milton* (c. 1804) when Blake describes Milton as "pond'ring the intricate mazes of Providence, / Viewing his Sixfold Emanation scatter'd thro' the deep / In torment!" (Book the First, Plate 2, lines 17–20). The irony of the "medicals," the anti-poets who are to take the "dictation," turns on Milton's prayer that the "Heav'nly Muse" dictate *Paradise Lost* to or through him, and on the fact that Milton, because he was blind, dictated *Paradise Lost* to his daughters.

9.18 (184:20). John Eglinton – Pseudonym of William Kirkpatrick Magee (1868–1961). He was born in Dublin, the son of a Protestant clergyman, and was educated at Trinity College where he read classics. He became an accomplished essayist and an influential figure on the Dublin literary scene. William Butler Yeats paid him the compliment of regarding him as "our one Irish critic." He was assistant librarian of the National Library in 1904 and remained so until 1922, when he resigned and retired to England in protest of the founding of the Irish Free State.

9.19 (184:22). *The Sorrows of Satan* – A novel (1897) by Marie Corelli (pseudonym of Mary MacKay; 1855–1924). She was notable for her outspoken prejudice that her critics were all blasphemers and for the fact that she regarded herself as a latter-day Shakespeare, retiring, as did Shakespeare, from London to Stratford-on-Avon. *The Sorrows of Satan* set new records as a best-seller; it was subtitled "Or the Strange Experience of one Geoffrey Tempest, Millionaire." Satan's sorrows derive somewhat sentimentally from the proposition that "everywhere and at all times, he is trying to find some human being strong enough to repulse him and all his works." The title mocks Stephen's intention (after Blake) to rewrite *Paradise Lost* so that Satan is portrayed as the romantic hero who champions the cause of man against Jehovah, the impersonal forces of the universe.

9.22–26 (184:24–28). *First he tickled . . . Jolly old medi* – A fragment of an unpublished bawdy poem, "Medical Dick and Medical Davy," by Oliver St. John Gogarty; see 9.908–9n.

9.27–28 (184:29–30). Seven is dear to the mystic mind – In Hebrew, Greek, Egyptian, and Eastern traditions, seven was regarded as the embodiment of perfection and unity, mystically appropriate to sacred things. Seven "was also used by early [Christian] writers as the number of completion and perfection" (George Ferguson, *Signs and Symbols in Christian Art* [New York, 1954], p. 154; cited by Joan Keenan). In its association with mystical experience it rivaled the number three in popularity.

9.28 (184:30). *The shining seven W B calls them – W. B. Yeats in "A Cradle Song"; second stanza (1895 version): "God's laughing in Heaven / To see you so good; / The Shining Seven / Are gay with his mood." The "seven" are the seven planets known in 1890, when the poem was written—Mercury, Venus, Mars, Saturn, Jupiter, Uranus, and Neptune—and they echo the "Starry Seven" ("The Seven Angels of the Presence") of another W.B., William Blake in *Milton* (Book the First, Plate 14, line 42).

9.29 (184:31). his rufous skull – Describing John Eglinton (W. K. Magee).

9.30 (184:32–33). an ollav, holyeyed – AE (George William Russell). The "ollaves" were pre-Christian Irish masters of learning and poetry.

9.31 (184:33). a sizar's laugh – A "sizar" at Trinity College in Dublin (as at Cambridge University in England) was a student whose fees were paid by the college he attended. The student wore a red cap, which identified him as a dependent; he waited on the fellows and performed other menial tasks.

9.32–33 (184:35–36). *Orchestral Satan . . . as angels weep* – These lines echo two lines from *Paradise Lost:* the first describes Satan "Prone on the flood" of the burning lake of hell: "Lay floating many a rood" (1:196); the second describes Satan as he is about to speak to the fallen angels: "and thrice in spite of scorn, / Tears such as Angels weep, burst forth" (1:619–20).

9.34 (184:37). *Ed egli avea del cul fatto trombetta* – Italian: "And of his arse he made a trumpet" (*Inferno* 21:139). Dante and Virgil are escorted through the Fifth Chasm by a squad of ten Barterers ("Those who made secret and vile traffic of their Public offices and authority, in order to gain money"). Dante regards them as demons: the ten men of the squad stick out their tongues at their captain and he answers their unruly conduct in the manner described in the quoted line.

9.36 (184:39). Cranly's eleven true Wicklowmen – After a remark by Joyce's friend J. F. Byrne (Cranly in fiction), who argued that twelve men with resolution could save Ireland and that they could be found in County Wicklow; eleven here, because presumably Cranly would be the twelfth.

9.36–37 (184:39–185:1). Gap-toothed Kathleen . . . in her house – In Yeats's play *Cathleen ni Houlihan* (1902), Cathleen appears as the Poor Old Woman, a traditional symbol of Ireland. She is gap-toothed (has spaces between her teeth) because of her great age. The setting of the play, "close to Killala, in 1798," echoes the theme of liberation of Ireland, since a French expeditionary force landed there in that year in what proved an ineffectual attempt to help the Irish in the rebellion. Stephen recalls phrases from a passage early in the play: "BRIDGET: What was it put you wandering? OLD WOMAN: Too many strangers in the house. BRIDGET: Indeed you look as if you'd had your share of trouble. OLD WOMAN: I have had trouble indeed. BRIDGET: What was it put the trouble on you? OLD WOMAN: My land was taken from me. PETER: Was it much land they took from you? OLD WOMAN: My four beautiful green fields" (*Collected Plays* [New York, 1934], p. 81). "Strangers in the house" is an Irish epithet for the English invaders, and the "four beautiful green fields" are the four provinces of pre-Norman Ireland: Ulster, Connacht, Munster, and Leinster.

9.37–38 (185:1). and one more to hail him: *ave, rabbi* – That is, one to act the part of Judas, as in Matthew 26:49 when Judas identifies and betrays Jesus to those who had come to capture him: "and forthwith he came to Jesus, and said, Hail, Master [*Ave, Rabbi*, in the Latin of the Vulgate]; and kissed him."

9.38 (185:1–2). The Tinahely twelve – Tinahely is a market town on the River Derry in southern County Wicklow.

9.38–40 (185:2–4). In the shadow . . . Good hunting – Stephen is, of course, thinking about Cranly, but his thoughts echo and parody plot elements in John Millington Synge's (1871–1909) one-act play *In the Shadow of the Glen* (1903). The scene of the play is "the last cottage at the head of a long glen in County Wicklow." The heroine of the play, Nora Burke, thinking her husband dead, goes outside to cooee (whistle) for a young herdsman, Michael Dara. Later in the play Nora discovers that her husband, Dan, has only been feigning death; she, however, complains that Dan has been "cold" and implies that he has put her in danger of losing her youth. At the play's end Dan Burke throws his wife out without so much as a "godspeed," and she goes off with the poetic, spirited Tramp ("good hunting") to seek a life of lyric freedom in nature.

9.41 (185:5). Mulligan has my telegram – See 9.548–52 (199:18–24).

9.45 (185:9–10). I admire him . . . this side idolatry – "Old Ben" is Ben Jonson, and the allusion is to what Brandes called the "noble eulogy prefixed to the First Folio" of Shakespeare's plays: "I remember the players have often mentioned it as an honour to Shakespeare, that in his writing (whatsoever he penned) he never blotted out a line. My answer hath been, Would he hath blotted a thousand. Which they thought a malevolent speech. I had not told posterity this but for their ignorance, who chose that circumstance to commend their friend by, wherein he most faulted; and to justify mine own candour: for I loved the man, and do honour his memory, on this side idolatry, as much as any. He was (indeed) honest, and of open and full nature; had an excellent phantasy, brave notions, and gentle expressions; wherein he flowed with that facility, that sometimes it was necessary he should be stopped: . . ." (quoted in Brandes, p. 20).

9.47 (185:12–13). whether Hamlet is Shakespeare or James I or Essex – Various attempts have been made by literary historians to identify the "model" for the character of Hamlet. Candidates have included Shakespeare (on the basis of the poet's self-doubt); James I of England, previously James VI of Scotland (on the basis of his well-known morbidity); and Robert Devereux (1566–1601), second earl of Essex, another of Shakespeare's contemporaries (on the basis of his peculiar combination of impetuous military leadership and inexplicable lassitude).

9.48 (185:13–14). the historicity of Jesus – In the nineteenth century considerable theological discussion focused on the question: What difference would it make to a church and its theology if the "real history" of Jesus could be researched and published?

9.49 (185:14). formless spiritual essences – One of George William Russell's favorite phrases, as in the following comment (on W. B. Yeats's power as a poet): "Spirituality is the power of apprehending formless spiritual essences, of seeing the eternal in the transitory, and in the things which are seen the unseen things of which they are the shadow" (in "Religion and Love" [1904], reprinted in *Imaginations and Reveries* [Dublin, 1915], pp. 122–23).

9.50 (185:15–16). out of how deep a life does it spring – After the romantic assumption that the artist is greater in soul than other men and that the greatness of a work of art is in direct proportion to the greatness of the artist's soul.

9.50 (185:16). Gustave Moreau – (1826–98), a French painter noted for his romantic and symbolic style. His weird, exotic renderings of biblical and classical myths were admired by the avant-garde of his time, and as a "literary" painter he had considerable influence on French symbolist poets. Yeats, in his *Autobiography* (New York, 1958), p. 163, speaks of Russell's "early admiration for the works of Gustave Moreau"; Russell himself tended to play down his admiration for Moreau after about 1905.

9.51 (185:17). the deepest poetry of Shelley – Shelley was widely regarded in the late nineteenth century as the ideal poet of metaphysical, "intellectual" beauty, capable of that Neoplatonic vision that penetrates the "veil" of the sensuous world to apprehend the spiritual truth beyond.

9.52–53 (185:19). Plato's world of ideas – Nineteenth-century transcendental interpretations of Plato asserted that to him "truth" was ultimate, inevitably ideal, and abstract and that the material forms in which truths were embodied inevitably corrupted and distorted the truths to some degree.

9.54 (185:21). A. E. has been telling some yankee interviewer – See 7.785n.

9.57 (185:24). Aristotle was once Plato's schoolboy – Aristotle (384–322 B.C.) was associated with the Academy in Athens 367–347 B.C. while Plato (c. 427–347 B.C.) was head of the Academy.

9.61 (185:29). Formless spiritual. Father, Word and Holy Breath – See 9.49n. In Theosophy, and particularly in that branch of it known as "esoteric Christianity," God was assumed to be without limit (i.e., "formless"). Only by limiting himself, "making as it were a sphere . . . Spirit within and limitation, or matter without," does God become manifest. "The veil of matter . . . makes possible the birth of the Logos . . . and the Trinity becomes Father, Word [Logos, Self-Limited God] and Holy Breath as a modification of Father, Son and Holy Ghost" (Annie Besant, *Esoteric Christianity* [1901; Madras, India, 1953], pp. 152–53).

A more orthodox version of "Father, Word and Holy Breath" is presented by Robert Boyle, S.J.: "And there are two processions—the procession of the Son from the Father, and the procession of the Holy Spirit from the Father and the Son. The first is properly a generation, since the Father, knowing Himself, generates in that knowing a Word expressive of that knowing, which reflects in total perfection the infinite

Being. The mutual love of Father and Word breathes forth the third Person, not a generation (since it does not produce a Word imaging the Father), but more properly a spiration, a breathing forth, which, as it were, brings into unity the Father and the Son" ("James Joyce and the Soul," in *A Starchamber Quiry*, ed. E. L. Epstein [London, 1982], pp. 110–11).

9.61–62 (185:29–30). Allfather, the heavenly man – In esoteric Christianity, the "Allfather" is Christ, dual in nature, both without limit and with limit. "Heavenly man" is "an appellation . . . in the Hermetic Schools for the Adam-Kadmon; the Son, the Third Person of the Trinity in the Secret Doctrine" (Powis Hoult, *A Dictionary of Some Theosophical Terms* [London, 1910], p. 55); see 3.41n.

9.62–63 (185:30–31). Hiesos Kristos . . . at every moment – *Hiesos Kristos*, Greek: "Jesus Christ." Theosophical lore maintained that Jesus was an initiate of "that one sublime Lodge . . . of the true Mysteries in Egypt," and thus he would have been what Stephen calls "magician of the beautiful," "as a rose tree strangely planted in a desert would shed its sweetness on the barrenness around" (Besant, *Esoteric Christianity*, p. 97). As such the historical Christ became identified "in Christian nomenclature with the Second Person in the [Theosophical] Trinity, the Logos, or Word of God" (p. 28). "The second aspect of the Christ of the Mysteries is then the life of the Initiate, the life which is entered on at the first great Initiation, at which Christ is born in man, and after which He develops [and suffers] in man" (p. 129).

In Christian orthodoxy the Logos is not analogous to the human word spoken or written but is, according to St. Augustine, "the *inner word*, the soul's knowledge of itself" (William T. Noon, S.J., *Joyce and Aquinas* [New Haven, Conn., 1957], p. 119).

9.63–64 (185:32). I am the fire . . . sacrificial butter – One aspect of Annie Besant's *The Ancient Wisdom* (London, 1897) is "the Law of Sacrifice." Sacrifice is conceived not as "suffering" but as the willingness of the Logos to circumscribe "His infinite Life in order that he might be manifest" (p. 328); but the circumscription is without loss of infinitude, and the Law of Sacrifice becomes "thus the law of life-evolution in the universe" (p. 332), embracing both that which sacrifices and that which is sacrificed. The lines Stephen quotes are from the *Bhagavadgītā:* "I am the ritual action, I am the sacrifice, I am the ancestral oblation, I am the (medicinal) herb, I am the (sacred) hymn, I am also the melted butter, I am the fire and I am the offering" (trans. S. Radhakrishnan [London, 1948], p. 245).

9.65 (185:33). Dunlop – Daniel Nicol Dunlop, an Irish editor and Theosophist. He edited the *Irish Theosophist* (c. 1896–1915) and contributed articles under the pseudonym Aretas; he edited another Theosophical journal, the *Path* (London, 1910–14). In 1896, at its second annual convention (in Dublin), the Theosophical Society of Europe selected him its permanent chairman.

9.65 (185:33). Judge – William Q. Judge (1851–96), an Irish-American Theosophist who assisted Helena Petrovna Blavatsky in founding the Theosophical Society in 1875. He was subsequently head of the "powerful" Aryan Theosophical Society in New York City.

9.65 (185:33). the noblest Roman of them all – Marc Antony, in the final speech of Shakespeare's *Julius Caesar,* praises the now-dead Brutus: "This was the noblest Roman of them all. / All the conspirators, save only he, / Did that they did in envy of great Caesar" (V.v.68–70). As applied to Judge, the line is ironic. After Blavatsky's death in 1891, Judge in America and Annie Besant (1847–1933) in England jointly succeeded her, both supposedly as mouthpieces of an unknown master who had evolved to a superhuman level and who was the real head of the Theosophical movement. Besant preferred charges against Judge for fraudulent use of this master's name. The charges were not proven, but the result of the accusation was a worldwide split of the Theosophical movement—one faction followed Judge; the other, Besant.

9.65 (185:33). Arval – The central ruling body of the Theosophical movement was composed of twelve members and was called the Esoteric Section or (mystically) Arval, after a Roman priesthood of twelve members who performed the fertility rites of a somewhat mysterious mother-goddess. Theosophical lore associated this twelve with the twelve disciples (both groups governed by a "master" whose identity was shrouded in mystery).

9.65–66 (185:34). The Name Ineffable . . . K. H. – The Name Ineffable, the name not to be uttered (as the Israelites were forbidden to utter the name Jehovah). Master K. H. was Koot Hoomi, one of Blavatsky's two "masters," or "mahatmas." He was a Tibetan who had evolved to a superhuman level. He was reputedly in direct communication with H.P.B. (and after her death with some of her followers). He "spoke" to H.P.B. at times; at other times he "precipitated" messages in crayon or watercolor on rice paper. There was considerable public skepticism and even controversy among Theosophists over this master's identity, presence, and messages. Blavatsky and her followers spoke and issued orders "in the name of the Master."

9.67 (185:35–36). Brothers of the great white lodge – After Judge's death, an American Theosophist, Katherine A. Tingley, reorganized Judge's worldwide branch of the movement as the Universal Brotherhood Organization. Its members regarded themselves as heirs apparent of what was variously called the Great White Lodge, the Great Aryan Lodge, or the Grand Lodge of Central Asia (the mythic Indo-European source of all Theosophical doctrine called the Hierarchy of Adept).

9.68–69 (185:36–38). The Christ with . . . plane of buddhi – A capsule version of the Theosophical reading of Christ's career. The Egyptian Gnostic theologian Valentius (d. c. 160) held that Sophia ("wisdom"), in the last "aeon" before Christ, fell "into chaos in her attempt to rise unto the Highest." Once fallen, she repented and cried out "to the Light in which she had trusted." Christ was then sent "to redeem her from chaos," to crown her "with his light" (i.e., to baptize her with light—thus "moisture of light") and to lead her, his "bridesister," forth from bondage (Annie Besant, *Esoteric Christianity* [1901; Madras, India, 1953], pp. 102–3). The "plane of buddhi" is the fourth plane, "in which there is still duality but where there is no separation. . . . It is a state of bliss in which each is himself, with a clearness and vivid intensity which cannot be approached on lower planes, and yet in which each feels himself to include all others, to be one with them, inseparate and inseparable" (Annie Besant, *The Ancient Wisdom,* [London, 1897], p. 197).

9.69 (185:38–39). The life esoteric – That is, life on or approaching the "plane of buddhi"; "From this plane only can man act as one of the Saviours of the world" (Besant, *The Ancient Wisdom,* p. 342).

9.70 (185:39–40). O.P. must work off bad karma first – *O.P.:* ordinary people. *Karma* (in Theosophy): "the law of moral retribution, whereby not only does every cause have an effect, but he who puts the cause in action suffers the effect" (Christmas Humphreys, *Karma and Rebirth* [London, 1943], p. 11). Thus there is karma in everything man does; and bad karma suggests either the refusal to accept the effect of one's actions or the reluctance to perform one's duties (in which one's karma resides). In the successive embodiments of transmigration, the soul is placed in bodies and life situations that will aid it to work off the accumulated bad karma of its former lives.

9.70–71 (185:40). Mrs Cooper Oakley – Isabel Cooper-Oakley (b. 1854) was a highly successful businesswoman in London and a close associate of Blavatsky, both in India (from 1884) and in London (from 1890). She was distinguished as the recipient of H.P.B.'s "last message" when H.P.B. was on her deathbed.

9.71 (185:41). H.P.B.'s elemental – Referring to Helena Petrovna Blavatsky. In Theosophy the "elemental" is essentially the "lower," or "mortal," nature of man, one-fourth of which is visible as the physical body, three-fourths invisible as the astral or design body, the life principle, and the principle of desire. The joke involves Blavatsky's disciples' claim that she would appear to them after her death; it also involves the non-Theosophical pun on genitals.

9.72 (185:42). O fie! Out on't – Approximations of phrases from two of Hamlet's soliloquies: "Oh, that this too too solid flesh would melt" (I.ii.129–59: "Fie on't! ah fie!" [I.ii.135]) and "O, what a rogue and peasant slave am I!" (II.ii.576–632: "Fie, upon 't! Foh! About, my brain!" [II.ii.617]).

9.72 (185:42). Pfuiteufel! – A German oath: *Pfui*—"fie, for shame"; *teufel*—"devil."

9.74 (186:2). Mr Best – Richard Irvine Best (1872–1959), assistant director (1904–23) and director (1924–40) of the National Library, and translator of *Le cycle mythologique irlandais* by Marie Henri d'Arbois de Joubainville (1827–1910). Best's translation appeared as *The Irish Mythological Cycle and Celtic Mythology* (Dublin, 1903). De Joubainville was professor of Celtic literature at the Collège de France. Best was one of the founders of the School of Irish Learning in Dublin (1903). Early in his life, and certainly through 1904, he was an enthusiastic admirer of Walter Pater's and Oscar Wilde's

aestheticism. Later in his career his emphasis shifted from aestheticism to scholarship.

9.76–78 (186:4–7). That model schoolboy . . . shallow as Plato's – One of Plato's "musings about the afterlife" occurs in the Myth of Er at the end of the *Republic*. In that myth several souls of the famous dead, including that of Odysseus, have to choose new lives as animals or men. All the other souls are eager to choose, but Odysseus temporizes and finally chooses last. "Now the recollection of former toils had disenchanted him of ambition, and he went about for a considerable time in search of the life of a private man who had no cares; he had some difficulty in finding this, which was lying about and had been neglected by everybody else; and when he saw it, he said that he would have done the same had his lot been first instead of last, and that he was delighted to have it." Hamlet's "musings about the afterlife" are central in the "To be, or not to be" soliloquy (III.i.56–58), where Hamlet (like Plato) implies a desire for an afterlife free from "cares." Hamlet remarks, "For in that sleep of death what dreams may come / When we have shuffled off this mortal coil, / Must give us pause," and asks why one should face the problems of life "But that the dread of something after death, / The undiscover'd country from whose bourn / No traveller returns, puzzles the will." Aristotle never directly criticizes Plato's view of the immortality of the soul, but Stephen's rhetorical flourish has some basis in Aristotle's heavily qualified views of immortality as expressed in what most commentators regard as a difficult passage in *De Anima* (On the Soul) 3:5: "Mind in this sense of it is separable, impossible, unmixed, since it is in its essential nature activity (for always the active is superior to the passive factor, the originating force to the matter which it forms)." This passage is often read as implying that the active intellect in the soul (free of any memory, affect, character, or content) is immortal in a *general* but not in a *personal* way. Thus Aristotle could be said to regard Plato's (and Hamlet's) "musings" as "shallow," since those musings regard the soul as immortal in a personal sense.

9.79 (186:8). waxing wroth – In the first of Edmund Spenser's (c. 1552–99) two cantos of *Mutabilitie* (usually assumed to be part of *The Faerie Queene*), Jove is told that he is as subservient to the God of Nature as men are: "Thereat Jove wexéd wroth, and in his spright / Did inly grudge, yet did it well conceale" (stanza 35).

9.82–83 (186:11–12). Which of the two . . . from his commonwealth? – Answer: Plato. Aristotle's *Poetics* can be regarded as proof of his affirmation of the poet. In a much-quoted passage in Plato's *Republic* 10:606–7, Socrates asserts that none of the "excellences" of the ideal state under discussion please him more than the exclusion of "all imitative poetry" and the retention only of "hymns to the gods and praises of famous men." While this passage can be regarded as ironic, it is often taken (as Stephen's remark implies) to be a direct statement of "what Plato thinks."

9.84 (186:13). dagger definitions – That is, Stephen's argument will be based on the Aristotelian distinction between nominal definitions and essential definitions (Aristotle, *Posterior Analytics* 2:8). The distinction is used to point out that the process of definition begins with the "nominal" and proceeds to the "essential": it moves in the direction of cause. For example, an eclipse is a loss of light (nominal); an eclipse is a shadow on the earth caused by the interposition of the moon between the earth and the sun (essential).

9.84–85 (186:13–14). Horseness is the whatness of allhorse – A Platonic proposition that implies that individual horses are imperfect approximations of the idea "horse." Stephen's phrase echoes a famous remark, apocryphally attributed to Plato's opponent Antisthenes (see 7.1035n): "O Plato, I see a horse, but I do not see horseness."

9.85 (186:14). Streams of tendency and aeons they worship – That is, the Neoplatonic Theosophists, such as AE (George William Russell) who concocted his pen name out of *Aeon;* see 8.527–28n. Some definitions from *A Dictionary of Some Theosophical Terms*, compiled by Powis Hoult (London, 1910): "*Aeon:* (1) In Gnosticism, an emanation from Deity, and the medium of its expression. (2) A *kalpa* [a period of activity or manifestation; a Day of Brahma or age]" (pp. 4, 64). "Streams of Tendency": the ascending and descending flow through the "Planetary Chain—a series of seven globes or worlds which form the field of evolution during the planetary cycle or *manvantara*" (p. 101). A manvantara is "the cycle of manifestation [or Aeon] as opposed to *pralaya* or non-manifesta-

tion. It includes the seven *rounds* of the great *life-wave* of the Logos" (p. 82); see 9.62–63n.

9.85–86 (186:15). God: noise in the street – See 2.386n.

9.86 (186:15–16). Space: what you damn well have to see – An Aristotelian proposition (3.1–9 [37:1–10]), as against the Platonic view of space in *Republic* 7: "The spangled heavens should be used as a pattern and with a view to that higher knowledge; their beauty is like the beauty of figures or pictures excellently wrought by the hand of Daedalus, or some other great artist, which we may chance to behold; any geometrician who saw them would appreciate the exquisiteness of their workmanship, but he would never dream of thinking that in them he could find the true equal, or the true double, or the truth of any proposition."

9.86–88 (186:16–19). Through spaces smaller . . . but a shadow – Combines allusions to Blake's *Milton* and Dante's *Inferno*. At the conclusion of the *Inferno* in canto 34, Dante and Virgil, his guide, come to Satan, who at the earth's center is waist-deep in the ice of Lake Cocytus. Dante and Virgil crawl down over Satan's buttocks and exit from Hell to begin their upward journey toward the surface of the earth and the Mount of Purgatory. From Book the First of Blake's *Milton:* "For every Space larger than a red Globule of Man's blood / Is visionary, and is created by the Hammer of Los: / And every Space smaller than a Globule of Man's blood opens / Into Eternity, of which this vegetable Earth is but a shadow" (Plate 29, lines 19–22). Cf. *CW*, p. 222. See 17.1243–44n.

9.89 (186:19–20). Hold to the now . . . to the past – After St. Augustine's (353–430) *De Immortalitate Animae* (On the Immortality of the Soul): "For what is done needs expectation, that it may be done, and memory, that it may be understood as much as possible. And expectation is of future things, and memory is of things past. But the intention to act is of the present, through which the future flows into the past" (after J. P. Migne, *Patrologia Latina* [Paris, 1844–64], 32:1023A).

9.93 (186:24). Jubainville's book – See 9.74n.

9.94 (186:25). Hyde's *Lovesongs of Connacht* – See 3.397–98n.

9.95 (186:27). Gill's – See 6.317n.

9.96–99 (186:28–31). *Bound thee forth . . . lean unlovely English* – The first stanza of a poem by Douglas Hyde; Hyde intended the poem's six stanzas as an example of a meter (the *deibhidh*) widely used by ancient Irish bards but subsequently lost. Hyde's first stanza reads: "Bound thee forth my Booklet quick. / To greet the Polished Public. / Writ—I ween't was not my Wish— / In Lean unLovely English." The poem, as *envoi,*concludes Hyde's *The Story of Early Gaelic Literature* (London, 1894), pp. 173–74.

9.102 (186:35–36). An emerald set . . . of the sea – The second line of a poem, "Cushla-ma Chree" (Pulse of My Heart), by John Philpot Curran (1750–1817). The poem begins: "Dear Erin, how sweetly thy green bosom rises, / An emerald set in the ring of the sea."

9.103 (186:38). auric egg – In Theosophy, "An appellation that has been given to the Causal Body owing to its form" (Powis Hoult, *A Dictionary of Some Theosophical Terms* [London, 1910], p. 20). The Causal Body is "the Immediate body of the . . . Thinker vibrating to the [highest] levels of the mental plane. It has been so named because it 'gathers up within it the results of all experiences and these act as causes, moulding future lives' " (p. 30).

9.104–8 (186:38–187:3). The movements which work . . . the musichall song – Recalls a passage in Russell's essay "Nationality and Imperialism," in *Ideals in Ireland* (Dublin, 1901). "The Police gazettes, the penny novels, the hideous comic journals, replace the once familiar poems and the beautiful and moving memoirs of classic Ireland. The music that breathed Tir na n-og [the afterlife, "Land of Youth," of Irish myth] and overcame men's hearts with all gentle and soft emotions is heard more faintly, and the songs of the London music halls may be heard in places where the music of faery enchanted the elder generations.

"The national spirit . . . is shy, hiding itself away in remote valleys, or in haunted mountains, or deep in the quiet of hearts that do not reveal themselves. Only to its own will it comes and sings its hopes and dreams." See also "our mighty mother," 1.85n, and "mother Dana," 9.376n.

9.107–8 (187:2–3). the sixshilling novel – Popular and commercially exploited fiction that began to flood the British book market in the 1880s and threatened to displace the standard "serious" novel (which sold in three volumes for 31s. 6d.). This new fiction found such success partly because of the rapid rise in literacy after the educational reforms of the 1870s.

9.108–9 (187:3–4). France produces . . . in Mallarmé – Stéphane Mallarmé (1842–98), a French poet, leader of the symbolist movement, and principal formulator of the symbolist aesthetic. He was regarded as the embodiment of late-nineteenth-century decadence. His works include *Le cygne, Hérodiade,* and *L'après-midi d'un faune.* The phrase "the finest flower of corruption" was in fact Best's praise of Mallarmé.

9.109–10 (187:5). the poor of heart – Recalls two of the beatitudes from Jesus' Sermon on the Mount: "Blessed are the poor in spirit: for their's is the kingdom of heaven. . . . Blessed are the pure in heart: for they shall see God" (Matthew 5:3, 8).

9.110 (187:5). the life of Homer's Phaeacians – The Phaeacians, on whose island Odysseus is beached after he leaves Calypso's island, are described as living equitably in peace, wealth, and happiness, with feasting, music, and dancing. The Phaeacians listen to Odysseus's stories of his wanderings and hardships and are extraordinarily generous to him, in effect replacing the treasures Odysseus would have brought home from Troy. They finally deliver Odysseus safely to Ithaca, with no further interference from Poseidon but against his wish. Ironically, the Phaeacians' generosity is their undoing. Their way of life is severely disrupted when Poseidon punishes them for comforting and aiding Odysseus.

9.113 (187:9). Stephen MacKenna – (1872–1954), an Irish journalist, linguist, and student of philosophy, noted for the brilliance of his conversation and for his painstaking translations of Plotinus.

9.113–14 (187:10). The one about *Hamlet* – "Hamlet et Fortinbras" by Mallarmé, in *Oeuvres complètes* (Paris, 1945), p. 1558. The prose-poem first appeared as a letter in *Revue Blanche,* 15 July 1896.

9.114 (187:10–11). *il se promène . . . de lui-même* – French: "he walks in a leisurely fashion, reading in the book of himself"; Mallarmé's prose-poem continues: "a high and living sign; he scorns to look at any other. Nor will he be content to symbolize the solitude of the Thinker among other men; he kills them off aloofly and at random, or at least, they die. The black presence of the doubter diffuses poison, so that all the great people die, without his even taking the trouble, usually, to stab them behind the arras. Then, evidently in deliberate contrast to the hesitator, we see Fortinbras in the role of general, but no more efficaciously lethal than he; and if Death deploys his versatile appliances—phial, lotus-pool, or rapier—when an exceptional person flaunts his sombre livery, that is the import of the finale when, as the spectator returns to his senses, this sumptuous and stagnant exaggeration of murder (the idea of which remains as meaning of the play, attached to Him who makes himself alone) so to speak achieves vulgar manifestation as this agent of military destruction clears the stage with his marching army, on the scale of the commonplace, amid trumpets and drums" (*Selected Prose Poems, Essays, and Letters,* trans. and ed. Bradford Cooke [Baltimore, 1956]).

9.118–20 (187:15–17). *HAMLET / ou / LE DISTRAIT* – French: "Hamlet; or, The Distracted One." Mallarmé cites this in his prose-poem as the title of a French provincial production of *Hamlet;* but *Le distrait* (1697) is also the title of a comedy by Jean François Regnard (1655–1709), the most successful of Molière's imitators. In Regnard's play, when Léandre, the *distrait,* first appears in Act II, scene iii, his valet says, "He is dreaming and talking to himself; he does not see me," and the stage directions describe Léandre as "se promenant sur le théâtre en révant" (strolling about the stage in a state of reverie). Léandre, at the center of Regnard's plot of tangled, half-thwarted loves, is "the most forgetful man in the world"; at the play's end he even forgets that he has just overcome all obstacles and achieved the marriage he has so much desired. The comic parallel to Hamlet's tragic forgetfulness of purpose is obvious. Cf. 9.114n.

9.121 (187:18). *Pièce de Shakespeare* – French: "Play by Shakespeare"; but since *de* also means "of," it is a pun for the English-speaking mind: "a piece of Shakespeare."

9.125 (187:22). The absentminded beggar – A propaganda poem by Rudyard Kipling (1865–1936). Set to music by Sir Arthur Sullivan, the song was intended to raise funds "to secure small comforts for the troops at the front" in the Boer War. "Will you kindly drop a shilling in my little tambourine / For a gentleman in khaki ordered South?" According to Kipling, "The Absent Minded Beggar Fund" raised "about a quarter of a million pounds" in the course of the

war. Stephen's retort derives from Irish sentiment, which was bitterly opposed to the English conduct of the Boer War. See *Rudyard Kipling's Verse* (New York, 1940), p. 457.

9.129 (187:26). Sumptuous and stagnant exaggeration of murder – From Mallarmé's "Hamlet et Fortinbras"; see 9.114n.

9.130 (187:27). A deathsman . . . called him – Robert Greene (c. 1558–92), an Elizabethan novelist, playwright, and pamphleteer. The pamphlet Stephen alludes to is *A Groat's Worth of Wit bought with a Million of Repentance* (1592), in which Greene calls lust, not Shakespeare, "the deathsman of the soul." The pamphlet does, however, include a letter to three brother dramatists in which Greene mocks Shakespeare as "an upstart Crow, beautified with our feathers . . . in his owne conceit, the only Shake-scene in a countrie."

9.131 (187:28). a butcher's son – Shakespeare's father, John Shakespeare (d. 1601), was variously, according to available records, yeoman (landowner), glover, and whitawer (one who cured glove skins). The tradition that John Shakespeare was a butcher was first reported and perpetuated by the English antiquarian John Aubrey (1629–97).

9.131 (187:28–29). wielding the sledded pole-axe – Horatio describes the ghost of Hamlet's father to the other guards on the platform: "So frown'd he once, when, in an angry parle, / He smote the sledded Polacks on the ice" (I.i.62–63). The Quarto version of *Hamlet* read "Sleaded Pollox," the First Folio "sledded Pollax." The passage has been much disputed: "poleaxe" versus "Polacks."

9.132 (187:29–30). Nine lives . . . his father's one – The score in the play is eight, not nine: Polonius, Ophelia, Rosencrantz, Guildenstern, Gertrude, Laertes, Claudius, and Hamlet. The unchallenged "nine" may be a rhetorical flourish on "every cat has nine lives," and it may be a forecast of Stephen's argument that Shakespeare's own son, Hamnet, also died in the cause.

9.132–33 (187:30–31). Our Father who art in purgatory – Echoes the opening phrase of the Lord's Prayer, "Our Father which art in Heaven" (Matthew 6:9), and alludes to the Ghost's speech to Hamlet in which the Ghost describes himself in purgatory, "Doom'd for a certain term to walk the night, / And for the day confined to fast in fires, / Till the foul crimes done in my days of nature / Are burnt and purged away" (I.v.10–13).

9.133 (187:31). Khaki Hamlets don't hesitate to shoot – Khaki, the drab uniform that was widely regretted as an unheroic novelty during the Boer War, was introduced into the British army in the 1840s. By 1900 it was the standard uniform for troops in the field because it was so much more inconspicuous than red coats criss-crossed with white webbing. The slogan "Don't hesitate to shoot" became a rallying cry for Irish anger at the English policy of coercion in the 1880s. According to Irish anecdotal history, the command was first used by a Capt. "Pasha" Plunkett, who was in charge of a police barracks at Mitchelstown, County Cork, during a riot in 1887; see 12.874n. The thrust of Stephen's remark is that the wholesale killing in modern warfare is not unlike the wholesale killing in *Hamlet*.

9.133–34 (187:31–32). The bloodboltered shambles in act five – Act V of *Hamlet* begins with the burial of Ophelia and ends with the violent onstage deaths of Gertrude, Claudius, Laertes, and Hamlet. In *Macbeth*, Macbeth revisits the witches in Act IV, scene i, and there encounters the ghost of Banquo, whom he has had murdered. Macbeth says: "Now, I see, 'tis true; / For the blood-bolter'd Banquo smiles upon me, / And points at them [a show of eight Kings, Banquo's heirs] for his" (lines 122–24).

9.134–35 (187:32–33). the concentration camp sung by Mr Swinburne – The "song" is Swinburne's sonnet "On the Death of Colonel Benson," published in the *Saturday Review* (London, 9 November 1901), p. 584. Benson had died in a Boer prison camp. "Northumberland, so proud and sad today, / Weep and rejoice, our mother, who no son / More glorious than this dead and deathless one / Brought ever fame whereon no time shall prey. / Nor heed we more than he what liars dare say / Of mercy's holiest duties left undone / Toward whelps and dams of murderous foes whom none / Save we had spared or feared to starve and slay. // Alone as Milton and as Wordsworth found / And hailed their England, when from all around / Howled all the recreant hate of envious knaves, / Sublime she stands: while, stifled in the sound, / Each lie that falls from German boors and slaves / Falls but as filth dropt in the wandering waves." The concentration camps Stephen accuses Swinburne of praising were established by the British under Kitchener for the retention of

Boer civilians, including women and children. The camps were widely regarded as cruel and inhuman and were the subject of considerable controversy in England (let alone in Ireland, which was bitterly pro-Boer). Swinburne's poem was regarded as a whitewash of the concentration camps, and two letterwriters promptly attacked Swinburne in the *Saturday Review* (16 November 1901). One letterwriter called him "unthinking" and "excessive"; the other remarked: "It is not necessary to call the women and children 'whelps and dams.'" Swinburne replied by citing a series of atrocity stories about the Boers, whom he described as "virtual slave drivers" (in other words, it was all right for the British to persecute the Boers by detaining them in concentration camps because the Boers persecuted their British prisoners).

9.136 (187:34). Cranly . . . battles from afar – See 1.159n; the historical Cranly watched the Wars of the Roses "from afar." The battles Stephen has watched with Cranly are not clear; they could be chess, handball, or horseraces or the battles of the Boer War.

9.137–38 (187:35–36). *Whelps and dams . . . we had spared . . .* – From Swinburne's controversial poem; see 9.134–35n.

9.139 (187:37). the Saxon smile and yankee yawp – For "Saxon smile," see 1.732n. "Yankee yawp" is after Walt Whitman's "Song of Myself" (1855, 1891–92), section 52, lines 2–3: "I too am not a bit tamed, I too am untranslatable, / I sound my barbaric yawp over the roofs of the world." A "yawp" is a loud cry or yell.

9.139–40 (187:37–38). The devil and the deep sea – A proverbial equivalent of the choice between Scylla and Charybdis (the expression dates from the early sixteenth century).

9.142 (188:1). behoof – This rare word appears once in Shakespeare in *II Henry VI*, when Lord Say is pleading in vain for his life to the rebel leader Jack Cade (d. 1450): "This tongue hath parleyed unto foreign kings / For your behoof—" (IV.vii.77–78).

9.142 (188:1). Like the fat boy in Pickwick – In Dicken's *Posthumous Papers of the Pickwick Club* (1836–37), Mr. Wardle's servant, Joe the fat boy, is always asleep to the tune of "Damn that boy, he's gone to sleep again." But in chapter 8 he is, somewhat inconveniently, wide awake enough to observe a love scene between Miss Wardle and one of the Pickwickians.

He reports his observation to Miss Wardle's mother; his opening line: "I wants to make your flesh creep."

9.144/46 (188:3/5). *List! List! O list! / **If thou didst ever . . .** "GHOST: List, list, O, list! / If thou didst ever thy dear father love—HAMLET: O, God! GHOST: Revenge his foul and most unnatural murder. HAMLET: Murder!" (I.v.22–26).

9.147–49 (188:6–8). What is a ghost? . . . change of manners – A nominal definition of a ghost; see 9.84n.

9.149 (188:9). Stratford – Stratford-on-Avon, seventy-five miles northwest of London, was Shakespeare's birthplace (April 1564), where he married Anne Hathaway (1582), which he left for London (c. 1585), and to which he retired (c. 1612). The literal sense of the passage: it took as long to travel from Stratford to London in Elizabethan times as it took to travel from Dublin to Paris in the early twentieth century.

9.150 (188:10). limbo patrum – Elizabethan slang for a lockup or jail, as in Shakespeare's *Henry VIII* (V.iv.67–68). In Roman Catholic theology, *Limbus Patrum* was the state in which the souls of the pre-Christian patriarchs and prophets of the Old Testament were held until after the Resurrection, when Christ "harrowed hell" and brought them to heaven.

9.154 (188:14). It is this hour of a day in mid June – Stephen's source is Brandes: "The time of beginning was three o'clock punctually" (p. 101). "It is afternoon, a little before three o'clock. Whole fleets of wherries are crossing the Thames, picking their way among the swans and other boats to land their passengers on the south bank of the river" (p. 302).

9.155 (188:15–16). The flag is . . . the bankside – "The days of performance at these theatres were announced by the hoisting of a flag on the roof" (Brandes, p. 101); "for the flag waving over the Globe Theatre announces there is a play today" (p. 302). The "Bankside" is the south bank of the Thames at Southwark between Blackfriars and Waterloo bridges, opposite the City of London.

9.155–56 (188:16–17). The bear Sackerson . . . Paris garden – "Close to the Globe Theatre lay the Bear Garden, the rank smell from which greeted the nostrils even before it came in sight. The famous bear Sackerson, who is mentioned in *The Merry Wives of Windsor*

[I.i.306], now and then broke his chain and put female theatregoers shrieking to flight" (Brandes, p. 302). *Paris Garden:* the bear garden on the Bankside maintained from the sixteenth to the eighteenth century as a place for bear and bull baiting and prizefighting.

9.156 (188:17). Canvasclimbers – Sailors, after Shakespeare's *Pericles*, when Marina says: "When I was born, / Never was waves or wind more violent, / And from the ladder tackle [rope ladder] washes off / A canvas-climber" (IV.i.59–62).

9.157 (188:17). Drake – Sir Francis Drake (c. 1540–96), the first Englishman to circumnavigate the earth (1577–80) and a vice-admiral who played a key role in the English defeat of the Spanish Armada in 1588.

9.157 (188:18). chew their sausages among the groundlings – "Groundlings" were the spectators who stood in the pit; Hamlet condemns them as "for the most part . . . capable of nothing but inexplicable dumb-shows and noise" (III.ii.12–13). "They all had to stand—coalheavers and bricklayers, dock-labourers, serving-men and idlers. Refreshment-sellers moved about among them, supplying them with sausages and ale, apples and nuts. They ate and drank, drew corks, smoked tobacco, fought with each other, and, often, when they were out of humour, threw fragments of food, and even stones, at the actors" (Brandes, p. 105).

9.158 (188:19). Local colour – The heading of a subchapter on *Hamlet* in Brandes, pp. 357–60.

9.159–60 (188:21–22). Shakespeare has left . . . along the riverbank – From Charles W. Wallace's "New Shakespeare Discoveries: Shakespeare as a Man Among Men," *Harper's Monthly Magazine* 120 (1910): 489–510. The article cites the discovery of legal papers (Belott v. Mountjoy) that fix Shakespeare's residence in London from 1598 to 1604 at 13 Silver Street, the house of Christopher Mountjoy, a Huguenot. Wallace adds "local colour" to his account: "By reference to a map of London you will see that the Globe Theatre is situated on the south side of the Thames just between the Bankside and Maiden Lane, almost directly South of Silver Street. You can see Shakespeare start out from Silver Street for the theatre. Sometimes he stops on the way for Hemings and Condell. A brisk walk of ten minutes, with lively talk, down Wood Street, past the old city prison called the Counter, across Cheapside near where Cheapside Cross stood, then through Bread Street past the Mermaid Tavern takes them to the river, where a waterman ferries them across" (p. 508). *Swanmews:* literally, "a stable for swans."

9.161 (188:24). The swan of Avon – Epithet for Shakespeare after Ben Jonson's "To the Memory of William Shakespeare," in the First Folio edition of Shakespeare's works (1623): "Sweet Swan of Avon! What a sight it were / To see thee in our waters yet appear, / And make those flights upon the banks of Thames, / That did so take Eliza, and our James!" (lines 71–74).

9.163 (188:25). Composition of place. Ignatius Loyola – St. Ignatius Loyola's (1491–1556) *Spiritual Exercises* (1548), "The First Exercise," item 47: "*First Prelude.* The first prelude is a composition, seeing the place. Here it is to be observed that in the contemplation or meditation of a visible object as in contemplating Christ our Lord, Who is visible, the composition will be to see with the eye of the imagination the corporeal place where the object I wish to contemplate is found. I say the corporeal place, such as the Temple or the mountain where Jesus Christ is found, or our Lady, according to that which I desire to contemplate. In a meditation on sins, the composition will be to see with the eyes of the imagination and to consider that my soul is imprisoned in this corruptible body, and my whole compound self in this vale (of misery) as in exile amongst brute beasts; I say, my whole self, composed of body and soul."

9.164 (188:27). under the shadow – The rear portion of the stage in the Elizabethan theater was protected by a roof or platform called the "shadow." It not only protected players from the weather but also provided, in a theater lit solely by daylight, a darker place appropriate to scenes such as the appearance of the Ghost in *Hamlet* (I.iv, I.v).

9.164–65 (188:28). made up in . . . court buck – The Ghost appears in full armor, as Horatio remarks (I.i.60 and I.ii.226–29). Brandes (pp. 104–5) gives evidence to show that acting companies purchased their costumes. Stephen is repeating the possibly apocryphal tradition that noblemen contributed support to the companies by giving them secondhand court costumes.

9.165 (188:28–29). a wellset man with a bass voice – Sources include Lee (p. 286): "Aubrey reported that Shakespeare was 'a handsome well shap't man'"; and Harris: "Shakespeare was probably of middle height, or below it, and podgy. I always picture him to myself as very like Swinburne" (p. 268); and "I can see him talking, talking with extreme fluency in a high tenor voice" (p. 367).

9.166 (188:29). a king and no king – Francis Beaumont (c. 1584–1616) and John Fletcher's (1579–1625) *A King and No King* (1611), a tragicomedy. Stephen's source was Brandes, p. 599: "*A King and No King,* the play which in all probability succeeds *Philaster,* contains the same merits and defects as the latter, and here also Shakespeare might find reminiscences of his own work."

9.166 (188:30). the player is Shakespeare – According to Lee (p. 44), "Rowe identified only one of Shakespeare's parts, 'the Ghost in his own "Hamlet," ' and Rowe asserted his assumption of that character to be 'the top of his performance.' " Nicholas Rowe (1674–1718) was an English poet and dramatist who also edited Shakespeare's plays.

9.167 (188:30–31). all the years . . . not vanity – After Ecclesiastes 11:10: "Therefore remove sorrow from thy heart, and put away evil from thy flesh; for childhood and youth are vanity."

9.168 (188:32). Burbage – Richard Burbage (c. 1567–1619), an English actor who built and operated the Globe Theatre. He appears to have been the chief actor and tragedian of his day; he apparently played major roles not only in Shakespeare's plays but also in those of Ben Jonson, and Beaumont and Fletcher. Stephen's source was Lee, p. 222: "Burbage created the title-part in Shakespeare's tragedy [*Hamlet*], and its success on the stage led to its publication immediately afterwards."

9.169 (188:33). beyond the rack of cerecloth – In this context "rack" means the clouds in the upper air (as it does in *Hamlet* II.ii.506); "cerecloth" is cloth impregnated with wax, used in embalming the illustrious dead. Thus, the sense of the phrase is "on the other side of the grave."

9.170 (188:35). *Hamlet I am thy father's spirit* – A misquotation. "HAMLET: What? GHOST: I am thy father's spirit, / Doom'd for a certain term to walk the night" (I.v.8–10).

9.171 (188:36). bidding him list – See 9.144/46n.

9.172 (188:37–38). Hamnet Shakespeare – "In the Parish Register of Stratford-on-Avon for 1596, under the heading of burials, we find this entry, in a clear and elegant handwriting: '*August 11, Hamnet filius William Shakespeare.*' Shakespeare's only son was born on the 2d of February 1585 [with a twin, a girl named Judith]; he was thus only eleven and a half when he died. We cannot doubt that this loss was a grievous one to a man of Shakespeare's deep feeling; doubly grievous it would seem because it was his constant ambition to restore the fallen fortunes of his family, and he was now left without an heir to his name" (Brandes, p. 140).

9.174–75 (189:2). in the vesture of buried Denmark – In *Hamlet*, when the Ghost first enters Horatio tries unsuccessfully to question it in order to learn the meaning of its "unnatural behavior." Horatio says, "What art thou that usurp'st this time of night, / Together with that fair and warlike form / In which the majesty of buried Denmark / Did sometimes march?" (I.i.46–49).

9.179–80 (189:8). your mother is the guilty queen – See 7.751–52n.

9.180 (189:8–9). Ann Shakespeare born Hathaway – (1556–1623).

9.183 (189:12). Art thou there, truepenny – The Ghost from underneath the stage demands ("Swear!") that Horatio and Marcellus swear themselves to secrecy as Hamlet has requested. Hamlet, on hearing the Ghost: "Ah, ha, boy! say'st thou so? art thou there, truepenny? / Come on—you hear this fellow in the cellarage— / Consent to swear" (I.v.150–52). *Truepenny:* a trusty person, an honest fellow.

9.186 (189:15–16). As for living . . . Villiers de l'Isle has said – Comte Jean Marie Mathais Philippe Auguste de Villiers de l'Isle Adam (1838–89) was a French poet and playwright, immediate precursor of the French symbolist movement. His plays combine a flamboyant, latter-day romanticism with fantastic and macabre tales. Russell quotes from Villiers de l'Isle Adam's last play, *Axel*, published posthumously in 1890. At the climax of the play, Count Axel, who has "a paleness almost radiant" and "an expression mysterious from thought," meets Sara, a daring beauty who has come to steal the count's hidden treasure. They experience a

lightning bolt of love at first sight and Sara proposes that they elope to a setting where they can live a life that will match the beauty of their love. The count replies: "Live? No. Our existence is full. . . . Sara, believe me when I say that we have just exhausted the future. All the realities, what will they be tomorrow in comparison with the mirages we have just lived? . . . To consent, after this, to live would be but sacrilege against ourselves. Live? our servants will do that for us." He proposes suicide; they share a goblet of poison and perish in a rapturous love-death. In context it is appropriate that Russell should quote this line, because Yeats used it as an epigraph to *The Secret Rose* (1897), which he dedicated to Russell.

9.187 (189:17). greenroom gossip – Actors' and playwrights' gossip; the "greenroom," a room where performers can relax, has been traditional in English theaters since about 1700.

9.190–91 (189:20–21). *Flow over them . . . Mananaan MacLir* – From George William Russell's three-act verse play *Deirdre* (first performed 1902; published Dublin, 1907): a chant in Act III (p. 49) spoken by the druid Cathvah (a part played by Russell himself when the play was first performed). The chant calls down a druid curse, the *Faed Fia* (which Russell took to mean the last flood, the end of the heroic age), on the Red Branch Knights just before those heroes begin to quarrel among themselves and destroy a comradeship-in-arms comparable to that of the Arthurian Round Table: "Let the Faed Fia fall / Mananaun MacLir / Take back the day / Amid days unremembered. / Over the warring mind, / Let thy Faed Fia fall, / Mananaun MacLir / Let thy waters rise, / Mananaun MacLir / Let the earth fail / Beneath their feet, / Let thy waves flow over them, / Mananaun: / Lord of Ocean!" Mananaan MacLir is the ancient Irish god of the sea.

9.192 (189:22). sirrah – A common Elizabethan form of address to a person who is inferior in station or who is being mocked.

9.194 (189:25). noble – An English coin used until 1461, worth 6s.8d.

9.195 (189:26). Georgina Johnson's – A prostitute, whether fictional or real is unknown.

9.196 (189:27). Agenbite of inwit – See 1.481n.

9.202 (189:33). I paid my way – Mr. Deasy's aphorism (see 2.251 [30:39]).

9.203 (189:34–35). He's from beyant . . . northeast corner – George William Russell was born in Lurgan, County Armagh, Ulster (the northern province of Ireland). Ulster is the predominantly Protestant, pro-British section of Ireland, and hence its motto: "I paid my way." The River Boyne, which enters the Irish Sea twenty-eight miles north of Dublin, is not so much a geographical as a historical dividing line between the Orange of Ulster and the Green of Ireland, since it was at the Battle of the Boyne, 1 July 1690, that William III (of Orange) defeated the Irish under the deposed King James II, thus ensuring the continuance of English rule in Ireland.

9.207 (189:38). Buzz. Buzz – Stale news. Hamlet uses this expression to mock Polonius when the latter announces the arrival of the traveling players (II.ii.412).

9.208 (189:39). entelechy, form of forms – Aristotle uses the word *entelechy* (actuality, complete reality) in two ways: (1) to mean form-giving cause or energy, as contrasted with mere potential existence; (2) to mean, in relation to the phenomena of living and mental existences, form-giving cause realized in a more or less perfect actuality, as in plants, animals, and men. In effect, entelechy in this second sense means not just actuality, but an actuality that has the power to produce other actualities of the same kind. For "form of forms," see 2.74–75n.

9.210 (189:41). I that sinned and prayed and fasted – As in *A Portrait*, from the closing pages of chapter 2 through to the opening pages of chapter 4.

9.211 (190:1). A child Conmee saved from pandies – A "pandybat" is a leather strap reinforced with whalebone; schoolboys were punished by being pandied, struck on the palms of their hands. For the episode Stephen recalls, see *A Portrait* 1:D.

9.212 (190:2). I, I and I. I – Suggests both the continuity of the Aristotelian soul ("by memory . . . under everchanging forms") and the discontinuity ("I am other I now") of the body and its molecules.

9.213 (190:3). A.E.I.O.U. – The five vowels spell out the legend that Stephen owes George Russell money. Ioanna Ioannudou (*JJQ* 12, no.

3 [1975]:317) suggests an allusion to the exchange in Shakespeare's *Love's Labour's Lost* in which the pert young Moth maintains that the pedant Holofernes is a sheep: "MOTH: What is *a, b*, spell'd backward, with the horn on his head? HOLOFERNES: *"Ba, pueritia* [childishness], with a horn added. MOTH: *Ba*, most silly sheep with a horn. You hear his learning. HOL.: *Quis* [who], *quis*, thou consonant [nonentity]? MOTH: The last of the five vowels, if 'you' repeat them; or the fift, if I. HOL.: I will repeat them— *a, e, I*—MOTH: The sheep: the other two concludes it [proves my contention, completes the list], *o, U"* (V.i.47–57).

9.217 (190:8–9). She died . . . sixtyseven years after she was born – Anne Hathaway was born in 1556 and died on 6 August 1623.

9.221 (190:13). The sheeted mirror – The mirrors in a chamber of death were removed or covered to prevent the ghost of the dead person from appearing or lingering as a reflection in a mirror.

9.222–23 (190:15). *Liliata rutilantium* – See 1.276–77n.

9.225 (190:17–18). the tangled glowworm of his lamp – See 2.72n and 8.589–90n.

9.228–29 (190:21–22). A man of genius makes no mistakes. His errors are volitional – In the *Lesser Hippias*, questionably attributed to Plato (in *The Dialogues of Plato*, trans. B. Jowett [New York, 1895], vol. 4), the Sophist Hippias argues that Homer "shows Achilles to be true and simple and Odysseus to be wily and false" (p. 495). Socrates traps Hippias into revising his phrase about Odysseus to "cunning and prudent," saying that Odysseus lies knowingly and that Achilles lies inadvertently; he then goes on to argue that the good man errs voluntarily, the bad man involuntarily, and concludes: "Then, Hippias, he who voluntarily does wrong and disgraceful things [as Odysseus when he lies], if there be such a man, will be the good man? HIPPIAS: There I cannot agree with you. SOCRATES: Nor can I agree with myself, Hippias; and yet . . ." (cited by Jean Kimball, "Brainsick Words of Sophists: Socrates, Antisthenes, and Stephen Dedalus," *JJQ* 16, no. 4 [1979]: 399–407). My colleague Laszlo Versenyi points out that volitional errors are an aspect of "the Socratic method itself as practiced in the early dialogues; in the ironic-maieutic method Socrates uses when he deceives in order to undeceive, he presents arguments he knows to be wrong in order to help his interlocutors to discover the truth for themselves."

9.233 (190:28). Socrates – (469–399 B.C.), the Greek teacher and philosopher whose image dominates the dialogues of his student and disciple Plato. He insisted that virtue derives from knowledge and that knowledge was to be pursued through dialectic, in the tensions of dialogue among men.

9.234 (190:28). Xanthippe – Socrates' wife, whose name has come to connote the typical shrew. Socrates, according to his pupil Xenophon, ascribed numerous domestic virtues to Xanthippe; some apologists excuse her ill temper on the basis that she may have been provoked by Socrates' impractical and unconventional behavior. One semifictional account quotes Socrates: "Xanthippe is irreplaceable. If I can stand it with her, I shall learn to stand it with anybody" (see Richard Steele, *Spectator,* essay 479 [9 September 1712]).

9.235–36 (190:29–30). from his mother . . . into the world – Socrates' mother, Phaenareté, was a midwife. Plato describes Socrates' behavior in a dialogue as "midwifery," since Socrates seemed to help his students "give birth" to understanding that they in fact already possessed before the dialogue began.

9.236 (190:31). Myrto – A daughter of one Arsteides was, according to some accounts, Socrates' first wife.

9.236 (190:31). (*absit nomen!*) – Latin: literally, "let the name be absent"; but the phrase also involves a pun on the stock phrase *absit omen:* "let there be (no) ill omen (in a word just used)."

9.237 (190:31). Socratididion's – The diminutive of Socrates, frequently translated as "Sweet Socrates." In Aristophanes' (c. 448–c. 380 B.C.) comedy *The Clouds* (423 B.C.), a country bumpkin whose prodigal son has taken to gambling comes to Socrates to learn "the unjust logic that can shirk debts" (i.e., sophistry). When Socrates enters overhead in a basket (symbolic of his remoteness from worldly concerns), the countryman calls, "Socrates, Socratididion" (lines 221–22).

9.237 (190:31–32). Epipsychidion – A poem (1821) by Percy Bysshe Shelley (1792–1822). The title is a coined word (Greek) usually translated as "this soul out of my soul" (line 238).

The poem articulates Shelley's concept of "true love," a transcendental (from Shelley's point of view, Platonic) identification with a sister spirit.

9.237 (190:32). no man, not a woman, will ever know – Recalls legends of the blind Greek prophet Tiresias, who was said to have been changed into a woman in the middle of his life by some prank of the gods. His special attributes resulted in his being called to settle a dispute between Zeus and Hera: Zeus had maintained that the sexual act is more pleasurable to women than to men; Hera had argued the contrary. Tiresias agreed with Zeus and was blinded by Hera for his pains; Zeus compensated by awarding him inward sight.

9.238 (190:33). *caudlelectures – The reference is to *Curtain Lectures* (1846), a collection of short, witty pieces by Douglas Jerrold (1803–57). Each "lecture" is the nightlong henpecking harangue that a Margaret Caudle delivers to her husband, Job Caudle. The patient Job usually replies with a plaintive rebuttal or a sigh of resignation. A "caudle" is a warm drink for sick persons.

9.238–39 (190:33–34). the archons of Sinn Fein – For "Sinn Fein," see 8.458n. The phrase recalls the archons of Athens (the ruling magistrates) who condemned Socrates to death for, they said, corrupting the youth of Athens. The sentence was carried out with a cup of hemlock.

9.243–44 (190:39–40). the baldpink lollard . . . guiltless though maligned – Thomas Lyster, who, as a Quaker, is a "lollard" and was subject to public suspicion about his loyalties because he was not a Roman Catholic; see 9.1n.

9.245 (190:41). a good groatsworth of wit – The phrase is from Robert Greene's *A Groat's Worth of Wit bought with a Million of Repentance* (1592). A groat (4d.) was regarded as a trivial sum. See 9.130n.

9.246 (190:42). He carried a memory in his wallet – Recalls Ulysses' assertion in Shakespeare's *Troilus and Cressida* that memories quickly fade: "Time hath, my lord, a wallet at his back, / Wherein he puts alms for oblivion" (III.iii.145–46).

9.246 (191:1). Romeville – Seventeenth-century cant: "London." See 3.375n and 3.381–84n.

9.246–47 (191:1). *★The Girl I left behind me* –
An Irish ballad with many variants, though one
by the Irish poet, novelist, and composer Samuel Lover (1797–1868) seems appropriate to this
context: "The dames of France are fond and
free, / And Flemish lips are willing, / And soft
the maids of Italy, / And Spanish eyes are thrilling; / Still though I bask beneath their smile, /
Their charms fail to bind me, / And my heart
falls back to Erin's isle, / To the girl I left behind
me."

**9.247 (191:1–2). If the earthquake did not time
it** – The reference is to Shakespeare's *Venus and
Adonis*, lines 1046–48: "As when the wind, imprisoned in the ground, / Struggling for passage, earth's foundation shakes, / Which with
cold terror doth men's minds confound." Many
scholarly attempts to date the poem by internal
evidence have focused on the poem's use of details from nature and on the reference to the
plague in lines 508–10. None, however, has focused on the earthquake, since the major quake
recorded in England during the period occurred
in 1580, when Shakespeare, at sixteen, was perhaps a bit too young to have managed this sophisticated poem. *Venus and Adonis* was registered at the Stationer's Office, London, on 18
April 1593.

**9.248 (191:3). poor Wat, sitting in his form,
the cry of hounds** – A "wat" is a hare; a
"form," its lair. "By this, poor Wat, far off upon
a hill, / Stands on his hinder legs with listening
ear, / To hearken if his foes pursue him still, /
Anon their loud alarums he doth hear; / And
now his grief may be compared well / To one
sore sick that hears the passing bell" (*Venus and
Adonis*, lines 697–702).

9.248–49 (191:3–4). the studded bridle –
"The studded bridle on a ragged bough / Nimbly she fastens" (*Venus and Adonis*, lines 37–38).

9.249 (191:4). and her blue windows – "The
night of sorrow now is turned to day. / Her two
blue windows faintly she upheaveth, / Like the
fair sun" (*Venus and Adonis*, lines 481–83).

9.249–50 (191:4–6). *Venus and Adonis . . .*
light-of-love in London – "In 'Venus and
Adonis' glows the whole fresh sensuousness of
the Renaissance and of Shakespeare's youth. It
is an entirely erotic poem, and contemporaries
aver that it lay on the table of every light woman
in London" (Brandes, p. 56). "Light o' Love"
was an Elizabethan dance tune traditionally associated with levity and inconstancy in love;

thus, the phrase came to mean a light, wanton,
or inconstant woman. There is an elaborate
witty exchange on this phrase in Shakespeare's
Much Ado About Nothing (III.iv.45ff.).

**9.250–51 (191:6–7). Is Katherine . . . young
and beautiful** – In *The Taming of the Shrew* Petruchio, the hero, tells his friend Hortensio that
he has come to Padua in quest of a wealthy
bride. Hortensio first reproves him: "Petruchio,
shall I then come roundly [speak plainly] to
thee / And wish thee to a shrewd ill-favour'd
[homely] wife?" (I.ii.59–60). But then Hortensio (with Katharina, the heroine-shrew in
mind): "I can, Petruchio, help thee to a wife /
With wealth enough and young and beauteous, / Brought up as best becomes a gentlewoman: / Her only fault, and that is fault
enough, / Is that she is intolerable curst / And
shrewd and froward" (lines 85–90).

9.252 (191:8). a passionate pilgrim – Refers to
*The Passionate Pilgrime. By W. Shakespeare. At
London Printed . . . 1599.* The volume contains
twenty (or twenty-one) poems, only four or five
of which are usually (and somewhat controver-
sially) attributed to Shakespeare; of those, two
are concerned with "a woman coloured ill" and
two with a woman who has forsworn herself in
love.

9.253 (191:9). Warwickshire – The county in
which Stratford-on-Avon is located.

**9.254 (191:10). he left her and gained the
world of men** – As the speaker in Browning's
paired poems "Meeting at Night / Parting at
Morning" (1845). The male speaker in the two
poems recalls being reunited with his beloved at
night and "Parting at Morning": "Round the
cape of a sudden came the sea, / And the sun
looked over the mountain's rim: / And straight
was a path of gold for him [i.e., for the sun], /
And the need of a world of men for me."

9.254 (191:11). his boywomen – Female characters were acted by boys on the Elizabethan
stage. It was not until forty-four years after
Shakespeare's death that an actress first played
a part (Desdemona in *Othello*) on the English
stage, 8 December 1660.

9.256 (191:12). He was chosen – According to
Brandes (p. 10): "In a document dated November 28, 1582, two friends of the Hathaway family give a bond to the Bishop of Worcester's
Court declaring . . . that there is no legal im-
pediment to the solemnisation of the marriage

after one publication of the banns, instead of the statutory three. . . . It was the bride's family that hurried on the marriage, while the bridegroom's held back, and perhaps even opposed it. This haste is less surprising when we find that the first child, a daughter named Susanna, was born May 1583, only five months and three weeks after the wedding." Harris, however, has a different view (p. 358): "The whole story . . . is in perfect consonance with Shakespeare's impulsive, sensual nature; is, indeed, an excellent illustration of it. Hot, impatient, idle Will got Anne Hathaway into trouble, was forced to marry her, and at once came to regret."

9.256–57 (191:13). If others have . . . hath a way – The others who have "their will" are presumably the person(s) to whom Shakespeare's sonnets 135 and 143 are addressed: "Whoever hath her wish, thou hast thy Will" (with the pun on Will Shakespeare and will, "desire") (135:1), and "So will I pray that thou mayst have thy Will" (143:13). The pun on Anne Hathaway's name dates at least from Charles Dibdin's (1745–1814) "A Love Dittie," in his novel *Hannah Hewit; or, The Female Crusoe* (1792): "Angels must love Ann Hathaway; / She hath a way so to control, / To rapture the unprisoned soul, / And sweetest heaven on earth display, / That to be heaven Ann hath a way; / She hath a way, / Ann Hathaway—To be heaven's self Ann hath a way." *The Cyclopedia of Practical Quotations* (ed. J. K. Hoyt [New York, 1896], p. 203b) includes a slightly different version of the poem and says that it is "attributed to Shakespeare."

9.257 (191:13–14). By cock, she was to blame – After a madsong of Ophelia: "By Gis and by Saint Charity, / Alack, and fie for shame! / Young men will do 't, if they come to 't; / By cock, they are to blame. / Quoth she, before you tumbled me, / You promised me to wed. / [He answers]: So would I ha' done, by yonder sun, / An thou hadst not come to my bed" (*Hamlet* IV.v.59–66).

9.258 (191:14–15). sweet and twenty-six – "Sweet and twenty" is slang for a merry girl, after the clown's song in *Twelfth Night:* "What is love? 'tis not hereafter; / Present mirth hath present laughter; / What's to come is still unsure: / In delay there lies no plenty; / Then come kiss me, sweet and twenty, / Youth's a stuff will not endure" (II.iii.48–53). When they were married in 1582 Anne Hathaway was twenty-six; Shakespeare, eighteen.

9.258 (191:15). The greyeyed goddess – In *Venus and Adonis,* Venus speaks to Adonis: "Mine eyes are gray and bright and quick in turning" (line 140). "Gray eyes" in Elizabethan English meant blue; but "greyeyed goddess" is also a Homeric epithet for Athena, the goddess of wisdom.

9.258 (191:15–16). the boy Adonis – In *Venus and Adonis,* Adonis is described as "the tender boy" (line 32), but Shakespeare's poem does not play on a disparity of ages as much as on the disparity between the immortal goddess and the mortal boy.

9.259 (191:16). stooping to conquer – After Oliver Goldsmith's (1728–74) play *She Stoops to Conquer; or, The Mistakes of a Night* (1773), in which the heroine, Miss Hardcastle, masquerades as a barmaid and a poor relation in order to disarm young Marlow's bashfulness and win his affection.

9.259 (191:16). as prologue to the swelling act – In *Macbeth,* the witches hail Macbeth as thane of Glamis (which he is), as thane of Cawdor, and as king. After the witches vanish, Ross and Angus enter and inform Macbeth that he has been made thane of Cawdor. Macbeth regards the news as confirmation of the witches' prophecy that he will become king; Macbeth, aside: "Two truths are told, / As happy prologues to the swelling act / Of the imperial theme" (I.iii.127–29).

9.259–60 (191:17–18). a boldfaced Stratford . . . younger than herself – For "tumbles," see Ophelia's madsong, 9.257n; for "cornfield," see the following note. Harris (p. 368) writes: "I, too, Shakespeare tells us practically, was wooed by an older woman against my will. He wished the world to accept this version of his untimely marriage. Young Shakespeare in London was probably a little ashamed of being married to some one whom he could hardly introduce or avow."

9.266–67 (191:24–25). *Between the acres . . . would lie* – From the second verse of the page's song in *As You Like It:* "Between the acres of the rye, / With a hey, and a ho, and a hey nonino, / These pretty country folks would lie" (V.iii.23–25). But while Best's emendation, "ryefield" (9.263 [191:21]), is supported by the second verse of the song, Stephen's "cornfield" (9.260 [191:17]) is supported by the first verse: "It was a lover and his lass / . . . / That o'er the green cornfield did pass" (lines 17–19).

9.268 (191:26). Paris: the wellpleased pleaser – See 3.215 (42:34). The pun turns on the Greek myth of Paris, who pleased Aphrodite by awarding her the prize in a beauty contest with Athena and Hera. Aphrodite in turn pleased Paris by awarding him Helen of Troy (and coincidentally rewarding Paris's father, Priam, and his house with destruction in the Trojan War).

9.269–70 (191:27–28). A tall figure . . . its co-operative watch – George William Russell (AE) is reported to have been a very kindly man and at the same time very punctual in his habits and commitments. The gesture of interruption he makes here was repeated often enough to become a minor legend in Dublin literary circles, and thus need not be read as an act of rudeness toward Stephen.

9.271 (191:29). the *Homestead* – See 2.412n.

9.274 (191:32). Moore's – George Moore (1852–1933), an Irish novelist, poet, dramatist, and man of letters. As a young man Moore studied painting in Paris and lived a bohemian life. He styled himself "as receptive to impressions as a sheet of wax" and indeed appears to have been so. In Paris he responded to the naturalism of Zola and became for a time a staunch advocate and practitioner of naturalism in fiction. But he also responded to Baudelaire, Huysmans, and Walter Pater, influences that are reflected in a late-nineteenth-century strain of decadence in his attitudes. Resident in England from 1880 to 1901, he declared himself alienated by the cruelty of Kitchener's Boer War concentration camps and left England for Ireland, where he lived until 1911. In this "Irish phase" of his career Moore advocated the revival of Irish language, literature, and mythology and associated himself with the Abbey Theatre and with figures prominent in the Irish literary renaissance (Yeats, Synge, Edward Martyn, Russell [AE], Lady Gregory, and others). The tone of Moore's recollections in his autobiographical trilogy, *Hail and Farewell* (1911, 1912, 1914), suggests that his disillusionment with the Irish renaissance was a function of his not having been lionized in Dublin so thoroughly as he thought he deserved. In effect, it appears that Moore returned to Ireland "to take over" an already vigorous movement, and those associated with the movement were not sufficiently docile in their responses. Moore lived at 4 Ely Place Upper, a fashionable cul-de-sac parallel to and just east of St. Stephen's Green East.

9.275 (191:33). Piper – In an unpublished article, "Piper and the Peas," Alf Mac Lochlainn, chief librarian at University College, Galway, identifies Piper as William J. Stanton Pyper (1868–1941), a graduate of Erasmus Smith High School (see 8.187n) and a figure on the periphery of the Dublin literary scene in the 1890s. He was an enthusiast of the Irish language and interested in Theosophy and vegetarianism. His less-than-notable career included a brief venture into literary journalism dedicated to the Stuart cause (*The Whirlwind*) in London, 1889–90. He traveled quite a bit and apparently did odd jobs, including translations from the Russian (1915) and some literary reminiscences (1923).

9.276 (191:34). Peter Piper . . . pickled pickled pepper – A tongue-twisting nursery rhyme: "Peter Piper picked a peck of pickled pepper; / A peck of pickled pepper Peter Piper picked; / If Peter Piper picked a peck of pickled pepper, / Where's the peck of pickled pepper Peter Piper picked?" Alf Mac Lochlainn says the "received" version in Dublin begins: "If Peter Piper picked a peck of pickled pepper off a pewter plate, where's. . . ."

9.277 (191:35). Thursday . . . our meeting – The Hermetic Society met on Thursday evenings in Dawson Chambers at 11–12 Dawson Street in Dublin. In Theosophy, *hermetic* is defined as "Pertaining to the founder of a school of initiation; hence *esoteric:* . . . the inner or hidden. Esoteric truth is that which underlies forms and dogmas; that which is veiled to the common people, but is revealed to the initiated" (Powis Hoult, *A Dictionary of Some Theosophical Terms* [London, 1910], pp. 56, 48).

9.279 (191:37). Yogibogeybox – Stanislaus Joyce recalls that "box" was Gogarty's word for a public establishment or meeting hall; see Adams, p. 208.

9.279 (191:37). *Isis Unveiled* – Subtitled "A Master Key to the Mysteries of Ancient and Modern Science and Theology" (1876), by Helena Petrovna Blavatsky, was regarded by her disciples as the accredited textbook of Theosophy.

9.279 (191:38). Pali book – Pali, a form of Sanskrit, was the written language of ancient Ceylon (modern Sri Lanka). In *Isis Unveiled* (New York, 1886), vol. 1, pp. 578ff., Blavatsky postulates Pali-Sanskrit as the Ur-language in which the Ur-myths of the ancient world were originally realized before they spread through migration and translation east into Burma, Indochina, and China and west into Egypt, Israel, and Greece. Thus the "Pali book" is the Ur-book, the fountainhead of universal Ur-myth.

9.280 (191:38). we – In real life, Joyce and Gogarty; see Ellmann, p. 174.

9.280 (191:38–39). umbrel umbershoot – Colloquialisms for umbrella; see 9.283n.

9.281 (191:39). Aztec logos – Blavatsky argues that there was a "perfect identity of the rites, ceremonies, traditions, and even the names of the deities among the Mexicans and ancient Babylonians and Egyptians" (*Isis Unveiled*, vol. 1, p. 557). She asserts that "among both peoples magic or the arcane natural philosophy was practiced to the highest degree" (1:560). Earlier Blavatsky established that "*there is a logos in every mythos* or a groundwork of truth in every fiction" (1:162); therefore, an Aztec logos is the groundwork of universal truth (the "one universal religion" [1:560]) with an Aztec flavor, in the final analysis Theosophically identical with the Babylonian-, Egyptian-, Hindu-logos.

9.281 (191:39–40). astral levels – In Theosophy, a supersensible substance, imperceptible to the uninitiated, above and more refined than the tangible world. Properly trained in Theosophical meditation, an individual could "function" on astral levels, perceiving the "substance" of the astral world in all about him. See 8.535–36n.

9.281 (191:40). oversoul – An all-pervasive transcendental presence similar to astral levels. As defined by Ralph Waldo Emerson (1803–82) in "The Over-Soul," *Essays, First Series* (Boston, 1841): "The Unity, that *Over-Soul*, within which every man's particular being is contained and made one with all other."

9.281 (191:40). mahamahatma – Sanskrit: *mahatma*, "great-souled, wise"; *maha*, "great"— thus, "great, great-soul." In Theosophy, a mahatma is "One who has attained *Nirvana*, or liberation, but retains his physical body for the purpose of helping forward the progress of humanity" (Hoult, *Theosophical Terms*, p. 78).

9.282 (191:41). chelaship – A "chela" in esoteric Buddhism is a novice in the process of being initiated into the Mysteries.

9.282 (191:41). ringroundabout him – Echoes the nursery rhyme: "Ring-a-round-a-roses, / A pocket full of posies; / Tisha! Tisha! [or, Ashes! Ashes!] / We all fall down!"

9.283 (191:41–192:1). Louis H. Victory – A minor Irish man of letters at the end of the nineteenth century; his works include *Essays for Ireland; The Higher Teaching of Shakespeare; Essays of an Epicure;* and his collected poems, *Imaginations in the Dust* (London, 1903); see 9.287–88n.

9.283 (192:1). T. Caulfield Irwin – (1823–92), an Irish poet and writer of tales who in his later days suffered from what one anonymous friend called "a gentle mania." A next-door neighbor of the poet in Dublin did not take such a charitable view: "He says I am his enemy, and watch him through the thickness of the wall which divides our houses. One of us must leave. I have a houseful of books; he has an umbrella and a revolver."

9.283 (192:1–2). Lotus ladies tend them i' their eyes – The "lotus ladies" are Apsaras, the attractive and amorous nymphs of Hindu mythology and the ultimate reward of those who (on earth) achieve a perfect asceticism. In *Antony and Cleopatra*, Enobarbus describes Cleopatra at her first meeting with Antony: "Her gentlewomen, like the Nereides [sea nymphs], / So many mermaids, tended her i' the eyes, / And made their bends adornings" (II.ii.211–13).

9.284 (192:2). pineal glands – In Theosophy, the pineal gland (or pineal body) is said to have once been the "third eye," capable of transcendent spiritual vision, but it "became transmuted into the body known to physiologists as the 'pineal gland.' The powers of this body are— with few exceptions—at present latent in man; but with his further evolution, it is stated, they will become active, and the higher consciousness of the mental world will then be able to express itself through the physical brain" (Hoult, *Theosophical Terms*, p. 99).

9.284 (192:3). Buddh under plantain – In the legend of Buddha, after he abandoned his worldly career he attempted an excessive asceticism. This he in turn abandoned (because it did not free his mind) in favor of contemplation under the tree of wisdom—not a plantain but a bo or peepul tree. In the course of this contemplation Buddha achieved enlightenment; in Theosophical terms, he achieved the astral level and so could become one of the saviors of the world.

9.285 (192:3). Gulfer of souls, engulfer – That is, God, who in Theosophical terms cast souls out of himself into himself, since all souls are one with God and came from him. The vast majority of souls in earthly life forget their God-source though still contained within him.

9.285–86 (192:3–5). Hesouls, shesouls . . . whirling, they bewail – Recalls Dante's description of the carnal sinners in canto 5 of the *Inferno*. They are whirled about by a "hellish storm which never rests" (5:30), "shrieking and moaning and lamenting" (5:35). Also reminiscent of the tongue twister: "She sells sea shells by the seashore."

9.287–88 (192:6–7). *In quintessential . . . a shesoul dwelt* – After the opening lines of "Soul-Perturbating Mimicry," a poem about the death of a child, by Louis H. Victory; see 9.283n. The first of the poem's four stanzas reads: "In quintessential triviality / Of flesh, for four fleet years, a she-soul dwelt. / Oft, unpremeditatedly, I knelt / In meads, where round this thought-refining she, / To sun me in the God-light mystery, / That I, love-chained and beauty-pinioned, felt / Flashed from her, hieroglyphically spelt, / Like gifts that fall from white Austerity" (*Imaginations in the Dust*, vol. 1, pp. 132–33).

9.290–91 (192:9–10). Mr Russell, rumour . . . younger poets' verses – *New Songs, a Lyric Selection; Made by AE from Poems by Padraic Colum, Eva Gore-Booth, Thomas Koehler, Alice Milligan, Susan Mitchell, Seamus O'Sullivan, George Roberts, and Ella Young* [frontispiece by Jack B. Yeats] (Dublin, 1904). AE's (George William Russell's) untitled foreword characterizes the poems as representing "a new mood in Irish Verse . . . some of the new ways the wind of poetry listeth to blow in Ireland today" (p. 5). That foreword is dated "Dublin, December, 1903," and *New Songs* was the subject of a "Literary Notice" by Oliver St. John Gogarty in the first (May 1904) issue of *Dana: A Magazine of Independent Thought*, edited by John Eglinton; thus the "literary surprise" had already happened. It is not clear whether Joyce meant to reveal the librarian as "behind the times," whether the volume had yet to appear, or whether it is simply a mistake. Russell did not include any of Joyce's verses in the collection. See Ellmann, p. 174.

9.295 (192:15). caubeen – Anglicized Irish: "an old, shabby cap or hat."

9.296–97 (192:16–17). Touch lightly . . . Aristotle's experiment – Aristotle, *Problemata* 35:10, "Problems Connected with the Effects of Touch": "Why is it that an object which is held between two crossed fingers appears to be two? Is it because we touch it at two sentient points? For when we hold the hand in its natural position, we cannot touch an object with the outer sides of the two fingers."

9.297–98 (192:18–19). Necessity is that . . . be otherwise – Aristotle, *Metaphysics*, Book Gamma, 3:1005b: "A principle that is the most certain of all is, that the same attribute cannot belong and not belong to the same subject and in the same respect"; and in 5:1015b: "We say that that which cannot be otherwise is necessarily as it is."

9.298 (192:19). Argal – A corruption of Latin: *ergo*, "therefore"; hence it implies a clumsy bit of reasoning. It is used liberally by the First Clown (gravedigger) in *Hamlet* (V.i) as he "reasons" about Ophelia's death (suicide?).

9.301 (192:21). Young Colum – Padraic Colum (1881–1972), an Irish poet, dramatist, and man of letters. As described in *Irish Literature* (ed. Justin McCarthy, Maurice Egan, and Douglas Hyde [New York, 1904], vol. 2, p. 612), "Padraic Colum is one of the latest of young Irishmen who have made a name for themselves in the literary world. His work has been published in *The United Irishman* and in an interesting anthology entitled *New Songs, a Lyric Selection*, made by George Russell." See Padraic and Mary Colum, *Our Friend James Joyce* (New York, 1958).

9.301 (192:21). Starkey – A poet and editor. Born James Sullivan Starkey (1879–1958), he changed his name to Seumas O'Sullivan. Russell included five of his poems in *New Songs*. His early verse was characterized by "subjective and tender melancholy"; his later verse added political urgency to the Celtic twilight mood.

9.301 (192:21). George Roberts – (d. 1952), "part literary man and part businessman" (Padraic and Mary Colum, *Our Friend James Joyce*, p. 60). Roberts eventually became managing editor of the Dublin publishing house Maunsel & Co. (in which capacity he contracted with Joyce for the publication of *Dubliners*, a contract that went unfulfilled in the midst of an impressive wrangle).

9.302 (192:22–23). Longworth . . . in the *Express* – Ernest Victor Longworth (1874–1935), editor of the conservative and pro-English Dublin newspaper the *Daily Express* from 1901 to 1904. See "The Dead," *Dubliners*, in which Gabriel Conroy writes reviews for the *Express* and as a result finds himself in difficulties with the nationalist Miss Ivors.

9.303 (192:23). Colum's *Drover* – Padraic Colum's "A Drover" (*New Songs*, p. 42). The poem begins: "To Meath of the Pastures, / From wet hills by the sea, / Through Leitrim and Longford / Go my cattle and me." The ninth and final stanza: "I will bring you, my kine, / Where there's grass to the knee, / But you'll think of scant croppings, / Harsh with salt of the sea."

9.304–5 (192:25). Yeats admired . . . *Grecian vase* – The poem is Padraic Colum's "A Portrait," the lead poem in *New Songs* (p. 9), later retitled "A Poor Scholar of the Forties" (*Wild Earth* [Dublin, 1907]), pp. 13–14). In the poem the "scholar" is reproached by "the young dreamer of Ireland" for teaching Greek and Latin. The scholar replies: "And what to me is Gael or Gall? / Less than the Latin or the Greek. / I teach these by the dim rush-light, / In smoky cabins night and week, / But what avail my teaching slight. / Years hence in rustic speech, a phrase / As in wild earth a Grecian vase!" The context in which Yeats expressed his admiration for Colum's line is unknown.

9.306–7 (192:28). Miss Mitchell's joke about Moore and Martyn – Susan Mitchell (1866–1926), Irish wit, parodist, and poet, was associate editor of the *Irish Homestead*. Edward Martyn (1859–1923), a wealthy Irish Catholic landlord, was George Moore's cousin and (briefly) a friend and associate, together with Yeats and Lady Gregory, in founding Dublin's Literary Theatre in 1899. Martyn's biographer, Edward Gwynn (*Edward Martyn and the Irish Revival* [London, 1930], p. 13) describes him as "the only Irishman with large private means who was in full sympathy with almost every phase of the Irish revival." He provided financial support for projects as varied as the Abbey Theatre (1903), Arthur Griffith's pamphlet *Sinn Fein* (1905), and the Palestrina Choir in the Metropolitan Procathedral (in the interest of reforming church music). The relationship of Martyn and Moore ran the gamut from cooperation to strain to qualified estrangement. Su-

san Mitchell recounts this process in her book *George Moore* (New York, 1916); one phase she calls "the spoliation of Edward Martyn" (p. 103) by Moore, whom she labels "a born literary bandit" because of his appropriation of Martyn's play *The Tale of a Town* (1902), which he rewrote and issued as his own under the title *The Bending of the Bough*. Martyn never effected an open break with Moore; even when Moore flayed him as the "Dear Edward" of *Ave* (*Hail and Farewell;* 1911), Martyn's reaction was that he would not read it, with the remark: "George is a pleasant fellow to meet, and if I read the book I might not be able to meet him again" (Mitchell, *George Moore*, p. 94). Martyn's only revenge was to list "Mr. George Augustus Moore" as his "recreation" in *Who's Who* (1913). Martyn's biographer describes him as "hating all women with an instinctive, almost perverted antipathy" (Gwynn, *Edward Martyn*, p. 18). As Moore put it, Martyn "was a bachelor before he left his mother's womb." Moore, on the other hand, was characterized by Mitchell as a lover who "didn't kiss but told." Yeats, in his *Autobiography* (New York, 1958), described Moore as "a peasant sinner," Martyn as a "peasant saint." Mitchell's remark about "Martyn's wild oats" was circulated widely in Dublin and has become "immortal" in the Dublin vocabulary of anecdote. The thrust of her remark plays first on the fact that Martyn was the last person in the world to sow "wild oats" and second on the similarity between Martyn's continued association with Moore and a young man's wild and imprudent pursuit of (sexual) adventures that threaten damage to his reputation (in part because Moore constantly maligned Martyn as a dreadful sinner).

9.308–9 (192:29–30). They remind of . . . Sancho Panza – The central characters in the Spanish "national epic," Miguel de Cervantes's *Don Quixote* (1605, 1615). Don Quixote is the slender and mildly deranged gentleman who imagines that he is living in a chivalric romance; in the tragicomedy of the novel, Don Quixote's chivalric world is variously juxtaposed with the earthy realities of early-seventeenth-century Spain, one of which is the former pig farmer Sancho Panza, who follows Don Quixote in the role of his "squire." As Don Quixote is thin, so Sancho Panza is fat; George Moore was slender, Martyn heavy-set. The parallel suggests that the earthy Martyn tagged around after the ethereal and imaginative Moore; but it is complicated by the fact that Martyn appears to have been more of a romantic idealist ("the peasant saint") than Moore ("the peasant sinner"). Moore's remark,

"John Eglinton toils at 'Don Quixote'" (*Vale* [*Hail and Farewell;* 1914], p. 3), suggests that this line is Eglinton's contribution to this paragraph of garbled conversation.

9.309 (192:30–31). Our national epic . . . Dr. Sigerson says – George Sigerson (1838–1925), was an Irish physician, biologist, poet, translator (from Irish), and man of letters. In an essay, "Ireland's Influence on European Literature" (*Irish Literature*, ed. Justin McCarthy, Maurice Egan, and Douglas Hyde [New York, 1904], vol. 4, pp. vii–xiii), Sigerson argues not that Ireland has never produced an epic but that Irish influences have produced (among other works) the *Nibelungenlied* and *The Lay of Gudrun* ("the *Iliad* and the *Odyssey* of Germany" [p. viii]), *Tristan and Isolde*, Spenser's *Faerie Queene*, several of Shakespeare's plays, etc. He cites Fergus's "famous Táin[1]—the lost Epic of a lost World"; and then in a peroration to his contemporaries: "We dare not stand still. Ireland's glorious literary past would be our reproach, the future our disgrace. . . . Therefore must we work . . . in vindication of this old land which genius has made luminous. And remember that while wealth of thought is a country's treasure, literature is its articulate voice by which it commands the reverence or calls for the contempt of the living and of the coming nations of the earth" (pp. xii–xiii). In effect, Sigerson encourages the champions of the Irish literary revival to produce epics because the epic traditions of Ireland are so rich. Also relevant to this passage in *Ulysses* is John Eglinton's essay "Irish Books" (*Anglo-Irish Essays* [Dublin and London, 1918], pp. 87–89): "Meanwhile if we ask whether the voluminous literary activity of the last twenty years has brought forth a book, we shall have difficulty in fixing on any one work which Ireland seems likely to take to its affections permanently. If a masterpiece should still come of this literary movement we would not be surprised if it appears by a kind of accident and in some unexpected quarter, and we have a fancy that appearances in modern Ireland point to a writer of the type of Cervantes rather than to an idealising poet or romance writer. A hero as loveable as the Great Knight of the Rueful Countenance might be conceived, who in some back street of Dublin had addled his brains with brooding over Ireland's wrongs, and that extensive but not always quite sincere literature which expresses the resentment of her sons towards the stranger. His library would be described, the books which had 'addled the poor gentleman's brain' . . . we can conceive him issuing forth, fresh-hearted as a child at the age of fifty, with glib and saffron-coloured kilt, to realise and incidentally to expose the ideals of present-day Ireland. What scenes might not be devised at village inns arising out of his refusal to parley in any but his own few words of Gaelic speech; what blanketings, in which our sympathies would be wholly with the rebel against the despotism of fact! His Dulcinea would be—who but Kathleen ni Houlihan herself, who is really no more like what she is taken for than the maiden of Toboso. . . . And such a book . . . need not really insult . . . the cause of Irish nationality any more than Cervantes laughed real chivalry away."

9.310–11 (192:32–33). A knight of the rueful . . . a saffron kilt? – See the passage from John Eglinton, preceding note. "Knight of the rueful countenance" is one of Cervantes's epithets for Don Quixote; and one of the recurrent comic images in Cervantes's novel is the figure Quixote cuts when he removes his armor and reveals his yellow "walloon breeches" (bloomers). Saffron kilts were assumed by some Irish nationalists to have been the standard dress in Golden Age Ireland. Fournier d'Albe, an assistant lecturer in physics at the College of Science in Dublin and an eccentric Celtic revivalist, created something of a sensation when he advocated the adoption of saffron kilts and plaids as Irish national dress in a speech to the Literary and Historical Society in January 1902. P. W. Joyce (*A Social History of Ancient Ireland* [Dublin, 1903]) offered scholarly support to the advocates of saffron kilts, but recent scholars have argued that the kilts have more basis in fiction than in the fact of Irish national heritage; see Thornton, p. 172.

9.311 (192:33). O'Neill Russell – Thomas O'Neill Russell (1828–1908), a Celtic revivalist and linguist who had an extensive command of the Irish language. He spent thirty years in self-imposed exile in the United States, lecturing and writing on language; he also wrote a novel, *Dick Massey; a Tale of Irish Life* (1860), and several plays.

---

1 The *Táin Bo Cuailnge* (Cattle Raid of Cooley) was not "lost," but it was not very well known. Lady Gregory paraphrased it in *Cuchulain of Muirthemne* (London, 1902), and Standish O'Grady had summarized it in his account of "The Heroic Period" in his *History of Ireland* (London, 1878). The poem is, according to one of its recent translators, "the centrepiece of the Ulster cycle—and the oldest vernacular epic in Western literature" (*The Tain*, trans. Thomas Kinsella [Dublin, 1969], p. vii).

9.311 (192:33–34). O, yes, he must . . . old tongue – That is, the hero of "our national epic" must speak Irish; see Eglinton, quoted in 9.309n.

9.312 (192:34). And his Dulcinea? – See Eglinton, quoted in 9.309n. In *Don Quixote*, Dulcinea is the object of Quixote's chivalric love and duty: "a very good-looking farm girl. . . . Her name was Aldonza Lorenzo, and she it was he thought fit to call the lady of his fancies; and, casting around for a name which should not be too far away from her own, yet suggest and imply a princess and great lady, he resolved to call her Dulcinea del Toboso" (Part I, chapter 1).

9.312 (192:34). James Stephens – (1882–1950), an Irish poet, folklorist, and fiction writer. His early "clever sketches" were of Irish peasant life.

9.314 (192:36). Cordelia. *Cordoglio* – Cordelia, the youngest of King Lear's daughters, in Shakespeare's play suffers a prolonged estrangement from her father because of his imperious demands for proof of her affection, proof which in honest modesty she cannot articulate. The estrangement is deepened by the machinations of her older sisters (who feel no scruples about giving their versions of *proof*). The estrangement is resolved at the play's end, but only with the final tragic irony of her death as prelude to her father's. *Cordoglio* looks like an Italian version of "Cordelia," but it is also a noun meaning "deep sorrow."

9.314 (192:36). Lir's loneliest daughter – Cordelia is, of course, Lear's loneliest daughter, but the Irish *lear* or *lir* means "the sea," and Mananaan MacLir is the ancient Irish god of the sea; see 9.190–91n. The phrase is, however, from the opening lines of Thomas Moore's "The Song of Fionnuala": "Silent, oh Moyle, be the roar of thy water, / Break not, ye breezes, your chain of repose, / While, murmuring mournfully, Lir's lonely daughter / Tells to the night-star her tale of woes." In Moore's version of the legend, Lir is the original sea-deity who is displaced by Mananaan, his foster son. In the displacement process Lir's daughter Fionnuala is transformed into a swan by her foster mother.

9.315 (192:37). Nookshotten – Archaic: "pushed into a corner"; therefore, rendered remote and barbarous.

9.315 (192:37). French polish – A polishing preparation for woodwork and furniture made of shellac and gums dissolved in alcohol. French polish is also the high-gloss finish produced by that preparation.

9.317 (192:39). to give the letter to Mr. Norman . . . – That is, give Garrett Deasy's letter to Harry Felix Norman (1868–1947), editor of the *Irish Homestead* (1899?–1905).

9.321 (193:2). God ild you – Touchstone, a clown in *As You Like It*, uses the expression "God 'ild you" twice (III.iii.74–75; V.iv.56). It means "God reward you."

9.321 (193:2). The pig's paper – The *Irish Homestead*; see 2.412n.

9.322 (193:3). Synge – John Millington Synge (1871–1909), an Irish dramatist who was encouraged by Yeats in the winter of 1896–97 to abandon Paris and the bohemian life for Ireland and the Aran Isles—for the wealth of literary material available in Irish peasant life and in Irish language and folklore. Synge took his advice and by 1904 had produced an impressive one-act play, *In the Shadow of the Glen* (1903) (see 9.38–40n), and a one-act masterpiece, *Riders to the Sea* (1904).

9.322 (193:3). Dana – *A Magazine of Independent Thought*, a "little magazine" in Dublin (1904–5) edited by John Eglinton and coedited by Fred Ryan; see 2.256n. For the ancient Irish goddess Dana, see 9.376n.

9.323 (193:4). The Gaelic league – (Established 1893) organized an effort that had been advocated in the independent work of many Irish writers and scholars in the latter half of the nineteenth century: to revive an interest in the original language and literature of Ireland in order to develop an Irish national character and heritage independent of English influence. Although on the surface the league's aims appeared to be cultural, its ramifications were decidedly political.

9.329–30 (193:11–12). tiptoeing up nearer . . . of a chopine – Hamlet, receiving the players, speaks to one of the boy actors who plays the parts of women: "What, my young lady and mistress! By'r lady, your ladyship is nearer to heaven than when I saw you last, by the altitude of a chopine. Pray God, your voice, like a piece of uncurrent gold, be not cracked within the ring" (II.ii.443–47). A "*chopine*" is a woman's shoe with a thick cork sole.

9.332–33 (193:15–16). Courtesy or an inward light? – George Fox (1624–91), the founder of the Society of Friends (the Quakers) preached faith in and reliance on "inward light" (the presence of Christ in the heart). Fox was also, according to William Penn, extremely courteous, "civil beyond all forms of breeding in his behaviour" ("The Testimony of William Penn Concerning the Faithful Servant George Fox," in *The Journal of George Fox*, ed. Rufus M. Jones [New York, 1963], p. 63).

9.337–40 (193:20–24). Christfox in leather . . . fox and geese – This passage conjoins the careers of Shakespeare and George Fox. *Christfox:* from the Quaker assertion that Christ is present as an "inner light" in the heart and thus is a subtle "fox"; also because George Fox was hunted and hounded. *Leather trews:* close-fitting trousers or breeches combined with stockings, once worn by the Irish and by Scottish highlanders; Fox dressed in a similarly simple manner, which came to be regarded as peculiar to him and his followers. In his autobiography (ed. Rufus M. Jones [Philadelphia, 1903], vol. 1, p. 139) Fox remarks that he was known as "the man in leathern breeches." Fox was repeatedly harassed, pursued, and imprisoned for his views: he did once elude pursuit by hiding from the "hue and cry" in a blighted tree, and he spoke of himself when young as having "walked solitary in the Chase to wait upon the Lord" (1:69) and as having sought "hollow trees and lonesome places" (1:79). Shakespeare was also a runaway (to London). *Knowing no vixen:* Fox was not married until he was forty-five; Shakespeare, of course, led a "bachelor life" in London; and Lyster was unmarried. *Women he won to him:* Fox was famous for his successes in making converts, particularly among women; "tender people" was his phrase for those seriously inclined toward the search for spiritual light. Shakespeare's speculative biographers, notably Harris, depict Shakespeare as "a loose-liver while in London" (p. 374). *A whore of Babylon:* appears in Revelation 17:5 as "THE MOTHER OF HARLOTS AND ABOMINATIONS OF THE EARTH." Fox did achieve the conversion of several women of ill repute. Harris offers the associative link between Shakespeare and Fox the preacher: "Shakespeare's 'universal sympathy'—to quote Coleridge—did not include the plainly-clad tub-thumper who dared to accuse him to his face of serving the Babylonish Whore" (p. 380). *Ladies of justices:* for an apocryphal episode in Shakespeare's life that might be construed to fit, see 9.632–37n. George Fox married Margaret, the widow of Judge Fell of Swarthmoor Hall, Lancashire (1669). *Bully tapsters' wives:* "bully" means heavy or beefy, and it was also a term of endearment. Another episode in the Shakespeare apocrypha: Shakespeare was rumored to have fathered Sir William Davenant by the wife of the "tapster" (innkeeper) John D'Avenant; see 9.643n. *Fox and geese:* in his journal Fox explicitly refutes the then-popular antifeminine contention that women were geese and argues that women are as "tender" and as whole-souled as men. "Fox and geese" is also a children's game in which the childfox tries to pick off the childgeese as they run from one goal to another; and it is a game for two played on a board with pegs or checkers in which the geese attempt to trap the fox, the fox to pick off the geese one by one.

9.340–42 (193:24–26). And in New Place . . . grave and unforgiven – "New Place" was the mature Shakespeare's residence in Stratford-on-Avon. "At New Place . . . the spirit prevailing . . . was not the spirit of Shakespeare. Not only the town of Stratford, but his own home and family were desperately pious and puritanical" (Brandes, p. 671). "His wife was extremely religious, as is often the case with women whose youthful conduct has not been too circumspect. When she captured her boy husband of eighteen, her blood was as warm as his, but now, on the eve of Shakespeare's return [1613], she was vastly his superior in matters of religion" (p. 672). For the tenuous link with George Fox, see 9.802–4n. Stephen's language suggests an allusion to an Irish folk song, "Fair Maiden's Beauty Will Soon Fade Away". The last stanza: "My love is as sweet as the cinnamon tree; / She clings to me as close as the bark to the tree; / But the leaves they will wither and the roots will decay, / And fair maiden's beauty will soon fade away."

9.347 (193:31). A vestal's lamp – See 7.923n and 7.937n.

9.348–49 (193:32–33). What Caesar would . . . the soothsayer – In Shakespeare's *Julius Caesar* (I.ii.12–24), a soothsayer interrupts a festival in Rome to warn Caesar: "Beware the ides of March" (15 March). Caesar dismisses the warning by calling the soothsayer "a dreamer." Caesar is warned by other "omens" (II.ii) and again by the soothsayer (III.i.1–2). Caesar disregards the warnings, though with some uneasiness, and is, of course, assassinated on the ides of March.

9.349–50 (193:34). possibilities of the possible as possible – After Aristotle; see 2.50–51n and 2.67n.

9.350–51 (193:35–36). what name Achilles . . . among women – A famous riddle with no answer, cited by Sir Thomas Browne (1605–82) in his treatise *Hydriotaphia, Urn-Burial* (1658), chapter 5: "What song the Syrens sang, or what name Achilles assumed, when he hid himself among women, though puzzling questions, are not beyond all conjecture." In an attempt to prevent Achilles from his heroic destiny and eventual death in the Trojan War, Thetis, his mother, disguised him as a girl and sent him to live with the daughters of a neighboring king. Odysseus exposed the disguise with a ruse, and Achilles joined the Greeks in their expedition against Troy.

9.353 (193:38–39). Thoth, god of . . . moony-crowned – Thoth, the Egyptian god of learning, invention, and magic, is usually depicted with an ibis's head crowned with the horns of the moon. In Egyptian myth he was keeper of the divine archives, patron of history, and the herald, clerk, and scribe of the gods. ("Ra has spoken, Thoth has written.") When the dead are judged before Osiris, it is Thoth who weighs the heart and proclaims it wanting or not wanting.

9.353–54 (193:39). And I heard . . . Egyptian highpriest – From John F. Taylor's speech, as recalled in Aeolus; see 7.838 (142:16–17).

9.354–55 (193:40). *In painted chambers loaded with tilebooks* – Apparently a quotation, source unknown.

9.360–61 (194:5). Others abide our question – From a sonnet by Matthew Arnold, 1 August 1844, in a letter to Jane Arnold: "I keep saying, Shakespeare, Shakespeare, you are obscure as life." "Others abide our question. Thou art free. / We ask and ask—Thou smilest and art still, / Out-topping knowledge. For the loftiest hill, / Who to the stars uncrowns his majesty, // Planting his steadfast footsteps in the sea, / Making the heaven of heavens his dwelling place, / Spares but the cloudy border of his base / To the foiled searching of mortality; // And thou, who didst the stars and sun beams know, / Self-schooled, self-scanned, self-honoured, self secure, / Didst tread on earth unguessed at. Better so! // All pains the immortal spirit must endure, / All weakness which impairs, all griefs which bow, / Find their sole speech in that victorious brow."

9.362–63 (194:7–9). *Hamlet* is so personal . . . private paper . . . of his private life – Nineteenth-century critics regarded Hamlet as "among all the characters of Shakespeare, . . . the most eminently a metaphysician and psychologist" (James Russell Lowell [1819–91], in an essay, "Shakespeare Once More" [1870], included in *Among My Books* [Boston, 1870]). From there it was but a short step to the assumption that Hamlet was the most subjective and most autobiographically revealing of all of Shakespeare's characters—an assumption encouraged by the nineteenth-century fascination with the personality of the poet and by the fact that so little is known about Shakespeare's personal life.

9.366–67 (194:12–13). *Ta an bad . . . Tiam in mo shagart – Irish: "The boat is on the land. I am a priest." The first sentence is almost, but not quite, a practice sentence from Father Eugene O'Growney's (1863–99) *Simple Lessons in Irish* (1897).

9.367 (194:13). beurla – Irish: "the English language," with a pun on the French *beurre*, "butter."

9.367 (194:13). littlejohn – An epithet coined by George Moore for John Eglinton (W. K. Magee) (*Vale* [*Hail and Farewell*; 1914], p. 260). Little John was one of Robin Hood's principal lieutenants in balladry and legend; far from "little" in stature, in some versions of the legend he is portrayed as "little" in intelligence.

9.372 (194:19). Bear with me – From Marc Antony's oration at Julius Caesar's funeral: "O judgment! thou art fled to brutish beasts, / And men have lost their reason. Bear with me, / My heart is in the coffin there with Caesar, / And I must pause till it come back to me" (III.ii. 104–7).

9.374–75 (194:21–22). A basilisk. *E quando . . . Messer Brunetto* – Brunetto Latini (c. 1210–c. 1295), a Florentine writer whose influence on Italian letters was praised by Dante (see *Inferno* 15). One of Latini's major works was his *Li livres dou trésor*, a prose compendium of medieval lore that Brunetto wrote in French (1262–66?) because he regarded French as a language more widely known than Italian (though his other earlier major poetic work, *Tesoro* or *Tesoretto*, had been written in Italian).

The *Trésor*, Book 1, contains among other things a bestiary (*Histoire Naturelle*), *Des Basiliques* (Of Basilisks). The line Stephen recalls is from an Italian translation of this section about the "king of serpents": "and when it [the basilisk] looks at a man, it poisons him."

9.376 (194:23). mother Dana – Or Danu, the triple goddess of Celtic mythology, regarded as the mother of earth, fertility, and plenty and of the forces of youth, light, and knowledge and of the forces of disintegration and death.

9.376–78 (194:23–25). weave and unweave . . . unweave his image – This passage is reminiscent of Pater's discussion of the impressionistic and evanescent nature of subjective experience in the conclusion to *The Renaissance* (1873): "It is with this movement, with the passage and dissolution of impressions, images, sensations, that analysis leaves off—that continual vanishing away, that strange, perpetual weaving and unweaving of ourselves." The passage also echoes a "weaving" image from AE's poem "Dana" (*Collected Poems* [London, 1926], p. 37).

9.378 (194:26). the mole on my right breast – Cf. 9.474n.

9.381–82 (194:30). the mind . . . a fading coal – Percy Bysshe Shelley (1792–1822), an English romantic poet, wrote in "A Defence of Poetry" (1821; published 1840): "Poetry is not like reasoning, a power to be exerted according to the determination of the will. A man cannot say, 'I will compose poetry.' The greatest poet cannot say it; for the mind in creation is as a fading coal, which some invisible influence, like an inconstant wind, awakens to transitory brightness; this power arises from within, like the color of a flower which fades and changes as it is developed, and the conscious portions of our natures are unprophetic either of its approach or its departure."

9.383–86 (194:32–35). So in the future . . . Drummond of Hawthornden – William Drummond (1585–1644) was a Scottish poet. The second edition of his *Flowers of Sion* (1630) contains a prose meditation on mortality and immortality, "A Cypress Grove." Stephen secularizes one phase of Drummond's meditation: "If thou dost complain that there shall be a Time in which thou shalt not be, why dost thou not also grieve that there was a time in which thou was not; and so that thou art not as old as that enlivening Planet of Time? . . . That will

be after us, which, long long before we were, was."

9.387 (194:36). I feel Hamlet quite young – The gravedigger says that he became a gravedigger on "that very day that young Hamlet was born" (V.i.163–64), and in line 177 he identifies the time of his employment as "thirty years"; so Hamlet is thirty years old.

9.390 (194:39). Has the wrong sow by the lug – A stock expression for "he has made the wrong choice"; a "lug" is an ear.

9.391 (194:41). That mole is the last to go – Mole in the sense of birthmark or blemish; as when Hamlet is philosophizing on Denmark and mankind while he and his companions wait to see if the Ghost will appear: "So, oft it chances in particular men, / That for some vicious mole of nature in them, / . . . the stamp of one defect, / . . . Their virtues else—be they as pure as grace, / As infinite as man may undergo— / Shall in the general censure take corruption / From that particular fault" (I.iv.23–36).

9.392 (194:42). mow – Rare for a grimace, a mocking expression. Hamlet uses the word in that sense when he describes the way the courtiers mocked Claudius before Claudius became king (II.ii.364). Modern editors are inclined to render what Stephen—and Joyce—would have known as mows into "mouths."

9.393 (195:1). If that were the birthmark of genius – That is, if youth-in-love were the birthmark of genius.

9.394 (195:3). Renan – Ernest Renan (1823–92), a French critic, writer, and scholar famous for the "Protean inconsistency" of his scepticism and theories. Renan admired Shakespeare's late plays as "mature philosophical dramas" and undertook in one of his own *Drames philosophiques* (1888) to write a sequel to *The Tempest*, called "Caliban." Renan considered Shakespeare (in his last plays) "the historian of eternity," composing "great battles of pure ideas"; thus: Ariel (spirit of the air), Caliban (raw earth of the body), Prospero (the magical spirit of practical human imagination).

9.396 (195:5). The spirit of reconciliation – A standard nineteenth-century outline of Shakespeare's career, or of his "spiritual odyssey": after the light-heartedness of the early comedies and histories (1590s) came a period of spiritual struggle and turmoil marked by the great trag-edies (1600 to c. 1608), and he finally emerged into a period of spiritual serenity, with a capac-ity for reconciling his tragic vision with an affir-mation of the human capacity for moral growth and forgiveness, imaged in the emphasis on rec-onciliation in the plots of the last plays, *Cymbe-line, The Winter's Tale*, and *The Tempest*.

9.402–4 (195:13–14). What softens the heart . . . prince of Tyre? – Ulysses is not only the Latin version of Odysseus but also a character in *Troilus and Cressida*. In *Pericles*, Pericles (not of Athens but of Tyre), forced by treachery to flee from Tyre, is shipwrecked on Pentapolis. Stephen's sources all agree that the "change of tone" in Shakespeare's late plays (including *Per-icles*) reflects a change in his outlook. Brandes (p. 585) quotes a line from *Pericles* and remarks: "The words are simple . . . but they are of the greatest importance as symptoms. They are the first mild tones escaping from an instrument which has long yielded only harsh and jarring sounds. There is nothing like them in the drama of Shakespeare's despairing mood. . . . When he consented to rewrite parts of this *Pericles*, it was that he might embody the feeling by which he is now possessed. Pericles is a romantic Ulys-ses, a far-travelled, sorely tried, much-enduring man, who has, little by little, lost all that was dear to him."

9.405 (195:15). Head, redconecapped, buf-feted, brineblinded – This image of John Eg-linton in the whirlpool suggests Odysseus when, after the destruction of his last ship and its crew in Book 12 of *The Odyssey*, he runs the gamut between Scylla and Charybdis for the second time, clinging to the keel of his broken ship. This time Odysseus takes the whirlpool (Charybdis) side of the passage and survives to be beached on Calypso's island, just as Pericles loses all but survives shipwreck in Shake-speare's play.

9.406 (195:16). A child, a girl placed in his arms, Marina – In *Pericles*, at the height of a storm at sea Pericles' wife gives birth to a child (Marina) and apparently dies. Lychordia, the nurse, presents the child to Pericles: "Here is a thing too young for such a place, / Who, if it had conceit, would die, as I / Am like to do. Take in your arms this piece / Of your dead queen" (III.i.15–18). Brandes (p. 572) writes: "What figures occupy the most prominent place in the poet's sumptuous harvest-home but the young womanly forms of Marina [*Pericles*], Im-ogen [*Cymbeline*], Perdita [*The Winter's Tale*],

Miranda [*The Tempest*]. These girlish and for-saken creatures are lost and found again, suffer grievous wrongs, and are in no case cherished as they deserve; but their charm, purity and no-bility of nature triumph over everything."

9.407 (195:17). the bypaths of apocrypha – It is notable in relation to this remark that there is considerable suspicion about Shakespeare's part in the composition of *Pericles;* thus *Pericles* is "apocrypha." Most scholars agree that "when Hemings and Condell issued the famous first folio of Shakespeare's work in 1623, they prob-ably knew better than we why they did not in-clude *Pericles*" (i.e., because as Shakespeare's associates they knew he had not written the play?) (Charles W. Wallace, "New Shakespeare Discoveries: Shakespeare as a Man Among Men," *Harper's Monthly Magazine* 120 [1910]: 509).

9.408–9 (195:18–19). the highroads are dreary but they lead to the town – Coleridge praised Shakespeare for keeping to "the regular high road of human affections" (*Coleridge's Shake-speare Criticism*, ed. Thomas Middleton Rayson [Cambridge, Mass., 1930], p. 228).

9.410 (195:20). Good Bacon: gone musty – Eglinton is paraphrasing Sir Francis Bacon and reducing him to a proverbial expression. Bacon, in Book 1 of *The Advancement of Learning* (1605), discusses at length "distempers of learn-ing," notably three: "vain affectations, vain dis-putes, and vain imaginations." He complains against "the affecting of two extremes: antiquity and novelty," and answers: "The advice of the prophet is just in this case: 'Stand upon the old ways, and see which is the good way, and walk therein'" (Jeremiah 6:16).

9.410 (195:20). Shakespeare Bacon's wild oats – Suggesting that the English lawyer, phi-losopher, and man of letters Francis Bacon, Baron Verulam, Viscount St. Albans (1561–1626), had "misspent his youth" writing plays, which he then published using Shakespeare as "pawn" (as Moore was Martyn's wild oats; see 9.306–7n). The theory that Bacon wrote Shake-speare, while not original with her, is usually associated with the American novelist Delia Sal-ter Bacon (1811–59), with her rather tenuous claim of kinship with Lord Bacon and her book *Philosophy of the Plays of Shakespeare Unfolded* (London, 1857). Positive argument in favor of the theory hinges on juxtaposing "passages of similar import" from the two writers, while negative argument in favor of the theory maintains that Shakespeare's plays must have been written by a man more knowledgeable than Shakespeare, with his background, could have been.

9.411 (195:21). Cypherjugglers – One way of "proving" Bacon's authorship of the plays was to "discover" in Bacon's letters or papers a numerical cipher that when applied to the First Folio edition of Shakespeare's plays would evoke letters (words, sentences) clearly stating Bacon's authorship. Delia Bacon claimed to have discovered such a cipher, but "she became insane before she had imparted this key to the world" (Brandes, p. 89). However, the American politician and essayist Ignatius Donnelly (1831–1901) finally succeeded in imparting the key in *The Great Cryptogram: Francis Bacon's Cipher in the Socalled Shakespeare Plays* (Chicago and London, 1887) and *Cipher in the Shakespeare Plays* (1900).

9.411–12 (195:22). What town, good masters? – Donnelly launched his "invasions" from his home in Hastings, Minnesota, and it was with the Battle of Hastings in 1066 that William the Conqueror (1027–87) began the conquest of Saxon England.

9.412 (195:22). Mummed in names – Since both men used pseudonyms, they remained "mum," silent in their identities; and both were "mummers," actors playing the parts of pseudonymous persons.

9.412 (195:22). A.E., eon – See 8.527–28n.

9.413 (195:23–24). East of the sun, west of the moon: *Tir na n-og* – *Tir na n-og*, Irish: "Land of Youth"; a mythical island to the west of Ireland envisioned as a realm where mortal perfection and timeless but earthly pleasures were the rule. "East of the Sun, West of the Moon" is the title story of a collection of Norse folktales (1842–45; trans. G. W. Dasant, 1859) by Peter Christen Asbjörnsen (1812–85). A young peasant girl is bought from her parents by a great white bear, who turns out to be a prince who has been bewitched by his stepmother so that he is a bear by day. When the girl discovers the prince's secret, the resentful stepmother spirits him away to a castle "east of the sun and west of the moon." The girl contrives to follow, and after many trials the prince is liberated with the girl into the "happily ever after."

9.413–14 (195:24). Booted the twain and staved – That is, Eglinton and AE are outfitted as pilgrims (with staves, or pilgrim staffs).

9.415–17 (195:25–27). *How many miles . . . by candlelight?* – Nursery rhyme: "How many miles to Babylon? / Three score and ten. / Can I get there by candlelight? / Yes, and back again, / If your heels are nimble and light, / You may get there by candlelight."

9.418 (195:28–29). Mr Brandes accepts . . . the closing period – Brandes did accept *Pericles*: "Let us anticipate the works yet to be written—*Pericles, Cymbeline, Winter's Tale*, and *The Tempest*. In this last splendid period of his life's young September, his dramatic activity . . . is more richly varied now than it has ever been" (p. 572). Brandes also regarded the play as "rewritten" by Shakespeare; see 9.402–4n.

9.419–20 (195:30–31). What does Mr Sidney Lee . . . say of it? – Lee groups *Pericles* not with the "last plays" but with *Antony and Cleopatra* and *Timon of Athens*: "Shakespeare contributed only Acts III and V and parts of IV, which together form a self-contained whole, and do not combine satisfactorily with the remaining scenes. . . . But a natural felicity of expression characterizes Shakespeare's own contributions. . . . At many points he anticipated his latest dramatic effects" (pp. 198–99). For Lee's change of name, see p. 192.

9.421–22 (195:32–33). Marina, Stephen said . . . which was lost – Marina, Pericles' daughter, was a "child of storm" (see 9.406n). Miranda is the daughter of Prospero in *The Tempest*; when her future husband, Ferdinand, first sees her, he exclaims: "O you wonder! / If you be maid or no?" (I.ii.426–27). Perdita ("loss") is lost and found again in *The Winter's Tale*.

9.422 (195:33–34). What was lost . . . his daughter's child – Susanna, the elder of Shakespeare's daughters, was married to a Dr. John Hall of Stratford. Her daughter Elizabeth was born in 1608; thus, the birth of Shakespeare's granddaughter coincides roughly with what Brandes regards as the beginning of the period of the last plays.

9.423 (195:34–35). *My dearest wife . . . this maid* – In the "recognition scene" of *Pericles*, when the lost child is restored, Pericles says: "My dearest wife was like this maid, and such a one / My daughter might have been" (V.i. 108–9).

9.423–24 (195:35–36). Will any man . . . the mother? – Brandes argues that Susanna was Shakespeare's "favorite daughter" (p. 677) because she was his "principal heiress" (p. 686). He also argues that Shakespeare did not "love" his wife.

9.425–26 (195:38). *L'art d'être grandp . . .* – Mr. Best begins to say *grandpère* (French: "grandfather"), but left incomplete the phrase means "the art of being great." *L'art d'être grandpère* is the title of a book of poems for children (1877) by the French poet and novelist Victor Hugo (1802–85).

9.429–30 (195:38//39). *Love, yes. Word known to all men – At two other points in the day Stephen seems to regard the question "What is the word known to all men?" as a mystery (3.435 [49:5] and 15.4192–93 [581:5–6]). The key to the mystery seems to be not the word itself but the word-made-manifest. Only in the experience of love can the word known to all men be truly *known*.

9.430–31 (195:38//39). *Amor vero aliquid alicui bonum vult unde et ea quae concupiscimus – The Latin conjoins two phrases from St. Thomas Aquinas's *Summa Contra Gentiles*, First Book, Chapter 91, "That in God There Is Love." Aquinas is distinguishing between "True love [which] requires one to will another's good" and self love, which wills another's good primarily as conducive to one's own good. The entire sentence from which the phrases are drawn (with the conjoined phrases capitalized) reads: "Per hoc enim quod intelligimus vel gaudemus, ad aliquod objectum aliqualiter nos habere oportet; AMOR VERO ALIQUID ALICUI VULT; hoc enim amare dicimur, cui aliquod BONUM volumus secundum modum praedictum; UNDE ET EA QUAE CONCUPISCUMUS, simplicter quidem et proprie desiderare dicimur, non autem amare, sed potius nos ipsos, quibus ea concupiscimus; et ex hoc ipsa per accidens, non proprie dicimur amare" (Ex Officina Libraria MARIETTI [1820, 1927], p. 82). The passage as translated by the English Dominican Fathers (New York, 1924), p. 193 (conjoined phrases capitalized), reads: "For if we understand or rejoice, it follows that we are referred somehow to some object: whereas LOVE WILLS SOMETHING TO SOMEONE, since we are said to love that to which we

WILL SOME GOOD, in the way aforesaid. Hence WHEN WE WANT A THING, we are said simply and properly to *DESIRE* IT, and not to love it, but rather to love ourselves for whom we want it: and in consequence we are said to love it accidentally and improperly."

9.439–40 (196:7). Mr George Bernard Shaw – (1856–1950), the Dublin-born critic and playwright. Shaw's "commentaries" on Shakespeare began to appear when he was drama critic on the *Saturday Review* in the 1890s. His attitude toward Shakespeare was characteristically irreverent. See *Shaw on Shakespeare*, ed. Edmund Wilson (New York, 1961). See also Shaw's comedy *The Dark Lady of the Sonnets* (1910). The play does depict an unhappy relationship between Shakespeare and the "dark lady," whom Shaw identifies as Mary Fitton in the play though he refutes the identification in the preface.

9.440 (196:8). Mr Frank Harris – (1856–1931), a jack-of-all-trades and self-styled "lover of letters." He was editor and proprietor of the *Saturday Review* (1894–99), in which he published a series of articles on Shakespeare, collected and first published as *The Man Shakespeare and His Tragic Life-Story* (London, 1898).

9.441 (196:8–9). the *Saturday Review* – A London weekly review of politics, literature, science, and art founded in 1855.

9.442–43 (196:9–12). he too draws . . . earl of Pembroke – According to Harris (p. 202), "The story is very simple: Shakespeare loved Mistress Fitton and sent his friend, the young Lord Herbert [William Herbert, earl of Pembroke (1580–1630)] to her on some pretext, but with the design that he should commend Shakespeare to the lady. Mistress Fitton fell in love with William Herbert, wooed and won him, and Shakespeare had to moan the loss of both friend and mistress." Brandes (pp. 279ff.) refutes the identification of the "dark lady" as Mary Fitton but argues nevertheless that the relationship was "unhappy." Oscar Wilde, in *The Portrait of Mr. W. H.* (see 9.523–24n), writes: "Pembroke, Shakespeare and Mrs. Mary Fitton are the three personages of the sonnets: there is no doubt at all about it."

9.443–45 (196:12–14). I own that if . . . not to have been – An allusion to another theory about Shakespeare's love life then current: that Shakespeare was "passionately" in love with

William Herbert (see Brandes, p. 714); thus, the "rejection" effected by Mary Fitton's relation with Herbert would have been on the other side of the triangle.

9.446 (196:16). auk's egg – The great auk was in the news in 1904 as a species once widely distributed but recently extinct. Each nesting season females of the various species of auk laid only a single egg, which was large for the size of the bird and was colorfully marbled. The thrust of Stephen's wit is that the upshot of their discussion is a head (an egg) that promises the birth of an extinct idea.

9.448–49 (196:17–18). He thous and thees . . . Dost love, Miriam? – As a Quaker, the unmarried Lyster would address his wife (or any other person with whom he was familiar) in the archaic second-person singular (to demonstrate the brotherhood of man). Miriam (the Hebrew form of Mary) is Moses' sister's name, "Miriam the prophetess." She supported Moses but eventually turned temporarily against him because he married a woman who was not an Israelite. Tentatively, then: Stephen's use of the name harks back to the Shakespeare–George Fox associations (9.337–40n). As Shakespeare might have addressed Mary Fitton, George Fox might have addressed his wife, Margaret—the Quaker "prophetess Miriam"? Lyster remained a bachelor until he retired from the National Library in 1920. Shortly after his retirement he married Jane Campbell.

9.451–52 (196:20–21). Beware of what . . . in middle life – After the German: "Was man in der Jugend wünscht, hat man im Alter die Fülle," the motto of Goethe's *Dichtung und Wahrheit* (1811–14), an autobiography. The word *beware* is not in the original passage.

9.452 (196:22). *buonaroba* – Italian: literally, "a commonplace thing." In Elizabethan slang (as *bona roba*) the term meant a showy or flashy girl, for example in *II Henry IV* III.ii.26.

9.452–53 (196:22–23). a bay where all men ride – From Shakespeare's Sonnet 137, lines 5–8: "If eyes, corrupt by over-partial looks, / Be anchor'd in the bay where all men ride, / Why of eyes' falsehood hast thou forged hooks, / Whereto the judgement of my heart is tied?" Harris (p. 213) cites this line in connection with Mary Fitton, and he adds another phrase from the same sonnet, "the wide world's common place" (line 10), for which Stephen substitutes the more suggestive *buonaroba*.

9.453 (196:23). a maid of honor with a scandalous girlhood – Harris (p. 213) writes: "Mary Fitton became a maid of honor to Queen Elizabeth in 1595 at the age of seventeen. From a letter addressed by her father to Sir Robert Cecil on January 29th, 1599, it is fairly certain that she had already been married at the age of sixteen; the union was probably not entirely valid, but the mere fact suggests a certain recklessness of character, or overpowering sensuality, or both, and shows that even as a girl Mistress Fitton was no shrinking, timid, modest maiden. . . . Though twice married, she had an illegitimate child by Herbert, and two later by Sir Richard Leveson." Harris argues that Shakespeare was "betrayed" by Lord Herbert and that Mistress Fitton is "the 'dark lady' of the sonnet-series from 128 to 152, [and] is to be found again and again in play after play" (p. 212).

9.453 (196:23). a lordling – A little or petty lord. William Herbert did not inherit his title until 1601, four years after the "betrayal" as Harris (and Stephen) date it.

9.454 (196:24). a lord of language – The phrase occurs in the second stanza of Tennyson's "To Virgil" (1882): "Landscape-lover, lord of language / More than he that sang the 'Works and Days' [the Greek poet Hesiod], / All the chosen coin of fancy / Flashing out from many a chosen phrase." It also occurs in Oscar Wilde's *De Profundis* (written 1897; published posthumously with excisions 1905): "A week later, I am transferred here. Three more months go over and my mother dies. No one knew better than you how deeply I loved her and honoured her. Her death was terrible to me; but I, once a lord of language, have no words in which to express my anguish and my shame" (p. 65).

9.455 (196:25). coistrel – Shakespeare uses this word as a noun meaning knave or ruffian.

9.455 (196:25–26). had written *Romeo and Juliet* – Modern scholarship dates the play c. 1596. Harris argues that the play was written in 1597, after Shakespeare had fallen in love with Mary Fitton but before the Herbert betrayal (Mistress Fitton, Harris speculates, appears in the play as Romeo's pre-Juliet love, Rosalind [pp. 214–15]).

9.455–56 (196:26). Belief in himself has been untimely killed – The phrase "untimely killed" echoes the description of Macduff's birth in *Macbeth*: "Macduff was from his mother's womb / Untimely ripp'd" (V.vii.15–16). The sentence also recalls Harris (p. 364): "Shakespeare's loathing for his wife was measureless, was part of his own self-esteem, and his self-esteem was founded on snobbish nonessentials for many years, if not indeed, throughout his life."

9.456–57 (196:26–27). He was overborne . . . (a ryefield I should say) – See 9.266–67n.

9.458 (196:29). the game of laugh and lie down – From *Songs Composed by the Choisest Wits of the Age*, compiled by Richard Head (see 3.381–84n); "The Art of Loving": "She'll smile and she'll frown, / She'll laugh and lie down, / At every turn you must tend her." Laugh-and-lay-down was also an Elizabethan game of cards.

9.458 (196:29–30). dongiovannism – Harris's argument is that Shakespeare attempted to compensate for the failure of his marriage by becoming a Don Giovanni, a Don Juan, and seducing a variety of women, but, Harris concludes, he basically failed in that role.

9.459–60 (196:31–32). The tusk of the boar . . . love lies ableeding – Compounded allusion: (a) To Shakespeare's *Venus and Adonis* and the description of Adonis's corpse as discovered by Venus: "the wide wound that the boar had trenched / In his soft flank whose wonted lily white / With purple tears, that his wound wept, was drenched" (lines 1052–54); the description is repeated with variations in lines 1115–16: "the loving swine / Sheathed unaware the tusk in his soft groin." (b) To *The Odyssey:* Odysseus in his youth was wounded in the thigh by a boar; it is this wound that enables Odysseus's nurse to recognize him (and vouch for him to Penelope) when he returns home from his wanderings. (c) To Beaumont and Fletcher's play *Philaster; or, Love Lies Ableeding* (1609), in which a rather febrile heroine longs to die at the hands of a lover who has deserted her.

9.460–61 (196:32). If the shrew is worsted – Katharina, the shrew, is at least tamed if not worsted in Shakespeare's *The Taming of the Shrew*.

9.461 (196:33). woman's invisible weapon – Woman's visible weapon is, as Lear remarks (II.ii.280), "waterdrops," tears. The implication is that woman uses her sexuality (invisible) to seduce and (secretly) betray her husband or lover.

9.462–64 (196:34–36). some goad of the flesh . . . own understanding of himself – That is, Shakespeare was emasculated by Anne Hathaway's aggressive seduction, just as Adonis is figuratively emasculated by Venus's aggression; and Shakespeare's complicity in that aggression had the effect of original sin as defined in Lesson 6, "On Original Sin," in *The Catechism Ordered by the National Synod of Maynooth and Approved by the Cardinal, the Archbishop and Bishops of Ireland for General Use Throughout the Irish Church* (Dublin, 1882), p. 14: "Q. What other particular effects follow from the sin of our first parents? A. Our whole nature was corrupted by the sin of our first parents—it darkened our understanding, weakened our will, and left in us a strong inclination to evil." The argument is that the "original sin" of Anne Hathaway's seduction of Shakespeare has been compounded by the "new passion" for Mary Fitton, the supposed dark lady of the sonnets.

9.464 (196:37). whirlpool – Charybdis; see headnote to this episode, p. 192.

9.465 (196:38). They list. And in the porches . . . I pour – After the Ghost in *Hamlet;* see 7.750n and 9.144/46n.

9.466–71 (196:39–197:3). The soul has been . . . by his creator – Lady Macbeth uses the word "quell" (murder) when she is urging Macbeth to the murder of King Duncan: "What cannot you and I . . . put upon / His spongy [hard-drinking] officers, who shall bear the guilt / Of our great quell?" (I.vii.69–72). But Stephen is also raising the question of how the Ghost (Hamlet's father) knew of his wife's adultery and knew the manner of his own murder; see 7.751–52n.

9.471–72 (197:4). (his lean unlovely English) – Namely, Shakespeare's; see 9.96–99n.

9.473 (197:5–6). what he would but would not – After Zerlina in *Don Giovanni;* see 4.327n.

9.473–74 (197:6–7). Lucrece's bluecircled ivory globes – After Shakespeare's *The Rape of Lucrece* (line 407): "Her breasts, like ivory globes circled with blue."

9.474 (197:7). Imogen's breast, bare, with its mole cinquespotted – Imogen, the daughter of Cymbeline and the chaste heroine of Shakespeare's play, is visually, though not physically, violated by the villain, Iachimo, as she sleeps:

"On her left breast / A mole cinque-spotted, like the crimson drops / I' the bottom of a cowslip" (II.ii.37–39).

9.474–76 (197:8–9). He goes back . . . an old sore – Brandes imagines Shakespeare as having retired to Stratford with the satisfaction of a life's work accomplished. Harris (p. 404) imagines it otherwise: "The truth is, that the passions of lust and jealousy and rage had at length worn out Shakespeare's strength, and after trying in vain to win to serenity in 'The Tempest,' he crept home to Stratford to die."

9.478 (197:12). His beaver is up – The "beaver" is the front part of a helmet, which could be raised to reveal the face. In *Hamlet*, Horatio informs Hamlet of what he has seen and describes the Ghost as armed from head to foot. "HAMLET: Then saw you not his face? HORATIO: O, yes, my lord; he wore his beaver up" (I.ii.229–30).

9.479 (197:13–14). Elsinore's rocks, or what you will, the sea's voice – "Or What You Will" is the subtitle of Shakespeare's play *Twelfth Night*. It is notable in light of the passage that follows that Twelfth Night marks the celebration of the Epiphany (6 January), when Christ became manifest and was revealed to the world as the Son of God, that is, "the son consubstantial with the father" (9.481 [197:15]). For Elsinore's rocks and the sea-sound's temptation to madness and suicide, see 1.567–68n.

9.483 (197:17). Hast thou found me, O mine enemy? – In I Kings 21, King Ahab's wife, Jezebel, conspires to destroy the owner of a vineyard that Ahab has coveted. When the conspiracy is successful and Ahab takes possession of the vineyard, the prophet Elijah is instructed to curse Ahab. He tells Ahab, "Dogs shall lick thy blood, even thine" (21:19); Ahab responds: "Hast thou found me, O mine enemy? And he [Elijah] answered, I have found thee: because thou hast sold thyself to work evil in the sight of the Lord" (21:20).

9.484 (197:18). *Entr'acte* – French: "interval between the acts"; also a musical number or skit performed during such an intermission.

9.486 (197:21). My telegram – See 9.548ff. (199:18ff.).

9.487 (197:22). the gaseous vertebrate – Having a spine but without substance, a ghost; in

this case, "the son consubstantial with the father."

9.491 (197:26–27). *Was Du verlachst wirst Du noch dienen* – German proverb: "What you laugh at, you will nevertheless serve."

9.492 (197:28). *Brood of mockers: Photius, pseudo Malachi, Johann Most – For "brood of mockers," see 1.656–57n; for Photius, see 1.656n. "Pseudo Malachi," that is, Mulligan (in contrast to Elijah), is a false prophet; see 1.41n. Johann Most (1846–1906) was a German-American bookbinder and anarchist whose newspaper *Die Freiheit* (Freedom) accompanied him from Berlin to London to New York. He won a place in the hearts of the Irish (and in an English jail) by violently condoning the Phoenix Park murders. His approach—down with everything—included even the pamphlet *Down with the Anarchists!* (1901), designed to dramatize the impartial universality of his pacifism.

9.493–99 (197:29–198:3). He who Himself begot . . . be dead already – A parody of the Apostles' Creed (see 1.653n), after the manner of Sabellius (1.659n), Valentine (1.658n), and other heretics. Cf. 9.61n. "Agenbuyer" is Middle English for Redeemer; cf. 1.481n. The parody is borrowed and improved from Johann Most's pamphlet *The Deistic Pestilence* (Hull, England, 1902), pp. 14–15. Most characterizes "the God of Jewish-Christian ideology" as "A Godly Charlatan who created himself through the Holy Ghost, and then sent himself a mediator between himself and others, and who held in contempt and derided by his enemies, was nailed to a cross, like a bat on a barndoor; who was buried—arose from the dead—descended to hell—ascended to Heaven; and since then for eighteen hundred years has been sitting at his own right hand to judge the living and the dead when the living have ceased to exist" (quoted in Dominic Manganiello, *Joyce's Politics* [London, 1980], pp. 101–2).

9.500 (197:34). *Glo-o-ri-a in ex-cel-sis De-o* – Latin: "Glory be to God on high" (Luke 2:14), the opening phrase of the Angelic Hymn sung or recited in the celebration of the Mass. Note (for 1961 Random House edition): the phrase and its musical annotation should occur after (198:3) and not in the midst of the paragraph (197:29–198:3), which it interrupts.

9.501–2 (198:4–5). He lifts hands . . . with bells acquiring – See 3.120ff. (40:9ff.) and 3.415ff. (48:25ff.).

9.510–11 (198:14–15). To be sure . . . writes like Synge – A Dublin literary joke that had its origin in Yeats's hyperbolic assertion that Synge was another Aeschylus. See Padraic Colum, *The Road Round Ireland* (New York, 1926), pp. 358–59; and Oliver St. John Gogarty, *As I Was Going Down Sackville Street* (New York, 1937), pp. 299–300.

9.514 (198:18). D.B.C. – Dublin Bakery Co.'s tearoom in Dame Street; see 8.510n.

9.514 (198:18). Gill's – A bookseller; see 6.317n.

9.514 (198:18–19). Hyde's *Lovesongs of Connacht* – See 3.397–98n.

9.517–18 (198:23–25). I hear that . . . night in Dublin – The actress was Mrs. Bandmann Palmer (see 5.194–95n and 5.195–96n); her performance was billed as the 405th professional presentation of *Hamlet* in Dublin.

9.518–19 (198:25–26). Vining held that the prince was a woman – Edward Payson Vining (1847–1920), in *The Mystery of Hamlet; An Attempt to Solve an Old Problem* (Philadelphia, 1881), theorized that Hamlet was a woman, educated and dressed as a man in a plot to secure the throne of Denmark for her family's lineage.

9.519–20 (198:26–27). Has no-one made . . . Judge Barton – The Right Honorable Sir Dunbar Plunket Barton (1853–1937), judge of the High Court of Justice in Ireland (from 1900), was apparently "searching," because he finally did publish *Links Between Ireland and Shakespeare* (Dublin, 1919). Barton was a bit too balanced and judicial to argue that Hamlet was an Irishman, but in chapter 5 he does point out that Danish dominion in Ireland coincides with the historical time during which Hamlet was prince (thus, Hamlet could have been a Danish prince in Ireland). In chapter 41 Barton speculates that there was some "Celt in Shakespeare" and in chapter 38 that Shakespeare did visit Ireland, but Barton does not interlink these aspects of Shakespeare's life with the possibility of Hamlet's presence in Ireland. In his introduction Barton asserts, "The idea of gathering these links . . . was suggested by an article . . . by Mr. Justice Madden [see 9.582–83n] . . . and was encouraged by a perusal of the Introduction to Dr. Sigerson's *Bards of the Gael and Gaul*" (p. vii).

9.520–21 (198:27–28). He swears . . . by saint Patrick – That is, Hamlet, not Judge Barton, swears by one of the three patron saints of Ireland. In Act I, scene v, after the Ghost has spoken to Hamlet and departed, Hamlet, in "wild and whirling words" (line 133), says, "Yes, by Saint Patrick, but there is [offense], Horatio" (line 136).

9.523–24 (198:30–32). *Portrait of Mr W. H.* . . . a man of all hues – Oscar Wilde's *The Portrait of Mr. W. H.* (London, 1889), a brief version, less than half the length of the rewritten version, which was "misplaced" in 1895 and not published until 1921; available in *The Riddle of Shakespeare's Sonnets* (New York, 1962). Wilde's dialogue appears, in a paradoxical way and with skillful manipulation of "internal evidence," to argue that the sonnets, dedicated "To. The. Onlie. Begetter. Of. / These. Insuing. Sonnets. / Mr. W. H. All. Happinesse . . . ," were not addressed to William Herbert, earl of Pembroke (as Brandes and others supposed), but to a boy actor named Willie Hughes (after Sonnet 20, line 7: "A man in hew, all *Hews* in his controwling"). Wilde's argument was first advanced by the English scholar Thomas Tyrwhett (1730–86).

9.525 (198:33). For Willie Hughes – That is, Wilde did not say that the sonnets were written "by" Willie Hughes, but "for" him, dedicated to him.

9.526 (198:34). *Or Hughie Wills? Mr William Himself – Speculative scholarship had produced an impressive list of candidates for the role of W. H., including, in addition to Willie Hughes and William Herbert, earl of Pembroke: William Hathaway, a bookseller and Shakespeare's brother-in-law; William Hart, Shakespeare's nephew (b. 1600); William Himself, that is, the poet as "onlie begetter"; and, by transposition of initials, Henry Wriothesley, earl of Southampton (1573–1624).

9.531 (198:41). ephebe – An "ephebus," a youth just entering manhood or just being enrolled as a citizen.

9.532 (198:41). Tame essence of Wilde – After a satiric rhyme about Wilde that appeared in *Punch* shortly after Wilde's downfall (see 3.451n), entitled "Swinburne on Wilde": "Aesthete of aesthetes / What's in a name? / The poet is Wilde / But his poetry's tame."

9.536 (199:4). a plump of pressmen – "Plump" is archaic English dialect for a cluster or group; "Pressmen" is slang for newspapermen or journalists.

9.536 (199:4). Humour wet and dry – The four humors of medieval physiology: melancholy, cold and dry; phlegm, cold and wet; blood, hot and wet; choler, hot and dry. In his broadside "Gas from a Burner" (1912), Joyce mocked his countrymen: "And in a spirit of Irish fun / Betrayed her own leaders, one by one. / 'Twas Irish humor, wet and dry, / Flung quicklime into Parnell's eye" (lines 17–20). The quicklime incident took place in Castlecomer, County Kilkenny, on 16 December 1890 during the intense political bitterness that followed the Great Split; see F. S. L. Lyons, *Charles Stewart Parnell* (London, 1977), p. 542.

9.537 (199:5). five wits – A colloquialism: as man has five senses, five members (head and four limbs), five fingers, etc., and as five is the number of Solomon's seal, the pentagon, so it is the number of dominion by knowledge. The five wits, Elizabethan style, were common wit, imagination, fantasy, estimation, and memory.

9.537–38 (199:5–6). youth's proud livery he pranks in – From Shakespeare's Sonnet 2, lines 1–4: "When forty winters shall besiege thy brow, / And dig deep trenches in thy beauty's field, / Thy youth's proud livery, so gazed on now, / Will be a tatter'd weed, of small worth held." To "prank" means to adorn or be adorned.

9.538 (199:6). Lineaments of gratified desire – From William Blake, in two short poems: "What is it men in women do require? / The lineaments of Gratified Desire. / What is it women do in men require? / The lineaments of Gratified Desire." And: "In a wife I would desire / What in whores is always found, / The lineaments of gratified desire."

9.539–40 (199:7–8). Jove, a cool ruttime send them – After Falstaff in *The Merry Wives of Windsor:* "Send me a cool rut-time, Jove, or who can blame me to piss my tallow? Who comes here? my doe?" (V.v.15–17).

9.541 (199:9). Eve. Naked wheatbellied . . . fang in's kiss – See Stephen's meditation on Eve (3.41–44 [38:6–9]), plus an allusion to the serpent's seduction of Eve in the Garden of Eden (Genesis 3:1–6).

9.550–51 (199:21–22). *The sentimentalist is he who would enjoy without incurring the immense debtorship for a thing done* – From George Meredith's (1828–1909) *The Ordeal of Richard Feverel* (London, 1859): " 'Sentimentalists,' says the PILGRIM'S SCRIPT, 'are they who seek to enjoy, without incurring the Immense Debtorship for a thing done.' " (As Hugh Kenner has pointed out to me, Joyce quotes not from the 1859 edition but from the 1875 Tauchnitz edition, for which Meredith revised the text [vol. 1, p. 262].) The passage continues: " 'It is,' the writer says of Sentimentalism elsewhere, 'a happy pastime and an important science, to the timid, the idle, and the heartless: but a damning one to them who have anything to forfeit.' "

9.552 (199:23). kips – See 1.293n.

9.552 (199:23–24). College Green – Branch Post Office, Money Order and Savings Bank Office, and Postal Telegraph Office, 29 College Green, west of the front of Trinity College.

9.558–66 (199:30–40). It's what I'm . . . for a pussful – Mulligan parodies the style of Synge's plays. Synge created a singularly poetic and dramatic language out of the peculiar combination of Irish syntax and archaic English diction that marks the spoken English of County Wicklow (where Synge grew up) and the west of Ireland.

9.560 (199:32–33). a gallus potion would rouse a friar – "Gallus" is a dialect variant of *gallows.* Mulligan's ribaldry turns on the commonplace that a man being hanged has an erection in the process.

9.561 (199:34). Connery's – W. and E. Connery were the proprietors of the Ship Hotel and Tavern at 5 Abbey Street Lower.

9.564 (199:37). mavrone – A variant of the Irish *mavourneen,* "my love, my darling."

9.569 (200:2). tramper – English dialect for vagrant or wanderer. Synge frequently so characterized himself, and he used the word at the end of *The Tinker's Wedding* (1907) when the priest who would have taken the tinkers' (gypsies') money has been foiled and they run off: "and we'll have a great time drinking that bit with the trampers on the green of Clash."

9.570 (200:3). Glasthule – Glasthule is a district in Kingstown (now Dun Laoghaire).

When Synge was in Dublin in 1904, he lived with his family at 31 Crossthwaite Park West in Kingstown until he took rooms of his own in 15 Maxwell Road, Rathmines (but not before 10 October). Crossthwaite Park is near but not strictly speaking in Glasthule.

9.570 (200:4). pampooties – Moccasins made of undressed cowhide and worn by Aran islanders. The implication is that Synge has gone native.

9.576–77 (200:10–11). *Harsh gargoyle face . . . Saint André des Arts – Stephen recalls meeting Synge in Paris. Synge is variously described as having a swarthy face with pronounced features and deeply etched lines. In *James Joyce* (New York, 1939), Herbert Gorman remarks: "They [Joyce and Synge] met seven or eight times, lunching in the humble bistro-restaurant in the Rue St.-André-des-Arts where a four-or-five-course meal could be procured for one franc ten centimes. Synge would thrust his dark crude face across the table and talk volubly, his subject always being literature. He was dogmatic in his convictions, argumentative to the point of rudeness and inclined to lose his temper" (p. 101). "Lights" are lungs; "hash of lights," the cheapest of meals—see 3.177n.

9.577 (200:12). palabras – Spanish: "words"; hence, palaver, talk.

9.578 (200:12). Oisin with Patrick – Oisin, the legendary poet-hero of the Fianna, was the son of the great, quasi-legendary third-century (?) chieftain Finn MacCool; see 12.910n. The legend is that Oisin lived on after the third-century collapse of the age of heroes, finally to experience conversion at the hands of St. Patrick in the fifth century. St. Patrick and Oisin met in a sacred wood and in exchange for his conversion the aged Oisin told St. Patrick the tales of the heroic age of the Fianna. See W. B. Yeats, *The Wanderings of Oisin* (1889); in *The Poems*, ed. Richard J. Finneran [New York, 1983]).

9.578 (200:12–13). Faunman he met in Clamart woods – Clamart is a small town south of Paris; Synge has told a story about a strange meeting in a woods (comparable to the meeting between St. Patrick and Oisin).

9.579 (200:13). *C'est vendredi saint!* – French: "It is Good Friday!"

9.580 (200:14–15). I met a fool i' the forest –

In *As You Like It*, the melancholy Jacques recounts a meeting with the clown, Touchstone: "A fool, a fool! I met a fool i' the forest, / A motley [professional] fool; a miserable world! / . . . I met a fool; / Who laid him down and bask'd him in the sun, / And rail'd on Lady Fortune in good terms, / In good set terms [carefully composed phrases]" (II.vii.12–17).

9.582–83 (200:17–19). So Mr Justice Madden . . . the hunting terms – The Right Honorable Dodgson Hamilton Madden (1840–1928), judge of the High Court of Ireland (from 1892), wrote *The Diary of Master William Silence; a Study of Shakespeare and of Elizabethan Sport* (London, 1897). Madden "searched" Shakespeare for all references to "field sports"— hunting, falconry, etc.—arguing on the basis of these "evidences" that Shakespeare's knowledge of field sports marks him as an aristocrat and not a commoner. Madden elaborates the argument via speculative analysis of the country comic Justice Shallow (*II Henry IV* and *The Merry Wives of Windsor*) and his "cousin," Justice Silence's son, an offstage character named William Silence, who is "a good scholar . . . at Oxford" in *II Henry IV* (III.ii.11–12). Madden concluded that Shakespeare's knowledge of the earl of Rutland's (1576–1612) (and Justice Shallow's) home county, Gloucestershire, together with his knowledge of field sports suggest the earl of Rutland as Shakespeare's ghostwriter.

9.586–87 (200:22). the *Kilkenny People* – See 7.975–76n.

9.592 (200:27). in a galliard – See 9.5n.

9.594 (200:29). broadbrim – Another reference to traditional Quaker costume.

9.598–99 (200:33–34). *Northern Whig, Cork Examiner, Enniscorthy Guardian* – Three provincial newspapers (on file in the National Library): the *Northern Whig*, a Belfast daily; the *Cork Examiner*, a Cork daily; and the *Enniscorthy Guardian*, a weekly published on Saturdays in Enniscorthy, a town in Wexford in southeastern Ireland.

9.599 (200:35). Evans – An assistant librarian, whether real or fictional is unknown.

9.605 (200:41). sheeny – Slang for a Jew; a term of opprobrium.

9.607 (201:1). Ikey Moses – A late-nineteenth-century comic type of the Jew who tries to ingratiate himself in middle-class Gentile society. In *Ally Sloper's Half-Holiday,* a London illustrated weekly (see 15.2152n), a character named Ikey Moses is portrayed as an unctuous pickpocket and small-time con man; he even picks his hostess's pocket during a Christmas party. The comic treatment of his image results in a thinly disguised anti-Semitism.

9.609 (201:3). collector of prepuces – See 1.394n.

9.610 (201:4–5). the foamborn Aphrodite – The Greek goddess of love and mirth (Venus in the Roman pantheon) was born of the sea foam near Cythera when the sea was impregnated by the fall of Uranus's genitals after he was castrated by his son Cronus.

9.610–11 (201:5–6). The Greek mouth that has never been twisted in prayer – Source unknown, but it sounds suspiciously like Swinburne.

9.612 (201:6–7). *Life of life, thy lips enkindle* – From Shelley's *Prometheus Unbound: A Lyrical Drama* (completed 1820; published 1839): "VOICE IN THE AIR (*singing* [to the heroine, Asia]): Life of Life! thy lips enkindle / With their love the breath between them; / And thy smiles before they dwindle / Make the cold air fire" (II.v.48–51).

9.614–15 (201:10). Greeker than the Greeks – In other words, he indulges in pederasty.

9.615 (201:10). pale Galilean – An allusion to Swinburne's "Hymn to Proserpine" (1866): "Thou hast conquered, O pale Galilean; the world has grown grey from thy breath" (line 35). Swinburne coined the line from the poem's epigraph, "Vicisti, Galilae" (Thou hast conquered, Galilean), reputed to have been the last words of the Emperor Julian the Apostate (d. 363), who renounced Christianity during his lifetime. Jesus was a native of the town of Nazareth in the province of Galilee; hence Galilean.

9.616 (201:11). Venus Kallipyge – A marble statue found in the Golden House of Nero at Rome, housed in the Museo Nazionale in Naples. *Kallipyge,* Greek: "beautiful buttocks."

9.616–17 (201:12). *The god pursuing the maiden hid* – A line from the first chorus of Swinburne's play *Atalanta in Calydon* (1865). The play opens with a long invocation, spoken by the Chief Huntsman; the chorus replies with

an ode that begins, "When the hounds of spring are on winter's traces." The sixth stanza includes the quoted line though the pun on "maidenhead" is Mulligan's, not Swinburne's. "And Pan by noon and Bacchus by night, / Fleeter of foot than the fleet-foot kid, / Follows with dancing and fills with delight / The Maenad and the Bassarid; / And soft as lips that laugh and hide / The laughing leaves of the trees divide, / And screen from seeing and leave in sight / The god pursuing, the maiden hid."

9.620 (201:15). a patient Griselda – The epitome of the patient and virtuous woman, she is prominent in one of the tales of Giovanni Boccaccio's (1313–75) *Decameron* (Day 10, story 10). Geoffrey Chaucer (c. 1340–1400) employs her in the "Clerk's Tale" (*The Canterbury Tales*) to personify the virtues of the Christian woman, suffering humbly and without complaint the indignities her husband heaps upon her.

9.620 (201:15–16). *a Penelope stay-at-home – Odysseus's wife, Penelope, another archetype of the patient and virtuous woman, waited nineteen years for her husband's return.

9.621–23 (201:17–20). Antisthenes, pupil of Gorgias . . . to poor Penelope – See notes to 7.1035. "Kyrios Menelaus" is Lord Menelaus. "Brooddam" is a term of contempt, more appropriate to animals than to a human. "The wooden mare of Troy" metaphorically identifies Helen (whose entrance into Troy spelled its doom) with the wooden horse that the Greeks, feigning departure, offered as a peace gift to the Trojans. The Trojans accepted the gift with its hidden bonus of "heroes" and thus contributed unwittingly to the destruction of their city. When the horse was about to be dragged into the city, Helen, suspicious of what it might contain, sweet-talked the prominent Greek heroes in turn, imitating the sounds of their wives' voices. The heroes were moved but managed to restrain themselves.

9.623–25 (201:20–22). Twenty years he . . . chancellor of Ireland – Stephen's sources among Shakespeare's biographers date his residence in London from 1592 to 1613. Lee (p. 203) remarks that "in the later period of his life Shakespeare was earning above £600 a year"; Harris (p. 377) translates this as "nearly five thousand a year of our money." The salary of the lord chancellor of Ireland in 1904 was £5,000 per annum.

9.626 (201:23–24). the art of feudalism . . . art of surfeit – In "A Backward Glance O'er Travel'd Roads," the preface to *November Boughs* (1888), Walt Whitman (1819–92) characteristically set the "New World," with its free political institutions and its "free" poetry, off against "the poems of the antique, with European feudalism's rich fund of epics, plays, ballads." He goes on to remark, "Even Shakspere, who so suffuses current letters and art . . . , belongs essentially to the buried past. Only he holds the proud distinction for certain important phases of the past, of being the loftiest of the singers life has yet given voice to. All, however, relate to and rest upon conditions, standards, politics, sociologies, ranges of belief, that have been quite eliminated from the Eastern hemisphere, and never existed at all in the Western." It is notable in relation to Stephen's phrase "art of surfeit" that Whitman, in "A Thought on Shakspere" (1886), would remark: "The inward and outward characteristics of Shakspere are his vast and rich variety of persons and themes, with his wonderful delineations of each and all—not only limitless funds of verbal and pictorial resource, but great excess, superfoetation—. . . holding a touch of musk." *Superfoetation:* conception after a prior conception but before the birth of any offspring.

9.626–28 (201:24–26). Hot herringpies . . . ringocandies – Rich and sweet Elizabethan dishes. "Marchpane" is almond paste or marzipan (*Romeo and Juliet* I.v.9); "ringocandies" or eringoes are candied roots believed to cause potency in love (Falstaff in *The Merry Wives of Windsor* V.v.22).

9.628–29 (201:26–28). Sir Walter Raleigh . . . of fancy stays – "Sir Walter Raleigh's dress was always splendid, and he loved, like a Persian Shah or Indian Rajah of our day, to cover himself . . . with the most precious jewels. When he was arrested in 1603, he had gems to the value of £4,000 (about £20,000 in modern money) on his breast" (Brandes, pp. 416–17). Since the exchange rate in 1904 was 25 francs to the pound, twenty thousand pounds was "half a million francs."

9.630–31 (201:28–29). *The gombeenwoman . . . her of Sheba – "Gombeen," from the Irish *goimbín*, means usury or a usurer, originally one who gave loans to small farmers at ruinous rates. Queen Elizabeth fits the role, since the "plantation system" (in effect, English exploitation of the Irish peasantry) was established during her reign. Stephen's source is not clear: Lee (p. ix)

and Brandes (p. 14) assert the extravagance of both the materials and the quantities of her clothing, but they are too decorous to itemize undergarments; the Bible (I Kings 10:2 and II Chronicles 9:1) gives an even more generalized account of the Queen of Sheba's possessions.

9.631–32 (201:30–31) *between conjugial love . . . and scortatory love – After the English title of one of Emanuel Swedenborg's (1688–1772) works, *Delights of Wisdom Concerning Conjugal Love: after which follow the pleasures of Insanity concerning Scortatory Love* (London, 1794). Scortatory derives from the Latin *scortator,* a fornicator or whore-monger, which in turn derives from *scortum,* a prostitute, harlot, or strumpet.

9.632–37 (201:31–37). You know Manningham's . . . before Richard III – The only anecdote about Shakespeare known to have been recorded in his lifetime. Among Stephen's sources, Harris, Lee, and Wilde paraphrase the story, each for his own purposes, and Brandes (p. 196) quotes it in full: "In the diary of John Manningham, of the Middle Temple, the following entry occurs, under the date of March 13, 1602 [actually 1601]:—Upon a tyme when Burbidge played Rich.3, there was a Citizen grone soe farr in liking with him, that before shee went from the play shee appointed him to come that night unto hir by the name of Richard the 3rd. Shakespeare overhearing their conclusion went before, and was intertained . . . ere Burbidge came. The message being brought that Richard the 3d was at the dore, Shakespeare caused returne to be made that William the Conqueror was before Richard the 3d. Shakespeare's name was William."

9.635 (201:34). more ado about nothing – After the title of Shakespeare's comedy *Much Ado About Nothing.*

9.635 (201:34–35). took the cow by the horns – Obvious variation of "taking the bull by the horns" (meeting a difficulty directly instead of trying to avoid it), but also an allusion to the horns that the cuckold "burgher" is acquiring.

9.636 (201:35). knocking at the gate – In *Macbeth* (II.iii), as "comic" prelude to the discovery of King Duncan's murder, a drunken porter is aroused by knocking at the gate. The porter complains that drink has intensified his sexual desires and at the same time deprived him of the capacity for sexual experience.

9.637–38 (201:37). *the gay lakin, mistress Fitton – See 9.442–43n and 9.453n. "Lakin" is a contraction of *ladykin,* little lady, a term of endearment.

9.638 (201:37–38). mount and cry O – Derives from *Cymbeline,* as Imogen's husband, Posthumus, soliloquizes on Iachimo's supposed "conquest" of Imogen (see 9.474n): "perchance he spoke not, but, / Like a full-acorn'd boar, a German one, / Cried 'O!' and mounted, found no opposition / But what he looked for should oppose and she / Should from encounter guard." (II.v.15–19).

9.638 (201:38). birdsnies – Literally, "birds' eyes," an Elizabethan term of endearment.

9.638–39 (201:38). lady Penelope Rich – (c. 1562–1607). Several nineteenth-century scholars assumed that she was the "dark lady" of Shakespeare's sonnets. The principal exponent of this view was the English poet-scholar Gerald Massey (1828–1907), whose *Shakespeare's Sonnets Never Before Interpreted* (London, 1866) presented a tangled argument to prove that Penelope Rich was the object of Pembroke's love and that Shakespeare wrote many of the sonnets not from his own point of view but as dramatic communications in an elaborate four-way love intrigue between Pembroke, Lady Penelope, Southampton, and one Elizabeth Vernon. Other writers elaborated Massey's fictions into different kinds of liaison between Shakespeare and Lady Penelope, none of them with any known basis in fact. See 7.1040n.

9.639–40 (201:39–40). the punks of the bankside, a penny a time – The Bankside on the Thames was the area around the theaters in Elizabethan London. "Punks" are prostitutes, in this case cheap, as "penny a time" suggests, since the going price for a prostitute with "class" was about six shillings (see *All's Well That Ends Well* II.ii.22–23).

9.641–42 (201:41–42). *Cours la Reine . . . Tu veux? – Cours-la-Reine (literally, "the queen's public walk" or "parade") combines with the Quai de la Conférence to form a broad avenue on the right bank of the Seine in Paris. The snatches of French are a bargaining prostitute's words in a street encounter: "Another twenty sous [one franc]. We will indulge in little nasty things. Pussy [darling]? Do you wish [it]?"

9.643 (202:1–2). sir William Davenant of Oxford's mother – An allusion to John Aubrey's apocryphal story that Shakespeare made an annual journey from London to Stratford, stopping en route at John D'Avenant's Crown Inn in Oxford. Shakespeare is supposed to have fallen in love with D'Avenant's wife and to have fathered the poet and dramatist Sir William Davenant (1606–68) by her. William Davenant at times entertained the legend, lending credence to it. Stephen's sources treat the legend variously: Lee gives it qualified rejection; Brandes, qualified acceptance; and Harris, full-spirited endorsement, since it fits his image of Shakespeare as Don Juan.

9.646 (202:4). Blessed Margaret Mary Anycock – A pun on Blessed Margaret Mary Alacoque (1647–90), a French nun whose experience of a revelation in 1675 led her to crusade for "public liturgical devotion to the Sacred Heart [of Christ]." She was beatified shortly after her death (hence "Blessed") and canonized in 1920.

9.647 (202:5). Harry of six wives' daughter – Namely, Henry VIII's daughter Elizabeth (by the second of his six wives, Anne Boleyn).

9.647–48 (202:5–6). other lady friends . . . Lawn Tennyson – In Tennyson's *The Princess; A Medley* (1847), Prologue, lines 96–98: "And here we lit on Aunt Elizabeth, / And Lilia with the rest, and lady friends / From neighbour seats." For "Lawn Tennyson," see 3.492n.

9.651 (202:9). Do and do – In *Macbeth,* as the witches gather on the heath to meet Macbeth, the First Witch proposes to revenge herself on a sailor's wife by drowning the absent husband: "I'll do, I'll do, and I'll do" (I.iii.10).

9.651 (202:9). Thing done – See 9.550–51n.

9.651–52 (202:9–10). In a rosery . . . he walks – The English herbalist John Gerard (1545–1612), superintendent of gardens for Queen Elizabeth's secretary of state, compiled a catalogue of English garden plants (1596) and prepared *The Herball or Generall Historie of Plantes* (1597). Gerard had a "rosery" (rose garden) in Fetter (Ffetter) Lane in London. Shakespeare's connection with Gerard, however, is not clear. The garden may have been "public"; but Shakespeare may have known Gerard personally, since Gerard was a prominent member of the Barber-Surgeons Company, which had its hall almost across the street from the Huguenot's house where Shakespeare lived. Stephen's (Joyce's) source for the Gerard-Shakespeare connection was Maurice Clare's (pseudonym of May Byron) *A Day with William Shakespeare* (London, 1913) (cited in Richard Ellmann, *The Consciousness of Joyce* [New York, 1977], pp. 60–61).

9.652 (202:10). greyedauburn – Both Harris (p. 367) and Lee (p. 286) report that the colored bust of Shakespeare in the Stratford church shows him with hazel eyes and auburn hair and beard. Stephen (following Maurice Clare? see preceding note) speculates that Shakespeare's hair was going grey when he was in his mid-thirties.

9.652 (202:10–11). An azured harebell like her veins – In *Cymbeline*, Cymbeline's son Arviragus speaks to his brother, Guiderius, of the "fairest flowers" with which he will "sweeten [the] sad grave" of the dead "boy," Fidele: "Thou shalt not lack / The flower that's like thy face, pale primrose, nor / The azured harebell, like thy veins, no, nor / The leaf of eglantine" (IV.ii.220–23). Fidele is neither dead nor a boy but their sister, Imogen, in disguise.

9.652–53 (202:11). Lids of Juno's eyes, violets – In *The Winter's Tale*, in a "pastoral" scene, Perdita, the heroine, gives summer flowers as compliments to a middle-aged lord and then wishes for spring flowers to compliment a young lord: "daffodils, / That come before the swallow dares, and take / The winds of March with beauty; violets dim, / But sweeter than the lids of Juno's eyes / Or Cytherea's [Venus's] breath" (IV.iv.118–22).

9.656 (202:15). Whom do you suspect? – The punch line of a well-known joke about an aging Oxford pedant who has a young wife. He confides his self-satisfaction to an old friend: "I have ground for thought; my wife tells me she's pregnant." And the friend replies: "Good God, whom do you suspect?" See 12.1657 (338:14) for a repeat performance.

9.658 (202:17–18). But the court wanton spurned him for a lord – See 9.442–43n.

9.659 (202:19). Love that dare not speak its name – That is, homosexuality; see 3.451n.

9.660–61 (202:20–21). As an Englishman . . . loved a lord – After the proverb "An Englishman loves a lord."

9.662 (202:22). Old wall where . . . at Charenton – Charenton is a town five miles southeast of Paris at the confluence of the Seine and the Marne, famous as the site of a key bridge over the Marne and attendant fortifications.

9.664 (202:25). uneared wombs – From Shakespeare's Sonnet 3, lines 1–6: "Look in thy glass, and tell the face thou viewest / Now is the time that face should form another; / Whose fresh repair [renewal] if now thou not renewest, / Thou dost beguile the world, unbless some mother. / For where is she so fair whose unear'd [unplowed] womb / Disdains the tillage of thy husbandry?"

9.664 (202:25–26). the holy office an ostler does for the stallion – That is, the ostler brings the stallion to the mare; "holy office" is a name for the Inquisition.

9.665 (202:26–27). Maybe, like Socrates . . . shrew to wife – See 9.234n and 9.235n. Shakespeare may have been "like" Socrates in having a shrew as a wife. Shakespeare's mother, Mary Arden, appears to have been a woman of property, but there is no evidence to suggest that she was a midwife as, according to Plato, Socrates' mother, Phaenarete, had been.

9.666 (202:27–28). But she, the giglot . . . break a bedvow – Spoken of Xanthippe. A "giglot wanton" is a lascivious woman or frivolous girl; Shakespeare uses it in this combined sense in *I Henry VI* (IV.vii.41) when it is applied ("giglot wench") to Joan of Arc. "Break a bedvow" comes from Shakespeare's Sonnet 152, lines 1–4: "In loving thee thou know'st I am forsworn, / But thou art twice forsworn, to me love swearing, / In act thy bed-vow broke and new faith torn, / In vowing new hate after new love bearing." (152 is the last in the sequence of "dark lady" sonnets.)

9.666–68 (202:28–30). Two deeds are . . . husband's brother – The Ghost in *Hamlet* is obsessed with Gertrude's "infidelity" and with the image of his brother, Claudius, as "that incestuous, that adulterate beast, / With wicked witchcraft of his wit, with traitorous gifts" (I.v.41–42). "Dull-brained yokel" does not fit Shakespeare's Claudius as well as it fits the future course of Stephen's argument.

9.672 (202:35). the fifth scene of *Hamlet* –
That is, Act I, scene v, when the Ghost first
speaks to Hamlet. Whether the Ghost's words
mean that Gertrude and Claudius were guilty of
adultery before the murder is still debated; see
7.751–52n.

**9.673–74 (202:36–38). no mention of her . . .
she buried him** – "The only contemporary
mention made of [Anne Hathaway Shake-
speare] between her marriage in 1582 and her
husband's death in 1616 is as the borrower at an
unascertained date (evidently before 1595) of
forty shillings from Thomas Whittington, who
had formerly been her father's shepherd" (Lee,
p. 187).

9.675 (202:39). Mary, her goodman John –
Shakespeare's father, John, died in 1601; Mary,
his mother, in 1608.

**9.675–76 (202:39–40). Ann, her poor dear
Willun** – Shakespeare died in 1616; Anne, his
wife, in 1623.

9.677 (202:41). Joan, her four brothers – Joan
Hart, Shakespeare's sister, died in 1646 at the
age of eighty-eight; his brothers were Edmund
(1569–1607), Richard (1584–1613), and Gilbert
(the date of his death is not known, though Lee
assumes [p. 283] that he, like Joan, lived "to
patriarchal age").

**9.677 (202:41–42). Judith, her husband and
all her sons** – Judith, Shakespeare's younger
daughter, "survived her husband, sons and sister" (Lee, p. 281).

9.677–78 (202:42). Susan, her husband too –
Susanna Hall, Shakespeare's older daughter,
died in 1649; her husband, Dr. John Hall, in
1635.

**9.678–79 (203:1–2). Elizabeth, to use . . .
killed her first** – According to Lee (p. 282),
"Mrs. Hall's only child, Elizabeth, was the last
surviving descendant of the poet. . . . Her first
husband, Thomas Nash, was a man of property,
and, dying childless . . . on April 4, 1647 . . .
Mrs. Nash married, as a second husband, a widower, John Bernard or Barnard of Abington,
Northamptonshire." In the play within the play
in *Hamlet*, the Player Queen "protests too
much": "In second husband let me be accurst! /
None wed the second but who kill'd the first"
(III.ii.189–90).

**9.679–81 (203:3–5). *O, yes, mention . . . fa-
ther's shepherd** – See 9.673–74n.

9.682 (203:6). the swansong – Shakespeare's
will, drafted in January 1616 and emended in
March of that year before his death on 23 April.
See notes on the will below.

**9.686–87 (203:11–12). She was entitled . . .
common law** – In one transaction with a portion of his estate in London (1613), Shakespeare
attempted (Lee argues, p. 274) to bar his wife's
dowry, that is, to prevent her from claiming a
portion of the estate equal to the dowry that she
brought to him in marriage and/or to a third
share for life in her husband's freehold estate.
See 9.691–95n.

**9.687–88 (203:12–13). His legal knowledge
. . . judges tell us** – The Irish jurists Judge
Barton (9.519–20n) and Justice Madden
(9.582–83n) supply the comment. Madden remarks on Shakespeare's legal knowledge in the
Diary of Master William Silence (London, 1897),
and Barton was eventually to publish *Links Between Shakespeare and the Law* (Dublin, 1919).

**9.691–95 (203:16–20). And therefore he . . .
And in London** – Lee (pp. 274–75), Harris (p.
362), and Brandes (p. 686) all make the point
that in the first draft of his will Shakespeare
made itemized bequests to his children and relatives and to others in Stratford and London
but omitted his wife. A sentence was later inserted: "Item, I gyve unto my wife my second
best bed with the furniture." Ownership of two
"great beds" (if that's what they were) could be
cited as evidence of affluence. See 9.801–2n.

9.700 (203:25). Punkt – German: "dot, full
stop"; figuratively, an item or point of discussion.

9.708 (203:32). Pretty countryfolk – See
9.266–67n.

9.709 (203:33). our peasant plays – Yeats,
Lady Gregory, and the other moving spirits in
the theater of the Irish revival argued for, created, and produced plays about peasant life. See
9.38–40n and 9.322n for two outstanding examples.

**9.710–12 (203:34–37). He was a rich . . . pro-
moter, a tithe-farmer** – Shakespeare, or more
correctly his father, after repeated application,
was granted a coat of arms in 1599. In 1602
Shakespeare purchased "New Place," then the

largest house in Stratford; and throughout his active career in London he continued to invest in landholdings in and near Stratford until he had a sizable estate. Lee (p. 267) records Shakespeare's purchase in 1613 of a house in Blackfriars (London), "now known as Ireland Yard." Shakespeare was a shareholder in the Globe Theatre (and possibly in the Blackfriars Theatre). Shakespeare also purchased, in 1605, a moiety of the tithes (similar to a mortgage on parish taxes) of Stratford and three neighboring parishes; and in 1612 he, with two other Stratford residents, promoted a bill of complaint in the court of chancery in an attempt to clarify the legal responsibilities involved in the tithe ownership; result unknown.

9.716 (204:1). *Separatio a mensa et a thalamo* – Latin: "Separation from board and bedchamber"; a variant of the legal phrase *Separatio a mensa et thoro* (Separation from board and bed), granted by English courts instead of a divorce before the divorce laws were reformed in 1857.

9.720–24 (204:5–10). Antiquity mentions that . . . live in his villa – Aristotle was born in Stagira (Macedonia) and would have been a "schoolurchin" there. A year before Aristotle's death, the death of Alexander the Great (323 B.C.) made Athens unsafe for him (he was charged with impiety) and so as not to meet the fate of Socrates, he exiled himself to Calchis. The "antiquity" Stephen cites is Diogenes Laertius (fl. third century B.C.), who reports in his *Lives of the Philosophers* that Aristotle's will freed and endowed some of his slaves, commissioned a statue of his mother, and directed that he be buried with his wife, Pythias, and that his concubine, Herpyllis (apocryphal?) was to be allowed to live out her life in one of his houses. Nell (Eleanor) Gwyn (c. 1650–87) was an English actress and the mistress of Charles II (1630–85; king 1660–85); his dying request was "Let not poor Nelly starve."

9.726 (204:13). He died dead drunk – Brandes (p. 685), Harris (p. 404), and Lee (p. 272) all refer to the recollection (fifty years after the fact) of John Ward, rector of Stratford: "Shakespeare, [Michael] Drayton, and Ben Jonson had a merry meeting, and, it seems, drank too hard, for Shakespeare died of a feavor there contracted" (quoted in Brandes).

9.726–27 (204:13–14). *A quart of ale is a dish for a king* – In *The Winter's Tale*, the rogue Autolycus sings a song celebrating the coming of

spring-summer as the season that "Doth set my pugging [thieving] tooth on edge / For a quart of ale is a dish for a king" (IV.iii.7–8).

9.729 (204:14). Dowden – Edward Dowden (1843–1913), professor of English literature and oratory at Trinity College, Dublin, and an eminent scholar and critic. Address: Highfield House, Highfield Road, Rathgar, County Dublin.

9.729 (204:16). William Shakespeare and company, limited – Joyce's *Ulysses* was published in 1922 by Sylvia Beach (1887–1962) under the imprint of her bookstore, Shakespeare & Co., 12 rue de l'Odéon, in Paris. She established the bookstore in 1919.

9.729 (204:16–17). The people's William – One of Dowden's favorite critical themes was that Shakespeare was a poet of the people and for the people.

9.732–33 (204:19–21). the charge of pederasty . . . high in those days – There has been endless speculation about the homosexual implications of several of Shakespeare's sonnets. Dowden approaches the "charge" with considerable circumspection: "In the Renascence epoch, among natural products of a time when life ran swift and free, touching with its current high and difficult places, the ardent friendship of man with man was one" (*The Sonnets of William Shakespeare* [London, 1881], p. 8). He then goes on to cite several examples of such "ardent friendships" in the attempt to contextualize (and in a sense neutralize) the charge. Hugh Kenner suggests that "Joyce's eye was on the first sentence of a *Shakespeare* Dowden published in 1877 for the use of schoolchildren: 'In the closing years of the sixteenth century the life of England ran high' " (*Ulysses* [London, 1980], p. 113).

9.735 (204:23). The sense of beauty leads us astray – An observation characteristic of Oscar Wilde in a melancholy mood. Wilde, in *The Portrait of Mr. W. H.* (*The Riddle of Shakespeare's Sonnets* [New York, 1962], p. 186), remarks in answer to the question, "What do the Sonnets tell us about Shakespeare?—Simply that he was the slave of beauty."

9.738 (204:26). The doctor can tell us what those words mean – Reference is to Sigmund Freud (1856–1939), the Austrian physiologist and psychiatrist who founded psychoanalysis, which Stephen calls "the new Viennese school"

(9.780 [205:32]). In Freudian terms the "words" would, of course, mean an attempt to disguise or sublimate or excuse a deeply rooted unconscious compulsion.[2]

9.738–39 (204:26–27). You cannot eat your cake and have it – A familiar English proverb that appears as early as Heywood's *Proverbs* (1546). In context, Eglinton obviously implies that one cannot both have a sense of beauty and go astray.

9.740 (204:28–29). Sayest thou so . . . palm of beauty? – In other words, will Freud and the psychoanalysts behave like Antisthenes and take "the palm of beauty" from beautiful Helen and award it to the moral and virtuous Penelope, that is, take it away from the artist and award it to the moralist? See 9.621–23 (201:17–20) and 7.1035n.

9.741–42 (204:30–31). He drew Shylock out of his own long pocket – Shylock is the vengeful Jewish moneylender in Shakespeare's *Merchant of Venice*. To have a "long pocket" is a colloquialism implying that someone has money and is "close" with it. Brandes (p. 151) argues that "Shakespeare was attracted by the idea of making a real man and a real Jew out of this intolerable demon [Barabas, in Christopher Marlowe's (1564–93) *The Jew of Malta*]. It took effect upon his mind because it was at that moment preoccupied with the ideas of acquisition, property, money-making, wealth."

9.742–44 (204:31–33). The son of a . . . famine riots – Lee (p. 4), Harris (p. 352), and Brandes (p. 6) all present John Shakespeare as involved in a variety of trades including "malt"; only Lee (p. 6) mentions his lending small sums

of money to the municipal corporation of Stratford. According to Brandes's circumstantial account (p. 154), Shakespeare himself lent money and "did not share that loathing of interest which it was the fashion of his day to affect." Brandes (p. 153) and Lee (p. 194) identify Shakespeare as the owner if not a jobber of corn: "For we see that during the corn-famine of 1598 [February], he appears on the register as owner of ten quarters of corn and malt" (Brandes). Neither Brandes nor Lee mentions riots. A "tod" is a weight for wool: twenty-eight pounds; a quarter, as a measure for grain, is eight bushels, twenty-five to twenty-eight pounds.

9.744–45 (204:33–35). His borrowers are . . . uprightness of dealing – "Chettle Falstaff" is Stephen's version of Henry Chettle (c. 1560–c. 1607), the London printer and playwright who published Greene's *Groat's Worth of Wit* (1592) and followed it three months later with his own *Kind-Hart's Dreame* (1592), in which he regrets having published Greene's attack on Shakespeare (see 9.130n): "I am as sorry as if the originall fault had beene my fault, because myselfe have seene his demeanor no lesse civill than he exelent in the qualitie he professes. Besides, divers of worship have reported his uprightnes of dealing, which argues his honesty, and his facetious grace in writing, that aprooves his Art." Brandes (p. 19), Lee (p. 58), and Harris (pp. 372–73) all quote Chettle's apology. Contemporary descriptions of Chettle as a fat man gave rise to speculations that Chettle appeared as Sir John Falstaff in Shakespeare's *I* and *II Henry IV*, *Henry V*, and *The Merry Wives of Windsor*. Brandes notes the speculation (p. 179); Harris accepts it (pp. 150–51).

9.745–47 (204:35–37). He sued a fellowplayer . . . for every money lent – Lee (p. 206) and Brandes (p. 155) cite Shakespeare's suit against one Philip Rogers (an apothecary) of Stratford for £1 15s. 10d. owed for malt purchased and monies lent. "Pound of flesh" is an allusion to Shylock's vengeful attempts to exact that forfeit from a delinquent Gentile debtor, Antonio, in *The Merchant of Venice*. Lee (p. 206) regards Shakespeare as one who "stood vigorously by his rights in his business relations." Brandes (p. 155) remarks that "Shakespeare seems to have charged the current rate of interest, namely, ten per cent." Elsewhere (p. 130) Brandes argues that Shakespeare had "a fierce instinct . . . which led him . . . to amass property without any tenderness for his debtors and . . . to understand and feel that passion for power

---

2 This passage in the text is the subject of some controversy. As Thornton points out (p. 199), the *Little Review* version of this episode does not contain Eglinton's remark about "the doctor" (9.738 [204:26]), but it does include Stephen's remark "the new Viennese school Mr. Magee spoke of" (9.780 [205:32–33]). Thornton argues that Joyce in amending the passage could not have meant an allusion to Freud. But on the contrary, since Eglinton-Magee nowhere else alludes to Freud, the emendation is necessary to make Stephen's remark about "the new Viennese school" dramatically valid as well as to add weight to Stephen's concern lest "the doctor," which he renders "they" (9.740 [204:28]), should prove another Antisthenes. The "doctor" could, of course, be Mulligan; but how then explain not only Stephen's "they . . . us" but also the irrepressible Mulligan's silence in the face of this opening for further ribaldry?

[*Richard III*] which defies and tramples upon every scruple."

9.747–48 (204:38). How else could . . . get rich quick? – John Aubrey's (1626–97) collection of anecdotes was finally edited as *Brief Lives and Other Selected Writings* (London, 1898). Aubrey says that Shakespeare's father was a butcher and that Shakespeare "when he was a boy . . . exercised his father's trade" and subsequently was "a schoolmaster in the country." According to Lee (pp. 33–34), "the compiler [Robert Shiels and others under the direction of Colly Cibber] of 'Lives of the Poets' (1753), was the first to relate the story that his original connection with the playhouse was as holder of the horses of visitors outside the doors." And Brandes (p. 13) writes: "Malone [Edmund (1741–1812)] reports 'a stage tradition that his first office in the theatre was that of prompter's attendant,'" or "callboy." Harris, Lee, and Brandes are all understandably circumspect about these and other anecdotal attempts to account for Shakespeare's early life.

9.748 (204:39). brought grist to his mill – Proverbial expression for "raw materials that he could turn to profit."

9.748–51 (204:39–42). Shylock chimes with . . . was yet alive – See 9.741–42n. Lee (p. 68) argues that the "inspiration" of Marlowe's *Jew of Malta* is only incidental to the creation of Shylock; rather, the real inspiration was the "popular interest" aroused by the trial in February 1594 and the execution in June "of the Queen's Jewish physician, Roderigo Lopez." Lopez was accused on slender evidence of having accepted a bribe from Spanish agents to poison the queen and one Antonio Perez, a renegade Spaniard. The parallel with *The Merchant of Venice* is presumed to be enforced not only by conjunction of Shylock and Lopez but also by the fact that Shylock's proposed victim in the play is the titular hero, Antonio. The execution of Lopez was the occasion for a violent outbreak of anti-Semitism in London. In the "ceremony" of being hanged, drawn, and quartered, the victim was hanged on a tilted ladder or in such a way that his feet touched the platform, so he was suffocating but not necessarily dead when the vivisection began. Stephen's flourish about the heart does not occur in any of his sources. For "sheeny," see 9.605n.

9.751–52 (204:42–205:2). *Hamlet* and *Macbeth* . . . **turn for witchroasting** – James I (1566–1625; as James VI of Scotland 1567–

1625; king of England 1603–25). Fascinated by witchcraft, he produced a textbook on the subject, *Daemonologie* (1597), and as king of Scotland he was actively involved in promoting large-scale witch-trials and executions. Brandes (p. 424) links *Hamlet* and *Macbeth* with King James's interest in witchcraft and demonology, but he is more guarded than Stephen about citing James as an inspiration for *Hamlet*, since he dates *Hamlet* early, 1603 (or before); *Macbeth* is "safer," dated 1605–6 by both Brandes and Lee. Lee (p. 239) makes a considerable point of the appeal Shakespeare's *Macbeth* would have had for James I, not only on account of its demonology but also on account of its Scottish sources and sympathetic treatment of Banquo, James's ancestor. *Philosophaster:* a pretender to or dabbler in philosophy.

9.752–53 (205:2–3). The lost armada . . . *Love's Labour's Lost* – The Armada, a full-scale Spanish invasion attempt, was partially defeated by the English and then dispersed and destroyed by storms in 1588. Lee (p. 52n) remarks, "The name Armado was doubtless suggested by the expedition of 1588." Don Adriano de Armado, in *Love's Labour's Lost*, is a "fantastical Spaniard," a caricature of what Elizabethans regarded as typically Spanish: vain, fastidious, and bombastic. It should be noted that the play is usually described as "difficult" because it is so larded with topical allusions.

9.753–54 (205:3–4). His pageants the histories . . . Mafeking enthusiasm – Mafeking, a town in South Africa, was an English strong point during the Boer War. The Boers besieged it for 217 days, but although the Boers cut Mafeking's supply lines, they never put any real pressure on the English garrison. The garrison held out as much because of Boer disinterest as of English heroics. A relief column forced the Boers to withdraw from the Mafeking area on 17 May 1900. The response in London was a riotous victory celebration out of all proportion to the military significance of the event. "Mafeking" later became a term for extravagant (and essentially unwarranted) display of enthusiasm for the British Empire and expansionist policy. It is a historical commonplace that after the defeat of the Armada Elizabethan England enjoyed an extended period of enthusiastic Renaissance nationalism.

9.754–55 (205:4–5). Warwickshire jesuits . . . theory of equivocation – On 5 November 1605 an English Catholic plot to blow up both houses of Parliament and the king as he addressed them was intercepted and foiled. One of the high-level Catholics tried as a member of the plot in 1606 was the Warwickshire Jesuit Henry Garnet, provincial of the then-underground order in England. He distinguished himself at the trial by defending the "doctrine of equivocation," that is, maintaining that his attempt to practice deliberate deception on his accusers (i.e., to lie under oath) was perfectly ethical if done "for the greater Glory of God" (Jesuit motto). The porter in *Macbeth*, aroused from a drunken sleep by a knocking at the gate, imagines that he is the porter at hell's gate and says: "Who's there, in the other devil's name? Faith, here's an equivocator, who could swear in both the scales against either scale; yet could not equivocate to heaven" (II.iii.8–12). Lee makes the connection between Father Garnet and the Porter (p. 239).

9.755–57 (205:5–7). The *Sea Venture* . . . our American cousin – Lee (p. 252) argues that *The Tempest* was in part inspired by the experiences of the crew of the *Sea Venture*, a ship lost in the Bermudas on a voyage to Virginia in 1609. Members of the crew, marooned for ten months in the previously unknown islands, made their way to Virginia and thence to England in 1610. The somewhat fanciful accounts of their adventures produced considerable excitement in England. For Renan, see 9.394n. Caliban, the grossly human earth spirit of Shakespeare's play, is dubbed "Patsy" in honor of nineteenth-century stage caricatures of the immigrant Irish. For *Our American Cousin*, see 7.733–34n.

9.757 (205:7–8). The sugared sonnets follow Sidney's – Shakespeare's sonnets were called "sugred sonnets" by Francis Meres (1565–1647) in his *Palladio Tamia, Wits Treasury* (1598); he speaks of the sonnets not as published but as known "among [Shakespeare's] private friends." Sir Philip Sidney's (1554–86) famous sonnet sequence *Astrophel and Stella* (composed 1581–83?) obviously precedes Shakespeare's, but both Lee and Brandes are guarded about attributing to Sidney a decisive influence on Shakespeare's sonnets. Lee (p. 61) lists Sidney as "among the rills which fed the mighty river," and Brandes (p. 300) cites the sonneteer Samuel Daniel (1562–1619) as Shakespeare's "immediate predecessor and master."

9.757–60 (205:8–11). As for fay Elizabeth . . . of the buckbasket – "Fay Elizabeth" after Edmund Spenser's allegorical rendition of her in

(and as) *The Faerie Queene;* "carrotty Bess" because good Queen Bess had red hair; "gross virgin" because she reputedly enjoyed coarse humor. The tradition that Elizabeth inspired, or rather commanded, Shakespeare to write *The Merry Wives of Windsor* was apparently well established by 1702, when the English playwright John Dennis (1657–1734) mentions it in the epistle dedicatory to his play *The Comical Gallant*, a rewrite of *The Merry Wives*. "Meinherr" is slang for a German gentleman, as "Almany" is Elizabethan for Germany. The "buckbasket" in which this overmeticulous scholar (or Freudian?) is to "grope" figures repeatedly in *The Merry Wives of Windsor;* in Act III, scene iii, Falstaff is hidden in one, covered with "foul linen" and pitched into the Thames. "Buck" involves a pun on "horned animal," and therefore on cuckold (an obvious theme of the play).

9.762 (205:13). *Mingo, minxi, mictum, mingere* – Latin, conjugation of the verb *to make water, to urinate*. See 17.1188n.

9.763 (205:14). Prove that he was a jew – Shakespeare's religion has been the topic of considerable speculation. "Evidence" has been found to identify him as Catholic, Anglican, Puritan, Pagan, and atheist, but I have found no source for the conjecture that he was a Jew, nor, apparently, has Samuel Schoenbaum (*Shakespeare's Lives* [New York, 1970]).

9.763–64 (205:15). Your dean of studies . . . holy Roman – Reference is to the dean of studies, University College, Dublin, Father Joseph Darlington, S.J. (1850–1939). An article of his, "The Catholicity of Shakespeare's Plays" (*New Ireland Review* (1897–98): 241–49, and 304–10), argues in a circumspect way that Shakespeare was a Catholic—perhaps not a practicing Catholic but certainly (like the medieval cathedrals) one of the great flowerings of that tradition "of Chivalry and Christian faith."

9.765 (205:16). *Sufflaminandus sum* – Latin: "I ought to be repressed [in speaking]." After Ben Jonson's comment on Shakespeare in *Timber; or, Discoveries Made Upon Men and Matter, as They Have Flowed Out of His Daily Reading* (published posthumously, 1641): "Hee was honest, and of an open, and free nature: had an excellent Phantsie; brave notions, and gentle expressions: wherein he flow'd with that facility, that sometime it was necessary he should be stop't: *Sufflaminandus erat* [he should be repressed]; as Augustus [Roman emperor] said of

Haterius [a particularly glib Roman orator]" (*Works* [Oxford, 1925–52], vol. 8, p. 584).

9.766 (205:17). made in Germany – A stock phrase, since German manufacturers began to flood European markets with their products around 1890; see 8.555–56n and 15.4455n. Also a witticism at the expense of German scholars, who had a tendency to expropriate Shakespeare as "unser [our] Shakespeare."

9.766–67 (205:18). French polisher – See 9.315n.

9.767 (205:18). Italian scandals – In Elizabethan caricature the Italians were a scandalous people: outrageously Machiavellian in their lust for power (Claudius in *Hamlet* is a "Machiavellian prince"); outrageously licentious (in *Othello*, even Desdemona's chaste behavior can be made to appear suspect because she is a Venetian); and all devious Borgias in a quarrel, inclined to poison rather than to healthy Elizabethan confrontation (witness Hamlet's father's death and Claudius's plans for the last scene of *Hamlet*).

9.768 (205:19–20). A myriadminded man . . . Coleridge called him – In chapter 15 of his *Biographia Literaria* (1817), Samuel Taylor Coleridge (1772–1834) undertakes to apply the "principles" he has developed in preceding chapters "to purposes of practical criticism." The first application will be "to discover what the qualities in a poem are, which may be deemed promises and specific symptoms of poetic power, as distinguished from general talent. . . . In this investigation, I could not, I thought, do better, than keep before me the earliest work [*Venus and Adonis*, "The Rape of Lucrece"] of the greatest genius, that perhaps human nature has yet produced, our *myriadminded* Shakespeare." In a footnote Coleridge says that he has coined the word from a Greek phrase and that it belongs to Shakespeare "by singular right and by natural privilege."

9.770–71 (205:21–22). Amplius. In societate . . . inter multos – Latin: "A broad assertion. In human society it is of the utmost importance that there be amicable relations among the many [among as many as possible]." Stephen implies that this is a quotation from St. Thomas Aquinas, but the source is unknown; see 9.778–83n.

9.773 (205:24). Ora pro nobis – Latin: "Pray for us."

9.775 (205:27). Pogue mahone! Acushla machree! – Irish: "Kiss my arse! Pulse of my heart!"; see 9.102n.

9.775–76 (205:27–28). It's destroyed . . . we are surely! – Lines from Synge's one-act play *Riders to the Sea* (first performed in Dublin, 25 February 1904). In the course of the play Maurya (an old woman), having lost one son to the sea, tries to prevent her remaining son from a similar fate, but he overrules her. Then she has a vision of the living son on horseback followed by the dead son on a pony, which she and her daughters recognize as a presentiment of another death. Cathleen, the older daughter, keens: "It's destroyed we are from this day. It's destroyed, surely." In the context of the play, "destroyed" means starved or destitute.

9.778–83 (205:30–36). Saint Thomas, Stephen . . . hungers for it – Freud and his "Viennese school" regarded incest, that is, an oedipal relationship, as a necessary and disturbing component of infantile sexuality; thus, the process of "growing up" was regarded as a process of being weaned from incestuous tendencies. It is not St. Thomas but St. Augustine who likens lust (not simply incest) to avarice or covetousness (*aviditate*), in *De Civitati Dei* (15:16). St. Thomas quotes Augustine to that effect in the *Summa Theologica*, Secunda Secundae, Query 154, article 10, "Whether Sacrilege Can Be a Species of Lust." In article 9, "Whether Incest is a Determinate Species of Lust," St. Thomas's primary reason for condemning incest is that incest is "contrary to the natural respect we owe persons related to us," a point he makes also in articles 1 and 12. "Gorbellied" means bigbellied. Falstaff uses the word in *I Henry IV* (II.ii.93); as applied to St. Thomas, see 3.385n.

9.783–84 (205:36–37). Jews, whom christians . . . given to inter-marriage – Jewish tradition, as articulated in the Old Testament and reinforced in practice, involved a sharp prejudice against marriage with a non-Israelite (subsequently, non-Jew).

9.784–86 (205:38–40). The christian laws . . . hoops of steel – The "Christian laws" were those laws that forbade the lending of money at interest; since Jewish law did not so forbid, Jews were consequently tolerated for the importance of their economic function, "sheltered in the midst of storm" (in England, protected specifically under the King's Judaism until their expulsion in 1290; see 2.442n). The Lollards, a semimonastic society of religious reformers (fourteenth and fifteenth centuries), are associated with the leadership of the famous English reformer, theologian, and translator of the Bible John Wycliffe (c. 1324–84). Although they were persecuted in the Low Countries and England, they did find shelter from storm in the late fourteenth century, when England was experiencing the troubles that would eventually erupt in the Wars of the Roses (mid-fifteenth century). John of Gaunt, duke of Lancaster (1340–99), himself involved in an underground contest with Church power, championed Wycliffe and protected his Lollard followers. In *Hamlet*, Polonius advises his son, Laertes, who is about to depart for France, on the techniques of worldly experience: "Be thou familiar, but by no means vulgar. / Those friends thou hast, and their adoption tried [friendship tested], / Grapple them to thy soul with hoops of steel" (I.iii.61–63).

9.787 (205:41). old Nobodaddy – Blake's characterization of a god of wrath and hellfire, a god jealous of the joy of his own creation (as is the Old Testament Jehovah). "To Nobodaddy": "Why art thou silent and invisible, / Father of Jealousy? / Why dost thou hide thyself in clouds / From every searching eye? // Why darkness and obscurity / In all thy words & laws, / That none dare eat the fruit but from / The wily serpent's jaws? / Or is it because Secresy gains females' loud applause?" In another poem, "Let the Brothels of Paris be opened," he enters (lines 13–16): "Then old Nobodaddy aloft / Farted & belched & coughed, / And said, 'I love hanging & drawing & quartering / Every bit as well as war & slaughtering.' "

9.787–88 (205:42). at doomsday leet – A "leet" is a manorial court; hence, at the Last Judgment.

9.790 (206:3). sir smile neighbour – In Shakespeare's *Winter's Tale*, the protagonist, Leontes, is the victim of a compulsive jealous suspicion: "Now while I speak this, holds his wife by the arm / That little thinks she has been sluiced in's absence / And his pond fish'd by his next neighbor, by / Sir Smile, his neighbor" (I.ii.193–96).

9.790–91 (206:3–4). shall covet his . . . or his jackass – After the tenth of the Ten Commandments: "Neither shalt thou desire thy neighbour's wife, neither shalt thou covet thy neigh-

bour's house, his field, or his manservant, or his maidservant, his ox, or his ass, or any thing that is thy neighbour's" (Deuteronomy 6:21).

9.793 (206:6). Gentle Will – After Ben Jonson's epithet "Gentle Shakespeare," which he used twice in dedicatory poems to the First Folio, *Mr. William Shakespeare's Comedies, Histories and Tragedies* (1623): in "To the memory of my beloved the author, Mr. William Shakespeare, and what he hath left us" (line 56) and in "To the Reader" (line 2).

9.795–96 (206:10–11). The will to live . . . will to die – As a Puritan "saint," Anne Hathaway Shakespeare would have looked forward to death as the entry into eternal life. Eglinton is also alluding to Freud's assertion that the two basic and conflicting urges in the unconscious are the will to live and the will to die.

9.797 (206:12). *Requiescat!* – Latin, from the prayer for the repose of the dead, *Requiescat in pace:* "May he (or she) rest in peace."

9.798–99 (206:13–14). *What of all . . . vanished long ago* – The opening lines of AE's (George William Russell's) poem "Sung on a By-Way." The first of the poem's four stanzas continues, "For a dream-shaft pierced it through / From the unknown Archer's bow" (*Collected Poems* [London, 1926], p. 128).

9.800–801 (206:16). the mobled queen – Hamlet asks the newly arrived First Player to repeat a speech describing "Priam's slaughter," that is, the death of the king of Troy. Queen Hecuba, who witnesses the death, is described as "the mobled [muffled] queen" (II.ii.524).

9.801–2 (206:16–18). a bed in those days . . . of seven parishes – While it is true that in Elizabethan England a "great bed" (a heavy and ornately carved four-poster) was a rarity and that most people slept on straw pallets, at least one "lesser bed" was a common feature of middle-class households. For "motorcar," see 7.341n.

9.802–4 (206:18–20). In old age . . . town paid for – "Gospeller" was a derisive term for a Puritan preacher. Brandes (p. 679), Harris (pp. 402–3), and Lee (pp. 268–69) all cite a 1614 entry in the Stratford municipal accounts: "Item, for one quart of sack and one quart of clarett wine given to a preacher at the New Place [Shakespeare's house], xx^d." Lee attributes this "civility" to the Puritan sympathies of Shakespeare's son-in-law; Brandes regards it as a "spiritual betrayal" of Shakespeare by his family, since Puritans were notorious enemies of poetry, theater, and the arts, including (for many radical Puritans) music.

9.805–6 (206:22). his chapbooks – Puritan religious tracts.

9.807 (206:23). the jordan – A chamber pot; also, short for "Jordan bottle," a bottle of water from the river Jordan in the Holy Land. Some Puritan sects regarded this water as symbolic of ultimate baptism and conversion.

9.807–9 (206:24–25). *Hooks and Eyes . . . Devout Souls Sneeze* – *Hooks and Eyes for Believers' Breeches* (London, c. 1650) was a Puritan pamphlet about works of charity; the other title seems to be an approximation of another Puritan pamphlet, *The Spiritual Mustard-Pot, to Make the Soul Sneeze with Devotion* (London, 1653).

9.809 (206:25–26). Venus has twisted her lips in prayer – Suggests Anne Hathaway in her role in *Venus and Adonis;* see 9.610–11 (201: 5–6).

9.810 (206:27–28). an age of . . . for its god – A commonplace about Jacobean London. Brandes develops this theme at some length (pp. 488–500).

9.811 (206:29–30). *inquit Eglintonus Chronolologus* – Latin: "cited Eglinton, the Chronologist." "Chronololologus" is a playful Latinization of a Greek word.

9.812–13 (206:31–32). a man's worst enemies . . . house and family – As Jesus teaches his disciples: "For I come to set a man at variance against his father, and the daughter against her mother, and the daughter in law against her mother in law. And a man's enemies shall be they of his own household" (Matthew 10:35–36 [Douay]).

9.815–16 (206:35). the fat knight – An epithet used repeatedly in reference to Falstaff in *Henry V* and *The Merry Wives of Windsor.*

9.817 (206:36). deny thy kindred – Juliet, "above at a window," speaks, unaware that Romeo is below in the orchard: "O Romeo, Romeo! wherefore art thou Romeo? / Deny thy father and refuse thy name" (II.ii.33–34).

9.817 (206:36). the unco guid – After the title

of Robert Burns's (1759–96) poem "Address to the Unco Guid, or the Rigidly Righteous" (1786, 1787). The poem attacks the self-righteous who regard themselves as holy or wise. "Unco" means uncouth, shy, awkward, or uncommon; "guid" means good.

9.817–18 (206:37). supping with the godless, he sneaks the cup – In *I Henry IV,* Act III, scene iii, Falstaff, in serio-comic fretfulness, complains that "villainous company" (i.e., Prince Hal and his friends) has kept him from repenting and from the "inside of a church." Later in the scene he accuses the absent Prince Hal of being a "sneak-cup," one who steals cups from taverns, the lowest kind of thief (lines 10, 9, 85).

9.818 (206:37–38). A sire in Ultonian Antrim – An Ultonian is an inhabitant of Ulster; Antrim is a county in Ulster in the northeast corner of Ireland. A sizable peninsula off the coast of County Antrim is called Island Magee, and the family name is associated with that district. However, Eglinton's father did not live in County Antrim. *Irish Literature* (ed. Justin McCarthy, Maurice Egan, and Douglas Hyde [New York, 1904]), in its biographical note on William K. Magee (pseudonym John Eglinton), remarks: "Mr. Magee is a native of Dublin and is the son of an Irish Protestant clergyman who died recently."

9.819 (206:38). quarter days – Obsolete for ember days; see 16.278n.

9.820 (206:40). Give me my Wordsworth – In *Two Essays on the Remnant* (1896), Eglinton describes the Remnant as those in the present "who feel prompted to perpetuate the onward impulse" of the "great literary period" of the early nineteenth century. He cites in particular Goethe, Schiller, Wordsworth, and Shelley and discusses at length Wordsworth's dominant contribution to that "onward impulse."

9.820–21 (206:40–207:1). Magee Mor Matthew – "Mor" is Irish for great, senior. Matthew appears as a character in several of Wordsworth's early poems. In "Expostulation and Reply" (1798), Matthew expostulates with William for dreaming his "time away," and William's reply argues the vitality of "dream." Wordsworth's note on Matthew: "A friend who was somewhat unreasonably attached to modern books of moral philosophy." In "Two April Mornings" he is described as "A village schoolmaster was he, / With hair of glittering grey."

9.821 (207:1). a rugged rough rugheaded kern – Richard II in Shakespeare's *The Tragedy of King Richard II* callously turns from the news of John of Gaunt's death: "Now for our Irish wars: / We must supplant those rough rugheaded [shaggy-haired] kerns [Irish foot soldiers]" (II.i.155–56).

9.821 (207:1). in strossers – In Shakespeare's *Henry V*, the dauphin, on the eve of his defeat at Agincourt, jokes with the constable of France, wittily combining allusions to his horse and his mistress: "O then belike she was old and gentle; and you rode, like a kern of Ireland, your French hose [baggy trousers] off, and in your strait strossers [underpants]" (III.vii.55–57).

9.821–22 (207:1–2). a buttoned codpiece – That is, crudely and suggestively detachable.

9.822 (207:2). netherstocks – Elizabethan stockings, cut out of material and sewed, not woven, together (*I Henry IV* II.iv.129 and *King Lear* II.iv.11).

9.822 (207:2–3). with clauber of ten forests – An allusion to Yeats's play *The Countess Cathleen* (1895 version). In scene I, Shemus's wife rails at him when he returns from hunting in the woods that she regards as haunted, and he answers: "I searched all day: the mice and rats and hedgehogs / Seemed to be dead, and I could hardly hear / A wing moving in all the famished woods, / Though the dead leaves and clauber [clabber, mud, mire] / Cling to my footsole."

9.822–23 (207:3). a wand of wilding in his hand – After the last stanza of "Two April Mornings" (1799, 1800), one of Wordsworth's "Matthew poems": "Matthew is in his grave, yet now, / Methinks, I see him stand, / As at that moment, with a bough / Of wilding in his hand." The "wilding" is wild- or crab-apple, a tree mythologically associated with laughter and with the Welsh and Irish goddesses cognate with Aphrodite.

9.824 (207:4). He knows your old fellow – What Mulligan has said about Bloom; see 9.614 (201:9).

9.826 (207:7). Dr Bob Kenny – Robert D. Kenny, surgeon to the North Dublin Poor Law Union Hospital; in other words, Stephen's mother was a charity case.

9.829 (207:10–11). He wrote the play . . . his father's death – John Shakespeare died 8 September 1601. Brandes argues (p. 341; on evidence of the Stationers' Register, 26 July 1602) that *Hamlet* was composed in 1601, a period when "many and various emotions crowded upon Shakespeare's mind" (as Brandes speculates about Shakespeare's reaction to the condemnations of Essex and Southampton early in 1601 and a possible crisis with the "Dark Lady of the Sonnets").

9.830 (207:11–12). two marriageable daughters – Susanna Shakespeare was born in May 1583; Judith, in 1585. Susanna was married in 1607; Judith, in 1616.

9.831 (207:12–13). *nel mezzo del cammin di nostra vita* – Italian: "in the middle of the journey of our life"; the opening line of canto 1 of Dante's *Inferno*. Dante (1265–1321) dates the vision of the *Divina Commedia* as 1300 (when he was thirty-five). The *Inferno* continues: "I came to myself in a dark wood where the straight way was lost."

9.832 (207:13–14). the beardless undergraduate from Wittenberg – In *Hamlet* (I.ii.112ff.), Claudius refuses to allow Hamlet to return to "school" at the University of Wittenberg. The First Quarto edition of *Hamlet* (1603) identifies Hamlet as a youth, "quite young, probably nineteen" (Brandes, p. 367). The Second Quarto (1604) modifies the emphasis on Hamlet's youth and implies that he was thirty; see 9.387n. Brandes stresses these changes as supportive of his argument that the thirty-five-year-old Shakespeare identified with and portrayed himself in the thirty-year-old Hamlet (pp. 367ff.).

9.833 (207:15). his seventyyear old mother – The date of Mary Arden Shakespeare's birth is unknown. She was married in 1557; therefore, by 1601 she would have been at least sixty.

9.833–34 (207:15–16). The corpse of John Shakespeare . . . walk the night – The Ghost speaks to Hamlet: "I am thy father's spirit, / Doom'd for a certain term to walk the night" (I.v.9–10); see 9.829n.

9.834–35 (207:16–17). From hour to hour it rots and rots – In *As You Like It*, Jacques tells the story of his meeting with "a fool i' the forest" (Touchstone) and quotes the fool as having said: "And so, from hour to hour, we ripe and ripe, / And then, from hour to hour, we rot and rot; / And thereby hangs a tale" (II.vii.26–28).

9.835 (207:18). mystical estate – That which, by definition, can only be spiritually, not physically, inherited.

9.836–37 (207:18–20). Boccaccio's Calandrino . . . himself with child – In Giovanni Boccaccio's (1313–75) *Decameron*, Day 9, story 3: the gullible Calandrino's friends fleece him by convincing him that he is great with child and then curing him for a price. *Calandrino*, Italian: a "level protractor"; figuratively, a ninny or simpleton.

9.838 (207:21). apostolic succession – The uninterrupted spiritual succession or descent from the apostles by regular and successive ordination of bishops; each bishop of the Church thus inherits the mystical estate of the apostles at his ordination.

9.838–39 (207:22). from only begetter to only begotten – After the Nicene Creed, which speaks of Christ as "the only begotten son of God"; see 3.45n. This phrase also recalls the dedication of Shakespeare's sonnets; see 9.523–24n.

9.839–40 (207:23–24). the madonna which . . . mob of Europe – Stephen argues that the Italian priesthood had substituted the "easy emotional" worship of the Virgin Mary for the difficult intellectual concept of the consubstantiality of father and son. There was considerable controversy about Mariolatry in the latter half of the nineteenth century, triggered by Pius IX's 1854 declaration (as dogma and an article of faith) that Mary was immaculately conceived.

9.840–42 (207:24–26). the church is founded . . . upon the void – In Catholic tradition, the founding of the Catholic church is identified with Matthew 16:18, when Jesus speaks to Simon Peter, since Peter was to be the first bishop of Rome (and the first pope): "And I say unto thee, that thou art Peter, and upon this rock I will build my church; and the gates of hell shall not prevail against it." The contrast between Jesus' "rock" and Stephen's "void" suggests the rock of Scylla and the whirlpool of Charybdis. (John Hunt, "Sundering and Reconciliation," unpublished paper, 1978.)

9.842–43 (207:27). *Amor matris*, subjective and objective genitive – *Amor matris*, Latin: "mother love." Stephen's comment implies that

the Latin phrase can be regarded as ambiguous: a mother's love for her child or the child's love for its mother. See 2.165n and 2.143n.

9.843 (207:27–28). the only true thing in life – In effect what Cranly has said about mother love in *A Portrait* 5:C.

9.848 (207:33). *Amplius. Adhuc. Iterum. Postea* – Latin: "Furthermore. Heretofore. Once again. Hereafter"; rhetorical terms associated with various phases of Scholastic argument.

9.852–53 (207:38–39). loves that dare not speak their name – Homosexual loves; see 3.451n.

9.854 (207:40). queens with prize bulls – In Greek mythology, Minos, king of Crete, offended Poseidon, who revenged himself by making Minos's wife, Pasiphaë, fall in love with a white bull. To fulfill her passion she concealed herself in a wooden cow that Daedalus prepared for her; the result of the union was the Minotaur—half bull, half man.

9.858 (208:3). *rue Monsieur le Prince – In early-twentieth-century Paris, a street in a red-light district.

9.862 (208:7). Sabellius, the African – See 1.659n.

9.862 (208:7–8). subtlest heresiarch of all the beasts of the field – After Genesis 3:1: "Now the serpent was more subtil than any beast of the field which the Lord God had made."

9.863–64 (208:9–10). The bulldog of Aquin . . . refutes him – St. Thomas Aquinas was a Dominican; thus the pun *Domini canis*, "dog of God": "bulldog" in honor of the tenacity of his grip; "of Aquin" since he came from the great Neapolitan family of Aquino. Among many "refutations" of Sabellius in the *Summa Theologica*, the principal one is Prima Secundae, Query 31, where St. Thomas pairs the heresies of Arius and Sabellius; he argues: "To avoid the heresy of Sabellius, we must shun the term *singularity*, lest we take away the communicability of the Divine Essence. . . . The word *solitary* is also to be avoided, lest we take away the society of the Three Persons; for, as Hilary says, *We confess neither a solitary nor a diverse god.*"

9.866 (208:12). Rutlandbaconsouthamptonshakespeare – Three leading candidates for the role of Shakespeare's ghostwriter: Roger

Manners (1576–1612), fifth earl of Rutland; Sir Francis Bacon (1561–1626); and Henry Wriothesley (1573–1624), third earl of Southampton. Many who have remained unconvinced that Shakespeare authored the plays have been what Samuel Schoenbaum has called "groupists" (*Shakespeare's Lives* [New York, 1970], pp. 591ff.)—among them are Delia Bacon, who imagined that in addition to Bacon, Raleigh and others were in on the deception (see 9.410n), and the New York City lawyer (James) Appleton Morgan (1846–1928), who believed that a consortium of noblemen, including Southamptom, Raleigh, Essex, Rutland, and Montgomery (ibid, p. 592), wrote the plays and used that prompt-book "copyist" Shakespeare as front man.

9.866–67 (208:12–13). another poet of the same name in the comedy of errors – In Shakespeare's *Comedy of Errors*, the comic confusion depends in part on the fact that two of the central characters are identical twins, both named Antipholus (their attendants are also identical twins, both named Dromio).

9.870–71 (208:17–18). nature, as Mr Magee understands . . . abhors perfection – W. K. Magee (pseudonym John Eglinton) in *Pebbles from a Brook* (Dublin, 1901), p. 45: "Nature abhors perfection. Things perfect in their way, whether manners, poetry, painting, scientific methods, philosophical systems, architecture, ritual, are only so by getting into some backwater or shoal out of eternal currents, where life has ceased to circulate. The course of time is fringed with perfections but bears them not upon its bosom."

9.873 (208:20–21). a merry puritan, through the twisted eglantine – "Puritan" involves not only another reference to Magee's bachelorhood and to his Protestant clergyman father, but also to Milton and the lines from "L'Allegro" that describe the lark at dawn, greeting the speaker: "Through the Sweet-Briar, or the Vine, / Or the twisted Eglantine."

9.875 (208:23). Himself his own father – See Sabellius, 1.659n.

9.876 (208:25). Pallas Athena! – In Greek mythology, the goddess of mother-wit and wisdom, born from Zeus's forehead. She is, of course, guardian angel and patron saint of Odysseus and his family in *The Odyssey*.

9.876–77 (208:25). The play's the thing! –

Hamlet soliloquizes on his improvised plot to trap the king into revealing himself; Hamlet plans to have some aspects of Claudius's murder of King Hamlet repeated in a play: "The play's the thing / Wherein I'll catch the conscience of the King" (II.ii.633–634).

9.877 (208:25–26). parturiate – Rare: "to bring forth young, to fructify."

9.879–80 (208:28–29). his mother's name lives in the forest of Arden – Mary Arden, Shakespeare's mother. The forest of Arden was both a real forest in England and the idealized pastoral-romantic setting of *As You Like It*. Shakespeare accepted the name Arden from his principal source for the play, Thomas Lodge's (c. 1558–1625) *Rosalynde, Euphues' Golden Legacy* (1590).

9.880–81 (208:29–30). Her death brought . . . Volumnia in *Coriolanus* – Mary Arden Shakespeare was buried 9 September 1608, and 1608 is generally accepted as the year when *Coriolanus* was first produced on stage. Volumnia, Coriolanus's mother, strikes the modern reader as the prideful, overbearing woman who will not relinquish her hold on her son. But times have changed: both Brandes (pp. 532–33) and Harris (p. 353) regard Volumnia as "sublime," "the most noble mother of the world" as Coriolanus calls her (V.iii.49), and both link the characterization of Volumnia with Shakespeare's affection for his mother. The scene to which Stephen refers is Act V, scene iii: Coriolanus, having defected from Rome, is on the verge of conquering the city for its enemies. Volumnia comes as a suppliant and appeals to Coriolanus's filial loyalty; that loyalty triumphs over his desire for revenge on Rome (and sends Coriolanus to his death).

9.881–82 (208:30–31). His boyson's death . . . in King John – Hamnet Shakespeare died in August 1596. Both Harris (pp. 58, 339–40) and Brandes (pp. 140–49) date *King John* 1596–97, and both link Shakespeare's treatment of the child Arthur with grief at the death of his son. Central to the play is the pathos of Arthur's innocence when he is at the mercy of his uncle, King John.

9.882 (208:31). Hamlet, the black prince – At his first appearance (I.ii), Hamlet, still mourning his father's death, is dressed in black. There is also a reference to Edward, the Black Prince of England (1330–76), who never succeeded to the throne because his father, Edward III (1312–77), outlived him.

9.882–83 (208:32–33). Who the girls . . . are we know – See 9.421–22n.

9.883–84 (208:33–34). Who Cleopatra, fleshpot . . . we may guess – That is, the three seductive heroines—Cleopatra in *Antony and Cleopatra*, Cressida in *Troilus and Cressida*, and Venus in *Venus and Adonis*—are all "modeled" on Anne Hathaway. For "fleshpot of Egypt" (Exodus 16:3), see 3.177–78n.

9.892 (208:42). mess – To "mess" is obsolete or dialect for to portion out food, to serve a dish.

9.894 (209:2). Gilbert, Edmund, Richard – Gilbert Shakespeare (b. 1566) apparently outlived William, but the date of his death was not recorded; Edmund Shakespeare (1580–1607); Richard Shakespeare (1574–1613).

9.894–97 (209:2–6). Gilbert in his old age . . . a man on's back – The spelling in this sentence imitates a Warwickshire dialect. "Maister Gatherer" is the collector of the entrance fee; "mass" is a dialect curse short for "by the mass." Lee (p. 42) repeats a story from William Oldys (1696–1761), the English antiquary, to the effect that one of Shakespeare's brothers, "presumably Gilbert," saw Shakespeare play the part of Adam, a servant, in *As You Like It*. The "cavaliers" are Stephen's "local color," emphasizing the disparity between Shakespeare's art and the philistinism of his "Puritan" family. Stephen also improves on the part Shakespeare was supposed to have played, casting him in the role of the more important Orlando, who, as a talented amateur, successfully wrestles with the old pro (I.ii.158–242). Needless to say, *As You Like It* is not a play about wrestling.

9.897 (209:6). The playhouse sausage – See 9.157n.

9.901 (209:10). What's in a name? – Juliet to Romeo when she discovers he is a Montague: "'Tis but thy name that is my enemy; / . . . O, be some other name! / What's in a name?" (II.ii.38–42).

9.908–9 (209:18–19). *Then outspoke . . . medical Davy* . . . – Another fragment from Oliver St. John Gogarty's unpublished bawdy poem "Medical Dick and Medical Davy." The poem plays Dick's extraordinary sexual prowess off against Davy's extraordinary financial prowess.

9.911–12 (209:21–22). In his trinity . . . in King Lear – "Black Wills" because all three villains assert that their villainies are willful, conscious acts. "Shakebags" is slang for thieves or pickpockets. Iago is the villain in *Othello;* Richard Crookback is Richard III in the play; and Edmund, the bastard son of Gloucester in *King Lear,* while hardly the play's only villain, still emerges as a central image of stark and willful human perversity. Black Will and Shakebag are the names of the hired killers in *Arden of Feversham* (1592), an anonymous tragedy of ordinary life in Elizabethan England (Heather Dukrow Ousby and Ian Ousby, *JJQ* 14, no. 4 [1977]: 482–83).

9.913–14 (209:23–24). that last play . . . dying in Southwark – The Stationers' Register, 26 November 1607, records *King Lear* as having been presented at court during Christmastime in 1606. Edmund Shakespeare was buried at St. Saviour's Church in Southwark, 31 December 1607.

9.919 (209:30). But he that filches . . . my good name . . . . – Iago to Othello: "Good name in man and woman, dear my lord, / Is the immediate jewel of their souls: / Who steals my purse steals trash; . . . / But he that filches from me my good name / Robs me of that which not enriches him / And makes me poor indeed" (III.iii.155–61).

9.921–22 (209:32–33). He has hidden . . . a clown there – Characters named William are impressive neither for their numbers nor their roles in Shakespeare's plays: William de la Pole, the earl of Suffolk, one of the contending lords in *I and II Henry VI;* two retainers, Sir William Lucy and Sir William Glansdale, in *I Henry VI,* and a William Stafford in *II Henry VI;* William Page, a boy, briefly the instrument of comedy at the expense of middle-class attitudes toward learning in *The Merry Wives of Windsor* (IV.i); William, a country bumpkin in love with Audrey, a country wench, in *As You Like It;* an offstage "cousin William" of Shallow's has become a "good scholar" at Oxford in *II Henry IV* (III.ii); and there is a cook named William in *II Henry IV*. "A fair name" is from *As You Like It:* "TOUCHSTONE: Is thy name William? WILLIAM: William, sir. TOUCHSTONE: A fair name" (V.i.23–25).

9.922–23 (209:33–34). as a painter of old . . . corner of his canvas – In Browning's dramatic monologue "Fra Lippo Lippi," from *Men and Women* (1855), as that painter describes the composition of a painting, "The Coronation of the Virgin," that he intends to complete: "Well, all these / Secured at their devotion, up shall come / Out of a corner when you least expect, / As one by a dark stair into a great light, / Music and talking, who but Lippo! I— / Mazed, motionless and moonstruck, I'm the man! / Back I shrink" (lines 359–64). Browning assumed that the figure in the "dark corner" was a self-portrait by Lippi; modern art historians think it portrays Lippi's patron.

9.923–24 (209:34–210:1). *He has revealed . . . will in overplus – As in Sonnet 135, lines 1–2: "Whoever hath her wish, thou hast thy 'Will,' / And 'Will' to boot, and 'Will' in overplus"; see also Sonnets 136 and 143.

9.924 (210:1–2). *Like John o'Gaunt – In *Richard II*, John of Gaunt on the eve of his death repeatedly puns on his name (II.i.73–83), as "Old Gaunt indeed, and gaunt in being old" (line 74).

9.924–25 (210:2–3). the coat of arms he toadied for – Both Harris (pp. 378–79) and Brandes (pp. 152–53) assert that the Shakespeares were not really entitled to a coat of arms and that John ("prompted" by his son) went through a variety of questionable maneuvers (1596–99) to secure the coat of arms and the social rank that it implied.

9.925 (210:3). on a bend sable a spear or steeled argent – Shakespeare's coat of arms: "Gold on a bend sable, a spear of the first, and for his crest or cognizance a falcon, his wings displayed argent, standing on a wreath of his colors, supporting a spear gold steeled as aforesaid." A "bend" is a diagonal bar, one-fifth the width of the shield, from upper left to lower right as one faces the shield. The motto: *Non sans droict* (Not without right).

9.926 (210:4). honorificabilitudinitatibus – Latin: "in the condition of being loaded with honors." The word, as the longest Latin word, is a scholarly joke. Shakespeare uses it once in a comic scene in *Love's Labour's Lost* (V.i.44).

9.926–27 (210:4–5). greatest shakescene in the country – From Robert Greene's denunciation of Shakespeare; see 9.130n.

9.927 (210:5). What's in a name – See 9.901n.

9.928–32 (210:7–12). A star, a daystar . . . eastward of the bear – The Danish astronomer Tycho Brahe (1546–1601) discovered a supernova above the small star Delta in the W-shaped constellation Cassiopeia, 11 November 1572, when Shakespeare was eight and a half years old. The nova, called Tycho's star, brightened rapidly until it outshone all the other stars and planets at night and was visible in daylight; it began to fade in December 1572. Delta is at the bottom of the left-hand loop of the W. "Firedrake" is an obsolete word for meteor. Raphael Holinshed (*Chronicles* [1587], vol. 3, p. 1257 [see 9.983–84n]) remarks that the phenomenon lasted "for the space of almost sixteen months," or until March 1574, when Shakespeare was almost ten years old. The supernova caused considerable imaginative excitement in Elizabethan England as a sort of Star of Bethlehem, heralding a new birth, the second coming of Christ. *Eastward of the bear:* when the Great Bear (or Big Dipper) is in the northwestern sky west of the North Star, Cassiopeia is in the southeast.

9.934 (210:13). Shottery – A village in Warwickshire in the parish of Stratford where Anne Hathaway lived before her marriage. According to Lee (p. 18), the village "was reached from Stratford by field-paths."

9.936 (210:15). he was nine years old when it was quenched – See 9.928–32n.

9.938 (210:17). to be wooed and won – The earl of Suffolk speaks to Reignier, the duke of Anjou, on behalf of Henry VI: "Thy daughter shall be wedded to my king; / Whom I with pain [difficulty] have woo'd and won thereto" (*I Henry VI* V.iii.137–38).

9.938 (210:17). meacock – An effeminate or spiritless man. Shakespeare uses the word once, in *The Taming of the Shrew*, when Petruchio is accounting for his sudden success in winning the shrew, Katharina: " 'Tis a world to see, / How tame, when men and women are alone, / A meacock wretch can make the curstest shrew" (II.i.313–15).

9.939 (210:19). *Autontimorumenos – Greek: "self-tormentor"; as *Heauton Timorumenos*, the title of a play (163 B.C.) by the Latin playwright Terence (c. 190–c. 159 B.C.). Terence's play was based on a similarly titled play by the Greek Menander (c. 342–291 B.C.), only fragments of which exist. Cf. Charles Baudelaire's "L'heautinouroumenos" from *Les fleurs du mal* [1857; trans. Robert Howard [Boston, 1982], p. 79), in which the speaker promises to butcher "you" without emotion, to "frolic in your tears," and to lacerate himself in "the greedy Irony" of the process (suggested by Theoharis Constantine Theoharis). See the self-lacerating Antisthenes, 7.1035n.

9.939 (210:19). *Bous Stephanoumenos* – Schoolboy Greek: "Ox- or bull-soul of Stephen"; what Stephen's school friends call to him as he passes on his way to the beach (and his decision to become an artist) in *A Portrait* 4:C. The friends link the phrase with "Bous Stephaneforos": "crowned ox or bull [as garland-bearer for a sacrifice]."

9.940 (210:20). configuration – In astrology, the relative position of planets and stars at an individual's birth; the configuration predetermines character and career.

9.940 (210:20–21). Stephen, Stephen, cut the bread even – Iona and Peter Opie list a variant of this ("loaf" for "bread") under "scraps of doggerel . . . associated with particular names" in *The Lore and Language of Schoolchildren* (London, 1959), p. 160.

9.940–41 (210:21–22). S.D: *sua donna . . . di non amare S.D.* – Italian: "S.D.: his woman. Oh sure—his. Gelindo [a man's name] resolves not to love S.D." The second "S.D." can be read as Stephen's initials but also as *sua donna*, "his woman"; that is, Stephen can be read as he who is cold and unloving.

9.944 (210:25). a pillar of cloud by day – From Exodus 13:21; see 7.865–66n.

9.947 (210:28). *Stephanos* – Greek: "crown or garland"; see 4.1n.

9.952 (210:35). Fabulous artificer – Daedalus, the mythological Greek inventor; see 1.34n.

9.953 (210:36). Newhaven-Dieppe – The route by which Stephen crossed the English Channel on his way from Dublin to Paris.

9.953 (210:36–37). Lapwing. Icarus – As Daedalus's "son," Stephen may well be Icarus, who pridefully flew too high and plunged to his death in the sea, but he may also be "Lapwing." Ovid, in his account of the flight of Daedalus and the fall of Icarus, concludes by describing Daedalus's mourning and his burial of his son:

"As he was consigning the body of his ill-fated son to the tomb, a chattering lapwing[3] looked out from a muddy ditch and clapped her wings uttering a joyful note" (Ovid, *Metamorphoses* 8:236–38). Ovid identifies the "lapwing" as Daedalus's nephew and apprentice, who showed so much inventive promise that Daedalus grew jealous and threw him from the Acropolis "with a lying tale that the boy had fallen." "Athena, who favors the quick-witted, caught the boy up and made him a bird, and clothed him with feathers in midair. His old quickness of wit passed into his wings and legs, but he kept the name which he had before. Still the bird does not lift her body high in flight . . . but she flutters along near the ground and lays her eggs in hedgerows; and remembering that old fall, she is ever fearful of lofty places" (8:252–59). The lapwing is so called in English after the jerky motions of its wings in flight. In the Bible it is listed, together with the bat, as a bird "to be held in abomination among the fowls" "and not to be eaten" (Leviticus 11:19 and Deuteronomy 14:18). According to Robert Graves (*The White Goddess* [New York, 1948], pp. 36–37), in Celtic mythology the lapwing, as "Disguise the Secret," is associated with the stag or roebuck ("Hide the Secret") and the dog ("Guard the Secret"). See 1.112n, 3.311n, and 3.336–37n.

In *Hamlet*, after the courtier-fop Osric delivers to Hamlet Laertes' challenge for a fencing

---

3 There is a potential confusion here, since Ovid's word is *perdix*, the Latin root for the French *perdrix* and the English *partridge*. Frank Justus Miller, in his translation of the *Metamorphoses* (London, 1916) renders the word *perdix* as "lapwing," as does *An Elementary Latin Dictionary*, by Charlton T. Lewis (New York, 1890). On the other hand, *A New Latin Dictionary*, edited by E. A. Andrews and revised by Charles Short and Charlton T. Lewis (!) (New York, 1888), lists *perdix* as "partridge." The confusion stems in part from the "imprecision" of bird names in classical Latin; there is no listed name for lapwing before Linnaeus, and the way Ovid describes the habits of the *perdix* (see above quotation) can apply equally well to both the lapwing and the partridge. As late as 1910 the French and Italian for *partridge* were locally applied to a wide variety of birds of similar habits but of different families, including not only partridges but also lapwings and plovers. Another potential confusion derives from the fact that some versions of the Daedalus story give the name *Perdix* to Daedalus's sister and the name *Talos* or *Talus* to the nephew; Ovid recounts the metamorphosis of the nephew into a *perdix*. Whether Joyce was aware of the confusion or not, we do not know; but *lapwing* (repeated five times in the space of a page) is easily the richer in suggestive connotations.

match, Horatio remarks: "This lapwing runs away with the shell on his head [he is so newly hatched]." Hamlet responds that Osric is merely a super-conformist to the self-serving manners of the courtier (V.ii.185–94). The fencing imagery (duel of wits) that follows in Scylla and Charybdis sustains the allusion to *Hamlet*.

9.954 (210:37). Pater, ait – Latin: "Father, he cries." Stephen imagines Icarus's cry as he falls. "His lips, calling to the last upon his father's name, were drowned in the dark blue sea" (Ovid, *Metamorphoses* 8:229, 235). In Luke 23:46, Jesus on the cross is described: "And Jesus crying with a loud voice, said Father, into thy hands I commend my spirit" (Douay; in the Latin Vulgate: *Et clamans uoce magna Iesus ait: Pater, in manus tuas commendo spiritum meum.*)

9.954 (210:37). Seabedabbled – In Shakespeare's *Venus and Adonis*, Venus describes a hare exhausted in the hunt as "dewbedabbled" (line 703) (Erlene Stetson, *JJQ* 19, no. 2 [1982]: 176).

9.954 (210:37). Weltering – In Book 1 of Milton's *Paradise Lost*, the "companions of [Satan's] fall" (line 76) are described as they begin to recover themselves on the burning lake of hell, and Satan "soon discerns, welt'ring by his side . . . Beelzebub" (lines 78–81).

9.956–57 (210:40–41). that brother motif . . . the old Irish myths – The story of three brothers, two of whom are cruel and vicious, the third, virtuous and successful, does recur in Irish mythology and folklore.

9.957–59 (210:42–211:2). The three brothers . . . wins the best prize – The two brothers Grimm, Jakob (1785–1863) and Wilhelm (1786–1859), were noted for their collection of medieval fairy and folk tales. The brother motif does recur in their stories but not in "The Sleeping Beauty," which Mr. Best cites.

9.960 (211:3). Best brothers – Best and Best, 24 Frederick Street, were among the most well known of Irish solicitors.

9.967 (211:10). Father Dineen – Father Patrick S. Dineen (1860–1934), an Irish-speaking writer, translator, editor, and philologist. *Irish Literature* (ed. Justin McCarthy, Maurice Egan, and Douglas Hyde [New York, 1904], p. 4025) describes him as "the most earnest writer of the Gaelic movement." By 1904 he had collected the works of several "classical" modern Irish poets,

written novels and plays in Irish, compiled an Irish–English dictionary, and collaborated in a translation of Geoffrey Keating's (c. 1570–c. 1644) *History of Ireland.*

9.969 (211:12). rectly – "Rect" is obsolete for right, straight, or erect, after the Latin *rectus,* "straight."

9.973 (211:16). two noble kinsmen – *The Two Noble Kinsmen* (c. 1613), by Shakespeare's "pupil" and "official successor" in the Globe Theatre, John Fletcher (1579–1625). It is generally assumed that Shakespeare had a minor role as collaborator with Fletcher in the composition of the play.

9.973 (211:17). nuncle – Obsolete or dialect: "uncle."

9.977 (211:21). Where is your brother? Apothecaries' hall – Stanislaus Joyce, who appears as Maurice Daedalus in *Stephen Hero* (but is phased out of *A Portrait*), had a clerkship at Apothecaries' Hall, 40 Mary Street; he quit 30 January 1904. See Ellmann (p. 144).

9.977–78 (211:21–22). My whetstone. Him, then Cranly, Mulligan – "Whetstone" continues the image of the duel of wits from 9.970 (211:13). The sequence represents the sequence of Stephen's intellectual companions: first Maurice, who is described in *Stephen Hero* (p. 26) as "having aided the elder Stephen bravely in the building of an entire science of aesthetic. . . . Stephen found Maurice very useful for raising objections." Maurice was then displaced from his role as discussant by Cranly (chapter 5, *A Portrait*), who in turn, suspected by Stephen of betrayal at the end of *A Portrait*, is displaced in favor of Mulligan; and now Mulligan has become suspect. Stephen omits one "whetstone" from his list: Lynch (see *A Portrait*, chapter 5, and *Ulysses*, Oxen of the Sun and Circe). Compare also Celia's remark in *As You Like It*, "for always the dullness of the fool is the whetstone of the wits" (I.ii.54–55).

9.981 (211:25–26). the voice of Esau. My kingdom for a drink – Richard III, unhorsed, his army crushed by the Tudors and their forces, shouts in desperation: "A horse! A horse! My kingdom for a horse!" (V.iv.7, 13). This in turn links with Esau, the older son of Isaac, who sold his birthright to his younger brother, Jacob, for "a mess of pottage" (Genesis 25:27–34). Jacob, encouraged and disguised by his mother, deceives his blind and dying father and receives the blessing that was rightfully Esau's as first-born son. "And Jacob went near unto Isaac his father; and he felt him, and said, The voice is Jacob's voice, but the hands are the hands of Esau" (Genesis 27:22).

9.983–84 (211:28–29). the chronicles from which he took the stuff of his plays – The data for most of Shakespeare's historical plays (including some aspects of *Macbeth, King Lear,* and *Cymbeline*) was derived from Raphael Holinshed's (d. c. 1580) *Chronicles* (1578), a history of England, Scotland, and Ireland.

9.985–86 (211:30–32). Richard, a whoreson . . . whoreson merry widow – In Shakespeare's *Richard III*, the hunchbacked Richard, duke of Gloucester and brother of Edward IV, is portrayed as having caused the deaths of Lady Anne's husband, Edward, Prince of Wales, and her father-in-law, Henry VI. In Act I, Gloucester intercepts Anne, who as chief mourner is following the corpse of Henry VI, and in a scene of ironic and shocking reversals takes "her in her heart's extremest hate" (I.ii.232) and achieves her promise of marriage—as he soliloquizes at the end of the scene: "Was ever woman in this humor woo'd? / Was ever woman in this humor won?" (lines 228–29). Anne was, of course, anything but a "merry widow." Shakespeare portrays her as sincere in her mourning and as embittered by her hatred of Gloucester; thus her "conversion" is reaction rather than a widow's traditional irresponsibility. For "What's in a name?" see 9.901n. A "whoreson" means literally a bastard; figuratively, a villainous person. *The Merry Widow* is the English title of *Die lustige Witwe* (1905), a light opera by the Hungarian composer Franz Lehar (1870–1948). The widow is truly merry, and the opera, truly light, became an international favorite immediately after its premiere.

9.987 (211:32–33). Richard the conqueror . . . William the conquered – A play on the anecdote about Shakespeare and Richard Burbage; see 9.632–37n. Richard III was the third of three brothers. He achieves the death of the second brother, Clarence, and when Edward IV, the first brother, dies, he maneuvers his way to the throne. Richard Shakespeare was also "a third brother" (since Stephen has eliminated Gilbert); and William Shakespeare was "conquered" by Anne Hathaway.

9.988 (211:34). The other four acts . . . from that first – That is, the initial explosion of Richard III's villainy and perversity in Act I (he

woos Anne, whom his treachery has widowed, and accomplishes fratricide) overshadows the sequence of villainies that follows—a partially defensible critical commonplace about the play.

9.988–89 (211:35–36). Of all his kings . . . Shakespeare's reverence – Another critical commonplace. The argument is that in the history plays, except *Richard III* (unless one also includes *Macbeth*), Shakespeare, while he hardly presents the kings as infallible, does essentially portray them in a sympathetic light.

9.989–90 (211:36). reverence, the angel of the world – In *Cymbeline*, Belarius speaks to Cymbeline's sons, Guiderius and Arviragus, about the burial of Cloten, Cymbeline's stepson and a villainous fool: "He was a queen's son, boys; / And though he came our enemy, remember / He was paid for that: though mean and mighty, rotting / Together, have one dust, yet reverence, / That angel of the world, doth make distinction / Of place 'tween high and low. Our foe was princely; / And though you took his life, as being our foe, / Yet bury him as a prince" (IV.ii.244–51).

9.990–92 (211:36–39). Why is the underplot . . . older than history? – Shakespeare combined the story of King Lear's pre-Christian reign as he found it in Holinshed's *Chronicles* with the story of an honorable duke who is deceived into repudiating his honest son in favor of the villainous son who reduces him to misery and blindness; the latter story Shakespeare lifted from Sir Philip Sidney's *Arcadia* (1590), Book 2, chapter 10: "The pitiful state and story of the Paphlagonian unkind king." Both Brandes (p. 453) and Lee (p. 241) remark on Shakespeare's indebtedness to Sidney, but only Brandes remarks that the Lear story "bears a distinctly Celtic impress" (p. 452). "Spatchocked" (usually spelled "spatchcock"), according to *A Classical Dictionary of the Vulgar Tongue* by Capt. Francis Grose (1785), involves an abbreviation of "dispatch cook," an Irish dish prepared in an emergency; thus it means to insert, interpolate, or sandwich (a phrase, sentence, etc.).

9.994 (211:42). George Meredith – English novelist and poet; see 9.550–51n.

9.995 (211:42). *Que voulez vous?* Moore would say – French: "What do you wish [one to do about it]?" For Moore, see 9.274n; one by-product of Moore's Paris period was his habit of larding his conversation with French phrases.

9.995 (211:42–212:1). He puts Bohemia on the seacoast – A much-cited boner in *The Winter's Tale* (see Brandes, p. 636, and Lee, p. 251). Shakespeare apparently accepted it from Robert Greene's *Pandosto, the Triumph of Time* (1588), which supplied the plot for the play.

9.995–96 (212:1–2). and makes Ulysses quote Aristotle – Another of Shakespeare's anachronisms, though it is Hector and not Ulysses who "quotes" Aristotle in *Troilus and Cressida* (II.ii.166). The joke is that Aristotle lived centuries after the Trojan War, which is the ostensible setting of the play.

9.999 (212:5–6). *what the poor are not, always with him – After Jesus, "For ye have the poor always with you; but me ye have not always" (Matthew 26:11; also Mark 14:7 and John 12:8).

9.999–1002 (212:6–10). The note of banishment . . . drowns his book – *The Two Gentlemen of Verona* has proved a difficult play to date, but it is assumed to be among the earlier plays and to have been written and performed before 1598. The plot of the play does hinge in part on the banishment of Valentine, one of the two gentlemen, by the duke of Milan, the father of Valentine's beloved, Sylvia. *The Tempest* is generally treated as the last of Shakespeare's plays, and it too involves banishment, in this case of Prospero, the rightful duke of Milan, by his brother Antonio. Prospero's white magic transforms the island of his exile into the scene of purgatorial punishment for Antonio and Alonso, king of Naples, who conspired in Prospero's banishment. Prospero is ultimately reconciled with the regenerated Alonso and restored to his dukedom. He concludes by relinquishing his magic: "I'll break my staff, / Bury it certain fathoms in the earth, / And deeper than did ever plummet sound / I'll drown my book" (V.i.54–57).

9.1003–4 (212:11–12). protasis, epitasis, catastasis, catastrophe – Critical terms, descriptive of various parts of a play as established by the Alexandrine school (a Greek culture that flourished at Alexandria after the decline of Athens and well into the Roman period). *Protasis*: the opening lines of a drama in which the characters are introduced and the argument explained; *epitasis*: that part of a drama that de-velops the main action; *catastasis*: the height or acme of the action, which is followed by the *catastrophe*, the final event in a drama, as death in a tragedy or marriage in a comedy.

9.1005–6 (212:12–14). when his married daughter . . . accused of adultery – Lee (pp. 266–67) is the only one of Stephen's sources who refers to this event. Susanna had married a Dr. John Hall: "On July 15, 1613, Mrs. Hall preferred, with her father's assistance, a charge of slander against one Lane in the ecclesiastical court at Worcester; the defendant, who had apparently charged the lady with illicit relations with one Ralph Smith, did not appear and was excommunicated." *Chip of the old block*: one who reproduces his father's (or mother's) peculiarities or characteristics; the phrase dates from at least 1626.

9.1006–8 (212:14–17). But it was the original . . . bishops of Maynooth – The clerical center of Ireland is located at St. Patrick's College in the town of Maynooth, fifteen miles northeast of Dublin. Stephen quotes from the *Maynooth Catechism* (Dublin, 1882), Lesson 6, "On Original Sin"; see 9.462–64n.

9.1008–9 (212:17–18). like original sin, committed by another in whose sin he too has sinned – From the *Maynooth Catechism*, Lesson 6, p. 14: "Q. What evils befell us in consequence of the disobedience of our first parents? A. We were all made partakers of the sin and punishment of our first parents, as we should be all sharers in their innocence and happiness, if they had been obedient to God (Rom. v. 12)."

9.1009–10 (212:18–19). It is between . . . last written words – Refers to the fact that Anne Hathaway Shakespeare was initially omitted from Shakespeare's will and inserted between the lines; see 9.691–95n.

9.1010–11 (212:19–20). it is petrified . . . not to be laid – The lines on Shakespeare's tombstone: "Good friend for Jesus sake forbeare, / To digg the dust encloased heare! / Bleste be ye man yt spares thes stones, / And curst be he yt moves my bones." Harris (p. 362) argues that "Shakespeare wrote the verses in order to prevent his wife being buried with him" (which, incidentally, she was not). *Four bones*: an Irish expression for the four cardinal points of the body, head, hands, and feet; in other words, the physicality of the body.

9.1011/1012 (212:20–21/21–22). Age has not withered it / infinite variety – From Enobarbus's much-quoted praise of Cleopatra in *Antony and Cleopatra*: "Age cannot wither her, nor custom stale / Her infinite variety" (II.ii.240–41).

9.1013–14 (212:22–24). in *Much Ado* . . . *Measure for Measure* – Apparently, what has not been "withered" is "an original sin . . . committed by another in which he too has sinned." In *Much Ado About Nothing*, Claudio, one of the heroes, is duped by the villainous half-brother of the duke of Aragon into believing that his fiancée, Hero, has been false to him on the eve of their wedding; the consequent suspicion and confusion (including Hero's "banishment") take the play to the brink of tragedy before it is pivoted back into comedy. In *As You Like It*, Frederick, the duke's brother, has usurped the duke's dominions and banished him (before the play begins); in Act I, scene iii, Rosalind, the duke's daughter, is in turn banished by her uncle; and in Act II, scene iii, the young hero, Orlando, excites the jealousy of his brother and is forced to flee into exile. For *The Tempest*, see 9.999–1002n. In *Hamlet* it is Claudius's murder of his brother and usurpation of his wife and throne that so infect Hamlet's life and world. And the central "original sin" of *Measure for Measure* is the perverse conscientiousness and austerity of Angelo, deputy to the duke of Vienna. When Angelo condemns Claudio to death for incontinence, Claudio's sister, Isabella, intercedes on her brother's behalf, only to excite incontinent desire in Angelo himself. Angelo then offers a bargain: Isabella's "honor" for Claudio's life. The potential destructiveness of this dilemma is rather arbitrarily resolved in what is, at best, a "dark" comedy.

9.1018–19 (212:29). He is all in all – Echoes Hamlet's appraisal of his father: "He was a man, take him for all in all, / I shall not look upon his like again" (I.ii.187–88). Stephen's repetition of John Eglinton's phrase implies that Shakespeare is God in his own creation, or the Holy Ghost; see 15.2118n.

9.1021 (212:31–32). In *Cymbeline* . . . bawd and cuckold – Both plays involve intense jealous suspicion: Othello's fatal suspicion of Desdemona and Posthumus Leonatus's ultimately dispelled suspicion of Imogen in *Cymbeline*. In both cases the suspicion of the woman's behavior is aroused by a "bawd" (one who procures

women for illicit purposes)—Iago in *Othello* and Iachimo in *Cymbeline*.

9.1022–23 (212:33). like José he kills the real Carmen – In George Bizet's (1838–75) opera *Carmen* (1857), the hero, Don José, is swept off his feet by the gypsy Carmen, and when she abandons him for the more romantic toreador Escamillo, he kills her in a fit of jealous rage.

9.1023 (212:34). the hornmad Iago – To be "hornmad" is to suffer excessive jealous suspicion of one's wife. Othello would seem to be the hornmad one in the play, but Iago is also a candidate for the disease, since he suspects on the basis of no evidence whatsoever that both Othello and Cassio have cuckolded him (I.iii.392–96 and again II.i.304–16).

9.1024 (212:34–35). the moor in him – That is, the Othello in him. Othello, though vulnerable to the tragic suspicion that unmans him, "Is of a constant, loving, noble nature," as Iago says (II.i.298).

9.1025 (212:36–37). Cuckoo! Cuckoo! . . . O word of fear – "Cuck," as a verb, means to sound the cuckoo's note. Mulligan quotes from the refrain of Spring's song (one of the paired songs that ends *Love's Labour's Lost*, V.ii.904–21). The refrain: "The cuckoo then, on every tree, / Mocks married men; for thus sings he, / Cuckoo; / Cuckoo, cuckoo: / O word of fear, / Unpleasing to a married ear!" "Cuckoo" equals, of course, "cuckold."

9.1026 (212:38). reverbed – The verb *to reverb* (reecho) occurs once in Shakespeare, when Kent reproves King Lear for his rashness in rejecting Cordelia: "Thy youngest daughter does not love thee least; / Nor are those empty-hearted whose low sound / Reverbs no hollowness" (I.i.154–56).

9.1028–29 (212:40–41). Dumas *fils* (or is it Dumas *père*) . . . created most – Magee's second thought is right; it was the elder Alexandre Dumas (1802–70) in an essay, "Comment je devins auteur dramatique" (How I Became a Playwright): "I realized that Shakespeare's works alone included as many types as the works of all other playwrights taken together. I realized finally that he was the one man who had, after God, created most" (in *Souvenirs dramatiques* [Paris, 1836]).

9.1030 (212:42). Man delights not him nor woman neither – Hamlet describes his melancholy distaste for man and the world to Rosencrantz and Guildenstern: "Man delights not me; no, nor woman neither, though by your smiling you seem to say so" (II.ii.321–22).

9.1032 (213:2). man and boy – The First Gravedigger in *Hamlet* (V.i.161–62): "I have been sexton here, man and boy, thirty years" (Patrick A. McCarthy, *JJQ* 13, no. 1 [1975]: 56).

9.1032–33 (213:3). his journey of life ended – See 9.831n.

9.1033 (213:3–4). he plants his mulberry tree – Both Brandes (p. 681) and Lee (p. 194) cite the tradition (apocryphal?) that Shakespeare planted a mulberry tree in his garden at New Place.

9.1033–34 (213:4). The motion is ended – Juliet, when she mistakenly believes Romeo has been killed in a duel with Tybalt: "O, break, my heart! poor bankrupt, break at once! / To prison, eyes, ne'er look on liberty! / Vile earth, to earth resign; end motion here; / And thou and Romeo press one heavy bier!" (III.ii.57–60).

9.1034 (213:5). Hamlet *père* and Hamlet *fils* – French: "father . . . son"; after Dumas *père* and Dumas *fils*; see 9.1028–29n.

9.1035–36 (213:6–7). And, what though murdered and betrayed, bewept by all frail tender hearts for – Source unknown.

9.1038–39 (213:10). prosperous Prospero, the good man rewarded – At the end of *The Tempest*, Prospero is restored to his dukedom and all is resolved on a positive note. Stephen is playing, however, on the tradition that equates the magician-playwright Shakespeare with the magician Prospero, since both practice dramatic deception; thus Prospero's final speech (see 9.999–1002n) has frequently been read as Shakespeare's farewell to his audience and his art.

9.1039 (213:11). Lizzie, grandpa's lump of love – Elizabeth Hall, Shakespeare's first grandchild, born in 1608. For "lump of love," see 3.88 (39:14).

9.1039 (213:11). nuncle Richie – Not only

Shakespeare's brother, who died in 1613; see also 3.76 (39:2).

9.1040 (213:12–13). where the bad niggers go – After the chorus of Stephen Foster's (1826–64) song "Old Uncle Ned": "Den lay down de shubble and de hoe, / Hang up de fiddle and de bow, / No more hard work for poor old Ned, / He's gone whar de good niggers [variants: darkies, people] go."

9.1041 (213:13). Strong curtain – In the tradition of the "well-made play," a "strong curtain" is a line that ends an act or scene with a surprise, thus building suspense for the next scene.

9.1042–44 (213:14–17). Maeterlinck says: . . . *his steps will tend* – Maurice Maeterlinck (1862–1949), a Belgian symbolist poet and dramatist, in *La sagesse et la destinée* (Wisdom and Destiny) (Paris, 1899): "Let us never forget that nothing happens to us which is not of the same nature as ourselves. . . . If Judas goes out this evening, he will move toward Judas and will have occasion to betray; but if Socrates opens his door, he will find Socrates asleep on the doorstep and will have the occasion to be wise" (p. 28).

9.1046–48 (213:20–22). The playwright who . . . two days later) – See 9.1028–29n. In the account of creation (Genesis 1:1–19), God creates light on the first day, the sun and the moon on the fourth day.

9.1048–50 (213:23–24). whom the most Roman . . . in all of us – *Dio boia*, Italian: literally, "hangman god"; figuratively, cruel god (or god of wrath), a common Roman expression for the force that frustrates human hopes and destinies. For "all in all," see 9.1018–19n.

9.1051–52 (213:25–27). economy of heaven . . . a wife unto himself – Combines allusions to *Hamlet* and to Matthew. In the "nunnery scene," Hamlet overscolds Ophelia: "Go to, I'll no more on't; it hath made me mad. I say, we will have no more marriages: those that are married already, all but one, shall live; the rest shall keep as they are. To a nunnery, go" (III.i.153–57). In Matthew, the Sadducees, "which say there is no resurrection" (22:23), attempt to trap Jesus by asking, If a woman has seven husbands, which will be her husband "in the resurrection?" Jesus answers, "In the resurrection they neither marry, nor are given in marriage, but are as the angels of God in heaven" (22:30).

9.1053 (213:28). *Eureka!* – Greek: "I have found (it)!"; what Archimedes is supposed to have said when, seated in his tub, he discovered the secret to determining specific gravity.

9.1056 (213:31). The Lord has spoken to Malachi – Recalls Malachi 1:1: "The burden of the word of the Lord to Israel by Malachi"; see 1.41n.

9.1059–60 (213:34–35). Those who are married . . . as they are – See 9.1051–52n.

9.1062–63 (213:38–39). they fingerponder . . . *Taming of the Shrew* – That is, they indulge minute examination of what might be considered an antifeminine play. The remark also recalls Swinburne's attack on Frederick J. Furnivall (1825–1910) and his New Shakespeare Society (1874): "metre-mongers, scholiasts, finger-counters, pedagogues, and figure-casters" ("The Three Stages of Shakespeare," *Fortnightly Review* 24 [1875]:615).

9.1065 (213:41–42). a French triangle – The relationship among the three people involved in an adultery; man-wife-lover, etc.

9.1065–67 (213:42–214:1). Do you believe your own theory? / —No, Stephen said promptly—See 9.228–29n.

9.1069 (214:3–4). the Platonic dialogues Wilde wrote – Two of the four essays in Oscar Wilde's *Intentions* (London, 1891)—"The Decay of Lying" and "The Critic as Artist"—are cast in the form of dialogue. *The Portrait of Mr. W. H.* (see 9.523–24n), Wilde's enigmatic study of the Shakespeare of the sonnets, is cast in the form of a prose narrative that recounts a dialogue. Wilde exploits the dialogue's potential for witty, enigmatic reversals, but only in the most superficial sense is his use of the dialogue "like Plato's." See 1.146n.

9.1070 (214:5). Eclecticon – The pun implies that John Eglinton's views are an eclectic compilation of then-current points of view.

9.1072–73 (214:8). Dowden believes . . . mystery in *Hamlet* – Edward Dowden, *Shakespeare: A Critical Study of His Mind and Art* (London, 1857), p. 126: "The mystery, the baffling vital obscurity of the play, and in particular of the character of its chief person, make it evident that Shakespeare had left far behind him that early stage of development when an artist obtrudes his intentions, or, distrusting his own ability to keep sight of one uniform design, deliberately and with effort holds that design persistently before him. . . . Hamlet might have been so easily manufactured into an enigma, or a puzzle; and then the puzzle, if sufficient pains were bestowed, could be completely taken to pieces and explained. But Shakespeare created it a mystery, and therefore it is forever suggestive; forever suggestive, and never wholly explicable."

9.1073–75 (214:9–11). Herr Bleibtreu . . . the Stratford monument – Karl Bleibtreu (1859–1928), a German poet, critic, and dramatist, argued in *Die Lösung der Shakespeare-Frage* (The Solution of the Shakespeare Question) (Berlin, 1907) that Shakespeare's plays were written by Roger Manners (1576–1612), the fifth earl of Rutland. Bleibtreu was hardly first in the field, but he was considerably more assertive than D. H. Madden (see 9.582–83n). From the outset the Baconians had argued that Shakespeare's epitaph "proved" that the secret of the authorship of his plays was buried with him in "the Stratford monument"; see 9.1010–11n. For a coincidence re Bleibtreu, see 4.199n. See also Ellmann, p. 411, and Adams, p. 8.

9.1075 (214:11–12). the present duke – John James Robert Manners (1818–1906), the seventh duke of Rutland (1888–1906) (dukedom created 1703), an English member of Parliament and statesman, published, among other things, *English Ballads*, "a volume of graceful verse."

9.1078 (214:15). I believe, O Lord, help my unbelief – From Mark 9:24: "Lord, I believe; help thou mine unbelief," said to Jesus by the father of a child about to be miraculously cured of a "dumb spirit."

9.1079 (214:16–17). *Egomen* – Greek: "I on the one hand." In context, "Egomen" involves a pun on the magazine the *Egoist*, which began installment publication of *A Portrait of the Artist as a Young Man* on 2 February 1914, thus helping Joyce "to believe" (in himself). This would make the "other chap" (9.1079–80 [214:17]), among others, George Roberts, the Dublin publisher and bookseller who had been so timid about publishing *Dubliners*. The *Egoist* was founded by Dora Marsden as the *Freewoman* in 1911; in 1913 she changed the title to the *New Freewoman*, and then, urged by Ezra Pound and other *men* to "mark the character of your paper as an organ of individualists of both sexes, and of the individualist principle in every department of life," she renamed it the *Egoist*, or Egomen.

9.1081 (214:18). the only contributor to *Dana* who – Joyce had a poem in the fourth issue of *Dana* (August 1904), printed over his own name: "Song" ("My love is in a light attire"). The poem is number 7 in *Chamber Music* (London, 1907).

9.1084 (214:21). Fraidrine. Two pieces of silver – "Fraidrine" mimicks Fred Ryan's pronunciation of his own name. Stephen recalls that he had borrowed "two shillings" from Ryan (2.256 [31:2–3]).

9.1088–89 (214:28). upper Mecklenburgh street – Tyrone Street Upper in 1904; now Railway Street—the heart of Dublin's red-light district in 1904.

9.1089–90 (214:29). the *Summa contra Gentiles* – Short title for St. Thomas Aquinas's *Summa de Veritate Catholicae Fidei contra Gentiles* (Comprehensive Treatise on the Truth of the Catholic Faith against Unbelievers).

9.1090–91 (214:30–31). Fresh Nelly and Rosalie, the coalquay whore – Two of Oliver St. John Gogarty's contributions to Irish folklore; their identities were established in unpublished materials, though "Fresh Nellie, / For she had as wild a belly" makes a brief appearance on p. 105 of Gogarty's *Collected Poems* (New York, 1954).

9.1093 (214:33). wandering Aengus of the birds – Aengus, son of Dagda, the supreme god of the Tuatha de Danaan (Tribes of Dana; see 9.376n), was the Irish god of youth, beauty, and love. He is portrayed with the birds of inspiration hovering about his head. Continually in search of his ideal mate, who had appeared to him in a dream, in some versions of the legend he discovers her as a swan, transforms himself into a swan, and flies away with her. Mulligan's phrase recalls Yeats's poem "The Song of the Wandering Aengus" from *The Wind Among the Reeds* (1899) (*Collected Poems* [New York, 1956], p. 57). It also echoes a phrase from Yeats's "The Old Age of Queen Maeve" (1903), "O Aengus of the birds" (line 101), when Maeve, the legendary mortal, promises the supernatural Aengus to aid him in carrying off his true love, the daughter of the "earthy house" (line 94) of Caer.

9.1098 (214:38–39). *Notre ami* Moore – The phrase recalls one of Edward Martyn's counterattacks on George Moore in which he remarks: "*Mon ami Moore* yearns to be *le génie de l'amitié*, but unfortunately he can never be looked upon as a friend. For he suffers from . . . a perennial condition of mental diarrhoea" (quoted in Edward Gwynn, *Edward Martyn and the Irish Revival* [London, 1930], p. 33).

9.1101 (214:41). French letters – Obviously French literature, but also slang for condoms.

9.1105 (215:4). Swill till eleven – 11:00 P.M. was closing time for Dublin pubs. The line recalls the weather forecaster's rhyme: "Rain after seven; rain till eleven."

9.1105 (215:4). *Irish nights entertainment – After Patrick J. McCall's (1861–1919) *The Fenian Nights' Entertainments* (1897), a collection of Ossianic legends written in peasant dialect and vaguely modeled on the *Arabian Nights*.

9.1106 (215:5). lubber – A clown, as well as a clumsy person.

9.1109 (215:8). I gall his kibe – Hamlet to Horatio about the gravedigger's verbal niceties: "the age is grown so picked [refined] that the toe of the peasant comes so near the heel of the courtier, he galls his kibe [he rubs a blister on the courtier's heel]" (V.i.151–54).

9.1110 (215:9). all amort – Elizabethan expression: "completely dejected." Used in *The Taming of the Shrew* (IV.iii.36) and *I Henry IV* (III.ii.124).

9.1111–12 (215:10–11). out of the vaulted cell into a shattering daylight – Out of the relatively dark interior of the librarian's office into the skylit foyer behind the circulation desk of the National Library.

9.1115–16 (215:14–15). Cashel Boyle . . . Tisdall Farrell – See 8.302n.

9.1116 (215:15). parafes – *Paraphs*: puts a flourish at the end of his signature to safeguard it against forgery.

9.1117 (215:17). priesteen – Irishism: "little priest."

9.1121 (215:21). A pleased bottom – Is Mulligan mocking Lyster as Bottom the Weaver in Shakespeare's *A Midsummer Night's Dream*—Bottom, "pleased" in converse with Titania, queen of the fairies, and all-unaware of his ass's head?

9.1122 (215:22). the turnstile – Gives access through the circulation desk in the main reading room to the library offices behind.

9.1123 (215:23). Blueribboned hat – Is this the Emma Clery of *Stephen Hero*, depersonalized to E. C., Emma, and "she" in *A Portrait?* At any rate, blue is a color-attribute of the Virgin Mary.

9.1124 (215:25). smoothsliding Mincius – Virgil mentions the Mincius River, near which he was born, as flowing among reeds on the plain of Lombardy (*Ecologues* 7:12). Milton, in "Lycidas" (lines 85–90), writes: "O Fountain *Arethuse*, and thou honor'd flood, / Smooth-sliding *Mincius*; crown'd with vocal reeds, / That strain I heard was of a higher mood: / But now my Oat proceeds, / And listens to the Herald of the Sea / That came in *Neptune's* plea" (i.e., Triton, Milton's "Herald of the Sea," had come to argue that the drowning of Lycidas was not Neptune's responsibility).

9.1125 (215:26). Puck – Or Robin Goodfellow, the mischievous but not malicious servant of Oberon, king of the fairies, in *A Midsummer Night's Dream*.

9.1126–27 (215:28–29). *John Eglinton . . . wed a wife?* – After Robert Burns's "John Anderson My Jo" (1789, 1790). The poem is addressed by a lover (wife) to her "jo," or sweetheart, Anderson, who is wrinkled and bald, and proposes that after many a happy day of climbing "the hill together . . . / We totter down, John, / And hand in hand we'll go, / And sleep thegither at the foot, / John Anderson my jo!"

9.1129 (215:31). Chin Chon Eg Lin Ton – After a song, "Chin Chin Chinaman," from the light opera *The Geisha* (see 6.355–57n). Chorus: "Chin Chin Chinaman / Muchee Muchee sad! / Me afraid allo trade / Wellee wellee bad! / Nose joke brokee broke / Makee shuttee shop! / Chin chin Chinaman / Chop, Chop, Chop" (sung by the proprietor of a tea shop).

9.1130 (215:32). plumber's hall – Local name for the Mechanic's Institute, 27 Abbey Street Lower. It was renovated during the summer of 1904 and opened in the fall as the Abbey Theatre, the new (and permanent) home of the Irish National Theatre Society.

9.1130–31 (215:33–34). Our players are creating . . . or M. Maeterlinck – Echoes remarks that Lady Gregory, Yeats, and others were making about the Irish National Theatre Society. See 9.1042–44n.

9.1132 (215:34–35). *the pubic sweat of monks – The Irish National Theatre Society fought running battles with Catholic (and Nationalist) objections and attempts to censor or suppress its plays.

9.1134 (215:37–38). the whipping lousy Lucy gave him – Lee (pp. 27–28), Brandes (pp. 10–11), and Harris (pp. 354–55) all affirm the tradition that Shakespeare was prosecuted, whipped, and perhaps imprisoned by Sir Thomas Lucy for deer stealing. Presumably Shakespeare fled to London to escape Lucy's continued attacks. Tradition also ascribes to Shakespeare a ballad at Lucy's expense; one recurrent line in the ballad: "Sing lowsie Lucy whatever befalle it."

9.1135 (215:38). *femme de trente ans* – French: "woman thirty years old"; figuratively, a woman of experience. The phrase is also the title of a novel (1831) by Honoré de Balzac (1799–1850).

9.1135 (215:38–39). And why no other children born? – Another speculative tradition is that Shakespeare visited Stratford at least once a year during the "London years" (1592?–1613). But the question remains: where was he after the births of his three children (Susanna in 1583, and the twins, Judith and Hamnet, in 1585, when Anne Hathaway Shakespeare was 29) and before he turned up in London? And if he was in or near Stratford, why no other children?

9.1137 (215:40). Afterwit – Obsolete for wisdom or perception that comes too late to be useful.

9.1139 (215:42). minion of pleasure – After Shakespeare's Sonnet 126 (sometimes regarded as the *envoi* of the "fair youth" sonnets): "Yet fear her [time-Nature], O thou minion of her pleasure!" (line 9).

9.1139 (215:42). Phedo's toyable fair hair – In Plato's *Phaedo*, Socrates fondles Phaedo's curls and teases him: "Tomorrow, I suppose, Phaedo, you will cut off this beautiful hair" (line 89). Socrates' tease involves the implication that

Phaedo's youthful arguments will go the way of the youth's hair.

9.1141 (216:2). Longworth and M'Curdy Atkinson – For Longworth, see 9.302n. F. M'Curdy Atkinson was one of the lesser of Dublin's literary lights; he, together with Longworth, shared a place in George Moore's "inner circle" and was on the periphery of the Irish National Theatre Society.

9.1142 (216:3). Puck Mulligan footed featly – Ariel is the "Puck" of *The Tempest;* he sings as he leads Ferdinand toward Prospero's cell: "Come unto these yellow sands, / And then take hands: / Curtsied when you have and kiss'd / The wild waves whist, / Foot it featly here and there; / And, sweet sprites, the burthen bear" (I.ii.376–81). Ferdinand wonders: "Where should this music be? i' the air or the earth?" (line 386).

9.1143–52 (216:4–13). *I hardly hear . . . they were worth* – A parody of the first stanza of Yeats's "Baile and Aillinn" (1903): "I hardly hear the curlew cry / Nor the grey rush when the wind is high, / Before my thoughts begin to run / On the heir of Uladh, Buan's son, / Baile, who had the honey mouth; / And that mild woman of the south, / Aillinn, who was King Lugaidh's heir, / Their love was never drowned in care / Of this or that thing, nor grew cold / Because their bodies had grown old. / Being forbid to marry on earth, / They blossomed to immortal mirth" (*Collected Poems* [New York, 1956], p. 393). *Purlieu:* a disreputable street or quarter; *Tommy:* a British soldier; *fillibeg:* a little kilt.

9.1153 (216:14). Jest on. Know thyself – For "Jest on," see 9.491n. "Know thyself" was one of the two mottoes on the temple of Apollo at Delphi; the other, "Nothing too much [or in excess]."

9.1155–56 (216:16–17). Synge has left off wearing black to be like nature – None of Synge's biographers is aware of this resolve and this change of habit, though Synge was impressed during his several visits to the Aran Isles by the colorful homespun dresses of the women and by the blue turtleneck sweaters and the grey homespun trousers and vests of the men. Sara Allgood, an actress at the Abbey Theatre during Synge's career there, said in retrospect that her abiding image of Synge was of him dressed in black cape and black stetson, as sketched by Jack B. Yeats during a rehearsal in 1907.

9.1158–60 (216:20–23). Longworth is awfully sick . . . her drivel to Jaysus – Joyce's review of Lady Gregory's *Poets and Dreamers*, "The Soul of Ireland," appeared in Longworth's *Daily Express*, 26 March 1903; Joyce took Lady Gregory to task for her explorations "in a land almost fabulous in its sorrow and senility," with the obvious twist that the senile dreams of the past were hardly sufficient to a vital national literature. Longworth "signed" the review "J.J." to qualify his responsibility for printing it; and Lady Gregory was offended, understandably, since it was she who had recommended Joyce to Longworth. "Hake" is dialect for gossiping woman. To "slate" is English dialect for to set a dog on; figuratively and colloquially, to criticize, censure, reprimand. See *CW*, pp. 102–5.

9.1161, 1164–65 (216:23–24, 27–28). the Yeats touch? / —the most beautiful book . . . thinks of Homer—Yeats, who also enjoyed Lady Gregory's patronage and friendship, gracefully praised her work. He wrote the preface to her *Cuchulain of Muirthemne: The Story of the Men of the Red Branch of Ulster* (London, 1902), with the assertion: "I think this book is the best that has come out of Ireland in my time" (p. vii). He compares the book favorably with other epic compilations, such as the *Mabinogian*, but Homer is Mulligan's contribution to the preface.

9.1162 (216:25). mopping – Obsolete or rare for a made-up face; pouting; grimacing. In *King Lear*, Edgar, pretending madness, claims that one of the "five fiends" that have possessed him was "Flibbertigibbet, of mopping and mowing, who since possesses chambermaids and waiting-women" (IV.i.57, 61–63).

9.1168 (216:32). the pillared Moorish hall – The central hall on the ground floor of the National Library does have a Moorish-Alhambra flavor, but in technical terms its contribution to the building's eclecticism is in the Renaissance style advocated by the Ecole des Beaux Arts in Paris, modified in this case by some Lombardo-Venetian elements reminiscent of the eldest Deane's style; see 8.1174n and 8.1180–81n.

9.1168–69 (216:32–33). Gone the nine men's morrice with caps of indices – "Nine men's morrice" (after the Morris dance) or "merrils" is a game remotely resembling checkers played with pegs or stones on a board or turf marked out in concentric squares. Stephen's remark echoes Titania's complaint to Oberon in *A Midsummer Night's Dream:* "The nine men's morris

is filled up with mud" (II.i.98). "Caps of indices" implies that Stephen is poeticizing some
change in the layout of the library, but just what
is unclear.

**9.1170 (216:34). Buck Mulligan read his tab-
let** – Since "the Lord has spoken to Malachi"
(9.1056 [213:30]), the implication is that Mulligan is playing the role of Moses returned from
Mount Sinai, bearing the "tables of the Law"
(Deuteronomy 10:5; Exodus 34:29).

9.1177 (217:1). patch's – "Patch" is Elizabethan for a fool, clown, or jester.

9.1179 (217:3). *marcato* – Italian (music): "in
a marked emphatic manner."

**9.1181–89 (217:5–13). TOBY TOSTOFF . . .
ROSALIE** – Toby and Crab are traditional in
English university bawdry; for the two medicals, see 9.908–9n; for Nelly and Rosalie, see
9.1090–91n; for Mother Grogan, see 1.352n.
"Tostoff" puns on *to toss off*, slang for to mas-
turbate; "crab" is, of course, the crab or body
louse that infects the pubic hair ("bush"), and
"bushranger" is Australian slang for bandit.

9.1192 (217:17). the Camden hall – A small
warehouse behind a produce shop in Camden
Street in south-central Dublin. It was one of the
temporary Dublin homes of the Irish National
Theatre Society before it moved into the Abbey
Theatre. For the autobiographical background
of this story, see Ellmann, pp. 160–61.

**9.1199–1200 (217:24–25). If Socrates leave
. . . go forth tonight** – See 9.1042–44n.

9.1202 (217:27). Seas between – Suggests that
Stephen and Mulligan pose as Scylla and Charybdis as Bloom (Odysseus) passes between
them.

**9.1206 (217:31). Here I watched . . . of the
birds** – Stephen watched the birds for an augury of his (failed) mission to the Continent
from the library steps in *A Portrait* 5:C; see
3.410–11n. For Aengus, see 9.1093n.

**9.1207–8 (217:32–34). Last night I flew . . .
held to me** – Stephen recalls his dream of the
previous night; in this phase he has played the
part of Daedalus or Icarus in flight as Ovid describes them before Icarus's folly carries him to
his death: "Now some fisherman . . . or a shepherd . . . or a plowman . . . spies them and
stands stupefied, and believes them to be gods

that they could fly through the air" (*Metamorphoses* 8:215–20). For the "creamfruit melon"
phase of the dream, see 3.367–69n.

9.1209 (217:35). The wandering jew – A legendary Jew doomed to wander the earth until
the Day of Judgment. There are various Christian and pre-Christian versions of the legend.
According to one traditional Christian account,
when Jesus was carrying his cross toward Calvary he paused to rest and was struck and
mocked by a Jew who said: "Go, why dost thou
tarry?" Jesus answered: "I go, but thou shalt
tarry till I return." Thus the Jew became un-
dying, suffering at the end of each century a
sickness that rejuvenated him to the age of
thirty. His fate also transformed his entire character; his cruelty became repentance, and he became gifted with supernatural wisdom. See
2.362n.

**9.1210 (217:36–37). He looked upon you to
lust after you** – After Jesus' definition of adultery in the Sermon on the Mount: "Ye have
heard that it was said by them of old time, Thou
shalt not commit adultery: But I say unto you,
That whosoever looketh on a woman to lust
after her hath committed adultery with her already in his heart" (Matthew 5:27–28).

**9.1210–11 (217:37). I fear thee, ancient mari-
ner** – In Coleridge's *Rime of the Ancient Mariner*
(1798), Part IV, gloss: "The Wedding-Guest
feareth that a spirit is talking to him; But the
ancient Mariner assureth him of his bodily life,
and proceedeth to relate his horrible penance."
Lines 224, 228: "I fear thee, ancient Mariner!
. . . I fear thee and thy glittering eye."

9.1212 (217:39). Manner of Oxenford – (Oxford), suggesting that homosexual preoccupation was, as Joyce put it, "the logical and inescapable product of the Anglo-Saxon college and
university system, with its secrecy and restrictions" (*CW*, p. 204).

9.1213 (217:40). Wheelbarrow sun – Recalls
the English critic and reformer John Ruskin
(1819–1900) by free association with Oxford; as
Joyce remarked, "At Oxford University . . . a
pompous professor named Ruskin was leading
a crowd of Anglo-Saxon adolescents to the
promised land of the future society—behind a
wheelbarrow" (*CW*, p. 202). The allusion is to
Ruskin's sending his pupils off to make roads in
order both to improve the country and to teach
them the virtues of productive labor as against

the pointless athleticism of running, rowing, etc.

9.1214 (218:1). Step of a pard – In medieval bestiaries, the pard is described as the most beautiful of all the four-footed animals. The name is regarded as deriving from the Greek πάν (*pan:* "all"), like Joseph's tunic "of every tinge in colors." The pard is "accustomed to feed itself on various foods and to eat the sweetest herbs"; after it eats, it sleeps for three days and wakes with a roar (therefore it is allegorically Christ). It is of a mild and good disposition, loved by all the animals except the dragon (foul breath as against the sweet breath of the pard). At 15.4326–27 (586:7–8) Bloom is described as moving *"with fleet step of a pard strewing the drag behind him, torn envelopes drenched in aniseed* [a sweet herb]."

9.1215 (218:2). portcullis barbs – The cast-iron grillwork in the arch over the Kildare Street gate to the National Library.

9.1218 (218:5–6). Kind air defined the coigns . . . Kildare street. No birds – As Duncan and the royal party reach Macbeth's castle Banquo praises its atmosphere: "This guest of summer, / The temple-haunting martlet [a swallow that makes mud-nests under eaves], does approve [demonstrate] / By his loved mansionary that the heaven's breath / Smells wooingly here. No jutty, frieze, / Buttress, nor coign of vantage [convenient corner], but this bird / Hath made his pendant bed and procreant cradle. / Where they most breed and haunt, I have observed / The air is delicate" (I.vi.3–10). Banquo's sentiments are a devastatingly mistaken anticipation of the climate-to-be within the castle. *No birds:* there will be no augury today—as in *A Portrait*

5:C, the augury was not promising; see 9.1206n.

9.1221 (218:8). Cease to strive – Cf. Blake's lyric, "And did those feet in ancient time," in the preface to *Milton:* "I will not cease from Mental Fight, / Nor shall my Sword sleep in my hand: / Till we have built Jerusalem / In England's green and Pleasant Land."

In *The Odyssey* Circe in effect counsels Odysseus to "cease to strive" when she advises him about the passage between Scylla and Charybdis. Odysseus asks how he can fight Scylla, and Circe rebukes him: "Must you have battle in your heart forever? / . . . Old contender, / Will you not yield to the immortal gods? / That nightmare cannot die, being eternal / evil itself . . . no power can fight her, / all that avails is flight" (12:116–21; Fitzgerald, p. 225).

9.1221 (218:8). Peace of the druid priests of Cymbeline – In the final scene of *Cymbeline* the soothsayer (Philarmonus) reads a prophecy: "When as a lion's whelp shall, to himself unknown, without seeking find, and be embraced by a piece of tender air; and when from a stately cedar shall be lopped branches, which, being dead many years, shall after revive, be jointed to the old stock, and freshly grow, then shall Posthumus [Leonatus] end his miseries, Britain be fortunate and flourish in peace and plenty" (V.v.435–42). The soothsayer then declares Leonatus "the lion's whelp" (443), Imogen "the piece of tender air" (446), and Cymbeline "the cedar" (453); thus the prophecy of peace is declared fulfilled.

9.1223–25 (218:10–12). *Laud we the gods . . . From our bless'd altars* – At the end of *Cymbeline;* see 7.835–36n.

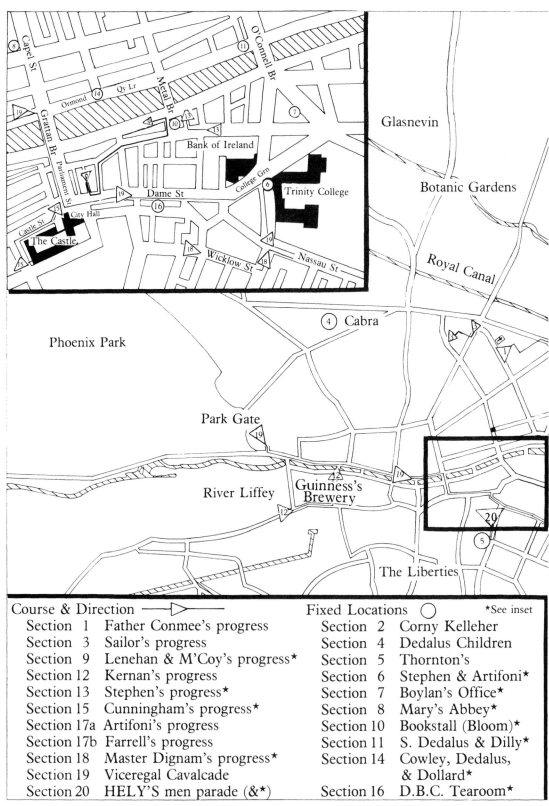

Course & Direction ──▷── Fixed Locations ○ ★See inset

Section 1	Father Conmee's progress		Section 2	Corny Kelleher
Section 3	Sailor's progress		Section 4	Dedalus Children
Section 9	Lenehan & M'Coy's progress★		Section 5	Thornton's
Section 12	Kernan's progress		Section 6	Stephen & Artifoni★
Section 13	Stephen's progress★		Section 7	Boylan's Office★
Section 15	Cunningham's progress★		Section 8	Mary's Abbey★
Section 17a	Artifoni's progress		Section 10	Bookstall (Bloom)★
Section 17b	Farrell's progress		Section 11	S. Dedalus & Dilly★
Section 18	Master Dignam's progress★		Section 14	Cowley, Dedalus,
Section 19	Viceregal Cavalcade			& Dollard★
Section 20	HELY'S men parade (&★)		Section 16	D.B.C. Tearoom★

EPISODE 10. *The Wandering Rocks*

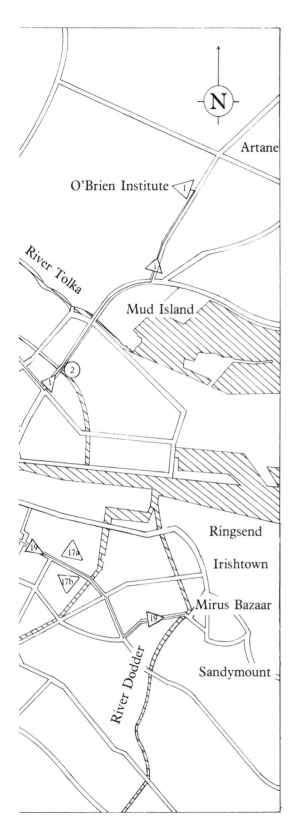

EPISODE 10

The Wandering Rocks

(10.1–1282, PP. 219–55)

Episode 10: *The Wandering Rocks,* **10.1–1282 (219–255).** In Book 12 of *The Odyssey,* Odysseus chooses to run the passage between Scylla and Charybdis rather than attempt the Wandering Rocks, which Circe describes as "drifters" with "boiling surf, under high fiery winds," remarking that only the *Argo* had ever made the passage, thanks to Hera's "love of Jason, her captain" (12:65–72; Fitzgerald, p. 223). Thus the episode does not occur in *The Odyssey.* The Wandering Rocks are sometimes identified with the Symplegades, two rocks at the entrance to the Black Sea that dashed together at intervals but were fixed when the *Argo* passed between them on its voyage to Colchis.

Time: 3:00 P.M. Scene: the streets of Dublin. Organ: blood; Art: mechanics; Symbol: citizens; Technique: labyrinth. Correspondences: *Bosphorus*—Liffey; *European Bank*—Viceroy; *Asiatic Bank*—Conmee; *Symplegades*—Groups of Citizens.

In the Linati schema Joyce lists the Persons as "Objects, Places, Forces, Ulysses" and remarks that the Sense (Meaning) of the episode is "The Hostile Environment."

The episode is composed of nineteen sections, which are interrupted by interpolated actions that are temporally simultaneous but spatially remote from the central action in which the interpolation occurs.

Section 1: 10.1–205 (pp. 219–24).
Intrusion: 10.56–60 (220:24–29). Mr Dennis J. Maginni . . . corner of Dignam's court – See Section 10, Intrusion.

10.1 (219:1). The superior, the very reverend John Conmee S.J. – See 5.322–23n.

10.2 (219:2–3). the presbytery steps – The presbytery is adjacent to the Jesuit Church of St. Francis Xavier in Gardiner Street Upper, north-central Dublin.

10.3 (219:3–4). Artane – On the northeastern outskirts of Dublin, approximately two and a half miles northeast of Father Conmee's church.

10.4 (219:4–5). *Vere dignum et iustum est – Latin: "It is indeed fitting and right"; the opening phrase of the preface, which begins the Eucharist (the canon or central section of the Mass). The Common Preface continues: "our duty and our salvation, always and everywhere to give thanks to you, Lord, Holy Father, Almighty and Eternal God."

10.4 (219:5). Brother Swan – Reverend Brother William A. Swan, director of the O'Brien Institute for Destitute Children (one hundred boys) in Fairview, in northeastern Dublin. The institute was maintained by the Christian Brothers, a teaching brotherhood of Catholic laymen; see 8.2n.

10.5–6 (219:6–7). Good practical Catholic: useful at mission time – For Martin Cunningham's practical Catholicism, see "Grace," *Dubliners.* "Mission time" refers to those annual periods when the Catholics of a parish rededicate themselves to their church and campaign to raise money for its support.

10.8–9 (219:10). the convent of the sisters of charity – In Gardiner Street Upper; the Jesuit fathers of Father Conmee's church were its chaplains.

10.11 (219:13). one silver crown – A former coin worth five shillings; a quarter of a pound sterling.

10.12 (219:14). Mountjoy square – A relatively fashionable area in the northeast quadrant of Dublin, now sliding into dereliction.

10.14–16 (219:17–19). cardinal Wolsey's words . . . in my old days – Thomas, Cardinal Wolsey (c. 1475–1530), an English churchman and statesman, was lord chancellor of England and one of Henry VIII's most powerful and guileful advisers. His resistance to Henry's first divorce eventually led to his downfall, and he died while being conveyed to London to stand trial for high treason. His "last words" to the captain of the guard, Sir William Kingston: "Had I served God as diligently as I have the king, he would not have given me over in my gray hairs" (Shakespeare, *Henry VIII* III.ii.455–57).

10.17 (219:20–21). the wife of Mr David Sheehy M. P. – Bessie Sheehy, whose husband, David (1844–1932), was member of Parliament (Nationalist) for South Galway (1885–90) and for South Meath (1903–18). The Sheehys lived at 2 Belvedere Place, a street that extends Mountjoy Square East toward the northwest.

10.19 (219:24). Buxton – A town in Derbyshire, England; its waters were famous as a curative aid for "indigestion, gout, rheumatism, and nervous and cutaneous diseases."

10.20–21 (219:24–25). And her boys, were they getting on well at Belvedere? – Richard and Eugene Sheehy were Joyce's friends and contemporaries at Belvedere. Richard graduated with Joyce in 1898, Eugene in 1899. Belvedere College is a Jesuit day school for boys, on Great Denmark Street in north-central Dublin. Belvedere House was itself a handsome eighteenth-century town-country house. The Jesuits acquired it in 1841 and expanded its facilities through the nineteenth century, until by 1890 it was a somewhat cramped quadrangle. Though the education was thorough and strictly Jesuit in character, the school was not so fashionable as Clongowes Wood College.

10.22 (219:27). The house was still sitting – Yes; see 7.75n.

10.24 (219:29). Father Bernard Vaughan – (1847–1922), an English Jesuit famous for his sermons. In a letter, 10 October 1906, Joyce remarked, "Fr. B. V. is the most diverting public figure in England at present. I never see his name but I expect some enormity" (*Letters* 2:182). Joyce said that Vaughan was the model for Father Purdon in "Grace," *Dubliners*.

10.32 (219:38). arecanut paste – *Areca* is a genus of palm tree; the *Areca catechu* yields a nut that Eastern peoples rolled in betel leaves to chew. The nut was advertised (and popularly believed) to aid in maintaining strong, bright teeth.

10.35 (219:41). Pilate! . . . that owlin mob? – Conmee recalls Father Vaughan's cockney accent. Pilate was the Roman military governor of Judea when Jesus was crucified; Mark 15, Luke 23, and John 18–19 all include versions of the story in which Pilate orders the crucifixion in response to a frenzy of public demand.

10.38 (220:2–3). Of good family . . . Welsh, were they not? – The Vaughans were a famous "good family" in Wales, but London-born Father Vaughan's connection seems to have been in name rather than heritage.

10.39 (220:4). father provincial – The Rome provincial of the Jesuit order in Ireland, the official to whom Father Conmee would report. The administrative and executive government of the society is entrusted under the general of the order to provincials, who in turn receive reports from superiors, and so forth.

10.41 (220:6–7). The little house – That is, the

lower grades at Belvedere, for boys seven to ten years of age.

10.43 (220:8). Jack Sohan – John Sohan, pawnbroker, 38 Townsend Street, Dublin.

10.43 (220:9). Ger. Gallaher – Gerald Gallaher, a brother of Ignatius Gallaher (and apparently similar in temperament); see 6.58n.

10.44 (220:10). Brunny Lynam – The name is associated with the bookmaker Lenehan visits (10.506 [233:12]).

10.47 (220:13). Fitzgibbon Street – Runs northeast from the northeast corner of Mountjoy Square.

10.56 (220:24). Mr Dennis J. Maginni – *Thom's* 1904 lists a Dennis J. Maginni as "professor of dancing &c.," 32 Great George's Street North. His flamboyant costume and manner rendered him a mobile Dublin landmark; see 8.98n.

10.58 (220:27). with grave deportment – Recalls Mr. Turveydrop, "a very gentlemanly man, celebrated for deportment" in Dickens's *Bleak House* (1852–53); his son, Prince Turveydrop, is a dancing master.

10.59 (220:28). lady Maxwell – *Thom's* 1904 lists a Lady Maxwell as residing at 36 Great George's Street North, which intersects the east end of Great Britain (now Parnell) Street.

10.60 (220:28–29). Dignam's court – Off Great Britain (now Parnell) Street, one-half mile southwest of where Father Conmee is.

10.61 (220:30). Mrs M'Guinness – Mrs. Ellen M'Guinness, pawnbroker, 38–39 Gardiner Street Upper, Dublin.

10.65 (220:34). Mary, queen of Scots – Mary Stuart (1542–87), the daughter of James V of Scotland. As against the dour Protestant Elizabeth, who had her beheaded, the Catholic Mary has been romantically portrayed as a woman of extraordinary grace and charm (as well, apparently, as ambition).

10.68 (220:37). Great Charles street – Runs northeast from the southeast corner of Mountjoy Square.

10.68–70 (220:38–39). the shutup free church ... will (D.V.) speak – Free Church, an extraparochial Church of Ireland chapel in Great Charles Street. The Reverend T. R. Greene, B.A., incumbent (i.e., the minister in charge). The church is "shutup" in that it is not open for prayer, as a Catholic church would be. "D.V." is an abbreviation for the Latin *Deo volente*, "God willing."

10.71 (220:41). Invincible ignorance – The Roman Catholic evaluation of Protestant faith, since the Protestant's commitment to his "heretical" faith commits him to "ignorance," which is "said to be invincible when the person is unable to rid himself of it notwithstanding the employment of moral diligence" (*Catholic Encyclopedia* [New York, 1910], vol. 7, p. 648).

10.73–74 (221:2). North Circular road – Described the half-circle of the northern boundary of 1904 metropolitan Dublin.

10.76 (221:5–6). Richmond street – A dead-end street off Richmond Place, a continuation of North Circular Road; see "Araby," *Dubliners.*

10.78 (221:7). Christian brother boys – There was a Christian Brothers School in Richmond Street; see 8.2n.

10.79–80 (221:9–10). Saint Joseph's church ... virtuous females – As he walks east and slightly south along Portland Row, Father Conmee passes St. Joseph's Roman Catholic Church and then St. Joseph's Asylum for Aged and Virtuous Females.

10.83–84 (221:13–14). Aldborough house ... that spendthrift nobleman – Lord Aldborough (d. 1801), who already had town houses in Dublin and London and country houses in England and Ireland, built the house in question—in what was then "the country"—for his wife, at a cost of forty thousand pounds (1792–98). This monumental extravagance was compounded by his wife's refusal to live in the house because she did not like its location.

10.84 (221:14). And now it was an office or something – In 1904 Aldborough House was surrounded by small cottages and occupied by the Stores Branch and Surveyor's Department of the General Post Office.

10.85 (221:15). North Strand road – Father

Conmee has turned northeast out of Portland Row.

10.86 (221:16). Mr William Gallagher – Purveyor, grocer, and coal and corn merchant, 4 North Strand Road.

10.88 (221:19). cools – "Cool" is a dialect English variant of *cowl*, or tub.

10.89 (221:19). *Grogan's the Tobacconist – R. Grogan, tobacconist, 16 North Strand Road.

10.89–90 (221:20–21). a dreadful catastrophe in New York – See 8.1146–47n.

10.91–92 (221:22–23). Unfortunate people to die ... perfect contrition – "Unprepared," that is, without benefit of extreme unction, but in exceptional cases an "act of perfect contrition" on the part of the individual (without the prayers of the Church) can "take away the effects of sin" and prepare the individual for his death. Father Conmee's *liberal* view is somewhat undercut by the fact that the "unfortunate people" were all "invincibly ignorant" Lutherans.

10.93 (221:24). Daniel Bergin's publichouse – Daniel L. Bergin, grocer, tea, wine, and spirit merchant, 17 North Strand Road.

10.96 (221:27). H. J. O'Neill's funeral establishment – Across the street from Bergin's, Harry J. O'Neill, undertaker and job carriage proprietor, 164 North Strand Road; Simon Kerrigan, manager. O'Neill's had the burying of Paddy Dignam.

10.99 (221:30–31). Youkstetter's – William Youkstetter, pork butcher, 21 North Strand Road.

10.101 (221:34). Charleville mall – On the south bank of the Royal Canal (which Father Conmee is approaching). The canal circles the northern outskirts of metropolitan Dublin and terminates near the mouth of the Liffey.

10.107 (221:42). Newcomen bridge – Continues North Strand Road over the Royal Canal.

10.110–11 (222:3–4). the reverend Nicholas Dudley ... north William street – *Thom's* 1904 lists the Reverend P. A. Butterly and the Reverend J. D. Dudley as curates of St. Agatha's Roman Catholic Church in William Street, north of North Strand Road. "C.C." is an abbreviation for curate-in-charge.

10.114 (222:8). Mud Island – Mud flats on the northeastern outskirts of Dublin (on the bay), now reclaimed as Fairview Park.

10.118 (222:12). the ivy church – North Strand Episcopal Church on North Strand Road (the tram carries Father Conmee northeast toward his destination).

10.133 (222:31). Annesley bridge – Continues North Strand Road over the River Tolka.

10.139–40 (222:38–39). *bless you, my child . . . pray for me* – Phrases the priest uses to reassure the penitent and to terminate the confession.

10.141 (222:41). Mr Eugene Stratton – See 6.184n.

10.144 (223:2). saint Peter Claver, S.J. – See 5.323n.

10.147–48 (223:6–7). that book by the Belgian jesuit *Le Nombre des Élus* – Father A. Castelein, S.J., *Le rigorisme, le nombre des élus et la doctrine du salut* (Rigorism, the Number of the Chosen and the Doctrine of Salvation) (Brussels, 1899). The book argued that the great majority of souls would be saved; it was immediately attacked as too "liberal" by the dogmatists, or "rigorists," who claimed that all who were not baptized as Catholics were subject to eternal damnation. The controversy was not confined to the Catholic church, since liberal Protestants in the late nineteenth century were also reacting against an inflexible doctrine of eternal damnation.

10.150 (223:9). (D.V.) – See 10.68–70n.

10.153 (223:13). Howth road – Runs northeast from the northern side of Mud Island to Howth. Father Conmee turns north at this point.

10.155 (223:15). Malahide road – Runs north-northeast toward the O'Brien Institute and Artane beyond.

10.156 (223:16). The joybells were ringing in gay Malahide – The opening line of the poem "The Bridal of Malahide," by the Irish poet Gerald Griffin (1803–40). The poem recounts the tangled story of Maud Plunkett's marriage

(see following note) as the "joybells" turn to "dead-bells . . . In sad Malahide." Final stanza: "The stranger who wanders / Along the lone vale / Still sighs while he ponders / On that heavy tale: / 'Thus passes each pleasure / That earth can supply— / Thus joy has its measure— / We live but to die!' "

10.156–58 (223:17–19). Lord Talbot de Malahide . . . widow one day – Henry II (1133–89), king of England (1154–89), granted Malahide (on the coast nine miles north of Dublin) to Richard Talbot, the first Lord Talbot of Malahide. The Talbots were later created hereditary lord admirals of Malahide and the seas adjoining by decree of Edward IV in 1476. A Talbot was not, however, the principal of the story Father Conmee recalls. The story is about Mr. Hussey, the son of Lord Galtrim, and his betrothed, Maud, the daughter of Lord Plunkett. The bridegroom was called from the altar to lead his troops against a marauding party and was killed; thus his bride was "maid, wife and widow in one day." She afterwards married twice; her third husband was Sir Richard Talbot of Malahide (d. 1329).

10.159 (223:20). townlands – See 7.91–92n.

10.161–62 (223:22–23). *Old Times in the Barony* – A book by Father Conmee (Dublin, n.d.), "a nostalgic but unsentimental recall of an older way of life, rural and uncomplicated, around the neighborhood of Luainford" (Kevin Sullivan, *Joyce Among the Jesuits* [New York, 1958], p. 17).

10.163 (223:24). Mary Rochfort – (1720–c. 1790) was married in 1736 to Col. Robert Rochfort (1708–74), who was created first earl of Belvedere in 1753. In 1743 she was accused of adultery with her brother-in-law, Arthur Rochfort; though apparently innocent, her unscrupulous husband blackmailed her into admitting guilt by promising a divorce. However, with the verdict in his favor and his brother in exile, Robert did not divorce his wife but rather imprisoned her on the Rochfort estate near Lough Ennel in County Westmeath. Mary Rochfort was released from her house arrest when her husband died in 1774, but she continued to live as a recluse. Although there is no evidence that she ever saw or entered Belvedere House, which was built by the second earl in 1786, Father Conmee thinks of her because she is commonly associated with that "Jesuit house."

10.167 (223:30). not her confessor – Something of an irony, since the Rochforts were Protestant.

10.168 (223:31). *eiaculatio seminis inter vas naturale mulieris* – Latin: "ejaculation of semen within the natural female organ"; a technical definition of complete sexual intercourse. The implication is that Lady Rochfort would have regarded her sin as less "serious" than adultery if intercourse was not complete, but had she been a Catholic, her catechism and her confessor would have made it quite clear that even the thought (or "almost-adultery") was every bit as serious as adultery itself.

10.171–73 (223:35–37). that tyrannous incontinence . . . the ways of God which were not our ways – With a shrug of near-fatalism (see 4.419n), Father Conmee sidesteps a much-questioned crux: If sexual satisfaction was sinful not only outside of wedlock but even in wedlock when the intent was not expressly that of procreation, why were human beings given such powerful sexual impulses and desires?

10.174 (223:38). Don John – That is, Don Juan.

10.176–77 (223:40–41). a beeswaxed drawing-room, ceiled with full fruit clusters – Before the development of petroleum-based waxes, beeswax was used on floors, wall paneling, and furniture. The ceiling of the drawing room Father Conmee imagines is decorated with stuccowork (as the ceilings of eighteenth-century Irish great houses usually were).

10.180 (224:4). lychgate – Or lich gate, a roofed gateway to a churchyard, originally a place where the bier could pause on its way to the grave (*lich*, Middle English: "body, corpse").

10.180–81 (224:5) cabbages, curtseying to him with ample underleaves – The question of the role of sex in childbirth can be avoided (primly) by meeting the child's question "Where did I come from?" with "We found you under a cabbage leaf."

10.182 (224:7). *Moutonner* – French: literally, "to render fleecy."

10.184 (224:9). reading his office – That is, the Divine Office, prayers for the different hours of the day, which monks and nuns celebrate in choir each day and priests recite daily from their breviary, "praying in the name of the Church and for the whole Church." There are eight canonical hours: four great (matins, about midnight; lauds, at dawn; vespers, at sunset; and compline, at bedtime) and four little (prime, the first hour in the early morning, 6:00 A.M.; terce, the third hour, in midmorning; sext, the sixth hour, at midday; and nones, the ninth hour, in the early afternoon, 3:00 P.M.).

10.186 (224:11). Clongowes field – Father Conmee recalls his "reign" as rector of Clongowes Wood College. See *A Portrait*, chapter 1.

10.187 (224:12). the boys' lines – The students at Clongowes were divided into three groups by age: those under thirteen were in the third line; from thirteen to fifteen, lower line; and fifteen to eighteen, higher line.

10.189 (224:16). breviary – Book containing the daily public or canonical prayers for the canonical hours. The daily recital of the breviary is obligatory for all those in major orders and for all choir members.

10.190 (224:16). An ivory bookmark – Inscribed with the beginnings and conclusions of the canonical hours.

10.191 (224:17). Nones – See 10.184n.

10.191 (224:17–18). lady Maxwell – See 10.59n.

10.193 (224:19). *Pater* and *Ave* – Father Conmee reads the Pater, the Lord's Prayer, and the Ave, "Hail, Mary, full of grace . . . ," as preludes to his reading of nones.

10.194 (224:20). *Deus in adiutorium* – Latin: "Oh God, to our aid [come]"; the opening phrase of Psalm 70 (Vulgate 69) and the direct beginning of nones.

10.196–98 (224:22–24). *Res in Beati . . . iustitioe tuoe* – Latin: "*Res* in *Blessed are the undefiled*" (*Res* is the Hebrew letter that heads the twentieth section of Psalm 119 [Vulgate 118], which is called "Blessed are the undefiled"): "Thy word is true from the beginning: and every one of thy righteous judgments endureth forever" (119:160). Father Conmee has already read three sections (lines 129–52) of the Psalm.

10.199 (224:25). A flushed young man – Stephen's friend Lynch; see 14.1154–55 (416:11–12).

10.204 (224:31–32). *Sin: Principes persecuti . . . cor meum* – *Sin* is the Hebrew letter that heads the twenty-first section of Psalm 119 (Vulgate 118). Latin: "Princes have persecuted me without a cause: but my heart standeth in awe of thy word" (119:161).

Section 2: 10.207–26 (pp. 224–25).
Intrusions: (a) 10.213–14 (225:1–2). Father John Conmee . . . on Newcomen Bridge – See Section 1. **(b) 10.222–23 (225:10–11). While a generous white . . . flung forth a coin** – (Molly Bloom), see Section 3.

10.213–14 (225:1–2). the Dollymount tram on Newcomen bridge – For Newcomen Bridge, see 10.107n. Dollymount was a suburban village three and a half miles northeast of the center of Dublin and just under three miles from Newcomen Bridge. Trams for Dollymount left Nelson's Pillar every five minutes during the day.

10.217 (225:5). Constable 57C – From C Division of the Dublin Metropolitan Police, headquarters in Store Street, north of the Liffey and 850 yards south-southeast of O'Neill's funeral establishment.

10.224 (225:12). What's the best news? – A stock phrase of greeting used by Bantam Lyons (5.520 [85:25]) and Simon Dedalus (10.886 [243:38]).

Section 3: 10.228–56 (pp. 225–26).
Intrusion: 10.236–37 (225:23–24). J. J. O'Molloy's white . . . warehouse with a visitor – See Section 8.

10.228 (225:15–16). MacConnell's corner – Andrew MacConnell, pharmaceutical chemist, 112 Dorset Street Lower, near the intersection with Eccles Street.

10.229 (225:16). Rabaiotti's icecream car – Antoni Rabaiotti, Madras Place (off North Circular Road), had a fleet of pushcarts that sold ices and ice cream in the Dublin streets.

10.230 (225:17). Larry O'Rourke – See 4.105n.

10.232, 235 (225:19, 22). *For England . . . home and beauty* – From a song, "The Death of Nelson," words by S. J. Arnold, music by John Braham. Refrain: " 'England expects that ev'ry man / This day will do his duty . . .' / At last the fatal wound, / Which spread dismay around, / The hero's breast . . . receiv'd; / 'Heav'n fights upon our side! / The day's our own,' he cried! / 'Now long enough I've lived! / In honor's cause my life was pass'd, / In honor's cause I fall at last, / For England, home and beauty, / For England, home and beauty.' / Thus ending life as he began, / England confess'd that ev'ry man / That day had done his duty."

Section 4: 10.258–97 (pp. 226–27).
Intrusions: (a) 10.264–65 (226:13–14). Father Conmee walked . . . tickled by stubble – See Section 1. **(b) 10.281–82 (226:31–32). The lacquey rang his bell—Barang!** – See Section 11. **(c) 10.294–97 (227:6–10). A skiff, a crumpled . . . and George's quay.**

10.260 (226:9). put in – Slang for to pawn.

10.267 (226:16). M'Guinness's – See 10.61n.

10.269 (226:18). Bad cess to – Slang: "bad luck to" (a "cess" is an imposed tax).

10.274 (226:23). Crickey – Dodging the curse *Christ* or *in Christ's name.*

10.280 (226:30). Sister Mary Patrick – In the convent of the Roman Catholic Sisters of Charity in Upper Gardiner Street.

10.291 (227:3). Our father who art not in heaven – After the opening of the Lord's Prayer: "Our Father, who art in Heaven, hallowed be thy name" (Matthew 6:9).

10.294 (227:6). throwaway, Elijah is coming – See 8.5–16 (151:6–19).

10.295 (227:7). Loopline bridge – See 5.138n.

10.295 (227:7). shooting the rapids – High tide was at 12:42 P.M.; since it is now after 3:00, the tide has turned and the current in the estuary of the Liffey is east-running.

10.297 (227:9–10). the Customhouse old dock and George's quay – The dock is on the north bank of the Liffey, the quay on the south bank, approximately one mile west of what was then the mouth of the Liffey and three-quarters of a mile east of the center of Dublin.

Section 5: 10.299–336 (pp. 227–28).
Intrusion: 10.315–16 (227:27–28). *A dark-backed figure . . . the hawker's car – (Bloom); see Section 10.

10.299 (227:11). Thornton's – James Thornton, fruiterer and florist to His Majesty the King and to His Excellency the Lord Lieutenant, etc., 63 Grafton Street; in other words, a very fashionable shop.

10.304 (227:16). game ball – The score when one side will win by making the next point.

10.310 (227:22). H.E.L.Y.'S – Five sandwich-board men who are advertising the stationery store where Bloom used to work; see 6.703n.

10.310 (227:22–23). past Tangier lane – The lane intersects Grafton street at 61; the men are moving south toward St. Stephen's Green, where (10.377–79 [229:19–22]) they turn to retrace their steps.

10.315 (227:27). Merchant's arch – A covered passageway from Temple Bar to Wellington Quay on the south bank of the Liffey. See J. F. Byrne, *The Silent Years* (New York, 1953), p. 19, for a description of the bookseller and his wares.

Section 6: 10.338–66 (pp. 228–29).

10.338 (228:13). *Ma!* – Italian: "But!"

10.338 (228:13). Almidano Artifoni – Takes his name from the owner of the Berlitz school of languages in Trieste and Pola, where Joyce taught. See *Letters* and Ellmann.

10.339 (228:14–15). Goldsmith's knobby poll – A statue of Oliver Goldsmith (1728–74), Irish man of letters, by the Irish sculptor John Henry Foley (1818–74), stands within the railings of Trinity College. The *Official Guide to Dublin* (1958) describes the statue as "an excellent study in tender and humorous meditation." Cf. David Garrick's (1717–79) "Impromptu Epitaph on Oliver Goldsmith": "Here lies Nolly Goldsmith, for shortness called Noll, / Who wrote like an angel, and talked like poor Poll."

10.341 (228:17). Palefaces – English tourists; see 1.166n.

10.342–43 (228:18–19). Trinity . . . bank of Ireland – The two institutions face each other across College Green; see 4.101–3n.

10.344–47 (228:21–24). *Anch'io ho avuto . . . Lei si sacrifica* – Italian: "I too had the same idea when I was young as you are. At that time I was convinced that the world is a beast [i.e., a pigsty]. It's too bad. Because your voice . . . would be a source of income, come now. But instead, you are sacrificing yourself."

10.348 (228:25). *Sacrifizio incruento* – Italian: "bloodless sacrifice."

10.350–51 (228:27–28). *Speriamo . . . Ma, dia: retta a me. Ci refletta* – Italian: "Let us hope . . . But, listen to me. Think about it."

10.352 (228:29). By the stern stone hand of Grattan – A bronze (not stone) statue of Henry Grattan (see 7.731n), also by Foley, stands in front of the Bank of Ireland, which was originally the Irish House of Parliament, where Grattan distinguished himself as orator and politician. Grattan is depicted with his right hand raised in a forensic gesture.

10.352 (228:29–30). Inchicore tram – That is, the soldiers have come from Richmond (now Clancy) Barracks in Inchicore, which is just south of Phoenix Park and the Liffey on the western outskirts of Dublin.

10.354 (228:31). *Ci rifletterò!* – Italian: "I'll think about it."

10.355 (228:33). *Ma, sul serio, eh?* – Italian: "Are you serious, eh?"

10.357 (228:35–36). Dalkey – A small town on the southeast headland of Dublin Bay; Mr. Deasy's school was in Dalkey.

10.358–59 (228:37–38). *Eccolo . . . pensi. Addio, caro* – Italian: "Here it is [the tram he is to take]. Come see me and think about it. Goodbye, dear fellow."

10.360–61 (229:1–2). *Arrivederla, maestro . . . E grazie* – Italian: "Goodbye, master . . . and thank you."

10.362 (229:3–4). *Di che? Scusi, eh? Tante belle cose!* – Italian: "For what? . . . Excuse me, eh? All the best!"

10.365 (229:8). gillies – Scots, originally the

Lowlanders' name for the followers of the Highland chiefs. The gillies in this case are members of the regimental band of the 2d Battalion of the Seaforth Highlanders (stationed in Dublin in 1904) on their way to Trinity College Park to play during the bicycle races; see 10.651–53n.

Section 7: 10.368–96 (pp. 229–30).
Intrusions: (a) 10.373–74 (229:15–16). The disk shot down . . . ogled them: six – See Section 9. **(b) 10.377–79 (229:19–22). Five tall-whitehatted . . . as they had come** – See Section 5.

10.368 (229:10). Miss Dunne – Boylan's secretary appears only in this section. She is mentioned by Corley (16.199–201 [618:19–22]).

10.368 (229:10). Capel street library – See 4.360n.

10.368 (229:10–11). *The Woman in White* – A novel (1860) of sensational intrigue by Dickens's associate Wilkie Collins (1824–89). The intricate plot involves madness, murder, confused identities, and delayed revelations.

10.371 (229:13–14). Is he in love with that one, Marion? – After Marian (not Marion) Halcombe, not the novel's heroine but easily its strongest and most striking woman character. The "he" is the Falstaffian villain, the Italian Count Fosco, of whom Marian Halcombe writes: "The one weak point in that man's iron character is the horrible admiration he feels for *me*." Count Fosco, though his projected villainies are being partially frustrated by Marian, says of her: "With that woman for my friend I would snap these fingers of mine at the world. . . . This grand creature . . . this magnificent woman, whom I admire with all my soul."

10.372 (229:14). Mary Cecil Haye – Mary Cecil Hay(e) (c. 1840–86), one of the more popular sentimental novelists of her time. Miss Dunne's preference for genteel sentimentality as against Collins's tougher fiber is not unlike Gertie McDowell's literary taste; see 13.633–34 (363:40–42).

10.377 (229:19–20). Monypeny's corner – R. W. Monypeny, designer and embroiderer of art needlework and white wool depot, 52–53 Grafton Street, at one of the corners across from St. Stephen's Green.

10.378 (229:20). the slab where Wolfe Tone's statue was not – In 1898 a foundation stone for the statue was laid at the northwest corner of St. Stephen's Green facing Grafton Street; the statue was never completed. Theobald Wolfe Tone (1763–98) was one of the great eighteenth-century Irish patriots and one of the principal founders of the Society of United Irishmen in 1791. The society at first envisioned the union of Protestant and Catholic Ireland to work toward constitutional independence as a republic on the model of the United States and revolutionary France. In 1795, however, the society shifted from a constitutional to a revolutionary approach and through Tone's leadership and diplomacy sought French aid for Irish rebellion. The French made several abortive attempts to send aid, particularly in support of the Rebellion of 1798. Wolfe Tone was captured at sea during one of these attempts and sentenced to death for high treason. He committed suicide in prison in Dublin. Tone is outside the mainstream of the Irish revolutionary tradition, since his republicanism would have appeared to Catholics (and in part to Protestants) as atheism. When the slab was swallowed up by street widening around the green early in the 1920s, little protest was raised, but when the present monument to Wolfe Tone was erected in the northeastern corner of the green a rather sharp protest ensued.

10.380 (229:23). Marie Kendall – (1874–1964), an English singer and comedienne, famous for her performances in pantomimes.

10.383–84 (229:27). at the band tonight – On the East Pier at Kingstown (now Dun Laoghaire)? See 2.33n.

10.385 (229:29). Susy Nagle's – For a possible identity, see 12.198n.

10.385 (229:29). Shannon – Apart from the context, identity and significance unknown.

10.385 (229:29–30). the boatclub swells – There were at least three fashionable yacht clubs in Kingstown (now Dun Laoghaire) in 1904.

10.391–92 (229:36). Twentyseven and six . . . one, seven, six – 27s., 6d., or £1 7s. 6d.

10.394 (229:38). *Sport* – See 7.387n.

10.395 (230:1–2). the Ormond – The Ormond Hotel, Mrs. De Massey, proprietor and wine and spirit merchant, 8 Ormond Quay Upper, on the north bank of the Liffey in the center of Dublin. The Sirens episode is to take place in this hotel.

Section 8: 10.398–463 (pp. 230–32).
The scene of this section is the old chapter house of St. Mary's Abbey. The tenth-century abbey, located on the north bank of the Liffey just west of the modern city center, was the oldest religious establishment in Dublin. It became a Cistercian abbey in the twelfth century, but it was dissolved in 1537 and later destroyed by fire; some of its stone was used to build Essex (now Grattan) Bridge over the Liffey. At the end of the nineteenth century what remained of the chapter house was part of the premises of Messrs. Alexander & Co., seed merchants. "The Chapter House, which must have been a lofty and splendid room, has been divided into two stories by the building of a floor half way up its walls. In the upper chamber, a loft used for storing sacks, the beautifully groined stone roof remains intact, looking very incongruous amidst its surroundings. The upper part of an old window is still visible. In the lower story the ancient architecture is concealed by the brickwork of wine vaults" (D. A. Chart, *The Story of Dublin* [London, 1907], pp. 276–77).

Intrusions: (a) 10.425 (230:36). From a long face . . . on a chess board – (John Howard Parnell); see Section 16. **(b) 10.440–41 (231: 16–17). The young woman . . . a clinging twig** – (Lynch's girlfriend); see Section 1.

10.399 (230:4). Crotty – "A singer at the Gaiety Theatre" (Shari Benstock and Bernard Benstock, *Who's He When He's at Home: A James Joyce Directory* [Urbana, Ill., 1980], p. 73).

10.400 (230:5). Ringabella and Crosshaven – Ringabella is a small bay and Crosshaven a village near the entrance to Cork Harbor, on the south coast of Ireland.

10.403 (230:10). vesta – A short wooden match, after Vesta, Roman goddess of the hearth and its fire.

10.407–9 (230:15–16). the historic council chamber . . . a rebel in 1534 – Silken Thomas (see 3.314n) did renounce his allegiance to Henry VIII in council in the chapter house of St. Mary's Abbey, flinging his sword of office "the English Thanes among."

10.411 (230:18–19). the old bank of Ireland . . . time of the union – The Bank of Ireland was originally located in what nineteenth-century guidebooks agree were "miserable premises" in St. Mary's Abbey, a street just north of the Liffey in central Dublin. After the Irish Parliament was dissolved in 1800 by the Act of Union, the House of Parliament was sold to the Bank of Ireland (1802) with the stipulation that the chamber of the House of Commons be altered so that it could not be used as a place for public discussion and debate.

10.411–13 (230:20–21). the original jews' temple . . . in Adelaide road – The first synagogue in Dublin was established in about 1650 in Crane Lane, just across the Liffey from the ruins of the abbey. The congregation moved north of the Liffey to Marborough Green in 1745 and in 1835 finally established a synagogue in what had been the chapter house of the abbey. In 1892 the congregation moved to a new synagogue, in Adelaide Road in southeastern Dublin.

10.415–16 (230:24–26). He rode down through . . . in Thomas court – Thomas Court was the main street of the walled city of medieval Dublin. It is at present a series of streets including Thomas Street. There is no record of a Kildare "mansion" in Thomas Court, but had there been one and had Silken Thomas been there, he might have approached the abbey by way of Dame Walk (except that the bridge that would have made that approach feasible was not constructed until the late seventeenth century). It is, however, historical fact that Silken Thomas and his retainers approached the abbey from Maynooth Castle, the Fitzgerald stronghold fifteen miles west of Dublin. He came with a considerable following of his retainers, and immediately after he renounced his allegiance to Henry VIII he laid siege to Dublin (unsuccessfully). See 3.314n.

10.433–34 (231:8). Mary's abbey – That is, the street; see 10.411n.

10.434 (231:9). floats – Large flatbedded wagons.

10.434–35 (231:9). carob and palm nut meal – Carob (locust beans or St. John's bread) from the Mediterranean and palm nut meal (a byproduct of the process of making coconut oil) were much in demand as cattle feed in the British Isles in the late nineteenth century.

10.435 (231:9–10). O'Connor, Wexford – The name of the transport company that owned the floats. Wexford is a county town on the east coast of Ireland seventy-two miles south of Dublin.

10.437–38 (231:12–13). The reverend Hugh . . . Saint Michael's, Sallins – Rathcoffey is a hamlet sixteen miles west of Dublin; Sallins is a town eighteen miles west-southwest of Dublin. St. Michael's was the residence of an Anglican archdeacon. The Reverend Love is essentially fictional. See Adams, pp. 29–35.

10.438–39 (231:14). the Fitzgeralds – (Or Geraldines), a powerful Anglo-Irish family that traces its heritage from the early twelfth century. By the early sixteenth century the family comprised two houses: the earls of Kildare and the earls of Desmond. By the eighteenth century they had become the dukes of Leinster.

10.442 (231:18). gunpowder plot – A conspiracy among English Catholics to destroy the English Parliament and King James I by springing a mine secreted under the House of Lords, 5 November 1605; see 9.754–55n.

10.444–48 (231:21–26). the earl of Kildare . . . the Fitzgerald Mor – Gerald Fitzgerald (1456–1513), eighth earl of Kildare (1477–1513), the most powerful Anglo-Irish lord of his time. His career was a stormy series of conflicts with jealous and powerful contemporaries. In the course of a conflict with Archbishop Creagh in 1495 he did set fire to Cashel Cathedral. The earl was charged in council before Henry VII (the archbishop present among his accusers), where he is supposed to have replied: "By Jesus, I would never have doone it, had it not beene told me that the archbishop was within." The last article of the accusation asserted: "All Ireland cannot rule this Earl"; and Henry VII is supposed to have replied: "Then in good faith shall the Earl rule all Ireland." The earl returned to Ireland as Henry VII's deputy. "Mor" is Irish for Great.

Section 9: 10.465–583 (pp. 232–35). Intrusions: (a) 10.470–75 (232:9–14). **Lawyers of the past . . . skirt of great amplitude** – See Section 10, Intrusion (b). **(b)** 10.515–16 (233:22–23). **The gates of the drive . . . the viceregal cavalcade. (c)** 10.534–35 (234:1–2). **Master Patrick Aloysius . . . half of pork-steaks** – See Section 18. **(d)** 10.542–43 (234:

10–11). **A card Unfurnished . . . number 7 Eccles street** – (Molly Bloom), see Section 3.

10.465 (232:4). Tom Rochford – See 8.989n.

10.467 (232:6). Turn Now On – A "turn" is a short theatrical act (dramatic, comic, musical, trained animal, etc.) in a variety show or vaudeville. Since such shows were often continuous from late afternoon through the evening (and were frequently offered in a café setting), members of the audience drifted in and out and could not always tell from the showbill posted beside the stage or from a program which turn was on. Rochfort's invention is designed to solve this "problem."

10.470–73 (232:9–13). Lawyers of the past . . . the court of appeal – The scene is the Four Courts, a large eighteenth-century building on the north bank of the Liffey near the center of Dublin. The building's great hall was dominated by statues of famous Irish lawyers and judges. The building housed, among other courts and offices: the Consolidated Taxing Office for the Supreme Court; King's Bench Division—Admiralty (judge of the High Court having admiralty jurisdiction); His Majesty's Court of Appeal in Ireland (the Supreme Court of Judicature); the late Consolidated Nisi Prius Court, now (1904) office for trials by jury in Dublin, in King's Bench Division. The Four Courts was gutted in the civil war (1922) and has been restored as the Irish Courts of Justice.

10.472 (232:11). costbag – Apparently Joyce's coinage from *costdrawer;* see 3.66n.

10.472 (232:11). Goulding, Collis and Ward – The fictional Goulding has been added to the real partnership of Collis and Ward, solicitors, 31 Dame Street.

10.490 (232:31). Tooraloo – See 5.13–16n.

10.491 (232:32–33). Crampton court – In central Dublin, just south of Grattan Bridge.

10.495 (232:37). Dan Lowry's musichall . . . Marie Kendall – The Empire Theatre of Varieties (late Star Music Hall), Dame Street and Crampton Court; for Marie Kendall, see 10.380n.

10.497 (233:1). Sycamore street – Runs parallel to Crampton Court from Dame Street to Essex Street East. Lenehan and M'Coy walk from Crampton Court east along Dame Street, then north through Sycamore Street.

10.500 (233:5). booky's vest – A vest with numerous outsized pockets designed to hold and keep on file betting slips.

10.504 (233:9). the Dolphin – The Dolphin Hotel and Restaurant, on the corner of Sycamore Street and Essex Street East. Lenehan and M'Coy turn and walk east into Temple Bar, which continues Essex Street to the east.

10.505 (233:10). for Jervis street – That is, for the hospital, Charitable Infirmary, Jervis Street (under the care of the Sisters of Mercy).

10.506 (233:12). Lynam's – *Thom's* 1904 lists no Lynam in the vicinity, but the implication is that the bookmaker's shop was in Temple Bar.

10.507 (233:12) Sceptre's starting price – Sceptre was a colt, not a filly, and his starting price in the Gold Cup Race was seven to four against. See 5.532n; and cf. 14.1128–33n.

10.508 (233:14). Marcus Tertius Moses' somber office – Marcus Tertius Moses, wholesale tea merchant, 30 Essex Street East, on the corner of Eustace Street. He was a Dublin politician, a magistrate (see 17.1610n), and a member of the board of directors of several charitable institutions in the city.

10.509 (233:15). O'Neill's clock – J. J. O'Neill, tea and wine merchant, 29 Essex Street East, across Eustace Street from Moses' office.

10.510 (233:16). After three – The Gold Cup Race was run at 3:08 P.M. Greenwich time on 16 June 1904. If it is after 3:00 in Dublin (Dunsink time), it is after 3:25 Greenwich time. Thus, the race has already been run; but the news, which was to come by telegraph, was not due to reach Dublin until 4:00, so Dublin bookmakers would still take bets at 3:00.

10.511 (233:17). O. Madden – See 7.388–89n.

10.512 (233:18). Temple bar – Continues eastward from Essex Street East.

10.515 (233:22). The gates of the drive – The Viceregal Lodge was in Phoenix Park on the western outskirts of Dublin, north of the Liffey.

10.520 (233:27). under Merchants' arch – They turn north through a passage that leads

from Temple Bar to the south bank of the Liffey; see 10.315n.

10.524 (233:31). *the Bloom is on the Rye* – From a song, "When the Bloom Is on the Rye" (or "My Pretty Jane"), words by Edward Fitzball, music by Sir Henry Bishop (1786–1855). First verse and chorus: "My pretty Jane, my pretty Jane / Ah! never, never look so shy / But meet me, meet me in the ev'ning / While the bloom is on, is on the rye. [Chorus:] The spring is waning fast, my love. / The corn is in the ear, / The summer nights are coming, love. / The moon shines bright and clear, / Then, pretty Jane, my dearest Jane, / Ah! never look so shy, / But meet me, meet me in the ev'ning / While the bloom, the bloom is on the rye."

10.526 (233:33). Liffey street – A street that runs north from the Metal Bridge, just across the Liffey from where Lenehan and M'Coy are walking.

10.532 (233:40). the metal bridge – Or Liffey Bridge, a footbridge over the Liffey in central Dublin.

10.532 (233:40–41). Wellington quay – On the south bank of the Liffey between Metal Bridge and Grattan Bridge to the west.

10.534–35 (234:1–2). Mangan's, late Fehrenbach's – P. Mangan, pork butcher, 1–2 William Street South (approximately a quarter-mile south of where Lenehan and M'Coy are walking).

10.536 (234:3). Glencree reformatory – St. Kevin's, a Roman Catholic reformatory, at the headwaters of the Glencree River in the hilly country ten miles south of the center of Dublin. The "annual dinner" was a fund-raising event. Since 1974 the institution has been called the Glencree Reconciliation Centre.

10.538 (234:5). Val Dillon – See 8.159n. (He was lord mayor in 1894–95.)

10.538 (234:5–6). sir Charles Cameron – (1841–1924), an Irish-born proprietor of newspapers in Dublin and Glasgow; Liberal M.P. for Glasgow (1874–1900).

10.538 (234:6). Dan Dawson – See 6.151n.

10.545 (234:14–15). Delahunt of Camden street – Joseph and Sylvester Delahunt, family grocers, tea, wine, and spirit merchants, 42 and 92 Camden Street Lower.

10.547 (234:16). Lashings – Plenty.

10.553–54 (234:23–24). it was blue o'clock in the morning after the night before – A parody of the opening lines of "Three O'Clock in the Morning" (1921), lyrics by Dorothy Terriss, music by Julian Robledo: "It's three o'clock in the morning, / We've danced the whole night thru, / And day-light will soon be dawning, / Just one more waltz with you, / That melody so entrancing, / Seems to be made for us two, / I could just keep right on dancing forever dear, with you."

10.555 (234:25–26). Featherbed Mountain – Featherbed Pass gives access through the Wicklow Mountains between Dublin and Glencree, ten miles to the south.

10.555 (234:26). Chris Callinan – See 7.690–91n.

10.555–56 (234:26). the car – See 5.98n.

10.557 (234:28). *Lo, the early beam of morning* – Not a duet but a quartet, from Michael William Balfe's opera *The Siege of Rochelle* (1835), libretto by Edward Fitzball. Clara, the opera's heroine, is wrongly accused of murdering a child and must flee Rochelle. The quartet occurs just before the end of Act I as the monk, Father Azino, and others aid her escape: "AZINO: Lo, the early beam of morning softly chides our longer stay; hark! the matin bells are chiming, / Daughter we must hence away, Daughter we must hence away. CLARA: Father, I at once attend thee, farewell, friends, for you I'll pray; / Lo! the early beam of morning softly chides our longer stay; / Hark! the matin bells are chiming, Father, we must hence away. MARCELLA: Lady, may each blessing wait thee, we for you will ever pray; / Hark! the matin bells are chiming, from all danger haste away."

10.569 (235:1). Hercules – The mention of the constellation is appropriate because Hercules was one of the heroes who accompanied Jason and the Argonauts, though he left the expedition before its successful attempt at passage through the Wandering Rocks.

10.582 (235:16). common or garden – Garden *variety*; that is, commonplace, usual.

Section 10: 10.585–641 (pp. 235–37). Intrusions: (a) 10.599–600 (235:34–36). On O'Connell bridge . . . professor of dancing &c – See Section 1, Intrusion. **(b) 10.625–31 (236:29–36). An elderly female . . . and Guarantee Corporation** – See Section 9, Intrusion (b).

10.585–86 (235:18–19). *The Awful Disclosures of Maria Monk* – (New York, 1836). Maria Monk (c. 1817–50), a Canadian, arrived in New York City in 1835 claiming that she had escaped from the nunnery of the Hôtel Dieu in Montreal. Her book and its sequel, *Further Disclosures* (also 1836), offered in lurid and fanciful detail the "revolting practices" that she had "witnessed." Two hundred thousand copies were sold, giving rise to violent anti-Catholic agitation; as early as 1836 she was convincingly revealed as a fraud, but the revelation had little effect on public response to her claims.

10.586 (235:19). Aristotle's *Masterpiece* – Or rather pseudo-Aristotle, purportedly clinical, mildly pornographic; one of the several listings after its initial appearance in 1694: "*Aristotle's masterpiece completed*: in two parts. The first containing the secrets of generation in the parts thereof. . . . The second part being a private looking glass for the female sex. Treating of the various maladies of the womb, and all other distempers incident to women. N.Y. printed for the Company of flying stationers, 1798." Apparently the most widely circulated work of pseudosexual and pseudomedical folklore in seventeenth- and eighteenth-century England.

10.591–92 (235:25–26). *Tales of the Ghetto* by Leopold von Sacher Masoch – Sacher-Masoch (1835–1895), the Austrian novelist who gave his name to *masochism*. The collection of stories, first published in 1885 in German, bore the English title *Jewish Tales* (Chicago, 1894). The tales are primarily concerned with anti-Semitic persecutions that recoil to the moral betterment of the persecutors and their victims.

10.599 (235:34). O'Connell bridge – Over the Liffey in east-central Dublin. Bloom is near the Metal Bridge; O'Connell Bridge is the next one to the east.

10.601–2 (235:37–38). *Fair Tyrants* by James Lovebirch – A James Lovebirch (pun intended) is listed as the author of several novels in the Bibliothèque National *Catalogue des livres imprimés* (Paris, 1930), vol. 100, pp. 1001–2; his most notable title: *Les cinq fessées de Suzette*

(Paris, 1910); trans. as *The Flagellation of Suzette* [Paris, 1925]). *Fair Tyrants* is not listed.

10.606 (236:5). *Sweets of Sin* – Unknown. It could have been soft-core dime-novel pornography, in which case it would not necessarily have found its way into nineteenth-century collections of pornography. Or it could have eluded search because it was a subtitle. Or it could be Joyce's own coinage.

10.607 (236:7). He read where his finger opened – Bloom is inadvertently practicing *sortes Biblicae* (or *Virgilianae* or *Homericae*), divination by the Bible (or Virgil or Homer), in which a passage is selected at random and treated as revelatory or prophetic.

10.625 (236:29). an elderly female – Reminiscent of Miss Flyte, "a curious little old woman," quite "mad," who haunts the court of chancery in Dickens's *Bleak House*.

10.625–41 (236:29–36). the building of . . . Guarantee Corporation – The Four Courts (see 10.470–73n). The *Freeman's Journal* for 16 June 1904 reports, on page 2 under "Law Intelligence . . . Law Notices This Day," that the lord chancellor, sitting in the High Court of Justice, Chancery Division "(Before the Registrar, 11:30 o'clock)," would hear among others "In Lunacy" the case of one "Potterton, of unsound mind, *ex parte* . . . Potterton, discharge queries, vouch account" (col. 4). "King's Bench Division—Admiralty—1:30 o'clock—*Ex Parte* Motions. Summons—The Owners of the Lady Cairns *v.* the Owners of the barque Mona" (col. 5); see 16.913–17n. "Yesterday, Court of Appeal," in column 1, contains the report of "LITIGATION ABOUT A POLICY. Re Arbitration between Havery and the Ocean Accident and Guarantee Corporation Limited—The Court reserved judgment."

Section 11: 10.643–716 (pp. 237–39).
Intrusions: (a) 10.651–53 (237:16–19). Bang of the lastlap . . . by the College Library. (b) 10.673–74 (238:3–4). Mr Kernan, pleased . . . along James's street – See Section 12. **(c) 10.709–10 (239:4–5). The viceregal cavalcade . . . out of Parkgate** – See Section 19.

10.643 (237:6). Dillon's auctionrooms – Joseph Dillon, auctioneer and valuer, 25 Bachelor's Walk (on the north bank of the Liffey between Metal Bridge and O'Connell Bridge).

10.651–53 (237:16–19). Bang of the lastlap bell . . . College Library – The "last pink" edition of the *Evening Telegraph*, Dublin, 16 June 1904, under the headline "CYCLING AND ATHLETICS / Dublin University [Trinity College] Bicycle Sports," reports the "combination meeting of the Dublin University Bicycle and Harrier Club . . . held this afternoon in College Park. . . . The weather, after a fine morning, broke down at the time of starting, but afterwards the atmospheric conditions improved. Sport opened with the Half-Mile Bicycle Handicap, and from that the events were rattled off in good order. The band of the Second Seaforth Highlanders was present during the afternoon.
"Details: Half-Mile Bicycle Handicap— J. A. Jackson, 10 yds., 1; W. H. T. Gahan, sch., 2. Also competed—T. W. Fitzgerald, 30; A. Henderson, 50. Time 1 min. 16 secs. Second heat—W. E. Wylie, 20 yds., 1; A. Munro, 35 yds., 2. Also competed—T. C. Furlong, sch. Won by three lengths. Time, 1 min. 17 secs."

10.654–55 (237:21). Williams's row – Off Bachelor's Walk.

10.658 (237:24). your uncle John – John Goulding, the brother of May (Goulding) Dedalus and Richie Goulding.

10.674 (238:4). James's street – On the western side of Dublin south of the Liffey (near the Guinness Brewery).

10.675 (238:5–6). the Scotch house – A pub; see 8.321n.

10.698 (238:33). where Jesus left the jews – That is, without hope of salvation because from a doctrinaire Christian point of view they are eternally damned for having refused to accept Jesus as the Messiah and for having demanded the Crucifixion.

10.703 (238:40). O'Connell street – The busy north–south thoroughfare just around the corner from Bachelor's Walk where Dilly and her father are talking.

10.710 (239:5). Parkgate – At the southeast entrance to Phoenix Park (on the western outskirts of Dublin north of the Liffey).

10.716 (239:11–12). little sister Monica – An allusion to St. Monica's Widow's Almshouse, 35–38 Belvedere Place, in northeastern Dublin, 500 yards east and slightly north of Bloom's house in Eccles Street.

Section 12: 10.718–98 (pp. 239–41).
Intrusions: (a) 10.740–41 (239:39–240:1).
Hello, Simon . . . Dedalus answered stopping – See Sections 11 and 14. **(b) 10.752–54 (240:14–16). North Wall . . . Elijah is coming** – See Section 4, Intrusion (c) and Section 16, Intrusion (b). **(c) 10.778–80 (240:40–42). Dennis Breen . . . Collis and Ward.**

10.718 (239:13). From the sundial towards James's Gate – Kernan is walking east along James's Street; see 10.674n. The sundial stands at the intersection of Bow Lane and James's Street; St. James's Gate is a court at the eastern end of James's Street, where James's Street becomes Thomas Street West.

10.719 (239:14). Pulbrook Robertson – Pulbrook, Robertson & Co., 5 Dame Street (where Kernan presumably works and toward which he is now walking).

10.720 (239:15). Shackleton's offices – George Shackleton & Sons, flour millers and corn merchants, 35 James's Street.

10.721 (239:16). Mr Crimmins – William C. Crimmins, tea, wine, and spirit merchant, 27–28 James's Street and 61 Pimlico (in the center of Dublin, south of the Liffey). Crimmins was a graduate of Trinity College and a Poor Law Guardian, that is, he was Protestant and Conservative.

10.725–26 (239:22). that General Slocum explosion – See 8.1146–47n.

10.731 (239:29). Palmoil – Graft. Kernan's prejudiced guess could not have been founded on news or fact on 16 June 1904, but time did tell that the *General Slocum* disaster was a function not only of the captain and crew's panicked ineptitude but also of corruption: the fire hoses on the ship were so rotten that they had been condemned and the ship immobilized by a $1,000 lien. Mysteriously, though, that lien was reduced to $25 on 14 June and promptly discharged so that the *Slocum* could sail (rotten hoses and all) on 15 June.

10.738 (239:37). frockcoat – Kernan is overdressed for his class and employment.

10.743 (240:3). Peter Kennedy, hairdresser – 48 James's Street.

10.743–44 (240:4). Scott of Dawson street – William Scott, fashionable and expensive tailor

and clothier, 2 Sackville (now O'Connell) Street Lower (formerly of Dawson Street).

10.744 (240:5). Neary – There was an Edward Neary, military and merchant tailor, 15 Anne Street South; but that doesn't seem to fit the used-clothes implication.

10.745 (240:6). Kildare street club toff – A "toff" is a dandy or swell. The Kildare Street Club was the most fashionable Anglo-Irish men's club in Dublin.

10.746 (240:7). John Mulligan, the manager of the Hibernian Bank – The Hibernian Bank, 23–27 College Green, manager, W. A. Craig; branch offices: 12 Sackville Street Lower, manager, Christopher Tierney; 84–85 Thomas Street, manager, Ignatius Spadscani; 85–86 Dorset Street Upper, manager, B. J. Lawless. There were two important John Mulligans in Dublin, but *Thom's* 1904 lists neither as a banker.

10.747 (240:8). Carlisle bridge – The original name for O'Connell Bridge, after Lord Carlisle, viceroy in 1791 when construction began. The name was officially changed to O'Connell Bridge in 1882. Kernan's "mistake" is consistent with his "west Briton" attitudes.

10.748 (240:10–11). Knight of the road – Kernan intends this as an epithet for salesman, but traditionally it is an epithet for highwayman. *The Knight of the Road* (Dublin, 1891) is also a comic opera by Percy French, music by Houston Colliston (subsequently retitled *The Irish Girl*). Set in post-1798 Ireland, the hero is a Robin Hood who bewilders his victims in a variety of disguises (Fritz Senn, *JJQ* 13, no. 2 [1976]: 244).

10.750 (240:12–13). The cup that cheers but not inebriates – The phrase occurs in Bishop Berkeley's praise of tar-water "of a nature so mild and benign and proportioned to the human constitution as to warm without heating, to cheer but not inebriate" (*Siris* [1744], par. 217). William Cowper (1731–1800) gave it the shape that Kernan misquotes; in praise of tea: "the cups that cheer but not inebriate" (*The Task* [1785], Part IV, line 34).

10.752 (240:14). North wall and Sir John Rogerson's quay – Respectively, the north and south banks of the Liffey near its mouth; Benson's ferry plied between the two quays. The throwaway is still moving eastward; see 10.294–97 (227:6–10).

10.756 (240:18). Returned Indian officer – An army officer who had done a tour of duty in India was popularly supposed to be recognizable from his sunburned face. Kernan has *not* been to India.

10.757–58 (240:20). *Ned Lambert's brother . . . Sam – For the fictional Ned Lambert, see 6.111n.

10.764 (240:27). Down there Emmet was hanged, drawn and quartered – Robert Emmet (see 6.977–78n) was hanged in front of St. Catherine's Church (Church of Ireland) in Thomas Street. He was then beheaded, not drawn and quartered. (Kernan is approaching Thomas Street West, which extends eastward from James's Street.)

10.765 (240:28). Dogs licking the blood off the street – A traditional "eye-witness" touch about Emmet's execution. In 1 Kings 21:19, the Lord directs Elijah to tell Ahab, "In the place where dogs licked the blood of Naboth shall dogs lick thy blood, even thine."

10.765 (240:29). the lord lieutenant's wife – The traditional eyewitness was "a woman who lived nearby"; Kernan upgrades her as the wife (Elizabeth) of Philipe Yorke (1757–1834), third earl of Hardwicke, lord lieutenant of Ireland from 1801 to 1806.

10.766 (240:29). noddy – A light two-wheeled hackney carriage.

10.767–68 (240:29//30). *topers . . . Fourbottle men – Kernan associates Emmet (probably mistakenly) with the rakish behavior of eighteenth-century gentlemen such as belonged to the "Order of Saint Patrick" or the "Monks of the Screw"; See 15.2653n.

10.769/770 (240:30/31). saint Michan's/Glasnevin – See 6.977–78n. St. Michan's Church, founded in 1095 by the Danish saint of that name, in Church Street near the Four Courts. Many heroes of the Rebellion of 1798, including the brothers Sheares (see 12.498–99n), were buried in its vaults, but a 1903 (centenary) search for Emmet's headless remains was unsuccessful, as was a similar search at Prospect Cemetery in Glasnevin; see headnote to Hades, p. 104.

10.773–74 (240:34–35). Watling street . . . visitor's waitingroom – The visitor's waiting room of the Guinness Brewery is on the corner of James's Street and Watling Street, which runs north to the Liffey. Kernan's direct route back to the office would have been to continue east through Thomas Street.

10.774–75 (240:36). Dublin Distillers Company's stores – (Warehouse), 21-32 Watling Street.

10.775 (240:36). an outside car – See 5.98n.

10.776–77 (240:38). Tipperary bosthoon – Tipperary is a rural county seventy-eight miles southwest of Dublin. A "bosthoon" is a flexible rod or whip made of green rushes laid together; contemptuously it means a soft, worthless, spiritless fellow.

10.778–79 (240:41). John Henry Menton's office – Solicitor, 27 Bachelor's Walk, on the north bank of the Liffey just west of O'Connell Bridge.

10.780 (240:42). Messrs Collis and Ward – Solicitors, 31 Dame Street, south of the Liffey in central Dublin.

10.781 (241:1). Island street – Parallel to the Liffey and one block south, Island Street runs east from Watling Street.

10.781 (241:2). Times of the troubles – The "times" Kernan contemplates are the Rebellion of 1798.

10.782 (241:3). those reminiscences of sir Jonah Barrington – (1760–1834), an Irish patriot, judge, and anecdotal historian. As a member of the Irish Parliament he held out staunchly against the Act of Union. He wrote two extensive books of "reminiscences": *Personal Sketches of His Own Time*, three volumes (1827–32), and *Historic Memoirs of Ireland*, two volumes (1809, 1833), later retitled *The Rise and Fall of the Irish Nation*.

10.784 (241:5). Gaming at Daly's – Daly's Club was located on what is now College Green, just southeast of the center of modern Dublin. It was founded in 1750, magnificently housed in 1790, and closed, thanks to competition from the Kildare Street Club, in 1823. The *Official Guide to Dublin* (1958) remarks that it was "a famous rendezvous for the 'bloods' of the early nineteenth century, dicing, duelling, and drinking being their main concern."

10.784–85 (241:5–6). One of those fellows . . . with a dagger – A commonplace story about irascible cardplayers.

10.785–86 (241:7–8). *lord Edward Fitzgerald . . . behind Moira house – Lord Edward Fitzgerald (1763–98) was president of the military committee of the United Irishmen and regarded as the master spirit behind the plans for the Rebellion of 1798. He was denounced by proclamation in March 1798 and went into hiding in Dublin; in May a £1,000 reward was offered for information regarding his whereabouts. Henry Charles Sirr (1764–1841), town major of Dublin in 1798, was notorious for his ruthless use of informers and for the brutality of the police he led. Apparently informed of Fitzgerald's intended movements, Sirr set a trap for him in Watling Street (where Kernan is walking) on the night of 17 May; Fitzgerald eluded the trap and escaped into the house of one of his supporters, Nicholas Murphy, 151–152 Thomas Street, where he was arrested the next day, suffering mortal wounds in the process. He died in prison on 1 June 1798. Murphy's house was near the junction of Thomas, James's, and Watling streets. Moira House belonged to Francis Rowden, the earl of Moira (1754–1824), a friend of Fitzgerald's who gave sanctuary to his wife, Pamela, while Fitzgerald was in hiding in 1798. The house was located on Usher's Quay, on the south bank of the Liffey, a quarter of a mile northeast of Kernan's position. Fitzgerald, after he went into hiding, occasionally stole back to the stables behind Moira House to meet his wife.

10.789 (241:11). that sham squire – Francis Higgins (1746–1802); see 7.348n.

10.789–90 (241:12). Course they were on the wrong side – That is, Kernan is a "west Briton," pro-English and against Irish independence.

10.790 (241:12–13). They rose in dark and evil days . . . Ingram – Line 33 of "The Memory of the Dead" (1843), by John Kells Ingram (1823–1907), an Irish poet and man of letters. The poem begins: "Who fears to speak of Ninety-Eight? . . . He's a knave or half a slave." The line Kernan remembers is followed by ". . . / To right their native land; / They kindled here a living blaze / That nothing can withstand."

10.791 (241:13). They were gentlemen – A typical "west Briton" phrase used to exonerate Anglo-Irish Protestant revolutionaries (such as Fitzgerald, Wolfe Tone, Emmet—and even Parnell) from the sort of blame due the croppies (see following note and 2.276n).

10.793 (241:16). At the siege of Ross did my father fall – From a song, "The Croppy Boy"; see 11.39n. Ross, in southeastern Ireland, was an English strongpoint in the opening phase of the Rebellion of 1798. The "siege" of 5 June 1798 was more properly an attack, in which a large but loosely organized and poorly armed force of "croppies" (Catholic peasant rebels) was finally routed after it all but overwhelmed the small but well-armed garrison. The defeat was a serious blow to rebel morale in southeastern Ireland.

10.794 (241:17). Pembroke quay – A section of what is now Ellis's Quay, on the north bank of the Liffey opposite Watling Street, where Kernan is walking.

**Section 13: 10.800–80 (pp. 241–43).
Intrusions: (a) 10.818–20 (242:7–10). Two old women . . . eleven cockles rolled** – See 3.29–36 (37:33–40). **(b) 10.842–43 (242:33–34). Father Conmee . . . murmuring vespers** – See Section 1; Section 2, Intrusion (a); and Section 4, Intrusion (a).

10.800 (241:23). the webbed window – Thomas Russell, lapidary and gem cutter, 57 Fleet Street, a street just south of and parallel to the Liffey, not far east of Merchant's Arch.

10.805–7 (241:29–32). Born all in the dark . . . wrest them – Echoes the description of Mammon's teaching to the fallen angels in Milton's *Paradise Lost* (1:670–92): "And with impious hands / Rifl'd the bowels of thir mother Earth / For treasures better hid." "Evil lights shining in the darkness" echoes John 1:5: "And the light shineth in the darkness; and the darkness comprehended it not." "Where fallen archangels flung the stars of their brows" recalls Revelation 12:4: "And his [the dragon's] tail drew the third part of the stars of heaven, and did cast them to the earth."

10.812 (241:38). old Russell – See 10.800n.

10.813–14 (242:2). Grandfather ape gloating on a stolen hoard – In "The Eaters of Precious Stones" in *The Celtic Twilight* (1893), Yeats describes a vision of "the Celtic Hell, and . . . the Hell of the artist": "One day I saw faintly an immense pit of blackness, round which went a circular parapet, and on this parapet sat innumerable apes eating precious stones out of the palms of their hands. The stones glittered green and crimson, and the apes devoured them with an insatiable hunger" (cited by James Penny Smith, *JJQ* 12, no. 3 [1975]: 314).

10.816 (242:4). Antisthenes – See 7.1035n.

10.816–17 (242:5–6). Orient and immortal . . . to everlasting – See 3.43–44n.

10.818–19 (242:8). through Irishtown along London bridge road – Irishtown is on the shore of Dublin Bay just south of the mouth of the Liffey and just north of Sandymount, where Stephen walked on the beach in Proteus. The two women who "came down the steps from Leahy's terrace" (3.29 [37:33]) have apparently walked north along the strand and are now walking west toward London Bridge (over the River Dodder) and toward south-central Dublin.

10.821–22 (242:12). the powerhouse – Dublin Corporation Electric Light Station, 49–56 Fleet Street, just east of the lapidary's. Stephen is moving west along Fleet Street.

10.822–23 (242:13). Throb always without . . . always within – Echoes the American novelist James Lane Allen's (1849–1925) *The Mettle of the Pasture* (New York, 1903). The hero of the novel confesses past immoralities to his fiancée, who rejects him; he then has a climactic scene with his mother, in which he refuses her wish (that he and the fiancée be married). The hero leaves, and the mother responds: "For her it was one of those moments when we are reminded that our lives are not in our keeping, and that whatsoever is to befall us originates in sources beyond our power. Our wills may indeed reach the length of our arms or as far as our voices can penetrate space; but without us and within moves one universe that saves us or ruins us only for its own purposes; and we are no more free amid its laws than the leaves of the forest are free to decide their own shapes and season of unfolding, to order the showers by which they are to be nourished and the storms which shall scatter them at last" (p. 125; see *CW*, pp. 117–18).

10.824 (242:14–15). Between two roaring worlds where they swirl – Recalls the famous lines from Matthew Arnold's "Stanzas from the Grande Chartreuse" (1855) as the speaker describes himself: "Wandering between two worlds, one dead, / The other powerless to be born" (lines 85–86). Stephen's words may also echo a stanza from the American poet Richard Henry Stoddard's "The Castle in the Air": "We have two lives about us, / Two worlds in which we dwell, / Within us and without us, / Alternate Heaven and Hell:— / Without, the somber Real, / Within, our heart of hearts, / The beautiful Ideal."

10.826 (242:17). Bawd and butcher – That is, god; see 9.1050 (213:24–25).

10.828 (242:19–20). Very large and . . . keeps famous time – Stephen passes the shop of William Walsh, clockmaker, at 1 Bedford Row.

10.828–29 (242:20). You say right . . .'twas so, indeed – Hamlet speaks to Rosencrantz and Guildenstern in mockery of Polonius: "I will prophesy he comes to tell me of the players; mark it. You say right, sir: o' Monday morning; 'twas so indeed" (II. ii. 405–7).

10.830 (242:21). down Bedford row – Bedford Row runs north to Aston Quay on the south bank of the Liffey from the west end of Fleet Street.

10.831 (242:22). Clohissey's window – M. Clohisey, bookseller, 10–11 Bedford Row.

10.831–32 (242:23). 1860 print of Heenan boxing Sayers – An international boxing match for the world championship (bare knuckles, wrestling and hugging permitted) between an American, John Heenan, and the world champion, an Englishman, Tom Sayers, Farnborough, England, 7 April 1860. The fight lasted thirty-seven rounds, each round ending when one of the boxers was knocked down. Finally Sayers's right arm was injured; the partisan crowd stormed the ring and the bout was declared a draw. In the history of boxing Heenan v. Sayers is regarded as a turning point, the end of old-style boxing, since after the fight boxing was suppressed in England and was subsequently allowed only under the marquess of Queensberry rules (formulated 1865).

10.832 (242:24). square hats – Silk, or stovepipe, hats.

10.838 (242:29). *The Irish Beekeeper* – The *Irish Beekeeper's Journal*, a serious and scientific publication, the official journal of the Irish Beekeeper's Association. It was published monthly at 15 Crowe Street in Dublin.

10.838–39 (242:29–30). *Life and Miracles of the Curé of Ars* – *Life of the Curé d'Ars*, from the French of Abbé Mounin (Baltimore, 1865). The phrase "life and miracles" was usually reserved for the lives of saints; since the curé of Ars, Jean-Baptiste Marie Vianney (1786–1859), was not canonized until 3 May 1925, Stephen apparently adds a rhetorical flourish to Mounin's simpler title. Vianney enjoyed considerable fame as a confessor during his lifetime (he was popularly regarded as capable of "reading hearts"). He was beatified on 8 June 1905.

10.839 (242:30). *Pocket Guide to Killarney* – There were a number of guides to Killarney current in the late nineteenth century, but none that we have seen bore this common "Pocket Guide" title. Killarney, in southwest Ireland's County Kerry, was at the turn of the century the most celebrated of Irish tourist resorts. The region was known for its "romantic" lake and mountain scenery.

10.840–41 (242:31–32). *Stephano Dedalo . . . palmam ferenti* – Latin: "To Stephen Dedalus, one of the best alumni, the class prize."

10.842–43 (242:33–34). **his little hours . . . murmuring vespers** – See 10.184n. Donnycarney was a village on Malahide Road.

10.844–45 (242:35–36). **Eighth and ninth book of Moses. Secret of all secrets** – The Pentateuch has traditionally been regarded as "the five books of Moses," and there is a legend dating at least from the medieval cabala that says the five books of the Pentateuch are the books only of Moses the Lawgiver, the books of Moses the Magician having been lost. One numerological version of the legend holds that since the forty-nine gates of wisdom were open to Moses, the complete number of his works should be nine; another version regards ten as the perfect number. At any rate, speculation about the "lost books" and "translations" purporting to be fragments of one or more of those books was not unusual in the world of nineteenth-century pamphlets.[1] What these publications have in common are compendia of magic formulae (Secret of all Secrets) of the sort Stephen reads below, though Joyce's actual source is not known.

10.845 (242:36). **Seal of King David** – The two interlaced triangles (six-pointed star), the emblem of Judaism, symbolic of divine protection.

10.849 (242:41–42). *Se el yilo . . . Sanktus! Amen* – *Se* reads *Sel* in the German version of the "Eighth and Ninth Books of Moses" (see this page, n. 1); thus, if the phrase were *Sel el yilo*, it could be regarded as a phonetic reproduction of the Spanish *Cielillo*, "Little Heaven"; and "*nebrakada*" could be Spanish-Arabic for "blessed". The whole charm would then read: "[My] little heaven of blessed femininity, love only me. Holy! Amen."

10.850–51 (243:1–2). **Charms and invocations of the most blessed abbot Peter Salanka** – The German version of the "Eighth and Ninth Books of Moses" identifies Salanka as "Pater [Father, not Peter] Salanka, Prior [not Abbot] of a famous Spanish Trappist Monastery." But we have been unable to trace Salanka and his peculiarly un-Spanish name (Salamanca?) beyond that.

10.852–53 (243:3–4). **Joachim's. Down, baldy-noddle, or we'll wool your wool** – See 3.108n and 3.113–14n.

10.858 (243:9). **A Stuart face of nonesuch Charles** – The face of Charles I (1600–49; king 1625–49), the second Stuart king of England,

---

1 See Viktor Link, "Ulysses and the 'Eighth and Ninth Books of Moses,'" *JJQ* 7, no. 3 [1970]: 199–203. Link argues that the book Joyce used may have been a nineteenth-century German publication, but Link also describes a number of differences between Joyce's materials and the German text (as though Joyce had just scanned the text and had at times mistranslated). On the other hand, Joyce may have used an English version, complete with mistranslations, corruptions, and additions; late in the nineteenth century the New York publisher W. W. Delany advertised in *Delany's Irish Song Book*, no. 2 (New York, n.d.), "The Sixth and Seventh Books of Moses as translated from a German translation under the personal supervision of W. W. Delany's corporation: the magic of the Israelites is fully explained—such as second sight, healing the sick . . . mesmeric clairvoyance, etc. . . . Beware of Humbugs." For a twentieth-century example, see Henri Gamache, *Mystery of the Long Lost 8th, 9th, and 10th Books of Moses; together with the legend that was of Moses and 44 Secret Keys to Universal Power* (Highland Falls, N.Y., 1967).

is depicted in the way Stephen describes Dilly's face. *Nonesuch:* in the rare sense of "most eminent."

10.861 (243:12). Dan Kelly's – Apart from the context, identity and significance unknown.

10.867–68 (243:19–20). Chardenal's French primer – C. A. Chardenal, *The Standard French Primer* (London, 1877).

10.875 (243:27). Agenbite – See "Agenbite of Inwit," 1.481n.

Section 14: 10.882–954 (pp. 243–45).
Intrusions: (a) 10.919–20 (244:40–41). Cashel Boyle . . . Kildare Street club. (b) 10.928–31 (245:8–11). The reverend Hugh . . . the Ford of Hurdles.

10.884 (243:35). Reddy and Daughter's – Richard Reddy (no "Daughter's"), antique dealer, 19 Ormond Quay Lower (on the north bank of the Liffey west of Dublin center).

10.884–85 (243:36). Father Cowley brushed his moustache – If he were properly a priest, he would not have a moustache.

10.890 (244:4). gombeen – Anglicized Irish for usurous.

10.892 (244:7). Reuben – Reuben J. Dodd; see 6.264–65n.

10.893 (244:9). *long John – John Fanning (fictional), subsheriff of Dublin, whose bailiffs have Cowley under siege. The high sheriff of Dublin was an honorary post; the subsheriff held the actual responsibility. See 10.934n.

10.897 (244:13). bockedy – From the Irish *bacach:* "lame, halt, clumsy."

10.899 (244:15). the metal bridge – A footbridge over the Liffey not far from where the two men are standing.

10.901 (244:18). square hat – See 10.832n.

10.901 (244:19). slops – Loose, baggy trousers.

10.916 (244:36). jewman – A term of abuse, apparently peculiar to Ireland; see Introduction, p. 5.

10.918 (244:38). *basso profondo* – Italian: "a very deep bass voice," or one who has such a voice.

10.920 (244:41). Kildare street club – See 5.560–61n.

10.929 (245:9). saint Mary's abbey – See p. 268 above.

10.929 (245:9). James and Charles Kennedy's – Rectifiers and wholesale wine and spirit merchants, 31–32 Mary's Abbey and 150–151 Capel Street. Love has turned south out of Mary's Abbey toward the Liffey.

10.930 (245:10). Geraldines – The Fitzgeralds; see 10.438–39n.

10.930–31 (245:10–11). toward the Tholsel beyond the Ford of Hurdles – The Tholsel (literally, "toll-collector's booth") was built 1307–27 (?) to house the courtroom, rooms for the Trinity Guild of Merchants, the Royal Exchange, and offices of the Dublin Corporation. Rebuilt in 1683 and 1783, it was demolished in 1806. It stood in Skinner's Row (now Christchurch Place), south of the Liffey in the center of Dublin. *Ath Cliath*, the Ford of Hurdles, is the ancient Irish name for the causeway of wicker hurdles that provided a ford across the Liffey before the Danes occupied the region and founded Dublin. The ford was located approximately where Queen Maeve Bridge now stands (somewhat to the west of the Reverend Love's position); it provided the Irish name for Dublin, Baile Átha Cliath—the Place of the Ford of Hurdles.

10.934 (245:14). the subsheriff's office – City of Dublin Sheriff's Office, J. Clancy, subsheriff, 30 Ormond Quay Upper (*Thom's* 1904, p. 1564), approximately 400 yards west of where the men are standing. They will double back to the Ormond Hotel, which is east of the office.

10.935 (245:15). Rock – See 8.687–88n.

10.935 (245:16). Lobengula – Zulu king of the Matabele (c. 1833–94), noted for the boldness of his opposition to European incursions on his territory. After the discovery of gold in his kingdom, he was induced to sign a treaty with the English (1888), but in 1893, provoked by "English insolence," he led a series of costly and futile attacks on the English, who had blandly regarded the treaty as evidence of their conquest of the Matabele's territory.

10.936 (245:16). Lynchehaun – An alias of one James Walshe, who assaulted and almost killed a woman on Achill Island, off the west coast of Ireland. Concealed by island peasants, he was finally captured, tried, and sentenced to life imprisonment (1895); but he escaped and fled to America where the British secret service tracked him down in Indianapolis. The American courts refused to extradite, however, accepting the Irish-American fiction that he was a political prisoner. Walshe subsequently visited Ireland disguised as a clergyman and again managed to escape before the police discovered his presence. Thus he passed into legend as a man so tough and resourceful the police were afraid to touch him, and he passed into literature as one of the models for Christy in John Millington Synge's *Playboy of the Western World* (1907).

10.937 (245:18). the Bodega – A pub; the Bodega Company, wine and spirit merchants and importers, in Commercial Buildings (off Dame Street).

10.938 (245:19). on the right lay – We have taken the right course.

10.942 (245:24). shraums – Matter running from weak or sore eyes.

10.946–47 (245:31). 29 Windsor avenue – Off Fairview Strand, on the northeastern outskirts of Dublin in 1904. See Ellmann, p. 68.

10.950 (245:35). Barabbas – See 6.274n.

Section 15: 10.956–1041 (pp. 246–48). Intrusions: (a) 10.962–63 (246:7–8). Bronze by gold . . . the Ormond hotel – See Sirens episode (11.1–1294 [pp. 256–91]). **(b) 10.970–71 (246:15–17). On the steps of . . . Abraham Lyon ascending. (c) 10.984–85 (246:33–35). Outside la Maison Claire . . . for the liberties.**

10.957 (246:2). Castleyard gate – In Cork Hill, the entrance to Dublin Castle; for the Castle, see 8.362n.

10.961 (246:6). towards Lord Edward street – 80 yards north of the castle; that is, Cunningham and company will walk that distance and there pick up their carriage.

10.962 (246:7). Miss Kennedy's . . . Miss Douce's – The barmaids in the Ormond Hotel; see 11.64n.

10.963 (246:8). the Ormond hotel – See 10.395n.

10.967 (246:12). Boyd? – William A. Boyd, general secretary of the Dublin Y.M.C.A.; see 8.5n.

10.967 (246:12). Touch me not – "For I am not yet ascended to my Father" (John 20:17): Jesus' words to Mary Magdalene after the Resurrection, when he discovers her weeping at the empty tomb.

10.968 (246:13). the list – Of those who have contributed to the temporary support of Dignam's widow and children.

10.969 (246:14). Cork hill – The slope from Castle Street to the junction of Dame and Lord Edward streets.

10.970 (246:15). City Hall – On Cork Hill, the seat of Dublin's municipal government is adjacent to the Castle. Cunningham and company are passing the front of the building when Nannetti appears.

10.971 (246:16). Alderman Cowley – There is no such name on the list of members, Corporation of Dublin, 1903–4.

10.971 (246:16). Councillor Abraham Lyon – Member for Clontarf West ward in 1903–4.

10.972 (246:18). The castle car . . . upper Exchange street – A streetcar routed to pass Dublin Castle. The street itself is another name for Cork Hill, along which Cunningham and his friends are walking.

10.973–74 (246:20). the *Mail* office – The *Dublin Evening Mail* (daily), 37–38 Parliament Street (which runs north from Cork Hill to Grattan Bridge over the Liffey).

10.980 (246:27). there is much kindness in the jew – From *The Merchant of Venice*. Shylock faces Antonio with the proposal that a pound of his flesh be exacted if he fails to repay a loan on time, and Antonio declares himself "Content, i' faith: I'll seal to such a bond, / And say there is much kindness in the Jew" (I. iii.153–54).

10.982 (246:30). Jimmy Henry – Assistant town clerk, James J. Henry, City Hall.

10.982 (246:31). Kavanagh's – James Kavanagh, justice of the peace and tea, wine, and spirit merchant, 27 Parliament Street (at the intersection of Essex Gate, from which the "winerooms" were entered).

10.984 (246:33). la maison Claire – See 8.586n.

10.984–85 (246:33–34). Jack Mooney's brother-in-law – Bob Doran, who is on a bender; see "The Boarding House," *Dubliners*.

10.985 (246:34–35). the liberties – See 3.33n.

10.987 (246:37–38). a shower of hail suit – Not unlike "pepper and salt," a kind of tweed with white knobs in the weave.

10.988 (246:39). Micky Anderson's watches – Michael Anderson, watchmaker, 30 Parliament Street, just short of Kavanagh's and Essex Gate.

10.1002 (247:11). Henry Clay – A popular cigar named after the American politician, orator, and statesman Henry Clay (1777–1852).

10.1004 (247:13). the conscript fathers – A name given to the Roman senators after the expulsion of the Tarquins in 510 B.C. Brutus, founder of the Roman Republic, added one hundred to the ranks of the senators, and the names of the newcomers were "written together" (*conscripta*) on the walls. Fanning is referring to a meeting of the Dublin City Council (the Corporation), composed of twenty aldermen and sixty councillors elected from the twenty wards of the city.

10.1006 (247:16). Hell open to Christians – After *Hell Opened to Christians; To Caution Them from Entering into It* (1688), by Giovanni Pietro Pinamonti (1632–1703), an Italian Jesuit. In translation (Dublin, 1868), the book was popular as a text for meditation. The sermons in *A Portrait*, chapter 3:B, are in part based on this tract.

10.1007 (247:17). Irish language – The movement to revive Irish as the cultural language of Ireland was echoed by frequent attempts to make it the official language of Dublin.

10.1007 (247:17–18). Where was the marshall – Answer: playing chess in the D.B.C. (Dublin Bakery Company) in Dame Street (about one block away). The city marshal was John Howard Parnell, one of whose duties was to keep order at meetings of the Dublin Corporation. See 8.500n and 8.504–5n.

10.1008–9 (247:19). old Barlow the macebearer – Macebearer and Officer of Commons John Barlow carried the mace as symbol of authority before the lord mayor or his deputy.

10.1010 (247:21). Hutchinson, the lord mayor – The Right Honorable Joseph Hutchinson, lord mayor of Dublin, 1904–5.

10.1010 (247:21). Llandudno – A fashionable watering place southwest of Liverpool in northern Wales.

10.1011 (247:21–22). Lorcan Sherlock – Secretary to the Dublin Corporation (in effect, deputy lord mayor). He was eventually lord mayor (1912–14).

10.1011 (247:22). locum tenens – Latin: "holding the place"; acting as a substitute.

10.1034–35 (248:5). pass Parliament street – The viceregal cavalcade can be seen from Parliament Street as it passes along the quays on the north bank of the Liffey.

Section 16: 10.1043–99 (pp. 248–49).
Intrusions: (a) 10.1063–64 (248:36–37). The onelegged sailor . . . England expects . . . – See Section 3. **(b) 10.1096–99 (249:33–36). Elijah, skiff . . . Bridgewater with bricks** – See Section 4, Intrusion (c), and Section 12, Intrusion (b).

10.1045 (248:15). Parnell's brother – See 10.1007n and 8.500n.

10.1050 (248:22). translated – That is, moved; specifically, to move a bishop from one see to another.

10.1053 (248:25–26). a working corner – In chess, a concentration of pieces in an attempt to develop control of the board.

10.1054 (248:27). mélange – French: literally, "mixture"; in this case, a mixture of fruits in thick cream.

10.1058 (248:31). D. B. C. – The Dublin Bakery Company's tearoom at 33 Dame Street.

10.1061–62 (248:34–35). Shakespeare is the happy . . . lost their balance – "Happy hunting ground" is patronizing slang for the American Indian paradise. Haines's remark is a reaction to the extraordinary wave of irresponsible speculation about Shakespeare in the latter half of the nineteenth century. Delia Bacon, whose mind did "lose its balance," provides a case in point; see 9.410n and 9.411n.

10.1063 (248:36). 14 Nelson street – Private Hotel, Mary M'Manus, proprietor. Nelson Street runs south-southeast from the middle of Eccles Street.

10.1064 (248:37). *England expects* . . . – From "The Death of Nelson"; see 10.232n.

10.1066–67 (249:2). Wandering Aengus – See 9.1093n.

10.1068 (249:3). *idée fixe* – French: literally, "fixed idea"; established as a technical term by the French psychologist Théodule Ribot (1839–1916) in *Les malades de la personalité* (Paris, 1885). An *idée fixe* was assumed to be an involuntary "dominant idea," usually delusional, "toward which a whole group of concordant ideas converges, all others being eliminated, practically annihilated" during prolonged periods, as in some forms of insanity (*The Diseases of the Personality* [Chicago, 1895], p. 81).

10.1072 (249:7). visions of hell – See *A Portrait*, chapter 3; see also 10.1006n.

10.1073 (249:8). the Attic note – That is, the note of Athenian culture in the fifth century B.C.

10.1073 (249:8). The note of Swinburne – A reference to Swinburne's preoccupation with what he took to be the "Attic note," the sensory freedom of classical Greek values as against what he portrayed as the repressive bent of Christian values; see his "Hymn to Proserpine" (1866). It is ironic that Mulligan consistently avoids another aspect of Swinburne's emphasis: "For there is no God found stronger than death; and death is a sleep" (line 110).

10.1073–74 (249:9). the white death and the ruddy birth – From Swinburne's "Genesis," in *Songs Before Sunrise* (1871), stanza 9: "For the great labour of growth, being many, is one; / One thing the white death and the ruddy birth; / The invisible air and the all-beholden sun, / And barren water and many-childed earth."

10.1074 (249:10). He can never be a poet – See 3.128n.

10.1078 (249:13–14). *professor Pokorny of Vienna – Julius P. Pokorny (b. 1887), a lecturer in Celtic philology in Vienna from 1914 and a professor of Celtic at the University of Berlin from 1921. In his *History of Ireland* (Vienna, 1916; trans. London, 1933), Pokorny argues, on the basis of an analytic treatment of Celtic mythology and philology, that the Celtic settlement of Ireland dates to 800 or 900 B.C. His preoccupation is with racial origins and racial longevity.

10.1082 (249:17). no traces of hell in ancient Irish myth – Pokorny did hold this view which has the merit of being half right. The otherworld of Celtic mythology, *Tir na n-og* (see 9.413n), has no trace of hell; but the mythology does include an underworld of phantoms and horrors, the ultimate test through which heroes like Cuchulin must pass before they can enter *Tir na n-og*.

10.1083–84 (249:18–19). The moral idea . . . of retribution – The idea that the Irish are amoral or immoral is not so much Pokorny's as it is the typical conservative English attitude. It dates at least from Giraldus Cambrensis's (Girald de Barri, c. 1146–c. 1220) *Topography of Ireland* (1188), which portrays the native Irish as infected with "abominable guile" and with "the pest of treachery."

10.1089–90 (249:26–27). He is going to write something in ten years – See John Keats's "Sleep and Poetry" (1817), lines 96–98: "O for ten years, that I may overwhelm / Myself in poesy; so I may do the deed / That my own soul has to itself decreed." Cf. the self-destructive vision of the fall of Icarus, lines 301–4.

10.1097–98 (249:34–35). beyond new Wapping street past Benson's ferry – The street is on the north bank of the Liffey near its mouth; the ferry was east of the street and nearer the river's mouth.

10.1098 (249:36). *Rosevean* from Bridgewater with bricks – See 3.504–5n.

Section 17: 10.1101–20 (pp. 249–50).

10.1101 (249:37). past Holles street – Artifoni is walking southeast along Mount Street Lower, a continuation of the northeast side of Merrion Square in the southeast quadrant of Dublin. The other two follow roughly the same course until Farrell turns back.

10.1101 (249:37–38). Sewell's yard – James Walter Sewell & Son and James Simpson, horse repository, commission, and livery establishment, 60 Mount Street Lower.

10.1103–4 (250:1). Mr Law Smith's house – Philip H. Law Smith, M.A., LL.D., barrister, 14 Clare Street (extends northwest from Merrion Square North, the northeast side of Merrion Square).

10.1105 (250:3). *College park – Of Trinity College, on the same northwest–southeast axis.

10.1107 (250:5). Mr Lewis Werner's cheerful windows – Louis Werner, surgeon oculist, ophthalmic surgeon to the Mater Misericordiae Hospital and Royal Victoria Eye and Ear Hospital. His "cheerful windows" were at 31 Merrion Square North on the corner of Holles Street.

10.1109 (250:8). *the corner of Wilde's house – Sir William and Lady Wilde, Oscar Wilde's parents, formerly lived at 1 Merrion Square North; Sir William, an oculist, was thus "at home" in this "medical area" of Dublin.

10.1109–10 (250:8–9). Elijah's name . . . Metropolitan Hall – For Elijah, see 8.13n. There is some confusion here, because Farrell is not looking at Metropolitan Hall, which is in Abbey Street (north of the Liffey), but at Merrion Hall, which is off to his left, on the corner of Denzille Lane (now Fenian Street) and Merrion Street Lower, the northerly extension of Merrion Square West. When Stephen and Lynch see the same poster (14.1579 [428:14]), it is on Merrion Hall and the confusion is resolved.

10.1111 (250:10). duke's lawn – The lawn of Leinster House, southeast of where Farrell is standing.

10.1113 (250:12). *Coactus volui* – Latin, literally, "having been forced, I was willing." R. J. Shork has located the phrase and its context in IV.2.21.5 of Justinian's *Digest,* the great legal compendium prepared at the behest of the Byzantine Emperor Justinian I (483–565) and published in 533. Shork says, "In this section of the . . . compendium the effect of force and fear on the validity of a contractual action is being discussed. An opinion by the jurisconsult Paulus is cited: '*Si metu coactus adii hereditatem, puto me heredem effici, qua quamvis si liberum esset noluissem, tamen coactus volui.*' (If I have been forced by fear to accept a legacy, I judge that I am made

a legatee because, although I would not have been willing had it been freely offered, nevertheless, having been forced, I was willing.)" See "Joyce and Justinian: U250 and 520," *JJQ* 23, (Fall 1985): 77.

10.1114 (250:13). Clare street – Extends Merrion Square North to the west-northwest (into Leinster and then Nassau Street, along the south side of Trinity College Park).

10.1115 (250:14). Mr Bloom's dental windows – Marcus J. Bloom, dental surgeon to Maynooth College, former lecturer on dental surgery, St. Vincent's Hospital, and ex-surgeon, Dental Hospital, Dublin, and St. Joseph's Hospital for Children, 2 Clare Street. No relation to Leopold Bloom.

Section 18: 10.1122–74 (pp. 250–52) – See Section 9, Intrusion (c).

10.1122 (250:20). Ruggy O'Donohoe's – M. O'Donohoe, international bar, 23 Wicklow Street, on the corner of William Street, where the pork butcher was located.

10.1123 (250:21–22). Mangan's, late Fehrenbach's – See 10.534–35n.

10.1124 (250:23). Wicklow street – In the southeast quadrant of Dublin 600 yards west of the scene of the previous action. Young Dignam is heading southeast. He will walk briefly north through Grafton Street and then turn east-southeast into Nassau Street (10.1154 [251:19]) toward his home in Sandymount near the bay, on the southeastern outskirts of metropolitan Dublin.

10.1125–26 (250:24–25). Mrs Stoer and Mrs Quigley and Mrs MacDowell – *Thom's* 1904 lists a John Stoer, Esq., 15 New Grove Avenue, and an F. H. Stoer, 83 Tritonville Road, both in *Sandymount. It lists no Quigleys in Sandymount, but it does list several MacDowells on Claremont Road, and one of those families may very well be Gerty MacDowell's (the heroine of Nausicaa).

10.1127 (250:26). uncle Barney – Bernard Corrigan, Mrs. Dignam's brother.

10.1128 (250:27). Tunney's – William J. Tunney, family grocer and tea, wine, and spirit merchant, 8 Bridge Street in Ringsend (just south of the mouth of the Liffey) and 10 Haddington Road (not far to the southwest).

10.1130 (250:29). Wicklow lane – Off the south side of Wicklow Street (at no. 31), near its western end.

10.1130 (250:29). Madame Doyle – Court dress and millinery warerooms, 33 Wicklow Street.

10.1131 (250:31). puckers – A "puck" is a blow; therefore, boxers.

10.1132 (250:31). putting up their props – Squaring off with clenched fists and flexed arms.

10.1133–34 (250:33–34). Keogh . . . Bennett – The match has some basis in fact, since an M. L. Keogh did box one Garry of the 6th Dragoons as the second event in a tournament in late April 1904. Percy Bennett, a member of the Zurich consular staff when Joyce lived in that city, is a grudge substitute for the more Irish Garry. Keogh knocked out Garry in the third round. See Ellmann.

10.1134 (250:34). Portobello – See 8.801–2n.

10.1034–35 (250:34–35). fifty sovereigns – Fifty pounds, a sizable purse for what would have amounted, in modern terms, to a semiprofessional bout.

10.1136 (250:37). Two bar – Two shillings.

10.1137 (250:37–38). do a bunk on – Deceive, run out on.

10.1141 (251:5). Marie Kendall – See 10.380n.

10.1142–43 (251:6–7). mots . . . in the packets of fags – A "mot" is a loose woman or prostitute. Cards with pictures of the sort Master Dignam is contemplating used to be enclosed as come-ons in packages of inexpensive cigarettes.

10.1143 (251:7). Stoer – See 10.1125–26n.

10.1146 (251:10). Fitzsimons – Robert Fitzsimmons (1862–1917), an English heavyweight boxer, won the world championship in 1897 by knocking out J. J. Corbett with a "solar plexus" punch. Fitzsimmons lost the title to the American heavyweight James J. Jeffries (1875–1953) in 1899.

10.1148 (251:12–13). Jem Corbett – James John "Gentleman Jim" Corbett (1866–1933), an American boxer noted for his skill. He became heavyweight champion of the world in 1892 by beating John L. Sullivan but lost the title to Fitzsimmons in 1897.

10.1150–52 (251:15–17). In Grafton street . . . grinning all the time – The "toff" (dandy, swell) is Boylan; the drunk is Bob Doran. See 10.984–85 (246:33–35).

10.1153 (251:18). No Sandymount tram – During the day, trams left Nelson's Pillar bound for Sandymount via Nassau Street and its southeasterly extensions every ten minutes (*Thom's* 1904, p. 1780).

10.1169 (251:37). butty – Thick and stout, after "butt," a large barrel or cask for wine or beer.

10.1173 (251:41–252:1). in purgatory . . . confession – The hope is that Dignam, having confessed his sins and been absolved, has not sinned mortally in the meantime and his soul has therefore been adjudged to purgatory, where he will complete his penance before entering heaven. It is significant that Dignam has sinned by going on at least one drunk, and also that Master Patrick does not recall his father's having received extreme unction, presumably because his death by "apoplexy" was sudden and unexpected. See 10.91–92n.

10.1173–74 (252:1). *father Conroy – The Reverend B. Conroy, C.C. (curate-in-charge) of Dignam's parish church, Mary, Star of the Sea, on Leahy's Terrace in Sandymount. See 13.448n.

Section 19: 10.1176–1282 (pp. 252–55).
The opening of the Mirus Bazaar took place not on 16 June but on 31 May 1904; nor was there a cavalcade, though the lord lieutenant did attend the opening. The fictional cavalcade starts at the Viceregal Lodge in Phoenix Park, exits at Park Gate, the southeastern entrance of the park, and proceeds east along the quays that line the northern bank of the Liffey. The cavalcade crosses the river at Grattan Bridge and proceeds east and south, past Trinity College and eventually across the Grand Canal and into Pembroke township (on the southeastern outskirts of Dublin, where the bazaar was located).

10.1176 (252:3). William Humble, earl of Dudley, and lady Dudley – William Humble Ward, second earl of Dudley (1866–1932), a Conservative and lord lieutenant of Ireland (1902–6). Married Rachel Gurney in 1891: two sons, three daughters.

10.1177 (252:4). *lieutenantcolonel Heseltine – Lt. Col. C. Heseltine was an extra aide-de-camp in the lord lieutenant's household in 1904.

10.1178–79 (252:6). the honourable Mrs Paget, Miss de Courcy – As Adams points out (p. 220n), the names have historical overtones: Sir John de Courcy was one of the Anglo-Norman heroes in the twelfth-century invasion of Ireland, and Henry William Paget (1768–1854), earl of Angelsey, was lord lieutenant of Ireland (1828–29; 1830–33); he, too, had been a military hero, in command of Wellington's cavalry at the battle of Waterloo.

10.1179 (252:6–7). the Honourable Gerald Ward A.D.C. – (Aide-de-camp); there is no such person listed in "The lord lieutenant's household" in *Thom's* 1904. But the *Irish Independent* (1 June 1904, pp. 4–5) reports "Lt. the Hon. Cyril Ward, R.N. [Royal Navy], A.D.C." in attendance on the lord lieutenant. See Adams, pp. 218–20.

10.1181 (252:9–10). Kingsbridge – Over the Liffey, just outside of Parkgate, was named in honor of George IV's visit to Dublin in 1821. It is now called Sean Heuston Bridge.

10.1183 (252:11–12). Bloody bridge – The next bridge in sequence east of Kingsbridge was called Barrack Bridge in 1904 (it is now Rory O'More Bridge, after a seventeenth-century Irish rebel leader). Bloody Bridge was a wooden bridge constructed on that site in 1670. The guildsmen of the Dublin Corporation evidently saw the bridge as a challenge to the profits from their ferries, wharves, and warehouses, and they communicated their disapproval of the bridge to their apprentices, who organized a wrecking expedition that was interrupted by the military. Four apprentices were killed; thus the name, Bloody Bridge.

10.1184 (252:13). Queen's and Whitworth bridges – In succession, east of Bloody Bridge. Queen's Bridge (1768) was named for George III's queen, Charlotte; it is now called Queen Maeve Bridge (after a first-century Irish queen). Whitworth Bridge was named for Earl Whit-

worth, lord lieutenant of Ireland 1813–17. It is now called Father Mathew Bridge, after the Reverend Theobald Mathew (1790–1856), "the apostle of temperance."

10.1185–86 (252:15). Mr Dudley White, B.L., M.A. – (Bachelor of Laws, Master of Arts), barrister, 29 Kildare Street, Dublin.

10.1186 (252:15). Arran quay – The north bank of the Liffey between Queen's (Queen Maeve) and Whitworth (Father Mathew) bridges.

10.1186–87 (252:16). Mrs M. E. White's, the pawnbroker's – 32 Arran Quay, on the corner of Arran Street West.

10.1188 (252:18). Phibsborough – A short street three-quarters of a mile north of where Mr. White stands; his dilemma: any of the three routes he contemplates will take from ten to fifteen minutes.

10.1190–91 (252:21). Four Courts – In Inns Quay, east of Whitworth (Father Mathew) Bridge; see 10.470–73n.

10.1191 (252:21–22). costsbag . . . Goulding, Collis and Ward – See 10.472n.

10.1192 (252:23). Richmond bridge – East of the Four Courts and next in the succession of bridges after Whitworth Bridge; it is now called O'Donovan Rossa Bridge, after Jeremiah O'Donovan (1831–1915), a Fenian leader whose advocacy of violence earned him the nickname Dynamite Rossa.

10.1193 (252:23–24). Reuben J Dodd, solicitor . . . Insurance Company – And Mutual Life Assurance Company of New York, 34 Ormond Quay Upper (east of Richmond Bridge).

10.1195 (252:26). King's windows – William King, printer and law stationer, 36 Ormond Quay Upper; thus, the "elderly female" turns back west toward the Four Courts, from which she had come.

10.1196 (252:27). Wood quay – On the south bank of the Liffey, opposite the western half of Ormond Quay Upper.

10.1196 (252:28). Tom Devan's office – Tom Devan worked in the Dublin Corporation Cleansing Department, 15–16 Wood Quay. The department was the focus of controversy because of repeated delays in the construction of a centralized sewage system for Dublin.

10.1196 (252:28). Poddle river – Has been moved for the convenience of fiction; it actually enters the Liffey from the south under Wellington Quay, approximately 350 yards east of the Dublin Corporation Cleansing Department in Wood Quay.

10.1197 (252:29). crossblind – See 7.440n.

10.1197 (252:29–30). the Ormond Hotel – At 8 Ormond Quay Upper.

10.1200 (252:32). the greenhouse – A public urinal stood at the eastern end of Ormond Quay Upper.

10.1200 (252:32–33). the subsheriff's office – See 10.934n.

10.1202 (252:35). Cahill's corner – Cahill & Co., letterpress printers, 35–36 Strand Street, on the corner of Capel Street just north of Grattan Bridge, where the cavalcade turns out of Ormond Quay Upper to cross the Liffey.

10.1204 (252:37). advowsons – In English law, the right to name the holder of a church benefice.

10.1204 (252:37). Grattan bridge – (Formerly Essex Bridge), after Richmond Bridge in the eastward succession of bridges. Named for Henry Grattan; see 7.731n.

10.1205–6 (252:39). Roger Greene's office – Roger Greene, solicitor, 11 Wellington Quay (on the south bank of the Liffey, east of Grattan Bridge).

10.1206 (252:39). Dollard's – Dollard Printing House, account-book manufacturer, 2–5 Wellington Quay (at the Grattan Bridge end of the quay).

10.1206 (253:1). Gerty MacDowell – See Nausicaa (13.1–771 [pp. 346–67]).

10.1207 (253:1–2). Catesby's cork lino – A linoleum manufactured by T. Catesby & Sons, Ltd., in Glasgow.

10.1209 (253:4). Spring's – Spring & Sons, coal factors and carriers, house agents, and furniture warehouse, 11 Granby Row Upper and 15–18 Dorset Street Upper.

10.1211 (253:6). Lundy Foot's – Lundy, Foot & Co., wholesale tobacco and snuff manufacturers, 26 Parliament Street (on the south corner of Essex Gate). The cavalcade moves down Parliament Street and turns east into Dame Street.

10.1211–12 (253:7). Kavanagh's winerooms – On the north corner of Essex Gate and Parliament Street; see 10.982n.

10.1214 (253:10). G.C.V.O – Knight, Grand Cross of Royal Victorian Order.

10.1214 (253:10–11). Micky Anderson's – See 10.988n.

10.1215 (253:11). Henry and James's – Clothiers, 1–3 Parliament Street and 82 Dame Street (on the corner where the cavalcade turns east).

10.1216 (253:12–13). Henry *dernier cri* James – *Dernier cri*, French: "the last word, the latest fashion." The repetition suggests an allusion to the American novelist Henry James (1843–1916), whose studied intricacies involved frequent use of French phrases.

10.1217 (253:13). Dame gate – A gate in the east wall of the medieval city of Dublin. It no longer exists, but it once stood off what is now Dame Street, across from and just east of the intersection with Parliament Street.

10.1220 (253:17–18). Marie Kendall – See 10.380n; her "poster" is on the Empire Palace Theatre, 72 Dame Street.

10.1227 (253:25). Fownes's street – Just short of the eastern end of Dame Street (where it becomes College Green).

10.1230 (253:28–29). Commercial Buildings – Off Dame Street at 41A (the intersection of Dame Street and College Green).

10.1231 (253:30). hunter watch – A watch having a hunting case, a hinged cover designed to protect the crystal from injury (as on the hunting field).

10.1232 (253:31). King Billy's horse – A much-vilified and frequently vandalized equestrian statue of King William III (William of Orange) (1650–1702; king 1689–1702) stood opposite Trinity College (one of the busiest intersections in Dublin). William defeated the Irish in the Battle of the Boyne (1690), suppressing yet another Irish bid for independence and reducing Ireland to the status of penal colony. He is remembered only a little more cordially than Cromwell as a great oppressor. The emphasis on the horse in this passage recalls a traditional Irish toast: "To the memory of the chestnut horse [that broke the neck of William of Orange]." (It was actually his collarbone, but that and a chill were the death of him.) The controversial statue was removed after an encounter with a land mine in 1929.

10.1236 (253:36–37). Ponsonby's corner – Edward Ponsonby, law and general bookseller, government agent and contractor, 116 Grafton Street, near its intersection with College Green. The cavalcade turns south into Grafton Street and then immediately east into Nassau Street.

10.1238–39 (253:39). Pigott's music warerooms – Pigott & Co., pianoforte and musical-instrument merchants, music sellers, and publishers, 112 Grafton Street.

10.1240–41 (253:41–42). the provost's wall – The provost's house in the Trinity College grounds is set behind a wall that angles from the west front of Trinity College into the north side of Nassau Street (through which the cavalcade will proceed east-southeast).

10.1241–42 (254:1). socks with skyblue clocks – See 4.282n, lines 19–20.

10.1242 (254:1–2). *My girl's a Yorkshire girl* – A song by C. W. Murphy and Dan Lipton: "Two fellows were talking about / Their girls, girls, girls / Sweethearts they left behind— / Sweethearts for whom they pined— / One said, My little shy little lass / Has a waist so trim and small— / Grey are her eyes so bright, / But best of all—[Chorus:] My girl's a Yorkshire girl, / Yorkshire through and through. / My girl's a Yorkshire girl, / Eh! by gum, she's a champion! / Though she's a fact'ry lass, / And wears no fancy clothes / I've a sort of Yorkshire Relish for my little Yorkshire Rose. [Stanza two:] When the first finished singing / In praise of Rose, Rose, Rose— / Poor Number Two looked vexed, / Saying in tones perplexed / My lass works in a factory too, / And also has eyes of grey / Her name is Rose as well, / And strange to say—[Stanza three:] To a cottage in Yorkshire they hied / To Rose, Rose, Rose / Meaning to make it clear / Which was the boy most dear. / Rose, their Rose didn't answer the bell, / But her husband did instead. / Loudly he sang to them / As off, off they fled—."

10.1249 (254:10). College park – In Trinity College north of Nassau Street and of its extension, Leinster Street.

10.1258–50 (254:19–21). the quartermile flat . . . W. C. Huggard – See 10.651–53n.

10.1260 (254:22). Finn's hotel – M. and R. Finn, private hotel and restaurant, 1–2 Leinster Street (where it becomes the eastward continuation of Nassau Street).

10.1262–63 (254:24–25). *Mr M. E. Solomons . . . viceconsulate – M. E. Solomons, a prominent member of Dublin's Jewish community, optician and manufacturer of spectacles and mathematical and hearing instruments, 19 Nassau Street; listed at the same address: the Austro-Hungarian vice-consulate, imperial and royal vice-consul, Maurice E. Solomons (justice of the peace in the City and County of Dublin). 19 Nassau Street is 350 yards west of where Farrell is "striding."

10.1264 (254:26). Trinity's postern – The south gate of Trinity College in Lincoln Place, just off Leinster Street at the southeastern corner of the college.

10.1264 (254:26–27). Hornblower – See 5.555n.

10.1264 (254:27). tallyho cap – The porters of Trinity College, Dublin, still wear black peaked caps not unlike those of the members of a fox hunt (whose traditional cry when the quarry is sighted is "Tallyho").

10.1265 (254:28). Merrion square – Leinster Street gives into Clare Street, which in turn becomes Merrion Square North.

10.1268–69 (254:32). Mirus bazaar – See headnote to Section 19, p. 283.

10.1269 (254:32). Mercer's hospital – In William Street, Dublin, incorporated by act of Parliament in 1734.

10.1270 (254:33). Lower Mount street – Continues Merrion Square North in an east-south-easterly direction.

10.1271 (254:34). Broadbent's – J. S. Broadbent, fruiterer, 2 Mount Street Lower.

10.1273 (254:36–37). the Royal Canal bridge – Curious, because Mount Street Lower, along which the procession has been moving, gives onto a bridge over the Grand (not the Royal) Canal and then into Northumberland Road. The Grand Canal circled the southern perimeter of metropolitan Dublin, the Royal Canal the northern. The bridge is now called McHenry Bridge.

10.1273 (254:37). Mr Eugene Stratton – See 6.184n.

10.1274 (254:38–39). Pembroke township – On the southeastern outskirts of Dublin.

10.1274–75 (254:39). Haddington road corner – The cavalcade is proceeding southeast along Northumberland Road; Haddington Road crosses it almost at right angles. The two old women (see 10.818–20 [242:7–10]) have continued walking west and south from London Bridge Road through Bath Avenue into Haddington Road.

10.1277 (255:1). without his golden chain – On state occasions the lord mayor of Dublin wore a gold chain as the emblem of his office.

10.1277–78 (255:1–2). Northumberland and Lansdowne roads – Lansdowne Road runs northeast from its intersection with Northumberland Road.

10.1279–81 (255:4–6). the house said . . . consort, in 1849 – Queen Victoria and her husband, Prince Albert, spent four days in Dublin, 6–10 August 1849, in the course of their first visit to Ireland. They entered the city from the southeast, via Pembroke Road, which angles through the intersection of Northumberland and Lansdowne roads. The *Freeman's Journal* for Tuesday, 7 August 1849, carried an incredibly detailed account of the royal couple's entry into Dublin. The account does not mention a specific "house . . . admired by the late queen," but it describes at length the scene on Pembroke Road: "This locality presented a very grand and animated appearance. Many of the houses were beautifully decorated, and the balconies, windows, and doorsteps were crowded with elegantly attired ladies and gentlemen." The account dwells at length on the queen's response to a cast-iron arch that spanned the intersection of Northumberland and Lansdowne roads, "tastefully covered with laurel and other evergreens, interspersed with blossoms of whitethorn . . . surmounted by an imperial crown about four feet in height."

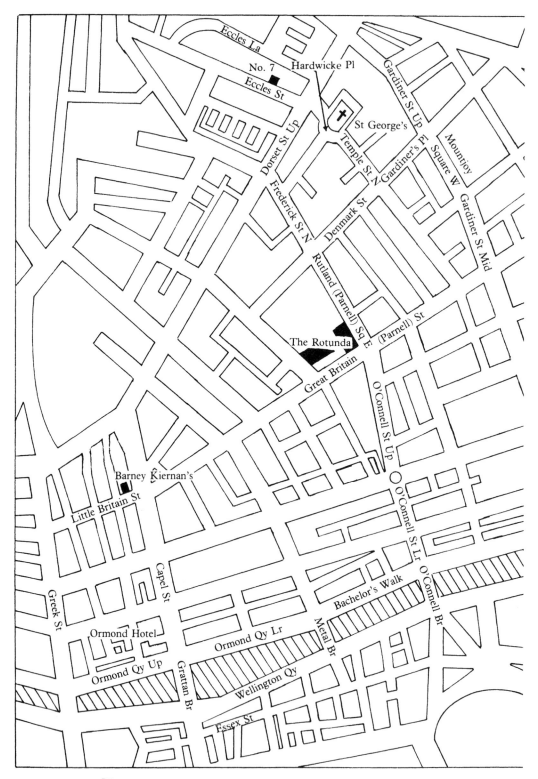

EPISODE 11. *Sirens*

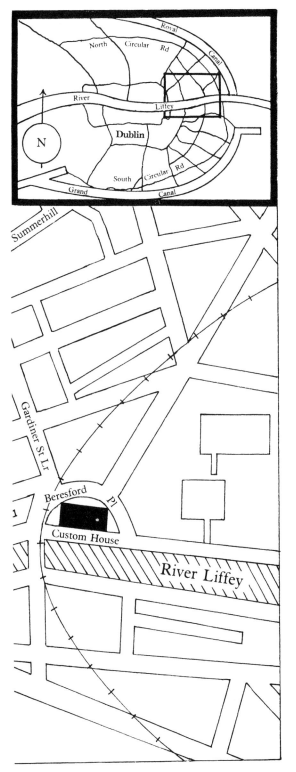

EPISODE 11

Sirens

(11.1–1294, PP. 256–91)

Episode 11: *Sirens*, 11.1–1294 (256–291). In Book 12 of *The Odyssey*, Circe, in the course of advising Odysseus about his voyage and its dangers, warns him about the two Sirens on their isle, "crying / beauty to bewitch men coasting by" (12:40; Fitzgerald, p. 222). She tells Odysseus that they will "sing [a man's] mind away on their sweet meadow lolling" (12:43; ibid.) so that he will be led to his death on the rocky shore of their isle. If, however, Odysseus wishes to "hear those harpies' thrilling voices" (12:60; Fitzgerald, p. 223) he must stop the ears of his men with wax and have himself tied to the mast, his men warned not to release him no matter how violently he protests. Later in Book 12 he follows Circe's advice and, without paying the penalty, hears the Sirens' song (promising pleasure and merriment after the perils of war and false-promising knowledge of the future to those who land on their rock). He then sails on to the passage between Scylla and Charybdis.

Time: 4:00 P.M. Scene: the Concert Room—the saloon at the bar and restaurant of the Ormond Hotel, 8 Ormond Quay Upper. The Ormond bar was a favorite haunt of Dublin's amateur musicians, and the saloon was frequently the setting for the small concerts that were popular in turn-of-the-century Dublin and in which the distinction between amateur and professional was not of much importance (see 11.275n). Organ: ear; Art: music; Color: none; Symbol: barmaids; Technique: *Fuga per canone*.[1] Correspondences: *Sirens*—barmaids; *the Isle*—the bar.

The Linati schema lists as "Colour, Coral," and as Persons, in addition to Ulysses and Menelaus: *Leucothea*: or Ino, the wife of Athamas, a king in Boeotia. When he went mad and killed one of their sons, she threw herself and her other son into the sea (to protect Athamas from further infanticide). The gods transformed her into the sea-deity Leucothea to aid men who were in peril at sea. In *The Odyssey* 5:333–53, she takes pity on Odysseus when he is storm-lashed by Poseidon after leaving Calypso's island. She speaks to him and lends him her magic veil for the swim to the island of the Phaeacians (Nausicaa's people). *Parthenope*: the siren who threw herself into the sea when the attempt to beguile Odysseus failed. *Orpheus and the Argonauts*: in Greek myth, Orpheus is the celebrated poet-musician whose lyre could charm into dance not only wild beasts but also trees and rocks. The Argonauts enlisted him for their expedition in quest of the Golden Fleece, and he was of considerable help: he charmed the Symplegades (Wandering Rocks) so that they were fixed in their places as the Argo passed through them, and he lulled to sleep the Colchian dragon that guarded the fleece. When his wife, Eurydice, died, he went down to Hades and almost succeeded in bringing her back to life, but, overcome by the anxiety of love, he broke the spell by looking back just before they passed the boundary of Hades. His grief at the second and final loss of Eurydice stunned him into treating the Thracian women with contempt. They revenged themselves by tearing him to pieces in a Bacchanalian orgy.

11.1–62 (256:1–257:24). Bronze by gold . . . Be pfrwritt. Done – This sequence of sixty fragments is usually described as an introductory announcement of the episode's musical motifs; the episode's musical "form" may also be developed by regarding this sequence as the "keyboard" on which the "fugue" is to be performed. The initial appearance in the episode of each of these "motifs" or "notes" is cited below.

11.1 (256:1). Bronze by gold heard the hoofirons, steelyringing – The barmaids in the Ormond Hotel, Miss Douce (bronze) and Miss Kennedy (gold), hear the viceregal procession (11.64–65 [257:26–28]). Bronze and gold were the principal metals in the world of Homer's epics; iron was the metal of Homer's own time.

11.2 (256:1–2). Imperthnthn thnthnthn – The "boots" (busboy) mimics Miss Douce's threat that she will report his "impertinent insolence" (11.99 [258:24]).

11.3 (256:3). Chips, picking chips off rocky thumbnail, chips – Simon Dedalus enters the bar (11.192–93 [261:4–5]).

11.4 (256:3–4). Horrid! And gold flushed – Miss Kennedy protests Miss Douce's "crude" remark (11.183–84 [260:34–36]).

11.5 (256:5). A husky fifenote blew – Simon

---

1 "A fugue according to rule." It involves three classes of subject: (1) *Andamenti*, a complete melody, beautiful in itself; (2) *Soggetti*, a short passage with a characteristic interval; and (3) *Attaco*, a short figure, usually *staccato*. In the opening section of the fugue the subject is presented together with the answer and a repetition of the subject in a different key (if there is to be a countersubject it is introduced in this section). The next section, the exposition, is a complete statement of the subject(s) and/or answer(s) by all the voices. This is followed by the "free" middle section; the climax then presents the subject in its most exciting aspect; and the coda concludes the fugue with the "desire for home."

Dedalus prepares his pipe for tobacco (11.218 [261:31]).

11.6 (256:6). Blew, Blue bloom is on the – From "When the Bloom Is on the Rye"; see 10.524n. Bloom decides to buy notepaper on which to write Martha Clifford (11.229–31 [262:1–2]).

11.7 (256:7). Gold pinnacled hair – Miss Kennedy's hair (11.166 [260:15]).

11.8 (256:8). *A jumping rose . . . rose of Castile – See 7.591n; Lenehan (and his pun) merge with descriptions of the barmaids (11.329ff. [264:28ff]).

11.9 (256:9). Trilling, trilling: Idolores – Miss Douce sings a line from the light opera *Floradora* (1899) (11.225–26 [261:38–39]), music by Leslie Stuart, book by Owen Hall, lyrics by E. Boyd-Jones and Paul Rubens. The opera takes place on a South Sea island that produces Floradora, a world-famous perfume. Idolores, the beautiful and flirtatious heroine, is being pursued (and spoiled) by a host of men, including the nasty villain, but her eventual salvation is ensured when she falls in love with Frank Abercoed (surprisingly enough, a lord in disguise). At the end of Act I they pledge their love, even though they have to part, and Abercoed sings "The Shade of the Palm." Refrain: "Oh Idolores, queen of the eastern sea, / Fair one of Eden look to the West for me, / My star will be shining, love, / When you're in the moonlight calm, / So be waiting for me by the Eastern sea, / In the shade of the sheltering palm."

11.10 (256:10). Peep! Who's in the . . . peepofgold? – Lenehan attempts to flirt with Miss Kennedy (11.242 [262:13]). "Peep! Who's in the corner?" is a traditional discovery question in a game of hide-and-seek.

11.11 (256:11). Tink cried to bronze in pity – Diners in the Ormond Hotel summoned a waiter by ringing a small bell. The pity is Miss Douce's for the "blind stripling" (11.286 [263:21]).

11.12 (256:12). And a call, pure, long and throbbing. Longindying call – The sound of the tuning fork that the blind stripling (piano tuner) has left behind in the bar (11.313–16 [264:11–15]).

11.13 (256:13–14). *Decoy. Soft word. But look: the bright stars fade. Notes chirping answer – Lenehan chats with the barmaids (11.320–32 [264:19–31]), and there is an allusion to the song "Goodbye, Sweetheart, Goodbye," words by Jane Williams (1806–85), music by John L. Hatton (1809–86): "The bright stars fade, the morn is breaking, / The dew-drops pearl each bud and leaf, / And I from thee my leave am taking, / Too brief with bliss, With bliss too brief. / How sinks my heart with fond alarms, / The tear is hiding in mine eye, / For time doth thrust me from thine arms, / Goodbye, sweetheart, goodbye. // The sun is up, the lark is soaring, / Loud swells the song of chanticleer, / The levret bounds o'er earth's soft flooring, / Yet I am here, yet I am here. / For since night's gems from heav'n did fade / And morn to floral lips doth hie, / I could not leave thee though I said, / Goodbye, sweetheart, goodbye."

11.14 (256:13–14). *O rose! Castile. The morn is breaking – Combines allusions to *The Rose of Castile* (see 7.591n) and "Goodbye, Sweetheart, Goodbye" (see preceding note).

11.15 (256:15). Jingle jingle jaunted jingling – Boylan approaches the Ormond Hotel (11.212 [261:25]). A "jingle" is a two-wheeled horse-drawn carriage; for "jaunted," see 5.98n. Also recalls the song "Jingle Bells" by John Pierpont (1785–1866), particularly the phrases "Laughing all the way" in the first verse and "Take the girls tonight" in the third. Chorus: "Jingle bells! Jingle bells! / Jingle all the way! / Oh, what fun it is to ride / In a one-horse open sleigh— / Jingle bells! Jingle bells! / Jingle all the way! / Oh, what fun it is to ride / In a one horse open sleigh!"

11.16 (256:16). Coin rang. Clock clacked – The clock strikes four as Boylan pays for his sloe gin (11.371–84 [265:31–266:4]).

11.17–18 (256:17–19). Avowal. *Sonnez*. I could . . . Sweetheart, goodbye – Miss Douce snaps her garter for Lenehan and Boylan. *Sonnez la cloche!* is French: "Sound the bell." See the song "Goodbye, Sweetheart, Goodbye," 11.13n.

11.19 (256:20). Jingle. Bloo – Boylan's and Bloom's notes are juxtaposed as Boylan leaves the Ormond for 7 Eccles Street (11.456–58 [267:42–268:3]).

11.20 (256:21–22). Boomed crashing chords . . . The tympanum – Simon Dedalus, Ben Dollard, and "Father" Cowley gather around the piano in the Ormond Hotel saloon (11.436–59 [267:19–268:5]). "When love absorbs my ardent soul. War! War!" after a duet for tenor (or soprano) and bass, by T. Cooke, "Love and War" or "When Love Absorbs My Ardent Soul." The core of the duet: "LOVER (Soprano or Tenor): While love absorbs my ardent soul, / I think not of the morrow . . . ; SOLDIER (Bass): While war absorbs my ardent soul, / I think not of the morrow." The mock contest of the duet is resolved when Love and War sing together: "Since Mars lov'd Venus, Venus Mars, / Let's blend love's wounds with battle's scars, . . . / And call in Bacchus all divine, . . . / To cure both pains with rosy wine, / . . . / And thus, beneath his social sway, / We'll sing and laugh the hours away." For "tympanum," see 11.536–37 (270:13–14).

11.21 (256:23). A sail! A veil awave upon the waves – Cowley sings to a picture, "A Last Farewell," on the wall (11.588–92 [271:26–31]). This passage, preceded as it is by "boomed crashing chords," also alludes to the opening scene of Verdi's *Otello* (1887). The orchestra announces a great storm at sea, and the chorus of Cypriots announces the sighting of Otello's ship, "una vela, una vela" (a sail, a sail) just before Otello's safe arrival and his proclamation ("Esultate!") of victory over the Turks. (T. C. Theoharis.) For "veil," see Leucothea, p. 290.

11.22 (256:24). Lost. Throstle fluted. All is lost now – Richie Goulding whistles a tenor air, "Tutto è sciolto" (Italian: "All Is Lost"), from Vincenzo Bellini's (1801–35) opera *La sonnambula* (The Sleepwalker) (1831) (11.610–41 [272:9–273:4]). The heroine, Amina, innocently sleepwalks her way into a situation that makes her appear faithless to her fiancé, the peasant Elvino. In Act II he laments: "All is lost now, / By all hope and joy / I am forsaken. / Nevermore can love awaken; / Past enchantment, no nevermore." Amina answers by assuring Elvino, "Thou alone hast all my heart," and condemns him as "faithless" because he will not "deign to hear" her.

11.23 (256:25). Horn. Hawhorn – Combines Lenehan's question "Got the horn or what?" (i.e., Are you sexually aroused?) (11.432 [267:15]) with Boylan's departure for Eccles Street (11.526–27 [270:1–2]).

11.24 (256:26). When first he saw. Alas! – Simon Dedalus is encouraged to sing "M'appari" from Flotow's opera, *Martha* (11.582ff. [271:25ff.]). The air for Lionel (tenor) begins: "M'appari, tutt' amor, il mio sguardo l'incontro." Italian: "All [perfect] love appeared to me, that encounter filled my eyes [completely won me]." Simon Dedalus sings one freely translated performing version (words by Charles Jeffreys): "When first I saw that form endearing; / Sorrow from me seem'd to depart: / Each graceful look, each word so cheering / Charmed my eye and won my heart. / Full of hope, and all delighted, / None could feel more blest than I; / All on Earth I then could wish for / Was near her to live and die: / But alas! 'twas idle dreaming, / And the dream too soon hath flown; / Not one ray of hope is gleaming; / I am lost, yes I am lost for she is gone. / When first I saw . . . won my heart. / Martha, Martha, I am sighing; / I am weeping still; for thee; / Come thou lost one, / Come thou dear one, / Thou alone can'st comfort me: / Ah Martha return! Come to me!" For the opera, see 7.58n.

11.25 (256:27). Full tup. Full throb – Bloom responds to "M'appari" (11.699–709 [274:30–40]). For "tup," see 11.706–7n.

11.26 (256:28). Warbling. Ah, lure! Alluring – Bloom recalls Molly singing a song (11.730–34 [275:23–28]).

11.27 (256:29). Martha! Come! – Again "M'appari," 11.24n (11.735, 740–41 [275:29, 35–36]).

11.28 (256:30). *Clapclap. Clipclap. Clappyclap – Simon Dedalus's performance of "M'appari" is applauded (11.754–60 [276:9–16]).

11.29 (256:31). Goodgod henev erheard inall – Richie Goulding recalls an occasion when his brother-in-law, Simon Dedalus, sang particularly well (11.778–83 [276:37–277:2]).

11.30 (256:32). Deaf bald Pat brought pad knife took up – Bloom asks the waiter for pen, ink, and blotter (11.822–23 [278:7–8]) and receives them (11.847–48 [278:36–37]).

11.31 (256:33). A moonlit nightcall: far: far – Simon Dedalus imitates the sounds of an Italian barcarole he once heard in Cork Harbor (11.854–55 [279:3–5]).

11.32 (256:34). I feel so sad. P. S. So lonely blooming – Bloom adds a postscript to his letter to Martha Clifford (11.894 [280:10–11]), echoing Thomas Moore's song "The Last Rose of Summer." The song is used extensively in Flotow's *Martha*. First verse: " 'Tis the last rose of summer / Left blooming alone; / All her lovely companions / Are faded and gone. / No flower of her kindred, / No rosebud is nigh, / To reflect back her blushes, / Or give sigh for sigh."

11.33 (256:35). Listen! – Miss Douce holds a seashell to George Lidwell's ear (11.923–25 [281:4–6]).

11.34–35 (256:36–37). The spiked and winding . . . and silent roar – The shell has various sounds (11.923–36 [281:4–19]), including an echo of Lenehan's question "Got the horn or what?" (11.432 [267:15]).

11.36 (256:38). Pearls: when she. Liszt's rhapsodies. Hisss – Bloom meditates on Molly and "chamber music" (11.979–85 [282:27–34]). Franz Liszt (1811–86), a Hungarian pianist and composer, wrote a popular series of virtuoso pieces for piano called "Hungarian Rhapsodies."

11.37 (256:39). You don't? – Miss Douce withdraws her arm from George Lidwell to the accompaniment of banter about believing and not-believing (11.814–20 [277:36–278:4]).

11.38 (256:40). Did not: no, no: . . . with a carra – The byplay between Lidwell and Lydia Douce ("Lidlyd") (11.814–20 [277:36–278:4]) is set in counterpoint against Boylan's rapping at the door of 7 Eccles Street (11.986–88 [282:35–37]).

11.39 (256:41–42). *Black. Deepsounding. Do, Ben, do – Ben Dollard is encouraged to sing as Cowley plays the opening chords of "The Croppy Boy" (11.998–99 [283:6–7]), a ballad about the Rebellion of 1798 by William B. McBurney (pseudonym Caroll Malone, d. c. 1902). A "croppy" was a Wexford or Irish rebel in 1798:

> "Good men and true! in this house who dwell,
> To a stranger *bouchal* [Irish: boy] I pray you tell
> Is the priest at home? or may he be seen?
> I would speak a word with Father Green."

> "The Priest's at home, boy, and may be seen: 5

> 'Tis easy speaking with Father Green;
> But you must wait, till I go and see
> If the holy father alone may be."

> The youth has entered an empty hall—
> What a lonely sound has his light footfall! 10
> And the gloomy chamber's still and bare,
> With a vested Priest in a lonely chair;

> The youth has knelt to tell his sins;
> "*Nomine Dei*" [Latin: "in God's name"], the youth begins:
> At "*mea culpa*" [Latin: "I am guilty"] he beats his breast, 15
> And in broken murmurs he speaks the rest.

> "At the siege of Ross did my father fall,
> And at Gorey my loving brothers all,
> I alone am left of my name and race,
> I will go to Wexford and take their place. 20

> "I cursed three times since last Easter day—
> At mass-time once I went to play;
> I passed the churchyard one day in haste,
> And forgot to pray for my mother's rest.

> "I bear no grudge against living thing; 25
> But I love my country above the king.
> Now, Father! bless me, and let me go
> To die, if God has ordained it so."

> The Priest said nought, but a rustling noise
> Made the youth look above in wild surprise; 30
> The robes were off, and in scarlet there
> Sat a yeoman captain with fiery glare.

> With fiery glare and with fury hoarse,
> Instead of blessing, he breathed a curse:—
> " 'Twas a good thought, boy, to come here and shrive, 35
> For one short hour is your time to live.

> "Upon yon river three tenders float,
> The Priest's in one, if he isn't shot—
> We hold his house for our Lord and King,
> And Amen! say I, may all traitors swing!" 40

> At Geneva Barrack that young man died,
> And at Passage they have his body laid.
> Good people who live in peace and joy,
> Breathe a prayer and a tear for the Croppy Boy.

11.40 (257:1). Wait while you . . . while you hee – Bloom improvises on Bald Pat, the waiter (11.915–19 [280:36–41]), incidentally echoing the mocking deception of line 7 of "The Croppy Boy" (see 11.39n).

11.41 (257:2). But wait! – Bloom decides not to leave the Ormond before the singing of "The Croppy Boy" (11.1005 [283:14]).

11.42 (257:3). Low in dark . . . Embedded ore – Bloom hears the opening chords of "The Croppy Boy" (11.1005–6 [283:14–15]). The phrases recall Stephen's musing (10.805–7 [241:29–32]) as well as scene iii of Wagner's *Das Rheingold* (The Rhinegold), the first of the four operas of *Der Ring des Nibelungen* (The Ring of the Nibelung) (1853–74). In scene iii, Wotan, the threatened king of the gods, descends into Nibelheim, the cavern residence of the dwarf Nibelungs. The Nibelungs have been enslaved by the dwarf Alberich, who has stolen the Rhinegold and suffered the curse of having to forswear love forever in order to rule the whole world through the magical power of a ring made out of the Rhinegold. In this phase of the fantastically complex Wagnerian plot, Wotan and his fellow gods trick Alberich and strip him of the ring and his power.

11.43 (257:4). *Naminedamine*. Preacher is he – Latin: "in the name of God"; the Croppy Boy does penance (see following note).

11.44 (257:4). All gone. All fallen – The Croppy Boy recounts the destruction of his family (11.1063–65 [285:1–3]); see "The Croppy Boy" (11.39n), stanzas 4 and 5. See also "The Last Rose of Summer," quoted in 11.32n.

11.45 (257:5). Tiny, her tremulous fernfoils of maidenhair – The singing of "The Croppy Boy" affects Miss Douce (11.1104–8 [286:8–13]).

11.46 (257:6). Amen! He gnashed in fury – The song reaches its climax (11.1120 [286:27]); see "The Croppy Boy" (11.39n), line 40.

11.47 (257:7). Fro. To, fro. A baton cool protruding – Miss Douce fondles the beerpull as she listens to the song (11.1112–17 [286:18–24]).

11.48 (257:8). Bronzelydia by Minagold – Miss Douce and Miss Kennedy are juxtaposed (11.1213 [289:4–5]).

11.49 (257:9–10). By bronze, by gold . . . Old Bloom – Bloom is leaving the hotel (11.1134–37 [287:1–4]).

11.50 (257:11). One rapped, one tapped with a carra, with a cock – The sound of the blind piano tuner's cane blends with the echo of Boylan's knocking and crowing (11.1118–19 [286:25–26]).

11.51 (257:12). Pray for him! Pray, good people! – Ben Dollard sings the closing lines of "The Croppy Boy" (11.1139–41 [287:6–8]); see 11.39n.

11.52 (257:13). His gouty fingers nakkering – Ben Dollard Spanish-dances his way to the bar after his song (11.1151–53 [287:18–20]); to "nakker" or "naker" is to sound a kettledrum.

11.53 (257:14). Big Benaben. Big Benben – Dollard is applauded (11.1154 [287:21]), with appropriate echoes of Big Ben, originally the name of the deep bell but applied now more generally to the clock in the clock tower of the Houses of Parliament, London.

11.54 (257:15). *Last rose Castile . . . so sad alone – Combines *The Rose of Castile* (see 7.591n) with "The Last Rose of Summer" (see 11.32n) as Bloom's meeting with "the whore of the lane" overlaps the continuing scene in the Ormond (11.1254, 1271 [290:9, 29]).

11.55 (257:16). Pwee! Little wind piped wee – Bloom's digestive processes as he leaves the Ormond (11.1203 [288:36]).

11.56–57 (257:17–18). True men, Lid . . . tschink with tschunk – Lidwell, Kernan, Cowley, Dedalus, and Dollard clink glasses (11.1269–72, 1280 [290:27–31, 40]). The fragment echoes lines 7–8 of Ingram's "The Memory of the Dead" (see 10.790n): "But a true man, like you, man, / Will fill your glass with us." It also echoes Timothy Daniel Sullivan's (1827–1914) "The Thirty-two Counties," a drinking song that names all the counties of Ireland. The chorus: "Then clink, glasses, clink, 'tis a toast we all must drink, / And let every voice come in at the chorus. / For Ireland is our home, and wherever we may roam / We'll be true to the dear land that bore us."

11.58 (257:19). Fff! Oo! – Bloom farts (11.1247, 1288 [290:1, 291:7]).

11.59 (257:20–21). Where bronze from . . . Where hoofs? – The sounds of the sirens (11.1269 [290:27]) and of the viceregal procession are fading.

11.60 (257:22). Rrrpr. Kraa. Kraandl – The sound of Bloom's fart is masked by the sound of a passing tram.

11.61 (257:23). *Then not till then . . . Be pfrwritt – Bloom reads Robert Emmet's last words (see 11.1275n) in the window of an antique shop (11.1289–92 [291:8–11]).

11.62 (257:24). Done – The last of Robert Emmet's last words (see 11.1275n) signals the end of this prologue of fragments and the beginning and end of the fugue (11.1294 [291:13]).

11.64 (257:26). *miss Douce's . . . miss Kennedy's – Lydia Douce and Mina Kennedy, the two barmaids in the Ormond Hotel, are apparently fictional, but Kennedy has a real address; see 11.517–18 (269:30–31).

11.67 (257:30). his ex – That is, his excellency, the lord lieutenant.

11.67 (257:30–31). *eau de Nil* – French: literally, "water of the Nile"; in this case, a cloth of a pale greenish-blue color.

11.70 (257:34). the fellow in the tall silk – The honorable Gerald Ward, A.D.C. (aide-de-camp); see 10.1179 (252:6–7).

11.77 (257:41). He's killed looking back – As Odysseus, tormented by the Sirens' song, struggles against the bonds that secure him to the mast.

11.79 (258:1). O wept! – Dodging the mild oath *Jesus wept;* see 3.68n.

11.86 (258:9). Bloowho – See 8.8ff. (151:9ff.).

11.86 (258:9). Moulang's pipes – Daniel Moulang, jeweler and pipe importer, 31 Wellington Quay; the quay is on the south bank of the Liffey east of Grattan (formerly Essex) Bridge. Bloom is walking west toward Grattan Bridge, which he will cross, turning west again along Ormond Quay Upper toward the Ormond Hotel.

11.86/88 (258:10/11). the sweets of sin/for Raoul – The novel Bloom has selected for Molly; see 10.606n.

11.87 (258:10). Wine's antiques – Bernard Wine, general dealer in jewelry and antiquities, 35 Wellington Quay (east of Moulang's).

11.88 (258:11). Carroll's – John Carroll, watchmaker and jeweler and dealer in old plate, 29 Wellington Quay (west of Moulang's).

11.89 (258:12). boots – The boy who polishes the hotel guests' boots at night and is an odd-jobber and busboy during the day.

11.93 (258:17). lithia crate – "Lithia" was a bottled spring water.

11.98 (258:22). Mrs de Massey – The proprietor of the Ormond Hotel, 8 Ormond Quay Upper.

11.110–11 (258:35). two and nine a yard – A moderately expensive material.

11.116–17 (259:2). the borax with cherry laurel water – (Sometimes with glycerine added), a popular cosmetic "remedy" for blemishes of the skin (including sunburn).

11.125 (259:10). Boyd's – Adams (p. 12) suggests Boileau and Boyd, Ltd., wholesale druggists, manufacturing chemists, and color merchants, 46 Mary Street (two blocks north and slightly east of the Ormond). But since both barmaids know "that old fogey" and since at least one of them (Miss Kennedy) lives in Drumcondra (a suburban area north of central Dublin), it could as easily be James Boyd, druggist, at 21 Grattan Parade, Drumcondra.

11.131 (259:17). No, don't, she cried – See 11.1201n.

11.139 (259:25). the Antient Concert Rooms – At 42 Great Brunswick (now Pearse) Street, a hall that private groups rented for concerts, plays, and other public gatherings.

11.144–45 (259:32). *like a snout in quest – As though she were a hunting dog baying on the trail of a quarry.

11.148 (259:36). And your other eye – A music-hall catch phrase of the 1890s, associated with the song "When [or Then] You Wink the Other Eye" and with the music-hall star Marie Lloyd (Matilda Alice Victoria Wood, 1870–1922), who "made appalling innuendoes with . . . apparently harmless ditties. . . . She may be said to have invented 'The Other Eye'" (Erlene Stetson, *JJQ* 19, no. 2 [1982]: 180).

11.149 (259:37). Aaron Figatner's – Diamond setter and jeweler, 26 Wellington Quay.

11.150 (259:38–39). Prosper Loré's – Wholesale hat manufacturer, 22 Wellington Quay.

11.151 (259:39). Bassi's blessed virgins – Aurelio Bassi, statue and picture-frame maker, 14 Wellington Quay.

11.151–52 (259:40). Bluerobed, white under – The traditional colors of the Virgin Mary's costume.

11.152 (259:40). come to me – This common phrase suggests both the Virgin's sympathy for the sinful and the heavily burdened and her role as intercessor with her son; in context, the phrase identifies the Virgin as another sort of Siren.

11.156 (260:4). The sweets of sin – See 10.606n.

11.175 (260:25). ringing in changes – The art of ringing a diatonically tuned set of bells (six, eight, or more) in continually varying order. It is an art-sport practiced enthusiastically by teams of change-ringers in the British Isles, particularly in England, where many parish churches have well-tuned rings of bells.

11.185 (260:37). Cantwell's offices – Cantwell and M'Donald, wholesale wine and whiskey merchants and rectifying distillers, 12 Wellington Quay.

11.185 (260:37). Greaseabloom – Involves a pun, "when it is remembered that *grease* is pronounced *grace* in Ireland" (P. W. Joyce, *English*, p. 137).

11.185 (260:37). Ceppi's virgins – Peter Ceppi & Sons, picture-frame and looking-glass factory and statuary manufacturers, 8–9 Wellington Quay.

11.186 (260:38–39). Nannetti's father hawked those things about – That is, Nannetti's father peddled religious objects from door to door.

11.189 (260:41–42). The Clarence – The Clarence Commercial Hotel, 6–7 Wellington Quay.

11.189 (260:42). Dolphin – The Dolphin Ho-

tel, restaurant and luncheon bar, 46–48 Essex Street (just off Wellington Quay to the south).

11.197 (261:9). Rostrevor – A town in the Mourne Mountains on the shore of Carlingford Lough, an arm of the sea fifty-five miles north of Dublin.

11.207 (261:20). simple Simon – After the nursery rhyme: "Simple Simon met a pieman, / Going to the fair. / Said Simple Simon to the pieman, / 'Let me taste your ware.' / Said the pieman to Simple Simon, / 'Show me first your penny.' / Said Simple Simon to the pieman, / 'Indeed, I haven't any.'"

11.208 (261:21). a doaty – Someone to doat (dote) on; a Dublin term of affection or endearment.

11.212 (261:25). Jingle – See 11.15n.

11.214–15 (261:27–28). Cantrell and Cochrane's – See 5.193n.

11.219 (261:32–33). the Mourne mountains – On the Irish Sea in County Down, about fifty miles north of Dublin.

11.222 (261:35–36). mermaid's – A popular brand of finely cut tobacco.

11.226 (261:39). O, Idolores . . . eastern seas! – See 11.9n.

11.227 (261:40). Mr Lidwell – J. George Lidwell (d. 1919), solicitor, 4 Capel Street, Dublin. See Ellmann, pp. 314, 329–31, 462.

11.229 (261:42). Essex bridge – The original name (1755) for Grattan Bridge; the name was officially changed before 1888.

11.230 (262:1). Daly's – Teresa Daly, tobacconist, 1 Ormond Quay Upper, at the foot of Grattan Bridge just east of the Ormond Hotel.

11.230–31 (262:2). *Blue bloom is on the rye – See "When the Bloom Is on the Rye," 10.524n.

11.241 (262:12). sandwichbell – A glass bell that protected and displayed sandwiches on the bar.

11.242 (262:13). Peep! Who's in the corner? – See 11.10n.

11.243–44 (262:15). To mind her stops – A

"stop" is a mark of punctuation; hence, "Be careful." But a stop is also a contrivance by which the pitch of an instrument is altered.

11.244 (262:15–16). To read only the black ones: round o and crooked ess – That is, to pay attention only to periods and question marks.

11.247 (262:19). solfa – The set of syllables (*do, re, mi, fa, sol, la, ti, do*) sung to the steps of the diatonic scale.

11.247 (262:20). plappering – Falling with a flat impact.

11.248–49 (262:21–22). Ah fox met ah stork . . . pull up ah bone? – Lenehan mixes the characters from two of Aesop's fables. In "The Wolf and the Crane," the wolf offers to pay a crane to remove a bone from his throat; when the crane removes the bone, he is told that his payment is that he has not been eaten. In "The Fox and the Stork," the fox invites the stork to dine and serves him soup in a flat plate so that the stork cannot eat; the stork invites the fox to dine and turns the tables by offering him mincemeat in a jar with a narrow neck.

11.258 (262:32). Dry – Lenehan is trying to cadge a drink.

11.264 (262:39). Mooney's *en ville* and in Mooney's *sur mer* – For "Mooney's *en ville*" (French: "in town"), see 7.892n. Mooney's *sur mer* (on the sea) was on the north quayside of the Liffey one short block south of the other Mooney's; Gerald Mooney, wine and spirit merchant, 3 Eden Quay.

11.264 (262:40). the rhino – Slang for ready money.

11.268–69 (263:3). that minstrel boy of the wild wet west – Burke is characterized as being from the west of Ireland, which Dubliners regard as both "wild" and "wet." "The Minstrel-Boy" (The Moreen) is a song from Thomas Moore's *Irish Melodies:* "The Minstrel-Boy to war is gone, / In the ranks of death you'll find him; / His father's sword he has girded on, / And his wild harp slung behind him. / Land of song! said the warrior-bard, / Though all the world betrays thee, / One sword at least, thy right shall guard, / One faithful harp shall praise thee! // The Minstrel fell!—but the foeman's chain / Could not bring his proud soul under; / The harp he lov'd ne'er spoke again /

For he tore its chords asunder; / And said, No chains shall sully thee, / Thou soul of love and bravery! / Thy songs were made for the pure and free, / They shall never sound in slavery." According to Zack Bowen (*Musical Allusions in the Works of James Joyce* [Albany, N.Y., 1974] p. 164), there may also be an allusion to "The Men of the West": "I give you the gallant old West, boys, / Where rallied our bravest and best: / When Ireland lay broken and bleeding; / Hurrah for the men of the West!"

11.273 (263:7). faraway mourning mountain eye – Suggests a Percy French (1854–1920) song, "The Mountains of Mourne," in which the speaker, an Irish laborer in London, insists that for all the sights of the city, the painted city girls, etc., he prefers his Mary "where the Mountains o' Mourne sweep down to the sea."

11.275 (263:9). the saloon door – The saloon is a large room in a one-story wing at the back of the hotel. In 1904 it was off the bar, which was then along the western side of the hotel (today it is off the dining room). The saloon's ceiling, a large mullioned window under a skylight, combines with the floor-to-ceiling paneling of the walls to make a resonant interior. In 1904 it was used for small, relatively informal concerts, song-fests, etc.

11.277–78 (263:12). the smoking concert – The sort of small-scale amateur-professional musical evening for which the Ormond was noted.

11.285 (263:20). God's curse on bitch's bastard – See 10.1119–20 (250:18–19).

11.286 (263:21). a diner's bell – See 11.11n.

11.287 (263:22). bothered – Deaf, after the Irish "*bodhar*, deaf, used both as a noun and a verb" in Irish English (P. W. Joyce, *English*, p. 221).

11.296 (263:33). Daly's – See 11.230n.

11.296–97 (263:34). Are you not happy in your home? – A question from Martha Clifford's letter (5.241–59 [77:32–78:13]).

11.297 (263:34–35). Flower to console me – In the language of flowers the appropriate flower for "consolation" is a scarlet geranium; see 5.261n.

11.297 (263:35). a pin cuts lo – See 8.630n.

11.298 (263:35–36). language of flow – See 5.261n.

11.298 (263:36). a daisy? Innocence that is – In the language of flowers a daisy does mean "innocence" unless it is colored, in which case it means "beauty."

11.300–301 (263:39). Smoke mermaids, coolest whiff of all – The advertising slogan for Mermaid cigarettes, ten for three pence. See 11.222n.

11.302 (263:41). *jaunting car – See 5.98n.

11.309–10 (264:7–8). Bloo smi qui go. Ternoon – "Bloom smiled quick go. Afternoon." But "qui" suggests a pun on the Latin and French word for "who." And "ternoon" is a printer's word for a group of three as well as the name for a triple chance in a numbers lottery.

11.310 (264:8–9). the only pebble on the beach – Proverbially, the sole desirable or remarkable person available or accessible.

11.320/322/327/344 (264:19/21/26/265:3). — *The bright stars fade . . . / —. . . the morn is breaking. / —The dewdrops pearl . . . / And I from thee . . .* – From "Goodbye, Sweetheart, Goodbye"; see 11.13n.

11.321 (264:20). A voiceless song – See 11.1092n.

11.329 (264:28). rose of Castile – See 7.591n.

11.335 (264:34). Ask no questions . . . hear no lies – After *She Stoops to Conquer; or, The Mistakes of a Night* (1773), by Oliver Goldsmith (1728–74). In Act III, Tony Lumpkin turns aside the question of how he "procured" his mother's jewels: "Ask me no questions, and I'll tell you no fibs."

11.340 (264:39). See the conquering hero comes – The opening line of a poem by Thomas Morell (1703–84): "See, the conquering hero comes! / Sound the trumpets, beat the drums; / Sports prepare, the laurel bring; / Sounds of triumph to him sing." Handel used the song in the oratorio *Judas Maccabaeus* (1747) and repeated it in Part III of *Joshua* (1748), where it is sung by a chorus of youths in celebration of Joshua's victory at Jericho. They are answered by a chorus of virgins: "See the godlike youth advance!"

11.350 (265:9). bitter – A type of English beer.

11.351 (265:10). Wire in yet? – Referring to the results of the Gold Cup at Ascot; see 10.510n.

11.353 (265:12). lugs – Ears.

11.353 (265:12–13). the sheriff's office – 30 Ormond Quay Upper; see 10.934n.

11.368 (265:28). Fine goods in small parcels – " 'Good goods are tied up in small parcels': said of a little man or a little woman, in praise or mitigation" (P. W. Joyce, *English*, p. 110).

11.374 (265:34). Sceptre – Lenehan's hot tip for the Gold Cup; see 10.507n.

11.379 (265:39). Idolores. The eastern seas – From "The Shade of the Palm"; see 11.9n.

11.383–84 (266:2–4). Fair one of Egypt . . . Look to the west . . . For me – After "The Shade of the Palm"; see 11.9n. "Egypt" implies the substitution of Cleopatra for the "Eve" of the song.

11.390 (266:10). ryebloom – Echoes "When the Bloom Is on the Rye," 10.524n.

11.396/402/425 (266:17/23/267:8). — . . . To *Flora's lips did hie / —I could not leave thee . . . / — . . . Sweetheart, goodbye!–*From "Goodbye, Sweetheart, Goodbye"; see 11.13n.

11.404 (266:25). Sonnez la cloche! – French: "Sound the bell!"

11.407 (266:30). lost chord – See 11.478n.

11.432 (267:15). Got the horn . . . ? – See 11.23n.

11.438 (267:21). the long fellow – John Fanning, in fiction the subsheriff.

11.438 (267:22). a barleystraw – Slang for a trifle; the word recalls the proverb "Thou knowest a barley straw / Will make a parish parson go to law."

11.438–39 (267:22). Judas Iscariot's – Judas, the man of Kerioth (in Judah), the disciple who betrayed Jesus for thirty pieces of silver (here, Reuben J. Dodd).

11.444 (267:27). Power – That is, Irish whiskey made by John Power & Son, Ltd., Dublin distillers.

11.449 (267:33). *Begone dull care – An anonymous drinking song first printed in Playford's *Musical Companion* (1687): "Begone, dull care! I prithee begone from me! / Begone, dull care! Thou and I shall never agree."

11.459 (268:4). *Love and war – See 11.20n.

11.463 (268:9–10). (why did he go so quick when I?) – Miss Douce is playing the part of the suicidally disappointed Siren Parthenope; see p. 290.

11.465 (268:12–13). *eau de Nil – See 11.67n.

11.468 (268:16). Collard grand – A middle-grade and relatively expensive English piano, priced from £110 in 1904.

11.473 (268:22). by Japers – Dodging the curse *by Jesus*.

11.473 (268:22–23). wedding garment – Slang for formal clothes.

11.478 (268:28). the lost chord – A song, words by Adelaide A. Procter (1825–64), music by Arthur Sullivan (1842–1900): "Seated one day at the Organ, / I was weary and ill at ease. / And my fingers wander'd idly / Over the noisy keys; / I know not what I was playing, / Or what I was dreaming then, / But I struck one chord of music, / Like the sound of a great Amen, / Like the sound of a great Amen. / It flooded the crimson twilight / Like the close of an Angel's Psalm, / And it lay on my fever'd spirit / With a touch of infinite calm; / It seem'd the harmonious echo / From our discordant life; / It linked all perplexed meanings / Into one perfect peace, / And trembled away into silence, / As if it were loth to cease. / I have sought, but I seek it vainly, / That one lost chord divine / Which came from the soul of an organ / And enter'd into mine. / It may be that Death's bright Angel / Will speak in that chord again; / It may be only in Heav'n / I shall hear that grand Amen."

11.486 (268:37). the coffee palace – The Dublin Temperance Institute and Coffee Booths and Restaurant, operated by the Dublin Total Abstinence Society, at 6 Townsend Street, just south of the Liffey in eastern Dublin.

11.487 (268:38). gave me the wheeze – Slang: "gave me the information."

11.487 (268:39). the other business – When they were "on the rocks" in Holles Street, Molly and Bloom collected and sold secondhand clothes and theatrical costumes.

11.489 (268:40). Keogh's – The implication is that Keogh's was a shop or a pub in the Holles Street neighborhood, but I have been unable to identify it.

11.493 (269:4). Merrion square style – Merrion Square was a fashionable (and expensive) residential area. Holles Street, where the Blooms lived, is off Merrion Square, but it was a "mixed" street with tenements as well as lower-middle-class housing and a hospital.

11.496–97 (269:7–8). has left off clothes of all descriptions – Vincent Deane reports, "A relative of mine claims that Dublin trams, at the beginning of the century, carried an advertisement which read 'Miss White has left-off clothes of every description.' The joke consisted in ignoring the hyphen."

11.500 (269:13–14). Paul de Kock – See 4.358n.

11.507 (269:20). Daughter of the regiment – *La fille du régiment* (1840), a French comic opera by the Italian Gaetano Donizetti (1797–1848). As the title suggests, the heroine is an orphan adopted by a regiment (in Napoleon's army). She falls in love with the opera's peasant hero, but their romance is interrupted by the disclosure that she is an aristocrat by birth. True love eventually crosses the class barriers.

11.508 (269:21). drummajor – In the British army, a bandmaster or drum major, in charge of a regimental fife and drum corps or band, is usually accorded the rank of warrant officer, entitling him to mess and associate with commissioned and noncommissioned officers as he chooses (with certain restrictions, depending on regimental tradition). There is also an allusion to *The Drum Major's Daughter* (*La fille du tambour-major* [1879] by Jacques Offenbach [1819–80]), a popular, light-opera adaptation of Donizetti's opera.

11.512–13 (269:26). My Irish Molly, O – A recurrent phrase in an anonymous Irish ballad, "Irish Molly O." "A poor unhappy Scottish youth" is brokenhearted because Molly's father has forbidden her to "wed a foreigner." As the youth puts it: "A poor forlorn pilgrim, I must wander to and fro, / And all for the sake of my

Irish Molly O!" The chorus describes Molly as "modest, mild and beautiful . . . / The primrose of Ireland."

11.516 (269:29). They pined in depth of ocean shadow – Saddened by their failure to lure Odysseus to their rocks? See Parthenope, p. 290.

11.517–18 (269:30–31). 4 Lismore Terrace, Drumcondra – Occupied in 1904 by a Mr. William Molony.

11.518 (269:31). Idolores, a queen, Dolores – After "The Shade of the Palm"; see 11.9n.

11.524 (269:40). Bachelor's walk – The northern quayside of the Liffey east of Ormond Quay Upper and Lower.

11.530, 551–52 (270:5, 29–30).—*When love absorbs my ardent soul . . . / . . . my ardent soul / I care not foror the morrow* – See 11.20n.

11.531 (270:7). roofpanes – In the ceiling of the saloon; see 11.275n.

11.532 (270:8). War! War! . . . You're the warrior – Ben Dollard is singing the wrong part. His heavy bass voice is not appropriate to the lighter tenor or soprano voice of Love in the "Love and War" duet (see 11.20n).

11.533 (270:9–10). your landlord – The Reverend Hugh C. Love.

11.533–34 (270:10). Love or money – Recalls the stock expression of absolute refusal: "not for love or money."

11.536–37 (270:13–14). you'd burst the tympanum . . . organ like yours – The remark refers to the soprano in the duet (see 11.20n) and recalls the medieval belief that the Virgin Mary conceived Jesus (by the Word of God) through the unbroken tympanum of her ear; see 15.2601–2 (521:23).

11.541 (270:18). *Amoroso ma non troppo* – Italian (music): "soft and tender, but not too much so."

11.547 (270:25). *Independent* – The *Irish Weekly Independent and Nation*, published Thursdays.

11.568 (271:5//6). *Jingle – See 11.15n.

11.569–70 (271:7). the Burton – See 8.369–70n.

11.580–82 (271:19–20). Poop of a lovely . . . Golden ship . . . Cool hands – Recalls Enobarbus's description of Cleopatra in *Antony and Cleopatra:* "The barge she sat in, like a burnished throne, / Burn'd on the water: the poop [stern] was beaten gold . . . at the helm / A seeming mermaid steers: the silken tackle / Swell with touches of those flower-soft hands, / That yarely [with a sailor's efficiency] frame the office [do their duty]" (II.ii.196–97, 213–16). For the ship *Erin's King*, see 4.434n.

11.581–82 (271:20). The harp that once or twice – See "The Harp that Once Through Tara's Halls," 8.606–7n.

11.587, 594–95 (271:25, 33–34).—*M'appari / M'appari tutt' amor: / Il mio sguardo l'incontr* . . . – See 11.24n.

11.590 (271:28–29). *A Last Farewell* – A print on the wall is appropriately an illustration of a song by John Willis, "The Last Farewell": "Farewell! and when the dark dark sea / Is wafting thee away / Then will you give one thought to me / As o'er the deep you stray. // Farewell, and when the sun's last rays / Sink down beneath the main / Thou'lt think of joys in other days / And sigh for home again."

11.591 (271:29–30). A lovely girl, her veil awave upon the wind – See 11.21n; also Leucothea, p. 290.

11.599 (271:38). Ah, sure, my dancing days are done – From the third verse of the song "Johnny, I Hardly Knew Ye" (see 5.551–52n): "Where are the legs with which you run / When you went to carry a gun? / Indeed your dancing days are done! / Faith, Johnny, I hardly knew ye."

11.602 (271:41–42). Play it in the original. One flat – In Flowtow's opera, "M'appari" is in the key of F major ("one flat"); see 11.24n; and cf. 7.59–60n.

11.606 (272:5). Graham Lemon's – Lemon & Co., Ltd., wholesale confection, lozenge, and comfit manufacturers to the queen, 49 Sackville (now O'Connell) Street Lower. Boylan has turned north from the Liffey side.

11.606 (272:5). Elvery's elephant – Elvery's Elephant House, John W. Elvery & Co., waterproof and gutta-percha manufacturers, 46–47 Sackville (now O'Connell) Street Lower (north of Lemon's).

11.610 (272:9–10). *Sonnambula* – See 11.22n.

11.611 (272:10). Joe Maas – Joseph Maas (1847–86), a famous English tenor (lyric rather than dramatic) who began his career as a choirboy and who starred in the German impresario Carl Rosa's (1842–89) opera company. Rosa's company was noted for its presentations of English versions of foreign operas.

11.611 (272:11). M'Guckin – Barton M'Guckin (1852–1913), an Irish tenor who also began his career as a choirboy and also sang in Rosa's company.

11.615 (272:14). Backache he. Bright's bright eye – Backache and bright eyes were commonly taken as "symptoms" of Bright's disease, a disease of the kidneys that could be caused by excessive consumption of alcohol.

11.615–16 (272:15). Paying the piper – After the common saying (c. 1681) "If you dance to the tune, you must pay the piper [fiddler]."

11.616 (272:15). Pills, pounded bread – Echoes the popular suspicion that most miracle-cure pills contained very little in the way of drugs or effective medication. In 1904 drugs were regarded as of very little help in the treatment of Bright's disease; change of climate, abstinence from alcohol, and a strict diet were usually recommended.

11.617 (272:16–17). *Down among the dead men* – Anonymous English song: "Here's a health to the Queen, and a lasting peace, / To faction an end, to wealth increase, / Come let's drink it while we have breath, / For there's no drinking after death. // And he that will this health deny / Down among the dead men, / Down among the dead men, / Down, down, down, down, / Down among the dead men let him lie!"

11.617 (272:17). Kidney pie. Sweets to the – A common joking use of Gertrude's line in *Hamlet* (V:i): "Sweets to the sweet. Farewell" (as she scatters flowers in Ophelia's grave); hence, as sweets to the sweet, so kidneys for those with kidney trouble.

11.619 (272:20). Vartry water – Dublin's public water supply was created by diverting the

River Vartry into a large reservoir, the Vartry or Roundwood Reservoir, eighteen miles south of Dublin.

11.619 (272:20). fecking – To "feck" is to discover a safe method of robbing or cheating.

11.621 (272:22). Screwed – Drunk.

11.624 (272:25). the gods of the old Royal – In other words, in the cheapest balcony seats. The old Royal Theatre in Hawkins Street was destroyed by fire in 1880, when Bloom was fourteen years old; it was replaced by a new Theatre Royal in 1884.

11.624 (272:25). little Peake – See 6.158 (91:17) and 6.157n.

11.627 (272:29–30). But want a good memory – It is proverbial wisdom that to be a successful liar one must have an extraordinary memory.

11.629 (272:32). *All is lost now* – See 11.22n.

11.630 (272:34). banshee – Irish: "a female fairy. . . . In modern times . . . a female spirit that attends certain families, and is heard *keening* or crying aloud at night round the house when some member of the family is about to die" (P. W. Joyce, *English*, p. 214).

11.633 (272:36). Blackbird – Similar in size and behavior to the American robin, with similar warning notes. The song is richer than a robin's, "deliberate, loud and melodious warbling" with "*lack of repetitive habit*" and with considerable improvisation on fragments of melody picked up from the surround (Roger Tory Peterson et al., *A Field Guide to the Birds of Britain and Europe* [Boston, 1967], p. 269).

11.633 (272:37). the hawthorn valley – Another name for the Furze or Furry Glen, a ravine in southwestern Phoenix Park near the Knockmaroon gate. It is "a deep hollow lined on either side with furze bushes and unnumerable hawthorn trees" (D. A. Chart, *The Story of Dublin* [London, 1907], p. 314).

11.634–35 (272:38–39). Echo. How sweet the answer – After Thomas Moore's "Echo," in *Irish Melodies*: "How sweet the answer Echo makes / To music at night, / When roused by lute or horn, she wakes, / And far away, o'er lawns and lakes, / Goes answering light. // Yet love hath echoes truer far, / And far more sweet, / Than e'er beneath the moon light's star, / Of horn or lute, or soft guitar, / The songs repeat. // 'Tis when the sigh, in youth sincere, / And only then,— / The sigh that's breath'd for one to hear, / Is by that one, that only dear, / Breathed back again!"

11.635 (272:39). All lost now – See 11.22n.

11.638–39 (272:42–273:1). In sleep she . . . in the moon – That is, the innocent heroine Amina of *La sonnambula*; see 11.22n.

11.640 (273:2). Call name. Touch water – Popular superstition held that there was danger of shock or injury to a sleepwalker who was abruptly awakened, with two exceptions: the sleepwalker could be softly called by name, or it could be arranged for the sleepwalker to touch water (in which case he or she would return to bed rather than risk drowning).

11.640 (273:3). She longed to go – Bloom interprets Amina's sleepwalking (dream) as an expression not of her innocence but of her desire.

11.644 (273:7–8). Still harping on his daughter – Hamlet ("mad") baits Polonius with crude jokes about his daughter. "POLONIUS (*aside*): How say you by that? Still harping on my daughter" (II.ii.188–89).

11.644–45 (273:8). Wise child that knows her father – See 6.53n.

11.648 (273:12). Crosseyed Walter sir I did sir – See 3.67–69 (38:35–37).

11.659 (273:24). a heart bowed down – "The Heart Bowed Down" is a song in Act II of Michael William Balfe's (1808–70) opera *The Bohemian Girl* (1843): "The heart bowed down by weight of woe, / To weakest hopes will cling, / To thought and impulse while they flow, / That can no comfort bring, / . . . / With those exciting scenes will blend, / O'er pleasure's pathway thrown; / But memory is the only friend, / That grief can call his own."

11.661 (273:26–27). in cool glaucous *eau de Nil* – In *The Odyssey*, the Sirens sing of the waters around their rock as "our green mirror" (12:186; Fitzgerald, p. 227). For *eau de Nil*, see 11.67n.

11.665–751 (273:30–276:6). *When first I saw . . .—To me!* – The italicized lines in these pages are from Lionel's air "M'appari" in *Martha;* see 11.24n.

11.668 (273:33). Braintipped – That is, the scalp tingles with pleasurable excitement.

11.681 (274:6). love's old sweet song – See 4.314n.

11.682–84 (274:7–10). the elastic band . . . in octave gyved them fast – Bloom, playing cat's cradle with the rubber band from his package of stationery, is cast in the role of Odysseus who, in the midst of the transit past the Sirens, is secured more firmly to the mast by his crew.

11.686 (274:12). Increase their flow – After the popular belief that intense sexual activity increased a singer's vocal capacity, and that more singing increased sexual desire.

11.687/688 (274:13/14–15). My head it simply/Your head it simply swurls – Boylan's song; see 4.282n.

11.688 (274:14). for tall hats – Implies an unfounded pretension to elegance or ability.

11.688–89 (274:15–16). What perfume does . . . want to know – From Martha Clifford's letter (5.258 [78:12–13]).

11.691 (274:18). kissing comfits – Various candies used to sweeten the breath.

11.692 (274:19). Hands felt for the opulent – From *Sweets of Sin;* see 10.606n.

11.696 (274:24–25). Singing wrong words – Simon Dedalus sings a popular version of "M'appari" (see 11.24n); but Bloom is right: Dedalus does half-remember and improvise some of the lines.

11.698 (274:26–27). Keep a trot for the avenue – That is, retain the ability to make a good appearance on occasion even though one is in decline, after the aging horse that can still show in competitive moments.

11.699–700 (274:28–29). Jenny Lind soup . . . pint of cream – Jenny Lind (1820–87) was a Swedish soprano whose abilities as a singer together with her personal qualities and generosity made her one of the most popular of nineteenth-century performers. She was noted for the abstemiousness of her diet; a bland but nourishing soup of the sort Bloom's recipe suggests, *Soup à la Cantatrice* (Professional Singer's Soup), was renamed in her honor. As Mrs. Isabella Beeton put it in *The Book of Household Management* (London, 1861), "Note: This is a soup, the principle ingredients of which, sago [not sage] and eggs, have always been deemed very beneficial to the chest and throat. In various quantities, and in different proportions, these have been partaken of by the principal singers of the day, including the celebrated Swedish Nightingale, Jenny Lind, and, as they have always avowed, with considerable advantage to the voice, in singing."

11.701 (274:30–31). That's the chat – Slang: "That's the right or correct thing."

11.706–7 (274:36–37). Tipping her tepping . . . topping her. Tup – All of these *t-p* "verbs" have in common the (archaic) meaning: to copulate as animals. To "tup" and to "tip" mean to copulate as a ram does. To "top" means to cover as an animal covers, and both "tap" and "tep" are dialect variants of "top." "Tipping" is also a musical term for double-tonguing.

11.722 (275:13). Drago's – Adolphe Drago, hairdresser and wigmaker, 36 Henry Street and 17 Dawson Street, Dublin.

11.725 (275:17). Mat Dillon's in Terenure – See 6.697n. Terenure is another name for Roundtown.

11.730 (275:23). *Waiting* – A song for soprano or tenor, words by Ellen H. Flagg, music by H. Millard (1867): "The stars shine on his pathway, / The trees bend back their leaves / To guide him to the meadow / Among the golden sheaves / Where I stand longing, loving / And list'ning as I wait / To the nightingale's wild singing, / Sweet singing to its mate, / Singing, singing, sweet singing to its mate. // The breeze comes sweet from heaven, / And the music in the air / Heralds my lover's coming, / And tells me he is there. / And tells me he is there, // Come for my arms are empty! / Come for the day was long! / Turn the darkness into glory, / The sorrow into song. / I hear his footfall's music, / I feel his presence near. / All my soul responsive answers / And tells me he is here. // O stars . . . shine out your brightest! / O night . . . ingale, sing sweet / To guide . . . him to me, waiting / And speed his flying feet, / To guide . . . him to me, waiting / And speed his flying feet."

11.733 (275:27). in old Madrid – A song with words by G. Clifton Bingham, music by Henry Trotere (Trotter): "Long years ago in old Madrid / Where softly sighs of love the light guitar, / Two sparkling eyes a lattice hid. / Two eyes as darkly bright as love's own star / There on a casement ledge when day was o'er, / A tiny hand lightly laid. / A face looked out, as from the river shore, / There stole a tender serenade. / Rang the lover's happy song, / Light and low from shore to shore, / But ah, the river flowed along / Between them evermore, / Come my love, the stars are shining, / Time is flying, love is sighing, / Come, for thee a heart is pining, / Here alone I wait for thee."

11.734 (275:27). Dolores shedolores – See 11.9n.

11.762–63 (276:18–19). by monuments of sir John . . . Theobald Mathew – In sequence up Sackville (now O'Connell) Street (as Boylan proceeds north). For Gray, see 6.258n; for Nelson, 6.293n; for Father Mathew, 6.319–20n.

11.764 (276:20–21). *Cloche. Sonnez la. Cloche. Sonnez la.* – See 11.17–18n.

11.765 (276:22). the Rotunda, Rutland square – At the top of Sackville (now O'Connell) Street, the Rotunda on Rutland (now Parnell) Square is an eighteenth-century building that housed a maternity hospital and a series of public rooms available for concerts, meetings, and exhibitions.

11.779–82 (276:39–277:1). *'Twas rank and fame . . . since love lives not* – See 7.471–72n.

11.789 (277:9). We never speak as we pass by – The title of a song (1882) by the American Frank Egerton: "The spell is past, the dream is o'er, / And tho' we meet, we love no more, / One heart is crush'd to droop and die, / And for relief must heav'nward fly, / The once bright smile has faded, gone, / And given way, to looks forlorn! / Despite her grandeur's wicked flame, / She stoops to blush beneath her shame. [Chorus:] We never speak as we pass by / Although a tear bedims her eye; / I know she thinks of her past life, / When we were loving man and wife. [Second verse:] In guileless youth, I sought her side, / And she became my virtuous bride, / Our lot was peace, so fair and bright, / One summer day, no gloomy night, / No life on earth more pure than ours / In that dear home midst field and flow'rs / Until the tempter came to Nell, / It dazzled her, alas! she fell."

11.789–90 (277:10). Rift in the lute – After Tennyson's song "The Rift within the Lute," in *Idylls of the King,* "Merlin and Vivien" (1859). The deceptive Vivien sings the song to the doubting Merlin in the attempt to convince him that she is trustworthy: "In love, if love be love, if love be ours, / Faith and unfaith can ne'er be equal powers: / Unfaith in aught is want of faith in all. // It is the little rift within the lute, / That by and by will make the music mute, / And ever widening slowly silence all. // The little rift within the lover's lute / Or little pitted speck in garner'd fruit, / That rotting inward slowly moulders all. // It is not worth the keeping: let it go. / But shall it? answer, darling, answer, no. / And trust me not at all or all in all."

11.797 (277:17). Barraclough's – Arthur Barraclough, professor of singing, 24 Pembroke Street Lower, Dublin.

11.798 (277:18–19). a retrospective sort of arrangement – See 6.150 (91:7).

11.802 (277:23). Thou lost one – "M'appari"; see 11.24n.

11.805–6 (277:27–28). *Corpus paradisum* – Latin: literally, "the body of paradise." The phrase combines two liturgical fragments that Bloom has heard: *Corpus* (5.350 [80:34]) and *In paradisum* (6.628 [104:25]).

11.812 (277:34). Dorset street – Boylan has continued from Sackville (now O'Connell) Street through its northwesterly extensions, Rutland (now Parnell) Square East and Frederick Street North, to Dorset Street Upper where he turns northeast, one short block from the east end of Eccles Street.

11.822 (278:7). A pad – A blotter.

11.844 (278:32). *Blumenlied* – German: "Flower Song." There are literally hundreds of songs so titled; the most famous is by the German lyric poet Heinrich Heine (1797–56).

11.845 (278:33–34). the stables near Cecilia street – There were stables at 5–6 Cecilia Street, in the midst of a commercial warehouse district just south of the Liffey in central Dublin.

11.850 (278:39). Ringabella, Crosshaven – See 10.400n.

11.851 (278:40). Queenstown harbour – Queenstown is now Cobh, the seaport of Cork, on the south coast of Ireland; the harbor is called either Cobh Harbor or Cork Harbor.

11.852 (278:41–279:1). those earthquake hats – When ashore, Italian sailors wore conical straw hats made of a straw similar to what the Irish would call "earthquake grass."

11.856 (279:6–7). your other eye – See 11.148n.

11.857–58 (279:7–8). Callan, Coleman . . . Fawcett – A fictional list of deaths in the obituary column of the day's *Freeman's Journal;* see 6.158 (91:16).

11.860 (279:11). Greek ees – Handwriting with Greek e's (ε) was thought to indicate an artistic temperament.

11.867 (279:19). Elijah is com – See 8.13n.

11.868 (279:20). p.o. – Post office; here, a postal money order.

11.868 (279:20–21). two and six – 2s. 6d., on the order of a ten-to-fifteen-dollar gift in 1985 values.

11.870 (279:23). O, Mairy lost the pin of her – See 5.281–84 (78:38–41).

11.877 (279:31). Sauce for the gander – "What's sauce for the goose is sauce for the gander." This proverbial attack on the double standard dates from at least 1671.

11.878–79 (279:32–34). A hackney car . . . avenue, Donnybrook – One James Barton is listed in *Thom's* 1904 as living at Rose Cottage, the first of three houses listed on Harmony Avenue in Donnybrook. *Thom's* does not list him as a "cab proprietor," and his role as driver of no. 324 is lost in "history."

11.881 (279:35). George Robert Mesias – See 6.831n.

11.882 (279:37). John Plasto – See 4.69n.

11.883–84 (279:38–39). This is the jingle that joggled and jingled – See 11.15n; and cf. 7.210–13n and 14.405–7n.

11.884 (279:39). Dlugacz' porkshop – Where Bloom purchased his breakfast kidney; see 4.46n.

11.884 (279:40). Agendath – See 4.191–92n.

11.887 (280:1). Town traveller – A traveling salesman.

11.888 (280:3). best references – A standard phrase used in letters by job applicants.

11.896 (280:13–14). Messrs Callan, Coleman and Co, limited – A nonexistent company that Bloom concocts out of the fictional obituary column (11.857 [279:8]).

11.898–99 (280:16–17). c/o P. O. Dolphin's barn lane – Bloom writes to Martha Clifford in care of a town sub–post office in what is now Dolphin Barn Street in southwestern Dublin.

11.901–3 (280:19–21). prize titbit . . . the laughing witch – See 4.502n.

11.904–5 (280:23–24). Music hath charms. Shakespeare said – No, it was William Congreve (1670–1729) in *The Mourning Bride* (1697), Act I, scene i: "Music hath charms to soothe the savage breast, / To soften rocks, and bend the knotted oak."

11.905 (280:24). Quotations every day in the year – Books and calendars of this sort were extraordinarily popular in the nineteenth century. William Schutte (*Joyce and Shakespeare* [New Haven, Conn., 1957], p. 126) cites *The Shakespeare Calendar; or, Wit and Wisdom for Every Day in the Year* (New York, 1850).

11.905 (280:25). To be or not to be – The opening line of Hamlet's famous soliloquy (III.i.56ff.).

11.907–8 (280:26–27). In Gerard's rosery . . . Do. But do – See 9.651–54 (202:9–12).

11.909 (280:28). Post office lower down – Town Sub–Post Office, Money Order and Savings Bank Office, 34 Ormond Quay Upper; west of the Ormond Hotel and just east of where Bloom would turn north toward Barney Kiernan's.

11.910 (280:29). Barney Kiernan's – Bernard Kiernan & Co., wholesale tea and spirit merchants, wine and brandy shippers, 8–10 Little Britain Street.

11.911 (280:30). House of mourning – "It is better to go to the house of mourning than to go to the house of feasting: for that is the end of all men; and the living will lay it to his heart" (Ecclesiastes 7:2).

11.911 (280:31). beetle – (Or beetlehead) is slang for blockhead.

11.927 (281:8). How Walter Bapty lost his voice – Walter Bapty (1850–1915) was a professor of singing in Dublin and one of the organizers of the Feis Ceoil (1897), the annual Dublin music festival and competition. Tom Kernan's story may be just that: Tom Kernan's story (see Adams, p. 73).

11.939/941 (281:22/24–25). Lovely seaside girls/Your head it simply – From Boylan's song; see 4.282n.

11.946 (281:30–31). Well, it's a sea. Corpuscle islands – A remote allusion to Phineas Fletcher's (1582–1650) allegorical poem *The Purple Island; or, The Isle of Man* (1633), a seventeenth-century layman's poeticized conception of the human body; see Adams, p. 150.

11.949 (281:34). What are the wild waves saying? – The title of a duet, words by Joseph Edwards Carpenter, music by Stephen Glover (1813–70): "BROTHER: What are the wild waves saying, Sister the whole day long, / That ever amid our playing, I hear but their low, lone song? / Not by the seaside only, / There it sounds wild and free; / But at night when 'tis dark and lonely, / In dreams it is still with me . . . SISTER: Brother! I hear no singing! / 'Tis but the rolling wave / Ever its lone course winging / Over some ocean cave! / 'Tis but the noise of water / Dashing ag'st the shore, / And the wind from bleaker quarter / Mingling with its roar . . . CHORUS: No! no, no, no! No, no, no! / It is something greater. / That speaks to the heart alone / The voice of the great Creator / Dwells in that mighty tone."

11.952 (281:38). Larry O'Rourke's – See 4.105n and 4.112–13n.

11.961–62 (282:7). *One: one, one, one, one, one: two, one, three, four – The numbers do not describe the music but "the step and motions of the dancers . . . the image of dancing couples which the music calls forth" (Zack Bowen, *Musical Allusions in the Works of James Joyce* [Albany, N.Y., 1974], p. 192).

11.965 (282:10). Ruttledge's door – See 7.28 (116:30).

11.965 (282:11). Minuet of *Don Giovanni* – First heard in Act I, scene iv of the opera; in the next scene it is played by an onstage band in the ballroom of Don Giovanni's house as Don Giovanni dances with Zerlina and then leads her offstage for an attempt at seduction.

11.967 (282:12–13). Peasants outside – Suggested by *Don Giovanni:* in Act I, scene iii, Don Giovanni has discovered Zerlina in a group of singing and dancing peasants near his house; in the next two scenes (see preceding note) there is the sense that the peasants, particularly Masetto, Zerlina's peasant-fiancé, are "outside" the house as Don Giovanni and his servants try to distract Masetto so that he won't interfere with the proposed seduction.

11.967 (282:13). eating dockleaves – A traditional image of the plight of the Irish peasantry during the Great Famine. The leaves of young plants can be used as potherbs, but mature plants can prove almost indigestible.

11.972 (282:19). My wife and your wife – From the American folksong "The Grey Goose." The song begins: "It was one Sunday mornin,' / Lawd, Lawd, Lawd, / The preacher went a-huntin' [Fifth verse:] And my wife and your wife, / . . . / They give a feather pickin'" (unsuccessfully, as it turns out, since the grey goose is inedible).

11.975 (282:22–23). *quis est homo:* Mercadante – Mercadante (see 5.402n) did not write a *Stabat Mater,* as this phrase suggests, though Bloom has earlier thought of Rossini's *Stabat Mater* in conjunction with Mercadante's *Seven Last Words;* see 5.397–98n and 5.403–4n.

11.977 (282:25). Dandy tan shoe of dandy Boylan – Echoes a nursery rhyme and its variant: "Handy-spandy, Jack-a-dandy, / Loves plum-cake and sugar candy. / He bought some at a grocer's shop, / And pleased, away he went, hop, hop." Variant: "Handy-dandy / Sugary candy— / Top or bottom. // Handy-spandy, / Jack a dandy— / Which good hand will you have?"

11.977–78 (282:26). socks skyblue clocks –See 4.282n, lines 19–20.

11.979 (282:27). Chamber music – The title of Joyce's first published book (London, 1907), a volume of thirty-six short lyrics.

11.981–83 (282:29–31). Empty vessels make . . . law of falling water – Bloom combines the acoustical principle that the resonance (and pitch) of a vessel changes as liquid is added with Archimedes' law of specific gravity (the ratio of the weight of water displaced by an object to the weight of the object).

11.983 (282:32). those rhapsodies of Liszt's Hungarian – See 11.36n.

11.986–87 (282:36). Paul de Kock – See 4.358n.

11.990 (282:39). *Qui sdegno* – Italian: "Here indignation"; in the Italian version of Mozart's opera *Die Zauberflöte* (The Magic Flute) (1791) these are the opening words of "In diesen heiligen Hallen" (In these sacred halls), an aria in Act II, scene iii. Shortly before the high priest of Isis and Osiris enters in this scene, the Queen of the Night has, in her "Revenge Aria," commanded her daughter, Pamina, to kill the high priest or be disowned. When the high priest enters, he is confronted by Pamina who, instead of assaulting him, confesses her dilemma and begs forgiveness for her mother. In his aria he comforts her and explains that "in these sacred halls" (in the halls of the temple of Light, over which he presides) there is no such thing as revenge: only love can bind human beings together.

11.991 (282:40). *The Croppy Boy* – The balance of this episode is larded with allusions to this song; see 11.39n.

11.991 (282:40–41). Our native Doric – See 7.326n.

11.992 (282:42). Good men and true – "The Croppy Boy" (11.39n), line 1.

11.996 (283:4). What key? Six sharps? – Six sharps is F-sharp major, as Dollard says.

11.1001 (283:9). on for a razzle – Slang: beginning a spree or a bender.

11.1004 (283:12–13). waiting Patty come home – See "Waiting," 11.730n.

11.1005–8 (283:14–17). In a cave of . . . from hoary mountains – See 11.42n.

11.1009 (283:18–19). The priest he sought . . . speak a word – "The Croppy Boy" (11.39n), lines 3–4.

11.1012–14 (283:23–25). Big ships' chandler's . . . ten thousand pounds – See Adams, p. 65.

11.1014–15 (283:25). the Iveagh home – In 1903 the Guinness Trust Dublin Fund ("for the amelioration of the poor laboring classes of Dublin") was amalgamated into the Iveagh Trust (Lord Iveagh being one of the principal heirs of the Guinness fortune). The Guinness f245Trust Buildings, a large charity lodging-house for men with 386 rooms or cubicles, off New Bride Street in central Dublin, thus became the Iveagh Trust Buildings or Iveagh House.

11.1015 (283:26). Number one Bass – See 8.121n.

11.1016–17 (283:27–28). The priest's at home . . . The holy father – "The Croppy Boy" (11.39n), lines 5–8.

11.1019 (283:30). Hushaby. Lullaby. Die, dog. Little dog, die – "This sounds like the end part of a song used to finish a child's turn on a swing. Usually it is a cat dying in such songs, but we have an example from Cheshire, c. 1900, which runs, 'An apple for the King, / And a pear for the Queen, / And a good toss over the bowling green. / Die, die, little dog, die, / Die for the sake of your mother's black eye. / Die, die-away'" (suggested by Iona Opie).

11.1020–22 (283:31–34). the youth had entered . . . sitting to shrive – "The Croppy Boy" (11.39n), lines 9–12.

11.1023–34 (283:35–36). *Answers* poet's picture puzzle – *Answers*, a popular and successful penny-weekly founded by Alfred Harmsworth (see 7.732–33n) in 1888. The magazine featured a weekly "picture puzzle" that, when deciphered, rendered the title of a famous poem; prize £5.

11.1025 (283:37). Lay of the last minstrel – The title of a poem (1802–4, 1805) by Sir Walter Scott (1771–1832).

11.1032–33 (284:3–5). *In nomine Domini* . . . confessing: *mea culpa* – "The Croppy Boy" (11.39n), lines 13–15.

11.1035–36 (284:8). coffin or coffey – See 6.595n.

11.1036 (284:8). *corpusnomine* – Another of Bloom's Latin compounds: "body-name," combining the *Corpus* he has heard (5.350 [80:34]) with *nominie* from "The Croppy Boy."

11.1040–43 (284:13–16). Since easter he had . . . had not prayed – "The Croppy Boy" (11.39n), lines 21–24. For "you bitch's bast," see 10.1119–20 (250:18–19).

11.1045 (284:19). dab – An expert.

11.1047 (284:22–23). to titivate – To make small alterations in one's toilet, etc. in order to add to one's attractions.

11.1049 (284:25–26). Way to catch rattlesnakes – Popular notion of a practical application of Indian snake-charming practices.

11.1050 (284:26). Michael Gunn – (d. 1901) was involved in the management of the Gaiety Theatre in Dublin from 1871 until his death. Even after his death the managers of the theater continued to be listed as "Michael Gunn Limited" (*Thom's* 1904). One measure of his reputation appears in R. M. Levey and J. O'Rorke, *Annals of the Theatre Royal, Dublin* (Dublin, 1880), with its dedication "To Michael Gunn, Esq., on whose sound Judgment the Future of the Drama in Dublin Hopefully Depends."

11.1050 (284:27). Shah of Persia – Nasr-al Din (d. 1896) made two state visits to England, in June 1873 and July 1889; the Prince of Wales (later Edward VII) was assiduous in his attentions to the shah's entertainment on both occasions. During the 1889 visit the shah caught the popular fancy and was "immortalized" in street songs and as the principal figure in innumerable stories of the sort Bloom recalls.

11.1051 (284:27–28). home sweet home – A song (1823), words by John Howard Payne, music by Henry Rowley Bishop: "'Mid pleasures and palaces though I may roam, / Be it ever so humble, there's no place like home; / A charm from the sky seems to hallow there, / Which, seek through the world, is ne'er met with elsewhere. // Home! Home! Sweet, sweet home! / There's no place like home."

11.1055 (284:32). music hath jaws – Cf. 11.904–5n.

11.1058 (284:36–37). what Spinoza says in that book of poor papa's – Baruch Spinoza (1632–77) was a famous Dutch-Jewish philosopher. On Bloom's bookshelf is *Thoughts from Spinoza* (17.1372 [708:26]). Molly (18.1115–16 [769:15–16]) recalls the incident and Bloom "talking about Spinoza and his soul thats dead I suppose millions of years ago." That is barely a hint, but as a guess: in the *Short Treatise on God, Man, and His Well-Being*, at the beginning of Appendix 2, "On the Human Soul," Spinoza comes close to suggesting that the soul is mortal—"What we call the Soul is a mode of the attribute which we call Thought, and that nothing else except this mode belongs to [man's essence]; so much so that when this mode comes to naught, the soul perishes also, although the above attribute remains unchanged." Nevertheless, Spinoza ends the appendix with the assertion that "knowledge of oneself" is distinctly possible: "And from all this (as also because our soul is united with God, and is a part of the infinite Idea, arising immediately from God) there can also be clearly seen the origin of clear knowledge, and the immortality of the soul." (The *Short Treatise* was written in the early 1660s but not published until 1862, trans. A. Wolf [London, 1910].)

11.1061–62 (284:40–41). God made the country man the tune – After William Cowper's (1731–1800) "God made the country, and man made the town" (*The Task* [1785], Book 1, line 749).

11.1063–65 (285:1–3). All gone. All fallen . . . name and race – "The Croppy Boy" (11.39n), lines 17–20. (Apparently Dollard alters the sequence of the poem's stanzas, reversing stanzas 5 and 6.) For the siege of Ross, see 10.793n. *Gorey:* after their defeat at Ross, the rebels regrouped at Gorey, ten miles south-southeast of Arklow (a town on the coast forty miles south of Dublin), and from there mounted on 9 June 1798 an attack on Arklow; the attack was another disaster for the rebels. *We are the boys of Wexford:* see 7.427–28n.

11.1068 (285:7). He bore no hate – "The Croppy Boy" (11.39n), line 25; and cf. 11.990n.

11.1072 (285:12). My country above the king – "The Croppy Boy" (11.39n), line 26.

11.1072–73 (285:13). Who fears to speak of nineteen four? – After "Who fears to speak of Ninety-eight"; see 10.790n.

11.1074 (285:15–16). *Bless me, father . . . let me go* – "The Croppy Boy" (11.39n), line 27.

11.1076–77 (285:18–19). eighteen bob a week – The barmaid's wage, 18s., can be translated as roughly $75–80 a week (U.S., 1985).

11.1077 (285:19). dibs – Slang for money.

11.1077–78 (285:20). Those girls, those lovely – Boylan's song; see 4.282n.

11.1078 (285:20–21). By the sad sea waves – A song from Sir Julius Benedict's (1804–85) opera *The Bride of Venice* (1843): "By the sad sea-waves / I listen, while they moan / A lament o'er graves / Of hope and pleasure gone. / I am young, I was fair, / I had once not a care / From the rising of the moon / To the setting of the sun. / Yet I pine like a slave / By the sad sea-wave. [Chorus:] Come again, bright days / Of hope and pleasure gone; / Come again, bright days, / Come again, come again."

11.1081–82 (285:24–26). The false priest . . . yeoman captain – "The Croppy Boy" (11.39n), lines 29–32.

11.1092 (285:37). *Songs without words – In German, *Lieder ohne Worte,* forty-eight piano pieces by Felix Mendelssohn (1809–47), published in eight groups of six (1834–45).

11.1093–94 (285:39). Understand animals . . . Solomon did – One popular bit of folklore about King Solomon was that he had a magic ring that enabled him to understand the language of animals.

11.1097–99 (286:1–3). With hoarse rude fury . . . to live, your last – "The Croppy Boy" (11.39n), lines 33–36.

11.1105–6 (286:10). On yonder river – "The Croppy Boy" (11.39n), line 37.

11.1106 (286:11). (her heaving embon) – From *Sweets of Sin;* see 10.606n.

11.1109 (286:14). The bright stars fade . . . The morn – From "Goodbye, Sweetheart, Goodbye"; see 11.13n.

11.1109 (286:14). O rose! Castile – See 7.591n.

11.1120 (286:27). I hold this house . . . Traitors swing – "The Croppy Boy" (11.39n), lines 39–40.

11.1126–27 (286:34–35). O'er ryehigh blue. Bloom – See "When the Bloom Is on the Rye," 10.524n.

11.1131–32 (286:39–40). At Geneva barrack . . . was his body laid – "The Croppy Boy" (11.39n), lines 41–42. Geneva Barrack was a depot for army recruits that was converted into a prison in 1798 for the confinement of rebels. It was on Waterford Harbor in southeastern Ireland; Passage is a village on the harbor north of the barrack. The location implies that the Croppy Boy was attempting to cross from Waterford into Wexford, the heartland of rebel insurgency in southern Ireland (1798).

11.1132 (286:40). Dolor! O, he dolores! – *Dolor*, Latin: "suffering, anguish"; see "The Shade of the Palm," 11.9n.

11.1139–41 (287:6–8). Pray for him . . . was the croppy boy – "The Croppy Boy" (11.39n), lines 43–44.

11.1150 (287:17). Lablache – Luigi Lablache (1794–1858), the Italian-born son of a French father and an Irish mother, was the most famous bass of his time in Europe. He was also noted for his acting, particularly as Leporello, the conniving servant in *Don Giovanni*. He gave Queen Victoria singing lessons off and on for over twenty years and was one of her "heroes."

11.1152 (287:20). nakkering – See 11.52n.

11.1154 (287:21). Big Benaben – See 11.53n.

11.1160 (287:28). Ben machree – *Machree*, Irish: "my heart." Thus *Ben machree* is "Mountain [of] my heart."

11.1164 (287:33). rift in the lute – See 11.789–90n.

11.1176 (288:5). *The Last Rose of Summer – See 11.32n.

11.1180 (288:10–11). Postoffice near Reuben J's – The post office at 34 Ormond Quay Upper was in the same building as Reuben J. Dodd's office; see 11.909n.

11.1181 (288:12). Greek street – Would be on Bloom's "indirect" route to Barney Kiernan's (see 11.910n) if he went around by the post office.

11.1183–84 (288:13–14). Her hand that rocks . . . rules the world – After William Ross Wallace's (1819–81) "What Rules the World?": "They say that man is mighty, / He governs land and sea; / He wields a mighty scepter / O'er lesser powers that be; / And the hand that rocks the cradle / Is the hand that rules the world."

11.1187 (288:17). Lionelleopold – Lionel is the character who sings "M'appari" in Flotow's *Martha*; see 11.24n and 7.58n.

11.1191–92 (288:23). Better give way . . . man with a maid – "The way of a man with a maid" is line 30 of Kipling's poem "The Long Trail," where it is included in a paraphrase of Solomon's questions (Proverbs 30:18–19): "There be three things which are too wonderful for me, yea, four which I know not: The way of an eagle in the air; the way of a serpent upon a rock; the way of a ship in the midst of the sea; and the way of man with a maid." But Bloom has in mind an anonymous late-nineteenth-century pornographic novel, *The Way of a Man with a Maid* (New York, 1968), in which the "heroine," prudish Alice, refuses the "hero," Jack, only to be trapped and debauched by him. Alice then "gives way," not "halfway" but all the way, abandoning all prudery for debauchery and joining Jack in a series of seductions of other women.

11.1197 (288:29–30). Organ in Gardiner . . . quid a year – See 5.396n.

11.1198–99 (288:31). Seated all day at the organ – See "The Lost Chord," 11.478n.

11.1199 (288:32). Maunder – Involves a pun on John Henry Maunder (1858–1920), a composer of sentimental church music.

11.1201 (288:34). no don't she cried – In *The Way of a Man with a Maid* (see 11.1191–92n), Jack and Alice (after her conversion) make use of his soundproof "snuggery" (a cozy little room) in their career of debauchery. "'No, don't,' she cried" functions as a refrain, recurring again and again to spice the novel's sequence of seductions and violations.

11.1210 (289:1–2). Simonlionel first I saw – Lionel's song "M'appari" begins with the phrase "When first I saw . . ."; see 11.24n.

11.1220–21 (289:12–13). one last, one lonely, last sardine of summer – See "'Tis the Last Rose of Summer," 11.32n.

11.1224 (289:16). Barry's – J. M. Barry & Co., merchant tailors and outfitters, 12 Ormond Quay Upper, just west of the Ormond Hotel.

11.1224 (289:16–17). that wonderworker – See 17.1819–39 (721:38–722:20).

11.1225 (289:17). Twenty-four solicitors in that one house – Bloom is right; *Thom's* 1904 lists twenty-four solicitors' offices at 12 Ormond Quay Upper.

11.1228–29 (289:20–21). the chap that wallops . . . Mickey Rooney's band – There are similar Irish and Irish-American songs ("McNamara's Band," for example), but the source of this one is unknown.

11.1231 (289:24). Asses' skins – Traditionally regarded as the finest material for drum heads.

11.1235 (289:28). Daly's – See 11.230n.

11.1235 (289:28). mermaid – See 11.222n.

11.1242 (289:36). Sweep! – The call of a chimney sweep advertising his services.

11.1242 (289:37). All is lost now – See "Tutto è sciolto," 11.22n.

11.1243 (289:38). bumbailiff – Contemptuous for a sheriff's deputy or assistant who pursues and catches from behind (after *bum*, buttocks).

11.1243 (289:38–39). Long John. Waken the dead – That is, Long John Fanning's name recalls the song "John Peel" (c. 1820) by John Woodcock Graves. John Peel was a master of hounds who lived in Cumberland, England; the chorus of the song asserts that his "'View hallo!' would waken the dead, / Or the fox from his lair in the morning."

11.1244 (289:39). *nominedomine* – See "The Croppy Boy" (11.39n), line 14.

11.1245 (289:41). *da capo* – Italian (music): "From the beginning," a direction to repeat a passage; hence the suggestion: over (and over) again.

11.1248 (290:2). shah of Persia – See 11.1050n.

11.1248–49 (290:2–4). Breathe a prayer . . . a yeoman cap – See "The Croppy Boy" (11.39n), line 44 and passim.

11.1253–54 (290:8–9). When first he saw that form endearing – See "M'appari," 11.24n.

11.1258 (290:14). we'd never, well hardly ever – Captain Corcoran in Gilbert and Sullivan's *H.M.S. Pinafore; or, The Lass that Loved a Sailor* (1878) qualifies from the absolute "never" to the relative "hardly ever" in a responsive song with his crew. In Act I he asserts, "I am never known to quail / At the fury of a gale, / And I'm never, never sick at sea! CREW: What, never? CAPT.: No, never! CREW: What, never? CAPT.: Hardly ever!" The routine is repeated in Act II when the Captain announces that he intends to marry and that he will never be "untrue" to his wife.

11.1258–59 (290:15). home sweet home – Song; see 11.1051n.

11.1259 (290:16). dip – "When the family dinner consisted of dry potatoes, . . . dip was often used, that is to say, gravy or broth, or water flavoured in any way in plates, into which the potato was dipped at each bite" (P. W. Joyce, *English*, p. 247). The implication is that this sort of "family dinner" was a mark of poverty.

11.1261 (290:18). Lionel Marks's – Lionel Marks, antique dealer, watchmaker, jeweler, and picture-frame maker, 16 Ormond Quay Upper.

11.1269–70 (290:27–28). they chinked their clinking glasses – See "The Thirty-two Counties," 11.56–57n.

11.1271 (290:29). last rose of summer – See "'Tis the Last Rose of Summer," 11.32n.

11.1271 (290:29). rose of Castile – See 7.591n.

11.1273 (290:32). A youth entered a lonely Ormond hall – See "The Croppy Boy" (11.39n), line 9.

11.1275 (290:34). Robert Emmet's last words – For Robert Emmet, see 6.977–78n. The last paragraph of Emmet's speech to the court that condemned him to death: "Let no man write my epitaph; for as no man who knows my motives dares now vindicate them, let not prejudice or ignorance asperse them. When my country takes her place among the nations of the earth then and not till then, let my epitaph be written. I have done."

11.1275 (290:34–35). Seven last words. Of Meyerbeer – Bloom has thought earlier of Mercadante's oratorio *The Seven Last Words* (see 5.403–4n) and of Meyerbeer's opera *Les Huguenots* (see 8.623–24n); Bloom's confusion resembles that noted in 11.975n.

11.1276–78 (290:36–38). True men like you . . . glass with us – See "The Memory of the Dead," 10.790n. The last two lines of the first stanza: "But a true man, like you, man, / Will fill your glass with us"; the last two lines of the poem: "And true men, be you, men, / Like those of Ninety-eight."

11.1280 (290:40). Tschink. Tschunk – See "The Thirty-two Counties," 11.56–57n.

11.1284 (291:3). greaseabloom – See 11.185n.

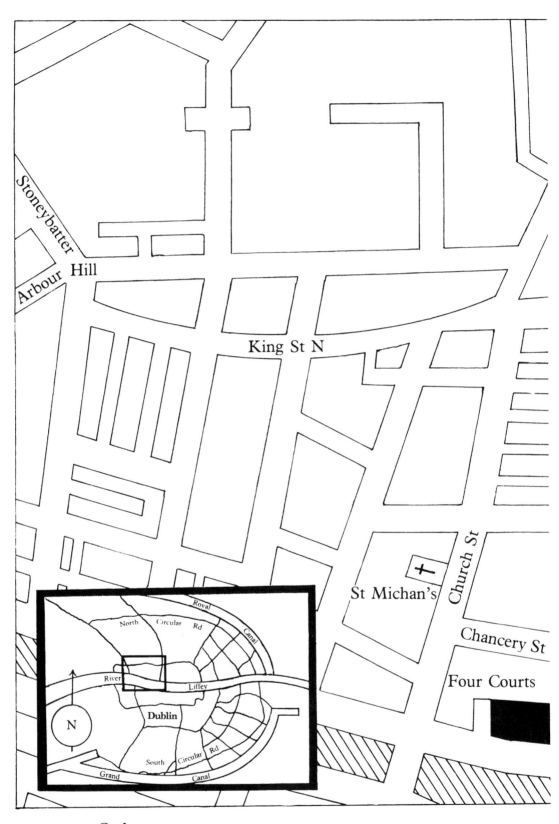

EPISODE 12. *Cyclops*

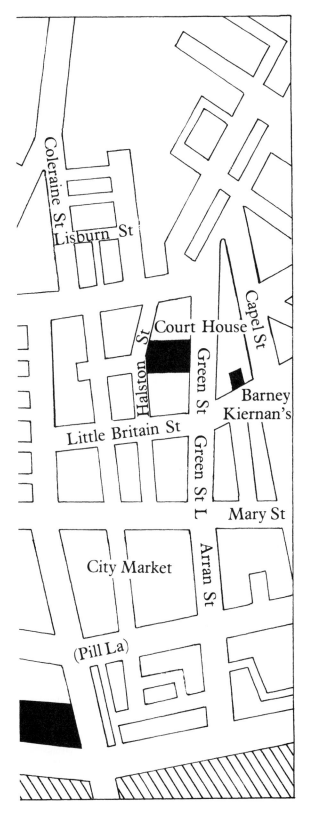

EPISODE 12

Cyclops

(12.1–1918, PP. 292–345)

Episode 12: *Cyclops,* **12.1–1918 (292–345).**
In Book 9 of *The Odyssey,* Odysseus describes
his adventures among the one-eyed Cyclopes,
who are "giants, louts, without a law to bless
them" (9:106; Fitzgerald, p. 160). They live in
a fertile land but are ignorant of agriculture;
they "have no muster and no meeting, / no consultation or old tribal ways, / but each one
dwells in his own mountain cave / dealing out
rough justice to wife and child, / indifferent to
what the others do" (9:112; ibid.). Odysseus
and a scouting party are trapped in the cave of
Polyphemus, one of the Cyclopes, who scoffs at
Zeus and at the laws of hospitality that govern
the "civilized" world, acting out his scorn by
devouring two of Odysseus's men. Polyphemus
imprisons Odysseus and his remaining companions, presumably to be eaten at the rate of two
a day. The second evening he "feasts" again,
and then Odysseus plies him with wine. In the
course of the drinking bout Odysseus announces that his name is "Noman," and when
the one-eyed giant collapses into drunken sleep,
Odysseus blinds him with a burning pike of olive wood. Polyphemus shouts that "Noman"
has ruined him, and his neighbors (taking him
literally) mock him and refuse to help. In the
morning Odysseus and his remaining men escape Polyphemus's search by hiding among his
sheep. Once free and launched in his ship,
Odysseus makes the mistake of revealing his
identity, taunting the blind Polyphemus, who
heaves a rock and almost sinks Odysseus's ship.
Then the blind giant calls on his father, Poseidon, to prevent Odysseus from returning home,
or, if "destiny / intend that he shall see his roof
again / . . . / far be that day, and dark the years
between. / Let him lose all companions, and return / under strange sail to bitter days at home"
(9:532ff; Fitzgerald, p. 173). Since destiny does
"intend" that Odysseus return home, Poseidon
is only able to grant the latter part of his son's
prayer.

Time: 5:00 P.M. Scene: the Tavern, Barney
Kiernan's pub, 8–10 Little Britain Street (i.e.,
Brittany Street). As a hobby, Kiernan collected
souvenirs of crime and punishment, which he
used to decorate his pub in a large and changing
display. Organ: muscle; Art: politics; Color:
none; Symbol: Fenian (see 2.272n); Technique:
gigantism.[1] Correspondences: *Noman*—I;[2]

Stake—cigar; *Challenge* [that the escaped Odysseus flings at Polyphemus]—Apotheosis.

The Linati schema lists as Persons: "No one
(I)," Ulysses, and two surprise entries (with no
specified correspondences), Galatea[3] and Prometheus.[4]

12.1 (292:1–2). old Troy of the D. M. P. – An
unidentified, possibly fictional, former inspector (now retired?) in the Dublin Metropolitan
Police.

---

passages are noted below as "Parody" with brief descriptions of the styles being lampooned.

2 Richard Ellmann (*Ulysses on the Liffey* [New
York, 1972], p. 110) remarks that Joyce privately
identified the anonymous narrator of this episode with
Thersites (*Iliad* 2:212), a deformed man who was the
most impudent talker among the Greeks. In post-
Homeric legend he is said to have ridiculed Achilles's
grief at having killed Pentesilea, the valorous queen of
the Amazons who had come to the aid of the Trojans.
Achilles found Thersites' remarks so grossly offensive
that he killed him on the spot. In *Troilus and Cressida,*
Shakespeare portrays Thersites as embittered and
foul-mouthed, cynically celebrating "war and lech-
ery" (II.iii.82) and calling the curse of "Neapolitan
boneache" [venereal disease] down on the whole camp
(II.iii.21).

3 *Galatea:* in Greek myth, Polyphemus the Cyclops falls in love with Galatea, a sea-nymph, but she
loves Acis, a Sicilian youth. Polyphemus discovers
Galatea and Acis in a grotto and crushes Acis with a
rock.

4 Clearly the Citizen is cast in the role of the Cyclops Polyphemus and Bloom in the role of Ulysses;
not so obviously, Bloom is also cast in the role of the
Prometheus of Shelley's *Prometheus Unbound* (1820).
Prometheus's name means "farsighted" or "prophetic," and Shelley said in his preface that Prometheus is, "as it were, the type of the highest perfection
of moral and intellectual nature." At the beginning of
Shelley's closet drama, Prometheus is being tortured
by command of Jupiter, the tyrannical High God who
is, from Shelley's point of view, irredeemable. In the
course of the drama, Prometheus (who abhors force,
"Power," tyranny) is "unbound" when he ceases to
hate Jupiter and seeks to withdraw the curse he has
flung at him: "I wish no living thing to suffer pain"
(I.306). In that apocalyptic moment, Jupiter's
"Power, which seems omnipotent" (IV.572), begins to
decline. As Demogorgon (who identifies himself as
"Eternity" III.i.52) describes the transformation in
what amounts to the play's epilogue: "Conquest [Ju-
piter] is dragged Captive through the deep" (IV.556)
(as Christ: "When he ascended up on high, he led
captivity captive" [Ephesians 4:8]). "Love, from its
awful throne of patient power / In the wise heart, from
the last giddy hour / Of dread endurance, from the
slippery, steep, / And narrow verge of crag-like agony,
springs / And folds over the world its healing wings"
(IV.558–561) (as, in Christian tradition, does the Holy
Ghost, the Paraclete or Comforter).

---

1 The narrative line of this episode is interrupted
by thirty-three passages that comment on the narrative by parodying various pompous, sensational, or
sentimental literary styles. In most cases the parodies
are "general"—parodies not of specific works but of
generalized stylistic conventions. The thirty-three

12.2 (292:2). Arbour hill – A street north of and parallel to the Liffey west of the center of Dublin.

12.2 (292:3). bloody – A mysteriously offensive curse to the Victorian and Edwardian ear that continued to be offensive into the 1930s; no one can quite explain how or why. Joyce thought, or at least said he thought, that it derived from *By Our Lady* (*Letters* 2:134); others suggest *By God's Blood*.

12.2–3 (292:3–4). sweep . . . near drove his gear into my eye – The near miss of the chimney sweep's broom and ladder (reminiscent of Odysseus's burning pike of olive wood) suggests that the narrator is one of the Cyclopes.

12.4 (292:5). Stony Batter – West of Dublin center, a section of the main road to the northwest from central Dublin.

12.8 (292:9). Soot's luck – From the Irish proverb "Where there's soot (or muck), there's luck."

12.8 (292:9). ballocks – Literally, testicles; figuratively, a crude, stupid, or clumsy person.

12.13–14 (292:16). *the garrison church at the corner of Chicken lane – Garrison Church, attached to Garrison Schools and a military hospital and the Provost Marshal's Prison (now the Arbour Hill Detention Barracks), was located on Arbour Hill at its intersection with Chicken Lane (now Manor Street).

12.15 (292:17). a wrinkle – Slang for special knowledge or experience (though usually implying a lie or an untruth).

12.16 (292:19). he had a farm – That is, he had a regular income from land rents.

12.16 (292:19). county Down – North-northeast of Dublin on the Irish Sea in what is now Northern Ireland. The southeastern half of the city of Belfast is in County Down.

12.17–18 (292:20–21). Moses Herzog over there near Heytesbury street – *Thom's* 1904 does not list a Moses Herzog as merchant, grocer, or tea merchant, but it does list an M. Herzog as resident at 13 St. Kevin's Parade. The parade in turn is not particularly "near Heytesbury Street" but is some distance to the west, off Clanbrassil Street Lower (near Bloom's former residence in Lombard Street West). Hy-

man identifies Herzog as "an authentic one-eyed Dublin Jew" (p. 186) and says that he "traded as an itinerant grocer" (p. 329), but he does not mention "trading without a license."

12.19 (292:22). *Circumcised? – In context (and in scorn), slang for Jewish.

12.20 (292:23). A bit off the top – Obviously an allusion to circumcision but slang for "some of the best"; the phrase was also part of the title of a music-hall song, "All I Want Is a Little Bit Off the Top," by Murray and Leigh. First verse: "Brown's a very old friend of mine, / And I went to his house to dine; / Some of the aristocracy were there; / Not a one of them came in late / And everyone of them piled his plate, / 'Twas fun to watch the animals, I declare. / The waiter came into the room with a pudding of wondrous size, / And tho' they ate enough to feed a town, / A leader of society completely lost his etiquette, / And yelled out to the host, Hey, Mr. Brown! [Chorus:] Carve a little bit off the top for me, for me! / Just a little bit off the top for me, for me, / Saw me off a yard or two, I'll tell you when to stop; / All I want is a little bit off the top!" In the second verse the speaker at a music hall finds himself behind a woman with a hat "three yards tall" and demands "a little bit off the top" or he'll call the police. In the third stanza the speaker goes to sleep in a haystack only to be awakened by a couple who have come to "segow" and have sat down on his head. He demands that they "move a little bit off the top for me" and then concedes, "the lady, she can stop / All I want is a little bit off the top!"

12.20 (292:23–24). plumber named Geraghty – *Thom's* 1904 does not list a Geraghty as a plumber, though it does list an M. E. Geraghty at 29 Arbour Hill. This would suggest that "plumber" is being used as slang for a clumsy, brutal person.

12.21 (292:24). hanging on to his taw – A "taw" is a whip; the expression means confronting someone without giving him a chance to strike back.

12.23 (292:26). lay – Slang for occupation (especially a criminal one).

12.24 (292:27). How are the mighty fallen! – A cliché from David's lament for the deaths of Saul and Jonathan: "The beauty of Israel is slain upon thy high places: how all the mighty are fallen!" (II Samuel 1:19; the exclamation is repeated in 1:25).

12.24–25 (292:27–28). Collector of bad and doubtful debts – Regarded in Ireland as the lowest of occupations, almost as bad as a career in petty crime.

12.29 (292:33). *trading without a licence* – The laws of the Dublin Corporation required that all merchants and traders obtain an annual license; see 12.17–18n.

Parody: 12.33–51 (292:37–293:16). For non-perishable goods . . . assigns of the other part – The style is that of a legal document in a civil suit for nonpayment of debts.

12.33–37 (292:37–41). Moses Herzog . . . Arran quay ward, gentleman – See 12.17–18n and 12.20n. Geraghty is nowhere listed as "Esquire" or "gentleman," only as plain Mr. M. E. Geraghty.

12.52 (293:17). t.t. – Teetotaler.

12.54 (293:19). What about paying our respects to our friend? – In other words, let's go have a drink at Mr. X's pub.

12.55 (293:20). John of God's – House of St. John of God, Stillorgan Park, County Dublin, was a "Licenced Private Asylum for the Insane" that advertised itself as "devoted to mentally affected Gentlemen."

12.58 (293:25). the citizen – Modeled on Michael Cusack (1847–1907), founder of the Gaelic Athletic Association (1884), which was dedicated to the revival of Irish sports such as hurling, Gaelic football, and handball. The association was notably contentious, "banning" as un-Irish those who participated in or watched such "English" games as association football (soccer), rugby, field hockey, and polo. Cusack styled himself "Citizen Cusack" and Ellmann (p. 61n) quotes as his standard greeting: "I'm Citizen Cusack from the Parish of Carron in the Barony of Burre in the County of Clare, you Protestant dog!"

12.59 (293:26). mavourneen's – Irish: "my love's."

12.60–62 (293:28–31). that meeting in the City Arms . . . Cattle traders – See 2.416–17n.

12.63 (293:32). the hard word – The inside story.

12.64 (293:33). the Linenhall barracks – An extensive range of buildings erected in 1715 to house the (English) government-sponsored manufacture of Irish linen. Deserted toward the end of the nineteenth century, it was occasionally used as a temporary barracks. It was bounded by King Street North, Coleraine Street, and Lisburn Street. The speaker and Joe Hynes walk east from Arbour Hill along King Street North and then turn south down Halston Street to Little Britain Street and Barney Kiernan's.

12.64–65 (293:33–34). the back of the court-house – They walk down Halston Street behind the courthouse that fronted at 26 Green Street and housed the Sessions House of the borough record and civil bill courts and the Office of the Clerk of the Crown and Peace, County and City of Dublin (i.e., the municipal courts).

Parody: 12.68–99 (293:38–294:32). In Inisfail the fair . . . raspberries from their canes – Parodies the style of nineteenth-century translations and revisions of Irish poetry, myth, and legend. This passage makes specific use of phrases from James Clarence Mangan's translation of "Aldfrid's Itinerary" (see following note) and in general lampoons the style of works such as Lady Gregory's *Gods and Fighting Men* (1904).

12.68 (293:38). In Inisfail the fair – *Inis* is Irish for island, and the *Fál* was the fetish stone, the stone of destiny at Tara; hence, the name means Island of Destiny (Ireland) and is associated with the Golden Age presided over by the high kings of Tara. The phrase is from the first line of James Clarence Mangan's (1803–49) translation of "Aldfrid's Itinerary," a poem in Irish by Aldfrid, a seventh-century king of Northumbria:

> I found in Innisfail the fair,
> In Ireland, while in exile there,
> Women of worth, both grave and gay men,
> Many clerics and many laymen.
>
> I traveled its fruitful provinces round,   5
> And in every one of the five I found,
> Alike in church and in palace hall,
> Abundant apparel and food for all.
>
> Gold and silver I found in money;
> Plenty of wheat and plenty of honey;   10
> I found God's people rich in pity,
> Found many a feast, and many a city.

I also found in Armagh the splendid,
Meekness, wisdom, and prudence
    blended,
Fasting as Christ hath recommended,   15
And noble councilors untranscended.

I found in each great church moreo'er,
Whether on island or on shore,
Piety, learning, fond affection,
Holy welcome and kind protection.   20

I found the good lay monks and
    brothers
Ever beseeching help for others,
And in their keeping the Holy Word,
Pure as it came from Jesus the Lord.

I found in Munster, unfettered of any,   25
Kings and queens and poets a many,
Poets well-skilled in music and measure,
Prosperous doings, mirth and pleasure.

I found in Connaught the just,
    redundance
Of riches, milk in lavish abundance;   30
Hospitality, vigor, fame
In Cruachan's land of heroic name.

I found in the country of Connall
    [Donegal] the glorious,
Bravest heroes, ever victorious;
Fair-complexioned men and warlike,   35
Ireland's lights, the high, the starlike!

I found in Ulster from hill to glen,
Hardy warriors, resolute men;
Beauty that bloomed when youth was
    gone,
And strength transmitted from sire to
    son.   40

I found in the noble district of Boyle
    [*MS here illegible*]
Brehons [lawyers, judges], Erenachs
    [archdeacons], weapons bright.
And horsemen bold and sudden in fight.

I found in Leinster the smooth and
    sleek,   45
From Dublin to Slewmargy's peak,
Flourishing pastures, valor, health
Song-loving worthies, commerce,
    wealth.

I found besides from Ara to Glea
In the blood rich country of Ossorie,   50
Sweet fruits, good laws for all and each,
Great chess-players, men of truthful
    speech.

I found in Meath's fair principality,
Virtue, vigor and hospitality;
Candor, joyfulness, bravery, purity—   55
Ireland's bulwark and security.

I found strict morals in age and youth
I found historians recording truth;
The things I sing of in verse unsmooth
I found them all I have written sooth.   60

12.68 (293:38). the land of holy Michan – Barney Kiernan's pub was in St. Michan's parish. The parish church, which dates from 1676, stands in Church Street, west of the Four Courts in central Dublin. The church was founded in 1095 by the Danish saint whose name it bears.

12.69 (293:39). a watchtower – The 100-foot-square tower of St. Michan's dates from the twelfth century and is considerably older than the church itself. Here the tower is associated with the fortified round towers that were a distinguishing feature of pre-Norman Irish religious communities.

12.69–70 (293:39–41). There sleep the mighty . . . princes of high renown – The vaults of St. Michan's church are famous for an "amazing preservation of the corpses" buried in them. "The skin of the corpses remains soft as in life. . . . Even facial characteristics may be distinguished" (*Official Guide to Dublin* [n.d.], pp. 51–52). Among the bodies buried in the vaults are "the Crusader" and several leaders of the Rebellion of 1798, including the brothers Sheares, Oliver Bond, and Dr. Charles Lucas.

12.72 (293:43). the gibbed haddock – That is, the haddock has a hooked and projecting lower jaw somewhat like that of an adult male salmon during and after the breeding season.

12.76–77 (294:4–6). the wafty sycamore . . . the eugenic eucalyptus – Wisdom, in Ecclesiasticus 24:16–23 (Douay), describes herself as a series of trees: "And I took root in an honorable people, and in the portion of my God his inheritance, and my abode is in the full assembly of saints. I was exalted like a cedar in Libanus [Lebanon] . . . and as a plane tree by the water in the streets was I exalted. . . . I gave a sweet smell like cinnamon, and aromatical balm." The sycamore native to Ireland is a species of maple; it is also called "planetree." The "Lebanonian cedar" is not native to Ireland, nor is the Australian eucalyptus ("eugenic" because a tincture made from opium, cinnamon, and kino, an exudation of the eucalyptus, was widely used as a douche in the early twentieth century).

12.81 (294:10). crans – A "cran" is a measure of fresh herrings (forty-five U.S. gallons).

12.81 (294:11). drafts – A "draft" is the quantity of fish taken in a net.

12.83 (294:13). *from Eblana to Slievemargy – Eblana was a place in Hibernia (as the Romans called Ireland) mentioned by the Greek geographer Ptolemy (second century A.D.) and subsequently identified with the site of Dublin. Slievemargy is a mountain approximately sixty miles southeast of Dublin, near the border of the ancient province of Leinster. See "Aldfrid's Itinerary" (12.68n), lines 45–46.

12.84 (294:14). unfettered Munster – Munster was (and still is) a province in southwestern Ireland; see "Aldfrid's Itinerary" (12.68n), line 25.

12.84 (294:14). Connacht the just – A province in western Ireland; see "Aldfrid's Itinerary" (12.68n), line 29.

12.85 (294:14–15). smooth sleek Leinster – The province that included Dublin; see "Aldfrid's Itinerary" (12.68n), line 45.

12.85 (294:15). Cruachan's land – Cruachan was the palace of Connacht; see 12.84n and "Aldfrid's Itinerary" (12.68n), line 32.

12.85 (294:15–16). Armagh the splendid – Armagh was the "metropolis" of ancient Ireland, the religious capital and a "world-famous" seat of learning. See "Aldfrid's Itinerary" (12.68n), line 13.

12.86 (294:16). the noble district of Boyle – Ninety miles west-northwest of Dublin; the town of Boyle was famous as the site of a great Norman abbey, and it figures in pre-Norman Irish history and legend. See "Aldfrid's Itinerary" (12.68n), line 41.

12.86 (294:16–17). the sons of kings – See 2.279–80n.

12.87 (294:18). a shining palace – The Dublin Corporation Fruit, Vegetable, and Fish Market, between St. Michan's and Arran streets, a block south of Barney Kiernan's pub in central Dublin.

12.89 (294:21). first fruits – A Jewish ceremonial offering; see 3.367–69n.

12.90 (294:21–22). O'Connell Fitzsimon – H.

O'Connell Fitzsimon ("son of Simon") was superintendent of the food market in 1904 (*Thom's* 1904, p. 1349).

12.91 (294:23). wains – Large open horse-drawn vehicles used for carrying heavy loads, especially of agricultural produce.

12.92 (294:24). floats – Large flat containers.

12.92–93 (294:25). Rangoon beans – A variety of muskmelon (sometimes called "snake melon"), two to three feet long, one to three inches in diameter; they resemble giant string beans and are used sometimes for preserves but more often as an oddity gourd.

12.93 (294:25). strikes – A local English measure that varies from half a bushel to four bushels.

12.93 (294:26). drills of Swedes – A "Swede" is a large variety of yellow turnip; a "drill" is the small furrow in which seed is sown.

12.94 (294:27). York and Savoy – Varieties of cabbage.

12.95 (294:27). pearls of the earth – An ancient Egyptian epithet for the onion, which was particularly venerated.

12.95 (294:28). punnets – A broad shallow basket for the display of fruits or flowers.

12.96 (294:29). bere – Barley.

12.97 (294:30). chips – A "chip" is a little box made of thin wood.

12.97 (294:31). sieves – A kind of coarse basket; or a measure, approximately a bushel.

12.98 (294:31). pelurious – Furry.

Parody: 12.102–17 (294:35–295:10). And by that way wend . . . agate with the dun – Continues the parody of Irish-revival legendry.

12.103 (294:36). flushed ewes – Ewes taken from pasture and fed on grain to prepare them for breeding.

12.103 (294:36–37). stubble geese – Dialect for greylag geese.

12.104 (294:37). roaring mares – "Roaring" is

a disease of horses; the principal symptom is loud, rasping breathing under exertion.

12.104 (294:38). storesheep – Animals kept for breeding or as part of the ordinary stock of a farm; also, lean animals sold to be fattened for market.

12.105 (294:38). Cuffe's – See 6.392n.

12.105 (294:38). springers – Cows or heifers near to calving.

12.105 (294:39). culls – Animals rejected from a herd or flock as being substandard.

12.105 (294:39). sowpigs – Spayed sows.

12.107 (294:41). polly – Dehorned.

12.107 (294:42). premiated – Prizewinning.

12.111 (295:3). *Lusk and Rush – Lusk is a parish and village eleven miles north of Dublin; Rush is a small seaport thirteen and a half miles northeast of Dublin in Lusk parish.

12.111 (295:4). Carrickmines – A village ten miles south-southeast of Dublin.

12.111 (295:4). Thomond – A small pre-Norman kingdom in North Munster.

12.112 (295:5). M'Gillicuddy's reeks – Mc-Gillicuddy's Reeks, the highest mountain range in Ireland, is in County Kerry, "the wild southwest." "Reek" is dialect for a heap or pile.

12.112 (295:5). lordly Shannon – The River Shannon runs south through central Ireland and then west to the Atlantic. The Irish rebel leader and journalist John Mitchel (1815–75) contemplates the river Shannon in Van Diemen's Land (Tasmania) and dreams of "its lordly namesake river in Erin" in his *Jail Journal* (1854).

12.113–14 (295:6–7). the gentle declivities of the place of the race of Kiar – Kiar was one of the three illegitimate sons of Queen Maeve of Connacht (quasi-legendary, first century A.D.) by the captain of her guard, Fergus MacRoy; Kiar's race became the residents of County Kerry in southwestern Ireland, hardly a land of "gentle declivities."

12.115 (295:9). targets of lamb – The neck or breast of lamb as a joint (without the shoulder).

12.116 (295:9). crannocks – After "curnoch," a local English measure, three or four bushels.

12.120 (295:13). Garryowen – A suburb of Limerick famous for its squalor and for the crudity and brutality of its inhabitants. It is also the title of a rollicking Irish drinking song with the refrain: "Instead of Spa we'll drink brown ale, / And pay the reckoning on the nail, / No man for debt shall go to gaol / From Garryowen in glory." A "famous Irish setter" of that name (b. 1876) was owned by J. J. Giltrap of Dublin (*Times Literary Supplement*, 9 January 1964, p. 27).

12.122 (295:15). gloryhole – A place where odds and ends are put away without order.

12.122 (295:15–16). cruiskeen lawn – Irish: "little full jug or flask"; the title of an Irish folksong: "Let the farmer praise his grounds, / Let the huntsman praise his hounds, / The shepherd his dew-scented lawn, / But I, more blessed than they, / Spend each happy night and day / With my charming little cruiskeen lawn, / Oh, my charming little cruiskeen lawn. [Chorus] Gra-ma-chree ma cruiskeen / Slainte geal mavourneen, / Gra-ma-chree a coolin bawn, bawn, bawn, / Oh! Gra-ma-chree a coolin bawn." Translation of the Irish chorus: "Love of my heart, my little flask, / Bright health, my darling. / Love of my heart, a long-haired girl, girl, girl, / Oh! Love of my heart, a long-haired girl // Immortal and divine, / Great Bacchus, God of wine, / Create me by adoption your son, / In hope that you'll comply, / That my glass shall ne'er run dry."

12.125 (295:18). a corporal work of mercy – See 17.487n.

12.127 (295:20). constabulary man – See 6.2n.

12.127 (295:20). Santry – A parish in the union of North Dublin, four miles north of the center of the city.

12.127 (295:21). a blue paper – A summons.

12.129 (295:22). Stand and deliver – The highwayman's command to his victim: halt and hand over your valuables.

12.134 (295:27). Doing the rapparee – The rapparees (Irish: "robbers, outlaws") were initially (from 1653) Irish Catholic landlords who had been dispossessed by Cromwell and who lived by blackmailing and plundering the

"Cromwellers," the Protestants established on their estates. After the Treaty of Limerick (1691), Irish soldiers who did not accept expatriation with Patrick Sarsfield, Lord Lucan, took to the hills as a new generation of rapparees. Sir Charles Gavan Duffy (1816–1903) wrote "The Irish Rapparees; a Peasant Ballad": "Righ Shemus [James II] he has gone to France and left his crown behind:— / Ill-luck be theirs, both day and night, put runnin' in his mind! / Lord Lucan followed after, with his slashers brave and true, / And now the doleful keen is raised—'What will poor Ireland do?' / 'What must poor Ireland do?' / 'Our luck, they say, has gone to France. What *can* poor Ireland do?' // 'Oh, never fear for Ireland, for she has so'gers still, / For Remy's boys are in the wood, and Rory's on the hill; / And never had poor Ireland more loyal hearts than these— / May God be kind and good to them, the faithful Rapparees!' / The fearless Rapparees! / The jewel waar ye, Rory with your Irish Rapparees!" The ballad continues in praise of the "changeless Rapparees" and their retributive violence and in condemnation of those "surly *bodachs*," the Cromwellers.

12.134 (295:27). Rory of the hill – The signature adopted in about 1880 by letterwriters who threatened landlords and others in the agitation for land reform. It is also the title of a poem by Charles Joseph Kickham (1830–82). Rory is characterized as a peasant patriot who saves a toothed rake for the day when he can lead a rebellion. The last of the poem's seven verses: "O! knowledge is a wondrous power / And stronger than the wind; / And thrones shall fall, and despots bow, / Before the might of mind; / The poet and the orator / The heart of man can sway, / And would to the kind heavens / That Wolfe Tone were here today! / Yet trust me, friend, dear Ireland's strength / Her honest strength—is still / The rough-and-ready roving boys, / Like Rory of the Hill."

12.140 (295:34). the Russians wish to tyrannise – In some quarters the Russo-Japanese War (1904–5) was regarded as evidence of Russian desire for world dominion.

12.141 (295:35). Arrah – Anglicized Irish: literally, "Was it?" or "Well, indeed!"; figuratively, "What nonsense."

12.141 (295:35). codding – Joking, talking nonsense.

12.146 (295:40). Ditto MacAnaspey – This peculiar name means "son of the bishop" in Irish. At the time of the great split over Parnell's leadership, a MacAnaspey, a member of a family of Dublin tombstone makers, made a lengthy speech in a public meeting. The speaker who followed him said simply: "Ditto MacAnaspey."

12.148 (296:1). *a chara* – Irish: "my friend."

Parody: 12.151–205 (296:5–297:27). The figure seated . . . of paleolithic stone – This description of the "Irish hero" further parodies late-nineteenth-century reworking of Irish legend, and it obviously owes a debt of "gigantism" to Homer's description of Polyphemus, the Cyclops in Book 9 of *The Odyssey*.

12.151 (296:5–6). a round tower – See 8.490–91n.

12.158 (296:13–14). mountain gorse (*Ulex europaeus*) – The common furze in Great Britain, two to three feet high, extremely branched, the branches terminating in spines.

12.161–62 (296:17–18). a tear and a smile – From Thomas Moore's poem "Erin, the Tear and the Smile in Thine Eyes," in *Irish Melodies*. "Erin, the tear and the smile in thine eyes / Blend like the rainbow that hangs in thy skies / Shining through sorrow's stream / Sad'ning through pleasure's beam / Thy suns, with doubtful gleam, / Weep while they rise."

12.169–70 (296:27). a girdle of plaited straw and rushes – A rope of that sort is called in Irish a *suguan;* figuratively, the word *suguan* is used as an epithet for a weak, flabby person; cf. 15.1960–62n.

12.176 (296:35). Cuchulin – (The Hound of Culan or Hound of Feats), a legendary figure, the great hero of the Red Branch Knights of Ulster, said to have flourished in the first century A.D. He excelled in every manly art and has been romanticized as the superhuman epitome of the Celtic hero, the defender of the realm who used his powers solely for the good of his people.

12.176–77 (296:35–36). Conn of hundred battles – King (A.D. 123–57), the first of the high kings of Ireland. Emerging from *Conn*acht, he defeated the forces of Leinster and Munster at Castleknock and divided Ireland with Mog Meadath, against whom Conn subsequently warred for fourteen years, until Mog was killed.

Conn is thus credited with having achieved a sort of national unity. He was murdered by a band of ruffians disguised as women.

12.177 (296:36). Niall of nine hostages – King of Ireland (379–405), regarded as the ancestor of the O'Neills. Little is known of him except that he invaded Britain and then Gaul, where he was killed. The "nine hostages" he exacted from the petty kings of Ireland to dissuade them from hostile acts.

12.177 (296:36). Brian of Kincora – Or Brian Boru; see 6.453n.

12.177 (296:36–37). *the ardri Malachi – That is, the high king Malachi; see 1.41n.

12.177–78 (296:37). Art MacMurragh – (1357–1417, king of Leinster 1377–1417). He was famous for his refusal to submit to Richard II's overlordship of Ireland, a refusal he backed more or less successfully with superior military skill. He is reputed to have been poisoned.

12.178 (296:37). Shane O'Neill – (c. 1530–67), elected "the O'Neill" in 1559. In 1556 he invaded the pale (the area of English control around Dublin) and burned Armagh. In 1562 he submitted to Queen Elizabeth, but his allegiance was somewhat questionable since he also supported Mary Queen of Scots and her claim to the English throne. However, even this latter allegiance was questionable, since he repeatedly raided Scots' settlements around Antrim. He was killed by the MacDonnells, a Scottish clan in exile in Ireland.

12.178 (296:37–38). Father John Murphy – (c. 1753–98), a priest and patriot, one of the first and principal leaders in the southeast during the Rebellion of 1798. He was initially successful, but his insurgent pikemen were defeated at Vinegar Hill, and he was subsequently captured and executed.

12.178 (296:38). Owen Roe – Owen Roe O'Neill (c. 1590–1649), an Irish soldier who served in the Spanish army. He returned to Ireland in 1642 as general in command of Irish forces loyal to Charles I. Successful at first against the English, who were preoccupied with the civil war in England, his forces were in the end brutally crushed by Cromwell's armies. He was supposedly poisoned by one of his own supporters.

12.178–79 (296:38). Patrick Sarsfield – (c. 1650–93), earl of Lucan, an Irish general who supported James II's claim to the English throne. In 1690 he defended Limerick against the invasion of William III and in a brilliant sally destroyed William's heavy artillery and forced his temporary withdrawal. After the Irish loss at the Battle of the Boyne on 1 July 1690, he is said to have regretted that they could not "change kings and fight it over again." After participating in the Treaty of Limerick (1691), which formalized the English reconquest of Ireland, he accepted exile to France, where he served in the French army and was killed at the battle of Landen (1693).

12.179 (296:38). Red Hugh O'Donnell – (c. 1571–1602), lord of Tyrconnell. He was imprisoned in Dublin Castle in 1587 but escaped. He was inaugurated as "the O'Donnell" and achieved a number of victories over the English, particularly in the west. In 1601 he laid siege to Kinsale and, failing to reduce it, went to Spain to seek aid from Philip III, but with no success. He died by poison administered by one James Blake, an agent of Queen Elizabeth.

12.179 (296:39). Red Jim MacDermott – An associate (and, in 1868, a betrayer) of Michael Davitt (see 15.4684n) and O'Donovan Rossa (see 12.199n) in the Irish Republican Brotherhood (Fenian Society).

12.179–80 (296:39). Soggarth Eoghan O'Growney – Father Eugene O'Growney (1863–99), one of the moving spirits of the Gaelic revival and a founder of the Gaelic League (1893). He was professor of Irish at Maynooth (1891); he edited the *Gaelic Journal* and wrote *Simple Lessons in Irish;* see 9.366–67n.

12.180 (296:39–40). Michael Dwyer – (1771–1816); a leader of the Rebellion of 1798, he eluded the English for five years. He intended to join Robert Emmet's revolt in 1803 but arrived too late and eventually surrendered voluntarily. He was transported to Australia, where he became high constable of Sydney.

12.180 (296:40). Francy Higgins – The sham squire; see 7.348n.

12.180 (296:40). Henry Joy M'Cracken – (1767–98), a leader of the United Irishmen in Ulster. He was commander-in-chief of the Ulster rebels at the battle of Antrim (1798). His forces were defeated, and he was captured and executed.

12.181 (296:40). Goliath – A famous giant of Gath, he was the Philistine champion who "morning and evening for forty days" defied the armies of Israel (I Samuel 17) until he was slain by David in single combat (1063 B.C.). His name means "splendor."

12.181 (296:40–41). Horace Wheatley – A music-hall performer, popular in pantomime roles in the 1890s. One of his more successful roles was as Baron O'Bounder in the pantomime *Cinderella*.

12.181 (296:41). Thomas Conneff – Unknown.

12.181 (296:41). Peg Woffington – Margaret Woffington (c.1720–60), a Dublin street child *whose career as one of the most successful ac*tresses of her time began in 1737 when she made her debut as Ophelia at the Smock Alley Theatre in Dublin. She took London by storm as "the handsomest woman that ever appeared on a stage." She was remembered sentimentally as kind to her relations and charitable to the poor.

12.181–82 (296:41–42). the Village Blacksmith – (1840), the title and hero of one of Henry Wadsworth Longfellow's "Psalms of Life": "toiling,—rejoicing,—sorrowing / Onward through life he goes" (lines 37–38).

12.182 (296:42). Captain Moonlight – A poison-pen name widely used to threaten (or forecast) retaliatory violence in the agitation for land reform in the 1870s and 1880s.

12.182 (296:42). Captain Boycott – Charles Cunningham Boycott (1832–97), an Englishman who was land agent in Ireland for an absentee landowner, the earl of Erne. He was a widely publicized victim of the treatment that subsequently bore his name. In 1880 he refused to accept rents at figures set by the tenants of the estates he managed and evicted them instead. He was ostracized by the Irish Land League; his life was threatened; servants were forced to leave his employ; his correspondence was intercepted, his food supplies curtailed, and the estates damaged by acts of sabotage. The proclamation against him: "Let every man in the parish turn his back on him; have no communications with him; have no dealings with him."

12.182 (296:42). Dante Alighieri – (1265–1321), the famous Florentine poet and patriot.

12.183 (297:1). Christopher Columbus – (1451–1506).

12.183 (297:1). S. Fursa – (d. c. 650), an Irish saint, festival 16 January. His mission founded a monastery in Ireland, another in England, and two on the Continent. Joyce remarks that he is "described in the hagiographic calendar of Ireland as the precursor of Dante Alighieri. A medieval copy of the Visions of Fursa depicts the voyage of the saint from hell to heaven. . . . This vision would have served as a model for the poet of the Divine Comedy, who . . . is honored by posterity because he was the last to visit and describe the three regions of the soul" (*CW*, p. 236).

12.183 (297:1). S. Brendan – (484–577), an Irish saint, festival 16 May. He founded monasteries in Ireland and in Brittany and was called Brendan the Navigator after his voyages, which became elaborately and fancifully transformed in myth: "Christopher Columbus, as everyone knows, is honoured by posterity because he was the last to discover America. A thousand years before . . . Saint Brendan weighed anchor for the unknown world [from the Aran Isles] . . . and, after crossing the ocean, landed on the coast of Florida" (*CW*, p. 235).

12.183 (297:1–2). Marshall MacMahon – See 3.164n.

12.184 (297:2). Charlemagne – Charles the Great (742–814), king of the Franks after 768 and Roman emperor (800–814). Irish tradition regarded Charlemagne as having sprung from the same Celtic stock as the ancestors of early Christian Ireland.

12.184 (297:2). Theobald Wolfe Tone – (1763–98), an Irish revolutionary and one of the founders of the United Irishmen. Tone was inspired with republican idealism by the successes of the American Revolution and by the apparent success of the French Revolution. He was instrumental in the abortive attempt to secure French support for Irish revolution in the 1790s, which ultimately led to his death; see 10.378n.

12.184 (297:2–3). the Mother of the Maccabees – The Maccabees were a Jewish family of great prominence who brought about a restoration of Jewish political life in the second and first centuries B.C. The mother in question, Salome, was, together with seven of her children, martyred (c. 168 B.C.) by the Syrian ruler Antiochus IV (king 175–164 B.C.) because the family resisted his attempts to substitute worship of the Greek gods for the Jewish religion. The mother and her children are the only Old Testament martyrs included in the hagiography of the Catholic church.

12.184–85 (297:3). the Last of the Mohicans – The title of a novel (1826) by the American James Fenimore Cooper (1789–1851).

12.185 (297:3). the Rose of Castile – See 7.591n.

12.185 (297:4). the Man for Galway – The title of a song by Charles James Lever (1806–72): "To drink a toast / A proctor roast, / Or bailiff, as the case is. / To kiss your wife, / Or take your life / At 10 or 15 paces, / To keep game cocks, to hunt the fox, / To drink in punch the Solway. / With debts galore, / But fun far more, / Oh, that's the man for Galway."

12.185–86 (297:4–5). the Man that Broke the Bank at Monte Carlo – The title of a music-hall song (1892) by Fred Gilbert (1850–1903). The song was based on the widely publicized gambling luck of one Charles "Monte Carlo" Wells, who broke the bank at Monte Carlo six times in 1892 before his luck turned and he lost it all. "[Chorus:] As I walk along the *Bois Boolong* / With an independent air / You can hear the girls declare / 'He must be a Millionaire,' / You can hear them sigh, / And wish to die, / You can see them wink the other eye / At the man who broke the Bank at Monte Carlo. [First verse:] I've just got here, through Paris, from the sunny southern shore; / I to Monte Carlo went, just to raise my winter's rent; / Dame Fortune smiled upon me as she'd never done before, / And I've now such lots of money, I'm a gent, / Yes, I've now such lots of money, I'm a gent. [Second verse:] I patronized the tables at the Monte Carlo hall, / Till they hadn't a sou for a Christian or a Jew; / So I quickly went to Paris for the charms of mad'moiselle / Who's the loadstone of my heart, what can I do, / When with twenty tongues she swears that she'll be true."

12.186 (297:5). the Man in the Gap – In ancient Ireland, a champion or military hero whose duties included avenging insults and offenses to his king and tribe; when the tribe's lands were threatened with invasion the champion kept "watch at the most dangerous ford or pass . . . the gap of danger." In modern Ireland the goalkeeper in hurling or football is often called "the man in the gap" (P. W. Joyce, *English*, p. 182).

12.186–87 (297:5). the Woman Who Didn't – After *The Woman Who Did* (1895), a novel by the Canadian Grant Allen (1848–99). The woman of Allen's novel attempts to emancipate herself in "free love."

12.187 (297:5–6). Benjamin Franklin – (1706–90), famous for, among other things, his "way with the ladies."

12.187 (297:6). Napoleon Bonaparte – (1769–1821), more successful as a conqueror than as a lover.

12.187 (297:6). John L. Sullivan – (1858–1918), the Irish-American heavyweight champion from Boston, Massachusetts, who was acknowledged as American champion (and billed as world champion) from 1882 until he lost the title to James J. Corbett in 1892.

12.188 (297:6–7). Cleopatra – (69–30 B.C.).

12.188 (297:7). Savourneen Deelish – Irish: "And my faithful darling"; the title of a ballad by George Colman (1762–1836), a pathetic lament about the parting of a young soldier and his love: "Ah! the moment was sad when my love and I parted / Savourneen Deelish, Eileen Oge! / As I kissed off her tears I was nigh broken-hearted! / Savourneen Deelish, Eileen Oge! / Wan was her cheek, which lay on my shoulder— / Damp was her hand, no marble was colder— / I felt that again I should never behold her, / Savourneen Deelish, Eileen Oge!"

12.188 (297:7). Julius Caesar – (100–44 B.C.).

12.188 (297:7). Paracelsus – Phillippus Aureolus Paracelsus Theophrastus Bombastus von Hohenheim (1493–1541), a German-Swiss alchemist and physician noted in medical history for his attention to pharmaceutical chemistry and famous as the author of a visionary Theosophical system.

12.188–89 (297:7–8). sir Thomas Lipton – (1850–1931), a Glasgow-born millionaire merchant of Irish parentage, known for the tea that still bears his name and for his unsuccessful and expensive attempts to win the America's Cup for England.

12.189 (297:8). William Tell – The hero of a Swiss legend, he was forced by a tyrant to prove his marksmanship by shooting an apple off his son's head. He is supposed to have succeeded, to have killed the tyrant, and to have led the revolt (c. 1307) that gained independence for the forest cantons of Switzerland.

12.189 (297:8). *****Michelangelo Hayes** – Michelangelo Buonarroti (1475–1564), the Florentine painter and sculptor, may seem obvious here, but Michelangelo Hayes (1820–77) was an Irish illustrator and caricaturist who became city marshal of Dublin.

12.189 (297:8–9). Muhammad – (570–632), the militant Arabian prophet who founded the Moslem religion.

12.189–90 (297:9). the Bride of Lammermoor – The title of a novel (1819) by Sir Walter Scott, one of the *Tales of My Landlord* series. The novel is regarded as a masterpiece of Gothic fiction, compounded of doom foretold and fulfilled. The bride's family rejects the bride's true love, Ravenswood, and imposes a husband of its own choice. The result is a curse and a malignant fate that dooms the bride, her husband, and her lover.

12.190 (297:9). Peter the Hermit – Peter of Amiens (c. 1050–c. 1115), the preacher and, for a time, the leader of the First Crusade (1095–99).

12.190 (297:9–10). Peter the Packer – A nickname for Lord Peter O'Brien of Kilfenora (1842–1914), crown counsel and eventually lord chief justice of Ireland. He was regarded as hostile to Land Leaguers and Irish Nationalists, and when he was acting for the Crown as attorney general he tended, particularly in political cases, to exercise his right to peremptory challenge of prospective jurors to an excessive degree. By thus attempting to ensure "unbiased" (or pro-English) juries, he earned a reputation for packing juries, whence his nickname.

12.190 (297:10). Dark Rosaleen – The title of an anonymous sixteenth-century Irish poem; the most famous translation is James Clarence Mangan's (1803–49). Rosaleen, the object of the speaker's love and devotion, is a personification of Ireland.

12.190–91 (297:10). Patrick W. Shakespeare – This combination obviously echoes speculation about Shakespeare's Irish background (see 9.519–20n); but it also involves a cryptogram:

Patrick W(eston) *Joyce* (1827–1914), no relation, was an Irish scholar and historian.

12.191 (297:10–11). Brian Confucius – Brian (like Patrick) is a familiar Irish given name and makes a Celt out of the famous Chinese philosopher Confucius (551–479 B.C.).

12.191 (297:11). Murtagh Gutenberg – Murtagh is another Irish given name. One of the better-known individuals to bear it was Murtagh O'Brien (d. 1119), a belligerent king of Munster. Johannes Gutenberg (1397–1468) was the German who received disputed credit for the invention of printing with movable type. It is notable in relation to the following note that Gutenberg, the son of Gensfleisch, assumed his mother's name.

12.191–92 (297:11). Patricio Velasquez – The Spanish painter Diego Rodríguez de Silva (1599–1660) also used his mother's name, Velázquez. "Patricio" is the Spanish form of Patrick.

12.192 (297:11–12). Captain Nemo – The hero of Jules Verne's (1828–1905) science-fiction novel *Twenty Thousand Leagues Under the Sea* (1870). "Nemo" is Latin for "no man" (the pseudonym Odysseus assumes during his escape from Polyphemus's cave).

12.192 (297:12). Tristan and Isolde – The hero and heroine of the legendary love story are associated with Ireland because Isolde, in all literary versions of the story, is an Irish princess, and in some versions their love was supposed to have been consummated in Chapelizod, a village just west of Dublin.

12.192 (297:12). the first Prince of Wales – Edward II of England (1284–1327; king 1307–27) was the first heir apparent of the English throne to bear the subsequently traditional title Prince of Wales (1301). He was one of the less attractive English kings, noted for his "weakness" and for the overtly homosexual nature of his behavior with "favorites." He was deposed and then murdered in 1327.

12.193 (297:12–13). Thomas Cook and Son – The travel agency, founded in 1841. By 1900 its name had become almost a generic term for travel agencies and guided tours. It was founded by Thomas Cook (1808–92) and his son, John Mason Cook (1834–99).

12.193 (297:13). the Bold Soldier Boy – "The Bowld Sojer Boy" is a poem by Samuel Lover;

typical of the poem's sixty lines are the following: "There's not a town we march through, / But ladies looking arch through / The window panes will sarch through / The ranks to find their joy. / While up the street / Each girl you meet / With look so sly / Will cry, 'My eye! / Oh! isn't he a darling, / The bowld sojer boy!'"

12.193 (297:13). Arrah na Pogue – Irish: "One given to kissing." *Arrah-na-Pogue; or, The Wicklow Wedding* (1864) was a play (with interpolated songs) by Dion Boucicault.

12.193–94 (297:13–14). Dick Turpin – A notorious English highwayman, executed in 1793. He is the hero of the anonymous ballad "Turpin Hero," sometimes called "Dick Turpin." The poem consists largely of a dialogue between Turpin and the lawyer whom he tricks and robs: "As Turpin was a-riding thro' Hounslow Moor, / He saw an old lawyer just trotting on before. / So he trots up to the old lawyer: / 'Good morning, Sir,' he says, / 'Aren't you afraid of meetin' Dick Turpin / O that such mischievous plays?' / Singing, hero, Turpiny hero." The lawyer responds that Turpin will never find his money because he's hidden it in his "coatcape"; at the top of the hill Turpin demands the coatcape, robs the lawyer, and advises him to say in the next town that he was robbed by Dick Turpin.

12.194 (297:14). Ludwig Beethoven – (1770–1827).

12.194 (297:14). the Colleen Bawn – Irish: "Fair-Haired Girl." She appears variously as the heroine of a novel, *Molly Bawn*, by Margaret Wolfe Hungerford (1855–97); in the title role of one of Dion Boucicault's plays, *The Colleen Bawn; or, the Brides of Garryowen* (1860) and in *The Lily of Killarney* (see 6.186n): "The Colleen Bawn, the Colleen Bawn / From childhood have I known, / I've seen that beauty in the dawn, / Which now so bright has grown. / Although her cheek is blanched with care, / Her smile diffuses joy. / Heaven formed her a jewel rare— / Shall I that gem destroy?"

12.194 (297:14–15). Waddler Healy – The Very Reverend John Healy (1841–1918), archbishop of Tuam, is described as having waddled in his gait (Adams, p. 154).

12.194–95 (297:15). Angus the Culdee – The Culdees (*céli dé*, Irish: "clients of God") were eighth-century Irish anchorites. Angus (or Aengus) the Culdee (d. 820) was noted for his self-

abnegation and humility and for a verse martyrology that he composed.

12.195 (297:15). Dolly Mount – Dollymount was a village on Dublin Bay on the northeastern outskirts of Dublin.

12.195 (297:15). Sidney Parade – Or Sydney Parade, an avenue and a suburban area near the shore of Dublin Bay just south of Sandymount.

12.195 (297:15–16). Ben Howth – The hill that dominates the northeast headland of Dublin Bay.

12.195 (297:16). Valentine Greatrakes – (1629–83), an Irish healer called "the stroker" because he was reputed to have effected cures by a combination of massage and hypnotic suggestion.

12.196 (297:16). Adam and Eve – Not only the biblical progenitors of humanity but also the popular Dublin name for the Church of St. Francis of Assisi off Merchant's Quay in central Dublin; see 17.757–58n.

12.196 (297:16–17). Arthur Wellesley – (1769–1852), duke of Wellington. The Dublin-born duke was not the soul of popularity in his native country, since as prime minister (1828–30), he symbolized rigorous English militarism and a conservative resistance to reform.

12.196 (297:17). Boss Croker – Richard Croker (1843–1922), an Irish-born American politician; he became leader of the Tammany Hall Democratic machine in New York City. He was "successful" enough to be able to retire in affluence in his native Cork in 1903.

12.196 (297:17). Herodotus – (c. 484–c. 425 B.C.), the Greek historian known as the Father of History.

12.196–97 (297:17). Jack the Giantkiller – The hero of the well-known nursery tale that celebrates the supremacy of skill over force.

12.197 (297:17–18). Gautama Buddha – Siddhartha Gautama (c. 563–c. 483 B.C.), the great religious teacher and reformer of early India; see 5.328n.

12.197 (297:18). Lady Godiva – (fl. 1040–80); see 8.449n.

12.197 (297:18). the Lily of Killarney – See 6.186n.

12.197–98 (297:18–19). Balor of the Evil Eye – In Irish legend, the leader of the Formorians, the gloomy giants of the sea who plagued other legendary prehistoric inhabitants of Ireland. He had an eye he opened only in battle, thus enfeebling his enemies. He was finally killed by his grandson, Lug of the Long Arm, who sent a sling ball through the eye and into Balor's brain.

12.198 (297:19). the Queen of Sheba – (Fl. tenth century B.C.), the biblical (quasi-legendary) queen of the Sabaeans who visited King Solomon (I Kings 10 and II Chronicles 9).

12.198 (297:19). Acky Nagle – John Joachim "Acky" Nagle, publican, of J. Nagle & Co., tea, wine, and spirit merchants, 25 Earl Street North.

12.198 (297:19). Joe Nagle – James Joseph Nagle, another of the brothers in J. Nagle & Co.

12.198–99 (297:19–20). Alessandro Volta – Count Alessandro Volta (1745–1827), an Italian physicist remembered for his research and inventions in electricity.

12.199 (297:20). Jeremiah O'Donovan Rossa – Jeremiah O'Donovan (1831–1915), a Fenian leader whose advocacy of violent measures in Ireland's struggle for independence earned him the nickname "Dynamite Rossa." A leader of the revolutionary Phoenix Society, he was tried for complicity in the "Phoenix conspiracy" but released in 1859. After a sojourn in the United States, he returned to Ireland in 1863 to become business manager of the radical newspaper *Irish People*. In 1865 the paper was seized and O'Donovan was convicted of treason-felony. He was treated somewhat inhumanely in prison, and his sufferings made him so famous that County Tipperary elected him to Parliament in 1869 while he was still in prison. His life sentence was commuted to banishment in 1870; he returned to the United States, where he edited the *United Irishman*. He was again in Ireland from 1891 until 1900, although at that time he was a symbol rather than an actor in the Irish political scene.

12.199 (297:20–21). Don Philip O'Sullivan Beare – (c. 1590–1660), the Irish-born Spanish soldier and historian who wrote *Historiae Catholicae Iberniae Compendium* (Lisbon, 1621), a valuable account of the Elizabethan wars.

12.210 (297:33). robbing the poorbox – A particularly low and unrewarding kind of thievery, since the poorbox in a church was an unguarded receptacle provided for small contributions to the poor.

12.211 (297:34). the prudent member – That is, Bloom. The *Old Charges* of the Masonic Order forbid "imprudent conversation in relation to Masonry in the presence of uninitiated strangers." The charges also forbid all "wrangling, quarrelling, backbiting, and slander."

12.213–14 (297:36–37). Pill lane and Greek street – On the western side of the Dublin Corporation Fruit, Vegetable, and Fish Market. By 1904 Pill Lane had been renamed Chancery Street.

12.214 (297:37). cod's eye – Slang: "fool's eye."

Parody: 12.215–17 (297:39–41). Who comes through . . . the prudent soul – Continues the parody of reworked Irish legend.

12.215 (297:39). Michan's land – Bloom is in St. Michan's parish; see 12.68n.

12.216 (297:40). O'Bloom, the son of Rory – From among the countless Rorys in Irish history, two possibilities: a Rory Oge O'More (d. 1578) who was head of his sept (clan) 1542–57. Rory Oge must have been "prudent," since he rebelled repeatedly and was repeatedly pardoned. Another Rory O'More (fl. 1641–1652) was the principal leader of the momentarily successful rebellion of 1641. He was noted for his courage and had the reputation among his Protestant enemies of being "reasonable and humane."

12.218–19 (297:42–298:1). the old woman of Prince's . . . subsidised organ – That is, the *Freeman's Journal*, which was regarded as the "official" newspaper of the Irish Nationalist cause. The relative pallor of the paper's nationalist sentiment encouraged radicals to regard it as "subsidised," compromised by the quasi-conservative political interests of the Irish Nationalist or Home Rule party.

12.219 (298:1–2). The pledgebound party on the floor of the house – In 1852, after considerable argument, fifty (about half) of the Irish members of the English Parliament pledged themselves to independent opposition to both major parties in the House of Commons and further pledged to throw their balance-of-power vote in support of the English party that undertook reforms in Ireland. The tactic was promising, but it collapsed when several of the Irish members broke their pledges. Parnell revived the tactic of a pledge-bound party with considerable success in the 1880s when the Irish party moved toward a working coalition with Gladstone's Liberal party. After Parnell's leadership collapsed in 1890, the coalition of Irish political parties that he had achieved disintegrated. A similar division also began to plague the English Liberal party, which, under Gladstone, had ruled with the support of Parnell's coalition. By the opening years of the twentieth century the English Liberal party was deeply split between pro-imperialists (led by Joseph Chamberlain; see 8.423–24n) and the anti-imperialists. As a result, the Liberal party's commitment to social reform and to a solution of the Irish question was virtually paralyzed, but the Irish Parliamentary or Nationalist party (Parnell's old party) continued to honor its pledge and to support the English Liberals even though the Liberals could or would do nothing for Ireland.

The Citizen's remark also echoes a parody of a song, "God Save Ireland," by Timothy Daniel Sullivan (1827–1914). The parody involves the "transmission" from the queen to the Irish people of a message from Lady Aberdeen, who was active in support of "good works." The message was that the home front could help the World War I effort by collecting socks for the troops at the front: "When you've gathered all the socks / Take them down to Dr. Cox, / Or to Dillon, or to Redmond, or myself; / For the party on the floor / Has agreed to look them o'er / While the Home Rule Bill is resting on the shelf. [Chorus:] Hell roast the king and God save Ireland! / Get a sack and start to work today! / Gather all the socks you meet / For the British Tommies' feet / When they're running from the Germans far away!" Dr. Alfred Cox was a prominent English medical politician. John Dillon (1851–1927) was second in command of the Irish Nationalist or Home Rule party during World War I; John Redmond (1856–1918) was the leader of that party. The grim joke is that parliamentary approval of Home Rule had been achieved on the eve of the war, but implementation was suspended for the duration of hostilities. To many Irish nationalists this suspension looked suspiciously like bad faith on England's part.

12.220–21 (298:3). *The Irish Independent . . . founded by Parnell* – The *Freeman's Journal* held to its support of Parnell long after most of his supporters had turned against him. It finally abandoned Parnell on 21 September 1891; by that time Parnell, with the help of those still loyal to him, was planning to found a new paper, the *Irish Daily Independent*, to support his cause; see 7.308n. Parnell was, however, mortally ill (he died on 5 October), and the paper did not begin publication until 18 December 1891. It quickly passed into the hands of anti-Parnellites and was acquired in 1900 by William Martin Murphy; see 12.237n.

12.225–36 (298:8–20). Gordon, Barnfield Crescent . . . Isabella Helen – The English names and addresses that the Citizen reads are selected from the columns of the *Irish Daily Independent* for 16 June 1904. Under Births the Citizen passes over the Irish-born (Bennett, Carr, and Coghill) in favor of "Gordon—11 June 1904, at 3 Barnfield Crescent, Exeter [England], the wife of W. Gordon, M.D., F[ellow] of the R[oyal] C[ollege] of P[hysicians], of a son. // Redmayne, 12 June 1904, of Ifficy, St. Anne's-on-the-Sea [England], the wife of William T. Redmayne, of a son." Under Marriages the Citizen skips three Irish matches (Figgis and Donnithorne, Neary and O'Neill, Wright and Flint) to concentrate on "Vincent and Gillett— 9 June 1904, at St. Margaret's, Westminster [London], by the Rev. T. B. F. Campbell, third son of Thomas Vincent, Whinburgh, Norfolk, to Rotha Marian Gillett, younger daughter of Rosa and the late George Alfred Gillett, 179 Clapham Road, Stockwell. // Haywood [not Playwood] and Ridsdale—8 June 1904, at St. Jude's, Kensington, by the Very Rev. Dr. Forrest, Dean of Worcester, assisted by the Rev. W. H. Bliss, Vicar of Kew, Charles Burt Haywood, only surviving son of the late Thomas Burt Haywood and Mrs. Haywood, of Woodhatch, Reigate, to Gladys Muriel, only daughter of Alfred Ridsdale, of Hatherly House, Kew Gardens." Under Deaths the Citizen omits six English entries (Johnston, Kennedy, Larkin, Lyon, Watson, and Young) and one Irish ("Howard—14 June 1904, at the City of Dublin Hospital, Steven Howard, President of the Dublin Branch of the Amalgamated Painters' Society, Aged 32 years"). The Citizen cites from the following entries: "Bristow—11 June 1904, at 'Fernleigh,' Whitehorse Lane, Thornton Heath, London, John Gosling Bristow. // Cann [not Carr]—12 June 1904, at Manor Road, Stoke Newington, Emma, daughter of the late W. A. Cann, of gastritis and heart disease. // Cockburn—10 June 1904, at the Moat House, Chepstow, after a short illness, Frances Mary Cockburn, in the 60th year of her age. // Dimsey—13 June 1904, at 4 Crouch Hall Road, Crouch End [England], Martha Elizabeth, the Wife of David Griffiths Dimsey, late of the Admiralty. // Miller—14 June 1904, at Northumberland Park, Tottenham, George Clark Miller, in the 85th year of his age. // Welsh—12 June 1904, at 35 Canning Street, Liverpool, Isabella Helen Welsh."

12.233 (298:17). that fellow – Venereal disease. In England, Cockburn is pronounced "Coburn."

12.236–37 (298:21). my brown son – Low slang for penis.

12.237 (298:21–22). Martin Murphy, the Bantry jobber – William Martin Murphy (1844–1921) was the owner of the *Irish Daily Independent*. He was born in Bantry on the southwest coast of Ireland and worked as a contractor (building railways and tramways); a member of Parliament (1885–92), he turned against Parnell in the Great Split of 1890. He distinguished himself as the chief opponent of the workers in the great Dublin strike of 1913. "Jobber" is slang for one who performs corrupt work in politics or intrigue.

12.238–39 (298:23–24). Thanks be to God . . . the start of us – After a popular drinking song, "One More Drink for the Four of Us": "I was drunk last night, drunk the night before. / Gonna get drunk tonight, if I never get drunk anymore, / 'Cause when I'm drunk I'm as happy as can be, / For I am a member of the souse familee. // Glorious, glorious, one keg of beer for the four of us. / Glory be to god there are no more of us, / For one of us could kill it all alone."

12.241 (298:26). And all down the form – Mourners at Irish wakes sat on long benches, or forms, usually supplied by the funeral parlor.

Parody: 12.244–48 (298:30–34). And lo, as they . . . fairest of his race – Continues the parodies of reworked Irish legend.

12.250 (298:36). snug – (Of a bar or pub) a small room or parlor behind the bar for private parties.

12.258 (299:4). u.p.: up – See 8.258n.

12.265 (299:13). *Bi i dho husht* – Irish: literally, "Silence!" but figuratively a somewhat impolite way of saying, "Shut up." The phrase is often used at public meetings, etc.

12.271 (299:20). Green street . . . G. man – The G (plainclothes) Division of the Dublin Metropolitan Police was located in Exchange Court off Dame Street. Green Street, around the corner from Little Britain Street, had two police stations: C Division at 25 and D Division at 11; 25 also housed the Sessions House (the chief judicial offices of the city) and the Office of the Clerk of the Crown and Peace, County and City of Dublin.

12.272 (299:21–22). to hang that fellow in Mountjoy – The real subsheriff in 1904, John Clancy, the prototype of the fictional Long John Fanning, was well known for his reluctance to fulfill his duty of preparing for the infrequent hangings that took place in Dublin. Mountjoy Government Prison, where long-term prisoners were held, was between North Circular Road and the Royal Canal on the northern outskirts of Dublin. There was no prisoner awaiting hanging in Mountjoy on 16 June 1904, but there was one awaiting retrial on a charge of murder. Thomas Byrne, a Dubliner, had allegedly beaten his wife to death on 27 March 1904. Byrne's first trial had ended in a hung jury on 9 June 1904, although the presiding judge, Lord O'Brien (see 12.190n), had virtually directed a verdict of guilty. There was considerable public controversy about the trial: against Lord O'Brien as a "hanging judge" and against Byrne as a brutal murderer who deserved immediate hanging. At the retrial on 2 August 1904 Byrne was found guilty; he was executed on 6 September 1904.

Parody: 12.280–99 (299:30–300:12). Terence O'Ryan . . . the ruddy and the ethiop – Continues the parodies of reworked Irish legend intermixed with retold stories from Greek mythology and medieval romance.

12.274 (299:25). pony – A glass of porter, half the standard pub measure of a pint.

12.280 (299:30). Terence O'Ryan – In 1904 a Reverend Terence W. O'Ryan was curate-in-charge of St. Vincent's Roman Catholic Church in Golden Bridge, a village three miles west of Dublin center (only appropriate, since "curate" was slang for bartender). Another O'Ryan is "immortalized" in a ballad by Charles Graham Halpine (1829–68), "Irish Astronomy; a Veritable Myth, Touching the Constellation of O'Ryan, Ignorantly and Falsely Spelled Orion." O'Ryan is characterized as a "man of might" whose "constant occupation" was poaching. St. Patrick visits him and asks modestly for food and water; O'Ryan responds, "'But here's a jug of mountain dew, / And there's a rattlin' hare, sir.'" St. Patrick rewards O'Ryan's generosity by promising him a permanent place in heaven as the constellation Orion.

12.281–82 (299:31–32). the noble twin brothers Bungiveah and Bungardilaun – Sir Edward Guinness, Lord Iveagh, and Sir Arthur Guinness, Lord Ardilaun, brothers though not twins, owned Guinness's Brewery; see 5.304n and 5.306n. "Bung" is slang for one who serves grog. The Irish journalist D. P. Moran attacked the liquor interests collectively and repeatedly as "Mr. Bung" in the pages of his weekly newspaper, the *Leader* (Dublin, established 1900).

12.282–83 (299:33). the sons of deathless Leda – In Greek mythology, Castor, the tamer of horses, and Pollux, the adept boxer, were the twin sons of Leda, who had been impregnated by Zeus disguised as a swan; Leda also gave birth to Helen and Clytemnestra. The twins were worshiped as aiders of men in war and on the sea, as the patrons of travelers, and as guardians of hospitality. Lord Iveagh was owner of a famous stable of thoroughbreds. Leda is "deathless" because immortalized in myth.

12.287 (299:38–39). to the manner born – As they wait for the appearance of the Ghost on the battlements, Horatio and Hamlet hear the sounds of the court's carouse. Horatio asks: "Is it a custom? HAMLET: Ay, marry is't. / But to my mind, though I am native here / And to the manner born, it is a custom / More honour'd in the breach than the observance. / This heavy-headed revel east and west / Makes us traduced and tax'd of [censured by] other nations" (I.iv.12–18).

12.291 (300:3). testoon – A silver-bronze shilling coin introduced in the reign of Henry VIII; it declined in value to sixpence in the course of the sixteenth century because it was debased metal. In this context it is a penny.

12.293–96 (300:4–8). a queen of regal . . . Empress of India – Queen Victoria was a granddaughter of George III of England, whose family had been the dukes of Brunswick in Germany. The titles were Victoria's official titles except for the phrase "and of the British dominions beyond the sea," a phrase first included in the royal formula at the coronation of Edward VII in 1902.

12.298 (300:10–11). from the rising . . . going down thereof – From Psalms 50:1: "The mighty God, even the Lord, hath spoken, and called the earth from the rising of the sun unto the going down thereof."

12.307 (300:21). codding – See 12.141n.

12.308 (300:22). Honest injun – American slang, a pledge of good faith. William S. Walsh (*Handy-Book of Literary Curiosities* [Philadelphia, 1892], p. 485) speculates, "Originally, no doubt, the reference to Indian honesty was sarcastic."

12.313 (300:27). Willy Murray – The name of one of Joyce's uncles; he worked for Collis and Ward, just as Richie Goulding does in the novel.

12.314 (300:28). Capel street – Just east of the Ormond Hotel in central Dublin. It gives north from Grattan Bridge.

12.323–24 (300:38). plain as a pikestaff – Proverbial at least since John Byrom (1691–1763), in *Epistle to a Friend*, "The point is plain as a pikestaff."

12.332–33 (301:6–7). They took the liberty . . . this morning anyhow – The joke derives from Jonathan Swift, *Complete Collection of Genteel and Ingenious Conversation* (1738), First Conversation: "COLONEL ATWIT: But is it certain that Sir *John Blunderbuz* is dead at last? LORD SPARKISH: Yes, or else he's sadly wronged; for they have buried him."

Parody: 12.338–73 (301:13–302:12). In the darkness spirit . . . had given satisfaction – Parodies a Theosophist's account of a spiritualist séance. The "scientific" exactitude of some of the phrases ("Communication was effected," "It was ascertained," etc.) lampoons the style of reports published by the Society for Psychical Research in London. The society was founded in 1882 for the purpose of making "an organized and systematic attempt to investigate that large group of debatable phenomena designated by such terms as mesmeric, psychical, and spiritualistic."

12.339 (301:14). tantras – In Hinduism, a ceremonial treatise related to the literature of magic and of the Puranas (sacred poetical works in Sanskrit that treat of the creation, destruction, and renovation of worlds, the deeds of gods and heroes, etc.). The tantras were widely used by Theosophists and spiritualists.

12.341 (301:16). etheric double – In Theosophy, the living human being is composed of a "dense body" and an "etheric body or double" "magnetically" bonded. In birth or rebirth the etheric double is fashioned in advance of its dense counterpart; the two bodies, once fused, shape the limits within which the human being as a conscious entity will have to live and work. At death the etheric double is separated from the dense body and gradually disintegrates; subsequently a new etheric body will be created for the rebirth of the soul, since one earth-life is not considered sufficient for the full evolution of the soul. In context, Dignam's etheric double is "particularly lifelike" because it is only just beginning to disintegrate.

12.341 (301:17). jivic rays – The *jiva* is the life energy, the vital principle of the individual soul.

12.343 (301:18–19). the pituitary body – Or gland, regarded by some Theosophists and spiritualists as that which unites the body with the soul (whose seat is in the pineal gland; see 9.284n). Since Dignam is but recently dead, the ties of his soul to his body are still strong though facing inevitable disintegration.

12.346 (301:22–23). on the path of prālāyā or return – *Prālāyā*, in Theosophy, is the period of the individual soul's reabsorption or rest after death and before rebirth. In this period the soul is supposed to divest itself of earthly concerns and concentrate on spiritual growth so that it will evolve toward rebirth in an improved state.

12.347 (301:23–24). certain bloodthirsty entities on the lower astral levels – The effort of the individual soul is to evolve through spiritual education toward higher and purer (less violent and earthy) astral levels; see 9.281n. In effect, Dignam's soul is threatened with spiritual retardation.

12.348 (301:25). the great divide – The phrase "to pass the great divide" was a stock nineteenth-century circumlocution for death; but see also 12.341n.

12.349 (301:26). *he had but seen as in a glass darkly – "For now we see through a glass, darkly; but then face to face: now I know in part; but then shall I know even as also I am known" (I Corinthians 13:12).

12.350 (301:27–28). atmic development – In Theosophy, the atmic plane is the plane of pure existence, where the soul's divine powers are in their fullest manifestation. Those who achieve this plane have completed the cycle of human evolution through a succession of lives and are perfect in wisdom, bliss, and power.

12.352 (301:30). more favoured beings – Those whose individual spiritual evolution has carried them through more stages on the journey to Atman than Dignam's has.

12.354 (301:32). tālāfānā, ālāvātār, hātākāldā, wātāklāsāt – Telephone, elevator, hot and cold (running water), water closet. The spelling parodies the Theosophists' predilection for Sanskrit terms (Sanskrit being regarded as the penultimate language [after Pali] of mysticism); see Pali, 9.279n.

12.354–55 (301:33–34). the highest adepts . . . volupcy of the very purest nature – The highest adepts have achieved existence on the atmic plane; see 12.350n. Earnest students of Theosophy realize "the supreme importance of the inner man over the outer case or body" and therefore practice a "moral" asceticism in this life (H. P. Blavatsky, *The Key to Theosophy* [London, 1893], pp. 174–75). When the ascetic has evolved to the atmic plane, the reward is *pure* "volupcy" (Joyce's coinage?) or bliss.

12.358 (301:36–37). the wrong side of Māyā – *Māyā* is the physical and sensuous universe conceived as a tissue of deceit and illusion. To be on the "wrong side of Maya" is not to have begun the Theosophical effort for spiritual evolution of the soul toward Atman.

12.359 (301:38). devanic circles – A *deva* is a divine being or deity; thus: among the divine ones, those who have achieved Atman.

12.359–60 (301:38–39). Mars and Jupiter . . . ram has power – In astrology, the planet Jupiter signifies a high-spirited, energetic mind, committed to new and progressive ideas and somewhat religiously inclined; Mars signifies a passionate, challenging temperament. The "ram" is Aries, the "eastern angle" his house in the heavens, his section of the zodiac; Aries marks the beginning, the spring of the zodiacal year. The qualities of Aries are dauntless courage, optimism, energy. In this case, since Mars and Jupiter are "out for mischief," their similar qualities are in conflict instead of in conjunction; the dark, destructive side of those qualities threatens to become manifest and to bring out the negative qualities of Aries: a tendency to bluff and heckle, to resent interference, and to indulge in temper tantrums.

12.368 (302:7). the return room – A small room added onto the wall of a house and projecting out from it.

12.369 (302:8). Cullen's – M. Cullen, bootmaker, 56 Mary Street, Dublin.

Parody: 12.374–76 (302:14–17). He is gone . . . with your whirlwind – Again parodies reworked Irish legend, the lament for the death of a hero.

12.375 (302:16). Banba – According to Geoffrey Keating's (c. 1570–c. 1644) *History of Ireland* (c. 1629), Banba was the eldest of the three daughters of Adam and Eve's son Cain. Banba and her sisters, Erin and Fotha, were the legendary first settlers of Ireland. Other versions of the legend style Banba as a queen of the Tuatha De Danaan (the legendary prehistoric race of heroes), and thus her name became (as did Erin) a poetic name for Ireland. In mythological terms, Banba and her two sisters apparently constituted a triple goddess (birth-love-death), with Banba functioning as goddess of death.

12.379 (302:20). point duty – The duty of a police constable stationed at a street or crossing to direct traffic.

12.382 (302:24). knocked bawways – Or bowways, from to bow, bend, or curve; similar to "knocked into a hoop" or "knocked arseways."

12.384 (302:26). poll – Slang for head; it originally meant a wig.

12.397 (303:1). The tear is bloody near your eye – See 12.161–62n.

12.398–402 (303:2–7). the little sleepwalking bitch . . . and no favour – The story of Bob Doran's shotgun courtship is told in "The Boarding House," *Dubliners*. For "bumbailiff," see 11.1243n. "Stravaging" means roaming about idly. "Fair field and no favour" is a phrase from horseracing used to describe a race in which there are no handicaps or favorites, in which all the horses are equally good. Hardwicke Street is in northeastern Dublin; its northern end is 75 yards east of the east end of Eccles Street.

Parody: 12.405–6 (303:10–11). And mournful . . . beam of heaven – Continues the previous parody; see 12.374–76n.

12.407 (303:13). skeezing – Slang for looking or ogling.

12.412 (303:17). O, Christ M'Keown – The connotations of this curse are unknown; for what it's worth, *Thom's* 1904 (p. 1945) lists "William M'Keown, G.P.O. [General Post Office], 15 Mount Street Lower," but the list of G.P.O. management and staff (p. 844) does not include him.

12.420 (303:23). *Joe Gann* – Derives his name not from the history of crime but from a British consular official in Zurich who offended Joyce; see Ellmann, pp. 427, 440, 441.

12.420 (303:23). *Bootle jail* – A maximum-security prison near Liverpool, England.

12.422 (303:26). *private Arthur Chace . . . Jessie Tilsit* – Mr. H. G. Pearson, departmental record officer at the Home Office in London, reports: "A careful search has been made of the Home Office record of capital cases for the period 1880 onwards but no mention has been found of the execution of Private Arthur Chace" (letter, 20 November 1970).

12.422–23 (303:27). *Pentonville prison* – A maximum-security prison in London.

12.425 (303:29). *Billington* – An English hangman named Billington did have the dubious distinction of hanging three Irish malefactors in one week in 1899; see Adams, p. 228.

12.425 (303:29–30). *Toad Smith* – A coworker with Joe Gann; see 12.420n.

12.430 (303:35). *H. Rumbold* – Sir Horace Rumbold, the British minister to Switzerland in 1918, appears by courtesy of Joyce's irritation with him; see Ellmann, p. 458.

12.431 (303:36). *Master Barber* – Barbers were originally surgeons and dentists as well as dressers of beards and hair. The Company of Barber-Surgeons was incorporated in 1461. The crafts were not formally separated until 1715.

Parody: 12.446–49 (304:15–18). In the dark land . . . saith the Lord – Parodies the style of popular "stories from medieval romance" as well as biblical prose.

12.447 (304:17). Erebus – In Greek mythology, a realm of darkness between the earth and Hades, the underworld.

12.451 (304:21). codology – Coined from *cod;* see 12.141n.

12.457 (304:27). The poor bugger's tool – It is a commonplace that a man who is hanged has an erection in the process.

12.460 (304:30). Kilmainham – Kilmainham Gaol, on the western outskirts of Dublin, was notorious for the generations of Irish patriots who were imprisoned and/or executed within its walls. It is now a museum.

12.460 (304:30–31). Joe Brady, the invincible – See 7.639n. He was hanged in Kilmainham, 14 May 1883.

12.463 (304:33). Ruling passion strong in death – From Alexander Pope's (1688–1744) *Moral Essays*, Epistle 1: "And you! brave COBHAM, to the latest breath / Shall feel your ruling passion strong in death: / Such in those moments as in all the past, / 'Oh, save my Country, Heav'n!' shall be your last" (lines 262–65).

Parody: 12.468–78 (304:39–305:9). The distinguished scientist . . . *per diminutionem capitis* – Parodies a medical journal's report of a medical society meeting.

12.468 (304:39–40). Luitpold Blumenduft – "Luitpold" is an archaic German form of Leopold; *Blumenduft*, German: "flower scent or fragrance."

12.474 (305:3). *corpora cavernosa* – Latin: "the cavernous bodies." In anatomy: masses of erectile tissue with large interspaces that may be distended with blood, especially those of the penis and clitoris.

12.478 (305:8). philoprogenitive – Having or tending to the love of offspring.

12.478 (305:8–9). *in articulo mortis per diminutionem capitis* – Medical Latin: "at the moment of death caused by breaking the neck."

12.480 (305:11). the invincibles – See 5.378n.

12.480 (305:12). the old guard – Presumably the "grand old men" of the Fenian movement (see 2.272n), among them John O'Leary (1830–1907), Charles Joseph Kickham (1826–82), and

Jeremiah O'Donovan (Rossa) (see 12.199n). Their careers began with involvement in the Young Ireland movement in the 1840s, then with the Fenians. In 1865 they were arrested, imprisoned, and transported in an English sweep designed to stifle the Fenian organization before it could mount a rebellion. They continued, however, to write and to crusade for Irish independence even though their revolutionary aims were overshadowed by Parnell's essentially constitutional attempts to achieve Home Rule.

12.481 (305:12). the men of sixty-seven – The Fenians made an attempt at rebellion in 1867, but it was abortive for various reasons: planned for 1865, it had to be delayed for lack both of weapons and of coordinated organization; furthermore, the English, in an effort to suppress dissent, arrested key Fenian spokesmen and moved Irish army units infiltrated by Fenians out of the country. Finally, the Fenian Society in America, on which the rebels were heavily dependent for support, was torn with dissension and so was ineffective in its partisan role. The rebellion itself, 5–6 March, took place without a chance of success and amounted to a bloodless failure.

12.481 (305:12–13). who fears to speak of ninety-eight – The Rebellion of 1798; see 10.790n.

12.483 (305:15). drumhead courtmartial – A summary trial conducted with an upturned drum as the "bench" for the purpose of judging offenses during military operations.

12.491 (305:24). Arrah! – See 12.141n.

12.494 (305:28). give you the bloody pip – To "give the pip" is slang for to depress, annoy, disgust.

12.495 (305:29). *a Jacobs' tin – W. and R. Jacobs & Co., Ltd., was a large biscuit (cookie) manufacturer in Dublin.

12.498–99 (305:34). the brothers Sheares – Henry (1755–98) and John (1766–98) Sheares were both members of the United Irishmen in the Rebellion of 1798. Betrayed by an informer, they were captured and went (so the sentimental story goes) hand in hand to their execution.

12.499 (305:34–35). Wolfe Tone beyond on Arbour Hill – Wolfe Tone is reported to have committed suicide in the Old Provost Marshal's

Prison on Arbour Hill, not far west of Barney Kiernan's pub; see 10.378n and 12.184n.

12.499–500 (305:35). Robert Emmet and die for your country – See 6.977–78n and the poem quoted in 12.500–501n.

12.500–501 (305:35–36). the Tommy Moore touch . . . far from the land – Sara Curran (d. 1808) was secretly engaged to Robert Emmet, and, on the evidence of letters found on him when he was captured, implicated in his plot (to such an extent that her father, John Philpot Curran [see 7.740n] was moved to disown her). The story that Emmet was captured in a stakeout when he went to bid her good-bye before fleeing into exile is apparently the embellishment of legend.

Thomas Moore's poem "She Is Far From the Land," in *Irish Melodies*, puts the sentimental touch on her: "She is far from the land where her young hero sleeps, / And lovers are round her, sighing: / But coldly she turns from their gaze, and weeps, / For her heart in his grave is lying. // She sings the wild song of her dear native plains, / Every note which he lov'd awaking;— / Ah! little they think who delight in her strains, / How the heart of the Minstrel is breaking. // He had liv'd for his love, for his country he died, / They were all that to life had entwin'd him; / Nor soon shall the tears of his country be dried, / Nor long will his love stay behind him. // Oh! make her a grave where the sunbeams rest, / When they promise a glorious morrow; / They'll shine o'er his sleep, like a smile from the West, / From her own lov'd island of sorrow."

12.504 (305:40). *the City Arms – The hotel where the Blooms lived when Bloom worked for the cattle trader Joseph Cuffe; see 2.416–17n.

12.504 (305:40–41). *pisser Burke – Andrew "Pisser" Burke, apparently fictional, another declining-and-falling, all-too-Irish member of the middle class. He was either living in or hanging around the City Arms Hotel when the Blooms lived there.

12.505 (305:41). an old one – Mrs. Riordan, who appears as the character "Dante" Riordan in chapter 1 of *A Portrait*.

12.505 (305:41–42). loodheramaun – Irish: "someone to be ashamed of."

12.508 (306:3). thumping her craw – See 5.382n.

12.510 (306:5). by the holy farmer – Or "by the holy father" (the pope), a low Dublin oath (Eric Partridge, *A Dictionary of Slang and Unconventional English* [London, 1937], p. 399).

12.513 (306:9). Mrs. O'Dowd – Elizabeth O'Dowd, proprietor of the City Arms Hotel.

12.516 (306:13). Power's . . . the blender's round in Cope street – John T. Power, wholesale spirit merchant, 18 Cope Street, just south of the Liffey in central Dublin.

12.519 (306:17). The memory of the dead – See 10.790n.

12.523 (306:22). *Sinn Fein! . . . Sinn fein amhain!* – Irish: "Ourselves! . . . Ourselves alone!"; a patriotic toast and the motto of the Gaelic League. The phrase is a refrain in the song "The West's Awake," by Timothy Daniel Sullivan (1827–1914): "Again through song-famed Innisfail / We wake the old tongue of the Gael: / The speech our fathers loved of yore / Makes music in our land once more! / Throughout a dark and doleful time / The stranger [England] made that speech a crime— / His might is passed; behold the dawn! / We've won the fight; *Sinn Fein Amhain!* // We found that dear tongue weak and low, / O'ermastered by its foreign foe; / Today both friends and foes can see / How strong and great 'tis bound to be! / Yes; soon again you'll rule and reign / Through Erin's fair and wide domain: / We bid you hail! *Mavourneen, slaun!* / And sing *Sinn Fein, Sinn Fein Amhain!*"

12.523–24 (306:22–23). The friends we love . . . hate before us – After Thomas Moore's "Where Is the Slave?" in *Irish Melodies*. "Oh, where's the slave so lowly, / Condemn'd to chains unholy, / Who could he burst / His bonds at first, / Would pine beneath them slowly? / . . . / We tread the land that bore us, / Her green flag glitters o'er us, / The friends we've tried / Are by our side, / And the foe we hate before us. // Farewell, Erin,—farewell, all, / Who live to weep our fall!" (lines 1–5, 18–24).

Parody: 12.525–678 (306:24–310:38). The last farewell was affecting . . . down Limehouse way – Parodies a newspaper's feature-story coverage of a large-scale public and social event. This "account" of the execution of Robert Emmet (see 6.977–78n) owes a debt of parody to Washington Irving's (1783–1859) story "The Broken Heart," in *The Sketch Book* (1819–20).

12.536 (306:37–38). the York street brass and reed band – Organized by the City and County of Dublin Conservative Workingman's Club, 38 York Street.

12.538–39 (306:39–41). the matchless melody . . . Speranza's plaintive muse – Speranza, the pseudonym of Jane Francisca Elgee, Lady Wilde (1826–96), Oscar Wilde's mother. "Plaintive" is hardly a fitting description of her "muse," however, since she was part of the literary-revolutionary movement of the Young Irelanders in 1848 and attempted a stirring, not to say incendiary, nationalist verse. The "matchless melody" is unknown, but Thornton (p. 269) quite plausibly suggests her poem "The Brothers. Henry and John Sheares," which does begin on a "plaintive" note of "lamp-light dull and sickly" and "gloom," though it shifts by the third stanza toward upbeat celebration of "the martyrs' glory." The brothers were, according to conflicting traditions, executed under circumstances either of "great barbarity" or of touching mutual affection; see 12.498–99n.

12.542–43 (307:3–4). The Night before Larry was stretched – An eighteenth-century Irish ballad that begins, "The night before Larry was stretched, / The boys they all paid him a visit." Larry and friends drink and play cards; Larry refuses the good offices of the clergy and worries that his "sweet Molly" will be frightened when his ghost visits her: "When he came to the nubbling chit / He was tucked up so neat and so pretty, / The rumbler jogged off from his feet / And he died with his face to the city; / He kicked too—but that was all pride, / For soon you might see 't was all over; / Soon after the noose was untied, / And at darky we walked him in clover, / And sent him to take a groundsweat."

12.547 (307:8–9). the Male and Female Foundling Hospital – *Thom's* 1904 lists no such "hospital," and all the orphanages that it does list are exclusively for either males or females.

12.549–50 (307:12). the Little Sisters of the Poor – A branch of the Roman Catholic Sisters of Charity; their only establishment in Dublin was St. Patrick's House, a home for aged males and females on South Circular Road in Kilmainham.

12.556 (307:20). Commendatore Bacibaci Beninobenone – Italian: "Commander (or Knight Commander) Kisskiss Pretty-well-verywell."

12.558 (307:22–23). Monsieur Pierrepaul Petitepatant – French: "Mr. Peterpaul Pittypat."

12.560 (307:24–25). Schwanzenbad-Hodenthaler – German: "Penis-in-bath–Inhabitant-of-the-valley-of-testicles."

12.560–61 (307:25). Countess Marha Virága Kisászony Putrápesthi – In addition to the obvious English puns, Hungarian: "Countess Cow [in contempt] Somebody's-flower Mademoiselle Putrapesthi." "Putrapesthi" conjoins *putrid pest* with *Budapest.*

12.561–62 (307:26). Count Athanatos Karamelopulis – Modern Greek: "Count Deathless Candy-vendor" (if *-pulis* is Joyce's way of rendering *-polis.*)

12.562 (307:26–27). Ali Baba Backsheesh Rahat Lokum Effendi – Ali Baba is a character in "Ali Baba and the Forty Thieves," one of the tales of the *Arabian Nights;* a poor peasant, he becomes rich by learning the password ("open sesame") of the thieves' cave. *Baksheesh,* Arabic: a tip, handout, or bribe; *rahat lokum effendi,* Albanian-Turkish: serene effulgent master (or gentleman).

12.562–64 (307:27–28). Senor Hidalgo Caballero Don Pecadillo y Palabras y Paternoster de la Malora de la Malaria – Spanish: "Sir Noble Knight Mr. Peccadillo and Words and Lord's Prayer of the Evil Hour of Malaria."

12.564 (307:29). Hokopoko – See 5.362n.

12.564 (307:29). Hi Hung Chang – Puns on Li Hung Chang (c. 1823–1901), a Chinese statesman of commanding ability, second in power only to the emperor for the then-remarkable period of twenty-five years (1870–1895).

12.564 (307:29). Olaf Kobberkeddelsen – Obviously, "O laugh, copper-kettle-son"; but Joan Keenan suggests that the pseudo-Danish is a reminder that *Hamlet* is set in Denmark (see following note) and may be an allusion to the Gundestrup Kedelen or the Rynkeby Kedelen, bronze Celtic caldrons discovered in 1891 and 1845, respectively, and now in the Danish National Museum. In Celtic tradition, the caldron for boiling meat was "a most important article in the household . . . the special property of the chief . . . much in the same way as his sword and shield" (P. W. Joyce, *A Social History of Ancient Ireland* [London, 1913], vol. 2, p. 124).

12.565 (307:30). Pan Poleaxe Paddyrisky – *Pan*, Polish: "Mr." or "Sir." The multilevel pun involves the famous Polish pianist Jan Paderewski (1860–1941); Paddy, the omnipresent stage-Irishman; and "Poleaxe," one editorial variant for the famous disputed passage in *Hamlet* of Horatio's description of the Ghost: "So frown'd he once, when, in an angry parle, / He smote the sledded Polacks [leaded poleaxe? Pollax?] on the ice."

12.565 (307:30). Goosepond – A pun on the Russian *gospodin*, mister.

12.566 (307:31). Borus Hupinkoff – The pun includes Boris Godunov (c. 1551–1605), virtual regent of Russia (1584–98) and then czar (1598–1605). The reign of the historical Boris was a mixed blessing for Russia. He undertook many "reforms," one of which miscarried into the introduction of serfdom in Russia. He is the subject of a play by Pushkin (1826, its performance delayed by censorship until 1831) and an opera (1874) by Modest Mussorgsky (1839–81), both of which turn on a sense of impending doom for Russia and on Boris's brooding and superstitious guilt over his murder of the rightful czarevitch Dmitri (whose throne he thus usurped, at least in fiction if not in history). An additional aspect of the pun: in May 1907 Joseph Conrad's son Borys had a severe and disturbing attack of whooping cough while Conrad was writing *Chance* and reading proof of *The Secret Agent*.

12.566–67 (307:31–32). Herr Hurhausdirektorpräsident Hans Chuechli-Steuerli – "Mr. Brothel-director-president Hans [short for Johannes (John)] Chuechli-Steuerli [suggesting 'Little-cake–Little-tax'; a Swiss-German family name]."

12.567–69 (307:32–34). Nationalgymnasium-museumsanatoriumandsuspensoriumsordinaryprivatedocentgeneralhistoryspecialprofessordoctor Kriegfried Ueberallgemein – The "title" is an obvious joke at the expense of German compounds (as in preceding note); *Kriegfried* means "War-peace" and is a pun on Siegfried (see 15.4242n); *Ueberallgemein* means, literally, "Overall, universal," but the pun also involves the German national anthem "Deutschland, Deutschland über Alles" (Germany, Germany over Everything) (1841) by A. H. Hoffmann von Falersleben.

12.573 (307:39). F.O.T.E.I. – Friends of the Emerald Isle.

12.573–74 (307:39–40). whether the eighth or ninth . . . Ireland's patron saint – St. Patrick (c. 385–c. 461). Not only is the day of his birth unknown but also the year and the place (Scotland? Wales? Gaul?). The comic solution (9 + 8 = 17) was proposed by Samuel Lover in "The Birth of St. Patrick." The poem asserts that the argument between believers in the eighth (as the day of St. Patrick's birth) and believers in the ninth was the occasion of "the first faction fight in owld Ireland," until one "Father Mulcahy" proposes the compromise: "Says he, 'Boys, don't be fightin' for eight or for nine, / Don't be always dividin'—but sometimes combine; / Combine eight with nine and seventeen is the mark, / So let that be his birthday.'— 'Amen,' says the clerk. / . . . / Then they all got blind dhrunk—which complated their bliss, / And we keep up the practice from that day to this" (lines 17–24).

But, humor aside, the uncertainties and controversies about the time and place of St. Patrick's birth and the beginning of his mission to Ireland have been taken so seriously that the *Maynooth Catechism* (Dublin, 1882), p. 23 (see 9.462–64n), saw fit to make the timing of St. Patrick's mission virtually an article of faith: "Q. By whom was Ireland converted to the true faith? A. Ireland was converted to the true faith by St. Patrick, who was sent by Pope Celestine, and came to our island in the year 432."

12.577–81 (308:2–7). The baby policeman, Constable MacFadden . . . Booterstown . . . readywitted ninefooter's – Booterstown, a village four miles southeast of the center of Dublin, prided itself on having a Metropolitan Police station (one of its few landmarks); the joke about the constable is that all Dublin police had to be at least five feet nine inches tall (and, by assumption, baby-faced country bumpkins).

12.586 (308:12). Avvocato Pagamimi – Italian: "Lawyer Paymimi," with a pun on Niccolò Paganini (1782–1840), the Italian virtuoso violinist.

12.586–87 (308:13). his thirty-two pockets – One for each of the thirty-two counties of Ireland.

12.593 (308:21). *Gladiolus Cruentus* – Botanical Latin for a fictional species of gladiolus, since the name of the genus derives from the

Latin for sword (after the shape of the leaves), and "Cruentus" means "spotted with blood."

12.600–601 (308:28–30). hoch, banzai, eljen, zivio, chinchin, polla kronia, hiphip, vive, Allah . . . evviva – "National" exclamations; variously: *hoch*, German ("high, noble, sublime"; a toast wishing a long life); *banzai*, Japanese ("May you live ten thousand years"—a battle cry and salutation to the emperor); *éljen*, Hungarian ("May he live long"); *zivio*, Serbo-Croatian ("Hail, may you live long"); *chinchin*, pidgin English (to salute ceremoniously, to greet or converse with polite inquiries; "I salute you"); *polla kronia*, modern Greek (literally, "Have many times"; or "Long life"); *hiphip*, American; *vive*, French ("long live"); *Allah*, Arabic ("God"); *evviva*, Italian ("hurrah").

12.602–3 (308:31–32). the eunuch Catalani – Angelica Catalani (1779–1849), an Italian soprano famous for her three-octave range (the normal soprano range is two octaves above middle C). Her range suggested that of a boy soprano or a castrato.

12.607 (308:37). the revolution of Rienzi – Cola di Rienzi (or Rienzo) (c. 1313–54) was a Roman popular leader. In 1347 he led a revolution in Rome, successfully displacing the ruling aristocracy and introducing governmental reforms. Placed at the head of the government, he assumed the title of tribune and became arrogant and arbitrary. He succeeded in alienating not only the populace, but also the papacy because of his visionary plans for restoring the secular "grandeur that was Rome." Expelled in 1348, in 1354 he returned at the request of Pope Innocent VI and provoked a riot in which he met his death.

12.608 (308:38). Dr Pippi – For P.P.: "Papa—Pope; Pontificum—Of the popes"; for *P.P.*, "Parochus—Parish Priest (used mostly in Ireland)" (*Catholic Encyclopedia* [New York, 1907], vol. 1, p. 25a; suggested by Joan Keenan).

12.618–19 (309:9–10). the quartering knife . . . disembowelling appliances – Except that Emmet was hanged and beheaded, not hanged, drawn, and quartered.

12.620–21 (309:11). Messrs John Round and Sons, Sheffield – Well-known nineteenth-century manufacturers of fine steel instruments and cutlery.

12.622 (309:12–13). blind intestine – Another name for the appendix.

12.624–25 (309:15–16). the amalgamated cats' and dogs' home – See 6.125n.

12.634–35 (309:27–28). the sick and indigent roomkeeper's association – The Sick and Indigent Roomkeeper's Society, 2 Palace Street, Dublin.

12.635–36 (309:28–29). nec and non plus ultra – Latin: *nec* (or *ne*) *plus ultra* and *non plus ultra* both mean "the uttermost point that can be attained."

12.640 (309:34). Sheila, my own – *Shiela-ni-Gara* is another of the many allegorical names for Ireland. Mrs. Seumas MacManus (pseudonym Ethna Carberry, 1866–1902), wrote a poem of that title that describes Shiela as "lonesome where [she] bides" but as looking forward to a "joy sadly won." The last stanza: "But, Shiela-ni-Gara, why rouse the stony dead, / Since at your call a living host shall circle you instead? / Long is our hunger for your voice—the hour is drawing near— / *O Dark Rose of Our Passion!* call and our *hearts shall hear.*" Robert Emmet's fiancée's name was not Shiela, but Sara Curran; see 12.500–501n.

12.645 (309:40–41). a hurling match – A rugged Irish game resembling a blend of field hockey, rugby, and lacrosse.

12.646 (309:41). Clonturk park – In Drumcondra, two miles north of Dublin on the banks of the River Tolka. Irish games such as hurling and Irish football were played there under the auspices of the Gaelic Athletic Association; see 12.58n.

12.647 (310:1). Anna Liffey – See 8.80n.

12.655–57 (310:10–12). Big strong men . . . frank use of their handkerchiefs – In Speranza's [Lady Wilde] poem "The Brothers: Henry and John Sheares," the spectators at the trial are described as "sobbing . . . And the strongest men can hardly see for weeping" (lines 10–11); see 12.538–39n. The Royal Irish Constabulary is not to be confused with the Dublin Metropolitan Police; see 6.2n.

12.658–59 (310:14). a handsome young Oxford graduate – In 1806 (three years after Robert Emmet's death) Sara Curran married Capt. Henry Sturgeon (c. 1781–1814) of the Royal

Army Staff Corps, a nephew of Lord Rock-ingham (1730–82), an English statesman and prime minister who was pro-American and pro-Irish in his sympathies. Sturgeon was Royal Military Academy, not Oxford, and he had a minor though distinguished military career in the Napoleonic Wars.

12.661–62 (310:17–18). solicited the hand . . . and was accepted on the spot – Sara Curran's marriage apparently offended Victorian and Na-tionalist sensibilities. Justin Huntly McCarthy (1830–1912), an Irish novelist and politician, noted in *Ireland Since the Union* (London, 1887): "It is curious to reflect that the three women whose names are associated with the three greatest figures of that revolutionary movement [the United Irishmen and the Rebel-lion of 1798]—the wife of Lord Edward Fitz-gerald, the wife of Wolfe Tone, and the affi-anced bride of Robert Emmet—should each have injured the memory of the great men with whose lives they were associated by consenting to accept the love and names of others" (quoted by Fritz Senn, *JJQ* 13, no. 2 [1976]: 244).

12.669–70 (310:27–28). provostmarshall, lieu-tenantcolonel Tompkin-Maxwell ffrenchmul-lan Tomlinson – A fictional name that suggests extraordinary pretension to "good family" backgrounds.

12.671–72 (310:29–30). blown . . . sepoys from the cannonmouth – Mutinous sepoys, Indian troops in the British army, were executed in this "exemplary" fashion. The punishment was inflicted in the days of the Mogul emperors (1526–1857) and was subsequently adopted by the British in India. Accounts of such atrocities were particularly prevalent during the Sepoy Mutiny (1857–58). "This was 'a frightful sight,' Dr. John Sylvester thought; and for the victims a peculiarly horrible punishment since, though hanging in itself was sufficient to make paradise very uncertain, death by mutilation after defile-ment made its attainment even less likely. The victim was lashed to a gun, the small of his back or the pit of his stomach against the muzzle, then 'smeared with the blood of someone mur-dered by a member of his race if such could be procured.' When the gun was fired the man's body was dismembered" (Christopher Hibbert, *The Great Mutiny: India 1857* [New York, 1978], pp. 124–25).

12.673 (310:31–32). a furtive tear – In Italian, *una furtiva lagrima*, a famous tenor aria in Act II, scene ii, of Donizetti's *L'elisir d'amore* (The

Elixir of Love) (1832). The wealthy young hero-ine, Adina, plays a reluctant Iseult to the timid peasant-hero Nemorino's stuttering Tristan. Ir-ritated by Nemorino's pathetic lovemaking, Adina agrees to marry a blustering soldier. Ne-morino tries to transform himself with a magical elixir of love (cheap wine), advertised as the love potion Tristan and Iseult shared. A comic tangle ensues. Just before the happy ending bestows an independent fortune and Adina's hand on Nemorino, that hero realizes that he has seen a "furtive tear" in Adina's eye, that she loves him and is unhappy at the prospect of marrying the soldier. Alone, Nemorino sings his aria. Adina returns, breaks down and admits she loves him, and, to cap the happy ending, everyone buys one more bottle of the elixir of love (Theoharis Constantine Theoharis).

12.676 (310:35). God blimey – A cockney curse: "God blame me."

12.676 (310:35). a clinker – Cockney slang for a clever, adept, or fashionable person.

12.678 (310:37). mashtub – A large tub used in brewing.

12.678 (310:38). Limehouse – A London slum, the cockney's heartland.

12.679–80 (310:40). the corporation meet-ing – See 10.1004–7 (247:13–17).

12.680 (310:40). shoneens – Irish: "would-be gentlemen."

12.683 (311:2). the Gaelic league – See 9.323n.

12.683 (311:2). the antitreating league – St. Patrick's Anti-Treating League, founded in 1902; its purpose was to promote temperance by combating the institution of "treating," by which each member of a drinking party felt it his "duty" to prove his generosity by taking his turn treating the others to drinks, thus prolong-ing drinking bouts beyond sobriety.

12.687–88 (311:7–8). she could get up . . . my Maureen Lay – Apparently from a version of "The Low-Backed Car." One version, by Sam-uel Lover, begins with the verse: "When I first saw sweet Peggy, / 'Twas on a market day. / A low-back'd car she drove, and sat / Up on a truss of hay: / But when that hay was blooming grass, / And decked with flow'rs of spring, / No flow'r was there, that could compare / To the blooming girl, I sing! / As she sat in her low-back'd car, / The man at the turnpike bar / Never ask'd for the toll, / But just rubb'd his auld poll, / And look'd after the low-back'd car!" For verse four, see 16.1886/87–88/94n. Another version, by John McCormack, substitutes "sweet Nellie" for "sweet Peggy" and "As she *lay* in her low-backed car."

12.689 (311:9). a Ballyhooly blue ribbon badge – Identifies the wearer as a member of a temperance brigade founded by the "apostle of temperance," the Reverend Theobald Mathew, in Ballyhooly, a village near Fermoy in County Cork, once notorious for its "faction-fights" (P. W. Joyce, *English*, p. 213). The phrase also recalls an Irish song: "The Ballyhooly Blue Ribbon Army": "There's a dashin' sowjer boy / And he's called his mother's joy, / And his ructions and his elegance they charm me— / He takes the chief command / In the water drinkin' band / Called the Ballyhooly Blue Ribbon Army. // With a Hey, Hi, Ho! / We'll all enlist, ye know! / His ructions and his elegance they charm me— / They don't care what they eat / If they drink their whiskey neat / In the Ballyhooly Blue Ribbon Army."

12.690 (311:10). colleen bawns – See 12.194n.

12.691 (311:12). flahoolagh – Anglicized Irish: literally, "chieftain-like"; figuratively, "plentiful."

12.692 (311:13). Ireland sober is Ireland free – This temperance slogan was coined by the Irish humorist-journalist Robert A. Wilson (pseudonym Barney Maglone, 1820–75). He produced a series of temperance "verses," apparently in a spirit of self-laceration, since his contemporaries observed that drink was his "besetting sin."

12.694 (311:15). the tune the old cow died of – This phrase commonly means unpleasant or deadening music, but in parts of Ireland and Scotland a further meaning has survived: a sermon delivered in lieu of a donation. There are several ballads and variants on this theme; a Scottish version seems appropriate here: "There was a piper had a cow / And he had nought to give her; / He took his pipe and played a spring, / And bade the cow consider. // The cow considered w' hersel' / That mirth wad never fill her: / 'Give me a pickle ait strae [a bundle of hay], / And sell your wind for siller [fodder].'"

12.694 (311:16). sky pilots – Clergymen or chaplains.

12.708 (311:30). *pro bono publico* – Latin: "for the public good."

Parody: 12.712–47 (311:34–312:32). All those who are . . . *After Lowry's lights* – Parodies the style of a newspaper's plug for a theatrical program (not dissimilar to the "paragraph" Bloom is trying to get to complement Keyes's ad).

12.712–16 (311:34–39). All of those who are interested . . . (and their name is legion) . . . recently rechristened – In the story of the Gaderene swine, Jesus meets a man possessed of an unclean spirit; "For he [Jesus] said unto him, Come out of the man, thou unclean spirit. And he [Jesus] asked him [the unclean spirit], What is thy name? and he answered, saying, My name is Legion: for we are many. . . . Now there was there nigh unto the mountains a great herd of swine feeding. And all the devils besought him, saying, Send us into the swine. . . . And forthwith Jesus gave them leave. And the unclean spirits went out, and entered into the swine: and the herd ran violently down a steep place into the sea, (they were about two thousand); and were choked in the sea" (Mark 5:8–13).

12.714 (311:37). cynanthropy – Literally, "of a dogman"; medically, a form of insanity in which the patient is convinced that he is a dog.

12.717 (311:40). Owen Garry – A semilegendary king of Leinster and contemporary of Finn MacCool's, third century A.D. In one of Patrick J. McCall's (1861–1919) versions of the Finn legends, in *The Fenian Nights' Entertainments* (see 9.1105n), Garry's daughter becomes Finn's wife.

12.722 (312:4). ranns – Irish: "verses, sayings, rhymes, songs."

12.725 (312:7–8). Little Sweet Branch – A translation of the Irish pseudonym, An Craoibhin Aoibhinn, of the poet, scholar, and translator Douglas Hyde (1860–1949), a founder (with W. B. Yeats) of the Irish Literary Society (1891), author of "The Necessity for de-Anglicising Ireland" (1892), one of the key promoters of the Gaelic League (founded in 1893), and, eventually, president of Ireland (1938–45).

12.726 (312:9) D.O.C. – Adams suggests that this is a cryptogram for "cod," a joke (p. 107n).

12.729 (312:12). Raftery – Anthony Raftery (c. 1784–1834), the blind Irish poet known as "the last of the bards." His works were rediscovered by Douglas Hyde and translated and praised by Hyde and Lady Gregory and others in the late nineteenth century. The reputation thus established was not only that of "satirical" poet but also of inspired composer of religious songs and repentant verse.

12.729 (312:12). *Donal MacConsidine – Dornhall Mac Consaidín (fl. mid–nineteenth century), a Gaelic scribe and poet who lived in County Clare in the west of Ireland.

12.734–35 (312:19–20). alliterative and isosyllabic rules of the Welsh englyn – The *englyn* is one of a group of meters, the most popular of which is the direct monorhyme *englyn*, a quatrain of thirty syllables distributed 10/6/7/7 between its lines. It has one end rhyme (which falls on the seventh or eighth syllable of the first line). The key syllables in each line are interlinked by alliteration and/or internal rhyme. The *englyn* was one of the established meters for "high poetry."

12.740–47 (312:25–32). *The curse of my curses . . . After Lowry's lights* – This "verse" is a parody of contemporary attempts to imitate classical Irish verse in English. *Lowry's lights:* the stage of Dan Lowry's Music Hall; see 10.495n.

12.751 (312:36). *a chara* – Irish: "my friend."

12.752 (312:37). not as green as he's cabbage-looking – Slang: "he's not as foolish as he looks."

12.753 (312:39). old Giltrap's – Gerty McDowell's maternal grandfather; see Nausicaa. See also 12.120n.

12.754 (312:39–40). ratepayers and corporators – "Ratepayers" were the residents of a parish who payed taxes and/or tithes; "corporators" were those enfranchised citizens in the city's wards who could vote for members of the Dublin Corporation (approximately 85,000 of Dublin's 287,000 residents were registered voters in 1903).

12.757 (313:1). Could a swim duck? – A variant of "Can a duck swim?"—in other words, an emphatic yes.

12.762–64 (313:7–9). didn't serve any notice . . . recover on the policy – Technically under British law, when an individual borrowed money, mortgaging his insurance policy as security, the mortgage was not valid unless the insurance company that issued the policy had been notified. This legal loophole was the source of considerable litigation, but attempts to void a mortgage based on the fact that the insuring company had not been notified of the mortgaging of its policy were rarely successful in the courts.

12.765 (313:11). old Shylock is landed – Shylock is the exacting Jewish moneylender in Shakespeare's *The Merchant of Venice;* to be "landed" is to be caught at one's own game.

12.773 (313:19). Bridgeman – Identity and significance unknown.

12.776–77 (313:23–24). Selling bazaar tickets . . . privileged lottery – For Bloom's "crime," see 8.184–85n.

12.778 (313:25). O, commend me to an israelite! – "Commend me to" (implying remembrance and good will) is a common turn of phrase in Shakespeare. The remark is, of course, anti-Semitic.

Parody: 12.785–99 (313:35–314:8). Let me, said he . . . me even of speech – Parodies the dialogue in sentimental-genteel nineteenth-century fiction.

12.801 (314:10). lagged – Originally, "transported as a convict"; subsequently, "arrested."

12.801–2 (314:11). the bobby, 14 A – The A Division of the Dublin Metropolitan Police had its headquarters in Kevin Street Upper, just around the corner from Bride Street in south-central Dublin.

12.802 (314:12). shebeen – Anglicized Irish for shop; slang for a shop or pub that sells liquor illegally, that is, without a license or after hours.

12.802 (314:12). Bride street – In the Liberties, the run-down section in south-central Dublin.

12.803 (314:13). shawls – Dublin slang for fisherwomen; hence, prostitutes.

12.803 (314:13). bully – A protector and exploiter of prostitutes.

12.804 (314:14–15). Joseph Manuo – One possibility for this un-French name: *Manu* is Sanskrit for the progenitor of the human race or for any person regarded as the human archetype.

12.805–6 (314:16). Adam and Eve's – See 17.757–58n.

12.807 (314:18). smugging – Toying amorously in secret (Joseph Wright, *English Dialect Dictionary* [London, 1904], vol. 5, p. 5622).

12.810 (314:21). *testament* – With a pun on "fundament"; also part of a verbal game similar to teapot (see 15.457n).

12.812 (314:24). the chapel – In Irish usage, a *chapel* is a Catholic church, a *church* is Church of Ireland.

12.816 (314:28). patch up the pot – Slang for marrying the woman a man had made pregnant.

12.819 (314:32). *Slan leat* – Irish: literally, "safe with you"; good-bye.

12.823 (314:36). Who is the long fellow running for the mayoralty – That is, who is Long John Fanning, the subsheriff, supporting? The lord mayor of Dublin was elected annually by the members of the Dublin Corporation. The subsheriff, by virtue of his duties as election supervisor, had considerable power as a "mayor-maker."

12.825 (314:39). Nannan – Joseph Nannetti; see 7.75n.

12.827–28 (314:42). William Field, M.P. – (b. 1848), a Dublin victualler, a member of Parliament from Dublin, and president and chief spokesman of the Irish Cattle Traders and Stockowners Association.

12.829 (315:1). Hairy Iopas – The poet who sings during a feast (and drinking bout) in Dido's palace at the end of Book 1 of Virgil's *Aeneid:* "Long-haired Iopas, one taught by mighty Atlas, makes the hall ring with his golden lyre. He sings of the wandering moon and the sun's toils; whence sprang human kind and the brutes, whence rain and fire; of Arcturus, the rainy Hyades and the twin Bears; why wintry suns make such haste to dip themselves in ocean, or what delay stays the slowly passing nights" (lines 740–46).

12.832–33 (315:5). sending them all to the rightabout – Slang for dismissing or turning away rudely.

12.833–34 (315:6). sheepdip for scab – "Scab" is a highly contagious skin disease suffered by sheep. The cure is immersion in a "dip" made of a solution of lime and sulfur.

12.834 (315:6–7). a hoose drench for coughing calves – "Hoose" is a cattle disease of the lungs and bronchial tubes caused by the thread or hair lungworm; a "drench" is a large quantity of fluid medicine given at one time.

12.834–35 (315:7–8). the guaranteed remedy for timber tongue – "Timber tongue," also called "wooden tongue" or "lumpy jaw," is a cattle disease, actinomycosis, caused by a fungus that encourages abnormal or tumorous growth of cells; it is similar to noninfectious foot-and-mouth disease. There was no known remedy in 1904.

12.835 (315:8). a knacker's yard – A "knacker" is one who buys worn-out horses and slaughters them for their hooves and hides and sells the flesh for dog meat. The term was derogatory, since it was associated with the popular (and well-founded) suspicion that much of what was sold as hamburger and sausage meat was in reality horse meat.

12.836–37 (315:9–10). here's my head and my heels are coming – A popular expression suggesting ill-coordinated haste or a person whose intentions are better than his performance.

12.845 (315:20). he'd have a soft hand under a hen – That is, he'd be good at stealing eggs from under a setting hen (without disturbing the hen so that she clucked a warning).

Parody: 12.846–49 (315:21–25). Ga Ga Gara . . . Klook Klook Klook – Parodies the style of a child's primer.

12.851 (315:27). to ask about it – Namely, to ask about methods of combating the threatened epidemic of foot-and-mouth disease. One normal method was to quarantine all the cattle of an infected area and then slaughter and bury them all. Another method was to quarantine all cattle but to destroy only the diseased. The timing of this "epidemic" and the discussion in Parliament are, of course, fictional. See 2.321–22n.

12.854 (315:31). by the mailboat – See 1.83–84n.

12.858–59 (316:36–37). the commissioner of police . . . in the park – See 7.75n.

12.859 (315:38). *The Sluagh na h-Eireann* – Irish: "the Army of Ireland"; an active patriotic society that complained to Parliament through Nannetti, 16 June 1904, that it was not allowed by the commissioners of police to play Gaelic games in Phoenix Park. The complaint noted that polo (presumably an English and foreign sport) was allowed.

Parody: 12.860–79 (315:39–316:19). Mr Cowe Conacre . . . (The house rises. Cheers.) – Parodies the minutes of proceedings of the House of Commons.

12.860 (315:39). Mr Cowe Conacre (Multifarnham. Nat) – The Conacre System (*con*, Irish: "common") was one method of exploiting the land and the poor in nineteenth-century Ireland (before the land reforms of the late nineteenth and early twentieth centuries). Technically, it referred to the practice of a wealthier tenant farmer's renting small patches of land (a half or a quarter of an acre) for an exorbitant price to his poorer neighbors. The peasants used these small patches to grow potatoes as a food crop, since they often could not grow both food crops and cash crops to pay the rent on their own small holdings. The Conacre System came to mean the whole exploitative system of absentee landlordism and the hierarchy of middlemen, sometimes as many as six or eight, who profited by renting and then subletting land, each in turn. Multifarnham, a village seven and a half miles northwest of Mullingar, is in the heart of the cattle country of County Westmeath; "Nat" is short for the (Irish) Nationalist party. County Westmeath had two representatives in Parliament, but needless to say, neither was from the village of Multifarnham.

12.861 (315:40). Shillelagh – *Síol Éalaigh*, Irish: "the descendants of Ealach [a village in County Wicklow]"; in reality County Wicklow had two representatives in Parliament. Shillelagh is famous for its oak trees; hence the use of its name for the Irish cudgel.

12.862–64 (315:42–316:2). orders that these animals . . . pathological condition – The conventional ,technique of preventing the spread of foot-and-mouth disease was to slaughter all the cattle in an infected district, regardless of the condition of individual animals.

12.865 (316:3). Mr Allfours (Tamoshant. Con.) – In addition to the pun, "Allfours" suggests the Right Honorable Arthur James Balfour, afterwards Earl Balfour (1848–1930), a Scot, first lord of the Treasury, leader of the House of Commons, and Conservative prime minister in 1904. He was in the Conservative cabinet as chief secretary for Ireland (1887–91), and through his commitment to the policy of "coercion" (instant and severe police measures against any expression of Irish Nationalist sentiment), he earned among the Irish the nickname Bloody Balfour. When the English imposed an embargo on Irish cattle in 1912 during an epidemic of foot-and-mouth disease, Balfour had temporarily retired from public life. "Tamoshanter" is not a place but the name of a Scottish wool cap; "Con", short for Conservative, is appropriate not only with respect to Balfour but also because the Irish assumed that Scots were Protestant-Conservative. In addition, Tam o' Shanter is the hero and title of a poem by Robert Burns; the hero is a drunken farmer who inadvertently interrupts a witch coven. The witches pursue him but are thwarted because they cannot follow him when he crosses running water; one of the witches manages, however, to snatch the tail off his horse.

12.869 (316:8). *Mr Orelli O'Reilly (Montenotte. Nat) – Myles George O'Reilly ("the O'Reilly," b. 1830) of County Cork; Montenotte is a suburb of the city of Cork, though O'Reilly was not an M.P., but only a pillar of the "old order." "Oh really, O'Reilly?" is a slangy expression of skepticism.

12.874 (316:13). Mitchelstown telegram – In September 1887, one of Parnell's associates, John Dillon (1851–1927), attempted to make a speech at Mitchelstown in County Cork. A riot erupted when the police tried to force an official recorder through the crowd in order to gather evidence for the prosecution of Dillon under the Act of Coercion; three men were killed by rifle fire from the police barracks (see 9.133n). So solid was Conservative sentiment for coercion in Parliament that Balfour, then chief secretary for Ireland (12.865n) could answer angry opposition questions in the House of Commons merely by quoting the cursory police report (a telegram). Gladstone subsequently used the slogan "Remember Mitchelstown" to rally the opposition.

12.874–75 (316:13–14). inspired the policy of gentlemen on the treasury bench – That is, has Balfour's commitment to the policy of coercion (violent police action) dictated a policy of economic suppression for Ireland (in this case an arbitrary embargo on Irish cattle)? In 1904 Balfour was first lord of the Treasury as well as prime minister.

12.876 (316:15). I must have notice of that question – The prime minister can refuse to answer a question in the House of Commons if he has not previously mentioned the subject and if he has not been given time to do his homework.

12.877 (316:16). Mr Staylewit (Buncombe. Ind) – Buncombe is a county in North Carolina; thanks to Felix Walker, a representative from that county in the Sixteenth Congress who felt bound to "make a speech for Buncombe," buncombe came to mean speechmaking or talk that is insincere or only for effect. "Ind" is short for Independent.

12.877 (316:16). Don't hesitate to shoot – See 9.133n.

12.880 (316:20–21). the man . . . that made the Gaelic sports revival – Michael Cusack; see 12.58n.

12.881 (316:21–22). The man that got away James Stephens – There is considerable evidence that Cusack was a Fenian, but there is no evidence that he was involved in Stephens's escape; the Fenian principals in that escape seem to have been John Devoy and Col. Thomas Kelley; see 3.241n.

12.881–82 (316:22–23). The champion of all Ireland . . . sixteen pound shot – The late-nineteenth-century record in Ireland was held by Denis Horgan: 46 feet 5½ inches. Cusack the Citizen, active from 1875 to 1885, never put the shot over 40 feet. In effect, Horgan was the great Irish athlete of his time; Cusack was the Irish spokesman for athletics.

12.884 (316:24). *Na bacleis* – Irish: "Don't bother about it."

12.889 (316:31). shoneen – See 12.680n.

12.890 (316:32). hurley – See 12.645n.

12.890 (316:32). putting the stone – Similar to putting the shot, except that expertise was established not merely by the greatest distance achieved with stones of the same weight, but by a series of distances achieved with stones of different weights. The Citizen's prowess with the shot and the stone mark him as Polyphemus, who breaks off a hilltop and heaves it after Odysseus's fleeing ship, almost sinking it (9:481ff.).

12.890 (316:33). racy of the soil – That is, characteristic of the people of a country (usually of Ireland).

12.891 (316:33). a nation once again – The title of a song by Thomas Osborne Davis (1814–45), an Irish poet and patriot. First verse: "When boyhood's fire was in my blood / I read of ancient freemen, / For Greece and Rome who bravely stood, / Three hundred men and three men, / And then I prayed I yet might see / Our fetters rent in twain, / And Ireland, long a province, be / A nation once again!"

Parody: 12.897–938 (316:40–318:5). A most interesting discussion . . . P. Fay, T. Quirke, etc., etc. – Parodies the minutes of a meeting written up as a disguised advertisement of a social or political organization (intended for insertion in the columns of a newspaper).

12.897–98 (316:41). *Brian O'Ciarnian's . . . Bretaine Bheag* – Irish: "Barney O'Kiernan's in Little Britain (i.e., Brittany) Street."

12.898–99 (316:42). *Sluagh na h-Eireann* – See 12.859n.

12.910 (317:14). Finn MacCool – (d. c. 284), Irish poet, warrior, and chieftain, the leader of the Fianna (from which the Fenians derived their name). He is a semilegendary figure, the central presence in the Ossian or Finn legends.

12.916–17 (317:21–22). Thomas Osborn Davis . . . *A nation once again* – See 12.891n. Davis's *Poems* (1846) were collected and edited by Charles Gavan Duffy, who praised them as "evergreen" in his introductory note.

12.919 (317:25). Caruso-Garibaldi – Enrico Caruso (1874–1921), the Italian dramatic tenor whose name was by 1910 a household word. He first attracted attention in Naples in 1896; after a series of tours, including London (1903), he went to New York (1904), where he was destined to become the chief attraction of the Metropolitan Opera Company. For Garibaldi, see 8.461n.

12.927–28 (317:34–35). the very rev. William Delany, S. J., L. L. D. – A Jesuit educator whose career was described as an "epoch in the history of Irish Catholic higher education" because he upgraded both academic and athletic performance as rector of Tullabeg College (1872–83). From 1883 to 1909 he was rector and subsequently president of University College in Dublin. From 1909 to 1912 he was provincial of the Jesuit order in Ireland.

12.928 (317:35). the rt rev. Gerald Molloy, D. D. – (1834–1906), theologian and educator, rector of the Catholic University of Ireland in Dublin (1883–1906).

12.928–29 (317:35–36). the rev. P. J. Kavanagh, C. S. Sp. – Patrick Fidelis Kavanagh (1834–1916), an Irish priest, poet, and historian known for his ability as an orator and for his *History of the Rebellion of 1798. C. S. Sp:* Congregation of the Holy Spirit; but Father Kavanagh was in actuality an O. F. M., a member of the Order of Friars Minor (Franciscans).

12.929 (317:36). the rev. T. Waters, C. C. – The Reverend Thomas Waters, curate-in-charge (1904), St. John the Baptist Roman Catholic Church, 35 Newtown Avenue, Blackrock.

12.929 (317:36–37). the rev. John M. Ivers, P. P. – The Reverend J. Michael Ivers was not parish priest (1904) but curate-in-charge, St. Paul's Roman Catholic Church, Arran Quay, Dublin.

12.929–30 (317:37). the rev. P. J. Cleary, O. S. F. – The Very Reverend P. J. Cleary, Order of St. Francis, vicar of the Franciscan church popularly known as Adam and Eve's, Merchant's Quay, Dublin.

12.930 (317:37–38). the rev. L. J. Hickey, O. P. – The Very Reverend Louis J. Hickey, Order of Friars Preachers, provincial of St. Saviour's Dominican Priory, Dominick Street Lower, Dublin.

12.930–31 (317:38). the very rev. Fr. Nicholas, O. S. F. C. – Friar Nicholas, Order of St. Francis Capuchin, vicar of the Franciscan Capuchin Monastery, St. Mary of the Angels, Church Street, Dublin.

12.931 (317:39). the very rev. B. Gorman, O. D. C. – Bernard Gorman, Order of Carmelites Discalced (i.e., barefooted), provincial of Discalced Carmelites Friary in Clarendon Street, Dublin.

12.931–32 (317:39). the rev. T. Maher, S. J. – A member of the Community of the Jesuit Church of St. Francis Xavier (Father Conmee's church) in Upper Gardiner Street, Dublin.

12.932 (317:40). the very rev. James Murphy, S. J. – Provincial of the Jesuit Church of St. Francis Xavier.

12.932–33 (317:40). the rev. John Lavery, V. F. – Vicar Forane (a priest appointed by a bishop to exercise a limited jurisdiction in a particular town or parish). The Reverend Lavery was a member of the Fathers of the Congregation of the Mission (C.M.), St. Peter's Presbytery, Phibsborough (on the western outskirts of Dublin).

12.933 (317:41). the very rev. William Doherty, D. D. – Curate-in-charge, St. Mary's Procathedral of the Immaculate Conception, Marlborough Street, Dublin.

12.933 (317:41–42). the rev. Peter Fagan, O. M. – A Marist father (Fathers of the Society of Mary, usually S.M.), resident at the Catholic University School in Upper Leeson Street.

12.934 (317:42). the rev. T. B. Brangan, O. S. A. – Thomas Brangan, Order of St. Augustine, a member of the community of Augustinian Friars, Augustinian Friary Chapel of St. Augustine and St. John, John Street West, Dublin.

12.934 (317:42). the rev. J. Flavin, C. C. – St. Mary's Procathedral of the Immaculate Conception, Marlborough Street, Dublin.

12.934–35 (318:1). the rev. M. A. Hackett, C. C. – The Reverend Martin Hacket was parish priest, St. Margaret's Roman Catholic Church, Finglas (a parish and village four miles north of the center of Dublin).

12.935 (318:1). the rev. W. Hurley, C. C. – Walter Hurley, St. James's Roman Catholic Church, James Street, Dublin.

12.935–36 (318:1–2). the rt rev. Mgr. M'Manus, V. G. – Monsignor Myles M'Manus, vicar general, canon, and parish priest, St. Catherine's Roman Catholic Church, Meath Street, Dublin.

12.936 (318:2). the rev. B. R. Slattery, O. M. I. – No B. R. Slattery is listed in the *Irish Catholic Directory* for 1904 as a member of the Order of Mary Immaculate or otherwise; hence, this seems to be either a coinage or an in-joke. Shari and Bernard Benstock (*Who's He When He's at Home: A James Joyce Directory* [Urbana, Ill., 1980], p. 154) suggest "possibly Rev. J. D. Slattery of St. Saviour's, Dublin." Another possible ringer: Robert Vincent Slattery, F.R.C.S.I. (Fellow of the Royal College of Surgeons in Ireland), educated at Clongowes Wood College and Catholic University Medical School, Dublin; Assistant Surgeon, Richmond Lunatic Asylum, Dublin.

12.936 (318:3). the very rev. M. D. Scally, P. P. – Michael D. Scally, parish priest, St. Nicholas's Roman Catholic Church, Francis Street in Dublin.

12.936–37 (318:3). the rev. F. T. Purcell, O. P. – *Thom's* 1904 lists a Thomas F. Purcell, Order of Friars Preachers, as a member of the Community of St. Saviour's Dominican Priory in Dominick Street Lower, Dublin.

12.937 (318:4). the very rev. Timothy canon Gorman, P. P. – SS. Michael and John's Roman Catholic Church, Exchange Street, Dublin.

12.937–38 (318:4–5). the rev. J. Flanagan, C. C. – John Flanagan, C. C., St. Mary's Pro-cathedral of the Immaculate Conception, Marlborough Street, Dublin.

12.938 (318:5). P. Fay – Of P. A. Fay & Sons, cattle salesmen, 36 Smithfield, Dublin.

12.938 (318:5). T. Quirke – Thomas G. Quirk, solicitor, 15 Frederick Street, Dublin; residence, Dalkey.

12.939 (318:7). Keogh-Bennett – See 10.1133–34n.

12.948 (318:16). and he swatting all the time – That is, Keogh was training as hard as he possibly could.

12.949 (318:17). The traitor's son – William Keogh, one of the Catholic Defence leaders in the 1850s, "honored, lauded by both lay and ecclesiastic sponsors" (and, ironically, "triumphantly contrasted with the base misleaders of Young Ireland of the decade before"), betrayed his supporters by accepting the solicitor-generalship of Ireland. Because of the vehemence of his protestations, Keogh was called "So-help-me-God Keogh." His name later became synonymous with betrayal and "rottenness" (Seumas MacManus, *The Story of the Irish Race* [New York, 1967], p. 611).

12.955 (318:23–24). Heenan and Sayers – See 10.831–32n.

12.956 (318:24–25). the father and mother of a beating – An Irish colloquialism for a severe beating; see P. W. Joyce, *English*, p. 198.

12.957 (318:25). kipper – A small person, a child.

12.958 (318:27). Queensberry rules – Namely: boxing with gloves; three-minute rounds (instead of rounds that ended only when there was a knockdown); no hugging or wrestling, etc. The rules, drawn up in 1865, were named for the English patron of boxing who encouraged their adoption, John Sholto Douglas, marquess of Queensberry (1844–1900).

Parody: 12.960–87 (318:29–319:19). It was a historic . . . mobbed him with delight – Parodies sports journalism.

12.972 (319:1). the bout – That is, the round.

12.976 (319:6). Eblanite – See 12.83n.

12.983 (319:15). Portobello – See 8.801–2n.

12.984 (319:16–17). Ole Pfotts Wettstein – A lawyer, Dr. Georg Wettstein, Norwegian vice-consul in Zurich, earned Joyce's enmity during a minor, but protracted litigation; see Ellmann, pp. 440, 452.

12.985 (319:17). Santry – A village and parish, three and a half miles north of Dublin center.

12.993 (319:25). the bright particular star – In Shakespeare's *All's Well that Ends Well*, Helena contemplates her love for Bertram, count of Rousillon, and their relative positions on the social scale: "'Twere all one / That I should love a bright particular star / And think to wed it, he is so above me" (I.i.96–98).

12.996 (319:28). says I to myself, says I – In Act I of Gilbert and Sullivan's *Iolanthe; or, The Peer and the Peri* (1882), the lord chancellor's song begins: "When I went to the bar as a very young man, / (Said I to myself, said I) / I'll work on a new and original plan / (Said I to myself, said I) / I'll never assume that a rogue or a thief / Is a gentleman worthy implicit belief, / Because his attorney has sent me a brief / (Said I to myself, said I)."

12.997–98 (319:30). the tootle on the flute – From the song "Phil the Fluter's Ball," by Percy French. Chorus: "With a tootle of the flute / And a twiddle of the fiddle—oh / Dancin' up the middle like a herrin' on the griddle— / Up! down! hands around! crossin' to the wall, / Oh, hadn't we the gaiety at Phil the Fluter's ball."

12.998–99 (319:30–32). Dirty Dan the dodger's . . . fight the Boers – The fictional Boylan's father, Daniel Boylan; a "dodger" is a shirker or malingerer; Island Bridge is an area south of the Liffey on the western outskirts of Dublin. The double-dealing in horses credited to him was a common way of exploiting the weaknesses of army procurement practices.

12.1000 (319:33). the poor and water rate – Two of the several overlapping taxes that collectively made up the "property taxes" in Dublin.

12.1002 (319:36). *Caddareesh – From the Irish *Cad arís:* "What, again?"

Parody: 12.1003–10 (319:37–320:3). Pride of Calpe's . . . line of Lambert – Parodies nineteenth-century reworkings of medieval romance.

12.1003 (319:37). Calpe's rocky mount – In Greek mythology, Calpe was one of the Pillars of Hercules, now the Rock of Gibraltar.

12.1005 (319:39). Alameda – In general, any large pleasure ground or park bordered with or in a grove of poplar trees. There is such a park in Gibraltar.

12.1023 (320:17). Stubb's – Stubb's *Weekly Gazette*, published by Stubb's Mercantile Offices, College Street, Dublin. Stubb's advertised itself as "a complete organization for the protection of Bankers, Merchants, Traders, and others against risk and fraud in their various commercial transactions." Stubb's offered a debt-recovery service, and its *Gazette* included "a weekly supplement giving lists of Creditors"

(i.e., very poor credit risks) (*Thom's* 1904, adv. p. 45).

12.1024 (320:17). flash toffs – Slang for ostentatiously showy would-be gentlemen.

12.1026 (320:20). Cummins of Francis street – M. Cummins, pawnbroker, had several branches in Dublin, including one in a slum area at 125 Francis Street in south-central Dublin.

12.1028 (320:22). pop – Slang for hock or pawn.

12.1029 (320:23–24). come home by weeping cross – Penances were done under "weeping cross"; thus, to regret a course of conduct.

12.1033 (320:28). right go wrong – Immediately, without hesitating to consider the consequences.

12.1039 (320:34). so help you Jimmy Johnson – After the Reverend James Johnson (fl. 1870–1900), a Scots Presbyterian who styled himself "the apostle of Truth" and produced a series of guides for Christian living: *Learning to Float; or, Saved through Faith* (Stirling, Scotland, 1890); *Learning to Fly; or, The Assurance of Faith* (Stirling, 1890); *Learning to Run in the Way of Holiness* (Stirling, 1890); *Learning to Walk in the Paths of Righteousness* (Stirling, 1890).

12.1041–42 (320:37–38). Whatever statement . . . evidence against you – The formula an arresting or investigating officer uses to remind a suspect of his legal rights.

12.1043 (320:40). *compos mentis* – Legal Latin: "sane in mind."

12.1052–53 (321:9). a half and half – Neither man nor woman.

12.1058 (321:14). A pishogue – Anglicized Irish: "charm or spell"; hence, one who is bewitched.

12.1064 (321:20–21). bringing down the rain – That is, it would make the heavens weep to see him.

12.1064 (321:21). cockahoop – Stuck up, nose in the air; after the practice of removing the cock (spigot) from a barrel and placing it on the hoop (top) in order to drain the barrel.

12.1065 (321:22). pewopener – One who directs parishioners to their seats in church; an usher.

12.1066 (321:23–24). Smashall Sweeney's moustaches – Sweeney was a pantomime figure who sported handlebar moustaches and played the comic Irishman as bull in a china shop.

12.1066–67 (321:24). signior Brini – Breen's father's cousin's name Italianized.

12.1067 (321:24). Summerhill – Continues Great Britain (now Parnell) Street to the east-northeast into a district of run-down houses and tenements.

12.1067 (321:25). *papal Zouave to the Holy Father – Early in 1860 a French general in exile, C. L. L. J. de Lamoricière (1806–65), was appointed commander of the papal troops by Pius IX. He recruited devout young Catholics as papal Zouaves to militarily restore the Pope's temporal power. However, Lamoricière's forces were defeated, and he surrendered in September 1860 and retired to France. The Zouaves continued for another decade to try, without much success, to help the pope resist the Italian occupation of Rome. The papal Zouaves affected flashy costumes and swaggering behavior after the French-recruited native Algerian infantry called Zouaves (1830–39).

12.1068 (321:26). Moss street – In 1904, a street of tenements and ruins just south of the Liffey in east-central Dublin.

12.1069 (321:26–27). two pair back and passages – That is, two rooms at the back (of a tenement); "passages" suggests that the rooms opened on a small court or airshaft.

12.1072 (321:31–32). Sadgrove v. Hole – Hole was the manager of a London company that wanted to make additions to its buildings. He hired an architect who in turn hired Sadgrove, a "quantities surveyor," to determine the costs of building; Sadgrove sent his estimates to seven builders. When Hole heard what the figures were, he thought them incorrect and sent postcards to two of the builders informing them that the "quantities were entirely wrong." Sadgrove's name was not mentioned in the postcards, but he brought an action, charging that the cards defamed him as a surveyor. The case turned on whether the cards were "publication" or "privileged communication" (a communica-

tion which by definition is not subject to charges of slander or libel). The trial judge ruled that the communication was not privileged, and the jury found for Sadgrove. On appeal, however, the judgment was reversed. The judges held that the communication to the builders *was* privileged since the builders had a vital interest in the communication. They also held that the postcards did not constitute "publication" even though the statements were "defamatory" because Sadgrove's name was not mentioned; therefore, no one except the "privileged" builders would be aware that the statements applied to Sadgrove. The judges also held that there was no malice on Hole's part (if malice could be proved, then the defamatory statements would constitute libel even if not "published") (*The Law Reports: King's Bench Division*, 2 K.B. 1 [1901]).

12.1074 (321:33). Six and eightpence, please – Eric Partridge cites this sum as "The usual Fee given to carry back the Body of the Executed Malefactor to give it Christian Burial" (from the seventeenth century) and, from the mid–eighteenth century, "A solicitor or attorney . . . because this was the usual fee" (*A Dictionary of Slang and Unconventional English* [London, 1937], p. 773).

12.1084–93 (322:3–13). that Canada swindle case . . . stuck for two quid – See 7.383n.

12.1086 (322:5). the bottlenosed fraternity – An anti-Semitic expression.

12.1088–89 (322:8–9). Do you see any green in the white of my eye? – That is, Do you regard me as gullible?

12.1089 (322:9). barney – Slang for foolery, humbug, cheat.

12.1090 (322:10). skivvies – See 1.138n.

12.1090 (322:10). badhachs – Anglicized Irish: "louts, churls, bumpkins."

12.1090 (322:10). county Meath – The county just north of County Dublin.

12.1095 (322:15). Recorder – Sir Frederick Falkiner; see 7.698–99n. The case was not heard in Falkiner's court but in the Southern Divisional Police Court before Earnest Godwin Swifte, divisional police magistrate.

12.1100 (322:21). Reuben J – Reuben J. Dodd.

12.1102 (322:23–24). Butt bridge – See 7.642n.

Parody:12.1111–40 (322:34–323:28). And whereas on the sixteenth . . . was a malefactor – Combines parodies of trial records and "high-classical" Irish legend.

12.1111 (322:34–35). the month of the oxeyed goddess – "Ox-eyed goddess" is a Homeric epithet for Juno; therefore, June.

12.1112 (322:35–36). the feast day of the Holy and Undivided Trinity – Sunday, 29 May 1904.

12.1113 (322:36–37). the virgin moon . . . first quarter – See 8.245n.

12.1115 (322:39). master Courtenay – Col. Arthur H. Courtenay (b. 1852), soldier and barrister, master of the High Court of Justice in Ireland, King's Bench Division, in 1904.

12.1116 (322:40). master Justice Andrews – William Drennan Andrews (1832–1924), judge of the Probate and Matrimonial Bench of the King's Bench Division in 1904.

12.1119 (323:2). Jacob Halliday – Grocer, tea, wine, and spirit merchant, 38A Main Street in Blackrock.

12.1120 (323:3). Livingstone – Apart from the context, identity and significance unknown.

12.1121 (323:4). the solemn court of Green street – See 12.64–65n.

12.1122–23 (323:6). the law of the brehons – The legal system of ancient Ireland; "brehons" were judges or lawyers.

12.1124–25 (323:9). the high sinhedrim – Or sanhedrin, the ancient Jewish high court of justice and supreme council in Jerusalem.

12.1125 (323:9). the twelve tribes of Iar – After the twelve tribes of Israel and the twelve persons on a jury. *Iar* means west or remote; hence, Ireland. Iar was also one of the three sons of Mileadh and is regarded as the legendary Milesian ancestor of the royal clans of Ireland. The "tribes" listed below suggest individual figures from Irish history and legend, but many of the names are common enough to be tribal.

12.1126 (323:10). Patrick – Among the host of

Irish Patricks there is always St. Patrick, one of the three patron saints of Ireland.

12.1126 (323:10). Hugh – One of the many Hughs in Irish legend was Hugh MacAnimire, a king (572–98) who summoned the first national assembly after the decline of Tara.

12.1126 (323:11). Owen – Or Eoghan: one was a second-century king of Munster who was defeated by Conn of the Hundred Battles; another was an Irish-born king of Scotland who invaded Ireland in the fourth century; and there was also a St. Eoghan (d. 618).

12.1127 (323:11). Conn – There were several, but the principal one was Conn of the Hundred Battles; see 12.176–77n.

12.1127 (323:12). Oscar – The son of Oisin and in legend one of the noblest of the third-century Fianna. He is the hero of the love story of Oscar and Aideen.

12.1127 (323:12). Fergus – The most famous of the Ferguses was Fergus Mac Roi, a legendary hero-king who became a druid poet and who was Cuchulin's "friend and master" (see 12.176n). It was Fergus who mistakenly led the legendary Deirdre to her death; see Yeats's play *Deirdre* (1907). See also 1.239–41n.

12.1128 (323:12). Finn – See 12.910n.

12.1128 (323:13). Dermot – See 2.393–94n.

12.1128 (323:13). Cormac – See 8.663–66n.

12.1129 (323:14). Kevin – St. Kevin of Glendalough (d. 618), one of the most famous of the Irish missionary saints.

12.1129 (323:14). Caolte – Caolte Mac Ronain, a legendary warrior-poet of the Fianna who lived to be over three hundred years old and who, at the end of his life, held a mystical dialogue with St. Patrick.

12.1129 (323:15). Ossian – Or Oisin, son of the legendary hero Finn MacCool, was the great poet of the Fianna. For Ossian's meeting with St. Patrick, see 9.578n.

12.1139 (323:26–27). ne bail ne mainprise – Middle English legal phrase for the refusal to grant bail; "mainprise" describes an individual who accepts the responsibility for a released prisoner's appearance in court.

12.1146 (323:34–35). do the devil – In legal slang, a "devil" is an unpaid junior counsel who helps to prepare a case; hence, to "do the devil" is to do hack work.

12.1151 (323:40). no more strangers in our house – See 9.36–37n and 7.87n.

12.1157 (324:4–5). the adultress and her paramour – Devorgilla and Dermot MacMurrough; see 2.393–94n.

12.1157–58 (324:5). the Saxon robbers – The phrase has the proper Celtic flourish (see 12.1296–98n), but the robbers were the Anglo-Norman overlords of an England they had conquered a hundred years before by defeating the Saxons at Hastings in 1066.

12.1159 (324:6). Decree *nisi* – In law, a decree that will take permanent effect at a specified time unless cause is shown why it should not or unless it is changed by further court proceedings.

12.1165 (324:13–14). the *Police Gazette* – The *National Police Gazette*, a New York weekly newspaper founded in 1846. Its heyday as the workingman's weekly ration of cheesecake, muckraking, high-society scandal, and sports (particularly boxing) began in 1879 when the paper came under the control of an Irish immigrant, Richard Kyle Fox (d. 1922). Brutal stories of the sort Alf Bergan reads (12.1321ff. [328.27ff.]) were typical of the paper's coverage. The *Gazette* is generally regarded as an important precursor of yellow journalism and the daily tabloid press in the 1890s.

12.1170–71 (324:18–20). Norman W. Tupper . . . officer Taylor – Apart from the context, the identity and significance of Mr. and Mrs. Tupper and Officer Taylor are unknown. For "Tupper" see "tup," 11.706–7n.

12.1172 (324:21). *fancyman – A sweetheart or a man who lives on the income of a prostitute.

12.1173 (324:21). tickles – Slang for erogenous zones.

12.1174 (324:23). the trick of the loop – A carnival game in which contestants try to win prizes by pitching small wooden hoops at a group of upright stakes.

12.1175 (324:24). *jakers, Jenny – Dodging the curse *Jesus, Jenny;* "jake" or "jakers" is also slang for "everything is all right, in order, perfect."

12.1176 (324:25). There's hair – Zack Bowen (*Musical Allusions in the Works of James Joyce* [Albany, N.Y., 1974], p. 220) cites this as "a popular music hall song" in which the singer's hair is "admired by girl friends, the Prince of Wales, and finally by an old orangutan in the zoo, each remarking 'there's hair!' "

12.1181 (324:30). tinkers – Literally, "tin-smiths," but "tinker" is also slang for Gypsy because tinkers, like Gypsies, were notorious for indigence, for cunning and thievery, and for a shiftless, nomadic way of life.

Parody: 12.1183–89 (324:32–40). O'Nolan, clad in . . . of the seadivided Gael – Continues the parody of medieval romance and "high-classical" Irish legendry.

12.1186 (324:36). the tholsel – See 10.930–31n.

12.1189 (324:39–40). the seadivided Gael – Since the Gaels (or Celts) were supposed to have invaded Ireland, Scotland, Wales, Brittany, and Cornwall from northern Spain, they were "seadivided." The Celtic or Gaelic languages as a group include, in addition to Irish, Welsh, Breton (Armoric), Scots, Cornish, and Manx.

12.1191 (324:42). Sassenachs – Irish: "Saxons."

12.1192 (325:1). doing the toff – Acting or speaking in a manner associated with fashionable and sophisticated gentlemen.

12.1193–94 (325:2–3). the Nelson policy . . . to the telescope – The English Admiral Horatio, Viscount Nelson (1758–1805), lost the sight of his right eye during the invasion of Corsica (1793). On 2 April 1801 an English fleet under Admiral Sir Hyde Parker attacked the Danish fleet at Copenhagen; early in the day Nelson, a vice-admiral in the fleet, was ordered to withdraw. Robert Southey, in his *Life of Nelson* (London, 1813), chapter 7, records the story of Nelson's refusal: "Nelson said, 'I have only one eye—I have a right to be blind sometimes':—and then, putting the glass to his blind eye . . . he exclaimed, 'I really do not see the signal!' " Nelson's insubordination led to a brilliant naval victory.

12.1194–95 (325:3–4). drawing up a bill of attainder to impeach a nation – One of the original policies of Arthur Griffith's Sinn Fein was to publish such a bill in order to impeach England in the court of "world opinion."

12.1198 (325:9). thicklugged – Thick-eared.

12.1205 (325:16–17). *cabinet d'aisance* – French: "water closet."

12.1207 (325:19). Full many a flower is born to blush unseen – From Thomas Gray's (1716–71) "Elegy Written in a Country Churchyard" (1742–50, 1751): "Full many a gem of purest ray serene / The dark unfathom'd caves of ocean bear; / Full many a flower is born to blush unseen, / And waste its sweetness on the desert air" (lines 53–56).

12.1209 (325:21). *Conspuez les anglais! Perfide Albion! – French: "Scorn the English! Perfidious England!" The latter phrase has been attributed to many irritated Frenchmen, including Napoleon on the occasion of his exile to St. Helena.

Parody: 12.1210–14 (325:22–26). He said and then . . . the deathless gods – Continues the parody of medieval romance and "high-classical" Irish legendry.

12.1211 (325:23). medher – Irish for a quadrangular one-piece wooden cup.

12.1211–12 (325:24). *Lamh Dearg Abu* – Irish: "Red Hand to Victory." The Red Hand is the heraldic symbol of Ulster and the O'Neills; it is also the symbol on the label of Allsop's bottled ale.

12.1213 (325:25). rulers of the waves – An allusion to England's preoccupation with and boast of its naval supremacy in the nineteenth and early twentieth centuries. See 1.574n and 12.1329n.

12.1213–14 (325:25–26). who sit on thrones of alabaster silent as the deathless gods – Source unknown.

12.1216 (325:28). a tanner – Slang for a sixpence.

12.1217 (325:29). Gold cup – See 5.532n.

12.1219–20 (325:32). And the rest nowhere – Fritz Senn quotes the *Annals of Sporting* 2:271;

"Captain Dennis Kelly at Epsom, May 3, 1769, after his horse had outdistanced the field: 'Eclipse first, the rest nowhere' " (*JJQ* 19, no. 2 [1982]: 166). Eclipse's reputation as an unbeatable horse (1769–70) led to the establishment of the Eclipse Stakes in 1884; see 15.2944–45n.

12.1221 (325:33). Bass's mare – Sceptre, a colt (not a mare) finished third behind Throwaway and Zinfandel; William Arthur Hamar Bass (b. 1879), English sportsman.

12.1225 (325:37). Lord Howard de Walden's – Thomas Evelyn Eelis (b. 1880), the eighth baron, divided his time between the army and horse racing.

12.1227 (325:39). takes the biscuit – Proverbial since 1610, well before "it takes the cake" (Eric Partridge, *A Dictionary of Slang and Unconventional English* [London, 1937], p. 1453).

12.1227–28 (325:40). Frailty, thy name is Sceptre – after Hamlet's line about his mother's inconstancy: "Frailty, thy name is woman!" (I.ii.146).

12.1230 (325:42). on the nod – On credit or for nothing.

12.1231 (326:1–2). *Old Mother Hubbard went to the cupboard – The first line of "Old Mother Hubbard," a fourteen-stanza nursery rhyme recorded or composed (c. 1804) by Sarah Catherine Martin (1768–1826); the first stanza continues: "Went to the cupboard, / To fetch her poor dog a bone; / But when she came there / The cupboard was bare / And so the poor dog had none."

12.1233 (326:4). pecker – Slang for courage, spirit.

12.1234 (326:5). dog – Slang for an inferior or broken-down racehorse.

12.1237–38 (326:8–9). the mote in others' . . . beam in their own – In Matthew 7:3, as Jesus brings the Sermon on the Mount to a close, he says, "And why beholdest thou the mote that is in thy brother's eye, but considerest not the beam that is in thine own eye?"

12.1239 (326:10). *Raimeis* – Irish: literally, "romance"; figuratively, "nonsense." It was made into a household word for cant by D. P. Moran in *The Leader* (Dublin, established

1900), a weekly newspaper dedicated to fighting pretense and humbug, which, from Moran's point of view, were everywhere on the Irish scene. See F. S. L. Lyons, *Culture and Anarchy in Ireland 1890–1939* (Oxford, 1979), pp. 58ff.

12.1240–41 (326:12–13). our missing twenty millions . . . instead of four – The most dramatic reduction in the population of Ireland occurred during the Great Famine of the 1840s as the result of starvation, disease, and emigration. The population of Ireland in 1841 was 8,196,000; by 1851 it had fallen to 6,466,000; and it continued to decline through the rest of the century until the population in 1901 was 4,459,000. If, however, population had continued to grow as it had in the two decades 1821 (6,800,000) to 1841 (8,196,000), the population at the end of the century would have been approximately 18,000,000. The U.S. census in 1900 estimated that approximately 4,000,000 Irish had immigrated to the United States in the course of the nineteenth century.

12.1241 (326:13). our lost tribes – In Jewish tradition, the ten tribes of Israel lost or dispersed in the course of the Assyrian conquests of Israel in the eighth century B.C. and again in the sixth century B.C. The Assyrians followed the policy of deporting the principal inhabitants of conquered districts, thus producing the "Babylonian captivity" of the Jews. The loss of ten of the original twelve tribes was regarded as Jehovah's punishment of his "chosen people" (Israel) because they were disobedient to his will.

12.1242–43 (326:14–15). our wool that was . . . time of Juvenal – The Roman poet and satirist Juvenal (c. 60–c. 140 A.D.). The Citizen's remark is something of an overstatement; there is little hard evidence about trade between Ireland and Rome, though historians assume that after the Roman conquest of England "there must have been" a significant increase of commerce, and Tacitus (c. 55–120 A.D.) in 100 A.D. remarks that Irish harbors "through commerce and merchants" were better known than English harbors. Trade and manufacturing in wool appear to have been of some importance in ancient Ireland, but the continental reputation of Irish woolens was not established until the sixteenth century; and from that time on, the English imposed a series of taxes and restrictions in the interest of preventing Irish competition with the English wool trade.

12.1243–44 (326:15–16). our flax and . . . looms of Antrim – Antrim, a county in northeastern Ireland, was the heart of the flax-growing, linen-weaving industry in Ulster as early as the mid–sixteenth century. Linen appears to have been the only Irish manufacture that the English encouraged, but even that encouragement was ambiguous, alternating with measures (as early as the 1690s) designed to suppress the Irish linen industry in favor of its English competition. The linen industry survived, however, to emerge as the most important Irish industry through the eighteenth century.

12.1244 (326:16). Limerick lace – Limerick, the capital of County Limerick, 120 miles west-southwest of Dublin, was famous for its handmade lace in the late seventeenth and the eighteenth centuries. The industry declined in the course of the nineteenth century, largely as a result of competition from machine-made lace.

12.1244–45 (326:17). our white flint glass down there by Ballybough – Ballybough, a small village two miles north of central Dublin (by 1900 absorbed into Fairview). Some pieces of glass, identified as pre-Norman and therefore associated with ancient Ireland, were found in caves near the village. The most famous glass factory in Ireland was at Waterford; it flourished from the 1690s until 1745, when it was suppressed, and then again briefly in the last quarter of the eighteenth century.

12.1245–46 (326:17–18). our Huguenot poplin that we have since Jacquard de Lyon – The manufacture of poplin was introduced into Dublin by Huguenot refugees in 1693. Joseph Marie Jacquard of Lyons (1752–1834) was the inventor of the Jacquard loom (c. 1801). The loom (not exclusively for poplin) made it possible to produce patterns of considerable complexity with a single, unvarying action on the weaver's part. The introduction of the Jacquard loom did increase the productivity of Dublin's poplin industry, but that industry was already firmly established.

12.1246 (326:19). our woven silk – Although silk culture was repeatedly attempted in Ireland with little success, the manufacture of silk (woven silk), introduced by Huguenot immigrants after 1685, enjoyed considerable prosperity until it died out in the first half of the nineteenth century (thanks to the technological advantage achieved by English and continental manufacturers during the Industrial Revolution).

12.1246 (326:19). our Foxford tweeds – Foxford is a village in County Mayo (in northwestern Ireland). A small but thriving handwoven tweed industry was established there in the course of the nineteenth century under the sponsorship of a local convent.

12.1246–47 (326:19–20). ivory raised point from the Carmelite convent in New Ross – New Ross is a village on the Barrow River in County Wexford; it was supposed to have taken its origins as the site of an ancient sixth-century monastery. P. W. Joyce (*The Story of Ancient Irish Civilization* [Dublin, 1907], p. 142) remarks on the painstaking and beautiful needlepoint work in ancient Ireland. The Carmelites at New Ross preserved some examples of ancient needlepoint and imitated them in a small but famous industry.

12.1248–50 (326:21–24). the Greek merchants that . . . the fair of Carmen – The ancient Irish fair of Carmen was held once every three years at Wexford. P. W. Joyce (*A Smaller Social History of Ireland* [London, 1906], pp. 494–95) asserts that Ireland was known to Phoenician merchants and through them to the Greeks, and he describes the "three principal markets" of the fair of Carmen "one of which was 'a market of foreigners selling articles of gold and silver . . . gold ornaments and noble clothes.'" Tyrian purple was the traditional dye of Greek "noble clothes."
  Gibraltar, one of the Pillars of Hercules, was captured from the Spanish in 1704 by a combined Dutch and British force, whereupon the British admiral "unscrupulously," or "cleverly," depending on the sympathies of the historian, seized it for the British Crown.

12.1251 (326:24). Tacitus – The Roman historian and orator, who does briefly mention Ireland in his life of *Agricola*, section 24, where he describes the passage of a ship around the island and observes that there was little difference between the religious practices of England and Ireland.

12.1251 (326:24). Ptolemy – (fl. 139–161 A.D.), an Alexandrian Greek astronomer and geographer. P. W. Joyce (*A Smaller Social History of Ireland* [London, 1906], p. 494) remarks that Ptolemy "is known to have derived his information from Phoenician authorities, and has

given a description of Ireland much more accurate than that which he has left us of Great Britain."

12.1251 (326:25). even Giraldus Cambrensis – Girald de Barri (c. 1146–c. 1220), a Welsh ecclesiast and chronicler, wrote two works on Ireland, *Topographia Hibernica* and *Expugnatio Hibernica*. Both works establish Giraldus as an apologist for the Anglo-Norman Conquest (at the expense of the Irish), though the first is somewhat the more factual account. Giraldus puts considerable emphasis on Irish import (not export) of wine, since that helped to establish his moral case against the Irish. See 10.1083–84n.

12.1252 (326:25). Connemara marble – Marble from this area on the west coast of Ireland was in considerable demand not as a building stone but as a variegated material from which small ornamental articles were made.

12.1252 (326:26). silver from Tipperary – Silver, zinc, and lead mines in this county in central Ireland enjoyed great productivity from the late seventeenth until the nineteenth century, when they began to suffer as a result of world competition.

12.1253 (326:27). hobbies – Strong, active middle-sized horses, said to have originated in Ireland.

12.1253–54 (326:27–28). King Philip of Spain . . . fish in our waters – In 1553 Philip II of Spain entered into a twenty-one-year agreement for the right to fish Irish coastal waters; a fee of £1,000 per year was to be paid into the Irish Treasury.

12.1255 (326:29). yellowjohns – A translation of the Irish epithet, "*Seán Buidhe*": "filthy John [Bull]"; in other words, filthy English.

12.1256–57 (326:30–32). the beds of the Barrow . . . marsh and bog – The Shannon (214 miles long) and the Barrow (100 miles long) rivers in the central lowlands of Ireland both flow through extensive bogs and marshes. In the latter half of the nineteenth century there was considerable public discussion of engineering projects designed to deepen the two rivers in order to drain the marshland and to develop peat bogs. Ironically, one of the principal private investors (and losers) in these schemes was Lord

Balfour (see 12.865n), but there was little progress made before World War I.

12.1258–60 (326:33–36). As treeless as Portugal . . . conifer family are going fast – The Irish Nationalist press consistently blamed English land policies for the deforestation of Ireland (by 1904 only a little more than one percent of Ireland was woodland). Demands for a reforestation program were a minor but significant part of Irish agitation for land reform. Helgoland (or Heligoland) is a pair of rocky, and in 1904 heavily fortified, German islands in the North Sea.

12.1260–61 (326:36–37). a report of Lord Castletown's – The Right Honourable Lord Castletown of Upper Ossory sat on an official committee of the Department of Agriculture and Technical Instruction for Ireland, appointed on 29 August 1907 and charged with inquiring into "the improvement of forestry in Ireland." Its report, presented to Parliament and simultaneously published in Dublin on 6 April 1908, reviews the destructive effects of the Land Purchase Acts (1882ff.) on Irish forests and submits statistical data to support its claim that the forests were being exhausted because the acts made no provision for replanting. The report goes on to demonstrate a decline in several Irish industries that had been occasioned by the denudation and argues at length, with specific recommendations, for "a national scheme of afforestation."

12.1262 (326:38). the giant ash of Galway – Unknown, but there are records of a number of giant ash trees in various parts of Ireland, trees apparently once associated with the inauguration places of local kings. According to P. W. Joyce (*A Social History of Ancient Ireland* [London, 1913], vol. 2, pp. 286–87), the ash was one of the seven "Chieftain Trees"; to desecrate such a sacred tree was "the crowning insult which could be inflicted on an enemy" (A. T. Lucas, "The Sacred Trees of Ireland," *Cork Historical and Archeological Society Journal* 68 [1963]: 25).

12.1262–63 (326:39–40). the chieftain elm of Kildare . . . acre of foliage – The elm was a "Common," not a "Chieftain," tree (see preceding note), and the name Kildare derives from the Irish *Cill-dair*, "the church of the oak." The oak was a "Chieftain" tree; the one in question was not renowned for the chieftain associated with it but for St. Brigid (see 12.1705n), a chieftain's daughter and one of the three patron saints of Ireland, who had her cell under the oak and who founded a religious community there. According to A. T. Lucas, several elms figure in the legends of Irish saints (including St. Patrick), but not at Kildare.

12.1264 (326:41). the fair hills of Eire, O – From a song, "The Fair Hills of Eiré, O," translated by James Clarence Mangan from the Irish of Donogh Mac Con-Mara (1738–1814). The poem begins, "Take a blessing from my heart to the land of my birth, / And the fair hills of Eiré, O! [Lines 13–14:] Her woods are tall and straight, grove rising over grove; / Trees flourish, in her glens below and on her heights above."

Parody: 12.1266–95 (327:1–36). The fashionable international world . . . in the Black Forest – Parodies newspaper accounts of important social events, in this case a high-fashion wedding. The parody also owes a debt of allusion to the catalogue of trees in Spenser's *The Faerie Queene*, a catalogue that has, in its turn, literary forebears in Chaucer's *Parliament of Fowls* (lines 176–82) and in Ovid's *Metamorphoses* (10:90–105). In Book 1, canto 1 of *The Faerie Queene*, Redcrosse (the ideal Christian knight) and Una (Truth, true faith) are threatened by a storm and take refuge in a forest: "Much can [did] they prayse the trees so straight and hy, / The sayling [for shipbuilding] Pine, the Cedar proud and tall, / The vine-prop Elme, the Poplar never dry, / The builder Oake, sole king of forrests all, / The Aspine good for staves, the Cypresse funerall. // The Laurell, meed [reward] of mightie Conquerours / And Poets sage, the Firre that weepeth still, / The Willow worne of forlorne Paramours, / The Eugh [yew] obedient to the benders will, / The Birch for shaftes, the Sallow for the mill, / The Mirrhe sweete bleeding in the bitter wound, / The warlike Beech, the Ash for nothing ill, / The fruitfull Olive, and the Platane [plane tree] round, / The carver Holme [holly], the Maple seldom inward sound" (stanzas 8 and 9).

At first the forest seems a realm of "delight" to Redcrosse and Una, but it is, as Una warns, an ambiguous realm that turns out to be the habitation of the Dragon-Error, who threatens to "strangle" Redcrosse and suffocate him with her vomit, "poyson horrible and blacke" (of false doctrine), before he overcomes her.

12.1267 (327:2–3). the chevalier Jean Wyse Neaulan – Nolan's name with a French accent, to fit the chivalric-romance allusions to Spenser as well as the allusions to Bellini's *Norma;* see 12.1277–78n.

12.1268 (327:3). the Irish National Foresters – A fraternal organization and benevolent society, avowedly nonpolitical and nonsectarian, but Catholic and Nationalist in practice. Its motto was "Unity, Nationality, and Benevolence." In 1904 Joseph Hutchinson (see 10.1010n) was general secretary of the Foresters; the organization had executive council offices at 9 Merchant's Quay and two branch halls in Dublin.

12.1268–69 (327:4). Miss Fir Conifer of Pine Valley – In the language of flowers, pine stands for philosophy.

12.1269 (327:4). Lady Sylvester Elmshade – Elmshade signifies dignity.

12.1269 (327:5). Mrs Barbara Lovebirch – Any relation to James Lovebirch (see 10.601–2n)? In the language of flowers, birch stands for meekness.

12.1269 (327:5). Mrs Poll Ash – A polled ash is a tree that has been cut back to promote a dense head, or "poll," of foliage. Ash signifies grandeur in the language of flowers; see 1.528n.

12.1270 (327:5). Mrs Holly Hazeleyes – Holly corresponds to foresight, hazel to reconciliation.

12.1270 (327:6). Miss Daphne Bays – A "bay" is a crown or wreath of laurel, signifying reward of merit. Daphne, when pursued by Apollo, prayed for aid and was metamorphosed into a laurel tree, which became Apollo's favorite tree.

12.1270 (327:6). Miss Dorothy Canebrake – Significance unknown.

12.1270–71 (327:6–7). Mrs Clyde Twelvetrees – See 6.219n.

12.1271 (327:7). Mrs Rowan Greene – The rowan (quicken or mountain ash) stands for prudence in the language of flowers; in Irish superstition it is regarded as a charm against the fairies and their pranks. It also is celebrated in Irish tradition as the first green of spring.

12.1271 (327:7). Mrs Helen Vinegadding – Helen of Troy did gad about, but her waywardness was inspired by Aphrodite (as she says in *The Odyssey,* Book 4) rather than by Dionysus,

god of wine; however, she does drug the wine she serves in Menelaus's court with "mild magic of forgetfulness" (4:221; Fitzgerald, p. 71). And as Fritz Senn points out, in Milton's "Lycidas" the pastoral landscape, "With wild Thyme and the gadding Vine o'ergrown" (line 40), mourns Lycidas's death (*JJQ* 19, no. 2 [1982]: 168).

12.1271–72 (327:8). Miss Virginia Creeper – Virginia creeper or woodbine means everchanging in the language of flowers.

12.1272 (327:8). Miss Gladys Beech – "Glady" is rare for resembling a glade, and beech signifies prosperity in the language of flowers. There must also be some allusion to the way Sylvia Beach gladdened the scene as the good angel who presided over publication of *Ulysses;* see 9.729n.

12.1272 (327:8). Miss Olive Garth – The olive signifies peace; "garth" is dialect English for a small yard or enclosure, or for a weir for catching fish.

12.1272–73 (327:9). Miss Blanche Maple – White maple is highly prized as a wood for furniture; maple stands for reserve in the language of flowers.

12.1273 (327:9). Mrs Maud Mahogany – Significance unknown.

12.1273 (327:9–10). Miss Myra Myrtle – Myrtle symbolizes love.

12.1273–74 (327:10). Miss Priscilla Elderflower – Elder signifies zealousness.

12.1274 (327:10). Miss Bee Honeysuckle – Recalls the music-hall song "The Honeysuckle and the Bee" (1901), by Albert H. Fitz and William H. Penn. Chorus: "You are my honey, honey suckle, I am the bee, / I'd like to sip the honeysweet from those lips, you see; / I love you dearly, dearly, and I want you to love me. / You are my honey, honey suckle, I am the bee." In the language of flowers, honeysuckle stands for bonds of love, sweetness of disposition.

12.1274 (327:10–11). Miss Grace Poplar – See "the Poplar never dry" (never spiritually thirsty?) in the passage from Spenser quoted under Parody: 12.1266–95n above.

12.1274–75 (327:11). Miss O Mimosa San – A geisha, one of the central figures in the light opera *The Geisha;* see 6.355–57n. In the language of flowers, mimosa signifies sensitiveness.

12.1275 (327:11). Miss Rachel Cedarfrond – A cedarleaf means "I live for thee."

12.1275 (327:12). the Misses Lilian and Viola Lilac – Lilian, after lily, for pure, white, delicate; Viola, after violet, for faithfulness, modesty; lilac for youthful innocence. Violet or purple lilac represents the first emotions of love.

12.1275–76 (327:12). Miss Timidity Aspenall – Aspen stands for lamentation and is associated with quaking, shivering.

12.1276 (327:13). Mrs Kitty Dewey-Mosse – Moss signifies maternal love, affection.

12.1276 (327:13). Miss May Hawthorne – Hawthorne blooms in May in Ireland; it stands for hope.

12.1276–77 (327:13–14). Mrs Gloriana Palme – In the language of flowers, the palm stands for victory; it appears as "the victor palm" in Chaucer's *The Parliament of Fowls* (line 182). In Spenser's *Faerie Queene*, "Gloriana" is the "greatest Glorious Queene of Faerie lond" (Book 1, canto 1, stanza 3); in "A Letter of the Authors" (1589) Spenser says she is the personification of "Glory in my general intention, but in my particular I conceive the most excellent and glorious person of our sovereign the Queene [Elizabeth]."

12.1277 (327:14). Mrs Liana Forrest – Significance unknown.

12.1277 (327:14). Mrs Arabella Blackwood – Blackwood or acacia = elegance, secret love. See 2.279n for a possible husband or family.

12.1277–78 (327:14–15). Mrs Norma Holyoake of Oakholm Regis – "Holm" is obsolete for the holm oak; so this fictional place is "double-oak king." Norma, the heroine of Vincenzo Bellini's opera *Norma* (1831), is high priestess of the temple of the druids in Gaul, which Caesar has just conquered. Act I of the opera takes place under the "Holy Oak" in the sacred forest of the druids, who plan a revolt against the Romans. Norma is reluctant to preach revolt because she is secretly in love with Pollione, the Roman proconsul in Gaul, and has borne him two children; but Pollione has fallen in love with Adalgisa, a virgin-deaconess of the druid temple. After triangular complications and a near-revolt against the Romans, Norma's noble, self-sacrificing spirit prevails, and she is reunited with Pollione as they are about to be burned at the stake for profaning the temple and violating her vows (suggested by T. C. Theoharis, letter, 6 May 1983.)

12.1279–80 (327:17). the M'Conifer of the Glands – "Gland" is archaic for an acorn. There are several figures in Irish history whose names have carried the epithet "of the Glens." Thornton mentions two: James MacDonnell (d. 1565), lord of the Glens; and the O'Donoghue of the Glens, a branch of the O'Donoghue family. A third possibility, Hugh Roe O'Donnell, was known as the O'Donnell of the Glens for his skillful retreat from Kinsale (1601) after the Irish collapse in that abortive siege; see 12.179n.

12.1283 (327:21). bretelles – Straps.

12.1284 (327:22–23). Larch ... Spruce – Larch stands for audacity or boldness, spruce for neatness.

12.1287 (327:26–27). heron feathers – The heron was sacred to the druids.

12.1288 (327:27). Senhor Enrique Flor – Portuguese: "Mr. Henry Flower."

12.1290 (327:30). *Woodman, spare that tree* – An American popular song by George P. Morris and Henry Russell. The first of its four verses: "Woodman, spare that tree! / Touch not a single bough, / In youth it shelter'd me, / And I'll protect it now; / 'Twas my forefather's hand / That placed it near his cot; / There, woodman, let it stand, / Thy axe shall harm it not."

12.1291–92 (327:31–32). the church of Saint Fiacre *in Horto* – For St. Fiacre, who is the patron saint of amateur horticulture and gardening, see 3.193n. "*In Horto*" is Latin for "in garden [enclosure]." There is a hermitage of St. Fiacre that would qualify as being *in Horto* at Kilfiachra (Kilfera) on the Nore, in southern Ireland.

12.1292 (327:32). the papal blessing – A letter from the pope conveying his blessing is, in Catholic tradition, a mark of the distinction of the couple and of the wedding's social significance.

12.1293 (327:33). hazelnuts – Emblematic of poetic wisdom in Irish mythology (Robert Graves, *The White Goddess* [New York, 1948], pp. 151–52). See 12.1270n.

12.1293 (327:33). beechmast – See 12.1272n.

12.1293 (327:33). bayleaves – See 12.1270n.

12.1293 (327:33–34). Catkins of willow – The significance of willow flowers depends on the species—for example, creeping willow means love forsaken; water willow, freedom; weeping willow, mourning; and French willow, bravery and humanity.

12.1293 (327:34). ivytod – The ivy plant was sacred to Dionysus, the god of wine. In the language of flowers it means assiduous to please.

12.1294 (327:34). hollyberries – Holly signifies enchantment; cf. 12.1270n.

12.1294 (327:34). mistletoe sprigs – In Act I of *Norma*, the archdruid says that the start of the revolt against the Romans will be signaled by Norma's ceremonial cutting of the sacred mistletoe; see 12.1277–78n.

12.1294 (327:35). quicken shoots – Rowan or mountain ash; see 12.1271n.

12.1295 (327:36). a quiet honeymoon in the Black Forest – Cf. the sojourn of Redcrosse and Una in the forest in Spenser's *Faerie Queene*, Parody: 12.1266–95n.

12.1296–98 (327:37–39). our trade with Spain . . . those mongrels were pupped – Irish trade with the Continent flourished before the Norman Conquest (1066) and before the Anglo-Norman invasion of Ireland (which began in 1169). There is some truth in the Citizen's overstatement, since there is evidence of considerable Irish trade with the Continent during the period of the great Irish missionaries in the seventh and eighth centuries. But as a Celtic epithet for the Saxons (or English), "mongrels" or "mongrel hosts" is at least as old as the Northern Welsh (Cumbric) poem, *The Gododdin*, an epic lament for the loss of a battle and the destruction of the men of Gododdin, written c. 600 (ed. and trans. Kenneth H. Jackson [Edinburgh, 1969], p. 105).

12.1298 (327:39). Spanish ale in Galway – By the sixteenth century Galway had become one of the principal ports in the British Isles, with particularly close trade ties with Spain. In an essay, "The City of the Tribes," Joyce asserts that by Cromwell's time Galway was the second most important harbor in the British Isles: "Almost all the wine imported into the United Kingdom from Spain, Portugal, the Canary Islands, and Italy passed through this port" (*CW*, p. 230). Cromwell's punitive conquest of Ireland was particularly hard on Galway and its merchant princes (1651) and began that city's decline as a port.

12.1298 (327:40). the winedark waterway – See 1.78n.

12.1302–3 (328:2–4). Queenstown, Kinsale, Galway . . . harbour in the wide world – All of them had been flourishing harbors in the sixteenth and seventeenth centuries but had fallen from prosperity in the course of the eighteenth and nineteenth centuries. Queenstown (now Cobh) (see 11.851n) had not suffered so much as the others. Kinsale Harbor is eighteen miles west-southwest of Cork Harbor (Queenstown). For Galway, see 12.1298n. Blacksod Bay is on the west-northwest coast of Ireland in County Mayo, sixty-five miles north of Galway Bay. Ventry and its relatively small Ventry Harbor are on the northern shore of Dingle Bay in County Kerry, southwestern Ireland. Killybegs is nineteen miles west of Donegal on Donegal Bay in County Donegal, northwestern Ireland; far from having the "third largest harbour in the world," Killybegs may have one of the smallest. It is more appropriately described as "a clean, pleasant little seaport where the tide comes up to the doors of the houses in the main street."

12.1304 (328:5). the Galway Lynches – Edward MacLysaght (*Irish Families* [Dublin, n.d.]) asserts: "The Norman family of Lynch . . . have been more prominent on account of their predominance in the affairs of Galway city, where they were the most influential of the 'Tribes.'" (Eighty-four different members of the "Tribe" held the office of mayor of Galway between 1484 and 1654; under Innocent VIII [1484–92] the Lynches became the ecclesiastical wardens of Galway.) See Joyce, "The City of the Tribes," *CW*, pp. 231–32.

12.1304 (328:5). the Cavan O'Reillys – An ancient and powerful house in County Cavan in central Ireland, northwest of Dublin. The family boasted that it was descended from Heremon, one of the three sons of Milesius (see 12.1308–10n).

12.1304–5 (328:6). the O'Kennedys of Dublin – More properly, the O'Kennedys of Ormond, a duchy with its power centered in Kilkenny in south-central Ireland. The O'Kennedys claimed descent from a nephew of Brian Boru (see 6.453n) and were the lords of Ormond from the eleventh century through the sixteenth, when they were overshadowed by the Norman-Irish Butlers. Brian Boru, himself a Kennedy, was *ardri*, or king, of Dublin (1002–14).

12.1305–6 (328:6–7). when the earl of Desmond . . . Charles the Fifth himself – James Fitzmaurice Fitzgerald (d. 1529), tenth earl of Desmond, one of the most powerful and independent of the Norman-Irish lords, bragged that he could field a household army of ten thousand men and launch his own fleet against England. In 1523, when Henry VIII was at war with France, the earl was negotiating an offer of aid to Francis I; Henry ordered him to submit to arrest, but the Earl was powerful enough to refuse with impunity. In 1529, on the eve of his death, the earl entered inconclusive negotiations with Charles V (1500–58), Holy Roman emperor and king of Spain as Charles I, to draw up a treaty of alliance against England.

12.1308 (328:9–10). Henry Tudor's harps – Henry VIII quartered (incorporated) a gold harp on a blue field into the royal arms of England as a symbol of his overlordship of Ireland.

12.1308–10 (328:10–12). the oldest flag afloat . . . sons of Milesius – The Province of Munster in southwestern Ireland was divided in ancient Ireland into Desmond (South Munster) and Thomond (North Munster). The last of the quasi-legendary invaders of Ireland were the Milesians, led by the three sons of Mileadh of Spain (Eber, Heremon, and Ith or Iar, the latter sometimes characterized as a brother of Mileadh rather than son). Legend has it that the Milesian flag had "three crowns on a blue field" and that it was "the oldest flag afloat" *in Ireland;* legend also regards the Milesians as the "ancestors" of the royal clans of Ireland.

12.1311 (328:13). Moya – Anglicized Irish: "as if it were" (ironic interjection).

12.1311–12 (328:13–14). All wind and piss like a tanyard cat – Proverbial: tannery cats are traditionally famed for their braggadocio and in-

effectuality, since tanneries never lack for rodents.

12.1312 (328:14). Cows in Connacht have long horns – Irish proverb. Since Connacht is in the far west, the implication is double: the farther away the cow is, the longer its horns (in reputation), together with the surprised provincial's discovery of the obvious. (The French edition renders this "Asses have ears.")

12.1314 (328:16). Shanagolden – A post town and parish in County Limerick, eighteen miles west of Limerick and 116 miles west-southwest of Dublin.

12.1314 (328:17). the Molly Maguires – By 1904 this was almost a generic term for anonymous groups of Irish terrorists. The original Molly Maguires were formed in 1641 by Cornelius Maguire to aid in the rebellion of that year; they were called Mollies because they disguised themselves in women's clothing. The Molly Maguires were "reactivated" during the Tithe War (1830–35), and provincial groups that actively terrorized land agents and landlords in the land-reform struggles in the latter half of the nineteenth century were often called Molly Maguires.

12.1315–16 (328:18–19). for grabbing the holding of an evicted tenant – In the struggle for land reform, groups of activists organized rent strikes and tried to prevent the then-endemic evictions. In the event that they could not prevent an eviction, they tried to prevent anyone else from profiting by seizing the evicted man's livestock and property or by occupying the vacant tenancy. Their aims were to keep the evicted man from being reduced to utter poverty and to reduce the landlord's income and thereby exact concessions by keeping the land vacant.

12.1318 (328:21–22). An imperial yeomanry . . . to celebrate the occasion – The Yeomanry was a British volunteer cavalry regiment raised by Yorkshire gentlemen to fight Bonnie Prince Charlie in 1745. It continued as a "semiformal" regiment, the members furnishing their own horses and training for fourteen days a year. The regiment distinguished itself in the Boer War and was awarded the title of Imperial Yeomanry in 1901. From the Irish point of view, the regiment was simply continuing the distinctively English practice of harassing and subjugating yet another free people. The phrase "imperial yeomanry" carried the slur that the

Yeomanry's amateur soldiers needed to fortify their courage with alcohol.

12.1319 (328:23). a hands up – The label on a bottle of Allsop's ale featured the Red Hand of Ulster, symbolic of the semilegendary heroes of that ancient Irish kingdom.

12.1324 (328:31). *Black Beast Burned in Omaha, Ga.* – The lynching, which immediately became national and international news, took place not in Omaha, Georgia, but in Omaha, Nebraska, 28 September 1919. The lynch mob hanged the victim (who had been accused of raping a young white woman), "riddled his body with bullets, and burned it." They then attempted to lynch the mayor, who tried to prevent the antiblack rampage that followed the lynching. The unaccountable substitution of Georgia for Nebraska was achieved by the *London Times*, 30 September 1919 (Timothy Weiss, *JJQ* 19, no. 2 [1982]: 183–86).

12.1325 (328:32). Deadwood Dicks – Deadwood Dick was the creation of the self-styled "sensational novelist" Edward L. Wheeler (c. 1854–c. 1885). Deadwood Dick, from Deadwood, South Dakota, careened his way through an advertised "122 Numbers" (dime novels), appearing variously as prospector, gambler, Robin Hood, semidesperado, and Indian fighter. In *Deadwood Dick, the Prince of the Road* (n.d.), he is described: "A broad black hat was slouched down over his eyes."

12.1325 (328:32). a Sambo – After the Spanish *zambo*, a negro or black; *Webster's New International* (Springfield, Mass., 1909), p. 1875, qualifies the word as "colloquial or humorous" (i.e., racist). In the nursery tale "Little Black Sambo," the child-hero is given a fine new suit of clothes and goes for a walk, but he is interrupted by a sequence of tigers, each of which exacts a piece of clothing for not eating the child. Eventually, stripped of his fine new clothing, he happens upon the tigers quarreling over the finery. In a frenzy, they run a ring around a tree so fast that they melt into a pool of butter ("or 'ghi' as it is called in India"). Little Black Sambo gets his clothes back, and the butter winds up on the family's pancakes.

12.1329 (328:36–37). the fighting navy . . . that keeps our foes at bay – From a song, "The Lads in Navy Blue": "It is the Navy, the British Navy / That keeps our foes at bay. / Our old song, Britannia rules the waves, / We still can sing today." See 1.574n and 12.1347n.

12.1330–32 (328:39–41). the revelations that's going . . . *Disgusted One* – Flogging in the Royal Navy was legally abolished in 1880, but the use of corporal punishment (i.e., just short of flogging) in naval discipline continued until at least 1906. The leading critic of such practices was the Irish Nationalist John Gordon Swift MacNeill (1849–1926), member of Parliament for Donegal. The questions he raised in the House of Commons in 1904 were widely echoed and debated in the correspondence columns of newspapers. One of the debaters was George Bernard Shaw: "In short, there are certain practices which, however expedient they may be, are instinctively barred by the humanity of the highest races; and corporal punishment is one of them. I should blush to offer a lady or a gentleman more reasons for my disgust at it. Yours truly, G. Bernard Shaw" (*Times* [London], 14 June 1904, p. 11:f).

12.1338 (329:5). A rump and dozen – There is no evidence that this was Sir John's expression for a flogging, but it was a proverbial Irish wager: a rump of beef and a dozen of claret; that is, the loser of the wager would provide the winner with a banquet.

12.1338–39 (329:6). sir John Beresford – The Citizen is apparently combining or confusing two John Beresfords: Sir John Poo Beresford (c. 1768–1844), Irish-born admiral in the British Navy and member of Parliament from an English constituency (1812–32). There is no evidence that Sir John had other than a "normal" attitude toward the practice of flogging. The other John Beresford (1738–1805) was commissioner of revenue in Ireland, and from an Irish point of view he comes much closer to qualifying for the epithet of "old ruffian," since his financial power made him "virtually king of Ireland." He motivated the building of the Custom House in Dublin, which became his "palace"; near it he established a riding school for the training of his horses. During the tension and rebellion of 1797–98 he was a staunch supporter of the English cause, and his riding school was the principal site of the floggings and other forms of torture inflicted on dissident Irish in Dublin.

12.1342 (329:9–10). 'Tis a custom more . . . than in the observance – See 12.287n.

12.1345 (329:13). meila – Anglicized Irish: "a thousand."

12.1347 (329:15). The fellows that never will be slaves – After the ode "Rule Britannia," words by James Thomson (1700–48), music by Thomas Arne (1710–78), first included in *The Masque of Alfred* (1740). The opening lines of the ode: "When Britain first, at Heav'n's command, / Arose from out the azure main, / Arose, arose, arose from out the azure main; / This was the charter, the charter of the land, / And guardian angels sung this strain: / Rule Britannia, Britannia rule the waves, / Britons never, never, never will be slaves."

12.1347–48 (329:16). the only hereditary chamber on the face of God's earth – The Citizen is, of course, referring to the English House of Lords, but that house was only predominantly, not exclusively, hereditary, since some of the membership was elected (from among the Scot and Irish peers), some included by virtue of ecclesiastical office, and the judicial members were appointed by the Crown. There were a number of other hereditary chambers in Europe, among them the House of Peers of the Prussian Landtag and the House of Lords of the Austro-Hungarian Reichsrat.

12.1349 (329:17). cottonball – Slang: having the appearance but not the actuality of being the real thing; thus, overpreoccupied with fashion, affected.

12.1351 (329:20). On which the sun never rises – See 2.249n.

12.1353 (329:22). yahoos – Creatures, essentially beasts in human form, in Swift's *Gulliver's Travels*, Part IV. See 3.111n.

Parody: 12.1354–59 (329:23–29). They believe in rod . . . living and be paid – Parodies the Apostles' Creed; see 1.653n.

12.1364–65 (329:37). our greater Ireland beyond the sea – An epithet for the United States; see 12.1240–41n. From the middle of the nineteenth century Irish-Americans continued to raise money and to train insurrectionists for the cause of Irish national independence.

12.1365–66 (329:38). the black 47 – The famine began in 1845 as the result of a potato blight that destroyed the staple food crop of the peasants. The famine increased in intensity, exacerbated by epidemics of typhoid, typhus, and cholera, to a climax in 1847; it finally began to be somewhat alleviated in the course of 1848. Peasants emigrated or stayed to die from starvation and disease; many were driven off their small holdings by landlords who refused to lower their rents or to attempt some kind of compensation for the disastrous failure of the potato crop. However, a great many landlords were far less callous than the Citizen's diatribe would suggest and ruined themselves in the effort to tide their peasants over.

12.1366 (329:39). shielings – Huts or small cottages.

12.1367 (329:39). the batteringram – When landlords or their agents drove the peasants off their small holdings (particularly when the object was to convert cultivated land to pasture), they frequently tore the roofs off the cottages or simply leveled the structures to prevent the peasants from hanging about.

12.1367–69 (329:40–42). the *Times* rubbed its hands . . . as redskins in America – Seumas MacManus (*The Story of the Irish Race* [New York, 1967], p. 610n) quotes the *London Times:* "They are going! They are going! The Irish are going with a vengeance. Soon a Celt will be as rare in Ireland as a Red Indian on the shores of Manhattan." No such quotation appears in the *Times* between 1845 and 1848, and yet the quotation effectively caricatures that newspaper's stance before its ("with great reluctance") change of heart on 8 February 1849. The English conservative Establishment's attitude toward Ireland was that it should be (and should remain) an *agrarian* state. This rationalized not only the continuing policy of suppression aimed at Irish industries but also the belief that, since by mid-nineteenth-century standards Ireland was overpopulated, depopulation, while regrettable, was in the long run a good thing.

12.1369 (329:42). *Even the Grand Turk sent us his piastres – T. O'Herlihy, in *The Famine (1845–47); A Survey of its Ravages and Causes* (Drogheda, 1950), p. 85: "Though the English government made no gestures of relief, the Society of Friends made more than a quarter of a million pounds available for relief. . . . Many other countries contributed their obole [coins], even the Turksman." The thrust here is that the English were more callous than the Turks, who themselves were notorious for their callous indifference to human suffering.

12.1369–71 (330:1–3). But the Sassenach tried to . . . sold in Rio de Janeiro – T. P. O'Connor, in *Gladstone, Parnell and the Great Irish Struggle* (Philadelphia, 1886), p. 366: "Testimony is as unanimous and proof as clear as to the abundance of the grain crop [in 1847] as they are to the failure of the potato crop. . . . John Mitchel quotes the case of the Captain who saw a vessel laden with Irish corn [wheat] at the Port of Rio de Janeiro." For John Mitchel, see 17.1648n.

12.1372 (330:4). Twenty thousand of them died in the coffinships – There is no evidence to support the Citizen's statistics one way or the other, but the appalling circumstances of the exodus from Ireland in 1846–48 are well documented and certainly warrant use of the phrase "coffin ships." This was particularly true of the innumerable, quasi-clandestine sailings from small ports where there was no inspection under the Passenger Act (1842). Ships—poorly appointed, poorly manned, and incompetently officered, with inadequate water, food, and space and no sanitation facilities—were overcrowded to the point where they were indeed more coffins than ships. But the term *coffin ship* was coined earlier, in the 1830s, to describe utterly unseaworthy ships, narrow and with deep holds designed to cheat on the registered-tonnage laws.

12.1373 (330:5). the land of the free – From "The Star-Spangled Banner."

12.1373 (330:5–6). the land of bondage – The phrase echoes Deuteronomy 5:6: "I am the Lord thy God, which brought thee out of the land of Egypt, from the house of bondage," making another analogue between the Irish and the Israelites.

12.1375 (330:7). Granuaile – The Irish name of Grace O'Malley (c. 1530–c. 1600), a chieftain from western Ireland whom her contemporary, Lord Henry Sidney, the lord deputy of Ireland, called "a most famous feminine sea captain." She was reputed to have nursed "all the rebellions in the province for 40 years."

12.1375 (330:7–8). Kathleen ni Houlihan – One of the traditional feminine embodiments of the "spirit of Ireland"; see 9.36–37n.

12.1377–78 (330:11–12). Since the poor old woman . . . on the sea – "Poor old woman" in Irish is *shan van vocht;* see 1.543–44n.

12.1378 (330:12). landed at Killala – A small expeditionary force of about a thousand French landed at Killala on the north coast of County Mayo in western Ireland in the autumn of 1798,

after the rebellion of that year had virtually collapsed. Although the French were initially successful, the Irish support they expected did not materialize, and the French were soon forced to surrender.

12.1379–80 (330:13–14). We fought for the royal . . . and they betrayed us – The Irish rose in support of James II, the last of the Stuart kings, when he was deposed in the "bloodless revolution" of 1688. In the war that followed (1689–91), the Irish held their own until they suffered a decisive defeat at the hands of William III of England in the Battle of the Boyne (1690). At that point James II "betrayed" his Irish allies by retiring into exile on the Continent.

12.1380–81 (330:14–15). Remember Limerick and the broken treatystone – After the defeat at Boyne, the Irish insurgents continued the war with French encouragement but with little hope of ultimate success. They made their final stand at Limerick, under the leadership of Patrick Sarsfield (see 12.178–79n). On 3 October 1691 the Treaty of Limerick was signed on a stone that later became a monument to the treaty. In substance, the treaty made some concessions to the Catholic Irish on the condition that Sarsfield and eleven thousand troops, the core of his army, accept exile to the Continent. In 1695ff. the Irish (Protestant) Parliament repudiated the treaty's concessions, with English connivance and consent.

12.1381–82 (330:16). to France and Spain, the wild geese – Sarsfield and the others who accepted (or fled into) exile in 1691 were called "the wild geese." Many of the wild geese enlisted in the armies of Catholic France or Spain.

12.1382 (330:16). Fontenoy – At the battle of Fontenoy (1745), the Irish Brigade distinguished itself fighting on the side of the victorious French against the allied armies of England, Holland, and Hanover.

12.1382 (330:17). Sarsfield – See 12.178–79n.

12.1382–83 (330:17). O'Donnell, duke of Tetuan in Spain – Leopold O'Donnell (1809–67), was a descendant of one of the wild-geese families and a marshal of Spain whose career was a checkerboard of military insurrections and counterinsurrections. He was prime minister of Spain, 1854–56, 1858–63, 1865–66.

12.1383–84 (330:18–19). Ulysses Browne of Camus that was fieldmarshal to Maria Teresa – Nolan is confusing two field marshals: Ulysses Maximilian, Count von Browne (1705–57), the Austrian-born son of one of the wild geese; he was one of the most distinguished field marshals in the army of Maria Theresa (1717–80), queen of Hungary and Bohemia and archduchess of Austria. He was killed while leading a bayonet charge at the battle of Prague. And George, Count de Browne (1698–1792), was born at Camus (thus "of Camus") in Limerick. He became a soldier of fortune and a field marshal in the Russian army and was a favorite of Maria Theresa and of Catherine the Great.

12.1387 (330:22). *entent cordiale – French: "Cordial understanding." The intense Anglo-French rivalry of the early twentieth century was resolved in such an "understanding" on 8 April 1904. Though not technically an "alliance," the *entente* implied a realignment of the European powers: France and England against the Triple Alliance of Germany, Austria-Hungary, and Italy. The agreement promised the French a free hand in Morocco; in return, the French recognized England's virtual conquest of Egypt.

12.1387–88 (330:23). Tay Pay's dinner party with perfidious Albion – "Tay Pay" was the nickname of Thomas Power O'Connor (see 7.687n), whose weekly *M.A.P.* (Mainly About People) was deprecated by some Irish radicals for having too much the tone of an English dinner party. For "perfidious Albion," see 12.1209n.

12.1389 (330:25). *Conspuez les Français* – French: "Scorn the French." Cf. 12.1209n.

12.1390–92 (330:26–29). the Prooshians and Hanoverians . . . old bitch that's dead – Hanover, an electorate of the Holy Roman Empire, was included as a province of Prussia in 1866. "George the Elector" (1660–1727) was hereditary ruler of the electorate of Hanover when he became heir to the English throne in 1714, and the German House of Hanover has continued on the English throne (the name was changed from Wettin to Windsor for patriotic reasons in World War I). The "German lad" is Albert, prince of Saxe-Coburg-Gotha, who added new German blood to the house when he became prince consort. Queen Victoria's mother was also a German princess; and although her parents lived in Germany, Victoria

was born on English soil in the expectation that she might become heir to the throne.

12.1394 (330:31). winkers – Dialect for eyelids or eyelashes, in this case an allusion to Queen Victoria's heavy-lidded eyes.

12.1394–98 (330:31–36). blind drunk in her royal . . . where the boose is cheaper – This is a flamboyant version of malicious gossip that was widely circulated toward the end of Queen Victoria's life. In part, it was a function of her idiosyncratic behavior (perpetual mourning and withdrawal from public life) after the death of Prince Albert; in part, it was a reaction to her reputation for excessive moral repressiveness. The "coachman" was the Scot John Brown (1826–83), the queen's gillie (attendant), upon whom she was extraordinarily dependent.

12.1397 (330:35). *Ehren on the Rhine* – American ballad by——Cobb and William H. Hutchinson. The ballad describes (since the soldier dies) the last parting of the soldier and his love. Chorus: "Oh love, dear love, be true, / This heart is only thine; / When the war is o'er, / We'll part no more / At Ehren on the Rhine."

12.1397–98 (330:35–36). come where the boose is cheaper – A parody, by George Dance (d. 1932), of Stephen Foster's song "Come Where My Love Lies Dreaming." Dance's parody begins: "Come where the booze is cheaper; / Come where the pots hold more, / Come where the boss is a deuce of a joss, / Come to the pub next door." The story goes that Queen Victoria admired the tune when a military band serenaded her with it at Windsor Castle and sent to ask the title and the words, to the embarrassment of the messenger and/or bandmaster (Fritz Senn, *JJQ* 13, no. 2 [1976]: 246).

12.1399 (330:37). Edward the peacemaker – What the French called Edward VII in the first blush of optimism about the *entente cordiale* (see 12.1387n). It was also a title that he coveted, as witness his efforts to establish peaceful relations with Austria (7.542–43n) and with his nephew, Kaiser Wilhelm II of Germany.

12.1400–1401 (330:39). more pox than pax – "More venereal disease than peace," an allusion to Edward VII's reputation as a ladies' man.

12.1401 (330:39). Edward Guelph-Wettin – The family name of the House of Hanover was

Guelph; Wettin is the Prussian version of the Swedish Wetter, Prince Albert's family name. Queen Victoria dropped the name Guelph when she married Prince Albert.

12.1402–4 (330:41–331:1). the priests and bishops of Ireland . . . the horses his jockeys rode – Edward VII was a horse fancier. During his state visit to Ireland in July of 1903 he was entertained by the Catholic University of Ireland at St. Patrick College, the clerical center of the Roman Catholic church in Ireland, in the town of Maynooth, fifteen miles west of Dublin. The supreme governing body of the university was made up of the Catholic archbishops and bishops of Ireland. For the reception, the college refectory was decorated with his *Britannic* majesty's racing colors and with engravings of two of his favorite horses, Diamond Jubilee and Ambush II. Monsignor Gerald Molloy (1834–1906), the rector of the university, gave an address of welcome. From an Irish point of view, the whole episode, including the unpriestly nature of the decorations, was an offensive demonstration of the Church's willingness to be subservient to the English Crown.

12.1404–5 (331:1). The Earl of Dublin – A title conferred on Edward VII when he was Prince of Wales by Queen Victoria on the occasion of her first state visit to Dublin, in 1849.

12.1406 (331:3). all the women he rode – Another reference to Edward VII's well-known free-wheeling behavior with women.

12.1412 (331:11–12). May your shadow never grow less – A common Irish salutation or toast, expressive of good will.

12.1415 (331:15). dunduckety – "Dun" means yellowish or grayish brown, and "duckety" means dark or gloomy.

12.1431 (331:31). Ireland . . . I was born here – See 7.87n.

12.1433 (331:33). a Red bank oyster – See 8.865–66n.

12.1434 (331:35). After you with the push – In other words, I'll go along with the crowd.

Parody: 12.1438–64 (331:39–332:28). The much-treasured and intricately . . . rich incrustations of time – Parodies a newspaper feature-story's description of a medieval tapestry or an illuminated manuscript.

12.1439–40 (331:40–41). Solomon of Droma . . . the Book of Ballymote – The 501 large folio pages of *The Book of Ballymote* (an anthology selected from older books) were produced in about 1391 in Sligo by several scribes, chief among them Solomon O'Droma and Manus O'Duigenan (together with Robert mac Sheehy). The book was written in the house of Tolmatoch mac Tadg (or mac Donogh or mac Dermond). Among other items, the book contains the ancient "Book of Invasions," genealogies of selected Irish families, histories and legends of early Irish kings, and an Irish translation of Nennius's *History of the Britons* (c. 800).

12.1443–46 (332:3–7). the four evangelists in turn . . . eagle from Carrantuohill – The iconographic symbols for the four evangelists after Revelation 4:7: Matthew, a winged man with a lance (in this case, "sceptre"); Mark, a lion; Luke, an ox; John, an eagle. The symbols are often winged after Revelation 4:8, "And the four beasts had each of them six wings about him." The "four masters" are the four Franciscan compilers of *The Annals of the Four Masters* (1632–36): Michael O'Clery, Conaire O'Clery, Cucoigcriche O'Clery, and Fearfeasa O'Mulchonry. Bogoak is oak that has been preserved in a peat bog; usually ebony in color, it was widely used for making ornaments in Ireland. The North American puma (cougar or mountain lion) is pitted against the lion because lions in various heraldic poses are included in the royal arms and crest of Great Britain. Kerry is the rough country in southwestern Ireland; Carrantuohill, the "inverted sickle," is, at 3,414 feet, the highest mountain in Ireland, the "grand master" of MacGillicudy's Reeks in County Kerry.

12.1447 (332:8). emunctory – Of or pertaining to the blowing of the nose.

12.1447 (332:8). duns – Irish: "forts," usually fortified hills.

12.1447 (332:8). raths – Irish: "ring-forts."

12.1448 (332:9). grianauns – *Grianaun*, Irish: sunroom of a medieval castle.

12.1448 (332:9). seats of learning – That is, monasteries.

12.1448 (332:9–10). maledictive stones – A heap of stones piled (and added to) as the monument to a disaster. It was traditional to add a stone as one passed such a monument in token of one's humility in the face of disaster; the superstition also suggested burying the disaster so that it would not rise again.

12.1449–50 (332:11). the Sligo illuminators – The scribes who wrote *The Book of Ballymote;* see 12.1439–40n.

12.1450–51 (332:12). in the time of the Barmecides – The subject and refrain of James Clarence Mangan's poem "The Time of the Barmecides." The Barmecides were the members of a powerful Persian family that flourished in the eighth century. "The Barber's Tale of His Sixth Brother" in the *Arabian Nights* tells of a Barmecide feast in which a member of the family gives a beggar an imaginary feast on magnificent dishes.

12.1451 (332:13). Glendalough – "The Valley of the Two Lakes," in County Wicklow twenty-five miles south of Dublin, is a short, deep valley noted for its beauty and its early monastic ruins. It is one of the most popular tourist sites in Ireland.

12.1451 (332:13). the lovely lakes of Killarney – In County Kerry; all guidebooks rhapsodize on the "multiform contrasts and endless variety" of the lakes and their mountain settings.

12.1451–52 (332:13–14). the ruins of Clonmacnois – Clonmacnois ("the Meadows of the Sons of Nos") is on the river Shannon in central Ireland; the ruins of seven churches, including a tenth-century cathedral, mark this site of the most remarkable of the religious schools, founded c. 544, devastated and ruined in 1552. Nineteenth-century guidebooks agree that the scenery was "lovely, sublime, and poetic."

12.1452 (332:14). Cong Abbey – Near Galway in County Galway. The abbey was founded in 624, destroyed by fire in 1114, and then rebuilt in Norman style in the course of that century. The abbey was disbanded in the sixteenth century, but considerable restoration of the building was undertaken in the nineteenth century.

12.1452 (332:14). Glen Inagh and the Twelve Pins – Glen Inagh is a long mountain valley in County Galway, flanked on one side by twelve conical domelike hills, the Twelve Pins or Bunnabeola ("the Peaks of Beola").

12.1452 (332:14–15). Ireland's Eye – A small island one mile north of the Howth promontory, the site of the ruins of a seventh-century chapel.

12.1453 (332:15). the Green Hills of Tallaght – South and west of Dublin, they afford a good view of the mountainous country to the south and were a favorite resort of the gentry in the seventeenth and eighteenth century.

12.1453 (332:15). Croagh Patrick – A 2,510-foot mountain on the coast in County Mayo; it was regarded as an enchanted hill. St. Patrick is said to have rung a bell at its summit to drive all venomous living things out of Ireland, and each time he tried to throw the bell away, it returned to his hand.

12.1453–54 (332:16–17). the brewery of Messrs . . . and Company (Limited) – In west-central Dublin south of the Liffey.

12.1454 (332:17). Lough Neagh's banks – Lough Neagh in northeastern Ireland is the largest lake in the British Isles; eighteen miles long and eleven miles wide, it has sixty-five miles of "banks." Thomas Moore "remembers" the banks in the second stanza of "Let Erin Remember the Days of Old" (see 3.302–3n): "On Lough Neagh's bank, as the fisherman strays, / When the clear cold eve's declining, / He sees the round towers of other days / In the wave beneath him shining; / Thus shall memory often, in dreams sublime, / Catch a glimpse of the days that are over; / Thus, sighing, look through the waves of time / For the long faded glories they cover."

12.1454–55 (332:17). the vale of Ovoca – Or Avoca, a picturesque junction of rivers in County Wicklow, south of Dublin. It is memorialized in Thomas Moore's poem "The Meeting of the Waters." For first verse, see 8.415–17n; the fourth and last stanza: "Sweet vale of Avoca! how calm could I rest / In thy bosom of shade, with friends I love best, / Where the storms that we feel in this cold world should cease / And our hearts, like thy waters, be mingled in peace."

12.1455 (332:17). Isolde's tower – A medieval tower with nine-foot walls, eighteen feet square in its interior, that stood until 1675 on the site of Essex Gate (Parliament Street) in central Dublin just south of the Liffey. There is no record of why the tower was so named, though it was near a spring called "Isod's Font" and all extant literary versions of the legend of Tristram and Isolde suggest that she was the king of Dublin's daughter.

12.1455 (332:18). the Mapas obelisk – A "folly" at Killiney, on the coast nine miles southeast of Dublin. It was constructed in 1741 on the grounds of Mr. Mapas's Killiney estate "with the benevolent intention of providing employment for the industrious poor." Guidebooks advertise "a remarkable view" from Obelisk Hill.

12.1455 (332:18). Sir Patrick Dun's hospital – On Grand Canal Street overlooking the Grand Canal, which circles south around Dublin. The hospital (built in 1803) was financed by the estate of Sir Patrick Dun (1642–1713), a famous and influential Scots-Irish physician and politician.

12.1455–56 (332:18). Cape Clear – On Clear Island, south of Bantry; the southernmost point of Ireland.

12.1456 (332:19). the glen of Aherlow – A valley eight miles long and two miles wide formed by the river Aherlow, famous for its beauty and, in history, as the contested major pass between County Tipperary and County Cork to the south. The phrase "the glen of Aherlow" functions as a refrain in Charles Joseph Kickham's (1830–82) ballad "Patrick Sheehan," a song about a peasant from the glen who goes blind in the Crimean War and then is jailed in Dublin; he laments his double loss (sight and freedom) with reference to the glen. (Kickham himself had also lost his eyesight while he was imprisoned.)

12.1456 (332:19). Lynch's castle – In Galway (see 12.1304n), the town residence of the famous James Lynch (Fitz-stephen), warden of Galway in the early sixteenth century. He condemned his own son to death (for conspiracy to mutiny on the high seas) and hanged him from a window to prevent his being rescued by other members of the family.

12.1456 (332:19). the Scotch house – A Dublin pub; see 8.321n.

12.1456–57 (332:19–20). Rathdown Union Workhouse at Loughlinstown – Loughlinstown was a hamlet eight and a half miles south-southeast of Dublin. *Thom's* 1904 (p. 1731) notes, as one of the hamlet's two distinguishing features: "On the brow of the hill [above Loughlinstown Green] stands the Rathdown

Union Workhouse [poorhouse], very prettily and most salubriously situated on a site of eight acres, erected in 1841 at an expense of £6,000."

12.1457 (332:20). Tullamore jail – Tullamore is a town in the bog of Allen; the jail is as undistinguished a building as the town itself. An Irish rhyme sums it up: "Great Bog of Allen, swallow down / That odious heap call'd Philipstown; / And if thy maw can swallow more, / Pray take—and welcome—Tullamore."

12.1457 (332:20–21). Castleconnel rapids – The broad weirs and rapids (the Falls of Doonas) on the Shannon in central Ireland; the Shannon is broad at this point and flows through innumerable rocky islets.

12.1458 (332:21). Kilballymachshonakill – Not a place but a name, in Irish: "Church (or Wood) of the town of the son of John of the Church." See 12.55n.

12.1458 (332:21–22). the cross at Monasterboice – Monasterboice, thirty-five miles northwest of Dublin, is the site of ecclesiastical ruins, a round tower and three stone crosses, two of which were regarded as among the finest in Ireland. The more important of the two is St. Boyne's Cross, which is reputed to be the most ancient Christian relic in Ireland.

12.1458 (332:22). Jury's Hotel – 6–8 College Green in Dublin.

12.1458–59 (332:22). S. Patrick's Purgatory – On Saints' Island in Lough Derg, County Donegal (northwestern Ireland). Tradition has held (from c. 1150) that St. Patrick had a vision of purgatory and hell in a cavern on the island and that properly prepared pilgrims could share that vision. The pilgrimage was wildly popular, inspiring excesses that brought it under papal ban in 1503; but the pilgrimage continued until the cave was desecrated and blocked up during Cromwell's "pacification" of Ireland in the 1650s (see 12.1507–9n). The lake (and particularly Station Island, three-quarters of a mile southeast of Saints' Island) later became and still is one of the most important sites of penitential pilgrimage in Ireland.

12.1459 (332:22). the Salmon Leap – A waterfall on the Liffey at Leixlip, eight miles west of Dublin. The name Leixlip derives from the Norse *Lax-Hlaup*, or Salmon Leap.

12.1459 (332:23). Maynooth college refectory – See 12.1402–4n.

12.1459 (332:23). Curley's hole – A bathing pool in Dollymount (northwestern outskirts of Dublin), dangerous to nonswimmers. In Joyce's satiric poem "Gas from a Burner" (1912), Maunsell's printer says: "Do you think I'll print / The name of the Wellington Monument, / Sydney Parade and the Sandymount tram / Downes's cakeshop and Williams's jam? / I'm damned if I do—I'm damned to blazes! / Talk about *Irish Names of Places* / It's a wonder to me upon my soul / He forgot to mention Curley's Hole."

12.1459–60 (332:23–24). the three birthplaces of the first duke of Wellington – Arthur Wellesley (1769–1852), the first duke of Wellington. Both the exact date (29 April?) and the place of his birth in Dublin are matters of controversy, though opinion seems to have settled on 24 Upper Merrion Street.

12.1460 (332:24). the rock of Cashel – Ninety-six miles southwest of Dublin in County Tipperary; the rock rises abruptly to a height of 300 feet out of an extensive plain. It is crowned by Cormac's Great Church or Cathedral (consecrated 1134), now called Cormac's Chapel, together with a round tower, a great stone cross, and the ruins of a medieval cathedral.

12.1460–61 (332:24–25). the bog of Allen – Begins twenty-five miles west-southwest of Dublin. Originally an extensive bog, it has been partially reclaimed.

12.1461 (332:25). the Henry Street Warehouse – Outfitters, silk mercers, and haberdashers, 59–62 Henry Street and 1–5, 36–39 Denmark Street, Dublin.

12.1461 (332:25). Fingal's cave – In Scotland, not Ireland; the largest of seven caves on the uninhabited island of Staffa in the Inner Hebrides. Fingal is portrayed as the father of Ossian by the Scot James Macpherson (1736–96) in his fictional versions of the Ossianic poems.

12.1465 (332:29). *Show us over the drink – Like the drunken Polyphemus in Book 9 of *The Odyssey*, the narrator cannot see to serve himself.

12.1471–72 (332:38–39). sold by auction off in Morocco like slaves or cattle – Jews were not technically slaves in Morocco in 1904, but the Moslem majority did subject them to "compulsory service"; both men and women were compelled to do all servile tasks, even on the Sabbath and holy days, and these services could apparently be bought and sold in the Moslem community. Compulsory service was abolished in 1907.

12.1473 (332:40). the new Jerusalem – Combines a reference to the ultimate Christian utopia (described in Revelation 21 and 22) with a reference to the Zionist movement and its dramatization of the Jewish desire for a "homeland" in Jerusalem. In context, the Citizen's question translates: "Are you advocating Zionism?" and encodes an anti-Semitic slur.

12.1476 (333:3). an almanac picture – That is, a picture to be "immortalized" on a calendar.

12.1476 (333:3–4). a softnosed bullet – These and other expanding bullets were developed in the late nineteenth century as particularly effective (and vicious) ammunition for military use. They were outlawed by the Hague conference on armaments and warfare of 1899 but continued in occasional use through World War I.

12.1485 (333:14). Love . . . the opposite of hatred – See note on Prometheus, p. 314, n. 4.

12.1486 (333:15). round to the court – See 12.271n.

12.1489 (333:20). apostle to the gentiles – St. Paul, who, after his conversion to Christianity, preached the gospel to all without distinction of race or nation; see I Timothy 2:7.

12.1490 (333:22–23). Love your neighbour – The second of Jesus' two commandments: "And the second is like unto it, Thou shalt love thy neighbour as thyself" (Matthew 22:39).

12.1491 (333:24). Beggar my neighbour – A card game for two children in which the object is to gain all the opponent's cards.

12.1492 (333:25). moya – See 12.1311n.

Parody: 12.1493–1501 (333:27–37). Love loves to love . . . God loves everybody – Sentimental adult child-talk.

12.1493 (333:27). Love loves to love love – Cf. St. Augustine, *Confessions* 3:1: "Not yet did I love, though I loved to love, seeking what I might love, loving to love." Augustine is describing his immersion in sexual desire before he discovered that God was the true and ultimate object of love and desire.

12.1493–94 (333:27–28). Constable 14 A loves Mary Kelly – For "14 A," see 12.801–2n; Mary Kelly is unknown, but her name is so common that it suggests "any Irish girl."

12.1495 (333:29–30). Li Chi Han . . . Cha Pu Chow – These Chinese lovers' names involve puns: the *Li Chi* (Book of Rites, a compilation of ceremonies) is one of the "five classics," the five sacred books of the Confucian canon; the *Han* dynasty reigned in China from 206 B.C. to 220 A.D. and was marked by a revival of letters. *Cha* is Mandarin Chinese for tea; a *Pu* is a measure of length (1.97 yards); and a *Chow* was a prefecture or district of the second rank or the chief city of such a district (as Foochow).

12.1496 (333:30/31). Jumbo, the elephant/Alice, the elephant – Jumbo (d. 1885) was a gigantic African elephant, a favorite with English children when he was at the Royal Zoological Gardens in London (1859–82). Acquired by P. T. Barnum in 1882 (Barnum's single greatest PR stroke), Jumbo was billed as "the world's largest elephant." Alice, a "nervous female" elephant at the London zoo, was so upset by the "swollen doleful crowds" mourning Jumbo's impending departure that her trumpeting upset the whole zoo—and contributed immeasurable free publicity for Jumbo and Barnum (J. Bryan III, *The World's Greatest Showman* [New York, 1956], p. 159).

12.1496–97 (333:31–32). Old Mr Verschoyle . . . with the turnedin eye – Mr. and Mrs. G. Verschoyle, 14 Sidney Avenue, Blackrock?

12.1497–98 (333:32–33). The man in the brown macintosh loves a lady who is dead – This can be read as a mocking identification of "Macintosh" as Mr. Duffy in "A Painful Case," *Dubliners.*

12.1502 (333:38). your very good health and song – Source unknown.

12.1506 (334:2). canters – That is, those who use religious cant; a seventeenth-century nickname for the Puritans.

12.1507–9 (334:3–6). sanctimonious Cromwell and his . . . mouth of his cannon – In 1649, after the resolution of the civil war in England, Oliver Cromwell (1599–1658) and his

highly disciplined and fanatically Protestant troops ("Ironsides") undertook to reduce the pro-Stuart resistance in Ireland. His campaign began with the reduction of Drogheda (on the coast thirty-two miles north of Dublin); the Ironsides massacred at least 2,800 men of the garrison. Many, though not all, accounts cite "thousands" of women and children as victims. Cromwell's dictum: "I am persuaded that this is the righteous judgment of God upon these barbarous wretches," and one massacre followed another on the principle that the bloodbath would break Irish resistance. The motto on the cannon's mouth is apparently apocryphal but an apt caricature.

12.1509–10 (334:6–7). that skit in the *United* . . . that's visiting England – The *United Irishman,* the weekly (Thursday) newspaper edited by Arthur Griffith, did print skits of the sort the Citizen reads but not the one that follows.

12.1515 (334:12). His Majesty the Alaki of Abeakuta – Abeakuta was a province in western Nigeria; the Alaki was the equivalent of the sultan of a small state. He was not a Zulu, but he was in fact visiting England in the summer of 1904.

12.1515–16 (334:13). *Gold Stick in Waiting, Lord Walkup of Walkup on Eggs – A gilded baton is the emblem of office of the Captain and Gold Stick of His Majesty's Body Guard of the Honourable Corps of Gentlemen-at-Arms (the ceremonial guard on state occasions). Gold Stick in 1904: the Right Honourable Baron Belper (presumably of Belper-on-Derwent in Derbyshire) (*Thom's* 1904, p. 106).

12.1520 (334:18). Ananias Praisegod Barebones – Praise-God Barebones (or Barbon) (c. 1596–1679), a London tanner, fanatic, and lay preacher. He was a member of the Parliament of 1653, called the Barebones Parliament in mockery of its alleged unpractical and sanctimonious nature. Ananias was one of the Jewish high priests who sat in judgment on St. Paul and "commanded them that stood by [Paul] to smite him on the mouth" (Acts 23:1–5). Ananias is also one of the Puritan preachers in Ben Jonson's *The Alchemist* (1610).

12.1523–25 (334:22–24). bible, the volume of the word . . . the great squaw Victoria – The Alaki discussed the Bible in question with Edward VII in the course of his visit to England.

12.1527 (334:27). *Black and White* – A brand of Scotch whiskey.

12.1528 (334:28). Kakachakachak – Does this coinage owe anything to *kakistocracy*, rare for government by the worst men?

12.1530 (334:29). Cottonopolis – An appellation for Manchester, the textile center of England.

12.1534–35 (334:34–35). Wonder did he put that bible to the same use as I would – A vulgar expression of Catholic contempt for Protestants and for the centrality of the Bible in Protestant tradition.

12.1538–39 (334:38–40). Is that by Griffith? . . . It's only initialled: P – Arthur Griffith did write "skits" of the sort quoted (see 12.1509–10n), at first under the pseudonym "Shanganagh" and subsequently simply initialed "P" (for the spirit of Parnell?). Brendan O Hehir (*A Gaelic Lexicon for "Finnegans Wake" and Glossary for Joyce's Other Works* [Berkeley, Calif., 1967]) defines the Irish *Shanganagh* as "antfull" or "old sand" (on the coast south of Dublin); P. W. Joyce (*English*, p. 319) defines it as "a friendly conversation," which seems more appropriate here.

12.1542–45 (335:3–6). those Belgians in the Congo . . . Casement . . . He's an Irishman – The Irish-born Sir Roger Casement (1864–1916) was in the British consular service (1895–1913). In February 1904, while serving as consul in the Congo, Casement filed a report on the forced labor in rubber plantations and other cruelties to natives under the Belgian administration there. The report was published, and the public reaction led in January to a reconvening of the Conference of Powers that had originally established Belgian control of the Congo; the conference resulted in a measure of reform. In 1914 Casement joined the then-militant Sinn Fein, negotiated with Germany for military support of an Irish revolt, and was hanged for high treason.

12.1552 (335:15). that whiteeyed kaffir – G. H. Chirgwin (1855–1922), a music-hall entertainer and multi-instrumentalist, performed in blackface with large white diamonds painted around his eyes, billing himself as the White-Eyed Kaffir (suggested by Vincent Deane).

12.1559 (335:22). Show us the entrance out – Blinded by Odysseus, Polyphemus the Cyclops can only grope his way out of his cave; see headnote to this episode, p. 314.

12.1561 (335:24). Goodbye Ireland I'm going to Gort – The usual form of this saying, "Good-bye, Dublin, I'm going to Gort," expresses the countryman's dissatisfaction with the city. Gort is a small village near Sligo in western Ireland.

12.1565 (335:28). Slattery's – A pub, William Slattery, grocer, tea, wine, and spirit merchant, 28 Ship Street Great (in central Dublin south of the Liffey).

12.1568 (335:33). tube – That is, a speaking tube, an intercommunications device.

12.1569–71 (335:33–37). (ow!) . . . (ow!) . . . (hoik! phthook!) . . . (ah!) – The sound effects that accompany this urination suggest that the nameless speaker has gonorrhea.

12.1571–72 (336:37). Jerusalem cuckoos – A disparaging nineteenth-century term for Zionists and, by late century, for all Jews on the assumption that all were involved in a Zionist conspiracy.

12.1574–77 (335:39–336:2). *Bloom gave the ideas for . . . selling Irish industries – As originally conceived, Sinn Fein did not contemplate violence (as Bloom thinks, 8.458–59 [163:38–39]), but intended the nonviolent subversion of English institutions in Ireland and the establishment of independent Irish political and economic institutions; see 8.458n. In part, the "idea" for Sinn Fein derived from a similar, and successful, Hungarian resistance to Austrian dominion in the latter half of the nineteenth century. Bloom's contemporaries (and "the Castle") believe this bit of gossip because Bloom has a Hungarian background and "because Griffith was persistently rumored to have a Jewish adviser-ghostwriter" (Hugh Kenner, *Ulysses* [London, 1980], p. 133).

12.1579 (336:4). God save Ireland – See 8.440n.

12.1580 (336:5). argol bargol – After *argáil* (Irish: "argument, discussion") but also after the Shakespearean "argal" (a corruption of *ergo*); therefore, "unsound reasoning, caviling."

12.1581 (336:6–7). Methusalem Bloom – That is, Rudolph (Virag) Bloom. Methuselah was the longest-lived man in the Bible: "And all the days of Methuselah were nine hundred sixty and nine years: and he died" (Genesis 5:27).

12.1581 (336:7). bagman – Commercial traveler.

12.1582 (336:8). prussic acid – No, it was an overdose of aconite (a cardiac and respiratory sedative when taken in small quantities); see 17.622–32 (684:33–685:8).

12.1585 (336:11–12). Lanty MacHale's goat . . . the road with everyone – An expression that usually involves MacHale's excessively friendly dog instead of a goat. Charles Lever (1806–72) memorializes Lanty or Larry M'Hale in a poem entitled "Larry M'Hale." The poem celebrates M'Hale's willingness to "ride with the rector [Protestant], and drink with the priest [Catholic]," his capacity for violence, and his even-handed indifference to debt and the law: "And, though loaded with debt, oh! the devil a thinner / Could law or the sheriff make Larry M'Hale."

12.1589 (336:16). Crofton – The Orangeman (Protestant and pro-English) appears as a character in "Ivy Day in the Committee Room," *Dubliners.*

12.1589–90 (336:17–18). pensioner out of the collector . . . have on the registration – Crofton once worked for the collector general of customs, but he has been pensioned from that service and now works (?) as an assistant to R. T. Blackburne, secretary to the Dublin County Council in 1904.

Parody: 12.1593–1620 (336:21–337:13). Our travellers reached . . . 'Tis a merry rogue – Parodies the style of late-nineteenth-century versions of medieval romance.

12.1599 (336:29). good den – Archaic: "good evening."

12.1605 (336:38). master Taptun – Joyce's coinage from tapster and tun?

12.1616 (337:8). a bason – Usually a tool used in felt forming (hat making), but here it stands in as archaic for "basin" to sustain the parody.

12.1616 (337:9). tansy – A pudding or omelet flavored with tansy juice.

12.1623–24 (337:18). about Bloom and the Sinn Fein – See 12.1574–77n.

12.1631 (337:26). a swaddler – A contemptuous Irish Catholic term, applied at first primarily to Wesleyan Methodists but then to all Protestants. Various derivations have been suggested, but the epithet remains stubbornly meaningless unless it is intended to suggest that Protestants are "swaddled" by rigid moral rules and restrictions.

12.1633 (337:31). Who is Junius? – Junius was the pseudonym of the unknown author of letters that appeared in the *Public Advertiser* in London between 1769 and 1772. The letters are biting and scurrilous attacks on George III and his ministers and contain considerable evidence that the writer had access to highly confidential government information. The answer to J. J. O'Molloy's question is still a riddle, though in 1904 (given an assist by Macaulay) the letters were often attributed to Dublin-born Sir Philip Francis (1740–1818).

12.1636 (337:33–34). according to the Hungarian system – Cunningham is alluding to Arthur Griffith's *The Resurrection of Hungary,* serialized in the *United Irishman* (January–June 1904). The book recounts the history of Hungary's struggle for a measure of independence from Austrian rule and presents that history as an appropriate model for Irish enterprise.

12.1638 (337:35). Bloom the dentist – Marcus J. Bloom, 2 Clare Street, Dublin.

12.1639 (337:37). Virag – Hungarian: "flower."

12.1642–43 (337:39–40). Island of saints and sages – See 3.128n.

12.1644 (337:41). They're still waiting for their redeemer – That is, the Jews, who believe that the Messiah is yet to come, as Christians of many sects and denominations await the Second Coming of Christ.

12.1646–48 (338:1–3). every male that's born . . . a father or a mother – Moslem rather than Jewish tradition. Many Jewish community traditions do heavily emphasize the desirability of male children, but the fundamental Jewish belief is that each married couple should perpetuate itself by achieving *both* a son and a daughter who live to be married and to produce children in their turn.

12.1651 (338:7). south city markets – The Dublin (South) City Market Company, fronting on Fade and Drury streets with a Market Arcade from George's Street South, in south-central Dublin.

12.1652 (338:7). Neave's food – Was advertised as a health food for "infants, invalids, growing children, and the aged."

12.1653 (338:9). *En ventre sa mère* – French: "In the belly of his mother."

12.1657 (338:14). And who does he suspect? – See 9.656n.

12.1658–59 (338:16). mixed middlings – A translation of the Irish phrase *eadar-mheadhon-aich:* "he is but very indifferent"; in context, his sexual identity is far from unambiguous.

12.1660 (338:17). a totty with her courses – Slang: a girl with her menstrual period.

12.1662 (338:20). sloping – To "slope" is slang for to disappear, to decamp, to run away.

12.1666 (338:26). A wolf in sheep's clothing – "Beware of false prophets, which come to you in sheep's clothing, but inwardly they are ravening wolves" (Matthew 7:15).

12.1667 (338:27–28). Ahasuerus I call him. Cursed by God – Ahasuerus was the name of two kings of Persia and Media (Esther, Ezra, Daniel), but the Citizen intends Ahasuerus as one of the traditional names for the Wandering Jew; see 9.1209n.

12.1671 (338:32). Saint Patrick would want to land again at Ballykinlar – As with the date and place of his birth, the date and the site of St. Patrick's landing in Ireland are a matter of contention. Two sites enjoy the reputation: the mouth of the Vantry River near Wicklow Head (on the coast south of Dublin) and Dundrum Bay (north of Dublin); Ballykinlar is a village on Dundrum Bay, five miles south of Downpatrick in County Down. See 12.573–74n.

Parody: 12.1676–1750 (338:39–340:42) And at the sound of . . . Christum Dominium Nostrum – This vision of the Island of Saints and Sages parodies "church news" accounts of religious festivals, in this case a procession that begins as the ceremonial blessing of a house and inflates to the consecration of a church and ultimately of a cathedral; see 12.1720–21n.

12.1676 (338:39). the sacring bell – Or Sanctus bell, rung at certain times during the Mass (be-

fore consecration of the elements and at the elevation of the host and of the chalice). In the Middle Ages, the bell was often mounted on the exterior of the church, and its ringing would announce the presence of the consecrated elements at the altar. In this case the sound of the bell announces that the procession is carrying the Blessed Sacrament.

12.1676 (338:39). a crucifer – One who carries the cross at the head of the procession.

12.1677 (338:40). thurifers – A thurifer carries the censer, or thurible, in which the incense is burned during the Mass.

12.1677 (338:40). boatbearers – The boatbearer carries the vessel containing the incense, which will be blessed and transferred to the censer by the celebrant.

12.1677 (388:40). readers – Those ordained to a minor order in the Catholic church and prepared for the office of reading the lessons.

12.1677 (338:40). ostiari – Ushers or doorkeepers, members of the lowest of the minor orders of the Catholic church.

12.1678 (338:42). guardians – A guardian is the superior of a Franciscan convent.

12.1679 (338:42–339:1). the monks of Benedict of Spoleto – The Benedictines. St. Benedict (c. 480–c. 543), who founded the order, was born in Nursia, an episcopal city in the Italian duchy of Spoleto. The Rule of St. Benedict, evolved by Benedict at Monte Cassino, formed and established the historical model for the monastic life of western Europe.

12.1679 (339:1). Carthusians – Founded in 1086 by St. Bruno (c. 1030–1101) at La Grande Chartreuse in France. The Carthusians were noted for the austerity of their adherence to the Rule of St. Benedict.

12.1680 (339:1). Camaldolesi – Founded in 1012 by St. Romuald (c. 950–1027), a Benedictine, on the plain of Camaldoli, near Arezzo in Italy. The monks wore white robes and were noted for the rigidity of their monastic rule.

12.1680 (339:2). Cistercians – Another offshoot of the Benedictine order, founded in 1098 by St. Robert, abbott of Molesme, at Citeaux near Dijon in France. The Cistercians also wore white habits and practiced a monastic rule of considerable severity.

12.1680 (339:2). Olivetans – Another offshoot of the Benedictine order, founded in 1319 at Monte Oliveto between Siena and Arezzo in Italy by Giovanni dé Tolomei (Blessed Bernard Ptolomei, 1272–1348).

12.1680 (339:2). Oratorians – The Fathers of the Oratory or the Oratory of St. Philip Neri (1515–95), founded at Rome by that saint in 1575. The priests of the congregation live in community but without monastic vows and under an essentially democratic constitution.

12.1680 (339:2). Vallombrosans – Founded (c. 1056) at Vallombrosa near Florence by St. John Gualbert (985–1073). The order was committed to austere observance of the Rule of St. Benedict.

12.1681 (339:3). the friars of Augustine – The Begging Friars or Hermits of St. Augustine or Austin Friars, founded by the union of several societies of recluses in the middle of the thirteenth century. They lived under the Rule of St. Augustine, derived from sermons attributed to St. Augustine (354–430).

12.1681 (339:3). Brigittines – The Order of Our Saviour, founded in 1346 by St. Bridgit (c. 1303–73) of Sweden and dedicated to the Rule of St. Augustine.

12.1681 (339:3). *Premonstratensians – The Order of Canons Regular, founded in 1120 at Premontré near Laon in France by St. Norbert (b. c. 1080). The order lived under an austere version of the Rule of St. Augustine.

12.1681 (339:4) Servi – The Servites or Servants of Mary, a monastic order founded in Florence in 1233 by seven wealthy Florentines. It was conducted under the Rule of St. Augustine.

12.1682 (339:4). Trinitarians – The Order of the Holy Trinity for the Redemption of Captives, founded in 1198 by St. John de Matha (1160–1213) and St. Felix of Valois (1127–1212). The order lived under the Rule of St. Augustine and was dedicated to the work of freeing Christians held in captivity in North Africa and the Middle East.

12.1682 (339:4). the children of Peter Nolasco – The Mercedarians, the Order of Our Lady of Mercy for the Ransom of Captives, initially a congregation of laymen founded by St. Peter Nolasco (1189–1256?) in 1218. The congregation lived under the Rule of St. Augustine and worked to ransom Christians held in captivity by the Moors.

12.1682–84 (339:5–6). from Carmel mount the children . . . Avila, calced and other – The Order of Our Lady of Mount Carmel. There has been some controversy over its origins (some of its early members believed that it was founded by the prophet Elijah), but apparently it was founded by Bertrand, count of Limoges, a soldier turned monk who with ten companions established a hermitage on Mount Carmel in 1156. St. Albert, the patriarch (bishop) of Jerusalem, gave them their "rule" in c. 1208. In the fourteenth and fifteenth centuries the order relaxed from the severities of the Rule of St. Albert; in the sixteenth century a sweeping reform was achieved by St. Theresa of Avila (1515–82) and St. John of the Cross. From that time the order had two branches: "discalced" (without shoes), following St. Theresa's strict adherence to the Rule of St. Albert; and "calced" (with shoes), adhering to the modification (relaxation) of the rule under Eugenius IV (pope 1431–47).

12.1684 (339:7). friars, brown and grey – The Dominicans and the Franciscans.

12.1684 (339:7). sons of poor Francis – The Franciscans, Order of Friars Minor, founded in 1209 by St. Francis of Assisi (1182–1226). The order was initially dedicated to the rule of poverty, but it rapidly became wealthy and powerful after the death of St. Francis.

12.1685 (339:7). capuchins – (After the Italian *cappuccio*, "cowl," of their habit), a branch of the Franciscans founded in 1525 in an effort to revive the dedicated simplicity of the Rule of St. Francis.

12.1685 (339:8). cordeliers – Franciscan friars who announced their strict adherence to the Rule of St. Francis by wearing knotted cords around their waists.

12.1685 (339:8). minimes – Mendicant friars, the Order of Minims (*Ordo Minimorum Eremitarum*), founded by St. Francis of Paola (1416–1507) in 1454.

12.1685 (339:8). observants – The Friars Minor of the Regular Observance (c. 1460), dedicated to strict observance of the Rule of St. Francis—as against the Conventuals, who observed a modified version of the rule.

12.1685 (339:8). the daughters of Clara – The Clares, Order of Poor Ladies, founded in 1212 by St. Clare of Assisi (1193–1253) and St. Francis as the feminine counterpart of the Friars Minor.

12.1686 (339:9). the sons of Dominic, the friars preachers – The Dominicans, Order of Friars Preachers (c. 1215), founded by St. Dominic (c. 1170–1221). The avowed purpose of the order was the salvation of souls, especially by means of preaching.

12.1686 (339:9–10). the sons of Vincent – The Vincentian Fathers, the Congregation of the Mission of St. Vincent de Paul (Order of Lazarists), founded in 1624 by St. Vincent de Paul (1576–1660) and dedicated to the relief of the poor under his *Constitutions of the Congregation of the Mission*.

12.1687 (339:10). the monks of S. Wolstan – St. Wolstan (1008–95), a Benedictine and bishop of Worcester, the last of the Saxon bishops of England, noted not for having founded an order but for the extraordinary devotion of his life to prayer and to the duties of his bishopric.

12.1687 (339:10–11). Ignatius his children – The Jesuits, the Society of Jesus, founded in 1534 by St. Ignatius Loyola (1491–1556) and noted for its commitment to missionary work and education.

12.1687–88 (339:11–12). the confraternity of the christian . . . Edmund Ignatius Rice – The Christian Brothers, a teaching brotherhood of Catholic laymen, bound under temporary vows. The original school was founded at Waterford in 1802 by Edmund Ignatius Rice (1762–1844), a layman who took religious vows in 1808 and whose organization was sanctioned by the pope in 1820.

12.1689 (339:13). S. Cyr – The French name for the child martyr St. Cyricus (d. c. 304). St. Cyr is also a military academy, the French equivalent of West Point.

12.1689–90 (339:13–14). S. Isidore Arator – St. Isidore ("belonging to tillage") the Farmer

(Spanish, 1070–1130), a confessor and the patron saint of peasants, farmers, and day laborers. Feast day: 25 October.

12.1690 (339:14). S. James the Less – One of the twelve Apostles and "a kinsman of the Lord," later bishop of Jerusalem (called "the Less" to distinguish him from the other apostle, St. James, the son of Zebedee). Feast day: 11 May.

12.1690 (339:14). S. Phocas of Sinope – St. Phocas the Gardener of Sinope (in Asia Minor), a martyr remembered for his hospitality to those who martyred him. Feast day: 22 September.

12.1690–91 (339:14–15). S. Julian Hospitator – Also noted for his hospitality, the patron saint of travelers, ferrymen, and wandering minstrels. His hospitality was his manner of penance for having killed his parents under the impression that they were his wife and a lover. Feast day: 12 February.

12.1691 (339:15). S. Felix de Cantalice – (1513–87), a peasant from the Abruzzi who became a Capuchin; he styled himself the Ass of the Capuchins and was noted for his simplicity and holiness. Feast day: 18 May.

12.1691 (339:15–16). S. Simon Stylites – St. Simon of the Pillar (388–459), an anchorite who dramatized his rigorous asceticism by spending over thirty-five years of his life on top of a pillar. He is said to have spent the entire forty days of Lent standing upright and abstaining from all food and drink. Feast day: 5 January.

12.1691–92 (339:16). S. Stephen Protomartyr – See 1.34n. Feast day: 26 December.

12.1692 (339:16). S. John of God – (1495–1550), Portuguese, the patron saint of hospitals for the needy poor and the founder of the Order of Brothers Hospitalers. Feast day: 8 March.

12.1692 (339:16–17). S. Ferreol – A legendary Spanish saint said to have been responsible for the conversion of Besançon in the early sixth century. Another St. Ferreolus (fl. third century) suffered martyrdom in southern France. Feast day: 18 September.

12.1692 (339:17). S. Leugarde – The French version of St. Lughaid (d. 608), an Irish abbot and missionary. Feast day: 4 August.

12.1692–93 (339:17). S. Theodotus – Martyred (c. 304) for giving Christian burial to seven martyred virgins. The patron saint of innkeepers, he was himself an innkeeper who refused to submit to a law requiring food served to guests to be presented to idols as votive offerings. Feast day: 18 May.

12.1693 (339:17). S. Vulmar – Or St. Wulmar (fl. seventh century), a French abbot and recluse who founded a monastery and a nunnery near Calais. Feast day: 20 July.

12.1693 (339:18). S. Richard – Richard de Wych (1197–1253), an English bishop and chancellor of Oxford, famous for his victory over Henry III (1207–72) in a Church-State power struggle.

12.1693 (339:18). S. Vincent de Paul – See 12.1686n. Feast day: 19 July.

12.1693–96 (339:18–21). S. Martin of Todi . . . S. Owen Caniculus – Martin Cunningham, Alfred Bergan, Joseph J. O'Molloy, Denis Breen, Cornelius Kelleher, Leopold Bloom, Bernard Kiernan, Terence Ryan, Edward Lambert, and the dog Garryowen join the company of the saints.

12.1693–94 (339:18). S. Martin of Todi – Martin I (d. 655), pope and martyr, was born at Todi in Umbria, Italy. His pontificate was marked by a struggle between the papacy (the bishop of Rome) and Constans II (Byzantine emperor 641–68) in Constantinople. Martin I refused a doctrinal compromise, was summoned to Constantinople, arrested for treason, maltreated, and banished into exile. Feast day: 12 November.

12.1694 (339:19). S. Martin of Tours – (c. 316–97) began life as a soldier, experienced conversion, and became a solitary with a following of monks. In humility he refused the bishopric of Tours but was made bishop by a ruse in 371. His leadership is credited with firmly establishing monasticism in western Europe. Feast day: 11 November. (St. Patrick [c. 373–c. 463] studied at Tours before his mission to Ireland.)

12.1694 (339:19). S. Alfred – Alfred the Great (849–99), king of the West Saxons, was not only a great military leader but also a great legalist, educator, and church reformer. His reputation is in part legendary as is his sainthood, which has never been formally conferred by the Church.

12.1694 (339:19). S. Joseph – Spouse of the Blessed Virgin Mary, confessor and patron of the Universal Church. Feast day: 19 March.

12.1694–95 (339:19). S. Denis – Or St. Dionysius, martyr (d. c. 275), bishop of Paris and one of the patron saints of France. He was beheaded because his success in making converts threatened to transform Paris into a Christian "island."

12.1695 (339:20). S. Cornelius – (d. 253), pope (251–53) and martyr who resisted the schism of Novatian and suffered banishment in the eighth persecution under the Roman emperors Valerian and Gallienus. He is commemorated for "his wisdom, for his works outshine the sun." Feast day: 16 September.

12.1695 (339:20). S. Leopold – Leopold the Good (1073–1136), an Austrian soldier-saint who founded several monasteries. Feast day: 15 November.

12.1695 (339:20). S. Bernard – Of Clairvaux (1090–1153), a Cistercian and abbot of Clairvaux; he is credited with having founded 163 monasteries and is remembered as one of the great doctors of the medieval Church.

12.1695 (339:20–21). S. Terence – (fl. first century), a little-known bishop and martyr.

12.1696 (339:21). S. Edward – Either St. Edward the Martyr (962–79), king of England; or, more probably, St. Edward the Confessor (c. 1003–66), king of England, noted for his innocence and humility and famous for the gift of prophecy. Feast day: 13 October.

12.1696 (339:21). S. Owen Caniculus – *Canicula*, Latin: "small dog, bitch"; thus, St. Owen of the Dogs, Garryowen.

12.1698 (339:23–24). S. Laurence O'Toole – (1132–80), archbishop of Dublin, an Irish soldier-saint who resisted the Norman invasion of Ireland but finally submitted to Henry II at the pope's insistence. He is the patron saint of Dublin. Feast day: 14 November.

12.1698–99 (339:24). S. James of Dingle and Compostella – The apostle and martyr, St. James the Great, the son of Zebedee; cf. 12.1690n (d. c. 44). He is said to have conducted a mission in Spain and, though he was beheaded in Jerusalem, his body was miraculously transported to Compostella in Spain;

Compostella thus became the most popular pilgrimage in western Europe. Feast day: 25 July. The Roman Catholic parish church of Dingle on Dingle Bay, southwestern Ireland, is the Church of St. James Compostella; Dingle Bay was the site of a sizable Spanish community in the sixteenth century.

12.1699 (339:24–25). S. Columcille and S. Columba – One Celtic saint with two names (521–97), the founder of several monastic churches and schools in Ireland, Scotland, and the Hebrides. He is (with St. Bridgid and St. Patrick) one of the three patron saints of Ireland. Feast day: 9 June.

12.1699 (339:25). S. Celestine – Celestine I (pope 422–32) defended the Church against the Pelagian Heresy. He is dear to the hearts of the Irish as the pope who sent St. Patrick on his mission to Ireland.

12.1699–1700 (339:25). S. Colman – One of three saints: (1) St. Colman of Cloyne (522–600), missionary and chief bard to the king of Munster (feast day: 24 November); (2) St. Elo (553–610), founder of several abbeys and monasteries (feast day: 26 September); or (3) St. Colman, bishop of Lindisfarne (d. 676), noted for his disputations (defeated) on the question of the date of Easter (feast day: 8 August).

12.1700 (339:26). S. Kevin – (d. 618), the founder and abbot of the monastery at Glendalough; see 12.1451n. Feast day: 3 June.

12.1700 (339:26). S. Brendan – See 12.183n.

12.1700 (339:26). S. Frigidian – (d. c. 558), an Irish saint who made a pilgrimage to Italy, where he became a hermit and subsequently bishop of Lucca. Feast day: 18 March.

12.1700 (339:26). S. Senan – The most famous of the twenty-odd Irish saints of this name is the S. Senan (c. 488–c. 544) after whom the River Shannon was named. He made a pilgrimage to Rome and returned to found several monastic churches in Ireland, among them a hermitage church on Scattery Island in the Shannon, chosen as a site "on which no female had ever trod." Immediately after the hermitage was founded, a female, St. Cannera, asked for sanctuary and could not be denied. Feast day: 8 March.

12.1700–1701 (339:27). S. Fachtna – (fl. sixth century), bishop of Ross and founder there of one of the great monastic schools of Ireland. Feast day: 14 August.

12.1701 (339:27). S. Columbanus – See 2.144n. Feast day: 21 November.

12.1701 (339:27). S. Gall – (c. 551–645), known as the "apostle of Switzerland," an Irish missionary to the Continent and a companion of St. Columbanus. Feast day: 16 October.

12.1701 (339:27). S. Fursey – St. Fursa; see 12.183n.

12.1701 (339:28). S. Fintan – (1) (d. 595), the founder of an influential monastery at Cloneagh in Ireland and known as "head of the monks of Ireland." Feast day: 17 February. (2) Munnu (d. 634), the founder of a monastery in County Wexford and a missionary to Scotland who died a leper. Feast day: 21 October.

12.1701–2 (339:28). S. Fiacre – See 3.193n. Feast day: 1 September.

12.1702 (339:28). S. John Nepomuc – (c. 1340–1393), confessor and martyr who was supposed to have been tortured and drowned by "good" King Wenceslaus of Bohemia because the saint refused to reveal the queen's confession. He is one of the patron saints of Bohemia and of confessors. Feast day: 16 May.

12.1702 (339:28–29). S. Thomas Aquinas – See 1.546–47n. Feast day: 7 March.

12.1702–3 (339:29). S. Ives of Brittany – Ivo or Yves Hélory (1253–1303), a confessor, bishop's judge, and lawyer who used his fees for philanthropy and defended the poor without charge. He is the patron saint of lawyers. Feast day: 19 May.

12.1703 (339:29). S. Michan – Little is known about this tenth- or eleventh-century Danish-Irish saint except that he is styled "bishop" and "confessor," and one of Dublin's more famous churches is named for him. Feast day: 25 August.

12.1703 (339:30). S. Herman-Joseph – The Blessed Herman-Joseph (1150–1241), the German mystic, was beatified but not canonized. Originally named Herman, the Virgin Mary bestowed the name Joseph on him in one of his many visions. Feast day: 7 April.

12.1703–4 (339:30). the three patrons of holy youth – The three youthful Jesuit saints noted below are regarded as the patron saints of Jesuit schools for boys ("holy youth").

12.1704 (339:30–31). S. Aloysius Gonzaga – (1568–91), Italian Jesuit saint, famous for his zeal for the virtue of chastity. Popularly regarded as a model of youthful purity, he died at the age of twenty-three from attending plague victims. He is one of the patron saints of youth. Feast day: 21 June.

12.1704 (339:31). S. Stanislaus Kostka – (1550–68), a Jesuit novice who overcame his family's resistance to his calling and demonstrated his faith by walking the 350 miles from Vienna to Rome to join the order. Feast day: 13 November.

12.1704–5 (339:31–32). S. John Berchmans – (1599–1621), another Jesuit devotee of the innocence and purity of youth. Feast day: 26 November.

12.1705 (339:32). Gervasius – (d. c. 165), a martyr, he was beaten with lead whips in Milan by the Roman general Astasius, who ordered the death of all Christians in his province. A brother (?) and fellow martyr, Protasius, was beheaded in the same purge. Feast day: 19 June.

12.1705 (339:32). Servasius – St. Servatius (d. 384), bishop of Tongres (in modern Belgium), commanded considerable reverence in medieval western Europe. Feast day: 13 May.

12.1705 (339:32). Bonifacius – The best known of the saints of this name was St. Boniface (c. 675–754), born Winfrid of England. He became the "apostle of Germany," archbishop of Mainz, and was martyred in a massacre of Christians in Friesland. Feast day: 5 June.

12.1705 (339:33). S. Bride – Or St. Bridgid (c. 453–c. 523), one of the three patron saints of Ireland. She founded several monasteries and is supposed to be buried in Downpatrick with SS. Patrick and Columcille, the other two patrons of Ireland. Feast day: 1 February.

12.1706 (339:33). S. Kieran – Among the several Irish saints of this name: (1) St. Kieran (c. 500–c. 560), bishop of Ossory and "One of the Twelve Apostles of Ireland." Feast day: 15 March. (2) St. Kieran of Clonmacnois (fl. sixth century), the founder of one of the most remarkable of the Irish monastic schools. Feast day: 9 September.

12.1706 (339:33). S. Canice of Kilkenny – See 3.259n. Feast day: 11 October.

12.1706 (339:33–34). S. Jarlath of Tuam – (d. c. 540) built a church in Tuam (County Galway) and established the first bishopric in Connacht; Tuam still retains its primacy in that province. Feast day: 6 June.

12.1706–7 (339:34). S. Finnbarr – The most famous of the five Irish saints of this name (c. 550–623) established the bishopric of Cork, founded a monastic school that dominated the district around Cork, and is the patron saint of that city. Feast day: 25 September.

12.1707 (339:34). S. Pappin of Ballymun – (fl. sixth century); little is known of him except that he was the abbot of a monastery at Ballymun (in the parish of Santry, four miles north of the center of Dublin; the parish church still bears his name, St. Papan, and presumably occupies the site of the monastery). In the *Martyrology of Tallaght*, St. Papan and his brother, St. Folloman, are commemorated on 31 July.

12.1707 (339:35). Brother Aloysius Pacificus – A brother and disciple of St. Francis of Assisi; see 12.1684n.

12.1708 (339:35). Brother Louis Bellicosus – Bellicosity to balance peacefulness?

12.1708 (339:36). Rose of Lima – (1586–1617), a virgin saint born in Lima, Peru, her face transformed by a mystical rose in childhood (hence her name) and her life transformed by many visions of Christ. She is the first American saint and thus the patroness of the Americas. Feast day: 30 August.

12.1708 (339:36). Rose . . . of Viterbo – (d. 1252), the patron saint of that Italian city. She was a member of the Third Order of St. Francis and was noted for the miracles associated with her and for the eloquence of her condemnation of the Holy Roman Emperor Frederick II's interference with the Church. Feast day: 4 September.

12.1708–9 (339:36–37). S. Martha of Bethany – One of Lazarus's sisters; see 5.289–91n. Feast day: 29 July.

12.1709 (339:37). S. Mary of Egypt – (fl. c.

400), a prostitute in Alexandria who made a pilgrimage to Jerusalem, where she was forbidden to enter the church but was admitted by the miraculous intervention of the Blessed Virgin Mary. After this experience, she is supposed to have spent forty-seven penitential years in the wilderness beyond the Jordan and attained such purity that she could walk on water. Feast day: 2 April.

12.1709 (339:37). S. Lucy – A virgin martyred at Syracuse at the end of the third century. There are a variety of legends about her career as a Christian virgin pledged to chastity in a pagan world. In one version she was denounced as a Christian by a suitor whom she had refused in favor of her vows. Brought before the emperor, she was condemned to exposure in a brothel, but the emperor's soldiers and magicians could not move her; they built a fire around her and she was unscathed until stabbed in the throat. Another version of the legend is that Lucy's eyes attracted a suitor, whereupon she plucked out her eyes only to have them miraculously restored. Feast day: 13 December.

12.1709 (339:37). S. Brigid – See S. Bride, 12.1705n.

12.1709–10 (339:38). S. Attracta – Or St. Araght (fl. fifth century). She was supposed to have received her veil from St. Patrick and to have divided her time between founding monastic houses in Galway and Sligo and praying in solitude. Feast day: 11 August.

12.1710 (339:38). S. Dympna – Virgin and martyr (seventh century), the Christian daughter of a pagan (Irish?) king who fled to the Continent to escape her father and/or his "unholy desires." He followed her and murdered her at Gheel near Antwerp. Miracles associated with her relics have made her the patron saint of the insane. Feast day: 15 May.

12.1710 (339:38). S. Ita – (c. 48–570), "the Mary or Brigid of Munster." She gave up the name Deidre for Ita (to assert her thirst for God) and was the founder of a religious community and school near Limerick. Feast day: 15 January.

12.1710 (339:38). S. Marion Calpensis – St. Marion of Calpe (Gibraltar); that is, Molly Bloom.

12.1710–11 (339:39). the Blessed Sister Teresa of the Child Jesus – (1873–97), beatified in 1923 and canonized in 1925. She was a member of the Order of Discalced Carmelites, noted for her dedication to the "spiritual way of childhood according to the teaching of the Gospels." Also known as St. Teresa of Lisieux. Feast day: 3 October.

12.1711 (339:39–40). S. Barbara – Virgin and martyr, a legendary saint, said to have been martyred in Bithynia (c. 236) or in Egypt (c. 306). The daughter of a "fanatic heathen," she was delivered to the law for torture by her father, who subsequently beheaded her when she refused to recant. Her father was struck by lightning on the spot; hence, she is the patron saint of those threatened by lightning and storms, of artillerymen, fireworks makers, etc. Feast day: 4 December.

12.1711 (339:40). S. Scholastica – (c. 480–c. 543), a sister of St. Benedict (see 12.1679n). She followed him to Monte Cassino, where she established a community of nuns governed according to her brother's rule. Feast day: 10 February.

12.1712 (339:40–41). S. Ursula with eleven thousand virgins – See 1.140n. day: 21 October.

12.1712–13 (339:41). nimbi and aureoles and gloriae – In art, the symbols of sanctity: the nimbus is represented as surrounding the head; the aureole, the body; and the glory combines nimbus and aureole. The nimbus is used in representations of saints and holy persons; the aureole is reserved for the three persons of the Godhead and for the Virgin Mary.

12.1713 (339:42). palms – Symbolic of martyrdom, the palm belongs to all the "noble army of martyrs."

12.1713 (339:42). harps – Symbolic of the Book of Psalms and of songs in praise of God. The harp is also the traditional symbol of Ireland, the Isle of Saints in procession.

12.1713 (339:42). swords – Symbolic of martyrdom and also associated with warrior-saints.

12.1713–14 (339:42). olive crowns – Symbolic of peace, used in representations of the Archangel Gabriel and several saints and on the tombs of martyrs.

12.1715 (340:2). Inkhorns – Symbolically an attribute of the doctors of the Church St. Augustine (see 7.842–44n) and St. Bernard (12.1695n) and of the evangelists Mark and Matthew.

12.1715 (340:2). arrows – Symbolic of spiritual weapons dedicated to the service of God, and also symbolic of the plague. St. Sebastian is depicted as pierced by arrows, and since he survived, he is one of the patron saints of those suffering from the plague. St. Ursula is also reputed to have survived torture by arrows (see 1.140n). St. Theresa is occasionally represented with a flaming arrow in her breast (see 12.1682–84n).

12.1715 (340:2). loaves – In general, the staff of life; symbolically, three loaves of bread are an attribute of St. Mary of Egypt (see 12.1709n), and a loaf is an attribute of St. Dominic because he is supposed to have fed his monastery by divine intervention (see 12.1686n).

12.1715 (340:2). cruses – (Bottles or jugs), an attribute of, among others, St. Benedict (see 12.1679n) and (on the end of a staff) of St. James the Great (see 12.1698–99n).

12.1715 (340:2). fetters – Symbols of the Passion, the flagellation of Christ by the soldiers; also an attribute of St. Leonard (d. c. 546) for his charitable work among the prisoners of King Clovis of France.

12.1715 (340:2). axes – Symbols of destruction; an axe is an emblem of St. Joseph (see 12.1694n) as carpenter, and it is also the emblem of the beheaded martyrs, St. John the Baptist, St. Matthew, and St. Mathias.

12.1715 (340:2). trees – Variously symbolic of lineage, as in the Tree of Jesse (the lineage of Christ), and of regenerative power, as the flowering tree is an attribute of the fourth-century Florentine St. Zenobius in commemoration of his power to restore dead things to life.

12.1715 (340:2). bridges – An attribute of (among others) St. John Nepomuc because he was martyred by being cast from a bridge to drown (see 12.1702n).

12.1716 (340:3). babes in a bathtub – An attribute of the legendary fourth-century St. Nicholas of Myra or Bari symbolizing his miraculous restoration of life to three dead children.

12.1716 (340:3). shells – A scallop shell is an attribute of St. James the Great (see 12.1698–99n) and was worn as an emblem by pilgrims to his shrine at Compostella.

12.1716 (340:3). wallets – Symbolic of pilgrim-saints; an attribute of St. Roch (together with the pilgrim staff and the shell of St. James of Compostella).

12.1716 (340:3). shears – Or pincers; an attribute of the third-century St. Agatha of Sicily, who was tortured by having her breasts torn with shears. Pincers are also an attribute of the third-century St. Apollonia of Alexandria, who had her teeth torn out in the process of her martyrdom; she is the patron saint of dentists.

12.1716 (340:3). keys – An attribute of St. Peter as guardian of "the keys of the kingdom of heaven" (Matthew 16:19) and of St. Martha (see 12.1708–9n) the patron saint of good housekeeping.

12.1716 (340:3). dragons – Symbolic of the devil and the attribute of the Archangel Michael and of several saints, including the second-century St. George of Cappadocia, the patron saint of England, and of St. Martha (see 12.1708–9n), who after the Crucifixion is supposed to have traveled to southern France and to have rid that region of a dragon.

12.1716 (340:3). lilies – Symbolic of purity and therefore the flower of the Virgin Mary; and as symbolic of chastity, the attribute of several saints, including St. Francis (see 12.1684n), St. Dominic (see 12.1686n), St. Clare (see 12.1685n), and St. Joseph (see 12.1694n).

12.1716 (340:4). buckshot – An obvious anachronism in this list of "symbolic attributes," but it may recall those Irish "martyrs" who benefited from William E. ("Buckshot") Forster's determination that the Royal Irish Constabulary (for humanitarian reasons) should use buckshot rather than ball cartridges when firing on crowds. Forster (1819–86) was chief secretary for Ireland (1880–82) and a Quaker.

12.1717 (340:4). beards – Apart from their general representational occurrence, beards are the particular attributes of several young minor saints who obtained beards by prayer; these latter are not mentioned in *Ulysses*.

12.1717 (340:4). hogs – Symbolic of sensuality and gluttony; one of the attributes of the fourth-century Egyptian hermit St. Anthony the Great, or Anthony Abbot, who spent twenty solitary years in the desert in a successful attempt to defeat the demons (temptations) of the flesh and to live for God alone.

12.1717 (340:4). lamps – Generally symbolic of wisdom and piety, specifically of the "wise virgins," and as such an attribute of St. Lucy (see 12.1709n).

12.1717 (340:4). bellows – Held by the devil (as a means of intensifying the flames of the flesh); an attribute of the early-sixth-century St. Genevieve.

12.1717 (340:4). beehives – Symbolic of great eloquence; an attribute of (among others) St. Bernard of Clairvaux (see 12.1695n), because "his eloquence was as sweet as honey."

12.1717 (340:4). soupladles – A spoon, held by a child near him, is an attribute of St. Augustine of Hippo (see 7.842–44n).

12.1717 (340:5). stars – Symbolic of divine guidance or favor; the Virgin Mary as Queen of Heaven is crowned with twelve stars (Revelation 12:1); the star is symbolic of her title Stella Maris (Star of the Sea); and a star on the forehead is an attribute of (among others) St. Dominic (see 12.1686n).

12.1717 (340:5). snakes – St. John, apostle and evangelist, was occasionally depicted with a cup (of poison) and a snake, symbolic of an attempt made on his life by the Roman emperor Domitian; St. Patrick is often depicted as treading on snakes to signify his having rid Ireland of venomous creatures; and St. Phocas (see 12.1690n) is depicted as entwined with snakes.

12.1717 (340:5). anvils – The martyr St. Adrian (d. 290) is depicted holding an anvil, since an anvil figured in his martyrdom.

12.1718 (340:5). boxes of vaseline – Secular and commercial reduction of box of ointment, symbolic of humble and costly affirmation, an attribute of Mary Magdalene and of Mary the sister of Lazarus (equated in medieval and Renaissance art) after John 12:3: "Then took Mary a pound of ointment of spikenard, very costly, and anointed the feet of Jesus, and wiped his feet with her hair." The box of ointment is also an attribute of the two surgeon-saints (see "forceps," 12.1718n).

12.1718 (340:5). bells – Symbolic of the power to exorcise evil spirits; one of the attributes of (among others) St. Anthony (see "hogs," 12.1717n).

12.1718 (340:5). crutches – Symbolic of age and feebleness; another of the attributes of St. Anthony.

12.1718 (340:5). forceps – Surgical instruments are attributes of the surgeon-brothers, the legendary third-century SS. Cosmas and Damian.

12.1718 (340:6). stag's horns – The stag is symbolic of piety and religious aspiration, of purity and solitude; the stag without a crucifix between its horns is an attribute of St. Julian Hospitator (see 12.1690–91n).

12.1718 (340:6). watertight boots – An "attribute" of Gabriel Conroy in "The Dead," *Dubliners.*

12.1719 (340:6). hawks – The wild falcon is symbolic of evil thought or action; the domestic falcon, of the holy man or the Gentile converted to Christianity.

12.1719 (340:6). millstones – Attributes of the fourth-century Spanish martyr St. Vincent of Sargossa and of the third-century Austrian martyr St. Florian of Noricum, because each suffered martyrdom by being thrown into the water with a millstone around his neck.

12.1719 (340:6–7). eyes on a dish – An attribute of St. Lucy (see 12.1709n).

12.1719 (340:7). wax candles – Play a great and varied role in Church symbolism and are universally used in shrines and in religious processions.

12.1719 (340:7). aspergills – The brushes with which holy water is sprinkled in Church ceremonies, symbolic of purification from and expulsion of evil. The aspergillum is an attribute of (among others) St. Anthony (see "hogs," 12.1717n), St. Benedict (see 12.1679n), and St. Martha (see 12.1708n and "dragons," 12.1716n).

12.1719 (340:7). unicorns – Symbolic of purity in general and of female chastity in particular. The unicorn is one of the attributes of the Virgin Mary and of several other virgin saints, notably those who were able to survive great temptation.

12.1720–21 (340:8–9). by Nelson's Pillar . . . Little Britain Street – Implies that the procession has formed at the Procathedral of the Immaculate Conception in Marlborough Street, a two-minute walk from the pillar, and that it takes a direct route west through Henry and Mary streets and north through Capel Street to Little Britain Street and to Barney Kiernan's. A procathedral is a parish church temporarily in use as a cathedral in a diocese that does not yet have a cathedral. It was a sore point with Dublin Catholics that the two "rightful" cathedrals in Dublin, St. Patrick's and Christ's Church, were (and are) in the hands of the Church of Ireland. The joke: Barney Kiernan's pub is to be consecrated as the long-awaited permanent cathedral in Dublin.

12.1721–22 (340:9–10). the introit in *Epiphania . . . Surge, illuminare* – The entrance chant of the mass for the Epiphany of Our Lord [Jesus Christ] (6 January). The introit does not, however, begin "Surge, illuminare" but "Ecce advenit Dominator Dominus" (See, he comes, the Lord and Conqueror); the lesson for that day does begin "Surge, illuminare, Jerusalem . . ." (Rise up in splendor, Jerusalem! Your light has come, the glory of the Lord shines upon you) (Isaiah 60:1–6).

12.1722–23 (340:11). the gradual *Omnes* which saith *de Saba venient* – The gradual of the Mass for the Epiphany begins "Omnes de Saba venient . . ." (All the people of Saba are coming with gifts of gold and incense, and singing the Lord's praises) (Isaiah 60:6) and continues "Surge, illuminare" (Isaiah 60:1).

12.1723–25 (340:12–13). casting out devils . . . halt and the blind – Various of the miracles of Jesus: "casting out devils" (Matthew 9:32ff.; Mark 5:1ff.; Luke 8:26ff.); "raising the dead" (Luke 7:11ff., 8:40ff.; Matthew 9:18ff.; Mark 5:21ff.); "multiplying fishes" (Matthew 14:13ff., 15:32ff.; Mark 6:34ff., 8:1ff.; Luke 9:12ff., John 6:1ff.); "healing the halt and the blind" (there are numerous instances in each of the four Gospels).

12.1725 (340:14). discovering various articles which had been mislaid – Miraculous aid of this sort is given by St. Anthony of Padua.

12.1726 (340:15). fulfilling the scriptures – Several times in the New Testament Jesus is said to have "fulfilled the scriptures," that is, to have acted or been treated in such a way as to fulfill Old Testament prophesies of the coming of the Messiah: Matthew 5:17; Luke 24:27; John 19:24; see 14.1577n; Acts 13:29; Hebrews 10:9.

12.1726–27 (340:16). beneath a canopy of cloth of gold – That is, beneath a *baldacchino*, the covering under which the Blessed Sacrament is borne in procession. It consists of a rich cloth (gold, silver, or white) on a rectangular framework supported by four, six, or eight staves, which are usually carried by high-ranking laymen. Father O'Flynn's presence under the *baldacchino* suggests that he is the highest ranking cleric in the procession (quite an honor, considering the assembled company).

12.1727 (340:17). Father O'Flynn – See 8.707, 713n.

12.1728 (340:17). Malachi – See 1.41n.

12.1728 (340:17). Patrick – See 5.330n.

12.1731–35 (340:22–26). the celebrant blessed the house . . . thereof with blessed water – An exaggeration of the ritual act of cleansing an edifice before entering it in the ceremony for the consecration of a house.

12.1735–37 (340:26–29). that God might bless . . . light to inhabit therein – A paraphrase of the closing lines of the *Alia Benedictio Domus* (Another Blessing for a House, outside of Eastertime), Rituale Romanum (Boston, 1926), title 8, chapter 7: "Therefore, at our entrance, Lord, bless and sanctify this house as you blessed the houses of Abraham, Isaac and Jacob: and cause the Angels of your light to inhabit this house and to protect those who dwell therein. Through Christ Our Lord." This blessing is no longer included in the Roman ritual.

12.1737–38 (340:29–30). he blessed the viands and the beverages – That is, he pronounced the *Benedictio Panis, Vini, Aquae et Fructum* from the ritual (Blessing of Bread, Wine, Water, and Fruits).

12.1740–43 (340:31–34). *Audiutorium nostrum . . . cum spiritu tuo* – Latin: "Our help is in the name of the Lord. / Who made heaven and earth. / The Lord be with you / And with thy spirit." A responsive formula of blessing that traditionally precedes a formal prayer.

378 Cyclops: 12.1746–1811

12.1746–50 (340:37–42). *Deus, cuius verbo sanctificantur . . . Christum Dominium nostrum* – Latin: "O God, by whose word all things are made holy, pour down your blessing on these which you created. Grant that whoever, giving thanks to you, uses them in accordance with your law and your will, may by calling on your holy name receive through your aid health of body and protection of soul, through Christ our Lord." This is the *Benedictio ad omnia*, the "Blessing for all [things]," which the priest uses on all occasions for which there is no specific blessing in a ritual.

12.1752 (341:2). Thousand a year – A toast, in effect: "wealth and good fortune."

12.1753 (341:3). John Jameson – An Irish whiskey: John Jameson & Son, Ltd., a Dublin distillery.

12.1753 (341:3–4). butter for fish – A lower-class Dublin toast, also meaning "wealth and good fortune."

12.1760 (341:12). scut – See 5.542n.

12.1770 (341:26). jaunting car – See 5.98n.

Parody: 12.1772–82 (341:28–40). The milk-white dolphin tossed . . . bark clave the waves – More parody of late-nineteenth-century romantic versions of medieval legend.

12.1779 (341:37). hosting – The raising of an armed force or military expedition.

12.1783 (341:41). lowering the heel of my pint – Drinking the last of what was left in the mug.

12.1785 (342:1–2). the curse of Cromwell – Calls the ruthlessness and brutality of Cromwell's suppression of Irish insurrection down on the head of the person cursed; see 12.1507–9n.

12.1785 (342:2). bell, book and candle – To curse "by bell, book, and candle" is to pronounce "major excommunication" (absolute and irrevocable exclusion of the offender from the Church). The bell calls attention; the book contains the sentence to be pronounced; the candle is extinguished to symbolize the spiritual darkness into which the excommunicant is cast.

12.1792 (342:9). Arrah – See 12.141n.

12.1792 (342:9). sit down on the parliamentary side of your arse – In other words, sit down and conduct yourself as you would in a parliamentary discussion.

12.1798 (342:16). whisht – Irish: "silence."

12.1801 (342:20). *If the man in the moon was a jew, jew, jew* – After the American popular song "If the Man in the Moon Were a Coon" (1905), by Fred Fisher. Chorus: "If the man in the moon were a coon, coon, coon, / What would you do? / He would fade with his shade the silv'ry moon, moon, moon / Away from you. / No roaming 'round the park in the bright moonlight, / If the man in the moon were a coon, coon, coon." For coon, see 6.704n.

12.1804 (342:24). Mendelssohn – Either the German philosopher Moses Mendelssohn (1729–86), a Jew who made impressive attempts to mitigate the brutal prejudice against Jews in eighteenth-century Berlin and who successfully broadened the outlook of his co-religionists, or Felix Mendelssohn-Bartholdy (1809–47), the German composer whose family had added the name Bartholdy when they renounced Judaism and embraced Christianity.

12.1804 (342:24). Karl Marx – (1818–83), the German social philosopher, was born of Jewish parents; he not only abandoned his faith but also replaced it with a rather shrill anti-Semitism.

12.1804 (342:24). Mercadante – See 5.403–4n; he was not a Jew but an Italian Catholic.

12.1804 (342:25). Spinoza – Baruch Spinoza (1632–77) was thoroughly educated in Jewish theology and speculation, but his philosophical views were so unorthodox that he was forced to withdraw from the synagogue. The Jewish community in Amsterdam did not, however, stop there but in 1656 achieved his excommunication and managed to have him banished from the city by the civil authority. See 11.1058n.

12.1808–9 (342:31). Christ was a jew like me – Of course, born into and brought up in a family portrayed in the Gospels as profoundly devout. The Gospels also suggest that his initial mission was to transform Judaism, not to displace it with a new religion. See 1.585n.

12.1811 (342:33). jewman – See 10.916n.

Parody: 12.1814–42 (342:37–343:28). A large and appreciative . . . Gone but not forgotten – Parodies a newspaper account of the departure of a royal foreign visitor.

12.1816 (342:39–40). Nagyaságos uram Lipóti Virag – If the order of the words has been Anglicized, then the Hungarian would mean: "Your greatness, my lord, Leopold Flower" (though *Lipóti* should be *Lipot*). If, on the other hand, the word order is Hungarian, then *Lipóti Virag* could mean "Virag of Lipot," that is, from the Jewish quarter of Budapest (and, by extension, of a number of other Hungarian towns and villages). (*Nagyaságos* should read *Nagyasàgos*.) See John Henry Raleigh, *The Chronicle of Leopold and Molly Bloom* (Berkeley, Calif., 1977), pp. 13ff.

12.1816–17 (342:40–41). Messrs Alexander Thom's, printers to His Majesty – Alexander Thom & Co., Ltd., printers and publishers, wholesale stationers and lithographers, agents for the sale of parliamentary papers and acts of Parliament, publishers of the *Dublin Gazette* ("published by the King's authority") and "Printers for His Majesty's Stationer's Office," 87–89 and 94–96 Abbey Street Middle.

12.1818 (342:42). Százharminczdrojúgulyás—Dugulás – Hungarian: "130-calf-shepherd [or soup]—Stopping up [sticking into]."

12.1822 (343:4). phenomenologist – The word was unusual enough in an early-twentieth-century context that it can be regarded here as almost a technical term, suggesting that Bloom is in the forefront of an important philosophical movement. Phenomenology is the study of all aspects of human experience in the course of which questions of objective reality and subjective response are to be held in abeyance; that is, phenomena are not to be prejudged as belonging to classes of differing importance or dismissed on metaphysical or ontological grounds.

12.1825 (343:8). Messrs Jacob *agus* Jacob – W. and R. Jacob & Co., Ltd., biscuit manufacturers in Dublin.

12.1828 (343:11). *Come Back to Erin* – A song by the English ballad composer "Claribel," Mrs. Charlotte Allington Barnard (1830–69). "Come back to Erin, Mavourneen, Mavourneen, / Come back, Aroon, to the land of thy birth: / Come with the shamrocks and springtime, Mavourneen, / And its Killarney shall ring with our mirth. / Sure, when we lent you to beautiful England, / Little we thought of the long winter days, / Little we thought of the hush of the starshine, / Over the mountains, the hills, and the braes."

12.1828 (343:12). *Rakoczy's March* – A song (1809) composed by Miklos Scholl and popularized by the army of Francis Rakoczy II of Transylvania. It was adopted by the Hungarians as their national march, and in the course of the nineteenth-century struggle between the Hungarians and the Austrians it assumed considerable political importance when the Austrians attempted to ban it. The song begins, "Light from Heaven guard our land," and appeals to "Men of proud Hungarian blood" to continue in this struggle for "Magyar glory."

12.1829 (343:13). the four seas – That bound Ireland: the North Channel to the northeast, the Irish Sea to the east, St. George's Channel on the southeast, and the Atlantic Ocean.

12.1830 (343:14). the Hill of Howth – See 3.133n.

12.1830 (343:14). Three Rock Mountain – At 1,469 feet, the mountain, which is south of Dublin, can be seen from the streets of the city.

12.1830 (343:14–15). Sugarloaf – See 8.166n.

12.1830–31 (343:15). Bray Head – See 1.181n.

12.1831 (343:15). the mountains of Mourne – See 11.219n.

12.1831 (343:15). the Galtees – A chain of mountains with some of the higher elevations in southwestern Ireland (in counties Limerick and Tipperary).

12.1831 (343:15–16). the Ox – Mountains in County Sligo in western Ireland.

12.1831 (343:16). Donegal – A mountainous county (rather than a range of mountains) in northwestern Ireland.

12.1832 (343:16). Sperrin peaks – In County Londonderry on the north coast of Ireland.

12.1832 (343:16–17). the Nagles and the Bographs – Two mountain ranges in northern County Cork in southern Ireland.

12.1832 (343:17). the Connemara hills – On the coast in County Galway, western Ireland.

12.1832–33 (343:17). the reeks of M'Gillicuddy – See 12.112n.

12.1833 (343:17–18). Slieve Aughty – A range of mountains between counties Galway and Clare in western Ireland.

12.1833 (343:18). Slieve Bernagh – The second largest of the Mourne Mountains at 2,449 feet.

12.1833 (343:18). Slieve Bloom – See 4.139n.

12.1835 (343:20–21). Cambrian and Caledonian hills – The hills of Wales and Scotland.

12.1839 (343:25). the Ballast office – See 8.109n.

12.1839 (343:25). Custom House – An imposing official building on the north bank of the Liffey, 400 yards downstream from the Ballast Office.

12.1840 (343:26–27). the Pigeonhouse – See 3.160n.

12.1841 (343:27). the Poolbeg light – See 3.279n.

12.1841 (343:27). *Visszontlátásra, Kedvés Barátom! Visszontlátásra!* – Hungarian: "See you again, my dear friend! See you again [Goodbye]!" This salutation is appropriate to a middle-class man, in contrast to the more formal salutation at 12.1816n. (The salutation should read: *Viszontlàtàsra kedevs baràton viszontlàtàsra*.)

12.1845–46 (343:32). Queen's royal theatre – See 6.184n.

12.1849 (343:35). in for the last gospel – Literally: in church before the end of the mass, in time to be credited as in attendance; figuratively: just in time to witness the climax of an action. The last Gospel is John 1:1–14; see 2.160n.

12.1855 (343:41). county Longford – Approximately ninety miles west-northwest of Dublin.

Parody: 12.1858–96 (344:3–345:6). The catastrophe was terrific . . . and F.R.C.S.I. – Parodies a newspaper account of a natural disaster.

12.1858–59 (344:4). The observatory of Dunsink – The astronomical observatory of Trinity College, built in 1785 on a low hill north of Phoenix Park and five miles from the center of Dublin. It became the Royal Observatory of Ireland in 1791. See 8.109n.

12.1859–60 (344:5). the fifth grade of Mercalli's scale – Giuseppe Mercalli (1850–1914), an Italian seismologist, invented a five-grade seismic scale that was highly empirical. It was regarded as particularly useful for the measurement of very severe shocks. "Fifth grade" meant that the shock was as heavy as any that had ever been recorded on a seismograph to that date.

12.1861 (344:7). the earthquake of 1534 – Mentioned in *Thom's* 1904, "Dublin Annals," p. 2093.

12.1861–62 (344:7–8). the rebellion of Silken Thomas – See 3.314n.

12.1863–65 (344:9–11). The Inn's Quay ward . . . square pole or perch – Barney Kiernan's pub was located in St. Michan's parish and in Inn's Quay ward. The ward and the parish are not, however, coextensive. The ward's 226 acres extend in a strip from the Liffey in central Dublin, north to the Royal Canal. The parish (126 acres, 36 square rods) is also north of the Liffey in central Dublin, but its northern boundary is less than halfway to the Royal Canal. The area that the parish and the ward have in common is 62 acres, 3 square rods, and Kiernan's pub was at the eastern edge of the common ground (map and letter, Dublin Valuation Office, A. K. Richardson for the secretary, 27 November 1970).

12.1865 (344:12). the palace of justice – See 12.64–65n.

12.1872 (344:20). Mr George Fottrell – Clerk of the Crown and Peace, Sessions House, Greene Street; see 12.64–65n.

12.1875 (344:23). sir Frederick Falkiner – See 7.698–99n.

12.1877 (344:26). the giant's causeway – A peninsula of basaltic columns (or ridges) that extends into the sea toward Scotland on the northeastern coast of Ireland.

12.1878–79 (344:27–28). Holeopen bay near the old head of Kinsale – Kinsale is on the southeastern coast of Ireland; Holeopen Bay is a small bay formed by two small strips of land that jut out into the Kinsale Harbor.

12.1884 (344:34–35). *missa pro defunctis* – Latin: "mass for the dead."

12.1889–90 (344:41). Messrs Michael Meade . . . Great Brunswick Street – (Now Pearse Street); builders and contractors, planing and molding mills, and joinery works.

12.1890–91 (344:42). Messrs T. C. Martin 77, 78, 79 and 80 North Wall – T. and C. Martin, Ltd., slate and tile yard.

12.1891–92 (345:1–2). the Duke of Cornwall's light infantry – Such a regiment did exist in 1904, but none of its three battalions was stationed in Dublin. However, the duchy of Cornwall was the legal appanage of the heir apparent to the Crown; H.R.H. George Frederic Ernest Albert, Prince of Wales and Duke of Cornwall and York, K.G., K.T., K.P., G.C.M.O., G.C.V.O., I.S.O., who was a general in the Royal army and a vice-admiral in the navy in 1904.

12.1892–96 (345:2–6). *H.R.H., rear admiral . . . and F.R.C.S.I. – Fictional, but see preceding note. *H.R.H.:* his royal highness; Hercules, after the Greek mythical hero-god; Hannibal, after the Carthaginian general (247–182 B.C.) famous for his leadership and for his near-success in a series of wars with Rome. *K.G.:* Knight of the Garter; *K.P.:* Knight of the Order of St. Patrick; *K.T.:* Knight Templar; *P.C.:* Privy Councilor; *K.V.B.:* Knight Commander of the Bath; *M.P.:* Member of Parliament; *J.P.:* Justice of the Peace; *M.B.:* Bachelor of Medicine; *D.S.O.:* Distinguished Service Order; *S.O.D.:* "sod"—a clod or sodomist; *M.F.H.:* Master of Fox Hounds; *M.R.I.A.:* Member of the Royal Irish Academy; *B.L.:* Bachelor of Laws or of Letters; *Mus. Doc.:* Doctor of Music; *P.L.G.:* Poor Law Guardian—from an Irish point of view, an oppressor of the poor; *F.T.C.D.:* Fellow of Trinity College, Dublin; *F.R.U.I.:* Fellow of the Royal University of Ireland; *F.R.C.P.I.:* Fellow of the Royal College of Physicians of Ireland; *F.R.C.S.I.:* Fellow of the Royal College of Surgeons in Ireland. See Adams, p. 201.

12.1897 (345:7). in all your born puff – Eric Partridge (*Dictionary of Slang and Unconventional English* [London, 1937], p. 665b) cites "puff" as being slang for "life, existence" from about 1880.

Parody: 12.1910–18 (345:22–32). When, lo, there came . . . shot off a shovel – Parodies biblical prose.

12.1910–12 (345:22–24). When, lo, there came . . . Him in the chariot – "And it came to pass, as they [Elijah and Elisha] still went on, and talked, that, behold, there appeared a chariot of fire, and horses of fire, and parted them both asunder; and Elijah went up by a whirlwind into heaven. And Elisha saw it, and he cried, My father, my father, the chariot of Israel and the horsemen thereof" (II Kings 2:11–12). See 8.13n.

12.1912–13 (345:24–25). clothed upon in the . . . raiment as of the sun – After the description of Jesus in Matthew 17:1–5: "And after six days Jesus taketh Peter, James, and John his brother, and bringeth them up into an high mountain apart, And was transfigured before them: and his face did shine as the sun, and his raiment was white as the light. And, behold, there appeared unto them Moses and Elias [Elijah] talking with him. Then answered Peter. . . . While he yet spake, behold, a bright cloud overshadowed them: and behold a voice out of the cloud, which said, This is my beloved son, in whom I am well pleased; hear ye him."

12.1913 (345:25–26). fair as the moon and terrible – After the Song of Solomon 6:10: "Who is she that looketh forth as the morning, fair as the moon, clear as the sun, and terrible as an army with banners?" (This passage is glossed in the Douay: "The spouse of Christ is but one: she is fair and terrible.")

12.1914–15 (345:27). And there came a . . . calling: *Elijah! Elijah!* – See 12.1910–12n.

12.1915 (345:28). *And He answered . . . *Abba! Adonai!* – Abba is a Syriac-Greek name for Father-God; Adonai (Lord) is a Hebrew name for God. During the agony in the garden of Gethsemane, Jesus prays, "And he said, Abba, Father, all things are possible unto thee; take away this cup from me: nevertheless not what I will, but what thou wilt" (Mark 14:36).

12.1916–17 (345:30). the glory of the brightness – See "gloriae," 12.1712–13n.

12.1917–18 (345:31). Donohoe's in Little Green Street – A pub, Donohoe and Smyth, grocers, tea, wine, and spirit merchants, 4–5 Green Street Little. (The street runs south at a right angle from Little Britain Street.)

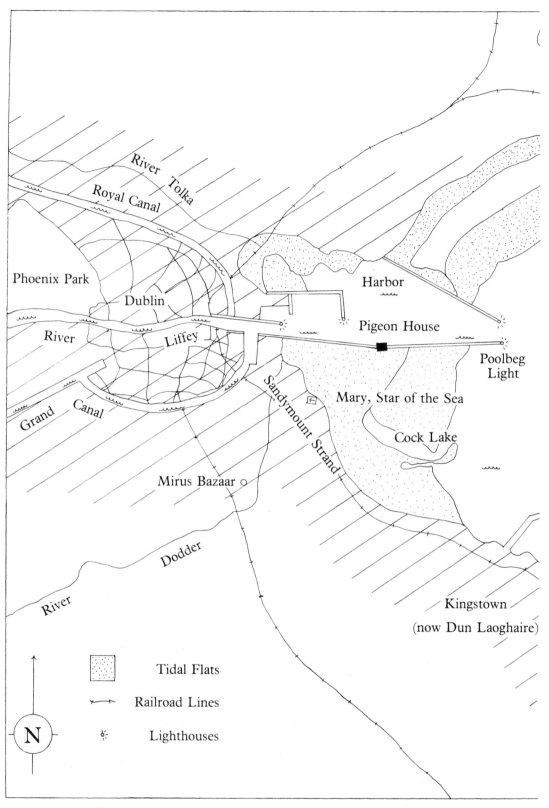

River Tolka

Royal Canal

Phoenix Park

Dublin

River

Liffey

Grand Canal

Harbor

Pigeon House

Poolbeg Light

Mary, Star of the Sea

Cock Lake

Sandymount Strand

Mirus Bazaar

Dodder

River

Kingstown
(now Dun Laoghaire)

Tidal Flats

Railroad Lines

Lighthouses

N

EPISODE 13. *Nausicaa*

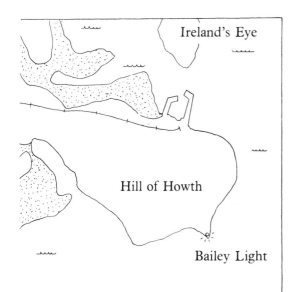

Ireland's Eye

Hill of Howth

Bailey Light

Kish Lightship

Dublin Bay

Kingstown Harbor

East Pier

Martello Tower

Sandycove

Dalkey

Dalkey Island

Dalkey Hill

EPISODE 13

Nausicaa

(13.1–1306, PP. 346–82)

Episode 13: *Nausicaa,* **13.1–1306 (346–382).** In Book 5 of *The Odyssey,* Odysseus leaves Calypso's island, is harassed by Poseidon (see headnote to Calypso, p. 70), and is finally beached at the mouth of a river in the land of a fabulous seafaring people, the Phaeacians. Odysseus hides in a thicket to sleep off his exhaustion and in Book 6 is eventually awakened by the activities of the Princess Nausicaa and her maids-in-waiting, who have come to the river to do the palace laundry. The specific incident that awakens Odysseus involves a ball lost in the course of a game (see 13.345ff. [355:34ff.]). Odysseus reveals himself to Nausicaa and decides not to grasp her knees as suppliant but to "let the soft words fall" (6:148; Fitzgerald, p. 115). He praises her beauty, likens her to a goddess, and pleads the hardship of his case. His appeal is successful; Nausicaa arranges for his safe conduct to the court, and eventually her parents arrange for his safe conduct home to Ithaca.

Time: 8:00 P.M. Scene: The rocks on Sandymount Strand where Stephen had paused in his morning's walk in Episode 3. Bloom has just come from his visit to Mrs. Dignam in Sandymount (a southeastern suburb of Dublin) and has retired to the beach beneath the seawall near the foot of Leahy's Terrace (3.29 [37:33], 13.1173 [379:14]). Organ: eye, nose; Art: painting; Color: gray, blue [blue is the color of beauty, chaste affections, and true love; it is an attribute of the Virgin Mary]; Symbol: virgin; Technique: tumescence, detumescence. Correspondences: *Phaeacia*—Star of the Sea (see 13.6–8n); *Nausicaa*—Gerty.[1]

The Linati schema lists as Persons in addition to Nausicaa: "Handmaidens, Alcinoos and Arete [Nausicaa's parents], Ulysses." Sense (Meaning): "The Projected Mirage." When Odysseus enters the walled city of the Phaeacians, Athena cloaks him in a fog so that he will not be interrupted and challenged by any of the Phaeacians. She does not dispel the fog until

Odysseus has knelt in the great hall of the palace and grasped Queen Arete's knees in supplication. The schema also lists "Onanism: Female: Hypocrisy" under Symbol.

13.2 (346:2). the sun was setting – Sunset in Dublin, 16 June 1904, was at 8:27 P.M. (*Thom's 1904,* p. 14).

13.4 (346:4). Howth – See 3.133n.

13.6–8 (436:6–10). the quiet church . . . Mary, star of the sea – The Roman Catholic Church of Mary, Star of the Sea, off Leahy's Terrace near Sandymount Strand, the Very Reverend John O'Hanlon, canon, parish priest. This is Dignam's parish church, where a temperance retreat is in progress in the course of this episode. "Star of the Sea" (Stella Maris) is an appellation of the Virgin Mary; see "stars," 12.1717n.

13.10 (346:13). Many a time and oft – Shylock complains to Antonio in *The Merchant of Venice:* "Signior Antonio, many a time and oft / In the Rialto you have rated [abused] me / About my moneys and my usances [usury]" (I.iii.107–9).

13.12 (346:14–15). beside the sparkling waves – Since the tide is out and only just turning, there would be a considerable expanse of mud flat between the young women and the waves.

13.12–13 (346:15–16). Cissy Caffrey and Edy Boardman – Apart from the fictional context and their Homeric role as "handmaidens," identity and significance unknown.

13.15 (346:18). *H.M.S. Belleisle* – His Majesty's Ship, Beautiful Island.

13.20 (346:24–25). happy as the day was long – A common saying since the sixteenth century.

13.24 (346:30). plucks – Close to the Irish for cheeks.

13.32 (346:38). scatty – Crumbled.

13.35 (346:42). Flora MacFlimsy – The flighty heroine of "Nothing to Wear" (1857), a poem by the American lawyer-poet William Allen Butler (1825–1902). "Miss Flora MacFlimsy of Madison Square" (the heart of fashionable New York in the 1850s) is mocked at length for the monied self-indulgence of her pursuit of

---

[1] Gerty derives her name from the heroine of Maria Cummins's (1827–66) sentimental novel *The Lamplighter* (1854), and the style associated with Gerty MacDowell owes a considerable debt of parody to the style of the novel. Gerty Flint, the heroine of *The Lamplighter,* begins life "neglected and abused . . . a little outcast," sweet, as expected, but vengeful and vindictive, capable of "exhibiting a very hot temper." She rapidly comes into possession of "complete self-control" and then of a sentimental religiosity that, combined with considerable coincidence, rewards her with the good life of self-sacrifice (and of affluence in her marriage to Willie, the love of her childhood, who has himself made it from rags to riches).

fashionable clothes until she ends "in utter despair / Because she had nothing whatever to wear."

13.37 (347:2–3). cherryripe red lips – From the refrain of a song in Thomas Campion's (1567–1620) *Fourth Book of Airs,* "There is a garden in her face." Lines 5–6: "There cherries grow which none can buy, / Till 'Cherry-ripe' themselves do cry." Robert Herrick worked a variant on Campion's song in "Cherryripe" (1648): "Cherry-ripe, ripe, I cry, / Full and fair ones; come and buy. / If so be you ask me where / They do grow, I answer: There, / Where my Julia's lips do smile; / There's the land, or cherry-isle, / Whose plantations fully show / All the year where cherries grow."

13.42 (347:7). golden rule – From the Sermon on the Mount: "Therefore all things whatsoever ye would that men should do to you, do ye even so to them: for this is the law and the prophets" (Matthew 7:12; also Luke 6:31).

13.42 (347:7). The apple of discord – In Greek mythology the proverbial name for the apple that Eris (goddess of discord) proposed as "for the fairest" (among Hera, Aphrodite, and Athena). Paris, called upon to judge in the beauty contest, awarded the apple to Aphrodite and was himself rewarded with Helen of Troy (and the Trojan War).

13.44–45 (347:10–11). the Martello tower – The one nearest at hand was not Stephen's residence but a similar tower in Sandymount, on the shore less than a mile south of Leahy's Terrace.

13.46–47 (347:12–13). every little Irishman's house is his castle – See 6.821–22n.

13.65 (347:35). What's your name? Butter and cream? – From oral tradition: "What's your name? / Butter an' crame / All the way from / Dirty Lane" (Leslie Daiken, *Out Goes She; Dublin Street Rhymes* [Dublin, 1963], p. 37).

13.84 (348:15). iron jelloids – Gelatinous lozenges containing iron, widely advertised as a cure for anemia (*Allbutt's Systematic Medical Volume* [1898], p. 514).

13.85–86 (348:16–17). the Widow Welch's female pills – A patent medicine advertised as a specific for "female troubles" and "that tired feeling."

13.88 (348:19). ivorylike – "Tower of Ivory" is an epithet for the Blessed Virgin Mary; see 13.287–89n.

13.90 (348:22–23). queen of ointments – An advertising slogan for Beetham's Larola: "Makes the skin as soft as velvet, Removes all Roughness, Redness, Heat Irritation, Tan and Keeps the Skin Soft, Smooth and White all the year round"; M. Beetham & Son, Cheltenham, England.

13.92 (348:25). Bertha Supple – Apart from the context, identity and significance unknown.

13.97 (348:31). queenly *hauteur* – In the Litany of Our Lady (called "of Loreto"), the Blessed Virgin Mary is eleven times addressed as Queen; see 13.287–89n. The French word *hauteur* means not only haughtiness, arrogance, but is also slang for wide awake, up to the job.

13.99–100 (348:33–35). Had kind fate but . . . benefit of a good education – Kind fate did will that Gerty Flint, the heroine of *The Lamplighter,* receive a good education (as the result of the sentimental patronage of a blind gentleman who recognizes Gerty's "good qualities") and also that she be born a gentlewoman, though fate withheld that good news for melodramatic revelation on Gerty's reaching maturity.

13.104 (348:39–40). the love that might have been – Recalls the concluding "moral" of John Greenleaf Whittier's (1807–92) narrative poem "Maud Muller": "For of all sad words of tongue or pen, / The saddest are these: 'It might have been!'" The poem is the pathetic story of a poor farm girl who meets a wealthy judge and is trapped for the rest of her "poor coarse life" in the "vague unrest" of daydream trust in romantic love and the "rags to riches" that "might have been."

13.109–10 (349:4–5). Madame Vera Verity . . . the Princess novelette – *The Princess's Novelettes* (1886–1904) was a weekly magazine published in London. Each issue included at least one complete "novelette" and an installment of a serialized story or novel. The magazine's weekly features included: A. A. P. (All About People); Beauty's Boudoir; Boudoir Gossip; Addressed to "Boudoir" Editor; and the Fashion Supplement. There was no Woman Beautiful page, and no Madame Vera Verity appears, but the magazine did advertise one G. *Vera Miller* as among the "Most Celebrated Writers of the Day" and carried her serialized "stories" almost continually from 1900 to 1904. The magazine's beauty and fashion pages were characterized by thinly disguised plugs for the magazine's advertisers and their products in prose of the sort Gerty echoes.

13.111 (349:6). eyebrowleine – Unknown.

13.117–18 (349:13–14). She had cut it . . . of the new moon – Popular superstition: "It is good to cut the hair at the new moon and by the light of the moon itself; but never should the hair be cut on Friday, for it is the most unlucky day of all the year" (Speranza [Lady Wilde], *Ancient Cures, Charms, and Usages of Ireland* [London, 1890], p. 63).

13.119 (349:15–16). Thursday for wealth – In astrology, Thursday (Jupiter's day) is a day for courage but it is also regarded as a favorable day on which to transact business.

13.120 (349:16–17). flush, delicate as the faintest rosebloom – "Mystical Rose" is another of the epithets for the Blessed Virgin Mary; see 13.287–89n.

13.130 (349:28). nose was out of joint – She had been crossed or was disconcerted or irritated; proverbial since the sixteenth century.

13.130–31 (349:29//). the London bridge road – Londonbridge Road is part of an east-west thoroughfare and is in Irishtown, 400 yards northwest of Tritonville Avenue in Sandymount, where Gerty and her family apparently live; see 13.631n. The choice of Londonbridge Road for the Wylie residence may also include an echo of the children's rhyme and game, "London Bridge is falling down."

13.132–33 (349:31–32). an exhibition in the intermediate – That is, to win the distinction of a cash prize at the end of his school year. The prizes were awarded on the results of competitive examinations set by the Intermediate Education Board for Ireland, established in 1878. Students in secondary and preparatory schools took intermediate examinations annually. To qualify for the second to the last (Middle Grade) examination a student had to be at least 15; for the last (Senior Grade), at least 16. The implication is that Reggie Wylie is at the most 16 or 17 years old.

13.133–34 (349:32). Trinity college – Was so consistently Anglo-Protestant in its orientation that "from about 1875 onwards the Irish Cath-

olic bishops [had forbidden] members of their Church to attend such an infidel College without a special dispensation" (F. S. L. Lyons, *Culture and Anarchy in Ireland 1890–1939* [Oxford, 1979], p. 20).

13.135 (349:33–34). W. E. Wylie – See 10.651–53n.

13.138–39 (349:38). They were protestants in his family – Gerty is hardly being realistic in what follows. The barriers to and prejudices against mixed marriages were formidable. Gerty would have had to obtain the permission of the bishop of her diocese, and before the marriage could take place, young Wylie would have been required to take instruction and be confirmed as a Catholic and to contract that any children of the marriage would be brought up as Catholics.

13.139–40 (349:39–40). Who came first and . . . then Saint Joseph – A delicate echo of the phrase "Jesus, Mary, and Joseph" (frequently used as half-prayer, half-oath). The Holy Family is traditionally invoked in prayer for order and concord in marriage and the family.

13.150 (350:10). dolly dyes – The brand name of a line of dyes packaged for home use.

13.151 (350:10). the *Lady's Pictorial* – "A weekly illustrated journal of fashion, society, art, literature, music and the drama" published in London on Thursday. The magazine had pretensions to fashionable upper-class tone, but the enervated sentimentality of its fiction betrays its essentially middle-class appeal. It asserted in its advertisements that it was "universally acknowledged to be the leading ladies' paper."

13.158 (350:19). Tuesday week – A week ago last Tuesday.

13.159 (350:20). Clery's – See 5.194n.

13.166 (350:29). a five – In American women's sizes a six and a half, a small foot.

13.167 (350:30). ash, oak or elm – A proverbial expression for eternity, echoed by Rudyard Kipling (1865–1936) in "A Tree Song": "England shall bide Judgement Tide / By oak and ash and thorn."

13.174 (350:38). dinky – Slang: small, neat, cute; in 1900 not deprecatory as now.

13.179 (351:3). blue for luck – Blue is a color-attribute of the Virgin Mary. It is the color of chaste affections, true love, and hope and thus is an appropriate good-luck charm for a bride, as in the rhyme for what a bride should wear: "Something old, something new, / Something borrowed, something blue, / And a silver sixpence in her shoe" (suggested by Joan Keenan).

13.181 (351:5–6). the green she wore . . . brought grief – In its negative aspect, green is regarded as the color of envy and jealousy, of love gone sour or thwarted, as in the proverbial saying: "Blue is love true, / Green is love deen [dying]."

13.182 (351:7). the intermediate exhibition – See 13.132–33n.

13.184–87 (351:9//11). *nearly slipped up the old . . . inside out or if they got untied that he was thinking about you so long as it wasn't of a Friday – "It is lucky to put a garment on inside out when dressing, if it is done accidentally, but it must be left as it is and worn inside out, otherwise the luck will be changed" (E. and M. A. Radford, *Encyclopedia of Superstitions*, ed. and rev. Christina Hole [London, 1961]). Also, if a shoe or garment comes untied, it means that someone is thinking of you. Friday "is the most unlucky day of the year" (see 13.117–18n), and consequently good luck omens tend to be reversed on Fridays.

13.192–93 (351:17–18). You are lovely, Gerty, it said – As the magic mirror in "Snow White and the Seven Dwarfs" responds to the wicked stepmother's question ("Mirror, mirror, on the wall, / Who's the fairest of them all?") until Snow White displaces her stepmother in the mirror's estimation.

13.196 (351:22). T.C.D. – Trinity College, Dublin; see 13.133–34n.

13.197–98 (351:23–24). the fashionable intelligence – That is, the society columns of the newspaper.

13.201 (351:28). Stoer's – See 10.1125–26n.

13.207 (351:35). a man among men – From Samuel Valentine Cole's (1851–1925) popular sentimental poem "Lincoln": "He who walked in our common ways, / With the seal of a king on his brow; / Who lived as a man among men his days, / And 'belongs to the ages' now."

13.208 (351:36). waiting, always waiting – See "Waiting," 11.730n.

13.208 (351:36). leap year – Traditionally it is supposed to be permissible for the woman to make the proposal of marriage during leap year.

13.209 (351:37). prince charming – Almost a generic name for the fairy-tale hero; a Prince Charming releases Snow White from the stepmother's spell in "Snow White and the Seven Dwarfs" (see 13.112–13n).

13.216–17 (352:4–5). for riches for poor . . . to this day forward – The vow from the Catholic Marriage Service that Gerty misquotes reads: "from this day forward, for better, for worse, for richer, for poorer, in sickness and in health, until death do us part."

13.225 (352:14). queen Ann's Pudding – A custard pudding thickened with bread crumbs and flavored with lemon rind and raspberry jam; see 7.90n.

13.232–33 (352:23–24). grandpapa Giltrap's lovely . . . that almost talked – See 12.120n.

13.234 (352:26). Clery's – See 5.194n.

13.247 (352:42). wigs on the green – An Irish colloquialism, originally for a faction fight and subsequently for any brawl.

13.250 (353:3). out of pinnies – That is, old enough to be dressed as a boy rather than in a baby's pinafore (roughly equivalent to "out of diapers").

13.256 (353:11). Anything for a quiet life – The title of a play (1626) by Thomas Middleton (c.1570–1627). The plot involves several houses in various states of comic disrepair; each of the houses is restored to "normal" by sons or servants whose slogan is "anything for a quiet life."

13.258–59 (353:13–15). here's the lord mayor . . . chinchopper chin – A variant of the nursery-rhyme game: "Here sits the Lord Mayor [*touch forehead*] / Here sit his two men [*eyes*] / Here sits the cock [*one cheek*] / Here sits the hen [*other cheek*] / Here sit the little chickens [*tip of nose*] / And here they run in [*mouth*] / Chin chopper, chin chopper, chin [*chuck under chin*]."

13.260 (353:15). as cross as two sticks – Irritated, annoyed; colloquial from about 1830.

13.270 (353:29). golliwog – A black doll with fuzzy hair and a grotesque appearance (implicitly racist).

13.277 (353:37–38). Tritonville road – One of the main north-south thoroughfares of Sandymount.

13.283 (354:2–3). the reverend John Hughes, S.J. – *Thom's* 1904 lists him as resident in the Presbytery House of the Church of St. Francis Xavier on Gardiner Street Upper.

13.283–84 (354:3–4). rosary, sermon . . . Most Blessed Sacrament – After reciting the rosary and hearing a sermon, the retreat is to celebrate benediction with the Blessed Sacrament, an evening service in honor of the Virgin Mary in the course of which the Litany of Our Lady (of Loreto) or a hymn in honor of Mary would be sung. The Blessed Sacrament is exposed for worship to the accompaniment of hymns and then the celebrant makes the sign of the cross over the participants with the monstrance after the host has been placed in it. The rosary is a form of prayer in which fifteen decades of Aves (a prayer to the Virgin Mary: "Hail Mary, full of Grace . . ."), each decade being preceded by a Pater (the Lord's Prayer) and followed by a Gloria ("Glory be to the Father, the Son, and the Holy Spirit . . ."), are recited on beads. A mystery is contemplated during the recital of each decade, and the rosary is divided into three parts, each consisting of five decades and known as a corona or chaplet. In the first chaplet the Five Joyful Mysteries are the subject: the Annunciation, Visitation, Birth of the Lord, Christ's presentation at the temple, his being found after three days' loss. The Five Sorrowful Mysteries contemplated in the second chaplet are the Agony in the Garden, the Scourging, the Crowning with Thorns, the Carrying of the Cross, the Crucifixion. The Five Glorious Mysteries, allotted to the third chaplet, are the Resurrection, the Ascension, the Descent of the Holy Ghost, the Assumption, and the Coronation of the Blessed Virgin.

13.286 (354:6). fane – Archaic or poetic for a temple or church (after the Latin *fanum*).

13.287 (354:7). the immaculate – The Blessed Virgin Mary.

13.287–89 (354:8–10). the litany of Our Lady . . . holy virgin of virgins – The Litany of Our Lady (of Loreto), a prayer of supplication appropriate to the occasion of this retreat both as part of the benediction ceremony and because the retreat is being held in the Church of Mary Star of the Sea. The litany begins with an appeal to the three persons of the Trinity ("Have mercy on us") and continues with a sustained supplication, "Holy Mary, Pray for us. / Holy Mother of God, / Holy Virgin of virgins, / . . . Mirror of justice, / Seat of wisdom, / Cause of our joy, / Spiritual vessel, // Vessel of honor, / Singular vessel of devotion, / Mystical rose, / Tower of David, / Tower of ivory, / House of gold, / Ark of the covenant, / Gate of Heaven, / Morning star, / Health of the sick, / Refuge of sinners, / Comforter of the afflicted." The litany ends with the prayer: "Grant that we thy servants, Lord, may enjoy unfailing health of mind and body, and through the prayer of the ever blessed Virgin Mary in her glory, free us from our sorrows in this world and give us eternal happiness in the next."

13.291 (354:11–12). taking the pledge – Making a religious vow to abstain from alcoholic beverages.

13.291–92 (354:12–13). or those powders . . . in Pearson's Weekly – *Pearson's Weekly* was a London penny-magazine published on Thursdays; its tone was set by sensational "inside" stories with a penchant for moral instruction of the poor (how to face poverty and how to get rich by means of hard work). Patent medicines and health gimmicks were significantly represented in its advertisements in 1904; several promised cures for alcoholism, typical among them: "TO CURE DRUNKARDS, with or without their knowledge, send stamp for Free Trial Package of a wonderful powdered remedy that has saved homes. . . . Address, in confidence, Ward Chemical Company, 53 Century House, Regent Street, London, W."

13.293–94 (354:15). in a brown study – Stock expression for deep in gloomy thought.

13.301–2 (354:24–25). the man who lifts . . . lowest of the low – After a speech in Act II, scene i of John Tobin's (1770–1804) play *The Honeymoon:* "The man that lays his hand upon a woman / Save in the way of kindness, is a wretch / Whom 'twere gross flattery to name a coward" (suggested by Vincent Deane).

13.303–4 (354:26–27). Virgin most powerful, Virgin most merciful – From the Litany of Our Lady; see 13.287–89n.

13.308 (354:32). screwed – Tipsy or drunk.

13.309–10 (354:34). a palpable case of doctor Fell – Dr. John Fell (1625–86), dean of Christ Church College, Oxford, and subsequently bishop of Oxford University, was a reactionary noted for his persecutions of liberal thinkers (notable among them, John Locke). Fell threatened the satirist Thomas (Tom) Brown (1663–1704) with expulsion from Christ Church unless he could adapt Martial's epigram 1:33 on the spot; Brown is supposed to have saved himself by responding: "I do not love thee, Dr. Fell / The reason why I cannot tell; / But this alone I know full well, / I do not love thee, Dr. Fell." (Martial's epigram: "Non amo te, Sabidi, nec possum dicere quare; / Hoc tantum possum dicere, non amo te.")

13.311–12 (354:36–37). With all his faults she loved him still – After a popular song, "With All Her Faults I Love Her Still" (1888), by Monroe H. Rosenfeld. First verse: "With all her faults I love her still, / And even though the world should scorn; / No love like hers, my heart can thrill, / Although she's made that heart forlorn!"

13.312 (354:37). *Tell me, Mary, how to woo thee* – A popular song by G. A. Hodson. First verse: "Tell me, Mary, how to woo thee, / Teach my bosom to reveal / All its sorrows sweet unto thee, / All the love my heart can feel."

13.313 (354:37–38). *My love and cottage near Rochelle* – From the refrain of an aria in Act II of Balfe's *The Siege of Rochelle* (see 10.557n), sung by Michel. The aria begins: "When I beheld the anchor weigh'd, / And with the shore thine image fade, / I deem'd each wave a boundless sea / That bore me still from love and thee; / I watched alone the sun decline, / And envied beams on thee to shine, / While anguish panted 'neath her spell, / My love and cottage near Rochelle."

13.314 (354:39). Lazenby's salad dressing – A prepared salad dressing manufactured by the soup maker F. Lazenby & Son, Ltd., London.

13.314–15 (354:40). *The moon hath raised* – From a song in *The Lily of Killarney* (see 6.186n). Opening lines of the duet: "The moon hath raised her lamp above, / To light the way to thee, my love."

13.317 (354:42–355:1). Charley . . . and Tom – Apparently Gerty MacDowell's brothers.

13.318 (355:1–2). Patsy and Freddy Dignam – Two of the five Dignam children.

13.318 (355:2). a group taken – A group photograph.

13.323 (355:8). Catesby's cork lino – See 10.1207n.

13.326 (355:11). a ministering angel – In *Hamlet*, Laertes replies to a priest who has objected that Ophelia as a suicide should not be buried in consecrated ground or given a requiem: "I tell thee, churlish priest, / A ministering angel shall my sister be, / When thou liest howling" (V.i.263–65). Sir Walter Scott uses the phrase in *Marmion* (1808), sending it on its way toward cliché: "O Woman! in our hours of ease, / Uncertain, coy, and hard to please, / And variable as the shade / By the light quivering aspen made; / When pain and anguish wring the brow, / A ministering angel thou!" (canto 6, stanza 30).

13.328 (355:13–14). the menthol cone – The cooling and aromatic effect of menthol rubbed on the forehead was used to relieve headache before aspirin came into widespread use.

13.331 (355:18). turned off the gas at the main every night – In houses lighted with gas, not only were individual jets turned off at night, but as an added (and fussy) safety precaution, all the gas supply was turned off at the main.

13.333 (355:20). the chlorate of lime – Was used as a disinfectant in outdoor toilets.

13.333 (355:20). Mr Tunney – See 10.1128n.

13.334 (355:21). christmas almanac – Christmas calendar.

13.341 (355:29–30). her own arms that were white – In *The Odyssey*, Nausicaa playing ball is described as "flashing first with her white arms" (6:101; Fitzgerald, p. 114).

13.342–43 (355:31–32). Walker's pronouncing dictionary – The English lexicographer John Walker's (1732–1807) *Critical Pronouncing Dictionary and Expositor of the English Language; . . . To which are prefixed principles of English pronunciation . . . rules to be observed by the natives of Scotland, Ireland, and London for avoiding their respective peculiarities* (London, 1791, repeatedly revised and reissued).

13.359 (356:9). If you fail try again – After "Try and Try Again," a poem (?) by William Edward Hickson (1803–70): "'Tis a lesson you should heed, / Try, try again. / If at first you don't succeed, / Try, try again."

13.372–73 (356:24–25). her who was conceived without stain of original sin – The Immaculate Conception of the Virgin Mary was raised from the status of "pious opinion" to that of dogma by Pope Pius IX in 1854. "The doctrine which holds the blessed Virgin Mary, from the first instant of her conception, to have been kept free from all stain of original sin, by the singular grace and privilege of Almighty God, in view of the merits of Jesus Christ the Saviour of mankind, is revealed by God, and therefore firmly and constantly to be believed by all the faithful."

13.373–74 (356:25–27). spiritual vessel, pray . . . for us, mystical rose – From the Litany of Our Lady; see 13.287–89n.

13.377–80 (356:31–34). what the great saint Bernard . . . ever abandoned by her – The "Memorare," a prayer attributed to St. Bernard of Clairvaux (see 12.1695n), who used it and admired it but did not compose it: "Remember, O most loving Virgin Mary, that it is a thing unheard of that anyone ever had recourse to thy protection, implored thy help, or sought thy intercession, and was left forsaken. Filled, therefore, with confidence in thy goodness, I fly to thee, O Mother, Virgin of virgins: to thee I come, before thee I stand a sorrowful sinner. Despise not my poor words, O mother of the Word of God, but graciously hear and grant my prayer. Amen."

13.395 (357:8). holy saint Denis – A mild oath; see 12.1694–95n.

13.395 (357:9). possing – To "poss" (dialect English) is to pound clothes in water in the process of washing.

13.409 (357:24). the Bailey light on Howth – The Bailey lighthouse on the southeast headland of the Hill of Howth.

13.417 (357:33–34). Martin Harvey – Sir John Martin-Harvey (1863–1944), an English actor and theatrical producer whose early-twentieth-century visits to Dublin were, according to his autobiography, "a series of triumphs" (somewhat marred in 1910 when he staged *Richard*

III and triggered a riot on the part of Irish Nationalists who wanted *Irish* plays).

13.418 (357:35). Winny Rippingham – Apart from the context, identity and significance unknown.

13.419 (357:36–37). two to always dress the same on account of a play – After the sentimental comedy *Two Roses* (1870), by James Albery (1838–99), in which the heroine sisters do dress alike.

13.420 (357:38). *retroussé* – French: "turned up, snub."

13.432 (358:10). more sinned against than sinning – A cliché; after King Lear, who rages against the gods ("these dreadful summoners") and against the storm on the heath: "I am a man / More sinn'd against than sinning" (III.ii.59–60).

13.436–37 (358:15–16). those cyclists showing off – Women on bicycles in 1904 were regarded as "scandalous" because they exposed the lower part of the calves of their legs.

13.438–39 (358:18). The memory of the past – From a song, "There Is a Flower That Bloometh," in Wallace's opera *Maritana* (see 5.563–64n); originally in Act III, some performing versions insert it in Act II, scene ii. In either case, the song is sung by the tenor-hero, Don Caesar, who has been tricked into marrying Maritana. But he doesn't know who his bride was, because she was veiled for the ceremony, and when he sings he assumes that both his bride and Maritana are gone forever. "There is a flower that bloometh / When autumn leaves are shed. / With the silent moment it weepeth, / The spring and summer fled. / The early frost of winter / Scarce one tint hath overcast. / Oh, pluck it ere it wither, / 'Tis the memory of the past! // It wafted perfume o'er us, / Of sweet, though sad regret / For the true friends gone before us, / Whom none would e're forget. / Let no heart brave its power, / By guilty thoughts o'ercast, / For then, a poison-flow'r / Is—the memory of the past!"

13.442 (358:22). Refuge of sinners . . . *Ora pro nobis* – From the Litany of Our Lady (see 13.287–89n); Latin: "Pray for us."

13.442–45 (358:23–26). Well has it been said . . . transpierced her own heart – A standard prayer in honor of the Virgin Mary; included in the "Official Edition" of *The Raccolta* at the turn of the century, it has since been dropped. "The seven dolors" are the Seven Sorrows of Mary: (1) her "suffering with" her Son, the Prophecy of Simeon "(Yea, a sword shall pierce through thy own soul also,) that the thoughts of many hearts may be revealed" (Luke 2:35); (2) the Flight into Egypt; (3) the Loss in the Temple (Luke 2:46–50); (4) the Carrying of the Cross; (5) the Crucifixion; (6) the Deposition; (7) the Entombment.

13.448 (358:29). Father Conroy – Father Bernard Conroy, 5 Leahy's Terrace, was curate at the Star of the Sea Church in Sandymount in 1904. He is apparently "no relation" to the fictional Gabriel Conroy, whose fictional brother Constantine is described as "senior curate in Balbriggan" in "The Dead," *Dubliners.*

13.448 (358:30). Canon O'Hanlon – See 13.6–8n.

13.451–53 (358:33–35). a Dominican nuṅ in their white . . . the novena of Saint Dominic – The Sisters of St. Dominic had two convents near Sandymount, one in Blackrock and one in Kingston. The habit of Dominican nuns in 1904: a white gown and scapular, symbolic of purity, *and* a black cloak and hood, symbolic of penance. The novena of St. Dominic, a nine-day devotion that would culminate in the celebration of that saint's feast on 4 August; St. Dominic was noted for his devotion to worship of the Virgin Mary and for his emphasis of the rosary as a form of worship.

13.453 (358:35–36). when she told him about that – Namely, about her first menstrual period.

13.458–59 (358:41–42). Our Blessed Lady herself . . . according to Thy Word – During the Annunciation Mary accepts the instruction of the Archangel Gabriel: "And Mary said, Behold the handmaid of the Lord: be it unto me accordingto thy word" (Luke 1:38).

13.463–64 (359:6–7). the forty hours adoration – The Forty Hours Prayer, or the Solemn Exposition of the Blessed Sacrament according to the Clementine Instruction (1592) of Pope Clement VIII. "The Blessed Sacrament is exposed to the public adoration of the faithful" from noon of the first day to noon of the third day following. The time is associated with the time that Jesus lay in the tomb before the Resurrection, though the devotion is celebrated throughout the year and not specifically in conjunction with Easter.

13.471 (359:16). the tide might come in on them – See 1.673–74n. The tide had turned just before 7:00 P.M.; the next high water was not due until 1:06 A.M. on the 17th. In Book 5 of *The Odyssey*, as Odysseus is about to arrive on Nausicaa's island: "Now even as he prayed the tide at ebb / had turned, and the river god made quiet water, / drawing him to safety in the shallows" (5:451–53; Fitzgerald, p. 106).

13.476 (359:22). thingamerry – Something one does not wish to or cannot specify; used before 1890.

13.478 (359:24). throw her hat at it – For a woman to throw her hat at a man is to attempt to attract his attention when her appearance, etc., would not otherwise have done so.

13.481 (359:28). piece – Uncomplimentary slang for a woman or girl.

13.485–86 (359:33–34). high crooked French heels – See 15.3119n and 15.3119–20n.

13.486 (359:35). *Tableau!* – French: literally, "picture, scene, sight"; it is the name of a parlor game in which the participants strike poses meant to symbolize a "message" and say, "Tableau," to announce that the pose is complete and ready to be observed and interpreted.

13.489–90 (359:37–38). Queen of angels . . . of the most holy rosary – From the Litany of Our Lady (see 13.287–89n): "Queen of angels, Queen of patriarchs, Queen of prophets, Queen of apostles, Queen of martyrs, Queen of confessors, Queen of virgins, Queen of all saints, Queen conceived without original sin, Queen assumed into Heaven, Queen of the most holy rosary."

13.491–92 (359:40). and censed the Blessed Sacrament – As prelude to the exposure of the Blessed Sacrament in the benediction ceremony; see 13.283–84n.

13.498 (360:6). *Tantum ergo* – A hymn (the last two verses of St. Thomas Aquinas's *Pange lingua gloriosi*) that is sung after the Blessed Sacrament has been exposed in the benediction ceremony (see 13.283–84n). Translation: "Falling in adoration down / Hail of all marvels this the crown; / The ancient rites are past; / Let the new covenant prevail / And faith, when all the senses fail, / Hold her fruition fast. // All height and depth of praise be done / To him the Father, him the Son, / And him proceeding thence; / Strength and salvation are of them, / And kingdom, and the diadem / Of One Omnipotence. Amen."

13.499 (360:7–8). *Tantumer gosa cramen tum* – Gerty's rhythmic version of the opening line of the *Tantum ergo*, "Tantum ergo Sacramentum"; Latin: "Falling in adoration down."

13.499–500 (360:8). Three and eleven – 3s. 11d., an unusually expensive pair of silk stockings.

13.500 (360:8–9). Sparrow's of George's street – Sparrow & Co., ladies' and gentlemen's outfitters and family linen warehouse, 16 Great George's Street South.

13.501 (360:10). Easter – Was on 3 April in 1904.

13.501 (360:10). a brack – A flaw in the fabric.

13.506 (360:17). a streel – Anglicized Irish for a lazy, untidy woman, a slattern.

13.519–20 (360:32–33). a glorious rose – Cf. "Mystical rose," 13.287–89n.

13.532–33 (361:5–6). half past kissing time, time to kiss again – A stock phrase, usually addressed to children who repeatedly ask what time it is.

13.535 (361:8). my uncle Peter – Slang for pawnbroker (after an appeal to a rich old uncle for financial aid).

13.536 (361:9). conundrum – Slang for a thing with an unknown or puzzling name.

13.547–48 (361:22). after eight because the sun was set – Sunset on 16 June 1904 in Dublin was at 8:27 P.M.

13.551 (361:26). waterworks – From the mid–eighteenth century, low slang for urinary organs.

13.552 (361:27). the second verse of the *Tantum ergo* – See 13.498n.

13.574 (362:11). *Panem de coelo proestitisti eis* – Latin: "You have given them bread from Heaven." The celebrant says this in the bene-

diction ceremony after the singing of the *Tantum ergo*. The response: "Having all sweetness in it."

13.601 (363:3). kinnatt – "An impertinent, conceited, impudent little puppy" (P. W. Joyce, *English*, p. 281).

13.604 (363:7). put that in their pipe and smoke it – After the whimsical English versifier and antiquarian Richard Harris Barham's (pseudonym Thomas Ingoldsby; 1788–1845) "Lay of St. Odille": "So put that in your pipe, my Lord Otto, and smoke it."

13.608 (363:11). *billy winks – A variant of "Wee Willie Winkie," a nursery rhyme: "Wee Willie Winkie runs through the town, / Upstairs and downstairs in his nightgown, / Rapping at the window, crying through the lock, / Are the children all in bed, for now it's eight o'clock."

13.613 (363:17). Puddeny pie – After the nursery rhyme: "Georgie Porgie, pudding and pie, / Kissed the girls and made them cry; / When the boys came out to play, / Georgie Porgie ran away."

13.619–23 (363:25–29). *the benediction because just then . . . Blessed Sacrament in his hands – In the benediction ceremony, after the responses (see 13.574n) and a prayer, the celebrant gives benediction with the Blessed Sacrament. "The veil . . . round his shoulders" is the humeral veil.

13.624–25 (363:30–31). the last glimpse of Erin – From the first line of a song by Thomas Moore: "Tho' the last glimpse of Erin with sorrow I see, / Yet wherever thou art shall seem Erin to me; / In exile thy bosom shall still be my home, / And thine eyes make my climate wherever we roam. // To the gloom of some desert or cold rocky shore, / Where the eye of the stranger can haunt us no more, / I will fly with my Coulin, and think the rough wind / Less rude than the foes we leave frowning behind. // And I'll gaze on thy gold hair as graceful it wreathes, / And hang over thy soft harp as wildly it breathes; / Nor dread that the cold-hearted Saxon will tear / One chord from that harp, or one lock from that hair."

13.625 (363:31). those evening bells – The title of a song by Thomas Moore: "Those evening bells! those evening bells! / How many a tale their music tells, / Of youth and home, and that sweet time, / When I last heard their soothing chime. // Those joyous hours have passed away, / And many a heart that then was gay, / Within the tomb now darkly dwells, / And hears no more those evening bells. // And so 'twill be when I am gone, / That tuneful peal will still ring on, / While other bards shall walk these dells, / And sing your praise, sweet evening bells."

13.625 (363:32). a bat – See 3.397–98n.

13.630 (363:37). the presbyterian church grounds – At the intersection of Tritonville and Sandymount roads in Sandymount.

13.631 (363:38). Tritonville avenue – A short, dead-end street just north of Leahy's Terrace in Sandymount.

13.632 (363:40). freewheel – In 1904, a relatively "modern" bicycle, equipped with a clutch that would disengage the rear wheel except when the driver was pedaling forward.

13.632–34 (363:40–42). like she read in . . . Vaughan and other tales – Gerty recalls the legend on the title page of a copy of Maria Cummins's *The Lamplighter*. Another of Maria Cummins's novels, *Mabel Vaughan* (1857), also has a girl-child as its heroine. In the opening pages of *The Lamplighter*, the orphan-heroine, Gerty, is fascinated by the lamplighter Trueman Flint and his activities; she is later rescued and adopted by him. See p. 384, n. 1.

13.639 (364:6–7). child of Mary badge – The Children of Mary, confraternities established in schools of the Sisters of Charity after 1847 in honor of the manifestation of the Miraculous Medal (1830). (The Sisters of Charity had a convent and school on Park Avenue in Sandymount.) The medal has an image of Mary with the words "O Mary, Conceived without Sin, Pray for Us Who Have Recourse to Thee"; the obverse, the letter *M* with a cross and twelve stars (an attribute of Mary as Queen of Heaven) above the hearts of Jesus and Mary.

13.642 (364:10). violet – Violet is the liturgical color for penitential occasions and for Lent; see p. 13, n. 4.

13.642–43 (364:10–11). Hely's of Dame Street – See 6.703n.

13.645–47 (364:14–16). Art thou real . . . twilight, wilt thou ever? – Louis J. Walsh (1880–1942), "boy orator" and amateur versifier. Joyce quotes the verse in question in *Stephen Hero*: "Art thou real, my ideal? / Wilt thou ever come to me / In the soft and gentle twilight / With your baby on your knee?" Magherafelt is a small village and parish on the shore of Lough Neagh in northeastern Ireland.

13.649–50 (364:19). but for that one shortcoming – Gerty's lameness may be much more of a disadvantage than she allows, given both male attitudes toward women in 1904 (Dublin) and the strikingly low marriage rate; see "*Ulysses* and Its Times," p. 6.

13.651 (364:21). Dalkey hill – On the coast eight miles southeast of Dublin, the site of what guidebooks describe as a "tastefully laid out public promenade."

13.653 (364:23–24). Love laughs at locksmiths – The title of a play (1803) by George Colman (1762–1836), and proverbial thereafter. The phrase was used in a music-hall song, "Linger Longer, Loo," in the Gaiety Burlesque's *Don Juan*. Opening lines: "Love laughs at locksmiths—so they say, / But don't believe it's true, / For I don't laugh when locked away / From my own darling Loo."

13.653–54 (364:24). the great sacrifice – A cliché for the loss of self that a woman was (ideally) supposed to experience in marriage.

13.657–59 (364:29–30). tragedy like the nobleman . . . put into a madhouse – Source unknown. "The land of song" is cliché for Italy.

13.659 (364:30–31). cruel only to be kind – Hamlet upbraids his mother: "I must be cruel, only to be kind: / Thus bad begins and worse remains behind" (III.iv.178–79).

13.662 (364:34–35). the accommodation walk beside the Dodder – A street where prostitutes solicit (as an "accommodation house" is a brothel). The river Dodder approaches the mouth of the Liffey from the south, flowing north past Sandymount and through Irishtown; the walk Gerty has in mind was in Irishtown not far from the Grand Canal docks and from Beggar's Bush Barracks, where part of the British garrison in Ireland was quartered.

13.666 (364:39). in spite of the conventions of Society with a big ess – Adultery was (from a lower-middle-class point of view) conventional in "high society" if "he" was married but separated by some "tragedy."

13.667 (364:40–41). from the days beyond recall – From "Love's Old Sweet Song"; see 4.314n.

13.669 (365:1). waiting, waiting – See "Waiting," 11.730n.

13.675 (365:8). *Laudate Dominum omnes gentes* – Latin: "Give praise to the Lord, O ye nations"; the opening line of Psalm 117 (Vulgate 116), the singing of which occurs while the Blessed Sacrament is being placed in the tabernacle. After this psalm, which concludes the benediction ceremony (see 13.283–84n), the celebrant says: "Let us adore the most holy Sacrament for ever."

13.686 (365:22). the bazaar fireworks – Of the Mirus Bazaar; see 8.1162n. The bazaar was held on grounds approximately 1,500 yards south-southwest of the strand at the foot of Leahy's Terrace, where this scene takes place.

13.688 (365:24). rossies – Anglicized Irish: "unchaste or wandering women."

13.703 (365:42–366:1). the Congested Districts Board – The board was established by the Land Purchase Act of 1891 in an attempt to resolve the problems of over-populated, poverty-stricken rural areas in the west of Ireland. In those areas where the population simply could not support itself on the infertile land, the board was empowered to enlarge small holdings by breaking up big estates, to encourage emigration to areas affording greater opportunities for being self-supporting, to introduce land resource development, and to encourage native industries. The board's methods were widely regarded as arbitrary, and its efforts did not meet with notable success.

13.708–9 (366:7–8). Besides there was absolution . . . before being married – Gerty thinks that to be sexually aroused is only a venial and not a mortal sin (in contrast to fornication), and thus she thinks it will be easy to confess and receive absolution. Her knowledge on these points is somewhat shaky; her catechism would have told her quite bluntly that "impurity" was a mortal sin, and that meant "any deliberate thought, word, look, or deed

with oneself or another by which the sexual appetite is aroused outside of marriage." Nor is there any reason for her to think that a mortal sin would mean that there was no absolution, since an individual who truly repents and confesses his mortal sin and undertakes penance for it can be absolved of "all eternal punishment," though not necessarily of "temporal punishment either in this life or in purgatory."

13.725 (366:27–28). pettiwidth – A brand name.

13.748 (367:13). an infinite store of mercy – "Mother of Mercy" is an epithet for the Blessed Virgin Mary.

13.752–53 (367:19). little bats don't tell – After the proverbial saying about the innocence of childhood: "Little birds don't tell." See 3.397–98n.

13.774 (368:2). the cut of her jib – Nautical and colloquial since about 1820: personal look or style, as the style of a ship can be read in the configuration of its sails.

13.780 (368:9–10). Tranquilla convent – See 8.143–44n.

13.781 (368:11). Sister? – The answer to Bloom's question is Sister Agatha, supplied by THE NYMPH (15.3435 [552:20]).

13.792 (368:25). Catch em alive, O – Echoes the anonymous Irish song "Sweet Molly Malone." First verse: "In Dublin's fair city, where girls are so pretty / I first set my eyes on sweet Molly Malone / As she wheel'd her wheelbarrow through streets broad and narrow / Crying, Cockles and Mussels! alive, alive, oh! / Alive, alive, oh! Alive alive, oh! Crying, / Cockles and Mussels, alive, alive, oh!"

13.794 (368:26–27). Mutoscope pictures in Capel street – A mutoscope was a device for exhibiting a series of photographs of objects in motion (taken by a mutograph); the effect was that of a rather jerky motion picture. The location in Capel Street in central Dublin north of the Liffey is unknown.

13.794 (368:27). Peeping Tom – See 8.449n.

13.796 (368:29–30). Felt for the curves inside her *deshabillé* – See *Sweets of Sin*, 10.606n.

13.800–801 (368:35). turnedup trousers –

Trousers with cuffs were a radical departure in men's fashions in the 1890s.

13.801–2 (368:35–37). He wore a pair of . . . his what? of jet – After a popular song, "She Wore a Wreath of Roses the Night That First We Met," by Thomas Haynes Bayly and J. Phillip Knight: "She wore a wreath of roses / The night that first we met, / Her lovely face was smiling / Beneath her curls of jet; / Her footstep had the lightness, / Her voice the joyous tone, / The tokens of a youthful heart / Where sorrow is unknown." Chorus: "I saw her but a moment, / Yet methinks I see her now, / With the wreath of summer flowers / Upon her snowy brow."

13.803 (368:38). O Mairy lost the pin of her – See 5.281–84n.

13.804 (368:38–39). Dressed up to the nines – That is, to perfection.

13.805 (368:40). on the track of the secret. Except the east – Echoes *In the Track of the Sun*; see 4.99–100n.

13.805–6 (368:41). Mary, Martha – See 5.289–91n.

13.806 (368:41). No reasonable offer refused – A common phrase in advertisements for the sale of personal property.

13.808 (369:1). on spec – On speculation, on the chance of finding something valuable or making a profit.

13.813 (369:7). Barbed wire – See 8.154n.

13.815 (369:10). *Tableau!* – See 13.486n.

13.825 (369:20–21). Wonder if it's bad to go with them then – The answer, of course, is no, but Jewish law is quite explicit in its prohibition of any contact with a menstruating woman; see Leviticus 15:19–33.

13.826 (369:21–22). Turns milk, makes . . . about withering plants – Popular superstitions about the presence of a menstruating woman.

13.827–28 (369:23–24). if the flower withers she wears she's a flirt – From the superstition that flowers, as simples (medicinal plants), could save maidens from spinsterhood and wives from barrenness; thus, if the flower withered, it implied imperfect womanhood.

13.832–33 (369:29–30). Kiss in the dark and never tell – A turn on "kiss and tell," proverbial from William Congreve's (1670–1729) comedy *Love for Love* (1695), Act II, scene x: "O fie, Miss, you must not kiss and tell."

13.837 (369:35). Beauty and the beast – The popular fairy story in which a beautiful daughter becomes the guest of a monster in order to save her father's life. The monster wins her love as a result of his kindness and intelligence, and her love in turn releases him from a spell and he becomes the handsome prince. The earliest of the many versions of this story is apparently in a collection of Italian stories, *Tredici Piacevoli Notti* (Facetious Nights) (1550), by Giovanni Straparola (d. c. 1557).

13.840 (369:38). Hair strong in rut – The odor of an animal's skin does change in rutting season, but the popular attribution of a similar change to human beings is somewhat fanciful.

13.845 (370:2). Drimmie's – David Drimmie & Sons, English and Scottish Law Life and Phoenix Fire offices, and National Guarantee and Suretyship Association, Ltd., 41 Sackville (now O'Connell) Street Lower, where Bloom was once employed.

13.847 (370:5). Shark liver oil – Before the development of fine petroleum oils and synthetic lubricants, sperm oil and shark-liver oil were used to lubricate delicate machinery.

13.857 (370:16). Nell Gwynn – See 9.720–24n.

13.857 (370:16). Mrs Bracegirdle – Anne Bracegirdle (1663–1748), a famous English actress and beauty in the Restoration theatre. In spite of rumors about her private life, she seems to have been the virtuous exception to Restoration expectations about actresses and their *amours*.

13.857 (370:16–17). Maud Branscombe – (fl. 1875–1910), an actress with an extraordinary reputation as a beauty. In 1877 alone over twenty-eight thousand copies of her photograph were sold; as one admirer put it, "Beauty and Maud Branscombe were synonymous." Her private life appears to have been not particularly flamboyant, though her divorce from Mr. Alexander Hamilton Gunn on the grounds of physical violence did receive considerable publicity in 1895.

13.862 (370:22). *Lacaus esant taratara* – That is, *La causa è santa, taratara;* see 8.623–24n.

13.865 (370:25). in a cart – Slang for in a quandary, not knowing which way to turn.

13.866–67 (370:27). the Appian way – In Ranelagh on the southern outskirts of Dublin.

13.867 (370:27). Mrs Clinch – A Mrs. Clinch lived at 24 Synnott Place, less than 200 yards north of Bloom's home in Eccles Street.

13.868 (370:28). Meath street – In the slums in south-central Dublin.

13.877 (370:39). French letter – Slang for a condom.

13.889 (371:12). lieutenant Mulvey – Harry Mulvey, lieutenant in the British Royal Navy (fictional).

13.889–90 (371:13). under the Moorish wall beside the gardens – The Moorish Wall and the Alameda Gardens were two landmarks in Gibraltar, where Molly grew up, but they are not adjacent to each other. The Moorish Wall is on the upper slopes or central plateau of the rock; the Alameda Gardens are a promenade-park in the town below.

13.891–92 (371:15–16). Glencree dinner . . . featherbed mountain – See 10.536n and 10.555n.

13.893 (371:17). Val Dillon – Lord mayor of Dublin, 1894–95; see 8.159n.

13.895 (371:19). Up like a rocket, down like a stick – A cliché, after Thomas Paine's (1737–1809) remark about Edmund Burke's turn from sympathy for the cause of the American Revolution to conservative opposition to the French Revolution: "The final event to himself has been, that as he rose like a rocket, he fell like a stick" ("Letter to the Addressers of the late Proclamation," 1792, p. 4; cited in Arlene Stetson, *JJQ* 19, no. 2 [1982]: 181).

13.900 (371:25). Jammet's – Jammet Brothers, proprietors of the Burlington Hotel and Restaurant, 26–27 St. Andrew's Street, in south-central Dublin not far from Trinity College and the Bank of Ireland.

13.901–2 (371:27). Say prunes and prisms – Overquoted into cliché, from Dickens's *Little Dorrit* (1857), Book 2, chapter 5; the officious Mrs. General counsels Amy, "Papa, potatoes, poultry, prunes, and prism, are all very good words for the lips: especially prunes and prism. You will find it serviceable, in the formation of a demeanor, if you sometimes say to yourself in company—on entering a room, for instance—Papa, potatoes, poultry, prunes and prism, prunes and prism."

13.906 (371:32–33). Those girls, those . . . seaside girls – See 4.282n.

13.909 (371:36). Wilkins – W. Wilkins, M.A., headmaster of High School of Erasmus Smith, 40 Harcourt Street, in southeastern Dublin. See 8.187n.

13.914 (371:42). Cuffe street – Where Harcourt Street meets St. Stephen's Green in southeastern Dublin.

13.916 (372:3). Roger Greene's – Solicitor, 11 Wellington Quay, in central Dublin.

13.921 (372:8). Prescott's – See 5.460n.

13.928 (372:17). Straight on her pins – Literally, "straight on her legs, not lame"; figuratively, "forthright, well-organized."

13.930–31 (372:20). that frump today. A.E. Rumpled stockings – See 8.542 (166:7–8).

13.931 (372:20–21). Or the one in Grafton street. White – See 8.616 (168:12–13).

13.931–32 (372:21). Beef to the heel – See 4.402–3n.

13.936 (372:26). She smelt an onion – From a joke about the man who determined to keep himself free from any entanglement with women. In order to fulfill his determination, he ate a raw onion whenever contact with women was imminent. His scheme and his self-discipline collapsed when he met a woman who found his oniony breath extraordinarily attractive.

13.939–40 (372:30). For this relief much thanks. In *Hamlet* – When Francisco, one of the guards, thanks Bernardo, another, for relieving him at his post (I.i.8).

13.942 (372:32–33). Your head it simply swirls – From Boylan's song; see 4.282n.

13.947–48 (372:38–39). *Her maiden name was . . . mother in Irishtown* – Irishtown is just north along the strand from where Bloom is resting. This Irish street-ballad has proved elusive, but there is an American version by the popular entertainer Harry Clifton called "Jemina Brown." The speaker meets Jemina by chance, finds her attractive, and eventually goes out on a date with her; then he sees her with another man, whom she passes off as "only brother Bill." She gets the speaker to lend her £50 and then disappears, finally to be discovered in one more chance meeting as coproprietor (with "brother Bill") of a grocery store in New Jersey. The speaker's £50 have, of course, purchased the store: "That shop was bought / And I was sold / By naughty Jemina Brown."

13.951 (373:1). Every bullet has its billet – That is, nothing occurs by chance, a saying attributed to King William III of England (1650–1702; king 1689–1702); also the title of a song by Charles Dibdin, music by Sir Henry R. Bishop. The song begins: "I'm a tough, true-hearted sailor, / Careless, and all that, d' ye see, / Never at the times a railer,— / What is time or tide to me? / All must die when fate shall will it, / Providence ordains it so; / Every bullet has its billet, / Man the boat, boys—Yeo, heave, Yeo!"

13.953–54 (373:4–5). and papa's pants will soon fit Willy – From an American nonsense song, "Looking Through the Knothole." The song begins: "We were looking through the knothole in father's wooden leg, / Oh, who will wind the clock while we are gone? / Go get the axe, there's a fly on baby's head / And papa's pants will soon be fitting Willie."

13.954 (373:5). fuller's earth – A material resembling clay in appearance but lacking plasticity; it was used for "fulling" cloth and wool, that is, for cleansing those materials of grease.

13.956 (373:7–8). washing corpse – Traditionally it was "woman's work" to prepare a corpse for burial.

13.957 (373:9). not even closed at first – At birth there is an open triangle in the top of a baby's skull.

13.959 (373:11). Mrs Beaufoy – See 4.502–3n.

13.960 (373:12). nurse Callan – At the National Maternity Hospital in Holles Street (fictional?).

13.961 (373:13.14). the Coffee Palace – See 11.486n.

13.961 (373:14). doctor O'Hare – In February 1904 he was on the staff of the National Maternity Hospital; see 3.181–82n. He died sometime between then and June, but we have been unable to confirm the date or cause of his death.

13.963–64 (373:16). Mrs. Duggan . . . in the City Arms – Mr. and Mrs. Joseph Duggan, 35 Prussia Street, not far from the City Arms Hotel, which was at 55.

13.968 (373:22–23). knock spots off them – Slang for to defeat or to be much better.

13.969–70 (373:24). Hands felt for the opulent – See *Sweets of Sin*, 10.606n.

13.975–76 (373:31). height of a shilling in coppers – That is, twelve thick copper pennies, a popular expression for a diminutive person.

13.976 (373:32). As God made them he matched them – A variant of Robert Burton's (1577–1640) proverb, "Marriage and hanging go by destiny; matches are made in heaven" (*Anatomy of Melancholy* [1621], part 3, sec. 2, mem. 5, subs. 5).

13.978–79 (373:35). Marry in May and repent in December – A variant of the proverb "Marry in haste, and repent at leisure."

13.984 (373:40). Wristwatches are always going wrong – Wristwatches were relatively new and undependable curiosities in 1904. After 1910, methods of reducing electrical disturbance (and consequent magnetic disturbance) in watches were developed, which led to dependable wristwatches.

13.986–87 (374:1). Pill lane – By 1904 renamed Chancery Street, in central Dublin just north of the Liffey; see 12.213–14n.

13.990 (374:5). ghesabo – Variant of *gazebo*, slang for "the whole show."

13.990–91 (374:6–7). Magnetic needle tells . . . sun, the stars – That is, a magnetometer, used to measure daily variations in the earth's magnetic field. By 1904 it had been established that periods of radical variation of that field (magnetic storms) coincided with periods of increased sunspot activity; thus, the "needle" would "tell" what's going on in the sun. The "stars" are Bloom's exaggeration of the capacity of an early-twentieth-century magnetometer.

13.991–92 (374:7). Little piece of steel iron – A compass needle.

13.992 (374:7–8). When you hold out the fork – A piece of iron or steel advanced toward a compass will cause the needle to deflect.

13.1000 (374:16). the horse show – See 7.193n.

13.1001 (374:18). How Giuglini began – Antonio Giuglini (1827–65), an Italian operatic tenor from a poor family who had considerable success in Dublin after 1857; his career was ended by insanity in 1864. The anecdote Bloom has in mind is unknown, but Giuglini was a great Dublin favorite, and anecdotes about him were current in Joyce's father's generation.

13.1004–5 (374:22). But lots of them can't kick the beam – That is, many women cannot experience orgasm. "Kick the beam" means literally that one arm of a scale is so lightly weighted that it strikes the beam or frame of the scales; hence, figuratively, to be light in weight, and in slang, to experience sudden emotion or orgasm.

13.1010 (374:29). opoponax – Or opopanax, the juice of the herb *Panax* (Hercules' Allheal).

13.1012 (374:31). dance of the hours – See 4.526n.

13.1013–14 (374:33). Good conductor, is it? Or bad? Light too – Black is a good conductor, that is, it absorbs heat (see 4.79–80 [57:10–11]). And black also absorbs light as Bloom suggests. In 1904 popular science classified both light and heat as "radiation" and explained them as different forms of "ether-waves" produced by "the vibration of atoms in all material bodies."

13.1018 (374:38). Cinghalese – See 5.32n.

13.1027 (375:7–8). Hyacinth perfume made of oil of ether or something – Compound ethers or esters were key components in the development of artificial perfumes in the latter half of the nineteenth century.

13.1028 (375:8). Muskrat – Muskrat scent was used as a substitute for the musk of the musk deer in the manufacture of perfumes. An artificial musk was developed in 1888.

13.1032 (375:13). hogo – Slang for a flavor, a taint (after the French, *haut goût*).

13.1036–37 (375:19–20). priests that are supposed to be are different – Popular superstition: priests, because they are celibate, have a different body odor.

13.1038–39 (375:21–22). The tree of forbidden priest – After the Tree of Forbidden Fruit, the Tree of the Knowledge of Good and Evil, attractive to Adam and Eve because it was the one thing forbidden them in the Garden (see Genesis 2:17 and 3:1–6).

13.1047 (375:31). Meagher's – See 7.119n.

13.1053 (375:38). Here's this nobleman passed before – See 13.305–7 (354:29–31).

13.1055 (375:40). tuck in – To "tuck in" is slang for to eat (from about 1838).

13.1056 (375:42). government sit – Government situation or employment (in context, a sinecure).

13.1058 (376:2). See ourselves as others see us – See 1.136n.

13.1060 (376:5). prize titbit story – See 4.502n.

13.1062 (376:7). Corns on his kismet – A terrible pun: kismet is, of course, fate, which in stage or rural Irish is pronounced *feet*.

13.1062–63 (376:7–8). Healthy perhaps absorb all the – Medical pathology describes a corn as a small local outgrowth of the outer skin with great enlargement of the horny layers (callosity). Most of the underlying nerve bulbs waste away; but if only one or two remain, pressure on the enlarged part can cause acute pain. Bloom reflects that a healthy body might absorb the callosity and reduce the outgrowth.

13.1063 (376:8). Whistle brings rain they say – Popular superstition: a whistling steam locomotive can cause rain on an otherwise dry but cloudy day.

13.1064–65 (376:10). Old Betty's joints are on the rack – Source unknown, but the context suggests that this is a line from a weather-prophecy jingle.

13.1065–66 (376:10–12). Mother Shipton's prophecy . . . Signs of rain it is – There is very little evidence other than tradition about the identity of the fabulous prophetess Mother Shipton. She is supposed to have lived in Tudor England (1486?–1561?) and is reputed to have prophesied the deaths of Cardinal Wolsey (c. 1475–1530) and other nobles in Henry VIII's court; however, *The Prophecie of Mother Shipton* was not published until 1641. Her prophecies enjoyed a revival of popularity and credibility in the nineteenth century, when they were reprinted with copious and fraudulent additions. The verse Bloom half-recalls reads, "Around the world thoughts shall fly / In the twinkling of an eye." It does not occur in the 1641 edition but was coined by Charles Hindley in 1862 for his hoax version, *The Wonderful History and Surprising Prophecies of Mother Shipton*. The lines are an obvious (retrospective) prophecy of the invention of the telegraph. Bloom's confusion about ships is logical because Hindley's next lines are "Water shall yet more wonders do, / Now strange, yet shall be true" (steam locomotion); the verses then continue through prophecies of railroads and railroad tunnels, submarines, iron steamships, and air travel by balloon.

13.1066–67 (376:12). The royal reader – The six volumes of the Royal Readers were a graded series of textbooks designed "to cultivate the *love of reading* by presenting interesting subjects treated in an attractive style." First published in the 1870s by Thomas Nelson & Sons of London, these texts formed part of the Royal School Series and were among the standard school texts on which the Intermediate Education Board for Ireland based its competitive examinations. In context, however, "royal reader" is a pun: Mother Shipton was a royal reader because she read and prophesied the fates of royalty.

13.1067 (376:12–13). And distant hills seem coming nigh – Source unknown.

13.1068 (376:14). Howth. Bailey light – See 13.409n.

13.1069 (376:15). Wreckers – Either those who are employed in saving lives or property from a wrecked vessel, or land-based pirates who wreck vessels by showing misleading lights.

13.1069 (376:15–16). Grace Darling – (1815–42), the daughter of William Darling, the lighthouse keeper on Longstone, one of the Farne Islands. On 7 September 1838 the steamer *For-*

farshire was wrecked near the lighthouse; all but nine of the sixty-three passengers perished. Grace and her father braved "dangerous seas" and made two trips to rescue the survivors. Grace became a national heroine and merited a commemorative poem, "Grace Darling" (1843), by Wordsworth on the occasion of her death. Wordsworth's poem was reprinted in the fifth Royal Reader (London, 1876).

13.1070 (376:16–17). cyclists: lighting up time – The *Evening Telegraph* for 16 June 1904 announced that "lighting-up time" for cyclists was 9:17 P.M.

13.1074 (376:21–22). Best time to spray . . . after the sun – Common advice to gardeners.

13.1075 (376:22). Red rays are longest – The wavelengths of light rays at the red end of the visible spectrum are longer than those of the other visible colors.

13.1075 (376:23). Roygbiv Vance – See 5.42–43n.

13.1076 (376:24). Venus? – The evening star on 16 June 1904 would have been Saturn, not Venus.

13.1077 (376:24–25). *Two. When three it's night – Jewish tradition as recorded in the *Tract Sabbath* (Babylonian Talmud), trans. M. L. Rockinson (1896), vol. 1, p. 61: "If only one star [can be seen in the sky] it is yet day; if two stars, it is twilight; three stars, it is night."

13.1079 (376:27). Land of the setting sun – Rarely, Japan (more often called the Land of the Rising Sun). But Walter G. Marshall (*Through America* [London, 1882], p. 257) wrote of "this 'Land of Setting Suns,' as California has been peculiarly and distinctly named."

13.1079 (376:27–28). Homerule sun setting in the southeast – As it rose in the northwest; see 4.101–3n.

13.1080 (376:28). My native land, goodnight – From an interpolated lyric in canto 1 of Byron's *Childe Harold's Pilgrimage* (1812). The lyric is a lament and celebration of Childe Harold's departure from England. First verse: "Adieu, adieu! my native shore / Fades o'er the waters blue; / The Night-winds sigh, the breakers roar, / And shrieks the wild sea-mew. / Yon sun that sets upon the sea / We follow in his flight; /

Farewell a while to him and thee, / My native Land—Good Night!" (1:118–25).

13.1081–82 (376:30). white fluxions – Vaginal discharge; the assumption was that sitting on a cold stone could cause such a discharge and that the discharge would threaten the health of an unborn child.

13.1083 (376:31). Might get piles myself – Another "popular medicine" reason for not sitting on a cold stone. Compare Odysseus's fears after his arrival on Nausicaa's island: "In vigil through the night here by the river / how can I not succumb, being weak and sick, / to the night's damp and hoarfrost of the morning" (5:466ff; Fitzgerald, p. 106).

13.1089–90 (376:39). sunflowers, Jerusalem artichokes – The two plants are similar in size and appearance.

13.1090 (376:40). Nightstock – A night-blooming stock.

13.1091 (376:41). Mat Dillon's garden – See 6.697n.

13.1093 (377:1–2). Ye crags and peaks I'm with you once again – From the Irish-born dramatist James Sheridan Knowles's (1784–1862) tragedy *William Tell* (1825). William Tell speaks in an impassioned monologue: "Ye crags and peaks, I'm with you once again! / I hold to you the hands you first beheld, / To show you they still are free. Methinks I hear / A spirit in your echoes answer me, / And bid your tenant welcome home again!" (I.ii.1–5).

13.1097 (377:6). The distant hills seem – See 13.1067n.

13.1098–99 (377:7–8). He gets the plums and I the plumstones – See 7.1021–22n.

13.1104–5 (377:14). Nothing new under the sun – "The thing that hath been, it is that which shall be; and that which is done is that which shall be done: and there is no new thing under the sun" (Ecclesiastes 1:9).

13.1112 (377:23). Rip van Winkle – The story "Rip Van Winkle," in *The Sketch Book* (1819–20) by Washington Irving. Rip does sleep for twenty years and he does awake to find his gun "incrusted with rust"; he returns home, to find "All changed. Forgotten."

13.1112 (377:24). Henny Doyle's – Apparently related to Luke and Caroline Doyle, friends of the Blooms; see 17.1260–61n.

13.1115 (377:27). Sleepy Hollow – "The Legend of Sleepy Hollow" is another of the stories in *The Sketch Book*, but it concerns Ichabod Crane, not Rip Van Winkle. Rip sleeps on an unnamed "green knoll" in "one of the highest parts of the Kaatskill mountains."

13.1117 (377:29). Ba – "The life-breath" (Powis Hoult, *A Dictionary of Some Theosophical Terms* [London, 1910], p. 21). In ancient Egyptian religion, Ba was "the soul, represented by a bird with a human head, supposed to leave the body at death, but expected eventually to return and, if the body be preserved (together with the *cher*, the transfigured soul or intelligence, and the *ka*, or genius of the body), to revivify it" (*Webster's New International Dictionary* [Springfield, Mass., 1909], p. 164; cited by John S. Rickard, *JJQ* 20, no. 3 [1983]: 357).

13.1117–18 (377:29–30). swallow . . . tree – In Plutarch's "On Isis and Osiris," Osiris's seventy-two murderers concealed his body in a chest, which they threw into the Nile so that Isis would not be able to recover her brother-husband's body. "The chest eventually came to rest under a tree which 'enfolded, embraced, and concealed the coffer within itself.' The tree was cut down and used as a pillar in a king's palace." But Isis's search was eventually successful; she found the pillar that concealed the body and "turned herself into a swallow and flew around the pillar." She eventually recovered the body only to lose it once again to the malice of "Typhon" (Osiris's brother Set) (Rickard, *JJQ* 20, no. 3 [1983]: 357). For "Bat," see 3.397–98n.

13.1118–19 (377:30–32). Metempsychosis. They believe . . . a tree from grief – The "they" suggests those who believed in Greek and Roman mythology; Daphne, for example, in her flight from Phoebus Apollo was transformed into a laurel tree that she might escape the "grief" of capture (Ovid, *Metamorphoses* 1). But the transformation of Daphne is *metamorphosis*, which Bloom here confuses with *metempsychosis*, the transmigration of souls.

13.1121 (377:34). odour of sanctity – A sweet or aromatic odor given off by the corpses of great saints either before burial or after exhumation. The odor is believed to be evidence of extraordinary sanctity.

13.1122 (377:35–36). Pray for us – Bloom has overheard the Litany of Our Lady (of Loreto); see 13.287–89n.

13.1124–26 (377:38–40). The priest's house . . . Twentyeight it is – Two houses on Leahy's Terrace were attached to the Mary Star of the Sea Church, nos. 3 and 5. Each was appraised at an annual rent of £28 in *Thom's* 1904. Bloom's fictional mistake apparently involved the valuation of one of these houses when he was working for *Thom's*.

13.1126–27 (377:40–41). Gabriel Conroy's brother is curate – Gabriel Conroy is the central character of "The Dead," *Dubliners*. The Reverend Bernard Conroy is listed as one of two curates-in-charge in 1904. In "The Dead," Gabriel's brother is named Constantine, not Bernard, and Gabriel thinks of him as "senior curate in Balbriggan." Balbriggan is a small town on the coast eighteen miles north of Dublin.

13.1129–30 (378:2–3). the bird in drouth . . . Throwing in pebbles – The crow in Aesop's fable "The Crow and the Pitcher" saves himself by this stratagem.

13.1130–31 (378:3–4). Like a little man . . . with tiny hands – See 13.1117n and 3.397–98n.

13.1132–33 (378:6). Stare the sun . . . like the eagle – In mythology, the eagle was supposed to be able to stare at the sun with impunity and to renew his sight in old age by flying up into the sun, where the dimness would be singed from his eyes.

13.1138–39 (378:13–14). That's how that wise man . . . the burning glass – Archimedes was celebrated for his application of mathematical theory to mechanics, but the story Bloom recalls is apocryphal: Archimedes was supposed to have delayed the Roman consul Marcellus's (c. 268–208 B.C.) conquest of Syracuse by setting the Roman fleet on fire with mirrors that concentrated the sun's rays.

13.1142 (378:17). Archimedes. I have it! – Bloom's "I have it!" echoes Archimedes' "Eureka!"; see 9.1053n.

13.1149 (378:26–27). *Faugh a ballagh* – Irish: "Clear the way." It was the battle cry of the Royal Irish Fusiliers and the motto of the Gough family (see 15.795n), and, as "Fág an Bealach" (1842), the title of a New Irelander's

patriotic song by Charles Gavan Duffy (1816–1903).

13.1151 (378:28). pitched about like snuff at a wake – See 6.235n.

13.1151 (378:29). when the stormy winds do blow – After a traditional song, "The Mermaid" (1840), attributed to one Parker. First verse and chorus: " 'Twas Friday morn when we set sail / And we were not far from the land, / When the captain spied a lovely mermaid / With a comb and glass in her hand. // Oh the ocean waves may roll / And the stormy winds may blow / While we poor sailors go skipping to the tops / And the landlubbers lie down below, below, below / And the landlubbers lie down below."

13.1154 (378:32). till Johnny comes marching home again – "When Johnny Comes Marching Home Again," by Patrick Sarsfield Gilmore (1829–92), was a Union army marching song in the Civil War. The song begins: "When Johnny comes marching home again, / Hurrah! hurrah! / We'll give him a hearty welcome then, / Hurrah! hurrah! / The men will cheer, the boys will shout, / The ladies, they will all turn out, / And we'll all feel gay, / When Johnny comes marching home."

13.1156 (378:34). The anchor's weighed –The title of a song by Arnold and Braham. The song begins: "The tear fell gently from her eye, / When last we parted on the shore. / My bosom beat with many a sigh, / To think I ne'er might see her more, / To think I ne'er might see her more. // 'Dear youth,' she cried, 'and canst thou haste away, / My heart will break; a little moment stay! / Alas I cannot part from thee!' // The anchor's weighed, the anchor's weighed, Farewell! farewell! Remember me."

13.1156 (378:35). with a scapular or medal on him – Catholic tradition: sailors wear sacred medals or cloth badges symbolic of a saint's protective presence.

13.1157–58 (378:35–37). the tephilim no what's . . . his door to touch – The word Bloom is seeking is *mezuzah* (Hebrew: "doorpost"); a piece of parchment inscribed with Deuteronomy 6:4–9 and 11:13–21 in twenty-two lines is rolled up and placed in a small case on the right-hand doorpost of Jewish households. It is touched or kissed by the devout as they enter or leave the house. The "tephilim" is a phylactery that contains four parts of the Pentateuch.

13.1158–59 (378:37–38). That brought us out . . . house of bondage – See 7.208–9n.

13.1160–61 (378:40). Hanging onto a plank or astride of a beam – The way Odysseus accomplishes the last leg of his voyage from Calypso's island to the island of the Phaeacians in Book 5 of *The Odyssey*. And in Book 12 after Odysseus's men have violated the cattle of the Sun God and ship and crew have been destroyed by Zeus, Odysseus binds the shattered mast and keel of the ship together, rides them toward Charybdis and, when the whirlpool sucks them down, leaps up and clings to "the great fig tree, / catching on like a bat under a bough" (12:433–34; Fitzgerald, p. 236). When the whirlpool stills and the beams surface, Odysseus rides them until he is beached on Calypso's island. For a possible coincidence, see "bat" at 13.1117 and at 13.1117n, 13.1117–18n, and 3.397–98n.

13.1161 (378:40–41). *lifebelt round him – In Book 5 of *The Odyssey*, the nereid Leukothea takes pity on Odysseus, being storm-buffeted on his raft, and advises him to shed Calypso's cloak and swim for it: "Here: make my veil your sash [lifebelt]; it is not mortal; / you cannot, now, be drowned or suffer harm" (5:345–47; Fitzgerald, p. 103).

13.1164 (379:4). Davy Jones' locker – Davy Jones was the sailor's traditional version of the spirit or devil of the sea; his "locker" was the bottom of the ocean, where all drowned things went for "safekeeping."

13.1165 (379:5). old cockalorum – Applied to a person it means "self-important little man."

13.1166 (379:6). A last lonely candle – See 11.32n.

13.1166–67 (379:6–7). Mirus bazaar . . . Mercer's hospital – See 8.1162n.

13.1168–69 (379:9–10). *The shepherd's hour: the hour of folding: hour of tryst – Source unknown; "folding" means putting sheep in a fold.

13.1170 (379:11). the nine o'clock postman – According to the "Postal Directory" in *Thom's* 1904, there were five deliveries of mail each weekday: at 7 A.M., noon, and 2:20, 6:10, and 8:00 P.M. There was one delivery on Sunday.

13.1170–71 (379:11–12). the glowworm's lamp . . . gleaming – See 8.589–590n.

13.1174–75 (379:15–16). *Evening Telegraph* . . . *Gold Cup* – See 2.412n and 5.532n.

13.1175 (379:17). Dignam's house – At 9 Newbridge Avenue in Sandymount, it was almost 500 yards inland and not visible from where Bloom is resting.

13.1180–81 (379:23–24). Kish bank the anchored lightship – See 3.267n.

13.1182–83 (379:26). Irish Lights board – The Commissioners of Irish Lights, with offices in the Carlisle Buildings, 27 D'Olier Street, Dublin, were charged with supervision and maintenance of lighthouses and lightships on the coast of Ireland.

13.1183 (379:26). Coastguards – The British coastguard service under the Admiralty had the character of a naval reserve, charged with the protection of customs revenue, lifesaving, and signal services.

13.1184 (379:27). lifeboat – See 16.643n.

13.1184–85 (379:27–28). Day we went out . . . in the Erin's King – See 4.434n. The excursion coasted Dublin Bay and rounded the Kish lightship.

13.1188 (379:32). funk – See 4.435n.

13.1190 (379:34). Crumlin – A parish and village three and a half miles southwest of the center of Dublin.

13.1190–91 (379:35). Babes in the wood – An English nursery tale (and ballad): two children are left to perish in the forest by an uncle who expects to profit from their death. In 1798, peasant rebels in the hills south of Dublin were also called "babes in the wood."

13.1194 (379:40). Calomel purge – Not as a purgative but after the practice of using Calomel as a lotion for the relief of mild skin irritations.

13.1200 (380:5). Left one is more sensitive – After the popular belief that a woman's left breast, because "nearer the heart," is the more sensitive of the two.

13.1204–5 (380:10–11). Gibraltar . . . Buena Vista. O'Hara's tower – South Sugar Loaf Hill (Buena Vista) at 1,361 feet is the highest point on Gibraltar; O'Hara's Tower formerly stood nearby on Wolf's Crag (1,337 feet).

13.1205 (380:11–12). Old Barbary ape that gobbled all his family – The Barbary ape, or macaque monkey, is a tailless terrestrial monkey that inhabits Algeria, Morocco, and the Rock of Gibraltar. The monkeys live in droves that are dominated by an old and fierce male. Presumably Bloom is recalling one of Molly's stories about her life on Gibraltar, but the source of Molly's story is unknown.

13.1206 (380:12). Sundown, gunfire for the men to cross the lines – At sundown on the Rock of Gibraltar the gates were shut so that no one could enter or leave the fortress-colony until sunrise the next day. Gunfire, just before sundown, warned the Rock's inhabitants and its garrison that the gates were about to be closed. The "lines" were the British positions on the Rock side of the neutral ground, a sandy isthmus that separates Gibraltar from Spain.

13.1208–9 (380:15–16). *Buenas noches, señorita . . . la muchacha hermosa* – Spanish: "Good evening, Miss. The man loves the beautiful young girl."

13.1212–13 (380:20). *Leah. Lily of Killarney* – For *Leah*, see 5.194–95n; for *Lily of Killarney*, see 6.186n. Both performances began at 8:00 P.M.

13.1213–14 (380:21). Hope she's over – That is, that Mrs. Purefoy has given birth to her child.

13.1223 (380:32–33). the sister of the wife . . . just come to town – From a progressive street rhyme: "The wild man of Borneo has just come to town. / The wife of the wild man of Borneo has just come to town" and so on through potentially endless improvisations.

13.1224–25 (380:34–35). Everyone to his taste . . . kissed the cow – A variant of the proverbial expression: "Why, everyone as they like; as the good Woman said, when she kiss'd the Cow" (Colonel Atwit in Dialogue 1 of Swift's *Complete Collection of Genteel and Ingenious Conversation* [1738]).

13.1225 (380:35–36). put the boots on it – Brought things to a (negative) climax.

13.1226 (380:36). Houses of mourning – See 11.911n.

13.1227 (380:37–38). *those Scottish Widows – The Scottish Widows' Fund (Mutual) Life Assurance Society, with home offices in Edinburgh, advertised "The Whole Profits are Divided Among the Policy Holders." *Thom's* 1904 (p. 1908) lists five Dublin agents for this insurance company.

13.1229 (380:40). Cramer's – Cramer, Wood & Co., Pianoforte Gallery and Music Warehouse, 4–5 Westmoreland Street, in east-central Dublin just south of the Liffey.

13.1230 (380:41–42). Her widow's mite – "And Jesus sat over against the treasury, and beheld how the people cast money into the treasury: and many that were rich cast in much. And there came a certain poor widow, and she threw in two mites, which make a farthing. And he called unto him his disciples, and saith unto them, Verily I say unto you, That this poor widow hath cast more in, than all they which have cast into the treasury: For all they did cast in of their abundance; but she of her want did cast in all that she had, even all her living" (Mark 12:41–44; cf. Luke 21:1–4).

13.1232–33 (381:1–2). Poor man O'Connor . . . by mussels here – The specific case Bloom recalls is unknown; but the inshore waters of Dublin Bay near the mouth of the Liffey were badly polluted at the beginning of the twentieth century, and there were frequent cases of hepatitis and other diseases caused by the eating of contaminated shellfish. For what it's worth: *Thom's* 1904 (p. 1482) lists a P. J. O'Conor, Esq. (and Mrs. O'Conor, presumably his mother), as resident at 75 Eccles Street, across the street from Bloom's house; see 4.77–78n.

13.1233 (381:3). The sewage – In 1904 there were no sewage treatment plants in Dublin and environs; the Liffey and its tributaries in Dublin were in effect open sewers, and the consequent pollution of the inner reaches of Dublin Bay was a matter of serious concern.

13.1237 (381:7–8). Love, lie and be . . . we die – See 8.754n.

13.1242–43 (381:14). Mailboat. Near Holyhead by now – The mailboat left Kingstown at 8:15 P.M.; the run to Holyhead, the terminus of the London and Northwestern Railroad in northwestern Wales, took about two and a half hours in 1904.

13.1251 (381:24–25). Bread cast on the waters – "Cast thy bread upon the waters: for thou shalt find it after many days" (Ecclesiastes 11:1).

13.1254–55 (381:28). Must come back. Murderers do – After the belief that the murderer always returns to the scene of the crime.

13.1258, 1264 (381:31, 38). I./AM. A – Just as it reads: "I am A" (the first letter of the alphabet). Also: "I am alpha" (the first letter in the Greek alphabet; hence, the first or the beginning); the phrase is repeated four times in Revelation (1:8 and 11, 21:6, and 22:13): "I am Alpha and Omega, the beginning and the ending, saith the Lord" (1:8). In *A Blakean Translation of Joyce's Circe* (Woodward, Penn., 1965), Frances M. Boldereff remarks that "AM.A. is a quote from *Annals of the Four Masters* [see 12.1443–46n]; it represents the way time was signified in the pagan world, it stands for 'Anima Mundi Anno': 'In the Universal mind [world soul], year . . .'" (p. 36). Alpha is also the sign of the fish, a traditional symbol for Christ; see 2.159n.

13.1267–68 (381:41–382:1). No fear of big . . . Guinness's barges – Dublin Bay was shallow off Sandymount Strand; at low water a large area of tidal flats would be exposed to the east of where Bloom is resting near the high-water line.

13.1268 (382:1–2). Round the Kish in eighty days – After the title of Jules Verne's (1828–1905) novel *Around the World in Eighty Days* (trans. 1873). For Kish, see 3.267n.

13.1274–75 (382:7–8). Liverpool boat long gone – Steamers for Liverpool sailed from the North Wall in Dublin twice daily, at noon and at 8:00 P.M.

13.1275 (382:9). Belfast – That is, the concert "tour" that Boylan has organized.

13.1276 (382:10). Ennis – Where Bloom is to observe the anniversary of his father's death on 27 June.

13.1276–77 (382:10–11). Just close my eyes a moment. Won't sleep, though – Odysseus, once safe on Nausicaa's island, hides himself, "While over him Athena showered sleep / that his distress should end, and soon, soon. / In quiet sleep she sealed his cherished eyes" (5:491ff.; Fitzgerald, p. 107).

13.1280 (382:14). Grace darling – See 13.1069n.

13.1281–82 (382:15–16). frillies for Raoul . . . heave under embon – See *Sweets of Sin*, 10.606n.

13.1282 (382:16). *señorita* – See 13.1208–9n.

13.1282–83 (382:17//). *Mulvey plump bubs me breadvan Winkle red slippers she rusty sleep wander years of dreams return – See 13.1112n.

13.1284 (382:17–18). Agendath – See 4.191–92n.

13.1284–85 (382:18–19). her next year . . . next her next – Cf. 7.207n.

13.1289–91 (382:23–25). *Cuckoo. / Cuckoo. / Cuckoo* – See 9.1025n. But in context the omen is ambiguous, because a young woman, hearing the bird, kisses her hand to it and says, "Cuckoo, cuckoo, / Tell me true, / When shall I be married?" The number of notes in the cuckoo's response gives her the answer. Here, the cuckoo responds with nine calls (for nine o'clock), which may suggest "nine years until marriage," but, since nine in numerology is the number of completeness and eternity, the answer may be "never."

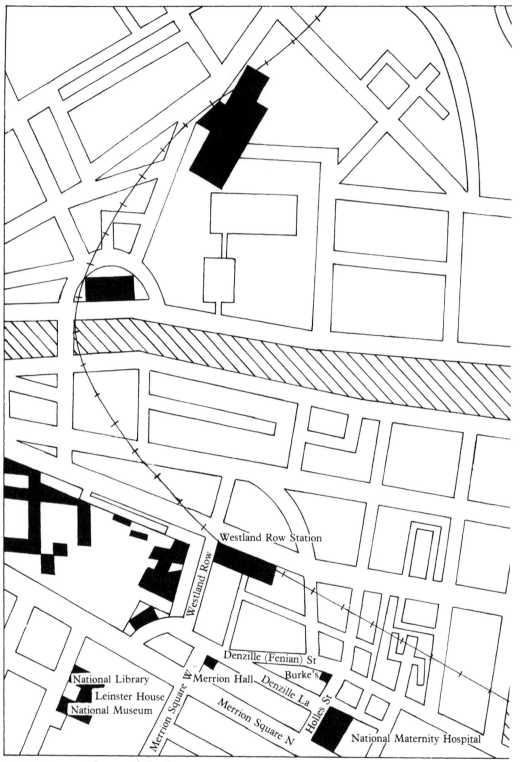

Westland Row Station

Westland Row

Denzille (Fenian) St

Burke's

Merrion Hall

Denzille La

Holles St

National Library

Leinster House

National Museum

Merrion Square W

Merrion Square N

National Maternity Hospital

EPISODE 14. *Oxen of the Sun*

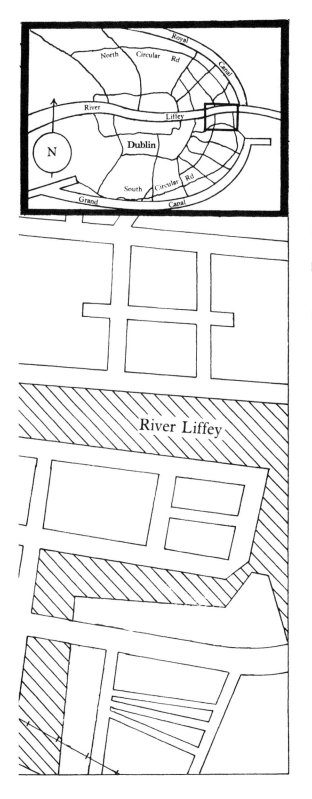

EPISODE 14

Oxen of the Sun

(14.1–1591, PP. 383–428)

Episode 14: *Oxen of the Sun*, 14.1–1591 (383–428). In Book 12 of *The Odyssey*, Odysseus and his men sail from Circe's island; they pass the Sirens, run the gamut of Scylla and Charybdis, and at nightfall are coasting the island of the sun-god Helios (Trinacria, modern Sicily). Both Circe and Tiresias have warned Odysseus to avoid the island and particularly to avoid harming the cattle sacred to Helios. But the crew, led by Eurylochus, refuse to spend the night at sea; Odysseus asks them to swear that they will not touch the sacred cattle, and when they agree, he reluctantly lands on the island. However, adverse weather maroons them on the island, and finally their provisions are exhausted. Odysseus goes inland to pray for relief but falls asleep. In the meantime, Eurylochus convinces the crew to forswear their oath, and they slaughter enough cattle for a six-day feast. Odysseus was in despair when he returned, but nothing could be done. On the seventh day, in deceptively fair weather, they embark. But Lampote has warned her father, Helios, who has appealed to Zeus. Zeus has promised retribution, and when the ship leaves the island, he makes good his word, destroying ship and crew with a lightning bolt and thus fulfilling the prophecies of Circe and Tiresias. Odysseus, once more frustrated and now condemned to further delay in his voyage home, lashes the mast and keel of his shattered ship together and endures the voyage through the whirlpool of Charybdis and past Scylla's rock. He is beached in exile on Calypso's island.

Time: 10:00 P.M. Scene: the National Maternity Hospital, 29–31 Holles Street, Dublin. Organ: womb; Art: medicine; Color: white; Symbol: mothers; Technique: embryonic development.[1] Correspondences: *Trinacria* [the island of the sun-god Helios, modern Sicily]—the hospital; *Lampote* and *Phaethusa* [daughters

of Helios entrusted with guarding the sacred cattle]—the nurses; *Helios*—Horne [Doctors Andrew J. Horne and Patrick J. Barry were the masters of the National Maternity Hospital in Holles Street in 1904]; *Oxen*—fertility; *Crime* [killing the oxen]—fraud [in the formal sense of breaking a vow].

The Linati schema lists as additional Persons: "Helios Hyperion" [Son and father together on one line];[2] Jove (Zeus), and Ulysses.

Style: 14.1–6 (383:1–8). *Deshil Holles Eamus . . . boyaboy hoopsa – Stuart Gilbert (James Joyce's "*Ulysses*" [New York, 1952], p. 296) says that this episode "begins with a set of three incantations, in the manner of the *Fratres Arvales*." The Arval Brethren were a Roman company of priests, twelve in number, whose principal function was to conduct public ceremonies in honor of the Roman goddess of plenty and fertility. An integral part of these ceremonies was the "Arval Hymn" (c. 218 A.D., discovered late nineteenth century). Each of the first five lines of the hymn was repeated three times; the final *Triumphe* ("Hurrah," "Hoopsa") was repeated six times. Translation: "Aid us, Lares / Nor suffer pestilence or destruction to come upon the people. / Be thou satiate, fierce Mars. / Leap over the Threshold! Halt! Beat [the ground]! / Call alternately the heroes all. / Aid us Mars. / Hurrah!"

14.1 (383:1). Deshil Holles Eamus – "Deshil" after the Irish *deasil, deisiol:* turning to the right, clockwise, sunwise; a ritual gesture to attract good fortune, and an act of consecration when repeated three times (P. W. Joyce, *A Social History of Ancient Ireland* [London, 1913], vol. 1, p. 301). "Holles" is Holles Street; the National Maternity Hospital stands on the corner of Holles Street and Merrion Square North. *Eamus*, Latin: "Let us go."

14.2 (383:3–4). Send us bright one . . . quickening and wombfruit – An invocation to the sun as a source of fertility. "Horhorn" suggests Dr. Andrew J. Horne, one of the two masters of the Hospital; it also suggests the horned cattle of the sun-god. See also 11.23n.

14.5 (383:7). *Hoopsa boyaboy hoopsa! – The cry with which a midwife celebrates the

---

[1] In structure this episode is a series of imitations of prose styles presented in chronological sequence from Latin prose to fragments of modern slang. Joyce remarked (jocoseriously?) in a letter to Frank Bugden, 20 March 1920, that "Bloom is the spermatozoon, hospital the womb, the nurses the ovum, Stephen the embryo." In effect, the sequence of imitations is a sustained metaphor for the process of gestation; Joyce would have assumed that in that process ontogeny (the development of the individual organism) recapitulates phylogeny (the evolutionary history of the species)—what Joyce called "the periods of faunal evolution in general" [*Letters* 1:140]); thus the development of the embryonic artist's prose style recapitulates the evolution of prose style in literary history. The stylistic imitations are noted below as "Style" with a brief description of the style being imitated.

---

[2] *Helios Hyperion:* in Greek myth, Hyperion is a Titan, the son of Gaea and Uranus and the father of Helios. In later myth Hyperion is identified with Apollo as the god of manly beauty.

birth of a male child as she bounces it to stabilize its breathing.

Style: 14.7–32 (383:9–39). Universally that person's . . . ever irrevocably enjoined? – An imitation of the Latin prose styles of the Roman historians Sallust (86–34 B.C.) and Tacitus (c. 1555–120 A.D.). The manner of this passage suggests a literal translation, without Anglicization of word usage and syntax.

14.16 (383:20–21). omnipollent – "Pollent," from the Latin *pollens*, is rare for powerful.

14.19 (383:24). lutulent – Rare: "muddy, turbid, thick."

14.25 (383:30–31). inverecund – Rare: "Immodest."

14.29–32 (383:35–39). that evangel simultaneously . . . ever irrevocably enjoined – "Evangel" would suggest the message or news of the Christian dispensation, but here it seems to have the more general meaning "message of God" to Adam and Eve (and hence all humankind): "Be fruitful, and multiply, and replenish the earth, and subdue it" (Genesis 1:28). The message is repeated (to Noah) in Genesis 9:1, 7 and (to Israel as a promise) in Leviticus 26:9. Leviticus 26:14ff. counters with the curse of destruction to those disobedient to this promise and injunction. See 8.33n.

Style: 14.33–59 (383:40–384:31). It is not why therefore . . . had been begun she felt – After the style of medieval Latin prose chronicles, again with the effect of a literal translation that does not Anglicize word usage and syntax.

14.35 (383:42–384:1). the art of medicine shall have been highly honoured – Ireland has an impressive history of accomplishments in medicine that dates from as early as the fifteenth century. This traditional commitment to medicine was particularly strong in the eighteenth century.

14.36 (384:2). sweating chambers – Or sweating houses, in which sweat was induced by hot air or steam; an ancient and traditional Irish cure, particularly for rheumatism (P. W. Joyce, *A Social History of Ancient Ireland* [London, 1913], vol. 1, pp. 625–26).

14.37 (384:2–3). the O'Shiels – A family of physicians that served the Mahoneys of Oriel. The most famous member of the family was Eoghan (Owen) O'Shiel, physician-in-chief to the armies of the Kilkenny Confederation in its campaigns for King Charles I and the House of Stuart against parliamentary forces (1642–50).

14.37 (384:3). the O'Hickeys – The Irish root of Hickey means "healer"; a family of hereditary physicians to the O'Briens of Thomond.

14.37 (384:3). the O'Lees – A family of hereditary physicians to the O'Flahertys of Connacht. The family produced a complete manual of medical studies in both Irish and Latin in the fifteenth century.

14.39 (384:5–6). trembling withering – St. Vitus's dance or chorea.

14.39–40 (384:6). loose boyconnell flux – "Loose flux" can be either a hemorrhage or severe diarrhea. "Boyconnell" is unknown.

14.41–46 (384:8–13). a plan was by them adopted . . . from all accident possibility removed – The "plan" was the establishment of maternity hospitals. The first maternity hospital in the British Isles was the Rotunda Hospital for the Relief of Poor Lying-in Women in Dublin. It was opened "in George's Lane, 15 March 1745, was incorporated by Royal Charter 1756 and was opened in Rutland [now Parnell] Square for the reception of patients, 8th December, 1757." In 1904 it was "the largest chartered Clinical School of Midwifery and Gynaecology in the United Kingdom" (*Thom's* 1904, p. 1380).

14.57–58 (384:28). that they her by anticipation went seeing mother – The National Maternity Hospital not only admitted "midwifery cases" but also conducted a dispensary and attended women "in their own homes, during their confinement, at all hours if notice was given at the Hospital" (*Thom's* 1904, p. 1381).

Style: 14.60–106 (384:32–386:4). Before born babe bliss had . . . sorrowing one with other – Imitates the style of Anglo-Saxon rhythmic alliterative prose, a style associated with Aelfric (c. 955–1022), the leading prose writer of his period. In his stylistic effects Aelfric was following a fashion of his time, one established in Latin prose in the tenth century and then carried over into Anglo-Saxon composition. The alliteration was also associated with Anglo-Saxon poetry, in which it was the dominant sound effect.

14.67 (384:39). sejunct – Obsolete for "sejoined": separated.

14.71 (385:3). Some man that wayfaring was – This line and the passage that follows (to 14.106 [386:4] sorrowing one with other) echo "The Wanderer," an Anglo-Saxon elegiac lament preserved in the *Exeter Book* (copied c. 975). The speaker of the poem, "deprived of my homeland, far from dear kinsmen," is a wanderer, an "earth-walker," in search of a new lord and hall. He moves through a perpetual winter, contemplates an endless sea voyage, and speaks his cares only to himself: "There is now none of the living to whom / I dare clearly say my heart's thought." In the second half of the poem the speaker turns from his personal lament to philosophize on "all the life of men—with what terrible swiftness they forgo the hall-floor, bold young retainers. . . . So the Creator of men's generations laid waste this dwelling-ground." The poem concludes with the assertion that the "wise in heart" never utters "too quickly the passion of his breast" and seeks his "support from the Father in heaven, where for us the only stronghold stands." At the line "Some man that wayfaring was," the first month of pregnancy apparently begins.

14.72 (385:4). Of Israel's folk – Recalls the Wandering Jew; see 9.1209n.

14.74 (385:7). Of that house A. Horne is Lord – Andrew J. Horne was one of the two masters of the National Maternity Hospital in 1904. Patrick J. Barry was the other.

14.74 / 77–78 (385:7 / 11). Seventy beds / in twelve moons thrice an hundred – *Thom's* 1904 (p. 1381) on the National Maternity Hospital: "This Hospital, reopened in 1894, contains 69 beds; there were 1,500 midwifery cases treated during the past year, and over 4,000 attendances at the Dispensary."

14.75–76 (385:9). so God's angel to Mary quoth – In the Annunciation (Luke 1:26–38), the Archangel Gabriel announces the birth of Jesus to the Virgin Mary.

14.81 (385:15). swire ywimpled – "Swire" is Anglo-Saxon for the neck or throat; "ywimpled" is Middle English (in Chaucer) for "covered with a wimple."

14.81 (385:16). levin – Archaic (from Anglo-Saxon): "lightning."

14.82–83 (385:17–18). God the Wreaker . . . water for his evil sins – In Genesis, God determines to destroy mankind (excepting Noah and his family) "for all flesh had corrupted his way upon the earth" (Genesis 6:12). In *The Odyssey* when Odysseus and his crew are marooned on Helios's island by storms, Odysseus suspects "the power of destiny devising ill" (12:295; Fitzgerald, p. 231); his suspicion seems to be confirmed by the gods' failure to intervene to allow him to depart the island. His men's violation of the sun-god's cattle then prepares for the entry of Zeus, "the Wreaker," when they finally do depart.

14.84 (385:19). rathe – Obsolete (from Anglo-Saxon): "quickly, speedily."

14.85 (385:20). thatch – Obviously roof, but also slang for female genitalia.

14.86 (385:23). stow – Obsolete (from Anglo-Saxon): "place."

14.87–88 (385:24–25). over land and seafloor . . . long outwandered – Odysseus was fated to be absent from home for twenty years: ten years in the Trojan War and ten years of wandering. This may also suggest the beginnings of life in the sea, the beginning of the process of "faunal evolution"; see p. 408, n. 1.

14.88 (385:25). townhithe – "Hithe" is archaic (from Anglo-Saxon) for a port or haven.

14.94 (382:32). O'Hare Doctor – See 13.961n.

14.95 (385:33). grameful – Archaic (from Anglo-Saxon): "full of grief or sorrow."

14.98 (385:36). algate – Obsolete or dialect: "always."

14.100 (385:38). housel – Archaic (from Anglo-Saxon): "the Eucharist," or the act of administering or receiving it (in this context: "in extreme unction").

14.100 (385:39). sick men's oil to his limbs – Anointing with holy oil is part of the sacrament of extreme unction.

14.101 (385:40). nun – In preference to "nurse" because *nun* derives from Latin through Anglo-Saxon whereas *nurse* enters Middle English from Old French. Nurse Callan does not belong to a religious order; the National Maternity Hospital was a secular institution.

14.102 (385:41). *Mona Island – An ancient name for Anglesey, an island county in northwestern Wales, a popular health resort in 1904.

14.102 (385:42). bellycrab – Cancer of the stomach.

14.103 (385:42). Childermas – 28 December, Holy Innocents Day, observed in commemoration of the children slain by Herod in Bethlehem; see Matthew 2:16–18.

14.105 (386:3). wanhope – Archaic: "want of hope; despair."

Style: 14.107–22 (386:5–386:22). Therefore, everyman, look to that . . . chiding her childless – Middle English prose. The opening paragraph echoes the opening speech of the medieval morality play *Everyman* (c. 1485). The Messenger announces the play's action and message: "The story saith: Man, in the beginning / Look well, and take good heed to the ending, / Be you never so gay. / You think sin in the beginning full sweet, / Which in the end causeth the soul to weep, / When the body lieth in clay. / Here shall you see how fellowship and jollity, / Both strength, pleasure, and beauty, / Will fade from thee as a flower in May. / For ye shall hear how our Heaven-King / Calleth Everyman to a general reckoning" (lines 10–20).

14.108 (386:6). every man that is born of woman – Echoes Job 14:1: "Man that is born of woman is of few days, and full of trouble."

14.108–10 (386:7–8). as he came naked forth . . . go as he came – Paraphrases Job 1:21: "Naked came I out of my mother's womb, and naked shall I return thither."

14.114 (386:13). unneth – That is, "uneath," obsolete: "not easy; difficult, hard."

14.121–22 (386:21). Nine twelve bloodflows – In other words, approximately nine years of menstruating. The implication is that Nurse Callan was at the hospital when the Blooms lived in Holles Street some nine years before. The reminder of menstruation also suggests that the first month of pregnancy is well-advanced.

Style: 14.123–66 (386:23–387:34). And whiles they spake . . . Thanked be Almighty God – Imitates the *Travels of Sir John Mandeville* (c. 1336–71), a medieval compilation of fantastic travel stories, apparently composed at Liège, Belgium, by one John of Burgundy or John with the Beard. The earliest manuscripts of English translations of the French original, and of a Latin translation of that original, date from the beginning of the fifteenth century.

14.125 (386:26). Dixon – The "Medical Directory" in *Thom's* 1904 (p. 872) lists a Joseph F. Dixon as a medical practitioner, residing at 12 Conyngham Road in Dublin (on the southeastern edge of Phoenix Park).

14.127 (386:28). the house of misericord – The Mater Misericordiae Hospital; see 6.375–76n.

14.129–30 (386:31). a horrible and dreadful dragon – In this case, a bee. Does this also suggest the age of dinosaurs in "faunal evolution"?

14.134 (386:36). cautels – Archaic: "caution, prudence"; also, "cunning, deceitful."

14.134 (386:37). avis – *Avys*, Middle English: "advice, counsel, opinion."

14.134 (386:37). *repreved – Archaic: "reproved, censured."

14.137 (386:40). mandement – A variant of *mandment*, obsolete: "command."

14.147 (387:10). Mahound – Mohammed was so called in the Middle Ages, when it was believed that his followers worshiped him as a god; the word was Middle English for a heathen god, an idol, a monster. The art of glass blowing did come from the East (China and India) to the West, but long before the time of Mohammed.

14.150–54 (387:14–19). strange fishes withouten heads . . . of the olive press – That is, canned sardines.

14.155–56 (387:20–21). *wheatkidneys out of Chaldee – That is, bread; see 3.118–19n. Chaldee, or Chaldea, was an ancient region in southwestern Asia on the Euphrates and the Persian Gulf.

14.157–59 (387:23–25). the serpents there to entwine . . . brewage like to mead – Describes the care of hop vines and the manufacture of beer.

14.160 (387:26). childe – Archaic: "a youth of noble birth."

14.161 (387:27). halp – Obsolete: past tense of *to help*.

14.162 (387:29). apertly – Archaic: "openly, publicly, plainly."

14.165 (387:32). nist – For *ne wist*, archaic: "knew not."

Style: 14.167–276 (387:35–391:2). This meanwhile this good . . . murdered his goods with whores – Imitates the fifteenth-century prose style of Sir Thomas Malory's (d. 1471) compilation of Arthurian legend, *Morte d'Arthur* (printed 1485).

14.168 (387:36). alther – Variant of *aller*, archaic: "of all."

14.178 (388:6–7). Expecting each moment to be her next – Lenehan's variant of the stock phrase for fear, "Expecting each moment to be his last."

14.184 (388:13). husbandly hand under hen – See 12.845n.

14.189 (388:20). saint Mary Merciable's – The Mater Misericordiae Hospital; see 6.375–76n.

14.190 (388:20). Lynch – Vincent Lynch appears as one of Stephen's close associates in *A Portrait*, chapter 5:A.

14.190 (388:21). Madden – William Madden, medical student; apart from the context, identity and significance unknown.

14.191 (388:22). Alba Longa – The most ancient town in Latium (the Latin colonies in ancient Italy), said to have been founded by Aeneas's son, Ascanius, to have been the mother-city of Rome, and to have been destroyed by Tullus Bostilius, the third king of ancient Rome, in 665 B.C. But "Alba" is also Irish for Scotland.

14.191 (388:22) Crotthers – J. Crotthers, med-ical student; apart from the context, identity and significance unknown.

14.193 (388:24). Punch Costello – Francis "Punch" Costello, medical student; apart from context, identity and significance unknown.

14.193 (388:25). gested – Archaic: "performed."

14.201 (388:34). red – Variant of *rede*, archaic: "(to) counsel, control."

14.202 (388:36–37). aresouns – Variant of *areason*, archaic: "a questioning, a calling to account."

14.205 (388:40). Eblana – A place in Hibernia (Ireland) mentioned by Ptolemy (see 12.1251n) and later identified with the site of Dublin (which was not established as a town until the time of the Vikings, c. 841). The name Dublin comes from the Irish *Duibhlinn*, "Dark Pool," after the peat-colored waters of the Liffey.

14.208–9 (389:2). the woman should bring forth in pain – After Genesis 3:16: "Unto the woman [the Lord God] said, I will greatly multiply thy sorrow and thy conception; in sorrow thou shalt bring forth children."

14.213–14 (389:7–8). but the law nor his judges did provide no remedy – Neither British civil law nor court precedent had established what choice was to be made when the mother's and/or the baby's life was endangered during delivery.

14.215 (389:10–11). *the wife should live (sith she was God's) and the babe to die – Roman Catholic doctrine held that if a medical choice had to be made between the life of the mother and the life of the child in the process of delivery, the life of the child was to take precedence.

14.220 (389:16). rede – See 14.201n.

14.221 (389:17–18). Saint Ultan of Arbraccan – (d. 656?), an Irish missionary to the Netherlands. In some versions of his life story he is described as the maternal uncle of St. Brigid (d. 523?) (see 12.1705n); in other versions he is said to have been the author of a *Life of St. Brigid*. He taught and fed orphans and came to be regarded in Ireland as the patron saint of sick and orphaned children.

14.222 (389:18). let – In the obsolete sense of "accept."

14.224–25 (389:22). *the one in limbo gloom, the other in purgefire – The baby, dead in childbirth, was presumably unbaptized and therefore destined for limbo; the mother, presumably baptized and possibly shriven, would be in purgatory.

14.226 (389:24). the sin against the Holy Ghost – Or "blasphemy against the Holy Spirit," frequently, and somewhat mysteriously, said to be the only unforgivable sin. It has a powerful grip on Stephen's imagination in *A Portrait*, 4:B. The *Catholic Encyclopedia* ([New York, 1910], vol. 7, pp. 414b–415a) says in effect that there is no real consensus among the church fathers; therefore, the "unforgivable" nature of the "blasphemy" cannot be explained. The mystery Stephen has in mind derives from St. Paul's question: "What? know ye not that your body is the temple of the Holy Ghost which is in you, which ye have of God, and are not your own?" (I Corinthians 6:19).

14.232 (389:31). spleen – Obsolete or rare for a fit of passion.

14.233–34 (389:33–34). the unicorn how once . . . cometh by his horn – The origin of this particular bit of medieval bestiology is obscure, but it may be the result of a (drunken) confusion of the legend of the unicorn with that of the phoenix. In some medieval bestiaries the unicorn is said to live a thousand years; this numerology links the unicorn with Christ and with the belief in thousand-year cycles of regeneration. The phoenix, the mythical bird that once in a millennium was consumed by fire and reborn from its own ashes, is also an emblem of Christ in medieval bestiaries.

14.236 (389:36). saint Foutinus – St. Foutin, the first bishop of Lyons in France (third century). Apparently the populace of Lyons and environs conjoined the image of this saint with that of certain pre-Christian priapic gods; as late as the sixteenth century, the worship of St. Foutin involved pouring wine over a representation of his genitalia, allowing it to sour, and then regarding the vinegar as a cure for barrenness.

14.241 (389:42). orgulous – Archaic: "proud, haughty."

14.242 (390:1). law of canons – Canonical law; collectively, the rules of doctrine and discipline enacted by Church councils and confirmed by the pope.

14.242 (390:1–2). Lilith, patron of abortions – The Hebrew "Lilith" is a night-hag, night-monster, night-fairy, a demon apparently of Babylonian origin. She is mentioned once in the Bible, in Isaiah's description of "the day of the Lord's vengeance" (Isaiah 34:14), where her name is rendered as "screech owl." Various legends depict her as Adam's sensual and animalistic first wife, who metamorphosed into a demon after she was replaced by Eve. Other legends portray her as a sensual temptress who becomes Adam's concubine after the Fall. She was regarded as particularly hostile to newborn children and to pregnant women, and amulets were worn to ward off her destructive influence.

14.242–43 (390:2–3). bigness wrought by wind of seeds of brightness – Stephen cites fabulous accounts of impregnation by wind as in Virgil (see 14.244n) and as in the legend of Zephyrus, the west wind, who fathered Achilles' horses. Other myths of impregnation involve a shower of seeds from the sun or the stars or the bright sky, as Zeus in the form of a shower of gold impregnated Danaë.

14.243–44 (390:3). potency of vampires mouth to mouth – Stephen recalls his "poem"; see 3.397–98n. The vampires of legend did not impregnate but fed on the blood of sleeping persons; another demon of the night, the incubus, was supposed to impregnate sleeping women.

14.244 (390:3–4). as Virgilius saith – Virgil, in the *Georgics* 3:271–77, describes the spring "excitement" of mares: "And as soon as the flame has stolen into their craving marrow . . . they all, with faces turned to the Zephyrs, stand on a high cliff, and drink in the gentle breezes. Then oft, without any wedlock, pregnant with the wind (a wondrous tale!) they flee over rocks and crags and lowly dales."

14.244 (390:4). by the influence of the occident – That is, of the West, Zephyrus, the west wind.

14.244–45 (390:4–5). by the reek of the moonflower – That is, by the presence of a menstruating woman. Pliny (23–79 A.D.), in his *Natural History*, gives long lists of a menstruating woman's powers for good or ill. One of the good powers is the ability to cure barrenness in other women.

14.245–46 (390:5–6). an she lie with . . . *effectu secuto* – The Latin, one of the basic principles of Scholastic philosophy, meaning "one performance following another." Stephen's source for this improbable mode of impregnation is unknown.

14.246–47 (390:6–7). in her bath according . . . Moses Maimonides – The two medieval philosophers have been previously linked in Stephen's mind (see 2.158n), but only Averroës appears to have held this opinion. In his medical work *Colliget*, he cites a "case history" of a woman impregnated in her bath by semen from a man bathing nearby. Sir Thomas Browne, in *Pseudodoxia Epidemica* (1646), Book 7, chapter 16, finds this impregnation a "new and unseconded way in History to fornicate at a distance, and much offendeth the rules of Physich."

14.247–48 (390:8–9). how at the end of the second month a human soul was infused – Aristotle argues in *On the Generation of Animals* that conception establishes a "nutritive soul" in the embryo and that the embryo has "sensitive soul" and "rational soul" "potentially but not actually," that is, the embryo will develop "soul" as the body develops. St. Thomas Aquinas, in *Summa Theologica*, Prima Primae, Query 118, adopts Aristotle's position and argues "that the intellectual soul is created by God at the end of human generation," that the nutritive and sensitive souls develop in the course of "human generation," and that the intellectual soul is "at the same time sensitive and nutritive, the preexisting forms being corrupted." The implication is that some time elapses between conception and the moment when the soul is "created" and "infused into" the body, but the "two months" is Stephen's (not Aquinas's) rhetorical flourish. Most modern Catholic theologians have been reluctant to follow Aquinas on this point, holding instead that the soul is present from the moment of conception.

14.248 (390:9). our holy mother – The Church.

14.250–52 (390:12–13). he that holdeth the fisherman's . . . for all ages founded – The fisherman's seal or ring is the papal seal (from c. 1265). Papal authority is derived from Jesus' words to Peter in Matthew 16:18: "Thou art Peter, and upon this rock [Petrus] I will build my church; and the gates of hell shall not prevail against it." Thus, the fisherman's seal is associated with Peter as the first "bishop of Rome." It also has its source in Jesus' words to the fishermen, Peter and his brother Andrew, "Follow me, and I will make you fishers of men" (Matthew 4:19).

14.258 (390:21). birth and death pence – The traditional donations or payments for the funeral mass (for the dead mother) and the baptismal service (for the newborn child).

14.261 (390:24–25). he who stealeth from the poor lendeth to the Lord – See 1.727n.

14.270 (390:36). akeled – Obsolete: "cooled, became cold."

14.276 (391:2). murdered his goods with whores – In Luke 15:30 the prodigal son's brother complains to his father that the prodigal "hath devoured thy living with harlots."

Style: 14.277–333 (391:3–395:15). About that present time . . . rest should reign – Imitates Elizabethan prose chronicles.

14.280–81 (391:7). the vicar of Christ – One of the pope's titles; refers to the assertion that the pope is to represent Christ as head of his Church on earth.

14.281 (391:8). vicar of Bray – The title of a song about a pliant clergyman who shifted nimbly with the winds of political and doctrinal change: "A zealous High Churchman" under Charles II, a "Jesuit" under James II, etc. Chorus: "And this is law I will maintain / Until my dying day, sir! / That whatsoever King may reign / Still I'd be Vicar of Bray, Sir!" The song concludes with the vicar's "allegiance" to George I: "And George my lawful King shall be / Until the times do alter." Bray is on the coast southeast of Dublin. The unflattering equation of the pope with the vicar of Bray echoes a common criticism of Pius X (1835–1914; pope 1903–14), who continued his predecessors' protests against the occupation of the Papal States by the Italian government but at the same time remained on remarkably friendly terms with that government.

14.281–83 (391:8–10). Now drink we, quod . . . my soul's bodiment – Parodies Jesus' words at the Last Supper: "And as they were eating, Jesus took bread, and blessed it, and brake it, and gave it to the disciples, and said, Take, eat: this is my body. And he took the cup, and gave thanks, and gave it to them, saying, Drink ye all of it; For this is my blood of the new testament, which is shed for many for the remission of sins" (Matthew 26:26–28).

14.283 (391:10). fraction – The breaking of bread in the Eucharist.

14.283–84 (391:11). them that live by bread alone – Jesus, fasting in the wilderness, refuses the devil's temptation, "command that these stones be made bread. But he answered and said, It is written [Deuteronomy 8:3], Man shall not live by bread alone, but by every word that proceedeth out of the mouth of God" (Matthew 4:3–4).

14.286 (391:13–14). coins of the tribute – See 2.86n.

14.289–90 (391:18). time's ruins build eternity's mansions – From a letter by William Blake to William Hayley, 6 May 1800: "Thirteen years ago I lost a brother, and with his spirit I converse daily and hourly in the spirit, and see him in my remembrance, in the regions of my imagination. I hear his advice, and even now write from his dictate. Forgive me for expressing to you my enthusiasm, which I wish all to partake, since it is to me a source of immortal joy, even in this world. By it I am the companion of angels. May you continue to be so more and more; and to be more and more persuaded that every mortal loss is an immortal gain. The ruins of Time build mansions in Eternity."

14.290–92 (391:19–21). Desire's wind blasts . . . the rood of time – A homily of St. Bernard of Clairvaux (1090–1153) is included in the Divine Office for 7 October, the Feast of the Blessed Virgin Mary of the Rosary: "To commend His grace to us and to destroy human wisdom, God was pleased to take flesh of a woman who was a virgin and so to restore like by like, to cure a contrary by a contrary, to draw out the poisonous thorn and most effectively to blot out the decree of sin. Eve was a thorn in her wounding; Mary is a rose in her sweetening of the affections of all. Eve was a thorn fastening death upon all; Mary is a rose giving the heritage of salvation back to all." As Thornton points out (p. 329), Stephen's imagery may also owe a debt to the *Divine Comedy;* in canto 13 of *Paradiso*, St. Thomas Aquinas warns Dante that obvious judgments may be hasty and false, "for I have seen first all the winter through the thorn display itself hard and forbidding and then upon its summit bear the rose" (lines 133–35). "To the Rose Upon the Rood of Time" is the dedicatory poem of Yeats's volume *The Rose* (1893)

(*Collected Poems* [New York, 1956], p. 31). The poem evokes the rose as muse and contemplates the rose as the intersection between temporal and eternal beauty, as what makes it possible to see "In all poor foolish things that live a day / Eternal beauty wandering on her way" (lines 11–12).

14.292–94 (391:21–23). In woman's womb word . . . shall not pass away – "And the Word was made flesh and dwelt among us, (and we beheld his glory, the glory as of the only begotten of the Father,) full of grace and truth" (John 1:14). The opening phrases of this passage follow St. Bernard's homily in the Feast of the Blessed Virgin Mary of the Rosary (see preceding note). See also John 1:1–5: "In the beginning was the Word, and the Word was with God, and the Word was God. The same was in the beginning with God. All things were made by him; and without him was not any thing made that was made. In him was life; and the life was the light of men. And the light shineth in darkness; and the darkness comprehended it not."

14.294 (391:23–24). *Omnis caro ad te veniet* – See 3.396–97n.

14.295–96 (391:24–25). who aventried the dear . . . Healer and Herd – "Aventre" is an obsolete word of obscure meaning, though the context of its use by Edmund Spenser suggests "to thrust forward (at a venture) as a spear." "Corse" is obsolete for body: "Agenbuyer" is Middle English for Christ, the Redeemer, as "Herd" is Christ as shepherd of God's flock, mankind.

14.296 (391:25–26). our mighty mother – See 1.85n.

14.296 (391:26). mother most venerable – One sequence of the Litany of Our Lady (of Loreto) begins, "Virgin most prudent, / Virgin most venerable"; see 13.287–89n.

14.297 (391:26–28). Bernardus saith aptly . . . *deiparae supplicem* – Source unknown; see 12.1695n and 13.377–80n.

14.298–301 (391:28–32). she is the second Eve . . . for a penny pippin – This theme is repeated several times in the Saturday Office of the Blessed Virgin Mary, notably in passages from SS. Irenaeus (second century), Augustine, and Bernard of Clairvaux. The relevant passage from St. Augustine: "Eve willingly accepted the drink offered by the serpent and handed it on to her husband; and by their action both deserved the penalty of death. Mary, filled with heavenly grace from above, brought forth life, by which mankind, already dead, can be revived." For "navel cords," see 3.37–40 (38: 1–5).

14.302 (391:33–34). Or she knew him . . . creature of her creature – In addition to the obvious pun on the biblical "to know" (to have sexual relations), this passage turns on the "mystery" of Mary's relation to God. This mystery is alluded to in a passage from St. Bernard in the Saturday Office of the Blessed Virgin Mary, but a more relevant passage from St. Bernard occurs in the Divine Office for the 11 October Feast of the Motherhood of the Blessed Virgin Mary: "But Mary knew herself to be His Mother and she trustfully calls Him her Son, whose majesty the Angels serve with awe. . . . God, I say, to whom the Angels are subject . . . He was subject to Mary. . . . That God should obey a woman is humility without precedent; that a woman should command God, exaltation without parallel."

14.303 (391:34). *vergine madre, figlia di tuo figlio* – Italian: "Virgin mother, daughter of thy son" (*Paradiso* 33:1; the opening line of St. Bernard's prayer to Mary on behalf of Dante).

14.303 (391:34–35). or she knew him not – The source of considerable heretical and theological contention: either Mary was not impregnated by the Holy Spirit or she was only the unwitting "vessel of flesh," not aware that it was the "Word" that "was made flesh" in her womb.

14.304 (391:35–36). the one denial or ignorancy with Peter Piscator – At the close of the Last Supper, Jesus predicts to Peter, "Verily I say unto thee, That this night, before the cock crow, Thou shalt deny me thrice" (Matthew 26:34). Peter protests that he will not, but each of the Gospels records his temporary defection and mortification. *Peter Piscator:* Peter the Fisherman; see 14.250–52n.

14.304–5 (391:36). who lives in the house that Jack built – The cumulative progression of the nursery rhyme "This is the house that Jack built" recalls the succession of bishops of Rome (popes) in "The house that Peter built" (as first bishop of Rome).

14.305–6 (391:37–38). *Joseph the joiner . . . all unhappy marriages – For "Joseph the joiner," see Mulligan's poem, 1.584–99 (19:3–

19). Joseph's doubts about Mary's pregnancy and its divine origin (Matthew 1:18–21) are allayed: "Behold, the angel of the Lord appeared unto him in a dream, saying, Joseph, thou son of David, fear not to take unto thee Mary thy wife: for that which is conceived in her is of the Holy Ghost" (1:20). In the Litany of St. Joseph, Joseph is variously addressed as "Glory of home life, / Guardian of virgins, / Pillar of families."

14.306–7 (391:38–40). *parceque M. Léo . . . ventre de Dieu! – French: "Because Mr. Léo Taxil has told us that the one who put her in this wretched position was the sacred pigeon, bowels of God [a curse]." For Léo Taxil, see 3.161–62n and 3.167n.

14.307–8 (391:40–41). *Entweder transubstantiality . . . no case subsubstantiality – *Entweder . . . oder*, German: "Either . . . or." The play on words recalls Stephen's earlier contemplation of heresies; see "Arius," 1.657n, and "Valentine," 1.658n. "Transubstantiation" is the miraculous change by which, according to Catholic doctrine, the eucharistic bread and wine become the body and blood of Christ, although their appearance remains unchanged. "Consubstantial" means sharing the same substance, as in theological terms the Father, the Son, and the Holy Spirit do. According to the Lutheran doctrine of "consubstantiation," the bread and wine do not become, but rather they coexist with, the body and blood of Christ during the Eucharist. "Subsubstantiality" (Joyce's coinage) suggests that the substance of bread and wine is debased (as implied by free association with Léo Taxil's crude accusation of bestiality, copulation with *le sacré pigeon;* see 3.50–52n).

14.309–11 (391:42–392:2). A pregnancy without joy . . . belly without bigness – Historically, the doctrine of Mary's immaculateness, her freedom from sin or fleshly taint, has been gradually enlarged: not only did she conceive without the "joy" (of copulation), but she also did not grow great with child, did not experience labor pains in giving birth (as Eve would not have had pain in childbirth had she not fallen), and Mary remained a virgin, her hymen intact, even after she had given birth. See 3.41–42n and 14.298–301n.

14.314, 317 (392:5, 7–8). *Staboo Stabella/The first three months she was not well, Staboo – The title and opening line of an unpublished bawdy ballad by Oliver St. John Gogarty; see Adams, p. 209.

14.314–15 (392:6). put in pod – Elizabethan slang: "made pregnant."

14.315 (392:6). Almany – Archaic: "Germany."

14.318 (392:8). nurse Quigley – Apart from the context, identity and significance unknown.

14.321 (392:12). gasteful – Obsolete: "wasteful."

14.326 (392:18). chode – Obsolete: past tense of *to chide*.

14.327–29 (392:19–21). thou chuff, thou puny . . . thou abortion thou – Recalls the name-calling contests between Prince Hal and Falstaff, particularly in *I Henry IV* (II.iv). *Chuff:* "a miser or rustic clown." *Got in the peasestraw:* figuratively, "illegitimate," since peasestraw was a cheap (and dishonest) substitute for hay. *Losel:* "a profligate, rake, or scoundrel." *Dykedropt:* "born in a ditch."

14.329–30 (392:22). like a curse of God ape – Source and connotations unknown.

14.330 (392:23). cognisance – In heraldry, a crest or badge worn to identify or distinguish the bearer.

14.331 (392:24). margerain gentle – A phrase from one of the verses of homage ("To mastres Margery Wentworthe") in John Skelton's (c. 1460–1529) *Garlande of Laurell* (1523): "With margerain ientyll, / The flowre of goodlyhede [goodliness], / Enbrowdred the mantill / Is of your maydenhede." In Elizabethan herbals, margerain (marjoram) was the herb of calm and gentleness, a remedy for diseases of the brain.

Style: 14.334–428 (392:27–395:15). To be short this passage . . . of a natural phenomenon – A composite imitation of late-sixteenth- and seventeenth-century Latinate prose styles, including those of John Milton (1608–74), Richard Hooker (1554–1600), Sir Thomas Browne (1605–82), and Jeremy Taylor (1613–67).

14.334–35 (392:28). Mary in Eccles – The Mater Misericordiae Hospital in Eccles Street; see 6.375–76n.

14.336–37 (392:30–31). obedience in the womb . . . poverty all his days – "By profession, members of the religious life publically as- sume the obligations of their state through the vows of poverty, chastity, and obedience" (*Maynooth Catechism* [Dublin, 1882]).

14.340 (392:35). intershowed – A Latin–Anglo-Saxon coinage: "demonstrated among (them)."

14.342–43 (392:37). the eternal son and ever virgin – Christ, who, though made flesh as man, was "free from all ignorance and error, from all sin and imperfection" (*Maynooth Catechism* [Dublin, 1882]).

14.343–48 (392:39–393:2). his curious rite of wedlock . . . she was there unmaided – Fantastic exemplary anthropology of this sort is characteristic of Sir Thomas Browne; see his *Pseudodoxia Epidemica* (Vulgar Errors) (1646). But the reference here is apparently to the suspicions indirectly suggested by the English Congregational minister William Ellis (1794–1872) in his *Three Trips to Madagascar* (London, 1838); see 17.1374n.

14.347 (393:1). kyries – See 7.559n.

14.347–48 (393:1–2). *Ut novetur sexus omnis corporis mysterium* – Latin: "That the whole mystery of physical sexuality may become known"; a mock anthem. Cf. *Pange lingua gloriosi*, 13.498n.

14.349–51 (393:3–6). Master John Fletcher . . . *To bed, to bed* – A song from Beaumont (c. 1584–1616) and Fletcher's (1579–1625) play *The Maid's Tragedy* (c. 1610): "To bed, to bed! Come, Hymen, lead the bride, / And lay her by her husband's side; / Bring in the virgins every one, / That grieve to lie alone, / That they may kiss while they may say a maid; / Tomorrow 'twill be other kiss'd and said, / Hesperus, be long a-shining, / While these lovers are a-twining" (I.ii.130–37).

14.353 (393:8). suadancy – A coinage from the obsolete *suade*, to persuade: "persuasiveness."

14.356 (393:12). Beau Mount – "Poetic" for the Mount of Venus.

14.358 (383:14–15). they had but the one doxy between them – John Aubrey (1626–97) wrote this about Beaumont and Fletcher in *Brief Lives* (edited 1898): "They lived together on the Banke side, not far from the Play-house, both bachelors; lay together; had one Wench in the house between them, which they did so admire;

the same cloathes and cloake, &c. between them." Aubrey's story had as its source not so much fact (Fletcher was married, Beaumont was not) as Ben Jonson's barb, said to have been at Beaumont and Fletcher's expense—spoken to a crude pair of puppets (Damon and Pythias) in *Bartholomew's Fair* (1614): "I say between you, you have both but one drab" (V.iv.223).

14.359–60 (393:16–17). life ran very high in those days – See 9.732–33n.

14.360 (393:17). custom of the country – The title of a play (c. 1628) by John Fletcher and Philip Massinger (1583–1640).

14.360–62 (393:17–19). Greater love than this . . . wife for his friend – Jesus preaches to his disciples in John 15:12–13: "This is my commandment, That ye love one another, as I have loved you. Greater love hath no man than this, that a man lay down his life for his friends."

14.362 (393:19). Go thou and do likewise – When a lawyer asks, "Who is my neighbour?" Jesus answers with the parable of the good Samaritan, a neighbor because he "shewed mercy," and then admonishes the lawyer, "Go, and do thou likewise" (Luke 10:25–37).

14.363 (393:20). Zarathustra – See 1.708n.

14.363 (393:21). French letters – Slang for condoms.

14.366 (393:24). the secondbest bed – See 9.691–95n.

14.366 (393:24). *Orate, fratres, pro memetipso* – Latin: "Brothers, pray for me myself." At the end of the offertory of the Mass the celebrant turns to the congregation and says, "Orate, fratres, ut meum ac vestrum sacrificium acceptabile fiat apud Deum Patrem omnipotentem" (Brothers [and sisters], pray that my sacrifice and yours may be acceptable to God the Almighty Father).

14.366–67 (393:24–25). And all the people shall say, Amen – Before the Amen, the response to the celebrant (see preceding note) is "May the Lord accept the sacrifice at your hands to the praise and glory of his name, for our good, and for the good of his holy Church everywhere. Amen."

14.367 (393:25–26). Remember, Erin, thy generations and thy days of old – Combines Thomas Moore's song "Let Erin Remember the Days of Old" (see 3.302–3n) with Moses' song in Deuteronomy 32:7, "Remember the days of old, consider the years of many generations."

14.368–69 (393:27–28). *and broughtedst in a stranger . . . fornication in my sight – The "stranger" in Moore's song (see 3.302–3n) is combined with several biblical echoes: "But the seventh day is the sabbath of the Lord thy God: in it thou shalt not do any work, thou . . . nor thy stranger that is within thy gates" (Exodus 20:10) and "thou mayest not set a stranger over thee, which is not thy brother" (Deuteronomy 17:15). The accusation of "fornication" is a frequent prophetic damnation; see Ezekiel 16:15, 26, 29.

14.369–70 (393:28). to wax fat and kick like Jeshurum – "But Jeshurun waxed fat, and kicked: thou art waxen fat, thou art grown thick, thou art covered with fatness; then he forsook God which made him, and lightly esteemed the Rock of his salvation" (Deuteronomy 32:15). Jeshurun (Hebrew: "righteous") is a poetic name for Israel.

14.370–71 (393:29–30). Therefore hast thou . . . the slave of servants – Again echoes several biblical passages, among them Lamentations 5:7–8: "Our fathers have sinned, and are not; and we have borne their iniquities. Servants have ruled over us: there is none that doth deliver us out of their hand."

14.371–72 (393:30–31). Return, return, Clan Milly . . . O Milesian – Among other possibilities, the Song of Solomon 6:13: "Return, return, O Shulamite; return, return, that we may look upon thee." "Clan Milly" is Irish for the race of Mileadh or the Milesians, the legendary ancestors of the royal clans of Ireland; see 12.1308–10n.

14.372–73 (393:31–33). Why hast thou done . . . merchant of jalaps – The question echoes the "reproaches" in the Mass for Good Friday, which begin: "My people, what have I done to you? How have I offended you?"; and, among other biblical sources, Deuteronomy 32:16: "They provoked him to jealousy with strange gods, with abominations provoked they him to anger." Cf. Ezekiel 5:8–11. (Apparently, the "strange gods" were as "merchant of jalaps," selling purgatives.) Compare Mulligan's remark that Haines's father had made his money "selling jalap to Zulus" (1.21–22 [7:11]).

14.373–75 (393:33–35). and didst deny me to . . . did lie luxuriously – That is, the Israelites "denied" their God in their subservience to the Romans and earlier in subservience to the princes of the East (India being mentioned only twice in the Old Testament, in Esther 1:1 and 8:9, where King Ahasuerus could be construed as the "Indian of dark speech"). The accusation that the daughters of Israel were misbehaving with "strangers" is frequent in prophetic condemnations of Israel; it is tempting here to make the Roman-English, Jewish-Irish links established in Aeolus (7.1–1075 [pp. 116–50]).

14.375–76 (393:35–36). Look forth now . . . Nebo and from Pisgah – Horeb (Sinai), Nebo, and Pisgah are three mountains associated with Moses' leadership of the children of Israel. At Horeb (Sinai), Moses receives "the law and the commandments" (Exodus 24–31) and the Lord's assurance of the promised land (Exodus 33:1–3). In Deuteronomy 32:48–52 the Lord tells Moses, "Get thee up . . . unto mount Nebo . . . and behold the land of Canaan, which I give unto the children of Israel for a possession: And die in the mount whither thou goest up." In Deuteronomy 34:1: "And Moses went up from the plains of Moab unto the mountain of Nebo, to the top of Pisgah," and from there he sees the promised land. See 7.873n.

14.376–77 (393:37). the Horns of Hatten – Or the Horns of Hittin, a mountain range west of the Sea of Galilee, associated by some seventeenth-century biblical geographers with the heights from which Moses viewed the promised land (partly because the promised land was described as "the whole land of the Hittites" in Joshua 1:4). Two thousand years of changing place names have compounded geographical confusion of this sort. Late nineteenth-century scholars rejected the Horns of Hittin in favor of a mountain range at the northeastern end of the Dead Sea, since that range commands the prospect described in Deuteronomy 34:1–3.

14.377 (393:37–38). a land flowing with milk and money – The promised land is repeatedly described as "a land flowing with milk and honey," as in the Lord's assurance to Moses in Exodus 33:3.

14.381 (394:1). the septuagint – A Greek translation of the Old Testament said to have been made in the third century B.C., called the "septuagint" because it was supposed to have been prepared in seventy days by seventy-two translators. It is the Old Testament used in the Eastern church, but it is not identical with the Old Testament in use among Jews and in Western Protestantism, which regards the additional books of the Septuagint as the Apocrypha.

14.382–83 (394:2–3). the Orient from on high . . . darkness that was foraneous – In the apocryphal gospel of Nicodemus, the two sons of Simon, risen from the dead as a result of Christ's resurrection, tell the story of Christ's descent into hell, where "the brazen gates were broken, and the iron bars were crushed, and all the dead that were bound were loosed from their bonds." Satan is bound and Christ removes Adam and "the righteous" to Paradise. "Foraneous" means utterly remote.

14.383–84 (394:3). Assuefaction minorates atrocities – That is, the act of becoming accustomed to atrocities diminishes their effect, after Sir Thomas Browne's argument in *Christian Morals*, Part III, section 10, that *memento mori* are not effective: "Forget not how assuefaction unto anything minorates the passion from it, how constant objects lose their hints, and steal an inadvertisement upon us."

14.384 (394:3–4). (as Tully saith of his darling Stoics) – In the *Tusculan Disputations* (45 B.C.), Marcus Tullius Cicero (106–43 B.C.) argues that "a human being should ponder all the vicissitudes that fall to man's lot" because "such events are cruel for those who have not reflected on them" and "everything which is thought evil is more grievous if it comes unexpectedly" (3:14).

14.384–85 (394:4–5). Hamlet his father showeth the prince no blister of combustion – The Ghost speaks to Hamlet: "But that I am forbid / To tell the secrets of my prison-house, / I could a tale unfold whose lightest word / Would harrow up thy soul. . . . But this eternal blazon [description of eternity] must not be / To ears of flesh and blood" (I.v.13–22).

14.385–86 (394:5–6). The adiaphane in the noon of life is an Egypt's plague – See Dante's *Inferno* 1:1–3, "In the middle of the journey of our life I came to myself in a dark wood where the straight way was lost." In Exodus 7–12 Egypt is visited with a series of plagues in punishment for the Pharaoh's refusal of Moses' demand for the freeing of the Israelites, among the plagues: "And the Lord said unto Moses,

Stretch out thine hand toward heaven, that there may be darkness over the land of Egypt, even darkness which may be felt" (Exodus 10:21). The final plague: "And it came to pass, that at midnight the Lord smote all the firstborn in the land of Egypt" (Exodus 12:29). For the adiaphane see 3.4n and 3.8–9n.

14.387 (394:7–8). ubi and quomodo – Latin: "the where and the manner."

14.387–89 (394:8–9). as the ends and ultimates . . . inceptions and originals – A paraphrase and summary of Aristotle's view of the relation between "seed" (origin) and the fully developed "animal" as that view is presented in *Physics* 2:8 and repeated in *On the Generation of Animals* 1:1. In the *Physics*, Aristotle quotes from Empedocles in the course of his argument; Empedocles had held a cyclical theory of creation—that once creation has been achieved, hate gradually disintegrates it to chaos and then love again begins the process of creation. In the first phases of creation love conjoins things at random, producing "monsters" such as the ox-man, but these cannot reproduce and hence cease to exist as creation clarifies itself. As Aristotle puts it, "Thus in the original combinations the 'ox-progeny' if they failed to reach a determinate end must have arisen through the corruption of some principle corresponding to what is now the seed [origin]."

14.392–93 (394:13–15). The aged sisters draw us . . . dead they bend – Combines the midwife with the woman who lays out the corpse, suggesting the three Fates of Greek mythology and the three phases—mother, lover, and hag of death—of the Triple Goddess, the goddess of the whole cycle of life. See Robert Graves, *The White Goddess* (New York, 1948); see also 9.376n.

14.394–95 (394:15–16). First saved from waters . . . bed of fasciated wattles – As Moses was found in Exodus 2:5: "And the daughter of Pharaoh came down to wash herself at the river; and her maidens walked along by the river's side; and when she saw the ark among the flags, she sent her maid to fetch it." See 3.298n. "Fasciated" means swaddled, enveloped with bands.

14.395 (394:17). at last the cavity of a mountain, an occulted sepulchre – As Moses was buried, Deuteronomy 34:5–6: "So Moses the servant of the Lord died there . . . according to the word of the Lord. And he buried him in a

valley in the land of Moab . . . but no man knoweth of his sepulchre unto this day." Sir Thomas Browne mentions this burial in chapter 1 of *Hydriotaphia: Urn-Burial* (1658). See 17.2000n.

14.396 (394:18). conclamation – An outcry or shout of many together.

14.396 (394:18). the ossifrage – Obsolete for the lammergeyer, the largest European bird of prey; also, osprey.

14.396–97 (394:19). the ubicity of his tumulus – The location of his sepulchral mound.

14.398 (394:20). Tophet – Traditionally regarded as an Old Testament "type" of hell. Tophet (literally, "place of burning") was located in the Valley of Hinnom, south of Jerusalem; there, corpses were burned (contrary to the law, as Jeremiah maintains [7:31–32]) and human sacrifices were performed in the worship of Moloch; thus its reputation as a place of evil and "hellfire." See Isaiah 30:33.

14.398 (394:20–21). Edenville – Stephen's version of the Garden of Eden; see 3.39 (38:4). To be "ushered" toward Tophet is to be sent to the inferno; toward Edenville is to be sent to purgatory. In Dante's *Purgatorio*, once the soul is purged by punishment, it passes through the Earthly Paradise (the Garden of Eden) on the summit of the Mount of Purgatory en route to Paradise.

14.399–400 (394:22–23). the whatness of our whoness – See 9.84–85 (186:13–14).

14.401 (394:24). *Etienne, Chanson – French: literally, "Stephen, Song."

14.402 (394:25). wisdom hath built herself a house – "Wisdom hath builded her house, she hath hewn out her seven pillars" (Proverbs 9:1).

14.403 (394:26). the crystal palace – An iron-and-glass exhibition building erected for the Great Exhibition (World's Fair) of 1851 in Hyde Park, London. Designed by the English engineers Sir Joseph Paxton (1801–65) and Sir Charles Fox (1810–74), it covered nineteen acres and was regarded as a "wonder of the world." In 1854 it was moved to Sydenham on the outskirts of London, where it was (until World War I) the site of a permanent fair. It was destroyed by fire in 1936. Fox was "immortalized" by one David Bogue in a parody of "The

House that Jack Built" entitled "The Crystal Palace that Fox Built" (1851).

14.404 (394:27–28). a penny for him who finds the pea – The "shell game," or "thimble-rigging," was popular at country fairs. The operator, talking and prestidigitating to confuse the players, hides a pea under one of a group of shells and then bets that the players cannot point out the right shell.

14.405–7 (394:29–31). *Behold the mansion . . . of Jackjohn's bivouac* – The opening lines of "The Domicile Erected by Jack" (1857) by George Shepard Burleigh, a parody of the nursery rhyme "The House that Jack Built." The third line of the parody reads "Ivan's Bivouac" instead of "Jackjohn's bivouac." The fun of the parody turns on the translation of the jingling nursery rhyme into an elaborate and heroic language. The cat, for example, is treated to the epithet "that sly / Ulysses quadrapedal."

14.408 (394:32). noise in the street – See 2.386n.

14.409 (394:33–34). Thor thundered . . . the hammerhurler – In Scandinavian mythology, Thor was the god of thunder and lightning and the son of Odin (chief of the gods). His hammer (the lightning bolt) always returned to his hand after he had thrown it; thunder was the rolling of his chariot.

14.413 (394:39). haught – Archaic: "high in one's estimation."

14.414 (394:40). his heart shook – The heartbeat of the unborn fetus begins in the fourth month of pregnancy.

14.417–18 (395:2–3). a word and a blow – Popular expression for "aggressive and volatile, not to be taken seriously."

14.418–19 (395:4). an old Nobodaddy – See 9.787n.

14.426–27 (395:13–14). the discharge of fluid from the thunderhead – Bloom's "explanation" echoes the eighteenth-century assumption that electricity was a "fluid," but it also owes something to Sir Thomas Browne, who attributed lightning and thunder to the explosion of "nitrous and sulphurous exhalations, set on fire in the clouds" and who remarked that if the exhalations were "spirituous" (fluid) "the noise

is great and terrible" (*Pseudodoxia Epidemica* [1646], Book 2, chapter 5).

Style 14.429–73 (395:16–396:27). But was Boasthard's . . . bring brenningly biddeth – An imitation of the style of John Bunyan (1628–88), a radical English preacher whose allegories, notably *Pilgrim's Progress* (1675), make extensive and successful use of proper names similar to Joyce's "Boasthard" and "Calmer."

14.436 (395:24). Bringforth – In Genesis 3:16 God says to fallen Eve, "in sorrow shalt thou bring forth children."

14.442–43 (395:32–33). which Phenomenon has . . . by the book Law – See 14.29–32n.

14.444 (395:34). Believe-on-Me – After John 6:35: "And Jesus said unto them, I am the bread of life: he that cometh to me shall never hunger; and he that believeth on me shall never thirst."

14.445–46 (395:36). no death and no birth neither wiving nor mothering – In Mark 12:25 Jesus answers the Sadducees (who did not believe in the Resurrection) and their trap-questions about who would be man and wife in heaven: "For when they shall rise from the dead, they neither marry, nor are given in marriage; but are as the angels which are in heaven."

14.450/453 (395:41/396:3). Bird-in-the-Hand/ Two-in-the-Bush – After the proverbial saying, "A bird in the hand is worth two in the bush," attributed as early as Plutarch (c.46–c.120 A.D.).

14.473 (396:27). brenningly – Archaic: "burningly."

Style: 14.474–528 (396:28–398:9). So Thursday sixteenth . . . queerities no telling how – After the style of the seventeenth-century diarists (and friends) John Evelyn (1620–1706) and Samuel Pepys (1633–1703), or rather after what Joyce thought to be Pepys's style, since he was working from a heavily edited selection; see J. S. Atherton, "Oxen of the Sun," in *James Joyce's "Ulysses": Critical Essays*, ed. Clive Hart and David Hayman (Berkeley, Calif., 1974), p. 324.

14.482–83 (396:38–39). the big wind . . . land so pitifully – An extraordinarily destructive and prolonged gale struck the British Isles and particularly Dublin and environs on 26 and 27 February 1903. See 1.366–67n. In *The Odyssey*, "a giant wind" (12:313; Fitzgerald, p. 232) drives Odysseus and his crew to seek shelter on the island of the sun-god, and "a month of onshore gales" (12:325; ibid.) keeps them pinned down on the island.

14.490–91 (397:5–7). In Ely place . . . up to Holles Street – Ely Place and Baggot Street are just southwest of Merrion Square. The Duke's Lawn is in front of Leinster House, just west of the square. The pattern also describes Mulligan's route from George Moore's (at 4 Ely Place Upper) to the Maternity Hospital.

14.493–94 (397:9–10). the Rt. Hon. Mr Justice Fitzgibbon's door – At 10 Merrion Square North. See 7.794n.

14.494–95 (397:10–11). (that is to sit . . . upon college lands) – Justice Fitzgibbon and Timothy Michael Healy (see 7.800n) were to sit together on the Trinity College Estates Commission (see 7.800–801n).

14.496–97 (397:13). (that was a papish . . . a good Williamite) – That is, George Moore, once a Roman Catholic, has become Protestant (and pro-English). George Moore's attitudes toward religion (as toward other matters of personal conviction) were somewhat equivocal. By his own account his family seems to have oscillated between Catholic and Protestant allegiances. His parents were Catholic, and in his *Confessions of a Young Man* (1888) Moore indulges modish and possibly insincere expressions of admiration for the Roman Catholic liturgy. "Lapsed Catholic," fascinated by the "new paganism," might be an apt description of Moore; or would it be his novel *The Lake* (1905), the story of a young priest's escape from "the prison-house of Catholicism"? Yeats, in *The Autobiography* (New York, 1958), describes Moore as "neither anticlerical nor anti-Catholic" and remarks that Moore did not go to mass "because his flesh was unwilling." Moore asserts in his autobiography, *Hail and Farewell* (3 vols.; 1911, 1912, 1914), that he formally became a Protestant. Atherton suggests that at this point Joyce's imitation of Daniel Defoe's (c. 1661–1731) style has already begun. ("Oxen of the Sun," in *James Joyce's "Ulysses,"* p. 324).

14.497 (397:14). a cut bob – With his hair cut short. This sort of sartorial observation is characteristic of Pepys's style.

14.500 (397:17). Saint Swithin – (d. 862), an English ecclesiastic, chaplain to King Egbert,

tutor to Egbert's son Ethelwulf, and subsequently Ethelwulf's chief councillor and bishop of Winchester. Feast day: 15 July.

14.503 (397:20–21). beef to the heel – See 4.402–3n.

14.505 (397:23). brangling – Archaic: "wrangling, brawling."

14.505–6 (397:24). scholar of my lady of Mercy – That is, Dixon received part of his medical training at the Mater Misericordiae Hospital in Eccles Street.

14.508–10 (397:27–30). *having dreamed tonight . . . to be for an omen of a change – See 15.3928n.

14.511 (397:31). pleading her belly – Granted a stay of execution on account of pregnancy, as in Defoe's *Moll Flanders* (1722): "My mother pleaded her belly, and being found quick with child, she was respited for about seven months."

14.511 (397:31). on the stools – In labor, with her feet supported to aid her efforts.

14.513 (397:33). riceslop – Or rice water, a drink for invalids made by boiling a small quantity of rice in water.

14.516 (397:36–37). Lady day – 25 March, the Feast of the Annunciation of the Blessed Virgin Mary.

14.516 (397:37). bit off her last chick's nails – After the Irish superstition that if a child's nails were cut before it was a year old, it would be "light-fingered and addicted to stealing" (Speranza [Lady Wilde], *Ancient Cures, Charms, and Usages of Ireland* [London, 1890], p. 68). The fetus begins to form nails in the fifth month of pregnancy.

14.517–18 (397:39). the king's bible – The King James Bible (indicating that the Purefoys are Protestant).

14.518 (397:39–40). *a methodist but takes the sacrament – That is, he is an old-fashioned Methodist. When John Wesley (1703–91) founded Methodism, he argued that Methodists should receive the sacraments in the established church rather than from their own ministers in their own chapels. This original relation to the established church was radically changed shortly after Wesley's death.

14.519 (397:41). Bullock harbour – See 1.671n.

14.520 (397:41–42). dapping on the sound – To fish by dropping the bait gently on the water.

14.523 (398:3–4). after wind and water fire shall come – This phrase, although not a quotation, has a biblical and prophetic ring to it: see 15.170–72 (434:27–30) and 15.4660ff. (598:11ff.).

14.524 (398:4). Malachi's almanac – Refers to the prophet Malachi's vision that closes the Old Testament (4:1): "For, behold, the day cometh, that shall burn as an oven; and all that do wickedly, shall be stubble: and the day that cometh shall burn them up, saith the Lord of hosts, that it shall leave them neither root nor branch." See 8.13n.

14.524–25 (398:5–6). Mr Russell has done . . . for his farmer's gazette – George William Russell's "farmer's gazette" was the *Irish Homestead* (see 2.412n). The "prophetical charm" recalls Russell's interest in the occult and in the mysteries of India, but, in the manner of Pepys's gossipy conjectures, it refers not to a real article but to Russell's personal and peculiar combination of interest in Theosophy and in agrarian reform.

Style: 14.529–81 (398:10–399:31). With this came up . . . sent the ale purling about – After the style of the English journalist, pamphleteer, and novelist Daniel Defoe (c. 1661–1731).

14.533 (398:15). that went for – That is, who styled himself as.

14.534 (398:16). pickle – A mischievous young man.

14.537 (398:20). Paul's men – Archaic: the nave of St. Paul's in London was once famous as a place to meet and lounge about; hence, "Paul's men" were loungers, hangers-on who did not work.

14.537 (398:20). flatcaps – Apprentices, after the distinctive round caps with low flat crowns that they wore in sixteenth- and seventeenth-century London.

14.537 (398:20). waistcoaters – Elizabethan slang, meaning either "gallants" (after their heavily ornamented sleeveless jackets) or "low-class prostitutes."

14.540 (398:23). sackpossets – A beverage made of raw eggs, sugar, and sack (a white wine imported to England from Spain in the sixteenth and seventeenth centuries).

14.540 (398:24). a boilingcook's – Slang for the poorest of restaurants or taverns.

14.542 (398:26). tester – Slang: "sixpence."

14.543 (398:27). punk – Slang: "prostitute."

14.546 (398:31). Kerry cows – An Irish breed of small, entirely black cattle, noted for the quality of their milk.

14.548 (398:33). There's as good fish in this tin – In *The Odyssey*, when Odysseus's provisions run out on the island of the sun-god, the men "scour the wild shore . . . for fishes and sea fowl" (12:330; Fitzgerald, p. 232) before they give in and slaughter the sacred cattle.

14.551 (398:37). *Mort aux vaches* – French: literally, "Death to the cows" (see p. 408); in French slang it means "Down with the cops!"

14.555 (398:41). headborough – A petty constable.

14.560 (399:6). bearpit – Wagers were made on contests between a bear and several dogs confined in a ring or a pit.

14.560 (399:6). cocking main – The ring established for a cockfight.

14.561 (399:7). *the romany folk – Gypsies.

14.569 (399:17). springers – See 6.392n.

14.569 (399:17). hoggets – Two-year-old boars.

14.570 (399:17). wether – A ram (especially, a castrated ram).

14.570 (399:18). actuary – A clerk.

14.570–71 (399:18). Mr Joseph Cuffe – See 6.392n.

14.571–72 (399:19). meadow auctions – Auctions of livestock that took place on farms rather than in markets.

14.572 (399:20). Mr Gavin Low's yard – Gavin Low, livestock agent, 47–53 Prussia Street, on the corner of North Circular Road opposite the cattle market, in the northwest quadrant of Dublin.

14.573 (399:21–22). *the hoose or the timber tongue – For "hoose," see 12.834n; for "timber tongue," see 12.834–35n.

14.576 (399:25). Doctor Rinderpest – See 2.333n.

14.579 (399:29). a bull that's Irish – A "bull" (or an "Irish bull") is a statement that makes logical sense to its innocent and wrongheaded speaker but that in objective and literal terms is nonsense. Typical examples: "Pat, do you understand French?" "Yes, if it's spoke in Irish." And, from an Irishman to a friend studying for the priesthood: "I hope I may live to hear you preach my funeral sermon." See 3.79n.

Style: 14.581–650 (399:31–401:30). An Irish bull in an . . . A man's a man for a' that – After the style of Jonathan Swift (1667–1745), particularly that of *A Tale of a Tub* (1704), Part IV, in which Swift lampoons Peter's (allegorically, the Roman Catholic church's) use of "papal bulls" in a rousing burlesque of the Church and its history.

14.581 (399:31). *an Irish bull in an English chinashop – A proverbial expression for blundering and destructive clumsiness, compounded here by the puns on Irish and papal bulls and by the reputation of England's china industry.

14.582–83 (399:32–33). that same bull . . . by farmer Nicholas – Nicholas Breakspear, Pope Adrian IV (pope 1154–59), was the only English pope. In a papal bull, *Laudabiliter* (1155)—of which, apparently, no verified copy survives—Adrian granted the overlordship of Ireland to Henry II of England (king 1154–89). Henry, in seeking the papal permission for invasion, had argued that Ireland was in a state of profound moral corruption and irreligion. The bull approved Henry's "laudable" determination "to extirpate certain vices which had taken root." Henry was, however, preoccupied on the Continent, and it was not until 1169 that he began to take up his option, encouraging "any of his subjects who were interested" to lend help to Dermod MacMurrough (see 2.393–94n). When this first "invasion" met with considerable success, Henry exacted pledges of allegiance from his venturesome subjects and took personal control of the invasion in 1171.

14.583 (399:34). an emerald ring – The English scholar and churchman John of Salisbury (c. 1115–80) records that in 1155 Pope Adrian gave Henry II an emerald (for "emerald isle") set in a gold ring as token of Henry's overlordship of Ireland.

14.589–90 (399:41–42). farmer Nicholas that was . . . a college of doctors – Nicholas II (pope 1058–61) undertook a series of reforms to suppress the practice of priests taking concubines and to restrict papal election to the college of cardinals. Thus, Adrian IV, a century later, could be expected to have remained celibate and to have been *elected* by the college.

14.592 (400:2). *the lord Harry – King Henry II of England; see 14.582–83n.

14.596–97 (400:7–8). whisper in his ear in the dark of a cowhouse – That is, whisper in the privacy of the confession box.

14.598–99 (400:10). the four fields of all Ireland – Traditionally, the four ancient kingdoms: Munster, Leinster, Ulster, and Connacht.

14.600 (400:11–12). a point shift – A shirtlike garment made of lace.

14.601 (400:14). spermaceti oil – Was used in the coronation of English monarchs.

14.604 (400:17). the father of the faithful – In the drunken whirl of Henrys in this passage, this seems to refer to Henry VIII (king 1509–47). In 1521, long before his break with Rome, Henry wrote a treatise, *Assertio Septem Sacramentorum*, defending the sacraments against Martin Luther's challenge. The book earned him the papal title Defender of the Faith, which English monarchs (as heads of the Church of England) have since retained.

14.613 (400:27). *By the Lord Harry – Henry VIII has metamorphosed into Henry VII (king 1485–1509). Henry VII reasserted English control of Ireland after the relapse occasioned by the Wars of the Roses. In 1494 English land-use laws were applied to Ireland, which, since English and Irish customs of land use were quite different, proved particularly onerous and detrimental to Irish agriculture. To swear "by the Lord Harry" is to swear by the devil.

14.614–15 (400:29–30). Roscommon . . . Connemara . . . Sligo – Roscommon is a county in central Ireland; Sligo, a county on the west coast; and Connemara is an area on the Atlantic coast in County Galway.

14.619 (400:35). the Lord Harry called farmer Nicholas – Henry VII has given way again to Henry VIII and a suggestion of his difficulties with Pope Clement VII (pope 1523–34) over Henry's attempt to divorce his first wife, Catharine of Aragon.

14.619 (400:35). the old Nicks – "Old Nick" and "old Harry" (or "Lord Harry") are common names for the Devil.

14.620 (400:36). an old whoremaster – Protestant churches consistently identified the Roman Catholic church as "the great whore that sitteth upon many waters: . . . MYSTERY, BABYLON THE GREAT, THE MOTHER OF HARLOTS AND ABOMINATIONS OF THE EARTH" (Revelation 17:1, 5).

14.620 (400:36). that kept seven trulls – Not to be outdone by Henry VIII, who had six wives, his papal adversary kept seven mistresses.

14.622 (400:39). pizzle – An animal's penis, often that of a bull.

14.623 (400:40). cleaning his royal pelt – After a parody (of his own poem "Moses") by the blind Dublin street-ballad singer Michael Moran (1794–1846), quoted in Yeats's *The Celtic Twilight* (London, 1893), pp. 72–73: "In Egypt's land, contagious to the Nile, / King Pharaoh's daughter went to bathe in style. / She tuk her dip, then walked unto the land, / To dry her royal pelt she ran along the strand. / A bulrush tripped her, whereupon she saw / A smiling babby in a wad o' straw / She tuk it up, and said with accents mild, / Tare-and-agers, girls, which au yez owns the child?" Yeats called Moran "The Last Gleeman" (p. 67).

14.626–27 (401:2). a blackthumbed chapbook – A slant allusion to Henry VIII's treatise *Assertio Septem Sacramentorum* (1521). See 14.604n.

14.627–28 (401:3–4). a left-handed descendant – That is, through an illegitimate line.

14.628 (401:4–5). the famous champion bull of the Romans – St. Peter, who is regarded as the one designated by Jesus to found "His Church" (Matthew 16:18) and who is believed to have been the first bishop of Rome (pope).

14.628–29 (401:5). *Bos Bovum* – Dog-Latin: "Bull of the Bulls."

14.630 (401:7). a cow's drinking trough – An allusion to Henry VIII's liaison with Irish-born Anne Boleyn (1507?–1536). She first appeared at court in 1522 and became queen (after all the machinations of Henry's divorce) in 1533.

14.631–32 (401:8). his new name – Defender of the Faith, still one of the royal titles of the reigning English monarch; see 14.604n.

14.633–34 (401:11). *the bulls' language – That is, the language in which papal bulls are written (Church Latin) combined in pun with the language of Irish bulls; see 14.579n.

14.638 (401:16–17). he and the bull of Ireland – Henry VIII was proclaimed Head of Church and State by act of Parliament in May 1536; in 1541 he was proclaimed King of Ireland (and thus Head of Church and State in Ireland). The Irish lords "diplomatically" accepted the Reformation of Ireland, but not without considerable dissension and violence.

14.643 (401:22–23). three sheets to the wind – A popular expression for "very drunk."

14.644–45 (401:24). ran up the jolly Roger – Proclaimed themselves pirates; the Jolly Roger flag of pirates is a white skull and crossbones on a black field.

14.645 (401:25). gave three times three – A standard form of giving a cheer in Ireland.

14.645 (401:25). let the bullgine run – The title of an English sea chanty: "We'll run from night til morning, / O run, let the bulgine run." "Bulgine" is navy slang for a bilge pump; the sense of the chanty is a devil-may-care "let's keep going even though the ship is sinking."

14.649–50 (401:29–30). *Pope Peter's but . . . man for a' that* – Combines a line from a Protestant street rhyme with a line from Robert Burns's poem "For A' That and A' That" (1795): "What though on homely fare we dine, / Wear hodden-grey, and a' that; / Gie fools their silks and knaves their wine, / A man's a man for a' that" (lines 9–12). The street rhyme is unknown, but it has relatives; for example, "Piss a bed, / Piss a bed, / Barley Butt, / Your Bum is so heavy, / You can't get up."

Style: 14.651–737 (401:31–404:10). Our worthy acquaintance . . . larum in the antechamber – In the style of Joseph Addison (1672–1719) and Richard Steele's (1672–1719) periodical essays in the *Tatler* (1709–11) and the *Spectator* (1711–12).

14.654–55 (401:35–36). to buy a colour or a cornetcy in the fencibles – The "fencibles" were military units organized and maintained for home service only. "A colour or a coronetcy" was the commissioned officer who carried the colors in a troop of cavalry, the lowest-ranking commissioned officer in the troop. Commissions in the British military were obtainable by purchase until the reforms of 1871.

14.659 (401:41). Mr Quinnell's – George Quinnell, printer, 45 Fleet Street, in central Dublin south of the Liffey.

14.660 (402:2). *Lambay Island* – Three miles off the coast nearly opposite Malahide, twelve miles east-northeast of Dublin. It is noted as a bird sanctuary.

14.662–63 (402:4–5). sir Fopling Popinjay and sir Milksop Quidnunc – Richard Steele made characters with similar names the butts of his satire in the *Tatler*, and the "man of mode" in George Etherege's (1634–91) comedy of that title (1676) is Sir Fopling Flutter.

14.666 (402:8–9). 'Tis as cheap sitting as standing – Lady Answerall to Colonel Atwit in Swift's *Complete Collection of Genteel and Ingenious Conversation* (1738), Part I: "Well, sit while you stay; 'tis as cheap sitting, as standing."

14.673 (402:17). dearest pledges – That is, children, as in Spenser's *Faerie Queene:* "But faire Charissa to a lovely fere [mate] / Was lincked, and by him had many pledges dere" (in contrast to her two sisters who "virgins were, / Though spoused") (1:10, stanza 4).

14.674 (402:19). bonzes – The Buddhist clergy of Japan (and sometimes of China and adjacent countries).

14.674–75 (402:19). who hide their flambeau under a bushel – In Matthew 5:14–15, Jesus says to the "multitudes": "Ye are the light of the world. . . . Neither do men light a candle and put it under a bushel, but on a candlestick; and it giveth light unto all that are in the house."

14.676 (402:21). some unaccountable muskin – "Muskin," meaning a pretty face, is a term of endearment for a woman, of contempt when said of a man. William Cowper (1731–1800) coined the phrase, and Dr. Johnson (1709–84) objected: "Those who call a man a cabbage, . . . an odd fish, and an unaccountable muskin, should never come into company without an interpreter" (*Connoisseur*, no. 138 [1756], p. 6; quoted in the *Oxford English Dictionary*).

14.682–84 (402:28–30). Lambay island from . . . our ascendency party – Richard Wogan Talbot, Lord Talbot de Malahide (b. 1846), was a retired army man and a landowner (3,600 acres) whose resistance to land reform was mild but firm. His family sold Lambay Island (see 14.660n) in 1878.

14.684–85 (402:31). national fertilising farm – An experiment in the then-controversial science of eugenics (to improve the hereditary qualities of the human race). The controversy began in the 1880s, when Sir Francis Galton (1822–1911), who had applied statistical methods to anthropological studies, turned his attention to the study of human heredity. A chair of eugenics was soon established at London University, intensifying the controversy, which peaked in 1910 and years following. Eugenics oversimplified the study of heredity by assuming that strong parents would produce strong children; intelligent parents, intelligent children; and so on with other traits. In practice, the near-impossibility of distinguishing between inherited and acquired characteristics proved too much for eugenics.

14.685 (402:31). *Omphalos* – See 1.176n.

14.685–86 (402:32). an obelisk . . . after the fashion of Egypt – Egyptian obelisks were phallic symbols dedicated to the sun-god and associated with fertility worship.

14.704 (403:12). to carry coals to Newcastle – A proverbial expression for a pointless and redundant enterprise, since Newcastle-upon-Tyne in England was noted for its concentration of blast furnaces.

14.705–10 (403:13–19). an apt quotation from . . . magnopere anteponunt – This "apt," Ciceronian quotation is apparently from a classic written specifically for the occasion by Mulligan. Latin: "Of such a kind and so great is the depravity of our generation, O Citizens, that our matrons much prefer the lascivious titillations of Gallic half-men to the weighty testicles and extraordinary erections of the Roman centurion."

14.720 (403:31). those loaves and fishes – Jesus fed the multitudes (which had followed him into the desert where he had gone to mourn the death of John the Baptist) with "five loaves and two fishes" (Matthew 14:13–21).

14.727 (403:40). ventripotence – Big-bellied, gluttonous.

14.728 (403:41–42). ovablastic gestation in the prostatic utricle – Literally, "the gestation of the germ layers of the embryonic egg in the vesicle of the prostate gland." The medical-student joke hinges on the assumption that the prostate gland is the male homologue of the uterus.

14.729 (404:1). Mr Austin Meldon – Dublin physician, fellow, counselor, and former president of the Royal College of Physicians in Ireland and senior surgeon to the Jervis Street Hospital.

14.730 (404:1). a wolf in the stomach – After the proverbial expression: "A growing boy has a wolf in his belly."

14.732 (404:4). Mother Grogan – See 1.357n.

14.733 (404:5). 'tis a pity she's a trollop – After the title of John Ford's (c. 1586–c. 1655) play *'Tis Pity She's a Whore* (1633).

Style: 14.738–98 (404:11–405:42). Here the listener who . . . of our store of knowledge – After the style of the Irish-born English novelist and cleric Laurence Sterne (1713–68), particularly his *Sentimental Journey Through France and Italy* (1768).

14.746–47 (404:21–22). Mais bien sûr . . . et mille compliments – French: "But certainly . . . and a thousand compliments (thanks)."

14.776 (405:15). marchand de capotes – French: literally, "a cloak merchant"; but *capote* is also slang for a condom. Since the sale of contraceptive devices was prohibited by law in Ireland, they had to be obtained on the sly or by mail order from England; see 17.1804–5 (721:19–21).

14.776 (405:15–16). Monsieur Poyntz – Two Dublin merchants might combine to qualify: B. Poyntz & Co., hosiers, glovers, and colonial outfitters, 105–106 Grafton Street; and Samuel Robert Poyntz, india-rubber warehouse and waterproofer, 20 Clare Street (*Thom's* 1904, p. 1989).

14.777 (405:16). livre – French: an obsolete French coin superseded by the franc and of slightly less worth than the franc. The livre is the coin "of record" in Sterne's *Sentimental Journey.*

14.778 (405:18). Le Fécondateur – French: "the impregnator."

14.780 (405:20). avec lui – French: "with him." The use of French phrases not only echoes Sterne, it also echoes George Moore's habit of salting his conversation with French phrases.

14.781 (405:21). ventre biche – French slang: "things go so well, with such vitality."

14.783 (405:23). sans blague – French: literally, "without nonsense"; thus, "no joke" or "all joking aside."

14.785 (405:26). umbrella – Slang for a diaphragm.

14.788 (405:29–30). ark of salvation – As Noah's ark was designed to save Noah and his family from the "deluge" (Genesis 6–8).

14.792 (405:34). il y a deux choses – French: "there are two things."

14.794–98 (405:36–42). The first, said she . . . our store of knowledge – The coy gesture of the kiss is reminiscent of Sterne's use of similar gestures, and the titillating "interruption" is one of his favorite satiric devices (see "The Temptation. Paris" and "The Conquest" in *A Sentimental Journey*).

Style: 14.799–844 (406:1–407:14). Amid the general vacant . . . on with a loving heart – After the style of the Irish-born man of letters (dramatist, poet, novelist, essayist) Oliver Goldsmith (1728–74).

14.808 (406:12). Gad's bud – "God's body," a mild eighteenth-century oath.

14.810 (406:14). Demme – A minced form of "damn," another mild eighteenth-century oath.

14.810 (406:14). Doctor O'Gargle – Apart from the context, significance unknown.

14.812 (406:17). Lawksamercy – A minced form of "Lord have mercy," an appropriately feminine eighteenth-century oath.

14.815–16 (406:21). Father Cantekissem – Apart from the context, significance unknown.

14.816 (406:21–22). pot of four – With a pun on the French *pot au feu* (stew).

14.821 (406:28). *enceinte* – French: "pregnant"; a genteel avoidance of the "gross" English equivalent.

14.826–27 (406:34). a cloud of witnesses – "Wherefore seeing we also are compassed about with so great a cloud of witnesses, let us lay aside every weight, and the sin which doth so easily beset us, and let us run with patience the race that is set before us" (Hebrews 12:1).

14.835 (407:2–3). on the by – Slang for standing around a counter or bar drinking.

14.839–40 (407:8). swore a round hand – Slang, after "to bet a round hand": to bet for (or against) several horses in one race.

14.840 (407:9). Stap – Obsolete: "stop" or "stuff."

14.842 (407:11–12). to honour thy father and thy mother – The fifth commandment: "Honour thy father and thy mother: that thy days may be long upon the land which the Lord thy God giveth thee" (Exodus 20:12).

Style: 14.845–79 (407:15–408:14). To revert to Mr Bloom . . . of the Supreme Being – After the style of Edmund Burke (1729–97), the Irish-born political philosopher who combined in his "conservatism" a practical and scholarly empiricism with a consistent veneration for and appeal to "the wisdom of our ancestors." Atherton also identifies traces of Dr. Johnson and the earl of Chesterfield (1694–1773) ("Oxen of the Sun," in *James Joyce's "Ulysses,"* eds. Clive

Hart and David Hayman [Berkeley, Calif., 1974], pp. 327–28).

14.854–56 (407:26–28). a cropeared creature . . . feet first into the world – In Shakespeare's *III Henry VI*, the hunchback, Gloucester (soon to become Richard III), stabs Henry VI (who has just compared himself to Daedalus, his son to Icarus) and then says: "Down, down to hell; and say I sent thee thither: / I, that have neither pity, love, nor fear. / Indeed, 'tis true that Henry told me of; / For I have often heard my mother say / I came into the world with my legs forward" (V.vi.67–71). Three times in the play Gloucester is called "crookback" and several times in *Richard III* he is described as "misshapen." "Gibbosity" is the condition of being hunchbacked.

14.857–59 (407:30–31). that missing link . . . late ingenious Mr Darwin – In *The Descent of Man and Selection in Relation to Sex* (1871), Charles Darwin (1809–82) postulated that a "missing link" had intervened between the apes and man in the process of evolution. In effect, the missing link was a way of accounting for the radical discontinuity between the two related species.

14.859 (407:32). the middle span of our allotted years – Born in 1866, Bloom was thirty-eight in 1904 and thus three years beyond the midpoint of his "allotted" "three score and ten."

14.873 (408:6–7). for eating of the tree forbid – See 13.1038–39n.

Style: 14.880–904 (408:15–409:3). Accordingly he broke his mind . . . feather laugh together – After the style of Dublin-born Richard Brinsley Sheridan (1751–1816), who, after a brief career as a successful dramatist (1775–79), had a distinguished career as a witty and resourceful member of Parliament. The style of this passage is closer to that of Sheridan's political oratory than it is to that of his plays.

14.886 (408:22–23). Ephesian matron – The "heroine" of this archetypal story was a widow of Ephesus, the intensity of whose mourning for her dead husband was matched by the alacrity with which she accepted the advances of a handsome new suitor. The most famous retelling of the story is in Petronius's (d. 66) *Satyricon*.

14.888 (408:24–25). *old Glory Allelujurum – This mocking name for Purefoy turns on the ejaculation "Glory Hallelujah" with which excited members of an American revivalist congregation would punctuate a sermon.

14.889 (408:26). dundrearies – Long sidewhiskers without a beard, a fashion set by the English comic actor Edward Askew Sothern (1826–81) in the part of the inane and fatuous Lord Dundreary in Tom Taylor's *Our American Cousin* (1858); see 7.733–34n.

14.891 (408:29). 'Slife – A petty oath: "God's life."

14.895 (408:33). the man in the gap – See 12.186n.

14.896–902 (408:35–42). Singular, communed the guest . . . esteemed the noblest – Atherton identifies this passage as an imitation of Dr. Johnson ("Oxen of the Sun," in *James Joyce's "Ulysses,"* ed. Clive Hart and David Hayman [Berkeley, Calif., 1974], p. 327).

14.897 (408:36–37). metempsychosis – See 4.339n.

14.904 (409:2–3). birds of a feather laugh together – After the nursery rhyme: "Birds of a feather flock together, / And so will pigs and swine; / Rats and mice will have their choice, / And so will I have mine."

Style: 14.905–41 (409:4–410:6). But with what fitness . . . acid and inoperative – After the style of the savage eighteenth-century satirist Junius; see 12.1633n.

14.905 (409:4–5). the noble lord, his patron – On the basis of the stylistic imitations in the preceding passage, Atherton suggests the earl of Chesterfield, whose belated offer of patronage to Dr. Johnson was so sternly rejected in Johnson's famous letter of 7 February 1755 ("Oxen of the Sun," in *James Joyce's "Ulysses,"* p. 328).

14.906–7 (409:5–6). this alien, whom the concession of a gracious prince has admitted to civic rights – Expelled in 1290, Jews were readmitted to the British Isles under Cromwell and Charles II, but they only very gradually (and from a series of grudging rather than "gracious" princes) were conceded civil rights: in 1723, the right to give evidence in courts of justice; in 1753, the right of naturalization; in 1830, the right to membership in civic corporations; in 1833, admission to the profession of advocate;

in 1845, to offices of alderman and lord mayor; and in 1858, to Parliament.

14.910 (409:10). granados – Archaic: "grenades."

14.912 (409:12–13). the security of his four per cents – That is, the security of his investments, which might be threatened if the English lost the Boer War or if the English government of Ireland were overthrown. Bloom owns "£900 Canadian 4% (inscribed) government stock" (17.1864–65 [723:12–13]).

14.921 (409:24). a very pelican in his piety – In heraldry, the pelican (a symbol of Christ) "represented as standing above its nest, having its wings addorsed [turned back to back] and nourishing its young with its blood is blazoned as *A Pelican in its Piety*" (Boutell, quoted in T. H. White, *The Bestiary: A Book of Beasts* [New York, 1960], p. 133n). In medieval bestiaries the pelican is described as particularly devoted to its children (apparently because adult pelicans feed their young by letting the young eat from their bills). Medieval legend developed the analogue to Christ: when the young pelicans begin to grow up, they strike their parents in the face with their wings and are killed in return. Three days later the mother pierces her side (as Christ's side was pierced on the cross) and pours her blood over the dead bodies, thus bringing them to life (as Christ's blood is the essence of man's regeneration).

14.925 (409:28–29). Hagar, the Egyptian – In Genesis 16, Abram (Abraham) and his wife Sarai (Sarah) are childless because Sarai is "barren." Sarai therefore "prays" Abram to "go in unto my maid" Hagar, the Egyptian. Hagar conceives and consequently "despises" her mistress, whereupon Sarai "dealt hardly" with her and Hagar "fled from her face." An "angel of the Lord" intervenes to restore order, and Hagar gives birth to Ishmael in Abram's house.

14.931 (409:36). balm of Gilead – Biblical Gilead (literally, "rocky region") was noted for the balm collected from "balm of Gilead" trees, a liquid resinous substance worth twice its weight in silver that was prized for its fragrance and for its medicinal virtues as a "heal-all." See Jeremiah 8:22.

Style: 14.942–1009 (410:7–412:4). The news was imparted . . . what God has joined – After the style of the English skeptical, anticlerical, and philosophical historian Edward Gibbon (1737–94).

14.943 (410:8). the Sublime Porte – Constantinople. Mohammed II (1430–81; sultan of Turkey 1451–81) styled his capital the Lofty (or Sublime) Gate of the Royal Tent. "Gate" is a metonym for courts of justice, since justice in the Near East was traditionally administered in the gate of a city or royal palace. The Turks were notorious in western Europe for the ceremonial and bureaucratic care with which they supervised and documented the legitimacy and precedence of the sultan's offspring.

14.951 (410:18). abigail – Slang for "lady's maid," after Abigail, the maid in Beaumont and Fletcher's play *The Scornful Lady* (1616).

14.952 (410:19). a strife of tongues – "Thou shalt hide them in the secret of thy presence from the pride of man: thou shalt keep them secretly in a pavilion from the strife of tongues" (Psalms 31:20).

14.956 (410:24). the prenatal repugnance of uterine brothers – The superstitious assumption that brothers born of the same mother but different fathers are innately antipathetic.

14.958 (410:27). the Childs murder – See 6.469n.

14.959 (410:28). Mr Advocate Bushe – See 6.470n.

14.961 (410:30). king's bounty touching twins and triplets – A sum of money from the royal purse (in England) given to a mother who has borne triplets; this particular bounty was not established until 1910.

14.962 (410:31–32). acardiac *foetus in foetu* – *Acardiac:* "lacking a heart"; *foetus in foetu,* medical Latin: "fetus at birth."

14.963 (410:32). aprosopia – Incomplete development or complete absence of the face.

14.963 (410:32). *agnathia – Absence or imperfect development of the jaws.

14.963 (410:33). chinless Chinamen – See 9.1129n.

14.966 (410:36–37). twilight sleep – See 8.378n.

14.970–71 (410:41–42). involution of the womb consequent upon the menopause – A popular medical superstition before the advent of modern medicine.

14.973 (411:3). *Sturzgeburt* – German: "sudden birth"; a medical term for the rare phenomenon of sudden, accidental birth.

14.973–75 (411:3–5). the recorded instances . . . or of consanguineous parents – More superstitious lore about multiple births and the births of monstrosities.

14.976 (411:6–7). which Aristotle has classified in his masterpiece – See 10.586n.

14.979–81 (411:10–12). the forbidding to a gravid . . . strangle her creature – In popular superstition, a pregnant woman was believed to endanger her unborn child if she stepped over a stile, a grave, a coil of rope, etc.

14.981–84 (411:12–15). the injunction upon her . . . seat of castigation – Superstition: a pregnant woman should not touch her genitalia lest her child be born malformed.

14.985 (411:16–17). negro's inkle, strawberry mark and portwine stain – Various popular expressions for birthmarks ("inkle" is a kind of linen tape or braid).

14.986–87 (411:19). swineheaded (the case of Madame Grissel Steevens – Miss Grissel Steevens (1653–1746) was the sister of a famous Dublin physician, Richard Steevens. Early in the eighteenth century Steevens died, leaving his money to his sister with the proviso that after her death the money would be used to found a hospital in Dublin. Such was her generosity that she immediately released the money for the hospital. She was apparently heavyset, and because she went veiled in public, gossip and rumor credited her (fancifully) with the features of a pig.

14.988 (411:21). a plasmic memory – In Theosophy, the total memory of the soul's metempsychosis, its journey through successive incarnations from lower forms through a succession of human forms toward the superhuman.

14.989–90 (411:22–23). the metaphysical traditions of the land he stood for – That is, the Scottish school of philosophy: Thomas Reid (1710–96), James Beattie (1735–1803), Dugald Stewart (1753–1828), Sir William Hamilton

(1788–1856), James McCosh (1811–94), and others. The central tenet of the school was that human beings are endowed with an immediate and intuitive knowledge of the world and of first principles.

14.994–96 (411:28–30). the Minotaur which . . . pages of his Metamorphoses – In Book 8 of the *Metamorphoses*, Ovid includes the story of the "foul adultery" of Minos's queen Pasiphaë and a bull. Pasiphaë's lust was consummated with the aid of a wooden cow fashioned by Daedalus. The issue of the "adultery" was the man-eating Minotaur, a creature with the body of a man and the head of a bull. Daedalus subsequently created the labyrinth as a "prison" for the Minotaur.

14.1000 (411:35). a nice clean old man – Recalls the refrain of an anonymous bawdy song: "If you can't get a woman, get a clean old man."

14.1002–3 (411:37–39). the juridical and theological . . . predeceasing the other – Whatever the merits of the "dilemma" as a subject for discussion, the "event" is usually considered a medical impossibility.

14.1008–9 (412:3–4). the ecclesiastical ordinance . . . what God has joined – In Matthew 19:4–6, Jesus answers the questions ("tempting") of the Pharisees regarding divorce: "Have ye not read, that he which made them at the beginning made them male and female, And said, For this cause shall a man leave father and mother, and shall cleave to his wife: and they twain shall be one flesh? Wherefore they are no more twain, but one flesh. What therefore God hath joined together, let not man put asunder." This passage comprises the gospel of the wedding mass.

Style: 14.1010–37 (412:5–39). But Malachias' tale began . . . Murderer's ground – After the style of Horace Walpole's (1717–97) Gothic novel *The Castle of Otranto* (1764). In this brief passage, Haines plays the part of Manfred, the bloodstained usurper in Walpole's novel. The passage also owes a debt of parody to a later Gothic novel, *The House by the Churchyard* (1863), by the Irish writer Joseph Sheridan Le Fanu (1814–73), as well as to the dialogue of Synge's plays.

14.1013 (412:8–9). a portfolio full of Celtic literature – Douglas Hyde's *Love Songs of Connacht*, which Haines left the library to buy; see 3.397–98n.

14.1016 (412:13). it seems, history is to blame – See 1.649 (20:40)

14.1017 (412:14). the murderer of Samuel Childs – See 6.469n.

14.1018 (412:15–16). This is the appearance is on me – A literal translation of the Irish expression "Seo é an chuma atá orm"; figuratively, "This is the condition I am in."

14.1018–19 (412:16). Tare and ages – A mild Irish-English oath from "Tare and ouns," the tears and wounds of Christ.

14.1020 (412:17–18). with my share of songs – A literal translation of the Irish expression "lem' chuid amhrán"; figuratively, "with the songs that I know."

14.1021 (412:18). soulth – Anglicized Irish: "an apparition or ghost."

14.1021 (412:19). bullawurrus – Brendan O Hehir (*A Gaelic Lexicon for "Finnegan's Wake," and Glossary for Joyce's Other Works* [Berkeley, Calif., 1967], p. 349) translates this Irish as "the smell of murder." P. W. Joyce (*English*, p. 227) defines it as "the spectral bull, with fire blazing from eyes and nose and mouth."

14.1022–23 (412:20–21). the Erse language – Technically, Scottish Gaelic; less properly, Irish Gaelic.

14.1025 (412:23–24). The black panther! – Cf. 9.1214n.

14.1026 (412:25). his head appeared – On the narrative level, Mina Purefoy's child has been born; on the level of "Technique: embryonic development," the process of birth has just begun; see p. 408, n. 1.

14.1027 (412:26). *Westland Row station – A railroad station not far from the hospital, where Mulligan and Haines will catch the last train to Sandycove, at 11:15 P.M.

14.1028 (412:27). the dissipated host – George Moore; see 9.274n.

14.1028–29 (412:28–29). The seer . . . murmuring: The vendetta of Mananaan! – AE (George William Russell) recites the chant from his play; see 2.257n and 9.190–91n. Mananaan MacLir was the sea-god of the Tuatha De Danaan (see 3.56–57n). His "vendetta" was with the dark and gloomy pirate-giants of the sea, the Formorians. Far from gloomy himself, Mananaan regarded the sea as a "plain of flowers."

14.1029 (412:29). The sage – John Eglinton (W. K. Magee); see 9.18n.

14.1029–30 (412:29). *Lex talionis* – See 7.755–56n.

14.1030–31 (412:29–31). The sentimentalist is he . . . for a thing done – See 9.550–51n.

14.1032 (412:32–33). the third brother – See 9.956–57n.

14.1033–34 (412:33–34). The black panther . . . of his own father – See 9.1214n and 1.555–57 (18:10–12).

14.1034 (412:35). For this relief much thanks – See 13.939–40n.

14.1034–35 (412:35–36). The lonely house by the graveyard – Cf. *The House by the Churchyard*, Style: 14.1010–37n.

Style: 14.1038–77 (412:40–414:2). What is the age . . . Leopold was for Rudolph – After the style (gentle pathos and nostalgia) of the English essayist Charles Lamb (1775–1834).

14.1042–43 (413:3–4). a modest substance in the funds – For Bloom's investments, see 17.1855–65 (723:2–13).

14.1047 (413:8). *Clanbrassil street – At 52 Clanbrassil Street Upper in south-central Dublin.

14.1047 (413:8). the high school – Bloom "attended" Erasmus Smith High School at 40 Harcourt Street, not far east of Clanbrassil Street in south-central Dublin. See 8.187n.

14.1049 (413:11). hard hat – A stiff felt hat, derby or bowler.

14.1055 (413:18). baisemoins – *Baisemains* is obsolete French for "compliments, respects."

14.1057 (413:20). Jacob's pipe – A large Continental pipe, with an underslung porcelain bowl usually carved in the shape of a human head; here associated with the patriarch, one of the three fathers (Abraham, Isaac, and Jacob) of Israel.

14.1063 (413:27). The wise father knows his own child – In Shakespeare's *The Merchant of Venice*, Shylock's clownish servant meets his father, who does not recognize him; in the comic banter that follows the son says to the "sandblind" father: "it is a wise father that knows his own child" (II.ii.75–76). Cf. 6.53n.

14.1064 (413:28). Hatch street, hard by the bonded stores – Hatch Street Upper is the southern boundary of University College. The "bonded stores" are W. and A. Gilbey, Ltd., distillers, across the street from the college.

14.1067 (413:32). the new royal university – In Earlsfort Terrace, just around the corner from Hatch Street, but not to be confused with University College; see 7.503n.

14.1068 (413:32–33). Bridie Kelly – Apart from the context, identity and significance unknown. "Bridie" is a diminutive form of Bridgid; see 12.1705n.

14.1070 (413:35–36). and in an instant . . . flood the world – In Genesis 1:1–3 God creates heaven and earth and light by "fiat": "In the beginning God created the heaven and the earth. And the earth was without form, and void; and darkness was upon the face of the deep. And the Spirit of God moved upon the face of the waters. And God said, Let there be light: and there was light."

Style: 14.1078–1109 (414:3–41). The voices blend and fuse . . . the forehead of Taurus – After the style of the English romantic Thomas De Quincey (1785–1859), particularly *The English Mail Coach* (1849), Part I[3] and Part III,

---

3 From Thomas De Quincey's *The English Mail Coach*, Part I: "Then comes a venerable crocodile [coachman] in a royal livery of scarlet and gold with sixteen capes; and the crocodile is driving four-in-hand from the box of the Bath mail. And suddenly we upon the mail are pulled up by a mighty dial sculptured with the hours that mingle with the heavens and the heavenly host. Then all at once we are arrived at Marlborough Forest, amongst the lovely households of the roe-deer; the deer and their fawns retire into the dewy thickets; the thickets are rich with roses; once again the roses call up the sweet countenance of Fanny; and she, being the granddaughter of a crocodile, awakens a dreadful legendary host of semi-legendary animals—griffins, dragons, basilisks, sphinxes—till at length the whole vision of fighting images crowds into one towering armorial shield, a vast emblazonry of human charities and human loveliness that have perished, but quartered heraldically

"Dream-Fugue Founded on the Preceding Theme of Sudden Death." The dream-fugue expands on kaleidoscopic visions of death and resolves on a note of "golden dawn" and "the endless resurrections of [God's] love."

14.1086/87 (414:12/14). Agendath/Netaim – See 4.191–92n.

14.1086 (414:13). screechowls – An English translation of the Hebrew *Lilith* (night-monster, night-fairy). When Isaiah prophesies the desolation of "all nations" during "the year of recompences for the controversy of Zion," he lists the inhabitants of the wasteland, including: "the screech owl also shall rest there, and find for herself a place of rest" (Isaiah 34:2, 8, and 14). See 14.242n.

14.1086 (414:13). the sandblind upupa – Or hoopoe, is described in medieval bestiaries as a bird that lives on the flesh of corpses and lines its nest with human excrement. "Sandblind" is archaic for "weak-sighted."

14.1087 (414:15–16). the ghosts of beasts – In *The Odyssey,* the sacred cattle of Helios begin to haunt Odysseus and his crew the minute they are dead: "cowhides began to crawl, and beef, both raw / and roasted, lowed like kine upon the spits" (12:395–96; Fitzgerald, p. 235). The ghosts also suggest that another age of "faunal evolution" is passing. Cf. 8.535–36n and 6.385–91n.

14.1088–89 (414:16–17). Huuh! Hark! Huuh! Parallax stalks behind and goads them – At the end of Yeats's play *The Countess Cathleen,* after the Angel has borne witness that the soul of the Countess "is passing to the floor of peace," Oona, the Countess's old nurse, speaks: "Tell them who walk upon the floor of peace / That I would die and go to her I love; / The years like great black oxen tread the world, / And God the herdsman goads them on behind, / And I am broken by their passing feet." For "parallax," see 8.110n.

with unutterable and demoniac natures, whilst over all rises, as a surmounting crest, one fair female hand with the forefinger pointing, in sweet sorrowful admonition, upwards to heaven, where is sculptured the eternal writing which proclaims the frailty of earth and her children" (quoted in George Saintsbury, *A History of English Prose Rhythm* [London, 1912], pp. 313–14—a book Joyce is known to have consulted in the composition of this episode).

14.1089–90 (414:17). the lacinating lightnings of whose brow are scorpions – De Quincey uses the verb to "lacinate" to mean tear, lacerate, pierce, stab. Parallax, the herdsman, marches under the eighth sign of the zodiac, Scorpio, the sign of "intensity of feeling, crusading, bold adventurer, . . . shrewd in attack, . . . [whose] weapon is the tongue" (Alexandra Kayhle, *Astrology Made Practical* [Hollywood, Calif., 1967], p. 44). A biblical reference is also urged by the context: in Revelation 9, the "fifth Angel" announces the opening of the "bottomless pit" and a consequent plague of smoke and darkness, locusts and scorpions.

14.1090–91 (414:18). the bulls of Bashan and of Babylon – "Many bulls have compassed me: strong bulls of Bashan have beset me round. They gaped upon me with their mouths, as a ravening and roaring lion" (Psalms 22:12–13). In Jeremiah 50:9–12 the Babylonians, "destroyers of mine heritage," are vilified "because ye are grown fat as the heifer at grass, and bellow as bulls." Jeremiah predicts that Babylon will be reduced to "a wilderness, a dry land, and a desert."

14.1092 (414:19–20). *Lacus Mortis* – Latin: "the lake, pit, or place of the dead"; combines with the Dead Sea.

14.1092 (414:20). zodiacal host – Both because animals comprise several of the signs of the zodiac and because the signs move westward toward the descent into the sea (of death), individually and in the process of extinction as a species in "faunal evolution."

14.1097–99 (414:27–29). And the equine portent . . . the house of Virgo – The constellation Pegasus (symbolic of poetic inspiration) would have been just visible above the horizon in Dublin on 16 June 1904 at 11:00 P.M. The heavens around are relatively "deserted," so it is particularly conspicuous as a constellation. As Pegasus rises above the horizon, Virgo (the zodiacal sign of the virgin) would begin its decline from the zenith, since Pegasus is "over" Virgo, or almost opposite in the heavens.

14.1099–1103 (414:29–34). wonder of metempsychosis . . . penultimate antelucan hour – As Virgo sets (toward dawn) the virgin (the Virgin Mary, via echoes of the Litany of Our Lady; see 13.287–89n) metamorphoses into Millicent (Milly) Bloom, who takes her place as Queen of Heaven (one of Mary's many titles) among the Pleiades, a cluster of stars in the constellation Taurus, which would have risen at 3:00 A.M., just before dawn, on 17 June. The Pleiades, the seven sisters, comprises six stars, the seventh, Merope, having hidden her face because she loved a mortal. As the rise of the Virgin Mary is a "harbinger" of Jesus as "daystar," so the "daystar" thus announced for Dublin during this night would have been Venus, on 17 June 1904. For "Martha, thou lost one," see 7.58n.

14.1103 (414:34). in sandals of bright gold – See 4.240–42n.

14.1104 (414:35). what do you call it gossamer – Bloom's phrase; see 13.1020 (374:40–41).

14.1105–6 (414:36–37). emerald, sapphire, mauve and heliotrope – According to the Doppler principle, the shift toward the blue end of the spectrum indicates that the star, or rather Milly's "pale blue scarf" (4.435 [67:4]), is approaching the earth.

14.1106 (414:37). cold interstellar wind – Not the modern concept but apparently Joyce's improvement on the early-twentieth-century idea of "ether-wind" or "ethereal wind," thought to be generated by the movement of celestial bodies through the "ether," the wave-transmitting medium that was assumed to permeate all space; see 17.263n. The modern concept of an interstellar medium of gas and dust particles dates from the 1930s, and hypotheses about interstellar wind were only made possible by the discovery that "the distribution of gas and dust is far from uniform" throughout the universe and that "the interstellar gas has quite different radial velocities in different regions" (Lyman Spitzer, Jr., *Diffuse Matter in Space* [New York, 1968], pp. 2–3).

14.1107 (414:38). simply swirling – See 4.282n.

14.1108–9 (414:40–41). Alpha, a ruby . . . forehead of Taurus – Just at dawn Aldebaran, Alpha Tauri, would have appeared above the horizon. It is a red-giant star in the triangle of stars that form the forehead of Taurus the Bull. As Alpha, it is, of course, the beginning (see 13.1258, 1264n); in astrology, Taurus is the zodiacal sign under which artistic consciousness, love, and money are furthered as dominating forces.

Style: 14.1110–73 (414:42–416:34). Francis was reminding . . . from the second constellation – After the style of Walter Savage Landor (1775–1864). The form of essay particularly associated with his name is characterized by the title of a series of volumes that appeared 1824–53, *Imaginary Conversations*. The conversations are between figures from classical literature and history. They do not attempt to re-create the historical past but rather to use that past to develop perspectives on the social, moral, and literary problems of Landor's own time.

14.1111 (415:1). Conmee's time – See 5.322–23n.

14.1111 (415:2). Glaucon – The straight man in Plato's *Republic*, was assumed in 1904 to have been Plato's brother.

14.1111 (415:2). Alcibiades – (c. 450–404 B.C.), Athenian politician and general, friend and pupil of Socrates. Alcibiades was noted for his talent, his insolence, and his capriciousness. His talent made him capable of brilliant political and military accomplishments; his insolence made him subject to exile and betrayal. "Alcibiades and Xenophon" is one of Landor's *Imaginary Conversations*.

14.1112 (415:2). Pisistratus – (c. 600–527 B.C.), tyrant of Athens who usurped power in 560 B.C. He was expelled twice but each time returned to regain his tyrannical hold on Athens. In his first years as tyrant he attempted to rationalize his position by paying court (as would-be friend) to the celebrated Athenian legislator Solon (c. 638–c. 558 B.C.). "Solon and Pisistratus" is another of Landor's *Imaginary Conversations*.

14.1113–14 (415:4–5). If I call them into . . . troop to my call? – As the shades of the dead have trooped to Odysseus's call in Hades (*The Odyssey*, Book 11); see p. 104.

14.1115 (415:6). Bous Stephanoumenos – See 9.939n.

14.1115 (415:6–7). bullockbefriending bard – See 2.431n.

14.1116 (415:7). lord and giver of their life – Odysseus in Hades "gives" the shades "life" by allowing them to drink of the blood of bullocks that has been poured into a trench; figuratively, of course, Odysseus gives the shades life by giving them some of his own lifeblood.

14.1116 (415:7). gadding – Archaic: "unkempt."

14.1116–17 (415:8). a coronal of vineleaves – Emblematic of poetic inspiration (as wine inspirits) and of poetic achievement.

14.1119 (415:10–11). a capful of light odes – See 9.1081n and 11.979n.

14.1121 (415:13//). *to acclaim you Stephenaforos – Schoolboy Greek for Stephen, the garland bearer (for sacrifice?).

14.1125 (415:17). his recent loss – Stephen's mother was buried 26 June 1903.

14.1127 (415:20). the rider's name – O. Madden (on Sceptre).

14.1128–33 (415:21–27). The flag fell and . . . reached, outstripped her – Lenehan's description of the Gold Cup Race is not particularly accurate; Sceptre, as the name suggests, was not a mare but a colt (cf. 8.829–31n). The account of the race is given in the *Evening Telegraph,* Dublin, 16 June 1904, p. 3: "(#1) Mr. F. Alexander's *Throwaway,* W. Lane (20 to 1 against); (2) Lord Howard de Walden's *Zinfandel,* M. Cannon (5 to 4); (3) Mr. W. Bass's *Sceptre,* O. Madden (7 to 4 against); (4) M. J. de Bremmond's *Maximum II,* G. Stern (10 to 1 against). The Race: Throwaway set fair pace to Sceptre, with Maximum II last, till fairly in the line for home, when Sceptre slightly headed Throwaway, and Zinfandel took close order with him. Throwaway, however, stayed on, and won cleverly at the finish by a length; three parts of a length divided second and third."

14.1130 (415:23). Phyllis – In pastoral poetry, a conventional name for a maiden. But the curse "Juno . . . I am undone" suggests the Phyllis in Greek myth who was married to and then abandoned by Demophon when he was on his way home from the Trojan Wars. Phyllis cursed him "by Rhea's daughter" (i.e., by Hera, the Greek counterpart of the Roman Juno) and then plotted his death.

14.1133 (415:27). All was lost now – See 11.22n.

14.1137 (415:32). W. Lane. Four winners yesterday and three today – At the Ascot Meeting on 15 June 1904, W. Lane won the Ascot Biennial Stakes on Mr. F. Alexander's Andover, the Coronation Stakes on Major Eustace Loder's Pretty Polly, the Fern Hill Stakes on Mr. P. Gilpin's Delaunay, and the Triennial Stakes on Mr. L. Neumann's Petit Bleu. On 16 June, in addition to the Gold Cup, Lane won the New Stakes on Mr. L. Neumann's Llangibby and the St. James's Place Stakes on Mr. S. Darling's Challenger.

14.1143 (415:40). Lalage – Another of the type names for classic beauties, after Horace (*Odes* II.v.15).

14.1148 (416:3). Corinth fruit – Currants (associated here with Corinth in classical Greece).

14.1148 (416:4). *Periplipomenes – A Greek coinage suggesting "itinerant fruit merchant."

14.1156 (416:13). Glycera or Chloe – Two more of the traditional names for classic or pastoral beauties. One famous Glycera was a Greek flower maiden and mistress of the Greek painter Pausias; another was a mistress of Menander. One famous literary Chloe is the pastoral maiden in the Greek romance *Daphnis and Chloe* (fourth or fifth century B.C.); another appears in Sir Philip Sidney's *Arcadia* (1590).

14.1157–58 (416:15). a slight disorder in her dress – After Robert Herrick's (1591–1674) "Delight in Disorder" (1648): "A sweet disorder in the dresse / Kindles in cloathes a wantonesse: / A lawn about the shoulders thrown / Into a fine distraction: / An erring lace, which here and there / Enthralls the Crimson Stomacher: / A Cuffe neglectful and thereby / Ribbands to flow confusedly: / A winning wave (deserving Note) / In the tempestuous petticote: / A carelesse shooe-string, in whose tye / I see a wilde civility: / Doe more bewitch me, then when Art / Is too precise in every part."

14.1161–62 (416:20–21). Bass's mare . . . this draught of his – Lenehan confuses William Arthur Hamar Bass (b. 1879), the owner of the colt Sceptre (see 14.1128–33n), with his uncle, Michael Arthur Bass, Baron Burton (1837–1909), director of Messrs. Bass & Co., Ltd., the manufacturers of Bass ale at Burton-on-Trent in England.

14.1164 (416:23). the scarlet label – The label

on a bottle of number-one Bass ale was a red triangle; see 14.1108–9n.

14.1165–66 (416:24–25). It is as painful perhaps to be awakened from a vision as to be born – This sounds suspiciously like AE (George William Russell), but the specific source remains unknown.

14.1166–67 (416:26–27). Any object, intensely regarded . . . incorruptible eon of the gods – A principle of Theosophy: since every object has a "soul," each soul properly contemplated, no matter what its degree, is equal to all others, or equally to be "loved."

14.1168 (416:28). Theosophus – Stephen's "master" in Theosophy; cf. 9.65–66n.

14.1168–69 (416:28–30). whom in a previous existence . . . karmic law – Typical credentials for a Theosophist's "master" involve the master's having been instructed in a previous incarnation by a mystical priesthood (Hindu, Tibetan, Egyptian?). For "karmic law," see 9.70n.

14.1169–70 (416:30). The lords of the moon – In Stephen's nonsense Theosophy, those presences that rule the twenty-eight phases of the moon and thus preside over the sequences of metempsychosis that the phases dictate for the growth of the individual human soul.

14.1170 (416:30–31). an orangefiery shipload from planet Alpha of the lunar chain – The "lunar chain" is the zodiac; Aries (Mars, energy in constructive process) is the first house of the zodiac; thus, "orangefiery" Mars is the "Alpha" (first) planet.

14.1171 (416:32). etheric doubles – See 12.341n.

14.1172–73 (416:33–34). incarnated by the rubycolored egos from the second constellation – That is, they came under the sign of the second house of the zodiac, the constellation Taurus; see 14.1108–9n.

Style: 14.1174–1222 (416:35–418:8). However, as a matter of fact . . . ages yet to come – After the style of the English essayist and historian Thomas Babington Macaulay (1800–59), a master of somewhat impetuous and unreliable history. He treated history with energy and verve to make it come out less sordidly and more reasonably than it does in the hands of most other historians.

14.1175 (416:36). some description of a doldrums – As Odysseus and his crew are pinned down by adverse winds on Helios's island.

14.1205–6 (417:31). the Mull of Galloway – An island in the Inner Hebrides, Argyllshire, Scotland.

14.1213 (417:40). Malachi Roland St John Mulligan – The full name makes the identity of Mulligan's real-life counterpart one-third clear (Oliver *St. John* Gogarty). Roland (d. 778) was the semilegendary nephew of Charlemagne and the hero of *Le chanson de Roland*. The clue to this name of Mulligan lies in the proverbial phrase "A Roland for an Oliver," meaning tit for tat; since Roland and Oliver were boon companions and peers in arms, the assumption was that there would be no choice between them in single combat.

14.1217–18 (418:3). that vigilant wanderer – See 14.71n.

14.1221 (418:8). Lafayette – James Lafayette, photographer to the queen and royal family, 30 Westmoreland Street, Dublin.

Style: 14.1223–1309 (418:9–420:29). It had better be stated . . . in which it was delivered – After the style of the English naturalist and comparative anatomist Thomas Henry Huxley (1825–95). Huxley is particularly noted for his contributions to and defense of the theory of evolution. He had an extraordinary ability to embody a disciplined scientific skepticism in a lucid expository prose.

14.1224 (418:10–11). (Div. Scep.) – *Divinitatis Scepticus*, Latin: Doubter of Divinity (suggested by Vincent Deane).

14.1230–31 (418:18). (Pubb. Canv.) – Public Canvasser (for advertisements).

14.1231–33 (418:19–22). the view of Empedocles . . . the birth of males – Empedocles (fl. 450 B.C.) was a native of Agrigentum in Sicily; Sicily is rendered under its ancient name, Trinacria, to reinforce the sustained allusion to *The Odyssey*. Empedocles did not hold the view stated here, but Aristotle, in *On the Generation of Animals*, Book 4, links the speculations of Empedocles with those of Anaxagoras (500–428 B.C.) and dismisses their views as "lightheaded." Anaxagoras, Aristotle says, held that "the germ . . . comes from the male, while the female only provides the place in which it is to be developed, and the male is from the right, the female from the left testis, and also that the male embryo is in the right of the uterus, the female in the left. Others, as Empedocles, say that the differentiation takes place in the uterus; for he says that if the uterus is hot or cold, what enters it becomes male or female, the cause of the heat or cold being the flow of the menstrual discharge, according as it is colder or hotter, more 'antique' or more 'recent.' "

14.1233–34 (418:22–23). or are the two long neglected . . . differentiating factors – Aristotle, in *On the Generation of Animals*, Book 4, argues that the male element (semen) is the active, formative principle, the female, the passive and receptive. The sex of the offspring is then determined by the principle that "prevails," that is, if the "spermatozoa" are "neglected," the passive, receptive principle would prevail and the offspring would be female. *Nemasperm:* literally, "threadlike sperm," in description of the shape of the spermatozoon.

14.1235 (418:24). Culpepper – Nicholas Culpeper (1616–54), an English physician and author of various works, including *The English Physitian* (London, 1648) and *A Directory for Midwives: or a Guide for Women in their Conception, Bearing, and Suckling Their Children* (London, 1651). Culpeper's concern is with practical medicine rather than with genetic theory.

14.1235 (418:24). Spallanzani – Lazzaro Spallanzani (1729–99), an Italian biologist and anatomist, noted for his pioneer work in disproving the doctrine of the spontaneous generation of life and for his investigation of the nature of the spermatic fluid and of the spermatozoa.

14.1236 (418:24). Blumenbach – Johann Friedrich Blumenbach (1752–1840), a German naturalist, physiologist, and anthropologist, noted as the founder of physiological anthropology and for his theory of the unity of the human race, which he divided into five physiological types: Caucasian, Mongolian, Malay, American, and Ethiopian. He speculated that a *nisus formativus*, "formative tendency," was inherent in all living things.

14.1236 (418:25). Lusk – William Thompson Lusk (1838–97), an American obstetrician whose book *The Science and Art of Midwifery* (New York, 1882) gained world renown as a standard medical text in the late nineteenth century.

14.1236 (418:25). Hertwig – Oscar Hertwig (1849–1922), a German embryologist who demonstrated that male and female sex cells are equivalent in their importance and that fertilization consists in the conjunction of equivalents. His brother, Richard Hertwig (1850–1937), was a co-worker who did considerable research on sex differentiation and on the relation between the nucleus and the cytoplasm in sex cells.

14.1236 (418:25). Leopold – Christian Gerhard Leopold (1846–1911), a German embryologist and gynecologist.

14.1236 (418:25). Valenti – Giulio Valenti (b. 1860), an Italian physician and embryologist.

14.1236–39 (418:25–29). a mixture of both? This . . . of the passive element – Aristotle's theory, as developed in *On the Generation of Animals*, is "a mixture of both," but nineteenth-century theory, as informed by Oscar Hertwig, is a radical departure from Aristotle's conception of the male as active, the female as passive. *Nisus formativus* means "formative tendency"; while the term is Blumenbach's (see 14.1236n), the context suggests that it is being used as an echo of Aristotle's male or "formative principle." *Succubitus felix* is Latin for "the fertile one who lies under"; this also echoes the Aristotelian concept of the passive receptivity of the female.

14.1243 (418:33). (Hyg. et Eug. Doc.) – Doctor of Hygienics and Eugenics.

14.1251 (418:42). Kalipedia – Greek: the study of beauty, or the achievement of learning by means of the contemplation of beauty.

14.1253–54 (419:2–4). plastercast reproductions . . . Venus and Apollo – Presumably like those Bloom has inspected in the National Museum; see 8.921–22n.

14.1257 (419:7). (Disc. Bacc.) – Bachelor of Discourse.

14.1268 (419:21). (Bacc. Arith.) – Bachelor of Arithmetic.

14.1270–73 (419:23–27). everything . . . is subject to a law of numeration as yet unascertained – This "law" became a cornerstone of late-nineteenth- and early-twentieth-century faith in the assumption that an absolute and knowable determinism would be found to govern not only the physical world but also human beings and their social organizations.

14.1276–77 (419:31–32). must certainly, in the poet's words, give us pause – That is, in Shakespeare's words; Hamlet, in the "To be or not to be" soliloquy: "For in that sleep of death what dreams may come / When we have shuffled off this mortal coil, / Must give us pause" (III.i.66–68).

14.1285 (419:42). the survival of the fittest – The phrase, coined by Herbert Spencer (1820–1903), became an aggressive slogan for a key concept in Darwin's theory of evolution as developed in *On the Origin of Species* (1859). Darwin argued that one aspect of the origin and perpetuation of a species was that those individuals best adapted to the environment in which the species found itself would survive to mate and have offspring. In popular terms, this concept was reduced to the simpleminded dictum "The strong survive, the weak perish."

14.1286–87 (420:1–2). an omniverous being – See 9.1048–50n.

14.1288 (420:3–4). pluterperfect imperturbability – A phrase from Mr. Deasy's letter; see 2.328 (33:6).

14.1292 (420:7–8). staggering bob – See 8.724n.

14.1302–3 (420:20–21). (Lic. in Midw., F.K.Q.C.P.I.) – Licensed in Midwifery, Former Knight of the Queen's College of Physicians in Ireland (since Horne is described as "ex-Vice President, Royal College of Physicians, Ireland" in *Thom's* 1904, p. 1381).

14.1304 (420:23). let the cat into the bag – After the proverbial "let the cat out of the bag"; disclosed a secret.

Style: 14.1310–43 (420:30–421:28). Meanwhile the skill and . . . good and faithful servant! – After the style of Charles Dickens; chapter 53, "Another Retrospect," of *David Copperfield* (1849–50) is particularly relevant.

14.1313 (420:34). She had fought the good fight – "Fight the good fight of faith, lay hold on eternal life, whereunto thou art also called, and hast professed a good profession before many witnesses" (I Timothy 6:12; see also II Timothy 4:7).

14.1320 (421:1). Doady – In *David Copperfield*, David's first wife, the "child-wife" Dora, calls him Doady.

14.1324–25 (421:5–6). Ulster bank, College Green branch – The Ulster Bank, Ltd., with home offices in Protestant Belfast, had branch offices throughout Ireland, including four in Dublin, one at 32–33 College Green.

14.1326 (421:7–8). that faroff time of the roses – Echoes James Clarence Mangan's lament "The Time of the Roses," from the Turkish of Meseeh (d. 1512). The phrase functions as a refrain in the poem, as at the end of the first stanza: "In, in at the portals that Youth uncloses, / It hastes, it wastes, the Time of the Roses." The poem develops the theme that the evanescence of youth demonstrates "that Life is a swift Unreality."

14.1326–27 (421:8). With the old shake of her pretty head – On her deathbed, in chapter 53 of *David Copperfield*, Dora recalls to David the relative failure of their marriage and mourns the eclipse of their "boy and girl" love "with the old shake of her curls."

14.1331–32 (421:13–15). our famous hero of . . . Waterford and Candahar – Sir Frederick Sleigh Roberts (1832–1914), first Earl Roberts of Kandahar, Pretoria, and Waterford (created 1901). Though born in India, Lord Roberts regarded himself as Anglo-Irish, as the Waterford in his title suggests. He had a military career of considerable distinction, highlighted by his defeat of the Ayub Khan at Kandahar in southern Afghanistan in 1880. He was commander in chief in South Africa during the Boer War; his successes there, commemorated by the Pretoria in his title, led to his earldom and to his appointment as commander in chief of the British army (1901–4).

14.1335–36 (421:18–19). the Treasury Remembrancer's office, Dublin Castle – The Office of the Lord Treasurer's Remembrancer and Deputy Paymaster for Ireland was responsible for the collection of debts (other than taxes) owed to the King's Treasury in Ireland. *Thom's* 1904, "Government Departments, Ireland," p. 834, is unaware of the presence of Mortimer Edward Purefoy in the office.

14.1336 (421:19). father Cronion – That is, Father Time, thanks to a confusion of the Greek god Cronus with the word *chronos* (time). Cronus was a god of harvests who overthrew his father, Uranus, and was in turn overthrown by his son, Zeus.

14.1339 (421:23). dout – Dialect: "put out, extinguish."

14.1341–42 (421:26). You too have fought the good fight – See 14.1313n.

14.1343 (421:27–28). Well done, thou good and faithful servant! – In Matthew 25:14–30, Jesus, in the parable of the talents, likens "the kingdom of Heaven" to "a man travelling in a far country" who delivers his goods to his servants for safekeeping. Two of the servants increase the goods (to their own benefit) by using them; one buries his share in the ground. The two who improve their master's goods are rewarded: "Well done, thou good and faithful servant." The third is "cast . . . into outer darkness."

Style: 14.1344–55 (421:29–421:42). There are sins or . . . silent, remote, reproachful –After the style of the famous English convert to Roman Catholicism John Henry Cardinal Newman (1801–90).

Style: 14.1356–78 (422:1–28). The stranger still regarded . . . in her glad look – After the style of the English aesthetician and essayist Walter Pater (1839–94); cf. particularly the imaginary portrait of his childhood in *The Child in the House* (1894). For the occasion Bloom recalls, see 6.1008–14 (115:14–20).

14.1363 (422:10). Roundtown – Where Bloom met Molly; see 6.697n.

14.1368 (422:15). Floey, Atty, Tiny – Mat Dillon's daughters.

14.1369 (422:17). Our Lady of the Cherries – There are many versions of this subject, among the most famous one by Titian (now in Vienna) and several by the early-sixteenth-century Netherland painter, Van Cleef. The allusion does not seem to be to a specific visual image but rather to the way Pater generalizes his aesthetic experience, particularly in *The Renaissance* (1873). In Christian art the cherry is one of the fruits of paradise, symbolic of sweetness of character and the delights of the blessed; as such, it is one of the attributes of the Virgin Mary.

14.1378 (422:27). (*alles Vergängliche*) – German: "All that is transitory"; the first line of the final chorus of Goethe's *Faust*, Part II (1832). The "immortal part" of Faust has been snatched from Mephistopheles and conducted toward "higher spheres," and the dramatic poem closes as the Mater Gloriosa speaks from above and Doctor Marianus ("worshiping prostrate") responds: "Look up to the glance of the savior, / All you tender penitents, / To transform yourselves with thanks / To the destiny of the Blessed. / May all higher meaning [consciousness] / Be at your service; / Virgin, mother, queen, / Goddess, remain merciful. [CHORUS MYSTICUS:] All that is transitory / Is only an image; / The insufficient / Here becomes an event [of importance]; / The indescribable / Here is achieved; / The eternal-feminine / Draws us upward" (lines 12096–111).

Style: 14.1379–90 (422:29–422:42). Mark this father . . . the utterance of the Word – After the style of the English art critic and reformer John Ruskin (1819–1900).

14.1382–83 (422:33–34). the vigilant watch of shepherds . . . of Juda long ago – The account of the Nativity in Luke 2:1–20 established Bethlehem in Judea as the place of Jesus' birth and describes "shepherds abiding in the field, keeping watch over their flock" who are informed by an "angel of the Lord" of the place and importance of the birth. The shepherds find "Mary, and Joseph, and the babe lying in a manger" and "make known abroad the saying which was told them concerning the child."

14.1390 (422:42). *the word – Recalls the metaphysical account of the Nativity in John 1:1–5: "In the beginning was the Word, and the Word was with God, and the Word was God."

Style: 14.1391–1439 (423:1–424:18). Burke's! Outflings my lord . . . *nunc est bibendum!* – After the style of the Scottish man of letters Thomas Carlyle (1795–1881).

14.1391 (423:1). Burke's – John Burke, tea and wine merchant, 17 Holles Street on the corner of Denzille (now Fenian) Street; a pub across the street and slightly north of the National Maternity Hospital.

14.1397 (423:8). placentation ended – In the narrative of the birth of Mina Purefoy's child, the afterbirth is complete. On the level of "Technique: embryonic development," it is about to begin.

14.1402 (423:14–15). Doctor Diet and Doctor Quiet – Two of a trilogy of physicians, proverbial from as early as the sixteenth century; the third is Doctor Merryman.

14.1404 (423:17). motherwit – In *The Odyssey*, Pallas Athena sustains in Odysseus this innate, intuitive ability to know.

14.1408 (423:22). *coelum* – Latin: "the vault of heaven."

14.1409 (423:23). cessile – Obsolete: "yielding."

14.1412 (423:26). farraginous – Rare: "formed of various materials; mixed."

14.1415 (423:30). Malthusiasts – Proponents of the doctrines of the English economist and statistician Thomas Robert Malthus (1766–1834). Malthus held that population increase inevitably outstripped the economies necessary for population support and that, in the absence of prudential restraints, war, famine, and disease would be the unavoidable (and necessary) population controls. The Malthusian League (1877) attempted to implement Malthus's doctrines by preaching contraception and planned parenthood. "Malthusiasts" also involves a pun on "enthusiasts" and the Latin *malus* (bad, evil).

14.1418 (423:34). homer – A Hebrew measure of from ten to twelve bushels.

14.1419 (423:34–35). thy fleece is drenched – "And Gideon said unto God, If thou wilt save Israel by mine hand, as thou hast said, Behold I will put a fleece of wool in the floor; and if the dew be on the fleece only, and it be dry upon all the earth beside, then shall I know that thou wilt save Israel by my hand, as thou hast said" (Judges 6:36–37).

14.1419 (423:35). Darby Dullman there with his Joan – Darby and Joan are an elderly couple who live in marital felicity, indifferent to the society of others, in Henry Sampson Woodfall's (1739–1805) ballad "The Happy Old Couple; or, The Joys of Love Never Forgot." The speaker tells his "Dear *Chloe*" that they must love in their youth in order to enjoy in old age the "current of fondness" that is shared by "dropsical" Darby and "sore-eyed" Joan, who still "possess" neither "beauty nor wit."

14.1419–20 (423:36). A canting jay – A caged bird that is an impertinent chatterer.

14.1422–23 (423:39–40). Herod's slaughter of the innocents – See 8.754n.

14.1426 (424:1–2). Derbyshire neck – A variety of goiter once endemic in Derbyshire, England.

14.1427 (424:3). threnes – A song of lamentation, a dirge, threnody; formerly applied specifically to the Lamentations of Jeremiah.

14.1427 (424:3). trentals – Archaic: dirges, elegies.

14.1428 (424:3). jeremies – After the French *Jérémie* (Jeremiah), for the Lamentations of Jeremiah.

14.1428 (424:4). defunctive music – That is, music belonging to the dead, a phrase from line 14 of Shakespeare's "The Phoenix and the Turtle."

14.1430 (424:6). Thou sawest thy America – In John Donne's (1573–1631) Elegie 19, "Going to Bed," the lover addresses his mistress: "O my America! my new-found-land" (line 27).

14.1431 (424:7). transpontine bison – That is, the bison on the other side of the "land-bridge" that nineteenth-century geologists assumed once linked North America, Europe, and Asia in the region of the Arctic Circle.

14.1431 (424:8). *Zarathustra – See 1.708n.

14.1431–32 (424:8–9). *Deine Kuh Trübsal . . . Milch des Euters* – German: "You are milking your cow [named] Affliction. Now you are drinking the sweet milk of her udder."

14.1434 (424:11). the milk of human kin – After Lady Macbeth's famous phrase for Macbeth's reluctance to kill his king: "the milk of human kindness" (I.v.18).

14.1436–37 (424:14). the honeymilk of Canaan's land – Canaan, the promised land; see 14.377n.

14.1438 (424:16). bonnyclaber – Irish: "thick curdled milk."

14.1439 (424:17–18). *Per deam Partulam . . . nunc est bibendum!* – Latin: "By the goddesses Partula and Pertunda now must we drink." Partula was the Roman goddess who presided over birth; Pertunda presided over the loss of virginity. *"Nunc est bibendum"* are the opening words of Horace's Ode 37.

Style: 14.1440–end (424:19–end). All off for a buster . . . Just you try it on – The style "disintegrates" into fragments of dialect and slang (including revival-preacher's rhetoric). As Joyce described it, "a frightful jumble of pidgin English, nigger English, Cockney, Irish, Bowery slang and broken doggerel" (*Letters* 1:138–39, 13 March 1920).

14.1440 (424:19). a buster – A drinking bout.

14.1440 (424:19). armstrong – With arms linked.

14.1440 (424:20). Bonafides – That is, bona fide travelers. The laws governing the times when alcoholic beverages could be served in public houses were subject to certain exceptions for individuals who could "prove" they were traveling and thus would not be able to "dine" (drink) during the legal hours.

14.1441 (424:20–21). Timothy of the battered naggin – Fritz Senn has discovered a source in a "paper read before the Irish National Literary Society, April 27, 1893" by Patrick J. McCall (b. 1861). The paper was a descriptive history of the area around St. Patrick's Cathedral. In part it dealt with one Dr. John Whalley (1653–1724), a Dublin astrologer, whose house in Patrick Street "was converted into an inn, which, at the beginning of the century, was owned by the popular Sir Timothy O'Brien. The worthy baronet appears to have been an eccentric character in his way, and among a certain class of his customers . . . he was invariably known as 'The Knight of the Battered Naggin,' recalling Cervantes's Knight of the Golden Basin in Don Quixote." The suspicion was that his battered cups enabled him to serve his customers less than full measure (*JJQ* 19, no. 2 [1982]: 172).

14.1441 (424:21). Like ole Billyo – Dialect (after "Billyhood"): "camaraderie."

14.1442 (424:21). brollies or gumboots – Rhyming slang for "breasts or bums [bottoms]."

14.1442 (424:22). Where the Henry Nevil's – Rhyming slang for "where the devil's". Two possible sources exist: (1) Dr. Henry Neville, "Rector of the Catholic University, ex-professor of Maynooth" (see 12.1402–4n), who in 1879 accomplished "a sudden lifting of the veil" and ignited considerable controversy by revealing the alarming extent to which the Irish priesthood had been imbued with what he called the "alien theology" of French Catholic refugees who fled the French Revolution and became professors and teachers at Maynooth (then newly founded). The refugees preached an antirevolutionary monarchism that included an unquestioning loyalty to the English Crown, and "in morals, they encouraged a repulsive rigour in the management of consciences" (Sean O'Faolain, *The Irish: A Character Study* [Old Greenwich, Conn., 1949], pp. 117–18). (2) The English actor and dramatic teacher, Henry Neville, noted for his roles in Dion Boucicault's (1822–90) plays and therefore popular in Dublin in the late nineteenth century.

14.1443 (424:22). old clo – Dialect: "old clothes"; apparently recalls Molly and Bloom's secondhand clothes business when they lived in Holles Street; see 11.487n. But in context the phrase also alludes to the tradition that dealing in old clothes was a Jewish (and somewhat deceptive or dishonest) trade.

14.1444 (424:23). the ribbon counter – See 6.70–71n.

14.1444 (424:24). Jay – Dodging the curse *Jesus*.

14.1444–45 (424:24). the drunken minister – Stephen, because he is dressed in black and wears a soft hat, in contrast to Bloom who wears a hard hat or bowler, which a Protestant minister would not wear.

14.1445–46 (424:25–26). *Benedicat vos omnipotens Deus, Pater et Filius* – Latin: "May almighty God, the Father and the Son . . . bless you." The "filial blessing" in the Dismissal portion of the Mass. The words *et Spiritus Sanctus* (and the Holy Spirit) are omitted.

14.1446 (424:26). A make – Slang for an easy mark, someone who can be cheated or exploited (Stephen).

14.1446 (424:26). The Denzille lane boys – A Dublin slang name for the Invincibles; see 5.378n.

14.1447 (424:27). Isaacs – Denigrating term

of address for someone presumed to be a Jew (Bloom).

14.1449 (424:29–30). *En avant, mes enfants!* – French: "Forward, my children!"

14.1450 (424:31). Thence they advanced five parasangs – A schoolboy cliché after the Greek historian Xenophon's (c. 430–c. 355 B.C.) *Anabasis*, an account of the ten thousand Greek troops in the Persian expedition under Cyrus the Younger against his brother Ataxerxes. In the first book, which deals with Cyrus's march up from the coast, Xenophon repeatedly uses the phrase to sum up a day's march; a parasang was approximately equal to three and a half miles.

14.1450 (424:31). Slattery's mounted foot – The title of a comic song by Percy French. The song begins: "You've heard of Julius Caesar, and of great Napoleon too, / And how the Cork Militia beat the Turks at Waterloo. / But there's a page of glory that, as yet, remains uncut, / And that's the warlike story of the Slattery Mounted Fut. / This gallant corps was organized by Slattery's eldest son, / A nobleminded poacher with a double-breasted gun." In the second stanza, "Slattery's Light Dragoons" approach a pub: "And there we saw a notice which the brightest heart unnerved: / 'All liquor must be settled for before the drink is served.' / So on we marched, but soon again each warrior's heart grew pale, / For rising high in front of us we saw the County Jail." In the third stanza Slattery's "heroes" are put to rout to the tune: "he that fights and runs away will live to fight again."

14.1451 (424:32). apostates' creed – In mockery of the Apostles' Creed; see 1.653n.

14.1453 (424:34). chuckingout time – Closing time for Dublin pubs in 1904 was 11:00 P.M.

14.1453 (424:34–35). *Ma mère m'a mariée* – The opening words of a bawdy French song: "Ma mère m'a mariée un mari / Mon Dieu, quel homme, qu'il est petit. // Je l'ai perdu au fond de mon lit / Mon Dieu, quel homme, qu'il est petit," etc. (My mother married me to a husband. My god, what a man, how small he is. I have lost him at the bottom of my bed. My god, what a man, how small he is).

14.1453–54 (424:35). British Beatitudes! – See 14.1459–60n.

14.1454 (424:35–36). *★Retamplatan digidi boumboum* – These nonsense words or something like them (though *rataplan* is French for "drumbeat") are occasionally added to "Ma mère m'a mariée" to reinforce its qualities as a marching song.

14.1455 (424:36–37). at the Druiddrum press by two designing females – See 1.366–67n.

14.1456–57 (424:38–39). Most beautiful book come out of Ireland my time – See 9.1161, 1164–65n.

14.1457 (424:39). *Silentium!* – Latin: "stillness, silence."

14.1458–59 (424:41). *★Tramp, tramp, tramp the boys are (atitudes!) parching* – After an American Civil War marching song, "Tramp, Tramp, Tramp," by George F. Root: "In the prison cell I sit, / Thinking, mother dear, of you, / And our bright and happy home so far away, / And the tears they fill my eyes, / Spite of all that I can do, / Though I try to cheer my comrades and be gay. [Chorus:] Tramp, tramp, tramp, the boys are marching, / Oh, cheer up, comrades, they will come, / And beneath the starry flag we shall breathe the air again, / Of freedom in our own beloved home." "Attitudes" is a military command that means "Correct your postures and alignment."

14.1459–60 (424:41–42). Beer, beef, business, bibles, bulldogs, battleships, buggery and bishops – The "British Beatitudes," a parody of line 138, canto 1 of Pope's *The Rape of the Lock* (1714), describing Belinda's dressing table: "Puffs, Powders, Patches, Bibles, Billetdoux." The "beatitudes" also play on British "apostasy" by amplifying "Beer and Bible," the nickname of a combination of High-Church Conservatives and English brewers who resisted Parliament's attempts to limit the sale of intoxicating beverages in and after 1873.

14.1460/61/62 (425:1/2/3). Whether on the scaffold high./When for Irelandear./We fall – From "God Save Ireland" (to the tune of "Tramp, Tramp, Tramp"); see 8.440n.

14.1462–63 (425:3). *★Bishops boosebox* – Another play on "Beer and Bible"; see 14.1459–60n.

14.1463 (425:4). Rugger. Scrum in. No touch kicking – They pause for a moment of rugby. In a "scrum," a huddle with arms locked over shoulders and heads down, they try to gain control of an imaginary ball in the scrum's center. "No touch kicking" means "Kick the ball and not the other players."

14.1465 (425:6). Who's astanding – To "stand" is to pay for the drinks.

14.1466 (425:7). Bet to the ropes – In other words, I have bet (and lost) all my money.

14.1466 (425:7). Me nantee saltee – Pidgin English: "I have no salt [money]."

14.1466 (425:8). a red – A red cent, a penny.

14.1467 (425:9). *Übermensch* – See 1.708n.

14.1468 (425:9). number ones – Number-one Bass ale; see 14.1164n.

14.1468 (425:9–10). Ginger cordial – Widely advertised as a temperance drink.

14.1469–70 (425:11–12). Stopped short never to go again when the old – From "My Grandfather's Clock" (1876), an American song by Henry C. Work, who advertised himself as one of the Christy Minstrels. "My grandfather's clock was too large for the shelf, / So it stood ninety years upon the floor; / It was taller by half than the old man himself, / Though it weighed not a pennyweight more. // It was bought on the morn of the day that he was born, / And was always his treasure and pride; / But it stopped short, never to go again, / When the old man died."

14.1470 (425:12). *Caramba!* – A Spanish exclamation of astonishment or vexation.

14.1470–71 (425:12–13). an eggnog or a prairie oyster – Traditional drinks for combating a hangover. A prairie oyster is one unbroken egg yolk seasoned with Worcestershire sauce, tomato catsup, vinegar, lemon juice, red pepper, salt, and Tabasco sauce.

14.1471 (425:13). Enemy? – "How goes the enemy?" is slang for "What's the time?"

14.1473 (425:16). Digs – Slang for a dwelling.

14.1474 (425:16). the Mater – The Mater Misericordiae Hospital in Eccles Street.

14.1474 (425:17). Buckled – Dialect: "married."

14.1474–75 (425:17–18). Full of a dure – That is, she would fill a door, she has an ample shape.

14.1476 (425:19). lean kine – In Genesis 41, the Pharaoh dreams of seven "ill-favoured and lean-fleshed kine," symbolic of seven years of famine.

14.1476 (425:19–20). Pull down the blind, love – A well-established music-hall gag line and the title of a song by Charles McCarthy: "Did you ever make love? If not, have a try / I courted a girl once, so bashful and shy / A fair little creature, who, by the by, / At coaxing and wheedling had such a nice way; / Ev'ry night to her house I went / In harmless delight our evenings were spent / She had a queer saying, whatever she meant, / For whenever I entered her house she would say, / [Chorus:] 'Pull down the blind, love, pull down the blind / Pull down the blind, love, come don't be unkind; / Though we're alone, bear this in mind / Somebody's looking, love, pull down the blind.'"

14.1476 (425:20). Two Ardilauns – Slang for two pints of Guinness; see 5.306n.

14.1477 (425:20–21). If you fall don't . . . Five. Seven. Nine – Mock advice to a boxer with a foreshortened knockdown count.

14.1478 (425:22). mincepies – Rhyming slang for eyes.

14.1478 (425:22). take me to rests – Rhyming slang for breasts.

14.1478–79 (425:22–23). anker of rum – Rhyming slang for a large bum or bottom (an anker is an eight-and-a-half-gallon measure).

14.1479–80 (425:23–24). Your starving eyes and allbeplastered neck you stole my heart – This apparently jumbles two or more songs, including the chorus of "Moonlight Bay" (1912), words by Edward Madden, music by Percy Wenrich: "We were sailing along on Moonlight Bay, / We could hear the voices ringing, / They seemed to say / 'You have stolen my heart, / Now don't go 'way!' / As we sang Love's Old Sweet Song, / On Moonlight Bay." (*Starving:* starry; *allbeplastered:* alabaster.)

14.1480 (425:24). gluepot – Low slang for the odor of a seminal emission.

14.1480–81 (425:24–25). Spud again the rheumatiz? – A potato talisman such as the one Bloom carries was superstitiously believed to protect the bearer from rheumatism.

14.1481–82 (425:26). I vear thee beest a gert vool – Dialect: "I fear you are a great fool."

14.1482 (425:27). Back fro Lapland – Slang: back from enforced seclusion at the end of the world, or back from jail.

14.1482–83 (425:27). Your corporosity sagaciating O K? – American slang: "corporosity" means literally bodily bulk; hence a person of impressive size. To "sagaciate" is Southern slang for to fare or to thrive.

14.1483–84 (425:28–29). Womanbody after going on the straw? – English dialect: "Is your woman about to give birth?"

14.1484 (425:29). Stand and deliver – See 12.129n.

14.1484 (425:29). There's hair – See 12.1176n.

14.1484–85 (425:29–30). Ours the white death and the ruddy birth – See 10.1073–74n.

14.1486 (425:31). Mummer's wire. Cribbed out of Meredith – See 9.550–51n.

14.1486 (425:31–32). orchidised – Medical: "having inflamed testicles."

14.1486 (425:32). polycimical – Rare: "full of a variety of bugs or insects."

14.1489 (425:34). Collar the leather – Slang: "grab the football."

14.1489 (425:34). nappy – Early-eighteenth-century slang for beer or ale.

14.1489–90 (425:35). Jock braw Hielentman's your barleybree – After one of the choruses in Robert Burns's "The Jolly Beggars; A Cantata" (1785, 1799): "Sing hey my braw John Highlandman! / Sing ho my braw John Highlandman! / There's not a lad in a' the lan' / Was match for my John Highlandman!" (lines 132–35). "Barleybree" (Scots: "barley brew") occurs in the chorus of Burns's song "Willie Brew'd a Peck of Maut [Malt]" (1789, 1790): "We are na that fou [full, drunk], / But just a drappie [small drop] in our e'e! / The cock may caw, the day may daw, / And ay we'll taste the barley-bree!"

14.1490–91 (425:35–36). Lang may your lum reck and your kailpot boil! – Scots dialect: "Long may your chimney smoke and your soup pot boil."

14.1491 (425:37). Leg before wicket – In cricket it is against the rules for the batsman to protect his wicket from the bowled ball with anything other than the bat. If the batsman interposes his body, the umpire rules "Leg before wicket," and the batsman is out.

14.1493 (425:38–39). Caraway seed – Traditionally used for disguising alcoholic breath.

14.1493 (425:39). Twig? – Slang: "Do you understand?"

14.1493–94 (425:39–40). Every cove to his gentry mort – Seventeenth-century underworld cant; see 3.381–84n.

14.1494 (425:40). Venus Pandemos – Venus or Aphrodite Pandemos (meaning "of all the people"), originally a goddess of all Greece, she evolved into the goddess of sensual lust and prostitution, in contrast to Aphrodite Urania, the goddess of the higher and purer love.

14.1494 (425:40). Les petites femmes – French: "The little women."

14.1494–95 (425:40–41). Bold bad girl from the town of Mullingar – Namely, Milly Bloom. After the chorus of an anonymous American song, "Desperado": "A bold bad man was this . . . desperado, / From Cripple Creek way down in . . . Colorado, / And he walked around like a . . . big tornado, / And everywhere he went he gave his war whoop!"

14.1495–96 (425:42). Haunding Sara by the wame – Scots dialect: "Holding Sarah by the waist or belly"; from stanza four of Robert Burns's poem "Ken ye ought o' Captain Grose?": "Is he to Abram's bosom gone? / I go and ago.— / Or haudin Sarah by the wame? / Iram coram dago."

14.1496 (425:42). On the road to Malahide – Combines suggestions of "The Bridal of Malahide" (see 10.156n) and Kipling's "Mandalay" (from *Barrack-Room Ballads*, 1892). The speaker of Kipling's poem dreams of being with a certain "Burma girl . . . On the road to Mandalay."

14.1496–97 (426:1). If she who seduced me had left but the name – After the opening lines of Thomas Moore's song "When He Who Adores Thee": "When he who adores thee, has left but the name / Of his fault and his sorrows behind, / O! say wilt thou weep, when they darken the fame / Of a life that for thee was resign'd?"

14.1497 (426:2). *Machree, macruiskeen – After "The Cruiskeen Lawn"; see 12.122n.

14.1498 (426:2–3). Smutty Moll for a mattress jig – "Moll Peatley's jig" was Dublin slang for copulation.

14.1498 (426:3). *And a pull all together – After one of several bawdy parodies of the "Eton Boat Song," by Johnson and Drummond. Chorus: "Jolly boating weather, Jolly sweet harvest breeze; / Oars clip and feather, cool 'neath the trees, / Yet swing, swing together with your backs between your knees" (some versions substitute "pull" for "swing"). The opportunities for parody are obvious.

14.1500 (426:5). shiners – Slang for coins, especially for sovereigns and guineas.

14.1500 (426:5–6). Underconstumble? – "Understumble," according to Eric Partridge, is a common pun on "understand," here combined with "underconstable."

14.1501 (426:6). chink – Cockney slang for money, especially coins.

14.1502 (426:8). ooff – Cockney slang for money.

14.1502–3 (426:8–9). two bar and a wing – Slang: "two shillings and a penny."

14.1503 (426:9). bilks – Cockney slang for swindlers or cheats.

14.1504 (426:11). coon – See 6.704n.

14.1505 (426:11–12). We are nae fou. We're nae tha fou – See 14.1489–90n.

14.1508 (426:14). teetee – Slang for teetotal, that is, not drinking.

14.1508 (426:14). Bowsing nowt but claret-wine – "Bowsing" is slang for drinking; after an Irish song, "The Rakes of Mallow": "Beaving, belle-ing, dancing, drinking / Breaking

windows, damning, sinking, / Ever raking, never thinking, / Live the rakes of Mallow. // One time nought but claret drinking, / Then like politicians thinking / To raise the sinking funds when sinking, / Live the rakes of Mallow."

14.1508 (426:15). Garn! – Cockney colloquialism: "Get away with you!"

14.1508 (426:15). glint – Slang for a look or glance.

14.1509 (426:15). Gum – A vulgar euphemism for God.

14.1509 (426:15). I'm jiggered – A colloquial oath approximate to "I'll be damned!"

14.1509 (426:15–16). been to barber – Bantam Lyons has just recently shaved off his moustache (5.521 [85:27]); but "been to barber" is also cockney slang for drunk and "shorn" of money.

14.1510 (426:17). *Rose of Castile – Lenehan recalls his pun; see 7.591n.

14.1511–12 (426:18–19). Look at Bantam's flowers – Does Lyons injure his nose or his lip when he "faints" (falls) and begin to bleed before he starts to "holler"? Or has he a bunch of flowers for his wife?

14.1512 (426:19–20). *The colleen bawn. My colleen bawn – See 12.194n.

14.1513 (426:20). Dutch oven – Boxing slang: "mouth."

14.1514 (426:21–22). The ruffin cly the nab – Seventeenth-century underworld cant: "The devil take the head," from the first line of "The Beggar's Curse" in Richard Head's *The Canting Academy* (London, 1673). The full line reads, "The Ruffin cly the nab of Harmanbeck"; "Harmanbeck" means a constable.

14.1514–17 (426:22–25). The ruffin cly the nab . . . form hot order – See following notes for annotation of verbal textures and allusions. Stephen Hand was a Dubliner whose misadventure Joyce clarified in a letter to Georg Goyert, the German translator of *Ulysses*, 6 March 1927: "Stephen Hand met a telegram boy who was bringing a private racing telegram from the stable of the celebrated English brewer Bass to the police depot in Dublin to a friend there to back Bass' horse *Sceptre* for the Cup. Stephen Hand gives boy 4 pence, opens the telegram over steam (grahamising), recloses it and sends the boy on with it, backs *Sceptre* to win and loses. (This really happened and his name was Stephen Hand though it was not the Gold Cup.)"

14.1515 (426:22–23). the jady coppaleen – "Jady" after "jade," a good-for-nothing or vicious horse; "coppaleen" is Anglicized Irish for a little horse.

14.1516 (426:23). Bass – See 14.1161–62n.

14.1516 (426:24). joey – Slang for a fourpenny piece from about 1855.

14.1516 (426:24). grahamise – Slang for to open letters that are en route to their destination. Sir James Graham (1792–1861) was an English statesman who as home secretary in 1844 procured a warrant to open the letters of the Italian patriot and revolutionary Giuseppe Mazzini, who had sought political asylum in England. Graham communicated the contents to the Austrian minister, which resulted in a public outcry against Graham's betrayal, in the course of which his name became a verb.

14.1516 (426:24). Mare on form – From a version of Bass's telegram; that is, Sceptre (though not a mare but a colt) is in top shape. See 14.1128–33n.

14.1517 (426:25). Guinea to a goosegog – A colloquial expression for overwhelming odds; a "goosegog" is a gooseberry.

14.1517 (426:25). a cram – Slang for something that fills the mind with false or exaggerated expectations.

14.1518 (426:27). chokeechokee – Slang for prison.

14.1519 (426:27). harman beck – Seventeenth-century underworld cant for a constable; see 14.1514n.

14.1519 (426:27). Madden – O. Madden was the jockey who rode Sceptre in the Gold Cup; see 14.1128–33n.

14.1520 (426:28–29). *O lust, our refuge and our strength – A parody of a phrase from one of the vernacular prayers prescribed for the end of low mass; see 5.420n.

14.1521–22 (426:30). Come ahome – For the song echoed here, see 18.1282–83n.

14.1522 (426:31). Horryvar, mong vioo – After the French *Au revoir, mon vieux* (Good-bye, old fellow).

14.1522 (426:31). the cowslips – In the language of flowers, the cowslip (or primrose) is symbolic of inconstancy.

14.1523 (426:32). Jannock – English dialect for honest, candid.

14.1523–24 (426:33). Of John Thomas, her spouse – Continues the parody from 14.1520 (426:28–29) above. "John Thomas" is slang for penis.

14.1526 (426:35–36). sheeny nachez – Slang: "Jew thing"; that is, what a Jew would do—opprobrious.

14.1526 (426:36). misha mishinnah – "A bad, violent and unprepared for death or end" (Joyce; see *JJQ* 4, no. 3 [1966]: 194).

14.1527 (426:36–37). Through yerd our lord, Amen – Continues the parody from 14.1523–24 (426:33). "Yerd" is slang for penis.

14.1528 (426:39). bluggy – A jocular and euphemistic twisting of *bloody*.

14.1531–32 (426:42–427:1). Landlord, landlord have you good wine, staboo? – See 14.314, 317n.

14.1532 (427:1). a wee drap to pree – Joyce intended this as an allusion to Burns's "Willie Brew'd a Peck of Maut" (14.1489–90n; see *JJQ* 4, no. 3 [1966]: 194), since in the lines "Willie brewed a peck of maut / And Rob and Allen came to see," the word "see" is sometimes varied as "pree," which Joyce defined as Scots for to examine and taste whiskey.

14.1533 (427:2). Right Boniface! – That is, right about-face, with a pun on "Boniface," slang for innkeeper and the name of nine popes and several saints; see 12.1705n.

14.1533 (427:2). Absinthe – See 3.217–18n.

14.1533–34 (427:2–3). *Nos omnes biberimus . . . capiat posteriora nostria – Latin: "We will all drink green poison [absinthe], and the devil take the hindmost."

14.1534 (427:3–4). Closing time, gents – The bartender announces that it is eleven o'clock, closing time for Dublin's fully licensed pubs.

14.1534–35 (427:4). Rome booze – Slang for wine.

14.1535 (427:4). toff – See 10.745n.

14.1535 (427:5). onions – A word difficult for drunks to pronounce and therefore used by the police as a sobriety test.

14.1535 (427:5). Cadges – See 5.392n.

14.1536 (427:6). Play low, pardner – From card games, slang for "Don't draw attention to yourself."

14.1536 (427:6). Slide – Slang for to disappear.

14.1536 (427:6). *Bonsoir la compagnie* – Hodgart and Worthington (*Song in the Works of James Joyce* [New York, 1959]) list this as the title of a song by Maud, but it also seems likely that it is an allusion to the drinking song "Vive l'Amour": "Let every good fellow now join in a song, / Vive la compagnie! / Success to each other and pass it along, / Vive la compagnie, / Vive la, Vive la, Vive l'amour / . . . Vive la compagnie."

14.1537 (427:6–7). And snares of the pox-fiend – Parodies a phrase from the second of the vernacular prayers prescribed for the end of low mass; cf. 14.1520n. The prayer is quoted at 5.442–47 (83:22–27).

14.1537 (427:7). Namby Amby – "Namby Pamby," from the English poet Ambrose Philips (1674–1749) and subsequently used by Pope and others to ridicule Philips's verse; hence, insipid, weakly sentimental, affectedly pretty.

14.1538 (427:7). Skunked? – Slang for betrayed, left in the lurch.

14.1538 (427:8). Leg bail – To "take leg bail" is to escape from custody (by running away).

14.1538 (427:8). Aweel, ye maun e'en gang yer gates – Scots: "Ah well, you must even go your own ways."

14.1539 (427:9). Kind Kristyann – Christian is the central pilgrim in Bunyan's *Pilgrim's Progress.* He lends a helping hand to other pilgrims, including Faithful and Hopeful and (unsuccessfully) Talkative.

14.1541 (427:11). sprung – Slang for drunk and exhausted.

14.1541 (427:11). Tarnally – As an oath, a dialect version of *eternally.*

14.1542 (427:12). longbreak – "Long break" is summer vacation for students in the British Isles.

14.1542 (427:12). curate – Slang for a bartender.

14.1542 (427:13). Cot's plood – Dialect for the oath *God's blood.*

14.1543 (427:13). prandypalls – A "pall" is an altarcloth or a square piece of cardboard covered with linen that is used for covering the chalice during mass. "Prandy" suggests *prandial,* an affected or humorous way of referring to a repast.

14.1543–45 (427:14–16). Thrust syphilis down to . . . wander through the world – Continues the parody of the vernacular prayers for the closing of low mass; see 14.1537n.

14.1545 (427:16). *Á la vôtre!* – French drinking salutation: "To your (health)!"

14.1546 (427:17). whatten tunket's – American dialect: "what in thunder."

14.1546 (427:17–18). Dusty Rhodes – "Dusty" was a common nickname for men named Rhodes; one Dusty Rhodes was an American comic-strip character from about 1900, the tramp who weathers continuous comic misfortune.

14.1547 (427:19). Jubilee Mutton – Dublin slang: "not much in contrast to his needs." In 1897, during the celebration of Queen Victoria's Jubilee, relatively small quantities of mutton were distributed free among the Dublin poor. The inadequacy of this gesture in contrast to the appalling need of the poor gave rise to this anti-English phrase.

14.1547 (427:19). Bovril – An English beef concentrate that becomes a kind of beef tea when water is added. It was widely advertised as a health food.

14.1548 (427:19–20). D' ye ken bare socks? –
After the opening line of the song "John Peel":
"D' ye ken John Peel with his coat so gay?"; see
11.1243n.

14.1548–49 (427:20). the Richmond – The
Richmond Lunatic Asylum; see 1.128n.

14.1550 (427:22). Bartle the Bread – Joyce
glossed this for the German translator: "Bartle
who delivers or eats the bread usually" (see *JJQ*
4, no. 3 [1966]: 194).

14.1551 (427:23). cit – Slang for citizen.

**14.1551 (427:23–24). Man all tattered . . .
maiden all forlorn** – See "The House That
Jack Built," 14.304–5n.

14.1552 (427:24). Slung her hook – Slang for
made off, ran away, died.

**14.1552–53 (427:24–25). Walking Mackintosh
of lonely canyon** – Parodies the titles of American dime-novel Westerns.

14.1553 (427:25). Tuck – Slang "drink, drink
up."

14.1553 (427:26). Nix for the hornies – Slang:
"Watch out for the cops."

14.1554 (427:27). passed in his checks –
American slang: "passed out; died."

14.1556 (427:29). Padney – A name that was
coined for Milly Bloom (or which she coined for
herself?). See 17.866 (693:3).

14.1558 (427:31). *Tiens, tiens* – French:
"Well, well."

**14.1558–59 (427:32). *O, get, rev on a gra-
dient one in nine** – In other words, "Oh, get
out, it's impossible for a racing car to accelerate
up an 11 percent grade." This assertion would
have been generally true in 1904, but the rapid
development of the automobile made it a fine
subject for irresolvable argument.

**14.1559 (427:32–33). Live axle drives are
souped** – That is, automobiles designed so that
the axle moves and imparts motion to the wheels
are doomed. There was a considerable argument in 1904 about whether axles should be
"fixed" (as they were in wagons) or "live," and
the speaker has chosen what has turned out to

be (since live-axle drives have long since become
standard) the wrong side of the argument.

14.1560 (427:33). Jenatzy licks him – Jenatzy,
a Belgian, was scheduled to drive for Germany
(a German Mercedes) in the Gordon Bennett
Cup Race in Germany, 17 June 1904. Jenatzy
had won the race in 1903, when it was held in
Ireland, and the *Evening Telegraph*, 16 June
1904, conceded him to be the favorite (though
he lost to Thery of France). The "him" Jenatzy
was to "lick" was, according to the *Evening Telegraph*, the other German driver, Baron de Ca-
ters. See 6.370n.

14.1560 (427:34). Jappies? high angle fire –
During the Russo-Japanese War (1904–5), naval supremacy was the key to Japanese military
success on the mainland. The Japanese fleet was
more powerful than Russia's Far Eastern fleet,
and in the first major naval engagement, 8–9
February 1904, the Japanese crippled several
Russian battleships and cruisers in an attack
launched by torpedo boats and pressed home by
long-range shelling. The high-angle fire of that
shelling was effective against the vulnerable
thinly armored decks of the Russian ships.
These early Japanese successes caused a lull in
the naval war while the Russians effected repairs. The *Evening Telegraph*, 16 June 1904, reported "a renewal of activity on the part of Russia's naval commanders" (though that renewal
was to lead to further Russian losses during the
summer of 1904).

14.1560 (427:34). inyah – Anglicized Irish: "Is
that so?"

14.1561 (427:34). war specials – Daily newspaper dispatches about the Russo-Japanese War
were printed in columns headed "War Specials."

**14.1563–64 (427:37–38). *May Allah the Ex-
cellent . . . ever tremendously conserve** – A
formal Arabic salutation (and prayer) pronounced at bedtime.

14.1565 (427:39). We're nae tha fou – See
14.1489–90n.

**14.1565 (427:39–40). The Leith police dis-
misseth us** – The first line of a tongue-twisting
nursery rhyme: "The Leith police dismisseth
us, / I'm thankful, sir, to say; / The Leith police
dismisseth us, / They thought we sought to
stay. / The Leith police dismisseth us, / We
both sighed sighs apiece, / And the sigh that we

sighed as we said goodbye / Was the size of the Leith police." In a letter to the German translator of *Ulysses* Joyce remarked, "the police sergeant asks drunks to repeat [this phrase] in order to test their sobriety."

14.1567 (427:41–42). Mona, my thrue love . . . Mona my own love – From a song, "Mona, My Own Love," by Weatherly and Adams. Chorus: "Mona, my own love, Mona my true love, / Art thou not mine thro' the long years to be? / By the bright stars above thee, / I love thee, I love thee, / Live for thee, die for thee, only for thee. / Oh, Mona, Mona, my own love, / Art thou not mine thro' the long years to be?"

14.1569 (428:1). obstropolis – Illiterate for "obstreperous."

14.1570 (428:2). Mount street – Just southeast of Burke's pub (see 14.1391n), from which the drinkers have exited.

14.1572 (428:5). Denzille lane – Denzille (Fenian) Street would have been a more direct route, but Stephen and Lynch, followed by Bloom, circle south on their way to the Westland Row station where they will entrain for the Amiens Street station on the edge of the red-light district in eastern Dublin, north of the Liffey.

14.1573 (428:6–7). We two, she said, will seek the kips where shady Mary is – In Dante Gabriel Rossetti's (1828–82) "The Blessed Damozel" (1850, 1856, 1870), the Damozel in heaven speaks and is overheard by her lover on earth: "'We two,' she said, 'will seek the groves / Where the lady Mary is, / With her five handmaidens, whose names / Are five sweet symphonies, / Cecily, Gertrude, Magdalen, / Margaret, and Rosalys'" (lines 103–8). For "kips," see 1.293n.

14.1574 (428:7–8). *Laetabuntur in cubilibus suis* – Latin: "Let them sing aloud upon their beds," from Psalms 149:5. The verse begins, "Let the saints be joyful in glory."

14.1575–76 (428:9–10). Sinned against the light – Namely, the Jews; see 2.361 (34:3).

14.1576–77 (428:10–11). that day is at hand . . . the world by fire – The traditional Christian version of the Last Judgment is that of a world consumed (and purified) by fire. On that day the Wandering Jew will be released from the bondage of his never-ending life; see 9.1209n.

14.1577 (428:11). *Ut implerentur scripturae* – Latin: "That the scriptures might be fulfilled." The phrase occurs several times in the Vulgate version of the Gospels; for example, in the description of the Crucifixion: "[The soldiers] said therefore among themselves, Let us not rend [the coat], but cast lots for it, whose it shall be: that the scripture might be fulfilled, which saith, They parted my raiment among them, and for my vesture they did cast lots. These things therefore the soldiers did" (John 19:24). The "scripture" referred to is Psalm 22:18. In any case, the phrase, which in the Vulgate is in the indicative, is changed to the subjunctive in *Ulysses;* that is, that which the Gospels assert as objective fact is rendered hypothetical (it might be, but not necessarily will be, fulfilled).

14.1578 (428:12–13). Then outspoke medical Dick to his comrade medical Davy – See 9.908–9n.

14.1579 (428:13). yellow – According to Joyce (*Letters* 3:130), Lynch's epithet is a substitute for the commonplace *bloody* and is a "proof of his culture." Cf. the epithet "yellowjohns," 12.1255n.

14.1579 (428:14). on the Merrion hall – See 10.1109–10n.

14.1580 (428:14). Elijah is coming – See 8.13n.

14.1580 (428:14–15). *Washed in the blood of the Lamb – See 8.9n.

14.1580–91 (428:15–27). Come on, you winefizzling . . . Just you try it on – This parody of an American evangelist's style is also reminiscent of the celebrated "raft passage" in chapter 3 of Mark Twain's *Life on the Mississippi* (1883).

14.1584 (428:19). *Alexander J Christ Dowie – See 8.13n.

14.1586 (428:21). bumshow – American slang for a carnival show that promises more (in the way of revealing glimpses of pretty girls, etc.) than it ever intends to deliver.

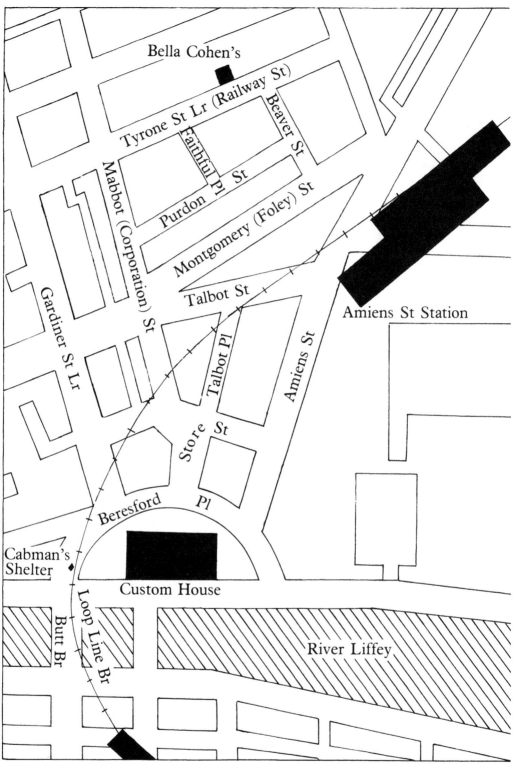

Bella Cohen's

Tyrone St Lr (Railway St)

Beaver St

Faithful Pl

Purdon St

Montgomery (Foley) St

Mabbot (Corporation) St

Talbot St

Amiens St Station

Gardiner St Lr

Talbot Pl

Amiens St

Store St

Beresford Pl

Cabman's Shelter

Custom House

Butt Br

Loop Line Br

River Liffey

EPISODE 15. *Circe*

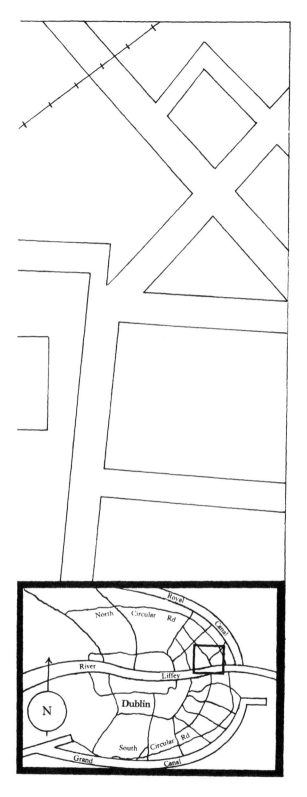

EPISODE 15

Circe

▬▬▬▬▬▬▬▬▬▬▬▬▬▬▬▬▬▬▬▬▬

(15.1–4967, PP. 429–609)

Episode 15: *Circe*, 15.1–4967 (429–609). In Book 10 of *The Odyssey*, Odysseus recounts his adventures with Aeolus and with the Lestrygonians and then describes his landing on Circe's island. Odysseus and his men are in a state of profound depression, "sick at heart, tasting our grief" (10:143; Fitzgerald, p. 181), as a result of the tantalizing view of Ithaca achieved with Aeolus's help and of the disastrous encounter with the Lestrygonians. They rest "cloaked in desolation / upon the waste sea beach" (10:179; Fitzgerald, p. 182), and Odysseus kills "a stag with noble antlers" (10:158; ibid.) on which they feast. Eventually Odysseus divides his crew into two platoons, one under his leadership, one led by Eurylochus. The leaders draw lots and the fate of exploring the island falls to Eurylochus. Eurylochus and his men discover Circe's hall, where all save Eurylochus are transformed into hogs by Circe's "foul magic" (10:247; Fitzgerald, p. 184). Eurylochus escapes to warn Odysseus, who then approaches Circe's hall alone. He is met by Hermes and accepts a magic herb, moly, to protect him from Circe's magic; Hermes also tells Odysseus that he must make Circe swear to release his men and to perform "no witches' tricks" (10:300; Fitzgerald, p. 186) lest he, too, be "unmanned" by her. Odysseus confronts Circe, whose magic fails, no match for his moly. Odysseus threatens her, and she swears that she will not harm him and that she will release his men. Not only does she keep her oath, but she also royally entertains Odysseus and his crew "until a year grew fat" (10:467; Fitzgerald, p. 191). Finally Odysseus's men urge him to "shake off this trance" (10:472; ibid.). He does, and Circe advises him to visit the underworld (Hades) to consult Tiresias. When Odysseus returns with Tiresias's prophecy, Circe helps him further with advice about the Sirens and Scylla and Charybdis.

Time: 12:00 midnight. Scene: the Brothel, Mrs. Cohen's establishment at 82 Tyrone Street Lower in the Dublin red-light district. Joyce called the district "nighttown"; Dubliners called it "Monto," after Montgomery (now Foley) Street, one of its central streets. The district lay just north of the Liffey and west of the Amiens Street railroad station. (See Ellmann, pp. 367–68.) Organ: locomotor apparatus; Art: magic; Color: none; Symbol: whore; Technique: hallucination.[1] Correspondences: *Circe*—Bella.

In the Linati schema, Joyce listed *L'Orca Antropofoba* as the Sense (Meaning) of the episode. It is not clear whether Joyce's Italian intended *antropofago*, "man-eating," or *antropophobia* (anthropophobia), a medical term for a morbid sensation of angst in the presence of other people. Probably the latter, but in either case there is an allusion to Ludovico Ariosto's (1474–1533) *Orlando Furioso* (1516, 1521, 1532), in which there are two orcs, a woman-eating seaborne one (cantos 8, 10, and 11) and a blind land-orc that eats only men (canto 17). The woman-eating orc is Proteus's revenge on an island people who have offended him; the man-eating orc resembles the Cyclops Polyphemus. The Linati schema also lists as Persons (without correspondences): "The Beasts, Telemachus, Ulysses, Hermes."

15.1 (429:1). *Mabbot street* – (Now Corporation Street), just north of the Liffey near the Amiens Street railway station.

15.1 (429:1). *nighttown* – Slang among Dublin journalists for the late shift on a newspaper. Here, the red-light district; see "Scene" in the headnote to this episode.

15.3 (429:3). *will-o-the-wisps* – In Goethe's *Faust* (I.xxi), a will-o'-the-wisp lights the way up the "magic-mad" mountain as Faust and Mephistopheles make their way toward the Walpurgisnacht (Witches' Sabbath) assembly. In folklore, the will-o'-the-wisp is considered ominous, often thought to be a soul rejected by hell and condemned to carry its own hellcoal on its wanderings (suggested by Joan Keenan).

15.5 (429:5). *Rabaiotti's . . . ice gondola* – See 10.229n.

---

1 The technique and some of the content of this episode can be informed by a variety of sources, among them: Gustave Flaubert's (1821–80) *The Temptation of Saint Anthony; or, A Revelation of the Soul* (1874; references below are to *The Complete Works of Gustave Flaubert* [London, 1904], vol. 7); Goethe's (1749–1832) *Faust* (1808), particularly, Part I, scene 21, "Walpurgisnacht"; Gerhard Hauptmann's (1862–1946) *Hanneles Himmelfahrt* (*The Assumption of Hannele: A Dream Poem*) (1892)—in the course of the play, apparitions seen by Hannele in her deathbed delirium are introduced as characters on stage; Henrik Ibsen's (1828–1906) *Ghosts; Spirits That Return* (1881); August Strindberg's (1849–1912) *The Ghost Sonata* (1907) and *The Dream Play* (1902); Leopold von Sacher-Masoch (1836–95), *Venus im Pelz* (written in 1870, published posthumously in 1904); references below are to *Venus in Furs* [New York, 1947]); and Richard von Krafft-Ebing (1840–1902), *Psychopathia Sexualis* (references below are to an edition published in Brooklyn, N.Y., 1937).

15.7–9 (429:8–10). *The swancomb of the gondola . . . under a lighthouse* – In Flaubert's *Temptation of Saint Anthony,* pp. 21ff. (see p. 452, n.1), gondolas, as "pleasure boats," and the Pharos lighthouse are aspects of Antony's resplendent vision of Alexandria before that vision metamorphoses into one of horror.

15.18 (429:19). **Kithogue** – Anglicized Irish: "A left-handed [and hence unlucky] person."

15.40 (430:13). *tatts* – Dialect: "tangles."

15.44–47, 56–59 (430:17–20, 29–32). **I gave it to Molly . . . the leg of the duck** – The sources of these bawdy rhymes are unknown.

15.48 (430:21). *Private Carr* – May very well owe his name to Joyce's irritation with one Henry Carr, a British consular official in Zurich. See Ellmann, index p. 823.

15.48 (430:21). *Private Compton* – Also owes his name to Joyce's enmity; see Ellmann, p. 459.

15.53 (430:26). **Signs on you** – Slang: "Bad luck to you."

15.53 (430:26). **More power the Cavan girl** – A cheer for a "wild one," because from a Dublin point of view County Cavan to the northwest is the nearest haven of the *wild* people.

15.55 (430:28). **Cootehill and Belturbet** – Small towns in County Cavan.

15.65 (431:2). **the parson** – Because Stephen is dressed in black and is wearing a soft hat, he looks like a Protestant minister.

15.70–72 (431:7–9). **She has it . . . leg of the duck** – See 15.44–47n.

15.74 (431:11). *the* **introit** *for paschal time* – The introit (entrance chant) of the Mass occurs near the beginning, just after the priest has recited the confiteor and ascended the altar steps. Paschal time, the period from Easter to Pentecost, is a season of joy, rebirth, and baptism (it is not a time for doing penance). The introit for Easter Day (when paschal time begins) is not what Stephen quotes in the passages that follow, but the introit reads in translation: "I have risen and now am I with you once more. Alleluia! You laid your hand upon me. Alleluia! You have shown how wonderful is your wisdom. Alleluia, alleluia! Lord you have proved me, and you know me. You saw me when I went to my rest, and you saw me rise again." The *Layman's Missal* remarks of this passage: "The risen Christ thanks his Father for rescuing him from the grave."

15.77 (431:15). *Vidi aquam egredientum de templo a latere dextro. Alleluia* – Latin: "I saw a stream of water welling forth from the right of the temple. Alleluia." This is the opening phrase of the antiphon used with asperges (the ceremony of sprinkling the altar) during paschal time. Its emphasis on joy contrasts with the antiphon used during the rest of the liturgical year, which begins: "If you sprinkle me with hyssop, Lord, I shall be cleansed." "Hyssop" is a bitter purgative.

15.84 (431:22). *(altius aliquantulum.) Et omnes ad quos pervenit aqua ista* – Latin: "(with considerable profundity.) And all among them came to that water." Stephen continues the antiphon from 15.77 (431:15).

15.86 (431:24). **Trinity medicals** – Students at the Medical School of the University of Dublin (usually called Trinity College after its only college).

15.91 (432:2). **Faithful place** – Off Tyrone Street Lower (in the heart of the red-light district).

15.92 (432:3). **squarepusher** – See 8.446n.

15.92 (432:3). **the greaser** – A person who lubricates machines, engines, railway carriages, etc.

15.93 (432:5). **mantrap** – Slang for a house of prostitution.

15.94 (432:6). **Stag** – Slang for an informer. See the headnote to this episode, p. 452.

15.96 (432:7–8). **Kilbride . . . Oliphant** – Apart from the context, identity and significance unknown (though the names were not unusual in 1904 Dublin).

15.98 (432:10). *(triumphaliter.) Salvi facti sunt* – Latin: "(triumphantly.) And they are made whole [saved]." This completes the quotation that Stephen began above (15.77 [431:15] and 15.84 [431:22]).

15.105–6 (432:18–19). So that gesture . . . would be a universal language – See "esperanto," 15.1691n.

15.106 (432:19). the gift of tongues – "And when the day of Pentecost was fully come, they [the Apostles] were all with one accord in one place. And suddenly there came a sound from heaven as of a rushing mighty wind, and it filled all the house where they were sitting. And there appeared unto them cloven tongues like as of fire, and it sat upon each of them. And they were all filled with the Holy Ghost, and began to speak with other tongues as the Spirit gave them utterance" (Acts 2:1–4). See 15.74n in re Pentecost.

15.107 (432:20). entelechy – See 9.208n.

15.109 (432:22). Pornosophical philotheology – Suggests "whore-wisdom love (of) theology."

15.109 (432:22–23). Mecklenburg street – The name of this notorious street in Dublin's red-light district was changed to Tyrone Street in 1887 (in a fanciful and unsuccessful attempt to upgrade the street). The name has been changed again and is now Railway Street.

15.111–12 (432:26–27). *Even the allwisest Stagyrite . . . by a light of love – The Stagyrite is Aristotle, who was born on the island of Stagyros. The print Stephen has in mind is in the Louvre and is by Hans Baldung (1476–1545), the Strasbourg painter and designer of woodcuts. Antifeminism is a recurrent theme in Baldung's work, and the clear suggestion is that even Aristotle could be rendered ignoble by a woman's power, presumably the power of his mistress, Herpyllis; see 9.720–24n. For "light of love," see 9.249–50n.

15.117 (433:3–4). the loaf and jug of bread and wine in Omar – Edward Fitzgerald (1809–83) translated and re-created *The Rubáiyát of Omar Khayyám* (1859). Stanza 12 reads: "A Book of Verse underneath the Bough, / A Jug of Wine, a Loaf of Bread—and Thou / Beside me singing in the Wilderness— / Oh, Wilderness were Paradise enow!" Stephen is also alluding to the bread and wine of the Mass.

15.120 (433:6). Damn your yellow stick – For Lynch's swearing in yellow instead of red ("bloody"), see 12.1255n.

15.122 (433:8). *la belle dame sans merci* –

French: "the beautiful woman without pity." Keats used this traditional phrase as the title of a poem (1819). "La Belle Dame" seems to hold out the promise of a transcendent love only to rob those she enthralls of their youth and vitality, the way Circe does (or threatens to do) in *The Odyssey*.

15.122 (433:8–9). Georgina Johnson – See 9.195n.

15.122–23 (433:9). *ad deam qui laetificat iuventutem meam* – Latin: "to the goddess who has gladdened the days of my youth." At the beginning of the Mass the celebrant says, "Introibo ad altare Dei" (I will go up to God's altar), and the minister or server replies, "Ad Deum qui laetificat iuventutem meam" (To God who has gladdened the days of my youth). See 1.5n.

15.129 (433:15–16). the customhouse – Stephen and Lynch are not far north of the Custom House. It is an impressive structure (1791) situated on the north bank of the Liffey east of the center of Dublin. It is surmounted by a colonnade and capped by a statue of Hope. The building housed not only custom and excise tax offices but also the Board of Public Works and the Poor Law Commission.

15.130 (433:16). take your crutch and walk – In John 5:8 Jesus heals "a certain man . . . which had an infirmity thirty and eight years" by saying, "Rise, take up thy bed, and walk."

15.142 (433:29–30). *under the railway bridge* – Where the Loop Line crosses Talbot Street. Bloom is at least 400 yards (and around two corners) behind Stephen and Lynch, but he, too, is approaching "the Mabbot Street entrance of nighttown." Mabbot Street is now Corporation Street.

15.144 (433:31). *Gillen's* – P. Gillen, hairdresser, 64 Talbot Street.

15.145 (433:32). *Nelson's* – See 7.1018n.

15.146 (434:1). *Gladstone* – See 5.323–24n.

15.148 (434:3). *Wellington* – See 12.1459–60n.

15.148 (434:4). *bonham* – English dialect: "a young pig."

15.149 (434:4–5). *****jollypoldy the rix-dix doldy** – A common form of child-rhyme play on names. A "doldy" is a stupid or impotent person.

15.150 (434:6). *Antonio Rabaiotti's* – In addition to his fleet of ice-cream "gondolas," Rabaiotti had a restaurant at 65 Talbot Street.

15.154 (434:10). fish and taters – Technically it is Friday, 17 June, a meatless day for Catholic Dublin in 1904.

15.154 (434:10). N.g. – Slang: "No good."

15.155 (434:11). *Olhausen's* – W. Olhansen, pork butcher, 72 Talbot Street (*Thom's* 1904, p. 1605).

15.158 (434:15). *crubeen* – A pig's foot.

15.168 (434:25). *Cormack's corner* – Thomas Cormack, grocer, tea, wine, and spirit merchant (a pub), 74 Talbot Street on the corner of Mabbot (now Corporation) Street.

15.170 (434:27). the brigade – The Dublin Metropolitan Fire Brigade.

15.171 (434:28). his house – Boylan's fictional residence?

15.171 (434:28–29). Beggar's bush – A suburban district two miles southeast of central Dublin. *Beggar's Bush* (1622) is also the title of a once-popular comedy by John Fletcher (1579–1625), Philip Massinger (1583–1640), and others. The plot turns on the usurpation of a maiden's throne and her restoration to it through the aid of her lover, a prince disguised as a merchant.

15.172 (434:29–30). London's burning . . . on fire! – After the popular old round: "Scotland's burning! Scotland's burning! Look out! Look out! Fire, fire! Fire, fire! Pour on water! Pour on water!"

15.174 (434:31–32). *Talbot street* – Runs west toward central Dublin from the Amiens Street (now Connolly) railroad station. Stephen and Lynch have turned north from Talbot Street, walked through Mabbot (now Corporation) Street, and turned east into Tyrone (once Mecklenburg, now Railway) Street.

15.185 (435:10). *sandstrewer* – An electric tram car designed to clean mud and refuse from the rails and to sand them.

15.190–91 (435:15–16). *a policeman's white-gloved hand* – Dublin police wore white gloves when directing traffic.

15.193 (435:18). *chains and keys* – Parts of a series of switches in a tramline.

15.195 (435:20). *the hat trick – As W. Y. Tyndall (*A Reader's Guide to James Joyce* [New York, 1959], p. 209) describes it: "An Irishman covers a turd on the street with his hat. He tells a policeman it is a bird and goes off for help, asking the policeman to stand guard in the meantime."

15.200 (435:25). Sandow's exercises – See 4.234n.

15.201 (435:26). The Providential – The Provident Clerks Guarantee and Accident offices (a London-based insurance firm with offices in Dublin) advertised "Guarantees for Fidelity, Accident Insurance, Combination Policies for Accidents and Disease, Insurances arranged under the Workmen's Compensation Act (1897), the Employer's Liability Act (1880) and at Common Law."

15.201–2 (435:27). Poor mamma's panacea – Bloom's potato talisman; see 14.1480–81n.

15.203 (435:29). Leonard's corner – At the intersection of Clanbrassil streets (Upper and Lower) with South Circular Road, so called after F. Leonard, grocer and ironmonger, 64–66 Clanbrassil Upper, near where Bloom lived when he was going to the high school; see 17.49–50n.

15.203–4 (435:29). Third time is the charm – After the popular belief that a third try at a difficult task or game (after two previous failures) is attended by special luck.

15.207 (436:5). Lad lane – In southeastern Dublin.

15.208 (436:5–6). Emblem of luck . . . Probably lost cattle – Cramps are a traditional sign of bad luck. Bloom speculates that the attack he recalls might have been the result of his having eaten bad meat, since "lost cattle" means either beef that has been illegally slaughtered or horse meat that has been substituted for beef.

15.209 (436:6). Mark of the beast – In Revelation, the Antichristian beast of the Apocalypse is given "power . . . over all kindreds, and tongues, and nations. . . . And [the beast] causeth all, both small and great, rich and poor, free and bond, to receive a mark in their right hand, or in their foreheads: And that no man might buy or sell save he that had the mark, or the name of the beast, or the number of his name" (13:7, 16–17).

15.212 (436:10). *O'Beirne's wall* – O'Beirne Brothers, tea and wine merchants, 62 Mabbot Street (on the corner of Talbot Street).

15.212–13 (436:11). *a visage unknown, injected with dark mercury* – In 1904, black lotion of mercury, or "black wash," was used in the treatment of syphilitic sores, and mercury or a combination of mercury and iodine was injected for cure of syphilis (over a period of at least two and a half years). As Odysseus approaches Circe's house in search of his men-turned-beasts, he is intercepted by Hermes (Mercury); see headnote to this episode, p. 452, and 15.4966–67n. In astrology, Mercury is identified as the voice of wisdom, the governor of intelligent speech. "Dark Mercury" would thus signify widespread infection (venereal), wisdom associated with devil worship, and evil counsel and betrayal.

15.216 (436:15). *Buenas noches, señorita Blanca. Que calle es esta?* – Spanish: "Good evening, Miss White. What street is this?"

15.218 (436:17). *Sraid Mabbot* – Irish: "Mabbot Street." In modern Dublin, street names are given in both English and Irish; but Mabbot Street is now Corporation Street.

15.220 (436:19). *Slan leath* – Irish: "Safe with you" (i.e., good-bye).

15.220 (436:19–20). Gaelic league – See 9.323n.

15.231–32 (436:27). the Touring Club – Touring clubs sponsored by the *Irish Cyclist* (see 15.233n) had been organized in various communities throughout Ireland. They put up signposts and route markers, sponsored tours, and worked to make the roads and paths in their communities safe for cyclists.

15.232 (436:27). Stepaside – A village crossroads seven miles south-southeast of Dublin.

15.233 (436:29). the *Irish Cyclist* – A weekly newspaper published at 2 Dame Court in Dublin, "devoted to the safe conduct and continued expansion of cycling in Ireland."

15.233–34 (436:29). *In darkest Stepaside* – After General William Booth's (1829–1912) Salvation Army diatribe *In Darkest England; and the Way Out* (1890), which was in turn named after Sir Henry Morton Stanley's *In Darkest Africa* (1890).

15.234 (436:30). Rags and bones – After the ragman's traditional cry: "Any rags, any bones, any bottles today?"

15.235–36 (436:31–32). Wash off his sins of the world – After John 1:29: "The next day John [the Baptist] seeth Jesus coming unto him [to be baptized], and saith, Behold the Lamb of God, which taketh away the sin of the world."

15.243 (437:7). *sweets of sin* – See 10.606n.

15.249 (437:13). *an elder in Zion* – The phrase does not appear anywhere in Jewish literature (where it would be "an elder in Israel" instead); thus, "an elder in Zion" suggests an allusion to *The Protocols of the Elders of Zion*, first published by the government press in Russia in 1905 and apparently plagiarized from several sources by Russian secret police in Paris. The result is the crudest sort of anti-Semitic calumny, but the protocols were eagerly devoured in Russia, and when they reached Western Europe at the end of World War I they had an extraordinary impact, which was to climax in the extreme—and deadly—anti-Semitism of the Nazis in the 1930s and 40s (in spite of well-publicized revelations of the hoax and its cynical cruelty in 1921). The protocols pretend to be a series of twenty-four lectures by the "elders" on how to gain control of the entire world and transform it into a Jewish state—by deadening the gentile mind with thought control and by infiltrating the press, financial institutions, and key government offices throughout the civilized world.

15.257 (437:22). *Ja, ich weiss, papachi* – German: "Yes, I know, father."

15.259–62 (437:24–28). (*With feeble vulture talons* . . . Abraham and Jacob – See 5.194–95n and 5.200–205n. In Exodus 3:6, God speaks to Moses: "I am the God of thy father, the God of Abraham, the God of Isaac and the God of Jacob."

15.264 (437:30). Mosenthal – See 5.194–95n.

15.270 (438:7). *Waterbury keyless watch* – An American machine-made watch manufactured in Waterbury, Connecticut. The watch with a built-in key was an American innovation in the latter half of the nineteenth century.

15.271 (438:7). *double curb Albert* – A watch chain colloquially named after Prince Albert, Queen Victoria's prince consort.

15.279 (438:17). *Goim nachez* – Yiddish: "The proud pleasure (special joy) of the Gentiles" (in scorn).

15.283–84 (438:23). *widow Twankey's crinoline and bustle* – The Widow Twankey was Aladdin's mother in popular pantomimes about Aladdin and his adventures.

15.288 (438:29). *blay* – English dialect: "blue linen."

15.289 (438:29). *an Agnus Dei* – *Agnus Dei*, Latin: "Lamb of God"; a medal bearing the image of a lamb as an emblem of Christ. See 15.235–36n. The triple prayer of the Agnus Dei is a central part of the Mass.

15.289 (438:29–30). *a shrivelled potato* – See 15.201–2n and 14.1480–81n.

15.290 (438:30). Sacred Heart of Mary – The more usual Irish Catholic invocation would be "Sacred Heart of Jesus." In invocations to Mary the emphasis is on "the Most Pure Heart of Mary"—one popular prayer addresses her: "O glorious Queen of Martyrs, whose sacred heart, in the passion of thy Son, was cruelly pierced by the sword" (Rev. Joseph P. Christopher and Very Rev. Charles E. Spence, *The Raccolta* [New York, 1943], pp. 264, 268).

15.297–302 (439:8–13). *Beside her mirage . . . eyes and raven hair* – The description of Molly echoes the description of the queen of Sheba as she appears to St. Anthony in chapter 2, "The Temptation of Love and Power," of *The Temptation of Saint Anthony* (see p. 452, n. 1). "Opulent curves" echoes a phrase from *The Sweets of Sin;* see 10.606n; and for "*mirage of datepalms,*" see "The Shade of the Palm," 11.9n.

15.306 (439:17). Mrs Marion – See 4.244n.

15.312–17 (439:24–30). *A coin gleams . . . scolding him in Moorish* – See 15.297–302n.

15.319 (440:2). *Nebrakada! Femininum* – See 10.849n.

15.330 (440:14). See the wide world – An echo from *Leah;* see 5.200–205n. This is, of course, what Bloom (as Odysseus) has been doing.

15.338–39 (440:23–24). We're a capital couple are Bloom and I; / He brightens the earth; I polish the sky – Thornton (p. 362) says this is a parody of an advertising slogan (?).

15.340 (440:25). *Sweny, the druggist* – See 5.463n.

15.340–41 (440:25–26). *in the disc of the soap sun* – In the closing paragraphs of *The Temptation of Saint Anthony:* "The dawn appears at last; and, like the uplifted curtains of a tabernacle, golden clouds, wreathing themselves into large volutes, reveal the sky. In the very middle of it, and in the disc of the sun itself, shines the face of Jesus Christ. Anthony makes the sign of the cross and resumes his prayers" (p. 170).

15.351 (441:8). *Ti trema un poco il cuore?* – Italian: "Does your heart tremble a little (beat a little faster)?" after Zerlina's "Mi trema . . ." ("My heart . . .") in Mozart's *Don Giovanni.* See 4.314n.

15.352 (441:9). *In disdain, she saunters away* – At the end of chapter 2 (see 15.297–302n), Anthony makes the sign of the cross and the queen of Sheba responds, "'So, then, you disdain me! Farewell!' She turns away weeping; then she returns. 'Are you quite sure? So lovely a woman?' She laughs, and the ape who holds the end of her robe lifts it up. 'You will repent, my fine hermit! You will groan; you will be sick of life! but I will mock at you. . . .' She goes off with her hands on her waist, skipping on one foot . . . with a spasmodic utterance which might be either a sob or a chuckle" (pp. 38–39).

15.355 (441:12). that *Voglio* – See 4.327n.

15.359–60 (440:18). There's no one in it – "In it" is a translation of "the Gaelic *Ann* . . . 'in existence'" (P. W. Joyce, *English,* p. 25).

15.362 (441:21). *Bridie Kelly* – See 14.1068n.

15.364 (441:23). Hatch street – See 14.1064n.

15.365 (441:24). *her bat shawl* – See 3.397–98n.

15.370 (442:3). the flash houses – Slang for the higher-class houses of prostitution where the women wore evening dresses, etc.

15.371 (442:4). Sixtyseven – That is, constable no. 67 of the Watch (the night police patrol).

15.375 (442:9). With all my worldly goods I thee and thou – Another fragment of Gerty's version of the Catholic marriage service; as the groom pledges the ring he says, "this gold and silver I thee give: and with all my worldly goods I thee endow." See 13.216–17n.

15.401 (443:8–9). Black refracts heat – See 4.79–80n.

15.402 (443:9–10). *Rescue of fallen women. Magdalen asylum – There were two Magdalen Asylums in Dublin in 1904. The Catholic one, under the care of the religious of Our Lady of Charity of Refuge, provided for "one hundred penitents" and was located at 104 Gloucester Street Lower. The Protestant asylum, at 8 Leeson Street Lower, advertised itself in 1904 as "the oldest Magdalen Asylum in Ireland" (established 1765) "intended only for young women who have for the first time fallen into vice." Bloom's self-designation as "secretary" would suggest he has the Protestant asylum in mind.

15.409 (443:18). Othello black brute – Bloom echoes Iago's suggestions that what attracts Desdemona to Othello is "animal," a suggestion picked up and extended by Desdemona's father, Brabantio, who claims that Desdemona has been corrupted by "magic" and "against nature."

15.410 (443:18). Eugene Stratton – See 6.184n.

15.410 (443:18–19). the bones and cornerman at the Livermore christies – Usually white entertainers in blackface. The Livermore Brothers World Renowned Court Minstrels appeared in Dublin in 1894. By that time the name "christies," after the Christy Minstrels (from c. 1843), had become a generic term for the minstrel show with its imitations of Southern Negro dialect and song. In the first part of the show, the performers were arranged in a semicircle with the white interlocutor in the middle and the blackface endmen or cornermen on the outside. The cornermen were armed with "bones" (castanets) and a tambourine. The second part, or

"olio," consisted of variety acts, not unlike vaudeville.

15.411 (443:19). Bohee brothers – Tom and Sam Bohee, another group of "christies," also appeared in Dublin in 1894. Their innovation appears to have been that they played banjos not only while they sang but also while they danced.

15.411 (443:20). Sweep – A chimney sweep, whose trade rendered him blackfaced.

15.413 (443:22). *Sambo* – See 12.1325n.

15.415–16 (443:25). *white kaffir eyes* – See 12.1552n.

15.420–23 (443:29–32). There's someone in the house . . . on the old banjo – From the nineteenth-century American popular song "I've Been Working on the Railroad": "Someone's in the kitchen with Dinah, / Someone's in the kitchen I know, / Someone's in the kitchen with Dinah, / Strummin' on the old banjo / Fee, fie, fiddlee eye oh . . . / Strummin' on the old banjo."

15.431 (444:9). ruck – In context, slang for a person who speaks and/or acts idiotically.

15.433 (444:11). a square party – A foursome (also slang for wife swapping).

15.435 (444:14). the dear gazelle – That is, the valentine quoted some lines from Thomas Moore's sentimental epic *Lalla Rookh* (1817). The lines appear in "The Fire-Worshippers," the third of the poem's four sections, and are spoken by a fair young maiden, Kanoon, to her hero-lover, Zali: "O ever thus, from childhood's hour, / I've seen my fondest hopes decay; / I never loved a tree or flow'r, / But 'twas the first to fade away. / I never nursed a dear gazelle, / To glad me with its soft black eye, / But when it came to know me well, / And love me, it was sure to die."

15.443 (444:22–23). Old Christmas night – Christmas Eve.

15.443 (444:23). Georgina Simpson's – Apart from the context, identity and significance unknown.

15.444 (444:24). the Irving Bishop game – A mind-reading (or guessing) game after Washington Irving Bishop (1847–89), an American mind reader (and performing magician) who enjoyed a brief success in the British Isles in the early 1880s before he became involved in a libel suit.

15.450–51 (445:3). *blue masonic badge* – Blue (for truth or fidelity) is the color of the first three degrees of Freemasonry. See 15.758–59n.

15.453 (445:5). Ireland, home and beauty – See 10.232, 235n.

15.455 (445:7). The dear dead days . . . old sweet song – See 4.314n.

15.457ff. (445:9ff.). teapot – A guessing game involving word substitutions; Bloom is saying, "I'm burning with curiosity," etc.

15.460 (445:13). London's teapot – See 15.172n.

15.462 (445:15). crackers – Party favors with a small explosive snapper inside.

15.465 (445:19). *an amber halfmoon* – In astrology, the sign that rules social companionship of a genial nature.

15.467 (445:21–22). The witching hour of the night – From *Hamlet;* see 6.750n.

15.469 (445:23–24). *Là ci darem la mano* – See 4.314n.

15.473 (445:29). *Voglio e non* – See 4.327n.

15.476 (446:2–3). beauty and the beast – See 13.837n.

15.487 (446:14). High jinks below stairs – "High jinks" is a parlor game in which contestants are elected by lot to perform ridiculous or obviously impossible feats. Thornton (p. 364) suggests an echo of James Townley's (1714–78) farce *High Jinks Below Stairs* (1759), but there may also be a nineteenth-century pornographic novel involved.

15.492–93 (446:21). The answer is a lemon – A "derisive reply" (Partridge, p. 477).

15.496 (446:25). *Leah* – See 5.194–95n.

15.496 (446:25–26). *Mrs Bandmann Palmer – See 5.194–95n and 5.195–96n.

15.500 (446:30–31). *Collis and Ward* – See 6.56n.

15.501 (446:31–447:1). *a skull and crossbones . . . white limewash* – "Limewash" suggests that the symbol is associated with Freemasonry. In the Scottish rites (which were observed in modified form by Irish Freemasons) a skull and crossbones, symbolic of mortality and death, were used in the Chamber of Reflection as a part of the preliminary ceremonies of initiation.

15.502 (447:1). *polonies* – Sausages made of partly cooked pork.

15.516 (447:15). Bright's! – See 11.615n.

15.518–19 (447:18–19). I am not on pleasure bent. I am in a grave predicament – Source unknown.

15.521 (447:21). deluthering – Anglicized Irish: "fawning, cringing, making up to."

15.534 (448:11). Jewman's melt – "Melt" is a dialect form of *milt*, secretion of the male reproductive glands of fishes. The low-slang application is hardly complimentary. For "Jewman," see 10.916n.

15.537 (448:14). *Saint Andrew's cross* – St. Andrew, one of the Twelve Apostles, was crucified on a cross shaped like an X. He is the patron saint of Scotland, and his X is the emblem of the highest order of Scottish knighthood.

15.541 (448:19). Fairyhouse races – Fairyhouse, fifteen miles northwest of Dublin, is the site of a popular steeplechase meeting on Easter Monday and Tuesday each year. The Irish Grand National is run at this meeting.

15.543 (448:21). Saxe tailormade – A suit or dress made from blue cloth (Saxon blue), possibly imported from Saxony.

15.544 (448:22). Leopardstown – A racetrack six miles south-southeast of Dublin; meetings on Saturdays.

15.546–47 (448:24–25). a three year old named Nevertell – An anachronism: the only Nevertell of record in the British Isles was foaled in 1910 by St. Primus or Oppressor out of Secret; Nevertell went to stud in 1912.

15.547 (448:26). Foxrock – A suburban district south of metropolitan Dublin and just east of the Leopardstown race track.

15.548 (448:26). shanderadan – Anglicized Irish for an old rickety rattle-trap of a car.

15.549–50 (448:28). Mrs Hayes – Apart from the context, identity and significance unknown.

15.557 (449:7). tammy – A fine worsted cloth, often with a glazed finish.

15.565 (449:15). Mrs Joe Gallaher's – A friend of the Joyce family; see Ellmann, p. 46n.

15.570 (449:21). Rogers – Apart from the context, identity and significance unknown.

15.570 (449:21–22). Maggot O'Reilly – "Maggot" is rare for an odd whim, caprice, or obsession; and for a person so possessed. Otherwise O'Reilly's identity and significance are unknown.

15.571 (449:23). Marcus Tertius Moses – See 10.508n. He lived at Liskeard House, Delgany, in County Wicklow, nineteen miles east-southeast of Dublin.

15.572 (449:24). Dancer Moses – Whether Dancer is a given name or a nickname is unknown; Hyman (p. 181) quotes this passage from *Ulysses*, but without comment about the daughter.

15.578 (449:30). hellsgates – That part of Tyrone Street at the intersection of Mabbot Street, so called because the "lower" whorehouses (rough and potentially violent) were concentrated there.

15.580 (450:3). gaffer – In Great Britain, the foreman of a gang of laborers, especially navvies or longshoremen.

15.584 (450:7). Cairns – Apart from the context, identity and significance unknown.

15.585 (450:8). Beaver street – Off Tyrone Street Lower.

15.586 (450:9). bucket of porter – The story of the workman or passerby who mistakes a bucket of beer at the foot of a ladder for a urinal is an old joke with many variants.

15.587 (450:10). Derwan's plasterers – A James Derwin, builder, 114 Drumcondra Terrace in Fairview, was alderman for Drumcondra ward, Dublin, in 1904.

15.589 (450:12). O jays! – Dodging the curse *O Jesus!*

15.590–91 (450:13–14). *Spattered with size and lime of their lodges* – That is, the loiterers become plasterers (masons) and their workshop or work group becomes a lodge, as in Freemasonry ("lodge" is obsolete or historical for a workshop). The size and lime are symbolic of the cement that binds Freemasons together in brotherhood.

15.596 (450:19). Glauber salts – Sodium sulfate used as a cathartic, named after the German chemist and physician Johann R. Glauber (1604–68), the discoverer of its medicinal properties.

15.604 (450:28). plodges – To "plodge" is to walk through mud or water.

15.606 (450:30–31). a shebeenkeeper – See 12.802n.

15.611 (451:4). Purdon street – Between Mabbot and Beaver streets in the red-light district.

15.611 (451:4). Shilling a bottle of stout – A legitimate pub pint would cost fourpence, one-third of a shilling.

15.620 (451:13). Portobello barracks – See 8.801–2n.

15.623 (451:17). We are the boys. Of Wexford – See 7.427–28n.

15.627 (451:21). Bennett? – For Sgt. Maj. Percy Bennett, see 10.1133–34n.

15.630–31 (451:24–25). The galling chain . . . our native land – See 7.427–28n.

15.635 (452:5). Wildgoose chase – See 3.163–64n.

15.636 (452:7). Westland row – Bloom followed Stephen and Lynch to the Westland Row station, where Stephen was given the slip by Mulligan and Haines (who apparently took the last of that night's trains south to Sandycove and the tower). Stephen and Lynch have taken a Loop Line train north to Amiens Street station, and then, with Bloom in pursuit, they have followed a circuitous route to Mrs. Cohen's.

15.638 (452:9). Malahide – See 3.243n.

15.642 (452:13). Relieving office – Bloom is punning on the Poor Relief Office, located nearby in the Custom House. Under certain rather strict conditions the office doled out money to the poor.

15.642 (452:14). cheapjacks – Dialect for traveling hawkers who offer apparent bargains by setting arbitrarily high prices and then offering to compromise.

15.642 (452:14). organs – Slang for workmen who lend money at very high rates of interest to fellow workmen.

15.645–46 (452:17–18). If I had passed . . . have been shot – Trulock, Harriss, and Richardson, Ltd., gun and rifle manufacturers and ammunition merchants, 9 Dawson Street; or Richard Trulock, gunsmith, 13 Parliament Street.

15.648 (453:20–21). Kildare street club – See 5.560–61n.

15.652 (452:26). *birdseye cigarettes* – Cigarettes made out of tobacco that has been cut with, rather than across, the fibers of the leaves.

15.655 (452:30). Sweets of sin – See 10.606n.

15.661 (453:3). *rencontres* – French: "meetings, adventures, coincidences."

15.661–62 (453:3–4). *Chacun son goût* – French: "Everyone to his own taste."

15.663 (453:5). Garryowen – See 12.120n.

15.672–73 (453:15–16). *he lets unrolled the crubeen . . . mastiff . . . gluts himself* – Reminiscent of the drugged bait the sibyl throws to the dog Cerberus in Book 6 of *The Aeneid* in order to slip Aeneas past his guard and into the Underworld.

15.677 (453:20). Bloom. Of Bloom. For Bloom. Bloom. – The Watch begin to decline Bloom's name as though it were a Latin noun: nominative, genitive (possessive), dative, accusative (where, appropriately, they stop).

15.686 (453:29). Kaw kave kankury kake – That is, "He gave Banbury cake." Cf. 8.84 (153:18–19).

15.694–95 (454:7). *Bob Doran falls silently into an area* – As Odysseus and his crew prepare to leave Circe's hall en route to Hades, Elpenor, "no mainstay in a fight nor very clever" who "fell asleep with wine" on the night before, awakes confused and falls to his death from the roof of the palace (10:153, 155; Fitzgerald, p. 194).

15.699–700 (454:12). Harold's cross bridge – (Now called Robert Emmet Bridge) over the Grand Canal, on the southern outskirts of Dublin.

15.700 (454:13). Bad french – Slang for obscene English.

15.703 (454:16). *Signor Maffei* – From *Ruby, Pride of the Ring;* see 4.346n.

15.709 (454:22). the bucking bronco Ajax – Unknown.

15.712 (454:25–26). *Leo ferox* . . . **the Libyan maneater** – Unknown.

15.713–14 (454:27–28). Fritz of Amsterdam, the thinking hyena – Unknown.

15.714 (454:28–29). the Indian sign – To have the "Indian sign" is to have the hypnotic ability to achieve ascendancy over animals or people.

15.721 (455:5). Dr. Bloom, Leopold, dental surgeon – See 12.1638n.

15.721–22 (455:6–7). *von Blum Pasha . . . half Austria. Egypt – See 17.1748n.

15.722 (455:6–7). *Donnerwetter* – German: literally, "thunderstorm"; figuratively, "Damn!"

15.728 (455:13). *cadi's dress* – In Islamic countries, a cadi is a minor magistrate or judge, usually of a small town or village.

15.729 (455:14). *the Legion of Honour* – A French order of merit founded by Napoleon in 1802 as an award for outstanding conduct in military or civilian life. The emblem of the order is a five-rayed star of white enamel edged with gold, surmounted by a wreath of oak and laurel.

15.730 (455:15–16). the Junior Army and Navy – One of the principal London clubs, located at 12 Grafton Street in London. Membership was limited to men who had served as middle-ranking officers in the military.

15.733 (455:19). No fixed abode – Legal phraseology: the charge is that Bloom may be a vagrant and therefore liable under British law to arrest and detention as a public burden or possibly as a menace to the public peace.

15.733–34 (455:19–20). Unlawfully watching and besetting – Legal phraseology: lying in wait to trap or ambush a victim.

15.740 (455:27). rose of Castile – See 7.591n.

15.741 (455:27). Virag – Hungarian: "flower."

15.745 (456:2). get your Waterloo – To suffer a serious defeat or reversal, after Napoleon's final defeat in the battle of Waterloo, 18 June 1815.

15.747 (456:4–5). inspector – Bloom is addressing a constable, not an inspector.

15.749 (456:7). THE DARK MERCURY – See 15.212–13n.

15.750 (456:8). The Castle – See 8.362n.

15.752 (456:11). *a crimson halter* – See 5.343n.

15.752 (456:11–12). *the* **Irish Times** – See 8.323n.

15.753–54 (456:13). Lionel, thou lost one! – See 7.58n and 7.59–60n.

15.758–59 (456:18–20). *plucking at his heart . . . dueguard of fellowcraft* – Bloom gives one of the Freemason's "signs of distress," a signal that makes "brothers immediately known to their brethren" so that they can claim assistance and protection. "Dueguard" of Freemasonry teaches every brother to keep watch over his words and actions, to remember his solemn obligations, and never to forget the penalty of broken vows and violated faith. "Fellowcraft" is the second degree of the first three degrees of Freemasonry; the others are (1) Apprentice and (3) Master. In context, the Masonic sign suggests an attempt to assert influence with or membership in the Anglo-Irish establishment, but in all probability the constables of the Dublin Metropolitan Police would be "good Catholics," suspicious and fearful of Freemasonry as some ultimate force of atheism and subversion.

15.760 (456:20–21). worshipful master, light of love – A Master is one who has attained the third degree of Freemasonry; as a Master Mason, he has reached the highest preferment within his lodge and has a voice in all the consultations of the officers of the lodge. For "light of love," see 9.249–50n.

15.760–61 (456:21–22). The Lyons mail. Lesurques and Dubosc – *The Lyons Mail* is the title of an English version of a French play, *The Courier of Lyons* (1850), as adapted by Charles Reade (1814–84) and popularized (from 1877) by the English actor-producer Sir Henry Irving (1838–1905). The plot hinges on a "real-life" story of "mistaken identity"; in 1796 a Frenchman Joseph Lesurques (1763–96) was accused of holding up the Lyons mail and executed for the crime. In 1800 it was revealed that the real criminal was one Dubosc, who bore a striking resemblance to Lesurques; Dubosc was subsequently apprehended and guillotined.

15.761 (456:22). the Childs fratricide case – See 6.469n.

15.763 (456:24–25). Better one guilty . . . wrongfully condemned – An inversion and exaggeration of the more usual axiom; see 6.474–75n.

15.765–66 (456:28). Peggy Griffin – Apart from the context, identity and significance unknown.

15.766–67 (456:29). the Bective rugger – The Bective Rangers was a rugby team named after the ancient parish of Bective Abbey (now a ruin fifteen miles northwest of Dublin). It played on a level comparable to that associated with semiprofessional sports in the United States and in 1904 had a history of relatively consistent success.

15.770 (457:3). ***the pass of Ephraim.*) Shitbroleeth** – In Judges 12:1–6, after Jephthah had won a victory over the Ephraimites, he stationed guards along the Jordan to prevent the escape of refugees. He gave the guards the password *shibboleth;* the Ephraimites could not pronounce the word and thus betrayed themselves and were slaughtered. In Freemasonry, in the ritual of the Fellowcraft degree (see 15.758–59n), the story of the Ephraimites is introduced and interpreted symbolically, *shibboleth* ("flood of waters") signifying the "plenty" that was denied the uninitiated Ephraimites.

15.775 (457:8). mare's nest – To "find a mare's nest" originally meant to imagine that one has made an extraordinary discovery when in fact the thing discovered is an illusion; hence, it became a phrase for finding oneself in a tangle of illusion.

15.776 (457:9). a scapegoat – In Jewish ritual, an annual "sacrifice" is made on Yom Kippur, the Day of Atonement, after Leviticus 16:21–22: "And Aaron shall lay both his hands upon the head of the live goat, and confess over him all the iniquities of the children of Israel, and all their transgressions in all their sins, putting them upon the head of the goat, and shall send him away by the hand of a fit man into the wilderness; And the goat shall bear upon him all their iniquities unto a land not inhabited: and he shall let go the goat in the wilderness." See 17.2058n and 8.752n.

15.779 (457:13). Majorgeneral Brian Tweedy – Bloom has promoted his father-in-law from sergeant major or major to the rank of another Tweedie, Maj. Gen. Willis Tweedie (b. 1836). The real-life Tweedie had a considerable reputation as an army commander in India. Cf. 18.766–67n.

15.780–81 (457:14–15). Got his majority for the heroic defence of Rorke's Drift – In January of 1879, at the beginning of the Zulu War, British troops invaded Zululand, and a force of about eight hundred was massacred by a Zulu army of over twenty thousand at Isandhlwana, 22 January. Later that same day a detachment of about four thousand troops of the Zulu army descended on the unfortified British communications post at Rorke's Drift. The post was manned by approximately 140 men, over thirty of them incapacitated. In a battle that lasted from late afternoon until almost dawn of the next day, the garrison successfully defended the outpost, and the Zulus withdrew. No Tweedy was among those present, but both of the officers in command, Lts. John Rouse Merriot Chard (1847–97) and Gonville Bromhead (1845–91), were promoted to the rank of major. The esteem in which the defenders were held is evidenced by the eleven Victoria Crosses (a record for a single, small-scale action) awarded to members of the garrison. See the English film *Zulu* (1964), directed by Cy Enfield.

15.785 (457:19). The royal Dublins – See 5.66–68n.

15.787 (457:21). The R.D.F. – The Royal Dublin Fusiliers.

15.788 (457:23). finest body of men, as physique – Minimum height for the Dublin Metropolitan Police in 1904 was five feet nine inches. The average height of Irish recruits entering British infantry regiments such as the R.D.F. in 1904 was five feet four and one-half inches.

15.791 (457:26). Up the Boers! – An anti-English slogan.

15.791 (457:26). Joe Chamberlain – See 8.423–24n.

15.793 (457:29). J.P. – Justice of the Peace.

15.795 (457:30–31). in the absentminded war under general Gough in the park – "The absentminded war" is the Boer War (1899–1902); see 9.125n. An equestrian portrait of the Irish-born General Hugh Gough (1779–1869), first Viscount Gough, stood in Phoenix Park in 1904. He distinguished himself in the Peninsular War against Napoleon (1808–14) and later in China (1841–42) and in India (1843–49). His statue was the target of frequent (and, in 1957, ultimately successful) anti-British demonstrations.

The Gough who fought in the Boer War was Sir Hubert de la Poer Gough (1870–1963), whose fame in that war was based on his daring in the relief of the key supply depot of Ladysmith (Natal), 28 February 1900, after a 118-day siege. Sir Hubert was eventually to gain some notoriety in early 1914 when, as a brigadier general stationed at the Curragh, he refused to command his troops in a police action against the violently pro-Union majority in Ulster.

15.796 (458:1). Spion Kop – A mountain in Natal, the scene of an important Boer victory over the British, 24 January 1900.

15.796 (458:1). Bloemfontein – Capital of the Orange Free State, South Africa. During the Boer War it was one of the principal centers of Boer strength. It fell to the British under Lord Frederick Roberts 13 March 1900; see 14.1331–32n.

15.797–98 (458:2–3). Jim Bludso. Hold her nozzle again the bank – From a ballad, "Jim Bludso (of the Prairie Belle)," in *Pike County Ballads and Other Pieces* (1871) by the American John Hay (1838–1905). The ballad tells the story of the heroic death of Jim Bludso, a Mississippi riverboat captain who "weren't no saint"—he had two wives in different river towns and was "A keerless man in his talk . . . / And an awkward man in a row." In lines 21–24 his "religion" is outlined: "And if ever the Prairie Belle took fire— / A thousand times he swore, / He'd hold her nozzle again the bank / Till the last soul got ashore." The *Prairie Belle* does catch fire, and Bludso is as good as his word at the price of his life.

15.813 (458:20). Bluebags – Slang for police constables (whose trousers were blue and often ill-fitting).

15.814/17 (458:21/24–25). *Mr Phillip Beaufoy/Matcham's Masterstrokes* – See 4.502–3n and 4.502n.

15.829–30 (459:6–7). the laughing witch hand in hand – See 4.513–15 (69:12–14).

15.834–35 (459:12). Mr J. B. Pinker – Joyce's literary agent in London; see Ellmann.

15.835–36 (459:13–14). the usual witnesses' fees – A cliché expression for the lowest possible pay for a respectable day's work.

15.836 (459:15). bally – Dodging the curse *bloody.*

15.837 (459:15). jackdaw of Rheims – "The Jackdaw of Rheims" is one of the verse legends in Richard Harris Barham's (1788–1845) *The Ingoldsby Legends* (1840). A jackdaw steals the cardinal's ring, admits the theft, and is canonized as "Jem Crow." "Jackdaw" is contemptuous for a talkative and foolish person.

15.840 (459:18). University of life. Bad art – The source for this cliché is not known.

15.844–45 (459:23). the hallmark of the beast – See 15.209n.

15.847–48 (459:25–26). Moses, Moses, king . . . in the *Daily News* – An obvious parody of "Moses," as recorded in Leslie Daiken, *Out Goes She; Dublin Street Rhymes* (Dublin, 1963), p. 17: "Holy Moses, King of the Jews, / Bought his wife a pair of shoes. / When the shoes began to wear, / Holy Moses began to swear. / When the shoes were quite worn out, / Holy Moses began to shout." The London-based *Daily News* was in the forefront of the "new" or yellow journalism at the beginning of the twentieth century.

15.854 (460:1). Street angel and house devil – A proverbial expression for a person who is courteous in public and boorish in his home.

15.861 (460:9). Mary Driscoll – The Blooms' maid when they lived in Ontario Terrace, Rathmines.

15.865 (460:14). of the unfortunate class – That is, a prostitute.

15.868–69 (460:18). six pounds a year and my chances – The average wage for a scullery maid at the turn of the century was four to six pounds a year, with an extra allowance for tea, sugar, and beer ("her chances").

15.878 (461:2). Play cricket – Slang: "play fair."

15.893 (461:18). *Your lord – The proper form of address to a judge in court is "My Lord"; to a member of the watch, "Constable."

15.895 (461:21). *George Fottrell – See 12.1872n.

15.898 (461:24–25). *water-lily* – In the language of flowers, symbolic of purity of heart or elegance.

15.902 (461:28–29). *the memory of the past* – See 13.438–39n.

15.903–4 (462:1). A sevenmonth's child – Popularly assumed to be at least a disadvantaged weakling, if not actually retarded.

15.910–11 (462:9). *the Loop line railway* – See 5.138n.

15.914–15 (462:13). *Dockrell's wallpaper at one and ninepence a dozen* – See 8.171n.

15.916 (462:16). *pensums* – Rare for school tasks or lessons.

15.919 (462:18). *boreens* – Anglicized Irish: "little roads or lanes."

15.920 (462:20–21). **Britanniametalbound*** – Britannia metal was an inexpensive alloy of tin, antimony, copper, and sometimes zinc used to give decorative "class" to inexpensive furniture. It could be tinted and would take a high luster.

15.931 (462:32). *A plasterer's bucket* – See 15.586n.

15.934 (462:36). Titbits – See 4.467n.

15.941 (463:7). disguised in liquor – Intoxicated.

15.941 (463:8). an Oxford rag – A hazing session (after "rag," for boisterous merrymaking).

15.942–47 (463:9–15). an infant, a poor foreign . . . land of the Pharaoh – See 3.298n.

15.951–52 (463:20). he could a tale unfold – See 8.420n.

15.954 (463:23). cobbler's weak chest – A cobbler's hunched posture at his workbench was regarded as a traditional image of the weakchested.

15.962–64 (463:33–35). Li li poo lil chile . . . Payee two shilly . . . – From song or pantomime, but specific source is unknown.

15.969 (464:4–5). The Mosaic code – See 7.755–56n.

15.975 (464:11–12). the hidden hand – See 8.458–59n.

15.978 (464:15–16). cast a stone . . . wrong turning – In John 8:3–7, the Pharisees tempt Jesus "that they might have to accuse him." They bring before him "a woman taken in adultery; and when they had set her in the midst, They said unto him, Master, this woman was taken in adultery, in the very act. Now Moses in the law commanded us, that such should be stoned: but what sayest thou? . . . he lifted up himself, and said unto them, He that is without sin among you, let him first cast a stone at her."

15.982 (464:20). Agendath Netaim – See 4.191–92n.

15.985 (464:24). A penny in the pound – Bloom promises to give his creditors a penny for each pound he owes.

15.986 (464:25). *the lake of Kinnereth* – See 4.155n.

15.991 (464:31). Bleibtreustrasse – See 4.199n.

15.995 (464:35). *John F. Taylor* – See 7.793n.

15.1000 (465:4). *avine* – Or avian: of or pertaining to birds.

15.1000 (465:4–5). *proboscidal* – Like a proboscis or pronounced nose.

15.1000–1001 (465:5). *Seymour Bushe* – See 6.470n.

15.1007 (465:12–13). Callan, Coleman – See 11.896 (280:13) and 6.158 (91:16).

15.1008 (465:13–14). Mr V. B. Dillon – Was buried 2 April 1904; see 8.159n.

15.1011 (465:17). sir Robert and lady Ball – See 8.110n.

15.1013 (465:19). Mrs Yelverton Barry – Derives her name from the Irish politician, judge, and orator Barry Yelverton (1736–1805), first Baron Avonmore.

15.1017 (465:23). prentice backhand – That is, "apprentice backhand," an obviously ineffectual attempt to disguise his handwriting.

15.1017–18 (465:24–25). North Riding of Tipperary on the Munster circuit – County Tipperary is in south-central Ireland. The Munster circuit, in southwestern Ireland, was the sequence of courts in various county locations over which a judge would preside in the course of his annual tour of duty in the provinces.

15.1018 (465:25). James Lovebirch – See 10.601–2n.

15.1019 (465:26). the gods – Slang for the upper balcony of a theater.

15.1019–20 (465:26–27). the *Theatre Royal* – See 6.184n.

15.1020 (465:27). a command performance of *La Cigale* – That is, at a performance requested by the lord lieutenant of Ireland. *La cigale* could be either a three-act comedy from the French of Henry Meilhac (1831–97) and Ludovic Halévy (1834–1908), translated and adapted for the American stage by John H. Delafield (1879), or the light opera *La cigale et la formi* (The Grasshopper and the Ant), by Henri-Alfred Duru (1829–89) and Henri Chivot, music by Edmond Andran (1840–1901), adapted into English by F. C. Burnand (1890).

15.1022 (465:30). Dunsink time – See 8.109n.

15.1023 (465:31). Monsieur Paul de Kock – See 4.358n.

15.1023–24 (465:32). *The Girl with the Three Pair of Stays* – The English title of a novel, *La femme aux trois corsets* (Paris, 1878), by Charles Paul de Kock.

15.1025 (465:33). MRS BELLINGHAM – As Adams suggests (p. 218), she probably owes her name to the fact that "on 11 June 1904 Charlotte Elizabeth, daughter of Alfred Payne and widow of Frederick Gough, was married" to Edward Bellingham (b. 1879), who subsequently became fifth baronet (second creation). In 1904 Bellingham was a lieutenant in the Royal Scots Guards.

15.1029–30 (466:3–4). sir Thornley Stoker's – Sir (William) Thornley Stoker (1845–1912), a prominent Dublin surgeon, lived at 8 Ely Place, Dublin.

15.1032 (466:7). edelweiss – German: literally, "noble-white"; an alpine perennial plant, it stands for nobility in the language of flowers.

15.1034–35 (466:9–10). blossom of the home-grown potato plant – The potato blossom stands for benevolence in the language of flowers.

15.1035 (466:10). a forcingcase – A small greenhouse or coldframe.

15.1035 (466:10). the model farm – In Glasnevin, was run by the joint enterprise of the Model Training School of the Board of Agriculture and the Botanic Gardens (founded by the Royal Dublin Society in 1790); in 1904 the gardens were under the supervision of the Royal Department of Agriculture and Technical Instruction for Ireland. Edelweiss could also be found in the Botanic Gardens not far from the Model Farm, in a small *cul-de-sac* (with greenhouse) called the "Alpine Yard."

15.1040 (466:15). Bluebeard – A legendary character who murders a succession of wives before he is finally exposed and slain. There are various late-medieval versions of the story, but final form seems to have been given to "the man with the blue beard" (c. 1697) by the French writer Charles Perrault (1628–1703).

15.1040–41 (466:16). Ikey Mo! – Ikey Moses; see 9.607n.

15.1043 (466:18). the darbies – Slang for handcuffs, from about 1660.

15.1046 (466:21). Venus in furs – The title of a novel by the Austrian Leopold von Sacher-Masoch (1836–95), *Venus im Pelz*. Severin, the masochistic hero of the novel, is described as a romantic "dreamer" who acts out his desires for total subjection to and enslavement by a woman he regards as "an Olympian deity." The heroine, Wanda, in love with Severin, reluctantly agrees to become his "cruel Northern Venus in Furs" and to accept him as her slave; gradually her imagination is "inflamed" by Severin's fantasies, and she evolves into the sadistic despot he has envisioned, humiliating him and whipping him; at the novel's end Wanda, "the lioness," meets her match in a leonine Greek lover and turns Severin over to him for his final punishment (and cure).

15.1046–49 (466:21–23). my frostbound coachman . . . wearing my livery – In *Venus in Furs* Severin, as "Gregor," Wanda's servant, delights "in serving as her coachman and footman." He also wears "her livery . . . a Cracovian costume in her colors, light-blue with red facings, and red quadrangle cap, ornamented with peacock-feathers. . . . The silver buttons bear her coat of arms" (p. 79).

15.1047 (466:22). *Palmer – Apart from the context, identity and significance unknown.

15.1049–51 (466:25–27). the armorial bearings . . . couped or – *Burke's Peerage, Baronetage and Knighthood* (London, 1949) lists the Bellingham escutcheon as arms: "argent [silver or white], 3 bugle horns, sable [black], stringed and garnished or [gold]: crest—A buck's head, couped, or."

15.1057 (467:1). THE HONOURABLE MRS. MERVYN TALBOYS – The Talboys baronetcy became extinct in 1560 when it passed into the female line.

15.1058 (467:2). hard hat – A bowler.

15.1061–62 (467:6–7). All Ireland versus the Rest of Ireland – Two all-star teams drawn from the armed forces stationed in Ireland.

15.1063 (467:8). Captain Slogger Dennehy of the Inniskillings – The "Army Directory" in *Thom's* 1904 lists no Dennehy among the officers of the 6th (Inniskilling) Dragoons, but there was a reasonably famous Anglo-Irish military

Dennehy, Major General Sir Thomas (b. 1829), who had a distinguished career in India and was made a knight commander of the Indian Empire (1896) and Extra Groom in Waiting to the king (1901). Whether he merited the nickname "Slogger" (one who hits hard) is not a matter of record.

15.1064 (467:10). Don Juan – See 4.314n.

15.1069–70 (467:16–17). He urged me to . . . officers of the garrison – In *Venus in Furs*, Severin dreams that Wanda will "have a circle of admirers . . . tread [him] underfoot and apply the lash." Wanda carries his "dreams to their realization" (pp. 70–71).

15.1086 (467:33). I love the danger – Bloom's response is similar to Severin's perverse combination of fear and pleasure in the face of Wanda's tortures in *Venus in Furs*.

15.1088 (468:2–3). I'll make you dance Jack Latten – The expression "I'll make you dance" is a stock threat of punishment, and the name "Jack Latten" intensifies the threat. P. W. Joyce (*English*, pp. 172–73) explains, "John Latten of Morristown House county Kildare . . . wagered he'd dance home to Morristown from Dublin— more than twenty miles—changing his dance step every furlong: and won the wager."

15.1100–1101 (468:16–17). You have lashed . . . nature into fury – In *Venus in Furs*, Wanda repeatedly complains that Severin has corrupted her by awakening "Dangerous potentialities that were slumbering" in her (p. 129) and transforming her into a "lionness" (p. 116).

15.1104 (468:20). Give him ginger – After the horse trader's practice of putting ginger under a dull horse's tail to make the animal look lively.

15.1109 (468:26–27). *He offers the other cheek. – Jesus, in the Sermon on the Mount, says: "Ye have heard that it hath been said, An eye for an eye, and a tooth for a tooth: But I say unto you, That ye resist not evil: but whosoever shall smite thee on thy right cheek, turn to him the other also" (Matthew 5:38–39).

15.1122 (469:12). Davy Stephens – See 7.28n.

15.1125 (469:15). Messenger of the Sacred Heart – Or the *Irish Rosary*, a devotional Catholic newspaper published monthly in Dublin.

15.1125 (469:15). Evening Telegraph – See 2.412n.

15.1128–30 (469:18–20). (The very reverend Canon . . . Hughes S.J. bend low.) – The three priests have celebrated benediction with the Blessed Sacrament (see 13.283–84n) at the temperance retreat in the course of the Nausicaa episode. For the priests, see 13.448n, 13.6–8n, and 13.283n.

15.1133–35 (469:23–25). *Cuckoo. / Cuckoo. / Cuckoo. – After the cuckoo clock in "the priest's house"; see 13.1289 (382:23–25) and 9.1025n.

15.1138 (469:28). *Jigjag. Jigajiga. Jigjag – Arabic and Mediterranean slang for copulation.

15.1143 (470:4). a Nameless One – After "The Nameless One," a poem by James Clarence Mangan. The speaker of the poem promises to "deliver" his "soul"; he asserts, "He would have taught men from wisdom's pages / The way to live," but found himself "trampled, derided, hated" instead. Thus he is "condemned . . . / To herd with demons from hell beneath." Subsequently, "with genius wasted" and full of revulsion at failures of love and friendship, he "pawned his soul for the Devil's dismal / Stock of returns." At the poem's end he repents: "He, too, had tears for all souls in trouble, / Here and in hell."

15.1145 (470:6). Weight for age – In horseracing, a weight (or handicap) apportioned to a horse according to its age.

15.1149 (470:10). tip – Slang for head.

15.1149 (470:10). Hundred shillings to five – The odds against Throwaway's winning the Gold Cup.

15.1153 (470:15). Another girl's plait cut – The loss of a girl's pigtail figuratively implies the loss of her virginity.

15.1153 (470:15–16). Jack the Ripper – The name given to an unknown London cutthroat who murdered and mutilated at least five and perhaps as many as ten prostitutes in London's East End between April and September 1888. His identity was and has continued to be the focus of considerable speculation and controversy in England. For example: The *Sunday Times* (London, 1 November 1970, p. 3, cols. 2–4) reports recent speculation that information about the killer was suppressed because he was a member of a socially prominent and powerful family and, further, that he was suffering from syphilis of the brain. The *Sunday Times* tentatively identifies this suspect as "Edward, Duke of Clarence, grandson of Queen Victoria, brother of George V, and heir to the throne of England." The Letters page of the *Sunday Times* (8 November 1970) carries a letter that specifically refutes this identification (though it does not challenge the broader assertions about social prominence and privilege), so the controversy continues.

15.1156 (470:18). And in black. A mormon. Anarchist – The Mormons did wear black; and the controversy over their belief in the practice of polygamy (from their beginnings in 1831 until the decline of the practice in the early years of the twentieth century) gave them considerable notoriety. Anarchists, though their political convictions were serious (if fanatical), were traditionally caricatured as wearing black clothes, black slouch hats, and carrying lighted black bombs.

15.1158 (470:20). no fixed abode – See 15.733n.

15.1162 (470:24). *sir Frederick Falkiner* – See 7.698–99n.

15.1164–65 (470:26–27). *From his forehead . . . Mosaic ramshorns* – Sir Frederick Falkiner appears as Michelangelo's *Moses;* see 7.756–57n. Michelangelo followed the tradition that depicted Moses as having horns. This tradition derived from a mistranslation in the Latin Vulgate of Exodus 34:29: "And it came to pass, when Moses came down from mount Sinai with the two tables of testimony in Moses' hand . . . that Moses wist not that the skin of his face shone." The Vulgate rendered "his face shone" as "his face was horned." See 7.854n.

15.1168 (471:3). *He dons the black cap.* – The ritual gesture of an English judge who is about to pronounce a death sentence.

15.1169–70 (471:5). Mountjoy prison – See 12.272n.

15.1173–74 (471:10). *The subsheriff Long John Fanning* – See 12.272n.

15.1174 (471:11). *Henry Clay* – See 10.1002n.

15.1176 (471:13–14). Who'll hang Judas Iscariot? – After Judas had betrayed Jesus, he attempted to return the money to "the chief priests and elders" and was refused. "And he cast down the pieces of silver in the temple, and departed, and went and hanged himself" (Matthew 27:3–5).

15.1177 (471:15). *H. Rumbold* – See 12.430n.

15.1182–83 (471:21–22). Hanging Harry . . . the Mersey terror – Liverpool is on the River Mersey, and the fictional Rumbold writes from Liverpool (12.415–31 [303:20–36]). The proper address to a judge is not "your Majesty" but "your Lordship."

15.1183 (471:22–23). Neck or nothing – In Swift's *Complete Collection of Genteel and Ingenious Conversation* (1738), a footman falls downstairs, and Lady Answerall responds, "Neck, or nothing. Come down, or I'll fetch you down. Well, but I hope the poor fellow has not saved the Hangman a Labour."

15.1184 (471:24). *George's church* – 1,000 yards northwest of Bella Cohen's; see 4.78n.

15.1189 (471:29). Zoo – The Zoological Gardens, in Phoenix Park not far from the main (southeastern) entrance.

15.1210 (472:21–22). Doctor Finucane – Thomas D. Finucane, licentiate of the Faculty of Physicians and Surgeons in Glasgow, apothecary and accoucheur (male midwife), 44 Main Street, Blackrock, a suburban village almost three miles southeast of Dignam's home in Sandymount.

15.1218 (473:2). Bloom, I am . . . list, O, list – After the Ghost in *Hamlet;* see 9.144n and 9.170n.

15.1220 (473:4). The voice is the voice of Esau – For "the voice of Esau," see 9.981n, and for the echo of *Leah,* see 5.200–205n.

15.222 (473:6). *Blesses himself.* – Makes the sign of the cross to defend himself against the presence of evil spirits.

15.1224 (473:8). It is not in the penny catechism – The *Shorter Catechism,* "a directory for catechising such as are of weaker capacity" (Dublin, 1886), does not mention the possibility of ghosts but does condemn "superstition" as a violation of the First Commandment and does list "spiritualism" as one of the principal forms of superstition.

15.1226 (473:10). metempsychosis – See 4.339n.

15.1230 (473:14). Mr J. H. Menton – See 6.568n.

15.1236 (473:21). *John O'Connell* – See 6.710n.

15.1237–38 (473:23). *Father Coffey* – See 6.595n.

15.1239 (473:24–25). *a staff of twisted poppies* – The staff of office of Morpheus, god of sleep; cf. 6.589n.

15.1241–42 (473:27–28). *Namine. Jacobs. Vobiscuits. Amen – Cf. 6.595n. "Jacob Vobiscuits" is Bloom-Latin for *Dominus vobiscum* (the Lord be with you). For "Jacobs," see 12.495n.

15.1247 (474:6). My master's voice! – The advertising trademark of Victrola (a phonograph) depicted a seated dog, listening at the horn of a gramophone, with the legend "His Master's Voice."

15.1249 (474:8). U.P. – See 8.258n.

15.1250 (474:9). House of Keys – See 7.141n.

15.1258–59 (474:18). Dignam's dead and gone below – After "Old Roger Is Dead," a child's singing game. The children stand in a circle and one (Old Roger) lies in the center; the circle chants, "Old Roger is dead and gone to his grave." A second child (apple tree) joins the first in the circle: "They planted an apple tree over his head. . . . The apples were ripe and ready to fall. . . . There came an old woman and picked them all up. . . . Old Roger jumped up and gave her a knock. . . . Which made the old woman go hippity hop."

15.1262 (474:22). Reuben J – See 6.264–65n.

15.1263–64 (474:24). Follow me up to Carlow – Title of a song by Dublin-born Patrick J. McCall about Feagh MacHugh O'Byrne (1544–97), a sixteenth-century hero who proved a hindrance to Queen Elizabeth's campaign for the subjugation of Ireland. He inflicted a very serious defeat on the English at Glenmalure in County Wicklow, made frequent and annoyingly successful raids into the pale, and ravaged counties Carlow and Kildare to the west of Wicklow. The chorus of McCall's song: "Curse and swear, Lord Kildare! / Feagh will do what Feagh will dare; / Now, Fitzwilliam, have a care— / Fallen is your star, low! / Up with halbert, out with sword, / On we go; for by the Lord, / Feagh McHugh has given the word: / Follow me up to Carlow!"

15.1265 (474:25). *a daredevil salmon leap* – A heroic feat performed several times by Cuchulain (see 12.176n), the first time in order to cross the "Pupil's Bridge" to the island of Scatach, the prophetess who is to teach him the arts of war: "Then he went into his warp-spasm. He stepped to the head of the bridge and gave his hero's salmon-leap onto the middle. He reached the far end of the bridge so quickly it had not time to fly up at him" (from "Before the Táin," in *The Táin*, trans. Thomas Kinsella [Dublin, 1969], p. 29).

15.1273 (475:3) Yummyumm – Plus "THE KISSES" suggest "Under the Yum Yum Tree" (1910), a popular American song by Harry Von Tilzer (1872–1946): "Under the yum yum tree, / That's the yummiest place to be, / When you take your baby by the hand / There'll be something doing down in Yum Yum land; / That is the place to play / With your honey and kiss all day, / When you're all by your lonely, / You and your only yum! yum! yummy, yummy, yum, / Under the Yum Yum tree."

15.1279 (475:10). *Zoe Higgins* – *Zoe* means "life" in Greek; and Bloom's mother's maiden name was Higgins.

15.1285 (475:16). Mrs Mack's – Mrs. Mack had two establishments, 85 and 90 Tyrone Street, and enjoyed such a reputation as a madame that the red-light district was sometimes called "Macktown."

15.1287 (475:18). eighty-one, Mrs Cohen's – Mrs. Cohen's house was at 82 (not 81) Tyrone Street. Ellmann says that Mrs. Cohen "was older than Mrs. Mack, and by 1904 had either retired or died" (p. 368).

15.1287–88 (475:19). Mother Slipperslapper – See 6.16n.

15.1302 (476:5). Mesias – See 6.831n.

15.1304 (476:7). a hard chancre – A hard, dull red, insensitive lesion—the first symptom of syphilis; cf. 15.212–13n.

15.1310 (476:13). potato – See 4.73n.

15.1323 (477:2). I never loved . . . it was sure to . . . – See 15.435n. Bloom's version of Moore's lines owes a debt to a parody by Lewis Carroll (Charles Lutwidge Dodgson, 1832–98), "Tema con Variazione," in *Rhyme? and Reason?* (London, 1883), lines 1–2, 5, 9, 13–16: "I never loved a dear Gazelle— / Nor anything that cost me much / . . . To glad me with his soft black eye / . . . But, when he came to know me well, / . . . And love me, it was sure to dye / A muddy green, or staring blue: / Whilst one might trace, with half an eye, / The still triumphant carrot through" (John A. Rea, *JJQ* 15, no. 1 [1977]: 87–88).

15.1327 (477:7). womancity – Solomon's Jerusalem, as evoked by a sensuous (rather than allegorical) reading of the biblical Song of Solomon. Cf. Blake, "Because the Lamb of God Creates himself a bride & wife / That we his Children evermore may live in Jerusalem / Which now descendeth out of heaven a City yet a Woman / Mother of myriads redeemed & born in her spiritual palaces / By a New Spiritual birth Regenerated from Death" (*The Four Zoas*, "Night the Ninth: Being the Last Judgment" [1797], p. 122, lines 16–20).

15.1333 (477:13). swinefat – In perverse contrast to the Hebrew she quotes (since Jewish law strictly prohibits pork and pork products), and also an allusion to Circe, since Circe in Book 10 of *The Odyssey* transformed the men of Odysseus's first exploratory patrol into swine.

15.1333–34 (477:14). Schorach ani wenowwach, benoith Hierushaloim – Hebrew: "I am black, but comely, O ye daughters of Jerusalem" (from the Song of Solomon 1:5).

15.1340–41 (477:21–22). a sepulchre of the gold of kings and their mouldering bones – A vision of the ancient tombs of the kings of Israel in the "city of David" (i.e., on the hill called Zion in Jerusalem). There was considerable speculation about the tombs at the beginning of this century, and the general opinion was that "the royal sepulchres were probably chambers containing separate recesses for the successive kings" (William Smith, *A Dictionary of the Bible* [Philadelphia, 1884], p. 298).

15.1347 (477:28). swaggerroot – The obvious pun on "cigarette" involves an echo of slang uses of "swagger," as in "swagger stick."

15.1355 (478:8). black gansy – A knitted woolen shirt or sweater worn instead of a jacket.

15.1356–57 (478:9–11). *Sir Walter Ralegh . . . potato and that weed – Raleigh (1552–1618) was generally credited with the introduction of the potato and tobacco from America into the British Isles after his unsuccessful attempts (1584–90) to found a colony on Roanoke Island off the Carolina coast. Raleigh's involvement in the enterprise was as sponsor rather than as participant, since Queen Elizabeth refused to let him leave England. The actual history of the introduction of the potato (regarded as cattle fodder until mid–eighteenth century) and tobacco into England and Ireland is considerably less clear than the Raleigh tradition would suggest; various English and Spanish explorers are now given prior credit.

15.1357–58 (478:11). a killer of pestilence by absorption – The potato; see 14.1480–81n.

15.1364 (478:18). Turn again, Leopold! Lord mayor of Dublin – What the bells of Bow Church said to Dick Whittington in the story "Dick Whittington and His Cat." Dick has come up to London to seek his fortune only to meet disappointment; as he leaves London, the bells call after him, "Turn again, Dick Whittington, thrice Lord Mayor of London." He turns and all goes well.

15.1366 (478:20). *in alderman's gown – The Municipal Council, the parliamentary ruling body of the Dublin Corporation, was composed of one alderman and three town councillors from each of the city's twenty wards. The council annually elected one of the aldermen to serve as lord mayor.

15.1366–68 (478:20–21). Arran Quay, Inns Quay . . . cattlemarket to the river – These five (of the Dublin Corporation's twenty) wards are in sequence from west to east along the north bank of the Liffey. Cattle from the cattle market in northwestern Dublin were driven through the streets of these wards on their way to the docks.

15.1369 (478:23). Cui bono? – Latin: "Who benefits by it?"; popularly, "Of what use is it?"

15.1369–70 (478:24–25). Vanderdeckens in their phantom ship of finance – In English versions of the legend of the Flying Dutchman, that unfortunate captain is named Vanderdecken. There are various versions of the legend, but in all the captain (for some affront to the eternal powers) is condemned to sail the seas forever in a phantom ship. In the version Wagner adopted for his opera *Der fliegenda Holländer* (1843), the condemned captain can only be saved from his eternal wandering by a woman's true love, and he is allowed on shore once every seven years to search for that woman (whom he eventually finds and loses through an irony of fate). In sailors' superstitions the sight of Vanderdecken's phantom ship is a particularly evil omen. The "of finance" links Vanderdecken with "Commodore" Cornelius Vanderbilt (1794–1877), the American financier and capitalist whose name, together with that of his heirs, became a household word for the "buccaneering" financier.

15.1373 (478:28). *the torchlight procession –* A common feature of election campaigns and victory celebrations.

15.1377–78 (479:5). *Timothy Harrington, late thrice Lord Mayor of Dublin –* Harrington (1851–1910), an Irish politician and patriot who was particularly close to Parnell in the 1880s, was lord mayor of Dublin three times (1901, 1902, 1903); see 15.1364n.

15.1379–80 (479:7). *councillor Lorcan Sherlock, locum tenens –* See 10.1011n. *Locum tenens,* Latin: "holding the place"; that is, deputy.

15.1385–86 (479:14–15). Cow Parlour off Cork street – Cork Street links Dolphin's barn (the village on the southwestern outskirts of Dublin where Bloom first met Molly) with Dublin proper. In 1904 Cow Parlour was a small lane of tenements off O'Curry Road, south of Cork Street.

15.1390 (479:19). These flying Dutchmen – See 15.1369–70n.

15.1397 (479:27–28). But their reign is . . . and ever and ev . . . – After Revelation 11:15, which forms part of the text of the Hallelujah Chorus of Handel's *Messiah* (see 8.1163–64n): "The kingdoms of this world are become the kingdoms of our Lord, and of his Christ; and he shall reign for ever and ever."

15.1398 (479:29). *Venetian masts –* Tall poles spiral-wound with multicolored ribbons, used to decorate streets on festive occasions.

15.1399 (479:30–31). Cead Mile Failte – Irish: "A Hundred Thousand Welcomes."

15.1400 (479:31). Mah Ttob Melek Israel – Hebrew: "How goodly are [thy tents] King of Israel"; after Balaam's praise of the Israelites in Numbers 24:5.

15.1402 (479:33). **the Royal Dublin Fusiliers –* See 5.66–68n. Three of the regiment's battalions were stationed in Ireland in 1904.

15.1402–3 (479:33–34). *the King's own Scottish Borderers –* Infantry. One of the regiment's battalions was stationed in Ireland in 1904.

15.1403 (479:34). *the Cameron Highlanders –* The Queen's Own Cameron Highlanders. None of the regiment's battalions was stationed in Ireland in 1904.

15.1403 (480:1). *the Welsh Fusiliers –* The Royal Welch Fusiliers. The regiment's fourth battalion was stationed in Ireland in 1904.

15.1407 (480:4–5). *The pillar of the cloud –* Guided the children of Israel as Moses led them out of Egypt toward the Promised Land; see 7.865–66n.

15.1408 (480:6). *the Kol Nidre –* Hebrew: "All our vows"; the title of a prayer that is recited (chanted to music) in synagogues on the eve of Yom Kippur, the Day of Atonement. The prayer celebrates a communal release from vows and oaths on the eve of the annual ceremony of cleansing and purification that is central to Yom Kippur.

15.1409 (480:7). *imperial eagles –* The principal of the military emblems of the Roman Empire.

15.1412 (480:10). *John Howard Parnell –* See 8.500n.

15.1413 (480:11–12). **the Athlone poursuivant and Ulster King of Arms –* The "poursuivant" was a junior officer of the College of Arms (Heralds' College, England, in charge of armorial bearings and genealogies), attached as an assistant to the Ulster king of arms, the chief official of the college in charge of Ireland and the Order of St. Patrick.

15.1414 (480:12–13). *the Right Honourable Joseph Hutchinson –* See 10.1010n.

15.1416–17 (480:15–16). *twentyeight Irish representative peers* – After Union (1801), twenty-eight of the Irish peers (who numbered ninety in 1904) were elected to sit in the House of Lords in London for life.

15.1418 (480:17). *the cloth of estate* – A rich cloth forming a canopy and background to the throne.

15.1420 (480:19). *the bishop of Down and Connor* – Church of Ireland; in 1904 the bishop was the Right Reverend Thomas James Welland (1830–1907).

15.1420–21 (480:19–20). *His Eminence Michael . . . of Armagh* – The Roman Catholic primate in Ireland, Michael, Cardinal Logue (1840–1924), the archbishop of Armagh (1887–1924), known for his guarded opposition to Parnell and his followers.

15.1422–23 (480:21–23). *His Grace, the most . . . of all Ireland* – (1824–1911), primate of the Church of Ireland (1893–1911).

15.1423 (480:23). *the chief rabbi* – The chief rabbinate for Ireland was not created until 1919.

15.1423–24 (480:23). *the presbyterian moderator* – The Reverend John MacDermott of Belfast was moderator of the general assembly of the Presbyterian church in Ireland in 1904.

15.1424 (480:24). *baptist* – The "head" of the Baptist Union of Ireland in 1904 was its president, Pastor J. Dinnin Gilmore of Dublin.

15.1424 (480:24). *anabaptist* – The sixteenth-century radical sect from which the modern Baptist church has derived.

15.1425 (480:24). *methodist* – The Reverend John Shaw Banks was president of the annual conference of the Methodist church in Ireland in 1903. The conference in 1904 was to begin on 20 June, at which time a new president was to be elected.

15.1425 (480:24). *Moravian* – The Protestant Episcopal Church of the United Brethren had eleven small congregations in Ireland; there was no "head."

15.1425–26 (480:25). *the honorary secretary of the society of friends* – The recording clerk (not the honorary secretary) of the Religious Society of Friends (the Quakers) in Ireland in 1904 was John Bewley Beale (1832–1910).

15.1426–27 (480:26). *the guilds and trades and trainbands* – These traditional groups enjoy special privileges in London, and they play a ceremonial part on occasions such as the installation of a new lord mayor or the coronation of a sovereign. In context, Bloom's installation as lord mayor has metamorphosed into a coronation procession.

15.1430 (480:30). *Italian warehousemen* – An "Italian warehouse" was an Italian grocery store.

15.1436–37 (480:37). **gentlemen of the bedchamber* – A sovereign's honorary attendants; the procession that follows is modeled on Edward VII's coronation procession.

15.1437 (480:37–38). *Black Rod* – The gentleman usher of the Black Rod, an official of the English House of Lords. His staff of office is an ebony rod surmounted by a lion. He is usher of the Garter and the personal attendant of the sovereign when the sovereign is present in the House of Lords.

15.1437 (480:38). *Deputy Garter* – Garter king of arms, the executive officer of the sovereign for the Order of the Garter, hence the sovereign's deputy since the sovereign is the grand master of the order.

15.1437 (480:38). *Gold Stick* – See 12.1515–16n.

15.1437–38 (480:38). *the master of horse* – An officer of the royal court responsible for the sovereign's horses. He rides next to the sovereign on all state occasions.

15.1438 (408:38–39). *the lord great chamberlain* – In England, a hereditary office formerly of great importance. He governs the palace at Westminster and has charge of the House of Lords during the sitting of Parliament.

15.1438 (480:39). *the earl marshal* – President of the English College of Heralds and the judge of courts of chivalry presiding over questions of honor and arms. Formerly judge of all courts martial, his office is now largely an obsolete decoration.

15.1438–39 (480:39–40). *the high constable carrying the sword of state* – The lord high constable of England was in effect the commander in chief of the army and navy and therefore the sovereign's "sword." The office was abolished by Henry VIII.

15.1439 (480:40). *saint Stephen's iron crown* – One of the central symbols of Hungarian sovereignty, presented by Pope Sylvester II (pope 999–1003) in 1000 to the first king of Hungary, Stephen I (c. 975–1038). The crown conferred the title of Apostolic Majesty on Stephen, who was to become the patron saint of Hungary. St. Stephen's crown here is substituted for St. Edward's crown, the comparable crown used in the English coronation procession.

15.1440 (480:40–41). *the chalice and bible* – Symbolic of the English sovereign's title Defender of the Faith and of that phase of the coronation oath in which the sovereign swears to uphold "the laws of God, the true profession of the Gospel, and the Protestant Reformed religion as it is established by law."

15.1443 (481:3). *Saint Edward's staff* – A silver gilt wand carried before the sovereign and symbolic of the justice and equity that were to be expected of the royal jurisprudence. The wand is supposed to recall the character of Edward the Confessor (St. Edward), king of England (1042–66).

15.1443–44 (481:4). *the orb and sceptre with the dove* – These important parts of the English royal regalia symbolize the fullness of the sovereign's power under God (since the orb is surmounted by a cross) and the peace that is the ideal use of that power (since the sceptre is surmounted by a cross and decorated with the image of a dove).

15.1444 (481:4). *the curtana* – A pointless sword, "the sword of Edward the Confessor," a symbol of mercy, carried before the English sovereign at his coronation.

15.1448–49 (481:9–10). *hawthorn and wrenbushes* – Hawthorn is a typical hedge plant; a wrenbush is a bunch of holly or gorse trimmed with ribbons, supposedly hiding the body of a dead wren. On St. Stephen's day, 26 December, Irish children go from door to door with wrenbushes, chanting, "Give us a penny to bury the wren": the wren, bird of the old year, is to be displaced in favor of the (English) robin, bird of the new.

15.1451–54 (481:12–15). **The wren, the wren . . . caught in the furze** – Part of a typical wrenbushers chant. (The wren became the "king of all birds" by secretly hitching a ride on the back of an eagle.)

15.1467 (482:1). **BELLHANGER** – One whose craft is the installation and maintenance of bells. It is a difficult craft, and its exponents are highly regarded in England, where bell ringing has evolved into an intricate national art.

15.1469 (482:3). *A sunburst appears in the northwest* – Emblematic of Home Rule; see 4.101–3n.

15.1470 (482:4). **THE BISHOP OF DOWN AND CONNOR** – See 15.1420n. At his coronation the English sovereign is attended by two "supporter bishops."

15.1477 (482:11). *dalmatic and purple mantle* – Garments worn by an English sovereign at his coronation.

15.1479 (482:13). **WILLIAM, ARCHBISHOP OF ARMAGH** – See 15.1422–23n.

15.1480–82 (482:14–16). **Will you to your power . . . thereunto belonging?** – Combines two parts of the oath the English sovereign takes at his coronation with, of course, the substitution of "Ireland" for "England." The oath of 1911 reads: "Will you solemnly promise and swear to govern the people of this United Kingdom of Great Britain and Ireland and the Dominions thereto belonging, according to the Statutes in Parliament agreed on and the respective Laws and Customs of the same?"
"I solemnly promise so to do."
"Will you to your power cause Law and Justice, in Mercy, to be executed in all your judgments?"
"I will."

15.1484 (482:18). **placing his right hand on his testicles, swears* – A form of oath-taking (signifying the sacred nature of man's reproductive capacities) recorded in Genesis 24:2–3: "And Abraham said unto his eldest servant of his house, that ruled over all that he had, Put, I pray thee, thy hand under my thigh: And I will make thee swear by the Lord, the God of heaven, and the God of the earth." Samuel Beckett (*Molloy* [New York, 1965], p. 167) cites it as Irish: "What is one to think of the Irish oath sworn by natives with the right hand on the relics of the saints and the left on the virile member?"

15.1484–85 (482:18–19). So may the Creator . . . promise to do – In answer to the final series of questions (about upholding religion) in the coronation oath, the sovereign says, "All this I promise to do."

15.1486 (482:20). MICHAEL, ARCHBISHOP OF ARMAGH – See 15.1420–21n.

15.1487 (482:21). *pours a cruse of hairoil over Bloom's head – In the coronation ceremony, after the coronation oath, the sovereign is anointed with holy oil to signify that his person is set apart and sanctified.

15.1487–88 (482:21–22). Gaudium magnum annuntio vobis. Habemus carneficem – Latin: "A great joy I announce to you. We have an executioner"; after the formula used to announce a new pope to the people of Rome: *Habemus pontificem* (We have a pope).

15.1490 (482:24). a mantle of cloth of gold – Several symbolic ceremonies follow the "solemn anointing" in the coronation ceremony, before the crown is placed on the sovereign's head. One of them involves investing the sovereign with the imperial mantle.

15.1490 (482:25). a ruby ring – The coronation ring of Scotland, bestowed on the sovereign in the sequence of ceremonies that immediately precede his being crowned.

15.1491 (482:25). the stone of destiny – Or the Stone of Scone, the coronation stone; traditionally it is under the coronation chair, in which the sovereign is seated when he is crowned by the archbishop.

15.1491–92 (482:26–27). The representative peers . . . their twentyeight crowns – See 15.1416–17n. After the king is crowned, the peers resume their coronets or caps.

15.1492 (482:27). Joybells – See 10.156n; when the king is crowned, the news is signaled from Westminster Abbey and broadcast by artillery salutes and churchbells.

15.1493 (482:27–28). Christ church, Saint Patrick's – Dublin's two great medieval cathedrals, now Church of Ireland.

15.1493 (482:28). George's – See 4.78n.

15.1493 (482:28). gay Malahide – See 10.156n.

15.1494 (482:28). Mirus bazaar – See 8.1162n.

15.1495 (482:30). The peers do homage – The next phase of the coronation ceremony after the king is crowned. The representative peers approach the sovereign in turn, genuflecting and repeating the Oath of Fealty.

15.1498 (483:2–3). I do become . . . to earthly worship – The opening sentence of the traditional Oath of Fealty.

15.1499–1500 (483:4–5). the Koh-i-Noor diamond – Persian: "Mountain of Light"; one of the largest known diamonds, it was added to the English crown jewels in 1894 through the conquest of the Punjab. At 102 carats, the stone would make something more than a modest ring.

15.1500 (483:5). palfrey – Usually defined as a small saddle horse for women (after Spenser), it can also mean a horse for state occasions, as distinguished from a warhorse (after Chaucer).

15.1500–1501 (483:6). Wireless intercontinental and interplanetary transmitters – By 1906 Marconi's "wireless telegraph" (radio) was capable of occasional transmission across the Atlantic, but dependable commercial transmission was limited to about 1,700 miles.

15.1504–5 (483:9–10). nominate our faithful . . . hereditary Grand Vizier – Bloom's "action" recalls an aberration of the Roman Emperor Caligula (12–41 A.D., emperor 37–41), who made his favorite horse, Incitatus ("swift one"), a member of the college of priests of his (Caligula's) cult and later a consul. *Copula felix,* Latin: "the fortunate bond or tie (of love)." The Grand Vizier was the chief officer of state of the Turkish Empire. Cf. Thornton, p. 376.

15.1507 (483:12). Selene – In Greek mythology, the sister of the sun-god Helios, she was the moon-goddess who illumined the night with her silver crown. Her image is subsumed in that of the Greek Artemis and the Roman Diana.

15.1517–18 (483:22–23). the promised land of our common ancestors – Combines the Promised Land of the Israelites with Ireland as "promised land"; see 12.1241n and 7.873n.

15.1520 (483:25). *The keys of Dublin, crossed* – See 7.141n and 7.142n.

15.1521 (483:26–27). *he is wearing green socks* – The joke is that Parnell, a profoundly superstitious man, was convinced that the color green was unlucky for him. His aversion to "Ireland's color" was a source of frequent embarrassment to him and his associates.

15.1525–26 (484:2–3). On this day twenty . . . enemy at Ladysmith – The relief of Ladysmith in the Boer War took place on 28 February 1900; see 15.795n. If we are to take Bloom's "twenty years" seriously, the major war news of 1884 was the siege of Khartoum, where the English general Charles George Gordon (1833–85) found his position under increasing pressure in the course of the year. Gordon's communications with the outside world were virtually suspended after April 1884, though two messages from him did come through in June 1884, asking the whereabouts of the relief expedition (which did not leave Cairo until 5 October and which was two days' march from Khartoum when that city fell in a massacre on 26 January 1885). The "hereditary enemy" (a traditional phrase for Moslems or Turks) in that case was the Mahdi, a Moslem coalition of religious fanatics and slave traders whose leader had taken the name Mahdi (the messenger of Allah who is supposed to complete Mohammed's work by converting or exterminating all remaining infidels). In 1881 the Mahdi proclaimed the jihad (the holy war of extermination) in the Sudan. After the fall of Khartoum, the English in effect abandoned the Sudan until Kitchener's successful reconquest of the area in 1898. And so back to Ladysmith, since Kitchener was chief of staff (1900) and subsequently the commander in chief of British forces during the Boer War (December 1900–1902).

15.1527 (484:4). Half a league onward! –From the opening lines of Tennyson's "The Charge of the Light Brigade" (1854), which memorializes the wrongheaded heroism of the Light Brigade's disastrous charge against entrenched Russian artillery at Balaclava (25 October 1854) during the Crimean War. The poem begins: "Half a league, half a league / Half a league onward, / All in the valley of Death / Rode the six hundred."

15.1527 (484:5). All is lost now! – See 11.22n.

15.1529 (484:7). Plevna – See 4.63n.

15.1530 (484:8). *Bonafide Sabaoth* – In addition to the standard meaning of *bona fide*, see 14.1440n. *Sabaoth* is the Greek form of the Hebrew word *tsebaoth* (armies); it occurs in Romans 9:29 and James 5:4. The phrase implied is *Yahweh-tsebaoth* (Lord God of Hosts), the spirit of God that guided his "chosen people" in battle.

15.1531 (484:9). CHAPEL – Guild or union; see 7.195n.

15.1534 (484:12). the man that got away James Stephens – See 12.881n and 3.241n.

15.1535 (484:13). A BLUECOAT SCHOOLBOY – See 8.1153n.

15.1542–43 (484:21). verily it is even now at hand – In the Gospels, Jesus repeatedly says, "Verily I say unto you," and less often, "The kingdom of heaven is at hand."

15.1544 (484:22). the golden city – After the hymn "Jerusalem the Golden," words by Bernard of Cluny (c. 1122–56), translated by John Mason Neale (1818–66), music by Alexander Ewing. First stanza: "Jerusalem the golden, / With milk and honey blest. / Beneath thy contemplation / Sink heart and voice oppressed. / I know not, O I know not / What joys await us there; / What radiance of glory, / What bliss beyond compare."

15.1544 (484:23). the new Bloomusalem – See 12.1473n.

15.1544–45 (484:23). Nova Hibernia – Latin: "New Ireland."

15.1546–47 (484:24–25). *Thirtytwo workmen . . . the counties of Ireland* – As Arthur Griffith recounts in *The Resurrection of Hungary* (see 12.1636n), in celebration of Hungary's achievement of qualified independence, the emperor Francis Joseph was cheered by "fifty-two working men from all the counties of Hungary."

15.1547 (484:25). *Derwan the builder* – See 15.587n.

15.1548 (484:26–27). (484:27). *with crystal roof* – See 12.87n.

15.1557 (485:7). *Morituri te salutant* – Latin: "They [who are] about to die salute thee"; the formula with which gladiators saluted the Roman emperor at the start of the gladiatorial games.

15.1561–62 (485:11–12). Leopold M'Intosh, the notorious fireraiser – Patrick J. McCall, in his account of the district around St. Patrick's Cathedral in Dublin, tells the story of a "Scotchman" named John M'Intosh who made gunpowder and kept a secret arsenal for Robert Emmet (see 6.977–78n) and who was taken by Major Sirr (see 10.785–86n) when the location of his powder manufactory was revealed by an accidental explosion. M'Intosh also led Sirr to a secret rebel arsenal and, as a reward for his information, was executed in front of his own house by the forces of the Crown (Fritz Senn, *JJQ* 19, no. 2 [1982]: 172). "Fireraiser" is a Scots term meaning an arsonist.

15.1562 (485:12). Higgins – Bloom's mother's maiden name was Ellen Higgins; Bloom is "talking" to Zoe Higgins. See also 7.348n.

15.1565–66 (485:16). with his sceptre strikes down poppies – Tarquinius Superbus (d. 495 B.C.), the last of the semilegendary tyrant-kings of Rome, was supposed to have prefigured the tyrannical nature of his reign when, as a child, he beheaded poppies with a toy sceptre.

15.1569 (485:19). Maundy money – Silver coins, worth 1d., 2d., 3d., and 4d., were annually distributed as alms to the poor on behalf of the English sovereign on Maundy Thursday (the day before Good Friday) in commemoration of the ancient but obsolete custom of washing the feet of the poor on this day (as Jesus washed his disciples' feet [John 13:5], counseled them to do likewise for one another [13:14], and commanded them "that ye love one another" [13:34]).

15.1569 (485:20). commemoration medals – Were traditionally struck and distributed on English state occasions such as coronations (or Queen Victoria's Jubilee, 1897).

15.1569 (485:20). loaves and fishes – See 14.720n; see also "Jubilee Mutton," 14.1547n.

15.1570 (485:21). Henry Clay cigars – See 10.1002n.

15.1571 (485:22). rubber preservatives – Contraceptive devices.

15.1573 (485:24–25). toad in the hole – A dish of meat baked or fried in batter.

15.1574 (485:25). Jeyes' fluid – A disinfectant for drains and sewers manufactured by Jeyes Sanitary Compounds Co., Ltd., London.

15.1574 (485:25). purchase stamps – Or trading stamps, issued by a merchant to be used instead of money when purchasing items from him.

15.1574 (485:25–26). 40 days' indulgences – In the Roman Catholic church, the remission of temporal punishment after the sinner's guilt has been confessed and forgiven. A forty days' indulgence remits as much temporal punishment as would be remitted by performing the ancient canonical penances for forty days. An indulgence diminishes the purgatorial penance due for a sin.

15.1576–77 (485:28). the royal and privileged Hungarian lottery – See 8.184–85n.

15.1577 (485:28–29). penny dinner counters – Tokens that entitled the bearer to a free dinner; see 8.237–38n.

15.1577–78 (485:29–30). the World's Twelve Worst Books – The books listed in the following lines may well be fictional, since only one of them (mercifully) appears in standard book catalogues.

15.1578 (485:30). Froggy and Fritz – Unknown.

15.1578 (485:30). Care of the Baby – J. P. Crozer Griffith (1856–1941), *The Care of the Baby: A Manual for Mothers and Nurses Containing Practical Directions for the Management of Infancy and Childhood in Health and in Disease*, 2d ed., rev. (Philadelphia, 1898).

15.1579 (485:31). 50 Meals for 7/6 – Unknown.

15.1579 (485:31). Was Jesus a Sun Myth? – Apparently fictional, but not entirely improbable. The sun is a traditional image of Christ (see 15.2118n), and interest in the sun-myth speculation could be supported by pointing to the coincidence of major Christian feasts with seasons of the sun: Christmas with the winter solstice; Easter with the vernal equinox; and by suggesting mythic parallels between Jesus and the Greek and Egyptian sun-gods, Apollo and Ra (suggested by Joan Keenan).

15.1580 (485:32). *Expel that Pain* – Unknown.

15.1580–81 (485:32–33). *Infant's Compendium of the Universe* – Unknown.

15.1581 (485:33). *Let's All Chortle* – Unknown.

15.1581–82 (485:33–34). *Canvasser's Vade Mecum* – Unknown.

15.1582 (485:34–35). *Love Letters of Mother Assistant* – Unknown, but a not-improbable contribution to anti-Catholic Victorian soft pornography.

15.1582–83 (485:35). *Who's Who in Space* – Unknown.

15.1583 (485:35–486:1). *Songs that Reached Our Heart* – Unknown.

15.1584 (486:1). *Pennywise's Way to Wealth* – Unknown, but with the comic inversion of the proverb: Penny-wise is pound-foolish.

15.1585 (486:2–3). *Women press forward . . . of Bloom's robe* – "And, behold, a woman, which was diseased with an issue of blood twelve years, came behind him [Jesus], and touched the hem of his garment: For she said within herself, If I may but touch his garment, I shall be whole. But Jesus turned about, and when he saw her, he said, Daughter, be of good comfort; thy faith hath made thee whole. And the woman was made whole from that hour" (Matthew 9:20–22).

15.1586 (486:3–4). *The lady Gwendolen Dubedat* – See 8.889n.

15.1588 (486:6–7). *Babes and sucklings* – "Out of the mouths of babes and sucklings hast thou ordained strength because of thine enemies, that thou mightest still the enemy and the avenger" (Psalms 8:2). In Matthew 21:15–16, Jesus quotes this passage in reproof of "the chief priests and scribes" who object to "the children crying in the temple, and saying, Hosanna to the son of David."

15.1591 (486:9). *Little father!* – A traditional Russian peasant epithet for the czar.

15.1593–94 (486:11–12). *Clap clap hands . . . for Leo alone* – A variant on a nursery rhyme: "Clap hands, clap hands / Till father comes home; / With his pockets full of plums / And a cake for Johnny."

15.1600 (486:18). *My more than Brother!* – Echoes Tennyson's *In Memoriam* (1850) 10:16–20: "My friend, the brother of my love; // My Arthur, whom I shall not see / Till all my widow'd race be run; / Dear as the mother to the son, / More than my brothers are to me."

15.1602 (486:20). *pussy fourcorners* – Or "Puss in the Corner," a children's game in which four children occupy the corners of a square; the fifth ("puss") attempts to secure a corner when the others change places.

15.1602 (486:21). *Peep! Bopeep!* – What an adult says when he plays with a baby by alternately hiding his face in his hands and then revealing it. Bopeep also figures in nursery rhyme: "Little Bo-Peep has lost her sheep, / And can't tell where to find them; / Leave them alone, and they'll come home, / Wagging their tails behind them."

15.1603 (486:22). *Ticktacktwo wouldyouseetashoe?* – From *Mother Goose's Melody* by Isaiah Thomas (Worcester, Mass., c. 1785), p. 31: "Is John Smith within? / Yes, that he is. / Can he set a shoe? / Aye, marry two. / Here a nail, and there a nail, / Tick, tack, too."

15.1605 (486:24). *Roygbiv* – See 5.42–43n.

15.1605 (486:24). *32 feet per second* – See 5.44n.

15.1606 (486:25). *Absence makes the heart grow younger* – After the proverb: "Absence makes the heart grow fonder."

15.1609 (486:28). **U.p: up* – See 8.258n.

15.1611 (486:31). *Maurice Butterly* – See 1.527n.

15.1619 (487:4). *The ram's horns . . . standard of Zion* – The *shofar,* made of ram's horns, was the battle trumpet of the ancient Israelites; it was also used by the priests to signal various religious festivals. It is associated with the Ark of the Covenant (Joshua 6:4) and with the Standard of Zion (the emblem of the Israelites as a chosen people) (Jeremiah 4:21). The *shofar* is still used in synagogues to proclaim such religious festivals as Yom Kippur and Rosh Hashanah (the Jewish New Year).

15.1623 (487:8). Aleph Beth Ghimel Daleth – The first four letters of the Hebrew alphabet (arithmetic values: 1, 2, 3, 4).

15.1623 (487:8). Hagadah – See 7.206n.

15.1623 (487:8–9). Tephilim – See 13.1157–58n.

15.1623–24 (487:9). Yom Kippur – See 8.35–36n.

15.1624 (487:9). Hanukah – The Feast of Dedication, instituted in 165 B.C. by Judas Maccabaeus to commemorate the dedication of the new altar of the Temple of Jerusalem set up to replace the altar that had been polluted by Antiochus Epiphanes. Hanukkah is celebrated for eight days because of the miracle that sustained the one-day supply of lamp oil for eight days. It occurs in December.

15.1624 (487:9). Roschaschana – Or Rosh Hashanah, the Jewish New Year, celebrated for two days at the beginning of the month of Tishri (September–October).

15.1624 (487:9). Beni Brith – Or B'nai B'rith (Hebrew: "Sons of the Covenant"), a Jewish fraternity founded in New York City in 1843. It admitted members without qualifications about dogma and ceremonial custom. By 1904 its international membership made it the most popular and most powerful Jewish fraternity.

15.1624 (487:10). Bar Mitzvah – Hebrew: "Son of Command"; the ceremony that celebrates a thirteen-year-old Jewish youth's coming of age.

15.1624 (487:10). Mazzoth – Hebrew: "unleavened"; unleavened bread, the eating of which is an important part of the celebration of the Feast of Passover.

15.1625 (487:10). Askenazim – After Ashkenaz, a biblical figure and great-grandson of Noah (Genesis 10:3), and after Ashchenaz, a kingdom allied with Israel against Babylon (Jeremiah 51:27). Ashkenaz became the medieval rabbinical name for Germany and eventually the name for the Jews of middle and northern Europe, as opposed to the Sephardim, the Jews of Spain and Portugal.

15.1625 (487:10). Meshuggah – See 8.314n.

15.1625 (487:10). Talith – A fringed shawl worn by Jewish men during morning prayer.

15.1626–27 (487:11–12). *Jimmy Henry, assistant town clerk* – See 10.982n.

15.1629 (487:14). The Court of Conscience – That is, the court of chancery (since descriptive of its original functions); also the court of requests, small local debt courts that fell into disuse toward the end of the nineteenth century.

15.1640 (487:26). Can I raise a mortgage on my fire insurance? – The answer in English law is No.

15.1642–43 (488:2–4). by the law of torts . . . sum of five pounds – What this legal tangle means is that Bloom lends them money without security other than their pledge to repay.

15.1645 (488:6). A Daniel did I say? – In Shakespeare's *The Merchant of Venice* (IV.i), Portia, disguised as her servant Balthasar, intervenes in the legal controversy between Antonio and Shylock. The shrewdness of her "judgments" leads first Shylock (line 223) and then Antonio's friend Gratiano (lines 333, 340) to call her a "Daniel": "A Daniel still say I, a second Daniel!" after the young "judge" Daniel in the History of Susanna in the Apocrypha. Daniel defends Susanna when the two elders whose advances she has refused try to revenge themselves by accusing her of adultery. Daniel questions them separately and develops conflicts in their testimony so that they are condemned and Susanna is exonerated.

15.1645 (488:6). A Peter O'Brien – Noted as an extraordinarily perceptive judge but not popular with the Irish; see 12.190n.

15.1651–54 (488:12–15). *Acid. nit. hydrochlor . . . ter in die* – *Acid. nit. hydrochlor dil*, 20 minims: dilute nitric and hydrochloric acid, twenty drops; *Tinct. mix vom.*, 4 minims: bitters, four drops; *Extr. taraxel. lig.*, 30 minims: extract of dandelion; *Aq. dis. ter in die.*, a solution that might possibly be used for the prevention of stomach disorders, if taken three times a day (*ter in die*). *Aq. dis.* is distilled water.

15.1655 (488:16). CHRIS CALLINAN – See 7.690–91n.

15.1656 (488:17). What is the parallax of the subsolar ecliptic of Aldebaran? – "Subsolar ecliptic" is a phrase no longer in use in astronomy. Callinan's question in effect means, "What is the angle between a line from the center of the earth to Aldebaran and a line from the center of the sun to Aldebaran?" See 14.1108–9n and 8.110n.

15.1658 (488:19). K. 11. – The correct answer to Callinan's question would have been 0.048 seconds of arc. Bloom's answer apparently owes a debt of improvisation to Kino's floating advertisement (8.90–92 [153:25–27]). But the *K* is also strangely relevant; in the Harvard system of classification of stars by temperature (1890), *K* would correctly identify Aldebaran as a somewhat cooler than average star.

15.1662–63 (488:23–24). When my progenitor . . . despot in a dark prison – If the uniform was a prison uniform, then the identity of this "progenitor" is unknown. If military uniform, cf. 17.869n.

15.1665 (488:26). Pansies? – For "thoughts," in the language of flowers.

15.1671 (489:6). Father . . . starts thinking – After the superstition that the birth of twins implies two fathers instead of one.

15.1673 (489:8). *An eightday licence – Publicans were licensed to sell alcoholic beverages six or seven days a week during rigidly specified hours; in effect, O'Rourke asks Bloom to declare an eight-day week.

15.1683 (489:19). our own house of keys – See 7.141n and 7.142n.

15.1685–86 (489:21–22). the plain ten commandments – See Exodus 20:3–17 and Deuteronomy 5:7–21.

15.1687 (489:23). Three acres and a cow – This phrase became the rallying cry for Irish land reform after its use by Jesse Collings (1831–1920), a member of Parliament, who coined the phrase in a successful effort to force a measure of land reform on Lord Salisbury's conservative and reluctant government in 1886.

15.1691 (490:1). esperanto – This relatively popular proposal for an international language was invented by L. L. Zamenhof, a physician in Warsaw, Poland, who signed his first publication on the subject (1887) "Dr. Esperanto" (Hopeful).

15.1701 (490:11). mixed bathing – Highly suspect and controversial in 1904.

15.1703–4 (490:13–14). *the Kildare street museum* – That is, the National Museum; see 8.921–22n.

15.1705 (490:15). *Venus Callipyge* – See 9.616n.

15.1705 (490:16). *Venus Pandemos* – See 14.1494n.

15.1706 (490:16). *Venus metempsychosis* – See 4.339n.

15.1707 (490:17). *the new nine muses* – (Expanded to twelve); in Greek mythology the nine muses were Calliope (epic poetry), Clio (history), Erato (erotic poetry), Euterpe (lyric poetry), Melpomene (tragedy), Polyhymnia (sacred song), Terpsichore (dance), Thalia (comedy and pastoral poetry), and Urania (astronomy).

15.1708 (490:19). *Plural Voting* – The right to cast more than one vote (or, in England, to vote in more than one constituency); the goal of plural voting was a form of proportional representation.

15.1711 (490:22). FATHER FARLEY – See 5.332–333n.

15.1712 (490:23). an anythingarian – That is, one who holds no particular creed or dogma.

15.1714 (490:25). MRS RIORDAN – See 6.378n.

15.1716 (490:27). MOTHER GROGAN – See 1.357n.

15.1720 (491:2). One of the old sweet songs – See 4.314n.

15.1723–25 (491:5–7). I vowed that . . . tooraloom, tooraloom – See 5.13–16n.

15.1726 (491:8). HOPPY HOLOHAN – See 5.96n.

15.1729 (491:11). Stage Irishman! – An Irishman who degrades himself by acting the clown because the Irish are popularly expected to be that way.

15.1731 (491:13–14). The Rows of Casteele – See 7.471–72n.

15.1748 (492:6). *Nelson's Pillar* – See 6.293n.

15.1752 (492:11). ALEXANDER J DOWIE – See 8.13n.

15.1755 (492:14–15). this stinking goat of Mendes – One of three sacred animals in Egyptian mythology; the others were Apis at Memphis (a bull regarded as a manifestation of that aspect of Osiris that rendered him immortal in the world of the dead) and Mnevis at Heliopolis (a bull as a manifestation of Ra, the sun-god). The goat whose cult was at Mendes in the Nile delta was held to be a manifestation of the generative forces that were another aspect of Osiris' divinity. The rites of the goat cult reportedly involved copulation between the sacred goat and women selected as outstandingly beautiful.

15.1756 (492:16). the cities of the plain – See 4.221–22n.

15.1757–58 (492:17–18). the white bull mentioned in the Apocalypse – There is no white bull in the Revelation of St. John the Divine, the best known Christian Apocalypse. In various mythologies a white bull occurs as a manifestation of a deity (Osiris, Egyptian; Zeus, Greek; Baal, Babylonian). Dowie may be making an inept attempt to identify Bloom with the "beast coming up out of the earth" in Revelation 13:11: "and he had two horns like a lamb, and he spake as a dragon." See 15.209n. Dowie may, however, be making a mistaken reference to one of the four mystic beasts (the four Evangelists) in Revelation 4:6ff.: "the second beast like a calf" is traditionally represented as a white bull-calf and read as the symbolic representation of Luke.

15.1758 (492:18–19). the Scarlet Woman – An opprobrious Protestant term for the Roman Catholic church, derived from "the woman arrayed in purple and scarlet colour" in Revelation 17:4. She is riding "upon a scarlet-coloured beast" (17:3), which Protestants identify as the beast of Revelation 13:11 (see 15.1757–58n): "And upon her forehead was a name written, MYSTERY, BABYLON THE GREAT, THE MOTHER OF HARLOTS AND ABOMINATIONS OF THE EARTH" (17:5).

15.1760 (492:20). Caliban – See 1.143n.

15.1762 (492:22). Parnell . . . Mr. Fox! – In his clandestine correspondence with Kitty O'Shea, Parnell used several assumed names, among them Fox and Stewart.

15.1763 (492:23). *Mother Grogan* – See 1.357n.

15.1764 (492:24). *upper and lower Dorset street* – Where Bloom had shopped for his pork kidney in the morning.

15.1765 (492:25–26). *condensed milk tins* – At the end of the last century producers of condensed milk in the British Isles stripped the milk of most of its fats and nutritive solids before it was condensed. The resulting malnutrition, particularly among the children of the poor, caused a scandal that led to legislation of regulatory standards (1901).

15.1768 (492:29). This is midsummer madness – In Shakespeare's *Twelfth Night*, Olivia comments on Malvolio's transformation from her "sad and civil" servant to her ludicrous and ardent lover: "Why, this is very midsummer madness" (III.iv.61).

15.1769 (492:30). guiltless as the unsunned snow – In Shakespeare's *Cymbeline*, Posthumus, duped by Iachimo, contemplates what he takes to be his wife Imogen's corruption and guilt: "I thought her / As chaste as unsunned snow" (II.v.12–13).

15.1770 (492:31–32). number 2 Dolphin's Barn – Occupied in 1904 by one Daniel Whelan, victualler.

15.1770 (492:32). Slander, the viper – In Shakespeare's *Cymbeline*, Posthumus sends a letter to his servant, Pisanio, commanding him to murder Imogen; Pisanio instead shows her the letter and contemplates her shock: "What shall I need to draw my sword? The paper / Hath cut her throat already. No, 'tis slander, / Whose edge is sharper than the sword, whose tongue / Outvenoms all the worms [serpents] of Nile . . . nay the secrets of the grave / This viperous slander enters" (III.iv.34–41).

15.1771–72 (492:33). *sgeul im barr bata coisde gan capall* – Garbled Irish for a phrase meaning: "A tale in the top of a stick [a pointless tale] is a horseless coach." See Brendan O Hehir, *A Gaelic Lexicon for "Finnegans Wake," and Glossary for Joyce's Other Works* (Berkeley, Calif., 1967), p. 350.

15.1776 (493:5–6). Dr Eustace's private asylum – Dr. Henry Eustace, 41 Grafton Street, maintained a private lunatic asylum for gentlemen and ladies in Glasnevin, north of Dublin.

15.1780–81 (493:10–11). prematurely bald from selfabuse – The moral prohibition of masturbation was backed up by bits of folk-wisdom such as that it would result in loss of hair.

15.1783 (493:14). more sinned against than sinning – See 13.432n.

15.1785–86 (493:17). *virgo intacta* – Medical Latin for a virgin with hymen intact.

15.1789 (493:20). Hypsospadia – Hypospadias is a malformation of the male genitourinary tract.

15.1793–94 (493:24–25). the patient's urine . . . reflex intermittent – This does not indicate an intimate knowledge of medicine, but vaguely implies kidney infection or insufficiency.

15.1796 (493:27). *fetor judaicus* – Latin: "Jewish stench."

15.1798–99 (493:30). the new womanly man – "Womanly man" is a phrase from Otto Weinenger's *Geschlecht und Charakter* (Sex and Character) (1903). Weinenger's anti-Semitic (and antifeminine) argument was that "Judaism is saturated with femininity" (p. 306), and Jewish men were therefore womanly, passive "nonmen" (cited in Ellmann, p. 463).

15.1802–3 (494:2–3). the Reformed Priests' Protection Society – With offices at 13 D'Olier Street in Dublin. "The primary object of the society is to extend a helping hand to priests of good character, who conscientiously abandon the Church of Rome for the pure faith of the Gospel; and to assist them to employment; also to assist young men originally intended for the priesthood" (*Thom's* 1904, p. 1389).

15.1808 (494:8). Glencree reformatory – See 10.536n.

15.1818 (494:21). MRS THORNTON – See 4.417n.

15.1827 (494:30). *Nasodoro* – Italian: "Nose of gold."

15.1827 (494:31). *Chrysostomos* – See 1.26n.

15.1827 (494:31). *Maindorée* – French: "Hand of gold."

15.1828 (494:31). *Silberselber* – German: "Silverself."

15.1828 (494:32). *Vifargent* – French: "Quicksilver."

15.1828 (494:32). *Panargyros* – Greek: "All-silver."

15.1834 (495:2). The Messiah ben Joseph or ben David – The Messiah of the House of Joseph, in some Jewish apocalyptic writings, is assigned various roles but principally that of heralding the coming of the Messiah of the House of David. The Messiah ben Joseph is to collect the Israelites together and establish their rule over Jerusalem; he will then be slain by the enemies of Israel, and the Messiah ben David will come as the force of resurrection that gives birth to the new world.

15.1836 (495:4). You have said it – In Luke 23:3, Jesus, having been accused by the elders and chief priests of identifying himself as "Christ a King" (the Messiah ben David), is questioned by Pilate: "And Pilate asked him, saying, Art thou the King of the Jews? and he answered him and said, Thou sayest it."

15.1837 (495:5). BROTHER BUZZ – See 5.450n.

15.1838 (495:6). ★Then perform a miracle like Father Charles – Significance unknown.

15.1840 (495:8). the Saint Leger – A race for three-year-old colts and fillies run annually in September at Doncaster, England.

15.1842 (495:10). Nelson's Pillar – See 6.293n.

15.1844 (495:12). king's evil – Scrofula (tuberculosis of lymph nodes, especially in the neck), so called because, according to medieval superstition, it was cured by the king's touch.

15.1845 (495:14). Lord Beaconsfield – Benjamin Disraeli (1804–81), English novelist and statesman, was created first earl of Beaconsfield in 1876.

15.1845–46 (495:14). Lord Byron – Molly recalls (18.209 [743:40]) that when he was court- ing her, Bloom was trying to look like the En- glish romantic poet (and lady-killer) George Gordon, Lord Byron (1778–1824).

15.1846 (495:14). *Wat Tyler* – (d. 1381), the principal leader of the ill-starred English peas- ant revolt of 1381.

15.1846 (495:14). *Moses of Egypt* – See 7.833n.

15.1846 (495:15). *Moses Maimonides* – See 2.158n.

15.1846–47 (495:15). *Moses Mendelssohn* – See 12.1804n.

15.1847 (495:15). *Henry Irving* – (1838– 1905), a distinguished English actor and theat- rical manager, known for the psychological force with which he projected his roles and fa- mous for the carefully elaborated stage settings of his productions.

15.1847 (495:15–16). *Rip van Winkle* – See 13.1112n.

15.1847 (495:16). *Kossuth* – Lajos (Louis) Kossuth (1802–94), a Hungarian liberal leader and reformer, a central figure in the Hungarian revolution (1848–49), and a staunch advocate of political freedom.

15.1847–48 (495:16). *Jean Jacques Rous- seau* – (1712–78), the French philosopher re- garded variously as the Father of Romanticism, of the French Revolution, and of modern peda- gogy.

15.1848 (495:16–17). *Baron Leopold Roth- schild* – The Rothschilds were a Jewish family of international bankers. Leopold de Roth- schild (1845–1917) was the third son of Baron Lionel de Rothschild (1808–79), the first Jewish member of the English Parliament.

15.1848 (495:17). *Robinson Crusoe* – The cast- away hero of Daniel Defoe's (1660–1731) novel (1719).

15.1848–49 (495:17). *Sherlock Holmes* – Sir Arthur Conan Doyle's (1859–1930) famous de- tective made his first appearance in *A Study in Scarlet* (1887).

15.1849 (495:17–18). *Pasteur* – Louis Pasteur (1822–95), the celebrated French scientist

known for his researches in microorganisms and for his practical application of those researches (pasteurization, etc.).

15.1850 (495:19). *bids the tide turn back* – A story told of (among others) Canute (c. 994– 1035), king of the English, Danes, and Norwe- gians. He is supposed to have had his throne placed on the seashore and to have commanded the tide to stand still; when it did not, he turned his inability to command the tide into a parable about the humility necessary to a king.

15.1850–51 (495:19–20). *eclipses the sun . . . his little finger* – See 8.566n.

15.1852 (495:21). BRINI, PAPAL NUNCIO – See 12.1066–67 (321:24).

15.1855 (495:24). *Leopoldi autem generatio* – Latin, after Matthew 1:18, which begins: "Christi autem generatio" (Now the generation of Christ was on this wise [Douay]). The non- sense genealogy that follows parodies biblical genealogies, particularly that of Jesus in Mat- thew 1:1–16.

15.1855 (495:24–25). Moses begat Noah – In the genealogy of Noah in Genesis 5, Lamech is the father of Noah. Moses' father is mentioned only as "a man of the house of Levi" (Exodus 2:1).

15.1855 (495:25). Noah begat Eunuch – The sons of Noah were Shem, Ham, and Japheth (Genesis 10:1). If "Eunuch" is punning on "Enoch," then Noah is the father of his own great-grandfather (Genesis 5).

15.1856 (495:25). O'Halloran – Unknown.

15.1856 (495:26). Guggenheim – Meyer Gug- genheim (1828–1905), the head of the well- known Philadelphia Jewish family of financiers and philanthropists.

15.1857 (495:27). Agendath begat Netaim – See 4.191–92n.

15.1858 (495:27–28). Le Hirsch – Baron Mau- rice de Hirsch (1831–96), an Austrian Jewish financier, was one of the outstanding philan- thropists of his time and deeply concerned about the plight of the Jews in anti-Semitic re- gions of Europe.

15.1858 (495:28). Jesurum – According to Eric

Partridge, "a distortion of Jesum, the accusative of Jesus." Cf. 14.369–70n.

15.1858 (495:28–29). MacKay – Unknown.

15.1859 (495:29). Ostrolopsky – Unknown.

15.1859 (495:30). Smerdoz – Or Smerdis, was the talented and promising but luckless brother of King Cambyses of Persia. Cambyses had him put to death in 523 B.C.

15.1860 (495:30). Weiss begat Schwartz – White begat Black (German pun).

15.1861 (495:31). Adrianopoli – Adrianople, the modern Edirne, is a city in Turkey.

15.1861 (495:31–32). Aranjuez – A city south of Madrid in central Spain.

15.1861–62 (495:32). Lewy Lawson – Unknown.

15.1862 (495:33). Ichabudonosor – Thornton (p. 384) suggests a combination of *Ichabod* and *Nebuchadnezzar*. Both imply the presence of Jewish misfortune. Ichabod (Hebrew: "no glory") was so named by his mother on her deathbed because "the glory is departed from Israel." The child's father had been killed in a losing cause against the Philistines; the Ark of the Covenant had been taken by the Philistines; and the child's grandfather had died on receipt of the news (I Samuel 4). Nebuchadnezzar, king of Babylon, besieged and reduced Jerusalem and carried the Israelites captive into Babylon (II Kings 24–25).

15.1863 (495:33). O'Donnell Magnus – The Great O'Donnell, Hugh Roe or Red Hugh; see 12.179n.

15.1863 (496:1). Christbaum – German: "Christmas tree."

15.1864 (496:2). ben Maimun – The Hebrew suggests "of the house of Maimun"; Thornton suggests "Maimonides." See 2.158n.

15.1864 (496:2). Dusty Rhodes – See 14.1546n.

15.1865 (496:3). Benamor – This combination of Hebrew *Ben* and Latin *Amor* suggests "Son of Love."

15.1865 (496:3–4). Jones-Smith – This com-

bination of the two most common family names in English suggests an everyman family.

15.1866 (496:4). Savorgnanovich – *Ovich* is the Russian suffix "son of," as in the familiar patronymic on the father's given name (Pavlovich, son of Paul). The suffix was also attached to many Jewish family names in Russia—as here, the sons of Savorgnan.

15.1866 (496:5). Jasperstone – The jasperstone in the high priest's breastplate (Exodus 28:17–21) is symbolic of the tribe of Asher, singled out in Moses' blessing of the twelve tribes of Israel: "Blessed above sons be Asher; let him be the favorite of his brothers" (Deuteronomy 33:24–25 RSV; suggested by Joan Keenan).

15.1867 (496:5). Vingtetunieme – French pun, "the twenty-first" (though it is the twenty-seventh generation in this geneological table); it may also be an allusion to the popular card game, twenty-one or blackjack.

15.1868 (496:6). Szombathely – Hungarian: "Saturday Place"; Bloom's father's birthplace, a small town in Hungary near the Austrian border, approximately 115 miles west of Budapest. In the Austro-Hungarian Empire it was known as Pinkafeld.

15.1868–69 (496:7–8). *et vocabitur nomen eius Emmanuel* – Latin: "and shall call his name Immanuel [God with us]"; from Isaiah 7:14: "Therefore the Lord himself shall give you a sign; Behold, a virgin shall conceive, and bear a son, and shall call his name Immanuel."

15.1870–71 (496:9–10). A DEADHAND (*Writes on the wall.*) – A "deadhand" (*mortmain*) is in effect the irreversible hand of ecclesiastical authority. During Belshazzar's "impious feast," the "fingers of a man's hand" appear and write a baffling message on the wall. Daniel interprets the message to mean "God hath numbered thy kingdom and finished it. . . . Thou art weighed in the balances, and art found wanting. . . . Thy kingdom is divided, and given to the Medes and Persians" (Daniel 5:26–28).

15.1871 (496:10). a cod – A joker or a fool.

15.1872–73 (496:11–12). CRAB / (*In bushranger's kit*) – For "Crab," see 9.1181–89n. A "bushranger" is one who lives in the bush, a backwoodsman. In Australia it refers particularly to an outlaw hiding in the bush.

15.1873 (496:12). the cattlecreep – A narrow opening for cattle to pass through.

15.1874 (496:13). Kilbarrack – A road in the village of Baldoyle, which is on the coast seven miles northeast of Dublin.

15.1876 (496:15). Ballybough bridge – Over the river Tolka in Fairview on the northeastern outskirts of Dublin.

15.1877 (496:16). A HOLLYBUSH – See 2.102–7n.

15.1878 (496:17). the devil's glen – Twenty-two miles south-southeast of Dublin, a picturesque glen one and a half miles long and hemmed in by rugged rock walls that reach 400 feet in height.

15.1880 (496:19). *frons* – Anatomically, the forehead or upper part of the head.

15.1883 (496:22). *Donnybrook fair* – See 5.561n.

15.1883 (496:23). Sjambok – South African: "to whip with a heavy leather whip" (and, as a noun, the name of the whip).

15.1885 (496:24). *with asses' ears* – In Greek mythology, Apollo imposed asses' ears on King Midas because Midas stupidly preferred Pan's music to his.

15.1886 (496:25–26). Don Giovanni, a cenar teco – See 8.1040–41n.

15.1887 (496:26). *Artane orphans* – See 6.537n.

15.1887–88 (496:27). *Prison Gate Mission* – The Dublin Prison Gate Mission, a Protestant institution "for the purpose of affording employment [in a laundry] and elementary instruction to women and young girls leaving the City Short Sentence Prisons" (*Thom's* 1904, p. 1372).

15.1890–91 (497:2–3). You hig, you hog . . . ladies love you! – The source of this street rhyme is unknown.

15.1893–96 (497:5–8). *If you see Kay . . . Tell him from me – An acrostic: F.U.C.K. / Tell him he may / C.U.N.T. / Tell him from me.

15.1897 (497:9). HORNBLOWER – See 5.555n.

15.1898 (497:10). *ephod* – A garment mentioned several times in the Old Testament, associated at times with the high priest, at other times with persons present at religious ceremonies, and in Judges with idolatrous worship. The *ephod* was draped with ornaments that symbolized the Urim and Thummim (doctrine and faith), the twelve tribes of Israel, etc. To wear the *ephod* was to be prepared for communion with God. See I Kings 23:11 (Douay), when the disposition of David's enemies is revealed to him through the priest's *ephod*.

15.1898–99 (497:10–12). And he shall carry . . . in the wilderness – Azazel (Hebrew: "dismissal") is the scapegoat (symbolically receiving the sins of the people). In Leviticus 16:8, 10: "And Aaron shall cast lots upon the two goats; one lot for the Lord, and the other lot for the scapegoat. . . . But the goat, on which the lot fell to be the scapegoat, shall be presented alive before the Lord, to make an atonement with him, and to let him go for a scapegoat into the wilderness." See 15.776n.

15.1899 (497:12). Lilith – See 14.242n.

15.1900–1901 (497:13). Agendath Netaim – See 4.191–92n.

15.1901 (497:13–14). Mizraim, the land of Ham – Mizraim is an Old Testament name for upper and lower Egypt. In Psalms 78:51, Egypt is called "the land of Ham," after the "younger" of Noah's three sons, who was "cursed" because he "saw the nakedness of his father" when Noah was drunk (Genesis 9:21–25). In Genesis 10:6, "Mizraim" is listed as one of "the sons of Ham."

15.1902–3 (497:16). *bonafide travellers* – See 14.1440n.

15.1904–5 (497:18). *long earlocks* – In observance of the Jewish prohibition against a man's touching his hair with a blade or a razor. Traditionally they are stroked or twirled during prayer and contemplation.

15.1907 (497:20). Belial – (Hebrew: literally, "worthless.") The "sons of Belial" are thus worthless, the wicked, or possibly the destructive ones, as in Deuteronomy 13:13. In the New Testament, II Corinthians 6:15, "Belial" becomes a name for Satan.

15.1907 (497:20). Laemlein of Istria – In 1502 an obscure Jewish heretic-prophet named Ascher Laemlein appeared in Istria (an Adriatic peninsula south of Trieste) and in effect proclaimed himself the Messiah ben Joseph; see 15.1834n.

15.1907 (497:20). Abulafia – Abraham Ben Samuel Abulafia (1240–c. 1291), a Jew from Saragossa, Spain, who proclaimed himself the Messiah and journeyed to Rome, where he attempted to convert Nicholas III (pope 1277–80) and barely escaped with his life.

15.1908 (497:21). *George R Mesias* – See 6.831n.

15.1914 (497:26//27). *Don Emile Patrizio Franz Rupert Pope Hennessy* – This collection of names suggests but does not specify several wild-geese families, such as the Taafes in Austria, the O'Donnells in Spain, the O'Briens in Russia, and the MacMahons in France. Sir John Pope Hennessy (1834–91), a conservative Irish Catholic politician, had a varied career as governor of several British colonies and was a successful anti-Parnellite candidate for Parliament in 1890.

15.1915 (497:26). two wild geese volant – For "wild geese," see 3.163–64n; "volant" in heraldry means in flight.

15.1916 (497:26). footboden – Anglicized German for floor or the ground at your feet.

15.1917 (497:26). Jude – In context, not the New Testament writer of the Epistle of Jude but slang for Jew.

15.1918 (497:27). *Iscariot* – The surname of Judas, the betrayer of Jesus.

15.1918 (497:27). *bad shepherd* – As Jesus is the "good shepherd" (John 10:14).

15.1922 (498:2). The squeak – Slang for a criminal who, once arrested, turns informer; and a piece of inside information that has been delivered to the police.

15.1922 (498:2). a split – Slang for a police spy, an informer.

15.1922 (498:2–3). the flatties – Slang for uniformed policemen.

15.1922 (498:3). Nip – Slang for to cheat, to steal; therefore, to catch.

15.1923 (498:3). rattler – Slang for a horse-drawn cab.

15.1926 (498:6). Brother Buzz – See 5.450n.

15.1927 (498:7). *a yellow habit* – What Jews were required to wear in some medieval and Renaissance Italian states. Heretics condemned by the Inquisition and turned over to the State to be burned at the stake also wore yellow gowns or gowns with a yellow cross; see 1.2n.

15.1928–29 (498:9). *hands him over to the civil power* – Heretics were tried (and condemned) by the Church, but the death sentence was carried out by the "civil power."

15.1929 (498:10). Forgive him his trespasses – After the Lord's Prayer: "And forgive us our trespasses, as we forgive those who trespass against us." Cf. Matthew 6:12 and Luke 11:4.

15.1930 (498:11). *Lieutenant Myers* – John J. Myers, in 1904 commander of the City of Dublin Fire Brigade, 12 Winetavern Street, Dublin.

15.1935 (498:16). *a seamless garment* – At the Crucifixion, Jesus' coat is described as "without seam, woven from the top throughout" (John 19:23).

15.1935 (498:16). I. H. S. – See 5.372n.

15.1936 (498:17). Weep not for me, O daughters of Erin – As Jesus was going to be crucified he said to the women who "bewailed and lamented him": "Daughters of Jerusalem, weep not for me, but weep for yourselves, and for your children" (Luke 23:27–28).

15.1941–52 (498:23–499:3). Kidney of Bloom . . . pray for us – This parodies a Catholic litany, particularly the Litany of the Sacred Heart with its refrain, "Heart of Jesus . . . have mercy on us"; cf. 13.287–89n. In biblical Hebrew the human kidney has metaphorical overtones, variously "mind, heart, soul" (*The Interpreter's Dictionary of the Bible* [New York, 1962]); cf. p. 70, n. 1 (suggested by Joan Keenan). The parody also reviews moments in Bloom's day; cf. 17.487n.

15.1947 (498:29). Sweets of Sin – See 10.606n.

15.1948 (498:30). Music without Words – See 11.1092n.

15.1952 (499:3). Potato Preservative – See 14.1480–81n.

15.1953 (499:4–5). *Vincent O'Brien – Irish composer and musician, the conductor (1898–1902) of the Palestrina Choir at the Metropolitan Procathedral in Dublin, known for his achievements in the reform of church music and its performance in Irish Roman Catholic churches.

15.1954–55 (499:5). *the chorus from Handel's . . . reigneth – See 15.1397n.

15.1955 (499:6). *Joseph Glynn – See 5.395n.

15.1960–62 (499:11–13). *in caubeen with clay . . . smile in his eye – Bloom's costume is patterned after that of the "stage Irishman" popularized by Dion Boucicault; see 8.601–2n. For *caubeen*, see 9.295n; *bogoak* is a piece of oak that has been preserved in a peat bog; *sugaun* is Irish for a rope made of twisted hay or straw. For "a smile in his eye," see 12.161–62n.

15.1962–64 (499:13–15). Let me be going . . . mother of a bating – The source of this apparent quotation from or parody of a stage-Irishman play is unknown.

15.1965 (499:17). To be or not to be – See 11.905n.

15.1983 (500:5). *Hog's Norton where the pigs plays the organs – Hog's Norton (or Hock-Norton), a village in Leicestershire, "where the organist once upon a time was named Piggs." Partridge dates the story and saying from the sixteenth century.

15.1984–85 (500:7). Tommy Tittlemouse – From the nursery rhyme: "Little Tommy Tittlemouse / Lived in a little house; / He caught fishes / In other men's ditches. // Little Tommy Tittlemouse / Lived in a bell-house; / The bell-house broke / And Tom Tittlemouse awoke."

15.1995 (500:19). The greeneyed monster – Iago warns Othello against jealousy: "O, beware, my lord, of jealousy; / It is the green-eyed monster which doth mock / The meat it feeds on" (III.iii.165–67).

15.2001 (500:25). Laughing witch? – From "Matcham's Masterstroke"; see 4.502n.

15.2001 (500:25). The hand that rocks the cradle – See 11.1183–84n.

15.2009 (501:7). Love me. Love me not. Love me – After the children's game, when the two formulas "She loves me; she loves me not" are repeated alternately in enumerating the petals of a flower or some other series of objects. The formula that coincides with the last petal is, of course, "true."

15.2011–12 (501:10–11). *Her forefinger giving . . . secret monitor – For the gesture, see 8.591n. The "passtouch of secret monitor" is also a Masonic sign to warn of moral or spiritual danger. The background of the sign is the warning with which Jonathan saved David's life in I Samuel 20. The signs Jonathan used were arrows, hence forefingers.

15.2013 (501:11). Hot hands, cold gizzard – After the proverbial saying "Cold hands, warm heart."

15.2020 (501:19). *their drugged heads – Like the members of Odysseus's crew, whom Circe has enchanted.

15.2025 (501:26–27). Don't fall upstairs – After the superstition that falling upstairs means one is entering where he is not welcome or where he will be unlucky.

15.2027 (501:29). The just man falls seven times – "For a just man falleth seven times, and riseth up again: but the wicked shall fall into mischief" (Proverbs 24:16). The traditional assumption is that the just man flirts once with each of the seven cardinal sins: pride, envy, wrath, lust, gluttony, avarice, and sloth.

15.2042–46 (502:19). *The floor is covered . . . Footmarks are stamped over it in all senses . . . a morris of shuffling feet . . . higgledypiggledy – At the beginning of Book 12 of *The Odyssey*, when Odysseus and his men return to Circe's island, "the Island of Aiaia" (line 3), Odysseus, describing the island at the Phaeacian court, remarks: "Summering Dawn / has dancing grounds there" (lines 3–4, Fitzgerald, p. 221). For "morris" see 2.155n. "Piggledy": at their first encounter with Circe in Book 10, half of Odysseus's men are turned into swine; see the headnote to this episode, p. 452.

15.2050 (502:24). *Kitty Ricketts – For a possible identity see Ellmann, p. 368.

15.2073 (503:12–13). the series of empty fifths – That is, the fifth without the third and therefore giving no indication of whether the key is major or minor. The open fifth is characteristic of the medieval and Renaissance tradition of modal music, which was conceived on the basis of what turns out to have been a misunderstanding of the seven modes of ancient Greek music. See 15.2090n.

15.2073–74 (503:13). *Florry Talbot* – See Ellmann, p. 368.

15.2087–88 (503:29–30). whether Benedetto Marcello found it or made it – Benedetto Marcello (1686–1739), an Italian composer particularly noted for his setting of Girolamo Giustiniani's Italian paraphrases of the first fifty psalms (1724–26). In his preface to the psalms Marcello says that he has limited his settings for the most part to two voices so that the words and sentiments would be clear as they were (he argues) in the "unisonous" music of the ancient Hebrews and Greeks, a music that he says had in its simplicity more power to affect the "passions" than "modern" music with its excessive ornament. He qualifies this distinction by saying that what he attempted in his settings of the psalms was to clothe "Ancient simplicity" in a garb of "modern harmony" so that the settings would not be "offensive" to a "modern" ear. The "it" that Marcello "found . . . or made" is presumably the melody for his setting of the psalm Stephen mentions. In his preface Marcello says that he visited several Jewish communities in search of examples of "ancient Hebrew" settings of the psalms; thus, he may have "found" the melody or he may have "made it," but Stephen argues that "it does not matter" because the melody has the true "ancient flavor." The melody of the setting for the psalm Stephen mentions does begin with an open fifth and does have the ancient or modal flavor that Stephen discusses.

15.2088 (504:1). an old hymn to Demeter – The fifth of the so-called Homeric Hymns (c. seventh century B.C.). Classical scholars of the late nineteenth century argued that "it seems to have been intended to state the mythical foundation of the Eleusinian Mysteries" (*Harper's Dictionary of Classical Literature and Antiquities* [New York, 1896]). Demeter (mother earth) was a fertility goddess, the Greek goddess of agriculture and of the civilization based on it.

15.2089 (504:1–2). *Coela enarrant gloriam Domini* – Latin: "The heavens declare the glory of the Lord"; the opening line of Psalm 19 (Vulgate 18), though Stephen substitutes *Domini* ("of the Lord") for the Vulgate's *Dei*

("of God"). Stephen uses a variant of the Latin name of the psalm; Marcello's versions were settings of an Italian text.

15.2089 (504:2). nodes – In music, the divisions that a plucked or vibrating string makes when it is "stopped" at a given point; for example, a string stopped at one-fourth of its length will vibrate in four sections and will produce a note a fifth above the note of the open string.

15.2090 (504:3). hyperphrygian and mixolydian – "Hyperphrygian" is more accurately "hypophrygian." Modes (four principal and three subordinate) were the patterned arrangements of ancient Greek music. The modes were descending minor scales with semisteps (halftones) between the third and fourth, and seventh and eighth degrees. The two modes Stephen mentions are as "far apart" as B and the G above in a modern scale; the Greeks assumed that particular modes conformed to or aroused particular emotional responses. Aristotle (*Poetics* VIII:7:1342a29–30) argues that the Lydian mode (and presumably the mixolydian) are "the gentle modes . . . suitable to children of tender age and [possessing] the elements both of order and education." The Phrygian (and hypophrygian) modes, on the other hand, are appropriate to "Bacchic frenzy and all similar emotions." The adaptation of the modal theory in medieval music used ascending rather than descending scales, and the halftones were not always between the third and fourth, and seventh and eighth degrees; that is, the scales of the medieval modes could start on tones other than the fundamental, and the position of semisteps would change each time the starting tone was shifted.

15.2091 (504:4). Circe's – See headnote to this episode, p. 452.

15.2092 (504:5). Ceres' – An ancient Roman goddess of grain and harvest, later identified with the Greek Demeter; see 15.2088n.

15.2092–93 (504:5–6). *David's tip from . . . about the alrightness of his almightiness* – Several of the psalms, including 19 (see 15.2089n), bear the heading "To the chief Musician." A "tip from the stable" is a horseracing term for inside and presumably dependable information. Cf. Stephen Hand, 14.1514–17n.

15.2093 (504:6–7). *Mais nom de nom* – French: "But, by George."

15.2094 (504:7–8). *Jetez la gourme . . . jeunesse se passe* – French: "Sow the wild oats. Youth must pass away."

15.2095 (504:9). **your knowledge bump** – Amateur phrenology; phrenologists assumed that particular mental faculties were localized in specific regions of the brain and that the strength of a given faculty was evidenced by the prominence of its region of the skull.

15.2097–98 (504:12). **Jewgreek is greekjew** – See 1.158n.

15.2101 (504:16–17). **Whetstone!** – See 9.977–78n.

15.2115 (504:31). **The Holy City** – A hymn (1892) by the English songwriter Frederic Weatherly (1848–1929), music by Stephen Adams: "Last night as I lay asleeping, / There came a dream so fair, / I stood in old Jerusalem / Before the temple there. / I heard the children singing, / And even as they sang, / Methought the voice of angels / From Heav'n in answer rang, / Methought the voice of angels / From Heav'n in answer rang, / Jerusalem, Jerusalem, / Lift up your gates and sing, / Hosanna in the Highest, / Hosanna to your King."

15.2118 (505:3). **God, the sun, Shakespeare** – A new Trinity. The sun is a traditional symbol for Christ, the second person of the Trinity, after Malachi 4:2: "But unto you that fear my name shall the sun of righteousness arise with healing in his wings" (cited by Joan Keenan). For Shakespeare as the Holy Ghost, see 9.1018–19n and 9.1028–29n.

15.2118–21 (505:4–7). **having itself traversed . . . preconditioned to become** – See 9.1042–44n. For "noise in the street," see 2.286n.

15.2121 (505:7). *Ecco!* – Latin: "Behold!" In medieval Scholastic argument the word meant: "It has been definitively stated."

15.2126 (505:12–13). **he knows more than you have forgotten** – An inversion of the saying "He has forgotten more than you'll ever know."

15.2129 (505:16). **the last day** – See 6.677–78n.

15.2135 (505:22). **Antichrist** – A great antagonist expected to fill the world with wickedness and to be conquered by Christ at the Second Coming. The Antichrist is mentioned in I John 2:18, 22 and is traditionally identified with the beast in Revelation (see 15.209n).

15.2140–41 (506:2–3). **Sea serpent in the royal canal** – Recalls all the speculation about sea serpents in Loch Ness, Scotland. It also recalls "the great dragon . . . that old serpent, called the Devil, and Satan, which deceiveth the whole world: he was cast out [of heaven] into the earth, and his angels were cast out with him" (Revelation 12:9). The "great dragon" is traditionally associated with the Antichrist. The Royal Canal skirted the northern border of metropolitan Dublin in 1904.

15.2144 (506:6). **A time, times and half a time** – From Revelation 12:13–14. After the "great dragon" or "serpent" is cast out of heaven, "he persecuted the woman which brought forth the man child. And to the woman were given two wings of a great eagle, that she might fly into the wilderness, into her place, where she is nourished for a time, and times, and half a time, from the face of the serpent."

15.2145 (506:7). **Reuben J Antichrist* – The metamorphoses of Reuben J. Dodd; see 6.264–65n.

15.2145 (506:7). *wandering jew* – See 9.1209n.

15.2149 (506:12). *his only son* – In Jeremiah 6:26 and Amos 8:10, the apocalyptic visitation of the wrathful judgment of God on a sinful people is predicted and compared to "mourning, as for an only son." It is notable that Bloom still mourns the death of his only son and that Reuben J. Dodd's son was "saved."

15.2152 (506:15). *Ally Sloper* – A caricature figure of the paterfamilias who presided over a penny illustrated-humor weekly, *Ally Sloper's Half-Holiday*, published by Gilbert Dalziel in London on Saturdays in the 1880s and 1890s. As drawn by W. F. Thomas, Ally Sloper had bulging eyes, a large, bulbous nose, and a spindle-shanked figure. Though obviously a solid member of the middle class, Sloper was represented as constantly embarrassing his family by his bumbling eccentricities and by his predilections for "Friv' girls" and the bottle.

15.2159–60 (506:23–24). *Il vient! . . . primigène* – French: "He comes [is here]! The man who laughs. The primordial man." *L'Homme qui rit* (1869) is a novel by Victor Hugo (1802–85). The central character in the novel is a boy whose face has been mutilated so that he always appears to be laughing; the novel develops the antithesis between his appearance and fluctuations in the boy's moral state.

15.2161 (506:25). *Sieurs et dames, faites vos jeux!* – French: "Gentlemen and ladies, place your bets!"; what the croupier at a roulette table says when he starts the wheel.

15.2162 (506:26). *Les jeux sont faits!* – French: "The bets are made!"

15.2163 (506:27–28). **Rien va plus* – French: "Nothing more goes"; that is, no more bets may be placed, since the roulette wheel is slowing down.

15.2171–73 (507:5–7). Jerusalem! / Open your gates and sing / Hosanna – See 15.2115n.

15.2175–76 (507:10). *second coming of Elijah* – See 8.13n.

15.2176–77 (507:11). *from zenith to nadir the End of the World* – In "Book the Second" of Blake's *Milton* (1804–8), the prophetic vision of a world in apocalyptic ruin is "view'd from Milton's Track" (plate 34:24). "Five females and the nameless Shadowy Mother, / Spinning it from their bowels with songs of amorous delight / And melting cadences that lure the Sleepers of Beulah down / . . . into the Dead Sea" (plate 34:27–30). The result: "Four universes round the Universe of Los remain Chaotic, / Four intersecting Globes, & the Egg form'd World of Los / In midst, stretching from Zenith to Nadir in midst of Chaos" (plate 34:32–34). Previously one of the songs of Beulah (female creative energy) has celebrated "the happy female joy" (plate 33:19) and continued "& Thou, O Virgin Babylon, Mother of Whoredoms, / Shalt bring Jerusalem in thine arms in the night watches, and / No longer turning her a wandering Harlot in the streets, / Shalt give her into the arms of God your Lord and Husband" (plate 33:20–23).

15.2177 (507:11–12). *a twoheaded octopus* – See 8.520–22n.

15.2179 (507:14). *the Three Legs of Man* – The triskele, three flexed legs joined at the thighs. It is a device of the Irish sea-god Mananaan MacLir (see 3.56–57n), and it is also the heraldic device of the Isle of Man (see 7.141n).

15.2181–82 (507:16–17). Wha'll dance . . . the keel row? – After a Scottish song, "Weel May the Keel Row": "Oh, who is like my Johnie, / Sae leish, sae blithe, sae bonnie! / He's foremost 'mang the mony / Keel lads o' coaly Tyne. / He'll set or row so tightly, / Or in a dance sae sprightly / He'll cut and shuffle slightly / 'Tis true, were he not mine. [Chorus:] Weel may the keel row, / The keel row, the keel row / Weel may the keel row, / That my lad's in."

15.2186 (507:21). *old glory* – The American flag.

15.2188 (507:23). ELIJAH – Cf. Elijah III, the Reverend Alexander J. Dowie; see 8.13nn.

15.2189 (507:24). Jake Crane – Identity and significance unknown.

15.2189 (507:24–25). Creole Sue – The title of an American popular song (1898), words and music by Gussie L. Davis.

15.2189–90 (507:25). *Dove Campbell, Abe Kirschner – Identity and significance unknown.

15.2191 (507:26). trunk line – The main through-line of a railroad system.

15.2191 (507:27). God's time – American slang for the various zones of standard time established in the United States and Canada in 1883 (for the convenience of the railroads).

15.2191–92 (507:27–28). Tell mother you'll be there – After the American popular song "Tell Mother I'll Be There" (1890) by Charles Fillmore, included in *Fillmore's Prohibition Songs* (New York, 1900): "When I was but a little child, how well I recollect, / How I would grieve my mother with my folly and neglect, / And now that she has gone to heav'n, I miss her tender care, / O angels, tell my mother I'll be there. [Chorus:] Tell mother I'll be there, in answer to her prayer, / This message, guardian angels, to her bear; / Tell mother I'll be there, heav'n's joys to share, / Yes, tell my darling mother I'll be there."

15.2194 (507:30–31). the second advent – The Second Coming of Christ; cf. 15.2135n.

15.2195 (507:31). Coney Island – In 1904, the most popular seaside resort in the vicinity of New York City.

15.2197–98 (507:34–508:1). Be on the side of the angels – Benjamin Disraeli (1804–81), speaking against Darwin's 1859 theory of evolution before the Oxford Diocescan Society in 1864: "What is the question which is now placed before society, with the glib assurance which to me is astounding? That question is this: is man an ape or an angel? I am on the side of the angels. I repudiate, with ignorance and abhorrence, these new-fangled theories."

15.2198 (508:1). Be a prism – Thornton (p. 391) suggests another allusion to Disraeli, from a speech before the House of Commons, 15 February 1849: "A man, always studying the subject, will view the general affairs of the world through the coloured prism of his own atmosphere." Cf. 13.901–2n.

15.2199 (508:2). a Gautama – That is, Gautama Buddha (Buddha of the Gautama family), the great religious teacher and reformer of early India.

15.2199 (508:2–3). Ingersoll – Robert Ingersoll (1833–99), an American politician, lawyer, orator, and evangelical agnostic. His "message" was humanistic and scientific (Darwinian) rationalism.

15.2200 (508:3). vibration – In occultism, a psychic pulsation felt and shared by the initiate.

15.2200 (508:4). nobble – English slang: "catch, seize."

15.2205 (508:9). A. J. Christ Dowie – See 8.13n.

15.2206 (508:10–11). Seventyseven west sixtyninth street – The context suggests that this is A. J. Dowie's New York City address or an address associated with his mission to New York City, but the city directories we have consulted give no evidence of any such connections; the address seems to have been fabricated for the dramatic occasion.

15.2207 (508:12). Bumboosers – Theatrical slang: "desperate drinkers."

15.2207 (508:12–13). save your stamps – For collection by the church mission to be sold to a stamp dealer to raise money.

15.2209/11 (508:14/16). Jeru . . . / . . . highhohhhh – See 15.2115n.

15.2216 (508:21). *black in the face* – Dowie has metamorphosed into Eugene Stratton; see 6.184n.

15.2223 (508:30). twig – Slang: "watch, inspect, understand."

15.2225–34 (508:31–509:6). KITTY-KATE . . . slipped into the bed – Public confessions of sin by the newly reformed were a staple of evangelical crusades of the sort Dowie ran, and confessions of reformed prostitutes were, for obvious reasons, particularly in demand.

15.2227 (508:33). Constitution hill – A short (and, in 1904, not very savory) section of the main north–south road in north-central Dublin. It was lined with tenements.

15.2227–28 (508:33). enrolled in the brown scapular – Enrolled in a sodality for young women dedicated to worship of the Blessed Virgin Mary. Its members wore brown scapulars as signs of their devotion (and, in popular superstition, as charms to protect their virginity).

15.2228 (508:34). a Montmorency – The De Montmorencys were a noble and fashionable Anglo-Irish family in County Dublin. In 1904 the head of the family was Willoughby John Horace, fourth Viscount Frankfort De Montmorency.

15.2233–34 (509:4–5). Hennessy's three stars – An excellent and expensive French Cognac.

15.2234 (509:5). Whelan – Cf. 8.353n.

15.2236 (509:8). In the beginning was the word – From John 1:1, which continues "and the Word was with God, and the Word was God."

15.2236 (509:8–9). world without end – See 2.200–204n.

15.2236–37 (509:9). Blessed be the eight beatitudes – In the Sermon on the Mount (Matthew 5:3–11) Jesus pronounces the beatitudes, each of which begins with the words "Blessed are." Roman Catholic catechisms list eight beatitudes, though the opening formula is repeated nine times in the passage in Matthew.

15.2242 (509:15). buybull – Puns "Bible" with

the slogan "Buy John Bull" (i.e., buy only English goods). See 14.1459–60n.

15.2242 (509:15). barnum – Phineas Taylor Barnum (1810–91), American showman, the opportunistic and inventive proprietor of a traveling circus billed as "The Greatest Show on Earth" (established 1871).

15.2245 (509:18). *In quakergrey kneebreeches and broadbrimmed hat* – That is, in seventeenth-century Quaker costume.

15.2246 (509:19–20). Seek thou the light – See 9.332–33n.

15.2247 (509:21). *He corantos by* – See 9.5n.

15.2254 (509:28–29). A thing of beauty – The opening phrase of Keats's poem *Endymion: A Poetic Romance* (1818): "A thing of beauty is a joy for ever: / Its loveliness increases; it will never / Pass into nothingness."

15.2256 (510:1). JOHN EGLINTON – W. K. Magee appears in the guise of Diogenes of Sinope (Diogenes the Cynic, 412–323 B.C.). Diogenes, to dramatize his philosophical doubts, carried a lighted lantern in broad daylight, ostensibly in search of an honest man.

15.2259 (510:5). Tanderagee – In 1904 a prosperous small market town in County Armagh, north of Dublin.

15.2261 (510:6–7). ollave – See 9.30n.

15.2262 (510:7). *Mananaun MacLir – AE (George William Russell) has metamorphosed into the figure of the Irish god of the sea, the legendary ancestor of the Isle of Man; see 3.56–57n. Oliver St. John Gogarty (*As I Was Going Down Sackville Street* [New York, 1937], p. 292) says that in AE's play *Deirdre* (written in 1901; first performed 1902; published Dublin, 1907), Russell himself appeared as Mananaan when the druid Cathvah invoked Mananaan MacLir that the sea might rise and cut off the flight of Deirdre and her love, Naisi. John Eglinton (W. K. Magee), however, says that AE's "mellow northern accent was heard behind the scenes intoning the prophecies of Cathvah the Druid" during the play's performance (*A Memoir of AE* [London, 1937], p. 54). For Mananaan MacLir, see also 9.190–91n.

15.2265 (510:11). *a bicycle pump* – See 8.533n.

15.2268 (510:14). Aum! Hek! Wal! Ak! Lub! Mor! Ma! – In *The Candle of Vision* (London, 1918), AE developed the mystical significance of the "roots of human speech" (p. 120) in two chapters, "The Language of the Gods" and "Ancient Intuitions." The first two words in this series are not given as examples by AE, though his discussion of "the sound correspondences of powers which in their combination and interaction make up the universe" (p. 120) suggests that *Aum*, composed of the roots A and M, would mean "A, the sound symbol for the self in man and Deity in the cosmos. Its form equivalent is the circle" (p. 121), and "M . . . is the close, limit, measure, end or death of things" (p. 125); thus, the syllable *Aum* is "the beginning and the end." It is also a variant spelling of the Sanskrit *Om*, a word believed to have magical powers and regarded as especially sacred by Hindus and Western occultists. *Hek:* "H is the sound correspondence of Heat" (p. 121); E, "where consciousness . . . has become passional" (p. 126); and K "is the symbol . . . of mineral, rock crystal or hardness of any kind" (p. 122). *Wal:* "if the fire acting on the water made it boil, they [the intuitive ancients] would instinctively combine the sound equivalents of water and fire, and 'Wal' would be the symbol" (p. 130). *Ak:* "would be to cut or pierce" (p. 130). *Lub* would be "the sound symbol . . . if the fire of life was kindled in the body to generate its kind" (p. 130). *Mor* would be said "if they saw death and felt it as the stillness or ending of motion or breath" (pp. 129–30). "'Ma' would . . . mean to measure, and as to think a thing is to measure it, 'Ma' would also come to be associated with thinking" (p. 130). In effect, Joyce has ordered AE's syllables in such a way as to suggest the sequence of sexual intercourse, appropriate since AE has transformed Mananaan MacLir in *The Candle of Vision:* "In the beginning was the boundless Lir, an infinite depth, an invisible divinity, neither dark nor light, in whom were all things past and to be" (p. 153).

15.2268–69 (510:15). *White yoghin of the gods – A "yoghin" is a person adept in Yoga (the development of the powers latent in man for achieving union with the Divine Spirit). The whole phrase refers to the *alba petra*, the white stone or white carnelian, "the stone of initiation, on which the word '*prize*' is generally found engraved, as it was given to the candidate who had successfully passed through all the preliminary trials of a neophyte" (H. P. Blavatsky, *Isis Unveiled* [New York, 1886], vol. 2, p. 351).

15.2269 (510:15–16). Occult pimander of Hermes Trismegistos – That is, of "Hermes thrice greatest," a late name of the Greek god Hermes conflated with the Egyptian god Thoth; see 9.353n. He was the fabled author of a number of works embodying Neoplatonic, Judaic, and cabalistic ideas together with astrological, alchemical, and magical doctrines. The *Poimandres* is one of these so-called Hermetic books; Poimandres is "a Higher Being that appears in a vision to Hermes Trismegistos and reveals to him a world of esoteric and occult knowledge" (Paul P. J. Van Caspel, *Bloomers on the Liffey* [Groningen, The Netherlands, 1980], p. 267).

15.2270 (510:16–17). Punarjanam patsy punjaub – "Punar-janman" is a Theosophical term for "1. A new or second birth. 2. The power of creating objective manifestations" (Hoult, p. 110). As a guess, "patsy" might refer to the stage Irishman; "punjaub" seems to be an approximation of "Pums"—the Supreme Spirit or the Divine Self in Man (pp. 109–110)—and "jaub" as a variant "Jaya (*Sans.*)—Conquering; being victorious" (p. 61).

15.2271 (510:18). beware the left, the cult of Shakti – "Shakti" in Hindu belief is the female generative energy in the universe; and the female is the left hand as the male is the right. The cult of Shakti (Shaktism) is one of the three great divisions of modern Hinduism; the other two are Saivism (the worship of Siva) and Vaishnavism (the worship of Vishnu). Shakti is usually worshiped as the wife of a male deity, particularly of Siva.

15.2272 (510:19). *Shiva! darkhidden Father! – In Hinduism Siva, the Destroyer, the ultimate ascetic, is worshiped as the destroyer of the earthly prison that holds man's soul in bondage. In the cult of Siva the universe is regarded as a play of appearance, a form that Siva assumes.

15.2275 (510:22). Aum! Baum! Pyjaum! – For "Aum," see 15.2268n; source and significance of "Baum" and "Pyjaum" unknown.

15.2275–76 (510:22–23). I am the light . . . creamery butter – A parody of the Hindu prayer quoted 9.63–64 (185:32). It also echoes Jesus' assertion: "I am the light of the world: he

that followeth me shall not walk in darkness, but shall have the light of life" (John 8:12). AE (George William Russell) was, of course, editor of the *Irish Homestead*, which had a lively interest in the improvement of Irish dairy production. See 2.412n.

15.2277 (510:24). A skeleton judashand strangles the light – The hand of Judas has betrayed Jesus, "the light of the world."

15.2288 (511:5). pot – French slang for a quick drink.

15.2292 (511:9). a nixie's green – In Teutonic mythology, a nixie is a female water sprite, sometimes portrayed as part woman, part fish. She is said to be given to soothsaying, fond of music and dancing, and treacherous.

15.2297 (511:14). *makes sheep's eyes – In affectation of her innocence she makes her eyes look large and soft.

15.2297–98 (511:14–15). Would you suck a lemon? – See 15.492–93n.

15.2304 (511:21). Lipoti Virag – "Leopold" Virag, Bloom's grandfather; see 12.1816n.

15.2304 (511:21–22). basilicogrammate – Paul P. J. Van Caspel (*Bloomers on the Liffey* [Groningen, The Netherlands, 1980], p. 267) suggests "secretary to a king" or "a royal scribe"; cf. Blum Pasha 17.1748n.

15.2307 (511:25). a roll of parchment – In Flaubert's *The Temptation of Saint Anthony*, chapter 3, Anthony's former disciple Hilarion enters to participate in the riot of torment that Anthony is experiencing. On his first appearance in chapter 3 Hilarion "grasps in his hand a roll of papyrus" (p. 40). Anthony quickly perceives that Hilarion "knows everything," and Hilarion responds, "Learn, too, that I have never left you. But you spend long intervals without perceiving me" (p. 41).

15.2308–9 (511:26–27). Cashel Boyle . . . Tisdall Farrell – See 8.302n.

15.2309 (511:27–28). an Egyptian pshent – The double crown of Egypt, combining that of Upper Egypt (a high conical white cap surmounted by a knob) with the red crown of Lower Egypt outermost.

15.2312 (511:30–31). Szombathely – See 15.1868n.

15.2318 (512:4). Granpapachi – Yiddish: "Grandfather."

15.2321 (512:7–8). our tribal elixir of gopherwood – Gopherwood is the unidentified wood with which Noah built the ark. "Make thee an ark of gopher wood; rooms shalt thou make in the ark, and shalt pitch it within and without with pitch" (Genesis 6:14).

15.2333 (512:21). Never put on you tomorrow what you can wear today – After the proverb "Never put off until tomorrow what you can do today."

15.2334 (512:21–22). Parallax! – See 8.110n.

15.2334–35 (512:22–23). (with a nervous twitch . . . brain go snap? – Stuart Gilbert (*James Joyce's "Ulysses"* [New York, 1952], p. 332n) notes: "One of Mrs. Piper's frequent remarks when 'coming out' of trance was, 'Did you hear something snap in my head?' and nervous twitching accompanied the process." Mrs. Leonora Piper, a spiritualist medium from Boston, Massachusetts, was the subject of extensive experiment and investigation from 1896 until World War I by the British Society for Psychical Research. Mrs. Piper's fame rested in part on the fact that many members of that more or less skeptical society thought that Mrs. Piper's experiences were valid confirmations of "the spiritistic theory" (i.e., of spiritualism).

15.2341 (512:30). Lily of the alley – Combines the titles of three songs: "Lily of the Valley" (1886), by L. Wolfe Gilbert and Anatol Friedland; another of the same name (1904) by George Cooper and Louis Tocaben; and "Sally in Our Alley," by Henry Carey. The Gilbert and Friedland "ditty": "Lily, Lily of the valley, / Dearie, dearie let's be pally / Sweetie, you're the nicest flower of the lot. / Be my Lily, oh be my Lily— / I'll be your forget-me-not." The first stanza of "Sally in Our Alley": "Of all the girls that are so smart / There's none like pretty Sally; / She is the darling of my heart, / And she lives in our alley. / There is no lady in the land / Is half so sweet as Sally, / She is the darling of my heart, / And she lives in our alley." The lily of the valley is also a traditional symbol for the Virgin Mary, after the Song of Solomon 2:1, "I am the rose of Sharon and the lily of the valleys."

15.2341–42 (512:31). bachelor's button discovered by Rualdus Colombus – That is, the clitoris, of which the anatomist Rualdus Columbus (1516–59) supposed himself to have been the discoverer.

15.2342 (512:31–32). Tumble her – See 9.257n.

15.2342 (512:32). Columble her – Literally, "make her into a dove."

15.2345 (513:3–4). What ho, she bumps! – The title of a music-hall song by Harry Castling and A. J. Mills. Chorus: "She began to bump a bit / Oh, she made a tremendous hit / When she kicked our villain in the threep'ny pit; / The actors guyed as she took running jumps, / And a boy in the gallery cried, 'Encore!' / What ho! she bumps."

15.2345–46 (513:4). The ugly duckling – The title of a story by Hans Christian Andersen (1805–75); the ugly duckling grows up to be a swan and thus outshines his duckling associates.

15.2346 (513:4). longcasted – Long-legged.

15.2346 (513:5). deep in keel – Having big buttocks.

15.2348 (513:7). When you come out without your gun – After the proverbial "What things [or ducks] you see when you come out without your gun."

15.2351 (513:10–11). How happy could you be with either . . . – In Act II of John Gay's (1685–1732) *The Beggar's Opera* (1728) Macheath sings, "How happy I could be with either, / Were t'other dear charmer away! / But while ye thus teaze me together, / To neither a word will I say."

15.2361–62 (513:23–24). When coopfattened . . . elephantine size – Geese are cooped in small cages and overfed to produce oversized livers for *pâté de foie gras*.

15.2363 (513:24–25). fennygreek and gumbenjamin – Actually, fenugreek and benzoin, but what the combination is supposed to do is unknown.

15.2365 (513:28). Fleshhotpots of Egypt – See 3.177–78n.

15.2366 (513:28–29). Lycopodium – Lycopodium powder has various uses, including treatment of excoriations of the skin.

15.2366–67 (513:29). Slapbang! There he goes again – After a music-hall song, "Slap Bang! Here We Are Again" (1866), by one Sheridan. First verse and chorus: "Long live our British Gentlemen / Who like a bit of sport, / Who smoke their weed and swig their stout / And won't have Gladstone's port! [Chorus:] For they always go a-rolling home, / They always go a-rolling home, / A jolly lot are they! / Tra, la la, Tra la la. / Slap bang, here we are again, / Slap bang, here we are again, / A jolly lot are we!"

15.2371 (514:2). Contact with a goldring – It was common superstition that contact with a gold ring would cure a sore eye.

15.2371–72 (514:2–3). *Argumentum ad feminam* – Latin: literally, "Argument to the woman"; after *argumentum ad hominem:* in logic, the fallacy of trying to refute an idea by discrediting the person who expresses it.

15.2373 (514:4). *Diplodocus and Ichthyosauros – Neither Greeks nor Romans, but dinosaurs.

15.2373 (514:5). Eve's sovereign remedy – Meaning unknown, but apparently the emphasis is on Eve as mother of nature, mother of actualities, in contrast to the Virgin Mary as mother of souls. See 17.2179n.

15.2374 (514:6). Huguenot – Means literally "oath companion."

15.2376–77 (514:9). Wheatenmeal with honey and nutmeg – Obviously a recipe for cookies and not the cure for warts that Virag is asking Bloom to remember.

15.2379 (514:11). Wheatenmeal with lycopodium and syllabax – A nonsense remedy composed by free association of 15.2366 (513:28–29) and 15.2335 (512:23).

15.2385 (514:18). mnemotechnic – The art of memory, mnemonics.

15.2385 (514:18–19). *La causa è santa*. Tara. Tara – See 8.623–24n.

15.2388 (514:21). Rosemary – Symbolizes remembrance in the language of herbs.

15.2389 (514:22–23). The touch of a deadhand cures – After the superstition that the touch of a dead man's hand would cure warts and other blemishes of the skin.

15.2394–95 (514:28). melancholy of muriatic – Muriatic acid; in the nineteenth century, the name for commercial forms of hydrochloric acid (incidentally, regarded as an effective suicide potion).

15.2395 (514:28). priapic pulsatilla – The European pasqueflower, *Anemone pulsatilla;* the pungent essential oil of the crushed plant was believed to be an aphrodisiac.

15.2395–97 (514:29–31). amputation. Our old . . . under the denned neck – Another treatment for warts: dry them out with applications of a caustic compound and then amputate them with a loop of horsehair. "Denned" in anatomy means a cavity or hollow.

15.2397 (514:31). the Bulgar and the Basque – The traditional costumes of Bulgar and Basque women include close-fitting trousers worn under wide-skirted and belted coats or dresses.

15.2400 (514:34–515:1). the religious problem – The impact of Darwinian evolution and absolute scientism had produced considerable skepticism about the claims of revealed religion in the late nineteenth century.

15.2400–2401 (515:1–2). to square the circle and win that million – One of the great mathematical problems of antiquity was the attempt to "square the circle," to transform a circle into a square so that its area could be determined. But the classical tools of elementary Euclidian geometry (the unmarked straightedge and the compass) could not perform this operation. Finally in 1882 the German mathematician Ferdinand Lindemann (b. 1852), using calculus, proved that π is a transcendental number and that therefore the circle cannot be squared. The problem nevertheless continued to have its devotees who were convinced that the circle could be squared and that the achievement would have incredible practical consequences (when, in fact, it would have virtually none). How the rumor of reward got launched and sustained, nobody knows. See Hugh Kenner, *Ulysses* (London, 1980), pp. 166–67.

15.2401 (515:2). Pomegranate! – The pomegranate figures variously in mythology. According to different versions of the myth of the fertility god Adonis, either he was conceived when his mother swallowed a pomegranate seed or the pomegranate sprang out of the hanged god's blood (and sometimes both). The pomegranate also had a special status in ancient Jewish rites. It "was the only fruit allowed to be brought inside the Holy of Holies—miniature pomegranates were sewn on the High Priest's robes when he made his yearly entry" (Robert Graves, *The White Goddess* [New York, 1948], p. 221).

15.2401–2 (515:2–3). From the sublime to the ridiculous is but a step – In this form the remark is attributed to Napoleon on the occasion of his 1812 near-victory that turned into disastrous defeat in Russia.

15.2404 (515:5). camiknickers – A woman's undergarment that combined a camisole (undershirt) with knickers (the forerunners of underpants).

15.2413 (515:16–17). lured by the smell – This "unscientific" generalization is true of many moths and echoes Charles Darwin's emphasis on "the instinctive recognition by smell for the choice of a suitable mate" (*On the Origin of Species* [New York, 1869], p. 414). Darwin was speaking of mammals, not insects.

15.2415–18 (515:19–23). They had a proverb . . . choice malt vinegar – Virag elaborates the proverb "Honey will draw more flies than vinegar." The Jewish year 5550 corresponds to 1789 A.D.

15.2421–22 (515:26–28). these night insects . . . complex unadjustable eye – That is, the eyes of many night insects have no way of adjusting to variations in light intensity; therefore they appear to be drawn toward light because they can in effect see nothing else when a strong light source is present.

15.2424 (515:30). Doctor L. B. – Bloom's namesake, the Dublin dentist? See 12.1638n.

15.2426–27 (515:33). Chase me, Charley! – A common Edwardian music-hall expression of female high spirits.

15.2427 (515:33). Buzz! – See 9.207n.

15.2433 (516:3). dibble – Slang for penis.

15.2434 (516:4). Bubbly jock! – Scots slang: "Turkey!"

15.2434 (516:5). Open Sesame! – See 12.562n.

15.2437 (516:8). Redbank oysters – See 8.865–66n.

15.2438–39 (516:10). the truffles of Perigord – Truffles were also regarded as an aphrodisiac.

15.2440 (516:12). viragitis – Or viraginity: masculine mentality and psychology in a woman.

15.2441–42 (516:13–14). Jocular. With my eyeglass in my ocular – In Gilbert and Sullivan's *Patience* (1881), Bunthorne blusters to Jane about his bohemian poet-rival: "I'll tell him that unless he will consent to be more jocular— / To cut his curly hair, and stick an eyeglass in his ocular, / To stuff his conversation full of quibble and quiddity, / To dine on chops and roly poly pudding with avidity, / He'd better clear away with all convenient rapidity" (II.6).

15.2445–46 (516:18). *Eve and the serpent contradicts – That is, in Genesis, Eve is not afraid of the serpent when he approaches to seduce her. But Bloom forgets the traditional assumption that the serpent that approached Eve was erect until *after* the seduction, when he is condemned: "upon thy belly shalt thou go" (Genesis 3:14).

15.2447 (516:19–20). Serpents too are gluttons for woman's milk – We have found no source for this bit of folklore, but it may be that Bloom is free-associating about the asp at Cleopatra's breast: "Dost thou not see my baby at my breast / That sucks the nurse asleep?" (*Antony and Cleopatra* V.ii.308–9).

15.2449 (516:22). Elephantuliasis – Bloom confuses elephantiasis with Elephantis, a Greek writer of erotica generally supposed to have been a woman. Her poems were quite famous; the Roman emperor Tiberius (42 B.C.–37 A.D.) is supposed to have kept them by his bedside as a how-to book "so that," as Pliny remarks, "he would not lack any precepts."

15.2457 (516:31). Instinct rules the world – Cf. 11.1183–84n.

15.2462 (516:35). Who's dear Gerald? – See 15.3009–13 (536:32–537:2).

15.2469–75 (517:6–12). I'm a tiny tiny . . . on the wing! Bing! – Source unknown.

15.2481 (517:18–19). *Jacob's pipe* – See 14.1057n.

15.2485 (517:23). *Mario, prince of Candai* – See 7.53n.

15.2489–90 (517:28). There is a flower that bloometh – See 13.438–39n.

15.2495–96 (517:33–35). Filling my belly . . . and go to my – In the parable of the prodigal son (Luke 15:13–32), the son is described as having "wasted his substance with riotous living," to the point where "he would fain have filled his belly with the husks that the swine did eat: and no man gave unto him. And when he came to himself, he said . . . I will arise and go to my father, and will say unto him, Father, I have sinned against heaven and before thee." Contrary to conventional expectations, the prodigal is not turned away but is welcomed as one who "was dead, and is alive again."

15.2504 (518:9). *Ci rifletta. Lei rovina tutto* – Italian: "Think it over. You ruin everything."

15.2506 (518:11). Love's old sweet song – See 4.314n.

15.2508–9 (518:14). the letter about the lute – A letter that Stephen has written to Arnold Dolmetsch; see 16.1765n.

15.2511 (518:16). The bird that can sing and won't sing – The proverb ends "must be made to sing."

15.2512 (518:17). *Philip Drunk and Philip Sober* – To appeal "from Philip Drunk to Philip Sober" is to ask reconsideration of a matter that has been decided in haste and on impulse. The saying comes from the story of the woman who, on receiving a bad judgment from Philip of Macedon when he was drunk, appealed to him sober and had the initial judgment reversed.

15.2514 (518:19). *Matthew Arnold's face* – See 1.173n and 1.158n.

15.2518 (518:23–24). if youth but knew – See 2.238n.

15.2518–19 (518:24). Mooney's en ville, Mooney's sur mer – See 11.264n and 7.892n.

15.2519 (518:24). the Moira – The Moira House and Tavern, a pub on the corner of Trin-

ity Street and Dame Lane in central Dublin south of the Liffey.

15.2519 (518:25). Larchet's – Larchet's Hotel and Restaurant, 11 College Green, just east of Moira House. The Moira and Larchet's not only add two more pubs to Stephen's day but also suggest that he has done some pub crawling on his way from the bookstalls in Wandering Rocks at 3:00-plus P.M. to the National Maternity hospital at 10:00-minus P.M.

15.2519 (518:25). Burke's – See 14.1391n.

15.2524 (519:1). *Zoe mou sas agapo* – Greek: "My life, I love you"; the epigraph and refrain of Byron's lyric "Maid of Athens, Ere We Part" (1810, 1812). First stanza: "Maid of Athens, ere we part, / Give, oh give me back my heart! / Or, since that has left my breast, / Keep it now, and take the rest! / Hear my vow before I go, / *Zoe mou sas agapo.*"

15.2525 (519:2). Atkinson – See 9.1141n.

15.2527 (519:4). Swinburne – See 1.77–78n.

15.2531 (519:8). Spirit is willing but the flesh is weak – Jesus reproves his disciples for falling asleep while he is praying in the garden of Gethsemane: "What, could ye not watch with me one hour? Watch and pray, that ye enter not into temptation: the spirit indeed is willing, but the flesh is weak" (Matthew 26:40–41).

15.2533 (519:10). Maynooth – The Royal College of St. Patrick (founded in 1795), for the education of young men destined for the Roman Catholic priesthood, was located in the town of Maynooth fifteen miles west-northwest of Dublin.

15.2545 (519:23). Fall of man – Contrary to the usual interpretation of Genesis 3, that the fall of man was a function of disobedience of a divine command, Virag treats the fall as literally a fall through sexual experience.

15.2546 (519:24–25). Nothing new under the sun – "The thing that hath been, it is that which shall be; and that which is done is that which shall be done: and there is no new thing under the sun" (Ecclesiastes 1:9).

15.2547 (519:25–26). *the Sex Secrets of Monks and Maidens – Source unknown, but no doubt another anti-Catholic, soft-pornography bit of Victoriana.

15.2547–48 (519:26). *Why I left the church of Rome – See 8.1070–71n.

15.2548 (519:27). the Priest, the Woman and the Confessional – A book (London, 1874) by Charles Pascal Telesphore Chiniquy; see 8.1070–71n. It had gone through twenty-four editions by 1883. Its central and prudish argument was that for women the experience of confession (opening "the secret recesses and sacred mysteries of their souls" to a man) was potentially corrupting.

15.2548 (519:27). Penrose – See 8.178 (156:3) and 8.1114 (181:32).

15.2549 (519:27–28). Flipperty Jippert – In *King Lear* during the storm on the heath, Edgar, disguised as the madman Poor Tom, "mistakes" his father, Gloucester, for "the foul fiend Flibbertigibbet" (III.iv.120), one of the minor agents of the Prince of Darkness.

15.2549 (519:29). pudor – Modesty, chastity, bashfulness.

15.2553 (520:1). *Coactus volui* – See 10.1113n.

15.2554 (520:3). spucks – From the German *spucken*, "to spit."

15.2555 (520:3–4). yadgana – After the Sanskrit for rump.

15.2558 (520:7). a penance. Nine glorias – An unlikely "penance" for the sin suggested; the "gloria," or Angelic Hymn, is Luke 2:14: "Glory to God in the highest, and on earth peace, good will toward men."

15.2558–59 (520:8). shooting a bishop – Or making a bishop: slang for sexual intercourse with the woman in the superior position.

15.2562 (520:11). A dry rush – Slang for sexual intercourse without emission (or, as in this case, without intromission).

15.2571 (520:20). *mooncalf* – A monster or a dolt, what Caliban is repeatedly called in *The Tempest;* see 1.143n.

15.2571–72 (520:21). *Verfluchte Goim!* – Yiddish: "Cursed Gentiles."

15.2572 (520:21). He had a father, forty fathers – In Flaubert's *The Temptation of Saint Anthony* (pp. 62–63), Anthony is plagued by a group of Heresiarchs who shout conflicting beliefs about the nature and origin of Jesus.

15.2572 (520:22). Pig God! – After the low Italian curse *Porco Dio*.

15.2572–73 (520:22). He had two left feet – One of the illustrations of the Virgin and Child in the *Book of Kells* depicts the Christ child with two left feet, the Virgin with two right feet. To "have two left feet" is slang for to be bumbling and inept.

15.2573 (520:22–23). *Judas Iacchia – The Cainites, an obscure sect of Gnostic heretics in the second century A.D., claimed to have a "Gospel of Judas," which inverted the Christian order (Judas became hero; Jesus, villain). Iacchia, that is, Bacchus in the Eleusinian mysteries, was (as the sacrificial fertility god) combined with Judas by the Cainites (and with Jesus by other inventive Heresiarchs). The Cainites and their "gospel" are mentioned in *The Temptation of Saint Anthony*, pp. 60–61, 64.

15.2573 (520:23). a Lybian eunuch – I wonder if this shouldn't be **a Lydian eunuch**, because then the epithet would fit the second-century Montanus, a convert from the cult of the earth mother Cybele (in whose worship he was castrated). He came from Phrygia-Lydia in Asia Minor and styled himself the Paraclete (cf. John 14:16) and claimed that divine revelation had not stopped with the Crucifixion and Resurrection. He was, of course, excluded as a heretic. He appears to Anthony in *The Temptation of Saint Anthony*, pp. 58–60.

15.2573 (520:23). the pope's bastard – The source for this speculation is unknown.

15.2575–76 (520:25–26). A son of a whore. Apocalypse – That is, Jesus was not Christ but the Antichrist, associated with the Scarlet Woman (see 15.1758n) and the forerunner of the Apocalypse described in Revelation; see 15.2135n.

15.2578–79 (520:28–29). Mary Shortall . . . Jimmy Pidgeon – Apart from the context, identity and significance unknown unless Mary Short/tall is all-things-to-all-men as, in prayer, the Blessed Virgin Mary is; in which case, see 3.161–62n for "the pigeon."

15.2578 (520:28). in the lock – Namely, in the Westmoreland National Lock (Government) Hospital, a hospital for the treatment of venereal diseases on Townsend Street in Dublin. The Contagious Diseases Acts of 1864, 1866, and 1869 made the lock hospitals virtual prisons for women suffering from venereal disease, or as *Thom's* 1904 discreetly puts it, "The institution is used not only as a means of curing physical disease, but as a reformatory for the moral reclamation of its patients" (p. 1380). The phrase *contagious diseases* is a Victorian euphemism for gonorrhea and syphilis.

15.2579 (520:29). the blue caps – The field caps of the Royal Dublin Fusiliers; see 5.66–68n.

15.2583–85 (521:2–4). *Qui vous a mis . . . le sacré pigeon* – See 3.161–62n.

15.2590 (521:10–11). Metchnikoff inoculated anthropoid apes – Ilya Metchnikoff (1845–1916), a Russian embryologist and cytologist, director of the Pasteur Institute (1895ff.), and Nobel Prize–winner (1908); he was famous for his demonstrations of the close relation between animal and human physiology. In 1904 he succeeded in infecting anthropoid apes with syphilis by inoculation.

15.2596 (521:17). Three wise virgins – See 7.937n.

15.2599–2600 (521:20–21). She sold love-philtres . . . the Roman centurion – Origen in *Contra Celsum* (1:32) refutes Celsus's (second century A.D.) anti-Christian argument that a Roman soldier named Panther fathered Jesus on Mary. In *The Temptation of Saint Anthony* "a Jew, with red beard, and his skin spotted with leprosy" mocks Antony, "his mother, the woman who sold perfumes, surrendered herself to Pantherus, a Roman soldier, under the corn sheaves, one harvest evening" (p. 63).

15.2601 (521:23). *fork* – Slang for crotch or penis.

15.2601–2 (521:23–24). He burst her tympanum – One medieval Scholastic tradition held that since Mary was impregnated by the Word (see 15.2236n), she was impregnated through the tympanum of her ear. See 11.536–37n.

15.2609 (522:2). *nakkering* – See 11.52n.

15.2610 (522:3). When love absorbs my ardent soul – See 11.20n.

15.2614 (522:8). *Ben my Chree!* – See 9.775n.

15.2621 (522:15–16). When first I saw . . . – See 11.24n.

15.2626 (522:22). *Dreck!* – Yiddish: "trash, junk, shit."

15.2628 (522:24–25). *Steered by his rapier* – The image suggests Henry Flower in the title role of Edmond Rostand's (1868–1918) *Cyrano de Bergerac* (1897). Cyrano is a swashbuckling poet-hero of the 1640s who compensates for his unfortunate physical appearance (a grotesquely long nose) with extraordinary romantic panache, but he never dares propose to (or even attempt to approach) his Roxanne.

15.2629 (522:25–26). *his wild harp slung behind him* – See 11.268–69n.

15.2633 (523:2). K. 11 – See 15.1658n.

15.2633 (523:2). Dr Hy Franks – See 8.97–98n.

15.2635 (523:4). All is lost now – See 11.22n.

15.2636 (523:5–6). *Virag unscrews his head . . . holds it under his arm* – In canto 28 of the *Inferno*, Dante meets those being punished for having sowed discord, including the Provençal troubadour-warrior Bertrand de Born (c. 1140–1215) who carries his head "like a lantern" (28:22). Bertrand tells Dante that his crime was giving evil counsel to the "young king," Prince Henry (d. 1183), the oldest son of Henry II of England (1133–89; king 1154–89). Bertrand says: "Because I parted persons thus united, I carry my brain, ah me! parted from its source which is in this trunk" (28:139–42). Virag's blasphemous accounts of the parentage of Jesus are in effect an attempt to separate the Father and the Son, two of the three persons of the Trinity.

15.2641–42 (523:11–12). the fighting parson who founded the protestant error – Namely, Martin Luther (1483–1546); but "the fighting parson" was also a nickname of William Gannaway Brownlow (1805–77), an American carpenter turned Methodist turned journalist. Proslavery but antisecession, he was expelled from the South during the Civil War; after the war he returned to Tennessee to become its governor and subsequently one of its U.S. senators.

15.2642 (523:13). Antisthenes, the dog sage – See 7.1035n. Antisthenes and his sect were called Cynics, after the Cynosarges Gymnasium, where Antisthenes taught. The Greek word *kynikos* means "doglike," a term appropriate not so much to Antisthenes as it was to later generations of his sect, noted for their insolent contempt of all human customs and values rather than for their adherence to virtue.

15.2643 (523:13–14). the last end of Arius . . . in the closet – See 1.657n and 3.50–52n.

15.2653 (523:24). Cardinal sin – The seven cardinal sins are pride, wrath, envy, lust, gluttony, avarice, and sloth.

15.2653 (523:24). Monks of the screw – An eighteenth-century society of Irish lawyers, statesmen, and intellectuals that also called itself the Order of Saint Patrick. The society met in its "convent" in Dublin or in "The Priory" near John Philpot Curran's (see 7.740n) country seat, since he was "prior" of the "order." The affectation of monkish habits was apparently a way of lending the spice of "violation" to the society's pursuit of pleasure. Cf. the first and third stanzas of Curran's "The Monks of the Screw": "When Saint Patrick our order created / And called us the Monks of the Screw, / Good rules he revealed to our abbot, / To guide us in what we should do. [Third stanza:] My children, be chaste—till you're tempted— / While sober, be wise and discreet: / And humble your bodies with fasting— / Whene'er you have nothing to eat."

15.2664–67 (524:10–13). Conservio lies, captured . . . upwards of three tons – Joyce (in his "Alphabetical Notebook," now in the Cornell University Joyce collection) cites these verses as the ones his father "quotes most," but the source of the verses remains unknown.

15.2671–76 (524:18–23). O, the poor little fellow . . . duckloving drake – An adaptation of the second stanza of "Nell Flaherty's Drake," an Irish ballad: "His neck was green—most rare to be seen, / He was fit for a queen of the highest degree; / His body was white—and would you delight— / He was plump, fat and heavy, and brisk as a bee. / The dear little fellow, his legs they were yellow, / He would fly like a swallow, and dive like a hake, / But some wicked savage, to grease his white cabbage, / Has murdered Nell Flaherty's beautiful drake."

15.2679 (524:27). By the hoky fiddle – An oath; for "hoky," see 5.362n.

15.2683 (524:31). the Easter kiss – The exchange of kisses is a solemnity in the high mass, often associated with Easter since a number of priests are necessary to its performance. The acolytes may be included in the solemnity and quite often are embarrassed into giggles.

15.2688–91 (525:3–6). Shall carry my heart . . . heart to thee – See 8.183n.

15.2717 (526:4). the bazaar – The Mirus Bazaar; see Section 19, p. 283 above.

15.2718 (526:5–6). the viceroy was there with his lady – See 10.1176n.

15.2718 (526:6). gas – Slang for excitement, pleasure.

15.2719 (526:6). Toft's hobbyhorses – A merry-go-round at the Mirus Bazaar. It was one of the pieces of equipment in a large traveling amusement park owned for generations by the Toft family of Cork.

15.2721 (526:9). Svengali's – Svengali is the archvillain of George DuMaurier's (1834–96) novel *Trilby* (1894). Svengali, a repulsive but musically gifted Austrian Jew, establishes a hypnotic hold over the beautiful Parisian laundress and model, Trilby. She is transformed into a great and famous singer under Svengali's influence; when Svengali dies, Trilby loses her voice but regains her warmth and humanity.

15.2721 (526:9–10). with folded arms and Napoleonic forelock – The stern and forbidding pose characteristic in portraits of Napoleon.

15.2724 (526:12–13). the sign of past master – Bloom identifies himself as the master of a Masonic lodge, since the title Master is conferred on a Mason as he assumes the duties of the chair. Only a Master or past Master can legally initiate, pass, or raise the members of a lodge.

15.2736–37 (526:24–25). *Aphrodisiac? Tansy and pennyroyal. But I bought it. Vanilla calms or? – Bloom tries to recall whether chocolate was regarded as an aphrodisiac; it was, since cocoa and its derivatives are mild stimulants. I have found no evidence that the combination of tansy and pennyroyal was so regarded as well, but tansy, which has a strong aromatic odor and a very bitter taste, was used in herbal medicine for a bitter tonic, and an infusion made from the pungently aromatic leaves of pennyroyal was used to promote perspiration. As for vanilla, it "calms" because, as another mild stimulant, it was thought useful in the treatment of nervous disorders.

15.2737–38 (526:25–26). Red influences lupus – *The New International Encyclopedia* ([New York, 1912] vol. 12, p. 548b) reports that the Danish physician Niels Finsen's (1860–1904) "phototherapy [had] proved successful in several cases" of lupus.

15.2741 (526:30). Try truffles at Andrews – Assuming truffles to be an aphrodisiac. Andrews & Co., a fashionable grocer and liquor merchant, 19–22 Dame Street, Dublin.

15.2745 (527:4). *Minnie Hauck in* **Carmen** – Minnie Hauck (1852–1929) was an American dramatic soprano who enjoyed a considerable reputation in Europe in the 1870s and 1880s, particularly in the title role of George Bizet's (1838–75) opera *Carmen* (1875), which she performed on tours that included the Gaiety Theatre in Dublin. The opera portrays the gypsy Carmen as a strong, ruthless, and capricious woman whose love is potentially destructive.

15.2746 (527:5). *keeper rings* – Or guard rings, to keep a valuable ring, especially a wedding ring, safely on a finger.

15.2772–73 (528:7–8). Powerful being . . . slumber which women love – In Leopold von Sacher-Masoch's *Venus in Furs*, the heroine, Wanda, repeatedly remarks on the dreaming (or slumbrous) look in Severin's (the hero's) eyes, and he repeatedly treats her to epithets of the "powerful being" sort. See 15.1046n. In the hallucination that follows, Bloom plays the part of Severin, Bella, that of a masculinized Wanda; in addition, the sequence is informed by Richard von Krafft-Ebing's (1840–1902) discussion of masochism (his coinage from Sacher-Masoch's name) in *Psychopathia Sexualis* (1886) (references in the notes below are to the 1937 Brooklyn [New York] edition). Krafft-Ebing's discussion and his case histories assume impotence to be a recurrent factor in masochism; he also develops implicit relations between masochism and foot-fetishism, clothes-fetishism,

and coprophilia, all of which take form in Bloom's hallucinations.

15.2779 (528:14–15). extra regulation fee – When the post office was closed, a letter could be posted for an extra fee in a railroad station. The sender chose the railroad station logically related to the letter's destination, and the letter was forwarded without having to be processed through the originating post office.

15.2779 (528:15). the too late box – A mailbox in front of the General Post Office in Dublin provided for those who wanted their letters canceled on a given day but who arrived after the post office had closed for that day.

15.2781–82 (528:17–18). a draught of thirtytwo feet . . . of falling bodies – Air currents do not, of course, follow that law; see 5.44n.

15.2785 (528:22–23). king David and the Sunamite – "Now king David was old and stricken in years; and they covered him with clothes, but he gat no heat. Wherefore his servants said unto him, Let there be sought for my Lord the king a young virgin . . . and [they] found Abishag a Shunamite, and brought her to the king. And the damsel was very fair, and cherished the king, and ministered to him: but the king knew her not" (I Kings 1:1–4).

15.2786 (528:23). Athos – See 6.125–27n.

15.2786 (528:23–24). A dog's spittle – Was assumed to carry rabies; Bloom is attempting to explain his father's death as caused by rabies rather than by self-administered poison.

15.2789 (528:26). Mocking is catch – After the proverb "Mocking is catching."

15.2794 (529:2–3). I should not have parted with my talisman – In contrast to Odysseus who does not part with the moly Hermes has given him to protect him from Circe's magic.

15.2805 (529:14). black knot – A fast or hard knot.

15.2806 (529:15). served my time – That is, as an apprentice.

15.2806 (529:16). *Kellett's – David Kellett, general draper, milliner, etc., 19–21 Great George's Street South, Dublin.

15.2807 (529:16). Every knot says a lot – Proverbial because the way a person ties a knot and the knot tied are supposed to reveal character much as handwriting does. The modern proverb and the belief it reflects have their roots in the ancient ritual use of knots as codes; for example, the Gordian knot, which Alexander the Great "cut," was apparently an elaborately encoded series of mystical propositions.

15.2814 (529:23). *Manfield's – Manfield & Sons, one of Dublin's more fashionable boot- and shoemakers, 78–79 Grafton Street.

15.2814–15 (529:23–24). my love's young dream – After Thomas Moore's song "Love's Young Dream." The first of the poem's three stanzas: "Oh! the days are gone, when Beauty bright / My heart's chain wove; / When my dream of life, from morn till night / Was love, still love. / New hope may bloom, / And days may come, / Of milder, calmer beam, / But there's nothing half so sweet in life / As love's young dream." Krafft-Ebing (pp. 173–76) provides two notable case histories of masochists whose foot-fetishism leads them to haunt woman's shoe stores, etc. As Krafft-Ebing puts it: "One of the most frequent forms of fetishism is that in which the female foot or shoe is the fetish. . . . The majority . . . of the cases of shoe fetishism rests upon a basis of more or less conscious masochistic desire for self-humiliation" (p. 172).

15.2817 (529:26). Clyde Road ladies – Clyde Road was in a fashionable upper-middle-class Anglo-Irish residential area south-southeast of metropolitan Dublin.

15.2817 (529:27). their wax model Raymonde – Before World War I clothes were shown not on living models but on miniature (and occasionally on life-size) wax figures.

15.2824 (530:4). If you bungle . . . football for you – Handy Andy is the bumbling antihero of Samuel Lover's 1842 novel of that name. Handy Andy's elaborate career of malfunction climaxes when his noble birth is revealed and he takes his place in the peerage as Lord Scatterbrain. Bella's (or The Hoof's) threat is a coarse rugby-field version of the way Wanda in *Venus in Furs* threatens "Gregor" (her lover, Severin, after he has become her "slave").

15.2827 (530:7). tache – Archaic: "that by which something is attached, a clasp."

15.2833 (530:14–15). Awaiting your further orders, we remain, gentlemen – A conventional ending for a business letter. It also describes "Gregor's" (Severin enslaved) relationship to Wanda in *Venus in Furs.*

15.2835 (530:17). basilisk – See 9.374–75n.

15.2839 (530:22–23). Adorer of the adulterous rump – Krafft-Ebing cites *oscula ad nates* (rump kissing) as a mild form of coprophilia (one of the symptoms of extreme masochism) (p. 194).

15.2843 (530:27). Dungdevourer! – Krafft-Ebing (pp. 193–94) cites several instances of this sort of coprophilia, which he regards as the ultimate in masochistic self-degradation.

15.2852–53 (531:10–11). on all fours, grunting, snuffling, rooting – Bella has transformed Bloom into a pig, as Circe transformed Odysseus's men into swine; see headnote to this episode, p. 452.

15.2854–55 (531:13). the attitude of most excellent master – In Freemasonry, during part of the ceremony of "raising" (i.e., elevating a lodge member to Master Mason), some forms of the ritual dictate that the individual lie prone as evidence of his humility.

15.2860 (531:18–19). places his heel on her neck – At the beginning of *Venus in Furs* the narrator, to whom Severin's story is about to be revealed, has a dream in which Venus visits him; she mocks him by saying that "as a rule" the man's neck will be under the foot of the woman (p. 17), as Severin is later to say he longs to be "the slave of a pitiless tyrant who treads us pitilessly underfoot" (p. 27). Krafft-Ebing (pp. 185 and 172–76) cites several cases in which masochistic fantasies and practices involve being trod upon.

15.2864 (531:23). I promise never to disobey – Since Bloom has assumed a Masonic "attitude," this could be taken as part of the apprentice Mason's oath of initiation, since in that oath he would promise not to reveal the secret (see 15.4951–52n) and would also promise absolute obedience to his master in Masonry. In *Venus in Furs* (pp. 90–91) Severin signs the "agreement" that makes him Wanda's servant-slave, Gregor; the agreement, of course, involves a similar promise.

15.2866 (531:25–26). You little know what's in store for you – Wanda repeatedly makes similar remarks to Severin in *Venus in Furs,* since she recognizes that his desire for subjugation is "romantic dreaming" even as she herself is being transformed into the "pitiless tyrant" whom Severin has "romantically" desired.

15.2867 (531:26–27). and break you in – At the climax of *Venus in Furs,* Wanda takes a Greek "lion" as a lover and abandons Severin; just before she abandons him, she betrays him into the ultimate cure of his masochistic fantasies by turning him over to the Greek to be whipped; as the Greek (with pleasure) accepts his role, he says, "Now watch me break him in" (p. 137).

15.2867–68 (531:27). Kentucky cocktails – What cocktails were called in the British Isles, since they, like bourbon, were regarded as an American invention.

15.2891–92 (532:21–23). The nosering, the pliers . . . Nubian slave of old – The "agreement" that Severin signs to formalize his role as Wanda's "slave" in *Venus in Furs* contains the stipulation: "Wanda is entitled not only to punish her slave as she deems best . . . but also is herewith given the right to torture him as the mood may seize her or merely for the sake of whiling away the time" (p. 90). "Nubian slave" suggests absolute slavery, since Nubia was the heart of Arab slave-trading territory from the fourteenth century until the beginning of the twentieth century.

15.2894–95 (532:25–26). *I shall sit on your ottoman saddleback – In his discussion of masochism (pp. 152–54), Krafft-Ebing cites the case history of an impotent man whose primary mode of sexual gratification was to be ridden as though he were a horse; while being ridden, he liked to be treated "without consideration."

15.2896 (532:27). Matterson's – Matterson & Sons, general commission agents, victuallers, and butter stores, 12 Hawkins Street, Dublin.

15.2897 (532:29). Stock Exchange cigar – Significance unknown.

15.2898 (532:29–30). *Licensed Victualler's Gazette* – A twopenny weekly trade newspaper, published in London. Catering to "licensed houses" (hotels, bars, etc.), it included "literary features" in the effort to broaden its advertising base by appealing to the victuallers'

customers as well as to the victuallers themselves.

15.2902 (533:3). *turning turtle* – Turning upside down (as a capsized ship with its bottom up); figuratively, becoming cowardly.

15.2916 (533:18). Hold him down, girls, till I squat on him – In *Venus in Furs,* Wanda has three Negro maids who bind Severin so that she can whip him (p. 92) or yoke him to a plow for her "amusement" (p. 102). Krafft-Ebing (pp. 137–38) includes the case history of a masochist who got his kicks by having women sit on his face.

15.2923 (533:25). *Mrs Keogh* – Apart from the context, identity and significance unknown, except that Circe is attended by four maids, nymphs "whose cradles were in fountains, under boughs, / or in the glassy seaward-gliding streams," and Mrs. Keogh (added to Zoe, Kitty, and Florry) makes the fourth (10:350–51; Fitzgerald, p. 188).

15.2932–33 (534:7–8). *Keating Clay . . . the Richmond asylum – The *Evening Telegraph* (Thursday, 16 June 1904, p. 4) reports that Richard Jones was reelected as chairman and Robert Keating Clay, a Dublin solicitor, as deputy chairman. For the Richmond Asylum, see 1.128n.

15.2933–34 (534:8–9). Guinness's preference shares are at sixteen three quarters – "Guinness . . . Preference shares maintained previous value, $16^{11}/_{16}$" (*Evening Telegraph,* 16 June 1904, p. 4).

15.2934–35 (534:10). Craig and Gardner – Craig, Gardner & Co., chartered accountants, 40–41 Dame Street, Dublin.

15.2936 (534:12). Throwaway – See 14.1128–33n and 5.532n.

15.2942 (534:18). *a figged fist* – An obscene Italian gesture common at least since the time of Dante (*Inferno,* 25:2) and still forceful: the thumb is protruded between the first and second fingers of the clenched fist. Symbolically, the fist (the fig) is the vulva, the thumb is phallic, and the combination, an outrageous "Fuck you!"

15.2944 (534:20–21). A cockhorse to Banbury cross – From a nursery rhyme usually said in accompaniment to a child's riding on an adult's knee (or a wooden horse). "Ride a cock-horse to Banbury Cross, / To see an old [or fine] lady upon a white horse; / Rings on her fingers and bells on her toes, / She shall have music wherever she goes." For Banbury, see 8.74–76n; a "cockhorse" is a child's hobby horse.

15.2944–45 (534:21). the Eclipse stakes – To be run on 16 July 1904 in Sandown Park on the Isle of Wight. See 12.1219–20n.

15.2947 (534:24). *cockhorse* – Astride; see 15.2894–95n.

15.2947–49 (534:24–26). The lady goes a pace . . . gallop a gallop – One among many versions of a nursery rhyme that accompanies a child being ridden in a sequence of different styles on an adult's knee.

15.2953 (534:32). suckeress – Bloodsucker, leech.

15.2958–59 (535:6). *farts stoutly* – See 15.2843n.

15.2959 (535:7). by Jingo – This mild oath picked up overtones of excessive chauvinism when "jingo" became the nickname for a supporter of Lord Beaconsfield's aggressive action of sending a British fleet to Turkish waters to oppose a Russian advance in 1878. This sense of the word was derived from a popular music-hall song. Chorus: "We don't want to fight, but by jingo if we do, / We've got the ships, We've got the men, We've got the money too."

15.2959–60 (535:7). sixteen three quarters – See 15.2933–34n; but in this horsey context the phrase could also mean "sixteen and three-quarters hands," a very large saddle horse.

15.2964–66 (535:12–14). No more blow hot . . . thing under the yoke – From *Venus in Furs:* Wanda repeatedly accuses Severin of vacillating in his "supersensual" desire to be her slave and in his willingness to be subjugated, humiliated, and injured. She also (and with increasing intensity) taunts him by pointing out that the treatment he is getting and the pain he is suffering are his romantic wishes come true. At one point (p. 102), Wanda has her three Negro maids yoke Severin–Gregor to a plow.

15.2973 (535:22). As they are now, so will you be – See 6.961n.

15.2976 (535:26). coutille – A close-woven soft canvas used for mattresses and pillows and in stays or corsets.

15.2980 (535:30). Alice – Repetition suggests an allusion to Lewis Carroll's (Charles L. Dodgson, 1832–98) heroine Alice in *Alice's Adventures in Wonderland* (1865) and *Through the Looking Glass* (1872): both focus on the elaborate metamorphoses that the heroine and her world undergo.

15.2981 (535:31–536:1). Martha and Mary – See 5.289–91n.

15.2985 (536:5). *charming soubrette* – See 10.380–81 (229:23–24).

15.2986 (536:6–7). I tried her things on – Krafft-Ebing, in his discussion of fetishism (which he links closely with masochism), cites several cases of otherwise heterosexual men who seek sexual gratification by dressing up in women's clothes and creating "beautiful women in imagination" (p. 251). One of the cases went in for corsets because masochistically he enjoyed "the pain of tight lacing" (p. 253).

15.2994–95 (536:16–17). Mrs Miriam Dandrade . . . Shelbourne Hotel – See 8.349–53 (160:38–161:1) and 8.351n.

15.3001–2 (536:24) *lieutenant Smythe-Smythe – The coinage is appropriate, since Smythe was a military name of some repute in 1904.

15.3002 (536:24–25). Mr Philip Augustus Blockwell, M.P. – Fictional. See 18.822n.

15.3002 (536:25). *signor Laci Daremo – See *Là ci darem*, 4.314n.

15.3003 (536:26). blueeyed Bert – Apart from the context, identity and significance unknown.

15.3003–4 (536:26–27). Henry Fleury of Gordon Bennett fame – Henry Fleury, no doubt one of Henry Flower's pseudonyms; see 14.1560n and 6.370n.

15.3004 (536:27). Sheridan; the quadroon Croesus – Croesus, king of Lydia in the sixth century B.C., the type of the infinitely wealthy man. "Sheridan" is unknown.

15.3004 (536:27–28). wetbob – A boy at Eton who devotes himself to boating.

15.3005 (536:28). old Trinity – Trinity College, Dublin.

15.3005–6 (536:29). Bobs, dowager duchess of Manorhamilton – Manorhamilton is a village in County Leitrim on the west coast of Ireland; "Bobs" is apparently fictional.

15.3010–11 (536:34). *Vice Versa – (Subtitled *A Lesson to Fathers*), a novel (1882) by the English writer Thomas Anstey Guthrie (pseudonym Francis Anstey, 1856–1934) with two stage versions, one by Edward Rose (1883), the other by Guthrie (1910). The central theme of the farce is father against son played out when the father's spirit inhabits the son's body, and vice versa. Since Bloom left high school in 1880, he couldn't have performed in the play (except in the anachronism of fiction).

15.3011–12 (536:34–537:2). He got that kink . . . gilds his eyelids – Krafft-Ebing reports the case of a transvestite who got his start by trying on his sister's "chemise" (pp. 251–52).

15.3024 (537:14). a jinkleman – A trickster, a cheat.

15.3024–25 (537:15). the ass of the Doran's – After "Doran's Ass," an Irish ballad about one Paddy Doyle who, drunk, mistakes Doran's ass for his sweetheart, Biddy Tool, and makes love to the ass. He comes to in a state of fright and runs to Biddy in time for the last stanza: "He told her his story mighty civil / While she prepared a whiskey glass: / How he hugged and smugged the hairy divil, / 'Go long,' says she, ''twas Doran's Ass!' / 'I know it was, my Biddy darling.' / They both got married the very next day, / But he never got back his ould straw-hat / That the jackass ate up on the way."

15.3029 (537:20–21). *the Black church – St. Mary's Chapel of Ease (Church of Ireland), so called because it was built of black Dublin stone. It is in Mountjoy Street in north-central Dublin, not far south of Bloom's home in Eccles Street. Legend had it that a person who circled the church three times at midnight would meet the devil.

15.3030–31 (537:21–22). *Miss Dunn at an address in D'Olier street – Two possibilities: Dunn's of 26 D'Olier Street was a fashionable shop (poulterer and fishmonger, game and venison dealer); or Boylan's secretary is named Miss Dunne (10.368 [229:10]), and though the address of his office is not given, there was the Advertising Company, Ltd., bill posters and advertising agents, at 15 D'Olier Street across from the Red Bank Restaurant, where Boylan is seen (6.196–99 [92:19–22]).

15.3036 (537:28). vitriol works – Dublin Vitriol Works Company, 17 Ballybough Road, on the northeastern outskirts of metropolitan Dublin.

15.3039 (537:32). a nasty harlot, stimulated by gingerbread – Krafft-Ebing cites the case of a similarly inclined Russian prince who "supported a mistress in unusually brilliant style, with the condition that she ate marchpane exclusively" (p. 193).

15.3045 (538:6). *Poldy Kock – See 4.358n.

15.3045 (538:6). *Bootlaces a penny – See 6.231 (93:17).

15.3045 (538:6–7). *Cassidy's hag – See 4.224 (61:15).

15.3046 (538:7). *Larry rhinoceros – A pun on "Larry O'Rourke"; see 4.105n. "Rhino" is slang for money.

15.3049 (538:10). Our mutual faith – Bloom assumes that Bella Cohen's name indicates that she is Jewish; Hyman (pp. 167–68) remains silent on this point.

15.3049 (538:10). Pleasants street – See 4.209–10n.

15.3062 (538:24). Mistress! – What Severin (as the slave-servant Gregor) is required to call Wanda in *Venus in Furs*.

15.3068 (539:2). With this ring I thee own – After the traditional line in the marriage service, "With this ring I thee wed." See 15.375n.

15.3077 (539:12). Miss Ruby – See 4.346n.

15.3084 (539:21). on the turf – Can be taken to mean that Marsh is in horse racing, but it is also slang for "in business as a prostitute."

15.3084 (539:21). Charles Alberta Marsh – Identity and significance unknown, except, as Adams suggests (p. 213), that he has a feminine middle name (as does Leopold *Paula* Bloom).

15.3085–86 (539:22–23). **the Hanaper and Petty Bag office** – In the Chancery Division of His Majesty's High Court of Justice in Ireland; its chief duties were secretarial to the lord chancellor.

15.3102 (540:6). **Two bar** – Two shillings.

15.3103 (540:7). **Fourteen hands high** – As a horse is measured; a small saddle horse.

15.3113 (540:19). *****the Caliph. Haroun Al Raschid** – See 3.366n.

15.3119 (540:26). *****four inch Louis Quinze heels** – Louis XV of France (1710–74; king 1715–74). Toward the end of his reign women's dresses were shortened to ankle length and high-heeled shoes became the fashion, though not quite so perversely high as four inches. Excessively high Louis XV heels were popularized during the Second Empire in France in the late 1860s.

15.3119–20 (540:26–27). **the Grecian bend** – A name for the stooped carriage with buttocks angled into prominence that became high fashion (partly as a result of excessively high heels) in France in the late 1860s. Zack Bowen (*Musical Allusions in the Works of James Joyce* [Albany, N.Y., 1974], p. 286) cites a song of that title popularized by William H. Lingard, a female impersonator of the 1860s: "The Grecian bend, as I now show, / You must admit is all the go; / The head well forward, and the body you extend, / To be perfect in the Grecian Bend."

15.3122 (540:29). **Gomorrahan vices** – The inhabitants of Sodom and Gomorrah (see 4.221–22n) are characterized in Genesis as indulging in unnatural sexual practices.

15.3129 (541:4). **Manx cat!** – A tailless cat from the Isle of Man.

15.3129–30 (541:5). **curly teapot** – Slang for penis (suggested by Eric Partridge).

15.3130 (541:6). **cockyolly** – A pet name for a small bird.

15.3131 (541:7). **doing his pooly** – Urinating.

15.3136ff. (541:12ff.). **I wouldn't hurt your feelings . . .** – Toward the end of *Venus in Furs*, Wanda, having met in her leonine Greek lover the man she "needs," similarly, but far less crudely, taunts her fawning slave-lover Severin.

15.3139 (541:15). **muff** – A foolish, silly person; in athletics, a clumsy person; a failure.

15.3149 (541:27). **lame duck** – A defaulter.

15.3154 (542:3–4). **in Sleepy Hollow your night of twenty years** – Combines allusions to two stories by Washington Irving; see 13.1112n and 13.1115n.

15.3158 (542:7). *****Rip van Winkle!** – In Irving's story, a ne'er-do-well plagued by a nagging wife; he beats frequent retreats into the Catskills on hunting expeditions. During the one on which the story focuses he is surprised by, among other things, a twenty-year sleep. He returns to his village to find his wife dead and himself virtually forgotten.

15.3168 (542:18). *simply swirling* – See 4.282n.

15.3173–74 (542:24). *****aunt Hegarty's** – Bloom's great-aunt on his mother's side.

15.3175 (542:26). **The *Cuckoo's Rest*** – See 9.1025n.

15.3178–79 (542:29–30). **Sauce for the goose, my gander, O** – See 11.877n.

15.3183 (543:4). **the Brusselette carpet** – An inexpensive imitation of Brussels carpet.

15.3184 (543:5). **Wren's auction** – See 6.446n.

15.3185–86 (543:7–8). **the little statue . . . art for art's sake** – For the statue of Narcissus, see 17.1428n. "Art for art's sake" became a rallying cry for late-nineteenth-century esthetes, characteristic of the reaction against the Victorian demand for moral realism in art. Oscar Wilde's stance was popularly regarded as a prototype of this anti-Victorian position.

15.3189 (543:11). **Hampton Leedom's** – Hampton Leedom & Co., wax and tallow chandlers, hardware, delft and china merchants, 50 Henry Street, Dublin.

15.3194 (543:16). **Swear!** – In *Hamlet*, as Hamlet attempts to swear Horatio and his companions to secrecy, the Ghost (in the "cellerage") repeatedly says, "Swear!" (I.v).

15.3198–99 (543:21). **secondbest bed** – See 9.691–95n.

15.3199 (543:21–22). Your epitaph is written – See 11.1275n.

15.3205–6 (543:29–544:1). I can give you . . . to hell and back – At the end of Book 10 in *The Odyssey*, Odysseus begs Circe to let him leave to continue his homeward voyage. She tells him, much to his distress, that he must first visit the land of the dead. He argues that no living man has ever visited that land, and she responds with directions for the voyage and for the sacrifices that will make the voyage successful; the latter include "sweet milk and honey, then sweet wine and last / clear water" (10:519; Fitzgerald, p. 193).

15.3208 (544:4). Cuck Cohen – Identity and significance unknown, though to "cuck" is obsolete for to defecate.

15.3215 (544:11). *My willpower! Memory! – Krafft-Ebing in his case histories of masochism repeatedly cites loss of willpower and memory as a result of this "disease."

15.3215 (544:11–12). I have sinned I have suff – See 5.372 (81:20–21).

15.3220 (544:17). *The passing bell* – A tolling bell to announce that a soul has passed or is passing from its body; the sound was to invoke prayers for the dying.

15.3220–21 (544:18–19). *the circumcised, in sackcloth and ashes, stand by the wailing wall* – Counting Bloom, ten Jews are present, constituting a *minyan*, the quorum of adult Jewish males required for communal services and for certain rituals, including the lament at the Wailing Wall, as here (except that Minnie Watchman, as a woman, could not be counted as one of the ten necessary to a minyan, although she could be present). The Wailing Wall in Jerusalem is the last remnant of the temple of Solomon, rebuilt by Herod and then destroyed by the Romans on Friday, 9 August 70 A.D.; it is thus the one remaining fragment of the holiest of Jewish sanctuaries, particularly revered as a place for mourning and lamentation, not just for personal loss but for the collective loss suffered by all Jews. *Anachronism:* before the British conquest of Palestine and capture of Jerusalem in 1917, Jews were prohibited by the Turkish government from holding a minyan at the wall, and afterwards permission to pray at the wall had the stipulation "quietly" attached because the wall was in a volatile Arab section of the city. Defiant Jews repeatedly caused newsworthy disturbances at the wall by lamenting loudly, blowing the *shofar* (see 15.1619n), etc. In present-day Israel a service is held at the wall three times a day. *Aside:* according to Hyman (p. 328), porters at the North Wall in Dublin used to call one section of the wharf where visitors gathered to lament the emigration of their relatives and friends the "wailing wall" as well.

15.3221–24 (544:19–22). *M. Shulomowitz . . . Leopold Abramowitz* – "Neighbors" of Bloom when Bloom lived in Lombard Street West. Incidentally, in 1904 a Mr. J. Bloom lived at 38 Lombard Street West. M. Shulomowitz (or Isaac Myer Shmulovitch, d. 1940) was secretary of the Jewish library at 57 Lombard Street West. Joseph Goldwater lived at 77 Lombard Street West. For Moses Herzog, see 12.17–18n. Harris Rosenberg lived at 63 Lombard Street West. For M. Moisel, see 4.209–10n. For J. Citron, see 4.205n. *Minnie Watchman:* a Morris Watchman lived at 77 Lombard Street West, according to *Thom's* 1904; *Thom's* 1905 lists a "Mr" Minnie Watchman at 20 St. Kevin's Parade; Hyman says that was Mrs. Minnie Watchman, his great-aunt (p. 329). The Reverend Leopold Abramowitz (more accurately, Abraham Lipman Abramovitz, d. 1907) was "An ordained rabbi, [who] arrived in Dublin in 1887 and served the community as *shochet* (ritual slaughterer), *chazan* (reader), *mohel* (circumciser) and Hebrew teacher" (Hyman, p. 329).

15.3227 (544:25). *dead sea fruit* – A common metaphor for hollow and unsatisfactory pleasures; after the apple of Sodom, which does grow near the Dead Sea—it is beautiful in appearance but bitter to the taste.

15.3227 (544:26). *no flowers* – Orthodox Jewish custom forbids flowers at funerals and on graves.

15.3228 (544:26). *Shema Israel . . . Adonai Echad* – See 7.209n; the Shema is ritually pronounced by or for a dying Jew.

15.3233–34 (544:33). *a nymph* – See 4.369 (65:11).

15.3235 (545:2). *interlacing yews* – The yew tree is traditionally associated with death and mourning.

15.3245 (545:12). highkickers – Dancers who, like can-can girls, showed their legs.

15.3245 (545:12–13). *coster picnicmakers – Costermongers, hawkers of fruits or vegetables.

15.3246 (545:13). panto boys – Pantomime performers.

15.3247 (545:14–15). La Aurora and Karini – Significance unknown.

15.3250 (545:18). transparencies – A piece of transparent material with a picture or design that is visible when light shines through it.

15.3250 (545:18). truedup dice – Dice that were geometrically perfect and therefore presumably "honest."

15.3250 (545:18–19). proprietary articles – Manufactured articles that some person or persons have the exclusive right to make and sell.

15.3258–59 (545:27–29). Professor Waldmann's wonderful . . . Rubin with photo – Significance unknown.

15.3261 (546:2). *Photo Bits* – See 4.370n.

15.3268 (546:10–11). a thing of beauty – See 15.2254n.

15.3274 (546:17). Steel wine – Wine, usually sherry, in which steel filings have stood for a considerable time; regarded as a medicine.

15.3277 (546:21). Frailty, thy name is marriage – See 12.1227–28n.

15.3295 (547:14). orangekeyed – See 4.330n.

15.3299 (547:18). Poulaphouca – A scenic waterfall on the upper Liffey, twenty miles southwest of Dublin. It is named after Phouka (Puck), a mischievous Celtic sprite allegedly trapped in a rock by St. Nessan.

15.3305 (547:25). *Irish National Forester's* – See 12.1268n.

15.3318 (548:8–9). *a red school cap with badge* – The school cap of the Erasmus Smith High School (see 8.187n) was black with a red, blue, and gold badge (?).

15.3321 (548:12). the old Royal stairs – See 11.624n.

15.3323 (548:14–15). the heat. There were sunspots that summer – Since the Old Royal Theatre was destroyed by fire in 1880, the sunspot activity would have to have been in the late 1870s. There was an outstanding minimum of sunspot activity in 1878 and no maximum between 1870 and 1883. Sunspot maximums were superstitiously supposed to account for eccentric behavior; cf. 8.568–69n.

15.3324 (548:15). tipsycake – A cake saturated with wine or spirits, stuck with almonds, and served with custard.

15.3325–26 (548:17–18). *blue and white football jerseys* – The football jerseys at the Erasmus Smith High School were black and red, not blue and white (?).

15.3326–28 (548:18–20). *Master Donald Turnbull . . . Percy Apjohn* – Bloom's schoolmates at the Erasmus Smith High School in Harcourt Street; all except Apjohn lived near the school. In 1904 Donald Turnbull lived at 53 Harcourt Street; Abraham Chatterton (b. 1862), educated at Erasmus Smith and Trinity College, Dublin, was registrar and bursar of Erasmus Smith in 1904 (Adams, p. 213); for Owen Goldberg, see 8.404n; John W. Meredith, 97 Haddington Road; for Percy Apjohn, see 8.404n.

15.3331 (548:23). Mackerel! – See 8.405n.

15.3335 (548:28). Montague street – A block north of the Erasmus Smith High School off Harcourt Street.

15.3354 (549:17). The flowers that bloom in the spring – In Act II of Gilbert and Sullivan's *The Mikado* (1885) Nanki-Poo sings: "The flowers that bloom in the spring, / Tra la, / Breathe promise of merry sunshine— / As we merrily dance and we sing, / Tra la, / We welcome the hope that they bring, / Tra la, / Of a summer of roses and wine." Ko-ko, in duet, answers: "The flowers that bloom in the spring, / Tra la, / Have nothing to do with the case. / I've got to take under my wing, / Tra la, / A most unattractive old thing, / Tra la, / With a caricature of a face."

15.3354–55 (549:18). Capillary attraction – The apparent attraction between a solid and a liquid caused by capillarity.

15.3355 (549:18–19). Lotty Clarke – Apart

from the context, identity and significance unknown.

15.3357 (549:21). *Rialto bridge – Over the Grand Canal on the western outskirts of metropolitan Dublin.

15.3360 (549:25). *Staggering Bob – See 8.724n.

15.3367 (550:4). *Ben Howth – See 8.900–902n.

15.3373 (550:10). Circumstances alter cases – "A comedietta in one act, adapted from *L'invitation à la valse* of Alexander Dumas" (New York, n.d.) by William Jones Hoppin (1813–95). The most strikingly altered case in the farce is that of Maurice, a "delicate hero of romance" with a "charming tenor" who, after seven years in the Algerian desert among "out and out savages," returns, having given up music and developed a gruff "deep bass" voice. His first love, the delicate older sister, is put off by this change, and her place is taken by the more robustly romantic younger sister (who has been writing her sister's letters to Maurice for seven years anyway). And all is well: the older sister has her all-too-faithful lawyer whom she finally accepts after his seven-year vigil.

15.3374 (550:11–12). Thirtytwo head over heels per second – See 5.44n.

15.3375 (550:12). Giddy Elijah – See 12.1910–12n.

15.3375–76 (550:13). government printer's clerk – That is, Bloom, who is imagining the newspaper account of his death. Bloom was for a time "clerk" in Alexander Thom's, "printers to his Majesty."

15.3378 (550:15). *the Lion's Head cliff – See 8.900–902n.

15.3382 (550:19–20). *Bailey and Kish lights the* Erin's King – The Bailey lighthouse is on the southeastern point of the Howth peninsula; the Kish lightship is anchored on Kish Bank off Dublin Bay; for "the Erin's King," see 4.434n.

15.3387–90 (550:24–28). When my country takes . . . written. I have . . . Done – See 11.1275n.

15.3392–93 (551:3). and no hair there either – This may be a reminder that Ruskin, apparently

instructed only by classical antiquity, was so shocked by the discovery on his wedding night that his wife had pubic hair that the marriage was never consummated.

15.3398 (551:10). quassia – An intensely bitter drug made from the wood of certain tropical American trees and used as a tonic.

15.3399 (551:11). Hamilton Long's – See 5.464–65n.

15.3405 (551:16). *Peccavi! – Latin: "I have sinned!"

15.3407 (551:18–19). the hand that rules – See 11.1183–84n.

15.3422 (552:6). Ware Sitting Bull! – That is, beware of the Sioux Indian chief Sitting Bull (c. 1831–90), one of whose exploits was the annihilation of General Custer and his forces at the battle of the Little Big Horn in 1876.

15.3434 (552:19). *in nun's white habit, coif and huge wingedwimple – The habit of a Carmelite nun.

15.3435 (552:20). Tranquilla convent. Sister Agatha – See 8.143–44n and 13.781n. Sister Agatha takes her name from St. Agatha of Sicily, virgin and martyr. Her martyrdom began when she was handed over to a house of prostitution and for a month subjected to "assaults and stratagems" (*Butler's "Lives of the Saints,"* ed. Herbert Thurston, S.J., and Donald Attwater [London, 1956], vol. 1, p. 256). When that didn't break her spirit, she was beaten and stretched on the rack, but she continued to respond with "cheerfulness"; so her breasts were crushed and then cut off, and finally she was "rolled naked over live coals mixed with potsherds." Her attributes are pincers and breasts "on a dish." She is patron of bell-founders and is "invoked against any outbreak of fire" (ibid.).

15.3435 (552:21). Mount Carmel – In ancient Palestine, associated with Elijah (I Kings 18:17–39) and Elisha (II Kings 2:25). It was in a fertile region and was regarded by Old Testament prophets as blessed of God. The Carmelite order was founded there in 1156; see 8.148n.

15.3435–36 (552:21). the apparitions of Knock and Lourdes – See 5.365n and 5.365–66n.

15.3442 (552:27). *the Coombe – A street in the

run-down area called the Liberties in south-central Dublin.

15.3444–47 (553:2–5). O Leopold lost . . . To keep it up – See 5.281–84 (78:38–41).

15.3461 (553:19). *an elected knight of nine* – One of the Knights Templar (emblem: a red cross on a white field). The order was founded by nine knights in 1118 to protect pilgrims on their way to the Holy Land; it was suppressed in 1312, in part because it had become too worldly and in part because it was a disruptive political power. The Freemasons regard themselves as the heirs apparent of the Knights Templar.

15.3461 (553:19). Nekum! – Meaning unknown.

15.3463 (553:21). Nebrakada! – See 10.849n.

15.3463 (553:21). *Cat o' nine lives! – Combines "cat of nine tails" with the proverbial "Every cat has nine lives."

15.3464 (553:22). The fox and the grapes – The title of one of Aesop's fables. The fox, hungry and thirsty, leaps at the grapes but is unable to reach them. He decides that he didn't want them anyway, since they were probably sour.

15.3465 (553:23). your barbed wire – See 8.154n.

15.3466 (553:25). Brophy, the lame gardener – Apart from the context, identity and significance unknown.

15.3466–67 (553:25–26). statue of the water-carrier – Aquarius, the eleventh sign of the zodiac, is the water bearer.

15.3467 (553:26). *good mother Alphonsus – Alphonsus is the Latin form of the masculine name Alphonso. Earlier in the day Bloom, speculating on the meaning of George William Russell's initials AE, had thought of Alphonsus as one possibility (8.529 [165:34]). The joke, of course, is that Mother Alphonsus is male, not female. There was a Monastery of St. Alphonsus (Church and Monastery of the Redemptoristines) in St. Alphonsus Road, Fairview, the Reverend Sister Mary Stanislaus, superior (1904).

15.3467 (553:26). Reynard – The fox in the medieval beast epic *Reynard the Fox*. Reynard's name derives from the Germanic *Raginohard*, "the wily, crafty one," and in the course of his enduring feud with the wolf he finally proves himself the real master of the beasts.

15.3468–70 (553:27–29). *THE NYMPH / (*with a cry flees from him unveiled . . . stench escaping from the cracks*) – In the *Purgatorio* 19 Dante, asleep, has a dream-vision of the siren who metamorphoses from ugly to attractive and enthralls him until Virgil intervenes: "He seized the other [the siren], and, rending her clothes, laid her open in front and showed me her belly; that awakened me with the stench which issued therefrom."

15.3474 (554:2). pay on the nail – That is, pay promptly and in cash.

15.3474–75 (554:2). You fee men dancers on the Riviera – Bloom has been reading "scandal" about wealthy women who hire gigolos at fashionable international resorts.

15.3481 (554:9). You'll know me the next time – Wanda in *Venus in Furs* repeatedly pleads with Severin to stop fawning on her and to assert his manhood; instead, he intensifies his masochistic infatuation. Finally, Wanda asserts her supremacy: "'Now play has come to an end between us,' she said with heartless coldness. 'Now we will begin in dead earnest. You fool, I laugh at you and despise you; you who in your insane infatuation have given yourself as plaything to *me*, the frivolous and capricious woman. You are no longer the man I love, but *my slave*, at my mercy even unto life and death.
    "'You shall know me!'" (p. 93).

15.3496 (554:25). Dead cod! – Incapable of sexual intercourse; "cod" is slang for the scrotum.

15.3498 (554:27). kipkeeper! Pox and gleet vendor! – Slang: "Brothelkeeper! Vendor of venereal disease [pox] and a morbid discharge from the urethra [gleet]."

15.3500 (555:2–3). the dead march from Saul – See 6.374n.

15.3502 (555:5). Mind your cornflowers – Punning slang for "tread warily": so that you don't step on the flowers and/or so that your toes (corns) aren't stepped on.

15.3503 (555:6–7). The cat's ramble through the slag – A piano routine, essentially tuneless and similar to "Chopsticks."

15.3511 (555:15). Forfeits – Penalties exacted for mistakes in ritual, as in children's games.

15.3515–18 (555:19–22). Give a thing . . . send you down below – Iona and Peter Opie (*The Lore and Language of Schoolchildren* [London, 1959], p. 133) cite an almost-identical verse from Laurencetown, County Galway. It occurs in children's games that involve rituals of giving or swapping.

15.3522 (555:26). To have or not to have, that is the question – After the opening line of Hamlet's over-quoted soliloquy, "To be, or not to be: that is the question" (III.i.56).

15.3536 (556:14–15). *Dans ce bordel où tenons nostre état* – French: "In this brothel where we hold our 'court'"; a variation of the refrain (*En ce bordeau où . . .*) of François Villon's (1431– c. 1463) *Ballade de la grosse Margot* (Ballad of Fat Margot).

15.3546 (556:26–27). *brevi manu* – Italian: "shorthanded" or "shortchanged."

15.3560 (557:12–13). drink . . . it's long after eleven – That is, it's long after the closing time of the pubs; something of a joke, since many Dublin brothels served drinks as a way of attracting after-hours clients.

15.3562–63 (557:16). What, eleven? A riddle – See 2.102–7n.

15.3577–81 (558:2–6). The fox crew . . . get out of heaven – See 2.102–7n.

15.3586 (558:12). slyboots – An apparently simple but actually subtle or shrewd person.

15.3588 (558:15). a drawwell – A well from which water is drawn by means of a bucket, rope, and pulley.

15.3594 (558:21). *The distrait or absent-minded beggar – See 9.118–20n and 9.125n.

15.3599 (558:27). Lucifer – The trade name of a friction match invented and marketed in England in 1827; subsequently a generic name for all matches. See 3.486–87n.

15.3604 (559:5). Be just before you are generous – In Richard Brinsley Sheridan's (1751– 1816) *The School for Scandal* (1777), the prodigal Charles Surface quotes this "old proverb" to his father's old and sober steward, rejecting justice as "an old, lame, hobbling beldame" in favor of his creed: "while I have, by heaven, I'll give" (IV.i.265–73).

15.3609 (559:10). Proparoxyton – In Greek, a word having an acute accent on the second syllable from the last.

15.3609 (559:10–11). Moment before the next Lessing says – Gotthold Lessing (1729–81) in his *Laocoön* (1766) attempted to distinguish between poetry and the plastic arts. One of these distinctions involves the "moment" (what Lessing called the *Augenblick*, the "blink of an eye"). The plastic artist chooses a single moment from the endless series of moments that is the natural world; the chosen moment cannot, however, simply record the transitory, it must imply a continuing action, the moment, the climax, the fulfillment to follow. The poet, on the other hand, faces the problem of describing consecutive actions, and so, for him, the "moment" in his medium (words) is different; see 3.13, 15n.

15.3610 (559:11). Thirsty fox – See 15.3464n.

15.3610 (559:11–12). Burying his grandmother – See 2.102–7n.

15.3629 (560:3). Sixteen years ago – Stephen recalls that sixteen years before, as a child at Clongowes Wood College, he had broken his glasses; see *A Portrait*, chapter 1:D.

15.3629–30 (560:3–5). Distance. The eye sees all flat. . . . Brain thinks. Near: far – See 3.416–17n.

15.3630–31 (560:5). Ineluctable modality of the visible – See 3.1n.

15.3631 (560:6). Sphinx – In Oscar Wilde's poem "The Sphinx" (1894), the Sphinx is addressed as "exquisite grotesque! half woman and half animal!" (line 12). The speaker of the poem questions the enigmatic and unanswering Sphinx about her prodigal and grotesque love life; he finally rejects her as the creature of a "songless, tongueless ghost of sin" (line 163) and because "You wake in me each bestial sense, you make me what I would not be" (line 168).

15.3631–32 (560:6). The beast that has two backs – See 7.751–52n.

15.3636 (560:12). Mr Lambe – Apart from the context, identity and significance unknown.

15.3638 (560:14). Lamb of London, who takest away the sins of our world – After John 1:29: "The next day John [the Baptist] seeth Jesus coming unto him, and saith, Behold the Lamb of God, which taketh away the sin of the world." The sentence "Behold . . . world" is the basis of the Agnus Dei; see next note.

15.3640 (560:16–17). *Dona nobis pacem* – Latin: "Give us peace"; the concluding phrase of the Agnus Dei (Lamb of God), which is sung or recited during the rites of Communion in the Mass.

15.3649–50 (560:26–27). *the bloodoath in The Dusk of the Gods* – That is, in Richard Wagner's opera *Die Götterdämmerung*, the last of the four-opera cycle *Der Ring des Nibelungen* (The Ring of the Nibelung) (1853–74). In the first act of *Die Götterdämmerung* the villain, Hagen, devises an elaborate plot to bring about the downfall of the gods. With a magic potion he makes the hero Siegfried forget Brunhilde, his true love, and the ring, his mission. Siegfried is manipulated so that he falls in love with Gutrune, Hagen's half-sister, and promises to woo Brunhilde for Gutrune's brother, Gunther. Gunther and Siegfried seal the compact with a blood oath of friendship, and, with the help of considerable Wagnerian plot elaboration, the doom of the gods is sealed.

15.3651–53 (560:28–30). *Hangende Hunger . . . Macht uns alle kaputt* – German: "Intense desire, questioning wife, destroys us all." In Act I of Wagner's *Die Walküre* (1854–56), the second of the four operas of the *Ring*, Siegmund arrives at the house of Hunding, whose wife is Siegmund's lost sister, Sieglinde. Brother and sister are eventually to elope and become Siegfried's parents, but first Sieglinde asks why Siegmund's name is "Woeful"; as he answers he calls her "Fragende Frau" and recounts the story of his life of woe, which incidentally reveals him as the enemy of her husband, Hunding.

15.3655 (561:2). Hamlet, I am thy father's gimlet! – See 8.67–68n.

15.3656–57 (561:4). No wit, no wrinkles – It was popular superstition that an unwrinkled brow signifies lack of intelligence.

15.3657 (561:4–5). Two, three, Mars, that's courage – Palmistry reads traits of character by the prominence of the various "mounts" on the hand; however, among handbooks on palmistry there is anything but universal agreement. Most texts do agree in locating one Mount of Mars below the Mount of Mercury (which is at the base of the little finger) and above the Mount of the Moon, which is at the heel of the hand. A prominent Mount of Mars is usually read as indicating courage and resolution. But Zoe counts, "Two, three, Mars," and it is not clear what her point of departure is: if she counts from the base of the thumb (1) to the Mount of the Moon (2), then Mars would be next (3); but if she counts from the base of the index finger (1), middle finger (2), ring finger (3), then she has confused the Mount of Apollo (a love of the beautiful and noble aspirations) for the Mount of Mars. If Zoe intends Mars as the fourth of the series, then either way she counts, the mount she has mistaken for Mars is Mercury (wit, industry, science).

15.3660 (561:7). Sheet lightning courage – Courage that is essentially passive or courage displayed by someone remote from danger, since sheet lightning does not strike.

15.3666 (561:14). Pandybat – See 9.211n.

15.3667–76 (561:15–25). *the coffin . . . flies open . . . Father Dolan springs up . . . very good little boy* – Stephen recalls an incident when he was at Clongowes: unfairly punished by Father Dolan, he asserted himself by complaining to Father Conmee, the rector; see 7.618n and chapter 1:D of *A Portrait*. In the Sixth Circle of the *Inferno* (canto 10), Dante encounters two "Epicurian Heretics" who are Florentines known to Dante. They are being roasted in their sepulchres, but the lids are open, and Dante's acquaintances sit up in their coffins and converse with him.

15.3681 (562:3–4). His criminal thumbprint on the haddock – Legend ascribes the black spots behind a haddock's pectoral fins to the imprint of the finger and thumb of St. Peter, who found "tribute money" in the mouth of a fish (as directed by Jesus in Matthew 17:24–27).

15.3685 (562:8). Thursday – Joyce was born on Thursday, 2 February 1882, and the presumption is that that is Stephen's birthday as well.

15.3687 (562:10). Thursday's child has far to go – After the nursery rhyme: "Monday's child is full of grace, / Tuesday's child is fair of face, / Wednesday's child is full of woe, / Thursday's child has far to go, / Friday's child is loving and giving, / Saturday's child must work for a living, / But the child that's born on the Sabbath Day, / Is bonny and blithe and good and gay."

15.3687–88 (562:11). Line of fate. Influential friends – The Line of Fate bisects the palm of the hand from the middle of the wrist toward the middle finger. If particularly well marked and colored with certain tributary hatchings, it indicates a life of good fortune as the result of association with "influential friends."

15.3690–92 (562:13–15). Imagination . . . Mount of the moon – If the Mount of the Moon at the base of the hand below the little finger is pronounced, it indicates imagination, a dreamy disposition, and/or outstanding morality.

15.3698–99 (562:22–23). Knobby knuckles, for the women – In palmistry, knobby knuckles are supposed to be the sign of a person who thinks and works systematically.

15.3701–2 (562:25–26). Gridiron. Travels beyond the sea and marry money – Cryptic and thus difficult to interpret from handbooks of palmistry.

15.3706 (563:4). Short little finger. Henpecked husband – Usually indicative of immaturity, lack of full development.

15.3707 (563:6). BLACK LIZ – See 12.846–49n.

15.3716 (563:15). I see, says the blind man – Various proverbial settings play on this: "I see, said the blind man, when he didn't see at all" or ". . . with his hammer and saw."

15.3718 (563:17). Moves to one great goal – Mr. Deasy's comment on history (2.380–81 [34:27–28]).

15.3726–28 (563:26–564:1). *A hackneycar, number . . . Harmony Avenue, Donnybrook* – See 11.878–79n.

15.3734 (564:7). have you the horn? – See 11.23n.

15.3744 (564:18). quims – Slang for vaginas.

15.3746 (564:20). Plucking a turkey – Low slang for sexual intercourse.

15.3760–61 (565:9–10). **in flunkey's prune . . . and powdered wig* – In Sacher-Masoch's *Venus in Furs*, the hero, Severin, is similarly costumed when he becomes Wanda's slave and servant (at his own insistence and finally with her compliance) (p. 79).

15.3763 (565:13). splash – A small quantity of soda water.

15.3764 (565:14). *antlered head* – The familiar caricature of the cuckold.

15.3767 (565:18). Madam Tweedy is in her bath – In *Venus in Furs*, Wanda bathes with Severin (as the slave Gregor) attending on her (pp. 107–10); at the end of the episode Wanda is posed in her furs with her foot on Severin's neck as she toys with her whip. They catch sight of themselves in a mirror and decide to introduce a German painter who has become enamored of Wanda to the scene that he might paint and "immortalize" it.

15.3770 (565:21). *Raoul darling – See 10.606n.

15.3770 (565:21–22). I'm in my pelt – With a pun on *Venus im Pelz* (Venus in Furs). See also 14.623n.

15.3778 (566:2). the pishogue – See 12.1058n.

15.3779 (566:3–4). Bartholomona, the bearded woman – Significance unknown.

15.3792–93 (566:15). Vaseline . . . Orangeflower – A vaseline perfumed with neroli (an essential oil distilled from orange flowers).

15.3804 (566:26). *Ride a cockhorse – See 15.2944n.

15.3820 (567:15). The mirror up to nature – Hamlet cautions the players against overacting in "The Mouse-Trap," saying, "For anything so overdone is from [contrary to] the purpose of playing, whose end, both at the first and now, was and is, to hold, as 't were, a mirror up to nature; to show virtue her own feature, scorn her own image, and the very age and body of the time his form and pressure" (III.ii.22–27).

15.3823 (567:19). *antlered* – See 15.3764n.

15.3826 (567:22–23). 'Tis the loud laugh bespeaks the vacant mind – After Oliver Goldsmith's (1728–74) idealization of and lament for English rural life, *The Deserted Village* (1770). In lines 113ff. he describes "the village murmur" "at evening's close"; among the sounds, "And the loud laugh that spoke the vacant [idle, at rest] mind" (line 122).

15.3828–29 (567:25). *Iagogo! How my Oldfellow chokit his Thursdaymornum – Iago's machinations in Shakespeare's *Othello* cause Othello to smother Desdemona in a climactic fit of jealous suspicion. "Oldfellow" is also slang for father. Stephen was born on Thursday; see 15.3685n and 15.3687n.

15.3835–36 (568:6–7). Even the great Napoleon . . . skin after his death . . . – The autopsy performed after Napoleon's death caused considerable political controversy; the three French surgeons in attendance asserted that his death was "premature" as a result of the climate of St. Helena and of the anguish caused by English harassment. The five English surgeons in attendance looked at the ulcerated and perforated wall of the stomach and declared it healthy. To cover their embarrassment (and obviously to further denigrate Napoleon), the English insisted on minute measurements of the body and remarked on its "womanly" form (particularly the overdeveloped breasts).

15.3838 (568:9). *Tunney's tawny sherry – From William James Tunney, family grocer and spirit dealer, 8 Bridge Street, Ringsend, and 10 Haddington Road. Both shops were quite near the Dignam "residence" in Sandymount.

15.3840 (568:11–12). *a pen chivvying her brood of cygnets* – See 9.160–61 (188:23).

15.3842 (568:14). *Scottish Widow's insurance policy* – See 13.1227n.

15.3851 (568:23). the beeftea is fizzing over – In Act II of Henrik Ibsen's (1828–1906) *Love's Comedy* (1862), the assembled company discusses love and elaborately develops its similarities to tea. One says, "There's beef tea too," and the poet-hero Falk replies, "And a beef love has equally been heard of, and still its trace may be detected among the henpecked of the mar-

ried state." The play develops the theme that, thanks to nineteenth-century morality and its repression of feminine vitality, love (together with the freedom necessary to it) and marriage are incompatible. The poet-hero (with his lover's help) decides to go it alone.

15.3853 (568:25). Weda seca whokilla farst – "None wed the second but who kill'd the first" (*Hamlet* III.ii.190); see 9.678–79n.

15.3857 (568:29). *merry widow hat – After the broad-brimmed hat worn by the flirtatious heroine of the popular light opera *The Merry Widow* (1905), from the German *Die lustige Witwe* by the Hungarian composer Franz Lehar. See 9.985–86n.

15.3861 (569:3). And they call me the jewel of Asia – See 6.355–57n.

15.3865 (569:8). *Et exaltabuntur cornua iusti* – Latin: "And the horns of the righteous shall be exalted"; from Psalms 75:10 (Vulgate 74:10): "All the horns of the wicked also will I cut off; but the horns of the righteous shall be exalted."

15.3865–67 (569:8–10). Queens lay with prize . . . the first confessionbox – See 14.994–96n. Pasiphaë's "foul adultery" was a function of Poseidon's wrath: Poseidon had given Minos (the king) a sacrificial "prize bull," which Minos hid, substituting an inferior one; Poseidon retaliated by arousing in Pasiphaë a passion for the prize bull.

15.3867 (569:10). Madam Grissel Steevens – See 14.986–87n.

15.3867–68 (569:11). the suine scions of the house of Lambert – "Evidently neither Sam nor Ned, but monsters; the phrase may refer either to Daniel Lambert, the English fat man (1770–1809), or to a family of Lamberts who for several generations were born with bristles all over their bodies" (Adams, p. 204). "Suine" is a mixture of oleomargarine with lard or other fatty ingredients.

15.3868–69 (569:11–12). And Noah was drunk with wine. And his ark was open – See 15.1901n. "Ark" puns on Noah's ark and the Ark of the Covenant, the gold-encrusted wooden box in which Moses placed the stone tablets bearing the Ten Commandments; the Ark of the Covenant occupied the most sacred place in the sanctuary of the temple at Jerusalem.

15.3875   (569:18–19).   parleyvoo – English slang for the French language, after the French question *"Parlez-vous . . . ?"* ("Do you speak . . . ?"), usually followed by the name of a language.

15.3889 (570:7). heaven and hell show – A Black Mass; see 15.4689–4711nn.

15.3893 (570:12). *dessous troublant* – French: "disordered underclothes."

15.3894 (570:13). *Ce pif qu'il a* – French slang: literally, "The nose he has"; figuratively, "The face he has (or makes)."

15.3896 (570:15). *Vive le vampire!* – French: "Long live the vampire!"

15.3909 (570:30). *pièce de Shakespeare* – See 9.121n.

15.3915 (571:3). *double entente cordiale . . . mon loup* – French: "double cordial understanding . . . my wolf [solitary man]." The phrase *entente cordiale* was generally used for a cordial understanding short of a formal alliance between two nations; see 12.1387n.

15.3915 (571:4). Waterloo – See 15.745n. In context, "loo" is British slang for water closet.

15.3922 (571:11). I dreamt of a watermelon – See 3.367–69n.

15.3928 (571:17). *Dreams goes by contraries – Popular superstition about the interpretation of dreams; for example, a dream of failure would portend success. Thus, Bloom's dream of Molly "wearing the pants" (14.508–10 [397:27–29]) is interpreted by the Pepys–Evelyn voice "to be for a change"—by contraries, then, Bloom is about to start wearing the pants in his family.

15.3930 (571:19). Street of harlots – See 3.366 (47:5).

15.3930 (571:19–20). *Serpentine avenue – See 3.130n.

15.3931 (571:20). Beelzebub – Hebrew: "Lord of Flies"; god of the Ekronites (II Kings 1:2) and a devil in the Gospels. In Milton's *Paradise*

Lost he is Satan's chief lieutenant among the fallen angels.

15.3935 (572:2). No, I flew. My foes beneath me – See 9.1207–8n.

15.3935 (572:2–3). And ever shall be. World without end – See 2.200–204n.

15.3936 (572:3). *Pater! Free!* – See 9.954n.

15.3940 (572:7). *O merde alors!* – French expletive equivalent to "damn and blast it" or "fuck it"; literally, "shit already."

15.3941 (572:8). Hola! Hillyho! – The call a falconer uses to retrieve his falcon. Hamlet, in extreme agitation after he has seen the Ghost, is summoned in this way by Marcellus ("Hillo, ho, ho, my lord!") and replies in kind ("Hillo, ho, ho, boy! come, bird, come") to Marcellus and Horatio (I.v.115–16).

15.3948–49 (572:16–17). An eagle gules volant in a field argent displayed – In heraldry, a red eagle in horizontal flight with its wings expanded ("displayed"), mounted on a silver background. It is the coat of arms of the Joyces of County Galway.

15.3949 (572:17). Ulster King at arms! – See 15.1413n.

15.3952–54 (572:21–23). *A stout fox drawn . . . earth, under the leaves* – Cf. Stephen's riddle, 2.102–7n; "badger earth" is a den a badger has dug.

15.3956 (572:25). *Ward Union* – See 8.341n.

15.3957 (572:27). *Six Mile Point, Flathouse, Nine Mile Stone* – Six Mile Point, where the hunt starts, is a headland on the east coast of Ireland in County Wicklow. It is six miles north of Wicklow and twenty-one miles south-southeast of Dublin. The hunt ranges north over the coastal plain past Flathouse (a country house no longer extant) to the Nine Mile Stone (nine miles north of Wicklow on the Wicklow–Dublin road, near Kilcoole).

15.3961 (572:31). *crown and anchor* – A game played with dice marked with crowns, anchors, hearts, etc., and a similarly marked board.

15.3961   (572:31–32).   thimbleriggers – See 2.310n.

15.3962 (572:32). *broadsmen* – Slang for card-sharpers.

15.3962 (572:32). *Crows* – Slang for those who keep watch while others steal.

15.3966 (573:3). Ten to one the field – Betting slang; see 2.309–10n.

15.3967 (573:4). Tommy on the clay – Betting slang: the bookie announces that money can be readily acquired at his place of business.

15.3968 (573:5). Ten to one bar one – Betting slang: the bookie announces that he will offer odds of ten to one against any single horse winning the race with the exception of one horse (usually the track or betting favorite).

15.3969 (573:6). *Spinning Jenny – A gambling machine that moves miniature horses over a table at random speeds.

15.3971 (573:8). Sell the monkey – Betting slang: the bookie proclaims that he can cover bets up to £500. ("Monkey" is slang for £500.)

15.3974 (573:11–12). *A dark horse, riderless . . . past the winningpost* – Throwaway wins this ghostly rerunning of the Gold Cup at Ascot; see 14.1128–33n and 5.532n.

15.3976–77 (573:14). *Sceptre, Maximum the Second, Zinfandel* – Other horses in the Gold Cup; see preceding note.

15.3977–78 (573:14–16). **the duke of Westminster's . . . prix de Paris* – See 2.301–3n.

15.3980 (573:18). *isabelle nag* – A brownish-yellow or light-buff-colored horse (after the French *jaune d'Isabeau*, "yellow of Isabel"), fancifully named for the underwear of Isabel of Austria, who had pledged not to change her clothes until the siege of Ostend was lifted (it lasted three years and ended by surrender in 1604). Another candidate is Isabella of Castile, who made the same pledge during the twelve-month-long siege of Granada in 1491.

15.3980 (573:18). *Cock of the North* – A nickname for the Scot George Gordon (1770–1836), the fifth and last duke of Gordon, whose Gordon Highlanders were instrumental in the suppression of the Catholic peasant insurrection in Wexford during the Rebellion of 1798.

15.3983 (573:21). *jogs along the rocky road* – See 2.284–85n.

15.3984 (573:22). THE ORANGE LODGES – See 2.270n.

15.3989 (573:30). *Per vias rectas!* – See 2.282n.

15.3993 (574:1). THE GREEN LODGES – The pro–Home Rule Irish, in contrast to the Orangemen; see 2.273–75n.

15.3994 (574:2). Soft day, sir John! – That is, Sir John Blackwood; see 2.279n and 2.286n.

15.3998 (574:6). noise in the street – See 2.386n.

15.4002–3 (574:10–11). *Yet I've a sort of a / Yorkshire relish for . . . – See 10.1242n.

15.4012 (574:21). augur's rod – See 3.410–11n.

15.4013 (574:22). *tripudium* – See 3.448n.

15.4019 (575:2). *Inverness cape* – A full sleeveless cape that fits closely about the neck.

15.4027 (575:11). My Girl's a Yorkshire Girl – See 10.1242n.

15.4038 (575:23). *dahlia* – In the language of flowers, the dahlia can represent either good taste or instability.

15.4042–43 (575:29). Madam Legget Byrne's – Mr. and Mrs. T. Leggett Byrne, teachers of dancing, 27 Adelaide Road and 68 Mountjoy Square West, Dublin.

15.4043 (575:29). *Levenstone's – Mrs. P. M. Levenston, dancing academy, 35 Frederick Street South, Dublin.

15.4043 (575:30). Deportment – See 10.58n.

15.4044 (575:30). Katty Lanner – Katti Lanner (1831–1915) was the daughter of the Austrian composer Joseph Lanner (1801–43), who created the Vienna waltz and revolutionized nineteenth-century dance music. Katti had a distinguished career as ballet mistress and choreographer of the English Theatre of Varieties in London. She retired to devote herself to private lessons in 1877.

15.4045–46 (575:32–33). *Tout le monde . . . monde en place!* – French: "Everyone move forward! Bow! Everyone to his place!"

15.4052–53 (576:2–3). Two young fellows . . . they'd left behind . . . – See 10.1242n.

15.4054 (576:4). the morning hours – For the ballet that follows, see 4.526n.

15.4060 (576:11). **Carré! Avant deux! . . . Balancé!* – French: "Form a square! Advance by twos! . . . Sway [from side to side]!"

15.4074 (576:26). My shy little lass has a waist – See 10.1242n.

15.4077 (576:29). *cipria* – Or cypre: henna. Extracts from the plant were used to color parts of the body.

15.4080 (577:2). *Avant huit! Traversé! Salut! Cours de mains! Croisé!* – French: "Four couples advance! Cross over [the men and women separate into two lines and face each other]! Nod! Exchange hands [the line of men passes down the line of women giving alternate hands to each in turn]! Exchange sides!"

15.4083 (577:5–6). *curchycurchy* – Curtsey-curtsey.

15.4090 (577:12). *Les tiroirs! Chaîne de dames! La corbeille! Dos à dos!* – French: "[Men] Form a middle rank! Women join hands to form a chain! Form a basket [the ends of the chain link to form a circle around the men]! Back to back!"

15.4092 (577:14). *simply swirling* – See 4.282n.

15.4098 (577:20). *Boulangère! Les ronds! Les ponts! Chevaux de bois! Escargots!* – French: "Bread-making [the heels of the hands are thrust out and down as though kneading bread]! In circles! Bridges [of hands]! Hobbyhorses! Corkscrew [or twirl, wind around]!"

15.4103–4 (577:25–26). *Dansez avec vos dames! . . . votre dame! Remerciez!* – French: "Dance with your partners! Change partners! Present the little bouquet to your partner. Thank each other [in parting]!"

15.4106 (577:28). Best, best of all – See 10.1242n.

15.4112 (578:6). *Toft's cumbersome whirligig* – The merry-go-round at the Mirus Bazaar; see 15.2719n.

15.4120 (578:15). *Pas seul!* – French: "Solo dance!"

15.4126 (578:21). *hornblower* – See 5.555n.

15.4130–31 (578:26–27). Though she's a factory . . . no fancy clothes – See 10.1242n.

15.4135 (579:2). Bis – French: "Over again!"

15.4139 (579:6). Dance of death – Literary or visual presentation of the power of death over the lives of all men. It had its origin in medieval church drama; the original plays began with an exhortation, then depicted the power of death over all classes of men from popes and emperors to serfs, and ended with an appropriate sermon. From these beginnings the subgenre of *danse macabre* was developed and proliferated in the medieval arts. Several nineteenth-century artists, among them Goethe, Saint-Saëns, and Strindberg, revived and reworked this subgenre.

15.4140 (579:7). *lacquey's bell* – At Dillon's auction rooms; see 10.643n.

15.4141 (579:8). *on Christass* – In John 12:12–15, Jesus enters Jerusalem in triumph: "On the next day much people that were come to the feast, when they heard that Jesus was coming to Jerusalem, Took branches of palm trees, and went forth to meet him, and cried, Hosanna: Blessed is the King of Israel that cometh in the name of the Lord. And Jesus, when he had found a young ass, sat thereon; as it is written [Zechariah 9:9], Fear not, daughter of Sion: behold, thy King cometh, sitting on an ass's colt."

15.4142–43 (579:10). through and through – See 10.1242n.

15.4143 (579:10). *bellhorses* – A horse wearing a bell and decorated with flowers and ribbons for May Day.

15.4143 (579:11). *Gadarene swine* – In Matthew 8:28–34, Jesus is met in Gadara, south of the Sea of Galilee, by "two [men] possessed with devils . . . exceeding fierce, so that no man might pass by that way." Jesus cast the devils out of the two men and allowed the devils to enter into a "herd of many swine feeding." The swine went berserk and "ran violently down a steep place into the sea, and perished in the waters." Similar accounts of the incident occur in Mark 5:1–20 and Luke 8:26–29.

15.4144 (579:11). *steel shark stone – Significance unknown.

15.4144 (579:11–12). onehandled Nelson – See 7.1018n.

15.4144–45 (579:12). two trickies Frauenzimmer – See 3.29–31 (37:33–35) and 7.1009 (147:31).

15.4145 (579:13). pram – Baby Boardman's from Nausicaa.

15.4145–46 (579:13). Gum, he's a champion – See 10.1242n.

15.4146 (579:13). Fuseblue – See Kevin Egan, 3.239 (43:22).

15.4146 (579:14). peer from barrel – As Lords Iveagh and Ardilaun have parlayed barrels of Guinness into peerages; see 5.303–12 (79:23–34).

15.4146 (579:14). rev. evensong Love – See 10.437–38n.

15.4147 (579:15). blind coddoubled bicyclers – See 5.551–52n.

15.4148 (579:15). snowcake – A cake topped with an icing of creamy whipped eggwhites.

15.4148 (579:15–16). no fancy clothes – See 10.1242n.

15.4149 (579:17). mashtub – See 12.678n.

15.4149–50 (579:17–18). sort of viceroy . . . bumpshire rose – When the Viceregal procession passed Trinity College en route from Phoenix Park to the Mirus Bazaar in The Wandering Rocks, its sounds were mingled with "My Girl's a Yorkshire Girl" (see 10.1242n) played by the regimental band of the 2nd Seaforth Highlanders (see 10.365n) at the bicycle races in Trinity College Park. *Reine*, French: "queen."

15.4157 (579:25). Stephen's mother . . . rises stark through the floor – As the ghost of Hamlet's father intervenes in Act III, scene iv when Hamlet is upbraiding his mother in her "closet." The Ghost intends "to whet [Ham-

let's] almost blunted purpose" (line 111) and is seen and heard only by Hamlet.

15.4164–65 (580:2–3). Liliata rutilantium . . . te virginum . . . – See 1.276–77n.

15.4170 (580:9–10). Mulligan meets the afflicted mother – As George Patrick Whelan has pointed out, this alludes to the fourth station of the cross as composed by St. Alphonsus Liguori (1696–1787): "Jesus meets His afflicted mother" (*JJQ* 17, no. 1 [1979]: 87). See 1.510n.

15.4171 (580:10). Mercurial Malachi – See 1.518n; and cf. 15.4966–67n.

15.4176 (580:15). Lemur – An interlink between the large-eyed nocturnal animal (nicknamed "ghost" by naturalists, as Walter W. Skeat points out in his *Etymological Dictionary of the English Language* [Oxford, 1909]) and the Roman Lemures, specters of the dead who wandered about at night to torment and frighten the living. The festival to propitiate them, the Lemuralia, occurred in May, and hence May was regarded as an unlucky month for marriages. John Joyce and Mary Jane Murray were married 5 May 1880. See Ellmann, p. 18.

15.4180 (580:20–21). Our great sweet mother! – See 1.77–78n.

15.4180 (580:21). Epi oinopa ponton – See 1.78n.

15.4183 (580:24–25). More women than men in the world – See 6.546–47n.

15.4190 (581:3). Love's bitter mystery – See 1.239–41n.

15.4192–93 (581:5–6). *Tell me . . . The word known to all men – See 9.429–30n.

15.4195–96 (581:8–9). at Dalkey with Paddy Lee – For Dalkey, see 2.25n; Paddy Lee appears only this one time, but in 1904 a Patrick J. Lee lived at 2 Convent Road in Dalkey.

15.4197–98 (581:10–12). Prayer for the suffering . . . forty days' indulgence – The Ursulines, a Roman Catholic religious order for women devoted to the teaching of young girls and the nursing of the sick. The lengthy prayer that Stephen's mother refers to begins, "Most holy Mary, Our Lady of Intercession," and focuses, "O Mary, countless souls await with unutterable anxiety the assistance of our prayers and the merits of our good works in that place of expiation [purgatory]." The prayer did merit an indulgence, but of five hundred, not forty days; see 15.1574n.

15.4200 (581:14). Hyena! – The hyena "is accustomed to live in the sepulchres of the dead and to devour their bodies. Its nature is that at one moment it is masculine and at another feminine, and hence it is a dirty brute" (T. H. White, *The Bestiary: A Book of Beasts* [New York, 1960], pp. 30–31).

15.4214 (581:28). His noncorrosive sublimate – That is, the fires of hell, which punish sinners without consuming or destroying them.

15.4214–15 (581:28). Raw head and bloody bones! – See 8.726n.

15.4219 (582:5). God's hand! – Traditionally symbolic of the almighty will and power of God, whose countenance "no man could behold and live" (Exodus 33:20).

15.4220 (582:5). A green crab – The crab is symbolic of the zodiacal house of Cancer; the color green is added, presumably from the green bile the mother vomited in her last illness.

15.4227 (582:13). Ah non, par exemple! – French exclamation, equivalent to "Good Heavens, no!"

15.4227 (582:13). The intellectual imagination! – Recalls Matthew Arnold's phrase "imaginative reason" in his inaugural lecture as professor of poetry at Oxford, "On the Modern Element in Literature" (1857). The opening sentence of the lecture is also relevant to the way Stephen contextualizes his outburst: "An intellectual deliverance is the peculiar demand of those ages which are called modern; and those nations are said to be imbued with the modern spirit most eminently in which the demand for such a deliverance has been made with most zeal, and satisfied with most completeness."

15.4227–28 (582:13–14). With me all or not at all – See 3.452n.

15.4228 (582:14). Non serviam! – Latin: "I will not serve." The phrase is traditionally assigned to Satan at the moment of his fall, after Jeremiah 2:20: "and thou saidst, I will not serve" (Douay). In chapter 3:B of *A Portrait*, Father Arnall uses the phrase to characterize

Lucifer's sin, and in chapter 5:C Stephen, in conversation with Cranly, says he will refuse his mother's request to make his "easter duty" and caps his remarks with the assertion, "I will not serve."

15.4232–33 (582:18–19). O Sacred Heart of Jesus, have mercy on him! – A variation of the invocation "Most Sacred Heart of Jesus, have mercy on us," which the devout, kneeling, were encouraged to repeat three times after the conclusion of a mass in which they had taken communion.

15.4239–40 (582:26–27). Inexpressible was my anguish . . . on Mount Calvary – The source of this prayer is unknown, but the vocabulary ("anguish," "love, grief and agony") is characteristic of prayers associated with "Jesus crucified" and with "the Blessed Virgin Mary sorrowing." Mount Calvary (Hill of the Skull, [Luke 23:33], after the Aramaic *Golgotha*) is the hill on which Jesus was crucified.

15.4242 (583:2). Nothung! – German: "Needful"; the magic sword in Wagner's *Der Ring des Nibelungen*. In *Die Walküre* (1854–56), the second of the four operas of the *Ring*, Wotan, the king of the gods, has planted it in the heart of a giant ash tree ("ashplant"). Siegmund, Siegfried's father, retrieves the sword, but when he attempts to defend himself with it against his sister's husband, Wotan withdraws the sword's magic power; the sword is shattered and Siegmund is killed. In the third opera, *Siegfried* (1856–69), Siegfried, because he does not know the meaning of fear, is able to reforge the sword. Ironically it is with this sword, its magic power restored, that Siegfried will unwittingly bring about *Die Götterdämmerung* (The Twilight of the Gods) in the final opera (1874) of the *Ring*. See 15.3649–50n and 15.3651–53n.

15.4244–45 (583:4–6). Time's livid final flame . . . and toppling masonry – See 2.9–10n.

15.4297 (585:4). Bulldog – Slang for a sheriff's officer.

15.4298 (585:5). Gentlemen that pay the rent – An Irish-English expression for pigs (suggested by Vincent Deane).

15.4298–99 (585:6). *he makes a masonic sign – As with the Watch (see 15.758–59n), Bloom uses his knowledge of Freemasonry to suggest an influential connection with the Protestant Anglo-Irish Establishment.

15.4299 (585:7). the vicechancellor – See 7.262n.

15.4302 (585:9). ragging – Slang for assailing roughly and noisily or tormenting someone as a practical joke; more generally, creating a disturbance.

15.4306 (585:14). your own son in Oxford – See 15.1289 (475:21).

15.4308 (585:17). *Incog – A colloquial abbreviation of *incognito;* also slang for intoxicated.

15.4324–25 (586:4–6). draws his caliph's hood . . . Haroun Al Raschid – See 3.366n; one of the legends about this ruler was that he went about in disguise through the streets of Baghdad in order to maintain an awareness of the mood of his subjects.

15.4326–27 (586:7–8). a pard strewing the drag . . . drenched in aniseed – See 9.1214n.

15.4329 (586:10). Hornblower of Trinity – See 5.555n.

15.4334 (586:16). woman's slipperslappers – See 6.16n.

15.4336 (586:18). 65 C, 66 C, night watch – Constables from the C Division of the Dublin Metropolitan Police; see 10.217n.

15.4338 (586:20). Mrs O'Dowd – See 12.513n.

15.4338–39 (586:21). the Nameless One – See 15.1143n.

15.4341 (586:23–24). sir Charles Cameron – See 10.538n.

15.4342 (586:25). red Murray – See 7.25n.

15.4342–43 (586:25). editor Brayden – See 7.38–39n.

15.4343 (586:25). T. M. Healy – See 7.800n.

15.4343 (586:25–26). Mr Justice Fitzgibbon – See 7.794n.

15.4343–44 (586:26). John Howard Parnell – See 8.500n.

15.4344 (586:26–27). the reverend Tinned Salmon – See 8.496n.

15.4344 (586:27). Professor Joly – See 8.573–74n.

15.4345–46 (586:28). the Westland Row Postmistress – Where Bloom has received his letter from Martha Clifford; see 5.53n.

15.4348 (586:31–32). Mrs Ellen McGuinness – See 10.61n.

15.4349 (586:32). Mrs Joe Gallaher – See 15.565n.

15.4349 (586:32). Jimmy Henry – See 10.982n.

15.4350 (586:33). *superintendent Laracy – Former superintendent and headmaster of the Hibernian Marine School in Grove Park, Rathmines. He was no longer there in 1904.

15.4350–51 (586:33–34). *Crofton out of the Collector-general's – See 6.247n.

15.4351 (586:34). Dan Dawson – See 6.151n.

15.4351 (586:34–35). dental surgeon Bloom – See 12.1638n.

15.4352 (586:35). Mrs Kennefick – "A total blank," as Adams says (p. 156).

15.4354 (586:37). Clonskeatram – See 7.4–5n.

15.4354–55 (586:38). Miss Dubedatandshedidbedad – See 8.889n.

15.4355–56 (586:38–39). Mesdames Gerald and Stanislaus Moran of Roebuck – That is, at an estate called Roebuck Hill, in Roebuck, a fashionable area in Dundrum, three miles south of central Dublin.

15.4356 (586:40). Drimmie's – See 13.845n.

15.4356–57 (586:40). colonel Hayes – "Colonel" Baxter Hayes, chief inspector of police for the Great Southern and Western Railway in Ireland, 23 Conyngham Road, Dublin.

15.4357 (586:40). Mastiansky – See 4.205n.

15.4357 (586:40). Citron – See 4.205n.

15.4357 (586:40–41). Penrose – See 8.178–79n.

15.4357 (586:41). *Aaron Figatner* – See 11.149n.

15.4357–57 (586:41). *Moses Herzog* – See 12.17–18n.

15.4358 (586:41). *Michael E Geraghty* – See 12.20n.

15.4358 (586:42). *Inspector Troy* – See 12.1n.

15.4358 (586:42). *Mrs Galbraith* – See 18.476n.

15.4359 (587:1). *old doctor Brady* – Dr. Francis F. Brady, Carnew, County Wicklow in 1904 (*Thom's* 1904).

15.4360–61 (587:2–3). *Mrs Miriam Dandrade and all her lovers* – See 8.349–50n and 15.3001–6 (536:23–29).

15.4365 (587:7). *Beaver street* – See 15.585n.

15.4371 (587:13–14). the fifth of George and seventh of Edward – George Frederick Ernest Albert (1865–1936), heir apparent in 1904, became king of England (1910–36) as George V on the death of his father, Edward VII (1841–1910; king 1901–10).

15.4372 (587:14–15). Fabled by mothers of memory – See 2.7n.

15.4387 (587:30). Sisyphus – In Greek mythology, a king of Corinth known as the craftiest of men. He was condemned in the underworld to roll a huge marble block up a hill only to be frustrated at the last moment as the block rolled back down and he was compelled to begin again. There are various legendary accounts (all of them emphasizing craft and betrayal) of why he was so condemned, and there are various accounts of his forebears and children, including post-Homeric legends in which he is the father of Odysseus by Anticlea. See headnote to Hades, p. 104.

15.4388 (587:31). *Uropoetic – Medical: favoring the production of urine.

15.4392 (588:6). blighter – A contemptible person; also, a euphemism for *bugger* (pederast).

15.4396 (588:12). *Union Jack blazer and cricket flannels* – The costume suggests the traditional caricature of Tennyson as pillar of the Establishment, optimistic chauvinist.

15.4397 (588:13). Theirs not to reason why – Line 14 of Tennyson's "The Charge of the Light Brigade"; see 15.1527n. The second stanza: "Forward, the Light Brigade! / Was there a man dismay'd? / Not tho' the soldier knew / Some one had blunder'd. / Theirs not to make reply, / Theirs not to reason why, / Theirs but to do and die. / Into the valley of Death / Rode the six hundred."

15.4402 (588:18–19). Doctor Swift says . . . men in their shirts – Jonathan Swift (1667–1745), in the persona of M. B. Drapier, wrote "A Letter to the Whole People of Ireland" (1724), a series of pamphlets commonly called *Drapier's Letters;* in Letter 4: "For, in reason, all government without the consent of the governed, is the very definition of slavery: but, in fact, eleven men well armed will certainly subdue one single man in his shirt."

15.4407 (588:24). The bold soldier boy – See 12.193n.

15.4413 (589:2–3). Noble art of selfpretence – After "the noble art of self-defense," a euphemism used to upgrade boxing when that sport was reintroduced into England in 1866 under the genteel supervision of the Amateur Athletic Club and the marquess of Queensberry; see 12.958n.

15.4415 (589:4). *Enfin, ce sont vos oignons* – French: literally, "After all, those are your onions"; figuratively, "It's your quarrel, not mine."

15.4417 (589:6). DOLLY GRAY – From the popular Boer War song "Good-bye, Dolly Gray," by Will D. Cobb and Paul Barnes. Refrain: "Good-bye, Dolly, I must leave you, / Though it breaks my heart to go. / Something tells me I am needed / In the front to face the foe. / Hark! I hear the bugles calling / And I must no longer stay. / Good-bye, Dolly, I must leave you, / Good-bye, Dolly Gray."

15.4418–19 (589:7–8). *the sign of the heroine of Jericho*) Rahab – In Joshua 2, Joshua, having taken over the leadership of the Israelites after Moses' death, prepares to cross the Jordan and destroy the city of Jericho. He sends two spies into Jericho, where their presence is suspected, but they are sheltered and helped to escape by the harlot Rahab, who is in awe of the power of the Israelites' God. In return they promise her safety when Jericho is destroyed (as it is in Joshua 6), and they instruct her to make a sign: "thou shalt bind this line of scarlet thread in the window which thou didst let us down by" (Joshua 2:18). William Blake, in *Vala; or, The Four Zoas* (an incomplete prophecy begun c. 1795), Night the Eighth, characterizes Rahab as "the false female" who condemns Jesus, "the Lamb of God," to death in her role as "Mystery, Babylon the Great, the Mother of Harlots"; see 15.1758n. Rahab combines worship and mockery, since her focus is on "Mystery" (religion that is abstract and nonexperiential) and on "Death, God of all from whom we rise, to whom we all return" (Blake's MS pp. 105–6).

15.4419 (589:8). Cook's son, goodbye – From Kipling's "The Absent-Minded Beggar": "Cook's son—Duke's son—son of a belted Earl— / Son of a Lambeth publican—it's all the same today!"; see 9.125n. The phrase includes a pun on the famous English travel agency Thomas Cook & Son; see 12.193n.

15.4419–20 (589:9). the girl you left behind – See 9.246–47n.

15.4435 (589:26). philirenists – Lovers of peace.

15.4435 (589:27). the tsar – Nicholas II (1868–1918; czar 1894–1917). His "peace rescript of 1898" solicited petitions from "the peaceloving peoples of the world." It resulted in the Hague Conference of 1899. The conference of national powers did not manage "universal disarmament" or even a plan for curtailment of armaments, but it did set up a tribunal for the arbitration of international disputes and it began to systematize international laws of war. It is something of an irony that Nicholas II's peace crusade was a prelude to the Russo-Japanese War of 1904–5. In retrospect the czar's motivation appears to have been to stall for time so that Russia could achieve an armament comparable to that of the Austro-Hungarian Empire.

15.4435–36 (589:27). the king of England – For Edward VII's role as lover of peace, see 12.1399n. In 1908 and 1909 Edward VII and Czar Nicholas II met twice, ostensibly in the interests of peace; but their meetings were not regarded with popular favor in England or on the Continent because they seemed to presage an alliance with Russia in aid of England's intensifying naval and colonial competition with Germany.

15.4436–37 (589:28–29). But in here it is . . . priest and the king – William Blake frequently yokes priest and king as a comprehensive image of oppression; cf. "Merlin's Prophecy": "The harvest shall flourish in wintery weather / When two virginities meet together. // The King & the Priest must be tied in a tether / Before two virgins can meet together."

15.4450 (590:16). the Sacred Heart – It is highly unlikely that the English sovereign, Defender of the Faith (of the Church of England), would wear this peculiarly Irish-Catholic symbol. See 6.954n.

15.4450–51 (590:17). the insignia of Garter and Thistle – That is, of the Knights of the Garter, the highest royal order in England, founded by Edward III in 1346. The insignia: a blue ribbon over the left shoulder bearing the image of St. George, and a blue garter on the left leg bearing the legend *Honi soit qui mal y pense* (Shamed be he who thinks evil of it). The Order of the Thistle was founded in Scotland in 809 by Archaicus, king of the Scots, and was renewed in Great Britain in the seventeenth century; its insignia: the image of St. Andrew (patron saint of Scotland) bearing a cross, imposed on a stylized thistle.

15.4451 (590:17–18). Golden Fleece – The Order of the Golden Fleece was founded in 1429 by Philip the Good, duke of Burgundy; it later existed in both Spain and Austria. Its insignia: a golden fleece hanging from an enameled flint stone emitting flames.

15.4451–52 (590:18). Elephant of Denmark – An order founded in 1189 by Knut VI, king of Denmark; its insignia: a blue moire cordon bearing a medallion with a white elephant, tower, and driver.

15.4452 (590:18). Skinner's and Probyn's horse – Skinner's Horse, an irregular cavalry regiment that distinguished itself in India under the command of James Skinner (1778–1841). The 11th Prince of Wales Own Lancers was nicknamed "Probyn's Horse," after its colonel, General Sir Deighton Macnaghten Probyn (1833–1924), who had a distinguished military career in India and (after his retirement from active duty) as a member of the royal household.

15.4452 (590:19). Lincoln's Inn bencher – A senior member of Lincoln's Inn, one of the four societies of lawyers that constitute the Inns of

Court in London. The inns have the exclusive right of admitting persons to the practice of law in England.

15.4453 (590:19–20). *ancient and honourable artillery company of Massachusetts* – Actually of Boston, a volunteer corps of artillery, infantry, and cavalry, the oldest regular military organization in America, founded in 1637 on the model of the Honorable Artillery Company (of London, founded in 1537). Purely military during the stresses of the colonial period, it evolved in the nineteenth century into a social organization that was only incidentally military.

15.4454–55 (590:21–22). *robed as a grand elect . . . with trowel and apron* – Freemasonry: Edward VII as prince of Wales was grand master of the Grand Lodge of England from 1874 until his accession to the throne in 1901. A portrait of him so robed is extant; see Eugen Lennhof, *The Freemasons* (New York, 1934), facing p. 181. The Masonic apron is symbolic of innocence and irreproachable conduct; the trowel, the peculiar working tool of the Master Mason's degree, is symbolic of the effort that cements the brotherhood into unity through brotherly love.

15.4455 (590:22). **made in Germany** – Suggests both Edward VII's lineage (see 12.1390–92n) and one of the varied lineages attributed to Freemasonry. "Made in Germany" was also a catch phrase for the shoddy or unfairly subsidized industrial products with which Germany was seeking to flood the world market in the late nineteenth and early twentieth centuries. The phrase was popularized by Ernest Williams in a short, racy, and alarming account of the impact of German industrial expansion on British industry, *Made in Germany* (London, 1896).

15.4457 (590:24). Défense d'uriner – French: "It is forbidden to urinate." See 15.586n.

15.4459 (590:26). Peace, perfect peace – The title of a popular hymn (1875) by Edward Henry Bickersteth (1825–1906), English bishop and poet. The opening lines: "Peace, perfect peace, in this dark world of sin? / The blood of Jesus whispers peace within."

15.4462 (590:30). *Mahak makar a bak – If this is an attempt at Arabic, it might mean "(You have) with you a sly one, your father."

15.4471–73 (591:10–12). You die for your country . . . let my country die for me – After Jesus raises Lazarus from the dead, the chief priests and Pharisees feel their "place and nation" threatened and take counsel. "And one of them named Caiaphas, being the high priest that same year, said unto them, Ye know nothing at all. Nor consider that it is expedient for us, that one man should die for the people, and that the whole nation perish not . . . he prophesied that Jesus should die for that nation" (John 11:48, 49–51).

15.4476 (591:17). *Joking Jesus* – See 1.584–87n and following notes.

15.4477 (591:17). *a white jujube* – See 8.4 (151:5).

15.4478–79 (591:18–19). My methods are new . . . dust in their eyes – See 1.584–87n.

15.4481 (591:21). Kings and unicorns! – After the nursery rhyme: "The lion and the unicorn / Were fighting for the crown; / The lion beat the unicorn / All round about the town. // Some gave them white bread, / And some gave them brown, / Some gave them plum cake, / And drummed them out of town." The lion and the unicorn are featured in the royal arms of England.

15.4484 (591:24). knackers – Testicles, usually of animals.

15.4484 (591:25). Jerry – English slang for a chamberpot or a penis.

15.4487 (591:28–29). *Absinthe. Greeneyed monster – Absinthe, a green and extraordinarily powerful liqueur, did produce severe nervous derangements; see 3.217–18n and 15.1995n.

15.4497 (592:9). Green rag to a bull – After the familiar assumption that red angers bulls; green is the color of Ireland, red of England (John Bull).

15.4499   (592:11).   *peep-o'-day-boy's* – See 3.241n.

15.4501 (592:13). The *vieille ogresse* **with the** *dents jaunes* – See 3.232–33n.

15.4502–3 (592:14–15). *nibbling a quince leaf* – Quince is symbolic of temptation in the language of flowers.

15.4505 (592:17). *Socialiste!* – See 3.169–72n.

15.4506 (592:18). DON EMILE PATRIZIO FRANZ RUPERT POPE HENNESSY – See 15.1914n.

15.4507 (592:19). *two wild geese volant* – See 15.1915n.

15.4508–9 (592:21–22). Werf those eykes . . . todos covered of gravy! – Polyglot: "Werf . . . eykes . . . footboden" is garbled German: "Throw those disgusting ones to the ground at your feet." "Porcos" (*puercos*), Spanish: "pigs"; *todos*, Spanish: "entirely, completely." For "johnyellows," see 12.1255n.

15.4517 (593:4). Green above the red – "The Green Above the Red" is a song by Thomas Osborne Davis. First stanza: "Full oft when our fathers saw the Red above the Green, / They rode in rude but fierce array, with sabre, pike, and sgian [knife]. / And over many a noble town, and many a field of dead. / They proudly set the Irish Green above the English Red."

15.4517 (593:4). Wolfe Tone – See 10.378n.

15.4522 (593:9). De Wet – See 8.435n.

15.4525–30 (593:12–17). *May the God above . . . a dove . . . our Irish leaders – Dublin informants have identified this as a Fenian ballad, but we have been unable to locate a copy in print. The "dove / With teeth as sharp as razors" is a striking image of the Holy Ghost as Comforter.

15.4531–35 (593:18–22). THE CROPPY BOY . . . country beyond the king – See the song "The Croppy Boy" (11.39n), lines 25–26.

15.4536 (593:23). RUMBOLD, DEMON BARBER – After the title of George Dibdin Pitt's (d. c. 1855) popular play *Sweeney Todd; the Demon Barber of Fleet Street* (1842). Todd's trick barber chair delivers his victims to the cellar where he "polishes them off" with his razor, robs them, and delivers their bodies to be "made into veal pies at Mrs. Lovett's in Bell Yard." Needless to say, Todd and Mrs. Lovett get their melodramatic comeuppance in the course of the play. See 12.430n.

15.4538–39 (593:25–26). cleaver purchased by Mrs Pearcy to slay Mogg – In a spectacular trial, 1–3 December 1890, Mary Eleanor Wheeler (otherwise Mrs. Pearcey) was con-victed of the murder of Mrs. Phoebe Hogg (not Mogg) and infant. The murder weapon (a cleaver) furnished one of the more lurid details of the trial.

15.4539–40 (593:26–28). Knife with which Voisin . . . sheet in the cellar – In October 1917 Louis Voisin, a French butcher living in London, murdered and dismembered Mrs. Emilienne Gérard. Part of her body was found in a meat sack in Regent Square, London; the remainder, in Voisin's cellar. He went to the gallows.

15.4541–42 (593:29–30). Phial containing arsenic . . . Seddon to the gallows – In September 1912 Mr. and Mrs. Frederick Seddon of London were charged with murdering their lodger Miss Barrow after it was discovered that what appeared to be a natural death had really been caused by arsenic. Mrs. Seddon was sent to prison; Mr. Seddon was hanged for the crime.

15.4547 (594:5). Horhot ho hray ho rhother's hest – That is, "Forgot to pray for [my] mother's rest"; see "The Croppy Boy" (11.39n), line 24.

15.4550 (594:8). *Mrs Bellingham* – See 15.1025n.

15.4550 (594:8). *Mrs Yelverton Barry* – See 15.1013n.

15.4550–51 (594:9). the *Honourable Mrs Mervyn Talboys* – See 15.1057n.

15.4555 (594:13–14). *Ten shillings a time. As applied to His Royal Highness – That is, Rumbold has the king's permission to sell pieces of the rope to interested spectators for souvenirs.

15.4562–64 (594:21–23). On coronation day . . . beer and wine! – See 1.300–305n.

15.4576 (595:5). *Ça se voit aussi à Paris* – French: "This [sort of thing] is also to be found in Paris."

15.4576–77 (595:6). *But by saint Patrick! – Horatio reproves Hamlet: "These are but wild and whirling words, my lord. HAMLET: I'm sorry they offend you. . . . HORATIO: There's no offence, my lord. HAMLET: Yes, by Saint Patrick, but there is, Horatio, / And much offence too" (I.v.133–37).

15.4578–80 (595:7–9). *Old Gummy Granny . . . blight on her breast* – Caricatures the Poor Old Woman image of Ireland as a death's head; see 1.403n and 1.543–44n. Leprechauns are traditionally depicted as seated on toadstools, with sugarloaf hats, shaped like slightly curved cones. The potato blight was the immediate cause of the great Irish famine; see 2.269n; and cf. 15.1034–35n.

15.4582 (595:11). Hamlet, revenge! – The Ghost speaks to Hamlet: "If thou didst ever thy dear father love—HAMLET: O God! GHOST: Revenge his foul and most unnatural murder" (I.v.23–25).

15.4582–83 (595:11–12). The old sow that eats her farrow! – That is, Ireland, as Stephen remarks in *A Portrait*, chapter 5:A.

15.4585 (595:14–15). the king of Spain's daughter – From the nursery rhyme: "I had a little nut tree, / Nothing would it bear / But a silver nutmeg / And a golden pear; // The King of Spain's daughter / Came to visit me, / And all for the sake of / My little nut tree."

15.4586 (595:15). *alanna* – *A leanbh*, Irish: "My child, my darling."

15.4586 (595:15). Strangers in my house – See 9.36–37n.

15.4587 (595:16). *banshee* – *Bean sí*, Irish: a female spirit being and death messenger.

15.4587 (595:16). Ochone! – *Ochón*, Irish: "Alas!"

15.4587 (595:16–17). Silk of the kine! – See 1.403n.

15.4587–88 (595:17–18). You met with poor . . . does she stand? – See 3.259–60n.

15.4590 (595:20). The hat trick! – See 15.195n. Also, in cricket a bowler accomplishes the hat trick when he knocks over or captures by means of catches three or more wickets with successive deliveries.

15.4590–91 (595:20–21). Where's the third person of the Blessed Trinity? – Literally: "Where is the Holy Ghost?" Figuratively, since Stephen is the son and Ireland is present (in the person of Old Gummy Granny), "Where is the Church?"

15.4591 (595:21). Soggarth Aroon? – *Sagart a rún*, Irish: "My Beloved Priest"; the title of a song by the Irish novelist John Banim (1798–1842). The song deals with the affection an Irish peasant feels for a patriot-priest. First stanza: "Am I a slave they say, Soggarth aroon? / Since you did show the way, Soggarth aroon, / Their slave no more to be, / While they would work with me, / Old Ireland's slavery, Soggarth aroon."

15.4591 (595:21–22). The reverend Carrion Crow – In Flaubert's *Madame Bovary* (1857), Part III, chapter 8, as Emma Bovary is dying from arsenic poisoning, Homais, the self-styled village "philosopher," "as was due to his principles compared priets to ravens [carrion-crows] attracted by the smell of death." The carrion crow also figures in a nursery rhyme, "Heigh-ho, the Carrion Crow": "A carrion crow sat on an oak, / . . . / Watching a tailor shape his cloak, / . . . / . . . // Wife! bring me my old bent bow, / . . . / That I may shoot yon carrion crow; / . . . // The tailor he shot, and missed his mark, / . . . / And shot his own sow quite through the heart." As a further irony, Stephen's question evokes a bird symbolic of death instead of the dove, the traditional symbol for the Holy Ghost.

15.4602 (596:10). *a proBoer** – As many Irish were; see 8.434n.

15.4606–7 (596:14–16). We fought for you . . . Honoured by our monarch – The first and second battalions of the Royal Dublin Fusiliers did campaign for the British in South Africa during the Boer War; they were singled out for special praise by Queen Victoria on St. Patrick's Day in 1900, when the queen announced her intention of raising a regiment of Irish guards to be added to the Household Brigade in honor of the loyal Irish troops in South Africa. "Missile troops" is obsolete for infantry armed with rifles (as is "fusiliers"). It is notable that Irish regiments fighting for the British were balanced by Irish brigades that fought on the side of the Boers.

15.4611 (596:20). *pentice* – That is, like a penthouse, projecting over something.

15.4612 (596:21–22). *Turko the terrible* – See 1.258n.

15.4612–14 (596:22–23). *in bearskin cap . . . chevrons and sabretache* – The uniform of an officer in the Royal Dublin Fusiliers; see 5.66–68n.

15.4615–16 (596:24–25). *the pilgrim warrior's sign of the knights templars* – The Knights Templar (the Knighthood of the Temple of Solomon) were a monastic and militant order founded in 1118 to protect Christians on pilgrimage to Jerusalem. The traditions of Freemasonry hold that modern Masons are the heirs apparent of the Knights Templar, and the Pilgrim Warrior's Sign indicates a readiness for militant action in support of the ideals of brotherhood. To become a Knight Templar in Freemasonry one must be a Royal Arch Mason; see 15.3461n.

15.4618 (596:27). Rorke's Drift – See 15.780–81n.

15.4618 (596:27). Up, guards, and at them! – What the duke of Wellington was supposed to have said at a critical juncture during the battle of Waterloo; Wellington himself claimed that while he did not say that, he might have ordered the devastating counterattack by saying "Stand up, Guards" and then giving their commanding officers the order to attack.

15.4618–19 (596:28). *Mahar shalal hashbaz – Hebrew: "Make haste to the prey" or "Fall upon the spoils." Isaiah is commanded to write these words on "a great roll" (Isaiah 8:1) and to give this name to his second son (8:3) as a prophetic reminder that the Assyrians will despoil Israel. In Freemasonry the words are used symbolically to suggest the readiness for action that is the ideal characteristic of a Masonic Knight Templar.

15.4621 (596:5). *Erin go bragh!* – *Éire go brách*, Irish: "Ireland until Judgment [day]!"; an Irish battle cry and the title of an anonymous Irish song. Chorus: "Oh then his shillelah he flourishes gaily, / With rattle 'em, battle 'em, crack and see-saw, / Och, liberty cheers him, each foe, too, it fears him, / While he roars out the chorus of Erin-go-Bragh!"

15.4630 (597:6). Garryowen – See 12.120n.

15.4630 (597:6). God save the king – See 8.4n.

15.4634 (597:10). The brave and the fair – Echoes a phrase in the opening lines of John Dryden's "Alexander's Feast; or the Power of Music; an Ode in Honor of St. Cecilia's Day" (1697), lines 15 and 19: "None but the brave deserve the fair." The ode was set to music by Jeremiah Clarke (1669–1707), by Thomas Clayton (1711), and (its most famous treatment) by Handel (1736).

15.4638 (597:15). *saint George – (d. 303), the dragon-slaying patron saint of England and the nation's spiritual leader in battle. "Follow your spirit, and upon this charge / Cry 'God for Harry, England, and St. George!'" (Henry V to his troops before Harfleur in Shakespeare's *Henry V* III.i.33–34).

15.4641–42 (597:17–18). The harlot's cry from . . . Ireland's windingsheet – After William Blake's "The Auguries of Innocence" (c. 1803), lines 115–16. Stephen substitutes "Ireland" for Blake's "England."

15.4648–49 (597:25). woman, sacred lifegiver – The phrase is characteristic of the way Michelet idealized Woman; see 3.167n.

15.4655–56 (598:6–7). White thy fambles . . . quarrons dainty is – See 3.381–84n.

15.4660 (598:11). Dublin's burning! . . . On fire, on fire! – See 15.172n.

15.4661ff. (598:12ff.). *Brimstone fires spring up . . .* – This stage direction describes an Armageddon, the great battle that is to destroy the world as prelude to the Last Judgment. The Black Mass at the end of the stage direction is appropriate, since Armageddon marks the climactic appearance of the Antichrist. On another level the scene is an anachronistic vision of Dublin during the Easter 1916 Uprising. A group of militant idealists, convinced that England's promise to Ireland of Home Rule after World War I was doomed to be broken, seized the General Post Office and ignited a general revolt in Dublin that raged through several days of street fighting, in the course of which the English overreacted and reduced the rebel strongholds with field artillery and Gatling guns.

15.4665 (598:16). *Pikes clash on cuirasses* – In the Rebellion of 1798, the Irish peasantry, poorly armed with (among other even less effective weapons) the traditional pike, was pitted against heavy cavalry well protected by cuirasses, a type of body armor.

15.4669 (598:21). *The midnight sun is darkened* – In the description of the Crucifixion: "And the sun was darkened, and the veil of the temple was rent in the midst" (Luke 23:45).

15.4670–72 (598:22–24). *The earth trembles . . . arise and appear to many* – In the description of the aftermath of the Crucifixion: "and the earth did quake, and the rocks rent; And the graves were opened; and many bodies of the saints which slept arose, And came out of the graves after his resurrection, and went into the holy city, and appeared unto many" (Matthew 27:51–53). For Prospect Cemetery, see p. 104; for Mount Jerome Cemetery, see 6.513n. The risen dead are already dressed for the Last Judgment, which Jesus describes (Matthew 25:31ff.) as a separation of the "sheep from the goats"—"the sheep on his right hand" to "inherit the kingdom prepared for you from the foundation of the world"; the goats "on the left hand, Depart from me, ye cursed, into everlasting fire, prepared for the devil and his angels."

15.4676–77 (598:29–30). *Factory lasses with . . . Yorkshire baraabombs* – See 10.1242n.

15.4678–79 (598:32–33). *Laughing witches in red . . . air on broomsticks* – In Robert Burns's poem "Tam o' Shanter" (1791), the hero is a drunken farmer who stumbles upon "Warlocks and witches in a dance!" (line 115), presided over by the devil in the shape of a shaggy dog. Coffins open (line 125); the "holy table" (altar) is defiled with a murderer's bones, dead babies, etc. (lines 130–42); the old women strip to their "sarks" (shirts) the better to dance, and Tam is on the verge of having his stomach turned (line 162) but is "bewitched" (line 183) by one "winsome wench" (line 164) in a "cutty sark" (short shirt) (line 171). His excitement gets the better of him and he shouts, "Weel done, Cutty-sark!" (line 189), revealing his presence and setting the witches in pursuit of him. He escapes because the witches cannot follow him over running water, though one of the witches manages to snatch the tail off his horse. See 4.513–14 (69:12–13).

15.4680–81 (598:33–34). **It rains dragons' . . . up from furrows* – Walter Hussey Burgh (1742–83), an Irish statesman and orator famous for his "power of stirring the passions," said in a speech in the Irish Parliament (1779): "Talk not to me of peace. Ireland is not at peace. It is smothered war. England has sown her laws as dragon's teeth, and they have sprung up as armed men." The allusion is to the Greek myth about Cadmus, the founder and king of Thebes. In the course of his wanderings he encountered and killed a dragon, whereupon Athena counseled him to sow its teeth in a field; armed men sprang up and immediately began to kill each other until only five were left. These five joined Cadmus in founding Thebes.

15.4681–82 (599:1). *the pass of knights of the red cross* – A password that identifies them as having been admitted to the Masonic degree Knight of the Red Cross (preliminary to that of Knight Templar). The Knights of the Red Cross are also known as the Knights of Babylon as a reflection of their mystic identity with the Jews who rebuilt Jerusalem and the temple after the Babylonian captivity; see 15.3461n and 15.4615–16n.

15.4682 (599:2). *Wolfe Tone* – See 10.378n.

15.4683 (599:2). *Henry Grattan* – See 7.731n.

15.4683 (599:3). *Smith O'Brien* – See 6.226n.

15.4683 (599:3). *Daniel O'Connell* – See 2.269n.

15.4684 (599:3). *Michael Davitt* – (1846–1906), the Irish patriot and politician who organized the Land League (1879) and who was instrumental in helping Parnell to fuse the two major political issues of the 1880s, Land Reform and Home Rule.

15.4684 (599:4). *Isaac Butt* – See 7.707n.

15.4684 (599:4). *Justin M'Carthy against Parnell* – A "real" contest, since the Irish writer and politician Justin McCarthy (1830–1912) led the majority anti-Parnellite wing of the Irish party after the Great Split over Parnell's leadership in 1890. McCarthy resigned his leadership in 1896.

15.4685 (599:4–5). *Arthur Griffith* – See 3.227n.

15.4685 (599:5). *John Redmond* – (1856–1918), an Irish politician who supported Parnell at the Great Split in 1890 and who worked to rally his broken party through the 1890s until it was reunited under his leadership in 1900.

15.4685 (599:5). *John O'Leary* – (1830–1907), characterized by Yeats in 1913 as the last representative of "Romantic Ireland." O'Leary began his career as a political radical with the Young Irelanders in 1848 and continued with the Fenians as editor of their paper, *The Irish People*. Deported in 1871, he was allowed to return in 1885, after which he was active in the literary movement and in radical politics.

15.4686 (599:6). *Lord Edward Fitzgerald* – See 10.785–86n.

15.4687 (599:7). *The O'Donoghue of the Glens* – A Celtic and Catholic family of Irish gentry who were an exception since they were not displaced or suppressed by English rule but continued to flourish in the wilds of County Kerry in southwestern Ireland until the beginning of the nineteenth century.

15.4688 (599:8–9). *the centre of the earth* – In Dante's *Inferno*, canto 34, the nethermost pit of hell, which contains the souls of those "who betrayed their masters and benefactors," notable among them Judas and, at the center, Satan.

15.4688–89 (599:9). *the field altar of Saint Barbara* – This legendary saint is associated with Heliopolis in Egypt or Nicomedia in Asia Minor. The daughter of a rich heathen, she was held in a tower by her father lest she be married without his permission. She was converted to Christianity and baptized during her father's absence. Once converted, she realized that her tower only had two windows, so she had a third cut that there might be one for each person of the Trinity. Her father was so outraged by her conversion that he delivered her up to public torture and finally beheaded her himself. On his way home he was struck down by a bolt of lightning out of a clear sky; thus St. Barbara became the patron saint of artillerymen, soldiers, and firefighters (also of architects). Her intercession was invoked as protection against lightning, explosives, and fire, and against accident and sudden death. Her central attribute is the three-windowed tower, and she was the only female saint to bear the attribute of the sacramental cup and wafer. The field altar appropriately bears her name as patron saint of those in battle.

15.4689–90 (599:9–10). *Black candles rise from its gospel and epistle horns* – Black candles are appropriate, since a Black Mass is about to be celebrated and black is Satan's color. The Black Mass in worship of Satan is associated with the witches' Sabbath and is performed as an elaborate series of inversions and perversions of the Christian Mass. It is traditionally performed on Thursday, possibly because the first mass (the Last Supper) occurred on Thursday, possibly because that supper was prelude to Judas's betrayal. The gospel side of the altar is on the congregation's left, where the Gospels are read; the epistle side is on the right.

15.4690 (599:11). *the tower* – Not only the Martello tower associated with Stephen, Mulligan, and Haines, but also St. Barbara's central attribute.

15.4691–93 (599:12–14). *On the altarstone . . . her swollen belly* – Black Mass is traditionally celebrated with the body of a naked woman as the altar. As "goddess of unreason," she is the inversion of the "Goddess of Reason," an abstraction set up in 1793 by the French Revolutionists to take the place of the Christian God as the supreme deity.

15.4693–94 (599:14–15). *Father Malachi O'Flynn . . . back to the front* – For Malachi, see 1.41n and 9.492n; for Father O'Flynn's reputation as a maker of fools, see 8.707n; the comic reversals of his costume follow the Black Mass emphasis on reversal; for the two left feet, see 15.2572–73n.

15.4695 (599:16–17). **The Reverend Mr Hugh C Haines Love M.A.* – See 1.49n and 10.437–38n.

15.4699 (599:21). *Introibo ad altare diaboli* – Latin: "I will go up to the devil's altar." Cf. 1.5n.

15.4701 (599:23). **To the devil which hath made glad my young days** – The Protestant Reverend Love responds as server in this Black Mass; cf. 1.5n.

15.4703 (599:25). *a blooddripping host* – The Black Mass is celebrated with blood, as against the wine that is transubstantiated into blood in the Christian Mass.

15.4703 (599:26). **Corpus meum* – Latin: "My body." As the priest begins that phase of the Mass called the Consecration, he repeats what Jesus said at the Last Supper: "Take it, all of you, and eat of it, *for this is my body.*"

15.4707/12 (599:31/600:3). THE DAMNED/ THE BLESSED – Are separated as they are to be at the Last Judgment, "When the Son of man shall come in his glory." See Matthew 25:31–46.

15.4708 (599:32). Htengier . . . Aiulella! – An inversion of "Alleluia, for the Lord God Omnipotent reigneth." Revelation describes the course of the Last Judgment: "And I heard as it were the voice of a great multitude, and as the voice of many waters, and as the voice of mighty thunderings, saying, Alleluia: for the Lord God omnipotent reigneth" (Revelation 19:6).

15.4711 (600:2). Doooooooooooog! – As "dog," an inversion of *God*.

15.4718 (600:9). Kick the Pope – One version of this Orange faction chant is a nagging street rhyme, "Tooral, looral, kick the Pope; / Hang him up wi' taury rope" (Leslie Daiken, *Out Goes She; Dublin Street Rhymes* [Dublin, 1963], p. 20). The "pope" is also Orangeman slang for a football, and "Kick the pope" for the ritual of kicking it around a field to taunt the Catholic Green.

15.4718 (600:9–10). Daily, daily sing to Mary – A Catholic hymn, "Omni die dic Mariae," called St. Casimir's hymn; as translated by Father Bittlestone: "Daily, daily sing to Mary, / Sing my soul, her praises due, / All her feasts, her actions worship, / With the heart's devotion true. / Lost in wond'ring contemplation, / Be her majesty confess'd: / Call her Mother, Call her Virgin, / Happy Mother, Virgin blest."

15.4726 (600:22). dialectic, the universal language – In contrast to Stephen's proposal, "So that gesture . . . would be a universal language" (15.105–6 [432:18–19]).

15.4730 (600:26). *Exit Judas. Et laqueo se suspendit* – Latin: "Judas left. And went and hanged himself." The last three Latin words quote Matthew 27:5 (Vulgate); the rest of Stephen's remark renders the sense of that passage.

15.4735 (601:5). This feast of pure reason – Alexander Pope, in *The First Satire of the Second Book of Horace Imitated* (1733), celebrates withdrawal from "all the distant Din that World can keep" into his "grotto . . . / There, my Retreat the best Companions grace, / Chiefs, out of War, and Statesmen, out of Place. / There St. John mingles with my friendly Bowl, / The Feast of Reason and the Flow of Soul" (lines 123–28). Henry St. John, Viscount Bolingbroke (1678–1751), was a controversial English statesman, orator, and author and a friend of Pope.

15.4737 (600:17). acushla – *A chuisle*, Irish: "O pulse"; a term of endearment.

15.4737–38 (600:17). At 8:35 a.m. you will be in heaven – Cf. Stephen's riddle (2.102–7 [26:33–38]). Executions in the British Isles were traditionally scheduled for 8:00 A.M.

15.4738 (600:17–18). Ireland will be free – Old Gummy Granny is speaking as a caricature of the Shan Van Vocht; see 1.543–44n.

15.4752 (601:19). Carbine in bucket! – Mili-

tary command. A "bucket" is the leather holster in which a cavalryman keeps his carbine (or lance).

15.4763 (602:6). *the coward's blow* – A blow struck to provoke someone else to fight or be considered a coward.

15.4793–94 (603:13–14). *Bennett'll shove you in the lockup – That is, Sergeant Major Bennett (see 10.1133–34n) would impose military punishment on a soldier who got in trouble with the civilian authorities.

15.4809 (604:3). sprung – Slang for exhausted or drunk.

15.4826 (604:22–23). wipe your name off the slate – That is, don't put him in charge (under arrest); to charge a drink in a bar is to put a man's name on a slate.

15.4827 (604:23–24). with my tooraloom tooraloom – See 5.13–16n.

15.4861–62 (606:6–7). Two commercials that were standing fizz in Jammet's – That is, two salesmen who were buying champagne for the other customers; for Jammet's, see 13.900n.

15.4864 (606:9–10). Behan's car – Significance unknown.

15.4866 (606:12). just going home by Gardiner street – This is plausible, since Gardiner Street slants north-northwest from the Custom House near the mouth of the Liffey and passes just west of "nighttown"; it would be Bloom's logical route home from east-central Dublin.

15.4868 (606:15). the mots – See 10.1142–43n.

15.4884 (607:2). Cabra – A small suburban district about two miles northeast of central Dublin; one of the residential waystations on Stephen's family's decline. *Thom's* 1904 lists no. 7 St. Peter's-terrace in Phibsborough (Cabra) under a Mr. John Joyce.

15.4886 (607:4). Sandycove – Where the Martello tower that Stephen has been sharing with Mulligan is located.

15.4926 (608:18). The name if you call. Somnambulist – After the common assumption that a sleepwalker may be safely aroused if he is gently called by his first name or an intimate nickname.

15.4930 (608:23). Black panther. Vampire – Haines's dream and Stephen's translation of Hyde's poem (3.397–98n) are obvious; cf. 9.1214n.

15.4932–33 (608:26–27). Who . . . drive . . . wood's woven shade? – Here and below, Stephen is reciting Yeats's "Who Goes with Fergus"; see 1.239–41n.

15.4951–52 (609:13–14). swear that I will . . . art or arts – This is from a version of the oath of secrecy required of all Freemasons as a condition of initiation into a lodge.

15.4953–54 (609:15–17). in the rough sands . . . ebbs . . . and flows – Source unknown.

15.4956 (609:19). *secret master* – The fourth degree in the Ancient and Accepted Scottish Rite of Freemasonry; the first of the so-called "Ineffable Degrees" (those principally engaged in contemplation of "the Ineffable Name [of the Deity]"). In the ritual of Freemasonry, "the true secret is just that which eternally surrounds you, but is seen by none, although it is there for all eyes to see."

15.4957 (609:20). *a fairy boy of eleven, a changeling* – In Celtic folklore, fairies plagued human beings by kidnapping particularly handsome and promising babies and leaving difficult and unresponsive (or cantankerous) fairy children in their places.

15.4957–58 (609:21). *an Eton suit* – See 6.76n.

15.4958 (609:21). *glass shoes* – In the fairy tale, Cinderella is transformed by her fairy godmother from a kitchen drudge into a princess in resplendent costume complete with glass shoes. One of the shoes is left behind at the ball when midnight strikes, and Cinderella's finery is replaced by her drudge's rags, but it is the fit of this shoe that enables the prince to identify Cinderella and rescue her from her slavery.

15.4959–60 (609:22–23). *He reads from right . . . kissing the page* – That is, in the attitude of a devout young Jewish scholar; compare with Bloom's memory of his father reading the *Haggadah* (7.206–7 [122:19–21]). The question of which sacred book Rudy is reading has been worried to little avail; it could be any Jewish religious text with the name of God in it.

15.4965–66 (609:29). *diamond and ruby buttons* – In the language of gems, the diamond has the power of making men courageous and of magnanimous and of protecting them from evil spirits. The ruby is symbolic of a cheerful mind, and it works as a preservative of health and as an amulet against poison, sadness, and evil thoughts.

15.4966–67 (609:30). *slim ivory cane . . . white lambkin* – These objects, together with the "bronze helmet" (15.4958 [609:22]), suggest that Rudy appears in the role of Hermes (Mercury). Hermes' "attributes are a hat with a wide brim . . . ; sandals which carried him swiftly on sea or land [see 4.240–42n] . . . ; and the herald's staff given him by Apollo, which in early art was adorned with white ribbons, but later twined with two serpents" (Clara Erskine Clement, *A Handbook of Legendary and Mythological Art* [Boston, 1881], p. 458). In ancient Rome, an ivory cane (*scipio eburneus*) was awarded to and carried by persons of distinction or royal authority. The "lambkin" is another of Hermes' attributes, since he was frequently represented as a shepherd with a single animal from his flock. In *The Odyssey*, when Hermes intercepts Odysseus as Odysseus approaches Circe's palace, he is described as "a boy whose lip was downy," and Odysseus says, "He took my hand and spoke as though he knew me" (10:278ff.; Fitzgerald, p. 185). See headnote to this episode, p. 452; and cf. 15.212–13n.

In the Old Testament/Jewish context suggested by Rudy's reading, the lamb is the "dominant sacrificial victim," symbolizing "innocence and gentleness"; it functions as "the central symbol of sacrifice in Passover." In the New Testament/Christian context Jesus is "the Lamb of God" (*The Interpreter's Dictionary of the Bible* [New York, 1962], s.v. "Lamb," vol. 3, pp. 58–59); see 15.235–36n and 15.289n. The "violet bowknot" on Rudy's cane finds its source in Catholic liturgy, where violet is the color of penitence and of the penitential seasons of Advent and Lent. In view of Rudy's name (from Old German *hrothi*, "fame," and *vulf*, "wolf"), the Biblical associations also suggest Isaiah's vision of "the peaceable kingdom" (11:1–10) when "The wolf shall dwell with the lamb," a passage read during Joyce's time in the mass for the first Tuesday in Advent. (For the biblical and liturgical citations in this note I am indebted to Joan Keenan.)

PART III

The Homecoming

(16.1–18.1609, PP. 612–783)

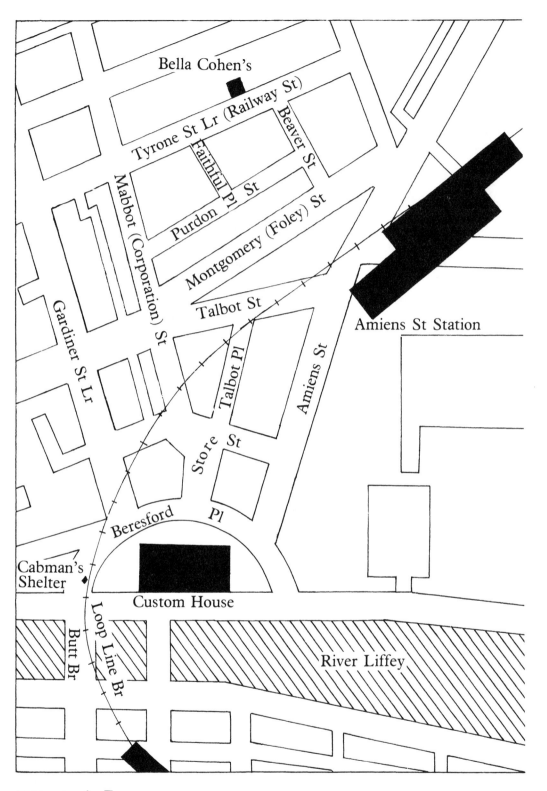

EPISODE 16. *Eumaeus*

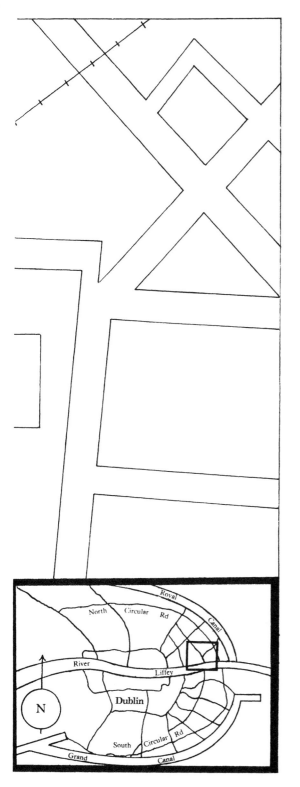

EPISODE 16

Eumaeus

(16.1–1894, pp. 612–65)

Episode 16: *Eumaeus*, **16.1–16.1894 (612–665)**.   In the course of Book 13 of *The Odyssey* Odysseus returns alone to Ithaca. He is in serious danger of suffering Agamemnon's fate (i.e., of being murdered on arrival) if he enters his house and announces his identity. He has a long consultation with Athena in which he gets news of his beleaguered house and of his son Telemachus's enterprise in searching for news of him on the mainland. Athena disguises Odysseus as an old man and counsels him to seek the dwelling of the swineherd Eumaeus, who "Of all Odysseus' field hands . . . cared most for the estate" (14:3–4; Fitzgerald, p. 259). In Book 14 Eumaeus receives the incognito Odysseus with a ready offer of hospitality and with sensible kindness and honesty. Book 15 is divided between a description of how Telemachus avoids the ambush the suitors have set for him as he returns to Ithaca and the development of the relationship between Odysseus and Eumaeus. In Book 16 Telemachus comes to Eumaeus's hut in search of news of his mother; Odysseus tests Telemachus's filial commitment and then reveals himself. Reunited, father and son plan an approach to their besieged house.

Time: 1:00 A.M. Scene: the cabman's shelter under the Loop Line bridge, just west of the Custom House, near Butt Bridge, (in 1904) the easternmost bridge over the Liffey. These coffeehouse shelters were relatively small eight-sided buildings, approximately ten feet by fifteen feet. Organ: nerves; Art: navigation; Color: none; Symbol: sailors; Technique: narrative (old). Correspondences: *Eumaeus*—Skin-the-Goat [i.e., James Fitzharris; see 7.640n]; *Ulysses, Pseudangelos*[1]—the Sailor; *Melanthious* [Odysseus's goatherd][2]—Corley.

The Linati schema adds Ulysses and Telemachus to the list of Persons and cites as Sense (Meaning): "The Ambush at Home"—the ambush that the suitors, led by Antinous, set to intercept Telemachus as he returns from the mainland to Ithaca and, presumably, the ambush the suitors would set if they knew that Odysseus was returning alone.

16.3 (613:3). orthodox Samaritan fashion – In Luke 10:30–37, Jesus answers a lawyer's question, "Who is my neighbour?" with the parable of the good Samaritan, which tells of a Samaritan who was willing to help a severely injured man whom the orthodox Jews ("a certain priest" and "a Levite") "passed by" and neglected.

16.6 (613:7). Vartry water – See 11.619n.

16.8–9 (613:9–11). *the cabman's shelter . . . near Butt bridge – See headnote to this episode.

16.17 (613:20). e.d.ed – Slang for finished, exhausted.

16.21 (613:25). along Beaver street – See 15.585n; Stephen and Bloom have turned south out of Tyrone Street, where the brawl took place. They are proceeding southeast toward the Amiens Street railroad station; eventually, they will turn southwest toward the cabman's shelter. Their route is thus circuitous, circumspect—as are both Odysseus's and Telemachus's approaches to Eumaeus's hut in *The Odyssey*.

16.21–22 (613:26). the farrier's – J. Kavanagh, horseshoer and farrier, 14–15 Beaver Street.

16.22–23 (613:26–27). the livery stables . . . Montgomery street – There was a livery stable at 42 Montgomery Street, on the corner of Beaver Street. Montgomery Street, which gave its

---

1 *Odysseus Pseudangelos* (Odysseus, the False Messenger) is the title of a lost Greek play cited by Aristotle in *The Poetics* as an example of a sort of "recognition" second only to that of Sophocles' *Oedipus*. Since the passage in Aristotle is far from easy, two translations:

"Again, there is a composite kind of recognition involving false inference on the part of one of the characters, as in the Odysseus Disguised as a Messenger. A said <that no one else was able to bend the bow; . . . hence B (the disguised Odysseus) imagined that A would> recognize the bow which, in fact, he had not seen; and to bring about a recognition by this means—the expectation that A would recognize the bow—is false inference" (S. H. Butcher [London, 1895; 4th ed., 1907], p. 61).

"There is also [a recognition] based on mistaken inference on the part of the audience, as in *Odysseus the False Messenger*. In that play, that he and no one else can string the bow is an assumption, a premise invented by the poet, and also his saying that he would

recognize the bow when in fact he had not seen it; whereas the notion that he (the poet) had made his invention for the sake of the other person who would make the recognition, that is a mistaken inference" (Gerald F. Else [Ann Arbor, Mich., 1970], pp. 46–47).

2 Melanthious persecutes his disguised master in Book 17 of *The Odyssey* and betrays him in Book 22 by supplying arms to some of the embattled suitors. He is caught and lashed to a plank and hoisted up to the roof beams to "Watch through the night." When the suitors are all slain, his nose, ears, hands, and feet are cut off and his genitals fed to the dogs (22:173, 475ff.; Fitzgerald, pp. 427, 436).

name (Monto) to the Dublin red-light district, is now Foley Street; it runs from Corporation Street (Mabbot Street in 1904) to Amiens Street, toward which Bloom heads in search of a cab.

16.24 (613:29). Dan Bergin's – Daniel L. Bergin, grocer, tea and wine merchant, 46 Amiens Street on the corner of Montgomery (now Foley) Street.

16.25 (613:30). a Jehu – Slang, originally for a fast or furious driver, after II Kings 9:20: "the driving is like the driving of Jehu the son of Nimshi; for he driveth furiously"; by 1904 it was simply cliché for any coachman or cab-driver.

16.27 (613:32–33). *the North Star hotel – At 26–30 Amiens Street, across the street from the railroad station.

16.33 (613:39). bevelling – Slang for moving or pushing.

16.33 (613:40). *Mullett's – John Mullett, tea, wine, and spirit merchant, 45 Amiens Street, next door to Bergin's.

16.33–34 (613:40). the Signal House – Thomas F. Hayden, family grocer and spirit merchant, the Signal House, 36 Amiens Street.

16.35 (613:41–42). Amiens street railway terminus – The Great Northern Railway terminus, trains to Belfast and northern Ireland.

16.37 (614:1). gone the way of all buttons – After the proverbial "Gone the way of all flesh."

16.41 (614:6). Jupiter Pluvius – Latin: "Jupiter the Rainmaker"; one of the many common epithets for the king of the Roman gods, emphasizing his role as lord of the weather. In context, the epithet is more cliché than allusion.

16.41 (614:6). dandered – Dialect for strolled, sauntered.

16.46–47 (614:12–13). Great Northern railway . . . point for Belfast – See 16.35n.

16.48 (614:15). the morgue – The Dublin City Morgue around the corner at 3 Store Street had a back entrance at 2–4 Amiens Street.

16.49–50 (614:16–17). the Dock Tavern – Mrs. M. A. Hall, proprietor, 1 Store Street, on

the corner of Amiens Street; Bloom and Stephen turn west into Store Street.

16.51 (614:18). C division police station – Dublin Metropolitan Police Barrack, C Division, was housed at 3 Store Street in the same complex of buildings as the morgue.

16.52 (614:19). *warehouses of Beresford place – Beresford Place curves from Store Street around the back of the Custom House toward Butt Bridge. There were several large warehouses in the street in 1904.

16.52–54 (614:19–21). *Stephen thought to think . . . in Talbot place – Stephen is recalling an association he established on his walk to the university in *A Portrait*, chapter 5:A; D. G. Baird and J. Paul Todd, the Talbot engineering works, mechanical engineers and founders, 20–25 Talbot Place, were just around the corner from its intersection with Store Street. Interestingly enough, in spite of all Joyce's admiration for Henrik Ibsen (1828–1906), this is the only direct mention of him in *Ulysses*. Ibsen, the great Norwegian dramatist, is regarded as one of the pioneers of modern drama. He is generally associated with "naturalism" in the theater and is credited with the origin of the play that treats social problems (the conflict between the individual and social norms or prejudices) in a blunt and outspoken manner. His later work combined realistic dialogue with a monolithic structuring of situation reminiscent of Greek tragedy. The association of Ibsen with the "stonecutter's" (converted for the purposes of fiction from what *Thom's* 1904 calls "engineers and founders") may pivot on Ibsen's play *When We Dead Awaken* (1899), which Joyce discussed at length in his essay "Ibsen's New Drama" (1900). Joyce described the sculptor Rubek's estranged (and awakened) wife: "Her airy freshness is as a breath of keen air. The sense of free, almost flamboyant, life, which is her chief note, counterbalances the austerity of Irene and the dullness of Rubek" (*CW*, p. 65).

16.54–55 (614:22–23). *fidus Achates – See 6.49n.

16.55–56 (614:23–24). James Rourke's city bakery – James Rourke, baker and flour merchant, 5–6 Store Street, on the corner of Mabbot (now Corporation) Street.

16.57 (614:25). our daily bread – See 4.82n.

16.58–59 (614:27–28). O tell me where is fancy bread – The opening line of a song that Portia sings while Bassanio is looking over a choice of caskets in Shakespeare's *The Merchant of Venice* (III.ii.63–71). The song begins, "Tell me where is fancy bred, / Or in the heart or in the head?"

16.63–64 (614:33). swell mobsmen – In context, slang for showily dressed pimps who double as pickpockets and thieves.

16.70–71 (614:42). that man in the gap – See 12.186n.

16.73 (615:2). bridewell – See 8.421n.

16.73 (615:3). Mr Tobias – Matthew Tobias, prosecuting solicitor for the Dublin Metropolitan Police; offices, Eustace Street, Dublin.

16.74 (615:3). old Wall – See 8.396n.

16.74 (615:4). *Mahony – Daniel Mahony, barrister and divisional police magistrate at the Central Metropolitan Police Court in the Four Courts.

16.74–75 (615:4–5). which simply spelt ruin for a chap when it got bruited about – See 16.209–10n.

16.77 (615:7). unscrupulous in the service of the Crown – A common Irish criticism of the Dublin Metropolitan Police who, while ostensibly Irish, were all too readily associated with the English Establishment.

16.78–79 (615:8–9). *the A division in Clanbrassil street – The A Division police barracks were in Kevin Street Upper, just off New Street, which is an extension of Clanbrassil Street; Clanbrassil Street and its extensions bisect south-central Dublin.

16.80 (615:11). *Pembroke road – In a fashionable area on the southeastern outskirts of metropolitan Dublin in 1904.

16.89–90 (615:22–23). the much vexed question of stimulants – Temperance (the prohibition of alcoholic beverages) was one of the great (and controversial) reform impulses of the late nineteenth and early twentieth centuries.

16.98 (615:33). that one was Judas – Namely, Lynch; see 15.4730n.

16.100–101 (615:36). the back of the Customhouse – Stephen and Bloom are in Beresford Place, which curves from Store Street around the north and west sides of the Custom House to end at Butt Bridge.

16.101 (615:36–37). the Loop Line bridge – The City of Dublin Junction Railway, an elevated railway that linked Westland Row station south of the Liffey with Amiens Street station north of the Liffey.

16.106 (615:42). the corporation watchman – That is, in the employ of the Dublin Corporation, the Dublin city government.

16.109 (616:4). Gumley – See 7.645n.

16.119 (616:13). funkyish – Elaborated from *funk*, slang for to be afraid, scared, depressed.

16.123 (616:18–19). the Thames embankment – An area in London once known for the indigents who congregated there; consequently, a stock phrase for indigence.

16.130 (616:26–27). Lord John Corley – Appears as a character in "Two Gallants," *Dubliners*.

16.130–31 (616:27–28). his genealogy came about in this wise – The archaic turn of phrase echoes Matthew 1:18, "Now the birth of Jesus Christ was on this wise," and suggests an irony at the expense of inflated genealogical claims to noble (if left-handed) lineage.

16.132 (616:29). *the G division – The plainclothes-detective branch of the Dublin Metropolitan Police. In 1904 the division was headed by a superintendent, a chief inspector, and two inspectors.

16.133 (616:29–30). Katherine Brophy, the daughter of a Louth farmer – Corley's mother. Louth is a county on the east coast of Ireland north of Dublin.

16.133–43 (616:30–41). His grandfather, Patrick Michael Corley . . . Katherine (also) Talbot . . . Lord John Corley – A breathtakingly circumstantial attempt to connect Corley's paternal grandmother to the Talbots of Malahide. New Ross is a town in County Wexford in southeastern Ireland.

16.136–37 (616:34–35). ***the house of the lords Talbot de Malahide** – Is located in the village of Malahide, nine miles north of Dublin. Called Malahide Castle, it is a large, square baronial mansion flanked by circular towers; it was first built in the twelfth century, though repeated reconstruction and updatings have effectively eliminated the original. The interior is richly overanimated with elaborate oak carvings and wainscoting. See 10.156–58n.

16.140 (616:38). **washkitchen** – A kitchen set aside for the washing of clothes; a laundry. The joke is that those who worked there would have virtually no contact with the family in the "big house."

16.147 (617:3). **swab** – A term of contempt for an idle, worthless person; especially, a drunkard.

16.158 (617:15). **a gentleman usher** – Obsolete for an assistant to a schoolmaster or to a head teacher.

16.161–62 (617:19–20). **stuck twice in the junior at the christian brothers** – For Christian Brothers, see 10.4n. Since their schools were more practically than academically demanding, Corley's failure to pass the second to the last year is not a very strong recommendation.

16.166 (617:24–25). **a dosshouse in Marlborough street, Mrs Maloney's** – A cheap lodging house; the street is just west of where the characters are standing. *Thom's* 1904 does not list a Mrs. Maloney on the street, but there are a number of "tenements" listed.

16.167 (617:25–26). **tanner** – Slang for sixpence.

16.167 (617:26). **M'Conachie** – Apart from the context, identity and significance unknown.

16.168–70 (617:27–29). **the Brazen Head . . . for friar Bacon** – The Brazen Head Hotel, the oldest hostelry in Dublin (established c. 1688), was not in Winetavern Street but a block west, at 20 Bridge Street Lower. Stephen is reminded of *The Honourable History of Friar Bacon and Friar Bungay* (c. 1589–92), a play by the English poet-dramatist-journalist Robert Greene (1558–92). The main plot of the play is a standard love triangle; the slapstick subplot involves a series of competitions in necromancy. In Act IV, Friar Bacon climaxes seven years of work with the creation of "the brazen head." Properly invoked, the head would have uttered great wisdoms and would have created a protective wall of brass around all of England. Unfortunately, the head utters its wisdom ("Time is! . . . Time was! . . . Time is past!") to Bacon's stupid servant Miles, who responds without the proper formulae of invocation; and at the words "Time is past!" a hammer appears and destroys the head.

16.175 (617:35). *haud ignarus malorum miseris succurrere disco* – Latin: "not at all ignorant of misfortune, I have learned to succor the miserable." This improves on Virgil's line in the *Aeneid* 1:630 when Dido says, "Non ignara mali miseris succurrere disco," to assure Aeneas of her willingness to comfort him (Not ignorant of misfortune . . .).

16.177 (617:37). **screw** – Slang for salary.

16.198–99 (618:19). **the Bleeding Horse in Camden street** – A pub in south-central Dublin, somewhat outside of Bloom's geographical patterns and rather low on the social scale, as Adams points out (pp. 205–6). Perhaps the reason for this relatively improbable meeting place lies in Adams's observation that the pub is important "as a center of low scheming" in James Sheridan Le Fanu's (1814–73) novel *The Cock and Anchor* (1845).

16.202 (618:24). **the Carl Rosa** – The Carl Rosa Opera Company, founded in 1873 by the German violinist and conductor Carl Rosa (born Rose, 1842–89). The company devoted itself to opera in English and toured extensively in the provinces; it established its popularity in Dublin in 1873 with the first of its many appearances in that city.

16.203 (618:25). **crossing sweeper** – The lowest of the low, but indispensable in a horse-drawn city. The most famous crossing sweeper in English literature is the pathetic Jo, a native of the slum "Tom-All-Alone's" in Dickens's *Bleak House* (1853).

16.205–6 (618:28). **Bags Comisky** – For what it's worth, *Thom's* 1904 lists a Mr. C. Comisky at 27 Effra Road in Rathmines. The nickname "Bags" suggests that he wore outsized trousers.

16.206–7 (618:29). **Fullam's, the shipchandler's** – John Fullam, shipchandler, bonded stores, rope, sail, and twine manufacturer, 6 Eden Quay, 4 Rogerson's Quay, and 54 Denzille Street.

16.207–8 (618:30). in Nagle's back – In the back room, or snug, of a pub managed by four Nagles; it had entrances at 9 Cathedral Street and 25 Earl Street North, not far northeast of where Stephen and Corley are talking.

16.208 (618:30). O'Mara – Apart from the context, identity and significance unknown.

16.208 (618:31). Tighe – Apart from the context, identity and significance unknown.

16.209 (618:31). lagged – Slang for arrested.

16.209–10 (618:32–33). fined ten bob . . . refusing to go with the constable – A conviction that would not only have been a disgrace but could have had serious social and economic consequences such as ostracism and loss of employment, particularly if the offender belonged to the middle class.

16.237 (619:24). Eblana – See 14.205n.

16.238 (619:24–25). Customhouse quay – In front of the Custom House on the north bank of the Liffey just a few yards from where Bloom and Stephen are standing.

16.247 (619:35–36). Everyone according to . . . to his deeds – Bloom's version of Karl Marx's (1818–93) socialist axiom "From each according to his ability; to each according to his needs."

16.251 (619:40). fag – Slang: "to do something fatiguing."

16.270 (620:20). the ingle – Obsolete for a fire burning on the hearth.

16.271 (620:21). Trinidad shell cocoa – A relatively inferior cocoa.

16.273 (620:23–24). the Friday herrings – Until 1967 Friday was a fast day (meatless) for Roman Catholics.

16.276–77 (620:27–28). the third precept of the church – "To observe the fasts on the days during the seasons appointed."

16.278 (620:29). *quarter tense or if not, ember days – The same thing, since "quarter tense," from the Latin *Quatuor Tempora* (Four Times), is Middle English for ember days, days of fast and abstinence at the beginning of various liturgical seasons. Ember days occur on the

Wednesday, Friday, and Saturday after 13 December, after Ash Wednesday (16 February in 1904), after Whitsunday (22 May in 1904), and after 14 September.

16.285 (620:38). pinch of tobacco – By 1900 tobacco was no longer used in medicine because of its unpredictable and "dangerous depressant action."

16.290 (621:1). tony – Slang for high on the social scale, fashionable.

16.292–94 (621:3–5). his rescue of that man . . . or Malahide was it? – It was at neither of these seaside resorts north of Dublin but from the Liffey in central Dublin that Mulligan's real-life counterpart, Oliver St. John Gogarty, rescued a bookmaker named Max Harris on Sunday, 23 June 1901.

16.309 (621:23). the men's public urinal – Under the Loop Line bridge just north of Butt Bridge and near the cabman's shelter.

16.314–19 (621:28–31 // 32).—*Puttana madonna, che ci dia i quattrini! Ho ragione? Culo rotto! / —Intendiamoci. Mezzo sovrano più . . . / —Dice lui, però! / —Mezzo. / —Farabutto! Mortacci sui! / —Ma ascolta! Cinque la testa più . . . – Italian: "—Whore of a Blessed Virgin, he must give us the money! Aren't I right? Busted asshole! / —Let's get this clear. Half a sovereign more . . . / —So that's what he says, however! / —Half. / —Blackguard! His filthy dead [ancestors]! / —But listen! Five more per person . . . "

16.320 (621:33). the cabman's shelter – See headnote to this episode, p. 534.

16.323–24 (621:37). Skin-the-Goat Fitzharris, the invincible – See 5.378n, 5.379n, and 7.640n. James Fitzharris was sentenced to life imprisonment as an accessory in the Phoenix Park murders, but he was released in 1902. There is no evidence to suggest that he was keeper of the cabman's shelter, but several Dubliners (1970) have suggested that the Dublin Corporation employed him as a nightwatchman after his release from prison; that is, Fitzharris had Gumley's job.

16.342 (622:16). voglio – See 4.327n.

16.346 (622:21). Bella Poetria! – Bloom's attempt at *Bella Poesia!*, Italian: "Beautiful Poetry!"

16.347 (622:22). *Belladonna. Voglio* – Bloom is attempting to say "I want a beautiful woman" in Italian; but "Belladonna" in Italian also means deadly nightshade.

16.363 (622:41–42). *Cicero, Podmore. Napoleon, Mr Goodbody. Jesus, Mr Doyle* – Adams (p. 223) suggests a solution to this word puzzle: "Cicero as a name comes from Latin *cicera*, chickpea, and might well be something like Podmore in English; Napoleon = Buonaparte = Goodbody; and Jesus = Christ = Anointed = oiled = Doyle."

16.364 (622:42–43). Shakespeares were as common as Murphies – If "common" in the sense of "not upper class," yes; but quantitatively, an exaggeration, though Shakespeare was not an unusual name.

16.364 (622:43). What's in a name? – In Shakespeare's *Romeo and Juliet*, Juliet discovers that Romeo is a Montague (and thus her family's enemy): "O, be some other name! / What's in a name? That which we call a rose / By any other name would smell as sweet" (II.ii.42–44).

16.376–77 (623:14). good old Hollands – Holland gin, formerly Holland geneva.

16.404–5 (624:1–2). *Buffalo Bill shoots . . . he never will* – Iona Opie (letter, 24 August 1970) suggests that this street rhyme is similar to a rhyme that appears in Carl Sandburg's *The American Songbag* (New York, 1927), pp. 384–85: "Bad Bill from Bunker Hill / Never worked (washed) and never will." Buffalo Bill was the American frontiersman and scout William F. Cody (1846–1917), who earned his reputation as a crack shot when he was a contractor supplying buffalo meat to workmen on the transcontinental railroad after the Civil War. He subsequently became an international figure as the head of a Wild West show in which he gave demonstrations of his marksmanship: one of his widely advertised feats was the shooting of clay pigeons with a revolver.

16.407 (624:5). the Bisley – The annual competitive meetings of the National Rifle Association (of England) were held in July on Bisley Common, twenty-nine miles southwest of London.

16.412 (624:11–12). Hengler's Royal Circus – See 4.349n.

16.415 (624:15–16). *D. B. Murphy of Carrigaloe* – This "commoner" (see 16.364n) says he is from Carrigaloe Station on Great Island on the passage between Cork (Queenstown, now Cobh) Harbor and Lough Mahon, the body of water that gives shipping access to Cork. The name Murphy means "sea-fighter" and, according to *Webster's New International Dictionary* (1909), is "jocose" for "a potatoe."

16.418 (624:18–19). Fort Camden and Fort Carlisle – The two forts that guarded the inner entrance to Cork (or Queenstown) Harbor; they are almost five miles south of Carrigaloe.

16.420 (624:20–21). *For England, home and beauty* – See 10.232, 235n.

16.423–24 (624:25). Davy Jones – See 13.1164n.

16.424 (624:25). a blind moon – That is, in the dark of the moon.

16.425 (624:27). Alice Ben Bolt – From the English popular song "Ben Bolt," by Thomas Dunn English and Nelson Kneass. Ben Bolt, a sailor faithful to his Alice, returns after a twenty-year absence to find Alice dead. First stanza: "Don't you remember, sweet Alice, Ben Bolt? / Sweet Alice with hair so brown, / Who blushed with delight if you gave her a smile, / And trembled with fear at your frown? / In the old church in the valley, Ben Bolt, / In a corner obscure and lone, / They have fitted a slab of granite so grey, / And Alice lies under the stones."

16.425–26 (624:27). Enoch Arden – A narrative poem (1864) by Tennyson. Enoch, the sailor-hero, happily weds Annie Lee; the luck of his small-boat enterprise eventually sours, and he determines to accept a position as boatswain on a ship bound for China in order to achieve security for his family. Enoch's absence is extended by shipwreck, and he finally returns "so brown so bow'd / So broken . . . " (lines 699–700), only to discover that his wife, having assumed him dead, has married Philip Ray, Enoch's and Annie's childhood friend. He struggles to conceal his identity, swearing the only person who knows to secrecy until after his death, and then dies brokenhearted, a "strong heroic soul" (line 909).

16.426 (624:27–28). Rip van Winkle – See 15.3158n.

16.426–27 (624:28). does anybody hereabouts remember Caoc O'Leary – "Caoch the Piper" ("Caoch" is Irish for one-eyed or blind), a ballad by John Keegan (1809–49). At the beginning of the poem the speaker recalls his childhood ("those happy times") and an overnight visit from the Piper, Caoch O'Leary; and when "twenty summers had gone past," the memory of the idyll remained, and "Old Caoch was not forgotten," even though the speaker's life has declined from "rosy childhood" to a sad and lonely maturity. Caoch reappears, weeping and on the verge of death. He asks, "Does anybody hereabouts / Remember Caoch the Piper?" (lines 59–60). He is, of course, remembered and welcomed by the solitary speaker, who suitably laments his state and Caoch's—and Caoch's death the next day.

16.427–28 (624:30). poor John Casey – Bloom confuses John Keegan, the author of "Caoch the Piper," with another Irish poet-patriot, John Keegan Casey (1846–70), who did merit the epithet "poor," since his imprisonment as a Fenian in 1867 and his consequent sufferings led to his premature death.

16.429–30 (624:32). The face at the window – If this is an anachronism, it may refer to a melodramatic novel, *The Face at the Window*, which appeared complete in *My Queen Novels* (a penny weekly), no. 951 (13 January 1914). The face, an omen of murder to come, appears out of a violent storm, "a white staring face, a man's face, pressed so close to her own that, though the glass divided them, she could almost fancy she felt his panting breath against her cheek. His hat was pulled low over his forehead; but she had a vivid expression of an ashen, death-like countenance—of a jaw dropping in the extremity of fear, and of wild, panic-stricken eyes."

16.433 (624:36). grasswidow – See 7.539n.

16.434 (624:37–38). Rocked in the cradle of the deep – A song (1832), by the American educator Emma Willard (1787–1870), music by Joseph Philip Knight. First stanza: "Rock'd in the cradle of the deep / I lay me down in peace to sleep; / Secure I rest upon the wave / For Thou, O Lord, Hast pow'r to save. / I know Thou wilt not slight my call, / For Thou dost mark the sparrow's fall! / And calm and peaceful is my sleep, / Rock'd in the cradle of the deep."

16.434–35 (624:38). uncle Chubb or Tomkin – "Chubb" is obsolete for a dull, spiritless person; "Tomkin" (Little Thomas), generically any Tom, Dick, or Harry.

16.435–36 (624:39). the Crown and Anchor – A common name for pubs frequented by sailors.

16.438 (624:42–625:1). With a high ro! . . . tearing tandy O! – These lines are the chorus of a sea chanty, "Galloping Randy Dandy O." First verse: "Now we're warping her into the docks, / Way-aye, roll and go! / Where the pretty girls come down in flocks, / My galloping Randy Dandy O!"

16.450 (625:14). *Rosevean* – See 3.504–5n.

16.452 (625:16). A.B.S. – Able-Bodied Seaman.

16.460 (625:24//25). *We was chased by pirates one voyage – Piracy between 1890 and 1910 was confined almost exclusively to the China seas.

16.462 (625:26). Captain Dalton – Apart from the context, identity and significance unknown.

16.462–63 (625:26–27). the best bloody man that ever scuttled a ship – See Byron's description of Haidee's pirate-father in *Don Juan* (1819, 1821, 1823), canto 3, stanza 41: "He was the mildest mannered man / That ever scuttled ship or cut a throat."

16.463 (625:27–28). *Gospodi pomilyou – Old Church Slavonic (the language of the Russian Orthodox church): "Lord have mercy on us" (cited by Joan Keenan).

16.470–71 (625:35–36). maneaters in Peru . . . livers of horses – Anthropologists have documented cannibal tribes at the headwaters of the Amazon in Bolivia and in western Brazil, but not among the extant mountain and coastal tribes of Peru.

16.474 (625:41). *Choza de Indios. Beni, Bolivia – Spanish: "Indian huts." Beni is a large province east of the Andes in northeastern Bolivia (for the most part unexplored in 1904); it is notable that Bolivia is landlocked, and it is unlikely that a late-nineteenth-century sailor would have penetrated so far east as Beni.

16.480 (626:5). diddies – "A woman's breast,

diminutive of the Irish, *did*, breast" (P. W. Joyce, *English*, p. 247).

16.486 (626:12). Glass. That boggles 'em – After the familiar stories of primitive peoples being baffled and fascinated by small mirrors.

16.489 (626:15–16). *Tarjeta Postal, Señor A. Boudin, Galeria Becchi, Santiago, Chile* – Spanish: "Postcard, Mr. A. Boudin, The Becchi Gallery. . . ." *Boudin* is French for blood sausage; *becchi* (or *becchino*) is Italian for gravedigger.

16.492 (626:19). William Tell – The hero of a fifteenth-century Swiss legend. Condemned to death by the Austrians (c. 1307), he is allowed to ransom his life if he will shoot an apple off his son's head; an excellent marksman, he succeeds, and then goes on to help the Swiss forest cantons win their independence from Austria.

16.492–93 (626:19–20). the Lazarillo-Don Cesar . . . depicted in *Maritana* – See 5.563–64n. Don Cesar, the hero of the opera, escapes the villain Don Jose's murderous plots. In Act II Don Cesar is condemned to death before a firing squad and is saved when his friend, the poor boy Lazarillo, removes the bullets from the firing squad's muskets. In Act III Don Jose forces Lazarillo to fire at Don Cesar; the bullet misses Don Cesar but lodges in his hat (as the audience discovers when he shakes it out on the stage).

16.496–97 (626:24). boxed the compass – To "box the compass" is to name the thirty-two points of the compass in their order. To qualify as an Able Seaman Murphy would have had to learn how to box the compass. Figuratively, the phrase means to make a complete about-turn or change of direction.

16.497 (626:25). q.t. – Slang for quiet (with emphasis on secrecy).

16.500–501 (626:28–29). Wednesday or Saturday . . . *via* long sea – The British and Irish Steam Packet Company's ships sailed between Dublin and London, calling at Falmouth, Plymouth, Southampton, and Portsmouth. From Dublin there were sailings each Wednesday and Saturday (approximately 640 miles by sea).

16.503 (626:33). going to Holyhead – Seventy miles from Dublin; see 13.1242–43n.

16.505 (626:34). Egan – Alfred W. Egan, secretary of the Dublin offices of the British and Irish Steam Packet Company.

16.507 (626:37). breaking Boyd's heart – A Dublin expression for taking a financial risk, after the Honourable Walter J. Boyd (b. 1833), who was a judge in Dublin's Court of Bankruptcy from 1885 to 1897.

16.512–13 (626:43–627:1). Plymouth, Falmouth, Southampton – See 16.500–501n.

16.515 (627:3–4). *the greatest improvement . . . wealth of Park lane – Improvements to the great tourist attractions, the Tower of London and Westminster Abbey, were widely advertised during the preparations (1901–2) for Edward VII's coronation. Park Lane is in the heart of Mayfair; in 1904 it was (and still is) one of London's most fashionable districts.

16.520 (627:9). hydros – Resorts that advertised rest and recuperation through mineral baths and other forms of hydrotherapy.

16.520–21 (627:10–11). Eastbourne, Scarborough, Margate . . . Bournemouth, the Channel Islands – For Margate, see 8.1064–65n; Eastbourne is a resort town on the English Channel in Sussex, sixty-six miles south-southeast of London; Scarborough is on the North Sea, forty-two miles northeast of York; Bournemouth is in the middle of the south coast of England on the Channel; the Channel Islands (Guernsey, Jersey, etc.) were in 1904 quiet, rural sea resorts off the west coast of Normandy at the southern entrance to the Channel.

16.526 (627:18). Elster Grimes – See 6.186n.

16.527 (627:18). Moody-Manners – The Moody-Manners Opera Companies, Ltd., formed in 1897 by the Irish bass Charles Manners (b. Southcote Mansergh, 1857–1935) and his wife, the English soprano Madame Fanny Moody; the "A" company (with Manners and his wife as stars) was in 1904 the largest English opera company in the world. There were also "B" and "C" companies for the lesser provinces.

16.533 (627:25–26). the Fishguard-Rosslare route – A steamship route between Rosslare, at the southeastern tip of Ireland, and Fishguard, in southwestern Wales. A regular service between the two ports was established in 1905.

16.534 (627:26). *tapis* – French: "carpet."

16.534 (627:26–27). the circumlocution departments – By 1904 a cliché for government offices snarled in red tape, from Dickens's satiric coinage in *Little Dorrit* (1857), chapter 10, "Containing the Whole Science of Government": "The Circumlocution Office was (as everybody knows without being told) the most important Department under Government."

16.551 (628:3). Poulaphouca – See 15.3299n.

16.551–52 (628:4). farther away from the madding crowd – After stanza 19 of Thomas Gray's (1716–71) "Elegy Written in a Country Churchyard" (1751): "Far from the madding crowd's ignoble strife / Their sober wishes never learned to stray; / Along the sequester'd vale of life / They kept the noiseless tenor of their way." Thomas Hardy used Gray's phrase as the title for a novel, *Far from the Madding Crowd* (1874).

16.552 (628:5). Wicklow . . . the garden of Ireland – What the narrator has in mind is a scenic area between Bray and Wicklow called the Garden of Wicklow; it is approximately twenty-five miles south of Dublin.

16.554 (628:7). the wilds of Donegal – The highlands of Donegal in northwestern Ireland—in guidebook prose, "second to none in the wildness of its scenery."

16.554 (628:8). coup d'oeil – French: "glance, view."

16.555–56 (628:9). not easily getatable – Bloom is right that few tourists visited Donegal in the early twentieth century. It was possible to travel by railroad from Dublin to Donegal, but the route was circuitous, and the lack of tourist accommodations in the thinly populated highlands was regarded by guidebooks as a discouragement to all but the hardy traveler.

16.557–58 (628:11–12). Howth with its historic associations – Howth and, to a lesser extent, Ringsend, at the mouth of the Liffey, were ports of entry for Dublin in the Middle Ages and became the principal Dublin–England packet stations until they were superseded by the artificial harbor at Kingstown (now Dun Laoghaire) in the 1830s.

16.558 (628:12). Silken Thomas – See 3.314n; during his ill-fated and short-lived rebellion, Thomas seized Howth and used it as a strong point in the hopes of preventing the English from landing reinforcements, because Howth was Dublin's main port of entry until the construction of Kingstown (Dun Laoghaire) Harbor.

16.558 (628:12). Grace O'Malley – See 12.1375n; her association with Howth derives from the story or legend that Lord Howth refused her hospitality when she was on her way home via Howth from a visit to Queen Elizabeth; she kidnapped Lord Howth's son and ransomed him on the condition that Lord Howth would open his doors to her at the dinner hour.

16.559 (628:12–13). George IV – (1762–1830), king of England (1820–30), landed at Howth on a visit to Ireland in August 1821; his visit was especially notable because he was the first English sovereign to land in Ireland in over a century.

16.559 (628:13). several hundred feet above sea level – The summit of the Hill of Howth is 563 feet above sea level.

16.560–61 (628:15). in the spring when young men's fancy – From Tennyson's "Locksley Hall" (1842), line 20: "In the spring a young man's fancy lightly turns to thoughts of love."

16.562 (628:17). on their left leg – Slang for "on the spur of the moment" (since it is traditional to start marching with the left foot).

16.563 (628:18). the pillar – Nelson's Pillar in central Dublin; see 6.293n. The pillar was the point of departure for trams from Dublin to Howth, nine miles to the north-northeast.

16.580 (628:38). knockingshop – Low slang for a brothel.

16.580 (628:38). tryon – Slang for an attempt to take advantage of someone.

16.581–82 (628:40). *Prepare to meet your God* – In Amos 4:12, the Lord promises to inflict elaborate punishment on the Israelites for their shortcomings: "Therefore thus will I do unto thee, O Israel: and because I will do thus unto thee, prepare to meet thy God, O Israel."

16.590–92 (629:8–10). That was why they . . . of them using knives – Immediately after the Phoenix Park murders on 6 May 1882 there was considerable speculation that the assassins might have been brought in from Europe or America. The principal reason for this speculation was not that the assassins used knives but that political assassination seemed so foreign in the midst of the optimism engendered by Parnell's release from prison on 2 May 1882. Parnell's release involved an agreement between Parnell and Gladstone (the so-called Kilmainham Treaty); Parnell was to use his political influence to reorganize the Land League so that he could control and diminish the violence of land-reform agitation; in return Gladstone was to push for serious parliamentary action on that reform.

16.593–94 (629:11–12). *where ignorance is bliss* – Thomas Gray's "Ode on a Distant Prospect of Eton College" (1742, 1747), lines 99–100: "Where ignorance is bliss, / Tis folly to be wise."

16.603 (629:22). *choza de* – See 16.474n.

16.606 (629:26). the days of the land troubles – See 16.590–92n.

16.608 (629:28–29). eightyone to be correct when he was just turned fifteen – No: it was 6 May 1882, and Bloom, who was born in 1866, would have been sixteen. It is tempting to use the phrase "when he was just turned fifteen" to establish a semiprecise date for Bloom's birth (late April or early May, which would make Bloom a Taurus; see 14.1108–9n), but elsewhere Joyce confuses the issue by suggesting that Bloom is an Aquarius (as Stephen presumably is). See 17.183n; and cf. John Henry Raleigh, *The Chronicle of Leopold and Molly Bloom: Ulysses as Narrative* (Berkeley, Calif., 1977), pp. 15–16, 27, and Hugh Kenner, *Ulysses* (London, 1980), p. 152.

16.614 (629:36–37). Europa point – The headland, of which the Rock of Gibraltar is the dominant feature.

16.615 (629:37–38). the rover . . . some reminiscences – *Some Reminiscences* is the title of a book of memoirs by Joseph Conrad, serialized in the *English Review* in 1908 and published as a book in 1912; it was later retitled *A Personal Record*. The not very revealing memoirs present a partial record of Conrad's youth in Poland and of his years in the French and British merchant marines. With the appearance of "the rover" in this passage, cliché becomes coincidence: in June 1922, five months after the publication of *Ulysses*, Conrad finished a novel entitled *The Rover* (London, 1923). The novel is set in Napoleonic France but makes considerable use of

Conrad's experience in the French merchant marine.

16.622 (630:3). I'm tired of all them rocks in the sea – Murphy's reluctance to acknowledge Gibraltar raises questions about the geography of his wanderings. If he never landed at or even saw Gibraltar, how did he get to many of the places he claims to have visited: the Red Sea, the Black Sea, and the Dardanelles (16.459–62 [625:23–26]), and Trieste (16.575 [628:33])?

16.622–23 (630:4). Salt junk – Hard, salted beef, a staple of the seafarer's diet at the turn of the century.

16.628–29 (630:11). to rule the waves – See 12.1347n.

16.629–30 (630:12). The North Bull at Dollymount – The North Bull is a sand island off Dollymount just northeast of Dublin. A wall across its southern end connects it to the mainland and prevents its sands from encroaching on Dublin Harbor.

16.632–33 (630:15–16). dreaming of fresh woods and pastures new – From Milton's "Lycidas"; see 2.57n.

16.634 (630:17–18). to find out the secret for himself – In Longfellow's "The Secret of the Sea" (1841), a landsman hears "the ancient helmsman" sing a "wondrous song" and asks to be taught it: "'Would'st thou,' so the helmsman answered, / 'Learn the secret of the sea? / Only those who brave its dangers / Comprehend its mystery!'" (lines 29–32).

16.643 (630:29). lifeboat Sunday – The Royal National Lifeboat Institution, Irish Auxiliary, Dublin Branch, was a volunteer lifesaving service that supported itself by private subscription. It held an annual and rather festive fundraising event that featured a demonstration of lifesaving skills.

16.648 (630:35). *Ireland expects that every man* – See 10.232, 35n.

16.650 (630:37). Kish – See 3.267n and 4.434n.

16.653 (630:40). the *Rover* – The ship's name and some of the circumstantial details of Murphy's story seem to derive from a popular song, "The Irish Rover," by J. M. Crofts: "On the fourth of July, eighteen hundred and six, / We set sail from the sweet cove of Cork, / We were sailing away with a cargo of bricks, / For the grand city hall in New York. / 'Twas a wonderful craft, she was rigged fore and aft, / And how the wild wind drove her. / She stood several blasts, she had twenty-seven masts, / And we called her the Irish Rover. [Chorus:] So fare thee well my own true love, / I'm going far from you, / And I will swear by the stars above / Forever I'll be true to you, / Tho' as I part, it breaks my heart, / Yet when the trip is over / I'll come back again in true Irish style / Aboard the Irish Rover." After seven years and a fog and a wreck, it turns out the singer is the sole survivor of the Irish Rover. See also 16.615n. The ship's name may also owe a debt of cliché to a popular light opera, *Black Rover* (1890). The Rover, the opera's pirate-hero, was one of William Ludwig's successful sequels to his role as the Flying Dutchman (see 16.859n). The opera, written by Seavelle and Luscombe, is set in mid-eighteenth-century Cuba; its melodramatic plot focuses on the young lovers Felix and Isadora, estranged because Felix has defied the Rover's curse. Felix endures shipwreck and rescue, voodoo enchantment, etc. before the spirit of the Rover blesses and reunites the lovers.

16.661 (631:6–7). Henry Campbell, the town-clerk – In 1904 he was, with offices in Dublin City Hall.

16.663 (631:9). nosepaint – Slang for a nose "painted" by alcoholism.

16.666 (631:12). The Skibbereen father – In "Old Skibbereen," an anonymous Irish ballad about the Great Famine, the father tells his son why they emigrated. The ballad begins: "It's well I do remember the year of '48, / When I arose with Erin's boys to battle 'gainst the fate. / I was hunted through the mountains like a traitor to the Queen, / And that's another reason why I left old Skibbereen."

16.675 (631:23). the figure 16 – In European slang and numerology the number sixteen meant homosexuality.

16.702–3 (632:10–11). *As bad as old . . . on my ownio* – See 6.374–75n.

16.709 (632:17–18). the Abbey street organ – The last pink edition of the *Evening Telegraph*, offices at 83 Abbey Street Middle.

16.718 (632:30). Bewley and Draper's – General merchants, manufacturers of mineral wa-

ters, wholesale druggists, wine merchants, and ink manufacturers, 23–27 Mary Street.

16.719–20 (632:31–32). *love me, love my dirty shirt – After the proverb "Love me, love my dog."

16.727 (632:41). gunboat – Slang for a thief, rascal, or beggar and, as in this case, for a beggarly prostitute.

16.729 (633:2–3). *the Lock hospital – See 15.2578n.

16.737 (633:11–12). Fear not them that . . . to buy the soul – After Matthew 10:28. Jesus counsels his disciples: "And fear not them which kill the body, but are not able to kill the soul: but rather fear him which is able to destroy both soul and body in hell."

16.752–53 (633:30–31). such inventions as X rays – Discovered in 1895 by Röntgen and so named because the cause of the rays was unknown; see 8.1029–30n.

16.756–60 (633:35–40). it is a simple substance . . . *corruptio per accidens* – "We must assert that the intellectual principle which we call the human soul is incorruptible. For a thing may be corrupted in two ways—[*corruptio per se*] of itself, and [*per accidens*] accidentally" (St. Thomas Aquinas, *Summa Theologica*, Prima Primae, Query 75, article 6). Aquinas then goes on to argue that neither mode of corruption can affect the soul, since "corruption is found only where there is contrariety," and since the soul is "simple," without contrariety, it is incorruptible.

16.763 (634:2). a demurrer – "*Law:* a pleading by a party to an action which, assuming the truth of the matter alleged by the opposite party, sets up that it is insufficient in law to sustain his claim or that there is some other defect on the face of the pleadings constituting a legal reason why the opposing party should not be allowed to proceed further" (*Webster's New International Dictionary* [1909]).

16.767 (634:8). Röntgen – See 8.1029–30n.

16.767 (634:8). Edison – The American inventor Thomas Alva Edison (1847–1931), who began his career with a series of inventions that significantly improved the telegraph. In the late 1870s he began to range through a variety of fields, inventing the phonograph (1878), the incandescent electric lamp (1879), the mimeograph, etc., etc., until by 1904 his name itself had come to mean "inventor."

16.768 (634:9). Galileo – (1564–1642), the Italian physicist and astronomer, is often credited with the invention of the telescope because he realized its importance to astronomy and hence described and exhibited a complete instrument in May 1609. The actual "invention" is far less clear; like printing, the telescope was probably developed simultaneously by several spectacle makers in Holland. Galileo apparently got the idea for the telescope by rumor rather than by "inspiration."

16.782 (634:28). our national poet – That is, Shakespeare (from a "west Briton" rather than an Irish point of view).

16.783 (634:27). like *Hamlet* and Bacon – On the Baconian controversy, see 9.410n.

16.792 (634:38). the Coffee Palace – See 11.486n.

16.801 (635:6). Sulphate of copper poisoning, SO$_4$ – Bloom's chemistry is shaky; copper sulfate is $CuSO_4$; SO_4 would be hopelessly unstable.

16.805–6 (635:11). Dr Tibble's Vi-Cocoa – Unidentified.

16.815–16 (635:25–26). that knife . . . reminds me of Roman history – See 2.48–49n.

16.821 (635:32). Our mutual friend's – The title of Dickens's novel *Our Mutual Friend* (1864–65) has come from and passed back into cliché.

16.831 (636:1). Sherlockholmesing – See 15.1848–49n.

16.833 (636:4). a jail delivery – Not an improbable notion; Bridgewater is on a fairly direct route from Dartmoor Prison in southwestern England to Dublin, so if Murphy was working his way home, the route would be a logical one. No explanation is proffered as to how Murphy came to change ships in Bridgewater, a small and far-from-busy port hampered by a tidal bore. Or is it that Murphy wanted to shun the publicity of the major port of Bristol thirty miles to the northeast?

16.835 (636:6–7). the oakum and treadmill fraternity – That is, prison, since picking oakum and walking a treadmill were two forms of hard labor in English prisons.

16.839–40 (636:11–12). the dramatic personage . . . of our national poet – In Shakespeare's *The Merchant of Venice*, Antonio is the merchant who befriends, to the verge of self-sacrifice, the young hero, Bassanio, in his love affair and monetary difficulties.

16.844–45 (636:17–18). any ancient mariner . . . about the schooner *Hesperus* – To "draw the long bow" is to tell a tall story, as the mariner does in Coleridge's narrative poem *The Rime of the Ancient Mariner* (1798); the *Hesperus* features in Longfellow's ballad "The Wreck of the Hesperus" (1840). The opening lines: "It was the schooner Hesperus, / That sailed the wintry sea." Longfellow's poem is not a "tall story" but a generalized narrative response to news of a December 1839 shipwreck.

16.850 (636:25). *Marcella the midget queen – Unknown.

16.851 (636:25–26). those waxworks in Henry street – World's Fair Waxwork Exhibition, 30 Henry Street, was not only a museum with a collection of wax figures; it also featured a changing program of variety acts, ballad singers, ventriloquists, etc.

16.851–56 (636:26–32). some Aztecs, as they . . . being adored as gods – Aztec kings were regarded as gods, but this seems closer to a confusion between *Aztec* and *ascetic*; if it is, then what Bloom has seen is a yogi ascetic or fakir whose musculature has been weakened by prolonged worship in one position.

16.858 (636:33). Sinbad – The wandering sailor-hero of several tall stories in the *Arabian Nights;* also the title figure of *Sinbad the Sailor,* a pantomime that enjoyed considerable popularity in Dublin during the 1890s. See 17.421–23nff.

16.859 (636:34). Ludwig, *alias* Ledwidge – William Ledwidge (1847–1923), a Dublin baritone whose stage name was Ludwig. He was featured with the Carl Rosa Opera Company and scored a popular success as Vanderdecken in *The Flying Dutchman* at the Gaiety Theatre in 1877. Thornton (pp. 439–40) assumes that this was Wagner's opera (see 15.1369–70n), but the opera with which Ludwig was most intimately identified was a musical version (by G. H. B. Rodwell) of *Vanderdecken; or, The Flying Dutchman* (1846), a popular play by the English playwright T. P. Taylor.

16.860–61 (636:35–36). the Gaiety when Michael Gunn was identified with the management – See 11.1050n.

16.868 (637:2–3). little Italy there, near the Coombe – There was a relatively small community of Italian immigrants in a tenement district just south of the Coombe in south-central Dublin.

16.870 (637:4). pothunting – That is, not hunting for sport but for something to eat.

16.870 (637:4–5). the harmless necessary animal of the feline persuasion – A cliché compounded from Shylock's explanation of his irrational hatred in Shakespeare's *The Merchant of Venice:* "Some men there are . . . that are mad if they behold a cat; . . . a harmless necessary cat" (IV.i.47–48, 55).

16.871 (637:6). tuckin – Irish slang for a good meal, a feast.

16.873 (637:8–9). Spaniards . . . passionate temperaments – The commonplace British prejudice that Mediterranean peoples are inclined to be hot-blooded, oversexed, and emotionally unrestrained.

16.875 (637:10). quietus – After Hamlet in the "To be or not to be" soliloqy: "For who would bear the whips and scorns of time . . . / When he himself might his quietus make / With a bare bodkin?" (III.i.70–76).

16.878–79 (637:14–15). Spanish nationality . . . technically Spain, i.e. Gibraltar – Molly's claim to Spanish citizenship might be made on the basis that her mother was Spanish, but Gibraltar was a Crown colony of Great Britain, and even though Spain argued then (as now) that Gibraltar should be part of Spain, the argument did not include an offer of citizenship to the children of the garrison on the Rock.

16.883 (637:20–21). *Roberto ruba roba sua* – Italian: "Robert stole his things."

16.886–87 (637:25–26). Dante and the isosceles . . . in love with – Beatrice Portinari (1266–90), a Florentine woman, identified on Boccaccio's authority as the object (or rather

image) of Dante Alighieri's (1265–1321) abstracted and spiritualized love. Beatrice was married to Simone de Bardi, hence the "triangle," presumably "isosceles" because Dante's idealization of Beatrice's image put him so far from the real marriage relationship at the triangle's base.

16.887 (637:26). Leonardo – Leonardo da Vinci (1452–1519), the painter, sculptor, and engineer, was another Florentine. The association of Leonardo's Mona Lisa (c. 1503) with Dante's Beatrice is an old tradition, frequently hinged on a passage in Dante's *Convivio* (3:8): "The soul operates very largely in two places because in those two places all the three natures of the soul have jurisdiction, that is to say in the eyes and mouth which it adorns most fully and directs its whole attention there to beautify them as far as possible. And in these two places I state these pleasures by saying 'in her eyes and in her sweet smile.' These two places, by a beautiful simile, may be called the balconies of the lady who dwells in the architecture of the body, that is to say the soul, because she often shows herself there as if under a veil."

16.887–88 (637:26). san Tommaso Mastino – Italian: "Saint Thomas [the] Mastiff"; that is, "bulldog Aquinas," who was born near Naples (1226–74); see 9.863–64n. The association of Dante and St. Thomas derives from the way Dante so thoroughly grounded the intellectual structure of *La divina commedia* on St. Thomas's philosophy and theology.

16.889–90 (637:27–28). All are washed in the blood of the sun – That is, in "sunny Italy," where popular mythology assumes all to be hot-blooded; see 8.9n.

16.890 (637:29). the Kildare street museum – The National Museum in Kildare Street; see 8.921–22n.

16.900–901 (637:40–41). ships lost in fog, collisions with icebergs – As in Coleridge's "The Rime of the Ancient Mariner," gloss to lines 71ff.: "And lo! the Albatross proveth a bird of good omen, and followeth the ship as it returned northward through fog and floating ice."

16.901 (637:42). Shipahoy – Music-hall and pantomime cliché for a sailor.

16.902 (637:42–43). *doubled the cape – The phrase could mean rounding the Cape of Good

Hope, but it usually means rounding Cape Horn, since that is the more dangerous passage.

16.906–13 (638:4–12). the wreck off Daunt's rock . . . petrified with horror – The Finnish (not Norwegian) ship *Palme* went aground off Blackrock, just south of Booterstown on the southern shore of Dublin Bay, during a severe storm on 24 December 1895. Two Irish lifeboats attempted to take the men off the *Palme*, but one of the boats capsized with the loss of its entire fifteen-man crew and the other could not reach the stranded ship. The *Palme*'s officers and crew were rescued without further loss on 26 December. Crowds did gather at Blackrock to view the wreck, but the visibility was poor and the wreck so distant that it was hard to see any detail without binoculars. Albert William Quill's memorial verse on the event, "The Storm of Christmas Eve, 1895," appeared under the headline "An Antispastic Dithyramb" in the *Irish Times*, 16 January 1896. The poem's second stanza is symptomatic of its quality: "Awake! to the sea! to the sea! raging, and surging, and eddying, / The billows gape in twain, yawning and fain for the sacrifice! / The crested dragon glares hitherward, hungry and ravening, / Befleck'd with the froth and the foam, back from the mouth of the fortalice." Daunt's Rock is not in Dublin Bay but off the coast of County Cork near the mouth of Cork Harbor.

16.913–17 (638:13–17). the case of the s.s. *Lady Cairns* . . . appears in her hold – The English bark (not steamship as "s.s." implies) *Lady Cairns* was rammed in rough and hazy weather by the German bark *Mona* off Kish Bank on 20 March 1904. The *Lady Cairns* capsized and sank "within two minutes," according to the *Freeman's Journal*, 22 March 1904; all hands were lost. The *Mona* was severely disabled and had to be towed into port (the "no water . . . in her hold" is an anti-German flourish). The admiralty court (*Freeman's Journal*, 27 June 1904) found the *Lady Cairns* at fault for not keeping effective lookout, since she was on the port tack and thus should have given the right of way to the *Mona*, which was on the starboard tack. The court in turn found no criminal negligence on the part of the master of the *Mona*, though he had been criticized for not immediately lowering all his lifeboats to search for survivors in the rough sea.

16.925 (638:26). *Ship's rum – Apparently the narrator's attempt at naval rum, 104-to-106 proof, manufactured in the British Virgin Islands for issue to the British navy and army.

16.933 (638:36). *the Loop line – See 16.101n.

16.945 (639:8). on the parish rates – Each parish in Ireland had a Poor Law Guardian who was responsible for the collection of the poor rate (taxes for support of the poor) and administration of the poor laws; in 1904 the system was anything but generous.

16.945 (639:8–9). Pat Tobin – In 1904 Patrick Tobin was secretary to the Paving Committee, one of the standing committees of the municipal council of the Dublin Corporation. He lived at 2 St. Vincent Street North, which extends Eccles Street west of Berkeley Road (*Thom's* 1904, pp. 1348, 1590).

16.951–52 (639:16). to make . . . ducks and drakes of – That is, to throw away money, after "ducks and drakes," a game in which players compete to see how many times they can skip a stone or a coin on water.

16.953 (639:18). stiver – After a small Dutch coin, slang for an English penny or any coin of small value.

16.957 (639:23–24). the falling off in Irish shipping – Statistics of Irish shipping in *Thom's* directories from 1890 to 1904 partially confirm this lament. The number and net tonnage of registered Dublin ships declined by more than nine percent between 1898 and 1902; Irish shipping as a whole apparently fared a bit better, but it could hardly be described as a growth industry at the turn of the century.

16.959 (639:25). A Palgrave Murphy boat – A steamship constructed for Palgrave, Murphy & Co., Dublin steamship owners.

16.959 (639:26). *Alexandra basin – A boat basin on the north bank of the Liffey at its mouth.

16.959–60 (639:26). the only launch that year – We have been unable to check the accuracy of this assertion.

16.963 (639:29). *au fait – French: "acquainted with [a subject]."

16.964–65 (639:30–32). *why that ship ran bang . . . harbour scheme was mooted – See 2.326n.

16.966 (639:32). a Mr Worthington – Robert Worthington, a Dublin railroad contractor whose railroad business would have benefited from increased Dublin–Galway traffic, was one of the leaders of a group of promoters who tried to revive the "Galway Harbor scheme" in 1912.

16.968 (639:35). Captain John Lever of the Lever line – John Orrell Lever, a Manchester, England, manufacturer and businessman who owned the ships in the Galway–Halifax experiment during the mid–nineteenth century.

16.978 (640:5). son of a seacook – Partridge (p. 741b) lists this as "a term of abuse: nautical . . . 1825."

16.979–82 (640:6–9). *The biscuits was as hard . . . Johnny Lever, O!* – Collections of sea chanties list at least twenty-five stanzas and many variations, since the song clearly lends itself to improvisatory talent. One version begins: "Oh the times are hard and the wages low, / Leave her, Johnny, leave her. / The bread is hard and the beef is salt, / But it's time for us to leave her. / It's growl you may, but go you must, / It matters not whether you're last or fust."

16.989 (640:18). with coal in large quantities – Coal deposits in Ireland were and are relatively meager; average annual Irish production in 1900–1902 was 112,000 tons per year as against England's average of 191 million tons. Average coal production in Ireland in 1962–66 was 200,000 tons, or one-eighth of its coal-energy needs.

16.989–90 (640:18–19). six million pounds . . . exported every year – The average annual export of pork from Ireland in 1898–1902 was worth £1,718,000.

16.990–91 (640:19–20). ten millions between butter and eggs – The average export of butter and eggs (1896–1902) was under £2.5 million.

16.996 (640:26–27). colonel Everard down there in Navan growing Tobacco – Navan was a small market town in County Meath, twenty-eight miles northwest of Dublin. Col. N. T. Everard was a gentleman farmer who in 1904 was conducting what he regarded as a successful twenty-acre experiment in tobacco growing.

16.1001 (640:32–33). The Germans and the Japs . . . their little lookin – In two interrelated ways: Japan was demonstrating that it had a powerful if limited navy in the Russo-Japanese War, and German naval power was beginning to

pose a serious threat to English sea power in the West. The corollary was that both the Germans and the Japanese were interested in a colonial expansion that threatened to bring them into conflict with the expansionist policies of the British Empire.

16.1002 (640:33–34). The Boers were the beginning of the end – That is, even though they lost their war for independence, the Boers demonstrated the tenuousness of England's hold over the 13 million square miles and 320 million subjects of its empire (1900).

16.1003 (640:35). Ireland, her Achilles heel – A phrase first applied to Ireland by George Bernard Shaw in the preface to *John Bull's Other Island* (1906): "The Irish coast is for the English invasion-scaremonger the heel of Achilles, and that they [the Anglo-Irish and Protestant Unionists] can use to make him pay the boot" (cited in Richard K. Bass, "Additional Allusions in 'Eumaeus,'" *JJQ* 10, no. 3 [1973]: 321–29). The allusion derives, of course, from the only vulnerable spot on Achilles' body—his right heel—which his mother, Thetis, held him by when she dipped him in the river Styx to make him invulnerable (and so the water did not touch it). In 1914 England suspended implementation of Home Rule for Ireland for the duration of hostilities of World War I; the argument was that an independent Ireland might be a threat to England. In 1916 Sir Roger Casement (see 12.1542–45n) and others tried to make that threat come true; they enlisted German support (a shipload of munitions, which the English intercepted) for the Easter 1916 Uprising.

16.1008–9 (640:41–42). Ireland, Parnell said . . . one of her sons – Source unknown.

16.1022 (641:14). Jem Mullins – A reference to the Irish patriot and physician James Mullin (1846–1920), who became a legendary image of peasant strength in his own lifetime, having begun life in abject poverty and been set to work in the fields at age eleven. He managed to teach himself and finally became an M.D. in 1881. He was friendly with and admired by Parnell and Davitt, among others.

16.1031 (641:24–25). pending that consummation . . . be wished for – Combines the opening phrases of Hamlet's much-quoted soliloquy (III.i.56) with his later remark: "'tis a consummation / Devoutly to be wish'd" (III.i.63–64).

16.1035–36 (641:30). the sister island – An epithet for England coined by Timothy Daniel Sullivan in a song, "Harp or Lion?" The song mocks the "west Briton" concept that "Ireland's love of liberty / . . . is dead and pass'd away" and that Ireland should apologize to "The rovers from our sister isle" who are in truth [and in sarcasm] Ireland's "'civilisers!'"

16.1041 (641:36–37). chummies – See 6.319n.

16.1045 (641:42). being on all fours with – To "be on all fours with" is slang for to square with, to conform, accord, agree, fit.

16.1052 (642:7). felonsetting – Richard K. Bass says "James Stephens coined this term in 1858 to describe Alexander Sullivan's activities. It means betraying rebels by publicizing their whereabouts" (*JJQ* 10, no. 3 [1973]: 325). For Stephens, the Fenian leader, see 2.272n and 3.241n. Alexander Martin Sullivan (1830–84) was against violence and strongly in favor of constitutional achievement of Home Rule, which led the Fenians to regard him as an informer.

16.1052 (642:8). Dannyman – Irish slang for a betrayer or informer, after Danny Mann, the servant in Gerald Griffin's (1803–40) popular novel *The Collegians* (1829). In the novel, with his master's connivance, he murders his master's wife, Eily. In Dion Boucicault's stage adaptation of the novel, *The Colleen Bawn* (1860), Danny attempts unsuccessfully and without his master's knowledge to murder Eily (the Colleen Bawn). See 12.194n.

16.1053–54 (642:9). Denis or Peter Carey – See 5.379n and 5.381n.

16.1066–67 (642:24–25). *Fitz, nicknamed Skin-the, merely drove the car for the actual perpetrators – No, he drove a decoy cab; see 7.640n.

16.1068–69 (642:27–28). the plea some legal luminary saved his skin on – Fitzharris was tried twice. In the first trial he was acquitted of a charge of murder. He was then tried and found guilty of being an accessory after the fact. The "legal luminary" was His Honour Richard Adams; see 7.679n.

16.1072 (642:31). on the scaffold high – See 8.440n.

16.1074–75 (642:35). snapping at the bone for the shadow – In Aesop's fable "The Dog and the Shadow," a dog with a piece of meat in his mouth catches sight of his reflection in a stream; the dog responds as though the reflection were real, dropping and losing his own piece of meat in the attempt to grab the shadow meat.

16.1076 (642:36). Johnny Lever – See 16.979–82n.

16.1077 (642:38). the *Old Ireland* tavern – The Old Ireland Hotel and Tavern, 10 North Wall Quay, Dublin; in 1904 it was one of the pubs nearest to the docks.

16.1078 (642:38–39). come back to Erin – See 12.1828n.

16.1085–86 (643:4–5). A soft answer turns away wrath – "A soft answer turneth away wrath: but grievous words stir up anger" (Proverbs 15:1).

16.1091–93 (643:11–13). *Ex quibus . . . Christus . . . secundum carnem – The whole phrase that Stephen quotes is from the Vulgate, Romans 9:5: "et ex quibus est Christus secundum carnem" (and from that race [the Israelites] is Christ, according to the flesh).

16.1096–98 (643:17–19). every country, they say . . . government it deserves – The saying originated with the French philosopher and political writer Count Joseph de Maistre (1753–1821). For "distressful country," see 3.259–60n.

16.1104 (643:26). bloody bridge battle – See 10.1183n.

16.1104–5 (643:26–27). seven minutes' war . . . between Skinner's alley and Ormond market – Skinner's Alley was off Cork Street, in central Dublin just south of the Liffey; Ormond Market (1682) was off King's Inn Quay, on the north bank of the Liffey just across from Skinner's Alley; the two locations were at either end of Richmond Bridge (1819), now O'Donovan Rossa Bridge, the previous site of Ormond Bridge (1684–1802). Ormond Bridge was the traditional battleground for faction fights between the artisans and apprentices of north and south Dublin in the eighteenth century. Which of these many minor "wars" Stephen has in mind is unknown.

16.1112 (643:35). bump of combativeness –

Located an inch or so behind the ears. Prominent bumps spelled combativeness to the phrenologist who accepted F. J. Gall's (1758–1828) hypothesis that mental faculties and traits of character could be read in the conformation of the skull.

16.1112 (643:35). gland of some kind – Glandular theory, thanks to the little that was known of the ductless glands and their functions in the nineteenth century, provided another popular set of hypotheses for biological determinants of human character and behavior.

16.1121–22 (644:3). *Spain decayed when the inquisition hounded the Jews out – The Inquisition did "hound" the Jews in Renaissance Spain, but they were expelled in 1492 by royal decree of Ferdinand V (known as "the Catholic"; 1452–1516). Unnoticed, Spain did begin a decline; many Jews had been in key political and economic administrative positions, and they were not easily replaced, since administrative expertise was despised as "Jewish" by Catholic Spain. The real decline of Spain's power did not become apparent until its costly overextension after the battle of Lepanto (1571), including the ruinous economic and military impact of the loss of the Armada (1588) and the debilitating cost of maintaining armies in the Low Countries during an extended period of Protestant revolt against Spanish rule (1567–1609).

16.1122–24 (644:4–5). England prospered when Cromwell . . . imported them – The Jews were expelled from England in 1290 during the reign of Edward I. Oliver Cromwell (1599–1658), as virtual dictator of England during the Protectorate (1653–60), vigorously supported religious liberty; in 1656 some Jewish families, encouraged by Cromwell's stand, petitioned for permission to enter England. Cromwell, lord protector, referred the petition to a commission of merchants and Puritan ministers, who recommended against it; but Cromwell persisted, for economic as well as religious reasons, and several important Jewish banking families were allowed to establish themselves in London and Oxford; thus "England prospered" because those select families with their international connections understood the economic terms of Cromwell's patronage and helped stabilize an economy disordered by civil war. As for the "much" that Cromwell has "to answer for," see 12.1507–9n for an example.

16.1128 (644:10–11). Spain again . . . with goahead America – During the Spanish-American War (23 April–12 August 1898), the Spanish, underequipped and demoralized, were no match for the United States; and the United States emerged from the war as a colonial power, having concluded the peace by dismembering what was left of the Spanish Empire.

16.1128–30 (644:11–13). *Turks. It's in the dogma . . . try to live better – Bloom attributes the backward conditions of the Turkish Empire and Turkish military vulnerability to the Islamic belief that death in battle was to be rewarded by immediate admission to heaven.

16.1130–31 (644:13–14). That's the juggle . . . false pretenses – That is, Roman Catholic parish priests raise money ("the wind") on their "false" argument that they have exclusive control over entry into heaven.

16.1135 (644:19). £300 per annum – Roughly equivalent to $18,000 to $20,000 a year (U.S., 1985).

16.1138–39 (644:23–24). Ubi patria . . . vita bene – Latin: "Where my country [is, there is] the good life." Bloom is apparently trying for the proverb "Ubi bene, ibi patria" (Where I am well or prosperous, there is my country).

16.1143–44 (644:29–30). changing colour like those crabs about Ringsend in the morning – During the Proteus episode, Stephen rests on a boulder in the sea wall that extends the south bank of the Liffey from Ringsend out to Poolbeg Light. He has watched the small crabs emerge as the tide came in beneath his feet. The crabs do appear to change color when they move. They can only be spotted by concentrated observation in the first place because they are so translucent as to be almost transparent; thus their color seems to change.

16.1161 (645:6–7). faubourg Saint-Patrice – French: "St. Patrick's Suburb."

16.1164–65 (645:9–10). Ireland . . . belongs to me – Could this be an allusion to the popular Scottish drinking song? "I belong to Glasgow, / Good old Glasgow town, / But what's the matter with Glasgow / For it's going round and round? / I'm only a common old working chap, / As anyone here can see, / But when I've had a couple of drinks of a Saturday, / Glasgow belongs to me."

16.1185–86 (645:36). *O'Callaghan . . . the halfcrazy faddist – See 6.236n.

16.1187 (645:38). rotto – Slang for drunk.

16.1191–92 (645:43–646:1). a strong hint to a blind horse – The traditional instrument for delivering such a hint is a club.

16.1192 (646:1). John Mallon of Lower Castle Yard – Assistant commissioner of the Dublin Metropolitan Police, with headquarters in Dublin Castle, Lower Castle Yard.

16.1193–94 (646:2–3). section two of the criminal law amendment act – (1885) forbids attempts to solicit or procure women for illicit sexual practices. As Thornton points out (pp. 447–48), there may be confusion here between sections two (II) and eleven (XI). Section XI provides against homosexuality and was the section under which Oscar Wilde was convicted. Did Joyce intend a linkage between the two Dublin "eccentrics"? The confusion can only be resolved by discovery of the nature of O'Callaghan's "eccentricity," if indeed there ever was an O'Callaghan.

16.1196 (646:6). six, sixteen – The number tattooed on the sailor's chest (see 16.675 [631:23]) is, of course, the number of this day, 16 June; according to Stuart Gilbert (*James Joyce's "Ulysses"* [New York, 1930], p. 351n), the numbers 6 and 16 were also Neopolitan argot for two forms of coition offered by prostitutes.

16.1197–1201 (646:7–12). the tattoo which was all . . . the head of the state – Tattooing was fashionable with nineteenth-century nobility, including Edward VII (of whom Bloom thinks) and George V of England, Nicholas II of Russia, and Alphonso XII of Spain. Since royalty set the fashion, the aristocracy was sure to follow, including even Lady Randolph Churchill, Sir Winston's mother. "The upper ten" is an on-the-spot cliché for high society, coined from "the submerged tenth" (see 16.1225–27n).

16.1202 (646:14). the Cornwall case – In 1870 Edward VII, then duke of Cornwall and Prince of Wales, was called to the witness stand in a divorce suit brought by Sir Charles Mordaunt against his wife. Two of the prince's friends were accused as correspondents. In view of the ambiguity at 16.1193–94n above, another Cornwall case may also be part of the allusion: in 1883 "two officials in Dublin Castle, named Cornwall and French were publically involved in an extensive homosexual circle" (H. Montgomery Hyde, ed., *The Three Trials of Oscar Wilde* [New York, 1956], p. 382).

16.1204 (646:16). Mrs Grundy – In Thomas

Moxton's (c. 1764–1838) play *Speed the Plough* (1798), Mrs. Grundy is an offstage rural oracle who is repeatedly invoked ("What will Mrs. Grundy say?") as the ultimate arbiter of stuffy middle-class propriety.

16.1212 (646:26). not caring a continental – After an essentially unsupported currency note issued by the Continental Congress in 1776; hence, a worthless coin.

16.1225–27 (646:43–647:1). the submerged tenth . . . under the microscope lately – General William Booth, the founder and leader of the Salvation Army, in his book *In Darkest England; and the Way Out* (1890) estimated that ten percent of the population of England lived in abject poverty and coined the phrase "the submerged tenth" to describe the political reality of poverty. The Salvation Army's campaign on behalf of that tenth did serve to sharpen public and official interest in the appalling problems of poverty in the British Isles. See 15.233–34n.

16.1227 (647:2). To improve the shining hour – From Isaac Watts's (1674–1748) hymn "Against Idleness." First stanza: "How doth the little busy bee / Improve each shining hour, / And gather honey all the day / From every opening flower!"

16.1228–29 (647:3–4). Mr Philip Beaufoy – See 4.502–3n.

16.1232 (647:8). *The pink edition extra sporting of the *Telegraph* – The pink edition of the *Evening Telegraph* was the latest evening paper of the Dublin dailies and hence had a more comprehensive coverage of the day's sports than any of the other newspapers.

16.1235 (647:12). the postcard was addressed A. Boudin – See 16.489n.

16.1237–38 (647:15). give us this day our daily press – See 4.82n.

16.1239 (647:17). H. du Boyes, agent for typewriters – There is no such advertisement in the *Evening Telegraph,* "Last Pink," 16 June 1904, but *Thom's* 1904, p. 1813, lists "H. Boyes, agent for Williams' Type Writer and Supplies, 5 Ormond quay, upper." Following Boyes's name in *Thom's* 1904 there are nine (but no Hugh) Boylans.

16.1240 (647:18). *Great battle, Tokio – "THE WAR. / BIG BATTLE AT TELISSA. / RUSSIAN DEFEAT. / Japs Take 300 Prisoners and 14 Guns. / Press Association War Special. / [datelined] Tokio, Thursday" (*Evening Telegraph*, 16 June 1904, p. 2, col. 9). Telissa is on the Liaotung Peninsula (in modern China) just west of North Korea. See 4.116–17n.

16.1240–41 (647:18). *Lovemaking in Irish, £200 damages – "GAELIC LEAGUE AND LOVE AFFAIRS. / Breách of Promise Action from Kilkenny. / Amusing Correspondence. / Verdict for £200" (*Evening Telegraph*, p. 3, cols. 3–5). The article describes in considerable detail the trial, the evidence of a rather circumstantial courtship, and Miss Maggie Delaney's successful suit against Frank P. Burke, a revenue officer and an enthusiast in the campaign to revive Irish as a language. In *The Odyssey*, at the hut of his swineherd, Eumaeus, Odysseus learns that the suitors in their "lovemaking" and feasting are doing considerable damage to his household and estate.

16.1241 (647:19). Gordon Bennett – "Gordon-Bennett Cup. / To-Morrow's Contest. / The Drivers and the Cars" (*Evening Telegraph*, p. 2, cols. 6–7); see 6.370n.

16.1241 (647:19). *Emigration Swindle – "Bogus Emigration Agent. / Case in the Police Court" (*Evening Telegraph*, p. 3, col. 2); see 7.383n.

16.1241–42 (647:19–20). Letter from His Grace. William ✠ – Does not appear; see 7.62n and 7.181n. The Cross Pattee (✠) is a sign used by the popes and Catholic archbishops and bishops immediately before the subscription of their names. It is also used in printed prayers and benedictions where the sign of the cross is to be made.

16.1242–44 (647:20–22). *Ascot meeting, the Gold Cup. Victory of outsider *Throwaway* . . . ribband at long odds – "Sporting. / ASCOT MEETING. / The Gold Cup. / The Outsider Wins" (*Evening Telegraph*, p. 3, col. 8); see 14.1128–33n. The article lists several of the "great horses" that had won the Gold Cup, but Sir Hugo, a horse that did win the English Derby in 1892 against forty to one odds, is not mentioned. Adams (p. 165) says that Sir Hugo was owned by Lord Bradford, not by Captain Marshall.

16.1244 (647:22). *New York disaster. Thousand lives lost – The disaster is the subject of an editorial, "The American Horror," *Evening Telegraph*, p. 2, cols. 3–4, and also of a news

story, p. 4, col. 2: "APPALLING AMERICAN DISASTER. / EXCURSION STEAMER ON FIRE. / 485 BODIES RECOVERED. / Victims Charred and Unrecognizable"; see 8.1146–47n and 10.731n.

16.1244–45 (647:23). Foot and Mouth. Funeral of the late Mr Patrick Dignam – Neither Deasy's "letter" nor Dignam's "funeral" managed to infiltrate the columns of the *Evening Telegraph*.

**16.1249–50 (647:28). *no 9 Newbridge Avenue, Sandymount* ** – Was vacant in 1904, according to *Thom's* 1904.

**16.1256 (647:36). *Bernard Corrigan* ** – Unknown, apart from his role in context as Dignam's brother-in-law.

16.1258–59 (647:38–39). Monks the dayfather about Keyes's ad – See 7.25n, 7.141n, and 7.195n.

16.1268–69 (648:7–9). Is that first epistle . . . thy foot in it – St. Paul wrote only one epistle to the Hebrews; Stephen's witticism implies that Mr. Deasy's letter is addressed to a chosen people in a promised land.

**16.1276–89 (648:17–32). the third event at Ascot . . . *Maximum II* ** – The whole account runs: "3.0—The GOLD CUP, value 1,000 sovs., with 3,000 sovs. in specie in addition, out of which the second shall receive 700 sovs., and the third 300 sovs., added to a sweepstake of 20 sovs. each, h. ft., for entire colts and fillies. Two miles and a half. Mr. F. Alexander's THROWAWAY, by Rightaway-Theale, 5 yrs, 9 st. 4 lb . . . W. Lane 1. Lord Howard de Walden's ZINFANDEL, 4 yrs, 9 st. . . . . M. Cannon 2. Mr. W. Bass's SCEPTRE, 5 yrs, 9 st. 11 lb. O. Madden 3. M. J. de Bremonds Maximum II, 5 yrs, 9 st. 4 lb. G. Stern O. (Winner trained by Braime.) Race started at 3.5 Betting—5 to 4 on Zinfandel, 7 to 4 against Sceptre, 10 to 1 agst Maximum II, 20 to 1 agst Throwaway (off). THE RACE. Throwaway set a fair pace to Sceptre with Maximum II last, till fairly in the line for home, when Sceptre slightly headed Throwaway, and Zinfandel took close order with him. Throwaway, however, stayed on and won cleverly at the finish by a length; three parts of a length divided second and third. Time—4 mins. 33 2-5 secs" (*Evening Telegraph*, 16 June 1904, p. 3, col. 8). For "buncombe," see 12.877n.

16.1289 (648:33). Lovemaking damages – See 16.1240–41n.

16.1298 (648:43). *Return of Parnell* – See 6.923–24n. The expectation that Parnell will return parallels the expectation in *The Odyssey* that Odysseus will return to Ithaca.

16.1298–99 (649:1–2). A Dublin fusilier . . . saw him in South Africa – See 15.4606–7n and 18.402–3n.

16.1301 (649:4). *committee room no 15 – In that room in the English Houses of Parliament on Saturday, 6 December 1890, an Irish Parliamentary party majority led by Timothy Michael Healy attempted to depose Parnell from leadership. But Parnell was in the chair and blocked the move on a parliamentary technicality. Healy and his allies managed only to split the party, forty-five to twenty-six, and the withdrawal of the forty-five left Parnell the leader of a truncated and embattled party.

16.1304–5 (649:8). The coffin they brought over – Parnell died at Brighton, England, on 6 October 1891; on Sunday, 11 October, his coffined body arrived at Kingstown and was moved through Dublin to the city hall, where it lay in state for several hours before burial in Glasnevin Cemetery.

16.1305 (649:9). De Wet, the Boer general – One of the more farfetched rumors about the second coming of Parnell; see 8.435n.

16.1306 (649:10). He made a mistake to fight the priests – During the political infighting that preceded the "split" in Committee Room 15, the Irish Roman Catholic hierarchy maintained a discreet silence until late November 1890; then Archbishops Croke and Walsh intervened, in effect publicly urging Parnell "to retire quietly and with good grace from the leadership" (Croke). They insisted that their interest was not "political" but "moral," but the net effect of their intervention was to speed Parnell's fall and to further confuse religion with politics. Parnell counterattacked vigorously, insisting on a separation of Church and State; and the hierarchy was just as vigorous in its insistence on its "moral" right to question the integrity of Parnell's leadership.

16.1308 (649:12–13). in nine cases out of ten it was a case of tarbarrels – That is, the population of Ireland was so bitterly anti-Parnell that he was to be burned at least in effigy (if not as a heretic). Tar barrels were used to make bonfires.

16.1309–10 (649:14). it was twenty odd years – Since Bloom must be aware that Parnell has only been dead thirteen years, he must be thinking of another controversial phase of Parnell's career in the early 1880s (when Parnell was in and out of prison and in danger of being linked to the Phoenix Park murders through Piggott's forgeries).

16.1313 (649:18–19). Either he petered out too tamely of acute pneumonia – Parnell's death seems to have been the result not of a single illness but of the cumulative impact of a number of causes. He did suffer from rheumatism, and he fearfully overextended himself in the effort to retrieve a lost cause; specifically, on Sunday, 27 September 1891, he spoke in the rain in County Galway and was forced to wear wet clothes for several hours. His condition worsened after that, and the final medical opinion that he died of rheumatic fever and a weak heart seems a rather vague description of the complex nature of his collapse.

16.1313–14 (649:19–20). just when his various political arrangements were nearing completion – A misleading statement, since Parnell's "political arrangements" (his attempts to put together a sizable Irish party) were in a state of galloping disintegration at the time of his death; in the attempt to recoup he was shifting from advocacy of constitutional reform toward advocacy of revolutionary violence. This shift in turn further alienated his former followers and admirers.

16.1316–17 (649:22–23). failing to consult a specialist – In the last few weeks of his life Parnell repeatedly refused to let his wife call in the London specialist Sir Henry Thompson, who had been attending him. Apparently Parnell was afraid that the precarious state of his health would force his retirement from politics.

16.1320 (649:26–27). nobody being acquainted with his movements even before – One aftermath of the divorce trial and its attendant publicity in 1890 was the shocking revelation that Parnell's "movements" for the ten years of his liaison with Mrs. O'Shea had been a well-kept open secret (see 16.1366–69n), unknown to the public even though his stature as a political leader led the public to assume that his life was in no way hidden.

16.1321–22 (649:29). *Alice, where art thou* –
A popular song by Wellington Guernsey and Joseph Ascher. The lover laments, "One year back this even, / And thou wert by my side," and repeatedly asks, "Alice, where art thou?" Finally, "looking heav'nward," he concludes, "Oh! There amid the starshine / Alice, I know art thou."

16.1322–23 (649:30). aliases such as Fox and Stewart – See 15.1762n.

16.1325–27 (649:33–35). a commanding figure . . . in his stockinged feet – Katherine O'Shea Parnell, in her *Charles Stewart Parnell; His Love Story and Political Life* (London, 1914), vol. 1, p. 135, describes him as "a tall gaunt figure, thin and deadly pale."

16.1327–29 (649:35–37). Messrs So-and-So . . . few and far between – The reference is to the leaders who emerged after Parnell's fall: Timothy Healy (7.800n), John Redmond (15.4685n), Justin M'Carthy (15.4684n), and others.

16.1329–30 (649:38). the idol with feet of clay – In Daniel, an image that Nebuchadnezzar had seen in a dream is described: "This image's head was of fine gold, his breast and arms of silver, his belly and his thighs of brass, His legs of iron, his feet part of iron and part of clay" (2:32–33). Daniel explains the dream: "And whereas thou sawest the feet and toes, part of potters' clay, and part of iron, the kingdom shall be divided; but there shall be in it of the strength of the iron. . . . And as the toes of the feet were part of iron, and part of clay, so the kingdom shall be partly strong, and partly broken" (2:41–42).

16.1330 (649:39). seventytwo of his trusty henchmen rounded on him – Counting Parnell, there were seventy-two people in Committee Room 15, and only forty-five "rounded on him"; cf. 16.1301n.

16.1334–35 (649:43–650:1). when they broke up . . . *United Ireland* – It was the *United Ireland*, established in 1881 as a vehicle for Parnell's views and policies. The acting editor during the December 1890 crisis was Matthew Bodkin, who first wavered and then took an anti-Parnell position on 6 December. When Parnell returned to Dublin on 10 December, he dismissed Bodkin as editor, but the anti-Parnellites reoccupied the newspaper offices while Parnell was at a mass meeting that night. Parnell and his followers literally stormed the building the next day and retook the paper. The anti-Parnellite faction, thus "suppressed," established the *Insuppressible* (December 1890–January 1891) to voice their opposition.

16.1338–39 (650:6). what's bred in the bone – Will not out of the flesh; proverbial.

16.1343–46 (650:11–15). *like the claimant in the Tichborne case . . . lord Bellew was it? – The claimant in this famous case was an Australian, Arthur Orton (1834–98), a coarse, ignorant butcher. Roger Charles Tichborne (1829–54), the heir presumptive of Sir James Francis Tichborne (1784–1862), was lost at sea on the *Bella* in 1854, but his mother refused to believe him dead and advertised for information of his whereabouts. Meanwhile, his younger brother, Alfred Joseph, had succeeded to the baronetcy upon the death of the father in 1862. In 1865 Orton announced his candidacy, claiming to be Roger Charles. He achieved considerable backing, including Lady Tichborne's, in spite of the fact that there was no physical or cultural similarity between the dead heir and the impostor. Orton brought suit to recover the estates in 1871 (103 days, denied). Lord Bellew, a schoolmate of Roger Charles, testified against Orton on the grounds that Roger Charles had tattoos to which he personally had added the letters "R.C.T." in Indian ink; Orton had no similar tattoo. In 1873 Orton was tried for perjury (188 days, guilty).

16.1349–51 (650:19–22). A more prudent course . . . lie of the land first – Precisely what Odysseus does when he reaches Ithaca; see headnote to this episode, p. 534.

16.1352 (650:23). That bitch, that English whore – Katherine O'Shea (1845–1921), whose ten-year liaison with Parnell was exposed in the divorce trial (1890) and resulted in the collapse of Parnell's career. She was English, the daughter of Sir John Page Wood, a chaplain to Queen Caroline (d. 1821) and later minister to the parish of Rivenhall, Essex; her mother was the daughter of the English admiral, Sampson Mitchell.

16.1352 (650:23). shebeen – See 12.802n.

16.1355 (650:26//). *She loosened many a man's thighs – Perhaps in daydream, but there is no evidence that her conduct, apart from her liaison with Parnell, was anything but virtuous, and when they married after her divorce from O'Shea they intended the marriage as a demonstration that their relationship had had a sort of legitimacy throughout their lives together. In *The Odyssey*, Eumaeus says of Odysseus (to Odysseus in disguise): "But the man's gone. / God curse the race of Helen and cut it down / that wrung the strength out of the knees of many" (14:68–69; Fitzgerald, p. 261). Butcher and Lang render the passage: "forasmuch as she hath caused the loosening of many a man's knees" (*The Odyssey of Homer* [New York, 1950], p. 211).

16.1356 (650:27). *The husband was a captain or an officer – William Henry O'Shea (1840–1905) entered the 18th Hussars at the age of eighteen, achieved the rank of captain, and sold his commission in 1867. His later life was spent variously on the fringes of political power.

16.1357 (650:28–29). a cottonball one – See 12.1349n.

16.1363 (650:36–37). with the usual affectionate letter that passed between them – Several of the "love letters" that passed between Parnell and Mrs. O'Shea were admitted into evidence at the divorce trial in November 1890.

16.1366–69 (650:40–43). the staggering blow came . . . public property all along – Parnell's liaison with Mrs. O'Shea was virtually a marriage (from 1881), complete with children, and as such it was a well-kept open secret, known to many of Parnell's associates and widely rumored, but not subject to political exploitation. When Captain O'Shea brought suit and Parnell refused to defend himself, the scandal became politically useful in that it revealed the mounting tensions within Parnell's own party and the increasing division between Parnell and Gladstone's Liberal party and within the Liberal party itself.

16.1376–77 (651:9–10). scrambling out of an upstairs . . . ladder in night apparel – An inaccurate version of a particularly damning story that went unchallenged at the trial (since Parnell refused to defend himself and the witness was not cross-examined). The maidservant's uncorroborated story was that three or four times Parnell had evaded discovery by Captain O'Shea by climbing out of Mrs. O'Shea's bedroom, descending a fire escape and then presenting himself at the door as if he had come to pay a call.

16.1379–80 (651:13–14). it was simply a case . . . being up to scratch – Nothing is simple in the Parnell-O'Shea affair, though the evidence suggests that the O'Sheas were estranged before Parnell came on the scene. Further, and in spite of O'Shea's unchallenged protestations of ignorance during the trial, it seems evident that he at first connived (grudgingly or indifferently) at a relationship that promised him political advantage and subsequently agreed to a de facto divorce (and to Mrs. O'Shea's de facto marriage to Parnell) from a complex of motives that included an interest in a share of the inheritance expected from Mrs. O'Shea's aunt.

16.1382–83 (651:17). falling a victim . . . forgetting home ties – In *The Odyssey*, Circe warns Odysseus that the Sirens will "sing his mind away" as they make men forget "home ties" (12:43; Fitzgerald, p. 222). Parnell was, of course, a bachelor when he met Mrs. O'Shea; thus, Parnell's "home ties" can only be construed as the fidelity he owed Irish political enterprise.

16.1390–91 (651:26–27). *farewell, my gallant captain – At the end of the first act of Wallace's opera *Maritana* (see 5.563–64n), Don Cesar, the hero, challenges the villainous captain of the guard to a duel and then sings: "Farewell, my valiant captain! / I told you how it would be; / You'll not forget, brave captain, / The lesson due to me! / Ha! Ha! Ha! Ha!" In the Parnell-O'Shea story, one significant (and much debated) turning point occurred in 1881 when the two men quarreled and O'Shea challenged Parnell to a duel; the duel never took place, and the treaty that resolved it seems to have been the basis for Mrs. O'Shea and Parnell's de facto marriage.

16.1395 (651:32). ministers of the gospel – There was considerable public outrage over Parnell's immorality, not only in Catholic Ireland but also in England where Dissenters put increasing pressure on Gladstone and threatened to topple his government if he did not act against Parnell.

16.1399–1400 (651:37–38). Heaping coals of fire on his head – "Therefore if thine enemy hunger, feed him; if he thirst, give him drink: for in so doing thou shalt heap coals of fire on his head" (Romans 12:20).

16.1400 (651:38). the fabled ass's kick – In Aesop's "The Ass and the Wolf," the ass distracts the wolf from his usual role as killer by complaining of a thorn in his hoof. The wolf tries to remove the thorn with his teeth and gets kicked for his pains. Moral: play the role you're intended for.

16.1404 (651:43). *Irishtown strand – The shore area just south of the Liffey on Dublin Bay. Since Bloom's house in Eccles Street is on the "north side," the strand would be out of Bloom's way except on rare occasions (such as that of Dignam's funeral).

16.1408–9 (652:6). she was also Spanish or half so – Mrs. Katherine Wood O'Shea Parnell was not (see 16.1352n), but she and O'Shea did spend some time in Spain after their marriage, and in her biography of her husband (*Charles Stewart Parnell* [London, 1914], vol. 1, p. 70) she remarks that "the admixture of Irish and Spanish blood is most charming in result."

16.1412 (652:10//). *about blood and the sun – See 16.873n.

16.1414 (652:12). The king of Spain's daughter – See 15.4585n.

16.1415–17 (652:13–15). farewell and adieu . . . to Scilly was so and so many . . . – Fragments of an anonymous ballad, "Spanish Ladies": "Farewell and adieu to you, gay Spanish ladies, / Farewell and adieu to you, ladies of Spain, / For we've received orders to sail to old England; / But we hope in short time to see you again. [Chorus:] We'll rant and we'll roar like true British sailors, / We'll rant and we'll roar across the salt seas, / Until we strike soundings in the channel of old England, / From Ushant to Scilly is 35 leagues. [Third verse:] Now the first land we made it is called the Deadman, / Then, Ramshead off Plymouth, Start, Portland and Wight; / We passed by Beechy, by Farleigh and Dungeness, / And hove our ship to, off South Foreland Light."

16.1419–20 (652:18). especially there it was, as she lived there. So, Spain – Shortly after their marriage in 1867 the O'Sheas moved to Madrid, where Captain O'Shea's Irish uncle, who had married a Spanish woman, had a bank. For roughly a year Captain O'Shea was a partner in his uncle's bank, but a dispute ended the partnership and the O'Sheas returned to England in 1868.

16.1421 (652:19). *Sweets of* – *Sin;* see 10.606n.

16.1422 (652:20). that Capel street library book – See 4.360n.

**16.1432 (652:32). *In Old Madrid – See 11.733n.

16.1435 (652:34–35). Lafayette of Westmoreland street – See 14.1221n.

16.1444 (653:1–2). barely sweet sixteen – From a popular song, "When You Were Sweet Sixteen" (1898), by James Thornton. Chorus: "I love you as I ne'er loved before / Since first I met you on the village green. / Come to me, or my dream of love is o'er. / I love you as I lov'd you / When you were sweet, / When you were sweet sixteen."

16.1448 (653:6–7). opulent curves – See 10.606n.

16.1452–54 (653:12//14). *Yes, puritanisme, it does though Saint Joseph's sovereign thievery alors (Bandez!) Figne toi trop – An obscure passage, but the French (coarse Parisian argot) may read, "puritanism . . . all right (Get a hard on!) Bugger yourself up to the neck [or, Go fuck yourself]." (Professor Hans Walter Gabler points out that in the French translation of *Ulysses* [*Ulysse*, trans. Auguste Morel (Paris, 1948), p. 338], "S.O.D." [12.1894 (345:5)] is rendered "Chevalier du Figne" [Knight of the Arsehole: "Sodomist, pederast"].) If that is the case, then "Saint Joseph's sovereign thievery" could involve a crude and blasphemous reference to St. Joseph's asexual relation to the Virgin Mary and to his usurpation of God's sovereignty as father, since Joseph as Mary's husband appeared to be Jesus' father on earth.

16.1456 (653:16). Jack Tar's – Humorous or affected for a sailor.

16.1468 (653:30). heaving *embonpoint* – See 10.606n.

16.1470–71 (653:33). I looked for the lamp which she told me – From Thomas Moore's "The Song of O'Ruark, Prince of Breffni," in *Irish Melodies*. The first two of the poem's four stanzas: "The valley lay smiling before me, / Where lately I left her behind; / Yet I trembled, and something hung o'er me, / That sadd'ned the joy of my mind. / I look'd for the lamp which, she told me, / Should shine, when her Pilgrim return'd; / But though darkness began to infold me, / No lamp from the battlements burn'd! // I flew to her chamber—'twas lonely, /

As if the lov'd tenant lay dead;— / Ah, would it were death, and death only! / But no, the young false one had fled. / And there hung the lute that could soften / My very worst pains into bliss; / While the hand, that had wak'd it so often, / Now throbb'd to a proud rival's kiss." See 2.393–94n.

16.1472–73 (653:35–36). the book about Ruby with met him pike hoses – See 4.346n and 4.339n.

16.1474–75 (653:38). with apologies to Lindley Murray – Lindley Murray (1745–1826) was an English grammarian whose *Grammar of the English Language* (1795) and other works on reading, spelling, and usage were standard nineteenth-century school texts. The apology due to Murray is obviously for "must have fell down," but in a broader sense an apology is due to Murray whose tone is highly moralistic: "If we lie no restraint against our lusts . . . they will hurry us into guilt and misery."

16.1490–92 (654:13–15). Then the decree *nisi* . . . *nisi* was made absolute – A divorce decree *nisi* is not final or absolute but is to take effect eventually unless (*nisi*) further cause is shown or a reason arises to prevent its taking effect. (Captain O'Shea was initially granted a decree *nisi*.) The king's (or in the O'Shea case, the queen's) proctor might best be described as the Crown's "district attorney" for probate court; he could and sometimes did intervene to reopen divorce cases after the decree *nisi* and before the decree became absolute. One such intervention occurred in 1886 in a case that had parallels to the Parnell case: the accused correspondent, Sir Charles Dilke (1843–1911), a radical English liberal politician, had his promising political career ruined. In the divorce trial itself, the accused wife, Mrs. Crawford, confessed that she had committed adultery with Dilke; her confession was not supported by other evidence, and Dilke was not allowed to protest his innocence; but a decree *nisi* was granted to Mr. Crawford. The queen's proctor intervened to reopen the trial, but Dilke was unable to prove his innocence, the decree *nisi* became absolute, and Dilke's career was ruined.

16.1496 (654:20–21). Erin's uncrowned king – An appellation for Parnell.

16.1500–1501 (654:25–26). penetrated into the printing . . . United Ireland – See 16.1334–35n.

16.1503 (654:29–30). the O'Brienite scribes – Matthew Bodkin, who had moved the *United Ireland* into an anti-Parnellite position (see 16.1334–35n), was acting editor while the editor, William O'Brien (1852–1928), was in America raising funds to aid evicted tenants in Ireland. O'Brien became one of the central figures of the anti-Parnellite coalition at the time of the split.

16.1505–6 (654:31–33). Though palpably a radically altered man . . . though carelessly garbed as usual – In December 1890 Parnell had apparently lost none of his charismatic vigor or sartorial fastidiousness. It was not until late June 1891 that Parnell's driven pace in the foredoomed attempt to recoup really began to take its toll on his health and to render him "pale and haggard" and disheveled in appearance. Later in that summer, "the deterioration in his physique was matched by the deterioration in what he had to say and how he said it" (Justin McCarthy, quoted in F. S. L. Lyons, *Charles Stewart Parnell* [London, 1977], p. 577).

16.1508 (654:35–36). their idol had feet of clay – See 16.1329–30n.

16.1520 (655:6–7). what's bred in the bone – See 16.1338–39n.

16.1526–27 (655:13–15). after the burial . . . alone in his glory – From "The Burial of Sir John Moore at Corunna" (1817), by the Irish poet the Reverend Charles Wolfe (1791–1823). The poem describes the silent and hasty burial of Gen. Sir John Moore by the English rearguard during the evacuation of La Coruña, Spain, in 1809. Moore was a great popular favorite in England and enjoyed considerable military success against Napoleon's forces in Spain. The poem ends: "We carved not a line, and we raised not a stone— / But we left him alone with his glory" (lines 31–32).

16.1533–34 (655:22–23). unless it ensued that . . . to be a party to it – There is considerable evidence to support the contention that Captain O'Shea was "party to" the relationship between Mrs. O'Shea and Parnell; see 16.1379–80n.

16.1534–35 (655:24). the usual boy Jones – That is, the usual informer; after one Bernard Duggan, a fellow student of Robert Emmet (see 6.977–78n) who joined Emmet's attempt to organize a rebellion in 1802–3 but who was said to have been a spy in the employ of the English.

Duggan's secret-service name has been known in anecdotal history as "the Trinity boy Jones." There is considerable disagreement among historians about "Jones" and the extent of his achievements, largely because the abortive rising, when it actually occurred, did, at least according to the English, come as a surprise.

16.1537–39 (655:27–29). a domestic rumpus and . . . his visits any more – Captain O'Shea testified at the divorce trial that he had exacted such a promise from Mrs. O'Shea in 1881, but the nature of that quarrel and its outcome remains ambiguous; see 16.1390–91n.

16.1558 (656:9). *conditio sine qua non* – Latin: stock phrase for "the indispensable condition."

16.1559–60 (656:11). Miss Ferguson – See 15.4950 (609:11) and 15.4932–33n.

16.1571 (656:25). Humpty Dumpty – Humorous or affected for an egg, after the well-known nursery-rhyme riddle.

16.1583 (656:39). the Buckshot Foster days – That is, 1880–82; see "buckshot," 12.1716n.

16.1585 (656:42). the evicted tenants' question – Refers to the social and political problems raised by the eviction from their holdings of extraordinary numbers of Irish peasants during the latter half of the nineteenth century. The majority of those evicted either would not or could not pay their rents; a sizable minority were evicted by landlords intent on agrarian reform. The crisis peaked in the poor harvest years 1879–80, and land reform emerged as a major political issue—in effect, what emerged was a crusade to achieve the peasant's ownership of the land he farmed.

16.1592–93 (657:7–9). *a step farther than Michael Davitt . . . as a backtothelander – Michael Davitt's (see 15.4684n) program of land reform advocated the use of public funds to achieve peasant ownership of the land; Bloom as "backtothelander" has gone "a step farther" by advocating an agrarian socialism in which all men would contribute by sharing agrarian labor.

16.1602 (657:18–19). destruction of the fittest – An inversion of Herbert Spencer's (1820–1903) summary phrase (slogan?) for Darwin's theory of natural selection, "survival of the fittest." Darwin's theory was based on the assumption that those forms of plants and ani-

mals best adapted to the conditions under which they were to live were the "fittest" and would survive, while poorly adapted forms would become extinct.

16.1609 (657:27). Ontario Terrace – In Rathmines just south of the Grand Canal; in 1904 the houses in Ontario Terrace were comparable in value to the houses in Eccles Street.

16.1611 (657:30). Sandymount or Sandycove – The Martello tower of the Telemachus episode is at Sandycove, seven miles southeast of Dublin center. Sandymount, just over two miles southeast of Dublin center, is the scene of the Proteus episode, of the beginning of Dignam's funeral, and of the Nausicaa Episode.

16.1621 (657:42–43). a cup of Epps's cocoa – Advertised in *The Weekly Freeman*, 18 June 1904, p. 13: "Epps's Cocoa; Grateful and Comforting; Nutritious and Economical; . . . The best suited for all ages and classes, The greatest invigorator for the fagged. Justly prized by Mothers for themselves and their children, who choose it eagerly."

16.1625–26 (658:5). that merry old soul – See 8.394n.

16.1629–30 (658:9–10). off Sheriff street lower – East of the Amiens Street railway station and north of the docks, a run-down area of tenements and relatively poor houses in 1904.

16.1638 (658:19–20). blood and ouns – See 1.22n.

16.1640 (658:22–23). The most vulnerable point of tender Achilles – See 16.1003n.

16.1642 (658:24). Carrick-on-Shannon – A market town in County Leitrim, ninety-eight miles west-northwest of Dublin (figuratively, a "backwoods" town).

16.1642 (658:25). county Sligo – On the west (Atlantic) coast of Ireland, regarded by Dubliners as picturesque and remote.

16.1650–51 (658:35). that Brazen Head – See 16.168–70n.

16.1653 (658:39). prize titbits – See 4.467n and 4.502n.

16.1662–64 (659:8–9). the former viceroy, earl Cadogan . . . dinner in London – The dinner for the Cabdrivers' Benevolent Association is not mentioned in the *Evening Telegraph* for 16 June 1904 for the very simple reason that it did not take place until 27 June. George Henry Cadogan (1840–1915), fifth Earl Cadogan, was lord lieutenant of Ireland 1895–1902.

16.1666–67 (659:12–13). sir Anthony Mac-Donnell had left Euston for the chief secre-tary's lodge – This item does not appear in the *Evening Telegraph*, but it is reported in the *London Times*, 17 June 1904, p. 6. The Right Honourable Sir Anthony Patrick MacDonnell (b. 1844) was under secretary (i.e., chief secretary) to the lord lieutenant of Ireland in 1904; and he did leave Euston station in London on 16 June to arrive at his residence, the under secretary's lodge in Phoenix Park, Dublin, on 17 June. The only news of Sir Anthony that appears in the *Evening Telegraph* for 16 June (p. 3, col. 2) is his ambiguous answer to Mr. Nannetti's question about the prohibition of Irish games in Phoenix Park. See 12.859n.

16.1669 (659:15–16). the ancient mariner – See 16.844–45n.

16.1680 (659:28). *The Arabian Nights Entertainment* – A loosely woven collection of Oriental stories in Arabic from c. 1100. In fragments, the stories were introduced into English in the first two decades of the nineteenth century; a complete, unexpurgated translation, *The Thousand Nights and a Night* (1885–88) was done by Sir Richard Burton (1821–90).

16.1680–81 (659:29). *Red as a Rose is She* – A novel (1870), by the English writer Rhoda Broughton (1840–1920). It is a bittersweet, sentimental love story in which the essentially truthful and courageous heroine slips into the practice of deception, suffers the melancholy consequences, and, morally purged by her trials, is rewarded with the good life.

16.1683 (659:31). found drowned – The stock phrase used by a coroner's jury that finds death to have been caused by accidental drowning; consequently, a standard newspaper heading. It does not appear in the *Evening Telegraph* for 16 June; the nearest thing is "Rescue from Drowning" (p. 3, col. 5), a brief story of "a young lad" rescued from the Liffey in Dublin at 4:00 P.M., 16 June 1904.

16.1683 (659:31–32). the exploits of King Willow – That is, of a champion cricket batsman, since cricket bats were made out of willow.

16.1683–84 (659:32–33). Iremonger having made . . . not out for Notts – The *Evening Telegraph*, 16 June 1904, p. 3, col. 6, under "Cricket," "Notts v. Kent," reports the day's progress of a match between the county teams of Nottingham and Kent: at the end of the day Iremonger, the Notts star batsman who had started the game, was still at bat having scored 155 runs with the loss of only two wickets (i.e., two of Iremonger's batting partners had been put out). The Notts total for two wickets: 290.

16.1698 (660:5). the last of the Mohicans – A novel (1826) by James Fenimore Cooper (1789–1851). It is the second of Cooper's *Leatherstocking Tales* in order of composition; the third in the narrative chronology of the five tales. As the title suggests, the novel deals with the extinction of an Indian tribe.

16.1699 (660:6–7). for all who ran to read – "And the Lord answered me, and said, Write the vision, and make it plain upon tables, that he may run that readeth it" (Habakkuk 2:2).

16.1701 (660:9). Wetherup – See 7.337n.

16.1705–6 (660:14). *dolce far niente* – See 5.32n.

16.1715–16 (660:25–26). *his right side being . . . his tender Achilles – See 16.1003n.

16.1727–28 (660:39). dreaming of fresh fields and pastures new – See 2.57n.

16.1728 (660:40). coffin of stones – Refers to the story that Parnell's body was not in the coffin but that the coffin was full of stones.

16.1729–30 (660:41–661:1). a stoning to death . . . time of the split – In 1890 there were 103 Parliamentary constituencies in Ireland, of which Parnellites held 86. When the split occurred (see 16.1301n), 72 of the 86 were present in Committee Room 15, and 45 turned anti-Parnellite. In the course of 1891 several of the loyal 26 either wavered or turned against Parnell. Thus Bloom's figures are impressionistic, but the assertion that Parnell's death was caused by the attacks of those who were previously his followers was widely accepted as valid, particularly by loyal Parnellites. Several times in the Bible, stoning to death is prescribed as the punishment for those who lead in the pursuit of false gods and for those who commit adultery.

16.1735 (661:5). across Beresford place – Bloom and Stephen walk northeast from the cabman's shelter, retracing their steps toward Gardiner Street Lower, which slants north-northwest toward Eccles Street.

16.1735 (661:5–6). Wagnerian music – At the end of the nineteenth century, Wagner (1813–83) was widely recognized as "one of the greatest of all musical geniuses," but his music was also popularly regarded as "heavy, difficult and avant-garde."

16.1737–38 (661:8–9). Mercadante's *Huguenots . . . Words on the Cross* – Bloom confuses the composers: for Mercadante's *Seven Last Words*, see 5.403–4n; for Meyerbeer's *Huguenots*, see 8.623–24n.

16.1738–39 (661:9–10). Mozart's *Twelfth Mass . . . the Gloria* – See 5.404n.

16.1742 (661:14). Moody and Sankey hymns – The Americans Dwight L. Moody (1837–99) and Ira D. Sankey (1840–1908), a team of evangelists. They enjoyed a considerable international popularity; Moody did most of the preaching at their meetings, while Sankey had charge of the singing. During the period of their cooperation Sankey compiled two volumes of hymns, *Sacred Songs and Solos* (1873) and *Gospel Hymns* (with P. P. Bliss, 1875). These collections became known as "Moody and Sankey hymns," though only a few of them were actually of Sankey's composition and none of them Moody's.

16.1742–43 (661:14–15). *Bid me to live . . . protestant to be* – The opening lines of Robert Herrick's (1591–1674) poem "To Anthea, who may command him anything," in *Hesperides* (1648). First stanza: "Bid me to live, and I will live / Thy Protestant to be: / Or bid me love, and I will give / A loving heart to thee." It is a Cavalier love lyric, not a Protestant hymn, and it was a popular Victorian drawing-room song in a setting by John L. Hatton (1809–86).

16.1744 (661:16). Rossini's *Stabat Mater* – See 5.397–98n.

16.1747–48 (661:20–21). *the jesuit father's church in upper Gardiner street – The Church of St. Francis Xavier; see 10.2n.

16.1752–53 (661:26–27). light opera of the *Don Giovanni* description – Mozart's opera has been on Bloom's mind all day (see 4.314n), and its general theme of the seducer and betrayer finally brought to justice obviously has its analogues to Bloom's domestic problems. From a late-twentieth-century point of view *Don Giovanni* is anything but "light opera," but late-nineteenth-century "appreciations" of Mozart's music (and personality) tended to emphasize "the buoyant nature which seemed to override misfortune and intrigue and to laugh at poverty" (*New International Encyclopedia* [New York, 1903], vol. 14, p. 846).

16.1753 (661:27). *Martha* – Comes much closer to being light opera; see 7.58n.

16.1754–55 (661:29). the severe classical school such as Mendelssohn – This misnomer for Felix Mendelssohn's (1809–47) light and popular romanticism matches calling *Don Giovanni* a light opera; see 11.1092n and 12.1804n.

16.1756–57 (661:31–32). Lionel's air in *Martha, M'appari* – See 11.24n.

16.1762 (661:37–38). Shakespeare's songs, at least of in or about that period – Most students of Shakespeare's songs are agreed that seventeenth-century transcriptions of the songs' music are Shakespearean rather than Shakespeare's own; that is, since most of the songs used popular tunes or folk tunes, the numerous transcriptions are assumed to be akin to but after the fact of the music as actually performed on Shakespeare's stage.

16.1762–64 (661:38–40). the lutenist Dowland . . . *ludendo hausi, Doulandus* – John Dowland (1563–1626), an English lutenist and composer of books of "Songs and Ayres." He is placed in Fetter Lane by the dating of the 1609 preface to his translation of the "Micrologus of Ornithoparcus," though much of his mature life before 1609 he spent traveling on the Continent and in residence as court lutenist in Denmark. His friends thought that he had missed many opportunities for advancing himself. One friend, Henry Peachem (1576–c. 1644), an English schoolmaster, traveler, draftsman, painter, and antiquary, gave Dowland an emblem of "a nightingale singing in the winter season on a leafless brier," with verses and the inscription, *Johannes Doulandus, Annos ludendo hausi* (Latin: "John Dowland, I used up my years in playing"); see Sir John Hawkins's (1719–89) *A General History of the Science and Practise of Mu-*

sic (1776; republished New York, 1963), vol. 1, pp. 481–83. For Gerard the herbalist in Fetter Lane, see 9.651–52n.

16.1765 (661:41). Mr Arnold Dolmetsch – A London musician connected with the London Academy of Music who made a psaltery for Yeats and whom Joyce approached with a request for a lute in 1904; see Ellman, pp. 154–55.

16.1766–67 (662:1–2). Farnaby and son with their *dux* and *comes* conceits – Giles Farnaby (c. 1565–1640) and his son Richard (b. 1590); the father was famous for his "Canzonets to 4 Voices, with a Song of Eight Parts" (1598). *Dux* is the proposition, theme, or subject in contrapuntal music of the sort the Farnabys composed; *comes* is the answer.

16.1767–68 (662:2–3). Byrd (William) who played the virginals . . . in the Queen's chapel – William Byrd (1543–1623), "the Atlas of English music," a composer of church music (and some secular music) who shared an appointment as organist of Queen Elizabeth's Chapel Royal from 1572 with Thomas Tallis (c. 1510–85). The "virginal" involves the fact that Queen Elizabeth owned and played one, that she was the "Virgin Queen," and that she was firm in her patronage of Tallis and Byrd, granting them in 1574 an exclusive twenty-one-year patent for (i.e., a monopoly on) the publication of music in England.

16.1768–69 (662:4). one Tomkins who made toys or airs – There were several musical Tomkins, Thomas, father and son, and brothers Giles, John, and Nicholas; the most well known was the younger Thomas (1572–1656), a student of William Byrd, organist at the Chapel Royal, and composer of some merit. A "toy" was a light or facetious composition in contradistinction to the somewhat more serious, though still secular, "air."

16.1769 (662:4). John Bull – (c. 1562–1628), an English organist, virginalist, composer, and professor of music at Oxford. (Also, of course, the traditional personification of the English nation, no relation, who derives from Dr. John Arbuthnot's [1667–1735] satirical *History of John Bull* [1712].)

16.1784 (662:21). a fourwalker – A horse whose four feet are never coordinated in a gait.

16.1784 (662:21). a hipshaker – That is, hipshot, with one hip lower than another.

16.1784 (662:21). a black buttocker – Since to "buttock" is to overtake in a horse race, a "black buttocker" is a horse that is always being overtaken.

16.1785 (662:22). putting his hind foot foremost – After the proverbial "putting one's best foot foremost" (to make a good impression).

16.1792–93 (662:31–32). like the camel, ship . . . potheen in his hump – Fanciful natural history, after the popular but mistaken assumption that the camel stores water in its hump—the fatty tissue of the hump is a reserve of food, not water. But the camel's stomach is peculiarly constructed to extract water from food and to retain it in significant quantities.

16.1794–95 (662:34). barring the bees – Refers to the popular late-nineteenth-century belief that the communal organization of bees was superior to man's communal arrangements.

16.1795 (662:34). Whale with a harpoon hairpin – In whale fishery, whales were frequently captured carrying bent and twisted harpoons from previous assaults.

16.1795–96 (662:34–35). *alligator tickle the small . . . sees the joke – After the popular assumption that an alligator could be hypnotized into quiescence by stroking it on its belly or throat.

16.1796 (662:35–36). chalk a circle for a rooster – A popular method of attempting to hypnotize a rooster.

16.1796 (662:36). *tiger my eagle eye – That is, a man masters a tiger by the hypnotic strength of his gaze.

16.1797 (662:37). the brutes of the field – "And Adam gave names to all cattle, and to the fowl of the air, and to the beasts of the field" (Genesis 2:20).

16.1800–1801 (662:42). *in medias res* – Latin: "in the middle of the thing [or story]"; the conventional opening of the epic after Homer's example.

16.1808–9 (663:9–10). Lady Fingall's Irish . . . the preceding Monday – The Irish Industries Association, 21 Lincoln Place in Dublin, under the aegis of the lord lieutenant's wife, Lady Dudley, and Elizabeth Mary Margaret (Burke) Plunkett, countess of Fingall (whose husband was a major Catholic landholder in County Meath). The association benevolently tried to encourage folk or cottage industry in Ireland; it did give occasional benefit concerts. The concert in question took place on Saturday, 14 May 1904 (and Joyce took part in it). The reason why Joyce moved it to "the preceding Monday" (13 June 1904) is not clear.

16.1810–11 (663:12–14). *Youth here has End . . . Dutchman of Amsterdam* – Jan Pieterszoon Sweelinck (1562–1621), a Dutch organist and composer, whose song "Mein junges Leben hat ein End" Stephen somewhat misrepresents in his translation, since the title means "My young life has an end," and the song (in rough translation) continues: "my joy and sorrow as well, / My poor soul will quickly / Part from my body. / My life can no longer stand firm; / It is very weak and must perish / In Death's conflict and struggle." Sweelinck's music shows considerable affinity with that of English composers of the Elizabethan period.

16.1811 (663:14). frows – English dialect for a Dutch or German woman; also, slang for an idle, dirty woman.

16.1812 (663:15). Johannes Jeep – (c. 1582–1650), a German composer and Kapellmeister who composed a book of psalms and several books of secular songs that were popular in the seventeenth century.

16.1815–16 (663:18–19). *Von der Sirenen . . . die Poeten dichten* – German: "From the Sirens' craftiness / Poets make poems." These are the opening lines of Johannes Jeep's song "Dulcia dum loquitur cogitat insidias" (Latin: "The charm while they are talking is thought treacherous"), which appeared in volume 2 of his *Studentengärtlein* (1614). The first verse of the song continues: "That they with their loveliness / Have drawn many men into the sea / For their song resounds so sweetly, / That the sailors fall asleep, / The ship is brought into misfortune, / And all becomes evil." The title of Jeep's song is apparently taken from a Renaissance Latin translation of *The Odyssey*.

16.1823 (663:26). Barraclough – See 11.797n.

16.1835 (663:41). *conversaziones* – In Italy (and by once-fashionable imitation elsewhere), a meeting, usually in the evening, for conversation, music, or discussion of some topic of literature, art, or science.

16.1836–37 (664:1–2). causing a slight flutter in the dovecotes of the fair sex – Fritz Senn suggests that this alludes to Coriolanus's "insolent" brag to the Volscians just before his death at their hands: "If you have writ your annals true, 'tis there / That, like an eagle in a dovecote, I / Flutter'd your Volscians in Corioles" (Shakespeare's *Coriolanus* V.vi.113–15; cited in *JJQ* 19, no. 2 [1982]: 176).

16.1851–52 (664:20). Ivan St Austell and Hilton St Just – Were featured with the Arthur Rousley Opera Company when that company made several appearances in Dublin in the 1890s. As Adams (p. 73) points out, both names are comically high-toned pseudonyms derived from towns (and their patron saints) in Cornwall, England.

16.1852 (664:21). *genus omne* – Latin: "all that sort."

16.1856 (664:25–26). the King street house – That is, the Gaiety Theatre, 46–49 King Street South.

16.1868 (664:40). *fools step in where angels* – A cliché after Alexander Pope's *Essay on Criticism* (1711), line 625: "For *Fools* rush in where *Angels* fear to tread."

16.1879 (665:11). his scythed car – The brushes of the sweeper are likened to the scythes the ancient Britons and Celts attached to the wheels of their war chariots.

16.1882 (664:15). Gardiner street lower – Gives northwest from behind the Custom House in the general direction of Eccles Street and Bloom's house.

16.1884 (665:17). *Und alle Schiffe brücken* – German: literally, "And all ships are bridged"; apparently Stephen mistakes *brücken* for "broken" in an attempt at Johannes Jeep's line "Welches das Schiff in Unglück bringt" (Which brings the ship into misfortune). See 16.1815–16n.

16.1886/87–88/94 (665:19–20/21/29). *as he sat in his lowbacked car* / *to be married by Father*

Maher / and looked after their lowbacked car – For the opening stanza of "The Low-Backed Car," see 12.687–88n; the concluding lines of the poem: "As we drove in the low-back'd car, / To be married by Father Maher— / Oh my heart would beat high / At her glance and her sigh— / Tho' it beat in a low-back'd car."

16.1889 (665:23). sirens – See 16.1382–83n.

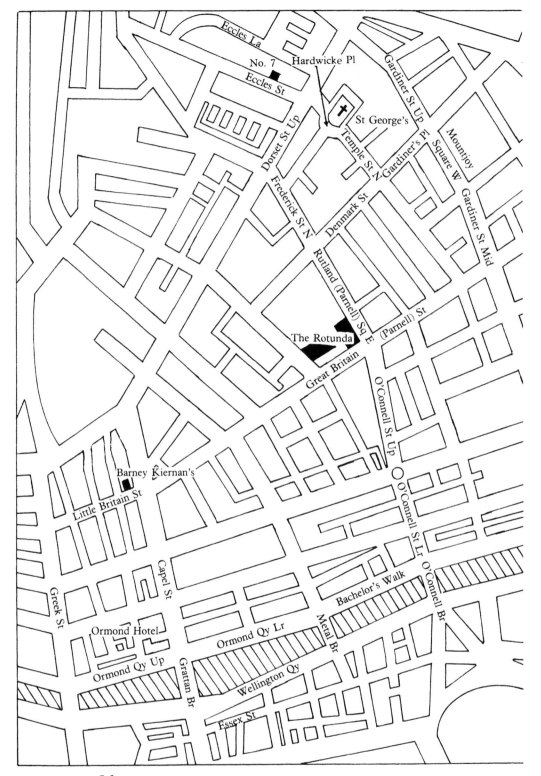

EPISODE 17. *Ithaca*

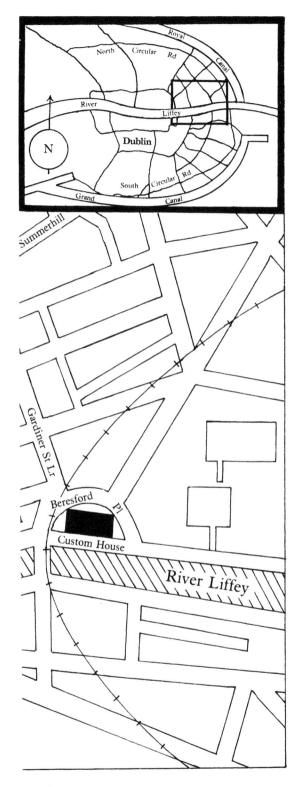

EPISODE 17

Ithaca

(17.1–2332, PP. 666–737)

Episode 17: *Ithaca,* **17.1–2332 (666–737).** In Book 17 of *The Odyssey,* Telemachus and Odysseus go their separate ways to Odysseus's palace. Odysseus is still in disguise as a beggar down on his luck. In Books 17–20 Odysseus—having entered his house "by a stratagem," as Bloom does (*Ulysses* 17.84 [668:20])—plots to kill the suitors. The state of his house "corrugates" his brow—as Bloom's brow is corrugated (17.322 [675:34]). Antinous, one of the chief suitors, is irritated by Odysseus and throws a stool at him (Book 17)—as Bloom runs into his displaced (by whom?) furniture (17.1274–78 [705:23–28]). On the morning of slaughter-day the suitors compete to see who can string Odysseus's great bow, but none can; the disguised Odysseus finally strings it with extraordinary ease, and Zeus reassures him with a thunderclap out of a cloudless sky (Book 21)—as the liturgical review of Bloom's day is rewarded by a "loud lone crack emitted by the insentient material of a strainveined timber table" (17.2061–62 [729:17–19]). Odysseus and Telemachus pen the suitors in the great hall of the palace—as Stephen helps lock the door (17.119 [669:27]). The slaughter of the suitors begins (Book 22) after Odysseus has strung the bow (correspondence: Reason), and Antinous (the part Mulligan is playing) is the first to be killed—as Bloom has already disposed of Mulligan (16.279–99 [620:31–621:11]). The second of the suitors to be killed is Eurymachus (Boylan's part), whom Athena has identified (Book 15) as the suitor on the verge of success because favored by Penelope's father and brothers. At the height of the killing in Book 22, the aegis of Athena shines under the roof of the hall, terrifying the suitors—as, at 17.1210 (703:23–27), a "celestial sign" appears. The lives of the poet and the herald are spared. When the killing is over, Telemachus is sent on an errand and Odysseus fumigates his house—as Bloom does (17.1321–29 [707:5–15]).

Penelope has slept through and is unaware of the slaughter. Odysseus's approach to Penelope is extraordinarily circumspect, not only when he is in disguise and wants to remain unknown to her (Book 19) but also when he reveals himself to her in Book 23. She in her turn is painfully slow to accept the ragged, bloodbegrimed "beggar" as her husband.

Time: 2:00 A.M. Scene: Bloom's house at 7 Eccles Street, N.E. Organ: skeleton; Art: science; Color: none; Symbol: comets; Technique: catechism (impersonal). Correspondences: *Antinous,* the first suitor—Buck Mulligan; *Eurymachus,* the second suitor—Boylan; *Bow*—reason; *Suitors*—scruples [it is of interest that the word "scruples" appears only once in *Ulysses* (17.1891 [724:5]), where it is used in its literal sense of "minute quantities"].

The Linati schema adds Eurycleia, Odysseus's old nurse, to Persons and lists *La Speranza Armata* (The Armed Hope) as the Sense (Meaning) of the episode.

17.2–9 (666:3–11). from Beresford place they . . . before George's church diametrically – Bloom and Stephen walk northeast along Beresford Place behind the Custom House to the foot of Lower Gardiner Street, then north-northwest along Lower Gardiner Street, its extension, Middle Gardiner Street, and the further extension, Mountjoy Square West; they turn left (west-southwest) down Gardiner's Place and pass Nerney Court on their right; they could have taken this right, turned left on St. Anthony's Place and then right into Hardwicke Place; instead, they continue to Temple Street North, turn right, and walk west-northwest toward Hardwicke Place, an extension of Temple Street North that curves ("circus") around the front of St. George's Church and leads directly into Eccles Street. See 4.78n.

17.13 (666:17). glowlamps – See 2.72n.

17.14 (666:17). paraheliotropic – In botany: "of leaves that turn their edges toward brilliant incident light." Paraheliotropism is the inhibition of leaf abscission due to light; a common example is a tree's retention of the leaves close to a streetlight (suggested by Roland McHugh).

17.14–15 (666:18). exposed corporation emergency dustbuckets – Outdoor trash baskets to be provided by the Dublin Corporation. This is one of Bloom's "civic self-help" ideas; the baskets did not exist in 1904.

17.16–17 (666:20–21). the maleficent influence of the presabbath – That is, Friday, the day before the Jewish Sabbath. Jews consider it an unlucky day because it is traditionally supposed to be the day on which Adam and Eve fell and were expelled from the Garden of Eden. In Christian tradition this is compounded by the fact that Jesus was crucified on Friday.

17.31–36 (666:37–667:3). the anachronism involved in assigning . . . interred at Rossnaree – The anachronism is that King Cormac Mac Art, who reigned from c. 254 until 277 (according to modern historians) or until 266 (according to *The Annals of the Four Masters*), was, at least in legend, supposed to have been converted to Christianity; see 8.663–66n. However, St. Patrick is credited with having brought Christianity to Ireland when Pope Celestine I sent him on his mission to Ireland in 432 (or 433). In his *Confession* St. Patrick says, "My father was Colpornius, a deacon, son of Potitus, a priest." *The Annals of the Four Masters* gives St. Patrick's great-grandfather as "Deisse" (= Odyssus = Odysseus = Ulysses?). *Butler's "Lives of the Saints"* (ed. Herbert Thurston, S. J., and Donald Attwater [London, 1956]) says of St. Patrick's arrival in Ireland: "It happened that at this very time the King Leogaire [Lear, Leary] and the assembled princes were celebrating a [druid] religious festival in honour of the return of the sun to power and heat." It was Easter eve; on Easter Day, St. Patrick preached before the king, and though there is no assertion that Leary was converted, he is supposed to have allowed St. Patrick to carry his mission to the people of Ireland unhindered.

17.40–42 (667:8–10). a matutinal cloud . . . than a woman's hand – In I Kings 16 Elijah prophesied against Ahab and in 17:1 proclaimed "As the Lord God of Israel liveth . . . there shall not be dew nor rain these years, but according to my word." When Elijah decided to call off this drought, he "went up to the top of Carmel . . . and put his face between his knees, And said to his servant, Go up now, look toward the sea. . . . And it came to pass at the seventh time, that [the servant] said, Behold, there ariseth a little cloud out of the sea, like a man's hand, and [Elijah] said, Go up, say unto Ahab, Prepare thy chariot, and get thee down, that the rain stop thee not" (I Kings 18:42–44). See 1.248–49 (9:32–33) and 4.218 (61:7–8).

17.48 (667:17). Owen Goldberg – See 8.404n.

17.48 (667:17). Cecil Turnbull – See 15.3326–28n.

17.49–50 (667:18–20). Longwood Avenue and Leonard's corner . . . Synge street . . . Bloomfield avenue – Longwood Avenue and Bloomfield Avenue in south-central Dublin are parallel to and respectively one and two blocks east of Clanbrassil Street, where Bloom was living when he attended the Erasmus Smith High School. Synge Street (which was named before and not after J. M. Synge; see 9.38–40n) is 350 yards east of Bloomfield Avenue. Leonard's Corner was the intersection of the Clanbrassil streets (Upper and Lower) and South Circular Road; see 15.203n.

17.51 (667:20). Percy Apjohn – See 8.404n. In 1904 a Thomas Barnes Apjohn lived in Rutland House, Crumlin; see following note.

17.52–53 (667:21–22). between Gibraltar villa . . . barony of Uppercross – Crumlin was a parish and village three and a half miles southwest of the center of Dublin. There was a Bloomfield House in Crumlin Road and a Gibraltar Villa (occupied in 1904 by Daniel Moulang; see 11.86n) in Dolphin's Barn Road just around the corner.

17.57 (667:27–28). in Matthew Dillon's house in Roundtown – See 6.697n.

17.58 (667:28–29). *Julius (Juda) Mastiansky – See 4.205n. Juda ("praised") is a biblical variant of Judah or Judas, but used especially as the name of one of the Twelve Apostles to distinguish him from Judas Iscariot, the traitor: "Judas [Juda] saith unto him, not Iscariot, Lord, how is it that thou wilt manifest thyself unto us, and not unto the world?" (John 14:22).

17.82 (668:18). To enter or not to enter – After the rhythms of Hamlet's soliloquy, "To be or not to be" (III.i.60).

17.84 (668:20). A stratagem – As Odysseus has entered his manor in Ithaca by the stratagem of his disguise as a beggar down on his luck.

17.86–87 (668:23). five feet nine inches and a half – Bloom is five inches taller than the average Dubliner, if the latter was the five feet four and one-half inches of the average Irish recruit to the British army in 1901.

17.93–94 (668:31–32). Francis Froedman . . . Frederick street, north – So listed in *Thom's* 1904, p. 1496.

17.94–96 (668:33–35). the last feast of the Ascension . . . of the christian era – The Feast of the Ascension occurs forty days after Easter and celebrates Christ's ascension into heaven after the Resurrection. Since Easter Sunday was 3 April in 1904, Ascension Day or Holy Thursday was 12 May (coinciding with the Jewish festival of Sukkoth; see 3.367–69n). The year 1904 was "bissextile," a leap year.

17.96 (668:35–36). jewish era five . . . and sixty-four – The Jewish calendar marked 10 September 1904 as the beginning of the year 5665.

17.97 (668:36–37). mohammedan era . . . hundred and twenty-two – The Islamic year 1322 began on 18 March 1904.

17.97–99 (668:37–669:1). golden number 5 . . . Julian period 6617 – All these except "Roman indiction 2" bear on methods of determining the date of Easter Sunday—an exercise of considerable importance, since the date of that movable feast determines the liturgical calendar of the Christian year. Part of the complexity derives from an elaborate effort to avoid the coincidence of Easter and the Jewish Passover. Easter Sunday is the first Sunday after the paschal full moon, the full moon that happens on or next after 21 March. Basic to this determination is the relationship of the lunar year (354 days) to the solar year (365.25 days); this relationship can be calculated as a nineteen-year (metonic) cycle, since nineteen solar years are nearly equal to 235 lunations—that is, once every nineteen years the new moon will fall on the same calendar day. "Golden number 5" means that 1904 was the fifth year of the nineteen-year metonic cycle that began in 1899; "epact 13" means that on any given date the moon would be thirteen days older than it would have been on the same date in the first year of the cycle (1899). The "solar cycle" is a period of twenty-eight years, since once every twenty-eight years Sunday falls on the same day of the month—"solar cycle 9" means that a cycle began in 1895. "Dominical letters CB" are a code means of describing the occurrence of Sundays within the years of the solar cycle: "C" means that the first Sunday of 1904 was 3 January; "B" means that since 1904 was a leap year, Sundays after 29 February would be determined as though 2 January had been the first Sunday of the year. "The Roman indiction" was a Roman cycle of fifteen years established in A.D. 313 for the purposes of taxation and accepted as an important Christian cycle (the Pontifical Indiction) during the Middle Ages; 1904 was the second year in this cycle. The Julian period is a cycle of 7,980 (365.25-day) Julian years, since once every 7,980 years the twenty-eight-year solar cycle, the nineteen-year lunar cycle and the fifteen-year Pontifical or Roman Indiction coincide. What it all adds up to is that the paschal full moon occurred on 31 March 1904 and Easter Sunday on 3 April 1904.

17.99 (669:2). *MCMIV – 1904.

17.103 (669:6–7). leverage of the first kind – In classical mechanics, the simplest of levers, the fulcrum at one end of the bar, the force exerted at the other end.

17.105 (669:8–9). a lucifer match – A friction match, first manufactured in England under the trade name "Lucifer Matches"; by 1900 the trade name had become generic.

17.110 (669:17). CP – Candlepower.

17.119 (669:27). he helped to close and chain the door – As Telemachus helps Odysseus pen the suitors in the house when the killing begins in Book 22 of *The Odyssey*.

17.128 (669:38). Abram coal – Advertised in 1904 as the finest A-brand coal in Dublin.

17.129–30 (670:1–2). Messrs Flower and M'Donald of 14 D'Olier street – Listed in *Thom's* 1904 as "coal importers, salt manufacturers, coke, charcoal, and corn merchants" (p. 1475).

17.136–38 (670:9–11). Brother Michael . . . the county of Kildare – For this episode in Stephen's life, see *A Portrait* 1:B.

17.138–39 (670:12–13). Simon Dedalus . . . number thirteen Fitzgibbon street – See *A Portrait* 2:B. Fitzgibbon Street is off Mountjoy Square, not far east of Eccles Street. In 1904, no. 13 was valued at £25 (as against Bloom's house at £28) annual rent.

17.140–41 (670:14–15). Miss Kate Morkan . . . 15 Usher's Island – The Misses Morkan appear as Gabriel Conroy's aunts in "The Dead," *Dubliners*, which apparently takes place in early January 1904. Usher's Island is in central Dublin on the south bank of the Liffey.

17.142 (670:15 //). *62 Clanbrassil street – In south-central Dublin. It is not clear whether the Gouldings lived in Upper or Lower Clanbrassil Street, but the two no. 62's were valued at £15 and £12 annual rent.

17.143 (670:16–17). number twelve North Richmond street – The residence of the boy-narrator of "Araby," *Dubliners*. In 1904 no. 12 was valued at an annual rent of £19; so though it was just east of the house in Fitzgibbon Street in northeastern Dublin, it was a step down in the housing scale.

17.144 (670:17–18). the feast of Saint Francis-Xavier in 1898 – 3 December, to celebrate the Spanish Jesuit St. Francis Xavier (1506–52), famous for his missionary work in India and the Far East. In *A Portrait* 3:C, that Saturday marks Stephen's release from the agony of guilt and fear provoked by the hellfire-and-damnation sermons of the retreat at Belvedere College.

17.144–46 (670:18–19). the dean of studies . . . 16 Stephen's Green, north – See *A Portrait* 5:A. The address is curious, since it is not the address of University College, which was at 84A–87 St. Stephen's Green South; no. 16 north is the address of the palace of the Church of Ireland archbishop of Dublin and primate of Ireland—in 1904, the most Reverend Joseph Ferguson Peacocke, D.D.

17.146–47 (670:20). his father's house in Cabra – Valued at £20; see 15.4884n.

17.164–70 (671:2–10). From Roundwood reservoir . . . upper Leeson street – This essentially accurate account is derived in large part from *Thom's* 1904, p. 2102. The course of the Dublin Water Works aqueduct from Roundwood (or Vartry) Reservoir, twenty-two miles south of Dublin, to Stillorgan (reading from south to north): east to Callowhill, north through the Glen of the Downs and across (not through) the Dargle (see 7.1008–9n). The barony of Rathdown includes almost the entire route of the aqueduct. The 250-foot gradient is not from Stillorgan to the "city boundary" but from Stillorgan to the quays in central Dublin.

17.170–75 (671:10–16). though from prolonged summer . . . other than those of consumption – Fiction: the spring of 1904 was normal Irish weather—far from dry. The Waterworks Committee was a standing committee of the Dublin Municipal Council; if the order for water conservation had been necessary, the committee would have been advised by its engineer, Harty, and the order would have been issued not by Harty but by the committee's secretary, Charles Power.

17.176–77 (671:16–18). recourse being had . . . Royal canals as in 1893 – *Thom's* 1904, p. 2105, notes this "recourse" taken on 16 October 1893 as the result of an "unprecedented drought." The waters of the two canals were quite polluted, hardly fit for swimming, and in retrospect the "recourse" seems an extreme measure.

17.177–82 (671:18–25). South Dublin Guardians . . . taxpayers, solvent, sound – In 1904 the municipal council's Waterworks Committee did bring an action through the council's law agent, Ignatius J. Rice, solicitor. The details as outlined here are derived from Rice's letter, which was published in the *Irish Independent*, 15 June 1904. The South Dublin Poor Law Union was an administrative grouping of Poor Law Guardians from Dublin City and County south of the Liffey. It levied a separate "poor rate" (tax) and had responsibility for the care and sustenance of the poor and indigent in its area.

17.183 (671:26–27). Bloom, waterlover, drawer of water, watercarrier – These phrases suggest that Bloom may be an Aquarius, as Stephen is (i.e., born under that sign of the zodiac, 20 January–19 February). Aquarius is the sign and house of altruism; traditionally, Aquarians are those who believe in and seek the welfare of others. But Bloom may also be a Taurus; see 16.608n and 14.1108–9n. In Deuteronomy, Moses exhorts all the children of Israel from the highest to the lowest, from "you captains of your tribes" to "the drawer of thy water," to obedience (29:10–11).

17.186 (671:29–30). its vastness in the ocean of Mercator's projection – The Flemish geographer and mathematician, Gerardus Mercator (Gerhard Kremer, 1512–94), is credited with deriving this two-dimensional projection from the three-dimensional globe. Since the lines of longitude and latitude meet at right angles in this projection, the polar regions (where the longitudinal lines on the globe converge) are amplified and the oceans appear far more vast than they actually are.

17.186–88 (671:30–31). its unplumbed profundity . . . exceeding 8000 fathoms – The Sundam or Sunda Trench off Sumatra was unsounded in 1904, but its depth turns out to be 3,158 fathoms (18,948 feet). In 1904 the greatest known depth was off Guam, 5,269 fathoms (31,614 feet). As of 1969 the greatest known depth was in the Mariana Trench in the Pacific, 6,033 fathoms (36,198 feet). In the late nineteenth century, oceanographers knew that mid-nineteenth-century soundings (which were supposed to have reached over 7,000 fathoms) were erroneous and that no such depths existed in the ocean: those earlier soundings had been made with rope and were effectively disproved by soundings made with wire after 1872. Nor were these facts the exclusive concern of oceanographers—they were common knowledge after the well-publicized oceanographic expedition of the British ship *Challenger*, 1873–76.

17.193 (671:37–38). its preponderance of 3 to 1 over the dry land of the globe – Best estimate as of 1900 was 72 percent.

17.195–96 (671:40–41). the multisecular stability of its primeval basin – *Multisecular:* "enduring over many centuries or ages." In 1900 the assumption that the pelagic deposits in intermediate depths were an ooze made up of dead microorganisms from the surface was common knowledge.

17.196 (671:41). its luteofulvous bed – "Luteofulvous" means reddish yellow. In 1900, thanks to the *Challenger*'s and other oceanographic studies, scientists assumed that the depths of the oceans had no pelagic ooze (see preceding note) but were shallow beds of reddish-yellow clay.

17.199 (672:3//). *homothetic – In mathematics: "similar and similarly placed"; as any two parallel plane sections of a cone or pyramid.

17.209–11 (672:15–16). *revealed by rhabdomatic or hygrometric instruments and exemplified by the well by the hole in the wall at Ashtown gate – See 5.296–97n.

17.213 (672:19–20). its buoyancy in the waters of the Dead Sea – The concentration of salts in the Dead Sea is so great that the specific gravity of its waters in 1906 was 1.16 (water = 1). Thus, a human body, which floats in water, more than floats in the Dead Sea.

17.217 (672:24–25). its strength in rigid hydrants – That is, as opposed to flexible hoses.

17.219 (672:27). minches – Channels between islands, such as the Little Minch between the Isles of Skye and Lewis in the Outer Hebrides off Scotland.

17.224–25 (672:33–34). its submarine fauna and flora (anacoustic, photophobe) – *Anacoustic:* "having no sense of hearing"; *photophobe:* "having an aversion to light." In 1900 scientists assumed (as in 1985 they do not) that the depths of the sea were utterly silent and that deep-sea creatures made and heard no sounds.

17.228 (672:37–38). stagnant pools in the waning moon – The waning moon is traditionally regarded as a sign of disintegration and decline on earth.

17.231 (672:42). Barrington's – John Barrington & Sons, Ltd., merchants and manufacturers, 201–202 Great Britain (now Parnell) Street.

17.238–39 (673:7–8). (his last bath having taken place in the month of October of the preceding year) – Another notable nonbathing poet was Dante Gabriel Rossetti; see 14.1573n.

17.249–51 (673:21–24). the respective percentage of protein . . . the latter in the firstnamed – Bacon, approximately 7,295 calories (uncooked) and nine grams of protein per pound; salt ling (cod), approximately 1,105 calories and 259 grams protein per pound; butter, 3,200 calories per pound, no protein.

17.263 (673:38–674:1). omnipresent luminiferous diathermanous ether – Late-nineteenth-century scientists regarded it as "proved" that light and thermal radiation were transmitted by wave motion; therefore, a medium through which the waves could pass was a theoretical necessity, a necessity met by postulating the universal presence of "luminiferous ether," a weightless substance like an elastic jelly that filled all the "empty" spaces of the universe and that transmitted light and other forms of radiant energy without impeding their passage. The "ether" hypothesis was by 1910 riddled with contradictions and ambiguities, but it remained in force until the impact of Einstein and the "new physics" in the 1920s and 1930s. "Diathermanous" means admitting the passage of heat. See 14.1106n.

17.270–71 (674:8–10). an expenditure of thermal units . . . to 212° Fahrenheit – A British thermal unit (Btu) is the amount of heat necessary to raise the temperature of one pound of water one degree Fahrenheit (under laboratory conditions at sea level); thus, 72° should read at least 162°, since Bloom cannot be heating much less than a pound (a pint) of water.

17.300 (675:7). Crown Derby – See 4.283–84n.

17.301 (657:8). shammy – Chamois.

17.304 (675:12). Plumtree's potted meat – See 5.144–47n.

17.306 (675:14–15). William Gilbey and Co's white invalid port – W. A. Gilbey, Ltd., wine growers and spirit merchants, distillers and importers, 46 and 71 Sackville (now O'Connell) Street Upper in Dublin.

17.307 (675:16). Epps's soluble cocoa – See 16.1621n.

17.308 (675:16–17). Anne Lynch's choice tea – Anne Lynch & Co., Ltd., at 69 George's Street South and several other addresses in Dublin.

17.311 (675:21). Irish Model Dairy's – From the Model Farm Dairy, operated by the Irish Department for Agriculture and Technical Instruction in Glasnevin.

17.312 (675:22). naggin – See 4.224n.

17.320 (675:32–33). two lacerated scarlet betting tickets – As Boylan has "plunged" (and lost) on Sceptre; see 5.532n, 16.1276–89n, and 18.1105n.

17.322 (675:34). corrugated his brow – Odysseus's brow is repeatedly "corrugated" as he witnesses the state of affairs in his besieged home; see headnote to this episode, p. 566.

17.329 (676:3). Bernard Kiernan's – See p. 314.

17.330 (676:4). David Byrne's – See 8.697n.

17.331 (676:5). Graham Lemon's – See 8.3–4n.

17.332–33 (676:7–8). Elijah, restorer of the church of Zion – See 8.13nn.

17.333–34 (676:8–9). F. W. Sweny and Co (Limited) – See 5.463n.

17.338–39 (676:14–15). Turkish and Warm Baths, 11 Leinster street – See 5.549n.

17.339–41 (676:15–17). with the light of inspiration . . . language of prediction – In the attitude of Moses when he came down from Mount Sinai with the tables of the Law, the secret of the Jews, and the prediction of their destiny; see 7.867–69n.

17.353 (676:30). Light to the gentiles – Isaiah predicts that the Messiah will be given "for a light to the Gentiles" (Isaiah 49:6); the prophecy is echoed by St. Paul (Romans 15:9–16).

17.354 (676:31). a collation – A light meal taken on fast days, appropriate since Stephen (as a nominal Catholic in Bloom's eyes) would have been expected to fast on Fridays.

17.361 (677:1). his symposiarchal right – His right as the master, director, or president of a symposium.

17.369 (677:10). jocoserious – Late in his career, Browning characterized himself as "jocoserious" and published a volume of poems called *Jocoseria* (London, 1883). The word was apparently coined by the minor English poet-critic Matthew Green in *Spleen* (1737): "Drink a jocoserious cup / With souls who took their freedom up" (lines 176–77).

17.369–70 (677:11). Epps's massproduct, the creature cocoa – "Massproduct" is an obvious pun suggesting the mass in which Bloom is functioning as priest, Stephen as communicant. "Creature" in context means food or drink that promotes human comfort, and, as W. Y. Tyndall points out (*A Reader's Guide to James Joyce* [New York, 1959], p. 222), cocoa is derived from the tree *Theobroma cacao*, "god-food cacao." See 16.1621n.

17.385–87 (667:28–30). had applied to the works of William Shakespeare . . . difficult problems – That is, Bloom has practiced *sortes Shakespearianae;* see 10.607n.

17.394–95 (678:2). the *Shamrock*, a weekly newspaper – An illustrated magazine, published weekly and monthly by the Irish National Printing and Publishing Company, 32 Abbey Street Lower in Dublin (1866ff.).

17.410 (678:19). kinetic poet – Stephen, in *A Portrait* 5:A, says: "The feelings excited by improper art are kinetic, desire or loathing. Desire urges us to possess, to go to something; loathing urges us to abandon, to go from something. These are kinetic emotions. The arts which excite them, pornographical or didactic, are therefore improper arts. The esthetic emotion (I use the general term) is therefore static. The mind is arrested and raised above desire and loathing."

17.417–18 (678:27). music by R. G. Johnston – Unknown.

17.419 (678:28–29). *If Brian Boru . . . old Dublin now* – For Brian Boru, see 6.453n. Bloom's proposed song sounds as though it were modeled on an extant song, but if it is, the original remains unknown.

17.421–23 (678:31–33). the sixth scene, the valley . . . *Sinbad the Sailor* – The first edition of the pantomime *Sinbad* made its Dublin debut 26 December 1892; the second, 30 January 1893. In both editions the sixth scene was advertised as "Grand Ballet of Diamonds and Serpentine Dance." See Adams, pp. 76–82.

17.423–27 (678:33–38). *produced by R Shelton . . . Bouverist, principal girl* – These details are historically accurate, with two exceptions; but they are also highly selective when one considers the wealth of detail at Joyce's disposal (see Adams, pp. 78–79). The exceptions: the pantomime was written by Greenleaf Withers, not by the American poet John Greenleaf Whittier (1807–92), whose didactic and sentimental rural verse is at a considerable remove from pantomimic improvisation; "Nelly Bouverist" intertwines two "principal girls," Kate Neverist and Nellie Bouverie.

17.429 (678:40). diamond jubilee of Queen Victoria – Was celebrated in 1897 to commemorate the sixtieth year of her reign. The celebration continued throughout the year, but the key date was 22 June 1897.

17.430 (679:1–2). opening of the new municipal fishmarket – At 4–33 St. Michan's Street, opened on 11 May 1897.

17.431–32 (679:2–5). opposition from extreme circles . . . duke and duchess of York – There were the usual patriotic mutterings and threats at the prospect of the visit of the duke and duchess of York to Dublin, 18–29 August 1897. *Thom's* 1904, p. 2105, asserts that Their Royal Highnesses were accorded "an enthusiastic welcome."

17.435 (679:7–8). *the Grand Lyric Hall on Burgh quay – On the south bank of the Liffey in east-central Dublin (formerly the Conciliation Hall), opened 26 November 1897.

17.435–36 (679:8–9). the Theatre Royal in Hawkins street – Opened 13 December 1897 (on the site of the old Royal); see 11.624n.

17.442 (679:16). *Everybody's Book of Jokes* –

Apparently a coinage or a generalization of a common sort of book title.

17.444 (679:18). the new lord mayor, Daniel Tallon – Lord mayor of Dublin 1898 and 1899 (elected in the fall of 1897). He owned and managed a pub on the corner of St. Stephen's Street and Great George Street South in south-central Dublin.

17.444–45 (679:19). the new high sheriff, Thomas Pile – Pile was high sheriff of Dublin in 1898; he became Sir Thomas Pile in 1900 and was lord mayor in 1900.

17.445 (679:19–20). the new solicitorgeneral, Dunbar Plunket Barton – Was solicitor general for Ireland from 1 January 1898 until 1900; see 9.519–20n.

17.455–56 (679:33). the maximum postdiluvian age of 70 – A reference to the traditional fundamentalist belief that before Noah's flood the average life span was hundreds of years, but that God in response to man's sinfulness imposed brevity as a continuing punishment after the flood. The scriptural basis for this belief is the contrast between the great ages of antediluvian figures such as Methuselah, 969 years (Genesis 5:27), and "The days of our years are three-score and ten" (Psalms 90:10; "A Prayer of Moses the man of God").

17.456–57 (679:33–34). Bloom, being 1190 years alive having been born in the year 714 – A miscalculation: if Bloom were 1190 years old in 1952, he would have been born in 762, not 714; what has happened is that Bloom's age (1190) has been subtracted from A.D. 1904 instead of A.D. 1952.

17.457–58 (679:35–36). the maximum antediluvian age, that of Methuselah, 969 years – See 17.455–56n.

17.458–61 (679:36–39). while if Stephen would . . . the year 81,396 B.C. – Another miscalculation: the proposition is that the ratio between their ages should remain seventeen to one, as it was in 1883; $17 \times 1190 = 20,230$ (Bloom's age when Stephen's age is 1190), and thus Bloom would have to have been born in 17,158 B.C. What has happened is that 70 has been substituted for 17, since $70 \times 1190 = 83,300$; and instead of subtracting the 83,300 from A.D. 3072 (when Stephen would be 1190 years old), it has been subtracted from 1904 to achieve the figure 81,396 B.C.

17.467–68 (680:6–7). Matthew Dillon's house . . . Kimmage road, Roundtown – The address did exist and was occupied in 1904 by an A. M'Dermott, Esq. By 1904 Roundtown had been renamed Terenure.

17.470 (680:10). Breslin's hotel – In Bray, thirteen miles southeast of central Dublin; by 1904 the name had been changed to the Station Hotel.

17.479–80 (680:20–22). *Mrs Riordan (Dante), a widow . . . 29 December 1891 – The memorable quarrel about Parnell that prompted Mrs. Riordan's removal from the Dedalus household is the dramatic burden of that family's Christmas dinner in *A Portrait* 1:C.

17.481–82 (680:23–24). the City Arms Hotel . . . 54 Prussia street – See 2.416–17n.

17.485–86 (680:27–29). Joseph Cuffe . . . the North Circular Road – See 6.392n.

17.487 (680:30). corporal work of mercy – The seven corporal works of mercy: (1) to bury the dead; (2) to clothe the naked; (3) to feed the hungry; (4) to give drink to the thirsty; (5) to harbor the houseless; (6) to visit those in prison; (7) to administer to the sick. The seven corporal works are paralleled by the seven spiritual works of mercy: (1) to admonish sinners; (2) to bear wrongs patiently; (3) to comfort the afflicted; (4) to counsel the doubtful; (5) to forgive offenses; (6) to instruct the ignorant; (7) to pray for the living and the dead.

17.490–91 (680:35–36). the corner of the North . . . place of business – See 14.572n.

17.495–96 (681:2). from the city to the Phoenix Park – North Circular Road looped around the northern limits of the inner city of Dublin in 1904 and ended at the eastern border of Phoenix Park.

17.506 (681:15). colza oil – Rapeseed oil, used for illumination and lubrication during the nineteenth century.

17.506–7 (681:16). the statue of the Immaculate Conception – Representing the Virgin Mary as she is told the news of her impending motherhood by her mother, St. Anne. It was not unusual for devout Catholics to keep a votive lamp burning before such statues (as Mrs. Riordan has done).

17.507–8 (681:16–18). her green and maroon . . . for Michael Davitt, her tissue papers – Mrs. Riordan's brushes turn up in *A Portrait* 1:A—the green for Parnell, the maroon for Michael Davitt (see 15.4684n); and she gave the child Stephen "a cachou every time he brought her a piece of tissue paper."

17.513–14 (681:23–24). *Eugene Sandow's *Physical Strength and How to Obtain It – See 4.234n.

17.518 (681:28–29). repristination – To "repristinate" is rare for to revive, to restore to an original condition.

17.520–23 (681:31–34). ringweight lifting . . . the full circle gyration . . . half lever movement on the parallel bars – Gymnastic exercises and equipment were widely advertised (and regarded) as essential to the well-organized curriculum in late-nineteenth-century schools. *Ringweight lifting:* lifting weights in competition. *Full circle gyration:* an exercise on the horizontal bar; *Half lever:* arms straight down at the sides, legs extended in front at right angles to the body.

17.534/538 (682:9/13–14). transubstantial heir/ consubstantial heir – Literally, Bloom's father is dead and Stephen's is living; figuratively, this recalls Stephen's preoccupation with the theological relation between the Father and the Son (cf. 1.656n, 1.656–57n, 1.657n, and 1.658n) and Stephen's treatise on Shakespeare as ghostfather to Hamlet as son in Scylla and Charybdis.

17.537 (682:12). Karoly – The Hungarian form (Károly) of Carl, Karl, Charles; a common name, but less common than in English (frequently, and somewhat erroneously, assumed to be a Hungarian Jewish name).

17.537 (682:13). (born Hegarty) – Bloom's maternal grandmother's maiden name was a fairly common Irish Catholic name; *Thom's* 1904, p. 1895, lists nine Hegartys under "Nobility, Gentry, Merchants and Traders" in Dublin.

17.539 (682:15). Christina Goulding (born Grier) – Stephen's maternal grandmother's maiden name is neither as common nor as Irish as Hegarty; *Thom's* 1904 lists one Grier, p. 1886.

17.540–41 (682:17). cleric or layman? – "Q. Can every body confer the Sacrament of Baptism? A. Yes, in time of need only, and when a priest cannot be had. . . . It is necessary that one should have the intention of conferring it in earnest, and that he should sprinkle natural water on the head (if possible) of the person to be baptized, pronouncing these words: 'I baptize thee in the name of the Father, and of the Son, and of the Holy Ghost. Amen'" (Rev. Andrew Donlevy, *The Catechism, or Christian Doctrine . . . Published for the Royal Catholic College of St. Patrick, Maynooth* [Dublin, 1848], pp. 211–13).

17.542–43 (682:18–20). the reverend Mr Gilmer Johnston . . . Nicholas Without, Coombe – Church of Ireland, St. Nicholas Without and St. Luke's was in the Coombe, but no record of the Reverend Johnston's incumbency has been discovered.

17.543–45 (682:20–21). James O'Connor, Philip Gilligan and James Fitzpatrick . . . village of Swords – Swords is a village eight miles north of Dublin. It takes its name from the Irish *Sórd Colaim Chille*, a pure well (*sórd*) said to have been blessed by St. Columcille; see 12.1699n. For Philip Gilligan, see 8.156–57n and 17.1252–53 (704:35). James O'Connor? James Fitzpatrick? It is ironic that baptism is the one sacrament that can, in an emergency, be performed by a layman.

17.545–46 (682:22–23). the reverend Charles Malone . . . Patrons, Rathgar – The Roman Catholic Church of the Three Patrons was in Rathgar Road, three miles south of the center of Dublin; *Thom's* 1904 lists the Reverend Charles Malone as one of the three curates in charge.

17.550 (682:28). a dame's school and the high school – See 5.237n and 8.187n.

17.552/53–54 (682:31/32). the intermediate/ the royal university – Not institutions of learning but rather examining and degree-granting institutions; see 7.503n and 13.132–33n.

17.566 (683:8–9). the aeronautic parachute – The first record of a descent from heights by parachute (or umbrella) is in Simon de Loubere's *History of Siam* (Paris, 1691); on 26 December 1783, Sebastian Lenormont made a descent with a semirigid 260-inch umbrella; and Jacques Garnerini is credited with the first non-rigid parachute descent, from a balloon in 1797.

17.566 (683:9). the reflecting telescope – Invented by the Scottish mathematician James Gregory (1638–75) in 1661 and adapted (from Gregory's description *Optica Promota*) by Sir Isaac Newton (1642–1727) in 1666.

17.566–67 (683:9). the spiral corkscrew – Corks were not used for stopping bottles until the seventeenth century, and though it is hardly proof positive, the first *patented* corkscrew is dated 1860.

17.567 (683:9–10). the safety pin – Invented "in three hours" on 10 April 1849 by the American Walter Hunt, who received $100 for the patent rights.

17.567 (683:10). the mineral water siphon – Patented in 1825 by the English inventor Charles Plinth as the "Regency portable fountain," and refined into what is essentially the modern siphon by the French inventor Antoine Perpigna in 1837.

17.567–68 (683:10–11). the canal lock with winch and sluice – The development of the canal lock with two gates is a matter of considerable controversy; it seems to have been one of those late-medieval, early-Renaissance "inventions" that happened in a variety of places at about the same time. Some historians suggest that locks were developed by the Dutch in the fourteenth century; others suggest the brothers Domenico of Viterbo in 1481. At any rate, locks were a universal feature of European canal engineering by 1500.

17.568 (683:11). the suction pump – The simple displacement or suction-lift pump was apparently known as early as the first century A.D. in Alexandria and by the late fourth century in various places in western Europe.

17.570 (683:13). kindergarten – The first kindergarten was established in 1840 by the German educator Friedrich Fröbel (1782–1852). His revolutionary ideas about child behavior and education spread rapidly through Western Europe and, after 1867, to the United States. By 1900 kindergartens were national institutions in many countries, but they remained local or philanthropic in England and Ireland; see 5.237n.

17.572–73 (683:16–17). the twelve constellations . . . Aries to Pisces – The progression of the twelve houses of the zodiac traditionally begins with the vernal equinox, so Aries (21 March–19 April) is first and Pisces (19 February–21 March) is last.

17.577/78 (683:21/22–23). *Ephraim Marks/1d bazaar at 42 George's street, South – A penny bazaar as listed in *Thom's* 1904, p. 1502.

17.577/79–80 (683:22/23–24). *Charles A. James/6½d shop . . . 30 Henry street – Charles Augustus James, hardware and fancy (notions) dealer, and Washington Hall (the "waxworks exhibition"); see 16.851n.

17.582 (683:27). monoideal – Apparently Joyce's coinage from the psychological term *monoideism* (1860), a state of prolonged fixation on one idea as a result of monomania or of artificial causes such as hypnotism. See 10.1068n.

17.586 (683:32). K. 11. Kino's 11/– Trousers – See 15.1658n and 8.90–92n.

17.587 (683:33). House of Keys. Alexander J. Keyes – See 7.141n and 7.25n.

17.590 (683:36). non-compo boots – Boots made out of real leather rather than composition materials.

17.591 (683:37–38). Barclay and Cook, 18 Talbot street – In 1904, 18 Talbot Street was occupied by S. Robinson, confectioner, and Dunlops, dyers and cleaners. An advertisement in the *Evening Telegraph* for 17 June 1904 locates Barclay and Cook, bootdealers, at 104 Talbot Street (Clive Hart and Leo Knuth, *A Topographical Guide to James Joyce's "Ulysses"* [Colchester, England, 1975], p. 15).

17.592 (683:39). Bacilikil (Insect Powder) – Unknown.

17.593 (684:1). Veribest (Boot Blacking) – Unknown.

17.594–95 (684:2–3). Uwantit (Combined pocket twoblade penknife with corkscrew, nailfile and pipecleaner) – Unknown.

17.597 (684:5). Plumtree's Potted Meat – See 5.144–47n.

17.601–2 (684:9–10). Councillor Joseph P. Nannetti . . . 19 Hardwicke street – *Thom's* 1904 lists Nannetti's residence as 18–19 Hardwicke Street, Rotunda Ward, in northeastern Dublin.

17.612–17 (684:22–28). Solitary hotel in mountain pass. . . . He reads. Solitary – This scene has a Hauptmannesque flavor, but it seems to remain more flavor than direct allusion; after Gerhart Hauptmann, German dramatist, novelist, and poet (1862–1946). Although frequently referred to as a "naturalist," his works are characterized by a vacillating combination of lyric romanticism and a tragic or pathetic realism, particularly noticeable in his treatment of women.

17.622 (684:33). *The Queen's Hotel, Ennis, county Clare – See 6.529–30n.

17.624 (684:36). aconite – A poison, but in small doses a cardiac respiratory sedative.

17.627 (685:1–2). the medical hall of Francis Dennehy, 17 Church street, Ennis – There is no record of an apothecary (or "medical hall") at 17 Church Street in Ennis.

17.631–32 (685:7–8). the general drapery store of James Cullen, 4 Main street, Ennis – Mr. Cullen's nonexistent store is located on a street that has never existed in Ennis.

17.640–41 (685:17–18). *A Pisgah Sight . . . of the Plums* – See 7.1057n and 7.1057–58n.

17.644 (685:21). *My Favorite Hero* – The title of an essay about Ulysses that Joyce wrote while he was at Belvedere; see Ellmann, p. 46.

17.644 (685:21–22). *Procrastination is the Thief of Time* – Line 390 in "Night I" of Edward Young's (1683–1765) *Night Thoughts* (1742); in context (lines 390–93): "Procrastination is the thief of time: / Year after year it steals, till all are fled, / And to the mercies of a moment leaves / The vast concerns of an eternal scene."

17.650 (685:28–29). Philip Beaufoy – See 4.502–3n.

17.650 (685:29). Doctor Dick – The pseudonym of a Dublin writer who provided and updated local and topical verses for pantomimes in the early years of the twentieth century.

17.650 (685:29). Heblon's *Studies in Blue* – Heblon is the pseudonym of the Dublin solicitor Joseph K. O'Connor (b. 1878). His *Studies in Blue* (Dublin, 1903) probes the underside of life in Dublin's slums from a police-court perspective.

17.654–56 (685:34–36). the summer solstice . . . sunset 8.29 p.m. – Summer solstice was at 9:00 P.M., Tuesday, 21 June 1904. The times of sunrise and sunset are correct as of *Thom's* 1904, p. 14. For St. Aloysius Gonzaga, whose feast day it was, see 12.1704n.

17.661 (686:2). halma – A game played on a checkerboard of 256 squares, by two with nineteen men apiece or four with thirteen apiece.

17.661 (686:2). *spilikins – Pickup sticks.

17.661 (686:3). nap – A card game in which each player receives five cards and calls the number of tricks he expects to win; if he wins all five, he has "made his nap."

17.662 (686:3). spoil five – A round game of cards that is "spoiled" if no player wins three of the possible five tricks.

17.662 (686:3). twenty-five – A variant of spoil five in which the winning score is twenty-five.

17.662 (686:3–4). beggar my neighbour – A game of cards in which the object is to gain all the opponent's cards.

17.663–64 (686:5). the policeaided clothing society – The Police Aided Children's Clothing Society, 188 Great Brunswick (now Pearse) Street, Dublin.

17.681 (686:25). balance of power – English diplomacy traditionally concentrated on balancing the Continental powers against one another (while sustaining friendly relations with "both sides") in the attempt to prevent any single Continental power from dominating all of Europe.

17.685 (686:29). nutgall – A dyestuff made from galls on the dyer's oak.

17.686 (686:31). metempsychosis – See 4.339n.

17.686–87 (686:32–33). *alias (a mendacious person mentioned in sacred scripture) – "Alias" echoes *Ananias*, a follower of the Apostles in Acts 5:1–11, who lies to Peter and drops dead as a consequence; hence, "Ananias" is colloquial for a liar.

17.690–91 (686:37–38). The false apparent parallelism . . . true by construction – The proof depends on a geometric construction that demonstrates that the two perpendicular arms of a balance are part of an enormous triangle, the apex of which is the center of the earth.

17.710–11 (687:20–21). postexilic . . . Moses of Egypt – In Jewish tradition the postexilic period begins after the Babylonian captivity (after 586 B.C.), and the semilegendary figure of Moses, the great lawgiver of the Old Testament, is preexilic. Clearly the term *postexilic* here implies both after Moses left Egypt and after the great dispersion of the Jews by the Romans in A.D. 70.

17.711–12 (687:21–22). Moses Maimonides, author of the *More Nebukim* – For Maimonides, see 2.158n; his *More Nebukim* (Hebrew: "Guide of the Perplexed") is a rational and philosophical work on biblical exegesis finished c. 1190. It is regarded as Maimonides' most important work, and, ironically enough, its attempt to reconcile Aristotelian reason and Hebraic revelation led to a long and bitter conflict between the orthodox and the liberal in Judaism.

17.712 (687:23). Moses Mendelssohn – See 12.1804n.

17.713–14 (687:23–25). from Moses . . . to Moses . . . there arose none like Moses – Proverbial Jewish encomium for Moses Maimonides (see 2.158n), after Deuteronomy 34:10: "And there arose not a prophet since in Israel like unto Moses, whom the Lord knew face to face" (Jacob Haberman, *JJQ* 19, no. 2 [1982]: 199).

17.716–18 (687:27–30). Aristotle . . . had been a pupil of a rabbinical philosopher – A Jewish legend (about both Aristotle and Plato) with practically no basis in fact, but it has flourished, particularly as a result of the impressively Aristotelian work of Moses Maimonides.

17.722 (687:33). Felix Bartholdy Mendelssohn – See 12.1804n.

17.722 (687:33). Baruch Spinoza – See 11.1058n and 12.1804n.

17.723 (687:34). Mendoza (pugilist) – Daniel Mendoza (1763–1836), "the Star of Israel," an English Jew who was champion of England (1792–95) and, therefore, with appropriate English modesty, "champion of the world."

17.723 (687:34). Ferdinand Lassalle – (1825–64), a German Jewish lawyer, Marxist socialist, and political reformer who began working in 1862 to form a worker's party; he was thus the virtual founder of the German Social Democratic party. He was killed in a duel over a love affair. His career was fictionalized by George Meredith in *The Tragic Comedians* (1880).

17.727 (688:3–4). *suil, suil, suil . . . suil go cuin* – Irish: "walk, walk, walk my dear, walk safely and walk calmly"; the first two lines of the Irish chorus of a ballad, "Shule Aroon." The four-line verses of the ballad are composed of three lines of English and one of Irish; the burden is a maiden's lament: "But now my love has gone to France, / To try his fortune to advance" (i.e., the loved one has gone to join the Irish Brigade to fight for the French).

17.729 (688:6). **kifeloch harimon . . . l'zamatejch* – Hebrew: "Thy temples are like a piece of pomegranate within thy locks" (Song of Solomon 4:3).

17.734 (688:11). **entituled** – Or intituled: "to entitle as a legislative act"; archaic: "to furnish with a name, title, or epithet [and the privileges or rights that it conveys]."

17.734 (688:11). *Sweets of Sin* – See 10.606n.

17.736–37 (688:14–15). the Irish characters for gee, eh, dee, em, simple and modified – Simple ꞅ, e, ꝺ, m; modified ꞅ́, é, ꝺ̇, ṁ—corresponding to the English letters *g, e, d, m* and compounds *gh, e, dh, mh*. In the Irish alphabet *g* is the seventh letter, *e* the fifth, *d* the fourth, and *m* the eleventh.

17.738–40 (688:15–18). *the Hebrew characters ghimel, aleph, daleth and (in the absence of mem) . . . qoph . . . 3, 1, 4, and 100 – Gimel, ג (g); aleph, א ('); daleth, ד (d); mem, מ (m); qoph, ק (q)—in order, the third, first, fourth, thirteenth, and nineteenth letters of the alphabet with numerical values 3, 1, 40, and 100.

17.741–42 (688:20). the extinct and the revived – That is, biblical Hebrew is "extinct" because in the postexilic period after the Babylonian captivity it gradually gave way to Aramaic for daily use, though it was retained as a learned language. Modern Hebrew, the language of the Jews of the Christian era, has been modified by Greek, Aramaic, and Latin influences; thus, biblical Hebrew, while still a language of scholarly study, is not a "living language." The Society for the Preservation of the Irish Language, founded in Dublin in 1877,

had made considerable progress in its efforts to revive the use of the Irish language by 1904, even though everyday use of the language had virtually disappeared in the course of the nineteenth century, except in the west of Ireland.

17.747–48 (688:26). servile letters – Inserted letters that do not belong to the original roots of words.

17.748–51 (688:27–30). both having been taught . . . progenitors of Ireland – This elaborate legend derives from the Reverend Geoffrey Keating (c. 1570–c. 1644), an Irish historian whose *Foras Feasa* (History of Ireland) (c. 1629) is an impressive collection of Irish legend-history, from the first arrivals (the three daughters of Cain; see 12.375n) to the Anglo-Norman invasion. Keating traces the Milesians Heber and Heremon (see 12.1308–10n) to Fenius Farsaigh (the son of Baoth, son of Magog, son of Japheth, son of Noah), and Fenius, the king of Scythia, is styled the ancestor of the Phoenicians and of the Milesians, who occupied Spain and then Ireland. In Book 1, section 15, Keating asserts that Fenius founded a school of languages on the plain of Shinar exactly 242 years after Noah's flood and 60 years after the "confusion of tongues" consequent on Nimrod's construction of the Tower of Babel (Genesis 11:1–9). Fenius sent scholars ("disciples") to learn each of the seventy-two languages of the confusion and based his school among the people on the plain of Shinar who still spoke the one ur-language, Hebrew. Thus, Fenius Farsaigh becomes the legendary ancestral link between Israel and the Milesians—between the Hebrew language and Irish.

17.752 (688:31–32). toponomastic – Coined from *toponymy,* the study of place names.

17.753 (688:33). culdees – See 12.194–95n.

17.753 (688:33). Torah – Literally, Genesis, Exodus, Leviticus, Numbers, and Deuteronomy, the first five books of the Old Testament, also called the Pentateuch, and traditionally ascribed to Moses. Figuratively, the Torah includes not only the five books of the Law of Moses, but also the so-called Oral Law and its ramifications in Talmudic law and commentaries.

17.754 (688:33–34). Talmud (Mischna and Ghemara) – The body of Jewish civil and ceremonial law and tradition. The Mishna of the Talmud sets forth the binding precepts of the elders as developed from the Pentateuch; and the Gemara comprises elaborate commentary on the Mishna. Two of these compilations exist: the Palestinian Talmud (fourth century) and the larger Babylonian Talmud (fifth century): both contain the same Mishna, but the Gemaras differ.

17.754 (688:34). Massor – The Masora or Masoretic text, developed between the sixth and the ninth centuries, is a system of vocalization and accentuation of biblical Hebrew (see 17.741–42n) together with a body of traditional information about the text of the Hebrew Bible.

17.754–55 (688:34). Book of the Dun Cow – Irish: *Leabhar na h-Uidhre;* the oldest (i.e., the earliest transcription) of miscellaneous Irish literature. It was compiled at the monastery of Clonmacnois by Mailmuri MacKelleher (d. 1106). Only a fragment (134 folio pages) remains, but that fragment contains sixty-five pieces: romantic tales in prose, an elegy on St. Columcille, a copy of the Voyage of Maelduin, etc.

17.755 (688:34–35). Book of Ballymote – See 12.1439–40n.

17.755 (688:35). Garland of Howth – Eighth or ninth century, an eighty-six-folio-page illuminated Latin manuscript now in Trinity College Library, Dublin. Splendidly ornamented and regarded as little inferior to the *Book of Kells*, it was found on Ireland's Eye, an island just north of Howth. It contains the four Gospels in Latin, partly in a pre-Jerome (pre-Vulgate) version.

17.755 (688:35). Book of Kells – c. eighth century. The most famous of Irish illuminated manuscripts, it contains the four Gospels in Latin and is the prize possession of Trinity College Library, Dublin.

17.755 (688:35). their dispersal – The Jews have experienced a sequence of great dispersions, including the Babylonian captivity (597 B.C., deportation of king and court; 586, second and larger deportation after the fall of Jerusalem; end of captivity, 538); the expulsion of Jews from Israel by the Romans under Emperor Vespasian (A.D. 70ff.); their expulsion from Spain (1492; see 16.1121–22n); and, under severe anti-Semitic pressure, the mass exodus of Jews from eastern Europe in the closing decades of the nineteenth century. The dispersions of the Irish have been endemic, beginning with the

"Flight of the Earls" in 1607; continuing when, under Sir Patrick Sarsfield (see 12.178–79n), almost the entire Irish army went into exile on the Continent after the Treaty of Limerick in 1691; and climaxing during and after the Great Irish Famine of the 1840s (see 2.269n).

17.756–57 (688:36–37). synagogical . . . rites in ghetto (S. Mary's Abbey) – See 10.411–13n.

17.757–58 (688:37–38). ecclesiastical rites in . . . masshouse (Adam and Eve's tavern) – The Franciscans in Dublin managed to survive English attempts to suppress Catholic worship in Ireland during the sixteenth and seventeenth centuries. In 1618 they established an "underground" church in Rosemary Lane, off Merchant's Quay just south of the Liffey; the lane was also the site of a tavern called Adam and Eve's, and since the tavern had its sign boards at each entrance to the lane, Catholic worshipers—ostensibly en route to the tavern when actually bound for church—could enter the lane without arousing suspicion. The present Franciscan Church of St. Francis of Assisi stands nearby, just off Merchant's Quay, and is still popularly called Adam and Eve's in memory of the seventeenth-century subterfuge.

17.758–59 (688:38–39). the proscription of their . . . jewish dress acts – The penal laws enacted in the years after and in contravention of the Treaty of Limerick (1691) were designed to suppress Catholicism and, in effect, Irish nationalism as well; they were impressively harsh, forbidding even (at least figuratively) the wearing of green, the Irish national color (see 3.259–60n; see also 1.403n). *Jewish dress acts:* there have been a wide variety of such laws in several countries, not only prohibiting Jews from wearing traditionally Jewish items of clothing but also requiring them to wear humiliating evidences of their Jewishness.

17.759 (688:39–689:1). *the restoration in Chanah David of Zion – That is, in King David's Land, Canaan, the land given by God to Abraham's posterity, the children of Israel. The growing anti-Semitism in nineteenth-century Europe forced many European Jewish communities to the verge of despair; thus, the appearance of Theodor Herzl's pamphlet "The Jewish State: An Attempt at a Modern Solution of the Jewish Question" (1896) caused a tremendous stir of interest and excitement with its proposal to obtain Palestine from the sultan of Turkey and to establish Zion, a Jewish homeland, under the guarantee of the Great Powers. See 4.156n and 4.192–93n.

17.763–64 (689:5–6). ***Kolod balejwaw . . . jehudi, homijah*** – Hebrew: loosely, "As long as deep within the heart / The soul of Judea is turbulent and strong"; the opening lines of "Hatikvah" (The Hope) (1878) by the Jewish poet Nephtali Herz Imber, set to music by Samuel Cohen, one of the pioneer settlers in Rishon Le Zion, Palestine, in the late 1890s. The song became the anthem of the Zionist movement in 1897, and today it is the anthem of Israel.

17.771–73 (689:15–17). the anticipation of modern . . . ogham writing (Celtic) – Both cuneiform and ogham inscriptions involve five figures ("quinquecostate"), and both are more like a cipher or a shorthand than they are like writing in the Greek or Roman alphabets. "Virgular" means having thin sloping or upright lines (as ogham does).

17.783 (689:29). The traditional figure of hypostasis – That is, the essential person of Christ in which his divine and human natures are united. Tradition held that Jesus was the only man who was ever exactly six feet tall and who ever had pure auburn hair.

17.784 (689:30). Johannes Damascenus – St. John of Damascus (c. 700–c. 754), an eloquent theologian, one of the doctors of the Latin church and one of the fathers of the Greek church. He was much concerned with the concept of hypostasis and argued that the divine and human in Christ were combined in one person without the possibility of conversion, confusion, or separation. He described Jesus as "tall . . . of a pale complexion, olive-tinted, and of the colour of wheat." This description was one feature of his resistance to the Greek emperor's order forbidding the worship of images.

17.784 (689:30). Lentulus Romanus – Fictional, supposed to have been the Roman governor of Judea before Pontius Pilate and supposed to have written a letter to the Roman Senate in which he described Jesus as "a man of tall stature" with "somewhat winecolored hair."

17.784 (689:31). Epiphanius Monachus – St. Epiphanius the Monk (c. 315–403), another of the fathers of the Greek or Eastern church and bishop of Constantia (ancient Salamis) in Cyprus. He is noted for his combative denunciations of Origen's stand on hypostasis in the course of which he described Jesus in much the same terms that John of Damascus later used.

17.785 (689:31–32). leucodermic, sesquipedalian with winedark hair – None of Stephen's "sources" uses these exact terms, but "leucodermic" means white-skinned; for "winedark," see 1.78n.

17.789–90 (690:4). the very reverend John Conmee, S.J. – See 5.322–23n.

17.790 (690:4–5). the reverend T. Salmon, D.D. – See 8.496n.

17.791 (690:5–6). Dr Alexander J. Dowie – See 8.13n.

17.792 (690:6–7). Seymour Bushe, K.C. – See 6.470n.

17.792 (690:7). Rufus Isaacs, K.C. – Rufus Daniel Isaacs, first marquis of Reading (1860–1935), a famous and popular Jewish lawyer in England.

17.793 (690:8). Charles Wyndham – Sir Charles Wyndham (1837–1919), one of the finer English actor-managers of the late nineteenth century. He was, as Bloom's phrase suggests, quite successful as "high comedian," but by no means limited to that genre.

17.794 (690:9). Osmond Tearle (†1901) – George Osmond Tearle (1852–1901), another English actor-manager, formed a succession of Shakespearean stock companies in London, New York, and Stratford-on-Avon.

17.802–28 (690:17–691:24). ***Little Harry Hughes . . . lies among the dead*** – *Child's Ballads*, ed. Helen Child Sargent and George Lyman Kittredge (Cambridge, 1904), number 155, "Sir Hugh; or, the Jew's Daughter"; variant N, p. 371, entitled "Little Harry Hughes and the Duke's Daughter," is closest to the variant Joyce uses. Apparently 155N substitutes "Duke's Daughter" for "Jew's Daughter" in genteel avoidance of the ballad's "anti-Semitism." The original story from which the ballad derives is of a boy, Hugh of Lincoln, supposedly crucified by Jews c. 1255. Apparently Joyce recalled his version from memory; the musical annotation was provided by Jacques Benoît-Méchin; see Ellmann, p. 521.

17.842 (692:12). the law of the conservation of energy – In 1904 that "law," as established in the course of the nineteenth century, held that mechanical work and the heat produced by that work can be compared as equivalent.

17.844 (692:14–15). ritual murder – See 6.771–72n.

17.860–61 (692:32–33). in Holles street and in Ontario . . . ages of 6 and 8 years – This places Bloom in Holles Street in 1895–96, in Ontario Terrace in 1897–98.

17.865 (693:2). 15 June 1889 – Milly Bloom's date of birth.

17.866 (693:3). Padney Socks – The stage-Irishman Paddy (plus to pad around in one's socks?).

17.869 (693:7). Herr Hauptmann Hainau, Austrian army – Julius Jakob, Baron Haynau (1786–1853), may be the model rapist Joyce had in mind. He was a notorious Austrian general, hated throughout western Europe (to the point of being in physical danger of mob violence when he traveled) for the cruelty and viciousness with which he put down the briefly successful revolutions of northern Italy (1848) and of Hungary (1849). Hauptmann is German for captain, a rank Haynau held before he was made colonel in 1830.

17.876 (693:14–15). the duke's lawn – A park-like area to the east of Leinster House off Merrion Street. Leinster House is part of the complex of buildings that includes the National Museum and the National Library.

17.879 (693:18). Elsa Potter – Apart from the context, identity and significance unknown.

17.880 (693:19). Stamer street – South of South Circular Road and just northwest of Ontario Terrace, where the Blooms were living in 1897–98.

17.891 (693:32–33). (valerian) – Herbs of the genus *Valeriana*, many of which have been used medicinally as stimulants or antispasmodics.

17.897–98 (694:4). the lake in Stephen's green – Along the northern side of St. Stephen's Green, a twenty-two-acre park in southeastern Dublin; it is an artificial lake with miniature islands and a sizable population of ducks.

17.913 (694:21). imbalsamation – Obsolete for embalming.

17.916–19 (694:25–29). the recurrence per hour . . . in arithmetical progression – The hour and minute hands on a fixed clock-dial coincide eleven times in the course of twelve hours; the eleventh coincidence occurs when the hands are at twelve/zero. Sixty minutes divided by eleven equals five and five-elevenths minutes.

17.921 (694:31). the 27th anniversary of his birth – In 1893 when Milly was three or four.

17.923 (694:33). quarter day – A day conventionally regarded as beginning a quarter-year; in England quarter days are 25 March (Lady Day), 24 June (Midsummer Day), 29 September (Michaelmas Day), and 25 December (Christmas Day).

17.929 (695:1). diambulist – A coinage for "daywalker," in contrast to somnambulist (sleepwalker) and noctambulist (nightwalker).

17.942 (695:15–16). a schoolfellow and a jew's daughter – That is, Stephen's "schoolfellow" Alec Bannon and Milly; cf. 17.802–28n.

17.947–48 (695:21–22). Mrs Emily Sinico . . . 14 October 1903 – Her death is central in "A Painful Case," *Dubliners* (though there the death occurs in November); see 6.997n.

17.952–53 (695:27). the anniversary of the decease of Rudolph Bloom – 27 June 1886.

17.966–67 (696:9–11). the Ship hotel . . . and E. Connery, proprietors – *Thom's* 1904, p. 1407, lists the Ship at no. 5, not at no. 6.

17.967–68 (696:11). the National Library of Ireland, 10 Kildare Street – 10 Kildare Street was occupied by the Church of Ireland Training College (Female Department); the library in Kildare Street is unnumbered, but the group of buildings in which it is housed is between nos. 6 and 10.

17.968–69 (696:12). the National Maternity Hospital, 29, 30 and 31 Holles street – As listed in *Thom's* 1904, p. 1519.

17.975–76 (696:20). Albert Hengler's circus – See 4.349n.

17.976 (696:20–21). the Rotunda, Rutland Square, Dublin – A maternity hospital on Rutland (now Parnell) Square in northeastern Dublin; it was financed by lotteries and by meetings, promenades, and entertainments given in the great rotunda room, eighty feet in diameter.

17.980 (696:25). imprevidibility – A coinage suggesting an unforeseeable nature.

17.982–83 (696:28–29). J. and T. Davy . . . Grand Canal – *Thom's* 1904, p. 1446, so lists these family grocers and wine and spirit merchants. Charlemont Mall was on the southern border of the inner city of Dublin, just across the Grand Canal from Ontario Terrace in Rathmines, where the Blooms once lived.

17.1014–15 (697:26). ineluctably constructed upon the incertitude of the void – Cf. 9.840–42n.

17.1021–22 (697:33–35). In what order of precedence . . . wilderness of inhabitation effected? – The ceremony that celebrates the exodus of the children of Israel out of Egypt into the wilderness of Sinai under Moses' leadership is Passover; see 7.206n, 7.207n, and 7.208–9n. In that ceremony the head of the house (Bloom) takes precedence, assisted by his mature son(s) (Stephen).

17.1023–25 (698:1–2). Lighted Candle in Stick borne by BLOOM – Since this is a ceremony, it suggests a celebration of Sunday vespers, the most solemn "hour" of the Divine Office; see 10.184n. It is a service of light (candle), and the Sunday vespers psalms are those of Easter vespers, since every Sunday is a celebration of the paschal mystery; the fifth and last of these psalms is Vulgate 113, which Stephen, as deacon, begins to recite below. See 15.74n.

17.1029 (698:5). secreto – Latin: literally, "set apart"; as the *"Prayer over the Offerings* ('secret'), the variable prayer, or prayers, in collect form that immediately precedes the preface [in the Mass]. The celebrant says it in a low voice" (*Layman's Missal* [Baltimore, Md., 1962], p. xlviii).

17.1030–31 (698:7–8). The 113th, *modus peregrinus* . . . *de populo barbaro* – Latin: "mode of going abroad: When Israel went out of Egypt, the house of Jacob from a people of strange language" (Vulgate, Psalms 113:1; King James, Psalms 114:1). The sentence continues: "Judah was his sanctuary, and Israel his dominion" (114:2). This verse is used in the Haggadah of Passover; see 7.206n and 17.1023–25n.

In Dante's *Purgatorio* 2:46ff., the psalm of exodus is sung by the souls of the fortunate dead whom Dante and Virgil see being ferried to the foot of the mountain of purification by Charon's angelic counterpart. This is also the psalm that Dante used in the letter to his patron, Can Grande della Scala, dedicating the *Paradiso* to him. Dante quotes the sentence above and then remarks, "If we consider the *literal* sense alone, the thing signified is the going out of the children of Israel from Egypt in the time of Moses; if the *allegorical*, our redemption through Christ; if the *moral*, the conversion of the soul from the grief and misery of sin to a state of grace; if the *anagogical*, the passage of the sanctified soul from the bondage of the corruption of this world to the liberty of everlasting glory."

17.1036–39 (698:14–18). What spectacle confronted them . . . humid nightblue fruit – An "improved" version of the closing lines of Dante's *Inferno*, 34:133–39: "The Guide [Virgil] and I entered by that hidden road to return into the bright world; and without caring for any rest, we mounted up, he first and I second, so far that I distinguished through a round opening the beauteous things which Heaven bears; and then we issued out, again to see the Stars."

17.1042–43 (698:21–22). the moon invisible . . . approaching perigee – The moon was in its first quarter and had risen at 6:40 P.M. and set at 10:17 P.M. on 16 June 1904. The moon was in apogee on Sunday, 5 June 1904, at 11:00 A.M.; perigee was to occur at noon on 17 June 1904, or in about nine hours.

17.1043–46 (698:22–26). the infinite lattiginous scintillating . . . centre of the earth – It is a commonplace that stars of the first and second magnitude are visible in the daytime from the bottom of a sufficiently deep shaft, but no matter how deep the shaft, the Milky Way is too dim to be visible; moreover, recent attempts to demonstrate the commonplace with far brighter stars have failed. "Lattiginous" is a coinage meaning "having the quality of a lattice." For "uncondensed," see 15.1765n.

17.1046–48 (698:26–28). *Sirius (alpha in Canis Maior . . . dimension of our planet – In 1905 Sirius was measured as 8.6 light-years distant from the earth (in 1970, 8.7); thus, Bloom's 10 is on the vague side, and the value he assigns to a light-year, 5.7×10^{12}, is low by 1905 standards (5.859×10^{12}) (as against 1970 [5.878×10^{12}]). Also, his estimate of Sirius's size (900 times that of earth) might be seen in the light of modern estimates that it is roughly 2,834,000 times that of earth. Sirius, the Dog Star, is Alpha (the brightest star) in the constellation Canis Major, the Big Dog.

17.1048 (698:28). Arcturus – In 1905 astronomers regarded Arcturus as the second brightest star visible in the northern hemisphere, after Sirius.

17.1049–50 (698:29–31). Orion with belt and sextuple . . . could be contained – What looks to an observer on earth like a blur in Orion's sword resolves telescopically into a star, the star into six stars, and behind those six stars the Great Nebula of Orion. Little was known before World War I about the size of and distance to nebulae, but Bloom's estimate (one hundred solar systems) is a radical understatement (on the order of one one-hundredth) of the assumptions astronomers contemporary with him were making. For example, Richard Hinkley Allen (*Star Names and Their Meanings* [1899], pp. 316–17) speaking of the Great Nebula of Orion: "A million globes, each equal in diameter to that of the earth's orbit, would not equal this in extent."

17.1050–51 (698:31–32). of moribund and of . . . Nova in 1901 – GK Persei, in the constellation Perseus, near Andromeda and Auriga, was a nova discovered 21–22 February 1901 by T. D. Anderson of Edinburgh; it flared briefly, becoming the brightest star visible in the northern hemisphere, and then declined.

17.1051–52 (698:32–33). our system plunging towards the constellation of Hercules – In 1905 astronomers estimated that the solar system was moving toward a point in the constellation Hercules at the rate of sixteen miles per second.

17.1052–53 (698:33–34). *of the parallax or parallactic . . . in reality evermoving wanderers – Since the stars remain apparently unmovable in the heavens (in contrast to the planets), they were called "fixed stars"; but by 1900 the fixity of numerous stars had been disproved, leading to the assumption that all stars moved. The German astronomer Friedrich Wilhelm Bessel (1784–1846) used "parallactic drift" (see "parallax," 8.110n) in 1838 to measure the first star parallax and to determine the first distance from earth to a star. That is, the apparent mo-

tion imparted to a star by what was actually the earth's motion in orbit (parallactic drift) could be measured (as the star appeared to describe the earth's orbit in the heavens), although it was not evidence that the star itself was in motion; that evidence came later when several star distances were known.

17.1054–55 (698:35–36). the years, three score and ten – See 17.455–56n.

17.1064–69 (699:10–16). themselves universes of void space . . . nowhere was never reached – Early-twentieth-century molecular physicists assumed that the spaces between molecules and the atoms and particles of which they were composed were infinitely vaster than the actual matter that made up the particles. They also assumed that the interspaces between particles were filled up with ether. These assumptions led, as here, to something like the Eleatic philosopher Zeno's (c. 490–c. 430 B.C.) second paradox: that Achilles cannot overtake the tortoise because at any moment in his pursuit he can only reach the place previously vacated by the tortoise.

17.1071–72 (699:20). the problem of the quadrature of the circle – See 15.2400–2401n.

17.1072–82 (699:21–32). the existence of a number computed . . . of any of its powers – What Bloom somewhat imperfectly recalls is a numerological exercise that is variously associated (by Madame Blavatsky and others) with the priesthoods of ancient Egypt, Babylon, etc. The exercise involved spelling out in an unending series $9^9 \times 9^9 \times 9^9$. . . . Each completed cycle would take several generations of priests to complete and would mark the climax of one era and the initiation of a new era. The mystic significance of the exercise derived from the assumption that nine was the perfect number, composed of three threes, the three unbreakable triangles that in turn composed a triangle: ⟁. The unending effort to spell out the ramifications of nine implied an extension toward the infinite of the divine order implicit in the number nine. Hugh Kenner has worked out a description of the number (*Ulysses* [London, 1980], pp. 167–68) and concludes that the number "which stupefied Bloom will commence with 4 and boast 369,693,099 additional digits"; Kenner concludes that the "thirty-three closely printed volumes of 1,000 pages each" would be "in the ball park." The number thirty-three also deserves attention as Jesus' age at the time of the Crucifixion and therefore as a number with significance in Christian tradition.

17.1087 (699:38–39). an atmospheric pressure of 19 tons – An essentially misleading calculation, since the atmospheric pressure at sea level is 14.6 pounds per square inch exerted *in every direction;* thus, attempts to calculate the total pressure exerted on all the body's surfaces render impressive figures of several tons but do not describe any real state.

17.1093–95 (700:5–8). a more adaptable and differently . . . Neptunian or Uranian – The combination of Darwinian evolution and the new astronomy led to considerable speculation about the existence of life forms on other planets of the solar system and, particularly among astronomers, about the possibility of life in other solar systems elsewhere in the universe.

17.1099–1100 (700:12–13). *to vanity, to vanities of vanities and to all that is vanity – "Vanity of vanities, saith the Preacher, vanity of vanities, all is vanity" (Ecclesiastes 1:2).

17.1102 (700:15). The minor was proved by the major – In other words, redemption was doubtful. The major premise of Bloom's answer: humanoid existence on other planets is possible, but if it exists, it will be human and therefore vain. The minor premise: since vain, redemption would be doubtful.

17.1104–5 (700:18–19). The various colours significant . . . vermillion, cinnabar – By 1910 spectroscopic analysis of the light emitted by various stars had been used to establish a direct relation between the color of the light and a star's temperature; see 15.1658n.

17.1105 (700:19–20). their degrees of brilliancy – In the first decade of the twentieth century the problem of degrees of brilliancy was a vexed one, since astronomers knew the distances to relatively few of the telescopically observable stars and therefore could not determine whether a star was relatively dim in itself or dim as a function of its distance. Stars were ranked according to their brightness as seen by the observer: magnitudes 1–5, visible to the naked eye; 6–7, visible to keen-sighted persons; 8–20, only visible by telescope.

17.1105–6 (700:20–21). their magnitudes revealed up to and including the 7th – See preceding note.

17.1106 (700:21). the waggoner's star – Either the star Capella in the constellation Auriga (the Charioteer) or the constellation Charles's Wain (Wagon), the Great Bear or Big Dipper (because a line through two of its stars points to the North Star, Polaris).

17.1107 (700:21). Walsingham way – Or Walsyngham Way: the Milky Way, from *The Vision of William Concerning Piers the Plowman* (fourteenth century). The Walsyngham Way as the path to the Virgin Mary's throne in heaven took its name from the path on earth to her shrine Our Lady of Walsyngham at Norfolk, also the Walsyngham Way.

17.1107 (700:22). the chariot of David – Ursa Minor, the Little Dipper, was variously identified in Jewish tradition as the chariot that Joseph sent to bring his father, Jacob, to him in Egypt (Genesis 45–46), the chariot in which Elijah was carried up to heaven (see 12.1910–12n), or the bear that David slew (I Samuel 17:34–36).

17.1108 (700:22–23). the condensation of spiral nebulae into suns – In 1905 astronomers thought that in studying the nebulae they were watching a process of "condensation," stars in the process of being formed out of plastic and gaseous material.

17.1108–9 (700:23–24). the interdependent gyrations of double suns – (Since they rotate about their common center of gravity); they were first observed by Galileo (1564–1642), and the nature of their rotation was established by Sir William Herschel (see 17.1110n).

17.1109–10 (700:24–25). the independent synchronous discoveries of Galileo, Simon Marius – Galileo and Simon Marius (1570–1624), a German astronomer, both discovered the four moons of Jupiter in 1610. (Galileo later accused Marius of pirating his discovery, but the simultaneity seems to have been genuine.)

17.1110 (700:25). Piazzi – Giuseppe Piazzi (1746–1826), an Italian astronomer noted for his discovery of the first asteroid, Ceres, in 1801 and for his publication in 1814 of a then-impressive catalogue of 7,646 stars.

17.1110 (700:25). Le Verrier – Urbain Jean Joseph Leverrier (1811–77), a French astronomer who did the mathematical calculations that determined the location of and led to the first observation of the planet Neptune by Galle (see below) in 1846. The English astronomer John Couch Adams (1819–92) had made similar calculations in 1845, but no telescopic search had been made to confirm his findings.

17.1110 (700:25). Herschel – Sir William Herschel (1738–1822), a German-English astronomer known for his discovery of Uranus (1781) and its satellites and for his extensive catalogue of nebulae (2,500), double-stars, etc. Cf. Piazzi above.

17.1110 (700:26). Galle – Johann Gottfried Galle (1812–1910), a German astronomer who made the telescopic confirmation of the existence of Neptune in 1846 (see Leverrier above). He also did extensive work on asteroids.

17.1110–12 (700:26–27). the systematizations attempted . . . of times of revolution – Johannes Kepler (1571–1630), a German astronomer and mathematician; the third of his "laws of planetary motion" (1619) determined a proportional relation between a planet's mean distance from the sun cubed and the time of one complete orbit squared. The German astronomer Johann Elert Bode (1747–1826) was known for his star charts (published 1801), which included 17,240 stars (12,000 more than any previous chart); he reproduced Johann Titius of Wittenburg's statement (published 1776) of the interrelations of planetary distances, subsequently called the "Titius-Bode law"; on the basis of this purely empirical numerical progression Bode predicted the existence of a "planet" (the asteroids) in the "gap" between Mars and Jupiter.

17.1112–13 (700:27–30). the almost infinite compressibility . . . perihelion to aphelion – Comets are "hirsute" because the word comet derives from the Greek *kometes*, "having long hair." Comets were assumed in 1910 to be "infinitely compressible" because not only their tails but also their nuclei appeared to have extremely low densities (very little mass in relation to quite impressive volumes). The distances involved in the orbits of comets were not known in 1904, but the periods of many orbits were and were assumed to reflect the distances involved. The period of Halley's Comet (76.08 years between perihelion passages) was at that time the longest known. Comets in orbit were by definition assumed not to leave the solar system; so "egressive and reentrant" would refer to visibility rather than to the solar system.

17.1113–14 (700:30). the sidereal origin of meteoric stones – Meteorites, because they were called "shooting stars," were popularly regarded as coming from the stars, but by 1910 astronomers were of the firm opinion that most if not all meteors had their origin within the solar system in particles in orbit around the sun that intersect with the earth in its orbit.

17.1114–15 (700:30–32). the Libyan floods on Mars . . . younger astroscopist – Libya is an equatorial region on Mars, so named by the Italian astronomer Giovanni Schiaparelli (1835–1910), whose work on the geography of Mars (1877ff.) and its "canals" led to considerable speculation about the possibility of life on Mars. It was established that the surface of the planet changed with its seasons. In 1894, twelve years after Stephen's birth, two American astronomers discovered that a month after the Martian vernal equinox there was a large dark belt extending from what they assumed to be the south polar "ice cap" north into the Libyan plains; they explained this color change as a flood resulting from the melting of the ice cap by summer heat. "Astroscopy" is obsolete for observation of the stars.

17.1115–17 (700:32–33). the annual recurrence of . . . S. Lawrence (martyr, 10 August) – Each year around 11 August a shower of meteors called the Perseids reaches a climax, apparently because the earth's orbit more or less regularly intersects an orbiting concentration of particles at that period. St. Lawrence (d. 258), whose feast day is 10 August, was an archdeacon and treasurer of the Church in Rome. He tricked the Roman prefect out of confiscating the Church's treasury (by giving it away to the poor) and was martyred by being roasted on a gridiron.

17.1117–18 (700:34–35). the monthly recurrence . . . moon in her arms – While the phenomenon does happen monthly, the dark disc of the old moon is rarely visible (unlike the bright crescent of the new); thus, when the old moon is visible, it is regarded as an evil omen. Cf. the seventh stanza of the anonymous ballad "Sir Patrick Spens" (Child, no. 58A): "Late, late yestre'en I saw the new moon / Wi' the auld moon in hir arm, / And I fear, I fear, my dear master, / That we shall come to harm."

17.1118–23 (700:36–41). the appearance of a star . . . constellation of Cassiopeia – For "magnitude," see 17.1105n; for "Shakespeare's birth star," see 9.928–32n. Tycho Brahe's star was "of the first magnitude" when he discovered it; after his discovery it continued to increase in brightness and thus no longer fit within the scale of magnitude: by 1905 it would have been classified as − 4 or − 5! By 1900 the theory that novas had their origin in stellar collision had been displaced by the theory that novas were in some way a function of and connected with nebulous matter.

17.1123–26 (700:41–701:3). *a star (2nd magnitude) . . . birth of Leopold Bloom – The constellation Corona Septentrionalis (Crown of Seven Stars) is Corona Borealis, the Northern Crown. A nova, T. Coronae Borealis, did appear in that constellation in May 1866, the year of Bloom's birth; it rose to the second magnitude before its decline; see 4.1n and 16.608n.

17.1126–29 (701:4–7). other stars of (presumably) . . . birth of Stephen Dedalus – Stephen was presumably born 2 February 1882 (see 15.3685n). The nova S. Andromedae (NGC 224) appeared in 1885 in the constellation Andromeda. In astrology the influence of Andromeda suggests rescue and release, as in Greek myth Andromeda was rescued from a monster by Perseus; see 17.1050–51n.

17.1129–30 (701:7–9). in and from the constellation . . . Rudolph Bloom, junior – Bloom's son, Rudy, was born in 1893; the nova T. Aurigae in the constellation Auriga was discovered by T. D. Anderson of Edinburgh in late January 1892; it rose to the fourth magnitude and then declined to the twelfth by the end of March. Auriga, the Charioteer, is near Perseus and Andromeda.

17.1140 (701:19). a Utopia – Capitalized it means the imaginary island of Sir Thomas More's (1478–1535) book (1516), and More's coinage in "New Latin" means No Place.

17.1149 (701:31–32). ardent sympathetic constellations – Such as the Tress of Berenice, which is said to be favorable to a lover's aspirations; see 17.1211–13n.

17.1149–50 (701:32). the frigidity of the satellite of their planet – The moon is not only lover's light, but also cold, as in the personifications of Artemis and Diana, the Greek and Roman goddesses of chastity.

17.1155–56 (701:38–39). the lake of dreams . . . the ocean of fecundity – These do not figure in astrology, but in selenography. They are prominent features on the moon's surface: the *marsh* of dreams, *Palus Somnii;* the sea of rains, *Mare Imbrium;* gulf of dews, *Sinius Roris;* and the *sea* of fecundity, *Mare Fecunditatis.*

17.1162 (702:7). the forced invariability of her aspect – Since the moon only rotates on its axis once each month, it always presents the same side toward the earth.

17.1165 (702:10). to render insane – See 8.245n.

17.1166 (702:12). terribility – Obsolete for terribleness.

17.1171–72 (702:17–18). What visible luminous sign attracted Bloom's who attracted Stephen's gaze? – As Dante and Virgil approach the Mount of Purgatory, they are challenged by Cato, who for the moment thinks they are fugitives from Hell: "Who hath guided you? or who was a lamp unto you issuing forth from the deep night that ever maketh black the infernal vale?" (*Purgatorio* 1:43–45). Virgil's answer begins: "Of myself I came not. A lady [Beatrice] came down from Heaven through whose prayers I succoured this man with my company" (1:52–54). Cf. 16.1470–71n.

17.1175–76 (702:21–23). Frank O'Hara . . . 16 Aungier street – As listed in *Thom's* 1904, p. 1418.

17.1188 (702:36). micturition – In *Finnegans Wake* (pp. 185–86), Joyce explicitly associates micturition with poetic creativity and with the writing of *Ulysses.*

17.1194–95 (703:5). High School – See 8.187n.

17.1203–5 (703:15–17). the problem of the sacerdotal . . . unnecessary servile work – The scholastic "problem" that Stephen raises is that since Jesus was both humanly and divinely complete (lacking nothing, having nothing in excess) (see 17.783n), does the fact that he "submitted" to circumcision call that completeness (integrity) into question? The Church's answer to Stephen's "problem" would hinge on Romans 4, where Paul argues that "unto Abraham faith was credited as justice. . . . And he received the sign of circumcision as the seal of the justice of faith." This passage is included in the Divine Office for 1 January with the clear implication that Jesus was not being "changed" but was receiving a "sign." The occasion of the circumcision is the Octave of the Nativity of Our Lord, celebrated 1 January; in 1904 the Roman Catholic church in Ireland did regard this day as a holy day of obligation, and Catholics were obliged to attend mass and to abstain from servile work as far as they were able.

17.1205–9 (703:17–22). the problem as to whether . . . hair and toenails – The prepuce as relic was originally in the Basilica of St. John Lateran in Rome; it was stolen and lost in the sixteenth century, but then found and placed in the Church of SS. Cornelius and Cyprian in Calcata outside of Rome. The "problem" Stephen poses: is this relic a part of the body of Jesus, in which case it is due latria, the highest kind of worship, paid to God only (i.e., to Christ as one of the three persons of the Trinity)? or is the relic "human," thus meriting hyperdulia, the veneration given to the Virgin Mary as the most exalted of human beings? Compare the "carnal bridal ring" with 14.250–52n.

17.1210 (703:23). celestial sign – At the climax of the execution of the suitors in *The Odyssey*, Book 22, Athena, having withheld her help while Odysseus and Telemachus proved "their mettle" as father and son, finally intervenes; "the aegis, Athena's shield, / took form aloft in the great hall." This celestial sign drives the remaining suitors "mad with fear" (22:297ff.; Fitzgerald, p. 430).

17.1211–13 (703:25–27). from Vega in the Lyre . . . the zodiacal sign of Leo – The constellation Lyra is the lyre of Orpheus; in Greek mythology the poetic power of Orpheus's lyre could charm beasts and make trees and rocks move. The Coma Berenices (Tress of Berenice) is so called after the legend that Berenice (d. 216 B.C.) pledged her hair to Aphrodite on the condition that her husband, Ptolemy III, return safely from a military expedition; when he did return, she sacrificed her beautiful head of hair, and it was translated into the heavens to commemorate the intensity of her love. (Joyce had his first date with his wife-to-be, Nora Barnacle, on 16 June 1904.) Leo (the Lion, 22 July–22 August) is the fifth house of the zodiac; Leo is the sign of those who are creative, authoritative, and kind, those who are strict individualists and who yet are expert at knowing the thoughts of others and intent on seeking the welfare of others as well as of themselves. They like to be good hosts and are profoundly loving and scrupulous in their homes.

17.1227 (704:7). the church of St. George – See 4.78n.

17.1230–31 (704:10–11). *Liliata rutilantium . . . Chorus excipiat* – Cf. 1.276–77n. Stephen alters the meaning by leaving out the phrase *te confessorum* (you, of confessors) and by altering the punctuation: "Bright [glowing] as lilies. A throng gathers about. Jubilant you of virgins. Chorus rescues [releases, exempts or receives]."

17.1233–34 (704:13–14). *Heigho, heigho / Heigho heigho* – The bells ring the half-hour (cf. 4.546–48 [70:11–13]); so according to the Linati schema it is 1:30 A.M.; according to the Stuart Gilbert schema it would be 2:30 A.M.; or, if the sun is about to rise (see 17.1257–58n), it is 3:30 A.M.

17.1240 (704:20–21). Bernard Corrigan – See 16.1256n.

17.1243–44 (704:24–26). The double reverberation . . . the resonant lane – Stephen leaves through the gate in the back wall of Bloom's garden. The gate gave into a lane that ran behind the houses on the north side of Eccles Street, from Eccles Place and the Mater Misericordia Hospital on the west to Dorset Street Lower on the east. When Virgil and Dante reach the bottom of the inferno at the center of the earth where Satan is embedded in the ice of Lake Cocytus, they turn head for heels and begin the ascent over Satan's buttock and along his leg toward the surface of the earth and the foot of the Mount of Purgatory. They climb through "a space, not known by sight but by the sound of a rivulet descending in it, along the hollow of a rock which it has eaten out with tortuous course and slow declivity" (*Inferno* 34:129–32). See 17.1036–39n. For "harp," see 7.370n. See also 9.86–88n.

17.1246–47 (704:28–30). The cold of interstellar space . . . Centigrade or Réaumur – Absolute zero, defined in 1904 as "the entire absence of heat," was theoretically fixed at −459.6°F (−273.1°C, −218.48°R). In the first decade of this century, astronomers assumed interstellar space to be very cold, but they theorized that the temperature approached but did not actually reach absolute zero. Modern physics has modified the temperature (−459.67°F, −273.15°C) and has come very close to those temperatures in the laboratory, though absolute zero has not yet actually been achieved.

17.1248 (704:30). proximate dawn – See 17.1257–58n.

17.1251–52 (704:34). Percy Apjohn (killed in action, Modder River) – There was considerable action along the Modder River in South Africa during the Boer War, particularly in 1899, when the British were defeated at Maagersfontein, and in 1900, when they achieved the surrender of Cronje at Paardeberg.

17.1252–53 (704:35). Philip Gilligan (phthisis, Jervis Street hospital) – In 1894 (see 8.156–57n and 8.159n) the Jervis Street Hospital and Charitable Infirmary, 14–20 Jervis Street, Dublin.

17.1253 (704:35–705:1). Matthew F. Kane (accidental drowning, Dublin Bay) – Kane was a friend of John Joyce's and chief clerk of the Crown Solicitor's Office in Dublin Castle. He was drowned on 10 July 1904 when he suffered a stroke while swimming off Kingstown. He was the prototype of the fictional Martin Cunningham, and his funeral cortege was remodeled to serve as Dignam's; see Adams, pp. 62–63.

17.1254 (705:1–2). Philip Moisel (pyemia, Heytesbury street) – Hyman (pp. 190–91) identifies him as the son of Nisan Moisel (see 4.209–10n) and says that he "resided in Heytesbury Street" until late in the nineteenth century, when "he emigrated to South Africa and died there about 1903." Heytesbury Street is in south-central Dublin.

17.1254–55 (705:2–3). Michael Hart (phthisis, Mater Misericordiae hospital) – (d. c. 1900), a friend of John Joyce's and the prototype of the fictional Lenehan.

17.1257 (705:5). The disparition of three final stars – See 13.1077n.

17.1257–58 (705:6). the apparition of a new solar disc – Scheduled for 3:33 A.M. in Dublin on 17 June 1904.

17.1260–61 (705:9). the house of Luke Doyle, Kimmage – Presumably in Kimmage Road, sections of which are in both Terenure (Roundtown) and Harold's Cross, villages south and west of Dublin, but *Thom's* 1904 lists no Doyle in residence there.

17.1262–63 (705:11). his gaze turned in the direction of Mizrach, the east – *Mizrach*, Hebrew: "the east"; Bloom assumes the attitude of a Jew at prayer, it being traditional for Jews west of Jerusalem to face east when they pray, particularly during the silent prayer called *Shmoneh Esreh* (Eighteen Benedictions).

17.1266 (705:14). avine music – Bird music.

17.1275–76 (705:24–25). The right temporal lobe . . . a solid timber angle – As Odysseus is conked by a stool thrown by the suitor Antinous in *The Odyssey*, Book 17.

17.1301 (706:18). supermanence – A coinage suggesting superpermanent.

17.1303 (706:21). (Cadby) – A relatively inexpensive piano manufactured in England.

17.1307 (706:26). *Love's Old Sweet Song* – See 4.314n.

17.1308–9 (706:27–28). Madam Antoinette Sterling – (1850–1904), an American-born contralto who married a Scot. She was very popular in the British Isles, particularly for her ballad singing.

17.1310 (706:29–30). *ritirando* – Italian: a coinage from "to retire," where one would expect the musical direction *ritardando* (retard).

17.1315–16 (706:37–38). Dr Malachi Mulligan's . . . gradation of green – See 14.1455–56 (424:37–38).

17.1321–22 (707:6). a black diminutive cone – Incense; Bloom fumigates his house, as Odysseus fumigates his after the slaughter of the suitors in Book 22 of *The Odyssey*.

17.1325 (707:9–10). Agendath Netaim – See 4.191–92n.

17.1333 (707:20). homothetic – See 17.199n.

17.1335 (707:22). Connemara marble – See 12.1252n.

17.1336 (707:23). 4.46 A.M. on the 21 March 1896 – In 1896 the vernal equinox occurred on 20 March at 2:02 A.M., Dublin time. (In Irish tradition, the first day of spring is St. Brigid's day, 1 February.)

17.1336 (707:24). Matthew Dillon – See 6.697n.

17.1338 (707:25–26). Luke and Caroline Doyle – See 17.1260–61n.

17.1338 (707:26). owl – Emblematic of wisdom and sacred to Pallas Athena; see 17.1210n.

17.1339 (707:26–27). Alderman John Hooper – See 6.950n.

17.1342 (707:30). pierglass – A large, high mirror, usually attached to the wall, often in the framed space, or "pier," between two windows or above a mantle.

17.1350 (708:1). ipsorelative – A reflexive, self-contained organization of cross-references.

17.1350 (708:1). aliorelative – An externally referential organization.

17.1352–53 (708:4–5). *Brothers and sisters . . . his grandfather's son* – That is, Bloom, assuming that Bloom was an only son and that Rudolph Virag, Bloom's father, was the only son of his father, Leopold Virag. There are many variants on this sort of riddle.

17.1361 (708:15). Catalogue these books – See 9.309n.

17.1362 (708:16). *Thom's Dublin Post Office Directory*, 1886 – This could be either of two publications: *The Post Office Directory and Calendar for 1886 . . .* printed by Alexander Thom; or the much more comprehensive *Thom's Official Directory of the United Kingdom of Great Britain and Ireland for 1886 comprising the 1886 Post Office Dublin City and County Directory.*

17.1363 (708:17). Denis Florence M'Carthy's *Poetical Works* – The Irish poet, scholar, and translator Denis Florence MacCarthy's (1817–82) *Ballads, Poems and Lyrics, Original and Translated* (Dublin, 1850); *Under-Glimpses and Other Poems* (1857); and *Bellfinder and Other Poems* (1857). Standard book catalogues do not list a *Poetical Works*.

17.1366 (708:20). *The Useful Ready Reckoner* – Unknown.

17.1367 (708:21). *The Secret History of the Court of Charles II* – *The Secret History of the Court and Reign of Charles II*, by a member of the Privy Council (London, 1792).

17.1368 (708:23). *The Child's Guide* – Titles that begin with this phrase are legion, among them, *The Child's Guide to Devotion* (London, 1850); *The Child's Guide to Knowledge; being a collection of useful and familiar answers on everyday subjects; adapted for youngsters. By a Lady* (London, 1878).

17.1369 (708:23//24). *The Beauties of Killarney* – Title unknown; for Killarney, see 12.1451n.

17.1370 (708:24). *When We Were Boys* by William O'Brien, M.P. – For O'Brien, see 16.1503n. *When We Were Boys* (London, 1890) is a novel O'Brien wrote while he was in jail. It is set in County Cork on the eve of the Fenian uprising of the 1860s.

17.1372 (708:26). *Thoughts from Spinoza* – This commonplace "thoughts from" suggests a coinage or generalization rather than the actual title of a book.

17.1373 (708:27). *The Story of the Heavens* by Sir Robert Ball – See 8.110n.

17.1374 (708:28). Ellis' *Three Trips to Madagascar* – William Ellis (1794–1872) was an English Congregationalist missionary; his *Three Visits to Madagascar during the years 1853–1854–1856. Including A Journey to the Capital; With Notices of the Natural History of the Country and of the Present Civilization of the People* (London, 1858), together with two of his other works on Madagascar, was regarded as the standard authority on the island in the nineteenth century.

17.1375 (708:30). *The Stark-Munro Letters* by A. Conan Doyle – An epistolary novel by Sir Arthur Conan Doyle (1859–1930). *The Stark Munro Letters; being a series of sixteen letters written by J. Stark Munro, M.B. (Bachelor of Medicine), to his friend and former fellow-student Herbert Swanborough, of Lowell, Massachusetts, during the years 1881–1884* (New York, 1895). The letters read as thinly disguised random lectures on topics that range from religion and politics to poverty and the practice of medicine. Central is Stark Munro's belief in the teleological presence of "the great Central Mind" (p. 47), "the all-wise Engineer" (p. 113) who presides over the evolution of the brain and man's spiritual progress (p. 50) and assures "the ultimate perfection of the race" (p. 112).

17.1375–76 (708:31). the City of Dublin . . . 106 Capel street – As listed in *Thom's* 1904, p. 1443.

17.1376–77 (708:32). 21 May (Whitsun Eve) 1904 – Whitsunday was 22 May 1904.

17.1379 (708:35). *Voyages in China by "Viator" – See 6.983n.

17.1380 (708:37). *Philosophy of the Talmud* – Again, a coinage or generalization of an actual title and apparently not the title itself.

17.1381 (708:38). Lockhart's *Life of Napoleon* – The Scottish novelist and man of letters John Gibson Lockhart (1794–1854), "the Scorpion," *Life of Napoleon Buonaparte, in Which the Atrocious Deeds, Which He Has Perpetrated, in order to Attain His Elevated Station, Are Faithfully Recorded; by Which Means Every Britain Will Be Enabled to Judge the Disposition of His Threatening Foe; and Have a Faint Idea of the Desolation Which Awaits This Country, Should His Menace Ever Be Realized* (1832), revised and reissued as *History of Napoleon* (1885).

17.1383 (709:3). *Soll und Haben* by Gustav Freytag – Gustav Freytag (1816–95) was a German novelist whose novels were extraordinarily popular in the nineteenth century. *Soll und Haben* (Debit and Credit) (1855) is a novel that studies the impact of the industrial revolution on middle-class Germans; the mercantile emphasis of the plot has anti-Semitic overtones.

17.1385 (709:5). Hozier's *History of the Russo-Turkish War* – Col. Sir Henry Montague Hozier (1842–1907), an English soldier and historian and editor-author of *The Russo-Turkish War: including an account of the rise and decline of the Ottoman power, and the history of the Eastern Question*, 2 vols. (London, 1877, 1879). The Russo-Turkish War took place in 1877 and 1878.

17.1386 (709:6–7). Garrison Library, Governor's Parade, Gibraltar – A combination library and club; in 1890 it was the "literary" resource of the Rock; it had 40,000 volumes and a pavilion, complete with billiard rooms and a bar. Governor's Parade was renamed Gunner's Parade in 1803, but both names persisted through the nineteenth century.

17.1388 (709:8). *Laurence Bloomfield in Ireland* by William Allingham – William Allingham (1824–89), Irish-born poet, editor and associate of the Pre-Raphaelites, *Laurence Bloomfield in Ireland: A Modern Poem* (London, 1864), reissued as *Laurence Bloomfield in Ireland; or, The New Landlord* (London, 1869). The preface to the second edition announces "that Ireland has a very different history and character from England, and needs a very different kind of management, and that Ireland has hitherto been lamentably mismanaged" (p. iv). In Irish politics "the chief binding element has been hatred," and Irish religion is characterized by "an aggravation of the evils of dogma and a suppression of the benevolence of religion." The result is "perpetual anger and conflict" (p. vi). These themes are deployed in a book-length poem (heroic couplets) focused on Bloomfield, the ideally compassionate landlord, and on the Dorans, the idealized peasant family. The supporting cast includes an assortment of tyrannical landlords, rapacious land agents, and sentimentalized if occasionally less-than-perfect peasants. With appropriate measures of agrarian violence and the beauties of nature, the outcome is quasi-utopian.

17.1391 (709:11). *A Handbook of Astronomy* – Another generalization rather than an actual title.

17.1394 (709:15). *The Hidden Life of Christ* – Unknown.

17.1395 (709:16). *In the Track of the Sun* – See 4.99–100n.

17.1397 (709:18). *Physical Strength and How to Obtain It by Eugen Sandow – See 4.234n.

17.1398–1402 (709:20–25). *Short but yet Plain* . . . the burgh of Southwark – This is apparently copied from an actual title page, since the British Museum catalogue does list the book (though not this particular edition) *Short but yet Plain Elements of Geometry and Plain Trigonometry*, and one Charles Cox was M.P. for Southwark in 1711.

17.1403–6 (709:27–31). Michael Gallagher . . . Enniscorthy, county Wicklow – Unknown, but one problem with Mr. Gallagher's hometown is that it is in County Wexford, some twenty-four miles south of the County Wicklow border.

17.1412 (709:36). incuneated – Wedged, impacted.

17.1413 (709:37). closestool – A utensil designed to hold a chamber pot.

17.1416 (709:41). Hozier's *History of the Russo-Turkish War* – See 17.1385n.

17.1422 (710:8). mnemotechnic – Systematic attempts to improve the efficiency of memory were much in the news in the late nineteenth century.

17.1425 (710:11). Plevna – See 4.63n.

17.1428 (710:15). Narcissus – In Greek myth, a beautiful young man who refused all love, even that of Echo, who pined away until only her voice remained. To punish his indifference, Nemesis made him fall in love with his own image reflected in a pool, whereupon he too pined away until he turned into the flower that bears his name. In the late nineteenth century Narcissus was frequently used as a metaphor for the self-preoccupation of the decadent romantic imagination.

17.1429 (710:15–16). P. A. Wren, 9 Bachelor's Walk – See 6.446n.

17.1448–49 (711:1–2). 2 weeks and 3 days previously (23 May 1904) – Monday, 23 May, is three weeks and four days from Friday, 17 June (?).

17.1453–54 (711:7–8). the occasion (17 October . . . Sinico, Sydney Parade) – See 17.947–48 (695:20–21), where Bloom dates her death as 14 October; see 6.997n. Sydney Parade is in Merrion, a village three miles south-southeast of Dublin center.

17.1456ff. (711:10ff.). *Debit* – Bloom's budget omits his expenditure of eleven shillings at Bella Cohen's; see 15.3556 (557:7–8).

17.1483 (711:42). disnoded – Unknotted, a coinage from node, knot, or entanglement.

17.1486 (712:2). effracted – Broken off.

17.1491 (712:9). *ungucal – Having nails or claws.

17.1494–95 (712:13). Mrs Ellis's juvenile school – See 5.237n.

17.1499 (712:19). borough English – A custom in English law under which lands and tenants descended to the youngest son or sometimes to the youngest daughter or a collateral heir.

17.1501 (712:21). (valuation £42) – Land values in Ireland were stated in terms of annual rental value (not of sale price).

17.1503 (712:24). *Rus in Urbe* – Latin: "The country in the city"; figuratively, combining the best of both worlds, after Martial's (c. 40–c. 102) *Epigrams* XII.xvii.21. Martial asks: "Do you [Sparsus] ask why I often resort to my small fields?" and argues that as "a poor man" his city home is noisy and he must retire to the country to find quiet because he cannot (as the wealthy Sparsus can) afford to have "country in the town."

17.1504 (712:24). *Qui si sana* – Italian: "Here one is healthy"; the motto on a house at 12 Newtown Avenue, Blackrock.

17.1516–17 (712:39–40). Dundrum, south, or Sutton, north – Dundrum, a village five miles south of Dublin center at the base of the Dublin Mountains. *Thom's* 1904 (p. 1693) remarks, "Dundrum is recommended for the purity of its air, and in summer is much resorted to by invalids." Sutton was a small coastal village on the isthmus connecting the headland of Howth with the mainland; it is eight miles north-northeast from Dublin center.

17.1519 (713:1). *feefarm grant – In English law, land held of another in fee simple subject to a fixed annual rent. Note that the annual rent that Bloom has proposed above (£42) is somewhat more affluent than Bloom's present annual rent (value) of £28.

17.1519 (713:2). 999 years – The customary English long-lease in 1900 was ninety-nine years.

17.1523–24 (713:6–7). *Encyclopedia Britannica and New Century Dictionary – In 1904, the most widely cited sources of middlebrow learning. The ninth edition of the *Britannica* (London, 1875–88) was twenty-four volumes; publication of an eleven-volume supplement began in 1900. *The Century Dictionary,* advertised as *The New C.D.* (London, 1889–95), was an encyclopedic lexicon of literary, scientific, and technological terms (7,046 pp.) plus a "Dictionary of proper names" (1,085 pp.).

17.1535 (713:20–21). embossed mural paper at 10/– per dozen – Not a dozen rolls of wallpaper, but a dozen flat sheets or "cut-out wallpaper motifs—flowers, birds, etc.—and it would have been very expensive, good quality paper." (This information from Mr. Hall of Cole & Son's wallpaper archives, London; as quoted in a letter, 15 July 1982, by Jean D. Hamilton, senior research assistant, Department of Prints and Drawings and Photographs, Victoria and Albert Museum, London.)

17.1544–46 (713:31–34). (salary, rising by biennial . . . after 30 years' service) – The salary arrangement is much more generous than it sounds. A cook who lived in and took her meals at the expense of a family would expect an annual wage of £12–26; a general maid, £10–17; the betweenmaid, £7½–11; and the whole provision for bonus and retirement is positively utopian for the period.

17.1552 (713:40). a tennis and fives court – A building for court tennis (in which the side and end walls are in-bounds, as in squash) and for English handball, called "fives."

17.1557–59 (714:4–7). sir James W. Mackey . . . 23 Sackville street, upper – As listed in *Thom's* 1904, p. 1585; Mackey had been prominent in Dublin political life, was lord mayor in 1866 and 1873, and was knighted for public service in 1874.

17.1565 (714:13). haytedder – A machine or tool for stirring and spreading hay that is in danger of rotting because it has been dampened by rain—a very useful tool in Ireland.

17.1578 (714:28–29). solidungular – Having a solid or uncloven hoof.

17.1579 (714:30). erigible – Rare: "capable of being erected."

17.1580 (714:32). Saint Leopold's – St. Leopold of Austria (1073–1125), distinguished for his charity and self-abnegation. As the brother-in-law of Henry V, Holy Roman emperor from 1106 to 1125, he was politically influential but always inconspicuous. Upon the death of Henry V he was offered the crown but refused, preferring instead to devote himself to charity and worship.

17.1604 (715:23). stripper cows – Cows that have almost stopped giving milk.

17.1604 (715:23). pike – A peaked and temporary stack of hay made up in a hayfield.

17.1610 (715:30). resident magistrate – In the last decade of the nineteenth century there were sixty-four resident magistrates functioning in all parts of Ireland except Dublin. The well-paid magistrates were popularly portrayed as living the ideal life of the hunting-shooting-fishing country gentleman.

17.1610 (715:30–31). justice of the peace – Appointed in Great Britain and Ireland by commission of the Crown to exercise a limited judicial and administrative authority in a county or borough. To qualify for appointment a person had to have an income from his estate of £100 a year, clear of all rents and charges (i.e., an unearned income of at least $11,000 after taxes [U.S., 1985]).

17.1611 (715:32). (*Semper paratus*) – Latin: "Always ready." See 8.934n.

17.1611–12 (715:32–33). recorded in the court directory – That is, registered in the office and Court Tower of the Ulster King of Arms in Dublin Castle; see 15.1413n.

17.1612–13 (715:33–34). M.P., P.C., K.P., L.L.D *honoris causa* – Member of Parliament, privy councillor, Knight of the Order of St. Patrick (the highest of the Irish orders of knighthood, as the Garter in England and the Thistle in Scotland; see 15.4450–51n), Doctor of Laws "for the sake of honor."

17.1613–14 (715:34–35). court and fashionable intelligence – The conventional newspaper heading for news of the socially prominent.

17.1627 (716:13). the letter of the law – Echoes St. Paul's famous distinction in II Corinthians 3:5–6: "but our sufficiency is of God; Who also hath made us able ministers of the new testament; not of the letter, but of the spirit: for the letter killeth, but the spirit giveth life."

17.1627–28 (716:14). law merchant – Commercial law, mercantile law, and the rules of evidence that obtain in that law.

17.1628 (716:14). covin – In law, a collusive agreement between two or more persons to prejudice a third; conspiracy.

17.1630 (716:17). venville rights – In English law, a certain kind of tenure peculiar to Dartmoor Forest; chief among its features are situation in an ancient village, suit at the lord's court, certain rights of common, and payment of fines.

17.1638–39 (716:26–27). *the Society for promoting Christianity among the jews – The Church of Ireland Auxiliary to the London Society for Promoting Christianity among the Jews was located at 45 Molesworth Street in Dublin.

17.1641 (716:29). Daniel Magrane and Francis Wade – Apart from the context, identity and significance unknown.

17.1643–44 (716:32–33). the political theory of colonial (e.g., Canadian) expansion – Before 1841, Canada had been a loose and divided grouping of provinces and territories; from that time through the rest of the nineteenth century Canada experienced "colonial expansion": the development of political integrity and independence of English rule. Many Irish saw emigration to Canada and other "expanding" colonies as a means of achieving the political independence denied Ireland.

17.1644–45 (716:33–35). the evolutionary theories . . . *Origin of Species* – Charles Darwin's (1809–82) *On the Origin of Species by Means of Natural Selection, or the Preservation of the Favored Races in the Struggle of Life* (1859) and *The Descent of Man and Selection in Relation to Sex* (1871). Darwin's theories were the subject of extraordinary controversy in the latter half of the nineteenth century, since they seemed so clearly to challenge man's pretensions to some order of divinity.

17.1647 (716:37). James Fintan Lalor – (1807–49), an Irish political writer who vigorously advocated republicanism and a radical program of land nationalization in the pages of the *Nation*, the *United Irishman*, and the *Irish Felon*, a magazine he edited. Even though crippled, he worked as a farmer to put his theories to the test. He was finally imprisoned for his opinions in 1849. His theories of land nationalization were taken up and promoted by the American economist Henry George (1839–97), whose *Progress and Poverty* (1879) enjoyed considerable popularity in Ireland.

17.1647–48 (716:37). John Fisher Murray – (1811–65), an Irish political writer and satirist, one of the radical Young Irelanders in the 1840s.

17.1648 (716:37). John Mitchel – (1815–75),

an Irish solicitor who gave up his profession for a career as a radical and a journalist. He took over the Young Irelanders' publication, the *Nation*, and then seceded from that journal to found the more radical *United Irishman* in 1848. The *United Irishman* was suppressed and Mitchel was sentenced to fourteen years penal servitude in Bermuda and then Tasmania. He escaped to America but eventually was allowed to return to Ireland in 1872. On the eve of his death in 1875 he was elected member of Parliament for Tipperary; see 12.112n.

17.1648 (716:37–38). J. F. X. O'Brien – See 4.491n.

17.1648–49 (716:38). the agrarian policy of Michael Davitt – See 16.1592–93n and 15.4684n.

17.1650 (716:39–40). (M. P. for Cork City) – Parnell was first returned to Parliament from Meath in 1875. In 1880 he won election in Meath, Mayo, and Cork City, and he held the latter seat for the rest of his career.

17.1650–51 (716:40–42). the programme of peace . . . for Midlothian, N.B. – Gladstone was member of Parliament for Midlothian, North Britain, from 1880 to 1894. As prime minister, he placed emphasis on international peace and on retrenchment in the British Empire (i.e., he argued against the acquisition of more territories and subjects). Gladstone was, perhaps somewhat conservatively, committed to reform, particularly to Irish land reform and the granting of a measure of Home Rule. But the slogan "peace, retrenchment, and reform" had already become a political bromide by the middle of the nineteenth century (Erlene Stetson, *JJQ* 19, no.2 [1982]: 181).

17.1653–56 (717:1–5). on Northumberland road . . . bearing 2,000 torches – Northumberland Road enters Dublin from the southeast and is part of the main thoroughfare from Kingstown (now Dun Laoghaire) to Dublin. The torchlight procession (as described) took place on 1, not 2, February 1888; fiction has moved it to coincide with Joyce's sixth birthday (see 15.3685n).

17.1656 (717:5). the marquess of Ripon – George Frederick Samuel Robinson, first marquess of Ripon (1827–1909), an English politician and statesman. He became a Catholic in 1874 and was popular in Ireland as a supporter of Gladstone's Irish policies, including Home Rule.

17.1656 (717:5). *(honest) John Morley – (1838–1923), an English statesman and author, was a consistent opponent of the English (Conservative) policy of coercion in Ireland and a dedicated Home Ruler; he was popular with the Irish even during his brief tenure as chief secretary for Ireland in 1886.

17.1658–59 (717:8–10). the Industrious Foreign Acclimatised . . . (incorporated 1874) – A joke at the expense of the compound names of building societies; *Thom's* 1904 (pp. 1352–54) lists several such societies in Dublin.

17.1666 (717:18). headrent – In English law, the rent payable to the freeholder of a property.

17.1672–78 (717:25–32). What rapid but insecure means . . . at 2:59 p.m. (Dunsink time) – Bloom's scheme for beating the system with private wireless telegraph is not all that farfetched. Race results were sent from England to Ireland by telegram in 1904, and results of the Gold Cup were not expected in Dublin until 4:00 P.M. Dunsink time. The race, which had been run at 3:08 Greenwich time, would have been over before 2:40 Dunsink time, but Dublin bookies did not close their books until 3:30 or 3:45. See 8.109n.

17.1680–81 (717:34–35). *7-schilling, mauve, imperforate, Hamburg, 1866 – Actually issued in 1865 (though 1866, the year of Bloom's birth, has apparently taken precedence). *Scott's Standard Postage Stamp Catalogue* (1969) lists this stamp as no. 20 and remarks that it is an "inversion," worth more canceled ($12.50) than uncanceled ($3.50).

17.1681–82 (717:35–36). 4 pence, rose, blue, paper perforate, Great Britain, 1855 – *Scott's* number 22, worth $200 uncanceled and $114 canceled.

17.1682–83 (717:36–37). *1 franc, stone, official, rouletted, diagonal surcharge, Luxemburg, 1879 – An overprint of 1 franc over 37½ centimes, *Scott's* number 28, color *bistre* (like stone), worth $135 uncanceled, $65 canceled; in sum, no one of these stamps is (or was) particularly valuable.

17.1687 (718:1–2). A Spanish prisoner's donation of a distant treasure – Owes a debt of imaginary happenstance to *The Count of Monte Cristo* (1844) by Alexandre Dumas *père* (1802–70). A dying fellow-prisoner (a "learned Italian") tells Edmund Dantes, the hero of the novel, of an immense fortune on the island of Monte Cristo. When the fellow-prisoner dies, Dantes arranges to be "buried" at sea in his place and then escapes to claim the fortune and his title.

17.1694 (718:10). to 32 terms – ¼d. projected to 32 terms in a geometrical progression of 2 would yield £2, 236, 962 2s. 8d.

17.1695–96 (718:11–12). to break the bank at Monte Carlo – See 12.185–86n.

17.1696–97 (718:12–13). problem of quadrature . . . £1,000,000 sterling – See 15.2400–2401n.

17.1699 (718:15). dunams – See 4.195n.

17.1700 (718:16). Agendath Netaim – See 4.191–92n.

17.1702–3 (718:19–20). human excrement possessing chemical properties – In Part III, chapter 5 of Swift's *Gulliver's Travels*, Gulliver is "permitted to see the Grand Academy of Lagado," where one of the "projectors" was intent on reducing "human excrement to its original food."

17.1707–8 (718:24–26). 4,386,035 the total population . . . returns of 1901 – *Thom's* 1904 (p. 611) lists the population of Ireland in 1901 as 4,458,775.

17.1710–11 (718:29). harbour commissioners – The commissioners of the Dublin Port and Docks Board, the office charged with the regulation of shipping, the collection of customs, and the management of the facilities of the Port of Dublin.

17.1712 (718:31). at Dublin bar – At the funnel-like entrance to Dublin Harbor where the two sea walls, the North Bull Wall and the South Wall, converge; the convergence of the two walls would make Bloom's scheme seem practicable, but it would have seriously impeded navigation.

17.1713 (718:31). at Poulaphouca – See 15.3299n; the Dublin hydroelectric scheme at Poulaphouca was begun in 1937.

17.1713 (718:32). Powerscourt – A famous estate on the Dargle twelve miles south of Dublin. There is an impressive three-hundred-foot waterfall on the estate.

17.1713 (718:32). catchment basins – The entire area from which drainage is received by a reservoir, a river, etc.

17.1714 (718:33). W.H.P. – Water horsepower.

17.1714–18 (718:33–38). A scheme to enclose . . . for mixed bathing – North Bull is a sandbar island in Dublin Bay off the village of Dollymount just northeast of Dublin. The southern end of the island was already "enclosed" by the North Bull Wall to keep the island's sands from encroaching on Dublin Harbor. Bloom's "scheme" is to "enclose," or stabilize with sea walls, the rest of the island, making it possible to erect permanent buildings on the island in place of or in addition to its golf course. "Mixed bathing" was unusual and the object of considerable suspicion in Ireland in 1904.

17.1722 (719:1–2). between Island bridge and Ringsend – There is a weir across the Liffey at Island Bridge, which is not quite four miles upstream from Ringsend at the mouth of the Liffey.

17.1724–26 (719:4–6). A scheme for the repristination . . . freed from weedbeds – Transport in Ireland was once heavily dependent on a well-developed system of canals, but in the latter half of the nineteenth century canal traffic began to decline not only as a result of competition with the railroad but also because the canals, subject to infestation with algae, were increasingly difficult and expensive to maintain. There is no commercial canal traffic in present-day Ireland. For "repristination," see 17.518n.

17.1726–31 (719:6–12). A scheme to connect by tramline . . . 43 to 45 North Wall – See 6.400–401n. Several links of the sort Bloom suggests were already in existence; the one Bloom refers to was the Drumcondra Link Railway, which looped around the northern outskirts of metropolitan Dublin, intersecting the Midland Great Western Railway at Liffey Junction northwest of the city and the Great Southern and Western Railway, which entered Dublin from the southwest and branched through a tunnel under Phoenix Park to join the Drumcondra Link and thence to the Midland and Great Western Railway's terminus on North Wall Quay near the mouth of the Liffey. Bloom proposes a line parallel with the Drumcondra

Link but nearer metropolitan Dublin to connect the cattle market with the East Wall, a quayside north of and perpendicular to the mouth of the Liffey.

17.1731–32 (719:13). Great Central Railway – William A. Wallis, general carrier and forwarding agent, agent for the Great Central Railway, at 5–6 North Wall Quay.

17.1732 (719:13–14). Midland Railway of England – Offices at 6 Eden Quay and 9 North Wall Quay.

17.1732–33 (719:14). City of Dublin Steam Packet Company – 15 Eden Quay and 13A and 19 North Wall Quay.

17.1733 (719:14–15). *Lancashire and Yorkshire Railway Company – Stores and offices, 13 North Wall Quay.

17.1733–34 (719:15–16). Dublin and Glasgow Steam Packet Company – The Duke Line, 70–72 North Wall Quay; cattle yard at 72.

17.1734–35 (719:16–17). *Glasgow, Dublin . . . (Laird line) – 73–75 North Wall Quay.

17.1735–36 (719:17–18). British and Irish Steam Packet Company – 3 North Wall Quay.

17.1736 (719:18). Dublin and Morecambe Steamers – Alex A. Laird & Co., 87–89 North Wall Quay.

17.1736–37 (719:18–19). London and Northwestern Railway Company – H. G. Burgess, general manager for Ireland, 48–57 North Wall Quay.

17.1737 (719:19–20). Dublin Port and Docks Landing Sheds – Nine landing sheds (unnumbered) at the outer end of the North Wall Quay.

17.1738–40 (719:20//22). *Palgrave, Murphy and Company . . . Holland and for Liverpool Underwriters' Association – Their transit shed was at the outer end of the North Wall Quay. Their office was at 17 Eden Quay. *Thom's* 1904 (p. 1981) describes them as "steamship owners, agents for steamers from Mediterranean, Spain, Portugal, France, Belgium, Holland &c. and for Liverpool Underwriter's association."

17.1742 (719:24). Dublin United Tramways Company, limited – See 7.6–7n.

17.1748 (719:31). Blum Pasha – Sir Julius Blum (b. 1843) was under secretary to the Egyptian Treasury, a position he filled with distinction, meriting him a Companion of the Bath in 1884 and Knight Commander of St. Michael and St. George in 1890. In that year, he left the civil service in Egypt, where he was called "Blum Pasha," to become manager of the Austrian Credit in Vienna. He was a man of considerable wealth.

17.1748 (719:31). Rothschild – A famous Jewish family of international bankers, founded by Mayer Anselm Rothschild (1743–1812) in Frankfurt, Germany. In the nineteenth century branches of the family founded banking houses in Vienna, Naples, Paris, and London. To say the least, they flourished; see 15.1848n.

17.1749 (719:31). Guggenheim – See 15.1856n.

17.1749 (719:31). Hirsh – See 15.1858n.

17.1749 (719:31). Montefiore – See 4.156n.

17.1749 (719:32). Morgan – A family of American financiers and bankers. Junius Spencer Morgan (1813–90) built his J. S. Morgan & Co. into one of the leading banking houses of the world. His son, John Pierpont Morgan (1837–1913), improved upon his father's modest ($10 million) success through his genius for financial reorganization and combination, a genius that achieved the United States Steel Corporation, the Northern Securities Company, and an Atlantic shipping combination.

17.1749 (719:32). Rockefeller – John Davison Rockefeller (1839–1937), an American capitalist who set out to achieve a monopoly on oil in the United States and did, gaining control not only of oil fields and refineries but also of the means of transportation (by forcing an alliance with the railroads). By the 1880s there was virtually no competition to Rockefeller's enterprises in the oil industry.

17.1750 (719:32). fortunes in 6 figures – Apparently the reckoning is in pounds (valued at five dollars in 1904), but even in the "poorest" of these cases, six figures is an underestimate, and in the richest, nine figures would be more like it.

17.1760 (720:7–8). the 70 years of complete human life – See 17.455–56n.

17.1775 (720:25). A Vere Foster's handwriting copybook – Anglo-Irish educator and philanthropist Vere Henry Lewis Foster (1819–1900) was interested in improving education and prepared a graded series of drawing and copybooks, *Vere Foster's Copy-Books, Bold Writing or Civil Service Series*, from which nineteenth-century English schoolchildren learned handwriting.

17.1779 (720:30). queen Alexandra of England – (1844–1925), a daughter of King Christian IX of Denmark, she married Albert Edward, Prince of Wales, in 1863 and became queen consort on his accession to the throne as Edward VII in 1901.

17.1779 (720:30). Maud Branscombe – See 13.857n.

17.1780 (720:31). Yuletide card – "Pictured souvenirs appropriate to Christmas" were introduced into the fashionable London world by J. C. Horsley, R.A., in 1846. By the 1890s the demand for them had become "enormous" in the British Isles and in the United States (*New International Encyclopedia* [New York, 1902], vol. 4, p. 719b).

17.1781 (720:32). a parasitic plant – That is, mistletoe, coincidentally sacred to the druids, since it was evergreen and presented a mystical contrast in midwinter to the sacred oaks on which it flourished.

17.1781 (720:32). *Mizpah* – Hebrew: "Watchtower"; the name of at least six different Old Testament towns or localities in Palestine; also in nineteenth-century usage, a parting salutation, after Genesis 31:49: "And Mizpah; for he said, The Lord watch between me and thee, when we are absent one from another." The salutation only works when the verse is taken out of context, since in context it is the fruit of the jealous suspicion between Jacob and his brother, Laban.

17.1782 (720:33–34). *Mr & Mrs M. Comerford – Lived at Neptune View, 11 Leslie Avenue, Dalkey, according to *Thom's* 1904, p. 1836.

17.1785 (720:37). Messrs Hely's, Ltd., 89, 90 and 91 Dame Street – A nonexistent address (the highest number in Dame Street in 1904 was 81); see 8.126n and 8.142n.

17.1786 (720:38). gilt "J" pennibs – Broadpointed pens stamped with the letter *J*.

17.1789–90 (721:3–4). William Ewart Gladstone's . . . (never passed into law) – The English Conservative party was in power at the end of 1885 thanks to Parnell's revolt against Gladstone and his Liberal party (over their reluctance to move toward Home Rule). The general election of late 1885 returned 251 Conservatives and 333 Liberals and gave Parnell's Home Rule party a solid 86 Irish delegates, an impressive balance of power. When Gladstone became prime minister on 1 February 1886, it was clear that he did so with the support of Parnell (and at the price of his commitment to Home Rule). Gladstone introduced a Home Rule bill on 13 April 1886 that was ultimately defeated 343 to 313 on 8 June 1886 by defections of 95 M.P.'s within his own party. Gladstone resigned on 26 June 1886, but when he was again returned to power in late 1892 he introduced a second Home Rule bill on February 1893, which was passed by the House of Commons by a majority of 43 votes at the beginning of September and rejected by the House of Lords 419 to 41 on 8 September 1893.

17.1791 (721:5). S. Kevin's Charity Fair – Sponsored by St. Kevin's (Church of Ireland) in South Circular Road, not far from the Blooms' residence in Lombard Street West.

17.1798–1801 (721:13–16). the transliterated name and address . . . MH/Y. IM – "Reserved" here means to keep from being known to others. The cryptogram is "boustrophedontic" in that it is formed by placing the alphabet A to Z in parallel with the alphabet Z to A and then substituting letters from the reversed alphabet for the letters of the message. It is "punctated" because marked by points or periods where the vowels are omitted, and "quadrilinear" because marked with four slant lines (/). Solved, it reads: "M RTH /DR FF LC/D LPH NS/B RN" (Martha Clifford's last name has been reversed as a double protection). The suppression of the vowels makes a simple code such as this harder to crack, since the patterned frequency of vowel recurrence makes the vowels relatively easy to spot.

17.1802 (721:17). *Modern Society* – Published weekly on Wednesday, dated Saturday; offices, 18 Kirby Street, Hatton Garden, London, E.C.

17.1804 (721:20). rubber preservatives – Condoms; see 14.776n.

17.1805 (721:21). Box 32, P.O. Charing Cross, London, W.C. – Not unlikely as an address for merchandisers of the sort implied, but whether the address was fact or fiction is unknown.

17.1808 (721:24–25). the Royal and Privileged Hungarian Lottery – See 8.184–85n.

17.1814–15 (721:32–33). a 1d adhesive stamp . . . of Queen Victoria – There were two "lilac" penny stamps bearing the image of Queen Victoria, both issued in 1881: *Scott's Standard Postage Stamp Catalogue* (1969) number 88 ($5 uncanceled, $1 canceled) and number 89 ($15 uncanceled, $3 canceled).

17.1815–17 (721:33–36). a chart of the measurements . . . 15/–, athlete's 20/– – Sandow (see 4.234n) did advertise exercising machines.

17.1817–19 (721:36–38). chest 28 in and 29½ . . . calf 11 in and 12 in – Compare with Bloom's neck size—17 (17.1431 [710:18])—and his build—"height 5 ft 9½ inches, full build" (17.2003 [727:25]).

17.1819–21 (721:38–40). Wonderworker, Coventry House, South Place, London, E C – Whether this product was fact or fiction is unknown.

17.1836 (722:15). absentminded beggar – See 9.125n.

17.1839 (722:19). the South African campaign – That is, the Boer War (1899–1902).

17.1855 (723:1). Paula – In Hungarian as in English, the feminine form of the name Paul.

17.1856 (723:2–3). the Scottish Widows' Assurance Society – See 13.1227n.

17.1857–60 (723:4–7). coming into force at 25 . . . £133–10–0 at option – This legal tangle describes the various conditions of Bloom's endowment insurance: twenty-five years from the date at which Bloom took out the insurance, he will have a "profit policy" of £430 and will begin to receive, in installments, the Mutual Fund's profit on that amount; when he is sixty (or if he dies between sixty and sixty-five), the profit policy will be £462 10s.; and after he is sixty-five, it will be £500. The final option is that, instead of the profit policy of £430 after twenty-five years, the policyholder or beneficiary can accept a smaller policy and cash; there would be similar options at sixty and sixty-five.

17.1861 (723:8). Ulster Bank, College Green branch – The Ulster Bank, Ltd., had a branch office at 32–33 College Green, where Bloom's acquaintance, Theodore Purefoy, was "conscientious second accountant" (14.1324 [421:5]).

17.1863 (723:10). £18–14–6 – Looks like an inconsiderable sum, but it is more than Stephen would earn in half a year of teaching school, and if Bloom's annual rent was £28, as his house is valued, it would pay for almost eight months of rent.

17.1864–65 (723:12–13). £900 Canadian 4% . . . (free of stamp duty) – *Moody's Manual of Corporate Securities; 1904* (New York, 1904), p. 315, lists, "*£12,000,000 Dominion of Canada 4 Per Cent. Bonds and Stock.* Due from June, 1904 to 1908. Interest payable May and November, at Bank of Montreal. Bonds are convertible into inscribed stock on payment of ⅛% of fee. Now outstanding, stock, £7,900,000; bonds £4,099,700." Bloom's annual income from the interest on the book value of his holdings would have been £36 and, since the shares are "free of stamp duty," tax exempt.

17.1865–66 (723:13–14). the Catholic Cemeteries' (Glasnevin) Committee – The Dublin Catholic Cemeteries Committee, founded by the Catholic Association in 1828 (the year before Catholic Emancipation), with offices at 4 Rutland (now Parnell) Square East, was charged with the management of Prospect Cemetery in Glasnevin.

17.1867 (723:16). deedpoll – In law, a deed executed by only one party.

17.1869 (723:18). no. 52 Clanbrassil street – 52 Clanbrassil Street Upper now sports a blue Bord Fáilte plaque announcing that it is the birthplace of Leopold Bloom.

17.1870 (723:19). Szombathely – See 15.1868n.

17.1875–77 (723:25–27). daguerreotype of Rudolf Virag and his father Leopold . . . (respectively) 1st and 2nd cousin, Stefan Virag – A highly improbable relationship unless Bloom's father and grandfather are interchanged. If Stefan Virag were Leopold's first cousin, he would be Rudolf's second cousin (?).

17.1877 (723:28). Szesfehervar – For Székesfehérvár, a town in Hungary thirty-five miles southwest of Budapest. In the Austro-Hungarian Empire it was known as Stuhlweissenburg (population in 1900, approximately 29,000).

17.1878 (723:28). *haggadah book – See 7.206n.

17.1879–80 (723:29–31). the passage of thanksgiving . . . for Pessach (Passover) – "We thank thee, Lord, our God, for that thou didst give our fathers a lovely, good and spacious land as an inheritance, and for that thou didst take us out, O Lord, our God, from the land of Egypt, and didst redeem us from the house of slavery, and for thy covenant which thou didst seal in our flesh, and for thy Torah which thou didst teach us, and for thy laws which thou didst make known to us, and for the life, grace, and lovingkindness, which thou didst bestow upon us, and for the repast of food wherewith thou dost feed and sustain us always—each day, and at all times, and in every hour. And for all these, Lord, our God, we thank thee and bless thee. May thy name be blessed in the mouth of every living thing, always and for ever and aye. As it is written: 'And thou shalt eat and be satisfied, then shalt thou thank the Lord, thy God, for the good land which He gave thee.' Blessed art thou, Lord, for the land and the food" (*The Haggadah of Passover,* English by Abraham Regelson [New York, 1944], p. 37).

17.1880 (723:31). the Queen's Hotel, Ennis – See 6.529–30n.

17.1885 (723:39). Athos – See 6.125–27n.

17.1885–86 (723:40). *das Herz . . . Gott . . . dein* – German: "the heart . . . God . . . your."

17.1897 (724:12–13). The prohibition of the use of fleshmeat and milk at one meal – The origin of this prohibition is obscure, but Jewish tradition ascribes it to the avoidance of idolatry of the sort practiced in heathen festivals; the specific source is Exodus 23: "Thou shalt not seethe a kid in his mother's milk." Traditional applications of this law have elaborate ramifications.

17.1897–98 (724:13). the hebdomadary – That is, once every seven days; in context, the Jewish Sabbath. In the Roman Catholic church the hebdomadary is that member of a chapter or a convent whose week it is to preside over the reading of the Divine Office; see 10.184n.

17.1899 (724:15). the circumcision of male infants – For devout Jews, a required ritual regarded as a consecration of male generative powers to God and as necessary for cleanliness. The scriptural basis for this ritual is Genesis 17:9–10: "And God said unto Abraham . . . This is my covenant, which ye shall keep between me and you and thy seed after thee; Every man child among you shall be circumcised."

17.1900 (724:15–16). the supernatural character of Judaic scripture – That is, the belief that the Pentateuch was the word of God as dictated to Moses: "And the tables [of Moses] were the work of God, and the writing was the writing of God, graven upon the tables" (Exodus 32:16). This belief was threatened if not shaken by nineteenth-century biblical scholarship and its demonstration of the composite nature of the text of the Pentateuch and of the essentially legendary identity of Moses, the Lawgiver.

17.1900–1901 (724:16). the ineffability of the tetragrammaton – The four consonants of the Hebrew "incommunicable name" of God, *JHVH* or *JHWH* or *YHVH* or *YHWH*. The vowels were originally suppressed to keep the name a secret from the enemies of Israel and to impress the faithful with the name "too secret to be pronounced." The original pronunciation of the word was lost, and it is now usually rendered *Yahweh*, Jehovah. See 17.1798–1801n.

17.1901 (724:16–17). the sanctity of the sabbath – Is enforced by elaborate and highly particularized Jewish legal traditions. The general prohibition of doing unnecessary work on this "day of rest and worship" has led to specific and often hairsplitting rules—two random examples: it is all right to tie a band of cloth around a pail but not to tie a rope around a pail; one letter of the alphabet can be written, but not two, and it is against the law to cheat by using an eraser.

17.1909–10 (724:27–28). *Maria Theresia, empress of Austria, queen of Hungary – (1717–80), queen of Hungary and Bohemia, archduchess of Austria, the daughter of Holy Roman Emperor Charles VI and wife of Holy Roman Emperor Francis I.

17.1938 (725:23). the poor rate – A special parish tax levied for the support of the poor.

17.1941 (725:27–28). bailiff's man – An indigent who hangs around the bailiff's office in hopes of being paid for running errands (usually unpleasant, having to do with debt collection, etc.).

17.1944–45 (725:30–31). Old Man's House (Royal Hospital) Kilmainham – The Royal Hospital for Ancient, Maimed, and Infirm Officers, in Kilmainham, just west of Dublin south of the Liffey.

17.1945 (725:31–32). Simpson's Hospital – For the reception of poor, decayed, blind, and gouty men, between 206 and 207 Britain Street Great (now Parnell Street) in Dublin.

17.1947 (725:34). disfranchised rate supported – The voting franchise in 1904 Dublin was accorded only to tax- and rate-payers; those being supported by the poor-law rates could not qualify.

17.1951 (726:2). latration – Barking (like a dog).

17.1974 (726:27). The cliffs of Moher – On the west coast of Ireland north and west of Ennis in County Clare. They extend along the coast for about five miles with an impressive 668-foot sheer precipice at Knockardakin. The base of the cliffs is washed by the Atlantic.

17.1974 (726:27). the windy wilds of Connemara – A mountainous lake country on the west coast of Ireland in County Galway, described by guidebooks as "forbidding" and "severe."

17.1974–75 (726:27–28). lough Neagh with submerged petrified city – See 12.1454n. Medieval tradition held that the lough was originally a small fountain that suddenly erupted, inundating a whole region with its villages and ecclesiastical towers.

17.1975 (726:28). the Giant's Causeway – See 12.1877n.

17.1975–76 (726:29). Fort Camden and Fort Carlisle – See 16.418n.

17.1976 (726:29). the Golden Vale of Tipperary – A fertile plain north of the Galtee Mountains in south-central Ireland; it is largely in County Tipperary but extends also into Counties Waterford and Limerick.

17.1976 (726:30). the islands of Aran – Off the west coast of Ireland. The properly patriotic Irish revivalist regarded the isles as a national utopia, since the natives still spoke Irish and lived in what was sentimentally regarded as true Irish fashion.

17.1976–77 (726:30). the pastures of royal Meath – County Meath is north of County Dublin on the east coast of Ireland; "royal" because it was one of the five original provinces of ancient Ireland. Its name comes from the Irish *Maith* or *Magh* (level country) and its pasturelands were (and are) famous.

17.1977 (726:30–31). Brigid's elm in Kildare – The name Kildare derives from the Irish *Cilldara*, "Church of the Oak" (not elm), where St. Brigid had her cell under an oak and founded a religious community in 490; see St. Bride, 12.1705n; and cf. 12.1262–63n.

17.1977–78 (726:31). the Queen's Island shipyard in Belfast – The shipyard of Harland and Wolff, Ltd., 150 acres in extent, employed at the height of its prosperity some ten thousand men.

17.1978 (726:31–32). the Salmon Leap – See 12.1459n.

17.1978 (726:32). the lakes of Killarney – See 12.1451n.

17.1981–82 (726:35–36). Pullbrook, Robertson . . . Dame Street, Dublin – As listed in *Thom's* 1904, p. 1991.

17.1982–83 (726:36–727:2). Jerusalem, the holy city . . . goal of aspiration – The Moslems under Caliph Omar (c. 582–644) conquered Jerusalem in 637; the Dome of the Rock (the Mosque of Omar) was built on the site of Solomon's temple in 688. The Gate of Damascus was the main gate in the ancient walled city of Jerusalem; hence, it is the "goal of aspiration" ("next year in Jerusalem"; see 7.207n).

17.1984–85 (727:3–4). *the Parthenon (containing statues of nude Grecian divinities) – The temple of Athena on the Acropolis overlooking Athens. Its interior main hall contained one statue (long since lost) by Phidias, of a fully clothed Athena in wood, gold, and ivory. Most of the other statuary on the two pediments and the Panathenaic frieze girdling the outside of the temple proper (inside the colonnade) has been either destroyed or removed; what has been preserved is in the British Museum among the Elgin Marbles.

17.1985–86 (727:4–5). Wall street . . . international finance – The concentration of banking institutions in New York's Wall Street did control American finance, but its world dominion was at least shared with the City (London's financial center) until after World War I.

17.1986–87 (727:5–6). the Plaza de Toros . . . had slain the bull) – La Línea de la Concepción, a town in Spain just over the border from the British colony of Gibraltar, had a bull ring that was a popular resort for the inhabitants and the garrison of Gibraltar. John O'Hara of the Royal Welch Fusiliers (not the Queen's Own Cameron Highlanders), garrisoned on the Rock, took up bullfighting as an amateur in the 1870s, enjoying remarkable success as Don Juan O'Hara.

17.1987–88 (727:6–7). Niagara (over which no human being had passed with impunity) – The first person to go over the falls in a barrel successfully (with impunity) was Anna Edson Taylor, who went over Horseshoe Falls on the Canadian side on 24 October 1901.

17.1989 (727:8–9). the forbidden country of Tibet (from which no traveller returns) – The Tibetan policy of exclusion effectively closed the country to most Western exploration, trade, and travel from 1792 until a British-Indian expedition under Colonel Younghusband crossed the border (in pursuit of "friendly relations") and fought its way to Lhasa, which it entered 3 August 1904. The net result was, of course, "friendly relations" with an "open country." At least ten intrepid travelers did enter Tibet in the closing years of the nineteenth century and did manage to return, despite Bloom's quote from Hamlet's "To be or not to be" meditation on death as "The undiscovered country from whose bourn / No traveller returns" (III.i.79–80).

17.1990 (727:9–10). the bay of Naples (to see which was to die) – After the Italian proverb about the beauty of Naples: "See Naples and then die."

17.1992 (727:12). septentrional – In the north; after Septentriones, a Roman name for Ursa Major.

17.1992–96 (727:12–17). the polestar, located at. . . delta of Ursa Maior – The seven stars of Ursa Major, the Big Dipper, are given Greek letters not in descending order of their magnitude but in sequence from north to south—alpha, beta, gamma, delta, epsilon, zeta, eta. The traditional way to find the polestar is to locate it on a line projected from beta through alpha. The rest of this passage is difficult, since there is no omega in the constellation, and substituting zeta (since Z is the last letter in the English alphabet as omega is in the Greek) does not help to clarify this inconclusive geometrical construction within Ursa Major. If, on the other hand, the polestar, Polaris, the fixed point in the night sky, is omega (the end), then the construction could be explained as extending beyond Ursa Major: the line alpha–delta passes close to Capella, alpha Aurigae, the brightest star in the Charioteer. A line projected from Polaris at right angles to the Ursa Major beta–alpha line also passes close to Capella; thus the right triangle of guidance: Ursa Major alpha to Polaris to Capella and back to Ursa Major alpha. See 13.1258, 64n.

17.1998 (727:19). carnose – Of, pertaining to, or like flesh; fleshy.

17.1998–99 (727:20). a pillar of cloud by day – See 7.865–66n.

17.2000 (727:21). occultation – Not in the astronomical sense of "in eclipse" but in the rarer sense of "hidden from the eye or understanding; secret, concealed; hence, mysterious, supernormal or supernatural" (*Webster's New International Dictionary* [Springfield, Mass., 1901], p. 1487b). (For example, the twelfth imam of Shia Islam, who disappeared in 678 A.D., is said to be "in occultation," his return expected at any moment.)

17.2001 (727:23). £5 reward – Compare the king's ransom of treasures and gifts that the Phaeacians lavish on Odysseus in Book 8 of *The Odyssey* (just before they discover who he is, hear the chronicle of his adventures, and deliver him home to Ithaca).

17.2008 (727:31). Everyman – In the morality play *Everyman* (c. 1485) the hero, Everyman, representing individually all men, is called to "a sure reckoning" (line 70) after a normally heedless life. His false friends—allegorically, Fellowship, Kindred, Cousin, and (Worldly) Goods—instantly abandon him. Knowledge, Confession, Beauty, Strength, Discretion, Five-

Wits, and Good Deeds accompany Everyman on his "pilgrimage" (line 68), but one by one they too fall away until Everyman faces his descent into the grave accompanied by Good Deeds alone. See 14.107–22n.

17.2008 (727:31). Noman – The name with which Odysseus disguises his identity when he is captive in Polyphemus's cave; see headnote to Cyclops, p. 314.

17.2010 (727:33). Honour and gifts of strangers, the friends of Everyman – As Odysseus is honored among the Phaeacians, see 17.2001n; and compare Everyman stripped down to Good Deeds en route to the grave, 17.2008n.

17.2010–11 (727:33–34). A nymph immortal, beauty, the bride of Noman – That is, Calypso, who in Book 5 of *The Odyssey* in effect offers Odysseus marriage and immortality. He refuses because it is his destiny to refuse, but also because he considers it nobler to fulfill his life as a mortal than it would be to avoid the dangers of that fulfillment by accepting Calypso's offer of immortality.

17.2014 (727:38). telescopic planets – To Bloom, the "asteroids" Uranus and Neptune, which are not visible to the naked eye.

17.2017–18 (728:3–4). the summons of recall – In the schema he gave to Stuart Gilbert, Joyce called Hermes' mission to Calypso's isle (to deliver the message from Zeus saying that it is time for Odysseus to return to Ithaca) "The Recall"; see headnote to Calypso, p. 70; and cf. 4.240–42n.

17.2018–19 (728:4–5). the constellation of the Northern Crown – See 17.1123–26n and 4.1n.

17.2019–20 (728:5–6). reborn above delta in the constellation Cassiopeia – See 9.928–32n and 17.1118–23n.

17.2020–21 (728:7–8). an estranged avenger, a wreaker of justice on malefactors, a dark crusader – As Odysseus upon his return; see headnote to this episode, p. 566. This passage also alludes to the romantic career of Edmund Dantes in *The Count of Monte Cristo*. Deprived by conspiracy of his fiancée and his liberty and legally forgotten for fourteen years, he escapes from prison, recovers the treasure of Monte Cristo, and returns in disguise as the count to avenge himself on the conspirators who betrayed him. In *A Portrait* 2:A, Dantes is called "that dark avenger" because he is repeatedly described as strikingly pale with dark eyes and jet-black hair and because the Byzantine plots of his revenges are "dark."

17.2021–22 (728:8). a sleeper awakened – Rip Van Winkle; see 13.1112n.

17.2023 (728:10). Rothschild – See 15.1848n.

17.2023 (728:10). the silver king – The title of a well-made melodrama (1882) by the English playwrights Henry Arthur Jones (1851–1929) and Henry Herman. The innocent hero, Denver, believes himself guilty of a crime of which he has been falsely accused. The heroine is persecuted and hungry. The landlord villain has a haughty, aristocratic manner and a penchant for evictions and murder. The final triumph of virtue is achieved when the landlord's accomplices confess and vindicate Denver.

17.2034 (728:23). the statue of Narcissus, sound without echo, desired desire – See 17.1428n.

17.2044 (728:35). *kidney burnt offering – In ancient Jewish ritual, the burnt offering or sacrifice at the temple corresponds to the morning prayer. The review of Bloom's day that follows is largely in terms of a quasi-schematic Jewish liturgical calendar, as his day has previously been reviewed in the form of a Roman Catholic litany; see 15.1940–52 (498:22–499:3). See p. 70, n. 1.

17.2045 (728:36). holy of holies – The innermost, most sacred part of a Jewish temple, entered only once a year by the high priest on the Day of Atonement; see 17.2058n below. In modern Jewish ritual the holy of holies is also a series of prayers with which every day's morning services begin and which has replaced the morning sacrifice of the ancient ritual. One of the prayers refers specifically to the orifices of the body, thanking God for the fact that they exist and are open.

17.2045 (728:36–37). the bath (rite of John) – Washing is part of the Jewish morning ritual. The "rite of John" suggests John the Baptist's mission and his baptizing of Jesus in Matthew 3.

17.2046 (728:37) rite of Samuel – A compound reference to Samuel's career, which involved the exorcism of witches, wizards, and familiar spirits, and to the circumstances of his death: "Now

Samuel was dead, and all Israel lamented him, and buried him in Ramah, even in his own city. And Saul had put away those that had familiar spirits, and the wizards, out of the land" (I Samuel 28:3).

17.2046–47 (728:37–38). *the advertisement of Alexander Keyes (Urim and Thummim) – For Keyes, see 7.25n and 7.141n. *Urim* and *Thummim*, Hebrew: "Light" and "Perfection" or "Fire" and "Truth"; these two symbols, which the priest wears on his breastplate of judgment, suggest doctrine and faith, the ever-present possibility of a revelatory perception of God's will.

17.2047 (728:38–729:1). the unsubstantial lunch (rite of Melchisedek) – The "unsubstantial lunch" recalls the Jewish priest's quasi-fast at noonday; Melchisedek is the archetypal priest of the Old Testament: "And Melchizedek king of Salem brought forth bread and wine: and he was the priest of the most high God" (Genesis 14:18). In Hebrews 5:6 and 10, St. Paul describes Jesus as a priest "after the order of Melchisedec."

17.2048 (729:2). holy place – The inner part of a Jewish temple where the ark of the Torah is housed and within which is the holy of holies; see 17.2045n.

17.2048–49 (729:2–3). Bedford row, Merchants' Arch, Wellington Quay – Bedford Row is off Crampton Quay on the south bank of the Liffey just east of the metal bridge and Wellington Quay; see 10.315n.

17.2049 (729:3). Simchath Torah – Hebrew: "Rejoice in the Law"; the last day of Sukkoth (see 4.210–11n), when the ritual reading of the Pentateuch, which forms part of the seven-day feast, is completed and the cycle of reading begins again.

17.2050 (729:4). Shira Shirim – Hebrew: "Song of Songs" (Song of Solomon), which is read on the Sabbath during Sukkoth; see 4.210–11n.

17.2051 (729:6). holocaust – Literally, "a burnt offering, total sacrifice"; figuratively, the ceremony that commemorates the destruction of the temple in Jerusalem by the Romans on the ninth day of Av (the eleventh month of the Hebrew year), 70 A.D. On that day Jews mourn the reduction of Jerusalem and Israel to a wilderness.

17.2051–53 (729:6–7). blank period of time . . . a leavetaking (wilderness) – Bloom has consistently been reluctant to recall the period between Cyclops and Nausicaa, the period that includes his charitable visit to Mrs. Dignam in Sandymount. *House of mourning:* see 11.911n. "Wilderness" recalls not only the Israelites' forty years of wandering in the wilderness after they "took leave" of Egypt, but also those wilderness periods of exile that the Jews have suffered ever since. Those periods are commemorated annually from the seventeenth day of Tamuz (the tenth month) to the ninth day of Av (eleventh month), when the temple was breached (see preceding note). The observance centers on the song the exiles sing, "By the rivers of Babylon, there we sat down, yea, we wept, when we remembered Zion" (Psalms 137:1).

17.2053–54 (729:8). rite of Onan – "And Judah said unto [his son] Onan, Go in unto thy [dead] brother's wife, and marry her, and raise up seed to thy brother. And Onan knew that the seed should not be his; and it came to pass, when he went in unto his brother's wife, that he spilled it on the ground, lest that he should give seed to his brother. And the thing which he did displeased the Lord: wherefore he slew him also" (Genesis 38:8–10).

17.2054 (729:9). heave offering – A ceremonial peace offering, based originally on several injunctions in the Pentateuch, including Leviticus 7:32: "And the right shoulder shall ye give unto the priest for an heave offering of the sacrifices of your peace offering." "Heave offering" is here used in the sense that the priest will lift up the meat and reserve it for his own use; see Numbers 5:9. The heave offering has since become a ceremonial contribution (obligatory or voluntary) for the use of priests and sacred persons.

17.2055 (729:10–11). Mrs Bella Cohen, 82 Tyrone street, lower – The mistaken address given in Circe (15.1287 [475:18]) has been corrected.

17.2056 (729:12). Armageddon – After the Hebrew name for Mount Megiddo ("the place of crowds") in Palestine. In Jewish tradition it is regarded as the site of a future and ultimate Messianic struggle. The Christian interpretation (after Revelation 16) puts it as the site of a conclusive battle on the occasion of the Second Coming.

17.2058 (729:13). atonement – The Day of Atonement, the Jewish Yom Kippur, is a fast day observed on the tenth day of Tishri (the seventh month). It is the great day of national humiliation and mourning, when the sins of the year are expiated. It is when the scapegoat is sacrificed (see 15.776n) and the only day of the year on which the high priest enters the holy of holies (see 17.2045n and 8.752n). In Christian terms, the atonement is the redemption of man and his reconciliation with God through Jesus Christ; as St. Paul puts it in Romans 5:11: "We also joy in God, through our Lord Jesus Christ, by whom we have now received the Atonement."

17.2061–62 (729:17–19). a brief sharp unforeseen heard . . . strainveined timber table – Bloom's "prayerful" review of his day is rewarded by a clap of thunder out of a cloudless sky, as Odysseus is rewarded in *The Odyssey* when he strings the bow, wins the bow-stringing contest against the suitors, and prepares to kill them: "Then Zeus thundered / overhead, one loud crack for a sign. / And Odysseus laughed within him that the son / of crooked minded Kronos had flung that omen down" (21:413–16; Fitzgerald, p. 416). Coincidentally, Carl Gustav Jung (1875–1961) recounts in *Memories, Dreams, Reflections* (recorded and edited by Aniela Jaffe [New York, 1961], pp. 104–7) two such occurrences of loud cracks from pieces of furniture in the summer of 1898—these turned him toward spiritualism and the occult and "wiped out all my earlier philosophy and made it possible for me to achieve a psychological point of view."

17.2066 (729:23). Who was M'Intosh? – See 15.1561–62n.

17.2070 (729:28). Where was Moses when the candle went out? – Two street-rhyme answers to this question from the early twentieth century: "Down in the cellar with his shirt tail out" and "Down in the cellar eating sauerkraut." Bloom's answer to the riddle: "In the dark."

17.2075–77 (729:33–34). Pulbrook, Robertson and Co . . . London, E.C. – See 17.1981–82n and 5.20n.

17.2079–80 (729:36–38). the performance of *Leah* . . . South King street – See 5.194–95n.

17.2083 (730:4–5). Rehoboth, Dolphin's Barn – Dolphin's Barn is a street and a section in southwestern Dublin; Rehoboth (Hebrew:

"wide places or streets") is the name of three sites in Genesis, and Rehoboth, Rehoboth Terrace, and Rehoboth Road were all in the Dolphin's Barn section of Dublin.

17.2092–95 (730:17–20). new violet garters . . . a long bright steel safety pin – In Book 18 of *The Odyssey*, Penelope rebukes the suitors (much to the disguised Odysseus's amusement), and they bring her gifts of jewelry and clothing, including "a wide resplendent robe, / embroidered fine, and fastened with twelve brooches, / pins pressed into sheathing tubes of gold" (18:292–94; Fitzgerald, p. 357).

17.2094 (730:19). Muratti's Turkish cigarettes – A popular and widely advertised brand in 1904.

17.2103 (730:29). Orangekeyed – See 4.330n.

17.2104–5 (730:29–31). Henry Price, basket . . . 23 Moore street – *Thom's* 1904 (pp. 1549, 1990) lists George, not Henry, Price at this business and address. Henry Price is listed (p. 1990) as a dealer in hardware, chandlery, and fancy goods, 27 South Great George's Street. Cf. 2.334n.

17.2115 (731:4). With circumspection, as invariably when entering an abode – As Odysseus approaches Penelope when he reveals himself to her in *The Odyssey*, Book 23.

17.2133ff. (731:25ff.). Assuming Mulvey to be the first term – This widely quoted and incomplete list of Molly's "adulteries" is troublesome if one expects it to be based on a technical definition of adultery, that is, "with ejaculation of semen within the natural female organ" (see 10.168n). Jesus, however, presents a far more rigorous definition of adultery in Matthew 5:27–28: "Ye have heard that it was said by them of old time, Thou shalt not commit adultery: But I say unto you, That whosoever looketh on a woman to lust after her hath committed adultery with her already in his heart."

17.2133 (731:25). Penrose – Fictional; he was boarding with the Citrons (see 4.205n) when the Blooms were in Lombard Street West. Cf. 18.572–75 (754:9–12).

17.2133 (731:26). Bartell d'Arcy – See 8.181n. Cf. 18.273–82 (745:31–43).

17.2134 (731:26). professor Goodwin – See 4.291n. Cf. 18.335–39 (747:21–26).

17.2134 (731:26). Julius Mastiansky – See 4.205n. Cf. 18.417–20 (749:35–39).

17.2134 (731:26–27). John Henry Menton – See 6.568n. Cf. 18.38–44 (739:3–9).

17.2134–35 (731:27). Father Bernard Corrigan – Apparently not Dignam's brother-in-law of 16.1256 (647:36) and 17.1240 (704:21); cf. 18.107–21 (741:2–19).

17.2135 (731:27–28). a farmer at the Royal Dublin Society's Horse Show – See 13.998–1000 (374:15–16) and 7.193n. Molly does not recall this incident.

17.2136 (731:28). Maggot O'Reilly – See 15.570 (449:20–21). Molly does not recall O'Reilly.

17.2136 (731:28–29). Matthew Dillon – See 6.697n. Cf. 18.721–22 (774:39–40) and 18.1312–13 (758:15–16).

17.2136–37 (731:29). Valentine Blake Dillon (Lord Mayor of Dublin) – See 8.159n. Cf. 18.429–30 (750:6–8).

17.2137 (731:30). Christopher Callinan – See 7.690–91n. Molly does not recall him.

17.2137 (731:30). Lenehan – Cf. 18.426–28 (750:3–5). See also 10.552–67 (234:22–40).

17.2137 (731:30). an Italian organgrinder – Cf. 11.1092–93 (285:37–38). Molly does not recall him.

17.2137–38 (731:30–31). an unknown gentleman in the Gaiety Theatre – Cf. 18.1109–14 (769:8–14).

17.2138 (731:31). Benjamin Dollard – Cf. 18.1285–90 (774:8–14).

17.2138–39 (731:32). Simon Dedalus – Cf. 18.1284–1300 (774:14–26) and 18.1088–90 (768:25–28).

17.2139 (731:32). Andrew (Pisser) Burke – See 12.504n. Cf. 18.965–67 (765:6–9).

17.2139 (731:32). Joseph Cuffe – See 6.392n. Cf. 18.510–16 (752:19–27).

17.2139 (731:32–33). Wisdom Hely – See 6.703n. Molly recalls that Bloom worked there, but she does not recall Hely himself.

17.2139–40 (731:33). Alderman John Hooper – See 6.950n. Molly does not recall him.

17.2140 (731:33). Dr Francis Brady – See 15.4359n. Cf. 18.576 (754:13–14).

17.2140 (731:33–34). Father Sebastian of Mount Argus – St. Paul's College of the Passionist Fathers, Mount Argus, off Kimmage Road in Harold's Cross, a village two and a quarter miles south-southwest of Dublin center. *Thom's* 1904 lists no Father Sebastian in residence, and Molly does not recall him.

17.2140–41 (731:34–35). a bootblack at the General Post Office – Molly has no recall of this incident.

17.2146 (732:2). a bester – Slang: "a cheat."

17.2163–64 (732:24). the agent and reagent of attraction – The chemical terms suggest an allusion to "elective affinity," the tendency of certain chemical substances to combine with certain particular substances in preference to others. The term was in use from the late eighteenth century, and Goethe appropriated it as a metaphor for human relationships in his novel *Die Wahlverwandtschaften* (Elective Affinities) (1809).

17.2171 (732:32–33). George Mesias . . . 5 Eden Quay – See 6.831n.

17.2179 (733:5). natured nature – A translation of the Medieval Latin *natura naturata*, the world considered as an effect of formal and material causes, the world of actualities—in contrast to *natura naturans*, the supreme or essential being of the world.

17.2196–97 (733:27–28). outrage . . . outrage . . . outrage – In addition to its contemporary meanings and usages, *outrage* has at least two obsolete meanings (Chaucer): excessive or extravagant indulgence, luxury; and a mad display, a violent expression of passion.

17.2202–3 (733:33–34). Exposure by mechanical artifice (mechanical bed) – As Hephaestus, the lame and ugly god of fire and its arts in Greek mythology, is cuckolded by his wife, Aphrodite, and Ares. Hephaestus revenges himself by weaving an invisible net of gold in which he traps the adulterous pair at their sport and exposes them to the laughter of the Olympians.

17.2212–13 (734:5–6). the presupposed intangibility of the thing in itself – The German philosopher Immanuel Kant (1724–1804) "presupposed" that reality existed on two levels, noumenal and phenomenal. The phenomenal level (the surface of things) could be known, and that knowledge, he argued, could be metaphysically validated; the noumenal level (the *Ding an Sich*, or "thing-in-itself") could be postulated, but knowledge of it had not been, and perhaps could not be, metaphysically demonstrated.

17.2218 (734:12). an aorist preterite proposition – "Aorist" is the tense of a Greek verb indicating that an action took place in an indefinite past time; "preterite" means belonging wholly to the past. The proposition Bloom has in mind is "He fucked her."

17.2226 (734:21). apathy – As the classicist W. B. Stanford of Trinity College, Dublin, points out, this is the Stoics' *apathia*, the extinction of the passions through the ascendancy of reason (in a lecture delivered at Williams College, 26 October 1983).

17.2230–31 (734:27). the land of the midnight sun – The polar regions, since the sun shines twenty-four hours a day at the height of the Arctic and Antarctic summers.

17.2231 (734:27–28). the islands of the blessed – In late classical mythology, the Fortunate Islands, somewhere in the unexplored western sea, where mortals favored by the gods went after death; cf. *Tir na n-og*, the Irish analogue, 9.413n.

17.2231 (734:28). the isles of Greece – From the first line of a lyric interpolated in Byron's *Don Juan*, "Canto the Third" (1821), between stanzas 86 and 87. The first stanza (of sixteen): "The Isles of Greece, the Isles of Greece! / Where burning Sappho loved and sung, / Where grew the arts of War and Peace, / Where Delos rose, and Phoebus sprung! / Eternal summer gilds them yet, / But all, except their Sun, is set."

17.2231–32 (734:28). the land of promise – Specifically, Canaan (see 7.1061n); figuratively, that better country (or condition of life) for which one has an unfulfilled yearning. See 14.375–76n.

17.2233 (734:29). milk and honey – In Exodus 3:8, God promises Moses "to bring them up out of that land [of Egypt] unto a good land and a large, unto a land flowing with milk and honey." See preceding note.

17.2241 (734:38–39). He kissed the plump . . . melons of her rump – In *The Odyssey*, when Odysseus arrives on Ithaca it is shrouded in mist, and he is skeptical when Athena tells him that it is indeed Ithaca. Eventually she dispels the mist "so all the island / stood out clearly. Then indeed Odysseus' / heart stirred with joy. He kissed the earth, / and lifting up his hands prayed to the nymphs" (13:352–55; Fitzgerald, p. 253). See 15.2839n.

17.2245 (735:4). velation – The act of veiling, concealment, secrecy. See 4.308n.

17.2250 (735:9). With what modifications did the narrator reply – In Book 19 of *The Odyssey*, Odysseus in disguise is questioned by Penelope. He responds with "lies he made appear so truthful / she wept as she sat listening" (19:203–4; Fitzgerald, p. 372) and with "details—minutely true" that also move her to tears (19:250; Fitzgerald, p. 373).

17.2256–57 (735:17–19). a performance by Mrs Bandmann . . . South King street – See 5.194–95n.

17.2258–59 (735:20). Wynn's (Murphy's) Hotel, 35, 36 and 37 Lower Abbey street – "Commercial and Family Hotel (late Wynn's), Mr. D. J. Murphy, proprietor" (*Thom's* 1904, p. 1408).

17.2259 (735:21). *entitled – See 17.734n.

17.2260 (735:22). Sweets of Sin – See 10.606n.

17.2262 (735:24). postcenal – After supper.

17.2275–76 (736:5). 8 September 1870 – Molly's birthday is also celebrated as the Feast of the Nativity of the Blessed Virgin Mary. Born under the zodiacal sign of Virgo, the Virgin (an earth sign), Molly could be expected to have quick and loving sympathies and to be interested in and skillful at physical methods of gratifying human needs.

17.2278–79 (736:8–9). with ejaculation of semen within the natural female organ – A technical definition of complete sexual intercourse; cf. 10.168n and 17.2133nff.

17.2280–81 (736:11). 29 December 1893 – Rudy's birthday is the feast day of St. Thomas à Becket, bishop and martyr. Becket (c. 1118–70), archbishop of Canterbury, was involved in a notable Church vs. State struggle with Henry II of England and was finally murdered by agents (or self-appointed agents) of the king.

17.2282 (736:13). a period of 10 years, 5 months, 18 days – From 27 November 1893 to 17 June 1904 is 10 years, 6 months and 21 days. From 9 January 1894 it is 10 years, 5 months, 8 days. In any event, ten years is the period of Odysseus' frustrated wanderings toward Ithaca and home after the fall of Troy, and ten years is the period of Dante's wanderings through sin toward spiritual crisis and the *Inferno* after his separation from Beatrice (by her death in 1290) (*Purgatorio* 32:2).

17.2288 (736:20). 15 September 1903 – Milly's first menstrual period occurs on the feast day of Our Lady of Sorrows when the Sorrowful Mysteries of the Virgin Mary are commemorated; see 13.283–84n.

17.2303–4 (736:36–37). on the 53rd parallel of latitude, N. and the 6th meridian of longitude, W – To be precise (since the Art of this episode is science), Dublin is 53°20' north, 6°15' west; 53° north, 6° west would place the Blooms in Tinahelly House just north of Wicklow.

17.2308–9 (737:2–3). both carried westward . . . proper perpetual motion of the earth – Curious, since the earth in fact rotates from west to east. Physically, then, they are moving eastward (toward Jerusalem and renewal); figuratively, to move westward is to move toward death.

17.2313 (737:8). Gea-Tellus – A combination of the Greek earth-goddess Gaea, the mother of all living creatures, and the Roman earthmother, Tellus Mater. Gaea was worshiped in Athens as the nourisher of children and at the same time as the goddess of death, who summoned all creatures back to her and hid them in her bosom. She is usually represented as reclining on her side, cradling two children in her free arm.

17.2314 (737:9). Narrator – In Book 23 of *The Odyssey*, Odysseus and Penelope exchange stories after they retire, and Odysseus is described as "Remembering, / he drowsed over the story's end. Sweet sleep / relaxed his limbs and his care-burdened breast" (23:342–44; Fitzgerald, p. 452).

17.2322 (737:17–18). Sinbad the Sailor . . . Tinbad . . . Whinbad – There were characters named Tinbad and Whinbad in the Dublin pantomime *Sinbad the Sailor;* see 17.421–23n.

17.2328–29 (737:24–25). a square round . . . roc's auk's egg – The roc was a mythical bird of Arabia, so huge that it carried off elephants to feed its young; Sinbad, in the "Second Voyage of Sinbad" in the *Arabian Nights,* discovers one of its eggs and finds it to be "fifty good paces" in circumference. He hitches a ride on the unwitting parent-bird's leg to escape the island on which he has been marooned. The great auk, a subarctic flightless bird (extinct 1844), laid a single outsized egg at each nesting. Since the egg is "square round," the circle has been squared; see 15.2400–2401n. When Dante experiences beatific vision, at the end of the *Paradiso,* he still finds that his human limitations prevent him from full comprehension and full expression of its mystery: "As the geometer who all sets himself to measure [square] the circle and who findeth not, think as he may, the principle he lacketh" (canto 33, lines 133–35).

In the first edition (as in the Critical Edition), a large dot or period ended this episode: the Q.E.D. (that which was to be proved) to indicate completion of the logical proposition *S-M-P;* see p. 12.

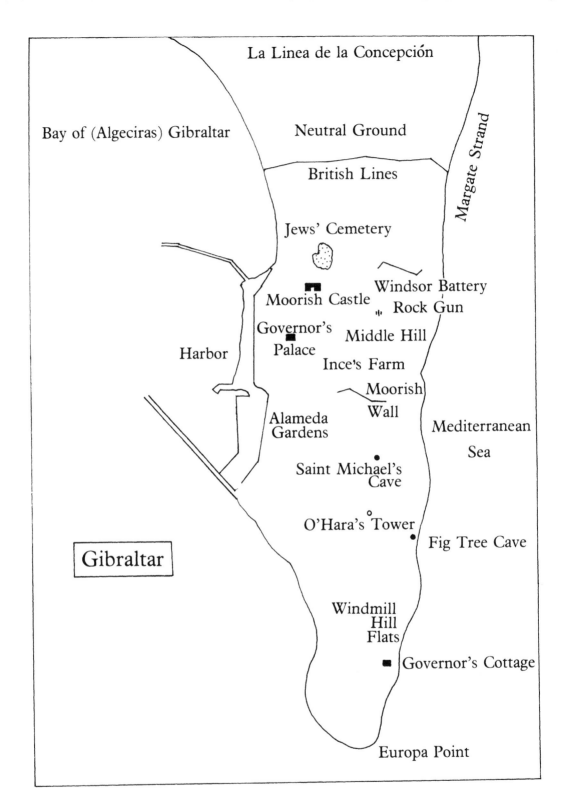

Gibraltar

EPISODE 18. *Penelope*

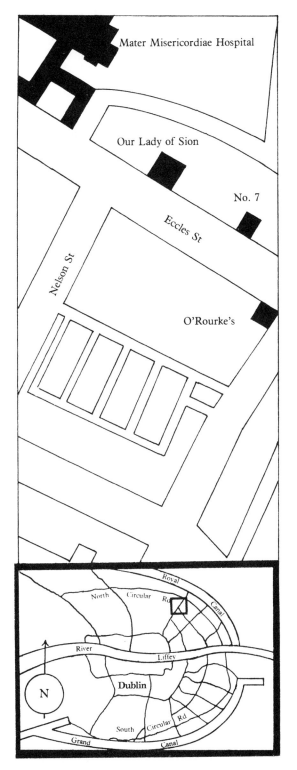

EPISODE 18

Penelope

(18.1–1609, PP. 738–83)

Episode 18: *Penelope*, 18.1–1609 (738–83). In Book 23 of *The Odyssey*, Penelope is awakened and informed by the nurse, Euryclea, that Odysseus has returned and slaughtered the suitors; at first she refuses to believe the nurse, saying that it must be some god in disguise who has killed the suitors for their presumption. When she descends into the hall to meet Odysseus, she is still reluctant, testing him, as he puts it, "at her leisure" (23:113; Fitzgerald, p. 445). What finally convinces Penelope that he is in fact Odysseus is his knowledge of the secret of the construction and the immovability of their bed. They retire, "mingled in love again" (23:300; Fitzgerald, p. 450), and then tell their stories to each other. In the morning Odysseus is up early to pacify the island, and the poem moves toward its close.

Time: none [Molly does not pattern her life by the clock]. Scene: the bed [as the sign of the bed is the key to the reunion of Odysseus and Penelope]. Organ: flesh; Art: none; Color: none; Symbol: earth (see 17.2313n); Technique: monologue (female), divided into eight sprawling, unpunctuated sentences (indicated below). Correspondences: *Penelope*—earth; *Web* [the shroud for Laertes, Odysseus's father, which Penelope weaves and unweaves in order to delay a decision among the suitors]—movement.

The Linati schema lists as Time, the recumbent 8, ∞, the sign for eternity as well as a symbol of female genitalia. It also lists as Persons, in addition to Ulysses and Penelope, Laertes [who is alive but "heartbroken" (15:360; Fitzgerald, p. 291) and retired from active life].

Sentence 1. 18.1–245 (pp. 738–44).

18.2 (738:2–3). the City Arms hotel – See 2.416–17n.

18.4 (738:5). faggot – English slang for an old, shriveled woman.

18.4 (738:5). Mrs Riordan – See 6.378n.

18.5 (738:5–6). had a great leg of – To "have a great leg of" is slang for to have considerable influence with.

18.5–6 (738:6–7). for masses for herself and her soul – See 6.857n. It was not uncommon for Catholics as devout as Mrs. Riordan considered herself to be to leave their money for such masses in order to relieve their sufferings and foreshorten their stay in purgatory.

18.8 (738:10). the end of the world – See 6.677–78n and 15.4670–72n.

18.19 (738:23). dring – To press, to squeeze.

18.25 (738:30). the south circular – The South Circular Road, which circled just inside the southern limits of metropolitan Dublin.

18.25–26 (738:31). the sugarloaf Mountain – See 8.166n.

18.26 (738:31–32). Miss Stack – Identity and significance unknown.

18.29 (738:35). to never see thy face again – Source in song or poem unknown.

18.36–37 (738:43–739:1). if it was down there he was really and the hotel story – Bloom has told Molly that he had "supper" at Wynn's Hotel in Lower Abbey Street (see 17.2257–58n); Molly wonders whether he is faking and has in fact been in the red-light district, which is not far to the northwest of Lower Abbey Street.

18.40 (739:5). Pooles Myriorama – A traveling show that appeared in Dublin approximately once a year in the 1890s, usually at the Rotunda (see 17.975n). A "myriorama" is a large picture or painting composed of several smaller ones that can be combined in a variety of ways. Pooles's show was a sort of travelogue with running commentary.

18.42 (739:8). mouth almighty – Slang: "he has a high opinion of himself."

18.56 (739:25). that Mary we had in Ontario Terrace – Mary Driscoll, the Blooms' servant when they lived in Ontario Terrace in Rathmines; see 15.861ff. (460:9ff.).

18.63 (739:34). oysters 2/6 per doz – An obvious exaggeration, three or four times the standard prices in 1900.

18.75 (740:5). singing about the place in the W C – *W. C.*: "water closet"; the song is unknown.

18.78 (740:10). the Tolka – See 8.588n.

18.78–79 (740:10). in my hand there steals another – Source in song or poem unknown.

18.80 (740:12). the young May Moon she's beaming love – See 8.589–90n.

18.91 (740:25). *the jews temples garden – On Adelaide Road between the Jewish synagogue and the Royal Victoria Eye and Ear Hospital near the Grand Canal.

18.95 (740:30–31). *who the german Emperor is – Wilhelm I (1797–1888), king of Prussia (1861–88) and German emperor (1871–88), died on 9 March 1888 and was succeeded by his son Frederick III (b. 1831), who died 15 June 1888 and was succeeded by his son, Wilhelm II (1859–1941), king of Prussia and German emperor (1888–1918). 1888 was the year of the Blooms' courtship.

18.107   (741:2).   Father   Corrigan – See 17.2134–35n.

18.115 (741:11–12). the bullneck in his horsecollar – A thick neck is popularly regarded as a sign of impressive sexual vitality; "horsecollar" is slang for a priest's reversed collar.

18.121 (741:19). give something to HH the pope for a penance – Molly's concept of the consequences of "sin" is about as sound as Gerty's (cf. 13.708–9n). Rev. Andrew Donlevy, *The Catechism, or Christian Doctrine . . . Published for the Royal Catholic College of St. Patrick, Maynooth* (Dublin, 1848), p. 103: "Q. Is it a more grievous offence to sin with a person in holy orders, or with a religious man or woman, than with another? A. Yes, it is much more grievous and more abominable; it is likewise a greater offence to sin with a kinsman or kinswoman, or with a married man or woman, than with others."

18.130 (741:30). talking stamps with father – See 4.65n.

18.132 (741:32). potted meat – See 5.144–47n.

18.136 (741:37). a Hail Mary – See 5.431n.

18.139 (741:40). an act of contrition – See 10.91–92n.

18.139 (741:40–41). the candle I lit . . . Whitefriars street chapel – That is, Molly has prayed for good luck and reinforced her prayer by placing a candle before a sacred image. The Convent and Church of the Calced Carmelites in Aungier and Whitefriar streets (central Dublin south of the Liffey) had a chapel in Whitefriar Street.

18.145–46 (742:5–6). Though his nose is not so big – In folklore, a large nose is supposed to indicate a large penis.

18.160 (742:23). give us a swing out of your whiskers – An expression from the west of Ireland meaning, "Preserve me from the story you're telling."

18.163 (742:27). Jesusjack the child is a black – Vincent Deane reports that this is still a popular Dublin catch phrase; its origin is unknown.

18.164–65 (742:28–29). you couldn't hear your ears – "An odd [Irish] expression:—'You are making such noise that I can't hear my ears'" (P. W. Joyce, *English*, p. 201).

18.168 (742:33). spunk – Slang for semen and also for courage.

18.169 (742:34). Josie Powell – Mrs. Denis Breen.

18.172 (742:38). Georgina Simpsons – See 15.443ff. (444:22ff.).

18.175–76 (742:42). about Our Lord being a carpenter – "And when the sabbath day was come, he [Jesus] began to teach in the synagogue: and many hearing him were astonished, saying . . . Is not this the carpenter, the son of Mary, the brother of James, and Joses, and of Juda, and Simon? and are not his sisters here with us? And they were offended at him" (Mark 6:2–3).

18.178 (743:2). the first socialist he said He was – A late-nineteenth-century commonplace among socialists, after Matthew 19:21: "Jesus said unto him, If thou wilt be perfect, go and sell that thou hast, and give to the poor, and thou shalt have treasure in heaven: and come and follow me."

18.181 (743:6). that family physician – *The Family Physician; a manual of domestic medicine by Physicians and Surgeons of the principal London Hospitals* (London, 1879), with four revised editions before 1895.

18.185 (743:10). Floey – One of Matthew Dillon's daughters.

18.195 (743:23). plabbery – From the Irish *plaboire*, "a fleshy-faced person with thick, indistinct speech."

18.204 (743:33). glauming – Grasping, clutching.

18.209 (743:40). trying to look like Lord Byron – Byron's (1788–1824) appearance and manner were widely publicized and imitated throughout his lifetime, and they remained images of romantic behavior and sensibility into the late nineteenth century. This was particularly true of his upswept hair, the air of delicate melancholy associated with his earlier poems, and his reputation as a dashing ladies' man.

18.214 (744:3). grigged – See 6.761n.

18.223 (744:14). when the maggot takes him – See 15.570n.

18.229 (744:21). *Up up – See 8.258n.

18.229 (744:21). *O sweetheart May – A song (1895) in which eight-year-old May asks the singer's promise of marriage. When, much later, he returns to marry her, she is betrothed to another. Chorus: "Sweetheart May, when you grow up, one day, / You may marry another and my love betray; / But I'll wait for you, and then we shall see / What you will do when I ask you to marry me."

18.234–45 (744:28–40). Mrs Maybrick that poisoned her husband . . . to go and hang a woman – James Maybrick (1839–89), a Liverpool cotton broker, died mysteriously in his home on 11 May 1889. Mrs. Florence Elizabeth Chandler Maybrick (1862–1941) was tried for his murder. At the trial it was established that she had had a lover or lovers and that she had quarreled with Maybrick; also that she had tried to obtain arsenic in the way Molly recalls—cleverly, but not cleverly enough to escape detection. There was some doubt about her guilt, since Maybrick was addicted to patent medicines that contained arsenic, but the jury was convinced that her flypaper trick had tipped the balance, and it found her guilty on 7 August 1889. She was condemned to death, but her sentence was commuted to life on 22 August 1889, and she was released on 25 January 1904.

Sentence 2. 18.246–534 (pp. 744–53).

18.247 (744:43). the D B C – See 8.510n.

18.255 (745:9). *the *Irish* times – See 8.323n.

18.261–62 (745:17). the stone for my month a nice aquamarine – The stone for Molly's month of September is chrysolite, symbolic of preservation from or the cure of folly; aquamarine, symbolic of hope, is the stone for October.

18.269 (745:26). Katty Lanner – See 15.4044n.

18.270 (745:28). the stoppress edition – An edition of the *Evening Telegraph* that hit the streets between 5:30 and 6:00 P.M. daily, called "stoppress" because the paper's central page carried a column labeled "Stop Press" that was held for the insertion of late news. More often than not the column appeared as a blank in the paper.

18.271 (745:29). the Lucan dairy – The Lucan Dairy Company had eighteen shops in Dublin and environs in 1904.

18.274–75 (745:33). Gounods Ave Maria – Charles François Gounod (1818–93), a French composer, set the Ave Maria (Hail Mary; see 5.431n) (1859) to a melody adapted from Bach. Scored for soprano and organ or orchestra, it was a very popular setting of the text.

18.275–76 (745:33–34). what are we waiting . . . the brow and part – From a song, "Good-Bye," by G. J. Whyte-Melville and F. Paolo Tosti. First and third verses: "Falling leaf and fading tree, / Lines of white in a sullen sea, / Shadows rising on you and me; / The swallows are making them ready to fly, / Wheeling out on a windy sky. / Good-bye, Summer! Good-bye. // What are we waiting for? Oh? My Heart! / Kiss me straight on the brows, and part! / Again, again! My Heart! My Heart! / What are we waiting for, you and I? / A pleading look, a stifled cry. / Good-bye, forever, Good-bye!"

18.282–83 (745:43). he hadnt an idea about my mother – Molly's mother, Lunita Laredo ("little moon" of Laredo, a town on the north coast of Spain), is something of a puzzle. She apparently deserted Tweedy and Molly or died early in Molly's life. What it was that Bloom "hadnt an idea about" remains a mystery. John Henry Raleigh (*The Chronicle of Leopold and Molly Bloom: Ulysses as Narrative* [Berkeley, Calif., 1977], p. 18) suggests that she was "evidently a demimondaine" and that "Molly might be illegitimate." Or it may be that Molly's mother was a Spanish Jew, a mystery that Bloom would value; see 18.1184 (771:14).

18.285 (746:4). Kenilworth square – A park or green just west of Rathmines and south of metropolitan Dublin, a little more than a mile southeast of the Tweedy home in Dolphin's Barn.

18.290 (746:9). skeezing – Slang for staring at covertly.

18.291–92 (746:11). the open air fete – A social event usually organized for the benefit of a charitable institution. The *Dublin Evening Mail* of Wednesday, 15 June 1904, carried an advertisement that was typical: "Titania Grand Open-Air Fete. In the Grounds of Blackrock House, Blackrock. (Kindly lent by T. C. McCormick, Esq.) Friday and Saturday, June 17, 18 (11:30 A.M. to 10 P.M.)." The fete was to feature "Boating, Steam Launch Trips, Swimming, Fireworks," etc.

18.295 (746:15). the Harolds cross road – A main road that leads south into the countryside from metropolitan Dublin. It passes near to Kenilworth square; see 18.285n.

18.296 (746:16). Zingari colours – Gypsy colors.

18.297 (746:17). slyboots – See 15.3586n.

18.306 (746:29). O Maria Santissima – Italian: "O Most Holy Mary."

18.307 (746:30). dreeping – Drooping or walking very slowly.

18.313 (746:37). Gardner – Lt. Stanley G. Gardner, of the 8th Battalion of the 2d East Lancashire Regiment. He is apparently fictional, though he may owe his name to Gardner's Battery, part of the complex of fortifications that commanded the landward approaches to Gibraltar. He is notably absent from the series of Molly's "lovers" (17.2133–42 [731:25–36]).

18.318 (746:43). what a Deceiver – While Penelope is still holding out in Book 23 of *The Odyssey*, Odysseus shows his artfulness as a deceiver; in order to keep the news of the suitors' deaths from the community, he stages what will appear to outsiders to be a wedding feast (as though Penelope had finally accepted one of the suitors).

18.322 (747:5). *Henny Doyle – See 13.1112n.

18.329 (747:14). eight big poppies – In the language of flowers: silence (if Oriental poppies), consolation (if red), fantastic extravagance (if scarlet), sleep (if white).

18.329–30 (747:14). because mine was the 8th – See 17.2275–76n.

18.344 (747:31–32). the 2 Dedalus girls coming from school – Katie and Boody apparently attend a school east or southeast of Eccles Street, which would then lie on their route home toward Cabra, not quite a mile to the northwest.

18.346–47 (747:35). for England home and beauty – See 10.232, 235n.

18.347–48 (747:36). there is a charming girl I love – "It is a charming girl I love" is a song in Act I of *The Lily of Killarney;* see 6.186n.

18.353 (747:42–43). some protestant clergyman – Belfast was then, as now, a notorious Protestant stronghold.

18.357–58 (748:5–6). *the Mallow concert at Maryborough – Maryborough, now Portlaoise, is a market and county town fifty-two miles southwest of Dublin in Queen's County (now County Laois). Apparently, when the Blooms were on their way to Mallow (a town twenty-two miles north of Cork), the Dublin–Cork train made a prolonged stop, and the Blooms got out for a snack (Roland McHugh, letter, 27 October 1984).

18.365 (748:14–15). theyd have taken us on to Cork – The Blooms would have taken the Great Southern and Western Railway, Dublin to Maryborough (52 miles); Cork is 112 miles beyond Maryborough. Molly's phrasing is reminiscent of the chorus to a popular music-hall song of the 1890s: "Oh, Mr. Porter what shall I do? / I want to go to Birmingham and they're taking me on to Crewe."

18.375 (748:27). St Teresas hall Clarendon St – St. Teresa's Total Abstinence and Temperance Loan Fund Society, 43–44 Clarendon Street, Dublin.

18.376 (748:28). Kathleen Kearney – Appears as a character in "A Mother," *Dubliners.* Kathleen's mother mounts her daughter's concert career by taking "advantage of her daughter's name," since Kathleen ni Houlihan is a traditional symbol of Ireland; see 1.403n.

18.376–77 (748:28–29). on account of father being in the army – Molly suspects that Irish nationalists are discriminating against her because of her father's army career (making him anti-Irish).

18.377 (748:29–30). the absentminded beggar – See 9.125n. During the Boer War intensely anti-British Irish nationalists were inclined to be as intensely pro-Boer, and this song of Kipling's was regarded as pro-British.

18.378 (748:30). *Lord Roberts – See 14.1331–32n.

18.378 (748:31). the map of it all – That is, she has the map of Ireland all over her face: colloquial for "it's obvious that she is Irish" (John Henry Raleigh, *The Chronicle of Leopold and Molly Bloom: Ulysses as Narrative* [Berkeley, Calif., 1977], p. 182).

18.380 (748:33). the Stabat Mater – See 5.397–98n.

18.381–82 (748:34–36). Lead Kindly Light . . . lead thou me on – See 4.347n.

18.383 (748:37). Sinner Fein – *Sinn Fein;* see 8.458n.

18.386 (748:40). *Griffiths – See 3.227n.

18.388 (748:43). Pretoria – The heavily fortified capital of the Boer republic of Transvaal in South Africa. It was the seat of the executive government of the coalition of Boer republics during the Boer War. Pretoria was not the scene of a battle; Boer general Paul Kruger abandoned it in May 1900, and the British occupied it without resistance.

18.388 (748:43). Ladysmith and Bloemfontein – See 15.1525–26n and 15.796n.

18.389 (749:1). 8th Bn 2nd East Lancs Rgt – See 18.313n.

18.392 (749:4–5). my Irish beauty – The phrase suggests a source in poem or song (unknown).

18.394–95 (749:8). *oom Paul and the rest of the other old Krugers – "Oom [uncle] Paul" was Stephanus Johannes Paulus Kruger (1825–1904), a Boer statesman and president of the South African republic of Transvaal from 1883 to 1900. His career was one long struggle, first against the contentious factions that divided his own people and later against the English, who put increasing pressure on the Boer republics to submit to annexation and English dominion; Kruger's opposition to annexation was determined (or obstinate), but the end result was the Boer War and annexation anyway.

18.398 (749:12–13). the Spanish cavalry at La Roque – At San Roque, rather, a town in Spain about seven miles from Gibraltar; it was a Spanish garrison town (against the foreign presence of the English on the Rock).

18.399 (749:14). Algeciras – A town in Spain on the western headland of the Bay of Algeciras; Gibraltar, the eastern headland, is some six miles away.

18.400 (749:15). the 15 acres – An area in Phoenix Park, Dublin. It was frequently used for military reviews and exercises of the sort Molly recalls.

18.400 (749:15). the Black Watch – The Royal Highlanders, a distinguished regiment of Scottish infantry, the 42d Regiment of the Line in the British army.

18.401–2 (749:16–17). the 10th hussars the prince of Wales own – The tenth of the cavalry regiments was the Prince of Wales Own Royal Hussars.

18.402 (749:17). the lancers – The 5th, the Royal Irish Lancers? the 9th, the Queen's Royal Lancers? the 12th, the Prince of Wales Royal Lancers? the 16th, the Queen's Lancers? the 21st, the Empress of India's Lancers?

18.402 (749:17). O the lancers theyre grand – Source unknown.

18.402–3 (749:17–18). the Dublins that won Tugela – The Tugela River valley was the scene of a Boer War campaign that was both frustrating and costly for the English. The point of the campaign was to relieve the pressure on Ladysmith (see 15.1525–26n). A force of British, including a battalion of Royal Dublin Fusiliers, crossed the Tugela on 18 February 1900 and, on the night of 23–24 February, stormed Spion Kop, the key of the enemy's position; but the next day the British were cut to ribbons in a murderous crossfire (the Dublins suffered thirty percent casualties). They were forced to abandon the position and retire beyond the Tugela on 27 February 1900.

18.403 (749:18–19). his father made his . . . horses for the cavalry – That is, Boylan's father; see 12.998–99n.

18.427 (750:4). the Glencree dinner – See 8.160n.

18.428 (750:5). featherbed mountain – See 10.555n.

18.428–29 (750:6–7). the lord Mayor . . . Val Dillon – See 8.159n.

18.441 (750:22). Manola – A loud and boisterous Spanish street song.

18.443 (750:24). Lewers – Mrs. R. G. Lewers, ladies' outfitting warehouse, 67 Grafton Street, Dublin (a fashionable shopping district in 1904).

18.446–47 (750:28). the Gentlewoman – A sixpenny weekly magazine published in London on Thursdays (dated Saturday). It advertised "'The Gentlewoman' is replete in every department with matter interesting to ladies. Its Fashions, English and French, are far in advance of its contemporaries both in artistic merit and reliability" (*Who's Who in Great Britain and Ireland* [London, 1906], p. 36).

18.451 (750:34). ORourkes – See 4.105n.

18.453 (750:36). a cottage cake – A cake without frosting.

18.454–55 (750:37–38). God spare his spit for fear hed die of the drouth – A west-of-Ireland expression of contempt for an ungenerous person.

18.455–56 (750:39). that antifat – In the late nineteenth century numerous patent medicines were advertised as ideal for those who wanted to reduce: "just keep on eating as much as you like," etc.

18.475 (751:20). Ill be 33 in September – No, Molly will be 34; cf. 17.2275–76 (736:5).

18.476 (751:21). Mrs Galbraith – Adams (p. 155) suggests "the spouse of H. Denham Galbraith, Esq., 58B Rathmines Road; the guess would be founded on her relative proximity to the Blooms' former neighborhood."

18.479 (751:24–25). Kitty O'Shea in Grantham street – "Kitty O'Shea in Grantham street is only the namesake of Parnell's lady; living at #3, . . . according to *Thom's Directory* for 1882, was Miss O'Shea" (Adams, p. 239).

18.481–82 (751:27–28). *that Mrs. Langtry the jersey lily the prince of Wales was in love with – Lillie (Mrs. Edward) Langtry (1852–1929) came from the obscurity of a parsonage in the Isle of Jersey to the London limelight (1874) by means of the wealthy elderly Irish widower Langtry (d. 1897). Her liaison with the Prince of Wales was widely publicized; she eventually left her husband (1881) and became an unsuccessful actress who nevertheless played to packed houses—thanks to her beauty and the prince's patronage. In 1899 she was married for a second time, to Sir Hugo Gerald de Bathe.

18.484–85 (751:31–33). some funny story about . . . he had the oyster knife – The story of the chastity belt and the oyster knife is apocryphal; its only basis in fact was Mr. Langtry's well-publicized jealousy of his young and beautiful wife.

18.488–90 (751:36–38). the works of Master Francois . . . because her bumgut fell out – François Rabelais (c. 1490–1553), the great French satirist, began his career as a Franciscan monk, switched to the more scholarly Benedictines, and eventually drifted into a sort of secular priesthood. In *The Histories of Gargantua and Pantagruel*, Book 1, chapter 6, "The very strange manner of Gargantua's birth," Rabelais describes how Gargantua's mother thinks she is about to give birth: "But it was the fundament slipping out, because of the softening of her right intestine—which you call the bum-gut—owing to her having eaten too much tripe." She is treated with an "astringent," and "By this misfortune the cotyledons of the matrix were loosened at the top, and the child leapt up through the hollow vein. Then, climbing through the diaphragm to a point above the shoulders, where this vein divides in two, he took the left fork and came out by the left ear" (trans. J. M. Cohen [London, 1955], p. 52).

18.493 (751:41). Ruby and Fair Tyrants – See 4.346n and 10.601–2n.

18.494–95 (751:42–752:1). page 50 the part about . . . a hook with a cord flagellate – Presumably from *Fair Tyrants*, which work remains unknown.

18.496 (752:2–3). about he drinking champagne out of her slipper – The particular source Molly has in mind for this bit of folklore is unknown.

18.496 (752:3). after the ball was over – From a sentimental ballad, "After the Ball" (1892), by Charles K. Harris. The ballad is the story of an old man who has remained celibate because long ago his "true love" apparently, but not really, deceived him: "I believ'd her faithless, after the ball." Chorus: "After the ball is over, / After the break of morn, / After the dancers' leaving, / After the stars are gone, / Many a heart is aching, / If you could read them all; / Many the hopes that have vanished, / After the ball."

18.497 (752:3–4). like the infant Jesus . . . in the Blessed Virgins arms – Attached to the Roman Catholic Church of Oblate Fathers of Mary Immaculate in Inchicore, on the western outskirts of Dublin, is a shrine of the Nativity, "with the wax figures of the Holy Family and Magi and the shepherds and horses and oxen, sheep and camels stretching all around the hall in cheap and dusty grandeur" (Stanislaus Joyce, *My Brother's Keeper* [New York, 1958], p. 10). The infant Jesus is unrealistically oversized, as Molly suggests.

18.499–500 (752:6–7). because how could she go . . . and she a rich lady – Back to Lillie Langtry and her chastity belt.

18.500–501 (752:8). H.R.H. he was in Gibraltar the year I was born – The *Gibraltar Directory and Guide Book*, published annually from 1873, contains a section on the history of Gibraltar that is meticulous in its record of royal favors, such as visits. The Prince of Wales did visit the Rock in 1859 and 1876, but not in 1870, the year of Molly's birth.

18.501–2 (752:9). lilies there too where he planted the tree – Cf. 18.481–82n. We can find no record of the Prince of Wales having been involved in a tree-planting ceremony on Gibraltar; but when he paid a ten-day visit in 1876, he did lay the cornerstone of the New Market, which opened on 1 November 1877.

18.507 (752:16). *plottering – Trifling, dawdling, lingering.

18.510 (752:19–20). Mr Cuffes – See 6.392n.

18.512 (752:22). mirada – Spanish: "look."

18.516–17 (752:27–28). Todd and Burns – Todd, Burns & Co., Ltd., silk mercers, linen and woolen drapers, tailors, etc., 17–18 and 47 Mary Street and 24–28 Jervis Street.

18.517 (752:28). Lees – Edward Lee, draper and silk mercer, 48 Mary Street and 6–7 Abbey Street Upper, with branches in Rathmines, Kingstown, and Bray.

18.520 (752:31). mathering – Irish dialect: "mothering."

Sentence 3. 18.535–95 (pp. 753–54).

18.542–43 (753:16). two bags full – After the nursery rhyme: "Baa, baa, black sheep, / Have you any wool? / Yes sir, yes sir, / Three bags full: / One for my master, / One for my dame, / But none for the little boy / Who cries in the lane."

18.545 (753:26). Cameron highlander – According to the *Gibraltar Directory and Guide Book*, the 79th Queen's Own Cameron Highlanders were stationed at Gibraltar from June 1879 to August 1882.

18.546 (753:27–28). where the statue of the fish used to be – Namely, in the center of the Alameda Gardens on Gibraltar. The statue was the figurehead of the *San Juan*, a Spanish ship of the line captured by the British at Trafalgar (1805). It represented a figure harpooning a fish and was, by 1884, in such a serious state of decay that it had to be removed.

18.548–49 (753:30–31). the Surreys relieved them – According to the *Gibraltar Directory and Guide Book*, a detachment of the 1st East Surreys relieved the Cameron Highlanders on Gibraltar in August 1882.

18.550 (753:32). greenhouse – A public urinal.

18.550–51 (753:32–33). the Harcourt street station – In southeastern Dublin, the terminus of the Dublin, Wicklow, and Wexford Railway.

18.552 (753:34). the 7 wonders of the world – Seven remarkable monuments in the ancient

Mediterranean world; usually: the pyramids of Egypt; the Pharos (lighthouse) at Alexandria; the walls and hanging gardens of Babylon; the temple of Artemis at Ephesus; the statue of Olympian Zeus by Phidias; the mausoleum erected by Artemisia at Halicarnassus; and the Colossus of Rhodes.

18.553 (753:36). the Comerfords party – See 17.1782n. The Blooms would have come up from Dalkey by the Dublin, Wicklow, and Wexford Railway; see 18.550–51n.

18.555 (753:38–39). 93 the Canal was frozen – It is unusual for the Royal and Grand canals to freeze over, but they did in 1893, according to John Garvin, the Dublin city commissioner (letter, 31 August 1970).

18.557 (753:41). meadero – Spanish: "urinal."

18.562 (753:22). the coffee palace – See 11.486n.

18.562–63 (753:22–23). bath of the nymph – See 4.369n.

18.565 (754:1). met something with hoses in it – Metempsychosis; see 4.339n.

18.573 (754:10–11). student that stopped in No 28 with the Citrons Penrose – See 4.205n and 8.178–79n.

18.576 (754:13). doctor Brady – See 15.4359n.

Sentence 4. 18.596–747 (pp. 754–59).

18.598 (754:40–41). *Loves old sweeeet sonnnng – See 4.314n.

18.601 (755:1). *Photo Bits – See 4.370n.

18.607 (755:9). levanter – A strong, raw easterly wind peculiar to the Mediterranean.

18.608–9 (755:10–11). like a big giant . . . their 3 Rock mountain – Gibraltar is 1,430 feet at its highest point and about three miles long from north to south. Three Rock Mountain, seven miles south of Dublin center, is 1,479 feet high. Of the two, Gibraltar is clearly the more impressive and dramatic.

18.612 (755:15). Mrs Stanhope – The fictional Hester Stanhope is named after Lady Hester Lucy Stanhope (1776–1839), an Englishwoman who had a remarkable career first as private sec-

retary to her uncle, William Pitt, and later as prophetess and head of a monastery on Mount Lebanon, where she evolved a religion of her own, a blend of Judaism, Christianity, and Islam.

18.613 (755:15). *the B Marche paris – Au Bon Marché, a famous department store in the Boulevard Haussmann in Paris.

18.616 (755:19). wogger – Or wog: uncomplimentary English slang for an Arab or dark-skinned person.

18.617 (755:21). Waiting – See 11.730n.

18.617 (755:21). in old Madrid – See 11.733n.

18.617–18 (755:21–22). Concone is the name of those exercises – Giuseppe Concone (1801–61), an Italian vocal teacher noted for his vocal exercises, "Thirty Daily Exercises for the Voice" (Opus 11); "These Exercises Form a Transition from the Grand Style to the Extreme Difficulties of Vocalization." The exercises were admired not only because they were effective but also because they were attractive (as exercises go).

18.623 (755:28). *captain Grove – Apart from the context, identity and significance unknown.

18.626 (755:31). the bullfight at La Linea – See 17.1986–87n.

18.626 (755:32). that matador Gomez was given the bulls ear – Molly may have a specific Gomez in mind (see Thornton, p. 491); but it is also possible that the name refers to the Gomez family that sent an unbroken sequence of distinguished performers into the bullring from the early 1870s through the 1930s. The president of a bullfight awards the bull's ear for an outstanding performance.

18.628 (755:34). Killiney hill – The southeastern headland of Dublin Bay (480 feet), affording a good view of Howth across the bay to the north.

18.635 (755:42). bell lane – Not on Gibraltar, as the context might suggest, but off Ely Place in Dublin.

18.643–44 (756:10). at the band on the Alameda esplanade – The Alameda on Gibraltar is a garden-promenade that functioned as something of an oasis on the desertlike rock. The regimental bands of the garrison gave concerts on Thursdays at 4:00 P.M. in winter and on Mondays and Thursdays at 9:00 P.M. in summer.

18.645 (756:11). the church – Molly is apparently no longer in the Alameda Gardens but some distance away, in the Church of St. Mary the Crowned, the Roman Catholic cathedral on Gibraltar.

18.650 (756:15). *like Thomas in the shadow of Ashlydyat – *The Shadow of Ashlydyat* (1863) by Mrs. Henry (Ellen Price) Wood (1814–87). Thomas Godolphin, grey by comparison with his "gay, handsome, careless" younger brother George, is a country gentleman and banker in his late thirties with "a quiet, pale countenance . . . a casual observer might have pronounced him 'insignificant.' . . . But there was a certain attraction to his face which won its way to hearts" ([London, 1902], p. 3). Thomas's "disappointments" consist in the loss of his young fiancée to typhus, brother George's dishonesty and the consequent loss of the family bank, fortune, and estate, and the lingering agony of a slow and premature death at the age of forty-five. Thomas can hardly be described as "gay" (a word Mrs. Wood uses repeatedly to characterize George); instead, he is "undemonstrative" (p. 198) and almost improbably saintly in his sustained refusal to complain.

18.653 (756:18–19). the Moonstone . . . of Wilkie Collins – *The Moonstone* (1868) by Wilkie Collins (1824–89) has been regarded by many, including T. S. Eliot and Dorothy Sayers, as "the first and most perfect detective story ever written." The novel's story is told in sequence by several eyewitnesses; the carefully elaborated plot involves the unraveling of a tangle of deceit that the Moonstone (properly the attribute of an Indian moon-god) engenders when it is inherited by (and immediately stolen from) a young English lady of fortune.

18.653 (756:19). East Lynne – *Or the Earl's Daughter* (1861), another novel by Mrs. Henry Wood. At the pathetic center of the novel's improbable plot is a woman wrongfully divorced who reenters her ex-husband's home in disguise so that, as governess, she can care for her own child; she dies, forgiven, on her deathbed. A dash of melodrama in the form of a murder trial completes the novel's popular appeal. Various stage versions have enjoyed extraordinary popularity.

18.654 (756:20). the shadow of Ashlydyat – See 18.650n.

18.654 (756:20). Henry Dunbar – A novel (1864) by the English novelist Mary Elizabeth Braddon (Mrs. John Maxwell, 1837–1915). The plot hinges on one character's impersonation of a dead millionaire and the gradual revelation of his identity and of the dead man's fate.

18.656 (756:22–23). Lord Lytton Eugene Aram – *The Trial and Life of Eugene Aram* (1832), by Edward Bulwer-Lytton, Baron Lytton (1803–73), an English politician and novelist. It is a romance of crime and social injustice in which the reader is asked to sympathize with the criminal (Aram) and his motive. Aram is portrayed as an ingenious and kindly teacher pressured by poverty into participating in a murder and robbery. Though Aram's motives are serious, he is nevertheless (and sentimentally) tried and condemned as a common criminal.

18.656–57 (756:23). Molly bawn . . . by Mrs Hungerford – Margaret Wolfe Hungerford (c. 1855–97), an Irish novelist who wrote, under the pseudonym "the Duchess," *Molly Bawn* (Irish: "Beautiful Molly") (1878). The title is derived from an Irish ballad that begins: "Oh, Molly Bawn! Why leave me pining, / All lonely waiting here for you?" Molly is the beautiful, well-meaning, but capricious Irish girl of good family who is wooed, almost lost, and finally won by the hero. The novel is notable only for its reproduction of the atmosphere and small talk of Irish high society.

18.658 (756:25). the one from Flanders – Daniel Defoe's (1660–1731) *The Fortunes and Misfortunes of the Famous Moll Flanders; Who was Born in Newgate, and during a Life of continu'd Variety for Threescore Years, besides her Childhood, was Twelve Year a Whore, five times a Wife (whereof once to her own Brother), Twelve Year a Thief, Eight Year a Transported Felon in Virginia, at last grew Rich, liv'd Honest and died a Penitent; Written from her own Memorandums* (1722).

18.673 (765:43). taittering – English dialect: "tilting, seesawing."

18.678–79 (757:6–7). *waiting always waiting . . . speeeed his flying feet – See 11.730n.

18.679–80 (757:7–8). their damn guns bursting . . . for the Queens birthday – One feature of life on Gibraltar was the daily gunfire that warned that the gates of the walled town were about to be shut and not opened until sunrise. The celebration of the queen's birthday was marked by the firing of every gun in the Rock's elaborate labyrinth of fortifications, in sequence from the "Rock Gun" at the top to the shore batteries at the bottom.

18.681–83 (757:10–12). when general Ulysses Grant . . . landed off the ship – Grant (1822–85), president of the United States from 1869 to 1877. At the close of his second term of office Grant made a world tour that included a visit by boat to Gibraltar on 17 November 1878. Grant's stature and bearing as soldier and former president won him universal acclaim abroad and technically would have merited a twenty-one-gun salute.

18.683 (757:12). old Sprague the consul – According to the *Gibraltar Directory and Guide Book*, Horatio Jones Sprague was the U.S. consul in Gibraltar from before 1873 (the first year of publication for the directory) until his death in 1902.

18.684 (757:13). in mourning for the son – Sprague's son, John Louis Sprague, was vice-consul with his father from 1877 until his death in 1886; see preceding note.

18.687 (757:17). jellibees – After the Arabic *jalab:* "a long cloak with a hood."

18.687–88 (757:17). levites assembly – The Levites are those devout Jews who aid the rabbi or high priest in the care of the tabernacle, the sacred vessels, and the temple.

18.688 (757:17). sound clear – The bugle call that instructs artillery to clear their guns for action.

18.688–89 (757:18–19). gunfire for the men . . . keys to lock the gates – See 18.679–80n.

18.690 (757:20). Rorkes drift – See 15.780–81n.

18.690 (757:21). Plevna – See 4.63n.

18.690–91 (757:21). sir Garnet Wolseley – Sir Garnet Joseph Wolseley, first Viscount Wolseley (1833–1913), was a Dublin-born British general of considerable distinction. The context suggests two of the actions in which he was involved: in 1879 he was commander in chief of the British army in South Africa, and he took

personal command in July of the Zulu War to avert further disasters of the sort that his subordinates had experienced at Isandhlwana (see 15.780–81n); Wolseley was also in command of the expedition that attempted (unsuccessfully) to relieve Gordon at Khartoum (see 15.1525–26n).

18.691 (757:21). Gordon at Khartoum – See 15.1525–26n.

18.696 (757:27). Bushmills whiskey – An Irish whiskey that was brewed in stone jars in Bushmills, a small town on the River Bush in northeastern Ireland.

18.704 (757:36–37). that medical in Holles street – Is notably absent from the list of suitors; see 17.2133–42 (731:25–36).

18.707–8 (757:41). if you shake hands twice with the left – To shake hands with the left hand is superstitiously regarded as an expression of hostility; what Molly has in mind is that a pointed gesture of this sort will draw attention and thus launch a flirtation.

18.709 (757:42–43). Westland row chapel – St. Andrews' (All Hallows') Roman Catholic Church in Westland Row; see 5.318n.

18.710–11 (758:2). Those country gougers up in the City Arms – See 2.416–17n.

18.714 (758:6). pots and pans and kettles to mend – The traditional self-advertising chant of a tinker has been elevated into a street rhyme: "Any pots, any pans, any kettles to mend?"

18.714–15 (758:6–7). any broken bottles for a poor man today – Has produced another street rhyme: "Any rags, any bones, any bottles today? / There's a poor old beggar man coming your way."

18.716 (758:8). that wonderworker – See 17.1819–39 (721:38–722:20).

18.718 (758:11). Mrs Dwenn – Mentioned only once; identity and significance unknown.

18.720 (758:13). pisto madrileno – A dish of tomatoes and red peppers in Madrid (Spanish) style.

18.721–22 (758:15). her father – Matthew Dillon; see 6.697n.

18.723 (758:17). Miss Gillespie – Mentioned only once; identity and significance unknown.

18.726 (758:20–21). Nancy Blake – Identity unknown.

18.736–37 (758:32–33). *in old Madrid . . . love is sighing I am dying – See 11.733n.

18.741–42 (758:39). the four courts – See 7.756–57n.

18.742 (758:40). the ladies letterwriter – *The Ladies' and Gentlemen's Model Letter Writer; (a complete guide to correspondences on all subjects)* (London, 1871).

18.744–45 (758:43). answer to a gentleman's proposal affirmatively – Obviously one of the headings in *The Ladies' Letter Writer*.

Sentence 5. 18.748–908 (pp. 759–63).

18.748 (759:5). Mrs Rubio – Apparently the Tweedy's Spanish housekeeper when they lived in Gibraltar. *Rubio*, Spanish: "blond, golden, fair."

18.751 (759:7–8). horquilla – Spanish: "pitchfork, hairpin, staple," etc.

18.754 (759:12). the Atlantic fleet coming in – In the late nineteenth century the British Royal Navy's Atlantic fleet was almost equal in size to the combined fleets of any one of the other naval powers. Ships and small flotillas from the Atlantic and Mediterranean fleets did call occasionally at Gibraltar, but the *Gibraltar Directory and Guide Book* lists only one visit of the Atlantic fleet, on 22 February 1912, when a force that included eight battleships put into Gibraltar in a display of naval power clearly designed to warn Germany that, in spite of the Balkan War, the Mediterranean was still a British lake.

18.756 (759:13). carabineros – Spanish: "a carbine-carrying cavalry soldier; an internal-revenue guard." In context, Mrs. Rubio is talking about the Spanish revenue guards whose territory was the "neutral ground" between Gibraltar and Spain. They were, of course, under considerable pressure when elements of the Atlantic or Mediterranean fleets called at Gibraltar.

18.756 (759:13–14). 4 drunken English sailors took all the rock from them – During the war of the Spanish succession (1700–1714) (England, Holland, Germany, and Portugal vs. France and Spain), Gibraltar, garrisoned by only 150 men, was attacked by a Dutch-English force of 1,800 men under Sir George Rooke and Prince George of Hesse Darmstadt. After Gibraltar was surrendered on 24 July 1704 following a three-day siege, the British managed to claim it for themselves and hold on to it.

18.757 (759:15). Santa Maria – The Roman Catholic Cathedral Church of St. Mary the Crowned in Main Street, Gibraltar.

18.760 (759:18–19). the sun dancing 3 times on Easter Sunday morning – A popular superstition in Ireland was that when the sun rose on Easter morning, it danced with joy at the birth of man's hope of salvation.

18.760–61 (759:19–20). when the priest was going . . . the vatican to the dying – "Vatican" is Molly's mistake for *viaticum* (the Eucharist given to a dying person or one in danger of death). It is traditional in Spain for a priest on his way to administer extreme unction to be preceded by an acolyte ringing a bell to announce the presence of the Eucharist.

18.761–62 (759:20–21). blessing herself for his Majestad – That is, blessing herself for the majesty of Christ because the Eucharist is passing.

18.763 (759:23). the Calle Real – The Spanish name for the English Waterport Street in Gibraltar.

18.764 (759:23–24). he tipped me just in passing – It is unclear which of several slang meanings of "tipped" Molly has in mind: he winked at her? or touched her lightly?

18.766–67 (759:26–27). father was up at the drill instructing – Suggests that Tweedy was not a "major" but a sergeant-major, one of whose principal duties in the British infantry of the 1880s would have been instruction in and supervision of drill (which was then regarded as the foundation of an army's tactics and of a soldier's unthinking obedience to command). Drill instruction would have been well beneath the duties of a major in the infantry. See Ellmann, p. 46n.

18.767 (759:27–28). the language of stamps – "When a stamp is inverted on the right-hand upper corner, it means the person written to is to write no more. If the stamp be placed on the left-hand upper corner, inverted, then the writer declares his affection for the receiver of the letter. When the stamp is in the center at the top it signifies an affirmative answer . . . when it is at the bottom, it is negative," and so forth through a number of other positions (*The Century Book of Facts* [Springfield, Mass., 1906], p. 658). Standardized postal practices have, of course, rendered the "language" all but obsolete.

18.768 (759:28). shall I wear a white rose – "Shall I Wear a White Rose or Shall I Wear a Red?" by H. S. Clarke and E. B. Farmer. The first of the song's three stanzas: "Shall I wear a white rose? / Shall I wear a red? / Will he look for garlands? / What shall wreathe my head? / Will a riband charm him, / Fair upon my breast? / Scarce I can remember / How he loves me best." By the third stanza the girl-speaker realizes that if he truly loves her, she won't need to be decorated.

18.769–70 (759:30). the Moorish wall – The upper slopes of the Rock form a plateau, with its long axis north and south; the Moorish Wall crosses that plateau from east to west just north of its center.

18.770 (759:30–31). my sweetheart when a boy – A song by Wilford Morgan and one Enoch: "Though many gentle hearts I've known / And many a pretty face / Where love sat gayly on his throne / In beauty and in grace: / Yet, never was my heart enthralled / With such enchanted joy / As by the darling whom I called / My sweet-heart, when a boy. // I hung upon her lightest word: / My very joys were fears / And fluttered timid as a bird / When sunshine first appears, / I never thought my heart could rove / Life then had no alloy: / With such a truth I seemed to love / My sweetheart, when a boy! // And yet, the dream has passed away / Though like it lived; it passed— / Each movement was too bright to stay, / But sparkled to the last. / Still on my heart the beams remain / In gay uncloudy joy, / When I remember her again / My sweet-heart—when a boy!"

18.774 (759:35). de la Flora – Spanish: "of the Flower."

18.775 (759:37). there is a flower that bloometh – See 13.438–39n.

18.779 (759:41–42). the pesetas and the perragordas – Spanish coins roughly equivalent to a sixpence and a penny; so colloquially, "nickels and dimes."

18.779–80 (759:42–43). *Cappoquin . . . on the black water – A small town on the River Blackwater in County Wexford in south-central Ireland.

18.781 (760:1–2). May when the infant king of Spain was born – 17 May 1886 was the birthday of Alfonso XIII (d. 1941), who was king of Spain at birth, since his father, Alfonso XII, had died in 1885.

18.782–83 (760:3). on the tiptop under the rockgun – The Rock Gun was a signal gun mounted on the highest point (1,356 feet) of the Rock in the northern face overlooking the neutral ground toward the mainland and Spain. It took precedence in all military ceremonies. *Murray's Handbook for Spain* (London, 1892), p. 421, remarks that in 1891 "the upper part of the Rock [was] no longer accessible to civilians, and only to officers under very stringent conditions." The restriction was imposed because an elaborate complex of heavy modern guns was being installed in new fortifications on the summit.

18.783–84 (760:3–4). OHaras tower . . . struck by lightning – The southern highpoint of the Rock (1,361 feet) was called O'Hara's Tower, after General O'Hara (d. 1802), military governor of Gibraltar 1787–91 and 1794–1802. O'Hara had the tower constructed in order to watch the movements of the Spanish fleet at Cadiz, fifty-eight miles overland to the west-northwest. The tower's obvious impracticality, which led to its being called "O'Hara's folly," was compounded by the fact that the tower was struck by lightning shortly after it was completed.

18.784 (760:4–5). the old Barbary apes they sent to Clapham – By 1889 only some twenty of the apes remained on Gibraltar, but even in those reduced numbers they were something of a nuisance as garden raiders. The *Gibraltar Directory and Guide Book* does not mention the export of apes to Clapham (a London suburb once famous for its fairs), but in 1882, when a full-grown male that was being harassed by the other apes took refuge in the Alameda Gardens, the governor of the Rock solved the problem by shipping the renegade ape off to the zoo in Regent's Park, London.

18.786 (760:7). rock scorpion – Garrison slang for a Spaniard born on Gibraltar.

18.786 (760:8). Inces farm – The upper slopes of the Rock, just north of the Moorish Wall; see 18.769–70.

18.790 (760:12). the firtree cove – None of the guidebooks we have consulted mention this cove, but several remark on Fig-Tree Cave, 790 feet above sea level in the eastern face of the Rock below the southern summit.

18.791 (760:13). the galleries and casemates – The Windsor and Union galleries, almost two miles in extent, were tunneled into the north face of the Rock as fortifications to command the land approaches to Gibraltar. The casemate batteries were installed to defend the harbor moles on the west side of the Rock in Gibraltar Bay.

18.791–92 (760:14). Saint Michaels cave – The largest of Gibraltar's caves, its entrance is about a thousand feet above the sea in the south face of the Rock. It has a large hall with stalactites and stalagmites that extend thirty to fifty feet from floor to roof, and there are several lower caverns that could be reached by ladders. *Murray's Handbook for Spain* (London, 1892), p. 421, notes that by 1891 the cave had been "permanently closed."

18.793–94 (760:16–17). the way down the monkeys . . . Africa when they die – Barbary apes (macaques) exist both in North Africa and on Gibraltar—two colonies of nonswimmers, separated by nine miles of water. The mystery of the separation, together with the labyrinth of caves and natural well-shafts on Gibraltar, has led to the sort of legend of a natural tunnel to Africa about which Molly is "sure." A more informed speculation is that the Roman soldiers who garrisoned the Rock brought the monkeys to Gibraltar from North Africa as pets.

18.795 (760:18). the Malta boat – In the 1880s the Peninsular and Oriental S. N. Company had a packet boat to Malta once a week on Tuesday mornings.

18.802 (760:26). embarazada – Spanish: "pregnant."

18.817 (761:2). Molly darling – A popular song (1871) by Will S. Hays: "Won't you tell me, Mollie Darling, / That you love none else but me? / For I love you, Mollie Darling, / You are all the world to me. / O! tell me, darling, that you love me, / Put your little hand in mine, / Take my heart, sweet Mollie darling, / Say that you will give me thine. [Chorus:] Mollie, fairest, sweetest, dearest, / Look up, darling, tell me this; / Do you love me, Mollie darling? / Let your answer be a kiss."

18.822 (761:18). block – To "block" is low slang for to have intercourse.

18.824 (761:10). firtree cove – See 18.790n.

18.826 (761:12–13). *the black water – See 18.779–80n.

18.830 (761:17). the Chronicle – The *Gibraltar Chronicle* (from 1801), a weekly newspaper published on Saturdays by the Printing Office, Garrison Library, Governor's (Gunner's) Parade. *The Traveller's Handbook for Gibraltar,* by an Old Inhabitant (London, 1884), p. 34, remarks that it was "a periodical of amusement, rather than of great interest to the public of Gibraltar."

18.831 (761:19). Benady Bros – Mordejai and Samuel Benadi, bakers, Engineer Lane, Gibraltar (in 1889).

18.833–34 (761:21–22). *over middle hill round . . . the jews burialplace – Molly and Mulvey walked north from the southern summit of the Rock, down past the Moorish Wall and Inces Farm over the sloping plateau of Middle Hill, and then down the northeast slopes toward the Jewish Cemetery, which was inside the British lines on the low-lying isthmus that connects the Rock to the mainland.

18.837 (761:25–26). HMS Calypso – *Thom's* 1904 lists this ship as a third-class cruiser of 2,770 tons in service as a drill ship for the Royal Naval Reserve in North American and West Indian waters, but its reality as a ship is hardly its significance; cf. the headnote to Calypso, p. 70.

18.837 (761:26). that old Bishop – The bishop of Lystra (the ancient city in Asia Minor where the New Testament Timothy was born and where St. Paul was stoned but miraculously not injured [Acts 14:6–21]). The bishop was Roman Catholic vicar apostolic of Gibraltar.

18.838 (761:27). womans higher functions – The catchphrase of conservative resistance to reforms aimed at achieving equal legal, political, economic, and cultural rights for women (one phase of which was reform of dress).

18.839 (761:28–29). the new woman bloomers – Designed by the American Elizabeth Smith Miller. They were called "bloomers" (1851) after the American reformer Amelia Jenks Bloomer (1818–94), who advocated them as sensible and hygienic clothing. They made their appearance on the English scene through the good offices of the Rational Dress Movement in the 1870s.

18.844 (761:34). brig – Slang for to pocket (i.e., steal) things.

18.848 (761:39). Lunita Laredo – See 18.282–83n.

18.848–49 (761:40). *along Williss road to Europa point – Europa Point is the southern tip of Gibraltar. Willis Road climbs the northwestern corner of the Rock in a series of switchbacks, ending at the Moorish Wall on the upper ridge; from there a series of paths lead over the southern summits and down toward Europa Point.

18.849 (761:41). the other side of Jersey – Meaning unknown.

18.856 (762:6). *up Windmill hill to the flats – Windmill Hill is the southernmost extension of the Gibraltar massif; it is topped by a plateau called Windmill Flats, which was used for parades and maneuvers by units of the British garrison.

18.857 (762:7). *captain Rubios that was dead – Identity and significance unknown.

18.858 (762:9). *the B Marche paris – See 18.613n.

18.859–60 (762:10–11). I could see over to Morocco . . . the Atlas mountain with snow – On a clear day Molly could easily see Morocco, but Tangiers, 35 miles through the straits to the southwest, would be masked by headlands, and the snowcapped Saharan Atlas Mountains in Algeria, 375 miles to the southeast, are clearly out of range.

18.861 (762:12). *Molly darling – See 18.817n.

18.862 (762:14). the elevation – At the climax of the Mass, when the Eucharist is elevated after the Consecration; the congregation stands and assents to the Eucharistic Prayer by singing, "Amen."

18.865 (762:17). *peau dEspagne – French: "skin of Spain."

18.866 (762:19). Claddagh ring – The Claddagh is a section of the city of Galway on the west coast of Ireland. A Claddagh ring, made of gold and decorated with a heart supported by two hands, was regarded as deriving from ancient Celtic design. It was the traditional wedding ring of Galway and the surrounding area from about 1784.

18.869 (762:22). an opal or a pearl – In the language of gems, the opal is traditionally symbolic of hope and pure thoughts; the pearl, of purity and innocence.

18.871 (762:23//). *the sandfrog shower from Africa – Meaning unknown.

18.871–72 (762:23//). *that derelict ship . . . the Marie whatyoucallit – The *Mary Celeste* remains one of the great unsolved sea mysteries. En route from New York to Genoa in 1872, the ship was abandoned off the Azores; several days later (4 December 1872) it was intercepted off the coast of Portugal, in good condition and still under sail. It was detained from mid-December until 1 March 1873 in Gibraltar pending settlement of insurance and salvage claims. Why captain and crew left an apparently sound ship and vanished has never been explained. The misspelling *Marie Celeste* was Sir Arthur Conan Doyle's contribution to the mystery in the *Cornhill Magazine* (January 1884). Also mysterious is Molly's memory: born 8 September 1870, she was just over two when the *Mary Celeste* "came up to the harbour" of Gibraltar.

18.874–77 (762:25–28). *once in the dear deaead . . . loves sweet soooooooong – See 4.314n.

18.878 (762:29). Kathleen Kearney – See 18.376n.

18.879 (762:31). skitting – "Laughing and giggling in a silly way" (P. W. Joyce, *English*, p. 325).

18.882–83 (762:35–36). I beg your pardon coach I thought you were a wheelbarrow – A west-of-Ireland expression of contempt for pretentious talk or behavior.

18.884–85 (762:37–38). the Alameda . . . on the bandnight – That is, in summer; see 18.643–44n.

18.896–97 (763:9). comes looooves old – See 4.314n.

18.897–99 (763:10–11). *My Ladys Bower . . . twilight and vaunted rooms – "My Lady's Bower" is a song by F. E. Weatherly and Hope Temple: "Thro' the moated Grange, at twilight, / My love and I we went, / By empty rooms and lonely stairs, / In lover's sweet content, / And round the old and broken casement / We watch'd the roses flow'r / But the place we lov'd best of all / Was called 'my Lady's bower.' / And with beating hearts we enter'd, / And stood and whisper'd low / Of the sweet and lovely lady / Who liv'd there years ago! / And the moon shone in upon us / Across the dusty floor / Where her little feet had wander'd / In the courtly days of yore. / And it touched the faded arras / And again we seem'd to see / The lovely lady sitting there / Her lover at her knee, / And we saw him kiss her fair white hand / And oh! we heard him say / I shall love thee, love, forever, / Tho' the years may pass away . . . / But then they vanish'd in a moment, / And we knew 'twas but a dream. / It was not they who sat there / In the silver moonlight gleam / Ah, no! 'twas we, we two together / Who had found our golden hour / And told the old, old story / Within 'My Lady's bow'r.'"

18.899 (763:12). Winds that blow from the south – See 8.183n.

Sentence 6. 18.909–1148 (pp. 763–70).

18.909 (763:24). wherever you be let your wind go free – The first line of a comic epitaph that concludes: "For holding my wind was the death of me" (Victor Pomerance, *JJQ* 15, no. 1 [1977]: 94).

18.911–12 (763:27). the porkbutchers – See 4.46n; and cf. 4.493n.

18.919 (763:36). sierra nevada – Spanish: "snowy range"; a mountain range in southern Spain 130 miles east-northeast of Gibraltar; it is the highest mountain range in Spain and ex-

tends for about 60 miles, 30 miles north of and parallel to the Mediterranean coast.

18.936 (764:14). lecking – English dialect: "to moisten, to water or sprinkle," especially clothes before ironing or a floor to lay dust.

18.941–42 (764:20–21). the London and Newcastle Williams and Woods – Manufacturers of confectionery, 205–206 Britain Street Great (now Parnell Street), with branches in London and Newcastle.

18.944 (764:24). Buckleys – See 4.45n.

18.947 (764:28). Mrs Fleming – See 6.17n.

18.948 (764:28–29). the furry glen or the strawberry beds – Two scenic recreation areas popular among Dubliners. The Furze, or Furry, Glen is just east of Knockmaroon Gate in the southwestern corner of Phoenix Park. It is a deep hollow lined with furze and hawthorne trees. The Strawberry Beds are outside Knockmaroon Gate on the steep north bank of the Liffey. The area is noted for what guidebooks call its "delightful views" as well as for the fruit in June and July.

18.950–51 (764:31–32). there are little houses down at the bottom of the banks there – That is, at the Strawberry Beds, where small thatched cottages served as summerhouse tearooms for visitors.

18.952 (764:34). ruck of Mary Ann coalboxes – A crowd of ordinary women dressed in costumes more appropriate to the music-hall stage than to the sort of outing Molly has in mind. A "Mary Ann" is a dress stand, and "coalbox" is slang for a music hall.

18.953 (764:34–35). Whit Monday is a cursed day – Whitmonday, a bank holiday (23 May in 1904), follows Whitsunday (also called Pentecost), the seventh Sunday after Easter, when the descent of the Holy Spirit is commemorated (see Acts 2:1–6). The source of the superstition that Whitmonday is a cursed day is unknown.

18.955 (764:37). Bray – See 1.181n.

18.956 (764:38). the steeplechase for the gold cup – Except that the Gold Cup was not a steeplechase; see 5.532n.

18.965 (765:6). Burke out of the City Arms hotel – Andrew ("Pisser") Burke; see 12.504n.

18.968–69 (765:10–11). Sweets of Sin by a gentleman of fashion – See 10.606n.

18.969 (765:11). Mr de Kock – See 4.358n.

18.973–76 (765:16–19). the sardines and the bream . . . said came from Genoa – Catalan Bay is a small bay and village under the cliffs on the east side of Gibraltar. According to the *Gibraltar Directory and Guide Book* (1954), p. 93, "it is inhabited chiefly by the descendents of Genoese fishermen." Their principal catch was sardines and bream, as Molly recalls.

18.979 (765:23–24). I never brought a bit of salt in – In Roman and many other mythologies, salt was regarded as a sacrificial substance sacred to the Penates, or household gods; hence, to bring "a bit of salt" into a new house before one moves in is to propitiate the household gods and to ensure good luck.

18.987–88 (765:33–34). will you be my man will you carry my can – Roland McHugh reports a children's game current in County Kerry: the children ask one another, "Will you be my man?" / "Yes." / "Will you carry my can?" / "Yes." / "Will you fight the fairies?" / "Yes." The children then blow in each other's faces until one gives in.

18.992 (765:39). *Lloyd's Weekly news – A Sunday newspaper published in London under various titles from 1842 to 1931. From November 1902 until May 1918 it was called *Lloyd's Weekly News*. It featured "All Saturday's News," a summary (in the form of telegrams) of the week's local and world news, and a wide variety of brief human-interest stories. Its general tone was that of conservative rather than yellow journalism.

18.1006 (766:13). Skerry's academy – George E. Skerry & Co., civil service, commercial, and university tutors, 76 St. Stephen's Green East and 10 Harcourt Street, Dublin. Milly would have attended the Harcourt Street branch, "shorthand, typewriting, and commercial college" (*Thom's* 1904, p. 1513).

18.1007 (766:14//). getting all 1s at school – The implication is that Milly has been at or near the top of her class in the national schools.

18.1012 (766:21). loglady – An inactive, stupid, or senseless woman.

18.1016 (766:25). teem – To empty or drain a vessel.

18.1023–24 (766:34). Tom Devans – See 10.1196n. *Thom's* 1904 lists no Devans in the immediate neighborhood of 7 Eccles Street, and Thomas J. Devan lived at 11 Leinster Street North, half a mile to the northwest.

18.1024 (766:35). Murray girls – A "John Murray, barrister" lived at 79 Eccles Street, across the street from the Blooms (*Thom's* 1904, p. 1482).

18.1026 (766:37). Nelson street – Just off Eccles Street and hence around the corner out of Molly's sight.

18.1031 (766:43–767:1). I oughtnt to have stitched . . . brings a parting – The superstition is that sewing or repairing a garment when a person is wearing it implies a parting (since that kind of sewing is so often a last-minute adjustment before some occasion).

18.1032 (767:1–2). the last plumpudding too split in 2 halves – It was Irish tradition to bake rings (or other symbolic objects) into cakes served at ceremonial occasions and to tell fortunes by the cake. For example, the person who found the ring in his slice could look forward to marriage. If the cake broke when being removed from its mold, the forecast was for a separation or a parting.

18.1038 (767:8–9). the Only Way in the Theatre Royal – For the theater, see 6.184n; *The Only Way* (1899), by the Irish cleric and dramatist Freeman Crofts Wills (c. 1849–1913), with the help of another cleric, Frederick Langbridge, is a stage version of Dickens's *A Tale of Two Cities* (1859). The play de-emphasizes the novel's dark, melodramatic concentration on the human cost of the French Revolution and concentrates instead on the pathos of the dissipated hero Sydney Carton's Platonic love for Lucie Manette (the Marchioness St. Evremonde), a love that prompts him to go to the guillotine in place of her condemned husband.

18.1041–42 (767:13–14). at the Gaiety for Beerbohm Tree in Trilby – On 10 and 11 October 1895, the English actor-manager Sir Herbert Beerbohm Tree (1853–1917) did stage a production of *Trilby* at the Gaiety in which he played Svengali; see 15.2721n.

18.1045 (767:18). Switzers window – Switzer

& Co., Ltd., drapers, silk mercers, upholsterers, and tailors, 88–93 Grafton Street, Dublin.

18.1047   (767:20).   the   Broadstone – See 5.117n.

18.1052   (767:26).   Conny   Connolly – Mentioned only once, identity and significance unknown.

18.1055   (767:29).   Martin   Harvey – See 13.417n; his first great success in London and Dublin was as Sydney Carton in *The Only Way;* see 18.1038n.

18.1068   (768:2).   Mrs   Joe   Gallaher – See 15.565n.

18.1069   (768:3).   the   trotting   matches – See 5.297–98n.

18.1070   (768:4).   Friery the solicitor – *Thom's* 1904 (p. 1876) lists Christopher Friery, solicitor (no address).

18.1075   (768:10).   not   to   leave   knives crossed – Robert Boyle, S.J., reports: "My Leitrim-bred grandmother, among numerous other superstitions, harbored one dealing with the impiety of crossed silverware, so that my sister, when she wished to annoy the ordinarily serene old lady, would cross the knives or the knife and spoon. Our grandmother, tight-lipped, would uncross them, cross herself, and sometimes, unable to suppress her irritation, object crossly" (*JJQ* 15, no. 4 [1978]: 384).

18.1091   (768:29).   the   intermediate – See 13.132–33n; one of Stephen's prizes figures in the last episode of chapter 2:E, *A Portrait.*

18.1105   (769:3).   that   thing   has   come   on   me – In Book 11 of *The Odyssey*, Tiresias prophesies that Odysseus will make the "insolent" suitors "atone in blood," as he eventually does (11:116, 118; Fitzgerald, p. 200).

18.1111   (769:10–11).   Michael   Gunn – See 11.1050n.

18.1111–12 (769:11). Mrs Kendal and her husband – Mr. and Mrs. William Hunter Kendal, the stage names of English actor-manager William Hunter Grimston (1843–1917) and the English actress Margaret (Madge) Robertson Grimston (b. 1849). Onstage Mrs. Kendal took the lead in the partnership, as offstage Mr. Kendal took the managerial lead.

18.1113 (769:12). Drimmies – See 13.845n.

18.1115 (769:15). Spinoza – See 11.1058n.

18.1117–18 (769:18). wife of Scarli – *The Wife of Scarli* (1897) by G. A. Greene, an English version of an Italian play, *Tristi amori* (Sorrows of Love), by Giuseppe Giacosa, was first performed in Dublin, 22 October 1897. Scarli, the husband, is portrayed as a pompous and relatively unattractive advocate. His wife, Emma, is shown in a more sympathetic and attractive light, as is her lover, Scarli's deputy and colleague, Fabrizio, who is virtuously paying his profligate father's debts and trying to keep the father (Count Arcieri) from falling into further excesses. Characteristically, Scarli, in Act I, praises Fabrizio's filial virtues; in Act II he puts the squeeze on Fabrizio for a check the count has forged. Later in Act II Scarli discovers Fabrizio and Emma's liaison and orders Emma out of the house. Act III begins with Scarli's internal debate about Emma's future; he is pompous and self-righteous but almost appealing in his uncertainty. Then Fabrizio and Emma have a big scene (should she leave or attempt to stay?); Emma finally thinks of "*the child*" and determines to sacrifice love for maternal duty; reconciliation; final curtain. The play was regarded as "daring," largely because it appeared to rationalize Emma's adultery by making Scarli an unattractive stuffed shirt; but it was not so daring as to let her leave her husband and get away with it.

18.1124–25 (769:26–27). the clean linen I wore brought it on too – Somewhat akin to the superstition that wearing a new hat will cause rain.

18.1128 (769:31). O Jamesy – Dodging the curse *O Jesus?* or calling on her maker?

18.1129 (769:32). sweets of sin – See 10.606n.

18.1131–32 (769:35). the other side of the park – The other side of Phoenix Park is over three and a half miles west of Eccles Street.

18.1141 (770:4). scout – English dialect: "to eject liquid forcibly, to squirt."

18.1143 (770:6). bubbles on it for a wad of money – It was popular superstition that coffee or tea (and also urine) that is covered with bubbles after it has been poured is a sign of money to come, provided the pourer has not tried to insure his own luck.

18.1148 (770:12). the jersey lily – See 18.481–82n.

18.1148 (770:12–13). O how the waters come down at Lahore – Molly's version of the opening lines of Robert Southey's (1774–1843) poem "The Cataract of Lodore; Described in Rhymes for the Nursery" (1823). This self-conscious nature-nursery poem begins: "How does the water / Come down at Lodore? / My little boy ask'd me / Thus, once on a time; / . . . / And 'twas in my vocation / For their recreation / That so I should sing; / Because I was laureate / To them and the King" (lines 1–4 and 19–23 of the poem's 121 lines). Southey's Lodore is a waterfall in Cumberland, England; Molly's Lahore was, in 1904, the capital of the Punjab, British India; today it is a city in West Pakistan.

Sentence 7. 18.1149–1367 (pp. 770–76).

18.1151 (770:16). Whit Monday – See 18.953n.

18.1153–54 (770:19–20). Dr Collins for womens diseases on Pembroke road – *Thom's* 1904 (p. 870) lists a J. H. Collins, Bachelor of Medicine, at 65 Pembroke Road in Dublin. He was the son of the Reverend T. R. S. Collins, chaplain and private secretary to the Church of Ireland archbishop of Dublin. But according to Ellmann (p. 516), another Dr. Joseph Collins (an American whom Joyce knew in Paris) sat for this portrait.

18.1155–56 (770:22). off Stephens green – An expensive and fashionable district in Dublin 1904.

18.1174 (771:2). strap – "A bold, forward girl or woman" (P. W. Joyce, *English*, p. 336).

18.1177–78 (771:6). it is a thing of beauty and a joy forever – See 15.2254n.

18.1182–83 (771:12). Rehoboth terrace – See 17.2083n. *Thom's* 1904 lists only two houses in this small street.

18.1185 (771:15). sloothering – Dublin slang for sloppy, slobbering.

18.1186 (771:16). the Doyles – See 8.274n.

18.1187 (771:18). blather – Anglicized Irish: "coaxing, flattery."

18.1187–88 (771:18). home rule and the land league – See 4.101–3n; see also "Home Rule" and "Irish Land League" in the index.

18.1188 (771:19). strool – Anglicized Irish: "untidy" or "confused."

18.1188–89 (771:19). the Huguenots – See 8.623–24n.

18.1189 (771:20). O beau pays de la Touraine – French: "O beautiful country of la Touraine"; an aria sung by Queen Marguerite de Valois at the beginning of Act II of Meyerbeer's *Les Huguenots*. She goes on to contrast the pastoral peace of the countryside with the "religious debates which make the land bloody."

18.1192 (771:24). Brighton square – In Rathgar, a townland three miles south of the center of Dublin. For townlands, see 7.91–92n.

18.1194 (771:25–26). the Albion milk and sulphur soap – Meaning unknown.

18.1200–1202 (771:34–36). breathing with his hand on his nose like that Indian god . . . museum in Kildare street – See 5.328n. S. Krishnamoorthy Aithal comments: "The Buddha and the breathing posture do not go together. *Pranayam*, breathing with hand on nose, is a Hindu ritual, and the Buddha, being a strong critic of Hinduism, will not have any truck with Hindu rituals and beliefs." He concludes that Molly must be "taking some other Indian god for the Buddha" (*JJQ* 16, no. 4 [1979]: 511).

18.1203–4 (771:37–38). a bigger religion than the jews and Our Lords put together – Either Bloom has been exaggerating or he is treating a number of Eastern religions as one. Such exaggerations were common in the late nineteenth century when westerners tended to inflate the populations of the East and to lump Eastern religions together without distinction. *The Century Book of Facts* (Springfield, Mass., 1906), p. 574, reports: Christianity, 477,080,158; Worship of Ancestors and Confucianism, 256,000,000; Hindooism, 190,000,000; Mohammedanism, 176,834,372; Buddhism, 147,900,000; Taoism, 43,000,000; Shintoism, 14,000,000; Judaism, 7,186,000; Polytheism, 117,681,669. Other authorities suggest that these figures are not well founded and cite late-nineteenth-century estimates that vary from 100,000,000 to 400,000,000 for Buddhism alone.

18.1213 (772:6). old Cohen – The *Gibraltar Directory and Guide Book* (1889) lists a David A. Cohen, boots and shoes, at 22 Engineer Lane, Gibraltar. In Book 23 of *The Odyssey*, Odysseus convinces Penelope that he is indeed Odysseus because he knows the secret of their bed and its construction (as Molly does, but Bloom does not, know the secret of the bed they share).

18.1214 (772:7). Lord Napier – Field Marshal Robert Cornelis Napier (1810–90), Lord Napier of Magdala (created 1868), had a distinguished career as a soldier in India and Abyssinia (Ethiopia). He was commander in chief in India (1869–75) and governor of Gibraltar (1876–83).

18.1218 (772:12–13). his huguenots – See 8.623–24n.

18.1218–19 (772:13). the frogs march – Slang for the way a drunken or violent person is carried face down by four men; the piece of music Molly has in mind is unknown.

18.1220 (772:14–15). worse and worse says Warden Daly – Source and connotations unknown.

18.1225 (772:20–21). his old lottery tickets – See 8.184–85n.

18.1227 (772:23–24). Sinner Fein – See 8.458n.

18.1228 (772:24). the little man – Arthur Griffith; see 3.227n.

18.1229 (772:26). Coadys lane – Off Bessborough Avenue on the northeastern outskirts of Dublin. In 1904 a John Griffith (an uncle of Arthur Griffith? a brother?) lived at 46 Bessborough Avenue in this relatively poor section of the city.

18.1235 (772:33). French letter – Slang for a condom.

18.1238 (772:37). the Aristocrats Masterpiece – That is, Aristotle's Masterpiece; see 10.586n.

18.1246–47 (773:4–5). naked the way the jews used when somebody dies belonged to them – During the *shivah*, the first phase of mourning after the burial of a relative, Jewish custom dictates that the mourners should strip themselves of adornment (though this does not mean all clothes) and that they should shun the comfort of furniture in favor of the earth or the floor.

18.1251 (773:9). *wethen – Or whethen, is "Used as an expostulatory exclamation; ? lit. 'why then'" (Joseph Wright, *English Dialect Dictionary* [London, 1905], vol. 6, p. 452a). P. W. Joyce (*English*, p. 350) says of "Why then" that it was "used very much in the South to begin a sentence, especially a reply, much as *indeed* is used in English:—. . . 'Which do you like best, tea or coffee?' 'Why then I much prefer tea.'"

18.1257 (773:17–18). the College races – The annual athletic meeting (track and field events) held under the auspices of Trinity College in Trinity College Park, Dublin. It was something of an event in the Dublin social calendar and was regarded as an annual reassertion and redefinition of the lines of demarcation between the "ins" and the "outs" in Dublin society.

18.1257 (773:18). Hornblower – See 5.555n.

18.1259 (773:19–20). sheeps eyes – See 15.2297n.

18.1259 (773:20). skirt duty – Army slang for the way women walk back and forth in a public place in the attempt (imagined or actual) to attract attention.

18.1264–65 (773:26–27). Tom Kernan . . . falling down the mens WC drunk – The opening incident in "Grace," *Dubliners*.

18.1282–83 (774:5). Bill Bailey wont you please come home – A popular American ragtime song (1902) by Hughie Cannon. Chorus: "'Won't you come home, Bill Bailey? / Won't you come home?' / She moans the whole day long, / 'I'll do the cooking, darling, / I'll pay the rent; / I knows I've done you wrong. / 'Member dat rainy eve dat I drove you out / Wid nothing but a fine tooth comb! / I know I's to blame. / Well, ain't it a shame? / Bill Bailey, won't you please come home?'"

18.1285 (774:7–8). the Glencree dinner – See 8.160n.

18.1291 (774:15). the old love is the new – Two possible sources exist: "Don't Give Up the Old Love for the New" (1896) by James Thornton, and "The Old Love and the New" by Alfred Maltby and Frank Musgrave (the more probable). Thornton's chorus: "Don't give up the old love for the new, / Stick to her who's proven good and true. / You may find a worse love; / Remember she's your first love, / And all her future life may rest with you. / When danger comes you'll find her by your side, / She'll cling to you whatever might betide, / Striving to cheer you / When trouble hovers near you. / Don't give up the old love for the new." The Maltby-Musgrave chorus: "Write those vows in water / Or trace them deep in snow, / The sunlight of a new love / Will melt them with its glow. . . . / Ah me, too true! / How very oft the old love / Will fade before the new."

18.1292 (774:16–17). so sweetly sang the maiden on the hawthorne bough – Source unknown.

18.1293 (774:17–18). Maritana – See 5.563–64n.

18.1293–94 (774:18). Freddy Mayers – Identity and significance unknown, unless Joyce is encoding Teodoro Mayer, a Hungarian Jew and newspaper publisher in Trieste who was one of the prototypes for Bloom; see Ellmann, pp. 196, 374n.

18.1294 (774:19). Phoebe dearest – "Phoebe Dearest, Tell O Tell Me" is a song by Claxon Bellamy and J. L. Hatton. The first of the song's three verses: "Phoebe, Dearest, tell, oh! tell me, / May I hope that you'll be mine? / Oh, let no cold frown repel me, / Leave me not in grief to pine. / Tho' tis told in homely fashion, / Phoebe, trust the tale I tell, / Ne'er was truer, purer passion, / Than within this heart does dwell. / Long I've watched each rare perfection, / Stealing o'er that gentle brow, / Till respect became affection, / Such as that I offer now. / If you love me and will have me, / True I'll be in weal or woe, / If in cold disdain you leave me, / For a soldier I will go."

18.1295/96 (774:19/20). goodbye sweetheart/ sweet tart goodbye – See 11.13n.

18.1297 (774:22). O Maritana wildwood flower – In Act III of Wallace's *Maritana* (see 5.563–64n), the hero, Don Caesar, and the heroine, Maritana (now husband and wife thanks to the villain's chicanery), sing this duet. When the duet begins, Don Caesar thinks that Maritana has been compromised as the king's mistress. He opens the duet "(*with grief*) Oh, Maritana . . . gilded shame." Needless to say, the mistake about her "shame" is resolved with sentimental alacrity.

18.1306 (774:33). the Kingsbridge station – Now Sean Heuston station, the terminus of the Great Southern and Western Railway on the western outskirts of metropolitan Dublin south of the Liffey.

18.1309 (774:36//). *the deathwatch too ticking in the wall – The deathwatch is any of various small beetles that bore into woodwork and furniture; the ticking sound comes from their knocking their heads against the wood. In superstition, the sound presages death.

18.1311–12 (774:38–39). lord Fauntleroy suit – A costume for little boys based on that worn by the child-hero of Frances Hodgson Burnett's (1849–1924) novel (and play) *Little Lord Fauntleroy* (1886). In the novel, the naïve but winning American-born boy becomes heir to an English title and estate.

18.1314–20 (774:41–775:6). he was on the cards this morning . . . and 2 red 8s for new garments – Molly's reading of cards is difficult to follow because (1) the nature of the layout she uses is not clear, though Bloom recalls "by sevens" (5.155 [75.15–16]) (but this makes the position of "the 7th card after that" obscure); (2) she overparticularizes her readings in the light of her own self-interest; and (3) characteristically, she projects her own wishes onto the cards. *Union with a young stranger neither dark nor fair:* apparently the jack of spades has appeared in the spread, indicating a young man who is dynamic, alert, and brilliant, but underdeveloped, in need of something to stabilize his life, in need of a *mentor. My face was turned the other way:* in most spreads one or more cards at the center represent the querent's present state and character, while the cards to left and right of center can be read as that which is to come and that which has been. *The 10 of spades for a journey by land then there was a letter on its way:* the ten of spades has apparently appeared among the cards Molly reads as the "guideposts to decision." In an oversimplified sense it could be read as "a journey by land" (Molly is to journey to Belfast anyway), but in a larger sense it indicates that important news will alter the course of her life (Molly oversimplifies this as Boylan's letter); the ten of spades can also mean a wall or barrier to be passed, the end of a period of delusion, the difficulty involved in facing the end of one phase of one's life. *Scandals too the 3 queens:* three queens implies meetings with important people and does warn the querent to beware of gossip. *The 8 of diamonds for a rise in society:* this is covered by the three queens; the eight of diamonds is more usually read as a card of balance, a card that will prevent excessive materialistic concern. In context with the three queens, the eight of diamonds would warn the querent to avoid any impetuous decisions and to rely more firmly on someone in authority who is close to her. *And 2 red 8s for new garments:* the two red eights could be read as forecasting a gift that causes pleasure, but usually a *spiritual* gift (restored health, love, wisdom, peace of mind) rather than a material (garments) gift. (Chief source for the above readings: Wenzell Brown, *How to Tell Fortunes with Cards* [New York, 1963].)

18.1333 (775:22). John Jameson – An Irish whiskey; see 12.1753n.

18.1355, 38–39/39–40/40–41 (775:23–24/28/30/31). where softly sighs of love the light guitar / two glancing eyes a lattice hid / two eyes as darkly bright as loves own star / as loves young star – See "In Old Madrid," 11.733n.

18.1357 (775:26). Tarifa – A Moorish town in Andalusia (Spain). It is the southernmost point in Europe, twenty-eight miles west-southwest of Gibraltar. The lighthouse at Europa Point is visible for fifteen miles on a clear night.

18.1342 (775:33). Billy Prescotts ad – See 5.460n.

18.1343 (775:33). Keyess ad – See 7.25n.

18.1345 (775:36). ruck – A throng of ordinary people.

18.1346 (775:37). Margate strand – On the North Front, the eastern side of the sandy isthmus that separates Gibraltar from the Spanish mainland. At specified hours it was a for-men-only bathing place; but there was also a bandstand on the strand, and it was a place of public resort on summer evenings.

18.1349–51 (775:41–43). that lovely little statue . . . real beauty and poetry – See 17.1428n.

18.1360 (776:11–12). if the wishcard comes out – The "wishcard" is the nine of hearts, "the most joyous card in the pack." "If the Querent has made a wish, the Nine of Hearts does not promise fulfillment of this wish as expressed in the Querent's mind. Instead, it represents something greater and more enduring, extending far beyond the realm of the Querent's imag-

ination" (Wenzell Brown, *How to Tell Fortunes with Cards* [New York, 1963], p. 50).

18.1360–61 (776:12–13). try pairing the lady herself and see if he comes out – Molly proposes to select a queen to represent herself, probably the queen of hearts (since she offers pleasure, joy, and unstinting love and acts instinctively rather than rationally). Molly will then pair her card with one or more cards chosen at random from the shuffled deck to see whether Stephen's card, the jack of spades, will turn up to fulfill her wish.

Sentence 8. 18.1368–1609 (pp. 776–83).

18.1374–75 (776:28–29). those old hypocrites in the time of Julius Caesar – Is Molly thinking about the moral tone of Roman rectitude as against Elephantis? See 15.2449n.

18.1377–78 (776:31–32). hed have something better to say for himself an old Lion would – In *The Odyssey*, Penelope repeatedly calls Odysseus "my lord, my lion heart" (4:724; Fitzgerald, p. 86).

18.1383–88 (776:38–777:1). my uncle John has a thing . . . the handle in a sweeping-brush – This street-rhyme-*cum*-riddle has not been identified. Marrowbone Lane in southeastern Dublin is part of a fairly direct route from Dolphin's Barn, where Molly lived with her father, toward the city center.

18.1390 (777:4). those houses round behind Irish street – That is, Irish Town in Gibraltar, one of the two main business streets in late-nineteenth-century Gibraltar. Whether the Rock's red-light district was then located off Irish Town (as Molly implies) is unknown. There was no Irish Street in Dublin.

18.1394 (777:9). coronado – Spanish: "tonsured as a Catholic monk." Molly (?) obviously intends *cornudo*, "horned, cuckolded."

18.1396 (777:11). the wife in Fair Tyrants – See 10.601–2n.

18.1397–98 (777:13). what else were we given all those desires for – See 10.171–73n.

18.1405 (777:22). I kiss the feet of you senorita – A direct translation of a Spanish expression of extreme courtesy.

18.1406 (777:23). didnt he kiss our hall door – Bloom has obviously secularized the ceremonial Jewish gesture of touching or kissing the *mezuzah;* see 13.1157–58n; and cf. 18.1595n.

18.1414 (777:32). Rathfarnham – A parish and village four miles south of the center of Dublin.

18.1414–16 (777:33–35). Bloomfield laundry . . . model laundry – Model Laundry, Bloomfield Steam Laundry Company, Ltd., proprietors, in Edmondstown, Rathfarnham.

18.1420 (777:40). that KC lives up somewhere this way – According to *Thom's* 1904 (p. 903), only three of the fifty-two king's counsels in Ireland lived in the northeast quadrant of Dublin (i.e., near the Blooms): Timothy Michael Healy, M.P. (see 7.800n), 1 Mountjoy Square; Michael C. Macinerney, 22 Mountjoy Square; and Denis B. Sullivan, 56 Mountjoy Square. Considering Joyce's enmity for Healy, Parnell's "betrayer," it would be Healy for choice.

18.1420 (777:41). Hardwicke lane – Just south of St. George's Church and just east of Bloom's house in Eccles Street.

18.1427 (778:5–6). the winds that waft my sighs to thee – The title of a song by H. W. Challis and William V. Wallace (the composer of *Maritana*): "The winds that waft my sighs to thee, / And o'er thy tresses steal; / Oh! let them tell a tale for me, / My lips dare not reveal! / And as they murmur soft and clear / The love I would impart. [Chorus:] Believe the whispers thou dost hear / Are breathings of my heart."

18.1427–28 (778:6–7). the great Suggester – In Book 23 of *The Odyssey*, Odysseus is repeatedly treated to an epithet that can be translated "the great tactician," "the man of many counsels," or simply "wise."

18.1429–30 (778:9). a dark man in some perplexity between 2 7s – In Molly's reading, Bloom is represented by the king of clubs, a lonely man of many talents, "of wide and diversified interests, outwardly sociable, but inwardly secretive and reserved. . . . The sympathetic understanding of a woman will be vital to his happiness, but he will have difficulty in making his wants known." Two (or usually three) sevens carry the "possibility of false accusations" and indicate perplexity about how the person (in this case, Bloom) can "benefit by his own integrity" (Wenzell Brown, *How to Tell Fortunes with Cards* [New York, 1963], pp. 85–86, 103).

18.1462 (779:6). arrah – Irish: "well, indeed."

18.1463–64 (779:7). Delapaz Delagracia – The *Gibraltar Directory and Guide Book* lists several "de la Paz" families and several "de Gracia."

18.1464–65 (779:8–9). *father Vilaplana of Santa Maria – The Reverend J. Vilaplana, Order of St. Benedict, was one of the ten priests associated with the Roman Catholic Cathedral Church of St. Mary the Crowned, but the *Gibraltar Directory and Guide Book* does not list that association until its 1912 and 1913 editions.

18.1465–66 (779:9–10). Rosales y OReilly in the Calle las Siete Revueltas – Spanish: "the Street of the Seven Turnings"—City Mill Lane to English-speaking Gibraltar. The *Gibraltar Directory and Guide Book* (1890) lists a James O'Reilly as resident in City Mill Lane.

18.1466 (779:10). Pisimbo – Not listed as a name in the *Gibraltar Directory and Guide Book*(s) we have consulted.

18.1466 (779:10–11). Mrs Opisso in Governor street – Mrs. Catherine Opisso, milliner and dressmaker, Governor's Street, Gibraltar.

18.1468 (779:13). Paradise ramp – Escalera de Cardona, one of the stairway side streets that slope up the Rock in Gibraltar.

18.1468 (779:13). Bedlam ramp – A local name for Witham's Ramp, running up the western slope of the Rock to the lunatic asylum, which was completed and occupied in 1884.

18.1468 (779:13). Rodgers ramp – Los Espinillos, another of the stairway streets on the western slopes of the Rock.

18.1469 (779:14). Crutchetts ramp – Or Portuguese Town (La Calera), another of the streets on the western slope of the Rock.

18.1469 (779:14). the devils gap steps – Ascending from the southwestern end of the town on Gibraltar toward the Devil's Bellows, a ravine that separates the upper slopes of the Rock from the southern plateau of Windmill Hill Flats.

18.1471–72 (779:17–18). como esta usted . . . y usted – Spanish: "How are you? Very well, thank you, and you?"

18.1475 (779:21). Valera – Juan Valera Y Alcalá Galiano (1824–1905), a Spanish novelist, poet, scholar, politician, and diplomat, generally regarded as a key figure in the late-nineteenth-century literary renaissance in Spain. Which of his many novels Molly attempted is not indicated by the context.

18.1475 (779:21–22). the questions in it all upside down the two ways – That is, it was in Spanish, since questions in Spanish begin ¿ and end ?.

18.1479–80 (779:27). so long as I didn't do it on the knife for bad luck – It is considered bad luck to use a knife as a substitute for a spoon ("to stir with a knife brings on strife").

18.1482 (779:30). Abrines – R. and J. Abrines, Ltd., Aix Bakery, 292 Main Street, Gibraltar.

18.1482–83 (779:31). the criada – Spanish: "the maid."

18.1486–87 (779:35–36). dos huevos estrellados senor – Spanish: "two fried eggs, sir."

18.1493 (779:43). gesabo – A vaguely pejorative term, as in "the whole gesabo," meaning the whole show or mess.

18.1497 (780:5–6). Walpoles – Walpole Brothers Ltd., linen drapers and damask manufacturers, 8–9 Suffolk Street, Dublin (with shops in London, Belfast, and elsewhere).

18.1498 (780:7). Cohens – See 18.1213n.

18.1499 (780:8). over to the markets – The Dublin Corporation Fruit, Vegetable, and Fish Market in Central Dublin, north of the Liffey, is bounded by Mary's Lane, Arran Street East, Chancery Street, and St. Michan's Street. It would have been a fifteen-minute walk from the Blooms' home.

18.1507–8 (780:18–19). mi fa pieta Massetto . . . presto non son piu forte – Italian: "I'm sorry for Masetto! . . . Quick, my strength is failing!" In Act I, scene iii of Mozart's *Don Giovanni*, Zerlina sings these lines in her duet with Giovanni, in response to his urging: "Come, my pretty delight! . . . I will change your fate." See 4.314n.

18.1516–17 (780:29–30). adulteress as the thing in the gallery said – At the performance of *The Wife of Scarli;* see 18.1117–18n.

18.1517–18 (780:31). this vale of tears – One much-quoted use of this stock phrase is in the Scot poet James Montgomery's (1771–1854) Hymn 214 in *The Issues of Life and Death:* "Beyond this vale of tears / There is a life above, / Unmeasured by the flight of years; / And all that life is love."

18.1535 (781:9–10). a mixture of plum and apple – This expression plays on the figurative use of "plum" as the best of good things and "apple" as the apple of discord, the reason for the Fall.

18.1541–42 (781:18). well soon have the nuns ringing the angelus – Namely, the nuns at the Dominican Convent of Our Lady of Sion, 18–21 Eccles Street, just west of the Blooms' house. The Angelus is a devotional exercise commemorating the Incarnation in which the Angelic Salutation (Hail Mary) is repeated three times. Occurring at sunrise, noon, and sunset, it is announced by a bell so that all the faithful can join.

18.1543 (781:19–20). an odd priest or two for his night office – Unlikely and irreverent; see 10.184n.

18.1548 (781:26). Lambes – Miss Alicia Lambe, fruiterer and florist, 33 Sackville (now O'Connell) Street Upper.

18.1548 (781:26–27). Findlaters – Alexander Findlater & Co., Ltd., tea, wine, and spirit merchants and provision merchants, 29–32 Sackville (now O'Connell) Street Upper, with several branches in Dublin City and County.

18.1550 (781:29). Fridays an unlucky day – See 17.16–17n.

18.1553–54 (781:32–33). shall I wear a white rose – See 18.768n.

18.1554 (781:33). Liptons – Lipton's Ltd., tea, wine, spirit, and provision merchants, 59–61 Dame Street, with several other shops in Dublin City and County and stores in London, Glasgow, and Liverpool.

18.1566 (782:5–6). go and wash the cobblestones off – "Cobbles" is dialect English for encrustations, lumps, and blemishes as well as for cobblestones.

18.1575 (782:16). leapyear like now yes 16 years ago – Bloom and Molly's courtship reached its climax on Howth, 10 September 1888, and 1888 was, as Molly recalls, a leap year.

18.1581–82 (782:24–25). looked out over the sea and the sky – In the *Paradiso* 27, Beatrice encourages Dante to look down from heaven to see how far the heavens have revolved around the earth. He does so and reports: "I saw beyond Cadiz the mad way which Ulysses took [out into the Atlantic and to his death, as Ulysses reported to Dante in the *Inferno* 26:90–142], and on this side, hard by the shore whereon Europa made herself a sweet burden [i.e., Phoenicia, from which Zeus in the form of a bull abducted Europa and carried her on his back to Crete]" (27:82–84). In effect, Dante imagines himself above the Mediterranean, seeing sunset on the coast of Phoenicia east of him and sunrise beyond Gibraltar in the no-man's ocean. He continues: "My enamoured mind, which held amorous converse ever with my Lady, burned more than ever to bring back my eyes to her" (27:99–100).

18.1584 (782:27). all birds fly – Iona Opie explains: "*All Birds Fly* is described under that title in Sean O Suilleabhain, *Irish Wake Amusements*, 1967, pp. 105–106, thus: 'A number of players sat in a semi-circle, hands resting on their knees. In front of them stood the leader; his assistant walked around at the back of the players. If the leader named some bird by saying, for example, "Crows fly," each player was supposed to simulate the flight of a crow by flapping his hands. In the midst of this, he would name another bird, and the flapping continued. But suddenly he might shout "Cats fly" or "Cows fly," and all hands had to remain still. Any player who was not alert enough to obey the change was slapped with a strap by the leader.' This game was not confined to wakes of course, and is typical of games played by sailors, in which alertness is the chief requirement and inattention is punished with the strap. The earliest recording we have found is in *The Girl's Own Book*, Mrs. Child, 1832, p. 29, 'Fly Away, Pigeon!' W. W. Newell includes a version in his *Games of American Children*, 1883, p. 119 (now in Dover paperback) 'Ducks Fly,' and gives analogues in German, French, and Swedish" (letter, 24 August 1970).

18.1584 (782:27). I say stoop – Iona Opie says: "We do not know a game of this name. It seems likely that it is a game of obeying commands or disregarding them according to the form in which the command is given; like 'O'Grady Says' . . . in which a command must not be obeyed unless prefaced by the words 'O'Grady says'" (letter, 24 August 1970).

18.1584 (782:28). washing up dishes – This may be another game, but Eric Partridge suggests "urinating" as a possibility.

18.1585 (782:29). the governors house – The governor of Gibraltar has two residences, a "palace" in town on the west side of the Rock and the governor's cottage, a seaside and secluded residence on the east side of the Rock.

18.1585–86 (782:29–30). with the thing around his white helmet – That is, a band with a badge identifying him as military police.

18.1587 (782:31–32). the auctions in the morning – The daily auction in Commercial Square in Gibraltar; colloquially, the Jews' Market. It was advertised as a tobacco auction, but the *Gibraltar Directory and Guide Book* (1889) remarks, "The goods sold at this Market are of great diversity and marvelous cheapness" (p. 45).

18.1589 (782:33). Duke street – There seems to be some confusion here: we find no evidence of a Duke Street in Gibraltar, and Duke Street in Dublin was halfway across the city from the egg, butter, and fowl market in Halston Street.

18.1590 (782:34). Larby Sharons – Does not appear in *Thom's* 1904 or in any of the *Gibraltar Directory and Guidebook*(s) (1889–1912) we have consulted.

18.1590 (782:35). the poor donkeys slipping half asleep – According to the *Gibraltar Directory and Guide Book* (1889), no more asses were to be used to carry supplies to the batteries on the upper slopes of the Rock—the men were to carry supplies themselves, on their backs. Apparently the "poor donkeys" had suffered several accidents.

18.1591–92 (782:36–37). the big wheels of the carts of the bulls – The two-wheeled carts with cages mounted on them used to transport fighting bulls.

18.1592 (782:37). the old castle – The Moorish Castle up against the northwest corner of the Rock of Gibraltar was built by Abu-Abul-Hajez in A.D. 725. Most of it is now in ruins, although a portion of the original wall is still standing.

18.1594 (782:40). Ronda – A mountain town in southern Spain forty-two miles northeast of Gibraltar. Guidebooks describe it as very old with well-preserved Moorish walls and towers and many Moorish buildings. The town is divided by a steep-sided gorge 300 feet wide and 600 feet deep. At the bottom of the gorge is the Guadalevin River.

18.1595 (782:40). posadas – Spanish: "inns or town houses."

18.1595 (782:41). glancing eyes a lattice hid – See 11.733n.

18.1595 (782:41). for her lover to kiss the iron – A Spanish colloquialism for a conventional gesture of courtship, since the ground-floor windows of Spanish town houses were usually defended by iron grilles.

18.1597 (782:43). Algeciras – See 18.399n.

18.1597 (783:1). serene – The Spanish *sereno*, what the unarmed nocturnal police in Spanish towns and cities call out as they make their rounds, and also what those police are called.

18.1597–98 (783:1). O that awful deepdown torrent O – Source in song or poem unknown. Molly may be recalling the gorge that bisects Ronda (see 18.1594n) or the waterfall Las Chorreas, four miles northwest of Algeciras and one of the scenic attractions of the region.

18.1598 (783:2). the sea the sea – Not that Molly is aware of it, but see 1.80n.

18.1599 (783:3). the Alameda gardens – See 18.643–44n.

18.1603 (783:8). or shall I wear a red – See 18.768n.

18.1603 (783:9). the Moorish wall – See 18.769–70n.

The "art" of the Aeolus episode is rhetoric, the form of linguistic manipulation Joyce considered closest to the heart of the working press. In its concentration on this self-conscious way of organizing language, Aeolus is the precursor of the more complicated use of imitation and parody in Cyclops (Episode 12) and Oxen of the Sun (Episode 14). The earlier manuscript drafts of Aeolus in *The Little Review* suggest that Joyce added a great number of rhetorical figures in his revisions, deliberately larding the chapter with as many devices as possible. What remains continually impressive is not simply the presence of practically every rhetorical figure outlined by Quintilian[1] and the classical rhetoricians, but the manner in which these contrivances are fitted into the chapter. The punnings of Lenehan, the pomposities of Professor MacHugh, the drunken ramblings of Myles Crawford, Stephen's literary high-seriousness, and Bloom's own idiosyncratic idiom are transformed into an encyclopedia of rhetorical devices. And, not unexpectedly, the speeches of Dan Dawson, Seymour Bushe, and John F. Taylor are examples of the three types of oratory outlined by Aristotle in his own *Rhetoric:* epideictic (the ceremonial display of oratory), forensic (legal), and deliberative (political).[2]

This appendix is by no means a complete catalogue of the rhetorical devices in Aeolus;[3] it is rather a suggestion of the range and exuberance of Joyce's celebration (and demolition?) of the art of rhetoric in this episode and throughout *Ulysses*. In attempting to arrange these figures in a rational order I have met with the fate of all other writers on rhetoric—the insufficiency, overlap, and reduplication of categories like Tropes or the Principal and Most Moving Figures of Speech. So, after exhaustive manipulation, I have decided to list these figures of rhetoric first serially, as they appear in Aeolus, then in alphabetical order, which seems as adequate a means of arrangement as any of the usual schemes that leave an overly large and ir-

APPENDIX: RHETORICAL FIGURES IN *AEOLUS*

---

1 Marcus Fabius Quintilian (A.D. 35–95), whose great work on rhetoric, *Institutio Oratoria,* is cast in the form of a training manual for public speaking.

2 Aristotle, *Rhetoric* 1:3:1358b.

3 For more on the rhetorical devices in Aeolus, see Stuart Gilbert, *James Joyce's "Ulysses"* (New York, 1952), pp. 195–98.

reducibly heterogeneous category called Miscellany.

Because the definitions of these forms were evolved from examples found in Greek and Roman literature—after the fact—even among the rhetoricians there was considerable uncertainty and much hairsplitting/headsplitting debate. If some of the definitions below seem redundant or in conflict with those of other authorities, it is not necessarily because I wish to continue the argument.

7.13 (116:14). Start, Palmerston Park! – *Ecphonesis:* exclamation, an exclamatory phrase.

7.14 (116:15). *THE WEARER OF THE CROWN* – *Metonymy:* the substitution of an attribute or adjunct of a thing for the thing itself.

7.21–22 (116:23–26). Grossbooted draymen rolled . . . stores! – *Chiasmus:* the inversion of the order of words in parallel clauses.

7.47 (117:20). All his brains are in the nape of his neck – *Diasyrm:* an expression of disparagement or ridicule.

7.48 (117:21–22). Fat folds of neck, fat, neck, fat, neck – *Epimone:* persistent use of the same word or words.

7.57–58 (117:35). Hand on his heart – *Ellipsis:* the deliberate omission of a word or words implied by context. "[His] hand on his heart."

7.59–60 (117:36–37). Co-ome thou lost one, / Co-ome thou dear one – *Diaeresis:* (1) the division of one syllable into two; (2) in prosody, the division made in a line or a verse when the end of a foot coincides with the end of a word; (3) the sign marking the division of one syllable into two, placed over the second of two vowels to indicate they should be sounded separately (¨).

7.61 (118:1). THE CROZIER AND THE PEN – *Metonymy:* substitution of the attribute for the person and institution signified: the crozier for the archbishop and the Church; the pen for the editor and journalism. See Appendix 7.14n.

7.63 (118:4). They watched the knees, legs, boots vanish – *Asyndeton:* the omission of conjunctions.

7.63 (118:4). Neck – *Synecdoche:* the use of a more comprehensive term for a less comprehensive, or vice versa—as whole for part or part for whole; in this case, the neck stands for the whole man, thanks to Simon Dedalus's sarcastic wit (see *sarcasm*, Appendix 7.991n).

7.83 (118:24–25). Working away, tearing away – *Epiphora:* the insistent repetition of one word at the end of several sentences.

7.100 (119:11–12). More Irish than the Irish – *Antanaclasis:* the repetition of a word in different senses (also called *antistasis*). "More Irish than the Irish" is also an example of *ploce:* the repetition of a word in an altered or pregnant sense, or for the sake of emphasis.

7.113 (119:27–28). If you want to draw the cashier is just going to lunch – *Enthymeme:* an argument based on a probable (i.e., implicit) premise (in this case: it is payday), as distinguished from a demonstration.

7.128 (120:1). Nannan – (For "Nannetti"), *apocope:* the omission of the last letter or syllable of a word.

7.128 (120:5). Hell of a racket they make – *Hyperbaton* (or *anastrophe*): the inversion of the natural order of words or phrases, especially for the sake of emphasis.

7.129 (120:5). Maybe he understands what I – *Anacoluthia:* a want of grammatical sequence; the passing from one construction to another before the former is completed.

7.168 (121:15). peeled pear – *Alliteration:* the repetition of similar consonant sounds at the beginning of words or stressed syllables.

7.174–75 (121:24). Sllt. Almost human the way it sllt to call attention – *Onomatopoeia:* the formation of a name or word by an imitation of the sound associated with the thing or action designated; this principle as a force in the formation of words; echoism.

7.176 (121:25–26). Doing its level best to speak – *Prosopopoeia* (personification): an imaginary or absent person is represented as speaking or acting; the introduction of a pretended speaker; also, investing abstractions with human qualities (as here).

7.206 (122:19). mangiD kcirtaP – *Metathesis:* a transposition of words; the interchange of position between sounds or letters in a word.

7.210–11 (122:25–26). And then the lamb and the cat and the dog and the stick and the water and the butcher . . . – *Polysyndeton:* the use of several conjunctions close together or the repetition of the same conjunction (as *and, or, nor*).

7.210–12 (122:25–28). And then the lamb and the cat and the dog and the stick and the water and the butcher and then the angel of death kills the butcher – *Climax:* arrangement of words, phrases, clauses in order of increasing importance.

7.218 (122:33–34). Now am I going to tram it out all the way . . . ? – *Anthimeria:* the substitution of one part of speech for another, as the substantive *tram* becomes a verb for Bloom.

7.226 (123:6). Citronlemon? – *Idiotism:* (1) an idiom; (2) the peculiar character or genius of a language; (3) a peculiarity of action, manner, or habit. An example of Bloom's talent for compounding; in this case, the name of his former neighbor combines with the citron-ethrog (see 4.210–11n) and with the odor of the soap in his pocket.

7.230–31 (123:10–12). I could go home still: tram: something I forgot. Just to see before dressing. No. Here. No – *Anacoluthia:* a want of grammatical sequence; the passing from one construction to another before the former is completed. The passage also suggests *ellipsis* (see Appendix 7.57–58n).

7.237 (123:18). The ghost walks – *Hypotyposis:* Gilbert defines hypotyposis as "the visionary imagination of things not present as being before the eyes." He also cites Stephen's vision of Dante's three rhymes as "three by three, approaching girls" (7.720 [138:26]).

7.237 (123:18–19). murmuring softly, biscuitfully – *Anthimeria:* the substitution of one part of speech for another.

7.241 (123:22–23). Agonising Christ, wouldn't it give you heartburn on your arse? – *Catachresis:* Gilbert calls it "metaphor bold to a degree of impropriety," but Quintilian defines it as "borrowing the word nearest the meaning intended" or "improper use of words; application of a term to a thing which it does not properly denote; abuse or perversion of a trope or metaphor." The phrase is also an example of *apostrophe:* a sudden break in discourse followed by the addressing of some person or thing, either present or absent; an exclamatory address.

7.246 (123:29). 'neath the shadows – *Aphaeresis:* the omission of a letter or syllable at the beginning of a word.

7.246 (123:29). o'er – *Syncope:* the loss of letters or sounds from the middle of a word; abbreviation, contraction.

7.246–47/53 (123:29–30/36). *its pensive bosom . . . overarching leafage/pensive bosom and the overarsing leafage* – *Paradiastole:* favorable turn is given to something unfavorable by the use of an expression that conveys only part of the truth (or vice versa?).

7.253 (123:36). *pensive bosom* – *Solecism:* a violation of the rules of grammar or syntax; properly, a faulty concord.

7.270–71 (124:20–21). A recently discovered fragment of Cicero's . . . *Our lovely land* – *Irony:* the intended meaning is the opposite of that expressed by the words used.

7.309 (125:19). Weathercocks – *Metaphor:* to Bloom, journalists are like the cocks that top weathervanes.

7.318 (125:31). Blessed and eternal God! – *Ecphonesis (ecphonema):* exclamation.

7.325 (126:2). The moon, professor MacHugh said – *Prolepsis:* the taking of the future as already done or existing. More specifically, in rhetorical grammar: (*procatalepsis*) (1) the anticipatory use of an attribute; (2) the anticipation and response to an opponent's objections. In his next words, Dan Dawson "features" the moon (7.327–28 [125:3]), which MacHugh anticipates. For *prolepsis*, see also Appendix 7.489n.

7.327 (126:3). *the vista far and wide* – *Synonymy:* the use of synonyms for the sake of amplification.

7.336 (126:13). Doughy Daw! he cried – *Hypocorism:* a pet name.

7.367–68 (127:10–12). Ohio—A perfect cretic! the professor said, Long, short and long – *Cretic:* a metrical foot.

7.370 (127:13). O, HARP EOLIAN – *Synaeresis:* contraction, especially of two vowels (the Greek æ) into a diphthong or a simple vowel.

7.380–81 (127:25–26). That'll be all right, Myles Crawford said more calmly. Never you fret . . . That's all right – *Exergasia:* Stuart Gilbert defines this as the "use of different phrases to express the same idea." Literally (Greek), "working out; to work out or perfect." "A figure when we abide still in one place, and yet seem to speak of diverse things, many times repeating one sentence, but yet with other words, sentences, and exhortations" (Quintilian).

7.393 (128:8). I hear feetstoops – *Anagram:* a transposition of the letters of a word, name, or phrase, whereby a new one is formed.

7.398 (128:14). It wasn't me sir. It was the big fellow shoved me, sir – *Epanaphora:* Stuart Gilbert suggests that epanaphora is a combined use of *anaphora* (the repetition of the same word or phrase in several successive clauses), *epiphora* (the impressive repetition of one word at the end of several sentences), and *epistrophe* (the repetition of the same word or groups of words at the end of successive clauses).

7.422 (129:7). The accumulation of the *anno Domini* – *Metalepsis:* the metonymical substitution of one word for another that was itself figurative (Quintilian). For *metonymy,* see Appendix 7.61n.

7.427–28 (129:13–14). *We are the boys of Wexford / Who fought with heart and hand* – *Zeugma:* the use of a single word to modify or govern two or more words, especially when applying in sense to only one of them or applying to them in different senses. See further discussion at Appendix 7.690–91n.

7.449 (129:36). Steal upon larks – *Truncated simile:* a comparison of one thing with another, especially as an ornament in poetry or rhetoric.

7.462–63 (130:16–17). Seems to be, J. J. O'Molloy said . . . but it is not always as it seems – *Epanalepsis:* repetition of a word or clause after intervening matter. *Symploce:* the repetition of one word or phrase at the beginning, and of another at the end, of successive clauses or sentences; a combination of *anaphora* and *epistrophe.*

7.471–72 (130:28–29). *'Twas rank and fame that tempted thee, / 'Twas empire charmed thy heart* – *Synoeceiosis:* contrasted or heterogeneous things are associated or coupled, such as contrary qualities attributed to the same sub-

ject. In early-twentieth-century Ireland it is conceivable that a disparity in scale between "empire" and "rank and fame" might have occasioned Gilbert's belief that this figure applies here. Myles Crawford's ironic jest at Mac-Hugh's expense is, in itself, comic enough.

7.486 (131:8). imperial, imperious, imperative – *Paregmenon:* the conjoining of words derived from one another, as "discrete and discretion."

7.489 (131:11). Vast, I allow: but vile – *Synchoresis:* concession, a rhetorical device for enlisting sympathy before a tirade.

7.489 (131:11). Vast, I allow – *Prolepsis* (also *procatalepsis*): the anticipation of and response to an opponent's objections.

7.489–95 (131:11–18). What was their civilization? . . . *It is meet to be here. Let us construct a watercloset* – *Epiphonema:* an exclamatory sentence or striking reflection that sums up or concludes a discourse or passage.

7.491–93 (131:14–16). The Roman . . . brought to every new shore on which he set his foot (on our shore he never set it) only his cloacal obsession – *Parenthesis:* an explanatory or qualifying word, clause, or sentence inserted into a passage with which it has not necessarily any grammatical connection and usually set off from it by round or square brackets, dashes, or commas.

7.494–95 (131:17–18). It is meet to be here. Let us construct a watercloset – *Tapinosis:* diminution, "humility, that is when the dignity or majesty of a high matter is much defeated by the baseness of a word; as to call the Ocean a stream, or the Thames a brook" (J. Smith, *The Mysteries of Rhetoric,* 1657).

7.496 (131:19–20). Our old ancient ancestors – *Tautology:* repetition of a word, phrase, idea, or statement; usually as a fault in style. Also, redundancy.

7.508–9 (131:35). Youth led by Experience visits Notoriety – *Allegory:* description of a subject under the guise of some other subject of a partly suggestive resemblance; an extended *metaphor.*

7.521 (132:9–10). Was he short taken? – *Anastrophe* (or *hyperbaton*): inversion of the usual order of words or clauses.

7.533–35 (132:23–25). **By Jesus, she had the foot and mouth disease and no mistake! The night she threw soup in the waiter's face in the Star and Garter, Oho!** – *Parataxis:* the placing of prepositions or clauses one after another, without indicating by connecting words (of coordination or subordination) the relationship between them.

7.555–57 (133:13–15). *****I speak the tongue of a race the acme of whose mentality is the maxim: time is money. Material domination. Domine! Lord!** – *Paralogism:* a piece of faulty reasoning—a faulty syllogism or a fallacy—especially (as distinct from a sophism) one of which the reasoner is himself unaware.

7.557 (133:15). ***Domine! Lord!** – *Metaphrase:* a translation; later, a word-for-word translation, as distinct from a paraphrase.

7.565–66 (133:25–26). **We are liege subjects of the catholic chivalry of Europe that foundered at Trafalgar** – *Enthymeme:* an argument based on a probable (i.e., implicit) premise; here: if the combined fleets of France and Spain had not been defeated at Trafalgar, Napoleon would have invaded and defeated England.

7.574 (133:34). **Boohoo! Lenehan wept** – *Mimesis:* imitation of the words or actions of another. Lenehan mimics the grief of Pyrrhus's followers.

7.582 (134:9). **I can't see the Joe Miller** – *Antonomasia:* substituting something for its proper name; more precisely, substituting a descriptive word or phrase for a proper name or a proper name for a quality associated with that name.

7.591 (134:19–20). **The Rows of Castile . . . Rose of cast steel** – *Paronomasia:* a play on words that sound alike; a pun.

7.594 (134:24). **I feel a strong weakness** – *Oxymoron:* the conjoining of contradictory terms so as to give point to the statement or expression, as in Milton's description of hell, "darkness visible."

7.601 (134:33–34). **Or was it you shot the lord lieutenant of Finland between you?** – *Erotesis (erotema):* the bold assertion in the form of a question of the opposite of what the question asks; as in "Shall I be frighted when a madman stares?"

7.605–9 (135:3–9). **Law, the classics . . . The turf . . . Literature, the press . . . the gentle art of advertisement . . . The vocal muse** – *Synathroesmus:* Gilbert calls this "accumulation by enumeration."

7.610 (135:9). **Dublin's prime favorite** – *Pleonasm:* the use of more words in a sentence than necessary to express the meaning; redundancy. Also, *paradiastole:* a favorable turn is given to something less favorable by the use of an expression that conveys only part of the truth, "prime" being the operative word and a juicy pun as well.

7.612 (135:11). **a fresh of breath air** – *Anagram:* a transposition of the letters of a word, name, or phrase, whereby a new one is formed.

7.612–13 (135:11–12). **I caught a cold in the park. The gate was open** – *Auxesis:* amplification, *hyperbole* (see Appendix 7.999n).

7.617–18 (135:18). **See it in your face. See it in your eye** – *Anaphora:* the repetition of the same word or phrase in several successive clauses.

7.622 (135:23–24). **Father Son and Holy Ghost and Jakes McCarthy** – *Anticlimax:* the opposite of *climax* (see Appendix 7.210–11n); a sentence in which the last part expresses something lower than the first. The addition of a particular that, instead of heightening the effect that has been building up, suddenly lowers it or makes it ludicrous.

7.630 (136:1). **That was a pen** – *Professional Jargon:* the terminology of a science or art, or the cant of a class, sect, trade, or profession. Also *metonymy:* the substitution of an attribute or adjunct of a thing for the thing itself.

7.650–51 (136:25). **Look at here. What did Ignatius Gallaher do?** – *Anacoensis:* the speaker applies to his hearers or opponents for their opinion on the point in question.

7.663 (136:37). **The loose flesh of his neck shook like a cock's wattles** – *Simile.*

7.674 (137:13). **CLEVER, VERY** – *Hysteron proteron:* a reversal of the natural or temporal order.

7.676–77 (137:15–16). **Gave it to them on a hot plate, the whole bloody history** – *Syllepsis:* a word, or a particular form or inflection of a word, is made to refer to two or more other words in the same sentence, while properly applying to or agreeing with only one of them (e.g., a masculine adjective qualifying two substantives, masculine and feminine, etc;) or applying them in different senses (e.g., literal and metaphorical) as here.

7.683 (137:22). Madam, I'm Adam. And Able was I ere I saw Elba – Two *palindromes:* a palindrome is a word, verse, or sentence that reads the same backwards as forwards.

7.690–91 (137:30–31). father of scare journalism and brother-in-law of Chris Callinan – Though Gilbert lists this as *zeugma,* it seems to me a little strained for the definition: the use of a single word to modify or govern two or more words, especially when applying in sense to only one of them or applying to them in different senses. Formerly it included more broadly the use of the same predicate, without repetition, with two or more subjects; and it is also sometimes applied to cases of irregular construction, in which a single word agrees grammatically with only one of the other words to which it refers (more properly called *syllepsis;* see Appendix 7.676–77n).

7.695 (137:36). Clamn dever – *Metathesis:* a transposition of words; the interchange of position between sounds or letters in a word.

7.723 (138:30–31). Underdarkneath – *Anastomosis:* insertion of a qualifying word between two parts of another word.

7.723–24 (138:31). mouth south: tomb womb – *Homoioteleuton:* a series of words with the same or similar endings.

7.729–30 (138:35–139:1). I hold no brief, as at present advised, for the third profession . . . but – *Epitrope:* permission is granted to an opponent, either seriously or ironically, to do what he proposed to do. Gilbert calls it "permission—a form of concession." Also *metabasis:* a transition from one subject or point to another. "A figure whereby the points of an oration . . . are knit together: and is, when we are briefly put in mind of what hath been said, and what remains further to be spoken" (J. Smith, *The Mysteries of Rhetoric,* 1657). "The passing from one indication to another, from one remedy to another" (*Blanchard's Physical Dictionary,* 1698).

7.730–31 (139:2). Your Cork legs are running away with you – *Hibernicism:* an idiom or expression characteristic of Irish speech.

7.736 (139:9). Sufficient for the day is the newspaper thereof – *Epigram:* a short poem leading up to an ending in a witty or ingenious turn of thought; a pointed or antithetical saying. In this case the epigram turns on Jesus' epigram "Sufficient unto the day is the evil thereof" (Matthew 6:34).

7.744–45 (139:19–20). He would have been on the bench long ago . . . only for . . . But no matter – *Aposiopesis:* breaking off as if unable or unwilling to proceed.

7.770–71 (140:15–16). *has wrought in marble of the soultransfigured and soultransfiguring* – *Polyptoton:* the repetition of a word or root in different cases or inflections in the same sentence.

7.771 (140:16). *deserves to live, deserves to live* – *Anaphora:* the repetition of the same word or phrase in several successive clauses.

7.787–88 (140:33–35). Magennis . . . Magennis – *Epanalepsis:* see Appendix 7.462–63n.

7.794 (141:4–5). Mr Justice Fitzgibbon, the present lord justice of appeal – *Apposition:* placing two coordinate elements together, the second as explanation or modification of the first.

7.804–7 (141:15–18). the speech . . . of a finished orator . . . pouring in chastened diction, I will not say the vials of his wrath but pouring the proud man's contumely upon the new movement – *Paralepsis:* emphasis by affecting to pass the point of interest by without notice, usually with such phrases as "not to mention" and "to say nothing of."

7.817–18 (141:31–32). He looked (though he was not) a dying man – *Epanorthosis:* a word or phrase is inserted to guard against or to correct a possible misunderstanding.

7.828–30 (142:5–7). *Great was my admiration in listening to the remarks addressed to the youth of Ireland a moment since by my learned friend.* – *Enantiosis:* meaning the opposite of what is said; a form of irony. See also *antithesis,* Appendix 7.846–49n.

7.839–40, 42 (142:18–19, 21). *I heard his words and their meaning was revealed to me. It was revealed to me* – *Anadiplosis* (*epanadiplosis*): duplication of a prominent, and usually the last, part of a sentence, line, or clause at the beginning of the next.

7.844 (142:23). **Ah, curse you!** – *Invective:* a sharp, bitter, or cutting expression or remark; a bitter gibe or taunt.

7.846–49 (142:26–29). *You are a tribe of nomad herdsmen; we are a mighty people. You have no cities nor no wealth: our cities are hives of humanity and our galleys . . . laden with all manner merchandise furrow the waters of the known globe* – *Antithesis:* the juxtaposition of contrasting ideas, often in parallel structure.

7.846–49 (142:26–31). *You are a tribe of nomad herdsmen . . . You have no cities nor no wealth . . . You have but emerged from primitive conditions* – *Incrementum:* an ascending toward a climax.

7.862–64 (143:7–9). *had the youthful Moses listened to . . . had he bowed his head and bowed his will and bowed his spirit* – *Anabasis* (*climax*).

7.864–67 (143:10–15). *he would never have brought the chosen people out of their house of bondage nor followed the pillar of cloud by day. He never would have spoken with the Eternal . . . nor ever have come down* – *Isocolon:* parallel elements similar in structure and length.

7.874–75 (143:22–24). **A sudden-at-the-moment-though-from-lingering-illness-often-previously-expectorated-demise** – *Polyhyphenation;* also *periphrasis:* substitution of many or several words where few or one would suffice; a wordy or roundabout way of speaking; circumlocution.

7.875 (143:23). **expectorated** – (for "expected"); *Paragoge:* the addition of a letter or syllable to a word, either inorganically, as in *oncet* for *once*, or, as in Semitic languages, to give emphasis or to modify the meaning.

7.888 (143:37–38). **'Tis the hour, methinks** – *Archaism:* the retention or imitation of what is old or obsolete.

7.890 (144:1). **That it be and hereby is resolutely resolved** – *Redundancy.* (In at least one of its dictionary senses, "resolute" means resolve.)

7.891–92 (144:3). **To which particular boosing shed?** – *Tapinosis:* diminution; "humility, that is when the dignity or majesty of high matter is much defeated by the baseness of a word" (J. Smith, *The Mysteries of Rhetoric*, 1657).

7.894–95 (144:6). **We will sternly refuse to partake of strong waters, will we not? Yes, we will not. By no manner of means** – *Litotes:* statement in which an affirmative is expressed by the negative of the contrary. Also *antimetabole:* repetition of the same words or ideas in transposed order; an *epanodos* (see Appendix 7.1040n) that is also an *antithesis.*

7.907 (144:21–22). **I hope you will live to see it published** – *Charientism:* gracefulness of style, expression of an unpleasant thing in an agreeable manner.

7.915 (144:31). **I have much, much to learn** – *Epizeuxis:* repetition of a word with vehemence or emphasis.

7.930 (145:10). **Let there be life** – *Parody* with substitution: "Let there be light!" (Genesis 1:3).

7.947 (145:30). **They had no idea it was that high** – *Oratio recta-obliqua:* Gilbert says, "giving, by quotation of a vulgar form, vivacity to the flatness of a third-personal report."

7.968–69 (146:18–19). **A newsboy cried in Mr Bloom's face:** – Terrible tragedy in Rathmines! A child hit by a bellows!—*Anticlimax.*

7.980 (146:31). **K.M.A.** – *Abbreviation:* "Kiss my arse."

7.991 (147:11). **he can kiss my royal Irish arse** – *Sarcasm:* a sharp, bitter, or cutting expression or remark.

7.999 (147:19–20). **With a heart and a half** – *Hyperbole:* an exaggerated statement used to express strong feeling or produce a strong impression and not intended to be taken literally.

7.1008–9 (147:31). **waxies' Dargle** – *Hibernicism.*

7.1018 (148:9). **onehandled adulterer** – *Par-*

onomasia (Pun): the use of words alike in sound but different in meaning: "onehandled" for "onehanded."

7.1022 (148:13–14). SPEEDPILLS VELOCI-TOUS AEROLITHS – *Neologism:* the use of, or practice of using, new words.

7.1040 (149:5). Poor Penelope. Penelope Rich – *Epanodos:* the repetition of a sentence in inverse order; a return to the regular thread of discourse after a digression. See also *antimetabole*, Appendix 7.894–95n.

7.1046–47 (149:13–14). Hackney cars, cabs, delivery wagons, mail-vans, private brough-ams – *Aparithmesis:* Gilbert says this is "enumeration in detail of things in corresponding words of the same grammatical character."

7.1055–56 (149:23–24). Call it, wait, the professor said opening his long lips to reflect. Call it, let me see – *Aporia:* doubt. "Aporia, or the Doubtfull. [So] called . . . because oftentimes we will seeme to cast perils, and make doubt of things when by a plaine manner of speech we might affirm or deny him" (Puttenham, *Arte of English Poesie*, 1589).

7.1070 (150:9–10). ANNE WIMBLES – Gilbert identifies "wimbles" as *Hapax Legomenon*, a term used in Greek lexicons to denote words found only once in extant literature. There are several words of this sort in Homer, and apparently "wimbles" is one of Joyce's contributions to the English lexicon; see 7.1070–71n.

Alphabetical Index of Rhetorical Figures in *Aeolus*

Abbreviation, 7.980 (146:31).
Allegory, 7.508–9 (131:35).
Alliteration, 7.168 (121:15).
Anabasis, 7.862–64 (143:7–9).
Anacoensis, 7.650–51 (136:25).
Anacoluthia, 7.129 (120:5); 7.230–31 (123:10–12).
Anadiplosis (Epanadiplosis), 7.839–40, 42 (142:18–19, 21).
Anagram, 7.393 (128:8); 7.612 (135.11).
Anaphora, 7.617–18 (135:18); 7.771 (140:16); in combination with Epiphora and Epistrophe (Epanaphora): 7.398 (128:14); in combination with Epistrophe (Symploce): 7.462–63n (130:16–17).

Anastomosis, 7.723 (138:30–31).
Anastrophe, 7.128 (120:5); 7.521 (132:9–10).
Antanaclasis (also called Antistasis), 7.100 (119:11–12).
Anthimeria, 7.218 (122:33–34); 7.237 (123:18–19).
Anticlimax, 7.622 (135:23–24); 7.968–69 (146:18–19).
Antimetabole, 7.894–95 (144:6).
Antithesis (see also Enantiosis), 7.846–49 (142:26–29).
Antonomasia, 7.582 (134:9).
Aparithmesis, 7.1046–47 (149:13–14).
Aphaeresis, 7.246 (123:29).
Apocope, 7.128 (120:1).
Aporia, 7.1055–56 (149:23–24).
Aposiopesis, 7.744–45 (139:19–20).
Apostrophe, 7.241 (123:22–23).
Apposition, 7.794 (141:4–5).
Archaism, 7.888 (143:37–38).
Asyndeton, 7.63 (118.4).
Auxesis, 7.612–13 (135:11–12).

Catachresis, 7.241 (123:22–23).
Charientism, 7.907 (144:21–22).
Chiasmus, 7.21–22 (116:23–26).
Climax, 7.210–12 (122:25–28); 7.862–64 (143:7–9).
Cretic, 7.367–68 (127:12).

Diaeresis, 7.59–60 (117:36–37).
Diasyrm, 7.47 (117:20).

Ecphonesis (Ecphonema), 7.13 (116:14); 7.318 (125:31).
Ellipsis, 7.57–58 (117:35); 7.230–31 (123:10–12).
Enantiosis, 7.828–30 (142:5–7).
Enthymeme, 7.113 (119:27–28); 7.565–66 (133:25–26).
Epanalepsis, 7.462–63 (130:16–17); 7.787–88 (140:33–35).
Epanaphora, 7.398 (128:14).
Epanodos, 7.1040 (149:5).
Epanorthosis, 7.817–18 (141:31–32).
Epigram, 7.736 (139:9).
Epimone, 7.48 (117:21–22).
Epiphonema, 7.489–95 (131:11–18).
Epiphora, 7.83 (118:24–25); in combination with Anaphora: 7.398 (128:14).
Epistrophe, in combination with Anaphora (Symploce): 7.462–63 (130:16–17); in combination with Anaphora and Epiphora (Epanaphora): 7.398 (128:14).
Epitrope, 7.729–30 (138:35–139:1).
Epizeuxis, 7.915 (144:31).
Erotesis (Erotema), 7.601 (134:33–34).
Exergasia, 7.380–81 (127:25–26).

This index is highly selective. Most of the people, pubs, shops, institutions, and landmarks that Joyce would have called "Dublin street furniture" have been omitted in favor of more public items and figures and in favor of cross-references. Joyce's fictional characters are listed only under first appearance in the notes unless further relevant information is presented in subsequent notes.

Most of the entries in this index are keyed to the episode and line number of the Critical and Synoptic Edition of *Ulysses* under which the note appears (for example, Aaron, 3.177–78; other entries refer to pages in this book (for example, Aeolus, p. 128).

INDEX

Eglinton, John, *see* Magee, William Kirkpatrick.
Egoist, 9.1079.
Elephantis, 15.2449; 18.1374–75.
Elijah, 8.13; 8.15; 8.57–58; 8.74–76; 9.483; 10.294;
   10.1109–10; 11.867; 12.1682–84; 12.1910–
   12; 12.1914–15; 14.1580; 15.2175–76;
   15.2188; 15.3375; 15.3435; 17.40–42;
   17.332–33.
Elijah III, *see* Dowie, John Alexander.
Elizabeth, of England, 9.630–31; 9.647; 9.757–60;
   10.392; 12.178; 12.1276–77; 15.1263–64;
   16.1767–68.
Ellis, Mrs., 5.237.
Ellis, William, *Three Trips to Madagascar*, 14.343–
   48; 17.1374.
Elpenor, p. 104; 6.510; p. 192; 15.694–95.
Elster-Grimes Grand Opera Company, 6.186;
   16.526.
Ember days, 16.278.
Emerson, Ralph Waldo, *Essays, First Series*, 9.281.
Emmanuel, 15.1868–69.
Emmet, Robert, 6.977–78; 10.764; 10.767–68;
   10.791; 11.61; 11.62; 11.1275; 12.180;
   12.500–501; 12.525–678; 12.618–19; 12.661–
   62; 15.1561–62; 15.3199; 15.3387–90;
   16.1534–35.
Empedocles, 14.387–89; 14.1231–33.
Empire Theatre of Varieties, 10.495; 12.740–47.
Encyclopedia Britannica, 17.1523–24.
Enniscorthy Guardian, 9.598–99.
Entente cordiale, 12.1387; 12.1399; 15.3915.
Epact, 17.97–99.
Ephesus, 14.886.
Ephod, 15.1898.
Epiphanies, 3.141.
Epiphanius, *see* St. Epiphanius the Monk.
Erasmus Smith High School, *see* High School of
   Erasmus Smith.
Erebus, 12.447–49.
Erin's King (ship), 4.434; 8.60; 11.580–82; 13.1184–
   85.
Eriphyle, p. 104.
Eris (goddess of discord), 13.42.
Esau, 4.22122; 9.981; 15.1220.
Etherege, George, *The Man of Mode*, 14.662–63.
Ethrog, *see* Citron (fruit).
Eucharist, 10.4; 18.760–61; *see also* Mass, ceremo-
   nies of the.
Eugamon of Cyrene, *The Telegonia*, p. 70.
Eugene Aram, *see* Bulwer-Lytton, Sir Edward.
Eugenics, 14.684–85.
Eumaeus, p. 534; 16.21; 16.1240–41; 16.1355.
Eurycleia, p. 566; p. 610.
Eurylochus, p. 84; p. 408; p. 452.
Eurymachos, p. 12; 1.744; p. 566.
Evangelists, the four, 12.1443–46.
Eve, 2.390; 3.41–42; 3.44; 3.391–92; 7.536–37;
   9.541; 12.1862; 14.29–32; 14.298–301;
   14.309–11; 15.2373; 15.2445–46.
Evelyn, John, *Diary*, 14.474–528.
Evening Mail (Dublin), 10.973–74.
Evening Telegraph (Dublin), 2.412; 6.370; 6.473;
   Aeolus passim; 10.651–53; 14.1560; 15.1125;
   15.2932–33; 15.2933–34; 16.709; 16.1232;
   16.1239 through 16.1244–45; 16.1276–89;
   16.1662–64; 16.1666–67; 16.1683; 16.1683–
   84; 18.270.
Everard, Col. N. T., 16.996.
Everyman (morality play), 14.107–22; 17.2008;
   17.2010.
Exeter Book, 14.71.
Extreme Unction, 1.421–22; 10.91–92; 14.100;

18.760–61.

Face at the Window, 16.429–30.
Fagan, Rev. Peter, 12.933.
Fair Tyrants, *see* Lovebirch, James.
Falkiner, Sir Frederick R., 7.698–99; 8.1151
   through 8.1158–59; 12.1095; 12.1875;
   15.1162; 15.1164–65.
Family Physician, 18.181.
Famine, The Great Irish, p. 6; 2.269; 3.306; 4.73;
   12.1365–66 through 12.1369–71; 15.4578–
   83; 17.755.
Famine riots (corn famine), 9.742–44.
Fanning, Long John (subsheriff), 7.106.
Farley, Rev. Charles, S.J., 5.332–33.
Farnaby, Giles, 16.1766–67.
Farrell, Cashel Boyle O'Connor Fitzmaurice Tisdall,
   9.1115–16.
Farrell, Sir Thomas, 6.226.
Faure, Felix, 3.233–34.
Feast of Our Lady of Mount Carmel, 8.148; *see also*
   Carmelites.
Feast of Tabernacles, 4.210–11; 7.226–27; 17.2049;
   17.2050; *see also* Citron (fruit).
Feast of the Ascension, 17.94–96.
Feast of the Epiphany, 9.479.
Feis Ceoil, 4.314; 6.222; 11.927.
Fell, Dr. John, 13.309–10.
Fencibles, 14.654–55.
Fenian Nights' Entertainments, *see* McCall, Patrick J.
Fenian Society (Irish Republican Brotherhood),
   2.272; 3.163–64; 3.241; 3.247; 4.491; 5.378;
   7.632–33; 7.707; 8.457–58; 8.459–61;
   12.179; 12.199; 12.480; 12.910.
Fenius Farsaigh, king of Scythia, 17.748–49.
Ferdinand V, of Spain, 16.1121–22.
Fergus mac Roy, 12.113–14; 12.1127.
Ferguson, Sir Samuel, "The Burial of King Cor-
   mac," 8.663–66.
Fianna, 9.578; 12.910; 12.1127; 12.1128; 12.1129.
Field, William, M. P., 2.415; 12.827–28.
Fille du régiment, *see* Donizetti, Gaetano.
Fingal's Cave, 12.1461.
Finn MacCool, 3.291–93; 9.578; 12.717; 12.910;
   12.1128.
Finsen, Dr. Niels, 15.2737–38.
Firstfruits (Jewish festival) 3.367–69; 9.1207–8;
   17.94–96.
Fitton, Mary, 9.442–43; 9.453; 9.462–64; 9.637–38.
Fitzball, Edward, "The Bloom Is on the Rye,"
   10.524; 11.6; 11.230–31; 11.390; 11.126–27;
   see Wallace, William Vincent—*Maritana;* and
   Balfe, Michael William—*The Siege of Ro-
   chelle.*
Fitzgerald, Edward (trans.), *The Rubáiyát of Omar
   Khayyám*, 15.117.
Fitzgerald, Lord Edward, 6.609; 7.348; 10.785–86;
   10.791; 12.661–62; 15.4686.
Fitzgerald, Gerald, 10.444–48.
Fitzgerald, James Fitzmaurice, 12.1305–6.
Fitzgerald, Thomas, Lord Offaly (Silken Thomas),
   3.314; 10.407–9; 10.415–16; 12.1861–62;
   16.558.
Fitzgeralds, the, 10.438–39; 10.930.
Fitzgibbon, Gerald (Lord Justice), 7.794; 7.807;
   14.494–95; 15.4343.
FitzGilbert, Richard (Richard de Clare), earl of
   Pembroke, 3.259.
Fitzharris, James ("Skin-the-Goat"), 7.640; 7.667–
   68; p. 534; 16.323–24; 16.1068–69.
Fitzsimmons, Robert, 10.1146.
Flanagan, Rev. J., 12.937–38.

Designer: Sandy Drooker
Compositor: Graphic Composition, Inc.
Text: Plantin
Display: Plantin